KU-314-193

DICK FRANCIS

DICK FRANCIS

WHIP HAND

RAT RACE

FORFEIT

HIGH STAKES

TWICE SHY

Whip Hand first published in Great Britain
in 1979 by Michael Joseph Limited
Rat Race first published in Great Britain
in 1970 by Michael Joseph Limited
Forfeit first published in Great Britain
in 1968 by Michael Joseph Limited
High Stakes first published in Great Britain
in 1975 by Michael Joseph Limited
Twice Shy first published in Great Britain
in 1981 by Michael Joseph Limited

This edition first published in Great Britain in 1985
by Octopus Books Limited
59 Grosvenor Street
London W1

in collaboration with:

William Heinemann Limited
10 Upper Grosvenor Street
London W1

and

Martin Secker & Warburg Limited
54 Poland Street
London W1

ISBN 0 86273 249 2

Printed and Bound in Great Britain by
Collins Glasgow

CONTENTS

WHIP HAND

This book is for
MIKE GWILYM
Actor
and
JACKY STOLLER
Producer
with gratitude and affection

PROLOGUE

I dreamed I was riding in a race.

Nothing odd in that. I'd ridden in thousands.

There were fences to jump. There were horses, and jockeys in a rainbow of colours, and miles of green grass. There were massed banks of people, with pink oval faces indistinguishable pink blobs from where I crouched in the stirrups, galloping past, straining with speed.

Their mouths were open, and although I could hear no sound I knew they were shouting.

Shouting my name, to make me win.

Winning was all. Winning was my function. What I was there for. What I wanted. What I was born for.

In the dream, I won the race. The shouting turned to cheering, and the cheering lifted me up on its wings, like a wave. But the winning was all; not the cheering.

I woke in the dark, as I often did, at four in the morning.

There was silence. No cheering. Just silence.

I could still feel the way I'd moved with the horse, the ripple of muscle through both of the striving bodies, uniting in one. I could still feel the irons around my feet, the calves of my legs gripping, the balance, the nearness to my head of the stretching brown neck, the mane blowing in my mouth, my hands on the reins.

There came, at that point, the second awakening. The real one. The moment in which I first moved, and opened my eyes, and remembered that I wouldn't ride any more races, ever. The wrench of loss came again as a fresh grief. The dream was a dream for whole men.

I dreamed it quite often.

Damned senseless thing to do.

Living, of course, was quite different. One discarded dreams, and got dressed, and made what one could of the day.

Chapter One

I took the battery out of my arm and fed it into the re-charger and only realized I'd done it when ten seconds later the fingers wouldn't work.

How odd, I thought. Recharging the battery, and the manoeuvre needed to accomplish it, had become such second nature that I had done them instinctively, without conscious decision, like brushing my teeth. And I realized for the first time that I had finally squared my subconscious, at least when I was awake, to the fact that what I now had as a left hand was a matter of metal and plastic, not muscle and bone and blood.

I pulled my tie off and flung it haphazardly onto my jacket, which lay over the leather arm of the sofa: stretched and sighed with the ease of homecoming: listened to the familiar silences of the flat; and as usual felt the welcoming peace unlock the gritty tensions of the outside world.

I suppose that that flat was more of a haven than a home. Comfortable certainly, but not slowly and lovingly put together. Furnished, rather, on one brisk unemotional afternoon in one store: 'I'll have that, that, that and that ... and send them as soon as possible.' The collection had gelled, more or less, but I now owned nothing whose loss I would ache over; and if that was a defence mechanism, at least I knew it.

Contentedly padding around in shirt sleeves and socks, I switched on the warm pools of tablelights, encouraged the television with a practised slap, poured a soothing Scotch, and decided not to do yesterday's washing up. There was steak in the fridge and money in the bank, and who needed an aim in life anyway?

I tended nowadays to do most things one-handed, because it was quicker. My ingenious false hand, which worked via solenoids from electrical impulses in what was left of my forearm, would open and close in a fairly vice-like grip, but at its own pace. It did *look* like a real hand, though, to the extent that people sometimes didn't notice. There were shapes like fingernails, and ridges for tendons, and blue lines for veins. When I was alone I seemed to use it less and less, but it please me better to see it on than off.

I shaped up to that evening as to many another. On the sofa feet up, knees bent, in contact with a chunky tumbler and happy to live vicariously via the small screen: and I was mildly irritated when halfway through a decent comedy the door bell rang.

With more reluctance than curiosity I stood up, parked the glass, fumbled through my jacket pockets for the spare battery I'd been carrying there, and snapped it into the socket in my arm. Then, buttoning the shirt cuff down over the plastic wrist, I went out into the small hall and took a look through the spyhole in the door.

There was no trouble on the mat, unless trouble had taken the shape of a middle-aged lady in a blue headscarf. I opened the door and said politely, 'Good evening, can I help you?'

'Sid,' she said. 'Can I come in?'

I looked at her, thinking that I didn't know her. But then a good many people whom I didn't know called me Sid, and I'd always taken it as a compliment.

Coarse dark curls showed under the headscarf, a pair of tinted glasses hid her eyes, and heavy crimson lipstick focussed attention on her mouth. There was embarrassment in her manner and she seemed to be trembling inside her loose fawn raincoat. She still appeared to expect me to recognize her, but it was not until she looked nervously over her shoulder, and I saw her profile against the light, that I actually did.

Even then I said incredulously, tentatively, 'Rosemary?'

'Look,' she said, brushing past me as I opened the door more widely. 'I simply must talk to you.'

'Well ... come in.'

While I closed the door behind us she stopped in front of the looking glass in the hall and started to untie the headscarf.

'My God, whatever do I look like?'

I saw that her fingers were shaking too much to undo the knot, and finally with a frustrated little moan she stretched over her head, grasped the points of the scarf, and forcefully pulled the whole thing forward. Off with the scarf came all the black curls, and out shook the more familiar chestnut mane of Rosemary Caspar, who had called me Sid for fifteen years.

'My God,' she said again, putting the tinted glasses away in her handbag and fetching out a tissue to wipe off the worst of the gleaming lipstick. 'I had to come, I had to come.'

I watched the tremors in her hands and listened to the jerkiness in her voice, and reflected that I'd seen a whole procession of people in this state since I'd drifted into the trade of sorting out trouble and disaster.

'Come on in and have a drink,' I said, knowing it was what she both needed and expected, and sighing internally over the ruins of my quiet evening. 'Whisky or gin?'

'Gin ... tonic ... anything.'

Still wearing the raincoat she followed me into the sitting room and sat abruptly on the sofa as if her knees had given way beneath her. I looked briefly at the vague eyes, switched off the laughter on the television and poured her a tranquillizing dose of mothers' ruin.

'Here,' I said, handing her the tumbler. 'So what's the problem?'

'Problem!' she was transitorily indignant. 'It's more than that.'

I picked up my own drink and carried it round to sit in an armchair opposite her.

'I saw you in the distance at the races today.' I said. 'Did the problem exist at that point?'

She took a large gulp from her glass. 'Yes, it damn well did. And why do you think I came creeping around at night searching for your damn flat in this ropey wig if I could have walked straight up to you at the races?'

'Well ... why?'

'Because the last person I can be seen talking to on a racecourse or off it is Sid Halley.'

I had ridden a few times for her husband away back in the past. In the days when I was a jockey. When I was still light enought for Flat racing and hadn't taken to steeplechasing. In the days before success and glory and falls and smashed hands ... and all that. To Sid Halley, ex-jockey, she could have talked publicly forever. To Sid Halley, recently changed into a sort of all-purpose investigator, she had come in darkness and fright.

Forty-fivish, I supposed, thinking about it for the first time, and realizing that although I had known her casually for years I had never before looked long enough or closely enough at her face to see it feature by feature. The general impression of thin elegance had always been strong. The drooping lines of eyebrow and eyelid, the small scar on the chin, the fine noticeable down on the sides of the jaw, these were new territory.

She raised her eyes suddenly and gave me the same sort of inspection, as if she'd never really seen me before: and I guessed that for her it was a much more radical reassessment. I was no longer the boy she'd once rather brusquely issued with riding instructions, but a man she had come to in trouble. I was accustomed, by now, to seeing this new view of me supplant older and easier relationships, and although I might often regret it, there seemed no way of going back.

'Everyone says ...' she began doubtfully. 'I mean ... over this past year, I keep hearing ...' She cleared her throat. 'They say you're good ... very good ... at this sort of thing. But I don't know ... now I'm here ... it doesn't seem ... I mean ... you're a jockey.'

'Was,' I said succinctly.

She glanced vaguely at my left hand, but made no other comment. She knew all about that. As racing gossip goes, it was last year's news.

'Why don't you tell me what you want done?' I said. 'If I can't help, I'll say so.'

The idea that I couldn't help after all reawoke her alarm and set her shivering again inside the raincoat.

'There's no one else,' she said. 'I can't go to anyone else. I have to believe ... I have to ... that you can do ... all they say.'

'I'm no superman,' I protested. 'I just snoop around a bit?

'Well ... Oh God ...' The glass rattled against her teeth as she emptied it to the dregs. 'I hope to God ...'

'Take your coat off,' I said persuasively. 'Have another gin. Sit back on the sofa, and start at the beginning.'

As if dazed she stood up, undid the buttons, shed the coat, and sat down again.

'There isn't a beginning.'

She took the refilled glass and hugged it to her chest. The newly revealed clothes were a cream silk shirt under a rust-coloured cashmere-looking sweater, a heavy gold chain, and a well cut black skirt: the everyday expression of no financial anxieties.

'George is at a dinner,' she said. 'We're staying here in London overnight. . . . He thinks I've gone to a film.'

George, her husband, ranked in the top three of British racehorse trainers and probably in the top ten internationally. On racecourses from Hong Kong to Kentucky he was revered as one of the greats. At Newmarket, where he lived, he was king. If his horses won the Derby, the Arc de Triomphe, the Washington International, no one was surprised. Some of the cream of the world's bloodstock floated by year by year to his stable, and even having a horse in his yard gave the owner a certain standing. George Caspar could afford to turn down any horse or any man. Rumour said he rarely turned down any woman: and if that was Rosemary's problem it was one I couldn't solve.

'He mustn't know,' she said nervously. 'You'll have to promise not to tell him I came here.'

'I'll promise provisionally,' I said.

'That's not enough.'

'It'll have to be.'

'You'll see,' she said. 'You'll see why. . . .' She took a drink. 'He may not like it, but he's worried to death.'

'Who . . . George?'

'Of course George. Who else? Don't be so damned stupid. For who else would I risk coming here on this damn charade?' The brittleness shrilled in her voice and seemed to surprise her. She visibly took some deep breaths, and started again. 'What did you think of Gleaner?'

'Er . . .' I said. 'Disappointing.'

'A damned disaster,' she said. 'You know it was.'

'One of those things,' I said.

'No, it was *not* one of those things. One of the best two-year-olds George ever had. Won three brilliant two-year-old races. Then all that winter, favourite for the Guineas and the Derby. Going to be the tops, everyone said. Going to be marvellous.'

'Yes,' I said. 'I remember.'

'And then what? Last Spring he ran in the Guineas. Fizzled out. Total flop. And he never even got within sight of the Derby.'

'It happens,' I said.

She looked at me impatiently, compressing her lips. 'And Zingaloo?' she said. 'Was that, too, just one of those things? The two best colts in the country, both brilliant at two, both in our yard. And neither of them won a damn penny last year as three-year-olds. They just stood there in their boxes, looking well, eating their heads off, and totally damn bloody useless.'

'It was a puzzler,' I agreed, but without much conviction. Horses which didn't come up to expectations were as normal as rain on Sundays.

'And what about Bethesda, the year before?' She glared at me vehemently. 'Top two-year-old filly. Favourite for months for the One Thousand and the Oaks. Terrific. She went down to the start of the One Thousand looking a million dollars, and she finished tenth. *Tenth*, I ask you!'

'George must have had them all *checked*,' I said mildly.

'Of course he did, Damn vets crawling all round the place for weeks on end. Dope tests. Everything. All negative. Three brilliant horses all gone useless. And no damned explanation. Nothing!'

I sighed slightly. It sounded to me more like the story of most trainers' lives, not a matter for melodramatic visits in false wigs.

'And now,' she said, casually dropping the bomb, 'there is Tri-Nitro.'

I let out an involuntarily audible breath, halfway to a grunt. Tri-Nitro filled columns just then on every racing page, hailed as the best colt for a decade. His two-year-old career the previous autumn had eclipsed all competitors, and his supremacy in the approaching summer was mostly taken for granted. I had seen him win the Middle Park at Newmarket in September at a record-breaking pace, and had a vivid memory of the slashing stride that covered the turf at almost incredible speed.

'The Guineas is only a fortnight away,' Rosemary said. 'Two weeks today, in fact. Suppose something happens ... suppose it's just as bad ... what if he fails, like the others ...?'

She was trembling again, but when I opened my mouth to speak she rushed on at a higher pitch. 'Tonight was the only chance ... the only night I could come here ... and George would be livid. He says nothing can happen to the horse, no one can get at him, the security's too good. But he's scared, I know he is. Strung up. Screwed up tight. I suggested he called you in to guard the horse and he nearly went berserk. I don't know why. I've never seen him in such a fury.'

'Rosemary,' I began, shaking my head.

'Listen,' she interrupted. 'I want you to make sure nothing happens to Tri-Nitro before the Guineas. That's all.'

'All....'

'It's no good wishing afterwards ... if somebody tries something ... that I'd asked you. I couldn't stand that. So I had to come. I had to. So say you'll do it. Say how much you want, and I'll pay it.'

'It's not money,' I said. 'Look ... there's no way I can guard Tri-Nitro without George knowing and approving. It's impossible.'

'You can do it. I'm sure you can. You've done things before that people said couldn't be done. I had to come. I can't face it ... George can't face it ... not three years in a row. Tri-Nitro has got to win. You've got to make sure nothing happens. You've got to.'

She was suddenly shaking worse than ever and looked well down the road to hysteria. More to calm her than from any thought of being able in fact to do what she wanted, I said 'Rosemary . . . all right. I'll try to do something.'

'He's got to win,' she said.

I said soothingly 'I don't see why he shouldn't.'

She picked up unerringly the undertone I hadn't known would creep into my voice: the scepticism, the easy complacent tendency to discount her urgency as the fantasies of an excitable woman. I heard the nuances myself, and saw them uncomfortably through her eyes.

'My God, I've wasted my time coming here, haven't I?' she said bitterly, standing up. 'You're like all bloody men. You've got menopause on the brain.'

'That's not true. And I said I'd try.'

'Yes.' The word was a sneer. She was stoking up her own anger, indulging an inner need to explode. She practically threw her empty glass at me instead of handing it. I missed catching it, and it fell against the side of the coffee table, and broke.

She looked down at the glittering pieces and stuffed the jagged rage halfway back into its box.

'Sorry,' she said shortly.

'It doesn't matter.'

'Put it down to strain.'

'Yes.'

'I'll have to go and see that film. George will ask . . .' She slid into her raincoat and moved jerkily towards the door, her whole body still trembling with tension. 'I shouldn't have come here. But I thought . . .'

'Rosemary,' I said flatly. 'I've said I'll try, and I will.'

'Nobody knows what it's like.'

I followed her into the hall, feeling her jangling desperation almost as if it were making actual disturbances in the air. She picked the black wig off the small table there and put it back on her head, tucking her own brown hair underneath with fierce unfriendly jabs, hating herself, her disguise and me: hating the visit, the lies to George, the seedy furtiveness of her actions. She painted on a fresh layer of the dark lipstick with unnecessary force, as if assaulting herself; tied the knot on the scarf with a savage jerk, and fumbled in her handbag for the tinted glasses.

'I changed in the lavatories at the tube station,' she said. 'It's all revolting. But I'm not having anyone see me leaving here. There are things going on. I know there are. And George is scared. . . .'

She stood by my front door, waiting for me to open it; a thin elegant woman looking determinedly ugly. It came to me that no woman did that to herself without a need that made esteem an irrelevance. I'd done nothing to relieve her distress, and it was no good realizing that it was because of knowing her too long in a different capacity. It was she who was subtly used to being in control, and I, from sixteen, who had respectfully followed her wishes. I thought that if tonight I had made her cry and given her warmth and contact and even a kiss, I could have done her more service; but the block was there, and couldn't be lightly dismantled.

'I shouldn't have come here,' she said. 'I see that now.'

'Do you want me ... to take any action?'

A spasm twisted her face. 'Oh God.... Yes I do. But I was stupid. Fooling myself. You're only a jockey ... after all.'

I opened the door.

'I wish,' I said lightly, 'that I were.'

She looked at me unseeingly, her mind already on her return journey, on her film, on her report of it to George.

'I'm not crazy,' she said.

She turned abruptly and walked away without a backward glance. I watched her turn towards the stairs and go without hesitating out of sight. With a continuing feeling of having been inadequate I shut the door and went back into the sitting room; and it seemed that the very air there too was restless from her intensity.

I bent down and picked up the larger pieces of broken glass, but there were too many sharp little splinters for total laziness, so I fetched the dustpan and brush from the kitchen.

Holding the dustpan could usefully be done left-handed. If I simply tried to bend backwards the real hand that wasn't there, the false fingers opened away from the thumb. If I sent the old message to bend my hand inwards they closed. There was always about two seconds' delay between mental instruction and electrical reaction, and taking that interval into account had been the most difficult thing to learn.

The fingers could not of course feel when their grip was tight enough. The people who fitted the arm had told me that success was picking up eggs: and I'd broken a dozen or two in practising, at the beginning. Absentmindedness had since resulted in an exploding light bulb and crushed-flat cigarette packets and explained why I used the marvels of science less than I might.

I emptied the bits of glass into the dustbin and switched on the television again; but the comedy was over, and Rosemary came between me and a cops-and-robbers. With a sigh I switched off, and cooked my steak, and after I'd eaten it picked up the telephone to talk to Bobby Unwin, who worked for the *Daily Planet*.

'Information will cost you,' he said immediately, when he found who was on his line.

'Cost me what?'

'A spot of quid pro quo.'

'All right,' I said.

'What are you after, then?'

'Um,' I said. 'You wrote a long piece about George Caspar in your Saturday colour supplement a couple of months ago. Pages and pages of it.'

'That's right. Special feature. In-depth analysis of success. The *Planet*'s doing a once-a-month series on high-flyers, tycoons, pop-stars, you name it. Putting them under the cliché microscope and coming up with a big yawn yawn exposé of bugger all.'

'Are you horizontal?' I said.

There was a short silence followed by a stifled girlish giggle.

'You just take your intuitions to Siberia,' Bobby said. 'What made you think so?'

'Envy, I dare say.' But I'd really only been asking if he was alone, without making it sound important. 'Will you be at Kempton tomorrow?'

'I reckon.'

'Could you bring a copy of that magazine, and I'll buy you a bottle of your choice.'

Oh boy, oh boy. You're on.'

His receiver went down without more ado, and I spent the rest of the evening reading the flat-racing form books of recent years, tracing the careers of Bethesda, Gleaner, Zingaloo and Tri-Nitro, and coming up with nothing at all.

Chapter Two

I had fallen into a recent habit of lunching on Thursdays with my father-in-law. To be accurate, with my *ex*-father-in-law; Admiral (retired) Charles Roland, parent of my worst failure. To his daughter Jenny I had given whatever devotion I was capable of, and had withheld the only thing she eventually said she wanted, which was that I should stop riding in races. We had been married for five years; two in happiness, two in discord, and one in bitterness; and now only the itching half-mended wounds remained. Those, and the friendship of her father, which I had come by with difficulty and now prized as the only treasure saved from the wreck.

We met most weeks at noon in the upstairs bar of the Cavendish Hotel, where a pink gin for him and a whisky and water for me now stood on prim little mats beside a bowl of peanuts.

'Jenny will be at Aynsford this weekend,' he said.

Aynsford was his house in Oxfordshire. London on Thursdays was his business. He made the journey between the two in a Rolls.

'I'd be glad if you would come down,' he said.

I looked at the fine distinguished face and listened to the drawling noncommittal voice. A man of subtlety and charm who could blast through you like a laser if he felt the need. A man whose integrity I would trust to the gates of hell, and whose mercy, not an inch.

I said carefully, without rancour, 'I am not coming to be sniped at.'

'She agreed that I should invite you.'

'I don't believe it.'

He looked with suspicious concentration at his glass. I knew from long experience that when he wanted me to do something he knew I wouldn't like, he didn't look at me. And there would be a pause, like this, while he found it in him to light the fuse. From the length of the pause, I drew no comfort of any sort. He said finally, 'I'm afraid she's in some sort of trouble.'

I stared at him, but he wouldn't raise his eyes.

'Charles,' I said despairingly, 'you *can't* ... you can't ask me ... You know how she speaks to me these days.'

'You give as good as you get, as I recall.'

'No one in their senses walks into a tiger's cage.'

He gave me a brief flashing upward glance, and there was a small twitch in his mouth. And perhaps it was not the best way of referring to a man's beautiful daughter.

'I have know you, Sid,' he said, 'to walk into tigers' cages more than once.'

'A tigress, then,' I amended, with a touch of humour.

He pounced on it. 'So you'll come?'

'No ... Some things, honestly, are too much.'

He sighed and sat back in his chair, looking at me over the gin. I didn't care for the blank look in his eyes, because it meant he was still plotting.

'Dover sole?' he suggested smoothly. 'Shall I call the waiter? We might eat soon, don't you think?'

He ordered sole for both of us, and off the bone, out of habit. I could eat perfectly well in public now, but there had been a long and embarrassing period when my natural hand had been a wasted, useless deformity, which I'd self-consciously hidden in pockets. At about the time I finally got used to it, it had been smashed up again, and I'd lost it altogether. I guessed life was like that. You gained and you lost, and if you saved anything from the ruins, even if only a shred of self-respect, it was enough to take you through the next bit.

The waiter told us our table would be ready in ten minutes and went quietly away, hugging menus and order pad to his dinner jacket and grey silk tie. Charles glanced at his watch and then gazed expansively round the big, light, quiet room, where other couples like us, sat in beige armchairs and sorted out the world.

'Are you going to Kempton this afternoon?' he said.

I nodded. 'The first race is at two-thirty.'

'Are you working on a job?' As an inquiry, it was a shade too bland.

'I'm not coming to Aynsford,' I said. 'Not while Jenny's there.'

After a pause, he said, 'I wish you would, Sid.'

I merely looked at him. His eyes were following the track of a bar waiter delivering drinks to distant customers: and he was taking a great deal too much time thinking out his next sentence.

He cleared his throat and addressed himself to nowhere in particular. 'Jenny has lent some money ... and her name, I'm afraid ... to a business enterprise which would appear to be fraudulent.'

'She's done *what*?' I said.

His gaze switched back to me with suspicious speed, but I interrupted him as he opened his mouth.

'No,' I said. 'If she's done that, it's well within your province to sort it out.'

'It's your name she's used, of course,' Charles said. 'Jennifer Halley.'

I could feel the trap closing round me. Charles studied my silent face and with a tiny sigh of relief let go of some distinct inner anxiety. He was a great deal too adept, I thought bitterly, at hooking me.

'She was attracted to a man,' he said dispassionately. 'I didn't especially like him, but then I didn't like you, either, to begin with . . . and I found that error of judgement inhibiting, as a matter of fact, because I no longer always trust my first instincts.'

I ate a peanut. He had disliked me because I was a jockey, which he saw as no sort of husband for his well-bred daughter: and I had disliked him right back as an intellectual and social snob. It was odd to reflect that he was now probably the individual I valued most in the world.

He went on, 'This man persuaded her to go in for some sort of mail order business . . . all frightfully up-market and respectable, at least on the surface. A worthy way of raising money for charity . . . you know the sort of thing. Like Christmas cards, only in this case I think it was a sort of wax polish for antique furniture. One was invited to buy expensive wax, knowing that most of the profits would go to a good cause.'

He looked at me sombrely. I simply waited, without much hope.

'The orders rolled in,' he said. 'And the money with them, of course. Jenny and a girl friend were kept busy sending off the wax.'

'Which Jenny,' I guessed, 'had bought ready, in advance?'

Charles sighed. 'You don't need to be told, do you?'

'And Jenny paid for the postage and packing and advertisements and general literature?'

He nodded. 'She banked all the receipts into a specially opened account in the name of the charity. Those receipts have all been drawn out, the man has disappeared, and the charity, as such, has been found not to exist.'

I regarded him in dismay.

'And Jenny's position?' I said.

'Very bad, I'm afraid. There may be a prosecution. And her name is on everything, and the man's nowhere.'

My reaction was beyond blasphemy. Charles observed my blank silence and nodded slowly in sympathy.

'She has been exceedingly foolish,' he said.

'Couldn't you have stopped her? Warned her?'

He shook his head regretfully. 'I didn't know about it until she came to Aynsford yesterday in a panic. She has done it all from that flat she's taken in Oxford.'

We went in to lunch, and I couldn't remember, afterwards, the taste of the sole.

'The man's name is Nicholas Ashe,' Charles said, over the coffee. 'At least that's what he said.' He paused briefly. 'My solicitor chap thinks it would be a good idea if you could find him.'

I drove to Kempton with visual and muscular responses on auto-pilot and my thoughts uncomfortably on Jenny.

Divorce itself, it seemed, had changed nothing. The recent antiseptic drawing of the line, the impersonal court to which neither of us had gone (no children, no maintenance disputes, no flicker of reconciliation, petition granted, next case please) seemed to have punctuated our lives not with a full stop but with hardly a comma. The legal position had not proved a great liberating open door. The recovery from emotional cataclysm seemed a long slow process, and the certificate was barely an aspirin.

Where once we had clung together with delight and passion, we now, if we chanced to meet, ripped with claws. I had spent eight years in loving, losing and mourning Jenny, and although I could wish my feelings were dead, they weren't. The days of indifference still seemed a weary way off.

If I helped her in the mess she was in, she would give me a rotten time. If I didn't help her, I would give it to myself. *Why*, I thought violently, in impotent irritation, had the silly bitch been so *stupid*.

There was a fair attendance at Kempton for a weekday in April, though as often before I regretted that in Britain the nearer a racecourse was to London, the more vulnerable it became to stay-away crowds. City-dwellers might be addicted to gambling, but not to fresh air and horses. Birmingham and Manchester, in days gone by, had lost their racecourses to indifference, and Liverpool had survived only through the Grand National. Most times it took a course in the country to burst at the seams and run out of racecards; the thriving plants still growing from the oldest roots.

Outside the weighing rooms there was the same old bunch of familiar faces carrying on chats which had been basically unchanged for centuries. Who was going to ride what, and who was going to win, and there should be a change in the rules, and what so-and-so had said about his horse losing, and wasn't the general outlook grim, and did you know young fella-me-lad has left his wife? There were the scurrilous stories and the slight exaggerations and the downright lies. The same mingling of honour and corruption, of principle and expediency. People ready to bribe, people with the ready palm. Anguished little hopefuls and arrogant big guns. The failures making brave excuses, and the successful hiding the anxieties behind their eyes. All as it had been, and was, and would be, as long as racing lasted.

I had no real right any longer to wander in the space outside the weighing room, although no one ever turned me out. I belonged in the grey area of ex-jockeys: barred from the weighing room itself but tolerantly given the run of much else. The cosy inner sanctum had gone down the drain the day half a ton of horse landed feet first on my metacarpals. Since then I had come to be glad simply to be still part of the brotherhood, and the ache to be riding was just part of the general regret. Another ex-champion had told me it took him twenty years before he no longer yearned to be out there on the horses, and I'd said thanks very much.

George Caspar was there, talking to his jockey, with three runners scheduled that afternoon; and also Rosemary, who reacted with a violent jerk when she saw me at ten paces, and promptly turned her back. I could imagine the waves of alarm quivering through her, although that day she looked her usual well-groomed elegant self: mink coat for the chilly wind, glossy boots, velvet hat. If she feared I would talk about her visit, she was wrong.

There was a light grasp on my elbow and a pleasant voice saying 'A word in your ear, Sid.'

I was smiling before I turned to him, because Lord Friarly, Earl, landowner, and frightfully decent fellow, had been one of the people for whom I'd ridden a lot of races. He was of the old school of aristocrats; stylish, beautifully mannered, genuinely compassionate, slightly eccentric, and more intelligent than people expected. A slight stammer was nothing to do with speech impediment but all to do with not wanting to seem to throw his rank about in an egalitarian world.

Over the years I had stayed several times in his house in Shropshire, mostly on the way to northern racemeetings, and had travelled countless miles with him in a succession of elderly cars. The age of the cars was not an extension of the low profile, but rather a disinclination to waste money on inessentials. Essentials, in terms of the Earl's income, were keeping up Friarly Hall and owning as many racehorses as possible.

'Great to see you, sir,' I said.

'I've told you to call me Philip.'

'Yes ... sorry.'

'Look,' he said, 'I want you to do something for me. I hear you're damned good at looking into things. Doesn't surprise me, of course, I've always valued your opinion, you know that.'

'Of course I'll help if I can,' I said.

'I've an uncomfortable feeling I'm being *used*,' he said. 'You know that I'm a sucker for seeing my horses run, the more the merrier, and all that. Well, during the past year I have agreed to be one of the registered owners in a syndicate ... you know, sharing the costs with eight or ten other people, though the horses run in my name, and my colours.'

'Yeah,' I said nodding. 'I've noticed.'

'Well ... I don't know all the other people, personally. The syndicates were formed by a chap who does just that – gets people together and sells them a horse. You know?'

I nodded. There had been cases of syndicate-formers buying horses for a smallish sum and selling them to the members of the syndicate for up to four times as much. A healthy little racket, so far legal.

'Those horses don't run true to form, Sid,' he said bluntly. 'I've a nasty feeling that somewhere in the syndicates we've got someone fixing the way the horses run. So will you find out for me? Nice and quietly?'

'I'll certainly try,' I said.

'Good,' he said, with satisfaction. 'Thought you would. So I brought the names for you, of the people in the syndicates.' He pulled a folded paper out of his inner pocket. 'There you are,' he said, opening it and pointing. 'Four horses. The syndicates are all registered with the Jockey Club, everything above board, audited accounts, and so on. It all looks all right on paper, but, frankly, Sid, I'm not *happy*.'

'I'll look into it,' I promised, and he thanked me profusely, and also genuinely, and moved away, after a minute or two, to talk to Rosemary and George.

Further away, Bobby Unwin, notebook and pencil in evidence, was giving a middle-rank trainer a hard-looking time. His voice floated over, sharp with northern aggression and tinged with an inquisitorial tone caught from tele-interviewers. 'Can you say, then, that you are perfectly satisfied with the way your horses are running?' The trainer looked around for escape and shifted from foot to foot. It was amazing, I thought, that he put up with it, even though Bobby Unwin's printed barbs tended to be worse if he hadn't had the personal pleasure of intimidating his victim face to face. He wrote well, was avidly read, and among most of the racing fraternity was heartily disliked. Between him and me there had been for many years a sort of sparring truce, which in practice had meant a diminution of words like 'blind' and 'cretinous' to two per paragraph when he was describing any race I'd lost. Since I'd stopped riding I was no longer a target, and in consequence we had developed a perverse satisfaction in talking to each other, like scratching a spot.

Seeing me out of the corner of his eye he presently released the miserable trainer and steered his beaky nose in my direction. Tall, forty, and forever making copy out of having been born in a back-to-back terrace in Bradford: a fighter, come up the hard way, and letting no one ever forget it. We ought to have had much in common, since I too was the product of a dingy back street, but temperament had nothing to do with environment. He tended to meet fate with fury and I with silence, which meant that he talked a lot and I listened.

'The colour mag's in my briefcase in the Press room,' he said. 'What do you want it for?'

'Just general interest.'

'Oh come off it,' he said. 'What are you working on?'

'And would you,' I said, 'give me advance notice of your next scoop?'

'All right,' he said. 'Point taken. And I'll have a bottle of the best vintage bubbly in the members' bar. After the first race. O.K.?'

'And for smoked salmon sandwiches extra, would I acquire some background info that never saw the light of print?'

He grinned nastily and said he didn't see why not: and in due course, after the first race, he kept his bargain.

'You can afford it, Sid, lad,' he said, munching a pink-filled sandwich and laying a protective hand on the gold-foiled bottle standing beside us on the bar counter. 'So what do you want to know?'

'You went to Newmarket . . . to George Caspar's yard . . . to do this article?' I indicated the colour magazine which lay, folded lengthwise, beside the bottle.

'Yeah. Sure.'

'So tell me what you didn't write.'

He stopped in mid-munch. 'In what area?'

What do you privately think of George as a person?'

He spoke round bits of brown bread. 'I said most of it in that.' He looked at the magazine. 'He knows more about when a horse is ready to race and what race to run him in than any other trainer on the Turf. And he's got as much feeling for people as a block of stone. He knows the name and the breeding back to the flood of every one of the hundred and twenty plus horses in his yard, and he can recognize them walking away from him in a downpour, which is practically impossible, but as for the forty lads he's got there working for him, he calls them all Tommy, because he doesn't know t'other from which.'

'Lads come and go,' I said neutrally.

'So do horses. It's in his mind. He doesn't give a bugger's damn for people.'

'Women?' I suggested.

'Uses them, poor sods. I bet when he's at it he's got his mind on his next day's runners.'

'And Rosemary . . . what does she think about things?'

I poured a refill into his glass, and sipped my own. Bobby finished his sandwich with a gulp and licked the crumbs off his fingers.

'Rosemary? She's half way off her rocker.'

'She looked all right yesterday at the races,' I said. 'And she's here today, as well.'

'Yeah, well, she can hold on to the grande dame act in public still, I grant you, but I was in and out of the house for three days, and I'm telling you, mate, the goings-on there had to be heard to be believed.'

'Such as?'

'Such as Rosemary screaming all over the place that they hadn't enough security and George telling her to belt up. Rosemary's got some screwy idea that some of their horses have been got at in the past, and I daresay she's right at that, because you don't have a yard that size and that successful that hasn't had its share of villains trying to alter the odds. But anyway . . .' he drank deep and tipped the bottle generously to replenish his supplies, '. . . she seized me by the coat in their hall one day . . . and that hall's as big as a fair-sized barn . . . literally seized me by the coat and said what I should be writing was some stuff about Gleaner and Zingaloo being got at . . . you remember, those two spanking two-year-olds who never developed . . . and George came out of his office and said she was neurotic and suffering from the change of life, and right then and there in front of me they had a proper slanging match.' He took a breath and a mouthful. 'Funny thing is, in a way I'd say they were fond of each other. As much as he could be fond of anybody.'

I ran my tongue round my teeth and looked only marginally interested, as if my mind was on something else. 'What did George say about her ideas on Gleaner and Zingaloo?' I said.

'He took it for granted I wouldn't take her seriously, but anyway, he said it was just that she had the heeby-jeebies that someone would nobble Tri-Nitro, and she was getting everything out of proportion. Her age, he said. Women always went very odd, he said, at that age. He said the security round Tri-Nitro was already double what he considered really necessary, because of her nagging, and when the new season began he'd have night patrols with dogs, and such like. Which is now, of course. He told me that Rosemary was quite wrong, anyway, about Gleaner and Zingaloo being got at, but that she'd got this obsession on the subject, and he was ready to humour her to some degree to stop her going completely bonkers. It seems that both of them ... the horses, that is ... proved to have a heart murmur, which of course accounted for their rotten performances as they matured and grew heavier. So that was that. No story.' He emptied his glass and refilled it. 'Well, Sid, mate, what is it you *really* want to know about George Caspar?'

'Um,' I said. 'Do you think there's anything he is afraid of?'

'George?' he said disbelievingly. 'What sort of thing?'

'Anything.'

'When I was there, I'd say he was about as frightened as a ton of bricks.'

'He didn't seem worried?'

'Not a bit.'

'Or edgy?'

He shrugged. 'Only with his wife.'

'How long ago was it, that you went there?'

'Oh ...' He considered, thinking. 'After Christmas. Yes ... second week in January. We have to do those colour mags such a long time in advance.'

'You don't think, then,' I said slowly, sounding disappointed, 'that he'd be wanting any extra protection for Tri-Nitro?'

'Is that what you're after?' He gave the leering grin. 'No dice, then, Sid, mate. Try someone smaller. George has got his whole ruddy yard sewn up tight. For a start, see, it's one of those old ones enclosed inside a high wall, like a fortress. Then there's ten-foot high double gates across the entrance, with spikes on top.'

I nodded. 'Yes ... I've seen them.'

'Well, then.' He shrugged, as if that settled things.

There were closed-circuit televisions in all the bars at Kempton to keep serious drinkers abreast of the races going on outside, and on the nearest of these sets Bobby Unwin and I watched the second race. The horse which won by six lengths was the one trained by George Caspar, and while Bobby was thoughtfully eying the two inches of fizz still left in the bottle, George himself came into the bar. Behind him, in a camel-coloured overcoat, came a subtantial man bearing all the stigmata of a satisfied winning owner. Cat-with-the-cream smile, big gestures, have this one on me.

'Finish the bottle, Bobby,' I said.

'Don't you want any?'

'It's yours.'

He made no objections. Poured, drank, and comfortably belched. 'Better go,' he said. 'Got to write up these effing colts in the third. Don't you go telling my editor I watched the second in the bar, I'd get the sack.' He didn't mean it. He saw many a race in the bar. 'See you, Sid. Thanks for the drink.'

He turned with a nod and made a sure passage to the door, showing not a sign of having despatched seven eighths of a bottle of champagne within half an hour. Merely laying the foundations, no doubt. His capacity was phenomenal.

I tucked his magazine inside my jacket and made my own way slowly in his wake, thinking about what he'd said. Passing George Caspar I said, 'Well done,' in the customary politeness of such occasions, and he nodded briefly and said 'Sid,' and, transaction completed, I continued towards the door.

'Sid ...' he called after me, his voice rising.

I turned. He beckoned. I went back.

'Want you to meet Trevor Deansgate,' he said.

I shook the hand offered: snow-white cuff, gold links, smooth pale skin, faintly moist; well-tended nails, onyx and gold signet ring on little finger.

'Your winner?' I said. 'Congratulations.'

'Do you know who I am?'

'Trevor Deansgate?'

'Apart from that.'

It was the first time I'd seen him at close quarters. There was often, in powerful men, a give-away droop of the eyelids which proclaimed an inner sense of superiority, and he had it. Also dark grey eyes, black controlled hair, and the tight mouth which goes with well-exercised decision-making muscles.

'Go on, Sid,' George said into my tiny hesitation. 'If you know, say. I told Trevor you knew everything.'

I glanced at him, but all that was to be read on his tough weathered countenance was a sort of teasing expectancy. For many people, I knew, my new profession was a kind of game. There seemed to be no harm, on this occasion, of jumping obligingly through his offered hoop.

'Bookmaker?' I said tentatively: and to Trever Deansgate directly, added, 'Billy Bones?'

'There you are,' said George, pleased. 'I told you so.'

Trevor Deansgate took it philosophically. I didn't try for a further reaction, which might not have been so friendly. His name at birth was reputed to be Shummuck. Trever Shummuck from Manchester, who'd been born in a slum with a razor mind and changed his name, accent and chosen company on the way up. As Bobby Unwin might have said, hadn't we all, and why not?

Trevor Deansgate's climb to the big league had been all but completed by buying out the old but ailing firm of 'Billy Bones', in itself a blanket pseudonym for some brothers called Rubenstein and their uncle Solly. In the past few years 'Billy Bones' had become big business. One could scarcely open a sports paper or go to the races without seeing the blinding fluorescent pink advertising, and slogans like 'Make no Bones about it, Billy's best' tended to assault one's peace on Sundays. If the business was as vigorous as its sales campaign, Trevor Deansgate was doing all right.

We civilly discussed his winner until it was time to adjourn outside to watch the colts.

'How's Tri-Nitro?' I said to George, as we moved towards the door.

'Great,' he said. 'In great heart.'

'No problems?'

'None at all.'

We parted outside, and I spent the rest of the afternoon in the usual desultory way, watching the races, talking to people, and thinking unimportant thoughts. I didn't see Rosemary again, and calculated she was avoiding me, and after the fifth race I decided to go.

A racecourse official at the exit gate stopped me with an air of relief, as if he'd been waiting for me for a shade too long.

'Note for you, Mr Halley.'

'Oh? Thanks.'

He gave me an unobtrusive brown envelope. I put it in my pocket and walked on, out to my car. Climbed in. Took out, opened, and read the letter.

Sid,

I've been busy all afternoon but I want to see you. Please can you meet me in the tea room? After the last?

Lucas Wainwright

Cursing slightly, I walked back across the car park, through the gate, and along to the restaurant, where lunch had given place to sandwiches and cake. The last race being just finished, the tea customers were trickling in in small thirsty bunches, but there was no sight of Commander Lucas Wainwright, Director of Security to the Jockey Club.

I hung around, and he came in the end, hurrying, anxious apologising and harassed.

'Do you want some tea?' He was out of breath.

'Not much.'

'Never mind. Have some. We can sit here without being interrupted, and there are always too many people in the bar.' He led the way to a table and gestured to me to sit down.

'Look, Sid. How do you feel about doing a job for us?' No waster of time, Commander Wainwright.

'Does "us" mean the Security Service?'

'Yes.'

'Official?' I said, surprised. The Racehorse Security people knew in moderate detail what I'd recently been doing and had raised no objections, but I hadn't imagined they actually approved. In some respects, I'd been working in their territory, and stepping on their toes.

Lucas drummed his fingers on the tablecloth.

'Unofficial,' he said. 'My own private show.'

As Lucas Wainwright was himself the top brass of the Security Service, the investigative, policing arm of the Jockey Club, even unofficial requests from him could be considered to be respectably well-founded. Or at least, until proved otherwise.

'What sort of job?' I said.

The thought of what sort of job slowed him up for the first time. He hummed and hah'ed and drummed his fingers some more, but finally shaped up to what proved to be a brute of a problem.

'Look, Sid, this is in strictest confidence.'

'Yes.'

'I've no higher authority for approaching you like this.'

'Well,' I said. 'Never mind. Go on.'

'As I've no authority, I can't promise you any pay.'

I sighed.

'All I could offer is . . . well . . . help, if you should ever need it. And if it was within my power to give it, of course.'

'That could be worth more than pay,' I said.

He looked relieved. 'Good. Now . . . this is very awkward. Very delicate.' He still hesitated, but at last, with a sigh like a groan, he said 'I'm asking you to make . . . er . . . discreet enquiries into the . . . er . . . background . . . of one of our people.'

There was an instant's silence. Then I said, 'Do you mean one of *you*? One of the Security Service?'

'I'm afraid that's right.'

'Enquiries into exactly what?' I said.

He looked unhappy. 'Bribery. Backhanders. That sort of thing.'

'Um,' I said. 'Have I got this straight? You believe one of your chaps may be collecting pay-offs from villains, and you want me to find out?'

'That's it,' he said. 'Exactly.'

I thought it over. 'Why don't you do the investigating yourselves? Just detail another of your chaps.'

'Ah. Yes.' He cleared his throat. 'But there are difficulties. If I am wrong, I cannot afford to have it known that I was suspicious. It would cause a great, a very great deal of trouble. And if I am right, which I fear I am, we . . . that is, the Jockey Club . . . would want to be able to deal with things quietly. A public scandal involving the Security Service would be very damaging to racing.'

I thought he was perhaps putting it a bit high, but he wasn't.

'The man in question,' he said miserably, 'is Eddy Keith.'

There was another countable silence. In the hierarchy of the Security Service then existing, there was Lucas Wainwright at the top, with two equal deputies one step down. Both of the deputies were retired senior-rank policemen. One of them was ex-Superintendent Eddison Keith.

I had a clear mental picture of him, as I had talked with him often. A big bluff breezy man with a heavy hand for clapping one on the shoulder. More than a trace of Suffolk accent in a naturally loud voice. A large flourishing straw-coloured moustache, fluffy light brown hair through which one could see the pink scalp shining, and fleshy-lidded eyes which seemed always to be twinkling with good humour, and often weren't.

I had glimpsed there occasionally a glint as cold and unmerciful as a crevasse. Very much a matter of sun on ice: pretty but full of traps. One for applying the handcuffs with a cheery smile; that was Eddy Keith.

But crooked ...? I would never have thought so.

'What are the indications?' I said at last.

Lucas Wainwright chewed his lower lip for a while and then said, 'Four of his enquiries over the past year have come up with incorrect results.'

I blinked. 'That's not very conclusive.'

'No. Precisely. If I were sure, I wouldn't be here talking to you.'

'I guess not.' I thought a bit. 'What sort of enquiries were they?'

'They were all syndicates. Enquiries into the suitability of people wanting to form syndicates to own horses. Making sure there weren't any undesirables sneaking into racing through the back door. Eddy gave all-clear reports on four proposed syndicates which do in fact all contain one or more people who would not be allowed through the gates.'

'How do you know?' I said. 'How did you find out?'

He made a face. 'I was interviewing someone last week in connection with a dope charge. He was loaded with spite against a group of people he said had let him down, and he crowed over me that those people all owned horses under false names. He told me the names, and I checked, and the four syndicates which contain them were all passed by Eddy.'

'I suppose,' I said slowly, 'they couldn't possibly be syndicates headed by Lord Friarly?'

He looked depressed. 'Yes, I'm afraid so. Lord Friarly mentioned to me earlier this afternoon that he'd asked you to take a look-see. Told me out of politeness. It just reinforced the idea I'd already had of asking you myself. But I want it kept quiet.'

'So does he,' I said reassuringly. 'Can you let me have Eddy's reports? Or copies of them? And the false and true names of the undesirables?'

He nodded. 'I'll see you get them.' He looked at his watch and stood up, the briskness returning to his manner like an accustomed coat. 'I don't need to tell you ... But do be discreet.'

I joined him on his quick march to the door, where he left me at an even faster pace, sketching the merest wave of farewell. His backview vanished uprightly through the weighing room door, and I took myself out again to my car, reflecting that if I went on collecting jobs at the present rate I would need to call up the troops.

Chapter Three

I telephoned the North London Comprehensive School and asked to speak to Chico Barnes.

'He's teaching judo,' a voice said repressively.

'His class usually ends about now.'

'Wait a minute.'

I waited, driving towards London with my right hand on the wheel and my left round the receiver and a spatter of rain on the windscreen. The car had been adapted for one-handed steering by the addition of a knob on the front face of the wheel's rim: very simple, very effective, and no objections from the police.

'Hullo?'

Chico's voice, cheerful, full even in one single word of his general irreverent view of the world.

'Want a job?' I said.

'Yeah.' His grin travelled distinctly down the line. 'It's been too dead quiet this past week.'

'Can you go to the flat? I'll meet you there.'

'I've got an extra class. They lumbered me. Some other guy's evening class of stout ladies. He's ill. I don't blame him. Where are you 'phoning from?'

'The car. From Kempton to London. I'm calling in at Roehampton, at the limb centre, as it's on the way, but I could be outside your school in . . . say . . . an hour and a half. I'll pick you up. O.K.?'

'Sure,' he said. 'What are you going to the limb centre for?'

'To see Alan Stephenson.'

'He'll have gone home.'

'He said he'd be there, working late.'

'Your arm hurting again?'

'No . . . Matter of screws and such.'

'Yeah,' he said. 'O.K. See you.'

I put the 'phone down with the feeling of satisfaction that Chico nearly always engendered. There was no doubt that as a working companion I found him great: funny, inventive, persistent, and deceptively strong. Many a rogue had discovered too late that young slender Chico with his boyish grin could throw a twenty stone man over his shoulder with the greatest ease.

When I first got to know him he was working, as I was, in the Radnor detective agency, where I had learned my new trade. At one point there had been a chance that I would become first a partner and eventually the owner of that agency, but although Radnor and I had come to an agreement, and had even changed the agency's name to Radnor-Halley, life had delivered an earthquake upheaval and decided things otherwise. It must have been only a day before the partnership agreements were ready to be signed, with finances arranged and the champagne approaching the ice, that Radnor himself sat down for a quiet snooze in his armchair at home, and never woke up.

Back from Canada, as if on stretched elastic, had immediately snapped an unsuspected nephew, brandishing a will in his favour and demanding his rights. He did not, he said forthrightly, want to sell half his inheritance to a one-handed ex-jockey, especially at the price agreed. He himself would be taking over and breathing new life into the whole works. He himself would be setting it all up in new modern offices, not the old crummy bomb-damaged joint in the Cromwell Road, and anyone who didn't like the transfer could vote with his feet.

Most of the old bunch had stayed on into the new order, but Chico had had a blazing row with the nephew and opted for the dole. Without much trouble he had then found the part-time job teaching judo, and the first time I'd asked for his help he'd joined up with enthusiasm. Since then I myself seemed to have become the most regularly employed investigator working in racing, and if Radnor's nephew didn't like it (and he was reputed to be furious) it was just too bad.

Chico bounced out through the swinging glass doors of the school with the lights behind him making a halo round his curly hair. Any resemblance to sainthood stopped precisely there, since the person under the curls was in no way long-suffering, god-fearing or chaste.

He slid into the car, gave me a wide grin, and said, 'There's a pub round the corner with a great set of bristols.'

Resignedly I pulled into the pub's car park, and followed him into the bar. The girl dispensing drinks was, as he'd said, nicely endowed, and moreover greeted Chico with telling warmth. I listened to the flirting chit chat and paid for the drinks.

We sat on a bench by the wall, and Chico approached his pint with the thirst brought on by too much healthy exercise.

'Ah,' he said, putting down the tankard temporarily. 'That's better.' He eyed my glass. 'Is that straight orange juice?'

I nodded. 'Been drinking on and off all day.'

'Don't know how you bear it, all that high life and luxury.'

'Easily.'

'Yeah.' He finished the pint, went back for a refill and another close encounter with the girl, and finally retracked to the bench. 'Where do I go then, Sid? And what do I do?'

'Newmarket. Spot of pub-crawling.'

'Can't be bad.'

'You're looking for a head lad called Paddy Young. He's George

Caspar's head lad. Find out where he drinks, and sort of drift into conversation.'

'Right.'

'We want to know the present whereabouts of three horses which used to be in his yard.'

'We do?'

'He shouldn't have any reason for not telling you, or at least, I don't think so.'

Chico eyed me. 'Why don't you ask George Caspar, right out? Be simpler, wouldn't it?'

'At the moment we don't want George Caspar to know we're asking questions about his horses.'

'Like that, is it?'

'I don't know, really.' I sighed. 'Anyway, the three horses are Bethesda, Gleaner, and Zingaloo.'

'O.K. I'll go up there tomorrow. Shouldn't be too difficult. You want me to ring you?'

'Soon as you can.'

He glanced at me sideways. 'What did the limb man say?'

'Hallo, Sid, nice to see you.'

He made a resigned noise with his mouth. 'Might as well ask questions of a brick wall.'

'He said the ship wasn't leaking and the voyage could go on.'

'Better than nothing.'

'As you say.'

I went to Aynsford, as Charles had known I would, driving down on Saturday afternoon and feeling the apprehensive gloom deepen with every mile. For distraction I concentrated on Chico's news from Newmarket, telephoned through at lunchtime.

'I found him,' he said. 'He's a much-married man who has to take his pay packet home like a good boy on Friday evenings, but he sneaked out for a quick jar just now. The pub's nearly next door to the yard; very handy. Anyway, if you can understand what he says, and he's so Irish it's like talking to a foreigner, what it boils down to is that all three of those horses have gone to stud.'

'Did he know where?'

'Sure. Bethesda went to some place called Garvey's in Gloucestershire, and the other two are at a place just outside Newmarket, which Paddy Young called Traces, or at least I think that's what he said, although as I told you, he chews his words up something horrible.'

'Thrace,' I said. 'Henry Thrace.'

'Yeah? Well, maybe you can make sense of some other things he said, which were that Gleaner had a tritus and Zingaloo had the virus and Bruttersmit gave them both the tums down as quick as Concorde.'

'Gleaner had a what?'

'Tritus.'

I tried turning 'Gleaner had a tritus' into an Irish accent in my head and came up with Gleaner had arthritis, which sounded a lot more likely. I said to Chico, '... and Brothersmith gave them the thumbs down ...'

'Yeah,' he said. 'You got it.'

'Where are you 'phoning from?'

'Box in the street.'

'There's a bit of boozing time left,' I said. 'Would you see if you can find out if this Brothersmith is George Caspar's vet, and if so, look him up in the 'phone book and bring back his address and number.'

'O.K. Anything else?'

'No.' I paused. 'Chico, did Paddy Young give you any impression that there was anything odd in these three horses going wrong?'

'Can't say he did. He didn't seem to care much, one way or the other. I just asked him casual like where they'd gone, and he told me, and threw in the rest for good measure. Philosophical, you could say he was.'

'Right, then,' I said. 'Thanks.'

We disconnected, but he rang again an hour later to tell me that Brothersmith was indeed George Caspar's vet, and to give me his address.

'If that's all, then, Sid, there's a train leaving in half an hour, and I've a nice little dolly waiting for me round Wembley way who'll have her Saturday night ruined if I don't get back.'

The more I thought about Chico's report and Bobby Unwin's comments the less I believed in Rosemary's suspicions; but I'd promised her I would try, and try I still would, for a little while longer. For as long as it took me, anyway, to check up on Bethesda, Zingaloo and Gleaner, and talk to Brothersmith the vet.

Aynsford still looked its mellow stone self, but the daffodil-studded tranquillity applied to the exterior only. I stopped the car gently in front of the house and sat there wishing I didn't have to go in.

Charles, as if sensing that even then I might back off and drive away, came purposefully out of his front door and strode across the gravel. Watching for me, I thought. Waiting. Wanting me to come.

'Sid,' he said, opening my door and stooping down to smile. 'I knew you would.'

'You hoped,' I said.

I climbed out onto my feet.

'All right.' The smile stayed in his eyes. 'Hoped. But I know you.'

I looked up at the front of the house, seeing only blank windows reflecting the greyish sky.

'Is she here?' I said.

He nodded. I turned away, went round to the back of the car, and lugged out my suitcase.

'Come on, then,' I said. 'Let's get it over.'

'She's upset,' he said, walking beside me. 'She needs your understanding.'

I glanced at him and said 'Mm.' We finished the short journey in silence, and went through the door.

Jenny was standing there, in the hall.

I had never got used to the pang of seeing her on the rare occasions we had met since she left. I saw her as I had when I first loved her, a girl not of great classical beauty, but very pretty, with brown curling hair and a neat figure, and a way of holding her head high, like a bird on the alert. The old curving smile and the warmth in her eyes were gone, but I tended to expect them, with hopeless nostalgia.

'So you came,' she said. 'I said you wouldn't.'

I put down the suitcase, and took the usual deep breath. 'Charles wanted me to,' I said. I walked the steps towards her, and as always, we gave each other a brief kiss on the cheek. We had maintained the habit as the outward and public mark of a civilized divorce; but privately, I often thought, it was more like the ritual salute before a duel.

Charles shook his head impatiently at the lack of real affection, and walked ahead of us into the drawing room. He had tried in the past to keep us together, but the glue for any marriage had to come from the inside, and ours had dried to dust.

Jenny said, 'I don't want any lectures from you, Sid, about this beastly affair.'

'No.'

'You're not perfect yourself, even though you like to think so.'

'Give it a rest, Jenny,' I said.

She walked abruptly away into the drawing room, and I more slowly followed. She would use me, I thought, and discard me again, and because of Charles I would let her. I was surprised that I felt no tremendous desire to offer comfort. It seemed that irritation was still well in the ascendancy over compassion.

She and Charles were not alone. When I went in she had crossed the room to stand at the side of a tall blond man whom I'd met before; and beside Charles stood a stranger, a stocky young-old man whose austere eyes were disconcertingly surrounded by a rosy country face.

Charles said in his most ultra-civilized voice, 'You know Toby, don't you Sid?', and Jenny's shield and supporter and I nodded to each other and gave the faint smiles of an acquaintanceship we would each have been happier without. 'And this, Sid, is my solicitor, Oliver Quayle. Gave up his golf to be here. Very good of him.'

'So you're Sid Halley,' the young-old man said, shaking hands. There was nothing in his voice either way, but his gaze slid down and sideways, seeking to see the half-hidden hand that he wouldn't have look at if he hadn't known. It often happened that way. He brought his gaze back to my face and saw that I knew what he'd been doing. There was the smallest flicker in his lower eyelids, but no other remark. Judgement suspended, I thought, on either side.

Charles's mouth twitched, and he said smoothly, 'I warned you, Oliver. If you don't want him to read your thoughts, you mustn't move your eyes.'

'Yours don't move,' I said to him.

'I learned that lesson years ago.'

He made courteous sit-down motions with his hands, and the five of us sank into comfort and pale gold brocade.

'I've told Oliver,' Charles said, 'that if anyone can find this Nicholas Ashe person, you will.

'Frightfully useful, don't you know,' drawled Toby, 'having a plumber in the family, when the pipes burst.'

It was a fraction short of offensiveness. I gave him the benefit of a doubt I didn't have, and asked nobody in particular whether the police wouldn't do the job more quickly.

'The trouble is,' Quayle said, 'that technically it is Jenny alone who is guilty of obtaining money by false pretences. The police have listened to her, of course, and the man in charge seems to be remarkably sympathetic, but ...' He slowly shrugged the heavy shoulders in a way that skilfully combined sympathy and resignation, '... one feels they might choose to settle for the case they have.'

'But I say,' protested Toby, 'it was that Ashe's idea, all of it.'

'Can you prove it?' Quayle said.

'Jenny says so,' Toby said, as if that were proof enough.

Quayle shook his head. 'As I've told Charles, it would appear from all documents that she signed that she did know the scheme was fraudulent. And ignorance, even if genuine, is always a poor, if not impossible, defence.'

I said, 'If there's no evidence against him, what would you do, even if I did find him?'

Quayle looked my way attentively. 'I'm hoping that if you find him, you'll find evidence as well.'

Jenny sat up exceedingly straight and spoke in a voice sharp with perhaps anxiety but certainly anger.

'This is all rubbish, Sid. Why don't you say straight out that the job's beyond you?'

'I don't know if it is.'

'It's pathetic,' she said to Quayle, 'how he longs to prove he's clever, now he's disabled.'

The flicking sneer in her voice shocked Quayle and Charles into visible discomfort, and I thought dejectedly that this was what I'd caused in her, this compulsive need to hurt. I didn't just mind what she'd said, I minded bitterly that because of me she was not showing to Quayle the sunny-tempered person she would still be if I wasn't there.

'If I find Nicholas Ashe,' I said grimly, 'I'll give him to Jenny. Poor fellow.'

None of the men liked it. Quayle looked disillusioned, Toby showed he despised me, and Charles sorrowfully shook his head. Jenny alone, behind her anger, looked secretly pleased. She seldom managed nowadays to goad me into a reply to her insults, and counted it a victory that I'd done it and earned such general disapproval. My own silly fault. There was only one way not to let her see when her barbs went in, and that was to smile ... and the matter in hand was not very funny.

I said, more moderately, 'There might be ways . . . if I can find him. At any rate, I'll do my best. If there's anything I can do . . . I'll do it.'

Jenny looked unplacated, and no one else said anything. I sighed internally. 'What did he look like?' I said.

After a pause Charles said, 'I saw him once only, for about thirty minutes, four months ago. I have a general impression, but that's all. Young, personable, dark haired, clean-shaven. Something too ingratiating in his manner to me. I would not have welcomed him as a junior officer aboard my ship.'

Jenny compressed her lips and looked away from him, but could not protest against this judgement. I felt the first faint stirrings of sympathy for her and tried to stamp on them: they would only make me more vulnerable, which was something I could do without.

I said to Toby, 'Did you meet him?'

'No,' he said loftily. 'Actually, I didn't.'

'Toby has been in Australia,' Charles said, explaining.

They all waited. It couldn't be shirked. I said directly to her, neutrally, 'Jenny?'

'He was *fun*,' she said vehemently, unexpectedly. 'My God, he was fun. And after you . . .' She stopped. Her head swung round my way with bitter eyes. 'He was full of life and jokes. He made me laugh. He was terrific. He lit things up. It was like . . . it was like . . .' She suddenly faltered and stopped, and I knew she was thinking, like us when we first met. Jenny, I thought desperately, don't say it, please don't.

Perhaps it was too much, even for her. How could people, I wondered for the ten thousandth useless time, how could people who had loved so dearly come to such a wilderness; and yet the change in us was irreversible, and neither of us would even search for a way back. It was impossible. The fire was out. Only a few live coals lurked in the ashes, searing unexpectedly at the incautious touch.

I swallowed. 'How tall was he?' I said.

'Taller than you.'

'Age?'

'Twenty-nine.'

The same age as Jenny. Two years younger than I. If he had told the truth, that was. A confidence trickster might lie about absolutely everything as a matter of prudence.

'Where did he stay, while he was . . . er . . . operating?'

Jenny looked unhelpful, and it was Charles who answered. 'He told Jenny he was staying with an aunt, but after he had gone, Oliver and I checked up. The aunt, unfortunately, proved to be a landlady who lets rooms to students in north Oxford. And in any case . . .' he cleared his throat, '. . . it seems that fairly soon he left the lodgings and moved into the flat Jenny is sharing in Oxford with another girl.'

'He lived in your flat?' I said to Jenny.

'So what of it?' She was defiant. And something else . . .

'So when he left, did he leave anything behind?'

'No.'

'Nothing at all?'

'No.'

'Do you want him found?' I said.

To Charles and Quayle and Toby the answer to that question was an automatic yes, but Jenny didn't answer, and the blush that started at her throat rose fast to two bright spots on her cheekbones.

'He's done you great harm,' I said.

With stubbornness stiffening her neck, she said, 'Oliver says I won't go to prison.'

'Jenny!' I was exasperated. 'A conviction for fraud will affect your whole life in all sorts of horrible ways. I see that you liked him. Maybe you even loved him. But he's not just a naughty boy who pinched the jampot for a lark. He has callously arranged for you to be punished in his stead. *That's* the crime for which I'll catch him if I damned well can, even if you don't want me to.'

Charles protested vigorously, 'Sid, that's ridiculous. Of course she wants to see him punished. She agreed that you should try to find him. She wants you to, of course she does.'

I sighed and shrugged. 'She agreed, to please you. And because she doesn't think I'll succeed; and she's very likely right. But even *talk* of my succeeding is putting her in a turmoil and making her angry ... and it's by no means unknown for women to go on loving scoundrels who've ruined them.'

Jenny rose to her feet, stared at me blindly, and walked out of the room. Toby took a step after her and Charles too got to his feet, but I said with some force, 'Mr Quayle, please will you go after her and tell her the consequences if she's convicted. Tell her brutally, make her understand, make it shock.'

He had taken the decision and was on his way after her before I'd finished.

'It's hardly kind,' Charles said. 'We've been trying to spare her.'

'You can't expect Halley to show her any sympathy,' Toby said waspishly.

I eyed him. Not the brightest of men, but Jenny's choice of undemanding escort, the calm sea after the hurricane. A few months earlier she had been thinking of marrying him, but whether she would do it post-Ashe was to my mind doubtful. He gave me his usual lofty look of non-comprehension and decided Jenny needed him at once.

Charles watched his departing back and said, with a tired note of despair, 'I simply don't understand her. And it took you about ten minutes to see ... what I wouldn't have seen at all.' He looked at me gloomily. 'It was pointless, then, to try to reassure her, as I've been doing?'

'Oh Charles, what a bloody muddle.... It won't have done any harm. It's just given her a way of excusing him ... Ashe ... and putting off the time when she'll have to admit to herself that she's made a shattering ... shaming ... mistake.'

The lines in his face had deepened with distress. He said sombrely,

'It's worse. Worse than I thought.'

'Sadder,' I said. 'Not worse.'

'Do you think you can find him?' he said. 'How on earth do you start?'

Chapter Four

I started in the morning, having not seen Jenny again, as she'd driven off the previous evening with Toby at high speed to Oxford, leaving Charles and me to dine alone, a relief to us both; and they had returned late and not appeared for breakfast by the time I left.

I went to Jenny's flat in Oxford, following directions from Charles, and rang the door-bell. The lock, I thought looking at it, would give me no trouble if there was no one in, but in fact after my second ring, the door opened a few inches, on a chain.

'Louise McInnes?' I said, seeing an eye, some tangled fair hair, a bare foot and a slice of dark blue dressing gown.

'That's right.'

'Would you mind if I talked to you? I'm Jenny's ... er ... ex-husband. Her father asked me to see if I could help her.'

'You're Sid?' she said, sounding surprised. 'Sid Halley?'

'Yes.'

'Well ... wait a minute.' The door closed and stayed closed for a good long time. Finally it opened again, this time wide, and the whole girl was revealed. This time she wore jeans, a checked shirt, baggy blue sweater, and slippers. The hair was brushed, and there was lipstick: a gentle pink, unaggressive.

'Come in.'

I went in and closed the door behind me. Jenny's flat, as I would have guessed, was not constructed of plasterboard and held together with drawing pins. The general address was a large Victorian house in a prosperous side street, with a semi-circular driveway and parking room at the back. Jenny's section reached by its own enclosed, latterly added staircase, was the whole of the spacious first floor. Bought, Charles had told me, with some of her divorce settlement. It was nice to see that on the whole my money had been well spent.

Switching on lights, the girl led the way into a large bow-fronted sitting room which still had its curtains drawn and the day before's clutter slipping haphazardly off tables and chairs. Newspapers, a coat, some kicked-off boots, coffee cups, an empty yoghurt carton in a fruit bowl, with spoon, some dying daffodils, a typewriter with its cover off, some scrunched-up pages that had missed the waste-paper basket.

Louise McInnes drew back the curtains, letting in the grey morning to dilute the electricity.

'I wasn't up,' she said unnecessarily.

'I'm sorry.'

The mess was the girl's. Jenny was always tidy, clearing up before bed. But the room itself was Jenny's. One or two pieces from Aynsford, and an overall similarity to the sitting room of our own house, the one we'd shared. Love might change, but taste endured. I felt a stranger, and at home.

'Want some coffee?' she said.

'Only if . . .'

'Sure. I'd have some anyway.'

'Can I help you?'

'If you like.'

She led the way through the hall and into a bare-looking kitchen. There was nothing precisely prickly in her manner, but all the same it was cool. Not surprising, really. What Jenny thought of me, she would say, and there wouldn't be much that was good.

'Like some toast?' She was busy producing a packet of white sliced bread and a jar of powdered coffee.

'Yes I would.'

'Then stick a couple of pieces in the toaster. Over there.'

I did as she said, while she ran some water into an electric kettle and dug into a cupboard for butter and marmalade. The butter was a half-used packet still in its torn greaseproof wrapping, the centre scooped out and the whole thing messy: exactly like my own butter packet in my own flat. Jenny had put butter into dishes automatically. I wondered if she did when she was alone.

'Milk and sugar?'

'No sugar.'

When the toast popped up she spread the slices with butter and marmalade and put them on two plates. Boiling water went onto the brown powder in mugs, and milk followed straight from the bottle.

'You bring the coffee,' she said, 'and I'll take the toast.' She picked up the plates and out of the corner of her eye saw my left hand closing round one of the mugs. 'Look out,' she said urgently, 'that's hot.'

I gripped the mug carefully with the fingers that couldn't feel.

She blinked.

'One of the advantages,' I said, and picked up the other mug more gingerly by its handle.

She looked at my face, but said nothing: merely turned away and went back to the sitting room.

'I'd forgotten,' she said, as I put the mugs on the space she had cleared for them on the low table in front of the sofa.

'False teeth are more common,' I said politely.

She came very near to a laugh, and although it ended up as a doubtful frown, the passing warmth was a glimpse of the true person living behind the slightly brusque facade. She scrunched into the toast and looked thoughtful, and after a chew and a swallow, she said: 'What can you do to help Jenny?'

'Try to find Nicholas Ashe.'

'Oh ...' There was another spontaneous flicker of smile, again quickly stifled by subsequent thought.

'You liked him?' I said.

She nodded ruefully. 'I'm afraid so. He is ... was ... such tremendous fun. Fantastic company. I find it terribly hard to believe he's just gone off and left Jenny in this mess. I mean ... he lived here, here in this flat ... and we had so many laughs ... What he's done ... it's incredible.'

'Look,' I said, 'would you mind starting at the beginning and telling me all about it?'

'But hasn't Jenny ...?'

'No.'

'I suppose,' she said slowly, 'that she wouldn't like admitting to you that he made such a fool of us.'

'How much,' I said, 'did she love him?'

'Love? What's love? I can't tell you. She was *in* love with him.' She licked her fingers. 'All fizzy. Bright and bubbly. Up in the clouds.'

'Have you been there? Up in the clouds?'

She looked at me straightly. 'Do you mean, do I know what it's like? Yes, I do. If you mean, was I in love with Nicky, then no I wasn't. He was fun, but he didn't turn me on like he did Jenny. And in any case, it was she who attracted him. Or at least ...' she finished doubtfully, '... it seemed like it.' She wagged her licked fingers. 'Would you give me that box of tissues that's just behind you?'

I gave her the box and watched her as she wiped off the rest of the stickiness. She had fair eyelashes and English rose skin, and a face that had left shyness behind. Too soon for life to have printed unmistakable signposts; but there did seem, in her natural expression, to be little in the way of cynicism or intolerance. A practical girl, with sense.

'I don't really know where they met,' she said, 'except that it was somewhere here in Oxford. I came back here one day, and he was *here*, if you see what I mean? They were already ... well ... interested in each other.'

'Er,' I said, 'have you always shared this flat with Jenny?'

'More or less. We were at school together ... didn't you know? Well, we met one day and I told her I was going to be living in Oxford for two years while I wrote a thesis, and she said, had I anywhere to stay, because she'd seen this flat, but she'd like some company.... So I came. Like a shot. We've got on fine, on the whole.'

I looked at the typewriter and the signs of effort. 'Do you work here all the time?'

'Here or in the Sheldonian ... er, the library, that is ... or out doing other research. I pay rent to Jenny for my room ... and I don't know why I'm telling you all this.'

'It's very helpful.'

She got to her feet. 'It might be as well for you to see all the stuff. I've put it all in his room ... Nicky's room ... to get it out of sight. It's all too boringly painful, as a matter of fact.'

Again I followed her through the hall, and this time on further down the wide passage, which was recognizably the first-floor landing of the old house.

'That room,' she said, pointing at doors, 'is Jenny's. That's the bathroom. That's my room. And this one at the end was Nicky's.'

'When exactly did he go?' I said walking behind her.

'Exactly? Who knows? Some time on Wednesday. Two weeks last Wednesday.' She opened the white painted door and walked into the end room. 'He was at breakfast, same as usual. I went off to the library, and Jenny caught the train to London to go shopping, and when we both got back, he was gone. Just gone. Everything. Jenny was terribly shocked. Wept all over the place. But of course, we didn't know then that he hadn't just left her, he'd cleared out with all the money as well.'

'How did you find out?'

'Jenny went to the bank on the Friday to pay in the cheques and draw out some cash for postage, and they told her the account was closed.'

I looked round the room. It has thick carpet, Georgian dressing chest, big comfort-promising bed, upholstered armchair, pretty, Jenny-like curtains, fresh white paint. Six large brown boxes of thick cardboard stood in a double stack in the biggest available space; and none of it looked as if it had ever been lived in.

I went over to the chest and pulled out a drawer. It was totally empty. I put my fingers inside and drew them along, and they came out without a speck of dust or grit.

Louise nodded. 'He had dusted. And hoovered, too. You could see the marks on the carpet. He cleaned the bathroom, as well. It was all sparkling. Jenny thought it was nice of him ... until she found out just why he didn't want to leave any trace.'

'I should think it was symbolic,' I said absently.

'What do you mean?'

'Well ... not so much that he was afraid of being traced through hair or fingerprints ... but just that he wanted to feel that he'd wiped himself out of this place. So that he didn't feel he'd left anything of himself here. I mean ... if you want to go back to a place, you subconsciously leave things there, you "forget" them. Well-known phenomenon. So if you subconsciously, as well as consciously, don't want to go back to a place, you may feel impelled to remove even your dust.' I stopped. 'Sorry. Didn't mean to bore you.'

'I'm not bored.'

I said matter-of-factly, 'Where did they sleep?'

'Here.' She looked carefully at my face and judged it safe to proceed. 'She used to come along here. Well ... I couldn't help but know. Most nights. Not always.'

'He never went to her?'

'Funny thing, I never ever saw him go into her room, even in the daytime. If he wanted her, he'd stand outside and call.'

'It figures.'

'More symbolism?' She went to the pile of boxes and opened the topmost. 'The stuff in here will tell you the whole story. I'll leave you to read it . . . I can't stand the sight of it. And anyway, I'd better clean the place up a bit, in case Jenny comes back.'

'You don't expect her, do you?'

She tilted her head slightly, hearing the faint alarm in my voice. 'Are you frightened of her?'

'Should I be?'

'She says you're a worm.' A hint of amusement softened the words.

'Yes, she would,' I said. 'And no, I'm not frightened of her. She just . . . distracts me.'

With sudden vehemence she said, 'Jenny's a super girl.' Genuine friendship, I thought. A statement of loyalties. The merest whiff of challenge. But Jenny, the super girl, was the one I'd married.

I said, 'Yes,' without inflection, and after a second or two she turned and went out of the room. With a sigh I started on the boxes shifting them clumsily and being glad neither Jenny nor Louise was watching. They were large, and although one or two were not as heavy as the others, their proportions were all wrong for gripping electrically.

The top one contained two foot-deep stacks of office-size paper, white, good quality, and printed with what looked like a typewritten letter. At the top of each sheet there was an impressive array of headings, including in the centre, an embossed and gilded coat of arms. I lifted out one of the letters, and began to understand how Jenny had fallen for the trick.

Research into Coronary Disability it said, in engraved lettering above the coat of arms, with, beneath it, the words *Registered Charity*. To the left of the gold embossing there was a list of patrons, mostly with titles, and to the right a list of the charity's employees, one of whom was listed as Jennifer Halley, Executive Assistant. Below her name, in small capital letters, was the address of the Oxford flat.

The letter bore no date and no salutation. It began about a third of the way down the paper and said:

So many families nowadays have had sorrowful first-hand knowledge of the seriousness of coronary artery disease, which even where it does not kill can leave a man unable to continue with a full, strenuous working life.

Much work has already been done in the field of investigation into the causes and possible prevention of this scourge of modern man, but much more remains still to be done. Research funded by Government money being of necessity limited in today's financial climate, it is of the utmost importance that the public should be asked to support directly the essential programmes now in hand in privately run facilities.

We do know, however, that many people resent receiving straightforward fund-raising letters, however worthy the cause, so to aid 'research into Coronary Disability' we ask you to buy something, along the same principle as Christmas cards, the sale of which does so much good work in so many fields. Accordingly the Patrons, after much discussion, have decided to offer for sale a supply of exceptionally fine wax polish, which has been especially formulated for the care of antique furniture.

The wax is packed in quarter-kilo tins, and is of the quality used by expert restorers and museum curators. If you should wish to buy, we are offering the wax at five pounds a tin; and you may be sure that at least threequarters of the revenue goes straight to Research.

The wax will be good for your furniture, your contribution will be good for the cause, and with your help there may soon be significant advances in the understanding and control of this killing disease.

If you should wish to, please send a donation to the address printed above. (Cheques should be made out to Research into Coronary Disability). You will receive a supply of wax immediately, and the gratitude of future heart patients everywhere.

Yours sincerely,
Executive Assistant

I said 'Phew' to myself, and folded the letter and tucked it into my jacket. Sob stuff; the offer of something tangible in return; and the veiled hint that if you didn't cough up it could one day happen to you. And, according to Charles, the mixture had worked.

The second big box contained several thousand white envelopes, unaddressed. The third was half full of mostly handwritten letters on every conceivable type of writing paper; orders for wax, all saying among other things, 'cheque enclosed'.

The fourth contained printed Compliments slips, saying that *Research into Coronary Disability* acknowledged the contribution with gratitude and had pleasure herewith in sending a supply of wax.

The fifth brown box, half empty, and the sixth, unopened and full, contained numbers of flat white boxes about six inches square by two inches deep. I lifted out a white box and looked inside. Contents, one flat round unprinted tin with a firmly screwed-on lid. The lid put up a fight, but I got it off in the end, and found underneath it a soft mid-brown mixture that certainly smelled of polish. I shut it up, returned the tin to its package, and left it out ready to take.

There seemed to be nothing else. I looked into every cranny in the room and down the sides of the armchair, but there wasn't as much as a pin.

I picked up the square white box and went back slowly and quietly towards the sitting room, opening the closed doors one by one, and looking at what they concealed. There had been two which Louise had not identified: one proved to be a linen cupboard, and the other a small unfurnished room containing suitcases and assorted junk.

Jenny's room was decisively feminine; pink and white, frothy with net and frills. Her scent lay lightly in the air, the violent scent of *Mille*. No use remembering the first bottle I'd given her, long ago in Paris. Too much time had passed. I shut the door on the fragrance and the memory and went into the bathroom.

A white bathroom. Huge fluffy towels. Green carpet, green plants.

Looking glass on two walls, light and bright. No visible tooth brushes: everything in cupboards, very tidy. Very Jenny. Roger & Gallet soap.

The snooping habit had ousted too many scruples. With hardly a hesitation I opened Louise's door and put my eyes round, trusting to luck she wouldn't come out into the hall and find me.

Organized mess, I thought. Heaps of papers, and books everywhere. Clothes on chairs. Unmade bed; not surprising, since I'd sprung her out of it.

A washbasin in a corner, no cap on the toothpaste, pair of tights hung to dry. An open box of chocolates. A haphazard scatter on the dressing chest. A tall vase with horsechestnut buds bursting. No smell at all. No long-term dirt, just surface clutter. The blue dressing gown on the floor. Basically the room was furnished much like Ashe's: and one could clearly see where Jenny ended and Louise began.

I pulled my head out and closed the door, undetected, Louise, in the sitting room, had been easily sidetracked in her tidying, and was sitting on the floor intently reading a book.

'Oh, hallo,' she said, looking up vaguely as if she had forgotten I was there. 'Have you finished?'

'There must be other papers,' I said. 'Letters, bills, cash books, that sort of thing.'

'The police took them.'

I sat on the sofa, facing her. 'Who called the police in?' I said. 'Was it Jenny?'

She wrinkled her forehead. 'No. Someone complained to them that the charity wasn't registered.'

'Who?'

'I don't know. Someone who received one of the letters, and checked up. Half those patrons on the letter-head don't exist, and the others didn't know their names were being used.'

I thought, and said, 'What made Ashe bolt just when he did?'

'We don't know. Maybe someone telephoned here to complain, as well. So he went while he could. He'd been gone for a week when the police turned up.'

I put the square white box on the coffee table. 'Where did the wax come from?' I said.

'Some firm or other. Jenny wrote to order it, and it was delivered here. Nicky knew where to get it.'

'Invoices?'

'The police took them.'

'These begging letters ... who got them printed?'

She sighed. 'Jenny, of course. Nicky had some others, just like them, except that they had his name in the space where they put Jenny's. He explained that it was no use sending any more letters with his name and address on, as he'd moved. He was keen, you see, to keep on working for the cause....'

'You bet he was,' I said.

She was half-irritated. 'It's all very well to jeer, but you didn't meet him. You'd have believed him, same as we did.'

I left it. Maybe I would have. 'These letters,' I said. 'Who were they sent to?'

'Nicky had lists of names and addresses. Thousands of them.'

'Have you got them? The lists?'

She looked resigned. 'He took them with him.'

'What sort of people were on them?'

'The sort of people who would own antique furniture and cough up a fiver without missing it.'

'Did he say where he'd got them from?'

'Yes,' she said. 'From the charity's headquarters.'

'And who addressed the letters and sent them out?'

'Nicky typed the envelopes. Yes, don't ask, on my typewriter. He was very fast. He could do hundreds in a day. Jenny signed her name at the bottom of the letters, and I usually folded them and put them in the envelopes. She used to get writers' cramp doing it and Nicky would often help her.'

'Signing her name?'

'That's right. He copied her signature. He did it hundreds of times. You couldn't really tell the difference.'

I looked at her in silence.

'I know,' she said. 'Asking for trouble. But, you see, he made all that hard work with the letters seem such fun. Like a game. He was full of jokes. You don't understand. And then, when the cheques started rolling in, it was so obviously worth the effort.'

'Who sent off the wax?' I said gloomily.

'Nicky typed the addresses on labels. I used to help Jenny stick them on the boxes and seal the boxes with sticky tape, and take them to the post office.'

'Ashe never went?'

'Too busy typing. We used to wheel them round the post office in those shopping bags on wheels.'

'And the cheques ... I suppose Jenny herself paid them in?'

'That's right.'

'How long did all this go on?' I said.

'A couple of months, once the letters were printed and the wax had arrived.'

'How much wax?'

'Oh we had stacks of it, all over the pace. It came in those big brown boxes ... sixty tins in each, ready packed. They practically filled the flat. Actually in the end Jenny wanted to order some more, as we were running very low, but Nicky said no, we'd finish what we had and take a breather before starting again.'

'He meant to stop anyway,' I said.

Reluctantly, she said, 'Yes.'

'How much money,' I said, 'did Jenny bank?'

She looked at me sombrely. 'In the region of ten thousand pounds. Maybe a bit more. Some people sent much more than a fiver. One or two sent a hundred, and didn't want the wax.'

'It's incredible.'

'The money just came pouring in. It still does, every day. But it goes direct to the police from the post office. They'll have a hell of a job sending it all back.'

'What about the box of letters in Ashe's room, saying "cheques enclosed"?'

'Those,' she said, 'are people whose money was banked, and who've been sent the wax.'

'Didn't the police want those letters?'

She shrugged. 'They didn't take them, anyway.'

'Do you mind if I do?'

'Help yourself....'

After I'd fetched them and dumped them in their box by the front door, I went back into the sitting room to ask her another question. Deep in the book again, she looked up without enthusiasm.

'How did Ashe get the money out of the bank?'

'He took a typewritten letter signed by Jenny saying she wanted to withdraw the balance so as to be able to give it to the charity in cash at its annual gala dinner, and also a cheque signed by Jenny for every penny.'

'But she didn't....'

'No. He did. But I've seen the letter and the cheque. The bank gave them to the police. You can't tell it isn't Jenny's writing. Even Jenny can't tell the difference.'

She got gracefully to her feet, leaving the book on the floor. 'Are you going?' she said hopefully. 'I've got so much to do. I'm way behind, because of Nicky.' She went past me into the hall, but when I followed her she delivered another chunk of dismay.

'The banks clerks can't remember Nicky. They pay out cash in thousands for wages every day, because there's so much industry in Oxford. They were used to Jenny in connection with that account, and it was ten days or more before the police asked questions. No one can remember Nicky there at all.'

'He's professional,' I said flatly.

'Every pointer to it, I'm afraid.' She opened the door while I bent down and awkwardly picked up the brown cardboard box, balancing the small white one on top.

'Thank you,' I said, 'for your help.'

'Let me carry that box downstairs.'

'I can do it,' I said.

She looked briefly into my eyes. 'I'm sure you can. You're too damned proud.' She took the box straight out of my arms and walked purposefully away. I followed her, feeling a fool, down the stairs and out onto the tarmac.

'Car?' she said.

'Round the back, but ...'

As well talk to the tide. I went with her, weakly gestured to the Scimitar, and opened the boot. She dumped the boxes inside, and I shut them in.

'Thank you,' I said again. 'For everything.'

The faintest of smiles came back into her eyes.

'If you think of anything that could help Jenny,' I said, 'will you please let me know?'

'If you give me your address.'

I forked a card out of an inner pocket and gave it to her. 'It's on there.'

'All right.' She stood still for a moment with an expression I couldn't read. 'I'll tell you one thing,' she said. 'From what Jenny's said ... you're not a bit what I expected.'

Chapter Five

From Oxford I drove west to Gloucestershire and arrived at Garvey's stud farm at the respectable visiting hour of eleven-thirty, Sunday morning.

Tom Garvey, standing in his stable yard talking to his stud groom, came striding across as I braked to a halt.

'Sid Halley!' he said. 'What a surprise. What do you want?'

I grimaced through the open car window. 'Does everyone think I want something, when they see me?'

'Of course, lad. Best snooper in the business now, so they say. We hear things, you know, even us dim country bumpkins, we hear things.'

Smiling, I climbed out of the car and shook hands with a sixty-year-old near-rogue who was about as far from a dim country bumpkin as Cape Horn from Alaska. A big strong bull of a man, with unshakable confidence, a loud domineering voice and the wily mind of a gypsy. His hand in mine was as hard as his business methods and as dry as his manner. Tough with men, gentle with horses. Year after year he prospered, and if I would have had every foal on the place exhaustively blood-typed before I believed its alleged breeding, I was probably in the minority.

'What are you after, then, Sid?' he said.

'I came to see a mare, Tom. One that you've got here. Just general interest.'

'Oh yes? Which one?'

'Bethesda.'

There was an abrupt change in his expression from half-amusement to no amusement at all. He narrowed his eyes and said brusquely, 'What about her?'

'Well ... has she foaled, for instance?'

'She's dead.'

'*Dead?*'

'You heard, lad. She's dead. You'd better come in the house.'

He turned and scrunched away, and I followed. His house was old and dark and full of stale air. All the life of the place was outside, in fields and foaling boxes and the breeding shed. Inside, a heavy clock ticked loudly into silence, and there was no aroma of Sunday roast.

'In here.'

It was a cross between a dining room and an office: heavy old table and chairs at one end, filing cabinets and sagging armchairs at the other. No attempts at cosmetic decor to please the customers. Sales went on outside, on the hoof.

Tom perched against his desk and I on the arm of one of the chairs: not the sort of conversation for relaxing in comfort.

'Now then,' he said. 'Why are you asking about Bethesda?'

'I just wondered what had become of her.'

'Don't fence with me, lad. You don't drive all the way here out of general interest. What do you want to know for?'

'A client wants to know,' I said.

'What client?'

'If I were working for you,' I said, 'and you'd told me to keep quiet about it, would you expect me to tell?'

He considered me with sour concentration.

'No lad. Guess I wouldn't. And I don't suppose there's much secret about Bethesda. She died foaling. The foal died with her. A colt, it would have been. Small, though.'

'I'm sorry,' I said.

He shrugged. 'It happens sometimes. Not often, mind. Her heart packed up.'

'Heart?'

'Aye. The foal was lying wrong, see, and the mare, she'd been straining longer than was good for her. We got the foal turned inside her once we found she was in trouble, but she just packed it in, sudden like. Nothing we could do. Middle of the night, of course, like it nearly always is.'

'Did you have a vet to her?'

'Aye, he was there, right enough. I called him when we found she'd started, because there was a chance it would be dicey. First foal, and the hear murmur, and all.'

I frowned slightly. 'Did she have a heart murmur when she came to you?'

'Of course she did, lad. That's why she stopped racing. You don't know much about her, do you?'

'No,' I said. 'Tell me.'

He shrugged. 'She came from George Caspar's yard, of course. Her owner wanted to breed from her on account of her two-year-old form, so we bred her to Timberley, which should have given us a sprinter, but there you are, best laid plans, and all that.'

'When did she die?'

'Month ago, maybe.'

'Well, thanks, Tom.' I stood up. 'Thanks for your time.'

He shoved himself off his desk. 'Bit of a tame turn-up for you, asking questions, isn't it? I can't square it with the old Sid Halley, all speed and guts over the fences.'

'Times change, Tom.'

'Aye, I suppose so. I'll bet you miss it though, that roar from the stands when you'd come to the last and bloody well lift your horse over it.' His face echoed remembered excitements. 'By God, lad, that was a sight. Not a nerve in your body ... don't know how you did it.'

I suppose it was generous of him, but I wished he would stop.

'Bit of back luck, losing your hand. Still, with steeplechasing it's always something. Broken backs and such.' We began to walk to the door. 'If you go jump-racing you've got accept the risks.'

'That's right,' I said.

We went outside and across to my car.

'You don't do too badly with that contraption, though, do you, lad? Drive a car, and such.'

'It's fine.'

'Aye, lad.' He knew it wasn't. He wanted me to know he was sorry, and he'd done his best. I smiled at him, got into the car, sketched a thank-you salute, and drove away.

At Aynsford they were in the drawing room, drinking sherry before lunch: Charles, Toby and Jenny.

Charles gave me a glass of fino, Toby looked me up and down as if I'd come straight from a pig sty, and Jenny said she had been talking to Louise on the telephone.

'We thought you had run away. You left the flat two hours ago.'

'Sid doesn't run away,' Charles said, as if stating a fact.

'Limps, then,' Jenny said.

Toby sneered at me over his glass: the male in possession enjoying his small gloat over the dispossessed. I wondered if he really understood the extent of Jenny's attachment to Nicholas Ashe, or if knowing, he didn't care.

I sipped the sherry: a thin dry taste, suitable to the occasion. Vinegar might have been better.

'Where did you buy all that polish from?' I said.

'I don't remember.' She spoke distinctly, spacing out the syllables, wilfully obstructive.

'Jenny!' Charles protested.

I sighed. 'Charles, the police have the invoices, which will have the name and address of the polish firm on them. Can you ask your friend Oliver Quayle to ask the police for the information, and send it to me.'

'Certainly,' he said.

'I cannot see,' Jenny said in the same sort of voice, 'that knowing who supplied the wax will make the slightest difference one way or the other.'

It appeared that Charles privately agreed with her. I didn't explain. There was a good chance, anyway, that they were right.

'Louise said you were prying for ages.'

'I liked her,' I said mildly.

Jenny's nose, as always, gave away her displeasure. 'She's out of your class, Sid,' she said.

'In what way?'

'Brains, darling.'

Charles said smoothly, 'More sherry, anyone?' and, decanter in hand, began refilling glasses. To me, he said, 'I believe Louise took a first at Cambridge in mathematics. I have played her at chess ... you would beat her with ease.'

'A Grand Master,' Jenny said, 'can be obsessional and stupid and have a persecution complex.'

Lunch came and went in the same sort of atmosphere, and afterwards I went upstairs to put my few things into my suitcase. While I was doing it Jenny came into the room and stood watching me.

'You don't use that hand much,' she said.

I didn't answer.

'I don't know why you bother with it.'

'Stop it, Jenny.'

'If you'd done as I asked, and given up racing, you wouldn't have lost it.'

'Probably not.'

'You'd have a hand, not half an arm ... not a stump.'

I threw my spongebag with too much force into the suitcase.

'Racing first. Always racing. Dedication and winning and glory. And me nowhere. It serves you right. We'd still have been married ... you'd still have your hand ... if you'd have given up your precious racing when I wanted you to. Being champion jockey meant more to you than I did.'

'We've said all this a dozen times,' I said.

'Now you've got nothing. Nothing at all. I hope you're satisfied.'

The battery charger stood on a chest of drawers, with two batteries in it. She pulled the plug out of the mains socket and threw the whole thing on the bed. The batteries fell out and lay on the bedspread haphazardly with the charger and its flex.

'It's disgusting,' she said, looking at it. 'It revolts me.'

'I've got used to it.' More or less, anyway.

'You don't seem to care.'

I said nothing. I cared, all right.

'Do you enjoy being crippled, Sid?'

Enjoy ... Jesus Christ.

She walked to the door and left me looking down at the charger. I felt more than saw her pause there, and wondered numbly what else there was left that she could say.

Her voice reached me quite clearly across the room.

'Nicky has a knife in his sock.'

I turned my head fast. She looked both defiant and expectant. 'Is that true?' I asked.

'Sometimes.'

'Adolescent,' I said.

She was annoyed. 'And what's so mature about hurtling around on horses and knowing ... *knowing* ... that pain and broken bones are going to happen?'

'You never think they will.'

'And you're always wrong.'

'I don't do it any more.'

'But you would if you could.'

There was no answer to that, because we both knew it was true.

'And look at you,' Jenny said. 'When you have to stop racing, do you look around for a nice quiet job in stockbroking, which you know about, and start to lead a normal life? No, you damned well don't. You go straight into something which lands you up in fights and beatings and hectic scrambles. You can't live without danger, Sid. You're addicted. You may think you aren't, but it's like a drug. If you just imagine yourself working in an office, nine to five, and commuting like any sensible man, you'll see what I mean.'

I thought about it, silently.

'Exactly,' she said. 'In an office, you'd die.'

'And what's so safe about a knife in the sock?' I said. 'I was a jockey when we met. You knew what it entailed.'

'Not from the inside. Not all those terrible bruises, and no food and no drink, and no damned sex half the time.'

'Did he show you the knife, or did you just see it?'

'What does it matter?'

'Is he adolescent ... or truly dangerous?'

'There you are,' she said. 'You'd prefer him dangerous.'

'Not for your sake.'

'Well ... I saw it. In a little sheath, strapped to his leg. And he made a joke about it.'

'But you told me,' I said. 'So was it a warning?'

She seemed suddenly unsure and disconcerted, and after a moment or two simply frowned and walked away down the passage.

If it marked the first crack in her indulgence towards her precious Nicky, so much the better.

I picked Chico up on Tuesday morning and drove north to Newmarket. A windy day, bright, showery, rather cold.

'How did you get on with the wife, then?'

He had met her once and had described her as unforgettable, the overtones in his voice giving the word several meanings.

'She's in trouble,' I said.

'Pregnant?'

'There are other forms of trouble, you know.'

'Really?'

I told him about the fraud, and about Ashe, and his knife.

'Gone and landed herself in a whoopsy,' Chico said.

'Face down.'

'And for dusting her off, do we get a fee?'

I looked at him sideways.

'Yeah,' he said. 'I thought so. Working for nothing again, aren't we? Good job you're well-oiled, Sid, mate, when it comes to my wages. What is it this year? You made a fortune in anything since Christmas?'

'Silver, mostly. And cocoa. Bought and sold.'

'Cocoa?' He was incredulous.

'Beans,' I said. 'Chocolate.'

'Nutty bars?'

'No, not the nuts. They're risky.'

'I don't know how you find the time.'

'It takes as long as chatting up barmaids.'

'What do you want with all that money, anyway?'

'It's a habit,' I said. 'Like eating.'

Amicably we drew nearer to Newmarket, consulted the map, asked a couple of locals, and finally arrived at the incredibly well-kept stud farm of Henry Thrace.

'Sound out the lads,' I said, and Chico said 'Sure', and we stepped out of the car onto weedless gravel. I left him to it and went in search of Henry Thrace, who was reported by a cleaning lady at the front door of the house to be 'down there on the right, in his office'. Down there he was, in an armchair, fast asleep.

My arrival woke him, and he came alive with the instant awareness of people used to broken nights. A youngish man, very smooth, a world away from rough, tough, wily Tom Garvey. With Thrace, according to predigested opinion, breeding was strictly big business: handling the mares could be left to lower mortals. His first words, however, didn't match the image.

'Sorry. Been up half the night . . . Er, who are you, exactly? Do we have an appointment?'

'No.' I shook my head. 'I just hoped to see you. My name's Sid Halley.'

'Is it? Any relation to . . . Good Lord. You're him.'

'I'm him.'

'What can I do for you? Want some coffee?' He rubbed his eyes. 'Mrs Evans will get us some.'

'Don't bother, unless . . .'

'No. Fire away.' He looked at his watch. 'Ten minutes do? I've got a meeting in Newmarket.'

'It's very vague, really,' I said. 'I just came to enquire into the general health and so on of two of the stallions you've got here.'

'Oh. Which two?'

'Gleaner,' I said. 'And Zingaloo.'

We went through the business of why did I want to know, and why should he tell me, but finally, like Tom Garvey, he shrugged and said I might as well know.

'I suppose I shouldn't say it, but you wouldn't want to advise a client to buy shares in either of them,' he said, taking for granted this was really the purpose of my visit. 'They might have difficulty in covering their full quota of mares, both of them, although they're only four.'

'Why's that?'

'They've both got bad hearts. They get exhausted with too much exercise.'

'Both?'

'That's right. That's what stopped them racing as three-year-olds. And I reckon they've got worse since then.'

'Somebody mentioned Gleaner was lame,' I said.

Henry Thrace looked resigned. 'He's developed arthritis recently. You can't keep a damn thing to yourself in this town.' An alarm clock made a clamour on his desk. He reached over and switched it off. 'Time to go, I'm afraid.' He yawned. 'I hardly take my clothes off at this time of the year.' He took a battery razor out of his desk drawer, and attacked his beard. 'Is that everything then, Sid?'

'Yes,' I said. 'Thanks.'

Chico pulled the car door shut, and we drove away towards the town.

'Bad hearts,' he said.

'Bad hearts.'

'Proper epidemic, isn't it?'

Let's ask Brothersmith the vet.'

Chico read out the address, in Middleton Road.

'Yes, I know it. It was old Follett's place. He was our old vet, still alive when I was here.'

Chico grinned. 'Funny somehow to think of you being a snotty little apprentice with the head lad chasing you.'

'And chilblains.'

'Makes you seem almost human.'

I had spent five years in Newmarket, from sixteen to twenty-one. Learning to ride, learning to race, learning to live. My old guv'nor had been a good one, and because I saw every day his wife, his lifestyle, and his administrative ability, I'd slowly changed from a boy from the backstreets into something more cosmopolitan. He had shown me how to manage the money I'd begun earning in large quantities, and how not to be corrupted by it; and when he turned me loose I found he'd given me the status that went with having been taught in his stable. I'd been lucky in my guv'nor, and lucky to be for a long time at the top of the career I loved; and if one day the luck had run out it was too damned bad.

'Takes you back, does it?' Chico said.

'Yeah.'

We drove across the wide Heath and past the racecourse towards the town. There weren't many horses about: a late morning string, in the distance, going home. I swung the car round familiar corners and pulled up outside the vet's.

Mr Brothersmith was out.

If it was urgent, Mr Brothersmith could be found seeing to a horse in a stable along Bury Road. Otherwise he would be home to his lunch, probably, in half an hour. We said thank you, and sat in the car, and waited.

'We've got another job,' I said. 'Checking on syndicates.'

'I thought the Jockey Club always did it themselves.'

'Yes, they do. The job we've got is to check on the man from the Jockey Club who checks on the syndicates.'

Chico digested it. 'Tricky, that.'

'Without him knowing.'

'Oh yes?'

I nodded. 'Ex-Superintendent Eddy Keith.'

Chico's mouth fell open. 'You're joking.'

'No.'

'But he's the fuzz. The Jockey Club fuzz.'

I passed on Lucas Wainwright's doubts, and Chico said Lucas Wainwright must have got it wrong. The job, I pointed out, mildly, was to find out whether he had or not.

'And how do we do that?'

'I don't know. What do you think?'

'It's you that's supposed to be the brains of this outfit.'

A muddy Range Rover came along Middleton Road, and turned into Brothersmith's entrance. As one, Chico and I removed ourselves from the Scimitar, and went towards the tweed-jacketed man jumping down from his buggy.

'Mr Brothersmith?'

'Yes? What's the trouble?'

He was young and harassed, and kept looking over his shoulder, as if something was chasing him. Time, perhaps, I thought. Or lack of it.

'Could you spare us a few minutes?' I said. 'This is Chico Barnes, and I'm Sid Halley. It's just a few questions ...'

His brain took in the name and his gaze switched immediately towards my hands, fastening finally on the left.

'Aren't you the man with the myoelectric prosthesis?'

'Er ... yes.' I said.

'Come in, then, Can I look at it?'

He turned away and strode purposefully towards the side door of the house. I stood still and wished we were anywhere else.

'Come on, Sid,' Chico said, following him. He looked back and stopped. 'Give the man what he wants, Sid, and maybe he'll do the same for us.'

Payment in kind, I thought: and I didn't like the price. Unwillingly I followed Chico into what turned out to be Brothersmith's surgery.

He asked a lot of questions in a fairly clinical manner, and I answered him in impersonal tones learned from the limb centre.

'Can you rotate the wrist?' he said at length.

'Yes, a little.' I showed him. 'There's a sort of cup inside there which fits over the end of my arm, with another electrode to pick up the impulses for turning.'

I knew he wanted me to take the arm off and show him properly, but I wouldn't have done it, and perhaps he saw there was no point in asking.

'It fits very tightly over your elbow,' he said, delicately feeling round the gripping edges.

'So as not to fall off.'

He nodded intently. 'Is it easy to put on and remove?'

'Talcum powder,' I said economically.

Chico's mouth opened, and shut again as he caught my don't-say-it stare, and he didn't tell Brothersmith that removal was often a distinct bore.

'Thinking of fitting one to a horse?' Chico said.

Brothersmith raised his still-harassed face and answered him seriously. 'Technically it looks perfectly possible, but it's doubtful if one could train a horse to activate the electrodes, and it would be difficult to justify the expense.'

'It was only a joke,' Chico said faintly.

'Oh? Oh, I see. But it isn't unknown, you know, for a horse to have a false foot fitted. I was reading the other day about a successful prosthesis fitted to the fore-limb of a valuable broodmare. She was subsequently covered, and produced a live foal.'

'Ah,' Chico said. 'Now that's what we've come about. A broodmare. Only this one died.'

Brothersmith detached his attention reluctantly from false limbs and transferred it to horses with bad hearts.

'Bethesda,' I said, rolling down my sleeve and buttoning the cuff.

'Bethesda?' He wrinkled his forehead and turned the harassed look into one of anxiety. 'I'm sorry. I can't recall . . .'

'She was a filly with George Caspar,' I said. 'Beat everything as a two-year-old, and couldn't run at three because of a heart murmur. She was sent to stud, but her heart packed up when she was foaling.'

'Oh dear,' he said, adding sorrow to the anxiety. 'What a pity. But I say, I'm so sorry, but I treat so many horses, and I often don't know their names. Is there a question of insurance in this, or negligence, even? Because I assure you . . .'

'No,' I said reassuringly, 'nothing like that. Can you remember, then, treating Gleaner and Zingaloo?'

'Yes, of course. Those two. Wretched shame for George Caspar. So disappointing.'

'Tell us about them.'

'Nothing much to tell, really. Nothing out of the ordinary, except that they were both so good as two-year-olds. Probably that was the cause of their troubles, if the truth were told.'

'How do you mean?' I said.

His nervous tensions escaped in small jerks of his head as he brought forth some unflattering opinions. 'Well, one hesitates to say so, of course, to top trainers like Caspar, but it is all too easy to strain a two-year-old's heart, and if they are good two-year-olds they run in top races, and the pressure to win may be terrific, because of stud values and everything, and a jockey, riding strictly to orders, mind you, may press a game youngster so hard that although it wins it is also more or less ruined for the future.'

'Gleaner won the Doncaster Futurity in the mud,' I said thoughtfully. 'I saw it. It was a very hard race.'

'That's right,' Brothersmith said. 'I checked him thoroughly afterwards, though. The trouble didn't start at once. In fact, it didn't show at all, until he ran in the Guineas. He came in from that in a state of complete exhaustion. First of all we thought it was the virus but then after a few days we got this very irregular heart beat, and then it was obvious what was the matter.'

'What virus?' I said.

'Let's see . . . The evening of the Guineas he had a very slight fever, as if he were in for equine 'flu, or some such. But it didn't develop. So it wasn't that. It was his heart, all right. But we couldn't have foreseen it.'

'What percentage of horses develop bad hearts?' I said.

Some of the chronic anxiety state diminished as he moved confidently onto neutral ground.

'Perhaps ten per cent have irregular heart beats. It doesn't always mean anything. Owners don't like to buy horses which have them, but look at Night Nurse which won the Champion Hurdle, that had a heart murmur.'

'But how often do you get horses having to stop racing because of bad hearts?'

He shrugged. 'Perhaps two or three in a hundred.'

George Caspar, I reflected, trained upwards of a hundred and thirty horses, year after year.

'On average,' I said, 'are George Caspar's horses more prone to bad hearts than any other trainer's?'

The anxiety state returned in full force. 'I don't know if I should answer that.'

'If it's "no",' I said, 'what's the hassle?'

'But your purpose in asking . . .'

'A client,' I said, lying with regrettable ease, 'wants to know if he should send George Caspar a sparkling yearling. He asked me to check on Gleaner and Zingaloo.

'Oh, I see. Well, no, I don't suppose he has more. Nothing significant. Caspar's an excellent trainer, of course. If your client isn't too greedy when his horse is two, there shouldn't be any risk at all.'

'Thanks, then.' I stood up and shook hands with him. 'I suppose there's no heart trouble with Tri-Nitro?'

'None at all. Sound, through and through. His heart bangs away like a gong, loud and clear.'

Chapter Six

'That's that, then,' Chico said over a pint and pie in the White Hart Hotel. 'End of case. Mrs Caspar's off her tiny rocker, and no one's been getting at George Caspar's youngsters except George Caspar himself.'

'She won't be pleased to hear it,' I said.

'Will you tell her?'

'Straight away. If she's convinced, she might calm down.'

'So I telephoned to George Caspar's house, and asked for Rosemary, saying I was a Mr Barnes. She came on the line and said hallo in the questioning voice one uses to unknown callers.

'Mr . . . Barnes?'

'It's Sid Halley.'

The alarm came instantly. 'I can't talk to you.'

'Can you meet me, then?'

'Of course not. I've no reason for going to London.'

'I'm just down the road, in the town,' I said. 'I've things to tell you. And I don't honestly think there's any need for disguises and so on.'

'I'm not being seen with you in Newmarket.'

She agreed, however, to drive out in her car, pick Chico up, and go where he directed: and Chico and I worked out a place on the map which looked a tranquillizing spot for paranoiacs. The churchyard at Barton Mills, eight miles towards Norwich.

We parked the cars side by side at the gate and Rosemary walked with me among the graves she was wearing again the fawn raincoat and a scarf, but not this time the false curls. The wind blew wisps of her own chestnut hair across her eyes, and she pulled them away impatiently: not with quite as much tension as when she had come to my flat, but still with more force than was needed.

I told her I had been to see Tom Garvey and Henry Thrace at their stud farms. I told her I had talked to Brothersmith; and I told her what they'd all said. She listened, and shook her head.

'The horses were nobbled,' she said obstinately. 'I'm sure they were.'

'How?'

'I don't know how.' Her voice rose sharply, the agitation showing in spasms of the muscles round her mouth. 'But I told you, I told you, they'll get at Tri-Nitro. A week today, it's the Guineas. You've got to keep him safe for a week.'

We walked along the path beside the quiet mounds and the grey weatherbeaten headstones. The grass was mown, but there were no flowers, and no mourners. The dead there were long gone, long forgotten. Raw grief and tears now in the municipal plot outside the town; brown heaps of earth and brilliant wreaths and desolation in tidy rows.

'George has doubled the security on Tri-Nitro,' I said.

'I know that. Don't be stupid.'

I said reluctantly, 'In the normal course of events he'll be giving Tri-Nitro some strong work before the Guineas. Probably on Saturday morning.'

'I suppose so. What do you mean? Why do you ask?'

'Well ...' I paused, wondering if indeed it would be sensible to suggest a way-out theory without testing it, and thinking that there was no way of testing it anyway.

'Go on,' she said sharply. 'What do you mean?'

'You could ... er ... make sure he takes all sorts of precautions when he gives Tri-Nitro that last gallop.' I paused. 'Inspect the saddle ... that sort of thing.'

Rosemary said fiercely, 'What are you saying? Spell it out, for God's sake. Don't pussyfoot round it.'

'Lots of races have been lost because of too-hard training gallops too soon beforehand.'

'Of course,' she said impatiently. 'Everyone knows that. But George would never do it.'

'What if the saddle was packed with lead? What if a three-year-old was given a strong gallop carrying fifty pounds dead weight? And then ran under severe pressure a few days later in the Guineas? And strained his heart?'

'My God,' she said. 'My God.'

'I'm not saying that it did happen to Zingaloo and Gleaner, or anything like it. Only that it's a distant possibility. And if it's something like that ... it must involve someone inside the stable.'

She had begun trembling again.

'You must go on,' she said. 'Please go on trying. I brought some money for you.' She plunged a hand into her raincoat pocket and brought out a smallish brown envelope. 'It's cash. I can't give you a cheque.'

'I haven't earned it,' I said.

'Yes, yes. Take it.' She was insistent, and finally I put it in my pocket, unopened.

'Let me consult George,' I said.

'No. He'd be furious. I'll do it ... I mean, I'll warn him about the gallops. He thinks I'm crazy, but if I go on about it long enough he'll take notice.' She looked at her watch and her agitation increased. 'I'll have to go back now. I said I was going for a walk on the Heath. I never do that. I'll have to get back, or they'll be wondering.'

'Who'll be wondering?'

'George, of course.'

'Does he know where you are every minute of the day?'

We were retracing our steps with some speed towards the churchyard gates. Rosemary looked as if she would soon be running.

'We always talk. He asks where I've been. He's not suspicious ... it's just a habit. We're always together. Well, you know what it's like in a racing household. Owners come at odd times. George likes me to be there.'

We reached the cars. She said goodbye uncertainly, and drove off homewards in a great hurry. Chico, waiting in the Scimitar, said, 'Quiet here, isn't it. Even the ghosts must find it boring.'

I got into the car and tossed Rosemary's envelope onto his lap. 'Count that,' I said, starting the engine. 'See how we're doing.'

He tore it open, pulled out a neat wad of expensive-coloured banknotes, and licked his fingers.

'Phew,' he said, coming to the end. 'She's bonkers.'

'She wants us to go on.'

'Then you know what this is, Sid,' he said, flicking the stack.

'Guilt money. To spur you on when you want to stop.'

'Well it works.'

We spent some of Rosemary's incentive in staying overnight in Newmarket and going round the bars, Chico where the lads hung out and I with the trainers. It was Tuesday evening and very quiet everywhere. I heard nothing of any interest and drank more than enough whisky, and Chico came back with hiccups and not much else.

'Ever heard of Inky Poole?' he said.

'Is that a song?'

'No, it's a work jockey. What's a work jockey? Chico my son, a work jockey is a lad who rides work on the gallops.'

'You're drunk,' I said.

'Certainly not. What's a work jockey?'

'What you just said. No much good in races but can gallop the best at home.'

'Inky Poole,' he said, 'is George Caspar's work jockey. Inky Poole rides Tri-Nitro his strong work at home on the gallops. Did you ask me to find out who rides Tri-Nitro's gallops?'

'Yes, I did,' I said. 'And you're drunk.'

'Inky Poole, Inky Poole', he said.

'Did you talk to him?'

'Never met him. Bunch of the lads, they told me. George Caspar's work jockey. Inky Poole.'

Armed with raceglasses on a strap round my neck I walked along to Warren Hill at seven-thirty in the morning to watch the strings out at morning exercise. A long time, it seemed, since I'd been one of the tucked-up figures in sweaters and skull cap, with three horses to muck out and care for, and a bed in a hostel with rain-soaked breeches for ever drying on an airer in the kitchen. Frozen fingers and not enough baths, ears full of four-letter words and no chance of being alone.

I had enjoyed it all well enough, when I was sixteen, on account of the horses. Beautiful, marvellous creatures whose responses and instincts worked on a plane as different from humans' as water and oil, not mingling even where they touched. Insight into their senses and consciousness had been like an opening door, a foreign language glimpsed and half learned, full comprehension maddeningly baulked by not having the right sort of hearing or sense of smell, nor sufficient skill in telepathy.

The feeling of oneness with horses I'd sometimes had in the heat of a race had been their gift to an inferior being; and maybe my passion for winning had been my gift to them. The urge to get to the front was born in them; all they needed was to be shown where and when to go. It could fairly be said that like most jump jockeys I had aided and abetted horses beyond the bounds of common sense.

The smell and sight of them on the Heath was like a sea breeze to a sailor. I filled my lungs and eyes, and felt content.

Each exercise string was accompanied and shepherded by its watchful trainer, some of them arriving in cars, some on horseback, some on foot. I collected a lot of 'Good morning, Sid's. Several smiling faces seemed genuinely pleased to see me; and some that weren't in a hurry stopped to talk.

'Sid!' exclaimed one I'd ridden on the flat for in the years before my weight caught up with my height, 'Sid, we don't see you up here much these days.'

'My loss,' I said, smiling.

'Why don't you come and ride out for me? Next time, you're here, give me a ring, and we'll fix it.'

'Do you mean it?'

'Of course I mean it. If you'd like to, that is.'

'I'd love it.'

'Right. That's great. Don't forget, now.' He wheeled away, waving, to shout to a lad earning his disfavour by slopping in the saddle like a disorganized jellyfish. 'How the bloody hell d'you expect your horse to pay attention if you don't?' The boy sat decently for all of twenty seconds. He'd go far, I thought, starting from Newmarket station.

Wednesday being a morning for full training gallops, there was the usual scattering of interested watchers: owners, pressmen, and assorted bookmakers' touts. Binoculars sprouted like an extra growth of eyes, and notes went down in private shorthand. Though the morning was cold the new season was warming up. There was a feeling overall of purpose, and the bustle of things happening. An industry flexing its muscles. Money, profit, and tax revenue making their proper circle under the wide Suffolk sky. I was still a part of it, even if not in the old way. And Jenny was right. I'd die in an office.

'Morning, Sid.'

I looked round. George Caspar, on a horse, his eyes on a distant string walking down the side of the Heath from his stable in Bury Road.

'Morning, George.'

'You staying up here?'

'Just for a night or two.'

'You should've let us know. We've always a bed. Give Rosemary a ring.' His eyes were on his string: the invitation a politeness, not meant to be accepted. Rosemary, I thought, would have fainted if she'd heard.

'Is Tri-Nitro in that lot?' I said.

'Yes, he is. Sixth from the front.' He looked round at the interested spectators. 'Have you seen Trevor Deansgate anywhere? He said he was coming up here this morning from London. Setting off early.'

'Haven't seen him.' I shook my head.

'He's got two in the string. He was coming to see them work.' He shrugged. 'He'll miss them if he isn't here soon.'

I smiled to myself. Some trainers might delay working the horses until the owner did arrive, but not George. Owners queued up for his favours and treasured his comments, and Trevor Deansgate for all his power was just one of a crowd. I lifted my raceglasses and watched while the string, forty strong, approached and began circling, waiting for their turn on the uphill gallop. The stable before George's had nearly finished, and George would be next.

The lad on Tri-Nitro wore a red scarf in the neck of his olive-green husky jacket. I lowered my glasses and kept my eye on him as he circled, and looked at his mount with the same curiosity as everyone else. A good-looking bay colt, well grown, with strong shoulders and a lot of heart room; but nothing about him to shout from the housetops that here was the wildly backed winter favourite for the Guineas and the Derby. If you hadn't known, you wouldn't have known, as they say.

'Do you mind photographs, George?' I said.

'Help yourself, Sid.'

'Thanks.'

I seldom went anywhere these days without a camera in my pocket. Sixteen millimetre, automatic light meter, all the expense in its lens. I brought it out and showed it to him, and he nodded. 'Take what you like.'

He shook up his patient hack and went away, across to the string, to begin the morning's business. The lad who rode a horse down from the stables wasn't necessarily the same one who rode it in fast work, and as usual there was a good deal of swapping around, to put the best lads up where it mattered. The boy with the red scarf dismounted from Tri-Nitro and held him, and presently a much older lad swung up onto his back.

I walked across to be close to the string, and took three or four photographs of the wonder horse and a couple of closer shots of his rider.

'Inky Poole?' I said to him at one point, as he rode by six feet away.

'That's right,' he said. 'Mind your back. You're in the way.'

A right touch of surliness. If he hadn't seen me talking to George first, he would have objected to my being there at all. I wondered if his grudging against-the-world manner was the cause or the result of his not getting on as a jockey, and felt sympathy for him, on the whole.

George began detailing his lads into the small bunches that would go up the gallops together, and I walked back to the fringes of things, to watch.

A car arrived very fast and pulled up with a jerk, alarming some horses alongside and sending them skittering, with the lads' voices rising high in alarm and protest.

Trevor Deansgate climbed out of his Jaguar and for good measure slammed the door. He was dressed in a city suit, in contrast to everyone else there, and looked ready for the boardroom. Black hair rigorously brushed, chin smoothly shaven, shoes polished like glass. Not the sort of man I would have sought as a friend, because I didn't on the whole like to sit at the feet of power, picking up crumbs of patronage with nervous laughter, but a force to be reckoned with on the racing scene.

Big scale bookmakers could be and often were a positive influence for good, a stance I thought sardonically that they had been pushed into, to survive the lobby that knew that a Tote monopoly (and a less greedy tax climate) would put back into racing what bookmakers took out. Trevor Deansgate personified the new breed; urbane, a man of the world, seeking top company, becoming a name in the City, the sycophant of earls.

'Hallo,' he said, seeing me. 'I met you at Kempton ... Do you know where George's horses are?'

'Right there,' I said, pointing. 'You're just in time.'

'Bloody traffic.'

He strode across the grass towards George, raceglasses swinging from his hand, and George said hallo briefly and apparently told him to watch the gallops with me, because he came straight back, heavy and confident, and stopped at my side.

'George says my two both go in the first bunch. He said you'd tell me how they're doing, insolent bugger. Got eyes, haven't I? He's going on up the hill.'

I nodded. Trainers often went up half way and watched from there, the better to see their horses' action as they galloped past.

Four horses were wheeling into position at the starting point. Trevor Deansgate applied his binoculars, twisting them to focus. Navy suiting with faint red pinstripes. The well-kept hands, gold cuff links, onyx ring, as before.

'Which are yours?' I said.

'The two chestnuts. That one with the white socks is Pinafore. The other's nothing much.'

The nothing much had short cannon bones and a rounded rump. Might make a 'chaser one day, I thought. I liked the look of him better than the whippet-shaped Pinafore. They set off together up the gallop at George's signal, and the sprinting blood showed all the way to the top. Pinafore romped it and the nothing much lived up to his owner's assessment. Trevor Deansgate lowered his binoculars with a sigh.

'That's that, then. Are you coming to George's for breakfast?'

'No. Not today.'

He raised the glasses again and focussed them on the much nearer target of the circling string, and, from the angle, he was looking at the riders, not the horses. The search came to an end on Inky Poole: he lowered the glasses and followed Tri-Nitro with the naked eye.

'A week today,' I said.

'Looks a picture.'

I supposed that he, like all bookmakers, would be happy to see the hot favourite lose the Guineas, but there was nothing in his voice except admiration for a great horse. Tri-Nitro lined up in his turn and at a signal from George set off with two companions at a deceptively fast pace. Inky Poole, I was interested to see, sat as quiet as patience and rode with a skill worth ten times what he would be paid. Good work jockeys are undervalued. Bad ones could ruin a horse's mouth and temperament and whole career. It figured that for the stableful he'd got, George Caspar would employ only the best.

It was not the flat-out searching gallop they would hold on the following Saturday morning over a long smooth surface like the Limekilns. Up the incline of Warren Hill a fast canter was testing enough. Tri-Nitro took the whole thing without a hint of effort, and breasted the top as if he could go up there six times more without noticing.

Impressive, I thought. The Press, clearly agreeing, were scribbling in their notebooks. Trever Deansgate looked thoughtful, as well he might, and George Caspar, coming down the hill and reining in near us, looked almost smugly satisfied. The Guineas, one felt, were in the bag.

After they had done their work the horses walked down the hill to join the still circling string where the work riders changed onto fresh mounts and set off again up to the top. Tri-Nitro got back his lad with the olive-green husky and the red scarf, and eventually the whole lot of them set off home.

'That's that, then,' George said. 'All set, Trevor? Breakfast?'

They nodded farewells to me and set off, one in the car, one on the horse. I had eyes mostly, however, for Inky Poole, who had been four times up the hill and was walking off a shade morosely to a parked car.

'Inky,' I said, coming up behind him, 'the gallop on Tri-Nitro ... that was great.'

He looked at me sourly. 'I've got nothing to say.'

'I'm not from the press.'

'I know who you are. Saw you racing. Who hasn't?' Unfriendly: almost a sneer. 'What do you want?'

'How does Tri-Nitro compare with Gleaner, this time last year?'

He fished the car keys out of a zipper pocket in his anorak, and fitted one into the lock. What I could see of his face looked obstinately unhelpful.

'Did Gleaner, a week before the Guineas, give you the same sort of feel?' I said.

'I'm not talking to you.'

'How about Zingaloo?' I said. 'Or Bethesda?'

He opened his car door and slid down into the driving seat, taking out time to give me a hostile glare.

'Piss off,' he said. Slammed the door. Stabbed the ignition key into the dashboard and forcefully drove away.

Chico had arisen to breakfast but was sitting in the pub's dining room holding his head.

'Don't look so healthy,' he said when I joined him.

'Bacon and eggs,' I said. 'That's what I'll have. Or kippers, perhaps. And strawberry jam.'

He groaned.

'I'm going back to London,' I said. 'But would you mind staying here?' I brought the camera out of my pocket. 'Take the film out of that and get it developed. Overnight if possible. There's some pictures of Tri-Nitro and Inky Poole on there. We might find them helpful, you never know.'

'O.K., then,' he said. 'But you'll have to ring up the Comprehensive and tell them that my black belt's at the cleaners.'

I laughed. 'There were some girls riding in George Caspar's string this morning,' I said. 'See what you can do.'

'That's beyond the call of duty.' But his eye seemed suddenly bright. 'What am I asking?'

'Things like who saddles Tri-Nitro for exercise gallops, and what's the routine from now until next Wednesday, and whether anything nasty is stirring in the jungle.'

'What about you, then?'

'I'll be back Friday night,' I said. 'In time for the gallops on Saturday. They're bound to gallop Tri-Nitro on Saturday. A strong work-out, to bring him to a peak.'

'Do you really think anything dodgy's going on?' Chico said.

'A toss-up. I just don't know. I'd better ring Rosemary.'

I went through the Mr Barnes routine again and Rosemary came on the line sounding as agitated as ever.

'I can't talk. We've got people here for breakfast.'

'Just listen, then,' I said. 'Try to persuade George to vary his routine, when he gallops Tri-Nitro on Saturday. Put up a different jockey, for instance. Not Inky Poole.'

'You don't think ...' her voice was high, and broke off.

'I don't know at all,' I said. 'But if George changed everything about, there'd be less chance of skulduggery. Routine is the robber's best friend.'

'What? Oh yes. All right. I'll try. What about you?'

'I'll be out watching the gallop. After that, I'll stick around, until after the Guineas is safely over. But I wish you'd let me talk to George.'

'No. He'd be livid. I'll have to go now.' The receiver went down with a rattle which spoke of still unsteady hands, and I feared that

George might be right about his wife being neurotic.

Charles and I met as usual at the Cavendish the following day, and sat in the upstairs bar's armchairs.

'You look happier,' he said, 'than I've seen you since ...' he gestured to my arm, with his glass. 'Released in spirit. Not your usual stoical self.'

'I've been in Newmarket,' I said. 'Watched the gallops, yesterday morning.'

'I would have thought ...' he stopped.

'That I'd be eaten by jealousy?' I said. 'So would I. But I enjoyed it.'

'Good.'

'I'm going up again tomorrow night and staying until after the Guineas next Wednesday.'

'And lunch, next Thursday?'

I smiled and bought him a large pink gin. 'I'll be back for that.'

In due course we ate scallops one-handedly in a wine and cheese sauce, and he gave me the news of Jenny.

'Oliver Quayle sent the address you asked for, for the polish.' He took a paper from his breast pocket and handed it over. 'Oliver is worried. He says the police are actively pursuing their enquiries, and Jenny is almost certain to be charged.'

'When?'

'I don't know. Oliver doesn't know. Sometimes these things take weeks, but not always. And when they charge her, Oliver says, she will have to appear in a magistrate's court, and they are certain to refer the case to the Crown Court, as so much money is involved. They'll give her bail, of course.'

'Bail!'

'Oliver says she is unfortunately very likely to be convicted, but that if it is stressed that she acted as she did under the influence of Nicholas Ashe, she'll probably get some sympathy from the judge and a conditional discharge.'

'Even if he isn't found?'

'Yes. But of course if he *is* found, and charged, and found guilty, Jenny would with luck escape a conviction altogether.'

I took a deep breath that was half a sigh.

'Have to find him then, won't we?' I said.

'How?'

'Well ... I spent a lot of Monday, and all of this morning looking through a box of letters. They came from the people who sent money, and ordered wax. Eighteen hundred of them, or thereabouts.'

'How do they help?'

'I've started sorting them into alphabetical order, and making a list.' He frowned sceptically, but I went on. 'The interesting thing is that all the surnames start with the letters L, M, N and O. None from A to K, and none from P to Z.'

'I don't see ...'

'They might be part of a mailing list,' I said. 'Like for a catalogue. Or even a charity. There must be thousands of mailing lists, but this one certainly did produce the required results, so it wasn't a mailing list for dog licence reminders, for example.'

'That seem reasonable,' he said dryly.

'I thought I'd get all the names into order and then see if anyone, like Christie's or Sotheby's, say – because of the polish angle – has a mailing list which matches. A long shot, I know, but there's just a chance.'

'I could help you,' he said.

'It's a boring job.'

'She's my daughter.'

'All right then. I'd like it.'

I finished the scallops and sat back in my chair, and drank Charles's good cold white wine.

He said he would stay overnight in his club and come to my flat in the morning to help with the sorting, and I gave him a spare key to get in with, in case I should be out for a newspaper or cigarettes when he came. He lit a cigar and watched me through the smoke. 'What did Jenny say to you upstairs after lunch on Sunday?'

I looked at him briefly. 'Nothing much.'

'She was moody all day, afterwards. She even snapped at Toby.' He smiled. 'Toby protested, and Jenny said "At least Sid didn't whine."' He paused. 'I gathered that she'd been giving you a particularly rough mauling, and was feeling guilty.'

'It wouldn't be guilt. With luck, it was misgivings about Ashe.'

'And not before time.'

From the Cavendish I went to the Portman Square headquarters of the Jockey Club, to keep an appointment made that morning on the telephone by Lucas Wainwright. Unofficial my task for him might be, but official enough for him to ask me to his office. Ex-Superintendent Eddy Keith, it transpired, had gone to Yorkshire to look into a positive doping test, and no one else was going to wonder much at my visit.

'I've got all the files for you,' Lucas said. 'Eddy's reports on the syndicates, and some notes on the rogues he O.K.'d.'

'I'll make a start then,' I said. 'Can I take them away, or do you want me to look at them here?'

'Here, if you would,' he said. 'I don't want to draw my secretary's attention to them by letting them out or getting them xeroxed, as she works for Eddy too, and I know she admires him. She would tell him. You'd better copy down what you need.'

'Right,' I said.

He gave me a table to one side of his room, and a comfortable chair, and a bright light, and for an hour or so I read and made notes. At his own desk he did some desultory pen-pushing and rustled a few papers, but in the end it was clear that it was only a pretence of being busy. He wasn't so much waiting for me to finish as generally uneasy.

I looked up from my writing. 'What's the matter?' I said.

'The . . . matter?'

'Something's troubling you.'

He hesitated. 'Have you done all you want?' he said, nodding at my work.

'Only about half,' I said. 'Can you give me another hour?'

'Yes, but . . . Look, I'll have to be fair with you. There's something you'll have to know.'

'What sort of thing?'

Lucas, who was normally urbane even when in a hurry, and whose naval habits of thought I understood from long practice with my Admiral father-in-law, was showing signs of embarrassment. The things that acutely embarrassed naval officers were collisions between warships and quaysides, ladies visiting the crew's mess deck with the crew present and at ease, and dishonourable conduct among gentlemen. It couldn't be the first two; so where were we with the third?

'I have not perhaps given you all the facts,' he said.

'Go on, then.'

'I did send someone else to check on two of the syndicates, some time ago. Six months ago.' He fiddled with some paperclips, no longer looking in my direction. 'Before Eddy checked them.'

'With what result?'

'Ah. Yes.' He cleared his throat. 'The man I sent – his name's Mason – we never received his report because he was attacked in the street before he could write it.'

Attacked in the street. . . . 'What sort of attack?' I said. 'And who attacked him?'

He shook his head. 'Nobody knows who attacked him. He was found on the pavement by some passer-by, who called the police.'

'Well . . . have you asked him – Mason?' But I guessed at something of the answer, if not all of it.

'He's, er, never really recovered,' Lucas said regretfully. 'His head, it seemed, had been repeatedly kicked, as well as his body. There was a good deal of brain damage. He's still in an institution. He always will be. He's a vegetable . . . and he's blind.'

I bit the end of the pencil with which I'd been making notes. 'Was he robbed?' I said.

'His wallet was missing. But not his watch.' His face was worried.

'So it might have been a straightforward mugging?'

'Yes . . . except that the police treated it as intended homicide, because of the number and target of the boot marks.'

He sat back in his chair as if he'd got rid of an unwelcome burden. Honour among gentlemen . . . honour satisfied.

'All right,' I said. 'Which two syndicates was he checking?'

'The first two that you have there.'

'And do you think any of the people on them – the undesirables – are the sort to kick their way out of trouble?'

He said unhappily, 'They might be.'

'And am I,' I said carefully, 'investigating the possible corruption of Eddy Keith, or Mason's semi-murder?'

After a pause, he said, 'Perhaps both.'

There was a long silence. Finally I said, 'You do realize that by sending me notes at the races and meeting me in the tearoom and bringing me here, you haven't left much doubt that I'm working for you?'

'But it could be at anything.'

I said gloomily, 'Not when I turn up on the syndicates' doorsteps.'

'I'd quite understand,' he said, 'if, in view of what I've said, you wanted to . . . er . . .'

So would I, I thought. I would understand that I didn't want my head kicked in. But then what I'd told Jenny was true: one never thought it would happen. And you're always wrong, she'd said.

I sighed. 'You'd better tell me about Mason. Where he went, and who he saw. Anything you can think of.'

'It's practically nothing. He went off in the ordinary way and the next we heard was he'd been attacked. The police couldn't trace where he'd been, and all the syndicate people swore they'd never seen him. The case isn't closed of course, but after six months it's got no sort of priority.'

We talked it over for a while, and I spent another hour after that writing notes. I left the Jockey Club premises at a quarter to six, to go back to the flat; and I didn't get there.

Chapter Seven

I went home in a taxi and paid it off outside the entrance to the flats, yet not exactly outside, because a dark car was squarely parked there on the double yellow lines, which was a towing-away place.

I scarcely looked at the car, which was my mistake, because as I reached it and turned away towards the entrance its nearside doors opened and spilled out the worst sort of trouble.

Two men in dark clothes grabbed me. One hit me dizzyingly on the head with something hard and the other flung what I later found was a kind of lasso of thick rope over my arms and chest and pulled it tight. They both bundled me into the back of the car where one of them for good measure tied a dark piece of cloth over my dazed half-shut eyes.

'Keys,' a voice said. 'Quick. No one saw us.'

I felt them fumbling in my pockets. There was a clink as they found what they were looking for. I began to come back into focus, so to speak, and to struggle, which was a reflex action but all the same another mistake.

The cloth over my eyes was reinforced by a sickly-smelling wad over my nose and mouth. Anaesthetic fumes made a nonsense of consciousness, and the last thing I thought was that if I was going the way of Mason they hadn't wasted any time.

I was aware, first of all, that I was lying on straw.

Straw, as in stable. Rustling when I tried to move. Hearing, as always, had returned first.

I had been concussed a few times over the years, in racing falls. I thought for a while that I must have come off a horse, though I couldn't remember which, or where I'd been riding.

Funny.

The unwelcome news came back with a rush. I had not been racing. I had one hand. I had been abducted in daylight from a London street. I was lying on my back on some straw, blindfolded, with a rope tied tight round my chest, above the elbows, fastening my upper arms against my body. I was lying on the knot. I didn't know why I was there ... and had no great faith in the future.

Damn, damn, *damn.*

My feet were tethered to some immovable object. It was black dark, even round the edges of the blindfold. I sat up and tried to get some part of me disentangled; a lot of effort and no results.

Ages later, there was a tramp of footsteps outside on a gritty surface, and the creak of a wooden door, and sudden light on the sides of my nose.

'Stop trying, My Halley,' a voice said. 'You won't undo those knots with one hand.'

I stopped trying. There was no point in going on.

'A spot of overkill,' he said, enjoying himself. 'Ropes *and* anaesthetic *and* blackjack *and* blindfold. Well, I did tell them of course, to be careful, and not to get within hitting distance of that tin arm. A villain I know has very nasty things to say about you hitting him with what he didn't expect.'

I knew the voice. Undertones of Manchester, overtones of all the way up the social ladder. The confidence of power.

Trevor Deansgate.

Last seen on the gallops at Newmarket, looking for Tri-Nitro in the string, and identifying him because he knew the work jockey, which most people didn't. Deansgate, going to George Caspar's for breakfast. Bookmaker Trevor Deansgate had been a question mark, a possibility, someone to be assessed, looked into. Something I would have done, and hadn't done yet.

'Take the blindfold off,' he said. 'I want him to see me.'

Fingers took their time over untying the tight piece of cloth. When it fell away, the light was temporarily dazzling; but the first thing I saw was the double barrel of a shotgun pointing my way.

'Guns too,' I said sourly.

It was a storage barn, not a stable. There was a stack of several tons of staw bales to my left, and on the right, a few yards away, a tractor. My feet were fastened to the trailer bar of a farm roller. The barn had a high roof, with beams; and one meagre electric light, which shone on Trevor Deansgate.

'You're too bloody clever for your own good,' he said. 'You know what they say? If Halley's after you, watch out. He'll sneak up on you when you think he doesn't know you exist, and they'll be slamming the cell doors on you before you've worked it out.'

I didn't say anything. What could one say? Especially sitting trussed up like a fool at the wrong end of a shotgun.

'Well, I'm not waiting for you, do you see?' he said. 'I know how bloody close you are to getting me nicked. Just laying your snares, weren't you? Just waiting for me to fall into your hands, like you've caught so many others.' He stopped and reconsidered what he'd said. 'Into your hand,' he said, 'and that fancy hook.'

He had a way of speaking to me that acknowledged mutual origins, that we'd both come a long way from where we'd started. It was not a matter of accent, but of manner. There was no need for social pretence. The message was raw, and between equals, and would be understood.

He was dressed, as before, in a City suit. Navy; chalk pin stripe this time; Gucci tie. The well-manicured hands held the shotgun with the expertise of many a weekend on country estates. What did it matter, I thought, if the finger that pulled the trigger was clean and cared for. What did it matter if his shoes were polished ... I looked at the silly details because I didn't want to think about death.

He stood for a while without speaking: simply watching. I sat without moving, as best I could, and thought about a nice safe job in a stockbroker's office.

'No bloody nerves, have you?' he said. 'None at all.'

I didn't answer.

The other two men were behind me to the right, out of my sight. I could hear their feet as they occasionally shuffled on the straw. Far too far away for me to reach.

I was wearing what I had put on for lunch with Charles. Grey trousers, socks, dark brown shoes; rope extra. Shirt, tie, and a recently bought blazer, quite expensive. What did that matter? If he killed me, Jenny would get the rest. I hadn't changed my will.

Trevor Deansgate switched his attention to the men behind me.

'Now listen,' he said, 'and don't snarl it up. Get these two pieces of rope and tie one to his left arm and one to the right. And watch out for any tricks.'

He lifted the gun a fraction until I could see down the barrels. If he shot from there, I thought, he would hit his chums. It didn't after all look like straight execution. The chums were busy tying bits of rope to both of my wrists.

'Not the left wrist, you stupid bugger,' Trevor Deansgate said. 'That one comes right off. Use your bloody head. Tie it high, above his elbow.'

The chum in question did as he said and pulled the knots tight, and almost casually picked up a stout metal bar, like a crowbar, standing their gripping it as if he thought that somehow I could liberate myself like Superman and still attack him.

Crowbar.... Nasty shivers of apprehension suddenly crawled all over my scalp. There had been another villain, before, who had known where to hurt me most, the one who had hit my already useless left hand with a poker, and turned it from a ruin into a total loss. I had had regrets enough since, and all sorts of private agonies, but I hadn't realized, until that sickening moment, how much I valued what remained. The muscles that worked the electrodes, they at least gave me the semblance of a working hand. If they were injured again I wouldn't have even that. As for the elbow itself... if he wanted to put me out of effective action for a long time, he had only to use that crowbar.

'You don't like that, do you, Mr Halley?' Trevor Deansgate said.

I turned my head back to him. His voice and face were suddenly full of a mixture of triumph and satisfaction, and what seemed like relief.

I said nothing.

'You're sweating,' he said.

He had another order for the chums. 'Untie that rope round his chest. And do it carefully. Hold onto the ropes on his arms.'

They untied the knot, and pulled the constricting rope away from round my chest. It didn't make much difference to my chances of escape. They were wildly exaggerating my ability in a fight.

'Lie down,' he said to me; and when I didn't at once comply, he said 'Push him down,' to the chums. One way or another, I ended on my back.

'I don't want to kill you,' he said. 'I could dump your body somewhere, but there would be too many questions. I can't risk it. But if I don't kill you, I've got to shut you up. Once and for all. Permanently.'

Short of killing me I didn't see how he could do it; and I was stupid.

'Pull his arm sideways, away from his body,' he said.

The pull on my left arm had a man's weight behind it and was stronger than I was. I rolled my head that way and tried not to beg, not to weep.

'Not that one, you bloody fool,' Trevor Deansgate said. 'The other one. The right one. Pull it out, to this side.'

The chum on my right used all his strength on the rope and hauled so that my arm finished straight out sideways, at right angles to my body, palm upwards.

Trevor Deansgate stepped towards me and lowered the gun until the black holes of the barrel were pointing straight at my stretched right wrist. The he carefully lowered the barrel another inch, making direct contact on my skin, pressing down against the straw-covered floor. I could feel the metal rims hard across the bones and nerves and sinews. Across the bridge to a healthy hand.

I heard the click as he cocked the firing mechanism. One blast from a twelve bore would take off most of the arm.

A dizzy wave of faintness drenched all my limbs with sweat.

Whatever anyone said, I intimately knew about fear. Not fear of any horse, or of racing, or falling, or of ordinary physical pain. But of humiliation and rejection and helplessness and failure ... all of those.

All the fear I'd ever felt in all my life was as nothing compared with the liquefying, mind-shattering disintegration of that appalling minute. It broke me in pieces. Swamped me. Brought me down to a morass of terror, to a whimper in the soul. And instinctively, hopelessly, I tried not to let it show.

He watched motionlessly through unccountable intensifying silent seconds. Making me wait. Making it worse.

At length he took a deep breath and said, 'As you see, I could shoot off your hand. Nothing easier. But I'm probably not going to. Not today.' He paused. 'Are you listening?'

I nodded the merest fraction. My eyes were full of gun.

His voice came quietly, seriously, giving weight to every sentence. 'You can give me your assurance that you'll back off. You'll do nothing more which is directed against me, in any way, ever. You'll go to France tomorrow morning, and you'll stay there until after the Guineas. After that, you can do what you like. But if you break your assurance ... well, you're easy to find. I'll find you, and I'll blow your right hand off. I mean it, and you'd better believe it. Some time or other. You'd never escape it. Do you understand?'

I nodded, as before. I could feel the gun as if it were hot. Don't let him, I thought. Dear God, don't let him.

'Give me your assurance. Say it.'

I swallowed painfully. Dredged up a voice. Low and hoarse. 'I give it.'

'You'll back off.'

'Yes.'

'You'll not come after me again, ever.'

'No.'

'You'll go to France and stay there until after the Guineas.'

'Yes.'

Another silence lengthened for what seemed a hundred years, while I stared beyond my undamaged wrist to the dark side of the moon.

He took the gun away, in the end. Broke it open. Removed the cartridges. I felt physically, almost uncontrollably sick.

He knelt on his pin-striped knees beside me and looked closely at whatever defence I could put into an unmoving face and expressionless eyes. I could feel the treacherous sweat trickling down my cheek. He nodded, with grim satisfaction.

'I knew you couldn't face that. Not the other one as well. No one could. There's no need to kill you.'

He stood up again and stretched his body, as if relaxing a wound-up inner tension. The he put his hands into various pockets, and produced things.

'Here are your keys. Your passport. Your cheque book. Credit cards.' He put them on a straw bale. To the chums, he said. 'Untie him, and drive him to the airport. To Heathrow.'

Chapter Eight

I flew to Paris and stayed right there where I landed, in an airport hotel, with no impetus or heart to go further. I stayed for six days, not leaving my room, spending most of the time by the window, watching the aeroplanes come and go.

I felt stunned. I felt ill. Disorientated and overthrown and severed from my own roots. Crushed into an abject state of mental misery, knowing that this time I really had run away.

It was easy to convince myself that logically I had had no choice but to give Deansgate his assurance, when he asked for it. If I hadn't, he would have killed me anyway. I could tell myself, as I continually did, that sticking to his instructions had been merely common sense: but the fact remained that when the chums decanted me at Heathrow they had driven off at once, and it had been of my own free will that I'd bought my ticket, waited in the departure lounge, and walked to the aircraft.

There had been no one there with guns to make me do it. Only the fact that Deansgate had truly said I couldn't face losing the other one. I couldn't face even the risk of it. The thought of it, like a conditioned response, brought out the sweat.

As the days passed, the feeling I had had of disintegration seemed not to fade but to deepen.

The automatic part of me still went on working: walking, talking, ordering coffee, going to the bathroom. In the part that mattered there was turmoil and anguish and a feeling that my whole self had been literally smashed in those few cataclysmic minutes on the straw.

Part of the trouble was that I knew my weaknesses too well. Knew that if I hadn't had so much pride it wouldn't have destroyed me so much to have lost it.

To have been forced to realize that my basic view of myself had been an illusion was proving a psychic upheaval like an earthquake, and perhaps it wasn't surprising that I felt I had, I really had, come to pieces.

I didn't know that I could face that, either.

I wished I could sleep properly, and get some peace.

When Wednesday came I thought of Newmarket and of all the brave hopes for the Guineas.

Thought of George Caspar, taking Tri-Nitro to the test, producing him proudly in peak condition and swearing to himself that this time nothing could go wrong. Thought of Rosemary, jangling with nerves, willing the horse to win and knowing it wouldn't. Thought of Trevor Deansgate, unsuspected, moving like a mole to vandalize, somehow, the best colt in the kingdom.

I could have stopped him, if I'd tried.

Wednesday for me was the worst day of all, the day I learned about despair and desolation and guilt.

On the sixth day, Thursday morning, I went down to the lobby and bought an English newspaper.

They had run the Two Thousand Guineas, as scheduled.

Tri-Nitro had started hot favourite at even money: and he had finished last.

I paid my bill and went to the airport. There were aeroplanes to everywhere, to escape in. The urge to escape was very strong. But wherever one went, one took oneself along. From oneself there was no escape. Wherever I went, in the end I would have to go back.

If I went back in my split-apart state I'd have to live all the time on two levels. I'd have to behave in the old way, which everyone would expect. Have to think and drive and talk and get on with life. Going back meant all that. It also meant doing all that, and proving to myself that I could do it, when I wasn't the same inside.

I thought that what I had lost might be worse than a hand. For a hand there were substitutes which could grip and look passable. But if the core of oneself had crumbled, how could one manage at all?

If I went back, I would have to try.

If I couldn't try, why go back?

It took me a long, lonely time to buy a ticket to Heathrow.

I landed at midday, made a brief telephone call to the Cavendish, to ask them to apologize to the Admiral because I couldn't keep our date, and took a taxi home.

Everything, in the lobby, on the stairs, and along the landing looking the same and yet completely different. It was I who was different. I put the key in the lock and turned it, and went into the flat.

I had expected it to be empty but before I'd even shut the door I heard a rustle in the sitting room, and then Chico's voice. 'Is that you, Admiral?'

I simply didn't answer. In a brief moment his head appeared, questioning, and after that, his whole self.

'About time too,' he said. He looked, on the whole, relieved to see me.

'I sent you a telegram.'

'Oh sure. I've got it here, propped on the shelf. *Leave Newmarket and go home stop shall be away for a few days will telephone*. What sort of telegram's that? Sent from Heathrow, early Friday. You been on holiday?'

'Yeah.'

I walked past him, into the sitting room. In there it didn't look at all the same. There were files and papers everywhere, on every surface, with coffee-marked cups and saucers holding them down.

'You went away without the charger,' Chico said. 'You never do that, even overnight. The spare batteries are all here. You haven't been able to move that hand for six days.'

'Let's have some coffee.'

'You didn't take any clothes, or your razor.'

'I stayed in a hotel. They had throwaway razors, if you asked. What's all this mess?'

'The polish letters.'

'What?'

'You know. The polish letters. Your wife's spot of trouble.'

'Oh . . .'

I stared at it blankly.

'Look,' Chico said. 'Cheese on toast? I'm starving.'

'That would be nice.' It was unreal. It was all unreal.

He went into the kitchen and started banging about. I took the dead battery out of my arm and put in a charged one. The fingers opened and closed, like old times. I had missed them more than I would have imagined.

Chico brought the cheese on toast. He ate his, and I looked at mine. I'd better eat it, I thought, and didn't have the energy. There was the sound of the door of the flat being opened with a key, and after that, my father-in-law's voice from the hall.

'He didn't turn up at the Cavendish, but he did at least leave a message.' He came into the room from behind where I sat and saw Chico nodding his head my direction.

'He's back,' Chico said. 'The boy himself.'

'Hallo, Charles,' I said.

He took a long slow look. Very controlled, very civilized. 'We have, you know, been worried.' It was a reproach.

'I'm sorry.'

'Where have you been?' he said.

I found I couldn't tell him. If I told him where, I would have to tell him why, and I shrank from why. I just didn't say anything at all.

Chico gave him a cheerful grin. 'Sid's got a bad attack of the brick walls.' He looked at his watch. 'Seeing that you're here, Admiral, I might as well get along and teach the little bleeders at the Comprehensive how to throw their grannies over their shoulders. And, Sid, before I go, there's about fifty messages on the 'phone pad. There's two new insurance investigations waiting to be done, and a guard job. Lucas Wainwright wants you, he's rung four times. And Rosemary Caspar has been screeching fit to blast the eardrums. It's all there, written down. See you, then. I'll come back here later.'

I almost asked him not to, but he'd gone.

'You've lost weight,' Charles said.

It wasn't surprising. I looked again at the toasted cheese and decided that coming back also had to include things like eating.

'Want some?' I said.

He eyed the congealing square. 'No thank you.'

Nor did I. I pushed it away. Sat and stared into space. 'What's happened to you?' he said.

'Nothing.'

'Last week you came into the Cavendish like a spring,' he said. 'Bursting with life. Eyes actually sparkling. And now look at you.'

'Well, don't,' I said. 'Don't look at me. How are you doing with the letters?'

'Sid ...'

'Admiral.' I stood up restlessly, to escape his probing gaze. 'Leave me alone.'

He paused, considering, then said, 'You've been speculating in commodities, recently. Have you lost your money, is that it?

I was surprised almost to the point of amusement.

'No,' I said.

He said, 'You went dead like this before, when you lost your career and my daughter. So what have you lost this time, if it isn't money? What could be as bad ... or worse?'

I knew the answer. I'd learned it in Paris, in torment and shame. My whole mind formed the word *courage* with such violent intensity that I was afraid it would leap out of its own accord from my brain to his.

He showed no sign of receiving it. He was still waiting for a reply.

I swallowed. 'Six days,' I said neutrally. 'I've lost six days. Let's get on with tracing Nicholas Ashe.'

He shook his head in disapproval and frustration, but began to explain what he'd been doing.

'This thick pile is from people with names beginning with M. I've put them in strictly alphabetical order, and typed out a list. It seemed to me we might get results from one letter only ... are you paying attention?'

'Yes.'

'I took the list to Christie's and Sotheby's, as you suggested, and persuaded them to help. But the M section of their catalogue mailing list is not the same as this one. And I found that there may be difficulties with this matching, as so many envelopes are addressed nowadays by computers.'

'You've worked hard,' I said.

'Chico and I have been sitting here in shifts, answering your telephone and trying to find out where you'd gone. Your car was still here, in the garage, and Chico said you would never have gone anywhere of your own accord without the battery charger for your arm.'

'Well ... I did.'

'Sid ...'

'No,' I said. 'What we need now is a list of periodicals and magazines dealing with antique furniture. We'll try those first with the M people.'

'It's an awfully big project,' Charles said doubtfully. 'And even if we do find it, what then? I mean, as the man at Christie's pointed out, even if we find whose mailing list was being used, where does it get us? The firm or magazine wouldn't be able to tell us which of the many people who had access to the list was Nicholas Ashe, particularly as he is almost certain not to have used that name if he had any dealings with them.'

'Mm,' I said. 'But there's a chance he's started operating again somewhere else, and is still using the same list. He took it with him, when he went. If we can find out whose list it is, we might go and call on some people who are on it, whose names start with A to K, and P to Z, and find out if they've received any of those begging letters recently. Because if they have, the letters will have the address on, to which the money is to be sent. And there, at that address, we might find Mr Ashe.'

Charles put his mouth into the shape of a whistle, but what came out was more like a sigh.

'You've come back with your brains intact, anyway,' he said.

Oh God, I thought, I'm making myself think to shut out the abyss. I'm in splinters.... I'm never going to be right again. The analytical reasoning part of my mind might be marching straight on, but what had to be called the soul was sick and dying.

'And there's the polish,' I said. I still had in my pocket the paper he'd given me the week before. I took it out and put it on the table. 'If the idea of special polish is closely geared to the mailing list, then to get maximum results the polish is necessary. There can't be many private individuals ordering so much wax in unprinted tins packed in little white boxes. We could ask the polish firm to let us know if another lot is ordered. It's just faintly possible that Ashe will use the same firm again, even if not at once. He ought to see the danger ... but he might be a fool.'

I turned away wearily. Thought about whisky. Went over and poured myself a large one.

'Drinking heavily, are you?' Charles said from behind me, in his most offensive drawl.

I shut my teeth hard, and said 'No.' Apart from coffee and water, it was the first drink for a week.

'Your first alcoholic blackout, was it, these last few days?'

I left the glass untouched on the drinks tray and turned round. His eyes were at their coldest, as unkind as in the days when we'd first met.

'Don't be so bloody stupid,' I said.

He lifted his chin a fraction. 'A spark,' he said sarcastically. 'Still got your pride, I see.'

I compressed my lips and turned my back on him, and drank a lot of the Scotch. After a bit I deliberately loosened a few tensed-up muscles, and said, 'You won't find out that way. I know you too well. You use insults as a lever, to sting people into opening up. You've done it to me in the past. But not this time.'

'If I find the right sting,' he said, 'I'll use it.'

'Do you want a drink?' I said.

'Since you ask, yes.'

We sat opposite each other in armchairs in unchanged companionship, and I thought vaguely of this and that and shied away from the crucifying bits.

'You know,' I said. 'We don't have to go trailing that mailing list around to see whose it is. All we do is ask the people themselves. Those ...' I nodded towards the M stack. 'We just ask some of them what mailing lists they themselves are on. We'd only need to ask a few ... the common denominator would be certain to turn up.'

When Charles had gone home to Aynsford I wandered aimlessly round the flat, tie off and in shirtsleeves, trying to be sensible. I told myself that nothing much had happened, only that Trevor Deansgate had used a lot of horrible threats to get me to stop doing something that I hadn't yet started. But I couldn't dodge the guilt. Once he'd revealed himself, once I knew he would do *something*, I could have stopped him, and I hadn't.

If he hadn't got me so effectively out of Newmarket I would very likely have still been prodding unproductively away, unsure even if there was anything to discover, right up to the moment in the Guineas when Tri-Nitro tottered in last. But I would also be up there now, I thought, certain and inquisitive; and because of his threat, I wasn't.

I could call my absence prudence, commonsense, the only possible course in the circumstances. I could rationalize and excuse. I could say I wouldn't have been doing anything that wasn't already being done by the Jockey Club. I came back, all the time, to the swingeing truth, that I wasn't there now because I was afraid to be.

Chico came back from his judo class and set to again to find out where I'd been; and for the same reasons I didn't tell him, even though I knew he wouldn't despise me as I despised myself.

'All right,' he said finally. 'You just keep it all bottled up and see where it gets you. Wherever you've been, it was bad. You've only got to look at you. It's not going to do you any good to shut it all up inside.'

Shutting it all up inside, however, was a lifelong habit, a defence learned in childhood, a wall against the world, impossible to change.

I raised at least half a smile. 'You setting up in Harley Street?'

'That's better,' he said. 'You missed all the fun, did you know? Tri-Nitro got stuffed after all in the Guineas yesterday, and they're turning George Caspar's yard inside out. It's all here, somewhere, in the *Sporting Life*. The Admiral brought it. Have you read it?'

I shook my head.

'Our Rosemary, she wasn't bonkers after all, was she? How do you think they managed it?'

'They?' I said.

'Whoever did it.'

'I don't know.'

'I went along to see the gallop on Saturday morning,' he said. 'Yeah, yeah, I know you sent the telegram about leaving, but I'd got a real little dolly lined up for a bit of the other on Friday night, so I stayed. One more night wasn't going to make any difference, and besides, she was George Caspar's typist.'

'She was ...'

'Does the typing. Rides the horses sometimes. Into everything, she is, and talkative with it.'

The new scared Sid Halley didn't even want to listen.

'There was a right old rumpus all day Wednesday in George Caspar's house,' Chico said. 'It started at breakfast when that Inky Poole turned up and said Sid Halley had been asking questions that he, Inky Poole, didn't like.'

He paused for effect. I simply stared.

'Are you listening?' he said.

'Yes.'

'You got your stone face act on again.'

'Sorry.'

'Then Brothersmith the vet turned up and heard Inky Poole letting off, and he said funny, Sid Halley had been around him asking questions too. About bad hearts, he said. Same horses as Inky Poole was talking about. Bethesda, Gleaner and Zingaloo. And how was Tri-Nitro's heart, for good measure. My little dolly typist said you could've heard George Caspar blowing up all the way to Cambridge. He's real touchy about those horses.'

Trevor Deansgate, I thought coldly, had been at George Caspar's for breakfast, and had heard every word.

'Of course,' Chico said, 'some time later they checked the studs, Garvey's and Thrace's, and found you'd been there too. My dolly says your name is mud.'

I rubbed my hand over my face. 'Does your dolly know you were working with me?'

'Do us a favour. Of course not.'

'Did she say anything else?' What the hell am I asking for, I thought.

'Yeah. Well, she said Rosemary got on to George Caspar to change all the routine for the Saturday morning gallop, nagged him all day Thursday and all day Friday and George Caspar was climbing the walls. And at the yard they had so much security they were tripping over their own alarm bells.' He paused for breath. 'After that she didn't say much else on account of three martinis and time for tickle.'

I sat on the arm of the sofa and stared at the carpet.

'Next morning,' Chico said, 'I watched the gallop, like I said. Your photos came in very handy. Hundreds of ruddy horses ... Someone told me which were Caspar's, and there was Inky Poole, scowling like in the pictures, so I just zeroed in on him and hung about. There was a lot of fuss when it came to Tri-Nitro. They took the saddle off and put a little one on, and Inky Poole rode on that.'

'It was Inky Poole, then, who rode Tri-Nitro, same as usual?'

'They looked just like your pictures,' Chico said. 'Can't swear to it more than that.'

I stared some more at the carpet.

'So what do we do next?' he said.

'Nothing . . . We give Rosemary her money back and draw a line.'

'But hey,' Chico said in protest. 'Someone got at the horse. You know they did.'

'Not our business, any more.'

I wished that he, too, would stop looking at me. I felt a distinct need to crawl into a hole and hide.

The doorbell rang with the long peal of a determined thumb. 'We're out,' I said; but Chico went and answered it.

Rosemary Caspar swept past him, through the hall and into the sitting room, advancing in the old fawn raincoat and a fulminating rage. No scarf, no false curls, and no loving kindness.

'So there you are,' she said forcefully. 'I knew you'd be here, skulking out of sight. Your friend kept telling me when I telephoned that you weren't here, but I knew he was lying.'

'I wasn't here,' I said. As well try damming the St Lawrence with a twig.

'You weren't where I paid you to be, which was up in Newmarket. And I told you from the beginning that George wasn't to find out you were asking questions, and he did, and we've been having one God-awful bloody row ever since, and now Tri-Nitro has disgraced us unbearably and it's all your bloody fault.'

Chico raised his eyebrows comically. 'Sid didn't ride it . . . or train it.'

She glared at him with transferred hatred. 'And he didn't keep him safe, either.'

'Er, no,' Chico said. 'Granted.'

'As for you,' she said, swinging back to me. 'You're a useless bloody humbug. It's all rubbish, this detecting. Why don't you grow up and stop playing games? All you did was stir up trouble, and I want my money back.'

'Will a cheque do?' I said.

'You're not arguing, then?'

'No,' I said.

'Do you mean you admit that you failed?'

After a small pause, I said, 'Yes.'

'Oh.' She sounded as if I had unexpectedly deprived her of a good deal of what she had come to say, but while I wrote out a cheque for her she went on complaining sharply enough.

'All your ideas about changing the routine, they were useless. I've been on and on at George about security and taking care, and he says he couldn't have done any more, no one could, and he's in absolute despair – and I'd hoped, I'd really hoped, what a laugh, that somehow or other you would work a miracle, and that Tri-Nitro would win, because I was so sure, so sure . . . and I was right.'

I finished writing. 'Why were you always so sure?' I said.

'I don't know. I just *knew*. I've been afraid of it for weeks ... otherwise I would not have been so desperate as to try you, in the first place. And I might as well not have bothered ... it's caused so much trouble, and I can't bear it. I can't bear it. Yesterday was terrible. He should have won.... I knew he wouldn't. I felt ill. I still feel ill.'

She was trembling again. The pain in her face was acute. So many hopes, so much work had gone into Tri-Nitro, such anxiety and such care. Winning races was to a trainer like a film to a film maker. If you got it right, they applauded: wrong, and they booed. And either way you'd poured your soul into it, and your thoughts and you skill and weeks of worry. I understood what the lost race meant to George, and to Rosemary equally, because she cared so much.

'Rosemary ...' I said, in useless sympathy.

'It's pointless Brothersmith saying he must have had an infection,' she said. 'He's always saying things like that. He's so wet, I can't stand him, always looking over his shoulder, I've never liked him. And it was his job anyway to check Tri-Nitro and he did, over and over, and there was nothing wrong with him, nothing. He went down to the post looking beautiful, and in the parade ring before that, there was nothing wrong, nothing. And then in the race, he just went backwards, and he finished ... he came back ... exhausted.' There was a glitter of tears for a moment, but she visibly willed them from overwhelming her.

'They've done dope tests, I suppose,' Chico said.

It angered her again. 'Dope tests! Of course they have. What do you expect? Blood tests, urine tests, saliva tests, dozens of bloody tests. They gave George duplicate samples, and that's why we're down here, he's trying to fix up with some private lab ... but they won't be positive. It will be like before ... absolutely nothing.'

I tore out the cheque and gave it to her, and she glanced at it blindly.

'I wish I'd never come here. My God, I wish I hadn't. You're a jockey. I should have known better. I don't want to talk to you again. Don't talk to me at the races, do you understand.'

I nodded. I did understand. She turned abruptly to go away. 'And for God's sake don't speak to George, either.' She went alone out of the room, and out of the flat, and slammed the door.

Chico clicked his tongue and shrugged. 'You can't win them all,' he said. 'What could you do that her husband couldn't, not to mention a private police force and half a dozen guard dogs?' He was excusing me, and we both knew it.

I didn't answer.

'Sid?'

'I don't know that I'm going on with it,' I said. 'This sort of job.'

'You don't want to take any notice of what she said,' he protested. 'You can't give it up. You're too good at it. Look at the awful messes you've put right. Just because of one that's gone wrong ...'

I stared hollowly at a lot of unseen things.

'You're a big boy now,' he said. And he was seven years younger than I, near enough. 'You want to cry on Daddy's shoulder?' He paused. 'Look, Sid mate, you've got to snap out of it. Whatever's happened it can't be as bad as when that horse sliced your hand up, nothing could. This is no time to die inside, we've got about five other jobs lined up. The insurance, and the guard job, and Lucas Wainwright's syndicates ...'

'No,' I said. I felt leaden and useless. 'Not now, honestly, Chico.'

I got up and went into the bedroom. Shut the door. Went purposelessly to the window and looked out at the scenery of roofs and chimney pots, glistening in the beginnings of rain. The pots were still there, though the chimneys underneath were blocked off and the fires long dead. I felt at one with the chimney pots. When fires went out, one froze.

The door opened.

'Sid,' Chico said.

I said resignedly, 'Remind me to put a lock on that door.'

'You've got another visitor.'

'Tell him to go away.'

'It's a girl. Louise somebody.'

I rubbed my hand over my face and head and down to the back of my neck. Eased the muscles. Turned from the window.

'Louise McInnes?'

'That's right.'

'She shares the flat with Jenny,' I said.

'Oh, that one. Well then, Sid, if that's all for today I'll be off. And ... er ... be here tomorrow, won't you?'

'Yeah.'

He nodded. We left everything else unsaid. The amusement, mockery, friendship and stifled anxiety were all there in his face and his voice.... Maybe he read the same in mine. At any rate he gave me a widening grin as he departed, and I went into the sitting room thinking that some debts couldn't be paid.

Louise was standing in the middle of things, looking around her in the way I had, in Jenny's flat. Through her eyes I saw my own room afresh: its irregular shape, high-ceilinged, not modern; and the tan leather sofa, the table with drinks by the window, the shelves with books, the prints framed and hung, and on the floor, leaning against the wall, the big painting of racing horses which I'd somehow never bothered to hang up. There were coffee cups and glasses scattered about, and full ashtrays, and the piles of letters on the coffee table and everywhere else.

Louise herself looked different: the full production, not the Sunday morning tumble out of bed. A brown velvet jacket, a blazing white sweater, a soft mottled brown skirt with a wide leather belt round an untroubled waist. Fair hair washed and shining, rose petal make-up on the English rose skin. A detachment in the eyes which said that all this honey was not chiefly there for the attracting of bees.

'Mr Halley.'

'You could try Sid,' I said. 'You know me quite well, by proxy.'

Her smile reached half-way. 'Sid.'

'Louise.'

'Jenny says Sid is a plumber's mate's sort of name.'

'Very good people, plumbers' mates.'

'Did you know,' she said, looking away and continuing the visual tour of inspection, 'that in Arabic "Sid" means "lord"?'

'No, I didn't.'

'Well, it does.'

'You could tell Jenny,' I said.

Her gaze came back fast to my face. 'She gets to you, doesn't she?'

I smiled. 'Like some coffee? Or a drink?'

'Tea?'

'Sure.'

She came into the kitchen with me and watched me make it, and made no funny remarks about bionic hands, which was a nice change from most new acquaintances, who tended to be fascinated, and to say so, at length. Instead she looked around with inoffensive curiosity, and finally fastened her attention on the calendar which hung from the knob on the pine cupboard door. Photographs of horses, a Christmas hand-out from the bookmaking firm. She flipped up the pages, looking at the pictures of the future months, and stopped at December, where a horse and jockey jumping the Chair at Aintree were sihouetted spectacularly against the sky.

'That's good,' she said, and then, in surprise, reading the caption, 'That's *you*.'

'He's a good photographer.'

'Did you win that race?'

'Yes,' I said mildly. 'Do you take sugar?'

'No thanks.' She let the pages fall back. 'How odd to find oneself on a calendar.'

To me, it wasn't odd. How odd, I thought, to have seen one's picture in print so much that one scarcely noticed.

I carried the tray into the sitting room and put it on top of the letters on the coffee table. 'Sit down,' I said, and we sat.

'All these,' I said, nodding to them, 'are the letters which came with the cheques for the wax.'

She looked doubtful. 'Are they of any use?'

'I hope so,' I said, and explained about the mailing list.

'Good heavens.' She hesitated, 'Well, perhaps you won't need what I brought.' She picked up her brown leather handbag, and opened it. 'I didn't come all this way specially,' she said. 'I've an aunt near here whom I visit. Anyway, I thought you might like to have this, as I was here, near your flat.'

She pulled out a paperback book. She could have posted it, I thought: but I was quite glad she hadn't.

'I was trying to put a bit of order into the chaos in my bedroom,' she said. 'I've a lot of books. They tend to pile up.'

I didn't tell her I'd seen them. 'Books do,' I said.

'Well, this was among them. It's Nicky's.'

She gave me the paperback. I glanced at the cover and put it down, in order to pour out the tea. *Navigation for Beginners*. I handed her the cup and saucer. 'Was he interested in navigation?'

'I've no idea. But I was. I borrowed it out of his room. I don't think he even knew I'd borrowed it. He had a box with some things in – like a tuck box that boys take to public school – and one day when I went into his room the things were all on the chest of drawers, as if he was tidying. Anyway, he was out, and I borrowed the book.... He wouldn't have minded, he was terribly easy-going ... and I suppose I put it down in my room, and put something else on top, and just forgot it.'

'Did you read it?' I said.

'No. Never got round to it. It was weeks ago.'

I picked up the book and opened it. On the fly-leaf someone had written 'John Viking' in a firm legible signature in black felt-tip.

'I don't know,' Louise said, anticipating my question, 'whether that is Nicky's writing or not.'

'Does Jenny know?'

'She hasn't seen this. She's staying with Toby in Yorkshire.'

Jenny with Toby. Jenny with Ashe. For God's sake, I thought, what do you expect? She's gone, she's gone, she's not yours, you're divorced. And I hadn't been alone, not entirely.

'You look very tired,' Louise said doubtfully.

I was disconcerted. 'Of course not.' I turned the pages, letting them flick over from under my thumb. It was, as it promised to be, a book about navigation, sea and air, with line drawings and diagrams. Dead reckoning, sextants, magnetism and drift. Nothing of any note except a single line of letters and figures, written with the same black ink, on the inside of the back cover.

$$\text{Lift} = 22.024 \times V \times P \times \left(\frac{1}{T1} - \frac{1}{T2}\right)$$

I handed it over to Louise.

'Does this mean anything to you? Charles said you've a degree in Mathematics.'

She frowned at it faintly. 'Nicky needed a calculator for two plus two.'

He had done all right at two plus ten thousand, I thought.

'Um,' she said. 'Lift equals 22.024 times volume times pressure, times.... I should think this is something to do with temperature change. Not my subject, really. This is physics.'

'Something to do with navigation?' I said.

She concentrated. I watched the way her face grew taut while she did the internal scan. A fast brain, I thought, under the pretty hair.

'It's funny,' she said finally, 'but I think it's just possibly something to do with how much you can lift with a gas bag.'

'Airship?' I said, thinking.

'It depends what 22.024 is,' she said. 'That's a constant. Which means,' she added, 'it is special to whatever this equation is all about.'

'I'm better at what's likely to win the three-thirty.'

She looked at her watch. 'You're three hours too late.'

'It'll come round again tomorrow.'

She relaxed into the armchair, handing back the book. 'I don't suppose it will help,' she said, 'but you seemed to want anything of Nicky's.'

'It might help a lot. You never know.'

'But how?'

'It's John Viking's book. John Viking might know Nicky Ashe.'

'But ... you don't know John Viking.'

'No,' I said, 'but he knows gas-bags. And I know someone who knows gas-bags. And I bet gas-bags are a small world, like racing.'

She looked at the heaps of letters, and then at the book. She said slowly, 'I guess you'll find him, one way or another.'

I looked away from her, and at nothing in particular.

'Jenny says you never give up.'

I smiled faintly. 'Her exact words?'

'No.' I felt her amusement. 'Obstinate, selfish and determined to get his own way.'

'Not far off,' I tapped the book. 'Can I keep this?'

'Of course.'

'Thanks.'

We looked at each other as people do, especially if they're youngish and male and female, and sitting in a quiet flat at the end of an April day.

She read my expression and answered the unspoken thought. 'Some other time,' she said dryly.

'How long will you be staying with Jenny?'

'Would that matter to you?', she said.

'Mm.'

'She says you're as hard as flint. She says steel's a pushover, beside you.'

I thought of terror and misery and self-loathing. I shook my head.

'What I see,' she said slowly, 'is a man who looks ill being polite to an unwanted visitor.'

'You're wanted,' I said. 'And I'm fine.'

She stood up, however, and I also, after her.

'I hope,' I said, 'that you're fond of your aunt?'

'Devoted.'

She gave me a cool, half ironic smile in which there was also surprise.

'Goodbye ... Sid.'

'Goodbye, Louise.'

When she'd gone I switched on a table light or two against the slow dusk, and poured a whisky, and looked at a pale bunch of sausages in the fridge and didn't cook them.

No one else would come, I thought. They had all in their way held off the shadows, particularly Louise. No one else real would come, but he would be with me, as he'd been in Paris.... Trevor Deansgate. Inescapable. Reminding me inexorably of what I would rather forget.

After a while I stepped out of trousers and shirt and put on a short blue bathrobe, and took off the arm. It was one of the times when taking it off really hurt. It didn't seem to matter, after the rest.

I went back to the sitting room to do something about the clutter, but there was simply too much to bother with, so I stood looking at it, and held my weaker upper arm with my strong whole, agile right hand, as I often did, for support, and I wondered which crippled one worse, amputation without or within.

Humiliation and rejection and helplessness and failure....

After all these years I would *not*, I thought wretchedly, I would damned well *not* be defeated by fear.

Chapter Nine

Lucas Wainwright telephoned the next morning while I was stacking cups in the dishwasher.

'Any progress?' he said, sounding very Commanderish.

'I'm afraid,' I said regretfully, 'that I've lost all those notes. I'll have to do them again.'

'For heaven's sake.' He wasn't pleased. I didn't tell him that I'd lost the notes on account of being bashed on the head and dropping the large brown envelope that contained them in the gutter. 'Come right away, then. Eddy won't be in until this afternoon.'

Slowly, absentmindedly, I finished tidying up, while I thought about Lucas Wainwright, and what he could do for me, if he would. Then I sat at the table and wrote down what I wanted. Then I looked at what I'd written, and at my fingers holding the pen, and shivered. Then I folded the paper and put it in my pocket, and went to Portman Square deciding not to give it to Lucas, after all.

He had the files ready in his office, and I sat at the same table as before and re-copied all I needed.

'You won't let it drag on much longer, will you, Sid?'

'Full attention,' I said. 'Starting tomorrow. I'll go to Kent tomorrow afternoon.'

'Good.' He stood up as I put the new notes into a fresh envelope and waited for me to go, not through impatience with me particularly, but because he was that sort of man. Brisk. One task finished, get on with the next, don't hang about.

I hesitated cravenly and found myself speaking before I had consciously decided whether to or not. 'Commander. Do you remember that you said you might pay me for this job not with money, but with help, if I should want it?'

I got a reasonable smile and a postponement of the goodbyes.

'Of course I remember. You haven't done the job yet. What help?'

'Er ... it's nothing much. Very little.' I took the paper out and handed it to him. Waited while he read the brief contents. Felt as if I had planted a landmine and would presently step on it.

'I don't see why not,' he said. 'If that's what you want. But are you on to something that we should know about?'

I gestured to the paper, 'You'll know about it as soon as I do, if you do that.' It wasn't a satisfactory answer, but he didn't press it. 'The only thing I beg of you, though, is that you won't mention my name at all. Don't say it was my idea, not to *anyone*. I ... er ... you might get me killed, Commander, and I'm not being funny.'

He looked from me to the paper and back again, and frowned. 'This doesn't look like a killing matter, Sid.'

'You never know what is until your dead.'

He smiled. 'All right. I'll write the letter as from the Jockey Club, and I'll take you seriously about the death risk. Will that do?'

'It will indeed.'

We shook hands, and I left his office carrying the brown envelope, and at the Portman Square entrance, going out, I met Eddy Keith coming in. We both paused, as one does. I hoped he couldn't see the dismay in my face at his early return, or guess that I was perhaps carrying the seeds of his downfall.

'Eddy,' I said, smiling and feeling a traitor.

'Hello, Sid,' he said cheerfully, twinkling at me from above rounded cheeks. 'What are you doing here?' A good-natured normal enquiry. No suspicions. No tremor.

'Looking for crumbs,' I said.

He chuckled fatly. 'From what I hear, it's us picking up yours. Have us all out of work, you will, soon.'

'Not a chance.'

'Don't step on our toes, Sid.'

The smile was still there, the voice devoid of threat. The fuzzy hair, the big moustache, the big broad fleshy face still exuded good will: but the arctic had briefly come and gone in his eyes, and I was in no doubt that I'd received a serious warning off.

'Never, Eddy,' I said insincerely.

'See you, fella,' he said, preparing to go indoors, nodding, smiling widely, and giving me the usual hearty buffet on the shoulder. 'Take care.'

'You too, Eddy,' I said to his departing back: and under my breath, again, in a sort of sorrow, 'You too.'

I carried the notes safely back to the flat, and thought a bit, and telephoned to my man in gas-bags.

He said hallo and great to hear from you and how about a jar sometime, and no, he had never heard of anyone called John Viking. I read out the equation and asked if it meant anything to him, and he laughed and said it sounded like a formula for taking a hot air balloon to the moon.

'Thanks very much,' I said sarcastically.

'No, seriously, Sid. It's a calculation for maximum height. Try a balloonist. They're always after records . . . the highest, the furthest, that sort of thing.'

I asked if he knew any balloonists but he said sorry, no he didn't, he was only into airships, and we disconnected with another vague resolution to meet somewhere, sometime, one of these days. Idly, and certain it was useless, I leafed through the telephone directory, and there, incredibly, the words stood out bold and clear: The Hot Air Balloon Company, offices in London, number provided.

I got through. A pleasant male voice at the other end said that of course he knew John Viking, everyone in ballooning knew John Viking, he was a madman of the first order.

Madman!

John Viking, the voice explained, took risks which no sensible balloonist would dream of. If I wanted to talk to him, the voice said, I would undoubtedly find him at the balloon race on Monday afternoon.

Where was the balloon race on Monday afternoon?

Horse show, balloon race, swings and roundabouts, you name it; all part of the May Day holiday junketings at Highalane Park in Wiltshire. John Viking would be there. Sure to be.

I thanked the voice for his help and rang off, reflecting that I had forgotten about the May Day holiday. National holidays had always been work days for me, as for everyone in racing; providing the entertainment for the public's leisure. I tended not to notice them come and go.

Chico arrived with fish-and-chips for two in the sort of hygienic greaseproof wrappings which kept the steam in and made the chips go soggy.

'Did you know it's the May Day holiday on Monday?' I said.

'Running a judo tournament for the little bleeders, aren't I?'

He tipped the lunch onto two plates, and we ate it, mostly with fingers.

'You've come to life again, I see,' he said.

'It's temporary.'

'We'd better get some work done, then, while you're still with us.'

'The syndicates,' I said; and told him about the luckless Mason having been sent out on the same errand and having his brains kicked to destruction.

Chico shook salt on his chips. 'Have to be careful then, won't we?'

'Start this afternoon?'

'Sure.' He paused reflectively, licking his fingers. 'We're not getting paid for this, didn't you say?'

'Not directly.'

'Why don't we do these insurance enquiries, then? Nice quiet questions with a guaranteed fee.

'I promised Lucas Wainwright I'd do the syndicates first.'

He shrugged. 'You're the boss. But that makes three in a row, counting your wife and Rosemary getting her cash back, that we've worked on for nothing.'

'We'll make up for it later.'

'You are going on, then?'

I didn't answer at once. Apart from not knowing whether I wanted to, I didn't know if I could. Over the past months Chico and I had tended to get somewhat battered by bully boys trying to stop us in our tracks. We didn't have the protection of being either in the Racecourse Security Service or the police. No one to defend us but ourselves. We had looked upon the bruises as part of the job, as racing falls had been to me, and bad judo falls to Chico. What if Trevor Deansgate had changed all that.... Not just for one terrible week, but for much longer; for always?

'Sid,' Chico said sharply. 'Come back.'

I swallowed. 'Well ... er ... we'll do the syndicates. Then we'll see.' Then I'll know, I thought. I'll know inside me, one way or the other. If I couldn't walk into tigers' cages any more, we were done. One of us wasn't enough: it had to be both.

If I couldn't ... I'd soon be dead.

The first syndicate on Lucas's list had been formed by eight people, of whom three were registered owners, headed by Philip Friarly. Registered owners were those acceptable to the racing authorities, owners who paid their dues and kept the rules, were no trouble to anybody, and represented the source and mainspring of the whole industry.

Syndicates were a way of involving more people directly in racing, which was good for the sport, and dividing the training costs into smaller fractions, which was good for the owners. There were syndicates of millionaires, coal miners, groups of rock guitarists, the clientele of pubs. Anyone from Aunty Flo to the undertaker could join a syndicate, and all Eddy Keith should have done was check that everyone on the list was who they said they were.

'It's not the registered owners we're looking at,' I said. 'It's all the others.'

We were driving through Kent on our way to Tunbridge Wells. Ultra-respectable place, Tunbridge Wells. Resort of retired colonels and ladies who played bridge. Low on the national crime league. Hometown, all the same, of a certain Peter Rammileese, who was, so Lucas Wainwright's informant had said, in fact the instigating member of all four of the doubtful syndicates, although his own name nowhere appeared.

'Mason,' I said, conversationally, 'was attacked and left for dead in the streets of Tunbridge Wells.'

'Now he tells me.'

'Chico,' I said. 'Do you want to turn back?'

'You got a premonition, or something?'

After a pause, I said 'No,' and drove a shade too fast round a sharpish bend.

'Look, Sid,' he said. 'We don't have to go to Tunbridge Wells. We're on a hiding to nothing, with this lark.'

'What do you think, then?'

He was silent.

'We do have to go,' I said.

'Yeah.'

'So we have to work out what it was that Mason asked, and not ask it.'

'This Rammileese,' Chico said. 'What's he like?'

'I haven't met him, myself, but I've heard of him. He's a farmer who's made a packet out of crooked dealings in horses. The Jockey Club won't have him as a registered owner, and most racecourses don't let him through the gates. He'll try to bribe anyone from the Senior Steward to the scrubbers, and where he can't bribe, he threatens.'

'Oh, jolly.'

'Two jockeys and a trainer, not so long ago, lost their licences for taking his bribes. One of the jockeys got the sack from his stable and he's so broke he's hanging around outside the racecourse gates begging for handouts.'

'Is that the one I saw you talking to, a while ago?'

'That's right.'

'And how much did you give him?'

'Never you mind.'

'You're a pushover, Sid.'

'A case of "but-for-the-grace-of-God",' I said.

'Oh, sure. I could just see you taking bribes from a crooked horse dealer. Most likely thing on earth.'

'Anyway,' I said, 'what we're trying to find out is not whether Peter Rammileese is manipulating four racehorses, which he is, but whether Eddy Keith knows it, and is keeping quiet.'

'Right.' We sped deeper into rural Kent, and then he said, 'You know why we've had such good results, on the whole, since we've been together on this job?'

'Why, then?'

'It's because all the villains know you. I mean, they know you by sight, most of them. So when they see you poking around on their patch, they get the heebies, and start doing silly things like setting the heavies on us, and then we see them loud and clear, and what they're up to, which we wouldn't have done if they'd sat tight.'

I sighed and said 'I guess so,' and thought about Trevor Deansgate; thought and tried not to. Without any hands one couldn't drive a car.... Just don't think about, it I told myself. Just keep your mind off it, it's a one way trip into Jellyfish.

I swung round another corner too fast and collected a sideways look from Chico, but no comment.

'Look at the map,' I said. 'Do something useful.'

We found the house of Peter Rammileese without much trouble, and pulled into the yard of a small farm that looked as if the outskirts of Tunbridge Wells had rolled round it like a sea, leaving it isolated and incongruous. There was a large white farmhouse, three storeys high, and a modern wooden stable block, and a long, extra large barn. Nothing significantly prosperous about the place, but no nettles either.

No one about. I put the brake on as we rolled to a stop, and we got out of the car.

'Front door?' Chico said.

'Back door, for farms.'

We had taken only five or six steps in that direction, however, when a small boy ran into the yard from a doorway in the barn, and came over to us, breathlessly.

'Did you bring the ambulance?'

His eyes looked past me, to my car, and his face puckered into agitation and disappointment. He was about seven, dressed in jodhpurs and T shirt, and he had been crying.

'What's the matter?' I said.

'I rang for the ambulance.... A long time ago.'

'We might help,' I said.

'It's Mum,' he said. 'She's lying in there, and she won't wake up.'

'Come on, you show us.'

He was a sturdy little boy, brown haired and brown-eyed and very frightened. He ran ahead towards the barn, and we followed without wasting time. Once through the door we could see that it wasn't an ordinary barn, but an indoor riding school, a totally enclosed area of about twenty metres wide by thirty five long, lit by windows in the roof. The floor, wall to wall, was covered with a thick layer of tan-coloured wood chippings, springy and quiet for horses to work on.

There was a pony and a horse careering about; and, in danger from their hooves, a crumpled female figure lying on the ground.

Chico and I went over to her fast. She was young, on her side, face half downwards; unconscious, but not, I thought deeply. Her breathing was shallow and her skin had whitened in a mottled fashion under her make-up, but the pulse in her wrist was strong and regular. The crash helmet which hadn't saved her lay several feet away on the floor.

'Go and ring again,' I said to Chico.

'Shouldn't we move her?'

'No ... in case she's broken anything. You can do a lot of damage moving people too much when they're unconscious.'

'You should know.' He turned away and ran off towards the house.

'Is she all right?' the boy said anxiously. 'Bingo started bucking and she fell off, and I think he kicked her head.'

'Bingo is the horse?'

'His saddle slipped,' he said: and Bingo, with the saddle down under his belly was still bucking and kicking like a rodeo.

'What's your name?' I said.

'Mark.'

'Well, Mark, as far as I can see, your Mum is going to be all right, and you're a brave little boy.'

'I'm six,' he said, as if that wasn't so little.

The worst of the fright had died out of his eyes, now that he had help. I knelt on the ground beside his mother and smoothed the brown hair away from her forehead. She made a small moaning sound, and her eyelids fluttered. She was perceptibly nearer the surface, even in the short time we'd been there.

'I thought she was dying,' the boy said. 'We had a rabbit a long time ago . . . he panted and shut his eyes, and we couldn't wake him up again, and he died.'

'Your Mum will wake up again.'

'Are you sure?'

'Yes, Mark, I'm sure.'

He seemed deeply reassured, and told me readily that the pony was called Sooty, and was his own, and that his Dad was away until tomorrow morning, and there was only his Mum there, and him, and she'd been schooling Bingo because she was selling him to a girl for show jumping.

Chico came back and said the ambulance was on its way. The boy, cheering up enormously, said we ought to catch the horses because they were cantering about and the reins were all loose, and if the saddles and bridles got broken his Dad would be bloody angry.

Both Chico and I laughed at the adult words, seriously spoken. While he and Mark stood guard over the patient, I caught the horses one by one, with the aid of a few horsenuts which Mark produced from his pockets and tied their reins to tethering rings in the walls. Bingo, once the agitating girths were undone and the saddle safely off, stood quietly enough, and Mark darted briefly away from his mother to give his own pony some brisk encouraging slaps and some more horsenuts.

Chico said the emergency service had indeed had a call from a child fifteen minutes earlier, but he'd hung up before they could ask him where he lived.

'Don't tell him,' I said.

'You're a softie.'

'He's a brave little kid.'

'Not bad for a little bleeder. While you were catching the bucking bronco he told me his Dad gets bloody angry pretty often.' He looked down at the still unconscious girl. 'You really reckon she's O.K., do you?'

'She'll come out of it. It's a matter of waiting.'

The ambulance came in due course, but Mark's anxiety reappeared, strongly, when the men loaded his mother into the van and prepared to depart. He wanted to go with her, and the men wouldn't take him on his own. She was stirring and mumbling, and it distressed him.

I said to Chico, 'Drive him to the hospital. . . . Follow the ambulance. He needs to see her wide awake and speaking to him. I'll take a look round in the house. His Dad's away until tomorrow.'

'Convenient,' he said sardonically. He collected Mark into the Scimitar, and drove away down the road, and I could see their heads talking to each other, through the rear window.

I went through the open back door with the confidence of the invited. Nothing difficult about entering a tiger's cage while the tiger was out.

It was an old house filled with brash new opulent furnishings, which I found overpowering. Lush loud carpets, huge stereo equipment, a lamp standard of a golden nymph and deep armchairs covered in black and khaki zig-zags. Sitting and dining rooms shining and tidy, with no sign that a small boy lived there. Kitchen uncluttered, hygienic surfaces wiped clean. Study ...

The positively aggressive tidiness of the study made me pause and consider. No horse trader that I'd ever come across had kept books and papers in such neat rectangular stacks; and the ledgers themselves, when I opened them, contained up-to-the-minute entries.

I looked into drawers and filing cabinets, being extremely careful to leave everything squared up after me, but there was nothing there except the outward show of honesty. Not a single drawer or cupboard was locked. It was almost, I thought with cynicism, as if the whole thing were stage dressing, orchestrated to confound any invasion of tax snoopers. The real records, if he kept any, were probably somewhere outside, in a biscuit tin, in a hole in the ground.

I went upstairs. Mark's room was unmistakable, but all the toys were in boxes, and all the clothes in drawers. There were three unoccupied bedrooms with the outlines of folded blankets showing under covers, and a suite of bedroom, dressing room and bathroom furnished with the same expense and tidiness as downstairs.

An oval dark red bath with taps like gilt dolphins. A huge bed with a bright brocade cover clashing with wall-to-wall jazz on the floor. No clutter on the curvaceous cream and gold dressing table, no brushes on any surface in the dressing room.

Mark's mum's clothes were fur and glitter and breeches and jackets. Mark's dad's clothes, thorn-proof tweeds, vicuna overcoat, a dozen or more suits, none of them hand made, all seemingly bought because they were expensive. Handfuls of illicit cash, I thought, and nothing much to do with it. Peter Rammileese, it seemed, was crooked by nature and not by necessity.

The same incredible tidiness extended through every drawer and even into the soiled linen basket, where a pair of pyjamas were neatly folded.

I went through the pockets of his suits, but he had left nothing at all in them. There were no pieces of paper of any sort anywhere in the dressing room.

Frustrated, I went up to the third floor, where there were six rooms, one containing a variety of empty suitcases, and the others, nothing at all.

No one, I thought on the way down again, lived so excessively carefully if they had nothing to hide; which was scarcely evidence to offer in court. The present life of the Rammileese family was an expensive vacuum, and of the past there was no sign at all. No souvenirs, no old books, not even any photographs except a recent one of Mark on his pony, taken outside in the yard.

I was looking round the outbuildings when Chico came back. There were no animals except seven horses in the stable and the two in the covered school. No sign of farming in progress. No rosettes in the tack room, just a lot more tidiness and the smell of saddle-soap. I went out to meet Chico and ask what he done with Mark.

'The nurses are stuffing him with jam butties and trying to ring his Dad. Mum is awake and talking. How did you get on? Do you want to drive?'

'No, you drive.' I sat in beside him. 'That house is the most suspicious case of no history I've ever seen.'

'Like that, eh?'

'Mm. And not a chance of finding any link with Eddy Keith.'

'Wasted journey, then,' he said.

'Lucky for Mark.'

'Yeah. Good little bleeder, that. Told me he's going to be a furniture moving man when he grows up.' Chico look across at me and grinned. 'Seems he's moved house three times that he can remember.'

Chapter Ten

Chico and I spent most of Saturday separately traipsing around all the London addresses on the M list of wax names, and met at six o'clock, footsore and thirsty, at a pub we both knew in Fulham.

'We never ought to have done it on a Saturday, and a holiday weekend at that,' Chico said.

'No.' I agreed.

Chico watched the beer sliding mouth-wateringly into the glass. 'More than half of them were out.'

'Mine too. Nearly all.'

'And the ones that were in were watching the racing or the wrestling or groping their girlfriends, and didn't want to know.'

We carried his beer and my whisky over to a small table, drank deeply, and compared notes. Chico had finally pinned down four people, and I only two, but the results were there, all the same.

All six, whatever other mailing lists they had confessed to, had been in regular happy receipt of *Antiques for All*.

'That's it, then,' Chico said. 'Conclusive.' He leaned back against the wall, luxuriously relaxing. 'We can't do any more until Tuesday.

Everything's shut.

'Are you busy tomorrow?'

'Have a heart. The girl in Wembley.' He looked at his watch and swallowed the rest of the beer. 'And so long, Sid boy, or I'll be late. She doesn't like me sweaty.'

He grinned and departed, and I more slowly finished my drink and went home.

Wandered about. Changed the batteries. Ate some cornflakes. Got out the form books and looked up the syndicated horses. Highly variable form: races lost at short odds and won at long. All the signs of steady and expert fixing. I yawned. It went on all the time.

I pottered some more, restlessly, sorely missing the peace that usually filled me in that place, when I was alone. Undressed, put on a bathrobe, pulled off the arm. Tried to watch the television: couldn't concentrate. Switched it off.

I usually pulled the arm off after I'd put the bathrobe on because that way I didn't have to look at the bit of me that remained below the left elbow. I could come to terms with the fact of it but still not really the sight, though it was neat enough and not horrific, as the messed up hand had been. I dare say it was senseless to be faintly repelled, but I was. I hated anyone except the limb man to see it; even Chico. I was ashamed of if, and that too was illogical. People without handicaps never understood that ashamed feeling, and nor had I, until the day soon after the original injury when I'd blushed crimson because I'd had to ask someone to cut up my food. There had been many times after that when I'd gone hungry rather than ask. Not having to ask, ever, since I'd had the electronic hand, had been a psychological release of soul-saving proportions.

The new hand had meant, too, a return to full normal human status. No one treated me as an idiot, or with the pity which in the past had made me cringe. No one made allowances any more, or got themselves tongue-tied with trying not to say the wrong thing. The days of the useless deformity seemed in retrospect an unbearable nightmare. I was often quite grateful to the villain who had set me free.

With one hand, I was a self-sufficient man.

Without any....

Oh God, I thought. Don't think about it. *There is nothing either good or bad, but thinking makes it so*. Hamlet, however, didn't have the same problems.

I got through the night, and the next morning, and the afternoon, but at around six I gave up and got in the car, and drove to Aynsford.

If Jenny was there, I thought, easing up the back drive and stopping quietly in the yard outside the kitchen, I would just turn right round and go back to London, and at least the driving would have occupied the time. But no one seemed to be about, and I walked into the house from the side door which had a long passage into the house.

Charles was in the small sitting room that he called the wardroom, sitting alone, sorting out his much-loved collection of fishing flies.

He looked up. No surprise. No effusive welcome. No fuss. Yet I'd never gone there before without invitation.

'Hallo,' he said.

'Hallo.'

I stood there, and he looked at me, and waited.

'I wanted some company,' I said.

He squinted at a dry fly; 'Did you bring an overnight bag?'

I nodded.

He pointed to the drinks tray. 'Help yourself. And pour me a pink gin, will you? Ice in the kitchen.'

I fetched him his drink, and my own, and sat in an armchair.

'Come to tell me?' he said.

'No.'

He smiled. 'Supper then? And chess.'

We ate, and played two games. He won the first easily, and told me to pay attention. The second, after an hour and a half, was a draw. 'That's better,' he said.

The peace I hadn't been able to find on my own came slowly back with Charles, even though I knew it had more to do with the ease I felt with him personally, and the timelessness of his vast old house, than with a real resolution of the destruction within. In any case, for the first time in ten days, I slept soundly for hours.

At breakfast we discussed the day ahead. He himself was going to the steeplechase meeting at Towcester, forty-five minutes northwards, to act as a Steward, an honorary job that he enjoyed. I told him about John Viking and the balloon race, and also about the visits to the M people, and *Antiques for All*, and he smiled with his own familiar mixture of satisfaction and amusement, as if I were some creation of his that was coming up to expectations. It was he who had originally driven me to becoming an investigator. Whenever I got anything right he took the credit for it himself.

'Did Mrs Cross tell you about the telephone call?' he said, buttering toast. Mrs Cross was his housekeeper, quiet, effective and kind.

'What telephone call?'

'Someone rang here about seven this morning, asking if you were here. Mrs Cross said you were asleep and could she take a message, but whoever it was said he would ring later.'

'Was it Chico? He might guess I'd come here, if he couldn't get me in the flat.'

'Mrs Cross said he didn't give a name.'

I shrugged and reached for the coffee pot. 'It can't have been urgent, or he'd have told her to wake me up.'

Charles smiled. 'Mrs Cross sleeps in curlers and face cream. She'd never have let you see her at seven o'clock in the morning, short of an earthquake. She thinks you're a lovely young man. She tells me so, every time you come.'

'For God's sakes.'

'Will you be back here, tonight?' he said.

'I don't know yet.'

He folded his napkin, looking down at it. 'I'm glad that you came, yesterday.'

I looked at him. 'Yeah,' I said. 'Well, you want me to say it, so I'll say it. And I mean it.' I paused a fraction, searching for the simplest words that would tell him what I felt for him. Found some. Said them. 'This is my home.'

He looked up quickly, and I smiled twistedly, mocking myself, mocking him, mocking the whole damned world.

Highalane Park was a stately home uneasily coming to terms with the plastic age. The house itself opened to the public like an agitated virgin only half a dozen times a year, but the parkland was always out for rent for game fairs and circuses, and things like the May Day jamboree.

They had made little enough effort on the roadside to attract the passing crowd. No bunting, no razzamatazz, no posters with print larg enough to read at ten paces; everything slightly coy and apologetic. Considering all that, the numbers pouring onto the showground were impressive. I paid at the gate in my turn and bumped over some grass to park the car obediently in a row in the roped off parking area. Other cars followed, neatly alongside.

There were a few people on horses cantering busily about in haphazard directions, but the roundabouts on the fairground to one side were silent and motionless, and there was no sight of any balloons.

I got out of the car and locked the door, and thought that one-thirty was probably too early for much in the way of action.

One can be wrong.

A voice behind me said, 'Is this the man?'

I turned and found two people advancing into the small space between my car and the one next to it: a man I didn't know, and a little boy, whom I did.

'Yes,' the boy said, pleased. 'Hallo.'

'Hallo, Mark,' I said. 'How's your Mum?'

'I told Dad about you coming.' He looked up at the man beside him.

'Did you, now?' I thought his being at Highalane was only an extraordinary coincidence, but it wasn't.

'He described you,' the man said. 'That hand, and the way you could handle horses.... I knew who he meant, right enough.' His face and voice were hard and wary, with a quality that I by now recognized on sight: guilty knowledge faced by trouble. 'I don't take kindly to you poking your nose around my place.'

'You were out,' I said mildly.

'Aye I was out. And this nipper, here, he left you there all alone.'

He was about forty, a wiry man with evil intentions stamped clearly all over him.

'I knew your car, too,' Mark said proudly. 'Dad says I'm clever.'

'Kids are observant,' his father said, with nasty relish.

'We waited for you to come out of a big house,' Mark said. 'And then we followed you all the way here.' He beamed, inviting me to enjoy the game. 'This is our car, next to yours.' He patted the maroon Daimler alongside.

The telephone call, I thought fleetingly. Not Chico. Peter Rammileese, checking around.

'Dad says,' Mark chatted on happily, 'that'll he'll take me to see those roundabouts while our friends take you for a ride in our car.'

His father looked down at him sharply, not having expected so much repeated truth, but Mark, oblivious, was looking at a point behind my back.

I glanced round. Between the Scimitar and the Daimler stood two more people. Large unsmiling men from a muscular brotherhood. Brass knuckles and toecaps.

'Get into the car,' Rammileese said, nodding to his, not to mine. 'Rear door.'

Oh sure, I thought. Did he think I was mad? I stooped slightly as if to obey and then instead of opening the door scooped Mark up bodily, with my right arm, and ran.

Rammileese turned with a shout. Mark's face, next to mine, was astonished but laughing. I ran about twenty paces with him, and set him down in the path of his furiously advancing father, and then kept on going, away from the cars and towards the crowds in the centre part of the showground.

Bloody hell, I thought. Chico was right. These days we only had to twitch an eyelid for them to wheel out the heavies. It was getting too much.

It had been the sort of ambush that might have worked if Mark hadn't been there: one kidney punch and into the car before I'd get my breath. But they'd needed Mark, I supposed, to identify me, because although they knew me by name, they hadn't by sight. They weren't going to catch me on the open showground, that was for sure, and when I went back to my car it would be with a load of protectors. Maybe, I thought hopefully, they would see it was useless, and just go away.

I reached the outskirts of the show-jumping arena, and looked back from over the head of a small girl sucking an ice-cream cornet. No one had called off the heavies. They were still doggedly in pursuit. I decided not to see what would happen if I simply stood my ground and requested the assorted families round about to save me from being frog-marched to oblivion and waking up with my head kicked in in the streets of Tunbridge Wells. The assorted families, with dogs and Grannies and prams and picnics, were more likely to dither with their mouths open and wonder what it had all been about, once it was over.

I went on, deeper into the show, circling the ring, bumping into children as I looked over my shoulder, and seeing the two men always behind me.

The arena itself was on my left, with show-jumping in progress inside, and ringside car encircling it outside. Behind the cars there was the broad grass walk-way along which I was going, and, on my right, the outer ring of the stalls one always gets at horse-shows. Tented shops, selling saddlery, riding clothes, pictures, toys, hot dogs, fruit, more saddles, hardwear, tweeds, sheepskin slippers ... an endless circle of small traders.

Among the tents, the vans: ice-cream vans, riding associations' caravans, a display of crafts, a fortune teller, a charity jumble shop, mobile cinema showing films of sheep dogs, a drop-sided juggernaut spilling out kitchen equipment in orange and yellow and green. Crowds along the fronts of all of them and no depth of shelter inside.

'Do you know where the balloons are?' I asked someone, and he pointed, and it was to a stall selling small gas balloons of brilliant colours: children buying them and tying them to their wrists.

Not those, I thought. Surely not those. I didn't stop to explain, but asked again, further on.

'The balloon race? In the next field, I think, but it isn't time yet.'

'Thanks,' I said. The posters had announced a three o'clock start, but I'd have to talk to John Viking well before that, while he was willing to listen.

What was a balloon race, I wondered? Surely all balloons went at the same speed, the speed of the wind.

My trackers wouldn't give up. They weren't running, and nor was I. They just followed me steadily, as if locked on to a target by a radio beam; minds taking literally an order to stick to my heels. I'd have to get lost, I thought, and stay lost until after I'd found John Viking, and maybe then I'd go in search of helpful defences like show secretaries and first aid ladies, and the single policeman out on the road directing traffic.

I was on the far side of the arena by that time, crossing the collecting ring area with children on ponies buzzing around like bees, looking strained as they went in to jump, and tearful or triumphant as they came out.

Past them, past the commentating box.... 'Jane Smith had a clear round, the next to jump is Robin Daly on Traddles' ... past the little private grandstand for the organizers and big-wigs – rows of empty folding seats – past an open-sided refreshment tent, full, and so back to the stalls.

I did a bit of dodging in and out of those, and round the backs ducking under guy ropes and round dumps of cardboard boxes. From the inside depths of a stall hung thickly outside with riding jackets I watched the two of them go past, hurrying looking about them, distinctly anxious.

They weren't like the two Trevor Deansgate had sent, I thought. His had been clumsier, smaller, and less professional. These two looked as if this sort of work was their daily bread; and for all the comparative safety of the show ground, where as a last resort I could get into the arena itself and scream for help, there was something daunting about them. Rent-a-thugs unsually came at so much per hour. These two looked salaried, if not actually on the Board.

I left the riding jackets and dodged into the film about sheep dogs, which I dare say would have been riveting but for the shepherding going on outside, with me as the sheep.

I looked at my watch. After two o'clock. Too much time was passing. I had to try another sortie outside and find my way to the balloons.

I couldn't see them. I slithered among the crowd, asking for directions.

'Up at the end, mate,' a decisive man told me, pointing. 'Past the hot dogs, turn right, there's a gate in the fence. You can't miss it.'

I nodded my thanks and turned to go that way, and saw one of my trackers coming towards me, searching the stalls with his eyes and looking worried.

In a second he would see me.... I looked around in a hurry and found I was outside the caravan of the fortune-teller. There was a curtain of plastic streamers, black and white, over the open doorway, and behind that a shadowy figure. I took four quick strides, brushed though the plastic strips, and stepped up into the van.

It was quieter inside and darker, with daylight filtering dimly through lace-hung windows. A Victorian sort of decor; mock oil lamps and chenille tablecloths. Outside, the tracker went past, giving the fortune-teller no more than a flickering glance. His attention lay ahead. He hadn't seen me come in.

The fortune-teller, however, had, and to her I represented business.

'Do you want your whole life, dear, the past and everything, or just the future?'

'Er ...' I said. 'I don't really know. How long does it take?'

'A quarter of an hour, dear, for the whole thing.'

'Let's just have the future.'

I looked out of the window. A part of my future was searching among the ring-side cars, asking questions and getting a lot of shaken heads.

'Sit on the sofa beside me here, dear, and give me your left hand.'

'It'll have to be the right,' I said absently.

'No, dear.' Her voice was quite sharp. 'Always the left.'

Amused, I sat down and gave her the left. She felt it, and looked at it, and raised her eyes to mine. She was short and plump, dark-haired, middle-aged, and in no way remarkable.

'Well, dear,' she said after a pause, 'it will have to be the right, though I'm not used to it, and we may not get such good results.'

'I'll risk it,' I said; so we changed places on the sofa, and she held my right hand firmly in her two warm ones, and I watched the tracker move along the row of cars.

'You have suffered,' she said.

As she knew about my left hand, I didn't think much of that for a guess, and she seemed to sense it. She coughed apologetically.

'Do you mind if I use a crystal?' she said.

'Go ahead.'

I had vague visions of her peering into a large ball on a table, but she took a small one, the size of a tennis ball, and put it in the palm of my hand.

'You are a kind person,' she said. 'Gentle. People like you. People smile at you wherever you go.'

Outside, twenty yards away, the two heavies had met to consult. Not a smile, there, of any sort.

'You are respected by everyone.'

Regulation stuff, designed to please the customers.

Chico should hear it, I thought. Gentle, kind, respected ... he'd laugh his head off.

She said doubtfully, 'I see a great many people, cheering and clapping. Shouting loudly, cheering you ... does that mean anything to you, dear?'

I slowly turned my head. Her dark eyes watched me calmly.

'That's the past,' I said.

'It's recent,' she said. 'It's still there.'

I didn't believe it. I didn't believe in fortune-tellers. I wondered if she had seen me before, on a racecourse or talking on television. She must have.

She bent her head again over the crystal which she held on my hand, moving the glass gently over my skin.

'You have good health. You have vigour. You have great physical stamina.... There is much to endure.'

Her voice broke off, and she raised her head a little, frowning. I had a strong impression what she had said had surprised her.

After a pause, she said. 'I can't tell you any more.'

'Why not?'

'I'm not used to the right hand.'

'Tell me what you see,' I said.

She shook her head slightly and raised the calm dark eyes.

'You will live a long time.'

I glanced out through the plastic curtain. The trackers had moved off out of sight.

'How much do I owe you?' I said. She told me, and I paid her, and went quietly over to the doorway.

'Take care, dear,' she said. 'Be careful.'

I looked back. Her face was still calm, but her voice had been urgent. I didn't want to believe in the conviction that looked out of her eyes. She might have felt the disturbance of my present problem with the trackers, but no more than that. I pushed the curtain gently aside and stepped from the dim world of hovering horrors into the bright May sunlight, where they might in truth lie in wait.

Chapter Eleven

There was no longer any need to ask where the balloons were. No one could miss them. They were beginning to rise like gaudy monstrous mushrooms, humped on the ground, spread all over an enormous area of grassland beyond the actual showground. I had thought vaguely that there would be two or three balloons, or at most six, but there must have been twenty.

Among a whole stream of people going the same way, I went down to the gate and through into the far field, and realized that I had obviously underestimated the task of finding John Viking.

There was a rope, for a start, and marshals telling the crowd to stand behind it. I ducked those obstacles at least, but found myself in a forest of half inflated balloons, which billowed immensely all around and cut off any length of sight.

The first clump of people I came to were busy with a pink and purple monster into whose mouth they were blowing air by means of a large engine-driven fan. The balloon was attached by four fine nylon ropes to the basket, which lay on its side, with a young man in a red crash helmet peering anxiously into its depths.

'Excuse me,' I said to a girl on the edge of the group. 'Do you know where I can find John Viking?'

'Sorry.'

The red crash helmet raised itself to reveal a pair of very blue eyes. 'He's here somewhere,' he said politely. 'Flies a Stormcloud balloon. Now would you mind getting the hell out, we're busy.'

I walked along the edge of things, trying to keep out of their way. Balloon races, it seemed, were a serious business and no occasion for light laughter and social chat. The intent faces leant over ropes and equipment, testing, checking, worriedly frowning. No balloons looked much like stormclouds. I risked another question.

'John Viking? That bloody idiot. Yes, He's here. Flies a Stormcloud.' He turned away, busy and anxious.

'What colour is it?' I said.

'Yellow and green. Look, go away, will you?'

There were balloons advertising whisky and marmalade and towns, and even insurance companies. Balloons in brilliant primary colours and pink-and-white pastels, balloons in the sunshine rising from the green grass in glorious jumbled rainbows. On an ordinary day, a scene of delight, but to me, trying to get round them to ask fruitlessly at the next clump gathered anxiously by its basket, a frustrating silky maze.

I circled a soft billowing black and white monster and went deeper into the centre. As if at a signal, there arose in a chorus from all around a series of deep throated roars, caused by flames suddenly spurting from the large burners which were supported on frames above the baskets. The flames roared into the open mouths of the half-inflated balloons, heating and expanding the air already there and driving in more. The gleaming envelopes swelled and surged with quickening life, growing from mushrooms to toadstools, the tops rising slowly and magnificently towards the hazy blue sky.

'John Viking? Somewhere over there.' A girl swung her arm vaguely. 'But he'll be as busy as we are.'

As the balloons filled they began to heave off the ground and sway in great floating masses, bumping into each other, still billowing, still not full enough to live with the birds. Under each balloon the flames roared, scarlet and lusty, with the little clusters of the helpers clinging to the baskets to prevent them escaping too soon.

With the balloons off the ground, I saw a yellow and green one quite easily; yellow and green in segments, like an orange, with a wide green band at the bottom. There was one man already in the basket, with about three people holding it down, and he, unlike everyone else in sight, wore not a crash helmet but a blue denim cap.

I ran in his direction, and even as I ran there was the sound of a starter's pistol. All around me the baskets were released, and began dragging and bumping over the ground; and a great cheer went up from the watching crowd.

I reached the bunch of people I was aiming for and put my hand on the basket.

'John Viking?'

No one listened. They were deep in a quarrel. A girl in a crash helmet, ski-ing jacket, jeans and boots stood on the ground, with the two helpers beside her looking glum and embarrassed.

'I'm not coming. You're a bloody madman.'

'Get in, get in dammit. The race has started.'

He was very tall, very thin, very agitated.

'I'm not coming.'

'You must.' He made a grab at her and held her wrist in a sinewy grip. It looked almost as if he were going to haul her wholesale into the basket, and she certainly believed it. She tugged and panted and screamed at him. 'Let go, John. Let go. I'm not coming.'

'Are you John Viking?' I said loudly.

He swung his head and kept hold of the girl.

'Yes, I am, what do you want? I'm starting this race as soon as my passenger gets in.'

'I'm not *going*,' she screamed.

I looked around. The other baskets were mostly airborne, sweeping gently across the area a foot or two above the surface, and rising in a smooth, glorious crowd. Every basket, I saw, carried two people.

'If you want a passenger,' I said. 'I'll come.'

He let go of the girl and looked me up and down.

'How much do you weigh?' And then, impatiently, as he saw the other balloons getting a head start, 'Oh, all right, get in. Get in.'

I gripped hold of a stay, and jumped, and wriggled, and ended standing inside a rather small hamper under a very large cloud of balloon.

'Leave go,' commanded the captain of this ship, and the helpers somewhat helplessly obeyed.

The basket momentarily stayed exactly where it was. Then John Viking reached above his head and flipped a lever which operated the burners, and there at close quarters, right above our heads, was the flame and the earfilling roar.

The girl's face was still on a level with mine. 'He's mad,' she yelled. 'And you're crazy.'

The basket moved away, bumped, and rose quite suddenly to a height of six feet. The girl ran after it and delivered a parting encouragement. 'And you haven't got a crash helmet.'

What I did have, though, was a marvellous escape route from two purposeful thugs, and a crash helmet at that moment seemed superfluous, particularly as my companion hadn't one either.

John Viking was staring about him the remnants of fury, muttering under his breath, and operating the burner almost non-stop. His was the last balloon away. I looked down to where the applauding holiday crowd were watching the mass departure and a small boy darted suddenly from under the restraining rope, and ran into the now empty starting area, shouting and pointing. Pointing at John Viking's balloon, pointing excitedly at me.

My pal Mark, with his bright little eyes and his truthful tongue. My pal Mark, whom I'd like to have strangled.

John Viking started cursing. I switched my attention from ground to air and saw that the reason for the resounding and imaginative obscenities floating to heaven was a belt of trees lying ahead which might prevent us going in the same direction. One balloon already lay in a tangle on the take-off side, and another, scarlet and purple, seemed set on a collision course.

John Viking yelled at me over the continuing roar of the burner, 'Hold on bloody tight with both hands. If the basket hits the top of the trees we don't want to be spilled right out.'

The trees looked sixty feet high and a formidable obstacle, but most of the balloons had cleared them easily and were drifting away skywards, great bright pear-shaped fantasies hanging on the wind.

John Viking's basket closed with a rush towards the tree tops with the burner roaring over our heads like a demented dragon. The lift it should have provided seemed totally lacking.

'Turbulence,' John Viking shrieked. 'Bloody turbulence. Hold on. It's a long way down.'

Frightfully jolly, I thought, being tipped out of a hamper sixty feet from the ground without a crash helmet. I grinned at him, and he caught the expression and looked startled.

The basket hit the tree tops, and tipped on its side, tumbling me from the vertical to the horizontal with no trouble at all. I grabbed right-handed at whatever I could to stop myself falling right out, and I felt as much as saw that the majestically swelling envelope above us was carrying on with its journey regardless. It tugged the basket after it, crashing and bumping through the tops of the trees, flinging me about like a rag doll with at times most of my body hanging out in space. My host, made of sterner stuff, had one arm clamped like a vice round one of the metal struts which supported the burner, and the other twined into a black rubber strap. His legs were braced against the side of the basket, which was now the floor, and he changed his footholds as necessary, at one point planting one foot firmly on my stomach.

With a last sickening jolt and wrench the basket tore itself free, and we swung to and fro under the wobbling balloon like a pendulum. I was by this manoeuvre wedged into a disorganized heap in the bottom of the basket, but John Viking still stood rather splendidly on his feet.

There really wasn't much room, I thought, disentangling myself and straightening upwards. The basket, still swaying and shaking, was only four feet square, and reached no higher than one's waist. Along two opposite sides stood eight gas cylinders, four each side, fastened to the wickerwork with rubber straps. The oblong space left was big enough for two men to stand in, but not overgenerous even for that: about two feet by two feet per person.

John Viking gave the burner a rest at last, and into the sudden silence said forcefully, 'Why the hell didn't you hold on like I told you to? Don't you know you damned nearly fell out, and got me into trouble?'

'Sorry,' I said, amused. 'Is it usual to go on burning, when you're stuck on a tree?'

'It got us clear, didn't it?' he demanded.

'It sure did.'

'Don't complain, then. I didn't ask you to come.'

He was of about my own age; perhaps a year or two younger. His face under his blue denim yachting cap was craggy with a bone structure that might one day give him distinction, and his blue eyes shone with the brilliance of the true fanatic. John Viking the madman, I thought, and warmed to him.

'Check round the outsides, will you,' he said. 'See if anything's come adrift.'

It seemed he meant the outside of the basket, as he was himself looking outwards, over the edge. I discovered that on my side, too, there were bundles on the outside of the basket, either strapped to it tight, or swinging on ropes.

One short rope, attached to the basket, had nothing on the end of it. I pulled it up and showed it to him.

'Damnation,' he said explosively. 'Lost in the trees, I suppose. Plastic water container. Hope you're not thirsty.' He stretched up and gave the burner another long burst, and I listened in my mind to the echo of his Etonian drawl and totally understood why he was as he was.

'Do you have to finish first, to win a balloon race?' I said.

He looked surprised. 'Not this one. This is a two and a half hour race. The one who gets furthest in that time is the winner.' He frowned. 'Haven't you ever been in a balloon before?'

'No.'

'My God,' he said. 'What chance have I got?'

'None at all, if I hadn't come,' I said mildly.

'That's true.' He looked down from somewhere like six feet four. 'What's your name?'

'Sid,' I said.

He looked as if Sid wasn't exactly the sort of name his friends had, but faced the fact manfully.

'Why wouldn't your girl come with you?' I said.

'Who? Oh, you mean Popsy. She's not my girl. I don't really know her. She was going to come because my usual passenger broke his leg, silly bugger, when we made a bit of a rough landing last week. Popsy wanted to bring some ruddy big handbag. Wouldn't come without it, wouldn't be parted from it. I ask you! Where is the room for a handbag? And it was heavy, as well. Every pound counts. Carry a pound less, you can go a mile further.'

'Where do you expect to come down?' I said.

'It depends on the wind.' He looked up at the sky. 'We're going roughly north-east at the moment, but I'm going higher. There's a front forecast from the west, and I guess there'll be some pretty useful activity high up. We might make it to Brighton.'

'*Brighton.*' I had thought in terms of perhaps twenty miles, not a hundred. And he must be wrong, I thought: one couldn't go a hundred miles in a balloon in two and a half hours.

'If the wind's more from the northwest we might reach the Isle of Wight. Or France. Depends how much gas is left. We don't want to come down in the sea, not in this. Can you swim?

I nodded. I supposed I still could: hadn't tried it onehanded. 'I'd rather not,' I said.

He laughed. 'Don't worry. The balloon's too darned expensive for me to want to sink it.'

Once free of the trees we had risen very fast, and now floated across country at a height from which cars on the roads looked like toys, though still recognizable as to size and colour.

Noises came up clearly. One could hear the cars' engines, and dogs barking, and an occasional human shout. People looked up and waved to us as we passed. A world removed, I thought. I was in a child's world, idyllically drifting with the wind, sloughing off the dreary earthbound millstones, free and rising and filled with intense delight.

John Viking flipped the lever and the flame roared, shooting up into the green-and-yellow cavern, a scarlet and gold tongue of dragon fire. The burn endured for twenty seconds and we rose perceptibly in the sudden ensuing silence.

'What gas do you use?' I said.

'Propane.'

He was looking over the side of the basket and around at the countryside, as if judging his position. 'Look, get the map out, will you. It's in a pouch thing, on your side. And for God's sake don't let it blow away.'

I looked over the side, and found what he meant. A satchel-like object strapped on through the wickerwork, its outward facing flap fastened shut with a buckle. I undid the buckle, looked inside, took a fair grip of the large folded map, and delivered it safely to the captain.

He was looking fixedly at my left hand, which I'd used as a sort of counterweight on the edge of the basket while I leaned over. I let it fall by my side, and his gaze swept upwards to my face.

'You're missing a hand,' he said incredulously.

'That's right.'

He waved his own two arms in a fierce gesture of frustration. 'How the *hell* am I going to win this race?'

I laughed.

He glanced at me. 'It's not damned funny.'

'Oh yes it is. And I like winning races ... you won't lose it because of me.'

He frowned disgustedly. 'I suppose you can't be much more useless than Popsy,' he said. 'But at least they say she can read a map.' He unfolded the sheet I'd given him, which proved to be a map designed for the navigation of aircraft, its surface covered with a plastic film, for writing on. 'Look,' he said. 'We started from here.' He pointed. 'We're travelling roughly north-east. You take the map, and find out where we are.' He paused. 'Do you know the first bloody thing about using your watch as a compass, or about dead reckoning?'

I had a book about dead reckoning, which I hadn't read, in a pocket of the light cotton anorak I was wearing; and also, I thanked God, in another zippered compartment, a spare fully charged battery. 'Give me the map,' I said. 'And let's see.'

He handed it over with no confidence and started another burn. I worked out roughly where we should be, and looked over the side, and discovered straight away that the ground didn't look like the map, they faded into the brown and green carpet of earth like patches of camouflage, the sunlight mottling them with shadows and dissolving them into ragged edges. The spread-vistas all around looked all the same defying me to recognize anything special, proving conclusively I was less use than Popsy.

Dammit, I thought. Start again.

We had set off at three o'clock, give a minute or two. We had been airborne for twelve minutes. On the ground the wind had been gentle and from the south, but we were now travelling slightly faster, and north-east. Say ... fifteen knots. Twelve minutes at fifteen knots ... about three nautical miles. I had been looking too far ahead. There should be, I thought, a river to cross; and in spite of gazing earnestly down I nearly missed it, because it was a firm blue line on the map and in reality a silvery reflecting thread that wound unobtrusively between a meadow and a wood. To the right of it, half hidden by a hill, lay a village, with beyond it, a railway line.

'We're there,' I said, pointing to the map.

He squinted at the print and searched the ground beneath us.

'Fair enough,' he said. 'So we are. Right. You keep the map. We might as well know where we are, all the way.'

He flipped the lever and gave it a long burn. The balloons ahead of us were also lower. We were definitely looking down on their tops. During the next patch of silence he consulted two instruments which were strapped onto the outside of the basket at his end, and grunted.

'What are those?' I said, nodding at the dials.

'Altimeter and rate-of-climb meter,' he said. 'We're at five thousand feet now, and rising at eight hundred feet a minute.'

'Rising?'

'Yeah.' He gave a sudden, wolfish grin in which I read unmistakably the fierce unholy glee of the mischievous child. 'That's why Popsy wouldn't come. Someone told her I would go high. She didn't want to.'

'How high?' I said.

'I don't mess about,' he said. 'When I race, I race to win. They all know I'll win. They don't like it. They think you should never take risks. They're all safety conscious these days and getting softer. Hah!' His scorn was absolute. 'In the old days, at the beginning of the century, when they had the Gordon Bennett races, they would fly for two days and do a thousand miles or more. But nowadays ... safety bloody first.' He glared at me. 'And if I didn't have to have a passenger, I wouldn't. Passengers always argue and complain.'

He pulled a packet of cigarettes out of his pocket and lit one with a flick of a lighter. We were surrounded by cylinders of liquid gas. I thought about all the embargoes against naked flames near any sort of stored fuel, and kept my mouth shut.

The flock of balloons below us seemed to be veering away to the left; but then I realized that it was we who were going to the right. John Viking watched the changing direction with great satisfaction and started another long burn. We rose perceptibly faster, and the sun, instead of shining full on our backs, appeared on our starboard side.

In spite of the sunshine it was getting pretty cold. A look over the side showed the earth very far beneath, and one could now see a very long way in all directions. I checked with the map, and kept an eye on where we were.

'What are you wearing?' he said.

'What you see, more or less.'

'Huh.'

During the burns, the flame over one's head was almost too hot, and there was always a certain amount of hot air escaping from the bottom of the balloon. There was no wind factor, as of course the balloon was travelling with the wind, at the wind's speed. It was sheer altitude that was making us cold.

'How high are we now?' I said.

He glanced at his instrument. 'Eleven thousand feet.'

'And still rising?'

He nodded. The other balloons, far below and to the left, were a cluster of distant bright blobs against the green earth.

'All that lot,' he said, 'will stay down at five thousand feet, because of staying under the airways.' He gave me a sideways look. 'You'll see on the map. The airways that the airlines use are marked, and so are the heights at which one is not allowed to fly through them.

'And one is not allowed to fly through an airway at eleven thousand feet in a balloon?'

'Sid,' he said, grinning. 'You're not bad.'

He flicked the lever, and the burner roared, cutting off chat. I checked the ground against the map and nearly lost our position entirely, because we seemed suddenly to have travelled much faster, and quite definitely to the south-east. The other balloons, when I next looked were out of sight.

In the silence John Viking told me that the helpers of the other balloons would follow them on the ground, in cars, ready to retrieve them when they came down.

'What about you?' I asked. 'Do we have someone following?' Did we indeed have Peter Rammileese following, complete with thugs, ready to pounce again at the further end? We were even, I thought fleetingly, doing him a favour with the general direction, taking him south-eastwards, home to Kent.

John Viking gave his wolfish smile, and said, 'No car on earth could keep up with us today.'

'Do you mean it?' I exclaimed.

He looked at the altimeter. 'Fifteen thousand feet,' he said. 'We'll stay at that. I got a forecast from the air boys for this trip. Fifty knot wind from two nine zero at fifteen thousand feet, that's what they said. You hang on, Sid, pal, and we'll get to Brighton.'

I thought about the two of us standing in a waist-high four foot square wicker basket, supported by terylene and hot air, fifteen thousand feet about the solid ground, travelling without any feeling of speed at fifty-seven miles an hour. Quite mad, I thought.

From the ground, we would be a black speck. On the ground, no car could keep up. I grinned back at John Viking with a satisfaction as great as his own, and he laughed aloud.

'Would you believe it?' he said. 'At last I've got someone up here who's not puking with fright.'

He lit another cigarette, and then he changed the supply line to the burner from one cylinder to the next. This involved switching off the empty tank, unscrewing the connecting nut, screwing it into the next cylinder, and switching on the new supply. There were two lines to the double burner, one for each set of four cylinders. He held the cigarette in his mouth throughout, and squinted through the smoke.

I had seen from the map that we were flying straight towards the airway which led in and out of Gatwick, where large aeroplanes thundered up and down not expecting to meet squashy balloons illegally in their path.

His appetite for taking risks was way out of my class. He made sitting on a horse over fences on the ground seem rather tame. Except, I thought with a jerk, that I no longer did it, I fooled around instead with men who threatened to shoot hands off ... and I was safer up here with John Viking the madman, propane and cigarettes, mid-air collisions and all.

'Right,' he said. 'We just stay as we are for an hour and a half and let the wind take us. If you feel odd, it's lack of oxygen.' He took a pair of wool gloves from his pocket and put them on. 'Are you cold?'

'Yes, a bit.'

He grinned. 'I've got long johns under my jeans, and two sweaters under my anorak. You'll just have to freeze.'

'Thanks very much.' I stood on the map and put my real hand deep into the pocket of my cotton anorak and he said at least the false hand couldn't get frostbite.

He operated the burner and looked at his watch and the ground and the altimeter, and seemed pleased with the way things were. Then he looked at me in slight puzzlement and I knew he was wondering, now that there was time, how I happened to be where I was.

'I came to Highalane Park to see you,' I said. 'I mean, you, John Viking, particularly.'

He looked startled. 'Do you read minds?'

'All the time.' I pulled my hand out of one pocket and dipped into another, and brought out the paperback on navigation. 'I came to ask you about this. It's got your name on the flyleaf.'

He frowned at it, and opened the front cover. 'Good Lord. I wondered where this had got to. How did you have it?'

'Did you lend it to anyone?'

'I don't think so.'

'Um ...' I said. 'If I describe someone to you, will you say if you know him?'

'Fire away.'

'A man of about twenty-eight,' I said. 'Dark hair, good looks, full of fun and jokes, easy-going, likes girls, great company, has a habit of carrying a knife strapped to his leg under his sock, and is very likely a crook.'

'Oh yes,' he said, nodding. 'He's my cousin.'

Chapter Twelve

His cousin, Norris Abbott. What had he done this time, he demanded, and I asked, what had he done before?

'A trail of bouncing cheques that his mother paid for.'

Where did he live, I asked. John Viking didn't know. He saw him only when Norris turned up occasionally on his doorstep, usually broke and looking for free meals.

'A laugh a minute for a day or two. Then he's gone.'

'Where does his mother live?'

'She's dead. He's alone now. No parents or brothers or sisters. No relatives except me.' He peered at me, frowning. 'Why do you ask all this?'

'A girl I know wants to find him.' I shrugged. 'It's nothing much.'

He lost interest at once and flicked the lever for another burn. 'We use twice the fuel up here as near the ground,' he said afterwards. 'That's why I brought so much. That's how some nosey parker told Popsy I was planning to go high, and through the airways.'

By my reckoning the airway was not that far off.

'Won't you get into trouble?' I said.

The wolf grin came and went. 'They've got to see us, first. We won't show up on radar. We're too small for the equipment they use. With a bit of luck, we'll sneak across and no one will be any the wiser.'

I picked up the map and studied it. At fifteen thousand feet we would be illegal from when we entered controlled airspace until we landed, all but the last two hundred feet. The airway over Brighton began at a thousand feet about sea level and the hills to the north were eight hundred feet high. Did John Viking know all that? Yes, he did.

When we had been flying for one hour and fifty minutes he made a fuel line change from cylinder to cylinder that resulted in a thin jet of liquid gas spurting out from the connection like water out of a badly joined hose. The jet shot across the corner of the basket and hit a patch of wickerwork about six inches below the top rail.

John Viking was smoking at the time.

Liquid propane began trickling down the inside of the basket in a stream. John Viking cursed and fiddled with the faulty connection, bending over it; and his glowing cigarette ignited the gas.

There was no ultimate and final explosion. The jet burnt as jets do, and directed its flame in an organized manner at the patch of basket it was hitting. John Viking threw his cigarette over the side and snatched off his denim cap, and beat at the burning basket with great flailing motions of his arm, while I managed to stifle the jet at source by turning off the main switch on the cylinder.

When the flames and smoke and cursing died down, we had a hole six inches in diameter right through the basket, but no other damage.

'Baskets don't burn easily,' he said calmly, as if nothing had happened. 'Never known one burn much more than this.' He inspected his cap, which was scorched into black-edged lace, and gave me a maniacal four seconds from the bright blue eyes. 'You can't put out a fire with a crash helmet,' he said.

I laughed quite a lot.

It was the altitude, I thought, which was making me giggle.

'Want some chocolate?' he said.

There were no signposts in the sky to tell us when we crossed the boundary of the airway. We saw an aeroplane or two some way off, but nothing near us. No one came buzzing around to direct us downward. We simply sailed straight on, blowing across the sky as fast as a train.

At ten past five he said it was time to go down, because if we didn't touch ground by five-thirty exactly he would be disqualified, and he didn't want that; he wanted to win. Winning was what it was all about.

'How would anyone know exactly when we touched down?' I said.

He gave me a pitying look and gently directed his toe at a small box strapped to the floor beside one of the corner cylinders.

'In here is a barograph, all stuck about with pompous red seals. The judges seal it, before the start. It shows variations in air pressure. Highly sensitive. All our journey shows up like a row of peaks. When you're on the ground, the trace is flat and steady. It tells the judges just when you took off and when you landed. Right?'

'Right.'

OK. Down we go, then.'

He reached up and untied a red cord which was knotted to the burner frame, and pulled it. 'It opens a panel at the top of the balloon,' he said. 'Let's the hot air out.'

His idea of descent was all of a piece. The altimeter unwound like a broken clock and the rate-of-climb meter was pointing to a thousand feet a minute, downwards. He seemed to be quite unaffected, but it made me queasy and hurt my eardrums. Swallowing made things a bit better, but no much. I concentrated, as an antidote, on checking with the map to see where we were going.

The Channel lay like a broad grey carpet to our right, and it was incredible but, whichever way I looked at it, it seemed that we were on a collision course with Beachy Head.

'Yeah,' John Viking casually confirmed. 'Guess we'll try not to get blown off those cliffs. Might be better to land on the beach further on . . .' He checked his watch. 'Ten minutes to go. We're still at six thousand feet . . . that's all right . . . might be the edge of the sea . . .'

'Not the sea,' I said positively.

'Why not? We might have to.'

'Well,' I said, 'this ...' I lifted my left arm. 'Inside this hand-shaped plastic there's actually a lot of fine engineering. Strong pincers inside the thumb and first two fingers. A lot of fine precision gears and transistors and printed electrical circuits. Dunking it in the sea would be like dunking a radio. A total ruin. And it would cost me two thousand quid to get a new one.'

He was astonished. 'You're joking.'

'No.'

'Better keep you dry, then. And anyway, now we're down here, I don't think we'll get as far south as Beachy Head. Probably further east.' He paused and looked at my left hand doubtfully. 'It'll be a rough landing. The fuel's cold from being so high ... the burner doesn't function well on cold fuel. It takes time to heat enough air to give us a softer touchdown.'

A softer touchdown took time ... too much time.

'Win the race,' I said.

His face lit into sheer happiness. 'Right,' he said decisively. 'What's that town just ahead?'

I studied the map. 'Eastbourne.'

He looked at his watch. 'Five minutes.' He looked at the altimeter and at Eastbourne, upon which we were rapidly descending. 'Two thousand feet. Bit dicy, hitting the roofs. There isn't much wind down here, is there.... But if I burn, we might not get down in time. No, no burn.'

A thousand feet a minute, I reckoned, was eleven or twelve miles an hour. I had been used for years to hitting the ground at more than twice that speed ... though not in a basket, and not when the ground might turn out to be fully inhabited by brick walls.

We were travelling sideways over the town, with houses below us. Descent was very fast. 'Three minutes,' he said.

The sea lay ahead again, fringing the far side of the town, and for a moment it looked as if it was there we would have to come down after all. John Viking, however, knew better.

'Hang on,' he said. 'this is it.'

He hauled strongly on the red cord he held, which led upwards into the balloon. Somewhere above, the vent for the hot air widened dramatically, the lifting power of the balloon fell away, and the solid edge of Eastbourne came up with a rush.

We scraped the eaves of grey slate roofs, made a sharp diagonal descent over a road and a patch of grass, and smashed down on a broad concrete walk twenty yards from the waves.

'Don't get out. Don't get out,' he yelled. The basket tipped on its side and began to slither along the concrete, dragged by the still half-inflated silken mass. 'Without our weight, it could still fly away.'

As I was again wedged among the cylinders, it was superfluous advice. The basket rocked and tumbled a few more times and I with it, and John Viking cursed and hauled at his red cord and finally let out enough air for us to be still.

He looked at his watch, and his blue eyes blazed with triumph.

'We've made it. Five twenty-nine. That was a bloody good race. The best ever. What are you doing next Saturday?'

I went back to Aynsford by train, which took forever, with Charles picking me up from Oxford station not far short of midnight.

'You went on the balloon race,' he repeated disbelievingly. 'Did you enjoy it?'

'Very much.'

'And your car's still at Highalane Park?'

'It can say there until morning,' I yawned. 'Nicholas Ashe now has a name, by the way. He's someone called Norris Abbott. Same initials, silly man.'

'Will you tell the police?'

'See if we can find him, first.'

He glanced at me sideways. 'Jenny came back this evening, after you'd telephoned.'

'Oh no.'

'I didn't know she was going to.'

I supposed I believed him. I hoped she would have gone to bed before I arrived, but she hadn't. She was sitting on the gold brocade sofa in the drawing room, looking belligerent.

'I don't like you coming here so much,' she said.

A knife to the heart of things from my pretty wife.

Charles said smoothly, 'Sid is welcome here always.'

'Discarded husbands should have more pride than to fawn on their fathers-in-law, who put up with it because they're sorry for them.'

'You're jealous,' I said, surprised.

She stood up fast, as angry as I'd ever seen her.

'How dare you!' she said. 'He always takes your side. He thinks you're bloody marvellous. He doesn't know you like I do, all your stubborn little ways and your meanness and thinking you're always *right*.'

'I'm going to bed,' I said.

'And you're a coward as well,' she said furiously. 'Running away from a few straight truths.'

'Goodnight, Charles,' I said. 'Goodnight, Jenny. Sleep well, my love, and pleasant dreams.'

'You ...' she said. 'You ... I hate you, Sid.'

I went out of the drawing room without fuss and upstairs to the bedroom I thought of as mine; the one I always slept in nowadays at Aynsford.

You don't have to hate me, Jenny, I thought miserably; I hate myself.

Charles drove me to Wiltshire in the morning to collect my car, which still stood where I'd left it, though surrounded now by acres of empty grass. There was no Peter Rammileese in sight, and no thugs waiting in ambush. All clear for an uneventful return to London.

'Sid,' Charles said, as I unlocked the car door. 'Don't pay any attention to Jenny.'

'No.'

'Come to Aynsford whenever you want.'

I nodded.

'I mean it, Sid.'

'Yeah.'

'Damn Jenny,' he said explosively.

'Oh no. She's unhappy. She ...' I paused. 'I guess she needs comforting. A shoulder to cry on, and all that.'

He said austerely, 'I don't care for tears.'

'No.' I sighed and got into the car, waved goodbye, and drove over the bumpy grass to the gate. The help that Jenny needed, she wouldn't take from me; and her father didn't know how to give it. Just another of life's bloody muddles, another irony in the general mess.

I drove into the city and around in a few small circles, and ended up in the publishing offices of *Antiques for All*, which proved to be only one of a number of specialist magazines put out by a newspaper company. To the *Antiques* editor, a fair-haired earnest young man in heavy-framed specs, I explained both the position and the need.

'Our mailing list?' he said doubtfully. 'Mailing lists are strictly private, you know.'

I explained all over again, and threw in a lot of pathos. My wife behind bars if I didn't find the con man, that sort of thing.

'Oh very well,' he said. 'But it will be stored in a computer. You'll have to wait for a print-out.'

I waited patiently, and received in the end a stack of paper setting out fifty-three thousand names and addresses, give or take a few dead ones.

'And we want it back,' he said severely. 'Unmarked and complete.'

'How did Norris Abbott get hold of it?' I asked.

He didn't know, and neither the name nor the description of Abbott/Ashe brought any glimmer of recognition.

'How about a copy of the magazine, for good measure?'

I got that too, and disappeared before he could regret all his generosity. Back in the car, I telephoned Chico and got him to come to the flat. Meet me outside, I said. Carry my bag upstairs and earn your salary.

He was there when I pulled up at a vacant parking meter and we went upstairs together. The flat was empty, and quiet, and safe.

'A lot of leg work, my son,' I said, taking the mailing list out of the package I had transported it in, and putting it on the table. 'All your own.'

He eyed it unenthusiastically. 'And what about you?'

'Chester races,' I said. 'One of the syndicate horses runs there tomorrow. Meet me back here Thursday morning, ten o'clock. O.K.?'

'Yeah.' He thought. 'Suppose our Nicky hasn't got himself organized yet, and sends out his begging letters next week, after we've drawn a blank?'

'Mm ... Better take some sticky labels with this address on, and ask them to send the letters here, if they get them.'

'We'll be lucky.'

'You never know. No one likes being conned.'

'May as well get started, then.' He picked up the folder containing the magazine and mailing list, and looked ready to leave.

'Chico ... Stay until I've repacked my bag. I think I'll start northwards right now. Stay until I go.'

He was puzzled. 'If you like, but what for?'

'Er ...'

'Come on, Sid. Out with it.'

'Peter Rammileese and a couple of guys came looking for me yesterday at Highalane Park. So I'd just like you around, while I'm here.'

'What sort of guys?' he said suspiciously.

I nodded. 'Those sort. Hard eyes and boots.'

'Guys who kick people half to death in Tunbridge Wells?'

'You dodged them, I see.'

'In a balloon.' I told him about the race while I put some things in a suitcase. He laughed at the story but afterwards came quite seriously back to business.

'Those buys of yours don't sound like your ordinary run-of-the-mill rent-a-thug,' he said. 'Here, let me fold that jacket, you'll turn up at Chester all creased.' He took my packing out of my hands and did it for me, quickly and neatly. 'Got all the spare batteries? There's one in the bathroom.' I fetched it. 'Look, Sid, I don't like these syndicates.' He snapped the locks shut and carried the case into the hall. 'Let's tell Lucas Wainwright we're not doing them.'

'And who tells Peter Rammileese?'

'We do. We ring him up and tell him.'

'You do it,' I said. 'Right now.'

We stood and looked at each other. Then he shrugged and picked up the suitcase. 'Got everything?' he said. 'Raincoat?' We went down to the car and stowed my case in the boot. 'Look, Sid, you just take care, will you? I don't like hospital visiting, you know that.'

'Don't lose that mailing list,' I said. 'Or the editor of *Antiques* will be cross.'

I booked unmolested into a motel and spent the evening watching the television, and the following afternoon arrived without trouble at Chester races.

All the usual crowd were there, standing around, making the usual conversations. It was my first time on a racecourse since the dreary week in Paris, and it seemed to me when I walked in that the change in me must be clearly visible. But no one, of course, noticed the blistering sense of shame I felt at the sight of George Caspar outside the weighing room, or treated me any differently from usual. It was I alone who knew I didn't deserve the smiles and the welcome. I was a fraud. I shrank inside. I hadn't known I would feel so bad.

The trainer from Newmarket who had offered me a ride with his string was there, and repeated his offer.

'Sid, do come. Come this Friday, stay the night with us, and ride work on Saturday morning.'

There wasn't much, I reflected, that anyone could give me that I'd rather accept: and besides, Peter Rammileese and his merry men would have a job finding me there.

'Martin ... Yes, I'd love to.'

'Great.' He seemed pleased. 'Come for evening stables, Friday night.'

He went on into the weighing room, and I wondered if he would have asked me if he'd known how I'd spent Guineas day.

Bobby Unwin buttonholed me with his inquisitive eyes. 'Where have you been?' he said. 'I didn't see you at the Guineas.'

'I didn't go.'

'I thought you'd be bound to, after all your interest in Tri-Nitro.'

'No.'

'I reckon you had the smell of something going on, there, Sid. All that interest in the Caspars, and about Gleaner and Zingaloo. Come clean, now, what do you know?'

'Nothing, Bobby.'

'I don't believe you.' He gave me a hard unforgiving stare and steered his beaky nose towards more fruitful copy in the shape of a top trainer enduring a losing streak. I would have trouble persuading him, I thought, if I should ever ask for his help again.

Rosemary Caspar, walking with a woman friend to whom she was chatting, almost bumped into me before either of us was aware of the other being there. The look in her eyes made Bobby Unwin seem loving.

'Go away,' she said violently. 'Why are you here?'

The woman friend looked very surprised. I stepped out of the way without saying a word, which surprised her still further. Rosemary impatiently twitched her onwards, and I heard her voice rising, 'But surely, Rosemary, that was Sid Halley....'

My face felt stiff. It's too bloody much, I thought. I couldn't have made their horse win if I'd stayed. *I couldn't* ... but I might have. I would always think I might have, if I'd tried. If I hadn't been scared out of my mind.

'Hallo Sid,' a voice said at my side. 'Lovely day, isn't it?'

'Oh lovely.'

Philip Friarly smiled and watched Rosemary's retreating back. 'She's been snapping at everyone since that disaster last week. Poor Rosemary. Takes things so much to heart.'

'You can't blame her,' I said. 'She said it would happen, and no one believed her.'

'Did she tell you?' he said curiously.

I nodded.

'Ah,' he said, in understanding. 'Galling for you.'

I took a deep loosening breath and made myself concentrate on something different.

'That horse of yours, today,' I said. 'Are you just giving it a sharpener, running it here on the Flat?'

'Yes,' he said briefly. 'And if you ask me how it will run, I'll have to tell you that it depends on who's giving the orders, and who's taking them.'

'That's cynical.'

'Have you found out anything for me?'

'Not very much. It's why I came here.' I paused. 'Do you know the name and address of the person who formed your syndicates?'

'Not off hand,' he said. 'I didn't deal with him myself, do you see? The syndicates were already well advanced when I was asked to join. The horses had already been bought, and most of the shares were sold.'

'They used you,' I said. 'Used your name. A respectable front.'

He nodded unhappily. 'I'm afraid so.'

'Do you know Peter Rammileese?'

'Who?' He shook his head. 'Never heard of him.'

'He buys and sells horses,' I said. 'Lucas Wainwright thinks it was he who formed the syndicates, and he who is operating them, and he's bad news to the Jockey Club and barred from most racecourses.'

'Oh dear.' He sounded distressed. 'If Lucas is looking into them. . . . What do you think I should do, Sid?'

'From your point of view,' I said. 'I think you should sell your shares, or dissolve the syndicates entirely, and get your name out of them as fast as possible.'

'All right, I will. And Sid . . . next time I'm tempted, I'll get you to check on the other people in the syndicate. The Security section are supposed to have done these, and look at them!'

'Who's riding your horse today?' I said.

'Larry Server.'

He waited for an opinion, but I didn't give it. Larry Server was middle ability, middle employed, rode mostly on the Flat and sometimes over hurdles, and was to my mind in the market for unlawful bargains.

'Who chooses the jockey?' I said. 'Larry Server doesn't ride all that often for your horse's trainer.'

'I don't know,' he said doubtfully. 'I leave all that to the trainer, of course.'

I made a small grimace.

'Don't you approve?' he said.

'If you like,' I said, 'I'll give you a list of jockeys for your jumpers that you can at least trust to be trying to win. Can't guarantee their ability, but you can't have everything.'

'Now who's a cynic?' He smiled, and said with patent and piercing regret, 'I wish you were still riding them, Sid.'

'Yeah.' I said it with a smile, but he saw the flicker I hadn't managed to keep out of my eyes.

With a compassion I definitely didn't want, he said, 'I'm so sorry.'

'It was great while it lasted,' I said lightly. 'That's all that matters.'

He shook his head, annoyed with himself for his clumsiness.

'Look,' I said, 'if you were *glad* I'm not still riding them I'd feel a whole lot worse.'

'We had some grand times, didn't we? Some exceptional days.'

'Yes, we did.'

There could be an understanding between an owner and a jockey, I thought, that was intensely intimate. In the small area where their lives touched, where the speed and the winning were all that mattered, there could be a privately shared joy, like a secret, that endured like cement. I hadn't felt it often, nor with many of the people I had ridden for, but with Philip Friarly, nearly always.

A man detached himself from another group near us, and came towards us with a smiling face.

'Philip. Sid. Nice to see you.'

We made the polite noises back, but with genuine pleasure, as Sir Thomas Ullaston, the reigning Senior Steward, head of the Jockey Club, head, more or less, of the whole racing industry, was a sensible man and a fair and openminded administrator. A little severe at times, some thought, but it wasn't a job for a soft man. In the short time since he'd been put in charge of things there had been some good new rules and a clearing out of injustices, and he was as decisive as his predecessor had been weak.

'How's it going, Sid?' he said. 'Caught any good crooks lately?'

'Not lately,' I said ruefully.

He smiled to Philip Friarly, 'Our Sid's putting the Security section's nose out of joint, did you know? I had Eddy Keith along in my office on Monday complaining that we give Sid too free a hand, and asking that we shouldn't let him operate on the racecourse.'

'Eddy Keith?' I said.

'Don't look so shocked, Sid,' Sir Thomas said teasingly. 'I told him that racing owed you a great deal, starting with the saving of Seabury racecourse itself and going right on from there, and that in no way would the Jockey Club ever interfere with you, unless you did something absolutely diabolical, which on past form I can't see you doing.'

'Thank you,' I said faintly.

'And you may take it,' he said firmly, 'that that is the official Jockey Club view, as well as my own.'

'Why,' I said slowly, 'does Eddy Keith want me stopped?'

He shrugged. 'Something about access to the Jockey Club files. Apparently you saw some, and he resented it. I told him he'd have to live with it, because I was certainly not in any way going to put restraints on what I consider a positive force for good in racing.'

I felt grindingly undeserving of all that, but he gave me no time to protest.

'Why don't both of you come upstairs for a drink and a sandwich? Come along, Sid, Philip . . .' He turned, gesturing us to follow, leading the way.

We went up the stairs marked 'Private' which on most racecourses lead to the civilized luxuries of the Stewards' box, and into a carpeted glass-fronted room looking out to the white-railed track. There were several groups of people there already, and a manservant handing around drinks on a tray.

'I expect you know most people,' Sir Thomas said, hospitably making introductions. 'Madelaine, my dear . . .' to his wife, '. . . do you know Lord Friarly, and Sid Halley?' We shook her hand. 'And oh yes, Sid,' he said, touching my arm to bring me around face to face with another of his guests . . .

'Have you met Trevor Deansgate?'

Chapter Thirteen

We stared at each other, probably equally stunned.

I thought of how he had last seen me, on my back in the straw barn, spilling my guts out with fear. He'll see it still in my face, I thought. He knows what he's made of me. I can't just stand here without moving a muscle . . . and yet I must.

My head seemed to be floating somewhere above the rest of my body, and an awful lot of awfulness got condensed into four seconds.

'Do you know each other?' Sir Thomas said, slightly puzzled.

Trevor Deansgate said, 'Yes. We've met.'

There was at least no sneer either in his eyes or his voice. If it hadn't been impossible, I would have thought that what he looked was *wary*.

'Drink, Sid?' said Sir Thomas; and I found the man with the tray at my elbow. I took a tumbler with whisky-coloured contents and tried to stop my fingers trembling.

Sir Thomas said conversationally, 'I've just been telling Sid how much the Jockey Club appreciates his successes, and it seems to have silenced him completely.'

Neither Trevor Deansgate nor I said anything. Sir Thomas raised his eyebrows a fraction and tried again. 'Well, Sid, tell us a good thing for the big race.'

I dragged my scattered wits back into at least a pretence of life going uneventfully on.

'Oh . . . Winetaster, I should think.'

My voice sounded strained, to me, but Sir Thomas seemed not to notice. Trevor Deansgate looked down to the glass in his own well-manicured hand and swivelled the ice cubes round in the golden liquid. Another of the guests spoke to Sir Thomas, and he turned away, and Trevor Deansgate's gaze came immediately back to my face filled with naked savage threat. His voice, quick and hard, spoke straight from the primitive underbelly, the world of violence and vengeance and no pity at all.

'If you break your assurance, I'll do what I said.'

He held my eyes until he was sure I had received the message, and then he too turned away, and I could see the heavy muscles of his shoulders bunching formidably inside his coat.

'Sid,' Philip Friarly said, appearing once more at my side. 'Lady Ullaston wants to know ... I say, are you feeling all right?'

I nodded a bit faintly.

'My dear chap, you look frightfully pale.'

'I ... er ...' I took a vague grip on things. 'What did you say?'

'Lady Ullaston wants to know ...' He went on at some length, and I listened and answered with a feeling of complete unreality. One could literally be torn apart in spirit while standing with a glass in one's hand making social chit chat to the Senior Steward's lady. I couldn't remember, five minutes later, a word that was said. I couldn't feel my feet on the carpet. I'm a mess, I thought.

The afternoon went on. Winetaster got beaten in the big race by a glossy dark filly called Mrs Hillman, and in the race after that Larry Server took Philip Friarly's syndicate horse to the back of the field, and stayed there. Nothing improved internally, and after the fifth I decided it was pointless staying any longer, since I couldn't even effectively think.

Outside the gate there was the usual gaggle of chauffeurs leaning against cars, waiting for their employers; and also, with them, one of the jump jockeys whose licence had been lost through taking bribes from Rammileese.

I nodded to him, as I passed. 'Jacksy.'

'Sid.'

I walked on to the car, and unlocked it, and flung my raceglasses onto the back seat. Got in. Started the engine. Paused for a bit, and reversed all the way back to the gate.

'Jacksy?' I said.'Get in, I'm buying.'

'Buying what?' He came over and opened the passenger door, and sat in beside me. I fished my wallet out of my rear trouser pocket and tossed it into his lap.

'Take all the money,' I said. I drove forward through the carpark and out through the distant gate onto the public road.

'But you dropped me quite a lot, not long ago,' he said.

I gave him a fleeting sideways smile. 'Yeah. Well ... this is for services about to be rendered.'

He counted the notes. 'All of it?' he said doubtfully.

'I want to know about Peter Rammileese.'

'Oh no.' He made as if to open the door, but the car by then was going too fast.

'Jacksy,' I said, 'no one's listening but me, and I'm not telling anyone else. Just say how much he paid you and what for, and anything else you can think of.'

He was silent for a bit. Then he said, 'It's more than my life's worth, Sid. There's a whisper out that he's brought two pros down from Glasgow for a special job and anyone who gets in his way just now is liable to be stamped on.'

'Have you seen these pros?' I said, thinking that I had.

'No. It just come through on the grapevine, like.'

'Does the grapevine know what the special job is?'

He shook his head.

'Anything to do with syndicates?'

'Be your age, Sid. Everything to do with Rammileese is always to do with syndicates. He runs about twenty. Maybe more.'

Twenty, I thought, frowning. I said, 'What's his rate for the job of doing a Larry Server, like today?'

'Sid,' he protested.

'How does he get someone like Larry Server onto a horse he wouldn't normally ride?'

'He asks the trainer nicely, with a fistful of dollars.'

'He bribes the *trainers*?'

'It doesn't take much, sometimes.' He looked thoughtful for a while. 'Don't you quote me, but there were races run last autumn where Rammileese was behind every horse in the field. He just carved them up as he liked.'

'It's impossible,' I said.

'No. All that dry weather we had, remember? Fields of four, five or six runners, sometimes, because the ground was so hard? I know of three races for sure when all the runners were his. The poor sodding bookies didn't know what had hit them.'

Jacksy counted the money again. 'Do you know how much you've got here?' he said.

'Just about.'

I glanced at him briefly. He was twenty-five, an ex-apprentice grown too heavy for the Flat and known to resent it. Jump jockeys on the whole earned less than the Flat boys, and there were the bruises besides, and it wasn't everyone who like me found steeplechasing double the fun. Jacksy didn't; but he could ride pretty well, and I'd raced alongside him often enough to know he wouldn't put you over the rails for nothing at all. For a consideration, yes, but for nothing, no.

The money was troubling him. For ten or twenty he would have lied to me easily: but we had a host of shared memories of changing rooms and horses and wet days and mud and falls and trudging back over sodden turf in paper-thin racing boots, and it isn't so easy, if you're not a real villain, to rob someone you know as well as that.

'Funny,' he said, 'you taking to this detecting lark.'

'Riotous.'

'No, straight up. I mean, you don't come after the lads for little things.'

'No,' I agreed. Little things like taking bribes. My business, on the whole, was with the people who offered them.

'I kept all the newspapers,' he said. 'After that trial.'

I shook my head resignedly. Too many people in the racing world had kept those papers, and the trial had been a trial for me in more ways than one. Defence counsel had revelled in deeply embarrassing the victim; and the prisoner, charged with causing grievous bodily harm with intent, contrary to section 18 of the Offences Against the Person Act 1861, (or in other words, bopping an ex-jockey's left hand with a poker) had been rewarded by four years in clink. It would be difficult to say who had enjoyed the proceedings less, the one in the witness box or the one in the dock.

Jacksy kept up his disconnected remarks, which I gathered were a form of time-filling while he sorted himself out underneath.

'I'll get my licence back for next season,' he said.

'Great.'

'Seabury's a good track. I'll be riding there in August. All the lads think it's fine the course is still going, even if . . .' He glanced at my hand. 'Well . . . you couldn't race with it anyway, could you, as it was?'

'Jacksy,' I said exasperated. 'Will you or won't you?'

He flipped through the notes again, and folded them, and put them in his pocket.

'Yes. All right. Here's your wallet.'

'Put it in the glove box.'

He did that, and looked out of the window. 'Where are we going?' he said.

'Anywhere you like.'

'I got a lift to Chester. He'll have gone without me by now. Can you take me south, like, and I'll hitch the rest.'

So I drove towards London, and Jacksy talked.

'Rammileese gave me ten times the regular fee, for riding a loser. Now listen, Sid, you swear this won't get back to him?'

'Not through me.'

'Yeah. Well, I suppose I do trust you.'

'Get on, then.'

'He buys quite good horses. Horses that can win. Then he syndicates them. I reckon sometimes he makes five hundred per cent profit on them, for a start. He bought one I knew of for six thousand and sold ten shares at three thousand each. He's got two pals who are O.K. registered owners, and he puts one of them in each syndicate, and they swing it so some fancy figurehead takes a share, so the whole thing looks right.'

'Who are the two pals?'

He gulped a lot, but told me. One name meant nothing, but the other had appeared on all of Philip Friarly's syndicates.

'Right,' I said. 'On you go.'

'The horses get trained by anyone who can turn them out looking nice for double the usual training fees and no questions asked. Then Rammileese works out what races they're going to run in, and they're all running way below their real class, see, so that when he says go, by Christ you're on a flyer.' He grinned. 'Twenty times the riding fee, for a winner.'

It sounded a lot more than it was.

'How often did you ride for him?'

'One or two, most weeks.'

'Will you do it again, when you get your licence back?'

He turned in his seat until his back was against the car's door and spent a long time studying the half he could see of my face. His silence itself was an answer, but when we had travelled fully three miles he sighed deeply and said, finally, 'Yes.'

As an act of trust, that was remarkable.

'Tell me about the horses,' I said, and he did, at some length. The names of some of them were a great surprise, and the careers of all of them as straightforward as Nicholas Ashe.

'Tell me how you got your licence suspended,' I said.

He had been riding for one of the amenable trainers, he said, only the trainer hadn't had an amenable wife. 'She had a bit of a spite on, so she shopped him with the Jockey Club. Wrote to Thomas Ullaston personally, I ask you. Of course, the whole bleeding lot of Stewards believed her, and suspended the lot of us, me, him, and the other jock who rides for him, poor sod, who never got a penny from Rammileese and wouldn't know a backhander if it smacked him in the face.'

'How come,' I said casually, 'that no one in the Jockey Club has found out about all these syndicates and done something positive about Rammileese?'

'Good question.'

I glanced at him, hearing the doubt in his voice and seeing the frown. 'Go on,' I said.

'Yeah.... This is strictly a whisper, see, not even a rumour hardly, just something I heard....' He paused, then he said, 'I don't reckon it's true.'

'Try me.'

'One of the bookies ... I was waiting about outside the gates at Kempton, see, and these two bookies came out, and one was saying that the bloke in the Security Service would smooth it over if the price was right.' He stopped again, and went on, 'One of the lads said I'd never have got suspended if that bitch of a trainer's wife had sent her letter to the Security Service and not to the big white chief himself.'

'Which of the lads said that?'

'Yeah. Well, I can't remember. And don't look like that, Sid, I really can't. It was months ago. I mean, I didn't even think about it until I heard the bookies at Kempton. I don't reckon there could be anyone that bent in the Security Service, do you? I mean, not in the Jockey Club.'

His faith was touching, I thought, considering his present troubles, but in days gone by I would have thought he was right. Once plant the doubt, though, and one could see there were a lot of dirty misdeeds that Eddy Keith might have ignored in return for a tax-free gain. He had passed the four Friarly syndicates: and he might have done all of the twenty or more. He might even have put Rammileese's two pals on the respectable owners' list, knowing they weren't. Somehow or other, I would have to find out.

'Sid,' Jacksy said. 'Don't you get me in bad with the brass. I'm not repeating what I just told you, not to no stewards.'

'I won't say you told me,' I assured him. 'Do you know those two bookies at Kempton?'

'Not a chance. I mean, I don't even know they were bookies. They just looked like them. I mean, I thought "bookies" when I saw them.'

So strong an impression was probably right, but not of much help; and Jacksy, altogether, had run dry. I dropped him where he wanted, at the outskirts of Watford, and the last thing he said was that if I was going after Rammileese to keep him, Jacksy, strictly out of it, like I'd promised.

I stayed in a hotel in London instead of the flat, and felt overcautious. Chico, however, when I telephoned, said it made sense. Breakfast, I suggested, and he said he'd be there.

He came, but without much hooray. He had trudged around all day visiting the people on the mailing list, but no one had received a begging letter from Ashe within the last month.

'Tell you what, though,' he said. 'People beginning with A and B and right down to K have had wax in the past, so it'll be the Ps and Rs that get done next time, which narrows the leg-work.'

'Great,' I said, meaning it.

'I left sticky labels everywhere with your address on, and some of them said they'd let us know, if it came. But whether they'll bother ...'

'It would only take one,' I said.

'That's true.'

'Feel like a spot of breaking and entering?'

'Don't see why not.' He started on a huge order of scrambled eggs and sausages. 'Where and what for?'

'Er ...,' I said. 'This morning you do a recce. This evening, after office hours but before it gets dark, we drift along to Portman Square.'

Chico stopped chewing in mid-mouthful, and then carefully swallowed before saying, 'By Portman Square, do you mean the Jockey Club?'

'That's right.'

'Haven't you noticed they let you in the front door?'

'I want a quiet look-see that they don't know about.'

He shrugged. 'All right then. Meet you back here after the recce?'

I nodded. 'The Admiral's coming here for lunch. He went down to the wax factory yesterday.'

'That should put a shine in his eyes.'

'Oh very funny.'

While he finished the eggs and attacked the toast I told him most of what Jacksy had said about the syndicates, and also about rumours of kickbacks in high places.

'And that's what we're looking for? Turning out Eddy Keith's office to see what he didn't do when he should've?'

'You got it. Sir Thomas Ullaston – Senior Steward – says Eddy was along complaining to him about me seeing the files, and Lucas

Wainwright can't let me see them without Eddy's secretary knowing, and she's loyal to Eddy. So if I want to look, it has to be quiet.' And would breaking in to the Jockey Club, I wondered, be considered 'absolutely diabolical' if I were found out?

'O.K.,' he said. 'I got the judo today, don't forget.'

'The little bleeders,' I said, 'are welcome.'

Charles came at twelve, sniffing the air of the unfamiliar surroundings like an unsettled dog.

'I got your message from Mrs Cross,' he said. 'But why here?' Why not the Cavendish, as usual?'

'There's someone I don't want to meet,' I said. 'He won't look for me here. Pink gin?'

'A double.'

I ordered the drinks. He said, 'Is that what it was, for those six days? Evasive action?'

I didn't reply.

He looked at me quizzically. 'I see it still hurts you, whatever it was.'

'Leave it, Charles.'

He sighed and lit a cigar, sucking in smoke and eyeing me through the flame of the match. 'So who don't you want to meet?'

'A man called Peter Rammileese. If anyone asks, you don't know where I am.'

'I seldom do.' He smoked with enjoyment, filling his lungs and inspecting the burning ash as if it were precious. 'Going off in balloons . . .'

I smiled. 'I got offered the post of regular co-pilot to a madman.'

'It doesn't surprise me,' he said dryly.

'How did you get on with the wax?'

He wouldn't tell me until after the drinks had come, and then he wasted a lot of time asking why I was drinking Perrier water and not whisky.

'To keep a clear head for burglary,' I said truthfully, which he half believed and half didn't.

'The wax is made,' he said finally, 'in a sort of cottage industry flourishing next to a plant which processes honey.'

'Beeswax!' I said incredulously.

He nodded. 'Beeswax, paraffin wax, and turpentine, that's what's in that polish.' He smoked luxuriously, taking his time. 'A charming woman there was most obliging. We spent a long time going back over the order books. People seldom ordered as much at a time as Jenny had done, and very few stipulated that the tins should be packed in white boxes for posting.' His eyes gleamed over the cigar. 'Three people, all in the last year, to be exact.'

'Three. . . . Do you think . . . it was Nicholas Ashe, three times?'

'Always about the same amount,' he said, enjoying himself. 'Different names and addresses, of course.'

'Which you did bring away with you?'

'Which I did.' He pulled a folded paper out of an inner pocket. 'There you are.'

'Got him,' I said, with intense satisfaction. 'He's a fool.'

'There was a policeman there on the same errand,' Charles said. 'He came just after I'd written out those names. It seems they really are looking for Ashe, themselves.'

'Good. Er ... did you tell them about the mailing list?'

'No, I didn't.' He squinted at his glass, holding it up to the light, as if one pink gin were not the same as the next and he wanted to memorize the colour. 'I would like it to be you who finds him first.'

'Hm.' I thought about that. 'If you think Jenny will be grateful, you'll be disappointed.'

'But you'll have got her off the hook.'

'She would prefer it to be the police.' She might even be nicer to me, I thought, if she was sure I had failed: and it wasn't the sort of niceness I would want.

Chico telephoned during the afternoon.

'What are you doing in your bedroom at this time of the day?' he demanded.

'Watching Chester races on television.'

'Stands to reason,' he said resignedly. 'Well, look, I've done the recce, and we can get in all right, but you'll have to be through the main doors before four o'clock. I've scrubbed the little bleeders. Look, this is what you do. You go in through the front door, right, as if you'd got pukka business. Now, in the hall there's two lifts. One that goes to a couple of businesses that are on the first and second floors, and as far as the third, which is all Jockey Club, as you know.'

'Yes,' I said.

'When all the little workers and Stewards and such have gone home, they leave that lift at the third floor, with its doors open, so no one can use it. There's a night porter, but after he's seen to the lift he doesn't do any rounds, he just stays downstairs. And oh yes, when he's fixed the lift he goes down your actual stairs, locking a door across the stairway at each landing, which makes three in all. Got it?

'Yes.'

'Right. Now there's another lift which goes to the top four floors of the building, and up there there's eight flats, two on each floor, with people living in them. And between those floors and the Jockey Club below, there's only one door locked across the stairway.'

'I'm with you,' I said.

'Right. Now I reckon the porter in the hall, or whatever you call him, he might just know you by sight, so he'd think it odd if you came after the offices were closed. So you'd better get there before, and go up in the lift to the flats, go right up to the top, and I'll meet you there. It's O.K., there's a sort of seat by a window, read a book or something.'

'I'll see you,' I said.

I went in a taxi, armed with a plausible reason for my visit if I should meet anyone I knew in the hall: but in fact I saw no one, and stepped into the lift to the flats without any trouble. At the top, as Chico had said, there was a bench by a window, where I sat and thought unproductively for over an hour. No one came or went from either of the two flats. No one came up in the lift. The first time its doors opened, it brought Chico.

Chico was dressed in white overalls and carried a bag of tools. I gave him a sardonic head-to-foot inspection.

'Well, you got to look the part,' he said defensively. 'I came here like this earlier, and when I left I told the chap I'd be back with spare parts. He just nodded when I walked in just now. When we go, I'll keep him talking while you gumshoe out.'

'If it's the same chap.'

'He goes off at eight. We better be finished before then.'

'Was the Jockey Club lift still working?' I said.

'Yeah.'

'Is the stairway door above the Jockey Club locked?'

'Yeah.'

'Let's go down there, then, so we can hear when the porter brings the lift up and leaves it.'

He nodded. We went through the door beside the lift, into the stair well, which was utilitarian, not plushy, and lit by electric lights, and just inside there dumped the clinking bag of tools. Four floors down we came to the locked door, and stood there, waiting.

The door was flat, made of some filling covered on the side on which we stood by a sheet of silvery metal. The keyhole proclaimed a mortice lock set into the depth of the door, the sort of barrier which took Chico about three minutes, usually, to negotiate.

As usual on these excursions, we had brought gloves. I thought back to one of the first times, when Chico had said, 'One good thing about that hand of yours, it can't leave any dabs.' I wore a glove over it anyway, as being a lot less noticeable if we were ever casually seen where we shouldn't be.

I had never got entirely used to breaking in, not to the point of not feeling my heart beat faster or my breath go shallow. Chico, for all his longer experience at the same game, gave himself away always by smoothing out the laughter lines round his eyes as the skin tautened over his cheekbones. We stood there waiting, the physical signs of stress with us, knowing the risks.

We heard the lift come up and stop. Held our breaths to see if it would go down again, but it didn't. Instead, we were electrified by the noise of someone unlocking the door we were standing behind. I caught a flash of Chico's alarmed eyes as he leapt away from the lock and joined me on the hinge side, our backs pressed hard against the wall.

The door opened until it was touching my chest. The porter coughed and sniffed on the other side of the barrier, looking, I thought, up the stairs, checking that all was as it should be.

The door swung shut again, and the key clicked in the lock. I let a long-held breath out in a slow soundless whistle, and Chico gave me the sickly grin that came from semi-released tension.

We felt the faint thud through the fabric of the building as the door on the floor below us was shut and locked. Chico raised his eyebrows and I nodded, and he applied his bunch of lock-pickers to the problem. There was a faint scraping noise as he sorted his way into the mechanism, and then the application of some muscle, and finally his clearing look of satisfaction as the metal tongue retracted into the door.

We went through, taking the keys but leaving the door unlocked, and found ourselves in the familiar headquarters of British racing. Acres of carpet, comfortable chairs, polished wood furniture, and the scent of extinct cigars.

The Security Section had its own corridor of smaller workadays offices, and down there without difficulty we eased into Eddy Keith's.

None of the internal doors seemed to be locked, and I supposed there was in fact little to steal, bar electric typewriters and other such trifles. Eddy Keith's filing cabinets all slid open easily, and so did the drawers in his desk.

In the strong evening sunlight we sat and read the reports on the extra syndicates that Jacksy had told me of. Eleven horses whose names I had written down, when he'd gone, so as not to forget them. Eleven syndicates apparently checked and accepted by Eddy, with Rammileese's two registered-owner pals appearing inexorably on all of them: and as with the previous four, headed by Philip Friarly, there was nothing in the files themselves to prove anything one way or the other. They were carefully, meticulously presented, openly ready for inspection.

There was one odd thing: the four Friarly files were all missing.

We looked through the desk. Eddy kept in it few personal objects: a battery razor, indigestion tablets, a comb, and about sixteen packs of book matches, all from gambling clubs. Otherwise there was simple stationery, pens, a pocket calculator and a desk diary. His engagements, past and future, were merely down as the race meetings he was due to attend.

I looked at my watch. Seven forty-five. Chico nodded and began putting the files back neatly into their drawers. Frustrating, I thought. An absolute blank.

When we were ready to go I took a quick look into a filing cabinet marked 'Personnel' which contained slim factual files about everyone present employed by the Jockey Club, and everyone receiving its pensions. I looked for a file marked 'Mason', but someone had taken that, too.

'Coming?' Chico said.

I nodded regretfully. We left Eddy's office as we'd found it and went back to the door to the stairway. Nothing stirred. The headquarters of British racing lay wide open to intruders, who were having to go empty away.

Chapter Fourteen

On Friday afternoon, depressed on many counts, I drove comparatively slowly to Newmarket.

The day itself was hot, the weather reportedly stoking up to the sort of intense heatwave one could get in May, promising a glorious summer that seldom materialized. I drove in shirtsleeves with the window open, and decided to go to Hawaii and lie on the beach for a while, like a thousand years.

Martin England was out in his stable yard when I got there, also in shirtsleeves and wiping his forehead with a handkerchief.

'Sid!' he said, seeming truly pleased. 'Great. I'm just starting evening stables. You couldn't have timed it better.'

We walked round the boxes together in the usual ritual, the trainer visiting every horse and checking its health, the guest admiring and complimenting and keeping his tongue off the flaws. Martin's horses were middling to good, like himself, like the majority of trainers, the sort that provided the bulk of all racing, and of all jockeys' incomes.

'A long time since you rode for me,' he said, catching my thought.

'Ten years or more.'

'What do you weigh, now, Sid?'

'About ten stone, stripped.' Thinner, in fact, than when I'd stopped racing.

'Pretty fit, are you?'

'Same as usual,' I said. 'I suppose.'

He nodded, and we went from the fillies' side of the yard to the colts. He had a good lot of two-year-olds, it seemed to me, and he was pleased when I said so.

'This is flotilla,' he said, going to the next box. 'He's three. He runs in the Dante at York next Wednesday, and if that's O.K. he'll go for the Derby.'

'He looks well,' I said.

Martin gave a carrot to his hope of glory. There was pride in his kind, fiftyish face, not for himself but for the shining coat and quiet eye and waiting muscles of the splendid four-legged creature. I ran my hand down the glossy neck, and patted the dark bay shoulder, and felt the slender, rock-hard forelegs.

'He's in grand shape,' I said. 'Should do you proud.'

He nodded with the thoroughly normal hint of anxiety showing under the pride, and we continued down the line, patting and discussing, and feeling content. Perhaps this was what I really needed, I thought: forty horses and hard work and routine. Planning and administering and paperwork. Pleasure enough in preparing a winner, sadness enough in seeing one lose. A busy, satisfying, out-of-doors lifestyle, a businessman on the back of a horse.

I thought of what Chico and I had been doing for months. Chasing villains, big and small. Wiping up a few messy bits of the racing industry. Getting knocked about, now and then. Taking our wits into minefields and fooling with people with shotguns.

It would be no public disgrace if I gave it up and decided to train. A much more normal life for an ex-jockey, everyone would think. A sensible, orderly decision, looking forward to middle and old age. I alone ... and Trevor Deansgate ... would know why I'd done it. I could live for a long time, knowing it.

I didn't want to.

In the morning at seven-thirty I went down to the yard in jodhpurs and boots and a pull-on jersey shirt. Early as it was, the air was warm, and with the sounds and bustle and smell of the stables all around my spirits rose from bedrock and hovered at somewhere above knee level.

Martin, standing with a list in his hand, shouted good morning, and I went down to join him to see what he'd given me to ride. There was a five-year-old, up to my weight, that he'd think just the job.

Flotilla's lad was leading him out of his box, and I watched him admiringly as I turned towards Martin.

'Go on, then,' he said. There was amusement in his face, enjoyment in his eyes.

'What?' I said.

'Ride Flotilla.'

I swung towards the horse, totally surprised. His best horse, his Derby hope, and I out of practice and with one hand.

'Don't you want to?' he said. 'He'd've been yours ten years ago as of right. And my jockey's gone to Ireland to race at the Curragh. It's either you or one of my lads, and to be honest, I'd rather have you.'

I didn't argue. One doesn't turn down a chunk of heaven. I thought he was a bit mad, but if that was what he wanted, so did I. He gave me a leg-up, and I pulled the stirrup leathers to my own length, and felt like an exile coming home.

'Do you want a helmet?' he said, looking around vaguely as if expecting one to materialize out of the tarmac.

'Not for this.'

He nodded. 'You never have.' And he himself was wearing his usual checked cloth cap, in spite of the heat. I had always preferred riding bareheaded except in races: something to do with liking the feel of lightness and moving air.

'What about a whip?' he said.

He knew that I'd always carried one automatically, because a jockey's whip was a great aid to keeping a horse balanced and running straight: a tap down the shoulder did the trick, and one pulled the stick through from hand to hand, as required. I looked at the two hands in front of me. I thought that if I took a whip and fumbled it, I might drop it: and I needed above all to be efficient.

I shook my head. 'Not today.'

'Right, then,' he said. 'Let's be off.'

With me in its midst the string pulled out of the yard and went right through Newmarket town on the horse-walks along the back roads, out to the wide sweeping Limekilns gallops to the north. Martin, himself riding the quiet five-year-old, pulled up there beside me.

'Give him a sharpish warm up canter for three furlongs, and then take him a mile up the trial ground, upsides with Gulliver. It's Flotilla's last work-out before the Dante, so make it a good one. O.K.?'

'Yes,' I said.

'Wait until I get up there,' he pointed, 'to watch.'

'Yep.'

He rode away happily towards a vantage point more than half a mile distant, from where he could see the whole gallop. I wound the left hand rein round my plastic fingers and longed to be able to feel the pull from the horse's mouth. It would be easy to be clumsy, to upset the lie of the bit and the whole balance of the horse, if I got the tension wrong. In my right hand, the reins felt alive, carrying messages, telling Flotilla, and Flotilla telling me, where we were going, and how, and how fast. A private language shared, understood.

Let me not make a mess of it, I thought. Let me just be able to do what I'd done thousands of times in the past, let the old skill be there, one hand or no. I could lose him the Dante and the Derby and any other race you cared to mention, if I got it really wrong.

The boy on Gulliver circled with me, waiting for the moment, answering my casual remarks in monosyllables and grunts. I wondered if he was the one who would have ridden Flotilla if I hadn't been there, and asked him, and he said, grumpily, yes. Too bad, I thought. Your turn will come.

Up the gallop, Martin waved. The boy on Gulliver kicked his mount into a fast pace at once, not waiting to start evenly together. You little sod, I thought. You do what you damned well like, but I'm going to take Flotilla along at the right speeds for the occasion and distance, and to hell with your tantrums.

It was absolutely great, going up there. It suddenly came right, as natural as if there had been no interval and no missing limb. I threaded the left rein through bad and good hands alike and felt the vibrations from both sides of the bit, and if it wasn't the most perfect style ever seen on the Heath, it at least got the job done.

Flotilla swept over the turf in a balanced working gallop and came upsides with Gulliver effortlessly. I stayed beside the other horse then for most of the way, but as Flotilla was easily the better I took him on from six furlongs and finished the mile at a good pace that was still short of strain. He was fit, I thought, pulling him back to a canter. He would do well in the Dante. He'd given me a good feel.

I said so to Martin, when I rejoined him, walking back. He was pleased, and laughed. 'You can still ride, can't you? You looked just the same.'

I sighed internally. I had been let back for a brief moment into the life I'd lost, but I wasn't just the same. I might have managed one working gallop without making an ass of myself, but it wasn't the Gold Cup at Cheltenham.

'Thanks,' I said, 'for a terrific morning.'

We walked back through the town to his stable and to breakfast, and afterwards I went with him, in his Land Rover to see his second lot work on the racecourse side. When we got back from that we sat in his office and drank coffee and talked for a bit, and with some regret I said it was time I was going.

The telephone rang. Martin answered it, and held out the receiver to me.

'It's for you, Sid.'

I thought it would be Chico, but it wasn't. It was, surprisingly, Henry Thrace, calling from his stud farm just outside the town.

'My girl assistant says she saw you riding work on the Heath.' he said. 'I didn't really believe her, but she was sure. Your head, without a helmet, unmistakable. With Martin England's horses, she said, so I rang on the off-chance.'

'What can I do for you?' I said.

'Actually it's the other way round,' he said. 'Or at least, I think so. I had a letter from the Jockey Club earlier this week, all very official and everything, asking me to let them know at once if Gleaner or Zingaloo died, and not to get rid of the carcass. Well, when I got that letter I rang Lucas Wainwright, who signed it, to ask what the hell it was all about, and he said it was really *you* who wanted to know if either of those horses died. He was telling me that in confidence, he said.'

My mouth went as dry as vinegar.

'Are you still there?'

'Yes,' I said.

'Then I'd better tell you that Gleaner has, in fact, just died.'

'When?' I said, feeling stupid. 'Er . . . how?' My heart rate had gone up to at least double. Talk about over-reacting, I thought, and felt the fear stab through like toothache.

'A mare he was due to cover came into use, so we put him to her,' he said, 'this morning. An hour ago, maybe. He was sweating a lot, in this heat. It's hot in the breeding shed, with the sun on it. Anyway, he served her and got down all right, and then he just staggered and fell and died almost at once.'

I unstuck my tongue. 'Where is he now?'

'Still in the breeding shed. We're not using it again this morning so I've left him there. I've tried to ring the Jockey Club, but it's Saturday and Lucas Wainwright isn't there, and anyway, as my girl said that you yourself were actually here in Newmarket . . .'

'Yes,' I said. I took a shaky breath. 'A post mortem. You would agree, wouldn't you?'

'Essential, I'd say. Insurance, and all that.'

'I'll try and get Ken Armadale,' I said. 'From the Equine Research Establishment. I know him ... Would he do you?'

'Couldn't be better.'

'I'll ring you back.'

'Right,' he said, and disconnected.

I stood with Martin's telephone in my hand and looked into far dark spaces. It's too soon, I thought. Much too soon.

'What's the matter?' Martin said.

'A horse I've been inquiring about has died.' ... Oh God Almighty ... 'Can I use your 'phone?' I said.

'Help yourself.'

Ken Armadale said he was gardening and would much rather cut up a dead horse. I'll pick you up, I said, and he said he'd be waiting. My hand, I saw remotely, was actually shaking.

I rang back to Henry Thrace, to confirm. Thanked Martin for his tremendous hospitality. Put my suitcase and myself in the car, and picked up Ken Armadale from his large modern house on the southern edge of Newmarket.

'What am I looking for?' he said.

'Heart, I think.'

He nodded. He was a strong dark-haired research vet in his middle thirties, a man I'd dealt with on similar jaunts before, to the extent that I felt easy with him and trusted him, and as far as I could tell he felt the same about me. A professional friendship, extending to a drink in a pub but not to Christmas cards, the sort of relationship that remained unchanged and could be taken up and put down as need arose.

'Anything special?' he said.

'Yes ... but I don't know what.'

'That's cryptic.'

'Let's see what you find.'

Gleaner, I thought. If there were three horses I should definitely be doing nothing about, they were Gleaner and Zingaloo and Tri-Nitro. I wished I hadn't asked Lucas Wainwright to write those letters, one to Henry Thrace, the other to George Caspar. If those horses died, let me know ... but not so soon, so appallingly soon.

I drove into Henry Thrace's stud farm and pulled up with a jerk. He came out of his house to meet us, and we walked across to the breeding shed. As with most such structures, its walls swept up to a height of ten feet, unbroken except for double entrance doors. Above that there was a row of windows, and above those, a roof. Very like Peter Rammileese's covered riding school, I thought, only smaller.

The day, which was hot outside, was very much hotter inside. The dead horse lay where he had fallen on the tan-covered floor, a sad brown hump with milky grey eyes.

'I rang the knackers,' Ken said. 'They'll be here pretty soon.'

Henry Thrace nodded. It was impossible to do the post mortem where the horse lay, as the smell of blood would linger for days and upset any other horse that came in there. We waited for not very long until the lorry arrived with its winch, and when the horse was loaded, we followed it down to the knackers' yard where Newmarket's casualties were cut up for dog food. A small hygienic place; very clean.

Ken Armadale opened the bag he had brought and handed me a washable nylon boiler suit, like his own, to cover trousers and shirt. The horse lay in a square room with whitewashed walls and a concrete floor. In the floor, runnels and a drain. Ken turned on the tap so that water ran out of the hose beside the horse, and pulled on a pair of long rubber gloves.

'All set?' he said.

I nodded, and he made the first long incision. The smell, as on past occasions, was what I liked least about the next ten minutes, but Ken seemed not to notice it as he checked methodically through the contents. When the chest cavity had been opened he removed its whole heart-lung mass and carried it over to the table which stood under the single window.

'This is odd,' he said, after a pause.

'What is?'

'Take a look.'

I went over beside him and looked where he was pointing, but I hadn't his knowledge behind my eyes, and all I saw was a blood-covered lump of tissue with tough looking ridges of gristle in it.

'His heart?' I said.

'That's right. Look at these valves . . .' He turned his head to me, frowning. 'He died of something horses don't get.' He thought it over. 'It's a great pity we couldn't have had a blood sample before he died.'

'There's another horse at Henry Thrace's with the same thing,' I said. 'You can get your blood sample from him.'

He straightened up from bending over the heart, and stared at me.

'Sid,' he said. 'You'd better tell me what's up. And outside, don't you think, in some fresh air.'

We went out, and it was a great deal better. He stood listening with blood all over his gloves and down the front of his overalls, while I wrestled with the horrors in the back of my mind and spoke with flat lack of emotion from the front.

'There are . . . or were . . . four of them,' I said. 'Four that I know of. They were all top star horses, favourites all winter for the Guineas and the Derby. That class. The very top. They all came from the same stable. They all went out to race in Guineas week looking marvellous. They all started hot favourites, and they all totally flopped. They all suffered from a mild virus infection at about that time, but it didn't develop. They all were subsequently found to have heart murmurs.'

Ken frowned heavily. 'Go on.'

'There was Bethesda, who ran in the One Thousand Guineas two years ago. She went to stud, and she died of heart failure this spring, while she was foaling.'

Ken took a deep breath.

'There's this one,' I said, pointing. 'Gleaner. He was favourite for the Guineas last year. He then got a really bad heart, and also arthritis. The other horse at Henry Thrace's, Zingaloo, he went out fit to a race and afterwards could hardly stand from exhaustion.'

Ken nodded. 'And which is the fourth one?'

I looked up at the sky. Blue and clear. I'm killing myself, I thought. I looked back at him and said, 'Tri-Nitro.'

'Sid!' He was shocked. 'Only ten days ago.'

'So what is it?' I said. 'What's the matter with them?'

'I'd have to do some tests to be certain,' he said. 'But the symptoms you've described are typical, and those heart valves are unmistakable. That horse died from swine erysipelas, which is a disease you get only in pigs.'

Ken said, 'We need to keep that heart for evidence.'

'Yes,' I said.

Dear God. . . .

'Get one of those bags, will you?' he said. 'Hold it open.' He put the heart inside. 'We'd better go along to the Research Centre, later. I've been thinking . . . I know I've got some reference papers there about erysipelas in horses. We could look them up, if you like.'

'Yes,' I said.

He peeled off his blood-spattered overalls. 'Heat and exertion,' he said. 'That's what did for this fellow. A deadly combination, with a heart in that state. He might have lived for years, otherwise.'

Ironic, I thought bitterly.

He packed everything away, and we went back to Henry Thrace. A blood sample from Zingaloo? No problem, he said.

Ken took enough blood to float a battleship, it seemed to me, but what was a litre to a horse which had gallons. We accepted reviving Scotches from Henry with gratitude, and afterwards took our trophies to the Equine Research Establishment along the Bury Road.

Ken's office was a small extension to a large laboratory where he took the bag containing Gleaner's heart over to the sink and told me he was washing out the remaining blood.

'Now come and look,' he said.

This time I could see exactly what he meant. Along all the edges of the valves there were small knobbly growths, like baby cauliflowers, creamy white.

'That's vegetation,' he said. 'It prevents the valves from closing. Makes the heart as efficient as a leaking pump.'

'I can see it would.'

'I'll put this in the fridge, then we'll look through those veterinary journals for that paper.'

I sat on a hard chair in his utilitarian office while he searched for what he wanted. I looked at my fingers. Curled and uncurled them. This can't all be happening, I thought. It's only three days since I saw Trevor Deansgate at Chester. *If you break your assurance, I'll do what I said.*

'Here it is,' Ken exclaimed, flattening a paper open. 'Shall I read you the relevant bits?'

I nodded.

'Swine erysipelas – in 1938 – occurred in a horse, with vegetative endocarditis – the chronic form of the illness in pigs.' He looked up. 'That's those cauliflower growths. Right?'

'Yes.'

He read again from the paper. 'During 1944 a mutant strain of erysipelas rhusiopathiae appeared suddenly in a laboratory specializing in antisera production and produced acute endocarditis in the serum horses.'

'Translate,' I said.

He smiled. 'They used to use horses for producing vaccines. You inject the horse with pig disease, wait until it develops antibodies, draw off blood, and extract the serum. The serum, injected into healthy pigs, prevents them getting the disease. Same process as for all human vaccinations, smallpox and so on. Standard procedure.'

'O.K.,' I said. 'Go on.'

'What happened was that instead of growing antibodies as usual, the horses themselves got the disease.'

'How could that happen?'

'It doesn't say, here. You'd have to ask the pharmaceutical firm concerned, which I see is the Tierson vaccine lab along at Cambridge. They'd tell you, I should think, if you asked. I know someone there, if you want an introduction.'

'It's a long time ago,' I said.

'My dear fellow, germs don't die. They can live like timebombs, waiting for some fool to take stupid liberties. Some of these labs keep virulent strains around for decades. You'd be surprised.'

He looked down again at the paper, and said, 'You'd better read these next paragraphs yourself. They look pretty straightforward.' He pushed the journal across to me, and I read the page where he pointed.

(1) 24–48 hours after intra-muscular injection of the pure culture, inflammation of one or more of the heart valves commences. At this time, apart from a slight rise in temperature and occasional palpitations, no other symptoms are seen unless the horse is subjected to severe exertion, when auricular fibrillation or interference with the blood supply to the lungs occurs; both occasion severe distress which only resolves after 2–3 hours rest.

(2) Between the second and the sixth day pyrexia (temperature rise) increases and white cell count of the blood increases and the horse is listless and off food. This could easily be loosely diagnosed as 'the virus'. However examination by stethoscope reveals a progressively increasing heart murmur. After about ten days the temperature returns to normal and, unless subjected to more than walk or trot, the horse may

appear to have recovered. The murmur is still present and it then becomes necessary to retire the horse from fast work since this induces respiratory distress.

(3) Over the next few months vegetations grow on the heart valves, and arthritis in some joints, particularly of the limbs, may or may not appear. The condition is permanent and progressive and death may occur suddenly following exertion or during very hot weather, sometimes years after the original infection.

I looked up. 'That's it, exactly, isn't it,' I said.

'Bang on the nose.'

I said slowly, 'Intra-muscular injection of the pure culture could absolutely not have occurred accidentally.'

'Absolutely not,' he agreed.

I said, 'George Caspar had his yard sewn up so tight this year with alarm bells and guards and dogs that no one could have got within screaming distance of Tri-Nitro with a syringeful of live germs.'

He smiled, 'You wouldn't need a syringeful. Come into the lab, and I'll show you.'

I followed him, and we fetched up beside one of the cupboards with sliding doors that lined the whole of the wall. He opened the cupboard and pulled out a box, which proved to contain a large number of smallish plastic envelopes.

He tore open one of the envelopes and tipped the contents onto his hand: a hypodermic needle attached to a plastic capsule only the size of a pea. The whole thing looked like a tiny dart with a small round balloon at one end, about as long, altogether as one's little finger.

He picked up the capsule and squeezed it. 'Dip that into liquid, you draw up half a teaspoonful. You don't need that much pure culture to produce a disease.'

'You could hold that in your hand, out of sight,' I said.

He nodded. 'Just slap the horse with it. Done in a flash. I use these sometimes for horses that shy away from a syringe.' He showed me how, holding the capsule between thumb and index finger, so that the sharp end pointed down from his palm. 'Shove the needle in and squeeze,' he said.

'Could you spare one of these?'

'Sure,' he said, giving me an envelope. 'Anything you like.'

I put it in my pocket. Dear God in heaven.

Ken said slowly, 'You know, we might just be able to do something about Tri-Nitro.'

'How do you mean?'

He pondered, looking at the large bottle of Zingaloo's blood, which stood on the draining board beside the sink.

'We might find an antibiotic which would cure the disease.'

'Isn't it too late?' I said.

'Too late for Zingaloo. But I don't think those vegetations would start growing at once. If Tri-Nitro was infected ... say ...'

'Say two weeks ago today, after his final working gallop.'

He looked at me with amusement. 'Say two weeks ago, then. His heart will be in trouble, but the vegetation won't have started. If he gets the right antibiotic soon, he might make a full recovery.'

'Do you mean ... back to normal?'

'Don't see why not.'

'What are you waiting for?' I said.

Chapter Fifteen

I spent most of Sunday beside the sea, driving north-east from Newmarket to the wide deserted coast of Norfolk. Just for somewhere to go, something to do, to pass the time.

Even though the sun shone, the wind off the North Sea was keeping the beaches almost empty; small groups were huddled into the shelter of flimsy canvas screens, and a few intrepid children built castles.

I sat in the sun in a hollow in a sand dune which was covered with coarse tufts of grass, and watched the waves come and go. I walked along the shore, kicking the worm casts. I stood looking out to sea, holding up my left upper arm for support, aware of the weight of the machinery lower down, which was not so very heavy, but always there.

I had often felt released and restored by lonely places, but not on that day. The demons came with me. The cost of pride ... the price of safety. If you didn't expect so much of yourself, Charles had said once, you'd give yourself an easier time. It hadn't really made sense. One was as one was. Or at least, one was as one was until someone came along and broke you all up.

If you sneezed on the Limekilns, they said in Newmarket, it was heard two miles away on the racecourse. The news of my attendance at Gleaner's post mortem would be given to George Caspar within a day. Trevor Deansgate would hear of it: he was sure to.

I could still go away, I thought. It wasn't too late. Travel. Wander by other seas, under other skies. I could go away and keep very quiet. I could still escape from the terror he induced in me. I could still ... run away.

I left the coast and drove numbly to Cambridge. Stayed in the University Arms Hotel and, in the morning, went along to Tierson Pharmaceuticals Vaccine Laboratories. I asked for, and got, a Mr Livingston, who was maybe sixty and greyishly thin. He made small nobbling movements with his mouth when he spoke. He looks a dried-up old cuss, Ken Armadale had said, but he's got a mind like a monkey.

'Mr Halley, is it?' Livingston said, shaking hands in the entrance hall. 'Mr Armadale has been on the 'phone to me, explaining what you want. I think I can help you, yes I do indeed. Come along, come along, this way.'

He walked in small steps before me, looking back frequently to make sure I was following. It seemed to be a precaution born of losing people, because the place was a labyrinth of glass-walled passages with laboratories and gardens apparently intermixed at random.

'The place just grew,' he said, when I remarked on it. 'But here we are.' He led the way into a large laboratory which looked through glass walls into the passage on one side, and a garden on another, and straight into another lab on the third.

'This is the experimental section,' he said, his gesture embracing both rooms. 'Most of the laboratories just manufacture the vaccines commercially, but in here we potter about inventing new ones.'

'And resurrecting old ones?' I said.

He looked at me sharply. 'Certainly not. I believe you came for information, not to accuse us of carelessness.'

'Sorry,' I said placatingly. 'That's quite right.'

'Well then. Ask your question.'

'Er, yes. How did the serum horses you were using in the nineteen forties get swine erysipelas?'

'Ah,' he said. 'Pertinent. Brief. To the point. We published a paper about it, didn't we? Before my time, of course. But I've heard about it. Yes. Well, it's possible. It's possible. It happened. But it shouldn't have done. Sheer carelessness, do you see? I hate carelessness. Hate it.'

Just as well, I thought. In his line of business, carelessness might be fatal.

'Do you know anything about the production of erysipelas anti-serum?' he said.

'You could write it on a thumbnail.'

'Ah,' he said. 'Then I'll explain as to a child. Will that do?'

'Nicely,' I said.

He gave me another sharp glance in which there was this time amusement.

'You inject live erysipelas germs into a horse. Are you with me? I am talking about the past, now, when they did use horses. We haven't used horses since the early nineteen fifties, and nor have Burroughs Wellcome, and Bayer in Germany. The past, do you see?'

'Yes,' I said.

'The horse's blood produces antibodies to fight the germ, but the horse does not develop the disease, because it is a disease pigs get and horses don't.'

'A child,' I assured him, 'would understand.'

'Very well. Now sometimes the standard strain of erysipelas becomes weakened, and in order to make it virulent again we pass it through pigeons.'

'Pigeons?' I said, very politely.

He raised his eyebrows. 'Customary practice. Pass a weak strain through pigeons to recover virulence.'

'Oh, of course,' I said.

He pounced on the satire in my voice. 'Mr Halley,' he said severely. 'Do you want to know all this or don't you?'

'Yes, please,' I said meekly.

'Very well, then. The virulent strain was removed from the pigeons and subcultured onto blood agar plates.' He broke off, looking at the blankness of my ignorance. 'Let me put it this way. The live virulent germs were transferred from the pigeons onto dishes containing blood, where they then multiplied, thus producing a useful quantity for injecting into the serum horses.'

'That's fine,' I said. 'I do understand.'

'All right.' He nodded. 'Now the blood on the dishes was bull's blood. Bovine blood.'

'Yes,' I said.

'But owing to someone's stupid carelessness, the blood agar plates were prepared one day with horse blood. This produced a mutant strain of the disease.' He paused. 'Mutants are changes which occur suddenly and for no apparent reason throughout nature.'

'Yes,' I said again.

'No one realized what had happened,' he said. 'Until the mutant strain was injected into the serum horses and they all got erysipelas. The mutant strain proved remarkably constant. The incubation period was always 24–48 hours after inoculation, and endocarditis ... that is, inflammation of the heart valves ... was always the result.'

A youngish man in a white coat, unbuttoned down the front, came into the room next door, and I watched him vaguely as he began pottering about.

'What became of this mutant strain?' I said.

Livingston nibbled a good deal with his lips, but finally said, 'We would have kept some, I dare say, as a curiosity. But of course it would be weakened by now, and to restore it to full virulence, one would have to ...'

'Yeah,' I said. 'Pass it through pigeons.'

He didn't think it was funny. 'Quite so,' he said.

'And all this passing through pigeons and subculture on agar plates, how much skill does this take?'

He blinked. 'I could do it, of course.'

I couldn't. Any injections I'd handled had come in neat little ampules, packed in boxes.

The man in the next room was opening cupboards, looking for something.

I said, 'Would there be any of this mutant strain anywhere else in the world, besides here? I mean, did this laboratory send any of it out to anywhere else?'

The lips pursed themselves and the eyebrows went up. 'I've no idea,' he said. He looked through the glass and gestured towards the man in the next room. 'You could ask Barry Shummuck. He would know. Mutant strains are his speciality.'

He pronounced 'Shummuck' to rhyme with 'hummock'. I know the name, I thought. I ... *oh my God.*

The shock of it fizzed through my brain and left me half breathless. I knew someone too well whose real name was Shummuck.

I swallowed and felt shivery. 'Tell me more about your Mr Shummuck,' I said.

Livingston was a natural chatterer and saw no harm in it. He shrugged. 'He came up the hard way. Still talks like it. He used to have a terrible chip on his shoulder. The world owed him a living, that sort of thing. Shades of student demos. He's settled down recently. He's good at his job.'

'You don't care for him?' I said.

Livingston was startled. 'I didn't say that.'

He had, plainly, in his face and in his voice. I said only, 'What sort of accent?'

'Northern. I don't know exactly. What does it matter?'

Barry Shummuck looked like no one I knew. I said slowly, hesitantly, 'Do you know if he has ... a brother?'

Livingston's face showed surprise. 'Yes, he has. Funny thing, he's a bookmaker.' He pondered. 'Some name like Terry. Not Terry ... Trevor, that's it. They come here together sometimes, the two of them ... thick as thieves.'

Barry Shummuck gave up his search and moved towards the door.

'Would you like to meet him?' Mr Livingston said.

Speechlessly, I shook my head. The last thing I wanted, in a building full of virulent germs which he knew how to handle and I didn't, was to be introduced to the brother of Trevor Deansgate.

Shummuck went through the door and into the glass-walled corridor, and turned in our direction.

Oh no, I thought.

He walked purposefully along and pushed open the door of the lab we were in. Head and shoulders leaned forward.

'Morning, Mr Livingston,' he said. 'Have you seen my box of transparencies, anywhere?'

The basic voice was the same, self-confident and slightly abrasive. Manchester accent, much stronger. I held my left arm out of sight half behind my back and willed him to go away.

'No,' said Mr Livingston, with just a shade of pleasure. 'But Barry, can you spare ...'

Livingston and I were standing in front of a work bench which held various empty glass jars and a row of clamps. I turned leftwards, with my arm still hidden, and clumsily, with my right hand, knocked over a clamp and two glass jars.

More clatter than breakage. Livingston gave a quick nibble of surprised annoyance, and righted the rolling jars. I gripped the clamp, which was metal and heavy, and would have to do.

I turned back towards the door.

The door was shutting. The back-view of Barry Shummuck was striding away along the corridor, the front edges of his white coat flapping.

I let a shuddering breath out through my nose and carefully put the clamp back at the end of the row.

'He's gone,' Mr Livingston said. 'What a pity.'

I drove back to Newmarket, to the Equine Research Establishment and Ken Armadale.

I wondered how long it would take chatty Mr Livingston to tell Barry Shummuck of the visit of a man called Halley who wanted to know about a pig disease in horses.

I felt faintly, and continuously, sick.

'It's been made resistant to all ordinary antibiotics,' Ken said. 'A real neat little job.'

'How do you mean?'

'If any old antibiotic would kill it, you couldn't be sure the horse wouldn't be given a shot as soon as he had a temperature, and never develop the disease.'

I sighed. 'So how do they make it resistant?'

'Feed it tiny doses of antibiotic until it becomes immune.'

'All this is technically difficult, isn't it?'

'Yes, fairly.'

'Have you ever heard of Barry Shummuck?'

He frowned. 'No, I don't think so.'

The craven inner voice told me urgently to shut up, to escape, to fly to safety ... to Australia ... to a desert.

'Do you have a cassette recorder here?' I said.

'Yes. I use it for making notes while I'm operating.' He went out and fetched it and set it up for me on his desk, loaded with a new tape. 'Just talk,' he said. 'It has a built-in microphone.'

'Stay and listen,' I said. 'I want ... a witness.'

He regarded me slowly. 'You look so strained ... It's no gentle game, is it, what you do?'

'Not always.'

I switched on the recorder, and for introduction spoke my name, the place, and the date. Then I switched off again and sat looking at the fingers I needed for pressing the buttons.

'What is it, Sid?' Ken said.

I glanced at him and down again. 'Nothing.'

I had got to do it, I thought. I had absolutely got to. I was never in any way going to be whole again, if I didn't.

If I had to choose, and it seemed to me that I did have to choose, I would have to settle for wholeness of mind, and put up with what it cost. Perhaps I could deal with physical fear. Perhaps I could deal with anything that happened to my body, and even with helplessness. What I could not forever deal with ... and I saw it finally with clarity and certainty ... was despising myself.

'I pressed the 'play' and 'record' buttons together, and irrevocably broke my assurance to Trevor Deansgate.

Chapter Sixteen

I telephoned Chico at lunchtime and told him what I'd found out about Rosemary's horses.

'What it amounts to,' I said, 'is that those four horses had bad hearts because they'd been given a pig disease. There's a lot of complicated info about how it was done, but that's now the Stewards' headache.'

'Pig disease?' Chico said disbelievingly.

'Yeah. That big bookmaker Trevor Deansgate has a brother who works in a place that produces vaccines for inoculating people against smallpox and diphtheria and so on, and they cooked up a plan to squirt pig germs into those red-hot favourites.'

'Which duly lost,' Chico said. 'While the bookmaker raked in the lolly.'

'Right,' I said.

It felt very odd to put Trevor Deansgate's scheme into casual words and to be talking about him as if he were just one of our customary puzzles.

'How did you find out?' Chico said.

'Gleaner died at Henry Thrace's, and the pig disease turned up at the post mortem. When I went to the vaccine lab I saw a man called Shummuck who deals in odd germs, and I remembered that Shummuck was Trevor Deansgate's real name. And Trevor Deansgate is very thick with George Caspar ... and all the affected horses, that we know of, have come from George Caspar's stable.'

'Circumstantial, isn't it?' Chico said.

'A bit, yes. But the Security Service can take it from there.'

'Eddy Keith?' he said sceptically.

'He can't hush this one up, don't you worry.'

'Have you told Rosemary?'

'Not yet.'

'Bit of a laugh,' Chico said.

'Mm.'

'Well, Sid mate,' he said. 'This is results day all round. We got a fix on Nicky Ashe.'

Nicky Ashe with a knife in his sock. A pushover, compared with ... compared with ...

'Hey,' Chico's voice said aggrievedly through the receiver. 'Aren't you pleased?'

'Yes, of course. What sort of fix?'

'He's been sending out some of those damn fool letters. I went to your place this morning, just to see, like, and there were two envelopes there with our sticky labels on.'

'Great,' I said.

'I opened them. They'd both been sent to us by people whose names start with P. All that leg work paid off.'

'So we've got the begging letter?'

'We sure have. It's exactly the same as the ones your wife had, except for the address to send the money to, of course. Got a pencil?'

'Yeah.'

He read the address, which was in Clifton, Bristol. I looked at it thoughtfully. I could either give it straight to the police, or I could check it first myself. Checking it, in one certain way, had persuasive attractions.

'Chico,' I said. 'Ring Jenny's flat in Oxford and ask for Louise McInnes. Ask her to ring me here at the Rutland Hotel in Newmarket.'

'Scared of your missus, are you?'

'Will you do it?'

'Oh sure.' He laughed, and rang off. When the bell rang again, however, it was not Louise at the other end, but still Chico.

'She's left the flat,' he said. 'Your wife gave me her new number.' He read it out. 'Anything else?'

'Can you bring your cassette player to the Jockey Club, Portman Square, tomorrow afternoon at, say, four o'clock?'

'Like last time?'

'No,' I said. 'Front door, all the way.'

* * *

Louise, to my relief, answered her telephone. When I told her what I wanted, she was incredulous.

'You've actually *found* him?'

'Well,' I said. 'Probably. Will you come, then, and identify him?'

'Yes.' No hesitation. 'Where and when?'

'Some place in Bristol.' I paused, and said diffidently, 'I'm in Newmarket now. I could pick you up in Oxford this afternoon, and we could go straight on. We might spot him this evening ... or tomorrow morning.'

There was a silence at the other end. Then she said, 'I've moved out of Jenny's flat.'

'Yes.'

Another silence, and then her voice, quiet, and committed.

'All right.'

She was waiting for me in Oxford, and she had brought an overnight bag.

'Hallo,' I said, getting out of the car.

'Hallo.'

We looked at each other. I kissed her cheek. She smiled with what I had to believe was enjoyment, and slung her case in the boot beside mine.

'You can always retreat,' I said.

'So can you.'

We sat in the car, however, and I drove to Bristol feeling contented and carefree. Trevor Deansgate wouldn't yet have started looking for me, and Peter Rammileese and his boys hadn't been in sight for a week, and no one except Chico knew where I was going. The shadowy future, I thought was not going to spoil the satisfactory present. I decided not even to think of it, and for most of the time, I didn't.

We went first to the country house hotel which someone had once told me of, high on the cliffs overlooking the Avon gorge, and geared to rich-American-tourist comfort.

'We'll never get in here,' Louise said, eying the opulence.

'I telephoned.'

'How organized! One room or two?'

'One.'

She smiled as if that suited her well, and we were shown into a large wood-panelled room with stretches of carpet, antique polished furniture, and a huge fourposter bed decked with American-style white muslin frills.

'My God,' Louise said. 'And I expected a motel.'

'I didn't know about the fourposter,' I said a little weakly.

'Wow,' she said, laughing. 'This is more *fun*.'

We parked the suitcases and freshened up in the modern bathroom tucked discreetly behind the panelling, and went back to the car: and Louise smiled to herself all the way to the new address of Nicholas Ashe.

It was a prosperous-looking house in a prosperous-looking street. A solid five-or-six-bedroomed affair, mellowed and white painted and uninformative in the early evening sun.

I stopped the car on the same side of the road, pretty close, at a place from where we could see both the front door and the gate into the driveway. Nicky, Louise had said on the way down, often used to go out for a walk at about seven o'clock, after a hard day's typing. Maybe he would again, if he was there.

Maybe he wouldn't.

We had the car's windows open because of the warm air. I lit a cigarette, and the smoke floated in a quiet curl through lack of wind. Very peaceful, I thought, waiting there.

'Where do you come from?' Louise said.

I blew a smoke ring. 'I'm the posthumous illegitimate son of a twenty-year-old window cleaner who fell off his ladder just before his wedding.'

She laughed. 'Very elegantly put.'

'And you?'

'The legitimate daughter of the manager of a glass factory and a magistrate, both alive and living in Essex.'

We consulted about brothers and sisters, of which I had none and she had two, one of each. About education, of which I'd had some and she a lot. About life in general, of which she'd seen a little, and I a bit more.

An hour passed in the quiet street. A few birds sang. Sporadic cars drove by. Men came home from work and turned into the driveways. Distant doors slammed. No one moved in the house we were watching.

'You're patient,' Louise said.

'I spend hours doing this, sometimes.'

'Pretty unexciting.'

I looked at her clear intelligent eyes. 'Not this evening.'

Seven o'clock came and went; and Nicky didn't.

'How long will we stay?'

'Until dark.'

'I'm hungry.'

Half an hour drifted by. I learned that she liked curry and paella and hated rhubarb. I learned that the thesis she was writing was giving her hell.'

'I'm so far behind schedule,' she said, 'and . . . oh my goodness, *there he is*.'

Her eyes had opened wide. I looked where she looked, and saw Nicholas Ashe.

Coming not from the front door, but from the side of the house. My age, or a bit younger. Taller, but of my own thin build. My colouring. Dark hair, slightly curly. Dark eyes. Narrow jaw. All the same.

He looked sufficiently like me for it to be a shock, but was nevertheless quite different. I took my baby camera out of my trouser pocket and pulled it open with my teeth as usual, and took his picture.

When he reached the gate he paused and looked back, and a woman ran after him calling, 'Ned, Ned, wait for me.'

'Ned!' Louise said, sliding down in her seat. 'If he comes this way, won't he see me?'

'Not if I kiss you.'

'Well, do it,' she said.

I took, however, another photograph.

The woman looked older, about forty; slim, pleasant, excited. She tucked her arm into his and looked up at his eyes, her own clearly, even from twenty feet away, full of adoration. He looked down and laughed delightfully, then he kissed her forehead and swung her round in a little circle onto the pavement, and put his arm round her waist, and walked towards us with vivid gaiety and a bounce in his step.

I risked one more photograph from the shadows of the car, and leaned across and kissed Louise with enthusiasm.

Their footsteps went past. Abreast of us they must have seen us, or at least my back, for they both suddenly giggled light-heartedly, lovers sharing their secret with lovers. They almost paused, then went on, their steps growing softer until they had gone.

I sat up reluctantly.

Louise said 'Whew!' but whether it was the result of the kiss, or the proximity of Ashe, I wasn't quite sure.

'He's just the same,' she said.

'Casanova himself,' I said dryly.

She glanced at me swiftly and I guessed she was wondering whether I was jealous of his success with Jenny, but in fact I was wondering whether Jenny had been attracted to him because he resembled me, or whether she had been attracted to me in the first place, and also to him, because we matched some internal picture she had of a sexually interesting male. I was more disturbed than I liked by the physical appearance of Nicholas Ashe.

'Well,' I said, 'that's that. Let's find some dinner.'

I drove back to the hotel, and we went upstairs before we ate, Louise saying she wanted to change out of the blouse and skirt she had worn all day.

I took the battery charger out of my suitcase and plugged it in: took a spent battery from my pocket, and rolled up my shirtsleeve and snapped out the one from my arm, and put them both in the charger. Then I took the charged battery from my suitcase and inserted it in the empty socket in the arm. And Louise watched.

I said, 'Are you ... revolted?'

'No, of course not.'

I pulled my sleeve down and buttoned the cuff.

'How long does a battery last?' she said.

'Six hours, if I use it a lot. About eight, usually.'

She merely nodded, as if people with electric arms were as normal as people with blue eyes. We went down to dinner and ate sole and afterwards strawberries, and if they'd tasted of seaweed I wouldn't have cared. It wasn't only because of Louise, but also because since that morning I had stopped tearing myself apart, and had slowly been growing back towards peace. I could feel it happening, and it was marvellous.

We sat side by side on a sofa in the hotel lounge, drinking small cups of coffee.

'Of course,' she said, 'now that we have seen Nicky, we don't really need to stay until tomorrow.'

'Are you thinking of leaving?' I said.

'About as much as you are.'

'Who is seducing whom?' I said.

'Mm.' She said, smiling. 'This whole thing is so unexpected.'

She looked calmly at my left hand, which rested on the sofa between us. I couldn't tell what she was thinking, but I said on impulse. 'Touch it.'

She looked up at me quickly. 'What?'

'Touch it. Feel it.'

She tentatively moved her right hand until her fingers were touching the tough, lifeless, plastic skin. There was no drawing back, no flicker of revulsion in her face.

'It's metal, inside there,' I said. 'Gears and levers and electric circuits. Press harder, and you'll feel them.'

She did as I said, and I saw her surprise as she discovered the shape of the inner realities.

'There's a switch inside there too,' I said. 'You can't see it from the outside, but it's just below the thumb. One can switch the hand off, if one wants.'

'Why would you want to?'

'Very useful for carrying things, like a briefcase. You shut the fingers round the handle, and switch the current off, and the hand just stays shut without you having to do it all yourself.'

I put my right hand over and pushed the switch off and on, to show her.

'It's like the push-through switch on a table lamp,' I said. 'Feel it. Push it.'

She fumbled a bit because it wasn't all that easy to find if one didn't know, but in the end pushed it both ways, off and on. Nothing in her expression but concentration.

She felt some sort of tension relax in me, and looked up, accusingly.

'You were testing me,' she said.

I smiled. 'I suppose so.'

'You're a pig.'

I felt an unaccustomed uprush of mischief. 'As a matter of fact,' I said, holding my left hand in my right, 'if I unscrew it firmly round this way several times the whole hand will come right off at the wrist.'

'Don't do it,' she said, horrified.

I laughed with absolute enjoyment. I wouldn't have thought I would ever feel that way about that hand.

'Why does it come right off?' she said.

'Oh . . . servicing. Stuff like that.'

'You look so different,' she said.

I nodded. She was right. I said, 'Let's go to bed.'

'What a world of surprises,' she said, a good while later. 'Almost the last thing I would have expected you to be as a lover is gentle.'

'Too gentle?'

'No. I liked it.'

We lay in the dark, drowsily. She herself had been warmly receptive and generous, and had made it for me an intense sunburst of pleasure. It was a shame, I thought hazily, that the act of sex had got so cluttered up with taboos and techniques and therapists and sin and voyeurs and the whole commercial ballyhoo. Two people fitting together in the old design should be a private matter, and if you didn't expect too much, you'd get on better. One was as one was. Even if a girl wanted it, I could never have put on a pretence of being a rough, aggressive bull of a lover, because, I thought sardonically, I would have laughed at myself in the middle. And it had been all right, I thought, as it was.

'Louise,' I said.

No reply.

I shifted a little for deeper comfort, and drifted, like her, to sleep.

A while later, awake early as usual, I watched the daylight strengthen on her sleeping face. The fair hair lay tangled round her head in the way I had seen it first, and her skin looked soft and fresh. When she woke, even before she opened her eyes, she was smiling.

'Good morning,' I said.

'Morning.'

She moved towards me in the big bed, the white muslin frills on the canopy overhead surrounding us like a frame.

'Like sleeping in clouds,' she said.

She came up against the hard shell of my left arm, and blinked from the awareness of it.

'You don't sleep in this when you're alone, do you?' she said.

'No.'

'Take it off, then.'

I said with a smile, 'No.'

She gave me a long considering inspection.

'Jenny's right about you being like flint,' she said.

'Well, I'm not.'

'She told me that at the exact moment some chap was smashing up your arm you were calmly working out how to defeat him.'

I made a face.

'Is it true?' she said.

'In a way.'

'Jenny said . . .'

'To be honest,' I said, 'I'd rather talk about you.'

'I'm not interesting.'

'That's a right come-on, that is,' I said.

'What are you waiting for, then?'

'I do so like your retreating maidenly blushes.'

I touched her lightly on her breast and it seemed to do for her what it did for me. Instant arousal, mutually pleasing.

'Clouds,' she said contentedly. 'What do you think of when you're doing it?'

'Sex?'

She nodded.

'I feel. It isn't thought.'

'Sometimes I see roses . . . on trellises . . . scarlet and pink and gold. Sometimes spiky stars. This time it will be white frilly muslin clouds.'

I asked her, after.

'No. All bright sunlight. Quite blinding.'

The sunlight, in truth, had flooded into the room, making the whole white canopy translucent and shimmering.

'Why didn't you want the curtains drawn, last night?' she said. 'Don't you like the dark?'

'I don't like sleeping when my enemies are up and about.'

I said it without thinking. The actual truth of it followed after, like a freezing shower.

'Like an animal,' she said, and then, 'What's the matter?'

Remember me, I thought, as I am. And I said, 'Like some breakfast?'

We went back to Oxford. I took the film to be developed, and we had lunch at *Les Quat' Saisons*, where the delectable pâté de turbot and the superb quenelle de brochet soufflée kept the shadows at bay a while longer. With the coffee, though, came the unavoidable minute.

'I have to be in London at four o'clock,' I said.

Louise said, 'When are you going to the police about Nicky?'

'I'll come back here on Thursday, day after tomorrow, to pick up the photos. I'll do it then.' I reflected. 'Give that lady in Bristol two more happy days.'

'Poor thing.'

'Will I see you, Thursday?' I said.

'Unless you're blind.'

Chico was propping up the Portman Square building with a look of resignation, as if he'd been there for hours. He shifted his shoulder off the stonework at my on-foot approach and said 'Took your time, didn't you?'

'The car park was full.'

From one hand he dangled the black cassette recorder we used occasionally, and he was otherwise wearing jeans and a sports shirt and no jacket. The hot weather, far from vanishing, had settled in on an almost stationary high pressure system, and I was also in shirtsleeves, though with a tie on, and a jacket over my arm. On the third floor all the windows were open, the street noises coming up sharply, and Sir Thomas Ullaston, sitting behind his big desk, had dealt with the day in pale blue shirting with white stripes.

'Come in, Sid,' he said, seeing me appear in his open doorway. 'I've been waiting for you.'

'I'm sorry I'm late,' I said, shaking hands. 'This is Chico Barnes, who works with me.'

He shook Chico's hand. 'Right,' he said. 'Now you're here, we'll get Lucas Wainwright and the others along.' He pressed an intercom button and spoke to his secretary. 'And bring some more chairs, would you?'

The office slowly filled up with more people than I'd expected, but all of whom I knew at least to talk to. The top administrative brass in full force, about six of them, all urbane worldly men, the people who really ran racing. Chico looked at them slightly nervously as if at an alien breed, and seemed to be relieved when a table was provided for him to put the recorder on. He sat with the table between himself and the room, like a barrier. I fished into my jacket for the cassette I'd brought, and gave it to him.

Lucas Wainwright came with Eddy Keith on his heels: Eddy looking coldly out of the genial face; big bluff Eddy whose warmth for me was slowly dying.

'Well, Sid,' Sir Thomas said. 'Here we all are. Now, on the telephone yesterday you told me you had discovered how Tri-Nitro had been nobbled for the Guineas, and as you see ... we are all very interested.' He smiled. 'So fire away.'

I made my own manner match theirs: calm and dispassionate, as if Trevor Deansgate's threat wasn't anywhere in my mind, instead of continually flashing through it like stabs.

'I've ... er ... put it all onto tape,' I said. 'You'll hear two voices. The other is Ken Armadale, from the Equine Research. I asked him to clarify the veterinary details, which are his province, not mine.'

The well-brushed heads nodded. Eddy Keith merely stared. I glanced at Chico, who pressed the start button, and my own voice, disembodied, spoke loudly into a wholly attentive silence.

'This is Sid Halley, at the Equine Research Establishment on Monday, May fourteenth. ...'

I listened to the flat sentences, spelling it out. The identical symptoms in four horses, the lost races, the bad hearts. My request, via Lucas Wainwright, to be informed if any of the three still alive should die. The post mortem on Gleaner, with Ken Armadale repeating in greater detail my own simpler account. His voice explaining, again after me, how horses had come to be infected by a disease of pigs. His voice saying, 'I found active live germs in the lesions on Gleaner's heart valves, and also in the blood from Zingaloo. ...' and my voice continuing, 'A mutant strain of the disease was produced at the Tierson Vaccine Laboratory at Cambridge in the following manner ...'

It wasn't the easiest of procedures to understand, but I watched the faces and saw that they did, particularly by the time Ken Armadale had gone through it all again, confirming what I'd said.

'As to motive and opportunity,' my voice said, 'we come to a man called Trevor Deansgate. ...'

Sir Thomas's head snapped back from its forward, listening posture, and he stared at me bleakly from across the room. Remembering, no doubt, that he had entertained Trevor Deansgate in the Stewards' box at Chester. Remembering perhaps that he had brought me and Trevor Deansgate there face to face.

Among the other listeners the name had created an almost equal stir. All of them either knew him or knew of him: the big up-and-coming influence among bookmakers, the powerful man shouldering his way into top-rank social acceptance. They knew Trevor Deansgate, and their faces were shocked.

'The real name of Trevor Deansgate is Trevor Shummuck,' my voice said. 'There is a research worker at the vaccine laboratory called Barry Shummuck, who is his brother. The two brothers, on friendly terms, have been seen together at the laboratories on several occasions. ...'

Oh God, I thought. My voice went on, and I listened in snatches. I've really done it. There's no going back.

'... This is the laboratory where the mutant strain originally arose

... unlikely after all this time for there to be any of it anywhere else. ...'

'Trevor Deansgate owns a horse which George Caspar trains. Trevor Deansgate is on good terms with Caspar ... watches the morning gallops and goes to breakfast. Trevor Deansgate stood to make a fortune if he knew in advance that the over-winter favourites for the Guineas and the Derby couldn't win. Trevor Deansgate had the means – the disease; the motive – money; and the opportunity – entry into Caspar's well-guarded stable. It would seem, therefore, that there are grounds for investigating his activities further.'

My voice stopped, and after a minute or two Chico switched off the recorder. Looking slightly dazed himself, he ejected the cassette and laid it carefully on the table.

'It's incredible,' Sir Thomas said, but not as if he didn't believe it. 'What do you think, Lucas?'

Lucas Wainwright cleared his throat. 'I think we should congratulate Sid on an exceptional piece of work.'

Except for Eddy Keith, they agreed with him and did so, to my embarrassment, and I thought it generous of him to have said it at all, considering the Security themselves had done negative dope tests and left it at that. But then the Security, I reflected, hadn't had Rosemary Caspar visiting them in false curls and hysteria: and they hadn't had the benefit of Trevor Deansgate revealing himself to them as a villain before they even positively suspected him, threatening vile things if they didn't leave him alone.

As Chico had said, our successes had stirred up the enemy to the point where they were likely to clobber us before we knew why.

Eddy Keith sat with his head held very still, watching me. I looked back at him, probably with much the same deceptively blank outer expression. Whatever he was thinking, I couldn't read. What I thought about was breaking into his office, and if he could read that he was clairvoyant.

Sir Thomas and the administrators, consulting among themselves, raised their heads to listen when Lucas Wainwright asked a question.

'Do you really think, Sid, that Deansgate infected those horses himself?' He seemed to think it unlikely. 'Surely he couldn't produce a syringe anywhere near any of those horses let alone all four.'

'I did think,' I said, 'that it might have been someone else ... like a work jockey, or even a vet. ...' Inky Poole and Brothersmith, I thought, would have had me for slander if they could have heard. '... But there's a way almost anyone could do it.'

I dipped again into my jacket and produced the packet containing the needle attached to the pea-sized bladder. I gave the packet to Sir Thomas, who opened it, tipping the contents onto his desk.

They all looked. Understood. Were convinced.

'He'd be more likely to do it himself if he could,' I said. 'He wouldn't want to risk anyone else knowing, and perhaps having a hold over him.'

'It amazes me,' Sir Thomas said with apparent genuineness, 'how you work these things out, Sid.'

'But I . . .'

'Yes,' he said, smiling. 'We all know what you're going to say. At heart you're still a jockey.'

There seemed to be a long pause. Then I said, 'Sir, you're wrong. This . . .' I pointed to the cassette, 'is what I am now. And from now on.'

His face sobered into a long frowning look in which it seemed that he was reassessing his whole view of me, as so many others had recently done. It was to him, as to Rosemary, that I still appeared as a jockey, but to myself, no longer. When he spoke again his voice was an octave lower, and thoughtful.

'We've taken you too lightly.' He paused. 'I did mean what I said to you at Chester about being a positive force for good in racing, but I also see that I thought it as something of an unexpected joke.' He shook his head slowly. 'I'm sorry.'

Lucas Wainwright said briskly, 'It's been increasingly clear what Sid has become.' He was tired of the subject and waiting as usual to spur on to the next thing. 'Do you have any plans, Sid, as to what to do next?'

'Talk to the Caspars,' I said. 'I thought I might drive up there tomorrow.'

'Good idea,' Lucas said. 'You won't mind if I come? It's a matter for the Security Service now, of course.'

'And for the police, in due course,' said Sir Thomas, with a touch of gloom. He saw all public prosecutions for racing-based crimes as sources of disgrace to the whole industry, and was inclined to let people get away with things, if prosecuting them would involve a damaging scandal. I tended to agree with him, to the point of doing the same myself, but only if privately one could fix it so that the offence wouldn't be repeated.

'If you're coming, Commander,' I said to Lucas Wainwright, 'perhaps you could make an appointment with them. They may be going to York. I was simply going to turn up at Newmarket early and trust to luck, but you won't want to do that.'

'Definitely not,' he said crisply. 'I'll telephone straight away.'

He bustled off to his own office, and I put the cassette into its small plastic box and handed it to Sir Thomas.

'I put it on tape because it's complicated, and you might want to hear it again.'

'You're so right, Sid,' said one of the administrators, ruefully. 'All that about pigeons . . .!'

Lucas Wainwright came back. 'The Caspars are at York, but went by air-taxi and are returning tonight. George Caspar wants to see his horses work, in the morning, before flying back to York. I told his secretary chap that it was of the utmost importance I see Caspar, so we're due there at eleven. Suit you, Sid?'

'Yes, fine.'

'Pick me up here, then, at nine?'

I nodded. 'O.K.'

'I'll be in my office, checking the mail.'

Eddy Keith gave me a final blank stare and without a word removed himself from the room.

Sir Thomas and all the administrators shook my hand and also Chico's; and going down in the lift Chico said, 'They'll be kissing you next.'

'It won't last.'

We walked back to where I had left the Scimitar, which was where I shouldn't have. There was a parking ticket under the wiper blade. There would be.

'Are you going back to the flat?' Chico said, folding himself into the passenger's seat.

'No.'

'You still think those boot men . . .?'

'Trevor Deansgate,' I said.

Chico's face melted into half-mocking comprehension.

'Afraid he'll duff you up?'

'He'll know by now . . . from his brother,' I shivered internally from a strong flash of the persistent horrors.

'Yeah, I suppose so.' It didn't worry him. 'Look, I brought that begging letter for you. . . .' He dug into a trouser pocket and produced a much folded and slightly grubby sheet of paper. I eyed it disgustedly, reading it through. Exactly the same as the ones Jenny had sent, except signed with a flourish 'Elizabeth More', and headed with the Clifton address.

'Do you realize they may have to produce this filty bit of paper in court?'

'Been in my pocket, hasn't it?' he said defensively. 'What else've you got in there? Potting compost?'

He took the letter from me and put it in the glove box, and let down the window.

'Hot, isn't it?'

'Mm.'

I wound down my own side window, and started the car, and drove him back to his place in Finchley Road.

'I'll stay in the same hotel,' I said. 'And look . . . come to Newmarket with me tomorrow.'

'Sure, if you want. What for?'

I shrugged, making light of it. 'Bodyguard.'

He was surprised. He said wonderingly, 'You can't really be afraid of him . . . this Deansgate . . . are you?'

I shifted in my seat a bit, and sighed.

'I guess so,' I said.

Chapter Seventeen

I talked to Ken Armadale in the early evening. He wanted to know how my session with the Jockey Club had gone, but more than that he sounded smugly self satisfied, and not without reason.

'That erysipelas strain has been made immune to practically every antibiotic in the book,' he said. 'Very thorough. But I reckon there's an obscure little bunch he won't have bothered with, because no one would think of pumping them into horses. Rare, they are, and expensive. All the signs I have here are that they would work. Anyway, I've tracked some down.'

'Great,' I said. 'Where?'

'In London, at one of the teaching hospitals. I've talked with the pharmacist there, and he's promised to pack some in a box and leave it at the reception desk for you to collect. It will have Halley on it.'

'Ken, you're terrific.'

'I've had to mortgage my soul, to get it.'

I picked up the parcel in the morning and arrived at Portman Square to find Chico again waiting on the doorstep. Lucas Wainwright came down from his office and said he would drive us in his car, if we liked, and I thought of all the touring around I'd been doing for the past fortnight, and accepted gratefully. We left the Scimitar in the car park which had been full the day before, a temporary open air affair in a cleared building site, and set off to Newmarket in a large, air conditioned Mercedes.

'It's too darned hot,' Lucas said, switching on the refrigeration. 'Wrong time of year.'

He had come tidily dressed in a suit, which Chico and I hadn't: jeans and sports shirts and not a jacket between us.

'Nice car, this,' Chico said admiringly.

'You used to have a Merc, Sid, didn't you?' Lucas said.

I said yes, and we talked about cars half the way to Suffolk. Lucas drove well but as impatiently as he did everything else. A pepper and salt man, I thought, sitting beside him. Brown and grey speckled hair, brownish eyes, with flecks in the iris. Brown and grey checked shirt, with a nondescript tie. Pepper and salt in his manner, in his speech patterns, in all his behaviour.

He said, as in the end he was bound to, 'How are you getting on with the syndicates?'

Chico, sitting in the back seat, made a noise between a laugh and a snort.

'Er ...' I said. 'Pity you asked, really.'

'Like that, is it?' Lucas said, frowning.

'Well,' I said. 'There is very clearly something going on, but we haven't come up with much more than rumour and hearsay.' I paused. 'Any chance of us collecting expenses?'

He was grimly amused. 'I suppose I could put it under the heading of general assistance to the Jockey Club. Can't see the administrators quibbling, after yesterday.'

Chico gave me a thumbs up sign from behind Lucas's head, and I thought I would pile it on a bit while the climate was favourable, and recover what I'd paid to Jacksy.

'Do you want us to go on trying?' I said.

'Definitely.' He nodded positively. 'Very much so.'

We reached Newmarket in good time and came to a smooth halt in George Caspar's well-tended driveway.

There were no other cars there; certainly not Trevor Deansgate's Jaguar. On that day he should be in the normal course of things at York, attending to his bookmaking business. I had no faith that he was.

George, expecting Lucas, was not at all pleased to see me, and Rosemary, coming downstairs and spotting me in the hall, charged across the parquet and rugs with shrill disapproval.

'Get out,' she said. 'How dare you come here?'

Two spots of colour flamed in her cheeks, and she looked almost as if she was going to try to throw me out bodily.

'No, no, I say,' Lucas Wainwright said, writhing as usual with naval embarrassment in the face of immodest female behaviour, 'George, make your wife *listen* to what we've come to tell you.'

Rosemary was persuaded, with a ramrod stiff back, to perch on a chair in her elegant drawing room, while Chico and I sat lazily in armchairs, and Lucas Wainwright did the talking, this time, about pig disease and bad hearts.

The Caspars listened in growing bewilderment and dismay, and when Lucas mentioned 'Trevor Deansgate' George stood up and began striding about in agitation.

'It isn't possible,' he said. 'Not Trevor. He's a friend.'

'Did you let him near Tri-Nitro, after that last training gallop?' I said.

George's face gave the answer.

'Sunday morning,' Rosemary said, in a hard cold voice. 'He came on the Sunday. He often does. He and George walked round the yard.' She paused. 'Trevor likes slapping horses. Slaps their rumps. Some people do that. Some people pat necks. Some people pull ears. Trevor slaps rumps.'

Lucas said, 'In due course, George, you'll have to give evidence in court.'

'I'm going to look a damned fool, aren't I?' he said sourly. 'Filling my yard with guards and taking Deansgate in myself.'

Rosemary looked at me stonily, unforgiving.

'I told you they were being nobbled. I told you. You didn't believe me.'

Lucas looked surprised. 'But I thought you understood, Mrs Caspar. Sid did believe you. It was Sid who did all this investigating, not the Jockey Club.'

Her mouth opened, and stayed open, speechlessly.

'Look,' I said awkwardly. 'I've brought you a present. Ken Armadale along at the Equine Research has done a lot of work for you, and he thinks Tri-Nitro can be cured, by a course of some rather rare antibiotics. I've brought them with me from London.'

I stood up and took the box to Rosemary: put it into her hands, and kissed her cheek.

'I'm sorry, Rosemary love, that it wasn't in time for the Guineas. Maybe the Derby ... but anyway the Irish Derby and the Diamond Stakes, and the Arc de Triomphe. Tri-Nitro will be fine for those.'

Rosemary Caspar, that tough lady, burst into tears.

We didn't get back to London until nearly five, owing to Lucas insisting on going to see Ken Armadale and Henry Thrace himself, face to face. The Director of Security to the Jockey Club was busy making everything official.

He was visibly relieved when Ken absolved the people who'd done blood tests on the horses after their disaster races.

'The germ makes straight for the heart valves, and in the acute stage you'd never find it loose in the blood, even if you were thinking of illness and not merely looking for dope. It's only later, sometimes, that it gets freed into the blood, as it had in Zingaloo, when we took that sample.'

'Do you mean,' Lucas demanded, 'that if you did a blood test on Tri-Nitro at this minute you couldn't prove he had the disease?'

Ken said, 'You would only find antibodies.'

Lucas wasn't happy. 'Then how can we prove in court that he has got it?'

'Well,' Ken said, 'you could do an erysipelas antibody count today and another in a week's time. There would be a sharp rise in the number present, which would prove the horse must have the disease, because he's fighting it.'

Lucas shook his head mournfully. 'Juries won't like this.'

'Stick to Gleaner,' I said, and Ken agreed.

At one point Lucas disappeared into the Jockey Club rooms in the High Street and Chico and I drank in the White Hart and felt hot.

I changed the batteries. Routine. The day crawled.

'Let's go to Spain,' I said.

'Spain?'

'Anywhere.'

'I could just fancy a señorita.'

'You're disgusting.'

'Look who's talking.'

We reordered and drank and still felt hot.

'How much do you reckon we'll get?' Chico said.

'More or less what we ask.'

George Caspar had promised, if Tri-Nitro recovered, that the horse's owner would give us the earth.

'A fee will do,' I'd said dryly.

Chico said, 'What will you ask, then?'

'I don't know. Perhaps five per cent of his prize money.'

'He couldn't complain.'

We set off southwards, finally, in the cooling car, and listened on the radio to the Dante Stakes at York.

Flotilla, to my intense pleasure, won it.

Chico, in the back seat, went to sleep. Lucas drove as impatiently as on the way up: and I sat and thought of Rosemary, and Trevor Deansgate, and Nicholas Ashe, and Trevor Deansgate, and Louise, and Trevor Deansgate.

Stab. Stab. '*I'll do what I said.*'

Lucas dropped us at the entrance to the car park where I'd left the Scimitar. It would be like a furnace inside, I thought, sitting there all day in the sun. Chico and I walked over to it across the uneven stone-strewn ground.

Chico yawned.

A bath, I thought. A long drink. Dinner. Find a hotel room again ... not the flat.

There was a Land Rover with a two-horse trailer parked beside my car. Odd, I thought idly, to see them in central London. Chico, still yawning, walked between the trailer and my car to wait for me to unlock the doors.

'It'll be baking,' I said, fishing down into my pocket for the keys, and looking downwards into the car.

Chico made a choking sort of noise. I looked up, and thought confusedly how fast, how very fast a slightly boring hot afternoon could turn to stone cold disaster.

A large man stood in the space between the trailer and my car with his left arm clamped around Chico, who was facing me. The man was more or less supporting Chico's weight, because Chico's head lolled forward.

In his right hand the man held a small pear-shaped black truncheon.

The second man was letting down the ramp at the rear of the trailer.

I had no difficulty in recognizing them. The last time I'd seen them I'd been with a fortune teller who hadn't liked my chances.

'Get in the trailer, laddie,' the one holding Chico said to me. 'The right hand stall, laddie. Nice and quick. Otherwise I'll give your friend another tap or two. On the eyes, laddie. Or the base of the brain.'

Chico, on the far side of the Scimitar, mumbled vaguely and moved his head. The big man raised his truncheon and produced another short burst of uncompromising Scottish accent.

'Get in the trailer,' he said. 'Go right in, to the back.'

Seething with fury, I walked round the back of my car and up the ramp into the trailer. The right hand stall, as he'd said. To the back. The second man stood carefully out of hitting distance, and there was no one else in the car park.

I found I was still holding my car keys, and put them back automatically into my pocket. Keys, handkerchief, money ... and in the left-hand pocket, only a discharged battery. No weapon of any sort. A knife in the sock, I thought. I should have learned from Nicholas Ashe.

The man holding Chico came round to the back of the trailer and half dragged, half carried Chico into the left hand stall.

'You make a noise, laddie,' he said, putting his head round to my side of the central partition, 'and I'll hit your friend here. On the eyes, laddie, and the mouth. You try and get help by shouting, laddie, and your friend won't have much face to speak of. Get it?'

I thought of Mason in Tunbridge Wells. A vegetable, and blind.

I said nothing at all.

'I'm travelling in here with your friend, all the way,' he said. 'Just remember that, laddie.'

The second man closed the ramp, shutting out the sunlight, creating instant night. Where many trailers were open at the top at the back, this one was not.

Numb, I suppose, is how I felt.

The engine of the Land Rover started, and the trailer moved, backing out of the parking slot. The motion was enough to rock me against the trailer's side, enough to show I wasn't going very far standing up.

My eyes slowly adjusted to a darkness which wasn't totally black owning to various points where the ramp fitted less closely than other against the back of the trailer. In the end I could see clearly, as if it mattered, the variations that had been done to turn an ordinary trailer into an escape proof transport. The extra piece at the back, closing the gap usually left open for air, and the extra piece inside, lengthways, raising the central partition from head height to the roof.

Basically, it was still a box built to withstand the weight and kicks of horses. I sat helplessly on the floor, which was bare of everything except muddy dust, and thought absolutely murderous thoughts.

After all that unpredictable travelling around I had agreed to go with Lucas and had stupidly left my car in plain vulnerable view all day. They must have picked me up at the Jockey Club, I thought. Either yesterday, or this morning. Yesterday, I thought, there had been no room in the car park, and I'd left my car in the street and got a ticket....

I hadn't been to my flat. I hadn't been back to Aynsford. I hadn't been to the Cavendish, or to any routine place.

I had, in the end, gone to the Jockey Club.

I sat and cursed and thought about Trevor Deansgate.

The journey lasted for well over an hour: a hot, jolting, depressing time which I spent mostly in consciously not wondering what lay at the end of it. After a while I could hear Chico talking, through the partition, though not the words. The flat, heavy, Glaswegian voice made shorter replies, rumbling like thunder.

A couple of pros from Glasgow, Jacksy had said. The one in with Chico, I thought, was certainly that. Not an average bashing mindless thug, but a hard man with brain power; and so much the worse.

Eventually the jolting stopped, and there were noises of the trailer being unhitched from the coupling: the Land Rover drove away, and in the sudden quiet I could hear Chico plainly.

'What's happening?' he said, and sounded still groggy.

'You'll find out soon enough, laddie.'

'Where's Sid?' he said.

'Be quiet, laddie.'

There was no sound of a blow, but Chico was quiet.

The man who had raised the ramp came and lowered it, and six-thirty, Wednesday evening, flooded into the trailer.

'Out,' he said.

He was backing away from the trailer as I got to my feet, and he held a pitchfork at the ready, the sharp tines pointing my way.

From deep in the trailer I looked out and saw where we were. The trailer itself, disconnected from the Land Rover, was inside a building, and the building was the indoor riding school on Peter Rammileese's farm.

Timber-lined walls, windows in the roof, open because of the heat. No way that anyone could see in, casually, from outside.

'Out,' he said, again, jerking the fork.

'Do what he says, laddie,' said the threatening voice of the man with Chico. 'At once.'

I did what he said.

Walked down the ramp onto the quiet tan-coloured riding-school floor.

'Over there.' He jerked the fork. 'Against the wall.' His voice was rougher, the accent stronger, than the man with Chico. For sheer bullying power, there wasn't much to choose.

I walked, feeling that my feet didn't belong to me.

'Back to the wall. Face this way.'

I turned with my shoulders lightly touching the wood.

Behind the man with the pitchfork, standing where from in the trailer I hadn't been able to see him, was Peter Rammileese. His face bore a nasty mixture of satisfaction, sneer, and anticipation, quite unlike the careful intentness of the two Scots. He had driven the Land Rover, I supposed; out of my sight.

The man with Chico brought Chico to the top of the ramp and held him there. Chico half stood and half lay against him, smiling slightly and hopelessly disorganized.

'Hallo, Sid,' he said.

The man holding him lifted the hand holding the truncheon, and spoke to me.

'Now listen, laddie. You stand quite still. Don't move. I'll finish your friend so quick you won't see it happen, if you move. Get it?'

I made no response of any kind, but after a moment he nodded sharply to the one with the pitchfork.

He came towards me slowly; warily. Showing me the prongs.

I looked at Chico. At the truncheon. At damage I couldn't risk.

I stood . . . quite still.

The man with the pitchfork raised it from pointing at my stomach to pointing at my heart, and from there, still higher. Slowly, carefully, one step at a time, he came forward until of the prongs brushed my throat.

'Stand still,' said the man with Chico, warningly.

I stood.

The prongs of the pitchfork slid past my neck, one each side, below my chin, until they came to rest on the wooden surface behind me. Pushing my head back. Pinning me by the neck against the wall, unharmed. Better than through the skin, I thought dimly, but hardly a ball for one's self-respect.

When he'd got the fork aligned as he wanted it, he gave the handle a strong thrusting jerk, digging the sharp tines into the wood. After that he put his weight into pushing against the handle, so that I shouldn't dislodge what he'd done, and get myself free. I had seldom felt more futile or more foolish.

The man holding Chico moved suddenly as if released, carrying Chico bodily down the ramp and giving him a rough overbalancing shove at the bottom. As weak as a rag doll, Chico sprawled on the soft wood shavings, and the man strode over to me to feel for himself the force being applied in keeping me where I was.

He nodded to his partner. 'And you keep your mind on your business,' he said to him. 'Never mind yon other laddie. I'll see to him.'

I looked at their faces, remembering them for ever.

The hard callous lines of cheekbone and mouth. The cold eyes, observant and unfeeling. The black hair and pale skins. The set of a small head on a thick neck, the ears flat. The heavy shape of a jaw blue with beard. Late thirties, I guessed. Both much alike, and both giving forth at great magnitude the methodical brutality of the experienced mercenary.

Peter Rammileese, approaching, seemed in comparison a matter of sponge. Despite his chums' disapproval he too put a hand on the pitchfork handle and tried to give it a shake. It seemed to surprise him that he couldn't.

He said to me, 'You'll keep your snotty nose out, after this.'

I didn't bother to answer. Behind them, Chico got to his feet, and for one surging moment I thought that he'd been fooling them a bit with the concussed act, and was awake and on the point of some effective judo.

It was only a moment. The kick he aimed at the man who had been holding him wouldn't have knocked over a house of cards. In sick and helpless fury I watched the truncheon land again on Chico's head, sending him down onto his knees, deepening the haze in his brain.

The man with the pitchfork was doing what he'd been told and concentrating on keeping up the pressure on the handle. I tugged and wrenched at it with desperation to get free, and altogether failed, and the big man with Chico unfastened his belt.

I saw with incredulity that what he'd worn round his waist was not a leather strap but a length of chain, thin and supple, like the stuff in grandfather clocks. At one end he had fixed some sort of handle, which he grasped; and he swung his arm so that the free end fizzed through the air and wrapped itself around Chico.

Chico's head snapped up and his eyes and mouth opened wide with astonishment, as if the new pain had cleared away the mists like a flamethrower. The man swung his arm again and the chain landed on Chico, and I could hear myself shouting, 'Bastards, bloody bastards ...' and it made no difference at all.

Chico swayed to his feet and took some stumbling steps to get away, and the man followed him, hitting him all over with unvarying ferocity, taking a pride in his work.

I yelled incoherently ... unconnected words, screaming at him to stop ... feeling anger and grief and an agony of responsibility. If I hadn't taken Chico to Newmarket ... if I hadn't been afraid of Trevor Deansgate ... as it was because of my fear that Chico was there ... on that day.... God.... Bastard. Stop it.... Stop.... Wrenched at the pitchfork and couldn't get free.

Chico lurched and stumbled and finally crawled in a wandering circle round the riding school, and ended lying on his stomach not far away from me. The thin cotton of his shirt twitched when the chain landed, and I saw dotted red streaks of blood in the fabric here and there.

Chico.... God....

It wasn't until he lay entirely still that the torment stopped. The man stood over him, looking down judiciously, holding his chain in a relaxed grasp.

Peter Rammileese looked if anything disconcerted and scared, and it was he who had got us there, he who had arranged it.

The man holding the pitchfork stopped looking at me for the first time and switched his attention to where Chico lay. It was only a partial shift of his balance, but it made all the difference to the pressure on my neck. I wrenched at the handle with a force he wasn't ready for, and finally got myself away and off the wall: and it wasn't the man with Chico I sprang at in bloodlusting rage, but Peter Rammileese himself, who was nearer.

I hit him on the side of the face with all my strength, and I hit him with my hard left arm, two thousand quids' worth of delicate technology packed into a built in club.

He screeched and raised his arms round his head, and I said 'Bastard' with savage intensity and hit him again, on the ribs.

The man with Chico turned his attentions to me, and I discovered, as Chico had, that one's first feeling was of astonishment. The sting was incredible: and after the lacerating impact, a continuing fire.

I turned on the man in a rage I wouldn't have thought I could feel, and it was he who backed away from me.

I caught the next swing of his chain on my unfeeling arm. The free end wrapped itself twice round the forearm, and I tugged with such fierceness that he lost his grip on the handle. It swung down towards me, a stitched piece of leather; and if there had been just the two of us I would have avenged Chico and fought our way out of there, because there was nothing about cold blood in the way I went for him.

I grasped the leather handle, and as the supple links unwound and fell off my arm I swung the chain in a circle above my head and hit him an almighty crack around the shoulders. From his wide opening eyes and the outraged Scottish roar I guessed that he was learning for the first time just what he had inflicted on others.

The man with the pitchfork at that point brought up the reserves, and although I might perhaps have managed one, it was hopeless against two.

He came charging straight at me with the wicked prongs and although I dodged them like a bullfighter the first man grabbed my right arm with both of his, intent on getting his chain back.

I swung round towards him in a sort of leap, and with the inside of my metal wrist hit him so hard on the ear and side of the head that the jolt shuddered up through my elbow and upper arm into my shoulder.

For a brief second I saw into his eyes at very close quarters: saw the measure of a hard fighting man, and knew he wasn't going to sit on the trailer and wail, as Peter Rammileese was doing.

The crash on the head all the same loosened his grasp enough for me to wrench myself free, and I lunged away from him, still clutching his chain, and turned to look for the pitchfork. The pitchfork man, however, had thrown the fork away and was unfastening his own belt. I jumped towards him while he had both his hands at his waist and delivered to him too the realities of their chosen warfare.

In the half-second in which both of the Scots were frozen with shock I turned and ran for the door, where, somewhere outside, there had to be people and safety and help.

Running on wood shavings felt like running through treacle, and although I got to the door I didn't get through it, because it was a large affair like a chunk of wall which pushed to one side on rollers, and it was fastened shut by a bolt which let down into the floor.

The pitchfork man reached me there before I even got the bolt up, and I found that his belt wasn't leather either, nor grandfather clock innards, but more like the chain for tethering guard dogs. Less sting. More thud.

I still had the stinger, and I swung round low from trying to undo the bolt and wrapped it round his legs. He grunted and rushed at me, and I found the other man right at my back, both of them clutching, and unfortunately I did them no more damage after that, though not for want of trying.

He got his chain back because he was stronger than I was and banged my hand against the wall to loosen my grasp, the other one holding on to me at the same time, and I thought well I'm damned well not going to make it easy for you and you'll have to work for what you want: and I ran round the place, and made them run, round the trailer, and round by the walls and down again to the door at the end.

I picked up the pitchfork and for a while held them off, and threw it at one of them, and missed; and because one can convert pain into many other things so as not to feel it, I felt little except rage and fury and anger, and concentrated on those feelings to make them a shield.

I ended as Chico had done, stumbling and swaying and crawling and finally lying motionless on the soft floor. Not so far from the door ... but a long way from help.

They'll stop now I'm still, I thought: they'll stop in a minute: and they did.

Chapter Eighteen

I lay with my face in the wood shavings and listened to them panting as they stood over me, both of them taking great gulps of breath after their exertions.

Peter Rammileese apparently came across to them, because I heard his voice from quite close, loaded with spite, mumbling and indistinct.

'Kill him,' he said. 'Don't stop there. Kill him.'

'Kill *him*?' said the man who'd been with Chico. 'Are you crazy?' He coughed, dragging in air. 'Yon laddie ...'

'He's broken my jaw.'

'Kill him yourself then. We're not doing it.'

'Why not? He's cut your ear half off.'

'Grow up, mon.' He coughed again. 'We'd be grassed inside five minutes. We've been down here too long. Too many people've seen us. And this laddie, he's won money for every punter in Scotland. We'd be inside in a week.'

'I want you to kill him,' Peter Rammileese said, insisting.

'You're not paying,' said the Scot, flatly, still breathing heavily. 'We've done what was ordered, and that's that. We'll go into your house now for a beer, and after dark we'll dump these two, as arranged, and then we're finished. And we'll go straight up north tonight, we've been down here too long.'

They went away, and rolled the door open, and stepped out. I heard their feet on the gritty yard, and the door closing, and the metal grate of the outside bolt, which was to keep horses in, and would do for men.

I moved my head a bit to get my nose clear of the shavings, and looked idly at the colour of them so close to my eyes, and simply lay where I was, feeling shapeless, feeling pulped, and stupid, and defeated.

Jelly. A living jelly. Red. On fire. Burning, in a furnace.

There was a lot of romantic rubbish written about fainting from pain, I thought. One absolutely tended not to, because there was no provision for it in nature. The mechanics were missing. There were no fail-safe cut-offs on sensory nerves: they went right on passing the message for as long as the message was there to pass. No other system had evolved, because through millennia it had been unnecessary. It was only man, the most savage of animals, who inflicted pain for its own sake on his fellows.

I thought: I did manage it once, for a short time, after very much too long. I thought: this isn't as bad as that, so I'm going to stay here awake, so I may as well find something to think about. If one couldn't stop the message passing, one could distract the receptors from paying much attention, as in acupuncture; and over the years I'd had a lot of practice.

I thought about a night I'd spent once where I could see a hospital clock. To distract myself from a high state of awfulness I'd spent the time counting. If I shut my eyes and counted for five minutes, five minutes would be gone: and every time I opened my eyes to check, it was only four minutes; and it had been a very long night. I could do better than that, nowadays.

I thought about John Viking in his balloon, and imagined him scudding across the sky, his blue eyes blazing with the glee of breaking safety regulations like bubbles. I thought about Flotilla on the gallops at Newmarket, and winning the Dante Stakes at York. I thought about races I'd ridden in, and won, and lost; and I thought about Louise, a good deal about Louise and fourposter beds.

Afterwards I reckoned that Chico and I had lain there without moving for over an hour, though I hadn't any idea of it at the time. The first sharp intrusion of the uncomfortable present was the noise of the bolt clicking open on the outside of the door, and the grinding noise as the door itself rolled partially open. They were going to dump us, they'd said, after dark; but it wasn't yet dark.

Footsteps made no sound on that soft surface, so that the first thing I heard was a voice.

'Are you asleep?'

'No,' I said.

I shifted my head back a bit and saw little Mark squatting there on his heels, in his pyjamas, studying me with six-year-old concern. Beyond him, the door, open enough to let his small body through. On the other side of the door, out in the yard, the Land Rover.

'Go and see if my friend's awake,' I said.

'O.K.'

He straightened his legs and went over to Chico, and I'd got myself up from flat to kneeling by the time he returned with his report.

'He's asleep,' he said, looking at me anxiously. 'Your face is all wet. Are you hot?'

'Does your Dad know you're down here?' I said.

'No he doesn't. I had to go to bed early, but I heard a lot of shouting. I was frightened, I think.'

'Where's your Dad now?' I said.

'He's in the sitting room with those friends. He's hurt his face and he's bloody angry.'

I practically smiled. 'Anything else?'

'Mum was saying what did he expect, and they were all having drinks.' He thought a bit. 'One of the friends said his ear-drum was burst.'

'If I were you,' I said, 'I'd go straight back to bed and not let them catch you out here. Otherwise your Dad might be bloody angry with you too, and that wouldn't be much fun, I shouldn't think.'

He shook his head.

'Goodnight, then,' I said.

'Goodnight.'

'And leave the door open,' I said. 'I'll shut it.'

'All right.'

He gave me a trusting and slightly conspiratorial smile, and crept out of the doorway to sneak back to bed.

I got to my feet and staggered around a bit, and made it to the door.

The Land Rover stood there about ten feet away. If the keys were in it, I thought, why wait to be dumped? Ten steps. Leant against the grey-green bodywork, and looked through the glass.

Keys. In the ignition.

I went back into the riding school and over to Chico, and knelt beside him because it was a lot less demanding than bending.

'Come on,' I said. 'Wake up. Time to go.'

He groaned.

'Chico, you've got to walk. I can't carry you.'

He opened his eyes. Still confused, I thought, but a great deal better.

'Get up,' I said urgently. 'We can get out, if you'll try.'

'Sid . . .'

'Yeah,' I said. 'Come on.'

'Go away. I can't.'

'Yes, you damned well can. You just say "Sod the buggers," and it comes easy.'

It came harder than I'd thought, but I half lugged him to his feet, and put my arm round his waist, and we meandered waveringly to the door like a pair of drunken lovers.

Through the door, and across to the Land Rover. No furious yells of discovery from the house: and as the sitting room was at the far end of it, with a bit of luck they wouldn't even hear the engine start.

I shovelled Chico onto the front seat and shut the door quietly, and went round to the driving side.

Land Rovers, I thought disgustedly, were made for left-handed people. All the controls, except the indicators, were on that side: and whether it was because I myself was weak, or the battery was flat, or I'd damaged the machinery by using it as a club, the fingers of my left hand would scarcely move.

I swore to myself and did everything with my right hand, which meant twisting, which would have hurt if I hadn't been in such a hurry.

Started the engine. Released the brake. Shoved the gear lever into first. Did the rest thankfully with my feet, and set off. Not the smoothest start ever, but enough. The Land Rover rolled to the gate, and I turned out in the opposite direction from London, thinking instinctively that if they found we'd gone and chased after us, it would be towards London that they would go in pursuit.

The 'sod the buggers' mentality lasted me well for two or three miles and through some dicey one-handed gear changing, but suffered a severe set-back when I looked at the petrol gauge and found it pointing to nearly empty.

The question of where we were going had to be sorted out, and immediately: and before I'd decided, we came round a bend and found in front of us a large garage, still open, with attendants by the pumps. Hardly believing it, I swerved untidily into the forecourt, and came to a jerking halt by the two-star.

Money in right hand pocket, along with car keys and handkerchief. I pulled all of them out in a handful and separated the crumpled notes. Opened the window beside me. Gave the attendant who appeared the money and said I'd have that much petrol.

He was young, a school kid, and he looked at me curiously.

'You all right?'

'It's hot,' I said, and wiped my face with the handkerchief. Some wood shavings fell out of my hair. I must indeed have looked odd.

The boy merely nodded however, and stuck the petrol nozzle into the Land Rover's filling place, which was right beside the driver's door. He looked across me to Chico, who was half lying on the front seats with his eyes open.

'What's wrong with him, then?'

'Drunk,' I said.

He looked as if he thought we both were, but he simply finished the filling, and replaced the cap, and turned away to attend to the next customer. I went again through the tedious business of starting right-handedly, and pulled out onto the road. After a mile I turned off the main road into a side road, and went round a bend or two, and stopped.

'What's happening?' Chico said.

I looked at his still wuzzy eyes. Decide where to go, I thought. Decide for Chico. For myself, I already knew. I'd decided when I found I could drive without hitting things, and at the garage which had turned up so luckily, and when I'd had enough money for the petrol, and when I hadn't asked the boy to get us help in the shape of policemen and doctors.

Hospitals and bureaucracy and questions and being prodded about; all the things I most hated. I wasn't going near any of them, unless I had to for Chico.

'Where did we go, today?' I said.

After a while he said, 'Newmarket.'

'What's twice eight?'

Pause. 'Sixteen.'

I sat in a weak sort of gratitude for his returning wits, waiting for strength to go on. The impetus which had got me into the Land Rover and as far as that spot had ebbed away and left room for a return of fire and jelly. Power would come back, I thought, if I waited. Stamina and energy always came in cycles, so that what one couldn't do one minute, one could the next.

'I'm burning,' Chico said.

'Mm.'

'That was too much.'

I didn't answer. He moved on the seat and tried to sit upright, and I saw the full awareness flood into his face. He shut his eyes tight and said '*Jesus*', and after a while he looked at me through slits, and said, 'You too?'

'Mm.'

The long hot day was drawing to dusk. If I didn't get started, I thought vaguely, I wouldn't get anywhere.

The chief practical difficulty was that driving a Land Rover with one hand was risky, if not downright dangerous, as I had to leave go of the steering wheel and lean to the left every time I changed gear: and the answer to that was to get the left hand fingers to grip the knob just once, and tightly, so that I could switch off the current, and the hand would stay there on the gear lever, unmoving, until further notice.

I did that. Then switched on the side-lights, and the headlights, dipped. Then the engine. I'd give anything for a drink, I thought, and set off on the long drive home.

'Where are we going?' Chico said.

'To the Admiral's.'

I had taken the southern route round Sevenoaks and Kingston and Colnbrook, and there was the M4 motorway stretch to do, and the cross at Maidenhead to the M40 motorway just north of Marlow, and then round the north Oxford ring road and the last leg to Aynsford.

Land Rovers weren't built for comfort and jolted the passengers at the best of times. Chico groaned now and then, and cursed, and said he wasn't getting into a mess like that again, ever. I stopped twice briefly on the way from weakness and general misery, but there wasn't much traffic, and we rolled into Charles's drive in three and a half hours, not too bad for the course.

I switched the Land Rover off and my left hand on, and couldn't get the fingers to move. That was all it needed, I thought despairingly, the final humiliation of that bloody evening, if I had to detach myself from the socket end and leave the electric part of me stuck to the gears. Why, *why*, couldn't I have two hands, like everyone else.

'Don't struggle,' Chico said, 'and you'll do it easy.'

I gave a cough that was somewhere between a laugh and a sob, and the fingers opened a fraction, and the hand fell off the knob.

'Told you,' he said.

I laid my right arm across the steering wheel and put my head down on that, and felt spent and depressed ... and punished. And someone, somehow, had got to raise the strength to go in to tell Charles we were there.

He solved that himself by coming out to us in his dressing gown, the light streaming out behind him from his open front door. The first I knew, he was standing by the window of the Land Rover, looking in.

'Sid?' he said incredulously. 'Is it you?'

I dragged my head off the steering wheel and opened my eyes, and said, 'Yeah.'

'It's after midnight,' he said.

I got a smile at least into my voice. 'You said I could come any time.'

An hour later, Chico was upstairs in bed and I sat sideways on the gold sofa, shoes off, feet up, as I often did.

Charles came into the drawing room and said the doctor had finished with Chico and was ready for me, and I said no thanks very much and tell him to go home.

'He'll give you some knock-out stuff, like Chico.'

'Yes, and that's exactly what I don't want, and I hope he was careful about Chico's concussion, with those drugs.'

'You told him yourself about six times, when he came.' He paused. 'He's waiting for you.'

'I mean it, Charles.' I said. 'I want to think. I want just to sit here and think, so would you please say goodbye to the doctor and go to bed.'

'No,' he said. 'You can't.'

'I certainly can. In fact, I have to, while I still feel...' I stopped. While I still feel *flayed*, I thought: but one couldn't say that.

'It's not sensible.'

'No. The whole thing isn't sensible. That's the point. So go away and let me work it out.'

I had noticed before that sometimes when the body was injured the mind cleared sharply and worked for a while with acute perception. It was a time to use, if one wanted to; not to waste.

'Have you seen Chico's skin?' he said.

'Often,' I said flippantly.

'Is your in the same state?'

'I haven't looked.'

'You're exasperating.'

'Yeah,' I said. 'Go to bed.'

When he'd gone I sat there deliberately and vividly remembering in mind and body the biting horror I'd worked so hard to blank out.

It had been to much, as Chico said.

Too much.

Why?

Charles came downstairs again at six o'clock, in his dressing gown, and with his most impassive expression.

'You're still there, then,' he said.

'Yuh.'

'Coffee?'

'Tea,' I said.

He went and made it, and brought two big steaming mugs, naval fashion. He put mine on the table which stood along the back of the sofa, and sat with his in an armchair. The empty-looking eyes were switched steadily my way.

'Well?' he said.

I rubbed my forehead. 'When you look at me,' I said, hesitatingly. 'Usually, I mean. Not now. When you look at me, what do you see?'

'You know what I see.'

'Do you see a lot of fears and self doubts, and feelings of shame and uselessness and inadequacy?'

'Of course not.' He seemed to find the question amusing, and then sipped the scalding tea, and said more seriously, 'You never show feelings like that.'

'No one does,' I said. 'Everyone has an outside and an inside, and the two can be quite different.'

'Is that just a general observation?'

'No.' I picked up the mug of tea, and blew across the steaming surface. 'To myself, I'm a jumble of uncertainty and fear and stupidity. And to others ... well, what happened to Chico and me last evening was because of the way others see us.' I took a tentative taste. As always when Charles made it, the tea was strong enough to rasp the fur off your tongue. I quite liked it, sometimes. I said, 'We've been lucky, since we started this investigating thing. In other words, the jobs we've done have been comparatively easy, and we've been getting a reputation for being successful, and the reputation has been getting bigger than the reality.'

'Which is, of course,' Charles said dryly, 'that you're a pair of dim-witted layabouts.'

'You know what I mean.'

'Yes, I do. Tom Ullaston rang me here yesterday morning, to arrange about stewards at Epsom, he said, but I gathered it was mostly to tell me what he thought about you, which was, roughly speaking, that if you had still been a jockey it would be a pity.'

'It would be great,' I said, sighing.

'So someone lammed into you and Chico yesterday to stop you chalking up another success?'

'Not exactly,' I said.

I told him what I had spent the night sorting out; and his tea got cold.

When I'd finished he sat for quite a while in silence, simply staring at me in best give-away-nothing manner.

Then he said, 'It sounds as if yesterday evening was ... terrible.'

'Well, yes, it was.'

More silence. Then, 'So what next?'

'I was wondering,' I said diffidently, 'if you'd do one or two jobs for me today, because I ... er ...'

'Of course,' he said. 'What?'

'It's your day for London. Thursday. So could you bear to drive the Land Rover up instead of the Rolls, and swap it for my car?'

'If you like,' he said, not looking enchanted.

'The battery charger's in it, in my suitcase,' I said.

'Of course I'll go.'

'Before that, in Oxford, could you pick up some photographs? They're of Nicholas Ashe.'

'Sid!'

I nodded. 'We found him. There's a letter in my car, too, with his new address on. A begging letter, same as before.'

He shook his head at the foolishness of Nicholas Ashe. 'Any more jobs?'

'Two I'm afraid. The first's in London, and easy. But as for the other ... Would you go to Tunbridge Wells?'

When I told him why, he said he would, even thought it meant cancelling his afternoon's board-meeting.

'And would you lend me your camera, because mine's in the car ... and a clean shirt?'

'In that order?'

'Yes, please.'

Wishing I didn't have to move for a couple of thousand years I slowly unstuck myself from the sofa some time later and went upstairs, with Charles's camera, to see Chico.

He was lying on his side, his eyes dull and staring vaguely into space, the effect of the drugs wearing off. Sore enough to protest wearily when I told him what I wanted to photograph.

'Sod off.'

'Think about barmaids.'

I peeled back the blanket and sheet covering him and took pictures of the visible damage, front and back. Of the invisible damage there was no measure. I put the covers back again.

'Sorry,' I said.

He didn't answer, and I wondered whether I was really apologizing for disturbing him at that moment or more basically for having tangled his life in mine, with such dire results. A hiding to nothing was what he'd said we were on with those syndicates, and he'd been right.

I took the camera out onto the landing and gave it to Charles. 'Ask for blownup prints by tomorrow morning,' I said. 'Tell him it's for a police case.'

'But you said no police ...' Charles said.

'Yes, but it he thinks it's already for the police, he won't go trotting round to them when he sees what he's printing.'

'I suppose it's never occurred to you,' Charles said, handing over a clean shirt, 'that it's your view of you that's wrong, and Thomas Ullaston's that's right?'

I telephoned to Louise and told her I couldn't make it, that day, after all. Something's come up, I said, in the classic evasive excuse, and she answered with the disillusion it merited.

'Never mind, then.'

'I do mind, actually,' I said. 'So how about a week tomorrow? What are you doing after that for a few days?'

'Days?'

'And nights.'

Her voice cheered up considerably. 'Research for a thesis.'

'What subject?'

'Clouds and roses and stars, their variations and frequency in the life of your average liberated female.'

'Oh Louise,' I said, 'I'll ... er ... help you all I can.'

She laughed and hung up, and I went along to my room and took off my dusty, stained, sweaty shirt. Looked at my reflection briefly in the mirror and got no joy from it. Put on Charles's smooth sea island cotton and lay on the bed. I lay on one side, like Chico, and felt what Chico felt; and at one point or other, went to sleep.

In the evening I went down and sat on the sofa, as before, to wait for Charles, but the first person who came was Jenny.

She walked in, saw me, and was immediately annoyed. Then she took a second look, and said, 'Oh no, not again.'

'I said merely, 'Hullo.'

'What is it this time? Ribs, again?'

'Nothing.'

'I know you too well.' She sat at the other end of the sofa, beyond my feet. 'What are you doing here?'

'Waiting for your father.'

She looked at me moodily. 'I'm going to sell that flat in Oxford,' she said.

'Are you?'

'I don't like it any more. Louise McInnes has left, and it reminds me too much of Nicky ...'

After a pause I said, 'Do I remind you of Nicky?'

With a flash of surprise she said, 'Of course not.' And then, more slowly, 'But he ...' she stopped.

'I saw him,' I said. 'Three days ago, in Bristol. And he looks like me, a bit.'

She was stunned, and speechless.

'Didn't you realize?' I said.

She shook her head.

'You were trying to go back,' I said. 'To what we had, at the beginning.'

'It's not true.' But her voice said that she saw it was. She had even told me so, more or less, the evening I'd come to Aynsford to start finding Ashe.

'Where will you live?' I said.

'What do you care?'

I supposed I would always care, to some extent, which was my problem, not hers.

'How did you find him?' she said.

'He's a fool.'

She didn't like that. The look of enmity showed where her instinctive preference still lay.

'He's living with another girl,' I said.

She stood up furiously, and I remembered a bit late that I really didn't want her to touch me.

'Are you telling me that to be beastly?' she demanded.

'I'm telling you so you'll get him out of your system before he goes on trial and to jail. You're going to be damned unhappy if you don't.'

'I hate you,' she said.

'That's not hate, that's injured pride.'

'How dare you!'

'Jenny,' I said. 'I'll tell you plainly, I'd do a lot for you. I've loved you a long time, and I do care what happens to you. It's no good finding Ashe and getting him convicted of fraud instead of you, if you don't wake up and see him for what he is. I wanted to make you angry with him. For your own sake.'

'You won't manage it,' she said fiercely.

'Go away,' I said.

'What?'

'Go away. I'm tired.'

She stood there looking as much bewildered as annoyed, and at that moment Charles came back.

'Hallo,' he said, taking a disapproving look at the general atmosphere. 'Hallo, Jenny.'

She went over and kissed his cheek, from long habit.

'Has Sid told you he's found your friend Ashe?' he said.

'He couldn't wait.'

Charles was carrying a large brown envelope. He opened it, pulled out the contents, and handed them to me: the three photographs of Ashe, which had come out well, and the new begging letter.

Jenny took two jerky strides and looked down at the uppermost photograph.

'Her name is Elizabeth More,' I said slowly. 'His real name is Norris Abbott. She calls him Ned.'

The picture, the third one I'd taken, showed them laughing and entwined, looking into each other's eyes, the happiness in their faces sharply in focus.

Silently, I gave Jenny the letter. She opened it and looked at the signature at the bottom, and went very pale. I felt sorry for her, but she wouldn't have wanted me to say so.

She swallowed, and handed the letter to her father.

'All right,' she said after a pause. 'All right. Give it to the police.'

She sat down again on the sofa with a sort of emotional exhaustion slackening her limbs and curving her spine. Her eyes turned my way.

'Do you want me to thank you?' she said.

I shook my head.

'I suppose one day I will.'

'There's no need.'

With a flash of anger she said, 'You're doing it again.'

'Doing what?'

'Making me feel guilty. I know I'm pretty beastly to you sometimes. Because you make me feel guilty, and I want to get back at you for that.'

'Guilty for what?' I said.

'For leaving you. For our marriage going wrong.'

'But it wasn't your fault,' I protested.

'No, it was yours. Your selfishness, your pigheadedness. Your bloody determination to win. You'll do anything to win, You always have to win. You're so hard. Hard on yourself. Ruthless to yourself. I couldn't live with it. No one could live with it. Girls want men who'll come to them for comfort. Who say, I need you, help me, comfort me, kiss away my troubles. But you ... you can't do that. You always build a wall and deal with your own troubles in silence, like you're doing now. And don't tell me you aren't hurt because I've seen it in you too often, and you can't disguise the way you hold your head, and this time it's very bad, I can see it. But you'd never say, would you, Jenny, hold me, help me, I want to cry?'

She stopped, and in the following silence made a sad little gesture with her hand.

'You see?' she said. 'You can't say it, can you?'

After another long pause I said, 'No.'

'Well,' she said, 'I need a husband who's not so rigidly in control of himself. I want someone who's not afraid of emotion, someone uninhibited, someone weaker. I can't live in the sort of purgatory you make of life for yourself. I want someone who can break down. I want ... an ordinary man.'

She got up from the sofa and bent over and kissed my forehead.

'It's taken me a long time to see all that,' she said. 'And to say it. But I'm glad I have.' She turned to her father. 'Tell Mr Quayle I'm cured of Nicky, and I won't be obstructive from now on. I think I'll go back to the flat now. I feel a lot better.'

She went with Charles towards the door, and then paused and looked back, and said, 'Goodbye, Sid.'

'Goodbye,' I said: and I wanted to say Jenny, hold me, help me, I want to cry: but I couldn't.

Chapter Nineteen

Charles drove himself and me to London the following day in the Rolls with me still in a fairly droopy state and Charles saying we should put it off until Monday.

'No,' I said.

'But even for you this is daunting ... and you're dreading it.'

Dread, I thought, was something I felt for Trevor Deansgate, who wasn't going to hold off just because I had other troubles. Dread was too strong a word for the purpose of the present journey; and reluctance too weak. Aversion, perhaps.

'It's better done today,' I said.

He didn't argue. He knew I was right, otherwise he wouldn't have persuaded to drive me.

He dropped me at the door of the Jockey Club in Portman Square, and went and parked the car, and walked back again. I waited for him downstairs, and we went up in the lift together: he in his City suit, and I in trousers and a clean shirt, but no tie and no jacket. The weather was still hot. A whole week of it, we'd had, and it seemed that everyone except me was bronzed and healthy.

There was a looking glass in the lift. My face stared out of it, greyish and hollow eyed, with a red streak of a healing cut slanting across near the hairline on my forehead, and a blackish bruise on the side of my jaw. Apart from that I looked calmer, less damaged and more normal than I felt, which was a relief. If I concentrated, I should be able to keep it that way.

We went straight to Sir Thomas Ullaston's office, where he was waiting for us. Shook hands, and all that.

To me he said, 'Your father-in-law told me on the telephone yesterday that you have something disturbing to tell me. He wouldn't say what it was.'

'No, not on the telephone,' I agreed.

'Sit down, then. Charles ... Sid ...' He offered chairs, and himself perched on the edge of his big desk. 'Very important, Charles said. So here I am, as requested. Fire away.'

'It's about syndicates,' I said. I began to tell him what I'd told Charles, but after a few minutes he stopped me.

'No. Look, Sid, this is not going to end here simply between me and you, is it? So I think we must have some of the others in, to hear what you're saying.'

I would have preferred him not to, but he summoned the whole heavy mob; the Controller of the Secretariat, the Head of Administration, the Secretary to the Stewards, the Licensing Officer, who dealt with the registration of owners, and the Head of Rules Department, whose province was disciplinary action. They came into the room and filled up the chairs, and for the second time in four days turned their serious civilized faces my way, to listen to the outcome of an investigation.

It was because of Tuesday, I thought, that they would listen to me now. Trevor Deansgate had given me an authority I wouldn't otherwise have had, in that company, in that room.

I said, 'I was asked by Lord Friarly, whom I used to ride for, to look into four syndicates, which he headed. The horses were running in his colours, and he wasn't happy about how they were doing. That wasn't surprising, as their starting prices were going up and down like yoyos, with results to match. Lord Friarly felt he was being used as a front for some right wicked goings on, and didn't like it.'

I paused, knowing I was using a light form of words because the next bit was going to fall like lead.

'On the same day, at Kempton, Commander Wainwright asked me to look into the same four syndicates, which I must say had been manipulated so thoroughly that it was a wonder they weren't a public scandal already.'

The smooth faces registered surprise. Sid Halley was not the natural person for Commander Wainwright to ask to look into syndicates, which were the normal business of the Security Section.

'Lucas Wainwright told me that all four syndicates had been vetted and OK'd by Eddy Keith, and he asked me to find out if there was any unwelcome significance in that.'

For all that I put it at its least dramatic, the response from the cohorts was of considerable shock. Racing might suffer from its attraction for knaves and rogues, as it always had, but corruption within the headquarters itself? Never.

I said, 'I came here to Portman Square to make notes about the syndicates, which I took from Eddy Keith's files, without his knowledge. I wrote the notes in Lucas's office, and he told me about a man he'd sent out on the same errand as myself, six months ago. That man, Mason, had been attacked, and dumped in the streets of Tunbridge Wells, with appalling head injuries, caused by kicks. He was a vegetable, and blind. Lucas told me also that the man who had formed the syndicates, and who had been doing the manipulating, was a Peter Rammileese, who lived at Tunbridge Wells.'

The faces were all frowningly intent.

'After that I ... er ... went away for a week, and I also lost the notes, so I had to come back here and do them again, and Eddy Keith discovered I'd been seeing his files, and complained to you, Sir Thomas, if you remember?'

'That's right. I told him not to fuss.'

There were a few smiles all around, and a general loosening of tension. Inside me, a wilting fatigue.

'Go on, Sid,' Sir Thomas said.

Go on, I thought. I wished I felt less weak, less shaky, less continuously sore. Had to go on, now I'd started. Get on with it. Go on.

I said, 'Well, Chico Barnes, who was here with me on Tuesday ...' They nodded. 'Chico and I, we went down to Tunbridge Wells, to see Peter Rammileese. He was away, as it happened. His wife and little son were there, but the wife had fallen off a horse and Chico went to the hospital with her, taking the little boy, which left me, and an open house. So I ... er ... looked around.'

Their faces said 'Tut, tut', but none of their voices.

'I looked for any possible direct tie-in with Eddy, but actually the whole place was abnormally tidy and looked suspiciously prepared for any searches any tax men might make.'

They smiled slightly.

'Lucas warned me at the beginning that as what I was doing was unofficial, I couldn't be paid, but that he'd give me help instead, if I needed it. So I asked him to help me with the business of Trevor Deansgate, and he did.'

'In what way, Sid?'

'I asked him to write to Henry Thrace, to make sure that the Jockey Club would hear at once if Gleaner died, or Zingaloo, and to tell me, so that I could get a really thorough post mortem done.'

They all nodded. They remembered.

'And then,' I said, 'I found Peter Rammileese on my heels with two very large men who looked just the sort to kick people's heads in and leave them blinded in Tunbridge Wells.'

No smiles.

'I dodged them that time, and spent the next week rolling around England in unpredictable directions so that no one could really have known where to find me, and during that time, when I was chiefly learning about Gleaner and heart valves and so on, I was also told that the two big men had been imported especially from Scotland for some particular job with Peter Rammileese's syndicates. There was also some rumour of someone high up in the Security Service who would fix things for crooks, if properly paid.'

They were shocked again.

'Who told you that, Sid?' Sir Thomas asked.

'Someone reliable,' I said, thinking that maybe they wouldn't think a suspended jockey like Jacksy as reliable as I did.

'Go on.'

'I wasn't really making much progress with those syndicates but Peter Rammileese apparently thought so, because he and his two men laid an ambush for Chico and me, the day before yesterday.'

Sir Thomas reflected. 'I thought that was the day you were going to Newmarket with Lucas to see the Caspars. The day after you were here telling us about Trevor Deansgate.'

'Yes, we did go to Newmarket. And I made the mistake of leaving my car in plain view near here all day. The two men were waiting beside it when we got back. And ... er ... Chico and I got abducted, and where we landed up was at Peter Rammileese's place at Tunbridge Wells.'

Sir Thomas frowned. The others listened to the unemotional relating of what they must have realized had been a fairly violent occurrence with a calm understanding that such things could happen.

There had seldom been, I thought, a more silently attentive audience.

I said, 'They gave Chico and me a pretty rough time, but we did get out of there, owing to Peter Rammileese's little boy opening a door for us by chance, and we didn't end up in Tunbridge Wells streets, we got to my father-in-law's house near Oxford.'

They all looked at Charles, who nodded.

I took a deep breath. 'At about that point,' I said, 'I ... er ... began to see things the other way round.'

'How do you mean, Sid?'

'Until then, I thought the two Scotsmen were supposed to be preventing us from finding what we were looking for, in those syndicates.'

They nodded. Of course.

'But supposing it was exactly the reverse.... Supposing I'd been pointed at those syndicates in order to be led to the ambush. Suppose the ambush itself was the whole aim of the exercise.'

Silence.

I had come to the hard bit, and needed the reserves I didn't have, of staying power, of will. I was aware of Charles sitting steadfastly beside me, trying to give me his strength.

I could feel myself shaking. It kept my voice flat and cold, saying the things I didn't like saying, that had to be said.

'I was shown an enemy, who was Peter Rammileese. I was given a reason for being beaten up, which was the syndicates. I was fed the expectation of it, through the man Mason. I was being given a background to what was going to happen; a background I would accept.'

Total silence and blank, uncomprehending expressions.

I said, 'If someone had savagely attacked me out of the blue, I wouldn't have been satisfied until I had found out who and why. So I thought, supposing someone wanted to attack me, but it was imperative that I didn't find out who or why. If I was given a false who, and a false why, I would believe in those, and not look any further.'

One or two very slight nods.

'I did believe in that who and that why for a while,' I said. 'But the attack, when it came, seemed out of all proportion ... and from something one of our attackers said I gathered it was not Peter Rammileese himself who was paying them, but someone else.'

Silence.

'So, after we had reached the Admiral's house, I began thinking, and I thought, if the attack itself was the point, and it was not Peter

Rammileese who had arranged it, then who had? Once I saw it that way, there was only one possible who. The person who had laid the trail for me to follow.'

The faces began to go stiff.

I said, 'It was Lucas himself who set us up.'

They broke up into loud, jumbled, collective protest, moving in their chairs with embarrassment, not meeting my eye, not wanting to look at someone who was so mistaken, so deluded, so pitiably ridiculous.

'No, Sid, really,' Sir Thomas said. 'We've a great regard for you . . .' The others looked as if the great regard was now definitely past tense. '. . . but you can't say things like that.'

'As a matter of fact,' I said slowly, 'I would much rather have stayed away and not said it. I won't tell you any more, if you don't want to hear it.' I rubbed my fingers over my forehead from sheer lack of inner energy, and Charles half made, and then stopped himself making, a protective gesture of support.

Sir Thomas looked at Charles and then at me, and whatever he saw was enough to calm him from incredulity to puzzlement.

'All right,' he said soberly, 'we'll listen.'

The others all looked as if they didn't want to, but if the Senior Steward was willing, it was enough.

I said, with deep weariness and no satisfaction, 'To understand the *why* part, it's necessary to look at what's been happening during the past months. During the time Chico and I have been doing . . . what we have. As you yourself said, Sir Thomas, we've been successful. Lucky . . . tackling pretty easy problems . . . but mostly sorting them out. To the extent that a few villains have tried to stop us dead as soon as we've appeared on the skyline.'

The disbelief still showed like snow in July, but at least they seemed to understand that too much success invited retaliation. The uncomfortable shiftings in the chairs grew gradually still.

'We've been prepared for it, more or less,' I said. 'In some cases it's even been useful, because it's shown us we're nearing the sensitive spot. . . . But what we usually get is a couple of rent-a-thug bullies in or out of funny masks, giving us a warning bash or two and telling us to lay off. Which advice,' I added wryly, 'we have never taken.'

They had all begun looking at me again, even if sideways.

'So then people begin to stop thinking of me as jockey, and gradually see that what Chico and I are doing isn't really the joke it seemed at first. And we get what you might call the Jockey Club Seal of Approval, and all of a sudden, to the really big crooks, we appear as a continuing, permanent menace.'

'Do you have proof of that, Sid?' Sir Thomas said.

Proof . . . Short of getting Trevor Deansgate in there to repeat his threat before witnesses, I had no proof. I said, 'I've had threats . . . only threats, before this.'

A pause. No one said anything, so I went on.

'I understand on good authority,' I said, with faint amusement, 'that there would be some reluctance to solve things by actually killing us, as people who had won money in the past on my winners would rise up in wrath and grass on the murderers.'

Some tentative half-smiles amid general dislike of such melodrama.

'Anyway, such a murder would tend to bring in its trail precisely the investigation it was designed to prevent.'

They were happier with that.

'So the next best thing is an ultimate deterrent. One that would so sicken Chico and me that we'd go and sell brushes instead. Something to stop us investigating anything else, ever again.'

It seemed all of a sudden as if they did understand what I was saying. The earlier, serious attention came right back. I thought it might be safe to mention Lucas again, and when I did there was none of the former vigorous reaction.

'If you could just imagine for a moment that there *is* someone in the Security Service who can be bribed, and that it is the Director himself, would you, if you were Lucas, be entirely pleased to see an independent investigator making progress in what had been exclusively your territory? Would you, if you were such a man, be pleased to see Sid Halley right here in the Jockey Club being congratulated by the Senior Steward and being given carte blanche to operate wherever he liked throughout racing?'

They stared.

'Would you, perhaps, be afraid that one of these days Sid Halley would stumble across something you couldn't afford for him to find out? And might you not, at that point, decide to remove the danger of it once and for all? Like putting weedkiller on a nettle, before it stings you.'

Charles cleared his throat. 'A pre-emptive strike,' he said smoothly, 'might appeal to a retired Commander.'

They remembered he had been an Admiral, and looked thoughtful.

'Lucas is only a man,' I said. 'The title of Director of Security sounds pretty grand, but the Security Service isn't that big, is it? I mean, there are only about thirty people in it full time, aren't there, over the whole country?'

They nodded.

'I don't suppose the pay is a fortune. One hears about bent policemen from time to time, who've taken bribes from crooks. Well ... Lucas is constantly in contact with people who might say, for instance, how about a quiet thousand in readies, Commander, to smother my little bit of trouble?'

The faces were shocked.

'It does happen, you know,' I said mildly. 'Backhanders are a flourishing industry. I agree that you wouldn't want the head of racing security to be shutting his eyes to skulduggery, but it's more a breach of trust than anything aggressively wicked.'

What he'd done to Chico and me was indeed aggressively wicked, but that wasn't the point I wanted to make.

'What I'm saying,' I said, 'is that in the wider context of the everyday immoral world, Lucas's dishonesty is no great shakes.'

They looked doubtful, but that was better than negative shakes of the head. If they could be persuaded to think of Lucas as a smallish scale sinner they would believe more easily that he'd done what he had.

'If you start from the idea of a deterrent,' I said. 'You see everything from the other side.' I stopped. The inner exhaustion didn't. I'd like to sleep for a week, I thought.

'Go on, Sid.'

'Well. . . .' I sighed. 'Lucas had to take the slight risk of pointing me at something he was involved in, because he needed a background he could control. He must have been badly shocked when Lord Friarly said he'd asked me to look into those syndicates, but if he had already toyed with the idea of getting rid of me, I'd guess he saw at that point how to do it.'

One or two of the heads nodded sharply in comprehension.

'Lucas must have been sure that a little surface digging wouldn't get me anywhere near him – which it didn't – but he minimized the risk by specifically directing my attention to Eddy Keith. It was safe to set me investigating Eddy's involvement with the shady side of the syndicates, because of course he wasn't involved. I could look for ever, and find nothing.' I paused. 'I don't think I was supposed to have much time to find out anything at all. I think that catching us took much longer than was intended in the original plan.'

Catching us . . . catching me. They'd have taken me alone, but both had been better for them . . . and far worse for me. . . .

'Took much longer? How do you mean?' Sir Thomas said.

Concentrate, I thought. Get on with it.

'From Lucas's point of view, I was very slow,' I said. 'I was working on the Gleaner thing, and I didn't do anything at all about the syndicates for a week after he asked me. Then directly I'd been told about Peter Rammileese and Mason, and could have been expected to go down to Tunbridge Wells, I went away somewhere else entirely, for another week; during which time Lucas rang Chico four times to ask him where I was.'

Silent attention, as before.

'When I came back, I'd lost the notes, so I did them again in Lucas's office, and I told him Chico and I would go down to Peter Rammileese's place the following day, Saturday. I think it's likely that if we had done so the . . . er . . . deterring . . . would have been done then, but in fact we went the same afternoon that I'd been talking to Lucas, on the Friday, and Peter Rammileese wasn't there.'

Weren't they all thirsty, I wondered? Where was the coffee? My mouth was dry, and a good deal of me hurt.

'It was on that Friday morning that I asked Lucas to write to Henry Thrace. I also asked him – entreated him, really – not to mention my name at all in connection with Gleaner, as it might get me killed.'

A lot of frowns awaited an explanation.

'Well . . . Trevor Deansgate had warned me in those sort of terms to stop investigating those horses.'

Sir Thomas managed to raise his eyebrows and imply a frown at one and the same time.

'Are those the threats you mentioned before?' he said.

'Yes, and he repeated them when you ... er ... introduced us, in your box at Chester.'

'Good God.'

'I wanted to get the investigation of Gleaner done by the Jockey Club so that Trevor Deansgate wouldn't know it had anything to do with me.'

'You did take those threats seriously,' Sir Thomas said thoughtfully.

I swallowed. 'They were ... seriously given.'

'I see,' said Sir Thomas, although he didn't. 'Go on.'

'I didn't actually tell Lucas about the threats themselves,' I said. 'I just begged him not to tie me in with Gleaner. And within days, he had told Henry Thrace that it was I, not the Jockey Club, who really wanted to know if Gleaner died. At the time I reckoned that he had just been careless or forgetful, but now I think he did it on purpose. Anything which might get me killed was to him a bonus, even if he didn't see how it could do.'

They looked doubtful. Doubts were possible.

'So then Peter Rammileese – or Lucas – traced me to my father-in-law's house, and on the Monday Peter Rammileese and the two Scots followed me from there to a horse show, where they had a shot at abduction, which didn't come off. After that I kept out of their way for eight more days, which must have frustrated them no end.'

The faces waited attentively.

'During that time I learned that Peter Rammileese was manipulating not four, but nearer twenty syndicates, bribing trainers and jockeys wholesale. It was then also that I learned about the bribable top man in the Security Service who was turning a blind eye to the goings on, and I regret to say I thought it must be Eddy Keith.'

'I suppose,' Sir Thomas said, 'that that was understandable.'

'So, anyway, on Tuesday Chico and I came here, and Lucas at last knew where I was. He asked to come to Newmarket with us on Wednesday, and he took us there in his own super four litre air conditioned highly expensive Mercedes, and although he's usually so keen to get on with the next thing, he wasted hours doing nothing in Newmarket, during which time I now think he was in fact arranging and waiting for the ambush to be properly set up, so that this time there should be no mistakes. Then he drove us to where the Scots were waiting for us, and we walked straight into it. The Scots did the special job they had been imported for, which was deterring Chico and me, and I heard one of them tell Peter Rammileese that now they had done what was ordered they were going north straight away, they'd been in the south too long.'

Sir Thomas was looking slightly strained.

'Is that all, Sid?

'No. There's the matter of Mason.'

Charles stirred beside me, uncrossing and recrossing his legs.

'I asked my father-in-law to go to Tunbridge Wells yesterday, to ask about Mason.'

Charles said, in his most impressive drawl, 'Sid asked me to see if Mason existed. I saw the police fellows in Tunbridge Wells. Very helpful, all of them. No one called Mason, or anything else for that matter, has been found kicked near to death and blinded in their streets, ever.'

'Lucas told me about Mason's case in great detail,' I said. 'He was very convincing, and of course I believed him. But have any of you ever heard of anyone called Mason who was employed by the Security Service, that was so badly injured?'

They silently, bleakly, shook their heads. I didn't tell them that I'd finally had doubts about Mason because there was no file for him in 'Personnel'. Even in a good cause, our breaking and entering wouldn't please them.

A certain amount of gloom had settled on their faces, but there were also questions they wanted to ask. Sir Thomas put their doubts into words.

'There's one obvious flaw in your reverse view of things, Sid, and that is that this deterrent . . . hasn't deterred you.'

After a pause I said, 'I don't know that it hasn't. Neither Chico nor I could go on, if it meant . . . if we thought . . . anything like that would happen again.'

'Like exactly what, Sid?'

I didn't reply. I could feel Charles glancing my way in his best noncommittal manner, and it was he, eventually, who got quietly to his feet, and walked across the room, and gave Sir Thomas the envelope which contained the pictures of Chico.

'It was a chain,' I said matter-of-factly.

They passed the photographs round in silence. I didn't particularly look to see what they were thinking, I was just hoping they wouldn't ask what I knew they would: and Sir Thomas said it baldly. 'Was this done to you as well?'

I reluctantly nodded.

'Will you take your shirt off, then, Sid?'

'Look,' I said. 'What does it matter? I'm not laying any charges of assault or grievous bodily harm, or anything like that. There's going to be no police, no court case, nothing. I've been through all that once, as you know, and I'm not, absolutely not, doing it again. This time there's to be no noise. All that's necessary is to tell Lucas I know what's been happening, and if you think it right, to get him to resign. There's nothing to be gained by anything else. You don't want any public scandal. It would be harmful to racing as a whole.'

'Yes, but . . .'

'There's Peter Rammileese,' I said. 'Perhaps Eddy Keith might really sort out those syndicates, now. It would only get Rammileese deeper in if he boasted that he'd bribed Lucas, so I shouldn't think he would. I doubt if he'd talk about Chico and me, either.'

Except perhaps, I thought sardonically, to complain that I'd hit him very hard.

'What about the two men from Glasgow?' Sir Thomas said. 'Are they just to get away with it?'

'I'd rather that than go to court again as a victim,' I said. I half smiled. 'You might say that the business over my hand successfully deterred me from that sort of thing for the rest of my life.'

A certain amount of urbane relief crept into both the faces and the general proceedings.

'However,' Sir Thomas said. 'The resignation of the Director of Security cannot be undertaken lightly. We must judge for ourselves whether or not what you said is justified. The photographs of Mr Barnes aren't enough. So please . . . take off your shirt.'

Bugger it, I thought. I didn't want to. And from the distaste in their faces, they didn't want to see. I hated the whole damn thing. Hated what had happened to us. Detested it. I wished I hadn't come to Portman Square.

'Sid,' Sir Thomas said seriously. 'You must.'

I undid the buttons and stood up and slid the shirt off. The only pink bit of me was the plastic arm, the rest being mottled black with dark red criss-crossed streaks. It looked by that time, with all the bruising coming out, a lot worse than it felt. It looked, as I knew, appalling. It also looked, on that day, the worst it would. It was because of that I'd insisted on going to Portman Square on that day. I hadn't wanted to show them the damage, yet I'd known they would insist, and I would have to: and if I had to, that day was the most convincing. The human mind was deviously ambivalent, when it wanted to defeat its enemies.

In a week or so, most of the marks would have gone, and I doubted whether there would be a single permanent external scar. It had all been quite precisely a matter of outraging the sensitive nerves of the skin, transient, leaving no trace. With such a complete lack of lasting visible damage, the Scots would know that even if they were brought to trial, they would get off lightly. For a hand, all too visible, the sentence had been four years. The going rate for a few days' surface discomfort was probably three months. In long robbery-with-violence sentences it was always the robbery that stretched the time, not the violence.

'Turn round,' Sir Thomas said.

I turned round, and after a while I turned back. No one said anything. Charles looked at his most unruffled. Sir Thomas stood up and walked over to me, and inspected the scenery more closely. Then he picked up my shirt from the chair, and held it for me to put on again.

I said 'Thank you,' and did up the buttons. Pushed the tails untidily into the top of my trousers. Sat down.

It seemed quite a long time before Sir Thomas lifted the inter-office telephone and said to his secretary, 'Would you ask Commander

Wainwright to come here, please?'

If the administrators still had any doubts, Lucas himself dispelled them. He walked briskly and unsuspectingly into a roomful of silence, and when he saw me sitting there he stopped moving suddenly, as if his brain had given up transmitting to his muscles.

The blood drained from his face, leaving the grey-brown eyes staring from a barren landscape. I had an idea that I must have looked like that to Trevor Deansgate, in the Stewards' box at Chester. I thought that quite likely, at that moment, Lucas couldn't feel his feet on to the carpet.

'Lucas,' Sir Thomas said, pointing to a chair, 'sit down.'

Lucas fumbled his way into the chair with his gaze still fixedly on me, as if he couldn't believe I was there, as if by staring hard enough he could make me vanish.

Sir Thomas cleared his throat, 'Lucas, Sid Halley, here, has been telling us certain things which require explanation.'

Lucas was hardly listening. Lucas said to me, 'You can't be here.'

'Why not?' I said.

They waited for Lucas to answer, but he didn't.

Sir Thomas said eventually, 'Sid has made serious charges. I'll put them before you, Lucas, and you can answer as you will.'

He repeated more or less everything I'd told them, without emphasis and without mistake. The judicial mind, I thought, taking the heat out of things, reducing passion to probabilities. Lucas appeared to be listening, but he looked at me all the time.

'So you see,' Sir Thomas said finally, 'we are waiting for you to deny – or admit – that Sid's theories are true.'

Lucas turned his head away from me and looked vaguely round the room.

'It's all rubbish, of course,' he said.

'Carry on,' said Sir Thomas.

'He's making it all up.' He was thinking again, fast. The briskness in some measure returned to his manner. 'I certainly didn't tell him to investigate any syndicates. I certainly didn't tell him I had doubts about Eddy. I never talked to him about this imaginary Mason. He's invented it all.'

'With what purpose?' I said.

'How should I know?'

'I didn't invent coming here twice to copy down notes of the syndicates,' I said. 'I didn't invent Eddy complaining because I'd seen those files. I didn't invent you telephoning Chico at my flat four times. I didn't invent you dropping us at the car park. I didn't invent Peter Rammileese, who might be persuaded to . . . er . . . talk. I could also find those two Scots, if I tried.'

'How?' he said.

I'd ask young Mark, I thought. He would have learnt a lot about the friends in all that time: little Mark and his accurate ears.

I said, 'Don't you mean, I invented the Scots?'

He glared at me.

'I could also,' I said slowly, 'start looking for the real reasons behind all this. Trace the rumours of corruption to their source. Find out who, besides Peter Rammileese, is keeping you in Mercedes.'

Lucas Wainwright was silent. I didn't know that I could do all I'd said, but he wouldn't want to bet I couldn't. If he hadn't thought me capable he'd have seen no need to get rid of me in the first place. It was his own judgement I was invoking, not mine.

'Would you be prepared for that, Lucas?' Sir Thomas said.

Lucas stared my way some more, and didn't answer.

'On the other hand,' I said, 'I think if you resigned, it would be the end of it.'

He turned his head away from me and stared at the Senior Steward instead.

Sir Thomas nodded. 'That's all, Lucas. Just your resignation, now, in writing. If we had that, I would see no reason to proceed any further.'

It was the easiest let-off anyone could have had, but to Lucas, at that moment, it must have seemed bad enough. His face looked strained and pale, and there were tremors round his mouth.

Sir Thomas produced from his desk a sheet of paper, and from his pocket a gold ball-point pen.

'Sit here, Lucas.'

He rose and gestured Lucas to sit by the desk.

Commander Wainwright walked over with stiff legs and shakily sat where he'd been told. He wrote a few words, which I read later. *I resign from the post of Director of Security to the Jockey Club. Lucas Wainwright.*

He looked around at the sober faces, at the people who had known him well, and trusted him, and had worked with him every day. He hadn't said a word, since he'd come into the office, of defence or appeal. I thought: how odd it must be for them all, facing such a shattering readjustment.

He stood up, the pepper and salt man, and walked towards the door.

As he came to where I sat he paused, and looked at me blankly, as if not understanding.

'What does it take,' he said, 'to stop you?'

I didn't answer.

What it took rested casually on my knee. Four strong fingers, and a thumb, and independence.

Chapter Twenty

Charles drove us back to Aynsford.

'You'll get a bellyful of courtrooms anyway,' he said. 'With Nicholas Ashe, and Trevor Deansgate.'

'It's not so bad just being an ordinary witness.'

'You've done it a good few times, now.'

'Yes,' I said.

'What will Lucas Wainwright do after this, I wonder.'

'God knows.'

Charles glanced at me. 'Don't you feel the slightest desire to gloat?'

'Gloat?' I was astounded.

'Over the fallen enemy.'

'Oh yes?' I said. 'And in your war at sea, what did you do when you saw an enemy drowning? Gloat? Push him under?'

'Take him prisoner,' Charles said.

After a bit I said, 'His life from now on will be prison enough.'

Charles smiled his secret smile, and ten minutes further on he said, 'And do you forgive him, as well?'

'Don't ask such difficult questions.'

Love thine enemy. Forgive. Forget. I was no sort of Christian, I thought. I could manage not to hate Lucas himself. I didn't think I could forgive: and I would never forget.

We rolled on to Aynsford, where Mrs Cross, carrying a tray upstairs to her private sitting room, told me that Chico was up, and feeling better, and in the kitchen. I went along there and found him sitting alone at the table, looking at a mug of tea.

'Hullo,' I said.

'Hullo.'

There was no need, with him, to pretend anything. I filled a mug from the pot and sat opposite him.

'Bloody awful,' he said. 'Wasn't it?'

'Yeah.'

'And I was dazed, like.'

'Mm.'

'You weren't. Made it worse.'

We sat for a while without talking. There was a sort of stark dullness in his eyes, and none of it, any longer, was concussion.

'Do you reckon,' he said, 'they let your head alone, for that?'

'Don't know.'

'They could've.'

I nodded. We drank the tea, bit by bit.

'What did they say, today?' he said. 'The brass.'

'They listened. Lucas resigned. End of story.'

'Not for us.'

'No.'

I moved stiffly on the chair.

'What'll we do?' he said.

'Have to see.'

'I couldn't...' He stopped. He looked tired and sore, and dispirited.

'No,' I said. 'Nor could I.'

'Sid ... I reckon ... I've had enough.'

'What, then?'

'Teach judo.'

And I could make a living, I supposed, from equities, commodities, insurance, and capital gains. Some sort of living ... not much of a life.

In depression we finished the tea, feeling battered and weak and sorry for ourselves. I couldn't go on if he didn't, I thought. He'd made the job seem worthwhile. His naturalness, his good nature, his cheerfulness: I needed them around me. In many ways I couldn't function without him. In many ways, I wouldn't bother to function, if I didn't have him to consider.

After a while I said, 'You'd be bored.'

'What, with Wembley and not hurting, and the little bleeders?'

I rubbed my forehead, where the stray cut itched.

'Anyway,' he said, 'it was you, last week, who was going to give up.'

'Well ... I don't like being ...' I stopped.

'Beaten,' he said.

I took my hand away and looked at his eyes. There was the same thing there that had suddenly been in his voice. An awareness of the two meanings of the word. A glimmer of sardonic amusement. Life on its way back.

'Yeah.' I smiled twistedly. 'I don't like being beaten. Never did.'

'Sod the buggers then?' he said.

I nodded. 'Sod 'em.'

'All right.'

We went on sitting there, but it was a lot better, after that.

Three days later, on Monday evening, we went back to London, and Chico, humouring the fears he didn't take seriously, came with me to the flat.

The hot weather had gone back to normal, or in other words, warm-front drizzle. Road surfaces were slippery with the oily patina left by hot dry tyres, and in west London every front garden was soggy with roses. Two weeks to the Derby ... and perhaps Tri-Nitro would run in it, if the infection cleared up. He was fit enough, apart from that.

The flat was empty and quiet.

'Told you,' Chico said, dumping my suitcase in the bedroom.

'Want me to look in the cupboards?'

'As you're here.'

He raised his eyebrows to heaven and did an inch by inch search.

'Only spiders,' he said. 'They've caught all the flies.'

We went down to where I'd parked at the front and I drove him to his place.

'Friday,' I said. 'I'm going away for a few days.'

'Oh yes? Dirty weekend?'

'You never know. I'll call you, when I get back.'

'Just the nice gentle crooks from now on, right?'

'Throw all the big ones back,' I said.

He grinned, waved, and went in, and I drove away with lights going on everywhere in the dusk. Back at the flats I went round to the lock-up garages to leave the car in the one I rented there, out of sight.

Unlocked the roll-up door, and pushed it high. Switched the light on. Drove the car in. Got out. Locked the car door. Put the keys in my pocket.

'Sid Halley,' a voice said.

A voice. *His* voice.

Trevor Deansgate.

I stood facing the door I'd just locked, as still as stone.

'Sid Halley.'

I had known it would happen, I supposed. Sometime, somewhere, like he'd said. He had made a serious threat. He had expected to be believed. I had believed him.

Oh God, I thought. It's too soon. It's always too soon. Let him not see the terror I feel. Let him not know. Dear God ... give me courage.

I turned slowly towards him.

He stood a step inside the garage, in the light, the thin drizzle like a dark grey-silver sheet behind him.

He held the shotgun, with the barrels pointing my way.

I had a brick wall on my left and another behind me, and the car on my right; and there were never many people about at the back of the flats, by the garages. If anyone came, they'd hardly dawdle around, in the rain.

'I've been waiting for you,' he said.

He was dressed, as ever, in city pinstripes. He brought, as always, the aura of power.

With eyes and gun facing unwaveringly my way, he stretched up behind him quickly with his left hand and found the bottom edge of the roll-up door. He gave it a sharp downward tug, and it rolled down nearly to the ground behind him, closing us in. Both hands, clean, manicured, surrounded by white cuffs, were back on the gun.

'I've been waiting for you, on and off, for days. Since last Thursday.'

I didn't say anything.

'Last Thursday two policemen came to see me. George Caspar telephoned. The Jockey Club warned me they were going to take proceedings. My solicitor told me I'd lose my bookmaking licence. I would be warned off from racing, and might well go to jail. Since last Thursday, I've been waiting for you.'

His voice, as before, was a threat in itself, heavy with the raw realities of the urban jungle.

'The police have been to the lab. My brother is losing his job. His career. He worked hard for it.'

'Let's all cry,' I said. 'You both gambled. You've lost. Too bloody bad.'

His eyes narrowed and the gun barrels moved an inch or two as his body reacted.

'I came here to do what I said I would.'

Gambled ... lost ... so had I.

'I've been waiting in my car around these flats,' he said. 'I knew you'd come back, some time or other. I knew you would. All I had to do was wait. I've spent most of my time here, since last Thursday, waiting for you. So tonight you came back ... with that friend. But I wanted you on your own ... I went on waiting. And you came back. I knew you'd come, in the end.'

I said nothing.

'I came here to do what I promised. To blow your hand off.' He paused. 'Why don't you beg me not to? Why don't you go down on your bloody knees and beg me not to?'

I didn't answer. Didn't move.

He gave a short laugh that had no mirth in it at all. 'It didn't stop you, did it, that threat? Not for long. I thought it would. I thought no one could risk losing both their hands. Not just to get me busted. Not for something small, like that. You're a bloody fool, you are.'

I agreed with him, on the whole. I was also trembling inside, and concerned that he shouldn't see it.

'You don't turn a hair, do you?' he said.

He's playing with me, I thought. He must know I'm frightened to death. He's making me sweat ... wanted me to beg him ... and I'm not ... *not* ... going to.

'I came here to do it,' he said. 'I've been sitting here for days, thinking about it. Thinking of you with no hands ... with just stumps ... with two plastic hooks.'

Sod you, I thought.

'Today,' he said, 'I started thinking about myself. I shoot off Sid Halley's right hand, and what happens to me?' He stared at me with increased intensity. 'I get the satisfaction of fixing you, making you a proper cripple instead of half a one. I get revenge ... hideous delightful revenge. And what else do I get? I get ten years, perhaps. You can get life for G.B.H., if it's bad enough. Both hands ... that might be bad enough. That's what I've been sitting here today thinking. And I've been thinking of the feeling there'd be against me in the slammer, for shooting your other hand off. Yours, of all people. I'd be better off killing you. That's what I thought.'

I thought numbly that I wasn't sure either that I wouldn't rather be dead.

'This evening,' he said, 'after you'd come back for ten minutes, and gone away again, I thought of rotting away in jail year after year wishing I'd had the bloody sense to leave you alone. I reckoned it wasn't worth years in jail, just to know I'd fixed you. Fixed you alive, or fixed you dead. So I decided, just before you came back, not to do that, but just to get you down on the ground squealing for me not to. I'd have my revenge that way. I'd remind you of it, all your life. I'd tell people I'd had you crawling. Make them snigger.'

Jesus, I thought.

'I'd forgotten,' he said, 'what you're like. You've no bloody nerves. But I'm not going to shoot you. Like I said, it's not worth it.'

He turned abruptly, and stooped, putting one hand under the garage door. Heaved; rolled it upwards and open.

The warm drizzle in the dark outside fell like shoals of silver minnows. The gentle air came softly into the garage.

He stood there for a moment, brooding, holding his gun: and then he gave me back what in the straw-barn he'd taken away.

'Isn't there *anything*,' he said bitterly, 'that you're afraid of?'

RAT RACE

Chapter One

I picked four of them up at White Waltham in the new Cherokee Six 300 that never got a chance to grow old. The pale blue upholstery still had a new leather smell and there wasn't a scratch on the glossy white fuselage. A nice little aeroplane, while it lasted.

They had ordered me for noon but they were already in the bar when I landed at eleven forty. Three double whiskies and a lemonade.

Identification was easy: several chairs round a small table were draped with four lightweight raincoats, three binocular cases, two copies of the *Sporting Life* and one very small racing saddle. The four passengers were standing nearby in the sort of spread-about group indicative of people thrown together by business rather than natural friendship. They were not talking to each other, though it looked as though they had been. One, a large man, had a face full of anger. The smallest, evidently a jockey, was flushed and rigid. The two others, an elderly man and a middle-aged woman, were steadfastly staring at nothing in particular in the way that meant a lot of furious activity was going on inside their heads.

I walked towards the four of them across the large lounge reception room and spoke to an indeterminate spot in mid air.

'Major Tyderman?'

The elderly man, who said 'Yes?', had been made a Major a good long time ago. Nearer seventy than sixty; but still with a tough little body, wiry little moustache, sharp little eyes. He had thin salt-and-pepper hair brushed sideways across a balding crown and he carried his head stiffly, with his chin tucked back into his neck. Tense: very tense. And wary, looking at the world with suspicion.

He wore a lightweight speckled fawn suit vaguely reminiscent in cut of his military origins, and unlike the others had not parked his binoculars but wore them with the strap diagonally across his chest and the case facing forwards on his stomach, like a sporran. Club badges of metal and coloured cardboard hung in thick clusters at each side.

'Your aeroplane is here, Major,' I said. 'I'm Matt Shore ... I'm flying you.'

He glanced over my shoulder, looking for someone else.

'Where's Larry?' he asked abruptly.

'He left,' I said. 'He got a job in Turkey.'

The Major's gaze came back from the search with a click. 'You're new,' he said accusingly.

'Yes,' I agreed.

'I hope you know the way.'

He meant it seriously. I said politely, 'I'll do my best.'

The second of the passengers, the woman on the major's left said flatly, 'The last time I flew to the races, the pilot got lost.'

I looked at her, giving her my best approximation to a confidence-boosting smile. 'The weather's good enough today not to have any fear of it.'

It wasn't true. There were cu-mins forecast for the June afternoon. And anyone can get lost any time if enough goes wrong. The woman give me a disillusioned stare and I stopped wasting my confidence builder. She didn't need it. She had all the confidence in the world. She was fifty and fragile looking, with greying hair cut in a straight-across fringe and a jaw-length bob. There were two mild brown eyes under heavy dark eyebrows and a mouth that looked gentle; yet she held herself and behaved with the easy authority of a much higher command than the Major's. She was the only one of the group not outwardly ruffled.

The Major had been looking at his watch. 'You're early,' he said. 'We've got time for the other half.' He turned to the barman and ordered refills, and as an afterthought said to me, 'Something for you?'

I shook my head. 'No, thank you.'

The woman said indifferently, 'No alcohol for eight hours before a flight. Isn't that the rule?'

'More or less,' I agreed.

The third passenger, the large angry looking man, morosely watched the barman push the measure up twice on the Johnnie Walker. 'Eight hours. Good God,' he said. He looked as if eight hours seldom passed for him without topping up. The bulbous nose, the purple thread veins on his cheeks, the swelling paunch, they had all cost a lot in Excise duty.

The atmosphere I wad walked into slowly subsided. The jockey sipped his low calorie lemonade, and the bright pink flush faded from his cheek bones and came out in fainter mottles on his neck. He seemed about twenty-one or two, reddish haired, with a naturally small frame and a moist looking skin. Few weight problems, I thought. No dehydration. Fortunate for him.

The Major and his large friend drank rapidly, muttered unintelligibly, and removed themselves to the gents. The woman eyed the jockey and said in a voice which sounded more friendly than her comment, 'Are you out of your mind, Kenny Bayst? If you go on antagonizing Major Tyderman you'll be looking for another job.'

Kenny Bayst flicked his eyes to me and away again, compressing his rosebud mouth. He put the half-finished lemonade on the table and picked up one of the raincoats and the racing saddle.

'Which plane?' he said to me. 'I'll stow my gear.'

He had a strong Australian accent with a resentful bite to it. The woman watched him with what would have passed for a smile but for the frost in her eyes.

'The baggage door is locked,' I said. 'I'll come over with you.' To the woman I said, 'Can I carry your coat?'

'Thank you.' She indicated the coat which was obviously hers, a shiny rust-coloured affair with copper buttons. I picked it up, and also the businesslike binoculars lying on top, and followed Kenny Bayst out of the door.

After ten fuming paces he said explosively, 'It's too damn easy to blame the man on top.'

'They always blame the pilot,' I said mildly. 'Fact of life.'

'Huh?' he said. 'Oh yeah. Too right. They do.'

We reached the end of the path and started across the grass. He was still oozing grudge. I wasn't much interested.

'For the record,' I said, 'What are the names of my other passengers? Besides the Major, that is.'

He turned his head in surprise. 'Don't you know her? Our Annie Villars? Looks like someone's cosy old granny and has a tongue that would flay a kangaroo. Everyone knows our little Annie.' His tone was sour and disillusioned.

'I don't know much about racing,' I said.

'Oh? Well, she's a trainer, then. A damned good trainer, I'll say that for her, I wouldn't stay with her else. Not with that tongue of hers. I'll tell you, sport, she can roust her stable lads out on the gallops in words a Sergeant-Major never thought of. But sweet as milk with the owners. Has them eating out of her little hand.'

'The horses, too?'

'Uh? Oh, yeah. The horses love her. She can ride like a jock, too, when she's a mind to. Not that she does it much now. She must be getting on a bit. Still, she knows what she's at, true enough. She knows what a horse can do and what it can't, and that's most of the battle in this game.'

His voice held resentment and admiration in roughly equal amounts.

I said, 'What is the name of the other man? The big one?'

This time it was pure resentment: no admiration. He spat the name out syllable by deliberate syllable, curling his lips away from his teeth.

'Mister Eric Goldenberg.'

Having got rid of the name he shut his mouth tight and was clearly taking his employer's remarks to heart. We reached the aircraft and stowed the coats and his saddle in the baggage space behind the rear seats.

We're going to Newbury first, aren't we?' he asked. 'To pick up Colin Ross?'

'Yes.'

He gave me a sardonic look. 'Well, you *must* have heard of Colin Ross.'

'I guess,' I agreed, 'That I have.'

It would have been difficult not to, since the champion jockey was twice as popular as the Prime Minister and earned six times as much.

His face appeared on half the billboards in Britain encouraging the populace to drink more milk and there was even a picture strip about him in a children's comic. Everyone, but everyone, had heard of Colin Ross.

Kenny Bayst climbed in through the rear end door and sat in one of the two rear seats. I took a quick look round the outside of the aircraft, even though I'd done a thorough pre-flight check on it not an hour ago, before I left base. It was my first week, my fourth day, my third flight for Derrydown Sky Taxis, and after the way Fate had clobbered me in the past, I was taking no chances.

There were no nuts loose, no rivets missing on the sharp-nosed little six seater. There were eight quarts of oil where there should have been eight quarts of oil, there were no dead birds clogging up the air intakes to the engine, there were no punctures in the tyres, no cracks in the green or red glass over navigation lights, no chips in the propellor blades, no loose radio aerials. The pale blue cowling over the engine was securely clipped down, and the matching pale blue cowlings over the struts and wheels of the fixed undercarriage were as solid as rocks.

By the time I'd finished the other three passengers were coming across the grass. Goldenberg was doing the talking with steam still coming out of his ears, while the Major nodded agreement in unhappy little jerks and Annie Villars looked as if she wasn't listening. When they arrived within earshot Goldenberg was saying '... can't lay the horse unless we're sure he'll pull it ...' But he stopped with a snap when the Major gestured sharply in my direction. He need hardly have bothered. I had no curiosity about their affairs.

On the principle that in a light aircraft it is better to have the centre of gravity as far forward as possible, I asked Goldenberg to sit in front in the righthand seat beside me, and put the Major and Anne Villars in the centre two seats, and left Kenny in the last two, with the empty one ready for Colin Ross. The four rear seats were reached by the port side door, but Goldenberg had to climb in by stepping up on the low wing on the starboard side and lowering into his seat through the forward door. He waited while I got in before him and moved over to my side, then squeezed his bulk in through the door and settled heavily into his seat.

They were all old hands at air taxis: they had their safety belts fastened before I did mine, and when I looked round to check that they were ready to go, the Major was already deep in the *Sporting Life*. Kenny Bayst was cleaning his nails with fierce little jabs, relieving his frustration by hurting himself.

I got clearance from the Tower and lifted the little aeroplane away for the twenty mile hop across Berkshire. Taxi flying was a lot different from the airlines, and finding racecourses looked more difficult to me than being radar vectored into Heathrow. I'd never before flown a racecourse trip, and I'd asked my predecessor Larry about it that morning when he'd come into the office to collect his card's.

'Newbury's a cinch,' he said offhandedly. 'Just point its nose at that vast runway the Yanks built at Greenham Common. You can practically see it from Scotland. The racecourse is just north of it, and the landing strip is parallel with the white rails to the finishing straight. You can't miss it. Good long strip. No problems. As for Haydock, it's just where the M6 motorway crosses the East Lancs road. Piece of cake.'

He took himself off to Turkey, stopping on one foot at the doorway for some parting advice. 'You'll have to practise short landings before you go to Bath; and avoid Yarmouth in a heatwave. It's all yours now, mate, and the best of British Luck.'

It was true that you could see Greenham Common from a long way off, but on a fine day it would anyway have been difficult to lose the way from White Waltham to Newbury: the main railway line to Exeter ran more or less straight from one to the other. My passengers had all flown into Newbury before, and the Major helpfully told me to look out for the electric cables strung across the approach. We landed respectably on the newly mown grass and taxied along the strip towards the grandstand end, braking to a stop just before the boundary fence.

Colin Ross wasn't there.

I shut down the engine, and in the sudden silence Anne Villars remarked, 'He's bound to be late. He said he was riding work for Bob Smith, and Bob's never on time getting his horses out.'

The other three nodded vaguely but they were still not on ordinarily chatty terms with each other, and after about five minutes of heavy silence I asked Goldenberg to let me out to stretch my legs. He grunted and mumbled at having to climb out onto the wing to let me past him and I gathered I was breaking Derrydown's number one rule: never annoy the customers, you're going to need them again.

Once I was out of their company, however, they did start talking. I walked round to the front of the aircraft and leant against the leading edge of the wing, and looked up at the scattered clouds in the blue-grey sky and thought unprofitably about this and that. Behind me their voices rose acrimoniously, and when they opened the door wide to get some air, scraps of what they were saying floated across.

'... simply asking for a dope test.' Anne Villars.

'... if you can't ride a losing race better than last time ... find someone else.' Goldenberg.

'... very difficult position ...' Major Tyderman,

A short sharp snap from Kenny, and Anne Villars' exasperated exclamation. 'Bayst!'

'... not paying you more than last time.' The Major, very emphatically.

Indistinct protest from Kenny, and a violently clear reaction from Goldenberg: 'Bugger your licence.'

Kenny my lad, I thought remotely, if you don't watch out you'll end up like me, still with a licence but with not much else.

A Ford-of-all-work rolled down the road past the grandstands, came through the gate in the boundary fence, and bounced over the turf towards the aircraft. It stopped about twenty feet away, and two men climbed out. The larger, who had been driving, went round to the back and pulled out a brown canvas and leather overnight grip. The smaller one walked on over the grass. I took my weight off the wing and stood up. He stopped a few paces away, waiting for the larger man to catch up. He was dressed in faded blue jeans and a whitish cotton sweater with navy blue edgings. Black canvas shoes on his narrow feet. He had nondescript brownish hair over an exceptionally broad forehead, a short straight nose, an a delicate feminine looking chin. All his bones were fine and his waist and hips would have been the despair of Victorian maidens. Yet there was something unmistakebly masculine about him: and more than that, he was mature. He looked at me with the small still smile behind the eyes which is the hallmark of those who know what life is really about. His soul was old. He was twenty six.

'Good morning,' I said.

He held out his hand, and I shook it. His clasp was cool, firm, and brief.

'No Larry?' he enquired.

'He's left. I'm Matt Shore.'

'Fine,' he said noncommittally. He didn't introduce himself. He knew there was no need. I wondered what it was like to be in that position. It hadn't affected Colin Ross. He had none of the 'I am' aura which often clings around the notably successful, and from the extreme understatement of his clothes I gathered that he avoided it consciously.

'We're late, I'm afraid,' he said. 'Have to bend the throttle.'

'Do my best . . .'

The larger man arrived with the grip, and I stowed it in the forward luggage locker between the engine wall and the forward bulkhead of the cabin. By the time the baggage door was securely fastened Colin Ross had found his empty seat and strapped himself into it. Goldenberg with heavy grunts moved out again so that I could get back to my lefthand place. The larger man, who was apparently the dilatory trainer Bob Smith, said his hellos and goodbyes to the passengers, and stood watching afterwards while I started the engine and taxied back to the other end of the strip to turn into wind for take-off.

The flight north was uneventful: I went up the easy way under the Amber One airway, navigating on the radio beacons at Daventry, Lichfield and Oldham. Manchester control routed us right round the north of their zone so that I had to drop down southwards towards Haydock racecourse, and there it was, just as Larry had said, near the interchange of the two giant roads. We touched down on the grass strip indicated in the centre of the course, and I taxied on and parked where the Major told me to, near the rails of the track itself, a mere hundred yards from the grandstand.

The passengers disembarked themselves and their belongings and Colin Ross looked at his watch. A faint smile hovered and was gone.

He made no comment. He said merely, 'Are you coming in to the races?'

I shook my head. 'Think I'll stay over here.'

'I'll arrange with the man on the gate to let you into the paddock, if you change your mind.'

'Thanks,' I said in surprise. 'Thanks very much.'

He nodded briefly and set off without waiting for the others, ducking under the white-painted rails and trudging across the track.

'Pilots' perks,' Kenny said, taking his raincoat from my hand and putting his arm forward for the saddle. 'You want to take advantage.'

'Maybe I will,' I said, but I didn't mean to. Horse racing began and ended with the Derby as far as I was concerned, and also I was a non-gambler by nature.

Anne Villars said in her deceptively gentle voice, 'You do understand that we're all going on to Newmarket after the races, and not back to Newbury?'

'Yes,' I assured her. 'That's what I was told.'

'Good.'

'If we don't go to jail.' Kenny said under his breath. Goldenberg looked at me sharply to see if I'd heard that, and I gave no sign of it. Whatever they were about, it was as little my concern as who killed Cock Robin.

Major Tyderman pushed at his moustache with a hand rigid with nervous energy and said, 'Last race at four thirty. Need a drink after that. Ready to start back at, say, five fifteen. That all right with you?'

'Perfectly, Major,' I nodded.

'Right,' he said. 'Good.' His gaze was flickering from one to another of his travelling companions, assessing and suspicious. His eyes narrowed fiercely at Kenny Bayst, opened and narrowed again rapidly on Goldenberg, relaxed on Anne Villars and went cold on the vanishing back of Colin Ross. The thoughts behind the outward physical reactions were unguessable, and when he finally looked back at me he didn't really see me, he was busy with the activity inside his head.

'Five fifteen,' he repeated vaguely. 'Good.'

Kenny said to me, 'Don't wast your money in the three thirty, sport;' and Goldenberg raised his fist with a face going purple with anger and nearly hit him.

Anne Villars' voice rapped into him, the steel sticking through the cream with a vengeance, the top-brass quality transcendent and withering.

'Control your temper, you stupid man.'

Goldenberg's mouth literally dropped open, to reveal a bottom row of unappetising brown stained teeth. His raised fist lowered slowly, and looked altogether foolish.

'As for you,' she said to Kenny. 'I told you to keep your tongue still, and that was your last chance.'

'Are you sacking me?' he asked.

'I'll decide that at the end of the afternoon.'

Kenny showed no anxiety about keeping his job, and I realized that in fact what he had been doing was trying to provoke them into getting rid of him. He'd got himself into nutrackers and while they squeezed he couldn't get out.

I became mildly curious to see what would happen in the three thirty. It would help to pass the afternoon.

They straggled off towards the stands, Kenny in front, the Major and Goldenberg together, with Annie Villars several paces behind. The Major kept stopping and looking back and waiting for her, but every time just as she reached him he turned and went off again in front, so that as a piece of courtesy, the whole thing was wasted. He reminded me vividly of an aunt who had taken me for childhood walks in just that way. I remembered quite clearly that it had been infuriating.

I sighed, shut the baggage doors and tidied up the aeroplane. Annie Villars had been smoking thin brown cigars. Goldenberg had been eating indigestion tablets, each from a square wrapper. The Major had left his *Sporting Life* in a tumbled heap on the floor.

While I was fiddling around with the debris, two more aeroplanes flew in, a four seat high winged Cessna and a six seat twin engined Aztec.

I watched their touchdowns with an uncritical eye, though I wouldn't have given the Aztec pilot a gold medal for his double bounce. Several small men disgorged themselves and made a dart like a flock of starlings across the track toward the paddock. They were followed by three or four larger and slower-moving people slung around with binoculars and what I later learned to be bags for carrying sets of racing colours. Finally out of each aircraft popped the most leisurely of all the inmates, a man dressed very much as I was, in dark trousers, white shirt, neat dark tie.

They strolled towards each other and lit cigarettes. After a while, not wanting to seem unsociable, I wandered across to join them. They turned and watched me come, but with no welcome in unsmiling faces.

'Hello,' I said moderately. 'Nice day.'

'Perhaps,' said one.

'You think so?' said the other.

They offered me fish-eyed stares but no cigarette. I had grown hardened to that sort of thing. I turned half away from them and read the names of the firms they flew for, which were painted on the tails of their aircraft. It was the same name on both. Polyplane Services.

How dreary of them, I thought, to be so antagonistic. I gave them the benefit of a very small doubt and made one more approach.

'Have you come far?'

They didn't answer. Just gave me the stares, like two cod.

I laughed at them as if I thought their behaviour pathetic, which in fact I did, and turned on my heel to go back to my own territory. When I'd gone ten steps one of them called after me, 'Where's Larry Gedge?' He didn't sound as if he liked Larry any better than me.

I decided not to hear: if they really wanted to know, they would come and ask nicely. It was their turn to cross the grass.

They didn't bother. I wasn't particularly sorry. I had long ago learned that pilots were not all one great happy brotherhood. Pilots could be as bloodyminded to each other as any group on earth.

I climbed back into my seat in the Cherokee and sorted out my maps and flight plans for the return journey. I had four hours to do it in and it took me ten minutes. After that I debated whether to go over to the stands and find some lunch, and decided I wasn't hungry. After that I yawned. It was a habit.

I had been depressed for so long that it had become a permanent state of mind. Expectations might lift the edge of the cloud every time one took a new job, but life never turned out to be as good as the hopes. This was my sixth job since I'd gone to learn flying with stars in my eyes, my fourth since the stars had faded for good. I had thought that taxi flying might be interesting, and after crop spraying, which I'd been doing last, anything would be; and perhaps it would indeed be interesting, but if I'd thought it might be free of gripe and bad temper I'd been kidding myself. For here it all was, as usual. Squabbling passengers and belligerent competitors and no discernible joy anywhere.

There was a small buffet on the side of the fuselage and the jar and sound of someone stepping up on to the wing. The slightly open door was pushed wide with a crash, and into its space appeared a girl, bending at the waist and knees and neck so that she could look inside and across at me.

She was slim and dark haired and she was wearing large square sunglasses. Also she had a blue linen dress and long white boots. She looked great. The afternoon instantly improved.

'You lousy bloody skunk,' she said.

It really was one of those days.

Chapter Two

'Wow,' she said. 'Wrong man.' She took off the sunglasses and folded them away in the white handbag which hung from her shoulder by a thick red, white and blue cord.

'Think nothing of it.'

'Where's Larry?'

'Gone to Turkey.'

'Gone?' she said blankly. 'Do you mean literally gone already, or planning to go, or what?'

'I looked at my watch. 'Took off from Heathrow twenty minutes ago, I believe.'

'Damn,' she said forcibly. 'Bloody damn.'

She straightened up so that all I could see of her was from the waist down. A pleasant enough view for any poor aviator. The legs looked about twenty-three years old and there was nothing wrong with them.

She bent down again. Nothing wrong with the rest of her, either.

'When will he be back?'

'He had a three year contract.'

'Oh, *hell*.' She stared at me in dismay for a few seconds, then said, 'Can I come in there and talk to you for a minute?'

'Sure,' I agreed, and moved my maps and stuff off Goldenberg's seat. She stepped down into the cockpit and slid expertly into place. By no means her first entrance into a light aircraft. I wondered about Larry. Lucky Larry.

'I suppose he didn't give you . . . a parcel . . . or anything . . . to give me, did he?' she said gloomily.

'Nothing, I'm afraid.'

'He's an absolute beast then . . . er, is he a friend of yours?'

'I've met him twice, that's all.'

'He's pinched my hundred quid,' she said bitterly.

'He pinched . . . ?'

'He bloody has. Not to mention my handbag and keys and everything.' She stopped and compressed her mouth in anger. Then she added, 'I left my handbag in this aeroplane three weeks ago, when we flew to Doncaster. And Larry has been saying ever since that he'll bring it on the next trip to the races and give it to Colin to give to me, and for three solid weeks he's kept on forgetting it. I suppose he knew he was going to Turkey and he thought if he could put it off long enough he would never have to give my bag back.'

'Colin . . . Colin Ross?' I asked. She nodded abstractedly.

'Is he your husband?'

She looked startled, then laughed. 'Good Lord, no. He's my brother. I saw him just now in the paddock and I said, 'Has he brought my handbag?' and he shook his head and started to say something, but I belted off over here in a fury without stopping to listen, and I suppose he was going to tell me it wasn't Larry who had come in the plane. . . . Oh damn it, I *hate* being robbed. Colin would have lent him a hundred quid if he was that desperate. He didn't have to pinch it.'

'It was a lot of money to have in a handbag.' I suggested.

'Colin had just given it to me, you see. In the plane. Some owner had handed him a terrific present in readies, and he gave me a hundred of it to pay a bill with, which was really sweet of him, and I can hardly expect him to give me another hundred just because I was silly enough to leave the first one lying about. . . .' Her voice tailed off in depression.

'The bill,' she added wryly. 'Is for flying lessons.'

I looked at her with interest. 'How far have you got?'

'Oh, I've got my licence,' she said. 'These were instrument flying lessons. And radio navigation, and all that jazz. I've done about ninety-five hours, altogether. Spread over about four years, though, sad to say.'

That put her in the experienced-beginner class and the dangerous time bracket. After eighty hours flying, pilots are inclined to think they know enough. After a hundred hours, they are sure they don't. Between the two, the accident rate is at its peak.

She asked me several questions about the aeroplane, and I answered them. Then she said, 'Well, there's no point in sitting here all afternoon,' and began to lever herself out on to the wing. 'Aren't you coming over to the races?'

'No,' I shook my head.

'Oh come on,' she said. 'Do.'

The sun was shining and she was very pretty. I smiled and said 'O.K.,' and followed her out on to the grass. It is profitless now to speculate on the different course things would have taken if I'd stayed where I was.

I collected my jacket from the rear baggage compartment and locked all the doors and set off with her across the track. The man on the gate duly let me into the paddock and Colin Ross's sister showed no sign of abandoning me once we were inside. Instead she diagnosed my almost total ignorance and seemed to be pleased to be able to start dispelling it.

'You see that brown horse over there,' she said, steering me towards the parade ring rails, 'That one walking round the far end, number sixteen, that's Colin's mount in this race. It's come out a bit light but it looks well in its coat.'

'It does?'

She looked at me in amusement. 'Definitely.'

'Shall I back it, then?'

'It's all a joke to you.'

'No,' I protested.

'Oh yes indeed,' she nodded. 'You're looking at this race meeting in the way I'd look at a lot of spiritualists. Disbelieving and a bit superior.'

'Ouch.'

'But what you're actually seeing is a large export industry in the process of marketing its wares.'

'I'll remember that.'

'And if the industry takes place out of doors on a nice fine sunny day with everyone enjoying themselves, well, so much the better.'

'Put that way,' I agreed, 'It's a lot more jolly than a car factory,'

'You will get involved,' she said with certainty.

'No.' I was equally definite.

She shook her head. 'You will, you know, if you do much racecourse taxi work. It'll bust through that cool shell of yours and make you feel something, for a change.'

I blinked. 'Do you always talk like that to total strangers?'

'No,' she said slowly, 'I don't.'

The bright little jockeys flooded into the parade ring and scattered to small earnest owner-trainer groups where there were a lot of serious conversations and much nodding of heads. On the instructions of Colin Ross's sister I tried moderately hard to take it all seriously. Not with much success.

Colin Ross's sister . . .

'Do you have a name?' I asked.

'Often.'

'Thanks.'

She laughed. 'It's Nancy. What's yours?'

'Matt Shore.'

'Hm. A flat matt name. Very suitable.'

The jockeys were thrown up like confetti and landed in their saddles, and their spindly shining long-legged transportation skittered its way out on to the track. Two-year-olds, Nancy said.

She walked me back towards the stands and proposed to smuggle me into the 'Owners and Trainers'. The large official at the bottom of the flight of steps beamed at her until his eyes disappeared and he failed to inspect me for the right bit of cardboard.

It seemed that nearly everyone on the small rooftop stand knew Nancy, and obvious that they agreed with the beaming official's assessment. She introduced me to several people whose interest collapsed like a soufflé in a draught when they found I didn't understand their opening bids.

'He's a pilot,' Nancy explained apologetically. 'He flew Colin here today.'

'Ah,' they said. 'Ah.'

Two of my other passengers were there. Annie Villars was watching the horses canter past with an intent eye and a pursed mouth: the field marshal element was showing strongly, the feminine camouflage in abeyance. Major Tyderman, planted firmly with his legs apart and his chin tucked well back into his neck, was scribbling notes into his racecard. When he looked up he saw us, and made his way purposefully across.

'I say,' he said to me, having forgotten my name. 'Did I leave my *Sporting Life* over in the plane, do you know?'

'Yes, you did, Major.'

'Blast,' he said. 'I made some notes on it . . . Must get it, you know. Have to go across after this race.'

'Would you like me to fetch it?' I asked.

'Well, that's very good of you, my dear chap. But . . . no . . . couldn't ask it. Walk will do me good.'

'The aircraft's locked, Major.' I said. 'You'll need the keys.' I took them out of my pocket and gave them to him.

'Right.' He nodded stiffly. 'Good.'

The race started away off down the track and was all over long before I sorted out the colours of Colin Ross. In the event, it wasn't difficult. He had won.

'How's Midge?' Annie Villars said to Nancy, restoring her giant raceglasses to their case.

'Oh, much better, thank you. Getting on splendidly.'

'I'm so glad. She's had a bad time, poor girl.'

Nancy nodded and smiled, and everyone trooped down the stairs to the ground.

'Well now,' Nancy said. 'How about some coffee? And something to munch, perhaps?'

'You must have others you'd prefer to be with . . . I won't get into trouble, you know, on my own.'

Her lips twitched. 'Today I need a bodyguard. I elected you for the job. Desert me if you like, but if you want to please, stick.'

'Not difficult,' I said.

'Great. Coffee, then.'

It was iced coffee, rather good. Half way through the turkey sandwiches the reason why Nancy wanted me with her drifted up to the small table where we sat and slobbered all over her. She fended off what looked to me like a random assembly of long hair, beard, beads, fringes and a garment like a table cloth with a hole in it, and yelled to me through the undergrowth, 'Buddy, your job starts right now.'

I stood up, reached out two hands, caught hold of an assortment of wool and hair, and pulled firmly backwards. The result resolved itself into a youngish man sitting down with surprise much more suddenly than he'd intended.

'Nancy,' he said in an aggrieved voice.

'This is Chanter,' she said to me. 'He's never grown out of the hippie thing, as you can see.'

'I'm an artist,' he said. He had an embroidered band across his forehead and round his head: like the horses' bridles, I thought fleetingly. All the hair was clean and there were shaven parts on his jaw just to prove that it wasn't from pure laziness that he let everything else grow. On closer inspection I was sure that it was indeed a dark green chenille table cloth, with a central hole for his head. Underneath that he wore low-slung buckskin trousers fringed from hip to ankle, and a creepy crepy dim mauve shirt curved to fit his concave stomach. Various necklaces and pendants on silver chains hung round his neck. Under all the splendour he had dirty bare feet.

'I went to art school with him,' Nancy said resignedly. 'That was in London. Now he's at Liverpool, just down the road. Any time I come racing up here, he turns up too.'

'Uh.' Chanter said profoundly.

'Do you get grants for ever?' I asked: not sneeringly; I simply wanted to know.

He was not offended. 'Look, man, like, up here I'm the fuzz.'

I nearly laughed. Nancy said, 'You know what he means, then?'

'He teaches,' I said.

'Yeah, man, that's what I said.' He took one of the turkey sandwiches. His fingers were greenish with black streaks. Paint.

'You keep your impure thoughts off this little bird,' he said to me, spitting out bits of bread. 'She's strictly my territory. But strictly, man.'

'Zat so?'

'Zat definitely, but definitely ... is ... so, man.'

'How come?'

He gave me a look which was as off beat as his appearance.

'I've still got the salt to put on this little bird's tail,' he said. 'Shan't be satisfied till it's there...'

Nancy was looking at him with an expression which meant that she didn't know whether to laugh at him or be afraid of him. She couldn't decide whether he was Chanter the amorous buffoon or Chanter the frustrated sex maniac. Nor could I. I understood her needing help when he was around.

'He only wants me because I won't,' she said.

'The challenge bit,' I nodded. 'Affront to male pride, and all that.'

'Practically every other girl has,' she said.

'That makes it worse.'

Chanter looked at me broodingly. 'You're a drag, man. I mean, cubic.'

'To each his scene,' I said ironically.

He took the last of the sandwiches, turned his back studiously towards me and said to Nancy, 'Let's you and me lose this dross, huh?'

'Let's you and me do nothing of the sort, Chanter. If you want to tag along, Matt comes in the deal.'

He scowled at the floor and then suddenly stood up so that all the fringes and beads danced and jingled.

'Come on then. Let's get a look at the horses. Life's a-wasting.'

'He really can draw,' Nancy said as we followed the tablecloth out into the sunshine.

'I wouldn't doubt it. I'll bet half of what he does is caricature, though, with a strong element of cruelty.'

'How d'you know?' she said, startled.

'He just seems like that.'

He padded along beside us in his bare feet and was a sufficiently unusual sight on a racecourse to attract a barrage of stares ranging from amusement to apoplexy. He didn't seem to notice. Nancy looked as if she were long used to it.

We came to a halt against the parade ring rails where Chanter rested his elbows and exercised his voice.

'Horses,' he said. 'I'm not for the Stubbs and Munnings thing. When I see a racehorse I see a machine, and that's what I paint, a horse-shaped machine with pistons thumping away and muscle fibres like connecting rods and a crack in the crank case with the oil dripping away drop by drop into the body cavity ...' He broke off abruptly but with the same breath finished. 'How's your sister?'

'She's much better,' Nancy said, not seeming to see any great change of subject. 'She's really quite well now.'

'Good,' he said, and went straight on with his lecture. 'And then I draw some distant bulging stands with hats flying off and everyone cheering and all the time the machine is bursting its gut. ... I see components, I see what's happening to the bits ... the stresses ... I see colours in components too ... nothing on earth is a whole ... nothing is ever what it seems ... everything is components.' He stopped abruptly, thinking about what he'd said.

After a suitably appreciative pause, I asked, 'Do you ever sell your paintings?'

'Sell them?' He gave me a scornful, superior stare. 'No, I don't. Money is disgusting.'

'It's more disgusting when you haven't got it,' Nancy said.

'You're a renegade, girl,' he said fiercely.

'Love on a crust,' she said, 'Is fine when you're twenty, but pretty squalid when you're sixty.'

'I don't intend to be sixty. Sixty is strictly for grandfathers. Not my scene at all.'

We turned away from the rails and came face to face with Major Tyderman, who was carrying his *Sporting Life* and holding out the aircraft's keys. His gaze swept over Chanter and he controlled himself admirably. Not a twitch.

'I locked up again,' he said, handing me the bunch.

'Thank's, Major.'

He nodded, glanced once more at Chanter, and retreated in good order.

Even for Nancy's sake the official wouldn't let Chanter up the steps to the Owners and Trainers. We watched at grass level with Chanter muttering 'stinking bourgeois' at regular intervals.

Colin Ross finished second. The crowd booed and tore up a lot of tickets. Nancy looked as though she were long used to that, too.

Between the next two races we sat on the grass while Chanter gave us the uninterrupted benefit of his views on the evils of money, racialism, war, religion and marriage. It was regulation stuff, nothing new. I didn't say I thought so. During the discourse he twice without warning stretched over and put his hand on Nancy's breast. Each time without surprise she picked it off again by the wrist and threw it back at him. Neither of them seemed to think it needed comment.

After the next race (Colin was third) Chanter remarked that his throat was dry, and Nancy and I obediently followed him off to the Tattersalls bar for lubrication. Coca Colas for three, splashed out of the bottles by an overworked barmaid. Chanter busily juggled the three glasses so that it was I who paid, which figured.

The bar was only half full but a great deal of space and attention was being taken up by one man, a large tough-looking individual with a penetrating Australian accent. He had an obviously new white plaster cast on his leg and a pair of crutches which he hadn't mastered. His loud laugh rose above the general buzz as he constantly apologized for knocking into people.

'Haven't got the hang of these props yet...'

Chanter regarded him, as he did with most things, with some

disfavour.

The large Australian went on explaining his state to two receptive acquaintances.

'Mind you, can't say I'm sorry I broke my ankle. Best investment I ever made.' The laugh rang out infectiously and most people in the bar began to grin. Not Chanter, of course.

'See, I only paid my premium the week before, and then I fell down these steps and I got a thousand quid for it. Now that ain't whistling, that ain't eh? A thousand bleeding quid for falling down a flight of steps.' He laughed again hugely, enjoying the joke. 'Come on mates,' he said, 'Drink up, and let's go and invest some of this manna from Heaven on my good friend Kenny Bayst.'

I jumped a fraction and looked at my watch. Coming up to three thirty. Kenny Bayst clearly hadn't told his good friend not to speculate. Absolutely none of my business. Telling him myself would be the worst favour I could do for Kenny Bayst.

The large Australian swung himself out of the bar, followed by the two mates. Chanter's curiosity overcame his disinclination to show himself at a loss.

'Who,' he said crossly, 'Is going to give that schmo a thousand quid for breaking his ankle?'

Nancy smiled. 'It's a new insurance fund, specially for people who go racing. Accident insurance. I don't really know. I've heard one or two people mention it lately.'

'Insurance is immoral,' Chanter said dogmatically, sliding round behind her and laying his hand flat on her stomach. Nancy picked it off and stepped away. As a bodyguard, I didn't seem to be doing much good.

Nancy said she particularly wanted to see this race properly, and left Chanter looking moody at the bottom of the staircase. Without asking her I followed her up the steps: a period alone with Chanter held no attractions.

Kenny Bayst, according to my slantways look at Nancy's racecard, was riding a horse called Rudiments: number seven, owned by the Duke of Wessex, trained by Miss Villars, carrying olive green with silver crossbelts and cap. I watched the horse canter down past the stands on the olive green grass and reflected that the Duke of Wessex had chosen colours which were as easy to distinguish as coal on a black night.

I said to Nancy, 'What did Rudiments do in his last race?'

'Hm?' she said absentmindedly, all her attention on the rose pink and white shape of her brother. 'Did you say Rudiments?'

'That's right. I brought Kenny Bayst and Annie Villars here, as well.'

'Oh. I see.' She looked down at her racecard. 'Last time out . . . it won. Time before that, it won. Time before that, it came fourth.'

'It's good, then?'

'Fairly, I suppose.' She wrinkled her nose at me. 'I told you you'd get involved.'

I shook my head. 'Just curious.'

'Same thing.'

'Is it favourite?'

'No, Colin is. But ... you can see over there, on that big board ... see? ... Rudiments is second favourite on the Tote at about three to one.'

'Well ...' I said. 'What does it mean, to lay a horse?'

'It means to stand a bet. It's what bookmakers do. What the Tote does, really, come to that.'

'Can people do it who aren't bookmakers?'

'Oh sure. They do. Say the bookmakers are offering three to one, and you yourself don't think the horse will win, you could say to your friends, I'll lay you four to one; so they'd bet with you because you were offering more. Also, no betting tax. Private wager, you see.'

'And if the horse wins, you pay out?'

'You sure do.'

'I see,' I said. And I did. Eric Goldenberg had laid Rudiments the last time it had run because Kenny Bayst had agreed to lose, and then he'd gone and won. Their tempers were still on the dicky side as a result: and they had been arguing today about whether or not to try again.

'Colin thinks he'll win this,' Nancy said. 'I do hope so.'

Bonanza for Bayst, I thought.

It was a seven furlong race, it seemed. The horses accelerated from standing to 30 m.p.h. in times which would have left a Porsche gasping. When they swung away round the far bend Rudiments was as far as I was concerned invisible, and until the last hundred yards I didn't see him once. Then all of a sudden there he was, boxed in in a bunch on the rails and unable to get past Colin Ross directly in front.

Kenny didn't find his opening. He finished the race in third place, still pinned in by Colin in front and a dappled grey alongside. I couldn't begin to tell whether or not he had done it on purpose.

'Wasn't that *great*?' Nancy exclaimed to the world in general, and a woman on the far side of her agreed that it was, and asked after the health of her sister Midge.

'Oh, she's fine, thanks,' Nancy said. She turned to me and there was less joy in her eyes than in her voice. 'Come over here,' she said. 'You can see them unsaddling the winner.'

The Owners and Trainers turned out to be on the roof of the weighing room. We leaned over the rails at the front and watched Colin and Kenny unbuckle the saddle girths, loop the saddles over their arms, pat their steaming horses, and disappear into the weighing room. The group in the winner's enclosure were busy slapping backs and unburdening to the Press. The group in the third enclosure wore small tight smiles and faraway eyes. I still couldn't tell if they were ecstatic and hiding it, or livid and ditto.

The horses were led away and the groups dispersed. In their place appeared Chanter, staring up and waving his arm.

'Come on down,' he shouted.

'No inhibitions, that's his trouble,' Nancy said. 'If we don't go down, he'll just go on shouting.'

He did. An official strode up manfully to ask him to belt up and buzz off, but it was like ripples trying to push over Bass Rock.

'Come on down, Nancy.' Fortissimo.

She pushed herself away from the rails and took enough steps to be out of sight.

'Stay with me,' she said. It was more than half a question.

'If you want it.'

'You've seen what he's like. And he's been mild, today. Mild. Thanks to you.'

'I've done absolutely nothing.'

'You're here.'

'Why do you come to Haydock, if he always bothers you too much?'

'Because I'm bloody well not letting him frighten me away.'

'He loves you.' I said.

'No. Can't you tell the difference, for God's sake?'

'Yes,' I said.

She looked startled, then shook her head. 'He loves Chanter, full stop.'

She took three more steps towards the stairs, then stopped again.

'Why is it that I talk to you as if I'd known you for years?'

To a certain extent I knew, but I smiled and shook my head. No one cares to say straight out that it's because one is as negative as wall paper.

Chanter's plaintive voice floated up the steps. 'Nancy, come on down. . . .'

She took another step, and then stopped again. 'Will you do me another favour? I'm staying up here a few more days with an aunt, but I bought a present for Midge this morning and I've given it to Colin to take home. But he's got a memory like a string vest for everything except horses, so would you check with him that he hasn't left it in the changing room, before you take off?'

'Sure,' I said. 'Your sister . . . I gather she's been ill.'

She looked away up at the sun-filled sky and down again and straight at me, and in a shattering moment of awareness I saw the pain and the cracks behind the bright public façade.

'Has been. Will be,' she said. 'She's got leukaemia.'

After a pause she swallowed and added the unbearable bit.

'She's my identical twin.'

Chapter Three

After the fifth race Chanter gloomily announced that about fifty plastic students were waiting for him to pat their egos and that although he despised the system he was likely to find eating a problem if he actually got the sack. His farewell to Nancy consisted in wiping his hands all over her, front and back, and giving her an open mouthed kiss which owing to her split-second evasive action landed on her ear.

He glared at me as if it were my fault. Nancy not relenting, he scowled at her and muttered something about salt, and then twirled around on his bare heel so that the tablecloth and all the hair and fringes and beads swung out with centrifugal force, and strode away at high speed towards the exit.

'The soles of his feet are like leather,' she said. 'Disgusting.' But from the hint of indulgence in her face I gathered that Chanter's cause wasn't entirely lost.

She said she was thirsty again and could do with a Coke, and since she seemed to want me still to tag along, I tagged. This time, without Chanter, we went to the members' bar in the Club enclosure, the small downstairs one that was open to the main entrance hall.

The man in the plaster cast was there again. Different audience. Same story. His big cheerful booming voice filled the little bar and echoed round the whole hall outside.

'You can't hear yourself think,' Nancy said.

In a huddle in a far corner were Major Tyderman and Eric Goldenberg, sitting at a small table with what looked like treble whiskies in front of them. Their heads were bent towards each other, close, almost touching, so that they could each hear what the other was saying amid the din, yet not be overheard. Relations between them didn't seem to be at their most cordial. There was a great deal of rigidity in their downbent faces, and no friendliness in the small flicking glances they occasionally gave each other.

'The *Sporting Life* man,' Nancy said, following my gaze.

'Yes. The big one is a passenger too.'

'They don't look madly happy.'

'They weren't madly happy coming up here, either.'

'Owners of chronic losers?'

'No - well, I don't think so. They came up because of that horse Rudiments which Kenny Bayst rode for Annie Villars, but they aren't down in the racecard as its owners.'

She flicked back through her card. 'Rudiments. Duke of Wessex. Well, neither of those two is him, poor old booby.'

'Who, the Duke?'

'Yes,' she said. 'Actually I suppose he isn't all that old, but he's dreadfully dim. Big important looking man with a big important looking rank, and as sweet as they come, really, but there's nothing but cotton wool upstairs.'

'You know him well?'

'I've met him often.'

'Subtle difference.'

'Yes.'

The two men scraped back their chairs and began to make their way out of the bar. The man in the plaster cast caught sight of them and his big smile grew even bigger.

'Say, if it isn't Eric, Eric Goldenberg, of all people. Come over here, me old sport, come and have a drink.'

Goldenberg looked less than enthusiastic at the invitation and the Major sidled away quickly to avoid being included, giving the Australian a glance full of the dislike of the military for the flamboyant.

The man in the cast put one arm clumsily round Goldenberg's shoulder, the crutch swinging out widely and knocking against Nancy.

'Say,' he said. 'Sorry, lady. I haven't got the hang of these things yet.'

'That's all right,' she said, and Goldenberg said something to him that I couldn't hear, and before we knew where we were we had been encompassed into the Australian's circle and he was busy ordering drinks all round.

Close to, he was a strange looking man because his face and hair were almost colourless. The skin was whitish, the scalp, half bald, was fringed by silky hair that had been fair and turning white, the eyelashes and eyebrows made no contrast, and the lips of the smiling mouth were creamy pale. He looked like a man made up to take the part of a large cheerful ghost. His name, it appeared, was Acey Jones.

'Aw, come on,' he said to me in disgust. 'Coke is for milk-sops, not men.' Even his eyes were pale: a light indeterminate bluey grey.

'Just lay off him, Ace,' Goldenberg said. 'He's flying me home. A drunken pilot I can do without.'

'A pilot, eh?' The big voice broadcast the information to about fifty people who weren't in the least interested. 'One of the fly boys? Most pilots I know are a bunch of proper tearaways. Live hard, love hard, drink hard. Real characters, those guys.' He said it with an expansive smile which hid the implied slight. 'C'm on now, sport, live dangerously. Don't disillusion all these people.'

'Beer, then, please.' I said.

Nancy was equally scornful, but for the opposite reasons. 'Why did you climb down?'

'Antagonizing people when you don't have to is like casting your garbage on the waters. One day it may come floating back, smelling worse.'

She laughed. 'Chanter would say that was immoral. Stands must be made on principles.'

'I won't drink more than half of the beer. Will that do?'

'You're impossible.'

Acey Jones handed me the glass and watched me take a mouthful and went on a bit about hell-raising and beating up the skies and generally living the life of a high-powered gypsy. He made it sound attractive and his audience smiled and nodded their heads and none of them seemed to know that the picture was fifty years out of date, and that the best thing a pilot can be is careful. There are old pilots and foolish pilots, but no old foolish pilots. Me, I was old, young, wise, foolish, thirty-four. Also depressed, divorced, and broke.

After aviation, Acey Jones switched back to insurance and told Goldenberg and Nancy and me and the fifty other people about getting a thousand pounds for breaking his ankle, and we had to listen to it all again, reacting with the best we could do in surprised appreciation.

'No, look, no kidding, sport,' he said to Goldenberg with his first sign of seriousness. 'You want to get yourself signed up with this outfit. Best fiver I've ever spent....'

Several of the fifty onlookers edged nearer to listen, and Nancy and I filtered towards the outside of the group. I put down the tasted beer on an inconspicuous table out in the hall while Nancy dispatched the bottom half of her coke, and from there we drifted out into the air.

The sun was still shining, but the small round white clouds were expanding into bigger round clouds with dark grey centres. I looked at my watch. Four twenty. Still nearly an hour until the time the Major wanted to leave. The longer we stayed the bumpier the ride was likely to be, because the afternoon forecast for scattered thunderstorms looked accurate.

'Cu-nims forming,' Nancy said, watching them. 'Nasty.'

We went and watched her brother get up on his mount for the last race and then we went up on the Owners and Trainers and watched him win it, and that was about that. She said goodbye to me near the bottom of the steps, outside the weighing room.

'Thanks for the escort duty ...'

'Enjoyed it ...'

She had smooth gilded skin and greyish brown eyes. Straight dark eyebrows. Not much lipstick. No scent. Very much the opposite of my blonde, painted, and departed wife.

'I expect,' she said, 'That we'll meet again, because I sometimes fly with Colin, if there's a spare seat.'

'Do you ever take him yourself?'

'Good Lord no.' She laughed. 'He wouldn't trust me to get him there on time. And anyway, there are too many days when the weather is beyond what I can do. Maybe one day, though....'

She held out her hand and I shook it. A grip very like her brother's, and just as brief.

'See you, then,' she said.

'I hope so.'

She nodded with a faint smile and went away. I watched her neat blue and white back view and stifled a sudden unexpected inclination to run after her and give her a Chantertype farewell.

When I walked across the track towards the aeroplane I met Kenny Bayst coming back from it with his raincoat over his arm. His skin was blotched pink again with fury, clashing with his carroty hair.

'I'm not coming back with you,' he said tightly. 'You tell Miss Annie effing Villars that I'm not coming back with you. There's no bloody pleasing her. Last time I nearly got the push for winning and this time I nearly got the push for not winning. You'd think that both times I'd had the slightest choice in the matter. I'll tell you straight, sport, I'm not coming back in your bloody little aeroplane having them gripe gripe gripe at me all the way back.'

'All right,' I said. I didn't blame him.

'I've just been over to fetch my raincoat. I'll go home by train ... or get a lift.'

'Raincoat ... but the aircraft is locked.'

'No it isn't. I just got my raincoat out of the back. Now you tell them I've had enough, right?' I nodded, and while he hurried off I walked on towards the aeroplane puzzled and a bit annoyed. Major Tyderman had said he had locked up again after he had fetched his *Sporting Life*, but apparently he hadn't.

He hadn't. Both the doors on the port side were unlocked, the passenger door and the baggage locker. I wasn't too pleased because Derrydowns had told me explicitly never to leave the aircraft open as they'd had damage done by small boys on several occasions: but all looked well and there were no signs of sticky fingers.

I did all the external checks again and glanced over the flight plan for the return. If we had to avoid too many thunderclouds it might take a little longer to reach Newmarket, but unless there was one settled and active over the landing field there should be no problem.

The passengers of the two Polyplane aircraft assembled by ones and twos, shovelled themselves inside, shut the doors, and were trundled down to the far end of the course. One after the other the two aeroplanes raced back over the grass and lifted away, wheeling like black darts against the blue, grey and white patchwork of the sky.

Annie Villars came first of my lot. Alone, composed, polite; giving nothing away. She handed me her coat and binoculars and I stored them for her. She thanked me. The deceptive mild brown eyes held a certain blankness and every few seconds a spasmodic tightening belied the gentle set of her mouth. A formidable lady, I thought. What was more, she herself knew it. She was so conscious of the strength and range of her power that she deliberately manufactured the disarming exterior in order not exactly to hide it, but to make it palatable. Made a nice change, I thought ironically, from all those who put up a big tough front to disguise their inner lack.

'Kenny Bayst asked me to tell you that he has got a lift home to Newmarket and won't be coming back by air.' I said.

A tiny flash of fire in the brown eyes. The gentle voice, completely controlled, said 'I'm not surprised.' She climbed into the aeroplane and strapped herself into her seat and sat there in silence, looking out over the emptying racecourse with eyes that weren't concentrating on the grass and the trees.

Tyderman and Goldenberg returned together, still deep in discussion. The Major's side mostly consisted of decisive nods, but it was pouring out of Goldenberg. Also he was past worrying about what I overheard.

'I would be surprised if the little shit hasn't been double crossing us all the time and collecting from some bookmaker or other even more than he got from us. Making fools of us, that's what he's been doing. I'll murder the little sod. I told him so, too.'

'What did he say?' the Major asked.

'Said I wouldn't get the chance. Cocky little bastard.'

They thrust their gear angrily into the baggage compartment and stood talking by the rear door in voices rumbling like the distant thunder.

Colin Ross came last, slight and inconspicuous, still wearing the faded jeans and the now crumpled sweat shirt.

I went a few steps to meet him. 'Your sister Nancy asked me to check with you whether you had remembered to bring the present for Midge.'

'Oh damn ...' More than irritation in his voice there was weariness. He had ridden six hard races, won three of them. He looked as if a toddler could knock him down.

'I'll get it for you, if you like.'

'Would you?' He hesitated, then with a tired flap of his wrist said, 'Well, I'd be grateful. Go into the weighing room and ask for my valet, Ginger Mundy. The parcel's on the shelf over my peg. He'll get it for you.'

I nodded and went back across the track. The parcel, easily found, proved to be a little smaller than a shoe box and was wrapped in pink and gold paper with a pink bow. I took it over to the aeroplane and Colin put it on Kenny Bayst's empty seat.

The Major had already strapped himself in and was drumming with his fingers on his binocular case, which was as usual slung around him. His body was still stiff with tension. I wondered if he ever relaxed.

Goldenberg waited without a smile while I clambered across into my seat, and followed me in and clipped shut the door in gloomy silence. I sighed, started the engine, and taxied down to the far end of the course. Ready for take-off I turned round to my passengers and tried a bright smile.

'All set?'

I got three grudging nods for my pains. Colin Ross was asleep. I took the hilarious party off the ground without enthusiasm, skirted the Manchester zone, and pointed the nose in the general direction of Newmarket. Once up in the sky it was all too clear that the air had become highly unstable. At lower levels, rising pockets of heat from the built-up areas bumped the aeroplane about like a puppet, and to enormous heights great heaps of cumulo-nimbus cloud were boiling up all round the horizon.

Airsick-making weather. I looked round to see if an issue of waterproof bags was going to be required. Needn't have bothered. Colin was still asleep and the other three had too much on their minds to worry about a few lurches. I told Annie Villars where the bags were to be found if wanted, and she seemed to think I had insulted her.

Although by four thousand feet the worst of the bumps were below us, the flight was a bit like a bending race as I tracked left and right to avoid the dark towering cloud masses. Mostly we stayed in the sunshine: occasionally raced through the small veiling clouds which were dotted among the big ones. I wanted to avoid even the medium sized harmless ones, as these sometimes hid a dangerous whopper just behind, and at a hundred and fifty miles an hour there was little chance to dodge. Inside every well grown cumulo-nimbus there were vertical rushing air currents which could lift and drop even an airliner like a yoyo. Also one could meet hailstones and freezing rain. Nobody's idea of a jolly playground. So it was a good idea to avoid the black churning brutes, but it was a rougher ride than one should aim for with passengers.

Everyone knows the horrible skin-prickling heart-thudding feeling when the normal suddenly goes wrong. Fear, its called. The best place to feel it is not with a jerk at four thousand feet in a battlefield of cu-nims.

I was used to far worse weather; so bad, beastly, even lethal weather. It wasn't the state of the sky which distracted me, which set the fierce little adrenalin-packed alarm bell ringing like crazy.

There was something wrong with the aeroplane.

Nothing much. I couldn't even tell what it was. But something. Something...

My instinct for safety was highly developed. Over-developed, many had said, when it had got me into trouble. Bloody coward, was how they'd put it.

You couldn't ignore it, though. When the instinct switched to danger you couldn't risk ignoring it, not with passengers on board. What you could do when you were alone was a different matter, but civil commercial pilots seldom got a chance to fly alone.

Nothing wrong with the instruments. Nothing wrong with the engine.

Something wrong with the flying controls.

When I swerved gently to avoid yet another lurking cu-nim the nose of the aircraft dropped and I had a shade of difficulty pulling it up again. Once level nothing seemed wrong. All the gauges seemed right. Only the instinct remained. Instinct and the memory of a slightly sluggish response.

The next time I made a turn, the same thing happened. The nose wanted to drop, and it needed more pressure than it should have done to hold it level. At the third turn, it was worse.

I looked down at the map on my knees. We were twenty minutes out of Haydock ... south of Matlock ... approaching Nottingham. Another eighty nautical miles to Newmarket.

It was the hinged part of the tailplane which raised or lowered the aircraft's nose. The elevators, they were called. They linked by wires to the control column in such a way that when you pushed the control column forward the tail went up and tipped the nose down. And vice versa.

The wires ran through rings and over pulleys, between the cabin floor and the outer skin of the fuselage. There wasn't supposed to be any friction.

Friction was what I could feel.

I thought perhaps one of the wires had somehow come off one of the pulleys during the bumpy ride. I'd never heard of it happening before, but that didn't mean it couldn't. Or perhaps a whole pulley had come adrift, or had broken in half ... If something was rolling around loose it could affect the controls fairly seriously.

I turned to the cheerful company.

'I'm very sorry, but there will be a short delay on the journey. We're going to land for a while at the East Midlands Airport, near Nottingham, while I get a quick precautionary check done on the aircraft.'

I met opposition.

Goldenberg said belligerently, 'I can't see anything wrong.' His eyes swept over the gauges, noticing all the needles pointing to the green safety segments on all the engine instruments. 'It all looks the same as it always does.'

'Are you sure it's necessary?' Annie Villars said. 'I particularly want to get back to see my horses at evening stables.'

The Major said 'Damn it all!' fiercely and frowned heavily and looked more tense than ever.

They woke up Colin Ross.

'The pilot wants to land here and make what he calls a precautionary check. We want to go straight on. We don't want to waste time. There isn't anything wrong with the plane, as far as we can see ...'

Colin Ross's voice came across, clear and decisive. 'If he says we're going down, we're going down. He's the boss.'

I looked round at them. Except for Colin they were all more moody and gloomy than ever. Colin unexpectedly gave me a flicker of a wink. I grinned as much to myself as to him, called up East Midlands on the radio, announced our intention to land, and asked them to arrange for a mechanic to be available for a check.

On the way down I regretted it. The friction seemed no worse: if anything it was better. Even in the turbulent air near the ground I had no great trouble in moving the elevators. I'd made a fool of myself and the passengers would be furious and Derrydowns would be scathing about the unnecessary expense, and at any time at all I would be looking for my seventh job.

It was a normal landing. I parked where directed on the apron and suggested everyone got out and went into the airport for a drink, as the check would take half an hour, and maybe more.

They were by then increasingly annoyed. Up in the air they must have had a lingering doubt that I was right about landing. Safe on the ground, they were becoming sure it was unnecessary.

I walked some of the way across the tarmac with them towards the airport passengers' doors, then peeled off to go to the control office for the routine report after landing, and to ask for the mechanic to come for a look-see as soon as possible. I would fetch them from the bar, I said, once the check was done.

'Hurry it up' Goldenberg said rudely.

'Most annoying. Most annoying indeed.' The Major.

'I was away last night ... particularly wanted to get back this evening. Might as well go by road, no point in paying for speed if you don't get it ...' Annie Villar's irritation overcoming the velvet glove.

Colin Ross said, 'If your horse coughs, don't race it.'

The others looked at him sharply. I said, 'Thanks' gratefully, and bore off at a tangent to the left. I saw them out of the side of my vision, looking briefly back towards the aircraft and then walking unenthusiastically towards the big glass doors.

There was a crack behind me like a snapping branch, and a monstrous boom, and a roaring gust of air.

I'd heard that sequence before. I spun round, appalled.

Where there had stood a smart little blue and white Cherokee there was an exploding ball of fire.

Chapter Four

The bomb had taken a fraction of a second to detonate. The public impact lasted three days. The investigations dragged on for weeks.

Predictably, the Dailies went to town on 'Colin Ross Escapes Death by One Minute' and 'Champion Jockey wins Race against Time'. Annie Villars, looking particularly sweet and frail, said in a television news interview that we had all been fantastically lucky. Major Tyderman was quoted as saying 'Fortunately there was something wrong with the plane, and we landed for a check. Otherwise ...' And Colin Ross had apparently finished his sentence for him; 'Otherwise we would all have been raining down on Nottingham in little bits.'

That was after they had recovered, of course. When I reached them at a run near the airport doors their eyes were stretched wide and their faces were stiff with shock. Annie Villars mouth had dropped open and she was shaking from head to foot. I put my hand on her arm. She looked at me blankly and then made a small mewing sound and crumpled against me in a thoroughly un-Napoleonic faint. I caught her on the way down and lifted her up in my arms to save her falling on the shower soaked tarmac. She weighed even less than she looked.

'God,' said Goldenberg automatically. 'God.' His mind and tongue seemed to be stuck on the single word.

The Major's mouth was trembling and he was losing the battle to keep it still with his teeth. Sweat stood out in fine drops on his forehead and he was breathing in short shocked gasps.

Holding Annie Villars I stood beside them and watched the death throes of the aeroplane. The first explosion had blown it apart and almost immediately the fuel tanks had ignited and finished the job. The wreckage lay strewn in burning twisted pieces over a radius of wet tarmac, the parts looking too small ever to have formed the whole. Rivers of burning petrol ran among them, and great curling orange and yellow flames roared round the largest piece, which looked like the front part of the cabin.

My seat. My hot, hot seat.

Trouble followed me around like the rats of Hamelin.

Colin Ross looked as shocked as the others but his nerves were of sterner stuff. 'Was that ... a bomb?'

'Nothing but,' I said flippantly.

He looked at me sharply. 'It's not funny.'

'It's not tragic, either,' I said. 'We're still here.'

A lot of the stiffness left his face and body. The beginnings of a smile appeared. 'So we are,' he said.

Someone in the control tower had pressed the panic button. Fire engines screamed up and foam poured out of the giant hoses onto the pathetic scraps. The equipment was designed to deal with jumbos. It took about ten seconds to reduce the Cherokee sized flames to black memories.

Three or four airport cars buzzed around like gnats and one filled with agitated officials dashed in our direction.

'Are you the people who came in that aircraft?'

The first of the questions. By no means the last. I knew what I was in for. I had been taken apart before.

'Which is the pilot? Will you come with us, then, and your passengers can go to the manager's office ... Is the lady injured?'

'Fainted,' I said.

'Oh ...' he hesitated. 'Can someone else take her?' He looked at the others. Goldenberg, large and flabby; the Major, elderly; Colin, frail. His eyes eyes passed over Colin and then went back, widening, the incredulity fighting against recognition.

'Excuse me ... are you ...?'

'Ross,' said Colin flatly. 'Yes.'

They rolled out the red carpet, after that. They produced smelling salts and a ground hostess for Annie Villars, stiff brandies for the Major and Goldenberg, autograph books for Colin Ross. The manager himself took charge of them. And someone excitedly rang up the national Press.

The board of Trade investigators were friendly and polite. As usual. And persistent, scrupulous, and ruthless. As usual.

'Why did you land at East Midlands?'

Friction.

'Had you any idea there was a bomb on board?'

No.

'Had you made a thorough pre-flight investigation?'

Yes.

'And no bomb?'

No.

Did I know that I was nevertheless responsible for the safety of the aircraft and could technically he held responsible for having initiated a flight with a bomb on board?

Yes.

We looked at each other. It was an odd rule. Very few people who took off with a bomb on board lived to be held responsible. The Board of Trade smiled, to show they knew it was silly to think anyone would take off with a bomb, knowing it was there.

'Did you lock the aircraft whenever you left it?'

I did.

'And did it remain locked?'

The knife was in. I told them about the Major. They already knew.

'He says he is sure that he relocked the doors,' they said, 'But even so wasn't it your responsibility to look after the safety of the aircraft, not his?'

Quite so.

'Wouldn't it have been prudent of you to accompany him to fetch the paper?'

No comment.

'The safety of the aircraft is the responsibility of the captain.'

Whichever way you turned, it came back to that.

This was my second interview with the Board of Trade.

The first, the day after the explosion, had been friendly and sympathetic, a fact-finding mission during which the word responsibility had not cropped up once. It had hovered delicately in the wings. Inevitably it would be brought on later and pinned to someone's chest.

'During the past three days we have interviewed all your passengers, and none of them has any idea who would have wanted to kill them, or why. We now feel we must go more carefully into the matter of opportunity, so we do hope you don't mind answering what may be a lot of questions. Then we can piece together a statement for you, and we would be glad if you would sign it ...'

'Do all I can,' I said. Dig my own grave. Again.

'They all agreed that the bomb must have been in the gift wrapped parcel which you yourself carried on board.'

Nice.

'And that the intended victim was Colin Ross.'

I sucked my teeth.

'You don't think so?'

'I honestly have no idea who it was intended for,' I said. 'But I don't think the bomb was in the parcel.'

'Why not?'

'His sister bought it, that morning.'

'We know.' He was a tall man, with inward looking eyes as if they wee consulting a computer in his head, feeding in every answer he was given and waiting for the circuits to click out a conclusion. There was no aggression anywhere in his manner, no vengeance in his motivation. A fact finder, a cause-seeker: like a truffle hound. He knew the sent of truth. Nothing would entice him away.

'And it sat on a shelf in the changing room all afternoon,' I said. 'And no one is allowed into the changing room except jockeys and valets.'

'We understand that that is so.' He smiled. 'Could the parcel have been the bomb? Weightwise?'

'I suppose so.'

'Miss Nancy Ross says it contained a large fancy bottle of bath oil.'

'No pieces in the wreckage?' I asked.

'Not a thing.' The tall man's nose wrinkled. 'I've seldom seen a more thorough disintegration.'

We were sitting in what was called the crew room in the Derrydown office on the old R.A.F. airfield near Buckingham. Such money as Derrydown spent on appearances began in the manager's office and ended in the passengers' waiting lounge across the hall. The crew room looked as if the paint and the walls were coming up to their silver wedding. The linoleum had long passed the age of consent. Three of the four cheap armchairs looked as if they had still to reach puberty but the springs in the fourth were so badly broken that it was more comfortable to sit on the floor.

Much of the wall space was taken up by maps and weather charts and various Notices to Airmen, several of them out of date. There was a duty roster upon which my name appeared with the utmost regularity and a notice typed in red capitals to the effect that anyone who failed to take the aircraft's documents with him on a charter flight would get the sack. I had duly taken all the Cherokee's records and maintenance certificates with me, as the Air Navigation Order insisted. Now they were burned to a crisp. I hoped someone somewhere saw some sense in it.

The tall man looked carefully round the dingy room. The other, shorter, broader, silent, sat with his green bitten HB poised over his spiral bound notebook.

'Mr Shore, I understand you hold an Airline Transport Pilot's

Licence. And a Flight Navigator's certificate.'

He had been looking me up. I knew he would have.

I said flatly, 'Yes.'

'This taxi work is hardly ... well ... what you were intended for.'

I shrugged.

'The highest possible qualifications ...' He shook his head. 'You were trained by B.O.A.C. and flew for them for nine years. First Officer. In line for Captain. And then you left.'

'Yes.' And they never took you back. Policy decision.

Never.

He delicately consulted his notes. 'And then you flew as Captain for a private British airline until it went into liquidation? And after that for a South American airline, who, I believe, dismissed you. And then all last year a spot of gun running, and this spring some crop spraying. And now this,'

They never let go. I wondered who had compiled the list.

'It wasn't guns. Food and medical supplies in, refugees and wounded out.'

He smiled faintly. 'To some remote African airstrip on dark nights? Being shot at?'

I looked at him.

He spread out his hands, 'Yes. I know. All legal and respectable, and not our business, of course.' He cleared his throat.... 'Weren't you the ... er ... the subject ... of an investigation about four years ago? While you were flying for British Interport?'

I took in a slow breath. 'Yes.'

'Mm.' He looked up, down, and sideways. 'I've read an outline of that case. They didn't suspend your licence.'

'No.'

'Though on the face of it one might have expected them to.'

I didn't answer.

'Did Interport pay the fine for you?'

'No.'

'But they kept you on as Captain. You were convicted of gross negligence, but they kept you on.' It was half way between a statement and a question.

'That's right,' I said.

If he wanted all the details, he could read the full report. He knew it and I knew it. He wasn't going to get me to tell him.

He said, 'Yes ... well. Who put this bomb in the Cherokee? When and how?'

'I wish I knew.'

His manner hadn't changed. His voice was still friendly. We both ignored this tentative shot at piling on the pressure.

'You stopped at White Waltham and Newbury ...'

'I didn't lock up at White Waltham. I parked on the grass outside the reception lounge. I could see the aeroplane most of the time, and it was only on the ground for half an hour. I got there early ... I can't see that anyone had a chance, or could rely on having a chance, to put a bomb on board at White Waltham.'

'Newbury?'

'They all stayed in their seats except me, Colin Ross came ... We put his overnight bag in the front baggage locker ...'

The tall man shook his head. 'The explosion was further back. Behind the captain's seat, at the very least. The blast evidence makes it certain. Some of the metal parts of the captain's seat were embedded in the instrument panel.'

'One minute,' I said reflectively. 'Very nasty.'

'Yes ... Who had an opportunity at Haydock?'

I sighed inwardly. 'I suppose anyone, from the time I gave the keys to Major Tyderman until I went back to the aircraft.'

'How long was that?'

I'd worked it out. 'Getting on for three hours. But ...'

'But what?'

'No one could have counted on the aircraft being left unlocked.'

'Trying to wriggle out?'

'Do you think so?'

He dodged an answer: said 'I'll give it to you that no one could have known whether it would be locked or unlocked. You just made it easy.'

'All right,' I said. 'If you'll also bear in mind that pickers and stealers unlock cars every day of the week, and that aircraft keys are the same type. Anyone who could manufacture and plant a bomb could open a little old lock.'

'Possibly,' he said, and repeated, 'But you made it easy.'

Damn Major Tyderman, I thought bleakly. Stupid, careless old fool. I stifled the thought that I probably would have gone across with him, or insisted on fetching his newspaper for him, if I hadn't been unwilling to walk away and leave Nancy.

'Who could have had access ... leaving the matter of locks?'

I shrugged one shoulder. 'All the world. They had only to walk across the track.'

'The aircraft was parked opposite the stands, I believe, in full view of the crowds.'

'Yes. About a hundred yards, in fact, from the stands. Not close enough for anyone to see exactly what someone was doing, if he seemed to be walking round peering in through the windows. People do that, you know, pretty often.'

'You didn't notice anyone, yourself?'

I shook my head. 'I looked across several times during the afternoon. Just a casual glance, though. I wasn't thinking about trouble.'

'Hm.' He reflected for a few seconds. Then he said 'Two of the Polyplanes were there as well, I believe.'

'Yes.'

'I think I'd better talk to the pilots, to see if they noticed anything.'

I didn't comment. His eyes suddenly focused on mine, sharp and black.

'Were they friendly?'

'The pilots? Not particularly.'

'How's the feud?'

'What feud?'

He stared at me assessingly. 'You're not that dumb. No one could work for Derrydown and not know that they and Polyplanes are permanently engaged in scratching each other's eyes out.'

I sighed. 'I don't give a damn.'

'You will, when they start reporting you.'

'Reporting me? For what? What do you mean?'

He smiled thinly. 'If you infringe the rules by as much as one foot, Polyplanes will be on to us before your wheels have stopped rolling. They're doing their best to put Derrydown out of business. Most of it we shrug off as simply spite. But if they catch you breaking the regulations, and can produce witnesses, we'd have to take action.'

'Charming.'

He nodded. 'Aviation will never need a special police force to detect crime. Everyone is so busy informing on everyone else. Makes us laugh, sometimes.'

'Or cry,' I said.

'That too.' He nodded wryly. 'There are no permanent friendships in aviation. The people you think are your friends are the first to deny they associate with you at the faintest hint of trouble. The cock crows until it's hoarse, in aviation.' The bitterness in his voice was unmistakable. But impersonal, also.

'You don't approve.'

'No. It makes our job easier, of course. But I like less and less the sight of people scrambling to save themselves at any cost to others. It diminishes them. They are small.'

'You can't always blame them for not always wanting to be involved. Aviation law cases are so fierce, so unforgiving . . .'

'Did your friends at Interport rally round and cheer you up?'

I thought back to those weeks of loneliness. 'They waited to see.'

He nodded. 'Didn't want to be contaminated.'

'It's a long time ago,' I said.

'You never forget rejection,' he said. 'It's a trauma.'

'Interport didn't reject me. They kept me on for another year, until they went bust. And,' I added, 'I didn't have anything to do with *that*.'

He gently laughed. 'Oh I know. My masters in that Government put on one of its great big squeezes and by one means or another forced them out of business.'

I didn't pursue it. The history of aviation was littered with the bodies of murdered air firms. Insolvency sat like a vulture in every boardroom in the industry and constantly pecked away at the bodies before they were dead. British Eagle. Handley Page, Beagle, the list of corpses was endless. Interport had been one of the largest, and Derrydowns, still struggling, one of the smallest, but their problems were identical. Huge inexorable costs. Fickle variable income. Write the sum in red.

I said, 'There is one other place, of course, where the bomb could have been put on board.' I stopped.

'Spell it out, then.'

'Here.'

The tall investigator and his silent friend with the pencil went down to the hangar to interview old Joe.

Harley called me into his office.

'Have they finished?'

'They've gone to ask Joe if he put the bomb in the Cherokee.'

Harley was irritated, which was with him a common state of mind. 'Ridiculous.'

'Or if Larry did.'

'*Larry . . .*'

'He left for Turkey that afternoon,' I pointed out. 'Would he have planted a legacy?'

'No.' Short, snappy and vehement.

'Why did he leave?'

'He wanted to.' He gave me a sharp glance bordering on dislike. 'You sound like the Board of Trade.'

'Sorry,' I said in conciliation. 'Must be catching.'

Harley's office dated back to a more prosperous past. There was a carpet of sorts on the floor and the walls had been painted within living memory, and his good quality desk had mellowed instead of chipping. Limp blue curtains framed the big window looking out over the airfield and several good photographs of aeroplanes had been framed and hung. Customers, when they visited him, were allowed the nearly new lightweight armchair. Crew sat on the wooden upright.

Harley himself was proprietor, manager, chief flying instructor, booking clerk and window cleaner. His staff consisted of one qualified mechanic past retiring age, one part-time boy helper, one full-time taxi pilot (me) and one part-time pilot who switched from taxiing to teaching, whichever was required, and on alternate days taught in a flying club twenty miles to the north.

Derrydown's other assets had been, before the Cherokee blew up, three useful aircraft and one bright girl.

The remaining two aircraft were a small single engined trainer, and a twin engined eight year old Aztec equipped with every possible flying aid, for which Harley was paying through the nose on a five year lease.

The girl, Honey, his brother's daughter, worked for love and peanuts and was the keystone which held up the arch. I knew her voice better than her face, as she sat up in the control tower all day directing such air traffic as came along. Between times she typed all the letters, kept the records, did the accounts, answered the telephone if her uncle didn't and collected landing fees from visiting pilots. She was reputed to be suffering from a broken heart about Larry and consequently came down from her crow's nest as seldom as possible.

'She's made puff balls out of her eyes, crying for that louse' was how my part-time colleague put it. 'But you wait just a week or two. She'll lie down for you instead. Never refused a good pilot yet, our Honey hasn't.'

'How about you?' I asked, amused.

'Me? She'd squeezed me like a lemon long before that Goddamned Larry ever turned up.'

Harley said crossly 'We've lost two charters since the bomb. They say the Aztec's too expensive, they would rather go by road.' He ran his hand over his head. 'There's another Cherokee Six up at Liverpool that's available to lease. I've just been talking to them on the phone. It sounds all right. They're bringing it across here tomorrow afternoon, so you can take it up when you get back from Newmarket and see what you think.'

'How about the insurance on the old one?' I asked idly. 'It would be cheaper in the long run to buy rather than lease.'

'It was on hire purchase,' he said gloomily. 'We'll be lucky if we get a penny. And it's not really your business.'

Harley was slightly plump and slightly bald and just not quite forceful enough to lift Derrydowns up by its bootstraps. His manner to me was more bossy than friendly, a reaction I understood well enough.

'The last person on earth to put a bomb on any aircraft would be Joe,' he said explosively. 'He looks after them like a mother. He *polishes* them.'

It was true. The Derrydown aircraft sparkled outside and were shampooed inside. The engines ran like silk. The general, slightly misleading, air of prosperity which clung around the public face of the firm was mostly Joe's work.

The Board of Trade came back from the hangar looking vaguely sheepish. The rough side of Joe's tongue, I guessed. At sixty-nine and with savings in the bank, he was apt to lay down his own laws. He had taken exception to my theory that a pulley on the elevator wires had come adrift. No such thing was possible in one of his aircraft, he had told me stiffly, and I could take my four gold rings away and I knew what I could do with them. As I hadn't worn my captain's jacket for nearly two years I told him the moths had beaten me to it, and although it was a feeble joke he gave me a less sour look and told me that it couldn't have been a broken pulley, he was sure it couldn't, and if it was, it was the manufacturer's fault, not his.

'It saved Colin Ross's life,' I pointed out. 'You should claim a medal for it.' Which opened his mouth and shut him up.

The Board of Trade trooped into Harley's office. The tall man sat in the armchair and Green Pencil on the hard one. Harley behind his desk. I leant against the wall, on my feet.

'Well now,' said the tall man. 'It seems as if everyone on this airfield had a chance to tamper with the Cherokee. Everyone in the company, and any customers who happened to be here that morning, and any member of the public wandering around for a look-see. We've assumed the bomb was aimed at Colin Ross, but we don't really know that. If it was, someone had a pretty accurate idea of when he would be in the aircraft.'

'Last race four thirty. He was riding in it,' Harley said. 'Doesn't take too much figuring to assume that at five forty he'd be in the air.'

'Five forty seven,' said the tall man, 'Actually.'

'Any time about then,' said Harley irritably.

'I wonder what the bomb was in,' said the tall man reflectively. 'Did you look inside the first aid tin?'

'No,' I said, startled. 'I just checked that it was there. I've never looked inside it. Or inside the fire extinguishers, or under the seats or inside the life jacket covers ...'

The tall man nodded. 'It could have been in any of those places. Or it could after all have been in that fancy parcel.'

'Ticking away,' said Harley.

I peeled myself slowly off the wall. 'Suppose,' I said hesitantly, 'Suppose it wasn't in any of those places. Suppose it was deeper, out of sight. Somewhere between the cabin wall and the outer skin ... like a limpet mine, for instance. Suppose that that bumpy ride ... and all those turns I did to avoid the cu-nims ... dislodged it, so that it was getting jammed in the elevator wires ... Suppose that was what I could feel ... and why I decided to land ... and that what saved us ... was the bomb itself.'

Chapter Five

The next day I took five jockeys and trainers from Newmarket to Newcastle races and back in the Aztec and listened to them grousing over the extra expense, and in the evening I tried out the replacement Cherokee, which flew permanently left wing down on the auto pilot, had an unserviceable fuel flow meter, and an overload somewhere on the electrical circuit.

'It isn't very good,' I told Harley. 'It's old and noisy and it probably drinks fuel and I shouldn't think the battery's charging properly.'

He interrupted me. 'It flies. And it's cheap. And Joe will fix it. I'm taking it.'

'Also it's orange and white, just like the Polyplanes.'

He gave me an irritable glare. 'I'm not blind. I know it is. And it's not surprising, considering it used to belong to them.'

He waited for me to protest so that he could slap me down, so I didn't. I shrugged instead. If he wanted to admit to his bitterest rivals that his standards were down to one of their third hand clapped out old buggies, that was his business.

He signed the lease on the spot and gave it to the pilot who had brought the aeroplane to take back with him on the train, and the pilot smiled a pitying smile and went off shaking his head.

The orange and white Cherokee went down to the hangar for Joe to wave his wand over, and I walked round the perimeter track to home sweet home.

One caravan, pilots' for the use of. Larry had lived in it before me, and others before him: Harley's taxi pilots stayed, on average, eight months, and most of them settled for the caravan because it was easiest. It stood on a dusty square of concrete which had once been the floor of a R.A.F. hut, and it was connected to the mains electricity, water and drainage which had served the long departed airmen.

As caravans go it must once have held up its head, but generations of beer drinking bachelors had left tiny teeth marks of bottle-caps along the edges of all the fitments, and circular greasy head marks on the wall above every seat. Airport dirt had clogged the brown haircord into a greyish cake, relived here and there by darker irregular stains. Shabby pin-ups of superhuman mammalian development were stuck to the walls with sellotape, and a scatter of torn-off patches of paint showed where dozens of others had been stuck before. Tired green curtains had opened and shut on a thousand hangovers. The fly-blown mirror had stared back at a lot of disillusion, and the bed springs sagged from the weight of a bored succession of pilots with nothing to do except Honey.

I had forgotten to get anything to eat. There was half a packet of cornflakes in the kitchen and a jar of instant coffee. Neither was much use, as yesterday's half pint of milk had gone sour in the heat. I damned it all and slouched on the two seat approximation to a sofa, and resignedly dragged out of my pocket the two letters which had lain unopened there since this morning.

One was from a television rental firm who said they confirmed that they were transferring the rental fron Larry's name to mine, as requested, and could I now be as good as to pay immediately the six weeks for which he was in arrears. The other, from Susan, said briefly that I was late with the alimony yet again.

I put down both the letters and stared unseeingly through the opposite window towards the darkening summer sky. All the empty airfield stretched away into the dusk, calm, quite, undemanding and shadowy, everything I needed for a few repairs to the spirit. The only trouble was, the process was taking longer than I'd expected. I wondered sometimes whether I'd ever get back to where I'd once been. Maybe if you'd hashed up your life as thoroughly as I had, there was never any going back. Maybe one day soon I'd stop wanting to. Maybe one day I would accept the unsatisfactory present not as a healing period but as all there ever was going to be. That would be a pity, I thought. A pity to let the void take over for always.

I had three pounds in my pocket and sixteen in the bank, but I had finally paid all my debts. The crippling fine, the divorce, and the mountainous bills Susan had run up everywhere in a cold orgy of hatred towards me in the last weeks we were together: everything had been settled. The house had always been in her name because of the nature of my job, and she had clung on to that like a leech. she was still living in it, triumphant, collecting a quarter of everything I earned and writing sharp little letters if I didn't pay on the nail.

I didn't understand how love could curdle so abysmally: looking back, I still couldn't understand. We had screamed at each other: hit each other, intending to hurt. Yet when we married at nineteen we'd been entwined in tenderness, inseparable and sunny. When it started to go wrong she said it was because I was away so much, long ten day tours to the West Indies all the time, and all she had was her job as a doctor's secretary and the dull endless housework. In an uprush of affection and concern for her I resigned from B.O.A.C. and joined Interport instead, where I flew short-haul trips, and spent most of my nights at home. The pay was a shade less good, the prospects a lot less good, but for three months we were happier. After that there was a long period in which we both tried to make the best of it, and a last six months in which we had torn each other's nerves and emotions to shreds.

Since then I had tried more or less deliberately not to feel anything for anybody. Not to get involved. To be private, and apart, and cold. An ice-pack after the tempest.

I hadn't done anything to improve the caravan, to stamp anything of myself upon it. I didn't suppose I would, because I didn't feel the need. I didn't want to get involved, not even with a caravan.

And certainly not with Tyderman, Goldenberg, Annie Villars and Colin Ross.

All of them except Goldenberg were on my next racing trip.

I had spent two more days in the Aztec, chauffeuring some business executives on their regular monthly visit to subsidiary factories in Germany and Luxembourg, but by Saturday Joe had tarted up the replacement Cherokee so I set off in that. The fuel meter still resolutely pointed to nought, which was slightly optimistic, but the electrical fault had been cured: no overload now on the generator. And if it still flew one wing low, at least the wing in question sparkled with a new shine. The cabin smelt of soap and air freshener, and all the ash trays were empty.

The passengers were to be collected that day at Cambridge, and although I flew into the aerodrome half an hour early, the Major was already there, waiting on a seat in a corner of the entrance hall.

I saw him before he saw me, and as I walked towards him he took the binoculars out of their case and put them on the low table beside him. The binoculars were smaller than the case suggested. In went his hand again and out came a silver and pigskin flask. The Major took a six second swig and with a visible sigh screwed the cap back into place.

I slowed down and let him get the binoculars back on top of his courage before I came to a halt beside him and said good morning.

'Oh ... Good morning,' he said stiffly. He stood up, fastening the buckle of the case and giving it a pat as it swung into its usual facing forwards position on his stomach. 'All set?'

'The others are not here yet. It's still early.'

'Ah. No. Of course.' He wiped his moustache carefully with his hand and tucked his chin back into his neck. 'No bombs today I hope?'

He wasn't altogether meaning to joke.

'No bombs,' I assured him.

He nodded, not meeting my eyes. 'Very upsetting, last Friday. Very upsetting, you know.' He paused. 'Nearly didn't come, today, when I heard that Colin ... er ...' He stopped.

'I'll stay in the aeroplane all afternoon,' I promised him.

The Major nodded again, sharply. 'Had a Board of Trade fellow come to see me. Did you know that?'

'They told me so.'

'Been to see you too, I suppose.'

'Yes.'

'They get about a bit.'

'They're very thorough. They'll go a hundred miles to get a single answer to a simple question.'

He looked at me sharply. 'Speaking from bitter experience?'

I hadn't known there was any feeling in my voice. I said, 'I've been told they do.'

He grunted. 'Can't think why they don't leave it to the police.'

No such luck, I thought. There was no police force in the world as tenacious as the British Board of Trade.

Annie Villars and Colin Ross arrived together, deep in a persuasive argument that was getting nowhere.

'Just say you'll ride my horses whenever you can.'

'... too many commitments.'

'I'm not asking a great deal.'

'There are reasons, Annie. Sorry, but no.' He said it with an air of finality, and she looked startled and upset.

'Good morning,' she said to me abstractedly. 'Morning Rupert.'

'Morning, Annie,' said the Major.

Colin Ross had achieved narrow pale grey trousers and a blue open necked shirt.

'Morning, Matt,' he said.

The Major took a step forward, bristling like a terrier. 'Did I hear you turning down Annie's proposition?'

'Yes, Major.'

'Why?' he asked in an aggrieved tone. 'Our money is as good as anyone else's, and her horses are always fit.'

'I'm sorry, Major, but no. Just let's leave it at that.'

The Major looked affronted and took Annie Villars off to see if the bar was open. Colin sighed and sprawled in a wooden armchair.

'God save me,' he said, 'From crooks.'

I sat down too. 'She doesn't seem crooked to me.'

'Who, Annie? She isn't really. Just not one hundred per cent permanently scrupulous. No, it's that crummy slob Goldenberg that I don't like. She does what he says, a lot too much. I'm not taking indirect riding orders from him.'

'Like Kenny Bayst?' I suggested.

He looked at me sideways. 'The word gets around, I see. Kenny reckons he's well out of it. Well I'm not stepping in.' He paused reflectively. 'The Board of Trade investigator who came to see me asked if I thought there was any significance in Bayst having cried off the return trip the other day.'

'What did you say?'

'I said I didn't. Did you?'

'I confess I wondered, because he did go across to the aeroplane after the races, and he certainly felt murderous, but ...'

'But,' he agreed, 'Would Kenny Bayst be cold blooded enough to kill you and me as well?' He shook his head. 'Not Kenny, I wouldn't have thought.'

'And besides that,' I nodded, 'He only came to the steaming boil after he lost the three thirty, and just how would he rustle up a bomb at Haydock in a little over one hour?'

'He would have to have arranged it in advance.'

'That would mean that he knew he would lose the race ...'

'It's been done,' said Colin dryly.

There was a pause. Then I said, 'Anyway, I think we had it with us all the time. Right from before I left base.'

He swivelled his head and considered it. 'In that case ... Larry?'

'Would he?'

'God knows. Sneaky fellow. Pinched Nancy's hundred quid. But a bomb ... and what was the point?'

I shook my head.

Colin said, 'Bombs are usually either political or someone's next of kin wanting to collect the insurance.'

'Fanatics or family ...' I stifled the beginnings of a yawn.

'You don't really care, do you?' he said.

'Not that much.'

'It doesn't disturb you enough to wonder whether the bomb merchant will try again?'

'About as much as it's disturbing you.'

He grinned. 'Yes ... well. It would be handy to know for sure whose name was on that one. One would look so damn silly taking fiddly precautions if it was the Major who finally got clobbered. Or you.'

'Me?' I said in astonishment.

'Why not?'

I shook my head. 'I don't stand in anyone's way to anything.'

'Someone may think you do.'

'Then they're nuts.'

'It takes a nut ... a regular psycho ... to put a bomb in an aeroplane ...'

Tyderman and Annie Villars came back from the direction of the bar with two more people, a man and a woman.

'Oh Christ,' Colin said under his breath. 'Here comes my own personal Chanter.' He looked at me accusingly. 'You didn't tell me who the other passengers were.'

'I don't know them. Who are they? I don't do the bookings.'

We stood up. The woman, who was in her thirties but dressed like a teenager, made a straight line for Colin and kissed him exuberantly on the cheek.

'Colin, darling, there was a spare seat and Annie said I could come. Wasn't that absolutely super of her?'

Colin glared at Annie who pretended not to notice.

The girl-woman had a strong upper class accent, white knee socks, a camel coloured high waisted dress, several jingling gold bracelets, streaky fair brown long hair, a knock-you-down exotic scent and an air of expecting everyone to curl up and die for her.

She latched her arm through Colin's so that he couldn't disentangle without giving offence, and said with a somehow unattractive gaiety, 'Come along everyone, let's take the plunge. Isn't it all just too unnerving, flying around with Colin these days.'

'You don't actually have to come,' Colin said without quite disguising his wishes.

She seemed oblivious. 'Darling,' she said. 'Too riveting. Nothing would stop me.'

She moved off towards the door, followed by the Major and Annie and the new man together, and finally by me. The new man was large and had the same air as the woman of expecting people to jump to it and smooth his path. The Major and Annie Villars were busy smoothing it, their ears bent deferentially to catch any falling crumbs of wisdom, their heads nodding in agreement over every opinion.

The two just-teenage girls I had stationed beside the locked aircraft were still on duty, retained more by the promise of Colin's autograph than by my money. They got both, and were delighted. No one, they anxiously insisted, had even come close enough to ask what they were doing. No one could possible have put a piece of chewing gum on to the aeroplane, let alone a bomb.

Colin, signing away, gave me a sidelong look of amusement and appreciation and said safety came cheap at the price. He was less amused to find that the affectionate lady had stationed herself in one of the rear seats and was beckoning him to come and sit beside her.

'Who is she?' I asked.

'Fenella Payne-Percival. Fenella pain in the neck.'

I laughed. 'And the man?'

'Duke of Wessex. Annie's got a horse running for him today.'

'Not Rudiments again?'

He looked up in surprise from the second autograph book.

'Yes. That's right. Bit soon, I would have thought.' He finished the book and gave it back. 'Kenny Bayst isn't riding it.' His voice was dry.

'You don't say.'

The passengers had sorted themselves out so that Annie and the Duke sat in the centre seats, with the Major waiting for me to get in before him into the first two. He nodded his stiff little nod as I stepped up on to the wing, and pushed at his moustache. Less tense, slightly less rigid, than last time. The owner was along instead of Goldenberg and Kenny wasn't there to stir things up. No coup today, I thought. No coup to go wrong.

The flight up was easy and uneventful, homing to the radio beacon on the coast at Ottringham and tracking away from it on a radial to Redcar. We landed without fuss on the racecourse and the passengers yawned and unbuckled themselves.

'I wish every racecourse had a landing strip,' Colin sighed. 'It makes the whole day so much easier. I hate all those dashes from airport to course by taxi.'

The racecourses which catered for aeroplanes were in a minority, which seemed a shame considering there was room enough on most, if anyone cared enough. Harley constantly raved in frustration at having to land ten or fifteen miles away and fix up transportation for the passengers. All the conveniently placed R.A.F. airfields with superb runways who either refused to let private aircraft land at all, or shut their doors firmly at 5 p.m. weekdays and all day on Saturdays had him on the verge of tears. As also did all the airfields whose owners said they wouldn't take the responsibility of having an aircraft land there or take off if they didn't have a fire engine standing by, even though Harley's own insurance didn't require it.

'The English are as air-minded as earth worms,' Harley said.

On the other hand Honey had tacked a list to the office wall which started in big red letters 'God Bless ...' and continued with all the friendly and accommodating places like Kempton Park, which let you land up the five furlong straight (except during five furlong races) and R.A.F. stations like Wroughton and Leeming and Old Sarum, who really tried for you, and the airfields who could let you land when they were officially shut, and all the privately owned strips whose owners generously agreed to you using them any time you liked.

Harley's view of Heaven was an open public landing field outside every town and a windsock and a flat four furlongs on every racecourse. It wasn't much to ask, he said plaintively. Not in view of the dozens of enormous airfields which had been built during world war two and were now disused and wasted.

He could dream, I thought. There was never any money for such schemes, except in wars.

The passengers stretched themselves on the grass. Fenella Payne-Percival made little up and down jumps of excitement like a small girl, the Major patted his binocular case reassuringly, Annie Villars efficiently picked up her own belongings and directed a look of melting feminine helplessness towards the Duke, Colin looked at his watch and smiled, and the Duke himself glanced interestedly around and said, 'Nice day, what?'

A big man, he had a fine looking head with thick greying hair, eyebrows beginning to sprout, and a strong square jaw, but there wasn't enough living stamped on his face for a man in his fifties, and I remembered what Nancy had said of him: sweet as they come, but nothing but cottonwool upstairs.

Colin said to me, 'Are you coming into the paddock?'

I shook my head. 'Better stay with the aeroplane, this time.'

The Duke said, 'Won't you need some lunch, my dear chap?.

'It's kind of you, sir, but I often don't have any.'

'Really?' He smiled. 'Must have my lunch.'

Annie Villars said, we'll leave soon after the last. About a quarter to five.'

'Right,' I agreed.

'Doesn't give us time for a drink, Annie,' complained the Duke.

She swallowed her irritation. 'Any time after that, then.'

'I'll be here,' I said.

'Oh do come on,' said Fenella impatiently. 'The pilot can look after himself, can't he? Let's get going, do. Come on, Colin darling.' She twined her arm in his again and he all but squirmed. They moved away towards the paddock obediently, with only Colin looking back. I laughed at the desperation on his face and he stuck out his tongue.

There were three other aircraft parked in a row. One private, one from a Scottish taxi firm, and one Polyplane. All the pilots seemed to have gone in to the races, but when I climbed out half way through the afternoon to stretch my legs, I found the Polyplane pilot standing ten yards away, staring at the Cherokee with narrowed eyes and smoking a cigarette.

He was one of the two who had been at Haydock. He seemed surprised that I was there.

'Hello,' I said equably. Always a sucker.

He gave me the old hard stare. 'Taking no chances today, I see.'

I ignored the sneer in his voice. 'That's right.'

'We got rid of that aircraft,' he said sarcastically nodding towards it, 'Because we'd flown the guts out of it. It's only suitable now for minor operators like you.'

'It shows signs of the way you flew it,' I agreed politely: and that deadly insult did nothing towards cooling the feud.

He compressed his lips and flicked the end of his cigarette away into the grass. A thin trickle of blue smoke arose from among the tangled green blades. I watched it without comment. He knew as well as I did that smoking near parked aircraft was incredibly foolish, and on all airfields, forbidden.

He said, 'I'm surprised you take the risk of flying Colin Ross. If your firm are proved to be responsible for his death you'll be out of business.'

'He's not dead yet.'

'If I were him I wouldn't risk flying any more with Derrydowns.'

'Did he, by any chance,' I asked, 'Once fly with Polyplanes? Is all this sourness due to his having transferred to Derrydowns instead?'

He gave me a bitter stare. 'No.' he said.

I didn't believe him. He saw that I didn't. He turned on his heel and walked away.

Rudiments won the big race. The dim green colours streaked up the centre of the track at the last possible moment and pushed Colin on the favourite into second place. I could hear the boos all the way from the stands.

An hour until the end of racing. I yawned, leaned back in my seat, and went to sleep.

A young voice saying 'Excuse me,' several times, woke me up. I opened my eyes. He was about ten, slightly shy, ultra well bred. Squatting down on the wing, he spoke through the open door.

'I say, I'm sorry to wake you, but my uncle wanted me to come over and fetch you. He said you hadn't had anything to eat all day. He thinks you ought to. And besides, he's had a winner and he wants you to drink his health.'

'Your uncle is remarkably kind,' I said, 'But I can't leave the aeroplane.'

'Well, actually, he thought of that. I've brought my father's chauffeur over with me, and he is going to sit here for you until you come back.' He smiled with genuine satisfaction at these arrangements.

I looked past him out of the door, and there, sure enough, was the chauffeur, all togged up in dark green with a shining peak to his cap.

'O.K.,' I said. 'I'll get my jacket.'

He walked with me along the paddock, through the gate, and across to the Members' bar.

'Awfully nice chap, my uncle,' he said.

'Unusually thoughtful,' I agreed.

'Soft, my mother says,' he said dispassionately. 'He's her brother. They don't get along very well.'

'What a pity.'

'Oh, I don't know. If they were frightfully chummy she would always be wanting to come with me when I go to stay with him. As it is, I go on my own, and we have some fantastic times, him and me. That's how I know how super he is.' He paused. 'Lots of people think he's terribly thick, I don't know why.' There was a shade of anxiety in his young voice. 'He's really awfully kind.'

I reassured him. 'I only met him this morning, but I think he's very nice.'

His brow cleared. 'You do? Oh, good.'

The Duke was knee deep in cronies all armed with glasses of champagne. His nephew disappeared from my side, dived through the throng, and reappeared tugging at his uncle's arm.

'What?' The kind brown eyes looked round; saw me. 'Oh yes.' He bent down to talk, and presently the boy came back.

'Champagne or coffee?'

'Coffee, please.'

'I'll get it for you.'

'I'll get it,' I suggested.

'No. Let me. Do let me. Uncle gave me the money.' He marched off to the far end of the counter and ordered a cup of coffee and two rounds of smoked salmon sandwiches, and paid for them with a well crushed pound note.

'There,' he said triumphantly. 'How's that?'

'Fine,' I said. 'Terrific. Have a sandwich.'

'All right.'

We munched companionably.

'I say,' he said, 'Look at that man over there, he looks like a ghost.'

I turned my head. Big blond man with very pale skin. Pair of clumsy crutches. Large plaster cast. Acey Jones.

Not so noisy today. Drinking beer very quietly in a far corner with a nondescript friend.

'He fell down some steps and broke his ankle and collected a thousand pounds from an insurance policy,' I said.

'Golly,' said the boy. 'Almost worth it.'

'He think's so, too.'

'Uncle has something to do with insurance. Don't know what, though.'

'An underwriter?' I suggested.

'What's that?'

'Someone who invests money in insurance companies, in a special sort of way.'

'He talks about Lloyds, sometimes. Is it something to do with Lloyds?'

'That's right.'

He nodded and looked wistfully at the sandwiches.

'Have another,' I suggested.

'They're yours, really.'

'Go on. I'd like you to.'

He gave me a quick bright glance and bit into number two.

'My name's Matthew,' he said.

I laughed. 'So is mine.'

'Is it really? Do you really mean it?'

'Yes.'

'Wow.'

There was a step behind me and the deep Eton-sounding voice said, 'Is Matthew looking after you all right?'

'Great sir, thank you,' I said.

'His name is Matthew too,' said the boy.

The Duke looked from one of us to the other. 'A couple of Matts, eh? Don't let too many people wipe their feet on you.'

Matthew thought it a great joke but the touch of sadness in the voice was revealing. He was dimly aware that despite his ancestry and position, one or two sharper minds had wiped their feet on *him*.

I began to like the Duke.

'Well done with Rudiments, sir,' I said.

His face lit up. 'Splendid, wasn't it? Absolutely splendid. Nothing on earth gives me more pleasure than seeing my horses win.'

I went back to the Cherokee just before the last race and found the chauffeur safe and sound and reading Doctor Zhivago. He stretched, reported nothing doing, and ambled off.

All the same I checked the aircraft inch by inch inside and even unscrewed the panel to the aft baggage compartment so that I could see into the rear part of the fuselage, right back to the tail. Nothing there that shouldn't be. I screwed the panel on again.

Outside the aircraft, I started in the same way. Started only: because when I was examining every hinge in the tail plane I heard a shout from the next aircraft.

I looked round curiously but without much haste.

Against that side of the Polyplane which faced away from the stands, two large men were laying into Kenny Bayst.

Chapter Six

The pilot of the Polyplane was standing aside and watching. I reached him in six strides.

'For God's sake,' I said. 'Come and help him.'

He gave me a cold stolid stare. 'I've got my medical tomorrow. Do it yourself.'

In three more steps I caught one of the men by the fist as he lifted it high to smash into the crumpling Kenny, bent his arm savagely backwards and kicked him hard in the left hamstring. He fell over on his back with a shout of mixed anger, surprise, and pain, closely echoed in both emotion and volume by his colleague, who received the toe of my shoe very solidly at the base of his spine.

Bashing people was their sort of business, not mine, and Kenny hadn't enough strength left to stand up, let alone fight back, so that I got knocked about a bit here and there. But I imagined that they hadn't expected any serious opposition, and it must have been clear to them from the beginning that I didn't play their rules.

They had big fists all threateningly bunched and the hard round sort of toecaps which cowards hide behind. I kicked their knees with vigour, stuck my fingers out straight and hard towards their eyes, and chopped the sides of my palms at their throats.

I'd had enough of it before they had. Still, I outlasted them for determination, because I really did not want to fall down and have their boots bust my kidneys. They got tired in the end and limped away quite suddenly, as if called off by a whistle. They took with them some damaged knee cartilage aching larynxes, and one badly scratched eye; and they left behind a ringing head and a set of sore ribs.

I leaned against the aeroplane getting my breath back and looking down at Kenny where he sat on the grass. There was a good deal of blood on his face. His nose was bleeding, and he had tried to wipe it with the back of his hand.

I bent down presently and helped him up. He came to his feet without any of the terrible slowness of the severely injured and there was nothing wrong with his voice.

'Thanks, sport.' He squinted at me. 'Those sods said they were going to fix me so my riding days were over ... God ... I feel crook ... here, have you got any whisky ... aah ... Jesus ...' He bent double and vomited rakingly onto the turf.

Straightening up afterwards he dragged a large handkerchief out of his pocket and wiped his mouth, looking in dismay at the resulting red stains.

'I'm bleeding ...'

'It's your nose, that's all.'

'Oh ...' He coughed weakly. 'Look, sport, thanks. I guess thanks isn't enough ...' His gaze sharpened on the Polyplane pilot still standing aloof a little way off. 'That bastard didn't lift a finger ... they'd have crippled me and he wouldn't come ... I shouted.'

'He's got his medical tomorrow,' I said.

'Sod his bloody medical ...'

'If you don't pass your medical every six months, you get grounded. If you get grounded for long in the taxi business you lose either your whole job or at least half your income ...'

'Yeah,' he said. 'And your own medical, when does that come up?'

'Not for two months.'

He laughed a hollow, sick sounding laugh. Swallowed. Swayed. Looked suddenly very small and vulnerable.

'You'd better go over and see the doctor,' I suggested.

'Maybe ... but I've got the ride on Volume Ten on Monday ... big race ... opportunity if I do well of a better job than I've had with Annie Villars ... don't want to miss it ...' He smiled twistedly. 'Doesn't do jockeys any good to be grounded either, sport.'

'You're not in very good shape.'

'I'll be all right. Nothing broken ... except maybe my nose. That won't matter; done it before.' He coughed again. 'Hot bath. Spell in the sauna. Good as new by Monday. Thanks to you.'

'How about telling the police?'

'Yeah. Great idea.' He was sarcastic. 'Just imagine their sort of questions. "Why was anyone trying to cripple you, Mr Bayst?" "Well, officer, I'd promised to fiddle their races see, and this sod Goldenberg, I beg his pardon, gentleman, Mr Eric Goldenberg, sticks these two heavies on to me to get his own back for all the lolly he had to cough up when I won ..." "And why did you promise to fiddle the race Mr Bayst?" "Well officer I done it before you see and made a handy bit on the side ..."' He gave me a flickering glance and decided he'd said enough. 'Guess I'll see how it looks tomorrow. If I'm in shape to ride Monday I'll just forget it happened.'

'Suppose they try again?'

'No.' He shook his head a fraction. 'They don't do it twice.'

He picked himself off the side of the fuselage and looked at his reflection in the Polyplane's window, licked his handkerchief and wiped most of the blood off his face.

The nose had stopped bleeding. He felt it gingerly between thumb and forefinger.

'It isn't moving. Can't feel it grate. It did, when I broke it.'

Without the blood he looked pale under the red hair but not leaden. 'Guess I'll be all right. Think I'll get into the plane and sit down, though ... Came in it, see ...'

I helped him in. He sagged down weakly in his seat and didn't look like someone who would be fit to ride a racehorse in forty-six hours.

'Hey,' he said, 'I never asked you ... are you O.K. yourself?'

'Yes ... Look, I'll get your pilot to fetch you some whisky.'

His reaction showed how unsettled he still felt. 'That would be ... fair dinkum. He won't go though.'

'He will,' I said.

He did. British aviation was a small world. Everyone knew someone who knew someone else. News of certain sorts travelled slowly but surely outwards and tended to follow one around. He got the message. He also agreed to buy the whisky himself.

By the time he came back, bearing a full quarter bottle and a scowl, the last race was over and the passengers for all the aeroplanes were turning up in little groups. Kenny began to look less shaky, and when two other jockeys arrived with exclamations and consolations, I went back to the Cherokee.

Annie Villars was waiting, not noticeably elated by her win with Rudiments.

'I thought you said you were going to stay with the plane,' she said. Ice crackled in her voice.

'Didn't take my eyes off it.'

She snorted. I did a quick double check inside, just to be sure, but no one had stored anything aboard since my last search. The external check I did more slowly and more thoroughly. Still nothing.

The thumping I'd collected started to catch up. The ringing noise in my head was settling into a heavy ache. Various soggy areas on my upper arms were beginning to stiffen. My solar plexus and adjacent areas felt like Henry Cooper's opponents on the morning after.

'Did you know,' I said to Annie Villars conversationally, 'That two men just had a go at beating up Kenny Bayst?'

If she felt any compassion she controlled it admirably. 'Is he badly hurt?'

'An uncomfortable night should see him through.'

'Well then ... I dare say he deserved it.'

'What for?'

She gave me a direct stare. 'You aren't deaf.'

I shrugged: 'Kenny thinks Mr Goldenberg arranged it.'

She hadn't known it was going to happen. Didn't know whether Goldenberg was responsible or not. I saw her hesitating, summing the information up.

In the end she said vaguely, 'Kenny never could keep his tongue still,' and a minute later, under her breath, 'Stupid thing to do. Stupid man.'

Major Tyderman, the Duke of Wessex and Fenella Payne-in-the-neck arrived together, the Duke still talking happily about his winner.

'Where's Colin?' asked Fenella. 'Isn't he here after all? What a frantic nuisance. I asked for him at the weighing room and that man, who did he say he was? His valet, oh yes, of course . . . his valet, said that he had already gone to the plane.' She pouted, thrusting out her lower lip. There was champagne in her eyes and petulance in her voice. The gold bracelets jingled. The heavy scent didn't seem to have abated during the afternoon. I thought Colin had dodged very neatly. The Major also had been included in the celebrations. He looked slightly fuzzy round the eyes and a lot less rigid everywhere else. The hand that pushed at the wiry moustache looked almost gentle. The chin was still tucked well back into the neck, but there was nothing aggressive any more: it seemed suddenly only the mannerism of one who used suspiciousness instead of understanding to give himself a reputation for shrewdness.

The Duke asked the Major if he minded changing places on the way home so that he, the Duke, could sit in front. 'I like to see the dials go round,' he explained.

The Major, full of ducal champagne, gracefully agreed. He and Fenella climbed aboard and I waited outside with the Duke.

'Is there anything the matter, my dear chap?' he said.

'No, sir.'

He studied me slowly. 'There is, you know.'

I put my fingers on my forehead and felt the sweat. 'It's a hot day,' I said.

Colin came eventually. He too was sweating: his now crumpled open shirt had great dark patches under the arms. He had ridden five races. He looked thin and exhausted.

'Are you all right?' he said abruptly.

'I *knew*,' said the Duke.

'Yes, thank you.'

Colin looked back to where the Polyplane still waited on the ground.

'Is Kenny bad?'

'A bit sore. He didn't want anyone to know.'

'One of the jockeys with him on the trip came back over and told us. Kenny said you saved him from a fate worse than death, or words to that effect.'

'What?' said the Duke.

Colin explained. They looked at me suspiciously.

'I'm fit to fly, if that's what's worrying you.'

Colin made a face. 'Yeah, boy, it sure is.' He grinned, took a deep breath, and dived into the back with the tentacly Fenella. The Duke folded himself after me into the front seats and we set off.

There was thick cloud over the Humber at Ottringham and all the way south to Cambridge. As he could see just about as far forward as the propeller, the Duke asked me what guarantee there was that we wouldn't collide with another aircraft.

There wasn't any guarantee. Just probability.

'The sky is huge,' I said. 'And there are strict rules for flying in clouds. Collisions practically never happen.'

His hands visibly relaxed. He shifted into a more comfortable position. 'How do you know where we are?' he asked.

'Radio,' I said. 'Radio beams from transmitters on the ground. As long as that needle on the dial points centrally downwards, we are going straight to Ottringham, where the signal is coming from.'

'Fascinating,' he said.

The replacement Cherokee had none of the sophistication of the one which had been blown up. That had had an instrument which locked the steering on to the radio beam and took the aircraft automatically to the transmitter. After the attentions of Kenny Bayst's assailants I regretted not having it around.

'How will we know when we get to Cambridge?' asked the Duke.

'The needle on that other dial down there will swing from pointing straight up and point straight down. That will mean we have passed over the top of the transmitter at Cambridge.'

'Wonderful what they think of,' said the Duke.

The needles came up trumps. We let down through the cloud over Cambridge into an overcast, angry looking afternoon and landed on the shower soaked tarmac. I taxied them over close to the buildings, shut down the engine, and took off my head set, which felt a ton heavier than usual.

'Wouldn't have missed it,' said the Duke. 'Always motored everywhere before, you know.' He unfastened his safety belt. 'Annie persuaded me to try flying. Just once, she said. But I'll be coming with you again, my dear chap.'

'That's great, sir.'

He looked at me closely, kindly. 'You want to go straight to bed when you get home, Matthew. Get your wife to tuck you up nice and warm, eh?'

'Yes,' I said.

'Good, good.' He nodded his fine head and began to heave himself cumbersomely out of the door and on to the wing. 'You made a great hit with my nephew, my dear chap. And I respect Matt's opinion. He can spot good'uns and bad'uns a mile off.'

'He's a nice boy,' I said.

The Duke smiled happily. 'He's my heir.'

He stepped down from the wing and went round to help Annie Villars put on her coat. No doubt I should have been doing it. I sat with my belt still fastened, feeling too rough to be bothered to move. I didn't relish the thought of the final hop back to Buckingham, up into the clouds again and with no easy well-placed transmitter to help me down at the other end. I'd have to go round the Luton complex ... could probably get a steer home from there, from the twenty-four hour radar....

I ached. I thought of the caravan. Cold little harbour.

The passengers collected their gear, shut the rear door, waved and walked off towards the buildings. I looked at the map, picked out a heading, planned the return journey in terms of time and the cross references I'd need to tell me when I'd got to Buckingham, if the radar should be out of service. After that I sat and stared at the flight plan and told myself to get on with it. After that I rested my head on my hand and shut my eyes.

Ridiculous wasting time, I thought. Cambridge airport charged extra for every minute they stayed open after six o'clock, and the passengers were already committed to paying for more than an hour. Every moment I lingered cost them more still.

There was a tap on the window beside me. I raised my head more quickly than proved wise. Colin Ross was standing there, watching me with a gleam of humour. I twisted the catch and opened the window flap on its hinge.

'Fit to fly, didn't you say?' he said.

'That was two hours ago.'

'Ah yes. Makes a difference.' He smiled faintly. 'I just wondered, if you don't feel like going on, whether you'd care to let me take you home for the night? Then, you can finish the trip tomorrow. It might be a fine day, tomorrow.'

He had flown a great deal and understood the difficulties. All the same, I was surprised he had troubled to come back.

'It might,' I agreed. 'But I could stay in Cambridge ...'

'Get out of there and fix the hangarage,' he said calmly.

'I'll have to check with Derrydowns ...'

'Check, then.'

I climbed too slowly out of the aeroplane and struggled into my jacket. We walked together across into the building.

'Call your wife, too,' he said.

'Haven't got one.'

'Oh.' He looked at me with speculative curiosity.

'No,' I said. 'Not that. Married twelve years, divorced three.'

Humour crinkled the skin round his eyes. 'Better than me,' he said. 'Married two years, divorced four.'

Harley answered at the first ring.

'Where are you? Cambridge? ... No, come back now, if you stay at Cambridge we'll have to pay the hangarage.' I hadn't told him about the fight, about the way I felt.

'I'll pay it,' I said. 'You can deduct it from my salary. Colin Ross has asked me to stay with him.' That would clinch it. Harley saw the importance of pleasing, and Colin Ross was his best customer.

'Oh ... that's different. All right then. Come back in the morning.'

I went into the Control office and arranged for the aircraft to be stowed under cover for the night, one last overtime job for the staff before they all went home. After that I sank into the Ross Aston Martin and let the world take care of itself.

He lived in an ordinary looking brick built bungalow on the outskirts of Newmarket. Inside, it was colourful and warm, with a large sitting-room stocked with deep luxurious velvet upholstered armchairs.

'Sit down,' he said.

I did. Put my head back. Shut my eyes.

'Whisky or brandy?' he asked.

'Whichever you like.'

I heard him pouring. It sounded like a tumblerful.

'Here,' he said.

I opened my eyes and gratefully took the glass. It was brandy and water. It did a grand job.

There were sounds of pans from the kitchen and a warm smell of roasting chicken. Colin's nose twitched.

'Dinner will be ready soon ... I'll go and tell the cooks there will be one extra.'

He went out of the room and came back almost immediately with his two cooks.

I stood up slowly. I hadn't given it a thought; was quite unprepared.

They looked at first sight like two halves of one whole: Nancy and Midge. Same dark hair, tied high on the crown with black velvet bows. Same dark eyes, straight eyebrows, spontaneous smiles.

'The bird man himself,' Nancy said. 'Colin, how did you snare him?'

'Potted a sitting duck ...'

'This is Midge,' she said. 'Midge ... Matt.'

'Hi,' she said. 'The bomb man, aren't you?'

When you looked closer, you could see. She was thinner than Nancy, and much paler, and she seemed fragile where Nancy was strong: but without the mirror comparison with her sister there was no impression of her being ill.

'First and last bomb, I hope,' I said.

She shivered. 'A lot too ruddy close.'

Colin poured each of them a Dubonnet and took whisky for himself. 'Bombs, battles ... some introduction you've had to racing.'

'An eventful change from crop spraying.' I agreed.

'Is that a dull job?' Midge asked, surprised.

'Dull and dangerous. You get bored to death trudging up and down some vast field for six hours a day ... It's all low flying, you see, so you have to be wide awake, and after a while you start yawning. One day maybe you get careless and touch the ground with your wing in a turn, and you write off an expensive machine, which is apt to be unpopular with the boss.'

Nancy laughed. 'Is that what you did?'

'No . . . I went to sleep for a second in the air one day and woke up twenty feet from a pylon. Missed it by millimetres. So I quit while everything was still in one piece.'

'Never mind,' Midge said. 'The next plane you touched disintegrated beautifully.'

They laughed together, a united family, close.

Colin told them about Kenny Bayst's fracas and they exclaimed sympathetically, which made me feel a humbug: Colin habitually drove himself to exhaustion and Midge was irretrievably afflicted, and all I had were a few minor bruises.

Dinner consisted simply of the hot roast chicken and a tossed green salad, with thick wedges of cheese afterwards. We ate in the kitchen with our elbows on the scarlet table, and chewed the bones. I hadn't passed a more basically satisfying evening for many a long weary year.

'What are you thinking?' Nancy demanded. 'At this moment?'

'Making a note to fall frequently sick at Cambridge.'

'Well,' said Midge. 'Don't bother. Just come any time.' She looked enquiringly at her sister and brother and they nodded. 'Just come,' she repeated. 'Whenever it's handy.'

The old inner warning raised its urgent head: don't get involved, don't feel anything, don't risk it.

Don't get involved.

I said, 'Nothing I'd like better,' and didn't know whether I meant it or not.

The two girls stacked the plates in a dishwasher and made coffee. Nancy poured cream carefully across the top of her cup.

'Do you think that bomb was really intended for Colin?' she asked suddenly.

I shrugged. 'I don't know. It could just as well have been intended for Major Tyderman or Annie villars or Goldenberg, or even Kenny Bayst, really, because it must have been on board before he decided not to come. Or it might have been intended for putting the firm out of action . . . for Derrydowns, itself, if you see what I mean, because if Colin had been killed, Derrydowns would probably have gone bust.'

'I can't see why anyone would want to kill Colin,' Midge said. 'Sure, people are jealous of him, but jealousy is one thing and killing five people is another . . .'

'Everyone seems to be taking it so calmly,' Nancy suddenly exploded. 'Here is this bloody bomb merchant running around loose with no one knowing just what he'll do next, and no one seems to be trying to find him and lock him up.'

'I don't see how they can find him,' Colin said. 'And anyway, I don't suppose he will risk trying it again.'

'Oh you . . . you . . . *ostrich*,' she said bitterly. 'Doesn't it occur to you that you don't just lightly put a bomb in an aeroplane? Whoever did it must have had an overwhelming reason, however mad it was, and since the whole thing went wrong they still have the same motive rotting away inside them, and what do you think Midge and I will do if next time you get blown to bits?.

I saw Midge looking at her with compassion and understood the extent of Nancy's fear. One day she was certainly going to lose her sister. She couldn't face losing her brother as well.

'It won't happen,' he said calmly.

They looked at him, and at me. There was a long, long pause. Then Midge picked up the wishbone of the chicken and held it out for me to pull. It snapped with the biggest side in her fist.

'I wish,' she said seriously, 'That Colin would stop cutting his toenails in the bath.'

Chapter Seven

I slept on a divan bed in Colin's study, a small room crammed with racing trophies, filing cabinets and form books. Every wall was lined with rows of framed photographs of horses passing winning posts and owners proudly leading them in. Their hooves thudded through my head most of the night, but all was peace by morning.

Colin brought me a cup of tea, yawning in his dark woolly bathrobe. He put the cup down on the small table beside the divan and pulled back the curtains.

'It's drizzling cats and dogs,' he announced. 'There's no chance of you flying this morning so you may as well relax and go back to sleep.'

I looked out at the misty rain. Didn't mind a bit.

'It's my day off,' I said.

'Couldn't be better.'

He perched his bottom on the edge of the desk.

'Are you O.K. this morning?'

'Fine,' I said. 'That hot bath loosened things a lot.'

'Every time you moved yesterday evening you could see it hurt.'

I made a face. 'Sorry.'

'Don't be. In this house you say ouch.'

'So I've noticed,' I said dryly.

He grinned. 'Everyone lives on a precipice. All the time. And Midge keeps telling me and Nancy that if we're not careful she'll outlive us both.'

'She's marvellous.'

'Yes, she is.' He looked out of the window. 'It was a terrible shock at first. Terrible. But now ... I don't know ... we seem to have accepted it. All of us. Even her.'

I said hesitantly, 'How long ...?'

'How long will she live? No one knows. It varies so much, apparently. She's had it, they think, for about three years now. It seems a lot of people have it for about a year before it becomes noticeable enough to be diagnosed, so no one knows when it started with Midge. Some people die within days of getting it. Some have lived for twenty years. Nowadays, with all the modern treatments, they say the average after diagnosis is from two to six years, but it will possibly be ten. We've had two ... We just believe it will be ten ... and that makes it much easier ...'

'She doesn't look especially ill.'

'Not at the moment. She had pneumonia a short while ago and the odd thing about that is that it reverses leukaemia for a while. Any fever does it, apparently. Actually makes her better. So do doses of radiation on her arms and legs, and other bones and organs. She's had several relapses and several good long spells of being well. It just goes on like that ... but her blood is different, and her bones are changing inside all the time ... I've seen pictures of what is happening ... and one day ... well, one day she'll have a sort of extreme relapse, and she won't recover.'

'Poor Midge ...'

'Poor all of us.'

'What about ... Nancy? Being her twin ...'

'Do identical bodies get identical blood diseases, do you mean?' He looked at me across the room, his eyes in shadow. 'There's that too. They say the chances are infinitesimal. They say there are only eighteen known cases of leukaemia occurring twice in the same family unit. You can't catch it, and you can't inherit it. A girl with leukaemia can have a baby, and the baby won't have leukaemia. You can transfuse blood from someone with leukaemia into someone without it, and he won't catch it. They say there's no reason why Nancy should develop it any more than me or you or the postman. But they don't *know*. The books don't record any cases of an identical twin having it, or what became of the other one.' He paused. Swallowed, 'I think we are all more afraid of Nancy getting it too than of anything on earth.'

I stayed until the sky cleared up at five o'clock. Colin spent most of the day working out which races he wanted to ride in during the coming week and answering telephone calls from owners and trainers anxious to engage him. Principally he rode for a stable half a mile down the road, he said, but the terms of his retainer there gave him a good deal of choice.

He worked at a large chart with seven columns, one for each day of the week. Under each day he listed the various meetings, and under each meeting he listed the names, prizes and distances of the races. Towards the end of the afternoon there was a horse's name against a fair proportion of races, especially, I noticed, those with the highest rewards.

He grinned at my interest. 'A business is a business,' he said.

'So I see. A study in time and motion.'

On three of the days he proposed to ride at two meetings.

'Can you get me from Brighton to Windsor fast enough for two races an hour and a half apart? Three o'clock race at Brighton. Four-thirty, Windsor. And on Saturday, three o'clock race at Bath, four-thirty at Brighton?'

'With fast cars both ends, don't see why not.'

'Good.' He crossed out a couple of question marks and wrote ticks instead. 'And next Sunday, can you take me to France?'

'If Harley says so.'

'Harley will say so,' he said with certainty.

'Don't you ever take a day off?'

He raised his eyebrows in surprise. 'Today,' he said, 'is off. Hadn't you noticed?'

'Er ... yes.'

'The horse I was going over to ride today went lame on Thursday. Otherwise I was going to Paris. B.E.A., though, for once.'

Nancy said with mock resignation, 'The dynamo whirs nonstop from March to November in England and Europe and then goes whizzing off to Japan and so on, and around about February there might be a day or two when we can all flop back in armchairs and put our feet up.'

Midge said, 'We put them up in the Bahamas last time. It was gorgeous. All that hot sun ...'

The others laughed. 'It rained the whole of the first week.'

The girls cooked steaks for lunch. 'In your honour,' Midge said to me. 'You're too thin.'

I was fatter than any of them; which wasn't saying much.

Midge cleared the things away afterwards and Nancy covered the kitchen table with maps and charts.

'I really am flying Colin to the races one day soon, and I wondered if you'd help ...'

'Of course.'

She bent over the table, the long dark hair swinging down over her neck. Don't get involved, I said to myself. Just don't.

'Next week, to Haydock. If the weather's good enough.'

'She's doing you out of a job,' Midge observed, wiping glasses.

'Wait till it thunders.'

'Beast,' Nancy said.

She had drawn a line on the map. She wanted me to tell her how to proceed in the Manchester control zone, and what to do if they gave her istructions she didn't understand.

'Ask them to repeat them. If you still don't understand, ask them to clarify.'

'They'll think I'm stupid,' she protested.

'Better that than barging on regardless and crashing into an airliner.'

'O.K.,' she sighed. 'Point taken.'

'Colin deserves a medal,' Midge said.

'Just shut up,' Nancy said. 'You're all bloody rude.'

When the drizzle stopped they all three took me back to Cambridge, squashing into the Aston Martin. Midge drove, obviously enjoying it. Nancy sat half on Colin and half on me, and I sat half on the door handle.

They stood in a row, and waved when I took off. I rolled the wings in salute and set course for Buckingham, and tried to ignore the regret I felt to be leaving.

Honey was up in the control tower at Derrydowns, Sunday or no Sunday, and Harley was aloft in the trainer giving someone a lesson. When he heard me on the radio he said snappily 'And about time to,' and I remembered the dimensions of my bank balance and didn't snap back. Chanter, I thought wryly, would have plain despised me.

I left the Cherokee Six in the hangar and walked round to the caravan. It seemed emptier, more sordid, more dilapidated than before. The windows all needed cleaning. The bed wasn't made. Yesterday's milk had gone sour again, and there was still no food.

I sat for a while watching the evening sun struggle through the breaking clouds, watching Harley's pupil stagger through some ropy landings, wondering how long it would be before Derrydowns went broke, and wondering if I could save enough before that happened to buy a car. Harley was paying me forty-five pounds a week, which was more than he could afford and less than I was worth. Of that, Susan, taxes and insurance would be taking exactly half, and with Harley deducting four more for my rent it wasn't going to be easy.

Impatiently I got up and cleaned all the windows, which improved my view of the airfield but not of the future.

When the light began to fade I had a visitor. A ripe shapely girl in the minimum of green cotton dress. Long fair hair. Long legs. Large mouth. Slightly protruding teeth. She walked with a man-eating sway and spoke with the faintest of lisps.

Honey Harley, come down from her tower.

She knocked on her way in. All the same if I'd been naked. As it was, I had my shirt off from the window cleaning and for Honey, it seemed, that was invitation enough. She came over holding out a paper in one hand and putting the other lightly on my shoulder. She let it slide down against my skin to half way down my back and then brought it up again to the top.

'Uncle and I were making out the list for the next week. We wondered if you fixed anything up with Colin Ross.'

I moved gently away, picked up a nylon sweater, and put it on.

'Yes ... he wants us Tuesday, Friday, Saturday and Sunday.'

'Great.'

She followed me across the small space. One step further backwards and I'd be in my bedroom. Internally I tried to stifle a laugh. I stepped casually round her, back towards the door. Her face showed nothing but businesslike calm.

'Look,' she said, 'Monday, that's tomorrow, then, you collect a businessman at Coventry, take him to Rotterdam, wait for him, and bring him back. That's in the Aztec. Tuesday, Colin Ross. Wednesday, nothing yet. Thursday, probably a trainer in Lambourn wanting to look at a horse for sale in Yorkshire, he'll let us know, and then Colin Ross again all the end of the week.'

'O.K.'

'And the Board of Trade want to come out and see you again. I told them early Tuesday or Wednesday.'

'All right.' As usual, the automatic sinking of the heart even at the words Board of Trade: though this time, surely, surely, my responsibility was a technicality. This time, surely, I couldn't get ground to bits.

Honey sat down on the two seat sofa and crossed her legs. She smiled.

'We haven't seen much of each other yet, have we?'

'No,' I said.

'Can I have a cigarette?'

'I'm sorry ... I don't smoke ... I haven't any.'

'Oh. Well, give me a drink, then.'

'Look, I really am sorry ... all I can offer you is black coffee ... or water.'

'Surely you've got some beer?'

'Afraid not.'

She stared at me. Then she stood up, went into the tiny kitchen, and opened all the cupboards. I thought it was because she thought I was lying. but I'd done her an injustice. Sex minded she might be, but no fool.

'You've no car, have you? And the shops and the pub are nearly two miles away.' She came back frowning, and sat down again. 'Why didn't you ask someone to give you a lift?'

'Didn't want to be a bother.'

She considered it. 'You've been here three weeks and you don't get paid until the end of the month. So ... have you any money?'

'Enough not to starve,' I said. 'But thanks all the same.'

I'd sent ten pounds to Susan and told her she'd have to wait for the rest until I got my pay cheque. She'd written back short and to the point. Two months, by then, don't forget. As if I could. I had under four pounds left in the world and too much pride.

'Uncle would give you an advance.'

'I wouldn't like to ask him.'

A small smile lifted the corners of her mouth. 'No, I can see that, as he's so intent on slapping you down.'

'Is he?'

'Don't pretend to be surprised. You know he is. You give him a frightful inferiority complex and he's getting back at you for it.'

'It's silly.'

'Oh sure. But you are the two things he longs to be and isn't, a top class pilot and an attractive man. He needs you badly for the business, but he doesn't have to like it. And don't tell me you didn't know all that, because it's been obvious all along that you understand, otherwise you would have lost your temper with him every day at the treatment he's been handing out.'

'You see a lot from your tower,' I said smiling.

'Sure. And I'm very fond of my uncle. And I love this little business, and I'd do anything to keep us afloat.' She said it with intense feeling. I wondered whether 'anything' meant sleeping with the pilots, or whether that came under the heading of pleasure, not profit. I didn't intend to find out. Not getting involved included Honey, in the biggest possible way.

I said, 'It must have been a blow to the business, losing that new Cherokee.'

She pursed her mouth and put her head on one side. 'Not altogether. In fact, absolutely the reverse. We had too much capital tied up in it. We had to put down a lump sum to start with, and the H.P. instalments were pretty steep ... I should think when everything's settled, and we get the insurance, we will have about five thousand pounds back, and with that much to shore us up we can keep going until times get better.'

'If the aircraft hadn't blown up, would you have been able to keep up with the H.P.?'

She stood up abruptly, seeming to think that she had already said too much. 'Let's just leave it that things are all right as they are.'

The daylight was fading fast. She came and stood close beside me, not quite touching.

'You don't smoke, you don't eat, you don't drink,' she said softly. 'What else don't you do?'

'That too.'

'Not ever?'

'Not now. Not here.'

'I'd give you a good time.' ...

'Honey ... I just ... don't want to.'

She wasn't angry. Not even hurt. 'You're cold,' she said judiciously. 'An iceberg.'

'Perhaps.'

'You'll thaw,' she said. 'One of these days.'

The Board of Trade had sent the same two men, the tall one and the silent one, complete with notebook and bitten green pencil. As before, I sat with them in the crew room and offered them coffee from the slot machine in the pasengers' lounge. They accepted, and I went and fetched three plastic cupfuls. The staff as well as the customers had to buy their coffee or whatever from the machine. Honey kept it well stocked. It made a profit.

Outside on the airfield my part-time colleague, Ron, was showing a new pupil how to do the external checks. They crept round the trainer inch by inch. Ron talked briskly. The pupil, a middle-aged man, nodded as if he understood.

The tall man was saying in effect that they had got nowhere with the bomb.

'The police have been happy to leave the investigation with us, but frankly in these cases it is almost impossible to find the identity of the perpetrator. Of course if someone on board is a major political figure, or a controversial agitator ... Or if there is a great sum of personal insurance involved ... But in this case there is nothing like that.'

'Isn't Colin Ross insured?' I asked.

'Yes, but he has no new policy, or anything exceptional. And the beneficiaries are his twin sisters. I cannot believe ...'

'Impossible' I said with conviction.

'Quite so.'

'How about the others?'

He shook his head. 'They all said, in fact, that they ought to be better insured than they were.' He coughed discreetly. 'There is, of course, the matter of yourself.'

'What do you mean?'

His sharp eyes stared at me unblinkingly.

'Several years ago you took out a policy for the absolute benefit of your wife. Although she is now your ex-wife, she would still be the beneficiary. You can't change that sort of policy.'

'Who told you all this?'

'She did,' he said. 'We went to see her in the course of our enquiries.' He paused. 'She didn't speak kindly of you.'

I compressed my mouth. 'No. I can imagine. Still, I'm worth more to her alive than dead. She'll want me to live as long as possible.'

'And if she wanted to get married again? Your alimony payments would stop then, and a lump sum from insurance might be welcome.'

I shook my head. 'She might have killed me in a fury three years ago, but not now, cold bloodedly, with other people involved. It isn't in her nature. And besides, she doesn't know anything about bombs and she had no opportunity ... You'll have to cross out that theory too.'

She has been going out occasionally with an executive from a firm specialising in demolitions.'

He kept his voice dead even, but he had clearly expected more reaction than he got. I wasn't horrified or even much taken aback.

'She wouldn't do it. Or put anyone else up to doing it. Ordinarily, she was too ... too kind hearted. Too sensible, anyway. She used to be so angry whenever innocent passengers were blown up ... she would never do it herself, Never.'

He watched me for a while in the special Board of Trade brand of unnerving silence. I didn't see what I could add. Didn't know what he was after.

Outside on the airfield the trainer started up and taxied away. The engine noise faded. It was very quiet. I sat. I waited.

Finally he stirred. 'All in all, for all our trouble, we have come up with only one probability. And even that gets us no nearer knowing who the bomb was intended for, or who put it on board.'

He put his hand in his inner pocket and brought out a stiff brown envelope. Out of that he shook onto the crew room table a twisted piece of metal. I picked it up and looked at it. Beyond the impression that it had once been round and flat, like a button, it meant nothing.

'What is it?'

'The remains,' he said, 'of an amplifier.'

I looked up, puzzled. 'Out of the radio?'

'We don't think so.' He chewed his lip. 'We think it was in the bomb. We found it embedded in what had been the tailplane.'

'Do you mean ... it wasn't a time bomb after all?'

'Well ... probably not. It looks as if it was exploded by a radio transmission. Which puts, do you see, a different slant on things.'

'What difference? I don't know much about bombs. How does a radio bomb differ from a time bomb?'

'They can differ a lot, though in many the actual explosive is the same. In those cases it's just the trigger mechanism that's different.' He paused. 'Well, say you have a quantity of plastic explosive. Unfortunately that's all too easy to get hold of, nowadays. In fact, if you happen to be in Greece, you can go into any hardware shop and buy it over the counter. On its own, it won't explode. It needs a detonator. Gunpowder, old-fashioned gunpowder, is the best. You also need something to ignite the gunpowder before it will detonate the plastic. Are you with me?'

'Faint but pursuing,' I said.

'Right. The easiest way to ignite gunpowder, from a distance, that is, is to pack it round a thin filament of fuse wire. Then you pass an electric current through the filament. It becomes red hot, ignites the gunpowder ...'

'And boom, you have no Cherokee Six.'

'Er, yes. Now, in this type of bomb you have a battery, a high voltage battery about the size of a sixpence, to provide the electric current. The filament will heat up if you bend it round and fasten one end to one terminal of the battery, and the other to the other.'

'Clear,' I said. 'And the bomb goes off immediately.'

He raised his eyes to Heaven. 'Why did I ever start this? Yes, it would go off immediately. So it is necessary to have a mechanism that will complete the circuit after the manufacturer is safely out of the way.'

'By a spring?' I suggested.

'Yes. You hold the circuit open by a hair spring on a catch. When the catch is removed, the spring snaps the circuit shut, and that's that. Right? Now, the catch can be released by a time mechanism like an ordinary alarm clock. Or it can be released by a radio signal from a distance, via a receiver, an amplifier and a solenoid, like mechanisms in a space craft.'

'What is a solenoid, exactly?'

'A sort of electric magnet, a coil with a rod in the centre. The rod moves up and down inside the coil, when a pulse is passed through the coil. Say the top of the rod is sticking up out of the coil to form the catch on the spring, when the rod moves down into the coil the spring is released.'

I considered it. 'What is there to stop someone detonating the bomb by accident, by unknowingly transmitting on the right frequency? The air is packed with radio waves ... surely radio bombs are impossibly risky?'

He cleared his throat. 'It is possible to make a combination type release mechanism. One could make a bomb in which, say, three radio signals had to be received in the correct order before the circuit could be completed. For such a release mechanism, you would need three separate sets of receivers, amplifiers and solenoids to complete the circuit ... We were exceptionally fortunate to find this amplifier. We doubt if it was the only one ...'

'It sounds much more complicated that the alarm clock.'

'Oh yes, it is. But also more flexible. You are not committed to a time in advance to set if off.'

'So no one had to know what time we would be leaving Haydock. They would just have to see us go.'

'Yes ... Or be told you had gone.'

I thought a bit. 'It does put a different slant, doesn't it?'

'I'd appreciate your thinking.'

'You must be thinking the same,' I protested. 'If the bomb could be set off at any hour, any day, any week even, it could have been put in the aircraft at any time after the last maintenance check.'

He smiled thinly. 'And that would let you half way off the hook?'

'Half way,' I agreed.

'But only half.'

'Yes.'

He sighed. 'I've sprung this on you. I'd like you to think it over, from every angle. Seriously. Then tell me if anything occurs to you. If you care at all to find out what happened, that is, and maybe prevent it happening again.'

'You think I don't care?'

'I got the impression.'

'I would care now,' I said slowly, 'If Colin Ross were blown up.'

He smiled. 'You are less on your guard, today.'

'You aren't sniping at me from behind the bushes.'

'No ...' He was surprised. 'You're very observant, aren't you?'

'More a matter of atmosphere.'

He hesitated. 'I have now read the whole of the transcript of your trial.'

'Oh.' I could feel my face go bleak. He watched me.

'Did you know,' he said. 'That someone had added to the bottom of it in pencil a highly libellous statement?'

'No.' I said. Waited for it.

'It says that the Chairman of Interport is of the undoubtedly correct opinion that the First Officer lied on oath throughout, and that it was because of the First Officer's own gross negligence, not that of Captain Shore, that the airliner strayed so dangerously off course.'

Surprised, shaken, I looked away from him, out of the window, feeling absurdly vindicated and released. If that postscript was there for anyone who read the transcript to see, then maybe my name hadn't quite so much mud on it as I'd thought. Not where it mattered anyway.

I said without heat, 'The Captain is always responsible. Whoever does what.'

'Yes.'

A silence lengthened. I brought my thoughts back from four years ago and my gaze from the empty airfield.

'Thank you.' I said.

He smiled very slightly. 'I wondered why you hadn't lost your licence ... or your job. It didn't make sense to me that you hadn't. That's why I read the transcript, to see if there was any reason.'

'You're very thorough.'

'I like to be.'

'Interport knew one of us was lying ... we both said the other had put the ship in danger ... but I was the Captain. It inevitably came back to me. It was, in fact, my fault.'

'He wilfully disobeyed your instructions ...'

'And I didn't find out until it was nearly too late.'

'Quite ... but he need not have lied about it.'

'He was frightened,' I sighed. 'Of what would happen to his career.'

He let half a minute slip by without comment. Then he cleared his throat and said 'I suppose you wouldn't like to tell me why you left the South American people?'

I admired his delicate approach. 'Gap in the dossier?' I suggested.

His mouth twitched. 'Well, yes.' A pause. 'You are of course not obliged ...'

'No' I said. 'Still ...' Something for something. 'I refused to take off one day because I didn't think it was safe. They got another pilot who said it was. So he took off, and nothing happened. And they sacked me. that's all.'

'But,' he said blankly, 'It's a Captain's absolute right not to take off if he thinks it's unsafe.'

'There's no B.A.L.P.A. to uphold your rights there, you know. They said they couldn't afford to lose custom to other airlines because their Captains were cowards. Or words to that effect.'

'Good gracious.'

I smiled. 'Probably the Interport business accounted for my refusal to take risks.'

'But then you went to Africa and took them,' he protested.

'Well ... I needed money badly, and the pay was fantastic. And you don't have the same moral obligation to food and medical supplies as to airline passengers.'

'But the refugees and wounded, coming out?'

'Always easier flying out than in. No difficulties finding the home base, not like groping for some jungle clearing on a black night.'

He shook his head wonderingly, giving me up as a bad job.

'What brought you back here to something as dull as crop spraying?'

I laughed. Never thought I could laugh in front of the Board of Trade. 'The particular war I was flying in ended. I was offered another one a bit further south, but I suppose I'd had enough of it. Also I was nearly solvent again. So I came back here, and crop spraying was the first thing handy.'

'What you might call a chequered career,' he commented.

'Mild compared with some.'

'Ah yes. That's true.' He stood up and threw his empty coffee beaker into the biscuit tin which served as a waste paper basket. 'Right then ... You'll give a bit of thought to this bomb business?'

'Yes.'

'We'll be in touch with you again.' He fished in an inner pocket and produced a card. 'If you should want me, though, you can find me at this number.'

'O.K.'

He made a wry face. 'I know how you must feel about us.'

'Never mind,' I said. 'Never mind.'

Chapter Eight

For most of that week I flew where I was told to, and thought about radio bombs, and sat on my own in the caravan in the evenings.

Honey didn't come back, but on the day after her visit I had returned from Rotterdam to find a large bag of groceries on the table: eggs, butter, bread, tomatoes, sugar, cheese, powdered milk, tins of soup. Also a pack of six half pints of beer. Also a note from Honey: 'Pay me next week.'

Not a bad guy, Honey Harley. I took up eating again. Old habits die hard.

Tuesday I took Colin and four assorted others to Wolverhampton races, Wednesday, after the Board of Trade departed, I took a politician to Cardiff to a Union strike meeting, and Thursday I took the racehorse trainer to various places in Yorkshire and Northumberland to look at some horses to see if he wanted to buy any.

Thursday evening I made myself a cheese and tomato sandwich and a cup of coffee, and ate them looking at the pin-ups, which were curling a bit round the edges. After I'd finished the sandwich I unstuck the sellotape and took all the bosomy ladies down. The thrusting pairs of heavily ringed nipples regarded me sorrowfully, like spaniels' eyes. Smiling, I folded them decently over and dropped them in the rubbish bin. The caravan looked just as dingy, however, without them.

Friday morning, when I was in Harley's office filing flight records, Colin rang Harley and said he wanted me to stay overnight at Cambridge, ready again for Saturday.

Harley agreed. 'I'll charge Matt's hotel bill to your account.'

Colin said 'Fine. But he can stay with me again if he likes.'

Harley relayed the message. Did I like? I liked.

Harley put down the receiver. 'Trying to save money,' he said disparagingly, 'Having you to stay.' He brightened: 'I'll charge him the hangarage, though.'

I took the Cherokee over to Cambridge and fixed for them to give it shelter that night. When Colin came he was with four other jockeys: three I didn't know, and Kenny Bayst. Kenny said how was I. I was fine, how was he? Good as new, been riding since Newbury, he said.

Between them they had worked out the day's shuttle. All to Brighton, Colin to White Waltham for Windsor, aeroplane to return to Brighton, pick up the others, return to White Waltham, return to Cambridge.

'Is that all right?' Colin asked.

'Sure. Anything you say.'

He laughed. 'The fusses we used to have when we used to ask this sort of thing ...'

'Don't see why' I said.

'Larry was a lazy sod ...'

They loaded themselves on board and we tracked down east of the London control zone and over the top of Gatwick to Shoreham airport for Brighton. When we landed Colin looked at his watch and Kenny nodded and said, 'Yeah, he's always faster than Larry. I've noticed it too.'

'Harley will give him the sack,' Colin said dryly, unfastening his seatbelt.

'He won't, will he?' Kenny sounded faintly anxious. Quicker journeys meant smaller bills.

'It depends on how many customers he pinches from Polyplanes through being fast.' Colin grinned at me. 'Am I right?'

'You could be,' I agreed.

They went off laughing about it to the waiting taxi. A couple of hours later Colin came back at a run in his breeches and colours and I whisked him over to White Waltham. He had won, it appeared, at Brighton. A close finish. He was still short of breath. A fast car drove right up to the aircraft as soon as I stopped and had him off down the road to Windsor in a cloud of dust. I went more leisurely back to Shoreham and collected the others at the end of their programme. It was a hot sunny day, blue and hazy. They came back sweating.

Kenny had ridden a winner and had brought me a bottle of whisky as a present. I said he didn't need to give me a present.

'Look, sport, if it weren't for you, I wouldn't be riding any more bleeding winners. So take it.'

'All right,' I said. 'Thanks.'

'Thanks yourself.'

They were tired and expansive. I landed at White Waltham before Colin arrived back from Windsor, and the other four yawned and gossiped, opening all the doors and fanning themselves.

'... gave him a breather coming up the hill.'

'That was no breather. That was the soft bugger dropping his bit. Had to give him a sharp reminder to get him going again.'

'Can't stand that fellow Fossel ...'

'Why do you ride for him then?'

'Got no choice, have I? Small matter of a retainer ...'

'... What chance you got on Candlestick?'

'Wouldn't finish in the first three if it started now ...'

'Hey,' said Kenny Bayst, leaning forward and tapping me on the shoulder. 'Got something that might interest you, sport.' He pulled a sheet of paper out of his trouser pocket. 'How about this, then?'

I took the paper and looked at it. It was a leaflet, high quality printing on good glossy paper. An invitation to all racegoers to join the Racegoers' Accident Fund.

'I'm not a racegoer,' I said.

'No, read it. Go on,' he urged. 'It came in the post this morning. I thought you'd be interested, so I brought it.'

I read down the page. 'Up to one thousand pounds for serious personal injury, five thousand pounds for accidental death. Premium five pounds. Double the premium double the insurance. The insurance everyone can afford. Stable lads, buy security for your missus. Jockeys: out of work but in the money. Race crowds, protect yourself against road accidents on the way home. Trainers who fly to meetings, protect yourself against bombs!'

'Damn it,' I said.

Kenny laughed. 'I thought you'd like it.'

I handed the leaflet back, smiling. 'Yeah. The so-and-sos.'

'Might not be a bad idea, at that.'

Colin's hired car drove up and decanted the usual spent force. He climbed wearily into his seat, clipped shut his belt, and said 'Wake me at Cambridge.'

'How did it go?' Kenny asked.

'Got that sod Export home by a whisker ... But as for Uptight,' he yawned, 'They might as well send him to the knackers. Got the slows right and proper, that one has.'

We woke him at Cambridge. It was a case of waking most of them, in point of fact. They stretched their way onto the tarmac, shirt necks open, ties hanging loose, jackets on their arms. Colin had no jacket, no tie: for him, the customary jeans, the rumpled sweat shirt, the air of being nobody, of being one in a crowd, instead of a crowd in one.

Nancy and Midge had come in the Aston Martin to pick us up.

'We brought a picnic,' Nancy said, 'as it's such a super evening. We're going to that place by the river.'

They had also brought swimming trunks for Colin and a pair of his for me. Nancy swam with us, but Midge said it was too cold. She sat on the bank wearing four watches on her left arm and stretching her long bare legs in the sun.

It was cool and quiet and peaceful in the river after the hot sticky day. The noise inside my head of engine throb calmed to silence. I watched a moorhen gliding along by the reeds twisting her neck cautiously to fasten me with a shiny eye, peering suspiciously at Colin and Nancy floating away ahead. I pushed a ripple towards her with my arm. She rode on it like a cork. Simple being a moorhen, I thought. But it wasn't really. All of nature had its pecking order. Everywhere, someone was the pecked.

Nancy and Colin swam back. Friendly eyes, smiling faces. Don't get involved, I thought. Not with anyone. Not yet.

The girls had brought cold chicken and long crisp cos lettuce leaves with a tangy sauce to dip them in. We ate while the sun went down, and drank a cold bottle of Chablis, sitting on a large blue rug and throwing the chewed bones into the river for the fishes to nibble.

When she had finished Midge lay back on the rug and shielded her eyes from the last slanting rays.

'I wish this could go on for ever,' she said casually. 'The summer, I mean. Warm evenings. We get so few of them.'

'We could go and live in the south of France, if you like,' Nancy said.

'Don't be silly ... Who would look after Colin?'

They smiled, all three of them. The unspoken things were all there. Tragic. Unimportant.

The slow dusk drained all colours into shades of grey. We lazed there, relaxing, chewing stalks of grass, watching the insects flick over the surface of the water, talking a little in soft summer evening murmuring voices.

'We both lost a stone in Japan, that year we went with Colin ...'

'That was the food more than the heat.'

'I never did get to like the food ...'

'Have you ever been to Japan, Matt?'

'Used to fly there for B.O.A.C.'

'B.O.A.C.?' Colin was surprised. 'Why ever did you leave?'

'Left to please my wife. Long time ago, now, though.'

'Explains how you fly.'

'Oh sure ...'

'I like America better,' Midge said. 'Do you remember Mr Kroop in Laurel, where you got those riding boots made in a day?'

'Mm ...'

'And we kept driving round that shopping centre there and getting lost in the one way streets ...'

'Super that week was ...'

'Wish we could go again ...'

There was a long regretful silence. Nancy sat up with a jerk and slapped her leg.

'Bloody mosquitoes.'

Colin scratched lazily and nodded. 'Time to go home.'

We wedged back into the Aston Martin. Colin drove. The twins sat on my legs, leaned on my chest and twined their arms behind my neck for balance. Not bad, not bad at all. They laughed at my expression.

'Too much of a good thing,' Nancy said.

When we went to bed they both kissed me goodnight, with identical soft lips, on the cheek.

Breakfast was brisk, businesslike, and accompanied throughout by telephone calls. Annie Villars rang to ask if there was still a spare seat on the Cherokee.

'Who for?' Colin asked cautiously. He made a face at us. 'Bloody Fenella,' he whispered over the mouthpiece. 'No, Annie, I'm terribly sorry. I've promised Nancy ...'

'You have?' Nancy said. 'First I've heard of it.'

He put the receiver down. 'I rescue you from Chanter, now it's your turn.'

'Rescue my foot. You're in and out of the weighing room all day. Fat lot of good that is.'

'Do you want to come?'

'Take Midge,' she said. 'It's her turn.'

'No, you go,' Midge said. 'Honestly, I find it tiring. Especially as it's one of those rush from course to course days. I'll go along to the meeting here next week. That will do me fine.'

'Will you be all right?'

'Naturally I will. I'll lie in the sun in the garden and think of you all exhausting yourselves racing round in circles.'

When it turned out that there were two other empty seats as well, in spite of Nancy being there, Annie Villars gave Colin a reproachful look of carefully repressed annoyance and said it would have been useful to have had along Fenella to share the cost. Why else did Colin think she had suggested it?

'I must have miscounted,' said Colin happily. 'Too late to get her now.'

We flew to Bath without incident, Nancy sitting in the righthand seat beside me and acting as co-pilot. It was clear that she intensely enjoyed it, and there was no pain in it for me either. I could see what Larry had meant about practising short landings, as the Bath runways were incredibly short, but we got down in fair order and parked alongside the opposition's Cessna.

Colin said 'Lock the aeroplane and come into the races. You can't forever stand on guard.'

The Polyplane pilot was nowhere to be seen. I hoped for the best, locked up, and walked with the others into the racecourse next door.

The first person we saw was Acey Jones, balancing on his crutches with the sun making his pale head look fairer than ever.

'Oh yes. Colin,' Nancy said. 'Do you want me to send a fiver to the Accident Insurance people? You remember, the leaflet which came yesterday? That man reminded me ... he got a thousand pounds from the fund for cracking his ankle. I heard him say so, at Haydock.'

'If you like,' he agreed. 'A fiver won't break the bank. May as well.'

'Bobbie Wessex is sponsoring it,' Annie commented.

'Yes,' Nancy nodded. 'It was on the leaflet.'

'Did you see the bit about the bombs?' I asked.

Annie and Nancy both laughed. 'Someone in insurance has got a sense of humour, after all.'

Annie hustled off to the weighing room to see her runner in the first race, and Colin followed her, to change.

'Lemonade?' I suggested to Nancy.

'Pints of it. Whew, it's hot.'

We drank it in a patch of shade, out on the grass. Ten yards away, loud and clear, Eric Goldenberg was conducting a row with Kenny Bayst.

'... And don't you think, sport, that you can set your guerrillas on me and expect me to do you favours afterwards, because if you think that you've got another think coming.'

'What guerrillas?' Goldenberg demanded, not very convincingly.

'Oh come off it. Set them to cripple me. At Redcar.'

'Must have been those bookmakers you swindled while you were busy double crossing us.'

'I never double crossed you.'

'Don't give me that crap,' Goldenberg said heavily. 'You know bloody well you did. You twisty little bastard.'

'If you think that, why the frigging hell are you asking me to set up another touch for you now?'

'Bygones are bygones.'

'Bygones bloody aren't.' Kenny spat on the ground at Goldenberg's feet and removed himself to the weighing room. Goldenberg watched him go with narrowed eyes and a venomous twist to his mouth. The next time I saw him he was holding a well-filled glass and adding substantially to his paunch, while muttering belligerently to a pasty slob who housed all his brains in his biceps. The slob wasn't one of the two who had lammed into Kenny at Redcar. I wondered if Goldenberg intended mustering reinforcements.

'What do you think of Kenny Bayst?' I asked Nancy.

'The big little Mister I-Am from Down Under,' she said. 'He's better than he used to be, though. He came over here thinking everyone owed him a living, as he'd had a great big successful apprenticeship back home.'

'Would he lose to order?'

'I expect so.'

'Would he agree to lose to order, take the money, back himself, and try to win?'

She grinned. 'You're learning fast.'

We watched Colin win the first race. Annie Villars' horse finished third from last. She stood glumly looking at its heaving sides while Kenny's successor made the best of explaining away his own poor showing.

'Annie should have kept Kenny Bayst,' Nancy said.

'He wanted out.'

'Like Colin doesn't want in,' she nodded. 'Annie's being a bit of a fool this season.'

Before the third race we went back to the aeroplane. The Polyplane pilot was standing beside it, peering in through the windows. He was not the stand off merchant from Redcar, but his colleague from

Haydock.

'Good afternoon,' Nancy said.

'Good afternoon, Miss Ross.' He was polite in the way that is more insolent than rudeness. Not the best method, I would have thought, of seducing Colin's custom back from Derrydowns. He walked away, back to his Cessna, and I went over the Cherokee inch by inch looking for anything wrong. As far as I could see, there was nothing. Nancy and I climbed aboard and I started the engine to warm it up ready to take off.

Colin and Annie arrived in a hurry and loaded themselves in, and we whisked off across southern England to Shoreham. Colin and Annie again jumped into a waiting taxi and vanished. Nancy stayed with me and the Cherokee, and we sat on the warm grass and watched little aeroplanes landing and taking off, and talked now and then without pressure about flying, racing, life in general.

Towards the end of the afternoon she asked 'Will you go on being a taxi pilot all your life?'

'I don't know. I don't look far ahead any more.'

'Nor do I,' she said.

'No.'

'We've been happy, these last few weeks, with Midge being so much better. I wish it would last.'

'You'll remember it.'

'That's not the same.'

'It's only special because of what's coming,' I said.

There was a long pause while she thought about it. At length she asked, disbelievingly, 'Do you mean that it is because Midge is dying that we are so happy now?'

'Something like that.'

She turned her head; considered me. 'Tell me something else. I need something else.'

'Comfort?'

'If you like.'

I said 'You've all three been through the classic progression, these last two years. All together, not just Midge herself. Shock, disbelief, anger and in the end acceptance . . .' I paused. 'You've come through the dark tunnel. You're out in the sun the other end. You've done most of your grieving already. You are a most extraordinary strong family. You'll remember this summer because it will be something worth remembering.'

'Matt . . .'

There were tears in her eyes. I watched the bright little dragonfly aeroplanes dart and go. They could heal me, the Ross family, I thought. Their strength could heal me. If it would take nothing away from them. If I could be sure.

'What was Colin's wife like?' I asked, after a while.

'Oh . . .' She gave a laugh which was half a sniff. 'A bit too much like Fenella. He was younger then. He didn't know how to duck. She was thirty-three and bossy and rich, and he was twenty and madly impressed by her. To be honest, Midge and I thought she was fabulous too. We were seventeen and still wet behind the ears. She thought it would be marvellous being married to a genius, all accolades and champagne and glamour. She didn't like it when it turned out to be mostly hard work and starvation and exhaustion . . . so she left him for a young actor who'd just had rave notices for his first film, and it took Colin months to get back to being himself from the wreck she'd made of him.'

'Poor Colin.' Or lucky Colin. Strong Colin. Months . . . it was taking me years.

'Yeah . . .' She grinned. 'He got over it. He's got some bird now in London. He slides down to see her every so often when he thinks Midge and I aren't noticing.'

'I must get me a bird,' I said idly. 'One of these days.'

'You haven't got one?'

I shook my head. I looked at her. Straight eyebrows, straight eyes, sensible mouth. She looked back. I wanted to kiss her. I didn't think she would be angry.

'No,' I said absentmindedly. 'No bird.'

Take nothing away from them. Nothing from Midge.

'I'll wait a while longer,' I said.

Several days, several flights later I telephoned the Board of Trade. Diffidently. Sneering at myself for trying to do their job for them, for thinking I might have thought of something they hadn't worked out for themselves. But then, I'd been on the flight with the bomb, and they hadn't. I'd seen things, heard things, felt things that they hadn't.

Partly for my own sake, but mainly because of what Nancy had said about the bomb merchant still running around loose with his motives still rotting away inside him. I had finally found myself discarding the thought that it was none of my business, that someone else could sort it all out, and coming round to the view that if I could in fact come up with anything it might be a profitable idea.

To which end I wasted a lot of brain time chasing down labyrinths of speculation, and fetched up against a series of reasons why not.

There was Larry, for instance. Well, what about Larry? Larry had had every chance to put the bomb on board, right up to two hours before I set off to collect the passengers from White Waltham. But however strong a motive he had to kill Colin or ruin Derrydowns, and none had so far appeared bar a few trivial frauds, if it was true it was a radio and a not a time bomb he couldn't have set it off because when it exploded he was in Turkey. If it had been Larry, a time bomb would have been the only simple and practical way.

Then Susan . . . Ridiculous as I thought it, I went over again what the Board of Trade man had said: she was going out occasionally with a demolitions expert. Well, good luck to her. The sooner she got married again the better off I'd be. Only trouble was, the aversion therapy of that last destructive six months seemed to have been just as successful with her as it had been with me.

I couldn't believe that any executive type in his right mind would bump off his occasional girl friend's ex-husband for the sake of about six thousand pounds of insurance, especially as the longer I lived, the greater would be the sum she eventually collected. I had three years ago stopped paying any more premiums, but the value of the pay-off automatically went on increasing.

Apart from knowing her incapable of the cold-blooded murder of innocent people, I respected her mercenary instincts. The longer I lived the better off she would be on all counts. It was as simple as that.

Honey Harley ... had said she would do 'anything' to keep Derrydowns in business, and the blowing up of the Cherokee had eased the financial situation. One couldn't sell things which were being bought on the hire purchase, and if one couldn't keep up the instalments the aircraft technically belonged to the H.P. company, who might sell it at a figure which did little more than cover themselves, leaving a molehill for Derrydowns to salvage. Insurance, on the other hand, had done them proud: paid off the H.P. and left them with capital in hand.

Yet killing Colin Ross would have ruined Derrydowns completely. Honey Harley would never have killed any of the customers, let alone Colin Ross. And the same applied to Harley himself, all along the line.

The Polyplane people, then? Always around, always belligerent, trying their damnedest to put Derrydowns out of business and win back Colin Ross. Well ... the bomb would have achieved the first object but have put the absolute dampers on the second. I couldn't see even the craziest Polyplane pilot killing the golden goose.

Kenny Bayst ... livid with Eric Goldenberg, Major Tyderman and Annie Villars. But as I'd said to Colin, where would he have got a bomb from in the time, and would he have killed Colin and me too? It didn't seem possible, any of it. No to Kenny Bayst.

Who, then?

Who?

Since I couldn't come up with anyone else, I went back over the possibilities all over again. Larry, Susan, the Harleys, Polyplanes, Kenny Bayst ... Looked at them up, down, and sideways. Got nowhere. Made some coffee, went to bed, went to sleep.

Woke up at four in the morning with the moon shining on my face. And one fact hitting me with a bang. Up, down and sideways. Look at things laterally. Start from the bottom.

I started from the bottom. When I did that, the answer rose up and stared at me in the face. I couldn't believe it. It was too darned simple.

In the morning I made a lengthy telephone call to a long lost cousin, and two hours later got one back. And it was then, expecting a flat rebuff that I rang up the Board of Trade.

The tall polite man wasn't in. He would, they said, call back later.

When he did, Harley was airborne with a pupil and Honey answered in the tower. She buzzed through to the crew room, where I was writing up records.

'The Board of Trade want you. What have you been up to?'

'It's only that old bomb,' I said soothingly.

'Huh.'

When the tall man came on the line, she was still listening on the tower extension.

'Honey,' I said. 'Quit.'

'I beg your pardon,' said the Board of Trade.

Honey giggled, but she put her receiver down. I heard the click.

'Captain Shore?' the voice said reprovingly.

'Er, yes.'

'You wanted me?'

'You said ... if I thought of any angle on the bomb.'

'Indeed yes.' A shade of warmth.

'I've been thinking,' I said, 'about the transmitter which was needed to set it off.'

'Yes?'

'How big would the bomb have been?' I asked. 'All that plastic explosive and gun powder and wires and solenoids?'

'I should think quite small ... you would probably pack a bomb like that into a flat tin about seven inches by four by two inches deep. Possibly even smaller. The tighter they are packed the more fiercely they explode.'

'And how big would the transmitter have to be to send perhaps three different signals?'

'Nowadays, not very big. If size were important ... a pack of cards, perhaps. But in this case I would have thought ... larger. The transmissions must have had to carry a fairly long way ... and to double the range of a signal you have to quadruple the power of the transmitter, as no doubt you know.'

'Yes ... I apologize for going through all this the long way, but I wanted to be sure. Because although I don't know *why*, I've a good idea of *when* and *who*.'

'What did you say?' His voice sounded strangled.

'I said ...'

'Yes, yes,' he interrupted. 'I heard. When ... when, then?'

'It was put on board at White Waltham. Taken off again at Haydock. And put back on again at Haydock.'

'What do you mean?'

'It came with one of the passengers.'

'Which one?'

'By the way,' I said. 'How much would such a bomb cost?'

'Oh ... about eighty pounds or so,' he said impatiently. 'Who ...?'

'And would it take a considerable expert to make one?'

'Someone used to handling explosives and with a working knowledge of radio.'

'I thought so.'

'Look,' he said, 'look, will you please stop playing cat and mouse. I dare say it amuses you to tease the Board of Trade ... I don't say I absolutely blame you, but will you please tell me which of the passengers had a bomb with him?'

'Major Tyderman,' I said.

'Major ...' He took an audible breath. 'Are you meaning to say now that it wasn't the bomb rolling round on the elevator wires which caused the friction which persuaded you to land ...? That Major Tyderman was carrying it around unknown to himself all the afternoon? Or what?'

'No,' I said. 'And no.'

'For God's sake ...' He was exasperated. 'I suppose you couldn't simplify the whole thing by telling me exactly who planted the bomb on Major Tyderman? Who intended to blow him up?'

'If you like.'

He took a shaking grip. I smiled at the crew room wall.

'Well, who?'

'Major Tyderman,' I said. 'Himself.'

Silence. Then a protest.

'Do you mean suicide? It can't have been. The bomb went off when the aeroplane was on the ground ...'

'Precisely,' I said.

'What?'

'If a bomb goes off in an aeroplane, everyone automatically thinks it was intended to blow up in the air and kill all the people on board.'

'Yes, of course.'

'Suppose the real intended victim was the aeroplane itself, not the people?'

'But why?'

'I told you, I don't know why.'

'All right,' he said. 'All right.' He took a deep breath. 'Let's start from the beginning. You are saying that Major Tyderman, intending to blow up the aeroplane for reasons unknown, took a bomb with him to the races.'

'Yes.'

'What makes you think so?'

'Looking back ... He was rigidly tense all day, and he wouldn't be parted from his binocular case, which was large enough to contain a bomb of the size you described.'

'That's absurdly circumstantial,' he protested.

'Sure,' I agreed. 'Then it was the Major who borrowed the keys from me, to go over to the aircraft to fetch the *Sporting Life* which he had left there. He wouldn't let me go, though I offered. He came back saying he had locked up again, and gave me back the keys. Of course he hadn't locked up. He wanted to create a little confusion. While he was over there he unscrewed the back panel of the luggage bay and put the bomb behind it, against the fuselage. Limpet gadget, I expect, like I said before, which came unstuck on the bumpy flight.'

'He couldn't have foreseen you'd land at East Midlands ...'

'It didn't matter where we landed. As soon as everyone was clear of the aircraft, he was ready to blow it up.'

'That's sheer guess work.'

'He did it in front of my eyes, at East Midlands. I saw him look round, to check there was no one near it. Then he was fiddling with his binocular case ... sending the signals. They could have been either very low or super-high frequencies. They didn't have very far to go. But more important, the transmitter would have been very low powered ... and very small.'

'But ... by all accounts ... and yours too ... he was severely shocked after the explosion.'

'Shocked by the sight of the disintegration he had been sitting on all day. And acting a bit, too.'

He thought it over at length. Then he said, 'Wouldn't someone have noticed that the Major wasn't using binoculars although he was carrying the case?'

'He could say he'd just dropped them and they were broken ... and anyway, he carries a flask in that case normally as well as the race glasses ... lots of people must have seen him taking a swig, as I have ... they wouldn't think it odd ... they might think he'd brought the flask but forgotten the glasses.'

I could imagine him shaking his head. 'It's a fantastic theory altogether. And not a shred of evidence. Just a guess.' He paused. 'I'm sorry, Mr Shore, I'm certain you've done your best, but ...'

I noticed he'd demoted me from Captain. I smiled thinly.

'There's one other tiny thing,' I said gently.

'Yes?' He was slightly, very slightly apprehensive, as if expecting yet more fantasy.

'I got in touch with a cousin in the army, and he looked up some old records for me. In World War II Major Tyderman was in the Royal Engineers, in charge of a unit which spent nearly all of its time in England.'

'I don't see ...'

'They were dealing,' I said, 'With unexploded bombs.'

Chapter Nine

It was the next day that Nancy flew Colin to Haydock. They went in the four seater 140 horse power small version Cherokee which she normally hired from her flying club for lessons and practice, and they set off from Cambridge shortly before I left there myself with a full load in the replacement Six. I had been through her flight plan with her and helped her all I could with the many technicalities and regulations she would meet in the complex Manchester control zone. The weather forecast was for clear skies until evening, there would be radar to help her if she got lost, and I would be listening to her nearly all the time on the radio as I followed her up.

Colin grinned at me. 'Harley would be horrified at the care you're taking to look after her. "Let them frighten themselves silly," he'd say, "Then he'll fly with us all the time, with none of this do-it-yourself nonsense".'

'Yeah,' I agreed. 'And Harley wants you safe, too, don't forget.'

'Did he tell you to help us?'

'Not actually, no.'

'Thought not.'

Harley had said crossly. 'I don't want them making a habit of it. Persuade Colin Ross she isn't experienced enough.'

Colin didn't need persuading: he knew. He also wanted to please Nancy. She set off with shining eyes, like a child being given a treat.

The Derrydowns Six had been hired by an un-clued-up trainer who had separately agreed to share the trip with both Annie Villars and Kenny Bayst. Even diluted by the hiring trainer, the large loud voiced owner of the horse he was running, and the jockey who was to ride it, the atmosphere at loading time was poisonous.

Jarvis Kitch, the hiring trainer, who could have helped, retreated into a huff.

'How was I to know,' he complained to me in aggrieved anger, 'That they loathe each other's guts?'

'You couldn't,' I said soothingly.

'They just rang up and asked if there was a spare seat. Annie yesterday, Bayst the day before. I said there was. How was I to know . . .?'

'You couldn't.'

The loud voiced owner, who was evidently footing the bill, asked testily what the hell it mattered, they would be contributing their share of the cost. He had a north country accent and a bullying manner, and he was the sort of man who considered that when he bought a man's services he bought his soul. Kitch subsided hastily: the small attendant jockey remained cowed and silent throughout. The owner, whose name I later discovered from the racecard was Ambrose, then told me to get a move on as he hadn't hired me to stand around all day on the ground at Cambridge.

Annie Villars suggested in embarrassment that the captain of an aircraft was like the captain of a ship.

'Nonsense,' he said, 'In a two bit little outfit like this he's only a chauffeur. Taking me from place to place isn't he? For hire?' He nodded. 'Chauffeur.' His voice left no one in any doubt about his opinion on the proper place of chauffeurs.

I sighed, climbed aboard, strapped myself in. Easy to ignore him, as it was far from the first time in my life I'd met that attitude. All the same, hardly one of the jolliest of trips.

The Cherokee Six cruised at fifty miles an hour faster than the One Forty, so that I passed Nancy somewhere on the way up. I could hear her calling the various flight information regions on the radio, as she could hear me. It was companionable, in an odd sort of way. And she was doing all right.

I landed at Haydock a few minutes before her, and unloaded the passengers in time to watch her come in. She put on a show to impress the audience, touching down like a feather on the grass. I grinned to myself. Not bad for a ninety-hour amateur. It hadn't been the easiest of trips either. There would be no holding her, after this.

She rolled to a stop a little way along the rails from me and I finished locking the Six and walked over to tell her she would smash the undercarriage next time she thumped an aeroplane down like that.

She made a face at me, excited and pleased. 'It was super. Great. The Liverpool radar people were awfully kind. They told me exactly which headings to fly round the control zone and then told me they would put me smack overhead the racecourse, and they did.'

Colin was proud of her and teased her affectionately. 'Sure, we've got here, but we've got to go home yet.'

'Going home's always easier,' she said confidently. 'And there are none of those difficult control zone rules round Cambridge.'

We walked together across the track to the paddock, ducking under the rails. Nancy talked the whole way, as high as if she'd taken benzedrine. Colin grinned at me. I grinned back. Nothing as intoxicating as a considerable achievement.

We left him at the weighing room and went off to have some coffee.

'Do you know it's only four weeks since we were at Haydock before?' she said. 'Since the bomb. Only four weeks. I seem to have known you half my life.'

'I hope you'll know me for the other half,' I said.

'What did you say?'

'Nothing ... Turkey sandwiches all right?'

'Mm, lovely.' She looked at me, unsure. 'What did you mean?'

'Just one of those pointless things people say.'

'Oh.'

She bit into the soft thick sandwich. She had good straight teeth. I was being a fool, I thought. A fool to get involved, a fool to grow fond of her. I had nothing but a lot of ruins to offer anyone, and she had the whole world to choose from, the sister of Colin Ross. If I was an iceberg, as Honey said, I'd better stay an iceberg. When ice melted, it made a mess.

'You've clammed up,' she said, observing me.

'I haven't.'

'Oh yes, you have. You do, sometimes. You look relaxed and peaceful, and then something inside goes snap shut and you retreat out into the stratosphere. Somewhere very cold.' She shivered. 'Freezing.'

I drank my coffee and let the stratosphere do its stuff. The melting edges safely refroze.

'Will Chanter be here today?' I asked.

'God knows.' She shrugged. 'Do you want him to be?'

'No.' It sounded more vehement than I meant.

'That's something, anyhow,' she said under her breath.

I let it go. She couldn't mean what it sounded like. We finished the sandwiches and went out to watch Colin ride, and after that while we were leaning against the parade ring rails Chanter appeared out of nowhere and smothered Nancy in hair and fringes and swirling fabric, as closely as if he were putting out a fire with a carpet.

She pushed him away, 'For God's sake ...'

He was unabashed. 'Aw Nancy. C'mon now. You and me, we'd have everything going for us if you'd just loosen up.'

'You're a bad trip, Chanter, as far as I'm concerned.'

'You've never been on any real trip, chick, that's your problem.'

'And I'm not going,' she said firmly.

'A little acid lets you into the guts of things.'

'Components,' I agreed. 'Like you said before. You see things in fragments.'

'Huh?' Chanter focussed on me. 'Nancy, you still got this creep in tow? You must be joking.'

'He sees things whole,' she said. 'No props needed.'

'Acid isn't a prop, it's a doorway,' he declaimed.

'Shut the door,' she said. 'I'm not going through.'

Chanter scowled at me. The green chenille tablecloth had been exchanged for a weird shapeless tunic made of irregular shaped pieces of fabrics, fur, leather and metal all stapled together instead of sewn.

'This is your doing, man, you're bad news.'

'It's not his doing,' Nancy said. 'The drug scene is a drag. It always was. Maybe at art school I thought getting woozy on pot was a gas, but not any more. I've grown up, Chanter. I've told you before, I've grown up.'

'He's brainwashed you.'

She shook her head. I knew she was thinking of Midge. Face something big enough, and you always grow up.

'Don't you have any classes today?' she asked.

He scowled more fiercely. 'The sods are out on strike.'

She laughed. 'Do you mean the students?'

'Yeah. Demanding the sack for the deputy Head for keeping a record of what demos they go to.'

I asked ironically, 'Which side are you on?'

He peered at me. 'You bug me, man, you do really.'

For all that, he stayed with us all afternoon, muttering, scowling, plonking his hands on Nancy whenever he got the chance. Nancy bore his company as if she didn't altogether dislike it. As for me, I could have done without it. Easily.

Colin won two races, including the day's biggest. Annie Villar's horse came second. Kenny Bayst won a race on an objection. The loud voiced Ambrose's horse finished fourth, which didn't bode well for sweetness and light on the way home.

The way home was beginning to give me faint twinges of speculation. The weak warm front which had been forecast for late evening looked as if it were arriving well before schedule. From the south-west the upper winds were drawing a strip of cloud over the sky like a sheet over a bed.

Nancy looked up when the sun went in.

'Golly, where did all that cloud come from?'

'It's the warm front.'

'Damn ... do you think it will have got to Cambridge?'

'I'll find out for you, if you like.'

I telephoned to Cambridge and asked them for their actual and forecast weather. Nancy stood beside me inside the telephone box and Chanter fumed suspiciously outside. I had to ask Cambridge to repeat what they'd said. Nancy smelled faintly of a fresh flowering scent. 'Did you say two thousand feet?' Yes, said Cambridge with exaggerated patience, we've told you twice already.

I put down the receiver. 'The front isn't expected there for three or four hours, and the forecast cloud base even then is as high as two thousand feet, so you should be all right.'

'Anyway,' she said, 'I've done dozens of practice let-downs at Cambridge. Even if it should be cloudy by the time we get back, I'm sure I could do it in earnest.'

'Have you ever done it without an instructor?'

She nodded. 'Several times. On fine days, of course.'

I pondered. 'You aren't legally qualified yet to carry passengers in clouds.'

'Don't look so fraught. I won't have to. They said it was clear there now, didn't they? And if the base is two thousand feet when I get there, I can keep below that easily.'

'Yes, I suppose you can.'

'And I've got to get back, haven't I?' she said reasonably.

'Mm ...'

Chanter pulled open the telephone box door. 'You taking a lease on that space, man?' he enquired. He put his arm forward over Nancy's chest a millimetre south of her breasts and scooped her out. She half disappeared into the enveloping fuzz and re-emerged blushing.

'Chanter, for God's sake, we're at the races!'

'Transfer to my pad, then.'

'No, thank you.'

'Women,' he said in disgust. 'Goddamn women. Don't know what's good for them.'

'How's that for a right-wing reactionary statement?' I enquired of the air in general.

'You cool it, man. Just cool it.'

Nancy smoothed herself down and said 'Both of you cool it. I'm going back to the aeroplane now to get set for going home, and you're not coming with me, Chanter. I can't concentrate with you crawling all over me.'

He stayed behind with a bad grace, complaining bitterly when she took me with her.

'He's impossible,' she said as we walked across the track. But she was smiling.

Spreading the map out on the wing I went through the flight plan with her, step by step, as that was what she wanted. She was going back as we'd come, via the radio beacon at Lichfield: not a straight line but the easiest way to navigate. As she had said, it was a simpler business going home. I worked out the times between points for her and filled them in on her planning sheet.

'You are five times as quick at it as I am,' she sighed.

'I've had a spot more practice.'

I folded the map and clipped the completed plan onto it. 'See you at Cambridge,' I said. 'With a bit of luck.'

'Meany.'

'Nancy ...'

'Yes?'

I didn't exactly know what I wanted to say. She waited. After a while I said earnestly. 'Take care.'

She half smiled. 'I will, you know.'

Colin came across the track dragging his feet. 'God, I'm tired,' he said. 'How's my pilot?'

'Ready, willing, and if it's your lucky day, able.'

I did the external checks for her while they climbed aboard. No bombs to be seen. Didn't expect any. She started the engine after I'd given her the all clear, and they both waved as she taxied off. She turned into wind at the far end of the field, accelerated quickly, and lifted off into the pale grey sky. The clouds were a shade lower than they had been. Nothing to worry about. Not if it was clear at Cambridge. I strolled across to the Derrydowns Six. Annie Villars and Kenny Bayst were both there already, studiously looking in opposite directions. I unlocked the doors, and Annie embarked without a word. Kenny gave her a sour look and stayed outside on the ground. I congratulated him on his winner. It all helped, he said.

Ambrose's trainer and jockey trickled back looking pensive, and finally Ambrose came himself, reddish in the face and breathing out beer fumes in a sickly cloud. As soon as he reached the aircraft he leaned towards me and gave me the full benefit.

'I've left me hat in the cloakroom,' he said. 'Hop over and fetch it for me.'

Kenny and the other two were all of a sudden very busy piling themselves aboard and pretending they hadn't heard. Short of saying 'Fetch it yourself' and losing Harley a customer, I was stuck with it. I trudged back across the track, through the paddock, into the Members' Gents, and collected the hat off the peg it was hanging on. Its band was so greasy that I wondered how Ambrose had the nerve to let anyone see it.

Turned, made for the door. Felt my arm clutched in a fiercely urgent grip.

I swung round. The hands holding onto my arm like steel grabs belonged to Major Tyderman.

'Major,' I exclaimed in surprise. I hadn't seen him there all through the afternoon.

'Shore!' He was far more surprised to see me. And more than surprised. Horrified. The colour was draining out of his face while I watched.

'Shore ... What are you doing here? Did you come back?'

Puzzled, I said, 'I came over for Mr Ambrose's hat.'

'But ... you flew ... you took off with Colin and Nancy Ross.'

I shook my head. 'No, I didn't. Nancy was flying.'

'But ... you came with them.' He sounded agonized.

'I didn't. I flew the Six here with five passengers.' The extreme state of his shock got through to me like a tidal wave. He was clinging on to my arm now more for support than to attract my attention.

'Major,' I said, the terrible, terrifying suspicion shaking in my voice, 'You haven't put another bomb on that aircraft? Not ... oh God ... another bomb?'

'I ... I ...' His voice strangled in his throat.

'Major.' I disengaged my arm and seized both of his. Ambrose's hat fell and rolled unnoticed on the dirty floor. 'Major.' I squeezed him viciously. '*Not another bomb*?'

'No ... but ...'

'But *what*?'

'I thought ... you were flying them ... I thought you were with them ... you would be able to cope ...'

'Major.' I shook him, gripping as if I'd pull his arms in two. 'What have you done to that aeroplane?'

'I saw you ... come with them, when they came. And go back ... and look at the map ... and do the checks ... I was sure ... it was you that was flying ... and you ... you ... could deal with ... but Nancy Ross ... Oh my God ...'

I let go one of his arms and slapped him hard in the face.

'*What have you done to that aeroplane*?'

'You can't ... do anything ...'

'I'll get her back. Get her down on the ground at once.'

He shook his head. 'You won't ... be able to ... She'll have no radio ... I put ...' He swallowed and put his hand to his face where I'd hit him. 'I put ... a plaster ... nitric acid ... on the lead ... to the master switch ...'

I let go of his other arm and simply looked at him, feeling the coldness sink in. Then I blindly picked up Ambrose's hat and ran out of the door. Ran. Ran across the paddock, across the track, down to the aircraft. I didn't stop to slap out of the Major what he'd done it for. Didn't think of it. Thought only of Nancy with her limited experience having to deal with a total electrical failure.

She could do it, of course. The engine wouldn't stop. Several of the instruments would go on working. The altimeter, the airspeed indicator, the compass, none of these essentials would be affected. They worked on magnetism, air pressure and engine driven gyroscopes, not electricity.

All the engine instruments would read zero, and the fuel gauge would register empty. She wouldn't know how much fuel she had left.

But she did know, I thought, that she had enough for at least two hours flying.

The worst thing was the radio. She would have no communication with the ground, nor could she receive any signals from the navigation beacons. Well ... dozens of people flew without radio, without even having it installed at all. If she was worried about getting lost, she could land at the first suitable airfield.

It might not have happened yet, I thought. Her radio might still be working. The nitric acid might not yet have eaten through the main electrical cable.

While I was on the ground I was too low down for them to hear me, but if I got up in the air fast enough I could tell the Manchester control people the situation, get them to relay the facts to her, tell her to land at an airfield as soon as she could ... A fairly simple matter to repair the cable, once she was safe on the ground.

I gave Ambrose his hat. He was still outside on the grass, waiting for me to climb through to the left hand seat. I shifted myself across on to it and with no seconds wasted and he hauled himself up after me. By the time he'd strapped himself in I had the engine running, my head-set in place, and the radios warming up.

'What's the rush?' Ambrose enquired, as we taxied at just under take-off speed down to the far end.

'Have to send a radio message to Colin Ross, who's in the air ahead of us.'

'Oh ...' He nodded heavily. He knew the Rosses had come up when we had, knew that Nancy was flying. 'All right then.'

I thought fleetingly that if he thought I couldn't even hurry without getting his permission first he was in for a moderate shock. I wasn't taking him back to Cambridge until I was certain Nancy and Colin were safe.

As there was only one head-set on board Ambrose couldn't hear any incoming transmissions, and with the microphone close against my lips I doubted if he could hear over the engine noise anything I sent outwards. I thought I would delay as long as possible inviting his objections.

Two hundred feet off the ground I raised the Air Traffic Controller at Liverpool. Explained that Nancy's radio might be faulty; asked if he had heard her.

Yes, he had. He'd given her radar clearance out of the control zone, and handed her on to Preston Information. Since I had to stay on his frequency until I was out of the zone myself, I asked him to find out from Preston if they still had contact with her.

'Stand by,' he said.

After a long two minutes he came back. 'They did have,' he said briefly. 'They lost her in the middle of one of her transmissions. They can't raise her now.'

Sod the Major, I thought violently. Stupid, dangerous little man. I kept my voice casual. 'Did they have her position?'

'Stand by.' A pause. He came back. 'She was on track to Lichfield,

E.T.A. Lichfield five three, flying visual on top at flight level four five.'

'On top?' I repeated with apprehension.

'Affirmative.'

We had been climbing steadily ourselves. We went into thin cloud at two thousand feet and came through it into the sunshine at four thousand. Everywhere below us in all directions spread the cotton-wool blanket, hiding the earth beneath. She would have to climb to that height as well, because the Pennines to the east of Manchester rose to nearly three thousand feet and the high ridges would have been sticking up into the clouds. With no room for her between the clouds and the hills she would have had either to go back, or go up. She wouldn't see any harm in going up. With radio navigation and a good forecast for Cambridge it was merely the sensible thing to do.

'Her destination is Cambridge,' I said. 'Can you check the weather there?'

'Stand by.' A much longer pause. Then his voice, dead level, spelling it out. 'Cambridge actual weather, cloud has spread in fast from the south west, now eight eighths cover, base twelve hundred feet, tops three thousand five hundred.'

I didn't acknowledge him at once: was digesting the appalling implications.

'Confirm weather copied,' he said baldly.

'Weather copied.'

'Latest meteorological reports indicate total cloud cover over the entire area south of the Tees.' He knew exactly what he was saying. The laconic non panic voice was deliberately unexcited. Nancy was flying above the cloud layer with no means of telling where she was. She couldn't see the ground and couldn't ask anyone for directions. Eventually she would have to come down, because she would run out of fuel. With the gauge out of action, she couldn't tell exactly how long she could stay airborne, and it was essential for her to go down through the clouds while the engine was still running, so that she could find somewhere to land once she was underneath. But if she went down too soon, or in the wrong place, she could all too easily fly into a cloud-covered hill. Even for a highly experienced pilot it was a sticky situation.

I said, with the same studied artificial calm, 'Can the R.A.F. radar stations find her and trace her where she goes? I know her flight plan ... I made it out for her. She is likely to stick to it, as she thinks it is still clear at Cambridge. I could follow ... and find her.'

'Stand by.' Again the pause for consultations. 'Change frequency to Birmingham radar on one eight zero five.'

'Roger,' I said. 'And thanks very much.'

'Good luck,' he said. 'You'll need it.'

Chapter Ten

He had explained the situation to Birmingham. I gave the radar controller Nancy's planned track and airspeed and estimated time for Lichfield, and after a few moments he came back and said there were at least ten aircraft on his screen which were possibles, but he had no way of telling who they were. 'I'll consult with the R.A.F. Wymeswold ... they may not be as busy as we are ... they can concentrate on it more.'

'Tell them that at about five three she will change her heading to one two five.'

'Roger,' he said. 'Stand by.'

He came back. 'R.A.F. Wymeswold say they will watch for her.'

'Great,' I said.

After a few moments he said in an incredulous voice, 'We have a report that Colin Ross is aboard the non-radio aircraft. Can you confirm?'

'Affirmative' I said. 'The pilot is his sister.'

'Good God' he said. 'Then we'd better find her.'

I had got them to route me straight through the control zone instead of round it, and was making for Northwich, and then the Lichfield beacon. We had taken off, I calculated, a good thirty minutes behind her, and in spite of the short cut and the Six's superior speed it would be barely possible to overtake her before Cambridge. I looked at my watch for about the twentieth time. Five fifty. At five fifty three she would be turning over Lichfield ... except that she wouldn't know she was at Lichfield. If she turned as scheduled, it would be on her part simply blind faith.

Birmingham radar called me up. 'Cambridge report a steady deterioration in the weather. The cloud base is now eight hundred feet.'

'Roger,' I said flatly.

After another five minutes, during which five fifty three came and went in silence, he said, 'Wymeswold report that an aircraft on their screen has turned from one six zero on to one two five, but it is five miles north east of Lichfield. The aircraft is unidentified. They will maintain surveillance.'

'Roger,' I said.

She could be drifting north east, I thought, because the wind from the south west was stronger than it had been on the northward journey, and I hadn't made enough allowance for it on the flight plan.

I pressed the transmit button and informed the radar man.

'I'll tell them,' he said.

We flew on. I looked round at the passengers. They looked variously bored, thoughtful and tired. Probably none of them would notice when we left our direct course to go and look for Nancy: but they'd certainly notice if or when we found her.

'Wymeswold report the aircraft they were watching has turned north on to zero one zero.'

'Oh no,' I said.

'Stand by ...'

Too easy, I thought despairingly. It had been too easy. The aircraft which had turned on to the right heading at the right time at roughly the right place hadn't been the right aircraft after all. I took three deep deliberate breaths. Concentrated on the fact that wherever she was she was in no immediate danger. She could stay up for more than another hour and a half.

I had over an hour in which to find her. In roughly three thousand square miles of sky as featureless as the desert. Piece of cake.

'Wymeswold report that the first aircraft has apparently landed at East Midlands, but that they have another possibility ten miles east of Lichfield, present heading one two zero. They have no height information.'

'Roger,' I said again. No height information meant that the blip on their screen could be flying at anything up to thirty thousand feet or more, not four thousand five hundred.

'Stand by.'

I stood by. Metaphorically bit my nails. Slid a sidelong glance at Ambrose and went unhurriedly about checking our own height, speed, direction. Lichfield dead ahead, eleven minutes away. Forty minutes to Cambridge. Too long. Have to go faster. Pushed the throttle open another notch and came up against the stops. Full power. Nothing more to be done.

'Possible aircraft now tracking steady one zero five. Present track if maintained will take it thirty miles north of Cambridge at estimated time two zero.'

'Roger.' I looked at my watch. Did a brief sum. Pressed the transmit button. 'That's the wrong aircraft. It's travelling too fast. At ninety knots she couldn't reach the Cambridge area before three five or four zero.'

'Understood.' A short silence. 'Retune now to R.A.F. Cottesmore, Northern Radar, one two two decimal one. I'm handing you on to them.'

I thanked him. Retuned. Cottesmore said they were in the picture, and looking. They had seven unidentified aircraft travelling from west to east to the south of them, all at heights unknown.

Seven. She could be any one of them. She could have gone completely haywire and turned round and headed back to Manchester. I felt my skin prickle. Surely she would have enough sense not to fly straight into a control zone without radio. And anyway, she still believed it was clear at Cambridge ...

I reached the Lichfield beacon. Turned on to course for Cambridge. Informed Cottesmore radar that I had done so. They didn't have me on their screen yet, they said: I was still too far away.

I tracked doggedly on towards Cambridge over the cottonwool wastes. The sun shone hotly into the cabin, and all the passengers except Ambrose went to sleep.

'One unidentified aircraft has landed at Leicester,' Cottesmore radar said. 'Another appears to be heading directly for Peterborough.

'That leaves five?' I asked.

'Six ... there's another now further to the west.'

'It may be me.'

'Turn left thirty degrees for identification.'

I turned, flew on the new heading.

'Identified,' he said. 'Return to former heading.'

I turned back on track, stifling the raw anxiety which mounted with every minute. They must find her, I thought. They *must*.

Cottesmore said, 'One aircraft which passed close to the south of us five minutes ago has now turned north.'

Not her.

'The same aircraft has now flown in a complete circle and resumed a track of one one zero.'

It might be her. If she had spotted a thin patch. Had gone to see if she could see the ground and get down safely to below the cloud. Had found she couldn't: had gone on again in what she thought was the direction of Cambridge.

'That might be her,' I said. Or someone else in the same difficulties. Or someone simply practising turns. Or anything.

'That particular aircraft has now turned due south ... slightly west ... now round again to south east ... back to one one zero.'

'Could be looking for thin patches in the cloud,' I said.

'Could be. Stand by.' A pause. Then his voice, remote and careful. 'Cloud base in this area is down to six hundred feet. Eight eighths cover. No clear patches.'

Oh Nancy ...

'I'm going to look for that one,' I said. 'Can you give me a steer to close on its present track?'

'Will do,' he said. 'Turn left on to zero nine five. You are thirty miles to the west. I estimate your ground speed at one fifty knots. The aircraft in question is travelling at about ninety five knots.'

In the twelve minutes it would take me to reach the other aircraft's present position, it would have shifted twenty miles further on. Catching up would take twenty-five to thirty minutes.

'The aircraft in question is circling again ... now tracking one one zero ...'

The more it circled, the sooner I'd catch it. But if it wasn't Nancy at all ... I thrust the thought violently out of my mind. If it wasn't we might never find her.

Ambrose touched my arm, and I had been concentrating so hard that I jumped.

'We're off course,' he said dogmatically. He tapped the compass. 'We're going due east. We'd better not be lost.'

'We're under radar control,' I said matter-of-factly.

'Oh ...' He was uncertain. 'I see.'

I would have to tell him, I thought. Couldn't put it off any longer. I explained the situation as briefly as I could, leaving out Major Tyderman's part in it and shouting to make myself heard over the noise of the engine.

He was incredulous. 'Do you mean we're chasing all over the sky looking for Colin Ross?'

'Directed by radar,' I said briefly.

'And who,' he asked belligerently, 'is going to pay for this? I am certainly not. In fact you have been totally irresponsible in changing course without asking my permission first.'

Cottesmore reported. 'The aircraft is now overhead Stamford, and circling again.'

'Roger,' I said. And for God's sake, Nancy, I thought, don't try going down through the cloud just there. There were some hills round about and a radio mast five hundred feet high.

'Steer one zero zero to close.'

'One zero zero.'

'Aircraft has resumed its former heading.'

I took a considerable breath of relief.

'Did you hear what I said?' Ambrose demanded angrily.

'We have a duty to go to the help of an aircraft in trouble,' I said.

'Not at my expense, we don't.'

'You will be charged,' I said patiently, 'only the normal amount for the trip.'

'That's not the point. You should have asked my permission. I am seriously displeased. I will complain to Harley. We should not have left our course. Someone else should have gone to help Colin Ross. Why should we be inconvenienced?'

'I am sure he will be pleased to hear your views,' I said politely. 'And no doubt he will pay any expenses incurred in his rescue.'

He glared at me speechlessly, swept by fury.

Annie Villars leaned forward and tapped me on the shoulder.

'Did I hear you say that Colin Ross is lost? Up here, do you mean? On top of the clouds?'

I glanced round. They were all awake, all looking concerned.

'Yes,' I said briefly. 'With no radio. The radar people think they may have found him. We're going over to see ... and to help.'

'Anything we can do ...' Annie said. 'Of course, call on us.'

I smiled at her over my shoulder. Ambrose turned round to her and started to complain. She shut him up smartly. 'Do you seriously propose we make no attempt to help? You must be out of your mind. It is our clear and absolute duty to do whatever we can. And a captain doesn't have to consult his passengers before he goes to help another ship in distress.'

He said something about expense. Annie said crisply, 'If you are too mean to pay a few extra pounds as your share of perhaps saving the life of Colin Ross, I shall be pleased to contribute the whole amount myself.'

'Atta girl,' Kenny Bayst said loudly. Annie Villars looked startled, but not displeased. Ambrose swivelled to face forwards. He had turned a dark purplish red. I hope it was shame and embarrassment, not an incipient thrombosis.

'The aircraft is circling again,' Cottesmore reported. 'Its position now is just south of Peterborough ... Remain on your present heading ... I am handing you on now to Wytton ... no need for you to explain to them ... they know the situation.'

'Thank you very much,' I said.

'Good luck ...'

Wytton, the next in the chain, the R.A.F. master station north east of Cambridge, was crisp, cool, efficient.

'Cloud base at Cambridge six hundred feet, no further deterioration in past half hour. Visibility three kilometres in light rain. Surface wind two four zero, ten knots.'

'Weather copied,' I said automatically. I was looking at the map. Another radio mast, this one seven hundred feet high, south of Peterborough. Go on, Nancy, I thought, go on, further east. Don't try there. Not there ...

Wytton said 'Aircraft now back on one one zero.'

I rubbed a hand round the back of my neck. I could feel the sweat.

'Steer zero nine five. You are now ten miles west of the aircraft.'

'I'm climbing to flight level eight zero. To see better.'

'Cleared to eight zero.'

The altimeter hands crept round to eight thousand feet. The blanket of white fleece spread out unbroken in all directions to the horizon, soft and pretty in the sun. The passengers murmured, perhaps realizing for the first time the extent of Nancy's predicament. Mile after mile after mile of emptiness, and absolutely no way of telling where she was.

'Aircraft's circling again ... Maintain zero nine five. You are now seven miles to the west.'

I said over my shoulder to Annie Villars, 'We'll see them soon ... Would you take this notebook ...' I handed her the spiral bound reporters' notebook I used for jotting during flights, 'and make some letters out of the pages? As big as you can. We will need, you see, to hold them up in the window, so that Nancy and Colin can read what we want them to do.'

And let it be them, I thought coldly. Just let it be them, and not some other poor lost souls. Because we'd have to stay to help. We couldn't leave them to struggle and look somewhere else for the ones we wanted ...

Annie Villars fumbled in her handbag and produced a small pair of scissors.

'Which letters?' she said economically. 'You say, and I'll write them down, and then make them.'

'Right … FOLWBASE. That will do to start with.'

I twisted my head and saw her start snipping. She was making them full page size and as bold as possible. Satisfied, I looked forward again, scanning the sunny waste, searching for a small black cigarette shape moving ahead.

'Turn on to one zero five' Wytton said. 'The aircraft is now in your one o'clock position five miles ahead.'

I looked down over to the right of the aircraft's nose. Ambrose reluctantly looked out of the window in sulky silence.

'*There*,' Kenny Bayst said. 'Over there, down there.' I looked where he was pointing … and there it was, slightly more over to our right, beginning another circling sweep over a darker patch of cloud which might have been a hole, but wasn't.

'Contact,' I said to Wytton. 'Closing in now.'

'Your intentions?' he asked unemotionally.

'Lead them up to the Wash, descend over the sea, follow the river and railway from King's Lynn to Cambridge.'

'Roger. We'll advise Marham. They'll give you radar coverage over the sea.'

I put the nose down, built up the speed, and overhauled the other aircraft like an E-type catching a bicycle. The nearer we got the more I hoped … it was a low winged aeroplane … a Cherokee … white with red markings … and finally the registration number … and someone frantically waving a map at us from the window.

The relief was overpowering.

'It's them,' Annie said, and I could only nod and swallow.

I throttled back and slowed the Six until it was down to Nancy's cruising speed, then circled until I came up on her left side, and about fifty yards away. She had never done any formation flying. Fifty yards was the closest it was safe to go to her and even fifty yards was risking it a bit. I kept my hand on the throttle, my eyes on her, and an extra pair of eyes I didn't know I had, fixed on the heading.

To Annie Villars I said, 'Hold up the letters for "follow". Slowly. One by one.'

'Right.' She held them flat against the window beside her. We could see Colin's head leaning back behind Nancy's. When Annie finished the word we saw him wave his hand, and after that Nancy waved her map against her window, which showed up better.

'Wytton,' I reported. 'It is the right aircraft. They are following us to the Wash. Can you give me a steer to King's Lynn?'

'Delighted,' he said. 'Steer zero four zero, and call Marham on frequency one one nine zero.'

'Thanks a lot,' I said with feeling.

'You're very welcome.'

Good guys, I thought. Very good guys, sitting in their darkened rooms wearing headsets and staring at their little dark circular screens, watching the multitude of yellow dots which were aircraft swimming slowly across like tadpoles. They'd done a terrific job, finding the Rosses. Terrific.

'Can you make a figure 4?' I asked Annie Villars.

'Certainly.' The scissors began to snip.

'When you have, would you hold up the O, then the 4, then the O again?'

'With pleasure.'

She held up the figures. Nancy waved the map. We set off north-eastwards to the sea, Nancy staying behind us to the right, with me flying looking over my shoulder to keep a steady distance between us. I judged it would take thirteen minutes at her speed to reach the sea, five to ten to let down, and twenty or so more to return underneath the cloud base to Cambridge. Her fuel by the time she got there would be low, but there was less risk of her running dry than of hitting a hill or trees or a building by going down over the land. Letting down over the sea was in these circumstances the best procedure whenever possible.

'We're going to need some more letters,' I told Annie.

'Which?'

'Um ... R, I, V, and N, D, C, and a T, and a nine.'

'Right.'

Out of the corner of my eye I could see Annie Villars snipping and Kenny Bayst, sitting behind her, sorting out the letters she had already made so that she could easily pick them out when they were needed. There was, I thought to myself, with a small internal smile, a truce in operation in that area.

Marham radar reported, 'You have four miles to run to the coast.'

'Hope the tide's in,' I said facetiously.

'Affirmative,' he said with deadpan humour. 'High water eighteen forty hours B.S.T.'

'And ... er ... the cloud base?'

'Stand by.' Down in his dark room he couldn't see the sky. He had to ask the tower dwellers above.

'Cloud base between six and seven hundred feet above sea level over the entire area from the Wash to Cambridge. Visibility two kilometres in drizzle.'

'Nice' I said with irony.

'Very.'

'Could I have the regional pressure setting?'

'Nine nine eight millibars.'

'Nine nine eight,' I repeated, and took my hand off the throttle enough to set that figure on the altimeter subscale. To Annie Villars I said, 'Can you make an 8, as well?'

'I expect so.'

'Crossing the coast,' Marham said.

'Right ... Miss Villars will you hold up SEA?'

She nodded and did so. Nancy waved the map.

'Now hold up SET, then 998, then MBS.'

'S ... E ... T,' she repeated, holding them against the window. 'Nine, nine, eight.' She paused 'There's no M cut out.'

'W upside down,' Kenny Bayst said, and gave it to her.

'Oh yes. M ... B ... S. What does mbs mean?'

'Millibars' I said.

Nancy waved the map, but I said to Annie, 'Hold up the nine nine eight again, it's very important.'

She held them up. We could see Nancy's head nodding as she waved back vigorously.

'Why is it so important?' Annie said.

'Unless you set the altimeter to the right pressure on the subscale, it doesn't tell you how high you are above the sea.'

'Oh.'

'Now would you hold up B A S E, then 6 0 0, then F T.'

'Right ... Base ... six hundred ... feet.'

There was a distinct pause before Nancy waved, and then it was a small, half hearted one. She must have been horrified to find that the clouds were so low: she must have been thanking her stars that she hadn't tried to go down through them. Highly frightening piece of information, that six hundred feet.

'Now,' I said to Annie, 'Hold up "Follow river and rail one nine zero to Cambridge".'

'Follow ... river ... and ... rail ... one ... nine ... zero ... to ... Cambridge ... no g ... never mind, c will do, then e.' She spelt it out slowly. Nancy waved.

'And just one more ... 40, then N, then M.'

'Forty nautical miles,' she said triumphantly. She held them up and Nancy waved.

'Now hold up "follow" again.'

'Right.'

I consulted Marham, took Nancy out to sea a little further, and led her round in a circle until we were both heading just west of south on one nine zero, and in a straight line to the railway and river from King's Lynn to Cambridge.

'Hold up D O W N,' I said.

She did it without speaking. Nancy gave a little wave. I put the nose of the Six down towards the clouds and accelerated to a hundred and forty knots so that there would be no possibility of her crashing into the back of us. The white fleecy layer came up to meet us, embraced us in sunlit feathery wisps, closed lightly around us, became denser, darker, an anthracite fog pressing on the windows. The altimeter unwound, the clock needles going backwards through 3,000 feet, 2,000 feet, 1,000 feet, still no break at 800 feet, 700 ... and there there at last the mist receded a little and became drizzly haze, and underneath us, pretty close underneath, were the restless rainswept dark greeny grey waves.

The passengers were all silent. I glanced round at them. They were all looking down at the sea in varying states of awe. I wondered if any of them knew I had just broken two laws and would undoubtedly be prosecuted again by the Board of Trade. I wondered if I would ever, ever learn to keep myself out of trouble.

We crossed the coast over King's Lynn and flew down the river to Ely and Cambridge, just brushing through the misty cloud base at seven hundred feet. The forward visibility was bad, and I judged it silly to go back and wait for Nancy, because we might collide before we saw each other. I completed the journey as briefly as possible and we landed on the wet tarmac and taxied round towards the airport buildings. When I stopped the engine, everyone as if moved by one mind climbed out and looked upwards; even Ambrose.

The drizzle was light now, like fine mist. We stood quietly in it, getting damp, listening for the sound of an engine, watching for the shadow against the sky. Minutes ticked past. Annie Villars looked at me anxiously. I shook my head, not knowing exactly what I meant.

She couldn't have gone down too far ... hit the sea ... got disorientated in the cloud ... lost when she came out of it ... still in danger.

The drizzle fell. My heart also.

But she hadn't made any mistakes.

The engine noise crept in as a hum, then a buzz, then a definite rhythm. The little red and white aeroplane appeared suddenly against the righthand sky, and she was circling safely round the outskirts of the field and coming sedately down to land.

'Oh ...' Annie Villars said, and wiped two surprising tears of relief out of her eyes.

Ambrose said sulkily, 'That's all right then. Now I hope we can get off home,' and stomped heavily away towards the buildings.

Nancy taxied round and stopped her Cherokee a short distance away. Colin climbed out on the wing, grinned hugely in our direction, and waved.

'He's got no bloody nerves,' Kenny said. 'Not a bleeding nerve in his whole body.'

Nancy came out after him, jumping down onto the tarmac and staggering a bit as she landed on wobbly knees. I began to walk towards them. She started slowly to meet me, and then faster, and then ran, with her hair swinging out and her arms stretched wide. I held her round the waist and swung her up and round in the air and when I put her down she wrapped her arms behind my neck and kissed me.

'Matt ...' She was half laughing, half crying, her eyes shining, her cheeks a burning red, the sudden release of tension making her tremble down to her fingertips.

Colin reached us and gave me a buffet on the shoulder.

'Thanks, chum.'

'Thank the R.A.F. They found you on their radar.'

'But how did you know ...?'

'Long story.' I said. Nancy was still holding on to me as if she would fall down if she let go. I made the most of it by kissing her again, on my own account.

She laughed shakily and untwined her arms. 'When you came ... I can't tell you ... it was such a relief ...'

Annie Villars came up and touched her arm and she turned to her with the same hectic over-excitement.

'Oh ... *Annie.*'

'Yes, dear,' she said calmly. 'What you need now is a strong brandy.'

'I ought to see to ...' she looked vaguely in my direction, and back to the Cherokee.

'Colin and Matt will see to everything.'

'All right, then ...' She let herself be taken off by Annie Villars, who had recovered her poise and assumed total command as a good general should. Kenny and the other jockey and trainer meekly followed.

'Now,' said Colin. 'How on earth did you know we needed you?'

'I'll show you,' I said abruptly. 'Come and look.' I walked him back to the little Cherokee, climbed up on to the wing and lay down on my back across the two front seats, looking up under the control panel.

'What on earth ...?'

The device was there. I showed it to him. Very neat, very small. A little polythene-wrapped packet swinging free on a rubber band which was itself attached to the cable leading to the master switch. Nearer the switch one wire of the two wire cable had been bared: the two severed ends of copper showed redly against the black plastic casing.

I left everything where it was and eased myself out on to the wing.

'What is it? What does it mean?'

'Your electric system was sabotaged.'

'For God's sake ... why?'

'I don't know,' I sighed. 'I only know who did it. The same person who planted the bomb a month ago. Major Rupert Tyderman.'

He stared at me blankly. 'It doesn't make sense.'

'Not much. No.'

I told him how the Major had set off the bomb while we were safely on the ground, and that today he had thought I was flying Nancy's Cherokee and could get myself out of trouble.

'But that's ... that means ...'

'Yes,' I said.

'He's trying to make it look as though someone's trying to kill me.'

I nodded. 'While making damn sure you survive.'

Chapter Eleven

The Board of Trade came down like the hounds of Hell and it wasn't the tall reasonable man I faced this time in the crew room but a short hard-packed individual with an obstinate jaw and unhumorous eyes. He refused to sit down: preferred to stand. He had brought no silent note-taker along. He was strictly a one man band. And hot on percussion.

'I must bring to your attention the Air Navigation Order Nineteen sixty six.' His voice was staccato and uncompromising, the traditional politeness of his department reduced to the thinnest of veneers.

I indicated that I was reasonably familiar with the order in question. As it ruled every cranny of a professional pilot's life, this was hardly surprising.

'We have been informed that on Friday last you contravened Article 25, paragraph 4, sub section a, and Regulation 8, paragraph 2.'

I waited for him to finish. Then I said 'Who informed you?'

He looked at me sharply. 'That is beside the point.'

'Could it have been Polyplanes?'

His eyelids flickered in spite of himself. 'If we receive a complaint which can be substantiated we are bound to investigate.'

The complaint could be substantiated, all right. Saturday's newspapers were still strewn around the crew room this Monday morning, all full of the latest attempt on Colin Ross's life. Front page stuff. Also minute details from all my passengers about how we had led him out to sea and brought him home under the 700 ft cloud base.

Only trouble was, it was illegal in a single engine aeroplane like the Six to take paying customers out over the sea as low as I had, and to land them at an airport where the cloud base was lower than one thousand feet.

'You admit that you contravened Section ...'

I interrupted him. 'Yes.'

He opened his mouth and shut it again. 'Er, I see.' He cleared his throat. 'You will receive a summons in due course.'

'Yes,' I said again.

'Not your first, I believe.' An observation, not a sneer.

'No,' I said unemotionally.

A short silence. Then I said, 'How did that gadget work? The nitric acid package on the rubber band.'

'That is not your concern.'

I shrugged. 'I can ask any schoolboy who does chemistry.'

He hesitated. He was not of the stuff to give anything away. He would never, as the tall man had, say or imply that there could be any fault in his Government or the Board. But having searched his conscience and no doubt his standing orders, he felt able after all to come across.

'The package contained fluffy fibreglass soaked in a weak solution of nitric acid. A section of wire in the cable to the master switch had been bared, and the fibreglass wrapped around it. The nitric acid slowly dissolved the copper wire, taking, at that concentration, probably about an hour and a half to complete the process.' He stopped, considering.

'And the rubber band?' I prompted.

'Yes ... well, nitric acid, like water, conducts electricity, so that while the fibreglass was still in position the electrical circuit would be maintained, even though the wire itself had been completely dissolved. To break the circuit the fibreglass package had to be removed. This was done by fastening it under tension via the rubber band to a point further up the cable. When the nitric acid dissolved right through the wire and the two ends parted, there was nothing to stop the rubber band contracting and pulling the fibreglass package away. Er ... do I make myself clear?'

'Indeed,' I agreed, 'you do.'

He seemed to give himself a little mental and physical shake, and turned with sudden energy towards the door.

'Right,' he said briskly. 'Then I need a word with Mr Harley.'

'Did you get a word with Major Tyderman?' I asked.

After the merest hiatus he said again, 'That is not your concern.'

'Perhaps you have seen him already?'

Silence.

'Perhaps, though, he is away from home?'

More silence. Then he turned to me in stiff exasperation. 'It is not your business to question me like this. I cannot answer you any more. It is I who am here to inquire into you, not the other way round.' He shut his mouth with a snap and gave me a hard stare. 'And they even warned me,' he muttered.

'I hope you find the Major,' I said politely, 'before he plants any more little devices in inconvenient places.'

He snorted and strode before me out of the crew room and along to Harley's office. Harley knew what he was there for and had been predictably furious with me ever since Friday.

'Mr Shore admits the contraventions,' the Board of Trade said.

'He'd be hard pushed not to,' Harley said angrily, 'considering every R.A.F. base across the country told him about the low cloud base at Cambridge.'

'In point of fact,' agreed the Board of Trade, 'he should then have returned immediately to Manchester which was then still within the legal limit, and waited there until conditions improved, instead of flying all the way to East Anglia and leaving himself with too small a fuel margin to go to any cloud-free airport. The proper course was certainly to turn back right at the beginning.'

'And to hell with Colin Ross,' I said conversationally.

Their mouths tightened in chorus. There was nothing more to be said. If you jumped red traffic lights and broke the speed limit rushing someone to hospital to save his life, you would still be prosecuted for the offences. Same thing exactly. Same impasse. Humanity versus laws, an age-old quandary. Make your choice and lie on it.

'I'm not accepting any responsibility for what you did,' Harley said heavily. 'I will state categorically, and in court if I have to, that you were acting in direct opposition to Derrydowns' instructions, and that Derrydowns disassociates itself entirely from your actions.'

I thought of asking him if he'd like a basin for the ritual washing of hands. I also thought that on the whole I'd better not.

He went on, 'And of course if there is any fine involved you will pay it yourself.'

Always my bad luck, I reflected, to cop it when the firm was too nearly bankrupt to be generous. I said merely, 'Is that all, then? We have a charter, if you remember ...'

They waved me away in disgust and I collected my gear and flew off in the Aztec to take a clutch of businessmen from Elstree to The Hague.

By the time, the previous Friday, that Colin and I had locked Nancy's Cherokee and ensured that no one would touch it, the first cohorts of the local press had come galloping up with ash on their shirt fronts, and the Board of Trade, who neither slumbered nor slept, were breathing heavily down the S.T.D.

Aircraft radios are about as private as Times Square: it appeared that dozens of ground-based but air-minded Midlands enthusiasts had been listening in to my conversation with Birmingham radar and had jammed the switchboard at Cambridge ringing up to find out if Colin Ross was safe. Undaunted, they had conveyed to Fleet Street the possibility of his loss. His arrival in one piece was announced on a television news broadcast forty minutes after we landed. The great British media had pulled out every finger they possessed. Nancy and Annie Villars had answered questions until their throats were sore and had finally taken refuge in the Ladies Cloaks. Colin was used to dealing with the press, but by the time he extricated himself from their ever increasing news hungry numbers he too was pale blue from tiredness.

'Come on,' he said to me. 'Let's get Nancy out and go home.'

'I'll have to ring Harley ...'

Harley already knew and was exploding like a firecracker. Someone from Polyplanes, it appeared, had telephoned at once to inform him with acid sweetness that his so highly qualified chief pilot had broken every law in sight and put Derrydowns thoroughly in the cart. The fact that his best customer was still alive to pay another day didn't seem to have got through to Harley at all. Polyplanes had made him smart, and it was all my fault.

I stayed in Cambridge by promising to foot the bill for hangarage again, and went home with Nancy and Colin.

Home.

A dangerous, evocative word. And the trouble was, it *felt* like home. Only the third time I'd been there, and it was already familiar, cosy, undemanding, easy ... It was no good feeling I belonged there, because I didn't.

Saturday morning I spent talking to the police face to face in Cambridge and the Board of Trade in London on the telephone. Both forces cautiously murmured that they might perhaps ask Major Rupert Tyderman to help them with their inquiries. Saturday afternoon I flew Colin back to Haydock without incident. Saturday night I again stayed contentedly at Newmarket, Sunday I took him to Buckingham, changed over to the Aztec, and flew him to Ostend. Managed to avoid Harley altogether until I got back Sunday evening, when he lay in wait for me as I taxied down to the hangar and bitched on for over half an hour about sticking to the letter of law. The gist of his argument was that left to herself Nancy would have come down safely somewhere over the flat land of East Anglia. Bound to have done. She wouldn't have hit any of the radio masts or power station chimneys which scattered the area and which had stuck up into the clouds like needles. They were all marked there, disturbing her, on the map. She had known that if she had to go down at random she had an average chance of hitting one. The television mast at Mendlesham stretched upwards for more than a thousand feet . . . But, said Harley, she would have missed the lot. Certain to have done.

'What would you have felt like, in her position?' I asked.

He didn't answer. He knew well enough. As pilot, as businessman, he was a bloody fool.

On Tuesday morning he told me that Colin had telephoned to cancel his trip to Folkestone that day, but that I would still be going in the Six, taking an owner and his friends there from Nottingham.

I imagined that Colin had changed his intention to ride at Folkestone and gone to Pontefract instead, but it wasn't so. He had, I found, flown to Folkestone. And he had gone in a Polyplane.

I didn't know he was there until after the races when he came back to the airport in a taxi. He climbed out of it in his usual wilted state, surveyed the row of parked aircraft, and walked straight past me towards the Polyplane.

'Colin,' I said.

He stopped, turned his head, gave me a straight stare. Nothing friendly in it, nothing at all.

'What's the matter?' I said puzzled. 'What's happened?'

He looked away from me, along to the Polyplane. I followed his glance. The pilot was standing there smirking. He was the one who had refused to help Kenny Bayst, and he had been smirking vigorously all afternoon.

'Did you come with him?' I asked.

'Yes, I did.' His voice was cold. His eyes also.

I said in surprise, 'I don't get it . . .'

Colin's face turned from cold to scorching. 'You . . . you . . . I don't think I can bear to talk to you.'

A feeling of unreality clogged my tongue. I simply looked at him in bewilderment.

'You've properly bust us up . . . Oh, I dare say you didn't mean to . . . but Nancy has lit off out of the house and I left Midge at home crying . . .'

I was appalled. 'But why? On Sunday morning when we left, everything was fine . . .'

'Yesterday,' he said flatly. 'Nancy found out yesterday, when she went to the airfield for a practice session. It absolutely overthrew her. She came home in a dreadful mood and raged round the house practically throwing things and this morning she packed a suitcase and walked out . . . neither Midge nor I could stop her and Midge is frantically distressed . . .' He stopped, clenched his jaw, and said with shut teeth, 'Why the hell didn't you have the guts to tell her yourself?'

'Tell her what?'

'*What*?' He thrust his hand into the pocket of his faded jeans and brought out a folded wad of newspaper. 'This.'

I took it from him. Unfolded it. Felt the woodenness take over in my face; knew that it showed.

He had handed me the most biting, the most damaging, of the tabloid accounts of my trial and conviction for negligently putting the lives of eighty seven people in jeopardy. A one-day wonder to the general public; long forgotten. But always lying there in the files, if anyone wanted to dig it up.

'That wasn't all,' Colin said. 'He told her also that you'd been sacked from another airline for cowardice.'

'Who told her?' I said dully. I held out the cutting. He took it back.

'Does it matter?'

'Yes, it does.'

'He had no axe to grind. That's what convinced her.'

'No axe . . . did he say that?'

'I believe so. What does it matter?'

'Was it a Polyplane pilot who told her? The one, for instance, who is flying you today?' Getting his own back, I thought, for the way I'd threatened him at Redcar.

Colin's mouth opened.

'No axe to grind,' I said bitterly. 'That's a laugh. They've been trying to prise you loose from Derrydowns all summer and now it looks as if they've done it.'

I turned away from him, my throat physically closing. I didn't think I could speak. I expected him to walk on, to walk away, to take himself to Polyplanes and my future to the trash can.

Instead of that he followed me and touched my arm.

'Matt . . .'

I shook him off. 'You tell your precious sister,' I said thickly, 'that because of the rules I broke leading her back to Cambridge last Friday I am going to find myself in court again, and convicted and fined and in debt again . . . and this time I did it with my eyes open . . . not like that . . .' I pointed to the newspaper clipping with a hand that trembled visibly, 'when I had to take the rap for something that was mostly not my fault.'

'Matt!' He was himself appalled.

'And as for the cowardice bit, she's got her facts wrong . . . Oh, I've no doubt it sounded convincing and dreadful . . . Polyplanes had a lot to gain by upsetting her to the utmost . . . but I don't see . . . I don't see why she was more upset than just to persuade you not to fly with me . . .'

'Why didn't you tell her yourself?'

I shook my head. 'I probably might have done, one day. I didn't think it was important.'

'Not important!' He was fierce with irritation. 'She seems to have been building up some sort of hero image of you, and then she discovered you had clay feet in all directions ... Of course you should have told her, as you were going to marry her. That was obviously what upset her most ...'

I was speechless. My jaw literally dropped. Finally I said foolishly, 'Did you say *marry* ...'

'Well, yes, of course,' he said impatiently, and then seemed struck by my state of shock. 'You were going to marry her, weren't you?'

'We've never ... even talked about it.'

'But you must have,' he insisted. 'I overheard her and Midge discussing it on Sunday evening, after I got back from Ostend. "When you are married to Matt," Midge said. I heard her distinctly. They were in the kitchen, washing up. They were deciding you would come and live with us in the bungalow ... They were sharing out the bedrooms ...' His voice tailed off weakly. 'It isn't ... it isn't true?'

I silently shook my head.

He looked at me in bewilderment. 'Girls,' he said. 'Girls.'

'I can't marry her,' I said numbly. 'I've hardly enough for a licence ...'

'That doesn't matter.'

'It does to me.'

'It wouldn't to Nancy,' he said. He did a sort of double take. 'Do you mean ... she wasn't so far out ... after all?'

'I suppose ... not so far.'

He looked down at the cutting in his hand, and suddenly screwed it up. 'It looked so bad,' he said with a tinge of apology.

'It was bad,' I said.

He looked at my face. 'Yes. I see it was ...'

A taxi drew up with a jerk and out piled my passengers, all gay and flushed with a winner and carrying a bottle of champagne.

'I'll explain to her,' Colin said. 'I'll get her back ...' His expression was suddenly horrified. Shattered.

'Where has she gone?' I asked.

He screwed up his eyes as if in pain.

'She said ...' He swallowed. 'She went ... to Chanter.'

I sat all evening in the caravan wanting to smash something. Smash the galley. Smash the windows. Smash the walls.

Might have felt better if I had.

Chanter ...

Couldn't eat, couldn't think, couldn't sleep.

Never had listened to my own advice: don't get involved. Should have stuck to it, stayed frozen. Icy. Safe.

Tried to get back to the Arctic and not feel anything, but it was too late. Feeling had come back with a vengeance and of an intensity I could have done without. I hadn't known I loved her. Knew I liked her, felt easy with her, wanted to be with her often and for a long time to come. I'd thought I could stop at friendship, and didn't realize how far, how deep I had already gone.

Oh Nancy ...

I went to sleep in the end by drinking half of the bottle of whisky Kenny Bayst had given me, but it didn't do much good. I woke up at six in the morning to the same dreary torment and with a headache on top.

There were no flights that day to take my mind off it.

Nancy and Chanter ...

At some point in the morning I telephoned from the coinbox in the customers' lounge to the Art School in Liverpool, to ask for Chanter's home address. A crisp secretarial female voice answered: very sorry, absolutely not their policy to divulge the private addresses of their staff. If I could write, they would forward the letter.

'Could I speak to him, then, do you think?' I asked: though what good that would do, Heaven alone knew.

'I'm afraid not, because he isn't here. The school is temporarily closed, and we are not sure when it will reopen.'

'The students,' I remembered. 'Are on strike?'

'That ... er ... is so,' she agreed.

'Can't you possibly tell me how I could get in touch with Chanter?'

'Oh dear ... You are the second person pressing me to help ... but honestly, to tell you the truth we don't know where he lives ... he moves frequently and seldom bothers to keep us up to date.' Secretarial disapproval and despair in the tidy voice. 'As I told Mr Ross, with all the best will in the world, I simply have no idea where you could find him.'

I sat in the crew room while the afternoon dragged by. Finished writing up all records by two thirty, read through some newly arrived information circulars, calculated I had only three weeks and four days to run before my next medical, worked out that if I bought four cups of coffee every day from Honey's machine, I was drinking away one fifteenth of my total week's spending money, decided to make it water more often, looked up when Harley came stalking in, received a lecture on loyalty (mine to him), heard that I was on the next day to take a Wiltshire trainer to Newmarket races, and that if I gave Polyplanes any more grounds for reporting me or the firm to the Board of Trade, I could collect my cards.

'Do my best not to,' I murmured. Didn't please him.

Looked at the door swinging shut behind his back.

Looked at the clock. Three twenty two.

Chanter and Nancy.

Back in the caravan, the same as the evening before. Tried turning on the television. Some comedy about American suburban life punctuated by canned laughter. Stood five minutes of it, and found the silence afterwards almost as bad.

Walked half way round the airfield, cut down to the village, drank half a pint in the pub, walked back. Total, four miles. When I stepped into the caravan it was still only nine o'clock.

Honey Harley was waiting for me, draped over the sofa with maximum exposure of leg. Pink checked cotton sun-dress, very low cut.

'Hi,' she said with self possession. 'Where've you been?'

'For a walk.'

She looked at me quizzically. 'Got the Board of Trade on your mind?'

I nodded. That, and other things.

'I shouldn't worry too much. Whatever the law says or does, you couldn't have just left the Rosses to flounder.'

'Your uncle doesn't agree.'

'Uncle,' she said dispassionately, 'is a nit. And anyway, play your cards right, and even if you do get a fine, Colin Ross will pay it. All you'd have to do would be to ask.'

I shook my head.

'You're daft,' she said. 'Plain daft.'

'You may be right.'

She sighed, stirred, stood up. The curvy body rippled in all the right places. I thought of Nancy: much flatter, much thinner, less obviously sexed and infinitely more desirable. I turned abruptly away from Honey. Like hitting a raw nerve, the thought of Chanter, with his hair and his fringes ... and his hands.

'O.K., iceberg,' she said, mistakenly, 'Relax. Your virtue is quite safe. I only came down, to start with, to tell you there was a phone call for you, and would you please ring back.'

'Who ...?' I tried hard to keep it casual.

'Colin Ross,' Honey said matter-of-factly. 'He wants you to call some time this evening, if you can. I said if it was about a flight I could deal with it, but apparently it's something personal.' She finished the sentence half way between an accusation and a question and left me ample time to explain.

I didn't. I said, 'I'll go up now, then, and use the telephone in the lounge.'

She shrugged. 'All right.'

She walked up with me, but didn't quite have the nerve to hover close enough to listen. I shut the lounge door in front of her resigned and humorously rueful face.

Got the number.

'Colin? Matt.'

'Oh good', he said. 'Look. Nancy rang up today while Midge and I were along at the races ... I took Midge along on the Heath because she was so miserable at home, and now of course she's even more miserable that she missed Nancy ... anyway, our cleaning woman answered the telephone, and Nancy left a message.'

'Is she ... I mean, is she all right?'

'Do you mean, is she with Chanter?' His voice was strained. 'She told our cleaner she had met an old art school friend in Liverpool and was spending a few days camping with her near Warwick.'

'*Her*?' I exclaimed.

'Well, I don't know. I asked our Mrs Williams, and she then said she *thought* Nancy said "her", but of course she would think that, wouldn't she?'

'I'm afraid she would.'

'But anyway, Nancy had been much more insistent that Mrs Williams tells me something else ... it seems she has seen Major Tyderman.'

'She didn't!'

'Yeah ... She said she saw Major Tyderman in the passenger seat of a car on the Stratford road out of Warwick. Apparently there were some roadworks, and the car stopped for a moment just near her.'

'He could have been going anywhere ... from anywhere ...'

'Yes,' he agreed in depression. 'I rang the police in Cambridge to tell them, but Nancy had already been through to them, when she called home. All she could remember about the driver was that he wore glasses. She thought he might have had dark hair and perhaps a moustache. She only glanced at him for a second because she was concentrating on Tyderman. Also she hadn't taken the number, and she's hopeless on the make of cars, so altogether it wasn't a great deal of help.'

'No ...'

'Anyway, she told Mrs Williams she would be coming home on Saturday. She said if I would drive to Warwick races instead of flying, she would come home with me in the car.'

'Well ... thank God for that.'

'If for nothing else,' he said aridly.

Chapter Twelve

I flew the customers from Wiltshire to Newmarket and parked the Six as far as possible from the Polyplane. When the passengers had departed standwards, I got out of the fuggy cabin and into the free air, lay propped on one elbow on the grass, loosened my tie, opened the neck of my shirt. Scorching hot day, a sigh of wind over the Heath, a couple of small cumulus clouds defying evaporation, blue sky over the blue planet.

A suitable day for camping.

Wrenched my thoughts away from the profitless grind: Nancy despised me, despised herself, had chosen Chanter as a refuge, as a steadfast known quantity, had run away from the near-stranger who had not seemed what he seemed, and gone to where she knew she was wanted. Blind, instinctive, impulsive flight. Reckless, understandable, forgivable flight . . .

I could take Chanter, I thought mordantly. I could probably take the thought and memory of Chanter, if only she would settle for me in the end.

It was odd that you had to lose something you didn't even know you had, before you began to want it more than anything on earth.

Down at the other end of the row of aircraft the Polyplane pilot was strolling about, smoking again. One of these fine days he would blow himself up. There was no smile in place that afternoon: even from a hundred yards one could detect the gloom in the heavy frowns he occasionally got rid of in my direction.

Colin had booked with Harley for the week ahead. Polyplanes must have been wondering what else they would have to do to get him back.

They played rough, no doubt of that. Informing on Derrydowns to the Board of Trade, discrediting their pilot, spreading smears that they weren't safe. But would they blow up a Derrydown aircraft? Would they go as far as that?

They would surely have had to be certain they would gain from it, before they risked it. But in fact they hadn't gained. No one had demonstrably been frightened away from using Derrydowns, particularly not Colin Ross. If the bomb had been meant to look like an attack on Colin's life, why should Colin think he would be any safer in a Polyplane?

If they had blown up the aircraft with passengers aboard, that would have ruined Derrydowns. But even if they had been prepared to go that far, they wouldn't have chosen a flight with Colin Ross on it.

And why Major Tyderman, when their own pilots could get near the Derrydown's aircraft without much comment? That was easier . . . they needed a bomb expert. Someone completely unsuspectable. Someone even their pilots didn't know. Because if the boss of Polyplanes had taken the dark step into crime, he wouldn't want chatty employees like pilots spilling it into every aviation bar from Prestwick to Lydd.

The second aeroplane, though, that Tyderman had sabotaged, hadn't been one of the Derrydowns at all. On the other hand, he had thought it was. I stood up, stretched, watched the straining horses scud through the first race, saw in the distance a girl with dark hair and a blue dress and thought for one surging moment it was Nancy. It wasn't Nancy. It wasn't even Midge. Nancy was in Warwickshire, living in a tent.

I thrust my balled fists into my pockets. Not the slightest use thinking about it. Concentrate on something else. Start from the bottom again, as before. Look at everything the wrong way up.

No easy revelation this time. Just the merest flicker of speculation.

Harley . . .?

He had recovered ill-invested capital on the first occasion. He had known Colin would not rely often on his sister's skill after the second. But would Harley go so far . . .? And Harley had known I wasn't flying Colin, though Tyderman had thought I was.

Rats on treadwheels, I thought, go round and round in small circles and get nowhere, just like me.

I sighed. It wasn't much use trying to work it all out when I obviously lacked about fifty pieces of vital information. Decision: did I or did I not start actively looking for some of the pieces? If I didn't, a successor to Major Tyderman might soon be around playing another lot of chemical tricks on aeroplanes, and if I did, I could well be heading myself for yet more trouble.

I tossed a mental coin. Heads you do, tails you don't. In mid-toss I thought of Nancy. All roads led back to Nancy. If I just let everything slide and lay both physically and metaphorically on my back on the grass in the sun, I'd have nothing to think about except what I hated to think about. Very poor prospect. Almost anything else was better.

Took the plunge, and made a start with Annie Villars.

She was standing in the paddock in a sleeveless dark red dress, her greying short hair curling neatly under a black straw hat chosen more for generalship than femininity. From ten paces the authority was clearly uppermost: from three, one could hear the incongruously gentle voice, see the non-aggression in the consciously curved lips, realize that the velvet glove was being given a quilted lining.

She was talking to the Duke of Wessex. She was saying, 'Then if you agree, Bobbie, we'll ask Kenny Bayst to ride it. This new boy had no judgement of pace, and for all his faults, Kenny does know how to time a race.'

The Duke nodded his distinguished head and smiled at her benevolently. They caught sight of me hovering near them and both turned towards me with friendly expressions, one deceptively, and one authentically vacant.

'Matt,' smiled the Duke. 'My dear chap. Isn't it a splendid day?'

'Beautiful, sir,' I agreed. As long as one could obliterate Warwickshire.

'My nephew Matthew,' he said, 'Do you remember him?'

'Of course I do, sir.'

'Well . . . it's his birthday soon, and he wants . . . he was wondering if for a birthday present I would give him a flight in an aeroplane. With you, he said. Especially with you.'

I smiled. 'I'd like to do that very much.'

'Good, good. Then . . . er . . . how do you suggest we fix it?'

'I'll arrange it with Mr Harley.'

'Yes. Good. Soon then. He's coming down to stay with me tomorrow, as it's the end of term and his mother is off somewhere in Greece. So next week, perhaps?'

'I'm sure that will be all right.'

He beamed happily. 'Perhaps I'll come along too.'

Annie Villars said patiently, 'Bobbie, we ought to go and see about saddling your horse.'

He looked at his watch. 'By jove, yes. Amazing where the afternoon goes to. Come along, then.' He gave me another large smile, transferred it intact to Annie, and obediently moved off after her as she started purposefully towards the saddling boxes.

I bought a racecard. The Duke's horse was a two year old maiden called Thundersticks. I watched the Duke and Annie watch Thundersticks walk round the parade ring, one with innocent beaming pride, the other with judicious non-commitment. The pace-lacking boy rode a bad race, even to my unpractised eye: too far out in front over the first furlong, too far out the back over the last. Just as well the Duke's colours were inconspicuous, I thought. He took his disappointment with charming grace, reassuring Annie that the colt would do better next time. Sure to. Early days yet. She smiled at him in soft agreement and bestowed on the jockey a look which would have bored a hole through steel plating.

After they had discussed the sweating colt's performance yard by yard, and patted him and packed him off with his lad towards the stables, the Duke took Annie away to the bar for a drink. After that she had another loser for another owner and another thoughtful detour for refreshment, so that I didn't manage to catch her on her own until between the last two races.

She listened without comment to me explaining that I thought it might be possible to do something positive about solving the Great Bomb Mystery, if she would help.

'I thought it was solved already.'

'Not really. No one knows why.'

'No. Well, I don't see how I can help.'

'Would you mind telling me how well Major Tyderman and Mr Goldenberg know each other, and how they come to have any say in how Rudiments should run in its various races?'

She said mildly, 'It's none of your business.'

I knew what the mildness concealed. 'I know that.'

'And you are impertinent.'

'Yes.'

She regarded me straightly, and the softness gradually faded out of her features to leave taut skin over the cheekbones and a stern set to the mouth.

'I am fond of Midge and Nancy Ross,' she said. 'I don't see how anything I can tell you will help, but I certainly want no harm to come to those two girls. That last escapade was just a shade too dangerous, wasn't it? And if Rupert Tyderman could do that ...' She paused, thinking deeply. 'I will be obliged if you will keep anything I may tell you to yourself.'

'I will.'

'Very well.... I've known Rupert for a very long time. More or less from my childhood. He is about fifteen years older.... When I was a young girl I thought he was a splendid person, and I didn't understand why people hesitated when they talked about him.' She sighed. 'I found out, of course, when I was older. He had been wild, as a youth. A vandal when vandalism wasn't as common as it is now. When he was in his twenties he borrowed money from all his relations and friends for various grand schemes, and never paid them back. His family bought him out of one mess where he had sold a picture entrusted to him for sake keeping and spent the proceeds ... Oh, lots of things like that. Then the war came and he volunteered immediately, and I believe all during the war he did very well. He was in the Royal Engineers, I think ... but afterwards, after the war ended, he was quietly allowed to resign his commission for cashing dud cheques with his fellow officers.'

She shook her head impatiently. 'He has always been a fool to himself... Since the war he has lived on some money his grandfather left in trust, and on what he could cadge from any friends he had left.'

'You included?' I suggested.

She nodded. 'Oh yes. He's always very persuasive. It's always for something extremely plausible, but all the deals fall through ...' She looked away across the Heath, considering. 'And then this year, back in February or March, I think, he turned up one day and said he wouldn't need to borrow any more from me, he'd got a good thing going which would make him rich.'

'What was it?'

'He wouldn't say. Just told me not to worry, it was all legal. He had gone into partnership with someone with a cast iron idea for making a fortune. Well, I'd heard that sort of thing from him so often before. The only difference was that this time he didn't want money....'

'He wanted something else?'

'Yes.' She frowned. 'He wanted me to introduce him to Bobbie Wessex. He said ... just casually ... how much he'd like to meet him, and I suppose I was so relieved not to find him cadging five hundred or so that I instantly agreed. It was very silly of me, but it didn't seem important ...'

'What happened then?'

She shrugged. 'They were both at the Doncaster meeting at the opening of the flat season, so I introduced them. Nothing to it. Just a casual racecourse introduction. And then,' she looked annoyed, 'the next time Rupert turned up with that man Goldenberg, saying Bobbie Wessex had given him permission to decide how Rudiments should be run in all his races. I said he certainly wasn't going to do that, and telephoned to Bobbie. But,' she sighed, 'Rupert had indeed talked him into giving him carte blanche with Rudiments. Rupert is an expert persuader, and Bobbie, well, poor Bobbie is easily open to suggestion. Anyone with half an eye could see that Goldenberg was as straight as a corkscrew but Rupert said he was essential as someone had got to put the bets on, and he, Rupert, couldn't, as no bookmaker would accept his credit and you had to have hard cash for the Tote.'

'And then the scheme went wrong,' I said.

'The first time Rudiments won, they'd both collected a lot of money. I had told them the horse would win. Must win. It started at a hundred to six, first time out, and they were both as high as kites afterwards.'

'And next time Kenny Bayst won again when he wasn't supposed to, when they had laid it?'

She looked startled. 'So you did understand what they were saying.'

'Eventually.'

'Just like Rupert to lie it out. No sense of discretion.'

I sighed. 'Well, thank you very much for being so frank. Even if I still can't see what connection Rudiments has with Major Tyderman blowing up one aircraft and crippling another.'

She twisted her mouth. 'I told you,' she said, 'Right at the beginning, that nothing I told you would be of any help.'

Colin stopped beside me in pink and green silks on his way from the weighing room to the parade ring for the last race. He gave me a concentrated inquiring look which softened into something like compassion.

'The waiting's doing you no good,' he said.

'Has she telephoned again?'

He shook his head. 'Midge won't leave the house, in case she does.'

'I'll be at Warwick races on Saturday ... flying some people up from Kent ... Will you ask her ... just to talk to me?'

'I'll wring her stupid little neck,' he said.

I flew the customers back to Wiltshire and the Six back to Buckingham. Harley, waiting around with bitter eyes, told me the Board of Trade had let him know they were definitely proceeding against me.

'I expected they would.'

'But that's not what I wanted to speak to you about. Come into the office.' He was unfriendly, as usual. Snappy. He picked up a sheet of paper from his desk and waved it at me.

'Look at these times. I've been going through the bills Honey has sent out since you've been here. All the times are shorter. We've had to charge less ... we're not making enough profit. It's got to stop. D'you understand? Got to stop.'

'Very well.'

He looked nonplussed: hadn't expected such an easy victory.

'And I'm taking on another pilot.'

'Am I out, then?' I found I scarcely cared.

He was surprised. 'No. Of course not. We simply seem to be getting too much taxi work just lately for you to handle on your own, even with Don's help.'

'Maybe we're getting more work because we're doing the trips faster and charging less,' I suggested.

He was affronted. 'Don't be ridiculous.'

Another long evening in the caravan, aching and empty.

Nowhere to go, no way of going, and nothing to spend when I got there. That didn't matter, because wherever I went, whatever I spent, the inescapable thoughts lay in wait. Might as well suffer them alone and cheaply as anywhere else.

For something to do, I cleaned the caravan from end to end. When it was finished, it looked better, but I, on the whole, felt worse. Scrambled myself two eggs, ate them unenthusiastically on toast. Drank a dingy cup of dried coffee, dried milk.

Switched on the television. Old movie, circa 1950, pirates, cutlasses, heaving bosoms. Switched off.

Sat and watched night arrive on the airfield. Tried to concentrate on what Annie Villars had told me, so as not to think of night arriving over the fields and tents of Warwickshire. For a long time, had no success at all.

Look at everything upside down. Take absolutely nothing for granted.

The middle of the night produced out of a shallow restless sleep a singularly wild idea. Most sleep-spawned revelations from the subconscious wither and die of ridicule in the dawn, but this time it was different. At five, six, seven o'clock, it still looked possible. I traipsed in my mind through everything I had seen and heard since the day of the bomb, and added a satisfactory answer to why to the answer to who.

That Friday I had to set off early in the Aztec to Germany with some television cameramen from Denham, wait while they took their shots, and bring them home again. In spite of breaking Harley's ruling about speed into pin-sized fragments it was seven-thirty before I climbed stiffly out of the cockpit and helped Joe push the sturdy twin into the hangar.

'Need it for Sunday, don't you?' he said.

'That's right. Colin Ross to France.' I stretched and yawned and picked up my heavy flight bag with all its charts and documents.

'We're working you hard.'

'What I'm here for.'

He put his hands in his overall pockets. 'You're light on those aeroplanes. I'll give you that. Larry, now, Larry was heavy-handed. Always needing things repaired, we were, before you came.'

I gave him a sketch of an appreciative smile and walked up to fill in the records in the office. Harley and Don were both still flying, Harley giving a lesson, and Don a sight-seeing trip in the Six, and Honey was still traffic-copping up in the tower. I climbed up there to see her and ask her a considerable favour.

'Borrow my Mini?' she repeated in surprise. 'Do you mean now, this minute?'

I nodded. 'For the evening.'

'I suppose I could get Uncle to take me home,' she reflected. 'If you'll fetch me in the morning?'

'Certainly.'

'Well ... all right. I don't really need it this evening. Just fill it up with petrol before you hand it back.'

'O.K. And thanks a lot.'

She gave me a frankly vulgar grin. 'Minis are too small for what you want.'

I managed to grin back. 'Yeah ...'

Given the wheels, make the appointment. A pleasant male voice answered the telephone, polite and quiet.

'The Duke of Wessex? Yes, this is his house. Who is speaking please?'

'Matthew Shore.'

'One moment, sir.'

The one moment stretched to four minutes, and I fed a week's beer money into the greedy box. At last the receiver at the other end was picked up and with slightly heavy breathing the Duke's unmistakable voice said, 'Matt? My dear chap, what can I do for you?'

'If you are not busy this evening, sir, could I call in to see you for a few minutes?'

'This evening? Busy? Hm ... Is it about Matthew's flight?'

'No, sir, something different. I won't take up much of your time.'

'Come by all means, my dear chap, if you want to. After dinner, perhaps? Nine o'clock, say?'

'Nine o'clock,' I confirmed. 'I'll be there.'

The Duke lived near Royston, west of Cambridge. Honey's Mini ate up the miles like Billy Bunter so that it was nine o'clock exactly when I stopped at a local garage to ask for directions to the Duke's house. On Honey's radio, someone was reading the news. I listened idly at first while the attendant finished filling up the car in front, and then with sharp and sickened attention. 'Racehorse trainer Jarvis Kitch and owner Dobson Ambrose, whose filly Scotchbright won the Oaks last month, were killed today in a multiple traffic accident just outside Newmarket. The Australian jockey Kenny Bayst, who was in the car with them, was taken to hospital with multiple injuries. His condition tonight is said to be fair. Three stable lads, trapped when a lorry crushed their car, also died in the crash.'

Mechanically I asked for, got, and followed, the directions to the Duke's house. I was thinking about poor large aggressive Ambrose and his cowed trainer Kitch, hoping that Kenny wasn't too badly hurt to race again, and trying to foresee the ramifications.

There was nothing else on the news except the weather forecast: heatwave indefinitely continuing.

No mention of Rupert Tyderman. But Tyderman, that day, had been seen by the police.

Chapter Thirteen

The Duke's manservant was as pleasant as his voice: a short, assured, slightly pop-eyed man in his later forties with a good deal of the Duke's natural benevolence in his manner. The house he presided over opened to the public, a notice read, every day between 1st March and 30th November. The Duke, I discovered, lived privately in the upper third of the south-west wing.

'The Duke is expecting you, sir. Will you come this way?'

I followed. The distance I followed accounted for the length of time I had waited for the Duke to come to the telephone and also his breathlessness when he got there. We went up three floors, along a two furlong straight, and up again, to the attics. The attics in 18th century stately homes were a long way from the front hall.

The manservant opened a white-painted door and gravely showed me in.

'Mr Shore, your Grace.'

'Come in, come in, my dear chap,' said the Duke.

I went in, and smiled with instant, spontaneous delight. The square low-ceilinged room contained a vast toy electric train set laid out on an irregular ring of wide green-covered trestle tables. A terminus, sidings, two small towns, a branch line, tunnels, gradients, viaducts, the Duke had the lot. In the centre of the ring, he and his nephew Matthew stood behind a large control table pressing the switches which sent about six different trains clanking on different courses round the complex.

The Duke nudged his nephew. 'There you are, what did we say? He likes it.'

Young Matthew gave me a fleeting glance and went back to some complicated point changing. 'He was bound to. He's got the right sort of face.'

The Duke said, 'You can crawl in here best under that table with the signal box and level crossing.' He pointed, so I went down on hands and knees and made the indicated journey. Stood up in the centre. Looked around at the rows of lines and remembered the hopeless passion I'd felt in toy shops as a child: my father had been an underpaid schoolmaster who had spent his money on books.

The two enthusiasts showed me where the lines crossed and how the trains could be switched without crashing. Their voices were filled with contentment, their eyes shining, their faces intent.

'Built this lot up gradually, of course,' the Duke said. 'Started when

I was a boy. Then for years I never came up here. Not until young Matthew got old enough. Now, as I expect you can see, we have great times.'

'We're thinking of running a branch line right through that wall over there into the next attic,' Matthew said. 'There isn't much room in here.'

The Duke nodded. 'Next week, perhaps. For your birthday.'

Young Matthew gave him a huge grin and deftly let a pullman cross three seconds in front of a chugging goods. 'It's getting dark,' he observed. 'Lighting up time.'

'So it is,' agreed the Duke.

Matthew with a flourish pressed a switch, and they both watched my face. All round the track, and on all the stations and signal boxes and in the signals themselves, tiny electric lights suddenly shone out. The effect, to my eyes, was enchanting.

'There you are,' said the Duke. 'He likes it.'

'Bound to,' young Matthew said.

They played with the trains for another whole hour, because they had worked out a timetable and they wanted to see if they could keep to it before they pinned it up on the notice board in the terminal. The Duke apologized, not very apologetically, for keeping me waiting, but it was, he explained, Matthew's first evening out of school, and they had been waiting all through the term for this occasion.

At twenty to eleven the last shuttle service stopped at the buffers in the terminal and Matthew yawned. With the satisfaction of a job well done the two railwaymen unfolded several large dustsheets and laid them carefully over the silent tracks, and then we all three crawled back under the table which held the level crossing.

The Duke led the way down the first flight and along the two furlongs, and we were then, it appeared, in his living quarters.

'You'd better cut along to bed, now, Matthew,' he said to his nephew. 'See you in the morning. Eight o'clock sharp, out in the stables.'

'Sure thing,' Matthew said. 'And after that, the races.' He sighed with utter content. 'Better than school,' he said.

The Duke showed me into a smallish white-painted sittingroom furnished with Persian rugs, leather armchairs, and endless sporting prints.

'A drink?' he suggested, indicating a tray.

I looked at the bottles. 'Whisky, please.'

He nodded, poured two, added water, gave me the glass and waved me to an armchair.

'Now, my dear chap . . .?'

It suddenly seemed difficult, what I had come to ask him, and what to explain. He was so transparently honest, so incapable of double dealing: I wondered if he could comprehend villainy at all.

'I was talking to Annie Villars about your horse Rudiments,' I said.

A slight frown lowered his eyebrows. 'She was annoyed with me for letting her friend Rupert Tyderman advise me . . . I do so dislike upsetting Annie, but I'd promised ... Anyway, she has sorted it all out splendidly, I believe, and now that her friend has turned out to be so extraordinary, with that bomb, I mean, I don't expect he will want to advise me about Rudiments any more.'

'Did he, sir, introduce to you any friend of his?'

'Do you mean Eric Goldenberg? Yes, he did. Can't say I really liked the fellow, though. Didn't trust him, you know. Young Matthew didn't like him, either.'

'Did Goldenberg ever talk to you about insurance?'

'Insurance?' he repeated. 'No, I can't remember especially that he did.'

I frowned. It had to be insurance.

It had to be.

'It was his other friend,' said the Duke, 'who arranged the insurance.'

I stared at him. 'Which other friend?'

'Charles Carthy-Todd.'

I blinked. 'Who?'

'Charles Carthy-Todd,' he repeated patiently. 'He was an acquaintance of Rupert Tyderman. Tyderman introduced us one day. At Newmarket races, I think it was. Anyway, it was Charles who suggested the insurance. Very good scheme. I thought it was. Sound. very much needed. An absolute boon to a great many people.'

'The Racegoers' Accident Fund,' I said. 'Of which you are Patron.'

'That's right.' He smiled contentedly. 'So many people have complimented me on giving it my name. A splendid undertaking altogether.'

'Could you tell me a little more about how it was set up?'

'Are you interested in insurance, my dear chap? I could get you an introduction at Lloyd's ... but ...'

I smiled. To become an underwriter at Lloyd's one had to think of a stake of a hundred thousand pounds as loose change. The Duke, in his quiet good natured way, was a very rich man indeed.

'No sir. It's just the Accident Fund I'm interested in. How it was set up, and how it is run.'

'Charles sees to it all, my dear chap. I can't seem to get the hang of these things at all, you know. Technicalities, and all that. Much prefer horses, don't you see?'

'Yes, sir, I do see. Could you perhaps, then, tell me about Mr Carthy-Todd? What he's like, and so on.'

'He's about your height but much heavier and he has dark hair and wears spectacles. I think he has a moustache ... yes, that's right, a moustache.'

I was jolted. The Duke's description of Charles Carthy-Todd fitted almost exactly the impression Nancy had had of Tyderman's companion. Dozens of men around, though, with dark hair, moustache, glasses ...'

'I really meant, sir, his ... er ... character.'

'My dear chap. Sound. Very sound. A thoroughly good fellow. An expert in insurance, spent years with a big firm in the city.'

'And ... his background?' I suggested.

'Went to Rugby. Then straight into an office. Good family, of course.'

'You've met them?'

He looked surprised at the question. 'Not actually, no. Business connection, that's what I have with Charles. His family came from Herefordshire, I think. There are photographs in our office ... land, horses, dogs, wife and children, that sort of thing. Why do you ask?'

I hesitated. 'Did he come to you with the Accident Scheme complete?'

He shook his fine head. 'No, no, my dear chap. It arose out of conversation. We were saying how sad it was for the family of that small steeplechase trainer who was drowned on holiday and what a pity it was that there wasn't some scheme which covered everyone engaged in racing, not just the jockeys. Then of course when we really went into it we broadened it to include the racing public as well. Charles explained that the more premiums we collected the more we could pay out in compensation.'

'I see.'

'We have done a great deal of good already.' He smiled happily. 'Charles was telling me the other day that we have settled three claims for injuries so far, and that those clients are so pleased that they are telling everyone else to join in.'

I nodded. 'I've met one of them. He'd broken his ankle and received a thousand pounds.'

He beamed. 'There you are, then.'

'When did the scheme actually start?'

'Let me see. In May, I should think. Towards the end of May. About two months ago. It took a little while to organize, of course, after we'd decided to go ahead.'

'Charles did the organizing?'

'My dear chap, of course.'

'Did you take advice from any of your friends at Lloyd's?'

'No need, you know. Charles is an expert himself. He drew up all the papers. I just signed them.'

'But you read them first?'

'Oh yes,' he said reassuringly, then smiled like a child, 'Didn't understand them much, of course.'

'And you yourself guaranteed the money?' Since the collapse of cut-price car insurance firms, I'd read somewhere, privately run insurance schemes had to show a minimum backing of fifty thousand pounds before the Board of Trade would give them permission to exist.

'That's right.'

'Fifty thousand pounds?'

'We thought a hundred thousand might be better. Gives the scheme better standing, more weight, don't you see?'

'Charles said so?'

'He knows about such things.'

'Yes.'

'But of course I'll never have to find that money. It's only a guarantee of good faith, and to comply with the law. The premiums will cover the compensation and Charles' salary and all the costs. Charles worked it all out. And I told him right at the beginning that I didn't want any profit out of it, just for lending it my name. I really don't need any profit. I told him just to add my share into the paying out fund, and he thought that was a most sensible suggestion. Our whole purpose, you see, is to do good.'

'You're a singularly kind, thoughtful and generous man,' I said.

It made him uncomfortable. 'My dear chap ...'

'And after tonight's news, I think several widows in Newmarket will bless you.'

'What news?'

I told him about the accident in which Kitch and Ambrose and the three stable lads had died. He was horrified.

'Oh, the poor fellows. The poor fellows. One can only hope that you are right, and that they had joined our scheme.'

'Will the premiums you have already collected be enough to cover many large claims all at once?'

He wasn't troubled. 'I expect so. Charles will have seen to all that. But even if they don't, I will make up the difference. No one will suffer. That's what guaranteeing means, do you see?'

'Yes, sir.'

'Kitch and Ambrose,' he said. 'The poor fellows.'

'And Kenny Bayst is in hospital, badly hurt.'

'Oh dear.' His distress was genuine. He really cared.

'I know that Kenny Bayst was insured with you. At least, he told me he was going to be. And after this I should think you would be flooded with more applications.'

'I expect you're right. You seem to understand things, just like Charles does.'

'Did Charles have any plans for giving the scheme a quick boost to begin with?'

'I don't follow you, my dear chap.'

'What happened to the Accident Fund,' I asked casually, 'After that bomb exploded in the aeroplane which had been carrying Colin Ross?'

He looked enthusiastic. 'Do you know, a lot of people told me they would join. It made them think, they said. I asked Charles if they had really done anything about it, and he said yes, quite a few inquiries had come in. I said that as no one had been hurt, the bomb seemed to have done the Fund a lot of good, and Charles was surprised and said so it had.'

Charles had met the Duke through Rupert Tyderman. Rupert Tyderman had set off the bomb. If ever there was a stone cold certainty, it was that Charles Carthy-Todd was the least surprised on earth that cash had followed combustion. He had reckoned it would.

He had reckoned right.

'Charles sent out a pamphlet urging everyone to insure against bombs on the way home,' I said.

The Duke smiled. 'Yes, that's right. I believe it was very effective. We thought, do you see, that as no one had been hurt, there would be no harm in it.'

'And as it was Colin Ross who was on board, the bomb incident was extensively covered on television and in the newspapers ... and had a greater impact on your Fund than had it been anyone else.'

The Duke's forehead wrinkled. 'I'm not sure I understand.'

'Never mind, sir. I was just thinking aloud.'

'Very easy habit to fall into. Do it myself, you know, all the time.'

Carthy-Todd and Tyderman's second sabotage, I thought to myself, hadn't been as good. Certainly by attacking Colin they'd achieved the same impact and national coverage, but I would have thought it was too obviously slanted at one person to have had much universal effect. Could be wrong, though ...

'This has been the most interesting chat,' said the Duke, 'But my dear fellow, the evening is passing. What was it that you wanted to see me about?'

'Er ...' I cleared my throat. 'Do you know, sir, I'd very much like to meet Mr Carthy-Todd. He sounds a most go-ahead, enterprising man.'

The Duke nodded warmly.

'Do you know where I could find him?'

'Tonight, do you mean?' He was puzzled.

'No, sir. Tomorrow will do.'

'I suppose you might find him at our office. He's sure to be there, because he knows I will be calling in myself. Warwick races, do you see?'

'The Accident Fund office ... is in Warwick?'

'Of course.'

'Silly of me,' I said. 'I didn't know.'

The Duke twinkled at me. 'I see you haven't joined the Fund.'

'I'll join tomorrow. I'll go to the office. I'll be at Warwick too, for the races.'

'Great,' he said. 'Great. The office is only a few hundred yards from the racecourse.' He put two fingers into an inside pocket and brought out a visiting card. 'There you are, my dear chap. The address. And if you're there about an hour before the first race, I'll be there too, and you can meet Charles. You'll like him, I'm sure of that.'

'I'll look forward to it,' I said. I finished my whisky and stood up. 'It was kind of you to let me come ... and I think your trains are absolutely splendid ...'

His face brightened. He escorted me all the way down to the front door, talking about young Matthew and the plans they had for the holidays. Would I fix Matthew's flight for Thursday, he asked. Thursday was Matthew's birthday. He would be eleven.

'Thursday it is,' I agreed. 'I'll do it in the evening, if there's a charter fixed for that day.'

'Most good of you, my dear chap.'

I looked at the kind, distinguished, uncomprehending face. I knew that if his partner Charles Carthy-Todd skipped with the accumulated premiums before paying out the Newmarket widows, as I was privately certain he would, the honourable Duke of Wessex would meet every penny out of his own coffers. In all probability he could afford it, but that wasn't the point. He would be hurt and bewildered and impossibly distressed at having been tangled up in a fraud, and it seemed to me especially vicious that anyone should take advantage of his vulnerable simplicity and goodness.

Charles Carthy-Todd was engaged in taking candy from a mentally retarded child and then making it look as though the child had stolen it in the first place. One couldn't help but feel protective. One couldn't help but want to stop it.

I said impulsively, 'Take care of yourself, sir.'

'My dear chap ... I will.'

I walked down the steps from his front door towards Honey's Mini waiting in the drive, and looked back to where he stood in the yellow oblong of light. He waved a hand gently and slowly closed the door, and I saw from his benign slightly puzzled expression that he was still not quite sure why I had come.

It was after one o'clock when I got back to the caravan. Tired, hungry, miserable about Nancy, I still couldn't stay asleep. Three o'clock, I was awake again, tangling the sheets as if in fever. I got up and splashed my itching eyes with cold water: lay down, got up, went for a walk across the airfield. The cool starry night came through my shirt and quietened my skin but didn't do much for the hopeless ache between my ears.

At eight in the morning I went to fetch Honey, filling her tank with the promised petrol at the nearest garage. She had made a gallon or two on the deal, I calculated. Fair enough.

What was not fair enough, however, was the news with which she greeted me.

'Colin Ross wants you to ring him up. He rang yesterday evening about half a hour after you'd buzzed off.'

'Did he say ... what about?'

'He did ask me to write you a message, but honestly, I forgot. I was up in the tower until nine, and then Uncle was impatient to get home, and I just went off with him and forgot all about coming down here with the message ... and anyway, what difference would a few hours make?'

'What was the message?'

'He said to tell you his sister didn't meet anyone called Chanter at Liverpool. Something about a strike, and this Chanter not being there. I don't know ... there were two aircraft in the circuit and I wasn't paying all that much attention. Come to think of it, he did seem pretty anxious I should give you the message last night, but like

I said, I forgot. Sorry, and all that. Was it important?'

I took a deep breath. Thinking about the past night, I could cheerfully have strangled her. 'Thanks for telling me.'

She gave me a sharp glance. 'You look bushed. Have you been making love all night? You don't look fit to fly.'

'Seldom felt better,' I said with truth. 'And no, I haven't.'

'Save yourself for me.'

'Don't bank on it.'

'Louse.'

When I rang Colin's number from the telephone in the lounge it was Midge who answered. The relief in her voice was as overwhelming as my own.

'Matt . . .!' I could hear her gulp, and knew she was fighting against tears. 'Oh, Matt . . . I'm so glad you've rung. She didn't go after Chanter. She didn't. It's all right. Oh dear . . . just a minute . . .' She sniffed and paused, and when she spoke again she had her voice under control. 'She rang yesterday evening and we talked to her for a long time. She said she was sorry if she had upset us, she had really left because she was so angry with herself, so humiliated at having made up such silly dreams about you . . . she said it was all her own fault, that you hadn't deceived her in any way, she had deceived herself . . . she wanted to tell us that it wasn't because she was angry with you that she ran out, but because she felt she had made such a fool of herself . . . Anyway, she said she had cooled off a good deal by the time the train got to Liverpool and she was simply miserable by then, and then when she found Chanter had gone away because of the strike she said she was relieved, really. Chanter's landlady told Nancy where he had gone . . . somewhere in Manchester, to do a painting of industrial chimneys, she thought . . . but Nancy decided it wasn't Chanter she wanted . . . and she didn't know what to do, she still felt muddled . . . and then outside the art school she met a girl who had been a student with us in London. She was setting off for a camping holiday near Stratford and . . . well . . . Nancy decided to go with her. She said a few days' peace and some landscape painting would put her right . . . so she rang up here and it was our cleaning woman who answered . . . Nancy swears she told her it was Jill she was with, and not Chanter, but of course we never got that part of the message . . .' She stopped, and when I didn't answer immediately she said anxiously, 'Matt, are you still there?'

'Yes.'

'You were so quiet.'

'I was thinking about the last four days.'

Four wretched, dragging days. Four endless grinding nights. All unnecessary. She hadn't been with Chanter at all. If she'd suffered about what she'd imagined about me, so had I from what I'd imagined about her. Which made us, I guessed, about quits.

'Colin told her she should have asked you about the court case instead of jumping to conclusions,' Midge said.

'She didn't jump, she was pushed.'

'Yes. She knows that now. She's pretty upset. She doesn't really want to face you at Warwick ... after making such a mess of things ...'

'I shan't actually slaughter her.'

She half laughed. 'I'll defend her. I'm driving over with Colin. I'll see you there too.'

'That's marvellous.'

'Colin's out on the gallops just now. We're setting off after he's come in and had something to eat.'

'Tell him to drive carefully. Tell him to think of Ambrose.'

'Yes ... Isn't it awful about that crash?'

'Have you heard what happened, exactly?'

'Apparently Ambrose tried to pass a slow lorry on a bend and there was another one coming the other way ... he ran into it head on and one of the lorries overturned and crushed another car with three stable lads in it. There's quite a lot about it in today's *Sporting Life*.'

'I expect I'll see it. And Midge ... thank Colin for his message last night.'

'I will. He said he didn't want you to worry any longer. He seemed to think you were almost as worried about her as we were.'

'Almost,' I agreed wryly. 'See you at Warwick.'

Chapter Fourteen

Honey had arranged for me to fly a Mr and Mrs Whiteknight and their two young daughters down to Lydd, where the daughters were to meet friends and leave on the car air ferry to Le Touquet for a holiday in France. After waving the daughters off, the Whiteknights wanted to belt back to see their horse run in the first race at Warwick, which meant, since there was no racecourse strip, landing at Coventry and hailing a cab.

Accordingly I loaded them up at Buckingham and pointed the nose of the Six towards Kent. The two daughters, about fourteen and sixteen, were world-weary and disagreeable, looking down their noses at everything with ingrained hostility. Their mother behaved to me with the cool graciousness of condescension, and autocratically bossed the family. Mr Whiteknight, gruff, unconsulted, a downtrodden universal provider, out of habit brought up the rear.

At Lydd, after carrying the daughters' suitcases unthanked into the terminal, I went back to the Six to wait through the farewells. Mr Whiteknight had obligingly left his *Sporting Life* on his seat. I picked it up and read it. There was a photograph of the Ambrose crash. The usual mangled metal, pushed to the side of the road, pathetic result of impatience.

I turned to the middle pages, to see how many races Colin was riding at Warwick. He was down for five, and in most of them was favourite.

Alongside the Warwick programme, there was an advertisement in bold black letters.

'Colin Ross has insured with us. Why don't you?' Underneath in smaller type it went on, '*You* may not be lucky enough to survive two narrow escapes. Don't chance it. Cut out the proposal form printed below and send it with five pounds to the Racegoers' Accident Fund, Avon Street, Warwick. Your insurance cover starts from the moment your letter is in the post.'

I put the paper down on my knee, looked into space, and sucked my teeth.

Major Tyderman had told Annie Villars that he and a partner of his had something going for them that would make them rich. She had thought he meant control of Rudiments, but of course it hadn't been that. The manoeuvring with Rudiments had come about simply because Tyderman couldn't resist a small swindle on the side, even when he was engaged in a bigger one.

Tyderman had got Annie to introduce him to the Duke so that he in his turn could produce Carthy-Todd. Goldenberg was incidental, needed only for placing bets. Carthy-Todd was central, the moving mind, the instigator. Everyone else, Tyderman, the Duke, Colin, Annie, myself, all of us were pieces on his chess-board, to be shoved around until the game was won.

Clean up and clear out, that was how he must have decided to play. He hadn't waited for the Fund to grow slowly and naturally, he'd blown up an aeroplane and used Colin Ross for publicity. He would only have stayed anyway until the claims began mounting, and if the crash victims at Newmarket were in fact insured he would be off within the week. He would stay just long enough to collect the crash-inspired rush of new premiums, and that would be that. A quick transfer to a Swiss bank. A one-way ticket to the next happy hunting ground.

I didn't know how to stop him. There would be no proof that he meant to defraud until after he'd done it. I could produce nothing to back up my belief. No one was going to lurch into drastic action on what was little more than a guess. I could perhaps telephone to the Board of Trade ... but the Board of Trade and I were hardly on speaking terms. The tall man might listen. He had, after all, once asked for my thoughts. Maybe the aircraft section had a hotline to the insurance section. And maybe not.

With a sigh I folded up Mr Whiteknight's newspaper and glanced again at the crash on the front page. Down in one corner in the left hand column, beside the account of the accident, a paragraph heading caught my eye.

Tyderman, it said. I read the dry meagre lines underneath with a vague and then mounting feeling of alarm.

'A man believed to be Major Rupert Tyderman was found dead

early yesterday beside the main London to South Wales railway line, between Swindon and Bristol. His death, at first attributed to a fall from a train, was later established as having been the result of a stab wound. The police, who had wanted to interview Major Tyderman, are making inquiries.'

The Whiteknight parents were walking back across the apron by the time I'd decided what to do. They were displeased when I met them and said I was going to make a telephone call. There wasn't time, they said.

'Check on the weather,' I lied. They looked up at the hazy heat-wave sky and gave me deservedly bitter looks. All the same, I went on my way.

The Duke's polite manservant answered.

'No, Mr Shore, I'm very sorry, His Grace left for Warwick half an hour ago.'

'Was young Matthew with him?'

'Yes, sir.'

'Do you know if he was planning to go to the Accident Fund office before he went to the racecourse?'

'I believe so, sir. Yes.'

I put the receiver down, feeling increasingly fearful. Rupert Tyderman's death put the game into a different league. Lives had been at risk before, in the aeroplanes; the basic callousness was there; but on those occasions the intention had been expressly not to kill. But now, if Carthy-Todd had decided to clear up behind him ... if Tyderman's blunder with Nancy's aeroplane, which had led to his uncovering, had also led directly to his death ... if Carthy-Todd had stopped Tyderman giving evidence against him ... then would he, could he possibly, also kill the simple, honest, truth-spilling Duke ... ?

He wouldn't, I thought coldly. He couldn't

I didn't convince myself one little bit.

The Whiteknights had no cause for complaint about the speed at which I took them to Coventry, though they consented only with bad grace when I asked to share their taxi to the races. I parted from them at the main gate and walked back towards the town centre, looking for the office of the Accident Fund. As the Duke had said, it wasn't far: less than a quarter of a mile.

It was located on the first floor of a small moderately well kept town house which fronted straight on to the pavement. The ground floor seemed to be uninhabited, but the main door stood open and a placard on the wall just inside announced 'Racegoers' Accident Fund. Please walk up.'

I walked up. On the first landing there was a wash room, a secretary's office, and, at the front of the house, a door with a yale lock and a knocker in the shape of a horse's head. I flipped the knocker a couple of times and the door came abruptly open.

'Hello,' said young Matthew, swinging it wide. 'Uncle was just saying you would miss us. We're just going along to the races.'

'Come along in, my dear chap,' said the Duke's voice from inside the room.

I stepped into the office. At first sight a plushy one: wall to wall plum coloured carpet, but of penny-pinching quality, two fat looking easy chairs with cheap foam seats, a pair of shoulder high metal filing cabinets and a modern afrormosia desk. The atmosphere of a solid, sober, long established business came exclusively from the good proportions of the bay windowed room, the mouldings round the nineteenth century ceiling, the carved wood and marble slab of the handsome fireplace, and some dark old gilt framed oils on the walls. The office had been chosen with genius to convince, to reassure, to charm. And as clients of insurance companies seldom if ever visited its office, this one must have been designed to convince, to reassure, to charm only the Duke himself.

The Duke introduced me to the man who had been sitting and who now stood behind the desk.

'Charles Carthy-Todd ... Matthew Shore.'

I shook his hand. He'd seen me before, as I'd seen him. Neither of us gave the slightest sign of it. I hoped he had not distinguished in me the minute subsidence of tension which I saw in him. The tension I felt hadn't subsided in the slightest.

He was all the Duke had said: a man with good presence, good voice, a thorough-going public school gent. He would have had to have been, to net the Duke; and there were all those silver framed photographs, which the Duke had mentioned, standing around to prove it.

He had dark hair with the merest sprinkling of grey, a compact little moustache, pinkish tan slightly oily-looking skin, and heavy black-framed glasses assisting his greyish blue eyes.

The Duke was sitting comfortably in an armchair in the bay window, his splendid head haloed by the shining day behind. His knees were crossed, his hands relaxed, and he was smoking a cigar. From his general air of pleased well-being, it was easy to see the pride he held in his beautiful benevolent fund. I wished sincerely for his sake that he wasn't going to have to wake up.

Charles Carthy-Todd sat down and continued with what he had been going to do when I arrived, offering young Matthew a piece of chocolate-covered orange peel from a half empty round red and gold tin. Matthew took it, thanked him, ate it, and watched him with anxious reserve. Like the Duke, I trusted young Matthew's instinct. All too clearly, it had switched to amber, if not to red. I hoped for all our sakes that he would have the good manners to keep quiet.

'Give Matthew a proposal form, Charles,' the Duke said contentedly. 'That's what he's come for, you know, to join the Fund.'

Carthy-Todd obediently rose, crossed to the filing cabinet, pulled open the top drawer, and lifted out two separate sheets of paper. One, it appeared, was the proposal form: the other, a lavishly curlicued certificate of insurance. I filled in the spaces on the ultra-simple proposal while Carthy-Todd inscribed my name and a number on the certificate; then I handed over a fiver, which left me with enough to live on cornflakes until pay day, and the transaction was complete.

'Take care of yourself now, Matt,' joked the Duke, and I smiled and said I would.

The Duke looked at his watch. 'Good gracious!' He stood up. 'Come along now, everybody. Time we went along to the racecourse. And no more excuses, Charles, I insist on you lunching with me.' To me he explained, 'Charles very rarely goes to the races. He doesn't much care for it, do you see? But as the course is so very close . . .'

Carthy-Todd's aversion to race meetings was to my mind completely understandable. He wished to remain unseen, anonymous, unrecognizable, just as he'd been all along. Charles would choose which meetings he went to very carefully indeed. He would never, I imagined, turn up without checking with the Duke whether he was going to be there too.

We walked back to the racecourse, the Duke and Carthy-Todd in front, young Matthew and me behind. Young Matthew slowed down a little and said to me in a quiet voice, 'I say, Matt, have you noticed something strange about Mr Carthy-Todd?'

I glanced at his face. He was half anxious, half puzzled, wanting reassurance.

'What do you think is strange?'

'I've never seen anyone before with eyes like that.'

Children were incredibly observant. Matthew had seen naturally what I had known to look for.

'I shouldn't mention it to him. He might not care for it.'

'I suppose not.' he paused. 'I don't frightfully like him.'

'I can see that.'

'Do you?'

'No,' I said.

He nodded in satisfaction. 'I didn't think you would. I don't know why Uncle's so keen on him. Uncle,' he added dispassionately, 'doesn't understand about people. He thinks everyone is as nice as he is. Which they're not.'

'How soon can you become his business manager?'

He laughed. 'I know all about trustees. I've got them. Can't have this and can't do that, that's all they ever say, Mother says.'

'Does your Uncle have trustees?'

'No, he hasn't. Mother's always beefing on about Uncle not being fit to control all that lucre and one day he'll invest the lot in a South Sea Bubble. I asked Uncle about it and he just laughed. He told me he has a stockbroker who sees to everything and Uncle just goes on getting richer and when he wants some money for something he just tells the stockbroker and he sells some shares and sends it along. Simple. Mother fusses over nothing. Uncle won't get into much trouble about money becaue he knows that he doesn't know about it, if you see what I mean?'

'I wouldn't like him to give too much to Mr Carthy-Todd,' I said.

He gave me a flashing look of understanding. 'So that's what I felt ... Do you think it would do any good if I sort of tried to put Uncle off him a bit?'

'Couldn't do much harm.'

'I'll have a go,' he said. 'But he's fantastically keen on him.' He thought deeply and came up with a grin. 'I must say,' he said, 'That he has awfully good chocolate orange peel.'

Annie Villars was upset about Kenny Bayst. 'I went to see him for a few moments this morning. He's broken both legs and his face was cut by flying glass. He won't be riding again before next season, he says. Luckily he's insured with the Racegoers' Fund. Sent them a tenner, he told me, so he's hoping to collect two thousand pounds at least. Marvellous thing, that Fund.'

'Did you join?'

'I certainly did. After that bomb. Didn't know it was Rupert, then, of course. Still, better to do things at once rather than put them off, don't you agree?'

'Were Kitch and the stable lads insured too, do you know?'

She nodded. 'They were all Kitch's own lads. He'd advised them all to join. Even offered to deduct the premium from their wages bit by bit. Everyone in Newmarket is talking about it, saying how lucky it was. All the stable lads in the town who hadn't already joined are sending their fivers along in the next few days.'

I hesitated. 'Did you read about Rupert Tyderman in the *Sporting Life?*'

A twinge of regret twisted her face: her mouth for the first time since I had known her took on a soft curve that was not consciously constructed.

'Poor Rupert ... What an end, to be murdered.'

'There isn't any doubt, then?'

She shook her head. 'When I saw the report, I rang the local newspaper down at Kemble ... that's where they found him. He was lying, they said, at the bottom of an embankment near a road bridge over the railway. The local theory is that he could have been brought there by car during the night, and not fallen from a train at all ...' She shook her head in bewilderment. 'He had one stab wound below his left shoulder blade, and he had been dead for hours and hours when he was found.'

It took a great deal of lying-in-wait to catch the Duke without Carthy-Todd at his elbow, but I got him in the end.

'I've left my wallet in the Accident Fund office,' I said. 'Must have left it on the desk when I paid my premium.... Do you think, sir, that you could let me have a key, if you have one, so that I can slip along and fetch it?'

'My dear chap, of course.' He produced a small bunch from his pocket and sorted out a bright new yale. 'Here you are. That's the one.'

'Very kind, sir, I won't be long.' I took a step away and then turned back, grinning, making a joke.

'What happens, sir, if it's you who gets killed in a car crash? What happens to the Fund then?'

He smiled back reassuringly in a patting-on-the-shoulder avuncular manner. 'All taken care of, my dear chap. Some of the papers I signed, they dealt with it. The Fund money would be guaranteed from a special arrangement with my estate.'

'Did Charles see to it?'

'Naturally. Of course. He understands these things, you know.'

Between the Duke and the main gate a voice behind me crisply shouted.

'Matt.'

I stopped and turned. It was Colin, hurrying towards me, carrying the saddle from the loser he'd partnered in the first race.

'Can't stop more than a second,' he said. 'Got to change for the next. You weren't leaving, were you? Have you seen Nancy?'

'No. I've been looking, I thought ... perhaps ...'

He shook his head. 'She's here. Up there, on the balcony, with Midge.'

I followed where he was looking, and there they were, distant, high up, talking with their heads together, two halves of one whole.

'Do you know which is Nancy?' Colin asked.

I said without hesitation. 'The one on the left.'

'Most people can't tell.'

He looked at my expression and said with exasperation, 'If you feel like that about her, why the bloody hell don't you let her know? She thinks she made it all up ... she's trying to hide it but she's pretty unhappy.'

'She'd have to live on peanuts.'

'For crying out loud, what does that matter? You can move in with us. We all want you. Midge wants you ... and now, not some distant time when you think you can afford it. Time for us is now, this summer. There may not be much after this.' He hitched the saddle up on his arm and looked back towards the weighing room. 'I'll have to go. We'll have to talk later. I came after you now, though, because you looked as though you were leaving.'

'I'm coming back soon.' I turned and walked along with him towards the weighing-room. 'Colin ... I ought to tell someone ... you never know ...' He gave me a puzzled glance and in three brief sentences I told him why the Accident Fund was a fraud, how he and the bomb had been used to drum up business, and in what way Carthy-Todd was a fake.

He stopped dead in his tracks. 'Good God,' he said. 'The Fund was such a great idea. What a bloody shame.'

Saturday afternoon. The Board of Trade had gone home to its lawn mowing and the wife and kids. I put down the telephone and considered the police.

The police were there, on the racecourse, all ready and able. But willing? Hardly. They were there to direct the traffic; a crime not yet committed would not shift them an inch.

Both lots, if they believed me, might eventually arrive on Carthy-Todd's doorstep. By appointment, probably; especially the Board of Trade.

There would be no Carthy-Todd to welcome them in. No records. No Fund. Possibly no Duke ...

I always told myself to stay out of trouble.

Never listened.

No clocks ticked in Carthy Todd's office. The silence was absolute. But it was only in my mind that it was ominous and oppressive. Carthy-Todd was safe at the races and I should have a clear hour at least: or so my brain told me. My nerves had other ideas.

I found myself tiptoeing across to the desk. Ridiculous. I half laughed at myself and put my feet down flat on the soundless carpet.

Nothing on the desk top except a blotter without blots, a tray of pens and pencils, a green telephone, a photograph of a woman, three children and a dog in a silver frame, a desk diary, closed, and the red and gold tin of chocolate orange peel.

The drawers contained stationery, paper clips, stamps, and a small pile of the 'insure against bombs on the way home' brochures. Two of the four drawers were completely empty.

Two filing cabinets. One unlocked. One locked. The top of the three drawers of the unlocked cabinet contained the packets of proposal forms and insurance certificates, and a third packet containing claim forms; in the second, the completed and returned forms of those insured, filed in a rank of folders from A-Z; and the third, almost empty, contained three folders only, one marked 'Claims settled'; one 'Claims pending', and the other 'Receipts.'

'Claims settled' embraced the records of two separate outgoing payments of one thousand pounds, one to Acey Jones and one to a trainer in Kent who had been kicked in the face at evening stables. Three hundred pounds had been paid to a stable girl in Newmarket in respect of fracturing her wrist in a fall from a two-year-old at morning exercise. The claim forms, duly filled in, and with doctor's certificates attached, were stamped 'paid' with a date.

'Claims pending' was fatter. There were five letters of application for claim forms, annotated 'forms sent', and two forms completed and returned, claiming variously for a finger bitten off by a hungry hurdler and a foot carelessly left in the path of a plough. From the dates, the claimants had only been waiting a month for their money, and few insurance companies paid out quicker than that.

The thin file 'Receipts' was in many ways the most interesting. The record took the form of a diary, with the number of new insurers entered against the day they paid their premiums. From sporadic twos and threes during the first week of operation the numbers had grown like a mushroom.

The first great spurt was labelled in the margin in small tidy handwriting. 'A.C. Jones, etc.' The second, an astronomical burst, was noted 'Bomb!' The third, a lesser spurt, 'Pamphlet'. The fourth, a noticeable upthrust, 'Electric failure'. After that, the daily average had gone on climbing steadily. The word, by then, had reached pretty well every ear.

The running total in two months had reached five thousand, four hundred and seventy-two. The receipts, since some insurers had paid double premiums for double benefits, stood at £28,040.

With the next inrush of premiums after the Kitch-Ambrose accident (which Carthy-Todd certainly had not engineered, as only non-claiming accidents were any good to him) there would almost have been enough in the kitty to settle all the claims. I sighed, frowning. It was, as Colin had said, a bloody shame. The Duke's view of the Fund was perfectly valid. Run by an honest man, and with its ratio of premiums to pay-off slightly adjusted, it could have done good all round.

I slammed the bottom drawer shut with irritation and felt the adrenalin race through my veins as the noise reverberated round the empty room.

No one came. My nerves stopped registering tremble; went back to itch.

The locked second cabinet was proof only against casual eyes. I tipped it against the wall and felt underneath, and sure enough it was the type worked on one connecting rod up the back: pushed the rod up from the bottom and all the drawers became unlocked.

I looked through all of them quickly, the noise I had made seeming to act as an accelerator. Even if I had all the time in the world, I wanted to be out of there, to be gone.

The top drawer contained more folders of papers. The middle drawer contained a large grey metal box. The bottom drawer contained two cardboard boxes and two small square tins.

Taking a deep breath I started at the top. The folders contained the setting-up documents of the Fund and the papers which the Duke had so trustingly signed. The legal language made perfect camouflage for what Carthy-Todd had done. I had to read them twice to make a strong grip and force myself to concentrate, before I understood the two convenants the Duke had given him.

The first, as the Duke had said, transferred one hundred thousand pounds from his estate into a guarantee trust for the Fund, in the event of his death. The second one at first sight looked identical, but it certainly wasn't. It said in essence that if the Duke died within the first year of the Fund, a further one hundred thousand pounds from his estate was to be paid into it.

In both cases, Carthy-Todd was to be sole Trustee.

In both cases, he was given absolute discretion to invest or use the money in any way he thought best.

Two hundred thousand pounds ... I stared into space. Two

hundred thousand pounds if the Duke died. A motive to make tongue-silencing look frivolous.

The twenty-eight thousand of the Fund money was only the beginning. The bait. The jackpot lay in the dead Duke.

His heirs would have to pay. Young Matthew, to be precise. The papers looked thoroughly legal, with signatures witnessed and stamped, and in fact it seemed one hundred per cent certain that Carthy-Todd wouldn't have bothered with them at all if they were not foolproof.

He wouldn't waste much more time, I thought. Not with the claims for the Ambrose accident coming in. With the Duke dead, the two hundred thousand would have to be paid almost at once, because the covenants would be a first charge on his estate, like debts. There would be no having to wait around for probate. If Carthy-Todd could stave off the claims for a while, he could skip with both the Duke's money and the whole Fund.

I put the papers back in their folder, back in the drawer. Closed it. Gently. My heart thumped.

Second drawer. Large metal box. One could open it without removing it from the cabinet. I opened it. Lots of space, but few contents. Some cottonwool, cold cream, glue, and half a used stick of greasepaint. I shut the lid, shut the drawer. Only to be expected.

Bottom drawer. Knelt on the floor. Two small square tins, one empty, one full and heavy and fastened all round with adhesive tape. Looked inside the two cardboard boxes first and felt the breath go out of my body as if I'd been kicked.

The cardboard boxes contained the makings of a radio bomb. Solenoids, transmitters, fuse wire, a battery and a small container of gunpowder in the first box. Plastic explosive wrapped in tin foil in the other.

I sat on my heels looking at the small square heavy tin. Heard in my mind the tall man from the Board of Trade: the tighter you pack a bomb the more fiercely it explodes.

Decided not to open the small square tin. Felt the sweat stand out in cold drops on my forehead.

I shut the bottom drawer with a caution which seemed silly when I remembered the casual way I'd tilted the whole cabinet over to open it. But then the bomb wouldn't get the signal where it was, not with those precious documents in the cabinet just above.

I wiped my hand over my face. Stood up. Swallowed.

I'd found everything I came to find, and more. All except for one thing. I glanced round the office, looking for somewhere else. Somewhere to hide something big ...

There was a door in the corner behind Carthy-Todd's desk which I assumed connected with the secretary's office next door. I went over to it. Tried the handle. It was locked.

I let myself out of Carthy-Todd's office and went into the secretary's room, whose door was shut but had no keyhole. Stared, in there, at an L-shaped blank wall. No connecting door to Carthy-

Todd. It was a cupboard, with the door on his side.

I went back to Carthy-Todd's office and stood contemplating the door. If I broke it open, he would know. If I didn't I could only guess at what was inside. Evidence of a fraud committed, that would spur the Board of Trade to action. Evidence that would make the Duke rescind his covenants, or at least rewrite them so that they were no longer death warrants . . .

Carthy-Todd hadn't been expecting trouble. He had left the key to the cupboard on his desk in the tray of pens and pencils. I picked up the single key which lay there, and it fitted.

Opened the cupboard door. It squeaked on its hinges, but I was too engrossed to notice.

There he was. Mr Acey Jones. The crutches, leaning against the wall. The white plaster cast lying on the floor.

I picked up the cast and looked at it. It had been slit neatly down the inside leg from the top to the ankle. One could put one's foot into it like a boot, with the bare toes sticking out of the end and the metal walking support under the arch. There were small grip-clips like those used on bandages sticking into the plaster all down the opening. Put your foot into the cast, fasten the clips, and bingo, you had a broken ankle.

Acey Jones, loudly drumming up business for the Fund.

Acey Jones, Carthy-Todd. Confidence tricksters were the best actors in the world.

I didn't hear him come.

I put the cast back on the floor just where it had been, and straightened up and started to shut the cupboard door, and saw him moving out of the corner of my eye as he came into the room. I hadn't shut the office door behind me, when I'd gone back. I hadn't given myself any time at all.

His face went rigid with fury when he saw what I'd seen.

'Meddling pilot,' he said. 'When the Duke told me he'd given you the key . . .' He stopped, unable to speak for rage. His voice was different, neither the Eton of Carthy-Todd, nor the Australian of Acey Jones. Just ordinary uninflected English. I wondered fleetingly where he came from, who he really was . . . a thousand different people, one for every crime.

Unblinking behind the black-frame glasses the pale blue grey eyes all but sizzled. The incongruous white eyelashes, which Matthew had noticed, gave him now a fierce fanatical ruthlessness. The decision he was coming to wasn't going to be for my good.

He put his hand into his trouser pocket and briefly pulled it out again. There was a sharp click. I found myself staring at the knife which had snapped out, and thought with a horrific shiver of Rupert Tyderman tumbling down dead beside the railway line . . .

He took a step sideways and kicked shut the office door. I twisted round towards the mantelshelf to pick up whatever I could find there . . . a photograph, a cigarette box . . . anything I could use as a weapon or a shield.

I didn't even get as far as taking anything into my hand, because he didn't try to stab me with the knife.

He threw it.

Chapter Fifteen

It hit me below the left shoulder and the jolt threw me forward on my twisting legs so that I hit my forehead solidly on the edge of the marble slab mantelshelf. Blacking out, falling, I put out a hand to stop myself, but there was nothing there, only the empty black hollow of the fireplace, and I went on, right down, smashing and crashing amongst the brass fire irons ... but I heard them only dimly ... and then not at all.

I woke up, slowly, stiffly, painfully, after less than a quarter of an hour. Everything was silent. No sound. No people. Nothing.

I couldn't remember where I was or what had happened. Not until I tried to get up. Then the tearing soreness behind my shoulder stung me straight back into awareness.

Had a knife sticking in my back.

Lying face down among the fire irons I felt gingerly round with my right hand. My fingers brushed like feathers against the hilt. I cried out at my own touch. It was frightful.

Stupid the things you think of in moments of disaster. I thought: damn it, only three weeks and one day to my medical. I'll never pass it.

Never pull knives out of wounds, they say. It makes the bleeding worse. You can die from pulling knives out of wounds. Well ... I forgot all that. I could see only that Acey-Carthy-Todd had left me for dead and if he found me alive when he came back he would most certainly finish the job. Therefore I had to get out of his office before he came back. And it seemed incongruous, really to walk round Warwick with a knife in one's back. So I pulled it out.

I pulled it out in two stages and more or less fainted after each. Kidded myself it was concussion from the mantelshelf, but I was crying as well. No stoic, Matt Shore.

When it was out I lay where I was for a while, looking at it, snivelling weakly and feeling the sticky warmth slowly spread, but being basically reassured because I was pretty sure by then that the knife had not gone through into my lung. It must have been deflected by hitting my shoulder blade: it had been embedded to three or four inches, but slanting, not straight in deep. I wasn't going to die. Or not yet.

After a while I got up on to my knees. I didn't have all the time in the world. I put my right hand on Carthy-Todd's desk: pulled myself to my feet.

Swayed. Thought it would be much much worse if I fell down again. Leant my hip against the desk and looked vaguely round the office.

The bottom drawer of the second filing cabinet was open.

Shouldn't be. I'd shut it.

Open.

I shifted myself off the desk and tried a few steps. Tottered. Made it. Leant gingerly against the wall. Looked down into the drawer.

The cardboard boxes were still there. The empty tin was still there. The small heavy tin wasn't.

Realized coldly that the future no longer meant simply getting myself to safety out of that office, but getting to the Duke before the bomb did.

It was only four hundred yards ... Only ...

I'd have to do it, I thought, because if I hadn't searched the office Carthy-Todd wouldn't now be in a tearing hurry. When I didn't turn up to ferry home the Whiteknights, or turn up anywhere again for that matter, except with a stab wound in a ditch, the Duke would say where I had been last ... and Carthy-Todd would want to avoid a police investigation like a slug shrinking away from salt. He wouldn't wait for that. He would obliterate my tracks.

There was something else missing from the office. I didn't know what it was, just knew it was something. It niggled for a moment, but was gone. Didn't think it could be important ...

Walked with deliberation to the door. Opened it, went outside. Stopped dead at the top of the stairs, feeling dizzy and weak.

Well. Had to get down them somehow. Had to.

The handrail was on the lefthand side. I couldn't bear to lift my left arm. Turned round, hung on tightly, and went down backwards.

'There you are,' I said aloud. 'You bloody can.' Didn't convince myself. It took Carthy-Todd to convince.

I laughed weakly. I was a fully paid up insurer with the Fund. Like to see Carthy-Todd pay my claim ... a thousand smackers for a knife in the back. Lovely.

Rolled out into the hot sunlit street as lightheaded as a blond.

Blond Acey Jones ...

Acey Jones was being pushed. Hurried. Knowing I'd found him out but still believing he could retrieve the situation. Still make his two hundred thousand. If he kept his nerve. If he killed the Duke immediately, this afternoon, and somehow made it look like an accident. If he dumped me somewhere later, as he had the Major ...

He would think he could still do it. He didn't know I'd told Colin, didn't know that Colin knew he was Carthy-Todd ...

The empty street had got much longer during the afternoon. Also it wouldn't stay absolutely still. It shimmered. It undulated. The pavement was uneven. Every time I put my foot down the paving stones reached up and stabbed me in the back.

I passed only an elderly woman on the way. She was muttering to herself. I realized that I was, too.

Half way. I squinted along at the gate of the car park. Had to make it. Had to. And that wasn't all. Had to find someone to go and fetch the Duke, so that I could explain ... explain ...

Felt myself falling and put a hand out towards the wall. Mustn't shut my eyes ... I'd be done for ... spun heavily against the bricks and shuddered at the result. Rested my head against the wall, trying not to weep. Couldn't spare the time. Had to get on.

I pushed myself back into a moderately upright walking position. My feet couldn't tell properly how far it was down to the pavement: half the time I was climbing imaginary steps.

Weird.

Something warm on my left hand. I looked down. My head swam. Blood was running down my fingers, dripping on to the pavement. Looked up again, along to the course. Head swam again. Didn't know if it was concussion or heat or loss of blood. Only knew it reduced the time factor. Had to get there. Quickly.

One foot in front of the other, I told myself... just go on doing that: one foot in front of the other. And you'll get there.

Concentrate.

I got there. Gate to the car park. And no official guarding it. At that time in the afternoon, they'd given up expecting further customers.

I said 'Ohh ...' in weak frustration. Have to go still further. Have to find someone ... I turned in to the car park. Through the car park there was a gate into the paddock. Lots of people there. Lots ...

I went between the cars, staggering, holding on to them, feeling my knees bending, knowing the dizzy weakness was winning and caring less and less about the jagged pain of every step. Had to find someone. Had to.

Someone suddenly came to me from quite close.

'Matt!'

I stopped. Looked slowly round. Midge was climbing out of Colin's parked Aston Martin down the row and running to catch me up.

'Matt,' she said, 'We've been looking for you. I came back to the car because I was tired. Where have you been?'

She put her hand with friendship on my left arm.

I said thickly, 'Don't ... touch me.'

She took her hand away with a jerk. 'Matt!'

She looked at me more closely, at first in puzzlement and then in anxiety. Then she looked at her fingers, and where she'd grasped my coat there were bright red smears.

'It's blood,' she said blankly.

I nodded a fraction. My mouth was dry. I was getting very tired.

'Listen ... Do you know the Duke of Wessex?'

'Yes. But ...' she protested.

'Midge,' I interrupted. 'Go and find him. Bring him here ... I know it sounds stupid ... but someone is trying to kill him ... with a bomb.'

'Like Colin? But that wasn't ...'

'Fetch him, Midge,' I said. 'Please.'

'I can't leave you. Not like this.'

'You must.'

She looked at me doubtfully.

'Hurry.'

'I'll get you some help, too,' she said. She turned lightly on her heel and half walked, half ran towards the paddock. I leant the bottom of my spine against a shiny grey Jaguar and wondered how difficult it would be to prevent Carthy-Todd from planting his bomb. That tin ... it was small enough to fit into a binocular case ... probably identical with the one which had destroyed the Cherokee. I would have sweated at the thought of so much confined explosive power if I hadn't been sweating clammily already.

Why didn't they come? My mouth was drier ... The day was airless ... I moved restlessly against the car. After I'd told the Duke, he'd have to go off somewhere and stay safely out of sight until the Board of Trade had dealt with Carthy-Todd ...

I dispassionately watched the blood drip from my fingers on to the grass. I could feel that all the back of my coat was soaked. Couldn't afford a new one, either. Have to get it cleaned, and have the slit invisibly mended. Get myself mended, to, as best I could. Harley wouldn't keep the job for me. He'd have to get someone else in my place. The Board of Trade doctors wouldn't let me fly again for weeks and weeks. If you gave a pint of blood as a donor, they grounded you for over a month ... I'd lost more than a pint involuntarily, by the looks of things ... though a pint would make a pretty good mess, if you spilled it.

I lifted my lolling head up with a jerk. Got to stay awake until they came. Got to explain to the Duke ...

Things were beginning to fuzz round the edges. I licked my dry lips. Didn't do much good. Didn't have any moisture in my tongue either.

I finally saw them, and it seemed a long way off, coming through the gate from the paddock. Not just Midge and the Duke, but two others as well. Young Matthew, jigging along in front.

And Nancy.

Chanter had receded into the unimportant past. I didn't give him a thought. Everything was as it had been before, the day she flew to Haydock. Familiar, friendly, trusting. The girl I hadn't wanted to get involved with, who had melted a load of ice like an acetylene torch.

Across the sea of cars Midge pointed in my direction and they began to come towards me, crossing through the rows. When they were only twenty or so yards away, on the far side of the row in front of me, they unaccountably stopped.

Come on, I thought. For God's sake come on.

They didn't move.

With an effort I pushed myself upright from the Jaguar and took the few steps past its bonnet, going towards them. On my left, six cars along, was parked what was evidently the Duke's Rolls. On the bonnet stood a bright red and gold tin. Matthew was pointing, wanting to cross over and fetch it, and Midge was saying urgently, 'No, come on, Matt said to come quickly, and he's bleeding ...'

Matthew gave her a concerned look and then nodded, but at the last second temptation was too much and he ran over and picked up the tin and started back to join them.

Bright red and gold tin. Containing sticks of orange peel dipped in chocolate. It had been on the desk. And afterwards ... not on the desk. Something missing. Red and gold tin.

Missing from Carthy-Todd's desk.

My heart bumped. I shouted, and my voice came out hopelessly weak.

'Matthew, throw it to me.'

He looked up doubtfully. The others began to walk through the rows of cars towards him. They would reach him before I could. They would be standing all together, Nancy and Midge and the Duke and young Matthew, who knew too that I'd been in Carthy-Todd's office that day.

I scanned the car park desperately, but he was there. He'd put the tin on the car and simply waited for them to come out of the races. The last race was about to start ... the horses had gone down to the post and at that moment the loudspeakers were announcing 'They're under starter's orders' ... He knew it wouldn't be long before they came ... He was standing over nearer the rails of the course with his black head showing and the sun glinting on his glasses. He had meant just to kill young Matthew and the Duke, but now there were Nancy and Midge as well ... and he didn't know he couldn't get away with it ... didn't know Colin knew ... and he was too far away for me to tell him ... I couldn't shout ... could barely talk.

'Matthew, throw me the tin.' It was a whisper, nothing more.

I began to walk towards him, holding out my right arm. Stumbled. Swayed. Frightened him.

The others were closing on him.

No more time. I took a breath. Straightened up.

'Matthew,' I said loudly. 'To save your life, throw me that tin. Throw it now. At once.'

He was upset, uncertain, worried.

He threw the tin.

It was taking Carthy-Todd several seconds to press the transmission buttons. He wasn't as adept at it as Rupert Tyderman. He wouldn't be able to see that he had missed his opportunity with the Duke, and that now there was only me. But whatever he did, he'd lost the game.

The red gold tin floated towards me like a blazing sun and seemed to take an eternity crossing the fifteen feet from Matthew. I stretched my right arm forward to meet it and when it landed on my hand I flung it with a bowling action high into the air behind where I was standing, back as far as I could over the parked rows, because behind them, at the rear, there was empty space.

The bomb went off in the air. Three seconds out of my hand, six seconds out of Matthew's. Six seconds. As long a time as I had ever lived.

The red and gold tin disintegrated into a cracking fireball like the sun, and the blast of it knocked both young Matthew and me with a screeching jolt flat to the ground. The windows in most of the cars in the car park crashed into splinters, and the two Fords just below the explosion were thrown about like toys. Nancy and Midge and the Duke, still sheltered between two cars, rocked on their feet and clung to each other for support.

Along in the stands, we heard later, no one took much notice. The race had started and the commentator's voice was booming out, filling everyone's ears with the news that Colin Ross was lying handy and going nicely on the favourite half a mile from home.

Young Matthew picked himself smartly up and said in amazement 'What was that?'

Midge completed the four bare steps to his side and held his hand.

'It was a bomb,' she said in awe. 'Like Matt said, it was a bomb.'

I was trying to get myself up off the grass. Even though the Duke was for the present safe, the Fund money was not. Might as well try for set and match ...

On my knees, I said to Matthew, 'Can you see Carthy-Todd anywhere? It was his tin ... his bomb ...'

'Carthy-Todd?' repeated the Duke vaguely. 'It can't be. Impossible. He wouldn't do a thing like that.'

'He just did,' I said. I was having no success in getting up any further. Had nothing much left. A strong arm slid under my right armpit, helping me. A soft calm voice said in my ear 'You look as if you'd be better staying down.'

'Nancy ...'

'How did you get into this state?'

'Carthy-Todd ... had a knife ...'

'There he is!' Matthew suddenly shouted. 'Over there.'

I wobbled to my feet. Looked where Matthew was pointing. Carthy-Todd, running between the rows, Nancy looked too.

'But that's,' she said incredulously, 'That's the man I saw in the car with Major Tyderman. I'd swear to it.'

'You may have to,' I said.

'He's running to get out,' Matthew shouted. 'Let's head him off.'

It was almost a game to him, but his enthusiasm infected several other racegoers who had come early out of the races and found their windows in splinters.

'Head him off,' I heard a man shout, and another 'There, over there. Head him off.'

I leaned in hopeless weakness against a car, and dimly watched. Carthy-Todd caught sight of the growing number converging on him. Hesitated. Changed course. Doubled back on his tracks. Made for the only free and open space he could see. The green grass behind him. The racecourse itself.

'Don't ...' I said. It came out a whisper, and even if I'd had a microphone he wouldn't have heard.

'Oh God,' Nancy said beside me. 'Oh no.'

Carthy-Todd didn't see his danger until it was too late. He ran blindly out across the course looking over his shoulder at the bunch of men who had suddenly, aghast, stopped chasing him.

He ran straight in front of the thundering field of three year olds sweeping round the last bend to their final flying effort up the straight.

Close bunched, they had no chance of avoiding him. He went down under the pounding hooves like a rag into a threshing machine, and a second later the flowing line of horses broke up into tumbling chaos ... crashing at thirty miles an hour ... legs whirling ... jockeys thudding to the ground like bright blobs of paint ... a groaning shambles on the bright green turf ... and side-stepping, swaying, looking over their shoulders, the rear ones in the field swerved past and went on to a finish that no one watched.

Nancy said in anguish, 'Colin!' and ran towards the rails. The pink and white silks lay still, a crumpled bundle curled in a protective ball. I followed her, plod by plod, feeling that I couldn't go any further, I simply couldn't. One car short of the rails, I stopped, I clung on to it, sagging. The tide was going out.

The pink and white ball stirred, unrolled itself, stood up. Relief made me even weaker. Crowds of people had appeared on the course, running, helping, gawping ... closing in like a screen round the strewn bodies ... I waited for what seemed an age, and then Colin and Nancy reappeared through a thronging wall of people and came back towards the car park.

'Only stunned for a second,' I heard him say to a passing inquirer. 'I shouldn't go over there ...' But the inquirer went on, looking avid.

Nancy saw me and waved briefly, and ducked under the rails with Colin.

'He's dead,' she said abruptly. She looked sick. 'That man ... he ... he was Acey Jones ... Colin said you knew ... his hair was lying on the grass ... but it was a wig ... and there was this bald white head and that pale hair ... and you could see the line of grease paint ... and the black moustache ...' Her eyes were wide. Full of horror.

'Don't think about it,' Colin said. He looked at me. 'She shouldn't have come over ...'

'I had to ... you were lying there,' she protested. He went on looking at me. His expression changed. He said 'Nancy said you were hurt. She didn't say ... how badly.' He turned abruptly to Nancy and said 'Fetch the doctor.'

'I tried to before,' she said. 'But he said he was on duty and couldn't see to Matt before the race in case he was needed ...' She tailed off and looked over at the crowd on the course. 'He'll be over there ... seeing to those two jockeys ...' She looked back at Colin with sudden fright. 'Midge said Matt had cut his arm ... Is it worse ...?'

'I'll fetch him,' Colin said grimly, and ran back to the battlefield. Nancy looked at me with such flooding anxiety that I grinned.

'Not as bad as all that,' I said.

'But you were walking . . . you threw that bomb with such force . . . I didn't realize . . . You do look ill . . .'

The Duke and young Matthew and Midge reappeared from somewhere. I hadn't seen them come. Things were getting hazier.

The Duke was upset. 'My dear chap,' he said over and over again. 'My dear chap . . .'

'How did you know it was a bomb?' Matthew asked.

'Just knew.'

'That was a pretty good throw.'

'Saved our lives,' said the Duke. 'My dear chap . . .'

Colin was back.

'He's coming,' he said. 'Immediately.'

'Saved our lives . . .' said the Duke again. 'How can we repay . . .'

Colin looked at him straightly. 'I'll tell you how, sir. Set him up in business . . . or take over Derrydowns . . . give him an air taxi business, based near Newmarket. He'll make you a profit. He'll have me for a customer, and Annie, and Kenny . . . and in fact the whole town, because the Fund can go on now, can't it?' He looked at me inquiringly, and I fractionally nodded. 'It may cost a bit to put right,' Colin said, 'But your Fund can go on, sir, and do all the good it was meant to . . .'

'An air taxi business. Take over Derrydowns,' the Duke repeated. 'My dear Colin, what a splendid idea. Of course. Of course.'

I tried to say something . . . anything . . . to begin to thank him for so casually thrusting the world into my fingers . . . but I couldn't say anything . . . couldn't speak. I could feel my legs collapsing. Could do nothing any more to stop them. Found myself kneeling on the grass, keeping myself from falling entirely by hanging on to a door handle of the car. Didn't want to fall. Hurt too much.

'Matt!' Nancy said. She was down on her knees beside me. Midge too. And Colin.

'Don't bloody die,' Nancy said.

I grinned at her. Felt light-headed. Grinned at Colin. Grinned at Midge.

'Want a lodger?' I asked.

'Soon as you like,' Colin said.

'Nancy,' I said. 'Will you . . . will you . . .'

'You nit,' she said. 'You great nit.'

My hand slipped out of the door handle. Colin caught me as I fell. Everything drifted quietly away, and by the time I reached the ground I couldn't feel anything at all.

FORFEIT

Chapter One

The letter from *Tally* came on the day Bert Checkov died. It didn't look like trouble; just an invitation from a glossy to write an article on the Lamplighter Gold Cup. I flicked it across the desk to the Sports Editor and went on opening the mail which always accumulated for me by Fridays. Luke-John Morton grunted and stretched out a languid hand, blinking vacantly while he listened to someone with a lot to say on the telephone.

'Yeah ... yeah. Blow the roof off,' he said.

Blowing the roof off was the number one policy of the *Sunday Blaze*, bless its cold heart. Why didn't I write for the *Sunday Times*, my wife's mother said, instead of a rag like the *Sunday Blaze?* They hadn't needed me, that was why. She considered this irrelevant, and when she couldn't actively keep it quiet, continued to apologize to every acquaintance for my employment. That the *Blaze* paid twenty-eight per cent more than the *Times*, and that her daughter was expensive, she ignored.

I slit open a cheap brown envelope and found some nut had written to say that only a vicious unscrupulous bum like myself would see any good in the man I had defended last Sunday. The letter was written on lavatory paper and spite oozed from it like marsh gas. Derry Clark read it over my shoulder and laughed.

'Told you you'd stir them up.'

'Anything for an unquiet life,' I agreed.

Derry wrote calm uncontroversial articles each week assessing form and firmly left the crusading rebel stuff to me. My back, as he constantly pointed out, was broader than his.

Eight more of my other correspondents proved to be thinking along the same general lines. All anonymous, naturally. Their problems, I reflected, dumping their work in the waste basket, were even worse than mine.

'How's your wife?' Derry said.

'Fine, thanks.'

He nodded, not looking at me. He'd never got over being embarrassed about Elizabeth. It took some people that way.

Luke-John's conversation guttered to a close. 'Sure ... sure. Phone it through by six at the latest.' He put down the receiver and focussed on my letter from *Tally*, his eyes skidding over it with professional speed.

'A study in depth ... how these tarty magazines love that phrase.

Do you want to do it?'

'If the fee's good.'

'I thought you were busy ghosting Buster Figg's autobiography.'

'I'm hung up on chapter six. He's sloped off to the Bahamas and left me no material.'

'How far through his horrid little life have you got?' His interest was genuine.

'The end of his apprenticeship and his first win in a classic.'

'Will it sell?'

'I don't know,' I sighed. 'All he's interested in is money, and all he remembers about some races is the starting price. He gambled in thousands. And he insists I put his biggest bets in. He says they can't take away his licence now he's retired.'

Luke-John sniffed, rubbing a heavily freckled hand across the prominent tendons of his scrawny neck, massaging his walnut sized larynx, dropping the heavy eyelid hoods while he considered the letter from *Tally*. My contract with the *Blaze* was restrictive: books were all right, but I couldn't write articles for any other paper or magazine without Luke-John's permission, which I mostly didn't get.

Derry pushed me out of his chair and sat in it himself. As I spent only Fridays in the office, I didn't rate a desk and usurped my younger colleague's whenever he wasn't looking. Derry's desk held a comprehensive reference library of form books in the top three drawers and a half bottle of vodka, two hundred purple hearts and a pornographic film catalogue in the bottom one. These were window dressing only. They represented the wicked fellow Derry would like to be, not the lawful, temperate, semi-detached man he was.

I perched on the side of his desk and looked out over the Friday morning clatter, a quarter acre of typewriters and telephones going at half speed as the week went on towards Sunday. Tuesdays the office was dead: Saturdays it buzzed like flies squirted with D.D.T. Fridays I felt part of it. Saturdays I went to the races. Sundays and Mondays, officially off. Tuesdays to Thursday, think up some galvanizing subject to write about, and write it. Fridays, take it in for Luke-John, and then for the Editor, to read and vet.

Result, a thousand words a week, an abusive mailbag, and a hefty cheque which didn't cover my expenses.

Luke-John said, 'Are you or Derry doing the Lamplighter?'

Without giving me a second Derry jumped in. 'I am.'

'That all right with you, Ty?' Luke-John asked dubiously.

'Oh sure,' I said. 'It's a complicated handicap. Right up his street.'

Luke-John pursed his thin lips and said with unusual generosity '*Tally* says they want background stuff, not tips ... I don't see why you shouldn't do it, if you want to.'

He scribbled a large O.K. at the bottom of the page and signed his name. 'But of course,' he added, 'if you dig up any dirt, keep it for *us*.'

Generous, be damned, I thought wryly. Luke-John's soul belonged to the *Blaze* and his simple touchstone in all decisions was, 'Could it possibly, directly or indirectly, benefit the paper?' Every member of the Sports section had at some time or other been ruthlessly sacrificed on his altar. For cancelled holidays, smashed appointments, lost opportunities, he cared not one jot.

'Sure,' I said mildly. 'And thanks.'

'How's your wife?' he asked.

'Fine thanks.'

He asked every week without fail. He had his politenesses, when it didn't cost the *Blaze*. Maybe he really cared. Maybe he only cared because when she wasn't 'fine' it affected my work.

I pinched Derry's telephone and dialled the number.

'*Tally* magazine, can I help you?' A girl's voice, very smooth, West Ken, and bored.

'I'd like to talk to Arnold Shankerton.'

'Who's calling?'

'James Tyrone.'

'One moment, please.' Some clicks and a pause. 'You're through.'

An equally smooth, highly sophisticated tenor voice proclaimed itself to be Arnold Shankerton, Features. I thanked him for his letter and said I would like to accept his commission. He said that would be very nice in moderately pleased tones and I gently added, 'If the price is right, naturally.'

'Naturally,' he conceded. 'How much do you want?'

Think of a number and double it. 'Two hundred guineas, plus expenses.'

Luke-John's eyebrows rose and Derry said, 'You'll be lucky.'

'Our profit margin is small,' Shankerton pointed out a little plaintively. 'One hundred is our absolute limit.'

'I pay too much tax.'

His sigh came heavily down the wire. 'A hundred and fifty, then. And for that it'll have to be good.'

'I'll do my best.'

'Your best,' he said, 'would scorch the paper. We want the style and the insight but not the scandal. Right?'

'Right,' I agreed without offence. 'How many words?'

'It's the main feature. Say three thousand five hundred, roughly speaking.'

'How about pictures?'

'You can have one of our photographers when you're ready. And within reason, of course.'

'Of course,' I said politely. 'When do you want it by?'

'We go to press on that edition ... let's see ... on November twentieth. So we'd like your stuff on the morning of the seventeenth, at the very latest. But the earlier the better.'

I looked at Derry's calendar. Ten days to the seventeenth.

'All right.'

'And when you've thought out how you'd like to present it, send us an outline.'

'Will do,' I said: but I wouldn't. Outlines were asking for trouble in the shape of editorial alterations. Shankerton could, and would, chop at the finished article to his heart's content, but I was against him getting his scissors into the embryo.

Luke-John skimmed the letter back and Derry picked it up and read it.

'In depth,' he said, sardonically. 'You're used to the deep end. You'll feel quite at home.'

'Yeah,' I agreed absentmindedly. Just what *was* depth, a hundred and fifty guineas worth of it?

I made a snap decision that depth in this case would be the background people, not the stars.

The stars hogged the headlines week by week. The background people had no news value. For once, I would switch them over.

Snap decisions had got me into trouble once or twice in the past. All the same, I made this one. It proved to be the most trouble-filled of the lot.

* * *

Derry, Luke-John and I knocked off soon after one and walked down the street in fine drizzle to elbow our way into the bar of the 'The Devereux' in Devereux Court opposite the Law Courts.

Bert Checkov was there, trying to light his stinking old pipe and burning his fingers on the matches. The shapeless tweed which swathed his bulk was as usual scattered with ash and as usual his toecaps were scuffed and grey. There was more glaze in the washy blue eyes than one-thirty normally found there: an hour too much, at a rough guess. He'd started early.

Luke-John spoke to him and he stared vaguely back. Derry bought us a half-pint each and politely asked Bert to have one, though he'd never liked him.

'Double scotch,' Bert mumbled, and Derry thought of his mortgages and scowled.

'How's things?' I asked, knowing that this too was a mistake. The Checkov grumbles were inexhaustible.

For once, however, the stream was dammed. The watery eyes focussed on me with an effort and another match sizzled on his skin. He appeared not to notice.

'Gi' you a piesh o' advish,' he said, but the words stopped there. The advice stayed in his head.

'What is it?'

'Piesh o' advish.' He nodded solemnly.

Luke-John raised his eyes to the ceiling in an exasperation that wasn't genuine. For old-time journalists like Bert he had an unlimited regard which no amount of drink could quench.

'Give him the advice, then,' Luke-John suggested. 'He can always do with it.'

The Checkov gaze lurched from me to my boss. The Checkov mouth belched uninhibitedly. Derry's pale face twisted squeamishly, and Checkov saw him. As a gay lunch, hardly a gas. Just any Friday, I thought: but I was wrong. Bert Checkov was less than an hour from death.

Luke-John, Derry and I sat on stools round the bar counter and ate cold meat and pickled onions, and Bert Checkov stood swaying behind us, breathing pipe smoke and whisky fumes down our necks. Instead of the usual steady rambling flow of grousing to which we were accustomed, we received only a series of grunts, the audible punctuation of the inner Checkov thoughts.

Something on his mind. I wasn't interested enough to find out what. I had enough on my own.

Luke-John gave him a look of compassion and another whisky and the alcohol washed into the pale blue eyes like a tide, resulting in pin-point pupils and a look of blank stupidity.

'I'll walk him back to his office,' I said abruptly. 'He'll fall under a bus if he goes on his own.'

'Serve him right,' Derry said under his breath, but carefully so that Luke-John shouldn't hear.

We finished lunch with cheese and another half-pint. Checkov lurched sideways and spilt my glass over Derry's knee and the pub carpet. The carpet soaked it up good-temperedly, which was more than could be said for Derry. Luke-John shrugged resignedly, half laughing, and I finished what was left of my beer with one swallow, and steered Bert Checkov through the crowd and into the street.

'Not closing time yet,' he said distinctly.

'For you it is, old chum.'

He rolled against the wall, waving the pipe vaguely in his chubby fist. 'Never leave a pub before closing. Never leave a story while it's hot. Never leave a woman on her doorstep. Paragraphs and skirts should be short and pheasants and breasts should be high.'

'Sure,' I said sighing. Some advice.

I took his arm and he came easily enough out on to the Fleet Street pavement. His tottering progress up towards the City end produced several stares but no actual collisions. Linked together we crossed during a lull in the traffic and continued eastwards under the knowing frontages of the *Telegraph* and the black glass *Express*. Fleet Street had seen the lot: no news value in an elderly racing correspondent being helped back from lunch with a skinful.

'A bit of advice,' he said suddenly, stopping in his tracks. 'A bit of advice.'

'Yes?' I said patiently.

He squinted in my general direction.

'We've come past the *Blaze*.'

'Yeah.'

He tried to turn me round to retrace our steps.

'I've business down at Ludgate Circus. I'm going your way today,' I said.

'Zat so?' He nodded vaguely and we shambled on. Ten more paces. He stopped again.

'Piece of advice.'

He was looking straight ahead. I'm certain that he saw nothing at all. No bustling street. Nothing but what was going on inside his head.

I was tired of waiting for the advice which showed no signs of materializing. It had begun to drizzle again. I took his arm to try and get him moving along the last fifty yards to his paper's florid front door. He wouldn't move.

'Famous last words,' he said.

'Whose?'

'Mine. Naturally. Famous last words. Bit of advice.'

'Oh sure,' I sighed. 'We're getting wet.'

'I'm not drunk.'

'No.'

'I could write my column any time. This minute.'

'Sure.'

He lurched off suddenly, and we made it to his door. Three steps and he'd be home and dry.

He stood in the entrance and rocked unsteadily. The pale blue eyes made a great effort towards sobering up, but the odds were against it.

'If anyone asks you,' he said finally, 'don't do it.'

'Don't do what?'

An anxious expression flitted across his pallid fleshy face. There were big pores all over his nose, and his beard was growing out in stiff black millimetres. He pushed one hand into his jacket pocket, and the anxiety turned to relief as he drew it out again with a half-bottle of scotch attached.

'Fraid I'd forgotten it,' he mumbled.

'See you then, Bert.'

'Don't forget,' he said. 'That advice.'

'Right.' I began to turn away.

'Ty?'

I was tired of him. 'What?'

'You wouldn't let it happen to you, I know that ... but sometimes it's the strong ones get the worst clobbering ... in the ring, I mean ... they never know when they've taken enough ...'

He suddenly leaned forward and grasped my coat. Whisky fumes seeped up my nose and I could feel his hot breath across the damp air.

'You're always broke, with that wife of yours. Luke-John told me. Always bloody stony. So don't do it ... don't sell your sodding soul ...'

'Try not to,' I said wearily, but he wasn't listening.

He said, with the desperate intensity of the very drunk, 'They buy you first and blackmail after ...'

'Who?'

'Don't know ... Don't sell. ... don't sell your column.'

'No,' I sighed.

'I *mean* it.' He put his face even closer. 'Never sell your column.'

'Bert ... Have you?'

He closed up. He pried himself off me and went back to rocking. He winked, a vast caricature of a wink.

'Bit of advice,' he said nodding. He swivelled on rubbery ankles and weaved an unsteady path across the lobby to the lifts. Inside he turned round and I saw him standing there under the light clutching the half-bottle and still saying over and over, 'Bit of advice, bit of advice.'

The doors slid heavily across in front of him. Shrugging, puzzled a little, I started on my way back to the *Blaze*. Fifty yards along, I stopped off to see if the people who were servicing my typewriter had finished it. They hadn't. Call back Monday, they said.

When I stepped out into the street again a woman was screaming.

Heads turned. The high-pitched agonized noise pierced the roar of wheels and rose clean above the car horns. With everyone else, I looked to see the cause.

Fifty yards up the pavement a knot of people was rapidly forming and I reflected that in this particular place droves of regular staff reporters would be on the spot in seconds. Nevertheless, I went back. Back to the front door of Bert's paper, and a few steps further on.

Bert was lying on the pavement. Clearly dead. The shining fragments of his half-bottle of whisky scattered the paving slabs around him, and the sharp smell of the spilt spirit mixed uneasily with the pervading diesel.

'He fell. He fell.' The screaming woman was on the edge of hysterics and couldn't stop shouting. 'He fell. I saw him. From up there. He fell.'

* * *

Luke-John said 'Christ' several times and looked badly shocked. Derry shook out a whole pot of paper clips on to his desk and absentmindedly put them back one by one.

'You're sure he was dead?' he said.

'His office was seven floors up.'

'Yeah.' He shook his head disbelievingly. 'Poor old boy.' Nil nisi bonum. A sharp change of attitude.

Luke-John looked out of the *Blaze* window and down along the street. The smashed remains of Bert Checkov had been decently removed. The pavement had been washed. People tramped unknowingly across the patch where he had died.

'He was drunk,' Luke-John said. 'Worse than usual.'

He and Derry made a desultory start on the afternoon work. I had no need to stay as the Editor had O.K.'d my copy, but I hung around anyway for an hour or two, not ready to go.

They had said in Bert's office that he came back paralytic from lunch and simply fell out of the window. Two girl secretaries saw him. He was taking a drink out of the neck of the bottle of whisky, and he suddenly staggered against the window, which swung open, and he toppled out. The bottom of the window was at hip height. No trouble at all for someone as drunk as Bert.

I remembered the desperation behind a bit of advice he had given me.

And I wondered.

Chapter Two

Three things immediately struck you about the girl who opened the stockbroker Tudor door at Virginia Water. First, her poise. Second, her fashion sense. Third, her colour. She had honey toast skin, large dark eyes and a glossy shoulder length bounce of black hair. A slightly broad nose and a mouth to match enhanced a landscape in which negro and Caucasian genes had conspired together to do a grand job.

'Good afternoon,' I said. 'I'm James Tyrone. I telephoned...'

'Come in,' she nodded. 'Harry and Sarah should be back at any minute.'

'They are still playing golf?'

'Mm.' She turned, smiling slightly, and gestured me into the house. 'Still finishing lunch, I expect.'

It was three thirty-five. Why not?

She led me through the hall (well-polished parquet, careful flowers, studded leather umbrella stand) into a chintz and chrysanthemum sitting-room. Every window in the house was a clutter of diamond shaped leaded lights which might have had some point when glass could only be made in six inch squares and had to be joined together to get anywhere. The modern imitation obscured the light and the view and was bound to infuriate window cleaners. Harry and Sarah had opted also for uncovered dark oak beams with machine-made chisel marks. The single picture on the plain cream walls made a wild contrast: a modern impressionistic abstract of some cosmic explosion, with the oils stuck on in lumps.

'Sit down.' She waved a graceful hand at a thickly cushioned sofa. 'Like a drink?'

'No, thank you.'

'Don't journalists drink all day?'

'If you drink and write, the writing isn't so hot.'

'Ah yes,' she said, 'Dylan Thomas said he had to be stone cold for any good to come of it.'

'Different class,' I smiled.

'Same principle.'

'Absolutely.'

She gave me a long inspection, her head an inch tilted to one side and her green dress lying in motionless folds down her slender body. Terrific legs in the latest in stockings ended in shiny green shoes with gold buckles, and the only other accessory on display was a broad strapped gold watch on her left wrist.

'You'll know me again.' she said.

I nodded. Her body moved subtly inside the green dress.

She said slowly, with more than simple meaning, 'And I'll know you.'

Her voice, face and manner were quite calm. The brief flash of intense sexual awareness could have been my imagination. Certainly her next remark held no undertone and no invitation.

'Do you *like* horses?'

'Yes, I do,' I said.

'Six months ago I would have said the one place I would never go would be to a race meeting.'

'But you go now?'

'Since Harry won Egocentric in that raffle life has changed in this little neck of the woods.'

'That,' I said, 'is exactly what I want to write about.'

I was on *Tally* business. Background to the Lamplighter. My choice of untypical racehorse owners, Harry and Sarah Hunterson, came back at that point from their Sunday golf course lunch, sweeping in with them a breeze compounded of healthy links air, expensive cigar smoke and half digested gin.

Harry was big, sixtyish, used to authority, heavily charming and unshakably Tory. I guessed that he read the *Telegraph* and drove a three litre Jaguar. With automatic tranmission, of course. He gave me a hearty handshake and said he was glad to see his niece had been looking after me.

'Yes, thank you.'

Sarah said, 'Gail dear, you didn't give Mr Tyrone a drink.'

'He didn't want one.'

The two women were coolly nice to each other in civilized voices. Sarah must have been about thirty years older, but she had worked hard at keeping nature at bay. Everything about her looked careful, from the soft gold rinse via the russet coloured dress to the chunky brown golfing shoes. Her well-controlled shape owed much to the drinking man's diet, and only a deep sag under the chin gave the game away. Neither golf nor gin had dug wrinkles anywhere except round her eyes. Her mouth still had fullness and shape. The wrappings were good enough to hold out hopes of a spark-striking mind, but these proved unrealistic. Sarah was all-of-a-piece, with attitudes and opinions as tidy and well-ordered and as imitative as her house.

Harry was easy to interview in the aftermath of the nineteenth hole.

'I bought this raffle ticket at the Golf Club dance, you see. Some chap was there selling them, a friend of a friend, you know, and I gave him a quid. Well, you know how it is at a dance. For charity, he said. I thought a quid was a bit steep for a raffle ticket, even if it was for a horse. Though I didn't want a horse, mind you. Last thing I wanted. And then damn me if I didn't go and win it. Bit of a problem, eh? To suddenly find yourself saddled with a racehorse?' He laughed, expecting a reward for his little joke.

I duly obliged. Sarah and Gail were both wearing the expressions which meant they had heard him say saddled with a racehorse so often that they had to grit their teeth now at each repetition.

'Would you mind,' I said, 'telling me something of your background and history?'

'Life story, eh?' He laughed loudly, looking from Sarah to Gail to collect their approval. His head was heavily handsome though a shade to fleshy round the neck. The bald sunburned crown and the well disciplined moustache suited him. Thread veins made circular patches of colour on his cheeks. 'Life story,' he repeated. 'Where shall I start?'

'Start from birth,' I said, 'and go on from there.'

Only the very famous who have done it too often, or the extremely introverted, or the sheer bloody-minded, can resist such an invitation. Harry's eyes lit up, and he launched forth with enthusiasm.

Harry had been born in a Surrey suburb in a detached house a size or two smaller than the one he now owned. He had been to a day school and then a minor public school and was turned down by the army because as soon as he left school he had pleurisy. He went to work in the City, in the head office of a finance company, and had risen from junior clerk to director, on the way using occasional snippets of information to make himself modest capital gains via the stockmarket. Nothing shady, nothing rash: but enough so that there should be no drop in his standard of living when he retired.

He married at twenty-four and five years later a lorry rammed his car and killed his wife, his three year old daughter, and his widowed mother. For fifteen years, much in demand at dinner parties, Harry 'looked around'. Then he met Sarah in some Conservative Party committee rooms where they were doing voluntary work addressing pamphlets for a by-election, and they had married three months later. Below the confident fruitiness of successful Harry's voice there was an echo of the motivation of this second marriage. Harry had begun to feel lonely.

As lives went, Harry's had been uneventful. No *Blaze* material in what he had told me, and precious little for *Tally*. Resignedly, I asked him if he intended to keep Egocentric indefinitely.

'Yes, yes, I think so,' he said. 'He has made quite a remarkable difference to us.'

'In what way?'

'It puts them several notches up in lifemanship,' Gail said coolly. 'Gives them something to boast about in pubs.'

We all looked at her. Such was her poise that I found it impossible to tell whether she meant to be catty or teasing, and from his uncertain expression, so did her uncle. There was no ducking it, however, that she had hit to the heart of things, and Sarah smoothly punished her for it.

'Gail dear, would you go and make tea for us all?'

Gail's every muscle said she would hate to. But she stood up ostentatiously slowly, and went.

'A dear girl,' Sarah said. 'Perhaps sometimes a little trying.' Insincerity took all warmth out of her smile, and she found it necessary to go on, to make an explanation that I guessed she rushed into with every stranger at the first opportunity.

'Harry's sister married a barrister ... such a clever man, you know ... but well ... *African*.'

'Yes,' I said.

'Of course we're *very* fond of Gail, and as her parents have gone back to his country since it became independent, and as she was born in England and wanted to stay here, well we ... well, she lives here with us.'

'Yes,' I said again. 'That must be very nice for her.'

Sad, I thought, that they felt any need to explain. Gail didn't need it.

'She teaches at an art school in Victoria,' Harry added. 'Fashion drawing.'

'Fashion *design*,' Sarah corrected him. 'She's really quite good at it. Her pupils win prizes, and things like that.' There was relief in her voice now that I understood, and she was prepared to be generous. To do her justice, considering the far-back embedded prejudices she clearly suffered from, she had made a successful effort. But a pity the effort showed.

'And you,' I said, 'How about your life? And what do you think of Egocentric?'

She said apologetically that her story wasn't as interesting as Harry's. Her first husband, an optician, had died a year before she met Harry, and all she had done, apart from short excursions into voluntary work, was keep house for the two of them. She was glad Harry had won the horse, she liked going to the races as an owner, she thought it exciting to bet, but ten shillings was her usual, and she and Gail had found it quite fun inventing Harry's racing colours.

'What are they?'

'White with scarlet and turquoise question marks, turquoise sleeves, red cap.'

'They sound fine,' I smiled. 'I'll look out for them.'

Harry said his trainer was planning to fit in one more race for Egocentric before the Lamplighter, and maybe I would see him then. Maybe I would, I said, and Gail brought in the tea.

Harry and Sarah rapidly downed three cups each, simultaneously consulted their watches, and said it was time to be getting along to the Murrows' for drinks.

'I don't think I'll come,' Gail said. 'Tell them thanks, but I have got some work to do. But I'll come and fetch you, if you like, if you think it might be better not to drive home. Give me a ring when you're ready.'

The Murrow drinks on top of the golf club gin were a breathalyser hazard in anyone's book. Harry and Sarah nodded and said they would appreciate it.

'Before you go,' I said, 'could you let me see any newspaper cuttings you have? And any photographs?'

'Certainly, certainly,' Harry agreed. 'Gail will show them to you, won't you honey? Must dash now, old chap, the Murrows, you know . . . President of the golf club. Nice to have met you. Hope you've got all the gen you need . . . don't hesitate to call if you want to know anything else.'

'Thank you,' I said, but he was gone before I finished. They went upstairs and down, and shut the front door, and drove away. The house settled into quiet behind them.

'They're not exactly alcoholic,' Gail said. 'They just go eagerly from drink to drink.'

Gail's turn to explain. But in her voice, only objectivity: no faintest hint of apology, as there had been in Sarah's.

'They enjoy life,' I said.

Gail's eyebrows rose. 'Do you know,' she said, 'I suppose they do. I've never really thought about it.'

Self-centred, I thought. Cool. Unaffectionate. Everything I disliked in a woman. Everything I needed one to be. Much too tempting.

'Do you want to see those photographs?' she asked.

'Yes, please.'

She fetched an expensive leather folder and we went through them one by one. Nothing in the few clippings that I hadn't learnt already. None of the photographs were arresting enough for *Tally*. I said I'd come back one day soon, with a photographer. Gail put the folder away and I stood up to go.

'It'll be two hours yet before they ring up from the Murrows. Stay and have that drink now?'

I looked at my watch. There was a train every thirty minutes. I supposed I could miss the next. There was Elizabeth. And there was Gail. And it was only an hour.

'Yes,' I said. 'I will.'

She gave me beer and brought one for herself. I sat down again on the sofa and she folded herself gracefully onto a large velvet cushion on the floor.

'You're married, of course?'

'Yes,' I agreed.

'The interesting looking ones always are.'

'Then why aren't you?'

Her teeth flashed liquid white in an appreciative smile. 'Ah . . . marriage can wait.'

'How long?' I asked.

'I suppose . . . until I find a man I can't bear to part with.'

'You've parted with quite a few?'

'Quite a few.' She nodded and sipped her beer, and looked at me over the rim. 'And you? Are you faithful to your wife?'

I felt myself blink. I said carefully, 'Most of the time.'

'But not always?'

'Not always.'

After a long considering pause she said one short word.

'Good.'

'And is that,' I asked, 'a philosophic comment, or a proposition?'

She laughed. 'I just like to know where I stand.'

'Clear eyed and wide awake...?'

'I hate muddle,' she nodded.

'And emotional muddle especially?'

'You're so right.'

She had never loved, I thought. Sex, often. Love, never. Not what I liked, but what I wanted. I battened down the insidious whisper and asked her, like a good little journalist, about her job.

'It serves.' She shrugged. 'You get maybe one authentic talent in every hundred students. Mostly their ambition is five times more noticeable than their ideas.'

'Do you design clothes yourself?'

'Not for the rag trade. Some for myself, and for Sarah, and for the school. I prefer to teach. I like being able to turn vaguely artistic ignorance into competent workmanship.'

'And to see your influence all along Oxford Street?'

She nodded, her eyes gleaming with amusement. 'Five of the biggest dress manufacturers now have old students of mine on their design staff. One of them is so individual that I can spot his work every time in the shop windows.'

'You like power,' I said.

'Who doesn't?'

'Heady stuff.'

'All power corrupts?' She was sarcastic.

'Each to his own corruption,' I said mildly. 'What's yours, then?'

She laughed. 'Money, I guess. There's a chronic shortage of the folding stuff in all forms of teaching.'

'So you make do with power.'

'If you can't have everything,' she nodded, 'you make do with *something*.'

I looked down into my beer, unable to stop the contraction I could feel in my face. Her words so completely summed up my perennial position. After eleven years I was less resigned to it than ever.

'What are you thinking about?' she asked.

'Taking you to bed.'

She gasped. I looked up from the flat brown liquid ready for any degree of feminine outrage. I could have mistaken her.

It seemed I hadn't. She was laughing. Pleased.

'That's pretty blunt.'

'Mm.'

I put down the beer and stood up, smiling. 'Time to go,' I said. 'I've a train to catch.'

'After that? You can't go after that.'

'Especially after that.'

For answer she stood up beside me, took hold of my hand, and put my fingers into the gold ring at the top of the zipper down the front of her dress.

'Now go home,' she said.

'We've only known each other three hours,' I protested.

'You were aware of me after three minutes.'

I shook my head. 'Three seconds.'

Her teeth gleamed. 'I like strangers.'

I pulled the ring downwards and it was clearly what she wanted.

Harry and Sarah had a large white fluffy rug in front of their fireplace. I imagined it was not the first time Gail had lain on it. She was brisk, graceful, unembarrassed. She stripped off her stockings and shoes, shook off the dress, and stepped out of the diminutive green bra and panties underneath it. Her tawny skin looked warm in the gathering dusk, and her shape took the breath away.

She gave me a marvellous time. A generous lover as well as practised. She knew when to touch lightly, and when to be vigorous. She had strong internal muscles, and she knew how to use them. I took her with passionate gratitude, a fair substitute for love.

When we had finished I lay beside her on the rug and felt the released tension weighing down my limbs in a sort of heavy languorous weakness. The world was a million light-years away and I was in no hurry for it to come closer.

'Wow,' she said, half breathless, half laughing. 'Boy, you sure needed that.'

'Mm.'

'Doesn't your wife let you . . .?'

Elizabeth, I thought. Oh God, Elizabeth. I must sometimes. Just sometimes.

The old weary tide of guilt washed back. The world closed in.

I sat up and stared blindly across the darkening room. It apparently struck Gail that she had been less than tactful, because she got up with a sigh and put her clothes on again, and didn't say another word.

For better or worse, I thought bitterly. For richer, for poorer. In sickness and in health keep thee only unto her as long as you both shall live. I will, I said.

An easy vow, that day I made it. I hadn't kept it. Gail was the fourth girl in eleven years. The first for nearly three.

'You'll miss your train,' she observed prosaically, 'if you sit there much longer.'

I looked at my watch, which was all I had on. Fifteen minutes.

She sighed, 'I'll drive you along to the station.'

We made it with time to spare. I stepped out of the car and politely thanked her for the lift.

'Will I see you again?' she said. Asking for information. Showing no anxiety. Looking out at me through the open window of the estate car outside Virginia Water station she was giving a close imitation of any suburban wife doing the train run. A long cool way from the rough and tumble on the rug. Switch on, switch off. The sort of woman I needed.

'I don't know,' I said indecisively. The signal at the end of the platform went green.

'Goodbye,' she said calmly.

'Do Harry and Sarah,' I asked carefully, 'always play golf on Sundays?'

She laughed, the yellow station lighting flashing on teeth and eyes. 'Without fail.'

'Maybe . . .'

'Maybe you'll ring, and maybe you won't.' She nodded. 'Fair enough. And maybe I'll be in, and maybe I won't.' She gave me a lengthy look which was half smile and half amused detachment. She wouldn't weep if I didn't return. She would accommodate me if I did. 'But don't leave it too long, if you're coming back.'

She wound up the window and drove off without a wave, without a backward glance.

The green electric worm of a train slid quietly into the station to take me home. Forty minutes to Waterloo. Underground to Kings Cross. Three quarters of a mile to walk. Time to enjoy the new ease in my body. Time to condemn it. Too much of my life was a battlefield in which conscience and desire fought constantly for the upper hand: and whichever of them won, it left me the loser.

Elizabeth's mother said with predictable irritation, 'You're late.'

'I'm sorry.'

I watched the jerks of her crossly pulling on her gloves. Overcoat and hat had already been in place when I walked in.

'You have so little consideration. It'll be nearly eleven when I get back.'

I didn't answer.

'You're selfish. All men are selfish.'

There was no point in agreeing with her, and no point in arguing. A disastrous and short lived marriage had left hopeless wounds in her mind which she had done her best to pass on to her only child. Elizabeth, when I first met her, had been pathologically scared of men.

'We've had our supper,' my mother-in-law said. 'I've stacked the dishes for Mrs Woodward.'

Nothing could be more certainly relied upon to upset Mrs Woodward than a pile of congealed plates first thing on Monday morning.

'Fine,' I said, smiling falsely.

'Goodbye, Elizabeth,' she called.

'Goodbye, Mother.'

I opened the door for her and got no thanks.

'Next Sunday, then,' she said.

'That'll be nice.'

She smiled acidly, knowing I didn't mean it. But since she worked as a receptionist-hostess in a health farm all week, Sunday was her day for seeing Elizabeth. Most weeks I wished she would leave us alone, but that Sunday it had set me free to go to Virginia Water. From the following Sunday, and what I might do with it, I wrenched my thoughts away.

When she had gone I walked across to Elizabeth and kissed her on the forehead.

'Hi,'

'Hi yourself,' she said. 'Did you have a good afternoon?'

Straight jab.

'Mm.'

'Good . . . Mother's left the dishes again,' she said.

'Don't worry, I'll do them.'

'What would I do without you!'

We both knew the answer to that. Without me, she would have to spend the rest of her life in a hospital ward, a prisoner with no possibility of escape. She couldn't breathe without the electrically driven pump which hummed at the foot of her high bed. She couldn't cut up her own food or take herself to the bathroom. Elizabeth, my wife, was ninety per cent paralysed from poliomyelitis.

Chapter Three

We lived over a row of lock-up garages in a mews behind Grays Inn Road. A development company had recently knocked down the old buildings opposite, letting in temporary acres of evening sunshine, and was now at the girder stage of a block of flats. If these made our place too dark and shut in when they were done, I would have to find us somewhere else. Not a welcome prospect. We had moved twice before and it was always difficult.

Since race trains mostly ran from London, and to cut my travelling time down to a minimum, we lived ten minutes' walk from the *Blaze*. It had proved much better, in London, to live in a backwater than in a main street: in the small mews community the neighbours all knew about Elizabeth and looked up to her window and waved when they passed, and a lot of them came upstairs for a chat and to bring our shopping.

The District Nurse came every morning to do Elizabeth's vapour rubs to prevent bed sores, and I did them in the evenings. Mrs Woodward, a semi-trained but unqualified nurse, came Mondays to Saturdays from nine-thirty to six, and was helpful about staying longer if necessary. One of our main troubles was that Elizabeth could not be left alone in the flat even for five minutes in case there was an electricity failure. If the main current stopped, we could switch her breathing pump over to a battery, and we could also operate it by hand: but someone had to be there to do it quickly. Mrs Woodward was kind, middle-aged, reliable, and quiet, and Elizabeth liked her. She was also very expensive, and since the Welfare State turns a fish-faced blind eye on incapacitated wives, I could claim not even so much as a tax allowance for Mrs Woodward's essential services. We had to have her, and she kept us poor: and that was that.

In one of the garages below the flat stood the old Bedford van which was the only sort of transport of any use to us. I had had it adapted years ago with a stretcher type bed so that it would take Elizabeth, pump, batteries and all, and although it meant too much upheaval to go out in it every week, it did sometimes give her a change of scenery and some country air. We had tried two holidays by the sea in a caravan, but she had felt uncomfortable and insecure, and both times it had rained, so we didn't bother any more. Day trips were enough, she said. And although she enjoyed them, they exhausted her.

Her respirator was the modern cuirass type: a Spirashell: not the old totally enclosing iron lung. The Spirashell itself slightly resembled the breastplate of a suit of armour. It fitted over the entire front of her chest, was edged with a thick roll of latex, and was fastened by straps round her body. Breathing was really a matter of suction. The pump, which was connected to the Spirashell by a thick flexible hose, alternately made a partial vacuum inside the shell, and then drove air back in again. The vacuum period pulled Elizabeth's chest wall outwards, allowing air to flow downwards into her lungs. The air-in period collapsed her chest and pushed the used breaths out again.

Far more comfortable, and easier for everyone caring for her than a box respirator, the Spirashell had only one drawback. Try how we might, and however many scarves and cardigans we might stuff in round the edges, between the latex roll and her nightdress, it was eternally draughty. As long as the air in the flat was warm it no longer worried her. Summer was all right. But the cold air continually blowing on to her chest not surprisingly distressed her. Cold also reduced to nil the small movements she had retained in her left hand and wrist, and on which she depended for everything. Our heating bills were astronomical.

In the nine and a half years since I had extricated her from hospital we had acquired almost every gadget invented. Wire and pulleys trailed all round the flat. She could read books, draw the curtains, turn on and off the lights, the radio and television, use the telephone and type letters. An electric box of tricks called Possum did most of these tasks. Others worked on a system of levers set off by the feather-light pressure of her left forefinger. Our latest triumph was an electric pulley which raised and rotated her left elbow and forearm, enabling her to eat some things on her own, without always having to be fed. And with a clipped on electric toothbrush, she could now brush her own teeth.

I slept on a divan across the room from her and with a bell beside my ear for when she needed me in the night. There were bells, too, in the kitchen and bathroom, and the tiny room I used for writing in, which with the large sitting-room made up the whole of the flat.

We had been married three years, and we were both twenty-four, when Elizabeth caught polio. We were living in Singapore, where I had a junior job in the Reuter's office, and we flew home for what was intended to be a month's leave.

Elizabeth felt ill on the flight. The light hurt her eyes, and she had a headache like a rod up the back of her neck, and a stabbing pain in her chest. She walked off the aircraft at Heathrow and collapsed half way across the tarmac, and that was the last time she ever stood on her feet.

Our affection for each other had survived everything that followed. Poverty, temper, tears, desperate frustrations. We had emerged after several years into our comparative calms of a settled home, a good job, a reasonably well-ordered existence. We were firm close friends.

But not lovers.

We had tried, in the beginning. She could still feel of course, since polio attacks only the motor nerves, and leaves the sensory nerves intact. But she couldn't breathe for more than three or four minutes if we took the Spirashell right off, and she couldn't bear any weight or pressure on any part of her wasted body. When I said after two or three hopeless attempts that we would leave it for a while she had smiled at me with what I saw to be enormous relief, and we had rarely even mentioned the subject since. Her early upbringing seemed to have easily reconciled her to a sexless existence. Her three years of thawing into a satisfying marriage might never have happened.

On the day after my trip to Virginia Water I set off as soon as Mrs Woodward came and drove the van north-east out of London and into deepest Essex. My quarry this time was a farmer who had bred gold dust in his fields in the shape of Tiddely Pom, ante-post favourite for the Lamplighter Gold Cup.

Weeds luxuriantly edged the pot-holed road wich led from a pair of rotting gateless gateposts into Victor Roncey's farmyard. The house itself, an undistinguished arrangement of mud-coloured bricks, stood in a drift of sodden unswept leaves and stared blankly from symmetrical grubby windows. Colourless paint peeled quietly from the woodwork and no smoke rose from the chimneys.

I knocked on the back door, which stood half open, and called through a small lobby into the house, but there was no reply. A clock ticked with a loud cheap mechanism. A smell of wellington boots richly acquainted with cowpat vigorously assaulted the nose. Someone had dumped a parcel of meat on the edge of the kitchen table from which a thread of watery blood, having by-passed the newspaper wrapping, was making a small pink pool on the floor.

Turning away from the house I wandered across the untidy yard and peered into a couple of outbuildings. One contained a tractor covered with about six years' mud. In another, a heap of dusty-looking coke rubbed shoulders with a jumbled stack of old broken crates and sawn up branches of trees. A larger shed housed dirt and cobwebs and nothing else.

While I hovered in the centre of the yard wondering how far it was polite to investigate, a large youth in a striped knitted cap with a scarlet pom-pom came round a corner at the far end. He also wore a vast sloppy pale blue sweater, and filthy jeans tucked into heavy-weight gum boots. Fair haired, with a round weather-beaten face, he looked cheerful and uncomplicated.

'Hullo,' he said. 'You want something?' His voice was light and pleasant, with a touch of local accent.

'I'm looking for Mr Roncey.'

'He's round the roads with the horses. Better call back later.'

'How long will he be?'

'An hour, maybe,' he shrugged.

'I'll wait, then, if you don't mind,' I said, gesturing towards my van.

'Suit yourself.'

He took six steps towards the house and then stopped, turned round, and came back.

'Hey, you wouldn't be that chap that phoned?'

'Which chap?'

'James Tyrone?'

'That's right.'

'Well for crying out loud why didn't you say so? I thought you were a traveller ... come on into the house. Do you want some breakfast?'

'Breakfast?'

He grinned. 'Yeah. I know it's nearly eleven. I get up before six. Feel peckish again by now.'

He led the way into the house through the back door, did nothing about the dripping meat, and added to the wellington smell by clumping across the floor to the furthest door, which he opened.

'Ma?' he shouted. 'Ma.'

'She's around somewhere,' he said, shrugging and coming back. 'Never mind. Want some eggs?'

I said no, but when he reached out a half-acre frying pan and filled it with bacon I changed my mind.

'Make the coffee,' he said, pointing.

I found mugs, powdered coffee, sugar, milk, kettle and spoons all standing together on a bench alongside the sink.

'My Ma,' he explained grinning, 'is a great one for the time and motion bit.'

He fried six eggs expertly and gave us three each, with a chunk of new white bread on the side.

We sat at the kitchen table, and I'd rarely tasted anything so good. He ate solidly and drank coffee, then pushed his plate away and lit a cigarette.

'I'm Peter,' he said. 'It isn't usually so quiet around here, but the kids are at school and Pat's out with Pa.'

'Pat?'

'My brother. The jockey of the family. Point-to-points, mostly, though. I don't suppose you would know of him?'

'I'm afraid not.'

'I read your column,' he said. 'Most weeks.'

'That's nice.'

He considered me, smoking, while I finished the eggs. 'You don't talk much, for a journalist.'

'I listen,' I said.

He grinned. 'That's a point.'

'Tell me about Tiddely Pom, then.'

'Hell, no. You'll have to get Pa or Pat for that. They're crazy on the horses. I just run the farm.' He watched my face carefully, I guessed for surprise, since in spite of being almost my height he was still very young.

'You're sixteen?' I suggested.

'Yeah.' He sniffed, disgusted. 'Waste of effort, though, really.'

'Why?'

'Why? Because of the bloody motorway, that's why. They've nearly finished that bloody three lane monster and it passes just over there, the other side of our ten-acre field.' He gestured towards the window with his cigarette. 'Pa's going raving mad wondering if Tiddely Pom'll have a nervous breakdown when those heavy lorries start thundering past. He's been trying to sell this place for two years, but no one will have it, and you can't blame them, can you?' Gloom settled on him temporarily. 'Then, see, you never know when they'll pinch more of our land, they've had fifty acres already, and it doesn't give you much heart to keep the place right, does it?'

'I guess not,' I said.

'They've talked about knocking our house down,' he went on. 'Something about it being in the perfect position for a service station with restaurants and a vast car park and another slip road to Bishops Stortford. The only person who's pleased about the road is my brother Tony, and he wants to be a rally driver. He's eleven. He's a nut.'

There was a scrunch and clatter of hooves outside, coming nearer. Peter and I got to our feet and went out into the yard, and watched three horses plod up the bumpy gravel drive and rein to a halt in front of us. The rider of the leading horse slid off, handed his reins to the second, and came towards us. A trim wiry man in his forties with thick brown hair and a mustard coloured moustache.

'Mr Tyrone?'

I nodded. He gave me a brisk hard handshake in harmony with his manner and voice and then stood back to allow me a clear view of the horses.

'That's Tiddely Pom, that bay.' He pointed to the third horse, ridden by a young man very like Peter, though perhaps a size smaller. 'And Pat, my son.'

'A fine looking horse,' I said insincerely. Most owners expected praise: but Tiddely Pom showed as much high quality to the naked eye as an uncut diamond. A common head, slightly U-necked on a weak shoulder, and herring gutted into the bargain. He looked just as uncouth at home as he did on a racecourse.

'Huh,' snorted Roncey. 'He's not. He's a doer, not a looker. Don't try and butter me up, I don't take to it.'

'Fair enough,' I said mildly. 'Then he's got a common head and neck, a poor shoulder and doesn't fill the eye behind the saddle either.'

'That's better. So you do know what you're talking about. Walk him round the yard, Pat.'

Pat obliged. Tiddely Pom stumbled around with the floppy gait that once in a while denotes a champion. This horse, bred from a thoroughbred hunter mare by a premium stallion, was a spectacular jumper endowed with a speed to be found nowhere in his pedigree. When an ace of this sort turned up unexpectedly it took the owner almost as long as the public to realize it. The whole racing industry was unconsciously geared against belief that twenty-two carat stars could come from tiny owner-trained stables. It had taken Tiddely Pom three seasons to become known, where from a big fashionable public stable he would have been newsworthy in his first race.

'When I bred him I was hoping for a point-to-point horse for the boys,' Roncey said. 'So we ran him all one season in point-to-points and apart from one time Pat fell off he didn't get beat. Then last year we thought we would have a go in hunter chases as well, and he went and won the Foxhunters' at Cheltenham.'

'I remember that,' I said.

'Yes. So last year we tried him in open handicaps, smallish ones . . .'

'And he won four out of six,' I concluded for him.

'It's your job to know, I suppose. Pat,' he shouted. 'Put him back in his box.' He turned to me again. 'Like to see the others?'

I nodded, and we followed Pat and the other two horses across the yard and round the corner from which Peter had originally appeared.

Behind a ramshackle barn stood a neat row of six well-kept wooden horse boxes with shingle roofs and newly painted black doors. However run down the rest of the farm might be, the stable department was in tip top shape. No difficulty in seeing where the farmer's heart lay: with his treasure.

'Well now,' Roncey said. 'We've only the one other racehorse, really, and that's Klondyke, that I was riding just now. He ran in hunter 'chases in the spring. Didn't do much good, to be honest.' He walked along to the second box from the far end, led the horse in and tied it up. When he took the saddle off I saw that Klondyke was a better shape than Tiddely Pom, which was saying little enough, but the health in his coat was conspicuous.

'He looks well,' I commented.

'Eats his head off,' said Roncey dispassionately, 'and he can stand a lot of work, so we give it him.'

'One-paced,' observed Pat regretfully over my shoulder. 'Can't quicken. Pity. We won just the two point-to-points with him. No more.'

There was the faintest glimmer of satisfaction in the laconic voice, and I glanced at him sideways. He saw me looking and wiped the expression off his face but not before I had seen for certain that he had mixed feelings about the horses' successes. While they progressed to

National Hunt racing proper, he didn't. Older amateur riders had been engaged, and then professionals. The father-son-relationship had needles in it.

'What do you have in the other boxes?' I asked Roncey, as he shut Klondyke's door.

'My old grey hunter at the end, and two hunter mares here, both in foal. This one, Piglet, she's the dam of Tiddely Pom of course; she's in foal to the same sire again.'

Unlikely, I thought, that lightning would strike twice.

'You'll sell the foal,' I suggested.

He sniffed. 'She's in the farm accounts.'

I grinned to myself. Farmers could train their horses and lose the cost in the general farm accounts, but if they sold one it then came under the heading of income and was taxed accordingly. If Roncey sold either Tiddely Pom or his full brother, nearly half would go to the Revenue.

'Turn the mares out, Joe,' he said to his third rider, a patient looking old man with skin like bark, and we watched while he set them loose in the nearest field. Peter was standing beside the gate with Pat: bigger, more assured, with far fewer knots in his personality.

'Fine sons,' I said to Roncey.

His mouth tightened. He had no pride in them. He made no reply at all to my fishing compliment, but instead said, 'We'll go into the house and you can ask me anything you want to know. For a magazine, you said?'

I nodded.

'Pat,' he shouted. 'You give these three horses a good strapping and feed them and let Joe get on with the hedging. Peter, you've got work to do. Go and do it.'

Both his boys gave him the blank acquiescing look which covers seething rebellion. There was a perceptible pause before they moved off with their calm accepting faces. Lids on a lot of steam. Maybe one day Roncey would be scalded.

He led the way briskly back across the yard and into the kitchen. The meat still lay there dripping. Roncey by-passed it and gestured me to follow him through the far door into a small dark hall.

'Madge?' he shouted. 'Madge?'

Father had as little success as son. He shrugged in the same way and led me into a living room as well worn and untidy as the rest of the place. Drifts of clutter, letters, newspapers, clothing, toys and indiscriminate bits of junk lay on every flat surface, including the chairs and the floor. There was a vase of dead and desiccated chrysanthemums on a window sill, and some brazen cobwebs networked the ceiling. Cold ash from the day before filled the grate. A toss-up I thought, whether one called the room lived-in or squalid.

'Sit down if you can find somewhere,' Roncey said. 'Madge lets the boys run wild in the house. Not firm enough. I won't have it outside, of course.'

'How many do you have?'

'Boys? Five.'

'And a daughter?' I asked.

'No,' he said abruptly. 'Five boys.'

The thought didn't please him. 'Which magazine?'

'*Tally*.' I said. 'They want background stories to the Lamplighter, and I thought I would give the big stables a miss and shine a bit of the spotlight on someone else for a change.'

'Yes, well,' he said defensively, 'I've been written up before, you know.'

'Of course,' I said soothingly.

'About the Lamplighter, too. I'll show you.' He jumped up and went over to a knee-hole desk, pulled out one of the side drawers bodily, and brought it across to where I sat at one end of the sofa. He put the drawer in the centre, swept a crumpled jersey, two beaten up dinky cars and a gutted brown paper parcel on to the floor, and seated himself in the space.

The drawer contained a heap of clippings and photographs all thrust in together. No careful sticking into expensive leather folders, like the Huntersons.

My mind leapt to Gail. I saw Roncey talking to me but I was thinking about her body. Her roundnesses. Her fragrant pigmented skin. Roncey was waiting for an answer and I hadn't heard what he'd asked.

'I'm sorry,' I said.

'I asked if you know Bert Checkov.' He was holding a lengthy clipping with a picture alongside and a bold headline, 'Back Tiddely Pom NOW.'

'Yes . . . and no,' I said uncertainly.

'How do you mean?' he said brusquely. 'I should have thought you would have known him, being in the same business.'

'I did know him. But he died. Last Friday.'

I took the clipping and read it while Roncey went through the motions of being shocked, with the indifference uppermost in his voice spoiling the effect.

Bert Checkov had gone to town with Tiddely Pom's chances in the Lamplighter. The way he saw it, the handicapper had been suffering from semi-blindness and mental blocks to put Tiddely Pom into the weights at ten stone seven, and all punters who didn't jump on the bandwaggon instantly needed to be wet nursed. He thought the ante-post market would open with generous odds, but urged everyone to hurry up with their shirts, before the bookmakers woke up to the bonanza. Bert's pungent phraseology had given Roncey's horse more boost than a four stage rocket.

'I didn't know he'd written this,' I admitted. 'I missed it.'

'He rang me up only last Thursday and this was in the paper on Friday. That must have been the day you said he died. In point of fact I didn't expect it would appear. When he telephoned he was, to my mind, quite drunk.'

'It's possible,' I conceded.

'I wasn't best pleased about it either.'

'The article?'

'I hadn't got my own money on, do you see? And there he went, spoiling the price. When I rang up my bookmaker on Friday he wouldn't give me more than a hundred to eight, and today they've even made him favourite at eight to one, and there's still nearly three weeks to the race. Fair enough he's a good horse, but he's not Arkle. In point of fact I don't understand it.'

'You don't understand why Checkov tipped him?'

He hesitated. 'Not to that extent, then, let's say.'

'But you do hope to win?'

'Hope,' he said. 'Naturally, I hope to win. But it's the biggest race we've ever tried ... I don't *expect* to win, do you see?'

'You've as good a chance as any,' I said. 'Checkov had his column to fill. The public won't read half-hearted stuff, you have to go all out for the positive statement.'

He gave me a small tight smile laced with a sneer for the soft option. A man with no patience or sympathy for anyone else's problems, not even his sons.

The sitting-room door opened and a large woman in a sunflower dress came in. She had thick fair down on her legs but no stockings, and a pair of puffed ankles bulged over the edges of some battered blue bedroom slippers. Nevertheless she was very light on her feet and she moved slowly, so that her progress seemed to be a weightless drift: no mean feat considering she must have topped twelve stone.

A mass of fine light brown hair hung in an amorphous cloud round her head, from which a pair of dreamy eyes surveyed the world as though half asleep. Her face was soft and rounded, not young, but still in a way immature. Her fantasy life, I guessed uncharitably, was more real to her than the present. She had been far away in the past hour, much further than upstairs.

'I didn't know you were in,' she said to Roncey.

He stood up several seconds after me. 'Madge, this is James Tyrone. I told you he was coming.'

'Did you?' She transferred her vague gaze to me. 'Carry on, then.'

'Where have you been?' Roncey said. 'Didn't you hear me calling?'

'Calling?' She shook her head. 'I was making the beds, of course.' She stood in the centre of the room, looking doubtfully around at the mess. 'Why didn't you light the fire?'

I glanced involuntarily at the heap of ashes in the grate, but she saw them as no obstacle at all. From a scratched oak box beside the hearth she produced three firelighters and a handful of sticks. These went on top of the ashes, which got only a desultory poke. She struck a match, lit the firelighters, and made a wigwam of coal. The new fire flared up good temperedly on the body of the old while Madge took the hearth brush and swept a few cinders out of sight behind a pile of logs.

Fascinated, I watched her continue with her housework. She drifted across to the dead flowers, opened the window, and threw them out. She emptied the water from the vase after them, then put it back on the window sill and shut the window.

From behind the sofa where Roncey and I sat she pulled a large brown cardboard box. On the outside was stencilled Kellogg's Cornflakes, 12 × Family Size and on the inside it was half filled with the same sort of jumble which was lying around the room. She wafted methodically around in a large circle taking everything up and throwing it just as it came into the box, a process which took approximately three minutes. She then pushed the box out of sight again behind the sofa and plumped up the seat cushions of two armchairs on her way back to the door. The room, tidy and with the brightly blazing fire, looked staggeringly different. The cobwebs were still there but one felt it might be their turn tomorrow. Peter was right. Ma had got the time and motion kick completely buttoned up; and what did it matter if the motive was laziness.

Roncey insisted that I should stay to lunch and filled in the time beforehand with a brisk but endless account of all the horses he had ever owned. Over lunch, cold beef and pickles and cheese and biscuits served at two-thirty on the kitchen table, it was still he who did all the talking. The boys ate steadily in silence and Madge contemplated the middle distance with eyes which saw only the scenes going on in her head.

When I left shortly afterwards Pat asked for a lift into Bishops Stortford and braved his father's frown to climb into the front seat of the van. Roncey shook hands firmly as before and said he hoped to receive a free copy of *Tally*. 'Of course,' I said. But *Tally* were notoriously mean: I would have to send it myself.

He waved me out of the yard and told Pat brusquely to come straight back on the four o'clock bus, and we were barely out through the sagging gateposts before Pat unburdened himself of a chunk of bottled resentment.

'He treats us like children ... Ma's no help, she never listens ...'

'You could leave here,' I pointed out. 'You're what – nineteen?'

'Next month. But I can't leave and he knows it. Not if I want to race. I can't turn professional yet, I'm not well enough known and no one would put me up on their horses. I've got to start as an amateur and make a name for myself, Pa says so. Well I couldn't be an amateur if I left home and got an ordinary job somehwere, I couldn't afford all the expenses and I wouldn't have any time.'

'A job in a stable ...' I suggested.

'Do me a favour. The rules say you can't earn a salary in any capacity in a racing stable and ride as an amateur, not even if you're a secretary or an assistant or anything. It's bloody unfair. And don't say I could get a job as a lad and do my two and have a professional licence, of course I could. And how many lads ever get far as jockeys, doing that? None. Absolutely none. You know that.'

I nodded.

'I do a lad's work now, right enough. Six horses, we've got, and I do the bloody lot. Old Joe's the only labour we've got on the whole farm, except us, believe it or not. Pa's always got a dozen jobs lined up for him. And I wouldn't mind the work, and getting practically no pay, I really wouldn't, if Pa would let me ride in anything except point-to-points, but he won't, he says I haven't enough experience, and if you ask me he's making bloody sure I never get enough experience . . . I'm absolutely fed up, I'll tell you straight.'

He brooded over his situation all the way into Bishops Stortford. A genuine grievance, I thought. Victor Roncey was not a father to help his sons get on.

Chapter Four

They held the inquest on Bert Checkov on that Monday afternoon. Verdict: Misadventure. Dead drunk he was, said the girl typist who saw him fall. Dead drunk.

And after he hit the pavement, just dead.

When I went into the office on Tuesday morning, Luke-John and Derry were discussing whether or not to go to the funeral on the Wednesday.

'Croxley,' Derry said. 'Where's that?'

'Near Watford,' I said. 'On the Metropolitan Line. A straight run into Farringdon Street.'

'What Fleet Street needs,' said Derry gloomily, 'is a tube station a lot nearer than blooming Farringdon. It's three quarters of a mile if it's an inch.'

'If you're right, Ty, we can manage it easily,' Luke-John said authoritatively. 'We should all go, I think.'

Derry squinted at the small underground map in his diary. 'Croxley. Next to Watford. What do you know?'

I'd had a girl at Watford once. The second one. I'd spent a lot of time on the Metropolitan Line while Elizabeth was under the impression I was extra busy in the *Blaze*. Guilt and deceit were old familiar travelling companions. From Watford, from Virginia Water, from wherever.

'Ty,' Luke-John was saying sharply.

'Huh?'

'The funeral is at two-thirty. An hour, say, to get there. . . ?'

'Not me,' I said. 'There's this *Tally* article to be done. It'll take me at least another two days in interviews.'

He shrugged. 'I'd have thought. . .'

'What depths have you plumbed so far?' Derry asked. He was sitting with his feet up on the desk. No work in a Sunday paper on Tuesday.

'The Roncey family,' I said. ''Tiddely Pom.'

Derry sniffed. 'Ante-post favourite.'

'Will he be your tip?' I asked with interest.

'Shouldn't think so. He's won a few races but he hasn't beaten much of any class.'

'Bert tipped him strongly. Wrote a most emphatic piece about catching the odds now before they shorten. He wrote it last Thursday; it must have been straight after the handicap was published in the racing calendar: and it was in his paper on Friday. Roncey showed me the clipping. He said Bert was drunk when he rang up.'

Luke-John sighed. Derry said decisively, 'That does it, then. If Bert tipped him, I'm not going to.'

'Why not?'

'Bert's heavy long-distance tips were nearly always nonstarters.'

Luke-John stretched his neck until the tendons stood out like strings, and massaged his nobbly larynx. 'Always the risk of that, of course. It happens to everyone.'

'Do you mean that seriously?' I asked Derry.

'Oh sure. Sorry about your *Tally* article and all that,' he grinned, 'but I'd say about the time it's published you'll find Tiddely Pom has been taken out of the Lamplighter.'

Derry twiddled unconcernedly with a rubber band and Luke-John shuffled absentmindedly through some papers. Neither of them felt the shiver travelling down my spine.

'Derry,' I said. 'Are you sure?'

'Of what?'

'That Bert always tipped nonstarters for big races.'

Derry snapped the band twice in his fingers. 'To be precise, if you want me to be precise, Bert tipped a higher percentage of big-race nonstarters than anyone else in the street, and he has been at his best in this direction, or worst, or at any rate his most consistent, during the past year. He'd blow some horse up big, tell everyone to back it at once, and then wham, a day or two before the race it would be scratched.'

'I've never noticed,' said Luke-John forbiddingly, as if it couldn't have happened without.

Derry shrugged. 'Well, it's a fact. Now, if you want to know something equally useless about that puffed up Connersley of the *Sunday Hemisphere*, he has a weird habit of always tipping horses which start with his own initial, C. Delusions of grandeur, I imagine.'

'You're having us on,' Luke-John said.

Derry shook his head. 'Uhuh. I don't just sit here with my eyes shut, you know. I read the newspapers.'

'I think,' I said suddenly, 'I will fetch my typewriter.'

'Where is it?'

Over my shoulder on the way back to the door I said, 'Being cleaned.'

This time the typewriter was ready. I collected it and went further along the street, to Bert's paper. Up in the lift, to Bert's department. Across the busy floor to the Sports Desk. Full stop beside the assistant sports editor, a constant racegoer, a long-known bar pal.

'Ty! What's the opposition doing here?'

'Bert Checkov,' I said.

We discussed him for a while. The assistant sports editor was hiding something. It showed in half looks, unfinished gestures, an unsuccessfully smothered embarrassment. He said he was shocked, shattered, terribly distressed by Bert's death. He said everyone on the paper would miss him, the paper would miss him, they all felt his death was a great loss. He was lying.

I didn't pursue it. Could I, I asked tentatively, have a look at Bert's clippings book? I would very much like to re-read some of his articles.

The assistant sports editor said kindly that I had little to learn from Bert Checkov or anyone else for that matter, but to go ahead. While he got back to work I sorted out the records racks at the side of the room and eventually found three brown paper clippings books with Bert's work stuck into the pages.

I took my typewriter out of its carrying case and left it lying on an inconspicuous shelf. The three clippings books went into the carrying case, though I had to squeeze to get it shut, and I walked quietly and unchallenged out of the building with my smuggled goods.

Luke-John and Derry goggled at the books of cuttings.

'How on earth did you get them out? And why on earth do you want them?'

'Derry,' I said, 'can now set about proving that Bert always tipped nonstarters in big races.'

'You're crazy,' Luke-John said incredulously.

'No' I said regretfully. 'If I'm right, the *Blaze* is on the edge of the sort of scandal it thrives on. A circulation explosion. And all by courtesy of the sports section.'

Luke-John's interest sharpened instantly from nil to needles.

'Don't waste time then, Derry. If Ty says there's a scandal, there's a scandal.'

Derry gave me a sidelong look. 'Our truffle hound on the scent, eh?' He took his feet off the desk and resignedly got to work checking what Bert had forecast against what had actually happened. More and more form books and racing calendars were brought out, and Derry's written lists slowly grew.

'All right,' he said at last. 'Here it is, just as I said. These books cover the last three years. Up till eighteen months ago he tipped runners and nonrunners in about the same proportion as the rest of us poor slobs. Then he went all out suddenly for horses which didn't run when it came to the point. All in big races, which had ante-post betting.' He looked puzzled. 'It can't be just coincidence, I do see that. But I don't see the point.'

'Ty?' said Luke-John.

I shrugged. 'Someone has been working a fiddle.'

'Bert wouldn't.' His voice said it was unthinkable.

'I'd better take these books back before they miss them,' I said, packing them again into the typewriter case.

'Ty!' Luke-John sounded exasperated.

'I'll tell you when I come back.' I said.

There was no denunciation at Bert's office. I returned the books to their shelf and retrieved my typewriter, and thanked the assistant sports editor for his kindness.

'You still here? I thought you'd gone.' He waved a friendly hand. 'Any time.'

'All right,' said Luke-John truculently when I got back to the *Blaze*. I won't believe Bert Checkov was party to any fiddle.'

'He sold his soul, I said plainly, 'Like he told me not to.'

'Rubbish.'

'He sold his column. He wrote what he was told to write.'

'Not Bert. He was a newspaper man, one of the old school.'

I considered him. His thin face looked obstinate and pugnacious. Loyalty to an old friend was running very strong.

'Well then,' I said slowly, 'Bert wrote what he was forced to write.'

A good deal of the Morton tension subsided and changed course. He wouldn't help to uncover a scandal an old friend was responsible for, but he'd go the whole way to upen up one he'd been the victim of.

'Clever beast,' said Derry under his breath.

'Who forced him?' Luke-John said.

'I don't know. Not yet. It might be possible to find out.'

'And *why*?'

'That's much easier. Someone has been making an ante-post book on a certainty. What Bert was doing ... being forced to do ... was persuading the public to part with their money.'

They both looked contemplative. I started again, explaining more fully. 'Say a villain takes up book-making. It can happen, you know.'

Derry grinned. 'Say one villain hits on a jolly scheme for making illegal gains in a fool-proof way with very little effort. He only works it on big races which have ante-post betting, because he needs at least three weeks to rake in enough to make it worth the risk. He chooses a suitable horse, and he forces Bert to tip it for all his column's worth. Right? So the public put their money on, and our villain sticks to every penny that comes his way. No need to cover himself against losses. He knows there won't be any. He knows he isn't going to have to pay out on that horse. He knows it's going to be scratched at or after the four day forfeits. Very nice fiddle.'

After a short silence Derry said, 'How does he know?'

'Ah well,' I said, shrugging, 'That's another thing we'll have to find out.'

'I don't believe it,' Luke-John said sceptically. 'All that just because Bert tipped a few nonstarters.'

Derry looked dubiously at the lists he had made. 'There were too many nonstarters. There really were.'

'Yes,' I said.

'But you *can't* have worked out all this just from what I said, from just that simple casual remark...'

'No,' I agreed. 'There was something else, of course. It was something Bert himself said, last Friday, when I walked back with him from lunch. He wanted to give me a piece of advice,'

'That's right,' Derry said. 'He never came out with it.'

'Yes he did. He did indeed. With great seriousness. He told me not to sell my soul. Not to sell my column.'

'No,' Luke-John said.

'He said "First they buy you and then they blackmail you".'

Luke-John said 'No,' again automatically.

'He was very drunk,' I said. 'Much worse than usual. He called the advice he was giving me his famous last words. He went up in the lift with a half-bottle of whisky, he walked right across his office, he drank from the bottle and without a pause he fell straight out of the window,'

Luke-John put his freckled fingers on his thin mouth and when he spoke his voice was low, protesting and thick, 'No ... my *God*'.

After leaving the *Blaze* I collected the van and drove down to a racing stable in Berkshire to interview the girl who looked after the best known horse in the Lamplighter.

Zig Zag was a household name, a steeplechaser of immense reputation and popularity, automatic headline material: but any day the cracks would begin to show, since he would be turning eleven on January the first. The Lamplighter, to my mind, would be his last bow as grand old man before the younger brigde shouldered him out. Until Bert Checkov had rammed home the telling difference in weights, Zig Zag, even allotted a punitive twelve stone ten pounds, had been the automatic choice for ante-post favourite.

His groom was earnest and devoted to him. In her twenties, unsophisticated, of middling intelligence, Sandy Willis's every sentence was packed with pithy stable language which she used unselfconsciously and which contrasted touchingly with her essential innocence. She showed me Zig Zag with proprietary pride and could recite, and did, his every race from the day he was foaled. She had looked after him always, she said, ever since he came into the yard as a leggy untried three year old. She didn't know what she'd do when he was retired, racing wouldn't be the same without him somehow.

I offered to drive her into Newbury to have tea in a café or an hotel, but she said no, thank you, she wouldn't have time because the evening work started at four. Leaning against the door of Zig Zag's box she told be about her life, hesitantly at first, and then in a rush. Her parents didn't get on, she said. There were always rows at home, so she'd cleared out pretty soon after leaving school, glad to get away, her old man was so mean with the houskeeping and her Mum did nothing but screech, nag, nag, at him mostly but at her too and her two kid sisters, right draggy the whole thing was, and she hoped Zig Zag would be racing at Kempton on Boxing Day so she'd have a good excuse not to go home for Christmas. She loved her work, she loved Zig Zag, the racing world was the tops, and no, she wasn't in any hurry to get married, there were always boys around if she wanted them and honestly whoever would swop Zig Zag for a load of draggy housework, especially if it turned out like her Mum and Dad...

She agreed with a giggle to have her photograph taken if Zig Zag could be in the picture too, and said she hoped that *Tally* magazine would send her a free copy.

'Of course,' I assured her, and decided to charge all free copies against expenses.

When I left her I walked down through the yard and called on the trainer, whom I saw almost every time I went racing. A businesslike man in his fifties, with no airs and few illusions.

'Come in, Ty,' he said. 'Did you find Sandy Willis?'

'Thank you, yes. She was very helpful.'

'She's one of my best lads.' He waved me to an armchair and poured some oak coloured tea out of a silver pot. 'Sugar?' I shook my head. 'Not much in the upstairs department, but her horses are always jumping out of their skins.'

'A spot of transferred mother love,' I agreed. I tasted the tea. My tongue winced at the strength of the tannin. Norton Fox poured himself another cup and took three deep swallows.

'If I write her up for *Tally*,' I said, 'You won't do the dirty on me and take Zig Zag out of the Lamplighter at the last minute?'

'I don't plan to.'

'Twelve stone ten is a prohibitive weight,' I suggested.

'He's won with twelve thirteen.' He shrugged. 'He'll never come down the handicap.'

'As a matter of interest,' I said, 'What happened to Brevity just before the Champion Hurdle?'

Norton clicked his tongue in annoyance. 'You can rely on it, Zig Zag will *not* be taken out at the last minute. At least not for no reason, like Brevity.'

'He was favourite, wasn't he?' I knew he was, I'd checked carefully from Derry's list. 'What exactly happened?'

'I've never been so furious about anything.' The eight month old grievance was still vivid in his voice. 'I trained that horse to the minute. To the minute. We always had the Champion Hurdle as his main target. He couldn't have been more fit. He was ready to run for his life. And then what? Do you know what? I declared him at the four day stage, and the owner, the *owner*, mark you, went and telephoned Weatherbys two days later and cancelled the declaration. Took the horse out of the race. I ask you! And on top of that, he hadn't even the courtesy, or the nerve probably, to tell me what he'd done, and the first I knew of it was when Brevity wasn't in the overnight list of runners. Of course I couldn't believe it and rang up Weatherbys in a fury and they told me old Dembley himself had struck his horse out. And I still don't know why. I had the most God almighty row with him about it and all he would say was that he had decided not to run, and that was that. He never once gave me a reason. Not one, after all that planning and all that work. I told him to take his horses away, I was so angry. I mean, how can you train for a man who's going to do that to you? It's impossible.'

'Who trains for him now?' I asked sympathetically.

'No one. He sold all three of his horses, including Brevity. He said he'd had enough of racing, he was finished with it.'

'You wouldn't still have his address?' I asked.

'Look here, Ty, you're not putting all that in your wretched paper.'

'No,' I assured him. 'Just one day I might write an article on owners who've sold out.'

'Well ... yes, I still have it.' He copied the address from a ledger and handed it to me. 'Don't cause any trouble.'

'Not for you,' I said. Trouble was always Luke-John's aim, and often mine. The only difference was that I was careful my friends shouldn't be on the receiving end. Luke-John had no such difficulties. He counted no one, to that extent, a friend.

Mrs Woodward and Elizabeth were watching the news on television when I got back. Mrs Woodward took a quick look at her watch and made an unsuccessful attempt at hiding her disappointment. I had beaten her to six o'clock by thirty seconds. She charged overtime by the half hour, and was a shade over businesslike about it. I never got a free five minutes: five past six and it would have cost me the full half hour. I understood that it wasn't sheer miserliness. She was a widow whose teenage son had a yearning to be a doctor, and as far as I could see it would be mainly Tyrone who put him through medical school.

The time-keeping war was conducted with maximum politeness and without acknowledgement that it existed. I simply synchronized our two clocks and my watch with the B.B.C. time signal every morning, and paid up with a smile when I was late. Mrs Woodward gave me a warmer welcome at ten past six than at ten to, but never arrived a minute after nine-thirty in the mornings. Neither of us had let on to Elizabeth how acutely the clock was watched.

Mrs Woodward was spare and strong, with a little of her native Lancashire in her voice and a lot in her character. She had dark hair going grey, rich brown eyes, and a determined jaw line which had seen her through a jilting fiancé and a work-shy husband. Unfailingly gentle to Elizabeth, she had never yet run out of patience, except with the vacuum cleaner, which occasionally regurgitated where it should have sucked.

In our flat she wore white nylon overalls which she knew raised her status to nurse from home help in the eyes of visitors, and I saw no reason to think any worse of her for it. She took off the overall and hung it up, and I helped her into the dark blue coat she had been wearing every single day for at least three years.

'Night, Mr Tyrone. Night, luv,' she said, as she always said. And always I thanked her for coming, and said I'd see her in the morning.

'Did you have a good day?' Elizabeth asked, when I kissed her forehead. Her voice sounded tired. The Spirashell tugged her chest up and down in a steady rhythm, and she could only speak easily on the outgoing breaths.

'I went to see a girl about a horse,' I said, smiling, and told her briefly about Sandy Willis and Zig Zag. She liked to know a little of what I'd been doing, but her interest always flagged pretty soon, and after so many years I could tell the exact instant by the microscopic relaxation in her eye muscles. She rarely said she was tired and had had enough of anything because she was afraid I would think her complaining and querulous and find her too much of a burden altogether. I couldn't persuade her to say flatly 'Stop, I'm tired.' She agreed each time I mentioned it that she would, and she never did.

'I've seen three of the people for the *Tally* article,' I said. 'Owners, owner-trainer, and stable girl. I'm afraid after supper I'd better make a start on the writing. Will you be all right watching television?'

'Of course ...' She gave me the sweet brilliant smile which made every chore for her possible. Occasionally I spotted her manufacturing it artificially, but no amount of reassurance seemed able to convince her that she needn't perform tricks for me, that I wouldn't shove her back into hospital if she lost her temper, that I didn't need her to be angelic, and she was safe with me, and loved, and, in fact, very much wanted.

'Like a drink?' I said.

'Love one.'

I poured us both a J and B wih Malvern Water, and took hers over and fastened it into the holder I'd rigged up, with the bent drinking straw near to her mouth. Using that she could drink in her own time, and a lot less got spilt on the sheets. I tasted appreciatively the pale fine Scotch, slumping into the big armchair beside her bed, sloughing off the day's travelling with a comfortable feeling of being at home. The pump's steady soft thumping had its usual soporific effect. It sent most of our visitors fast asleep.

We watched a brain-packed quiz game on television and companionably answered most of the questions wrong. After that I went into the kitchen and looked at what Mrs Woodward had put out for supper. Plaice coated with bread crumbs, a bag of frozen chips, one lemon. Stewed apples, custard. Cheddar cheese, square crackers. The Woodward views on food didn't entirely coincide with my own. Stifling thoughts of underdone steak I cooked the chips in oil and the plaice in butter, and left mine to keep hot while I helped Elizabeth. Even with the new pulley gadget some foods were difficult: the plaice broke up too easily and her wrist got tired, and we ended up with me feeding her as usual.

While I washed the dishes I made coffee in mugs, fixed Elizabeth's into the holder, and took mine with my typewriter into the little room which would have been a child's bedroom if we'd ever had a child.

The *Tally* article came along slowly, its price tag reproaching me for every sloppy phrase. The Huntersons, The Ronceys, Sandy Willis. Dissect without hurting, probe but leave whole. Far easier, I thought resignedly, to pick them to bits. Good for *Tally's* sales too. Bad for the conscience, lousy for the Huntersons, the Ronceys, Sandy Willis. To tell all so that the victim liked it ... this was what took the time.

After two hours I found myself staring at the wall, thinking only of Gail. With excruciating clearness I went through in my mind every minute of that uninhibited love making, felt in all my limbs and veins an echo of passion. Useless to pretend that once was enough, that the tormenting hunger had been anaesthetized for more than a few days. With despair at my weakness I though about how it would be on the next Sunday. Gail with no clothes on, graceful and firm. Gail smiling with my hands on her breasts. Gail fluttering her fingers on the base of my spine.

The bell rang sharply above my head. One ring: not urgent. I stood up slowly, feeling stupid and ashamed. Day-dreaming like Madge Roncey. Just as bad, Probably much worse.

Elizabeth was apologetic. 'Ty, I'm sorry to interrupt you...'

How can I do it, I thought. And knew I would.

'My feet are awfully cold.'

I pulled out the hot water bottle, which had no heat left. Her feet were warm enough to the touch, but that meant nothing. Her circulation was so poor that her ankles and feet ached with cold if not constantly warmed from outside.

'You should have said,' I protested.

'Didn't want to disturb you.'

'Any time,' I said fiercely. 'Any time.' And preferably twenty minutes ago. For twenty minutes she'd suffered her cold feet and all I'd done was think of Gail.

I filled her bottle and went through her evening routine. Rubs with surgical spirit. Washing. Bed pan.

Her muscles had nearly all wasted to nothing so that her bones showed angularly through the skin, and one had to be careful when lifting her limbs, as pressure in some places hurt her. That day Mrs Woodward had painted her toe nails for her instead of only her finger nails as usual.

'Do you like it?' she said. 'It's a new colour, Tawny Pink.'

'Pretty,' I nodded. 'It suits you.'

She smiled contentedly. 'Sue Davis brought it for me. She's a pet, that girl.'

Sue and Ronald Davis lived three doors away: married for six months and it still showed. They had let their euphoria spill over on to us. Sue brought things in to amuse Elizabeth and Ronald used his rugger-bred strength to carry the pump downstairs when we went out in the van.

'It matches my lipstick better than the old colour.'

'Yes it does,' I agreed.

When we married she had had creamy skin and hair as glossy as new peeled conkers. She had sun-browned agile limbs and a pretty figure. The transition to her present and forever state had been as agonizing for her mentally as it had been physically, and at one point of that shattering progress I was aware she would have killed herself if even that freedom hadn't been denied her.

She still had a good complexion, fine eyebrows, and long lashed eyes, but the russet lights had turned to grey in both her irises and her hair, as if the colour had drained away with the vitality. Mrs

Woodward was luckily expert with shampoo and scissors and I too had long grown accurate with a lipstick, so that Elizabeth always turned a groomed and attractive head to the world and could retain at least some terrifically important feminine assurance.

I settled her for the night, slowing the rate of the beathing pump a little and tucking the covers in firmly round her chin to help with the draught. She slept in the same half sitting propped up position as she spent the days: the Spirashell was too heavy and uncomfortable if she lay down flat, besides not dragging as much air into her lungs.

She smiled when I kissed her cheek. 'Goodnight, Ty.'

'Goodnight, honey.'

'Thanks for everything.'

'Be my guest.'

Lazily I pottered round the flat, tidying up, brushing my teeth, re-reading what I'd written for *Tally* and putting the cover on the typewriter. When I finally made it to bed Elizabeth was asleep, and I lay between the lonely sheets and thought about Bert Checkov and the nonstarters like Brevity in the Champion Hurdle, planning in detail the article I would write for the *Blaze* on Sunday.

Sunday.

Inevitably, inexorably, every thought led back to Gail.

Chapter Five

I telephoned to Charles Dembley, the ex-owner of Brevity, on Wednesday morning, and a girl answered, bright fresh voice, carefree and inexperienced.

'Golly, did you say Tyrone? *James* Tyrone? Yes, we do have your perfectly frightful paper. At least we used to. At least the gardener does, so I often read it. Well, of course come down and see Daddy, he'll be frightfully pleased.'

Daddy wasn't.

He met me outside his house, on the front step, a smallish man nearing sixty with a grey moustache and heavy pouches under his eyes. His manner was courteous stone-wall.

'I am sorry you have had a wasted journey, Mr Tyrone. My daughter Amanda is only fifteen and is apt to rush into things . . . I was out when you telephoned, as I expect she told you. I hope you will forgive her. I have absolutely nothing to say to you. Nothing at all. Good afternoon, Mr Tyrone.'

There was a tiny twitch in one eyelid and the finest of dews on his forehead. I let my gaze wander across the front of his house (genuine Georgian, not too large, unostentatiously well kept) and brought it gently back to his face.

'What threat did they use?' I asked. 'Amanda?'

He winced strongly and opened his mouth.

'With a fifteen-year-old daughter,' I commented, 'one is dangerously vulnerable.'

He tried to speak but achieved only a croak. After clearing his throat with difficulty he said, 'I don't know what you're talking about.'

'How did they set about it?' I asked. 'By telephone? By letter? Or did you actually see them face to face?'

His expression was a full giveaway, but he wouldn't answer.

I said, 'Mr Dembley, I can write my column about the last-minute unexplained withdrawal of favourites, mentioning you and Amanda by name, or I can leave you out of it.'

'Leave me out,' he said forcefully. 'Leave me out.'

'I will,' I agreed, 'if in return you will tell me what threat was made against you, and in what form.'

His mouth shook with a mixture of fear and disgust. He knew blackmail when he heard it. Only too well.

'I can't trust you.'

'Indeed you can,' I said.

'If I keep silent you will print my name and they will think I told you anyway ...' He stopped dead.

'Exactly,' I said mildly.

'You're despicable.'

'No,' I said. 'I'd simply like to stop them doing it to anyone else.'

There was a pause. Then he said 'It *was* Amanda. They said someone would rape her. They said I couldn't guard her twenty-four hours a day for years on end. They said to make her safe all I had to do was call Weatherbys and take Brevity out of the Champion Hurdle. Just one little telephone call, against my daughter's ... my daughter's health. So I did it. Of course I did. I had to. What did running a horse in the Champion Hurdle matter compared with my daughter?'

What indeed.

'Did you tell the police?'

He shook his head. 'They said ...'

I nodded. They would.

'I sold all my horses, after,' he said. 'There wasn't any point going on. It could have happened again, any time.'

'Yes.'

He swallowed. 'Is that all?'

'No ... Did they telephone, or did you see them?'

'It was one man. He came here, driven by a chauffeur. In a Rolls. He was, he seemed to me, an educated man. He had an accent, I'm not sure what it was, perhaps Scandinavian, or Dutch, something like that. Maybe even Greek. He was civilized ... except for what he said.'

'Looks?'

'Tall ... about your height. Much heavier, though. Altogether thicker, more flesh. Not a crook's face at all. I couldn't believe what I was hearing him say. It didn't fit the way he looked.'

'But he convinced you,' I commented.

'Yes.' He shuddered. 'He stood there watching me while I telephoned to Weatherbys. And when I'd finished he simply said "I'm sure you've made a wise decision, Mr Dembley", and he just walked out of the house and the chauffeur drove him away.'

'And you've heard no more from him at all?'

'No more. You will keep your bargain, too, like him?'

My mouth twisted. 'I will.'

He gave me a long look. 'If Amanda comes to any harm through you, I will see it costs you . . . costs you . . .' He stopped.

'If she does,' I said, 'I will pay.'

An empty gesture. Harm couldn't be undone, and paying wouldn't help. I would simply have to be careful.

'That's all,' he said. 'That's all.' He turned on his heel, went back into his house and shut the front door decisively between us.

* * *

For light relief on the way home I stopped in Hampstead to interview the man who had done the handicap for the Lamplighter. Not a well-timed call. His wife had just decamped with an American colonel.

'Damn her eyes,' he said. 'She's left me a bloody note.' He waved it under my nose. 'Stuck up against the clock, just like some ruddy movie.'

'I'm sorry,' I said.

'Come in, come in. What do you say to getting pissed?'

'There's the unfortunate matter of driving home.'

'Take a taxi, Ty, be a pal. Come on.'

I looked at my watch. Four thirty. Half an hour to home, counting rush hour traffic. I stepped over the threshold and saw from his relieved expression that company was much needed. He already had a bottle out with a half-full glass beside it, and he poured me one the same size.

Major Colly Gibbons, late forties, trim, intelligent, impatient and positive. Never suffered fools gladly and interrupted rudely when his thoughts leaped ahead, but was much in demand as a handicapper, as he had a clear comprehensive view of racing as a whole, like a master chess player winning ten games at once. He engineered more multiple dead heats than anyone else in the game; the accolade of his profession and a headache to the interpreters of photo finishes.

'A bloody colonel,' He said bitterly. 'Out-ranked, too.'

I laughed. He gave me a startled look and then an unwilling grin.

'I suppose it is *funny*,' he said. 'Silly thing is, he's very like me. Looks, age, character, everything. I even like the guy.'

'She'll probably come back,' I said.

'Why?'

'If she chose a carbon copy of you, she can't hate you all that much.'

'Don't know as I'd have her,' he said aggressively. 'Going off with a bloody colonel, and a Yank at that.'

His pride was bent worse than his heart: none the less painful. He sloshed another stiff whisky into his glass and asked me why, as a matter of interest, I had come. I explained about the *Tally* article, and, seeming to be relieved to have something to talk about besides his wife, he loosened up with his answers more than I would normally have expected. For the first time I understood the wideness of his vision and the grasp and range of his memory. He knew the form book for the past ten years by heart.

After a while I said, 'What can you remember about ante-post favourites which didn't run?'

He gave me a quick glance which would have been better focussed three drinks earlier. 'Is this for *Tally*, still?'

'No,' I admitted.

'Didn't think so. Question like that's got the *Blaze* written all over it.'

'I won't quote you.'

'Too right you won't.' He drank deeply, but seemed no nearer oblivion. 'Put yourself some blinkers on and point in another direction.'

'Read what I say on Sunday,' I said mildly.

'Ty,' he said explosively. 'Best to keep out.'

'Why?'

'Leave it to the authorities.'

'What are they doing about it? What do they know?'

'You know I can't tell you,' he protested. 'Talk to the *Blaze!* I'd lose my job.'

'Mulholland went to jail rather than reveal his sources.'

'All journalists are not Mulholland.'

'Same secretive tendencies.'

'Would you,' he said seriously, 'go to jail?'

'It's never cropped up. But if my sources want to stay unrevealed, they stay unrevealed. If they didn't who would tell me anything?'

He thought it over. 'Something's going on,' he said at last.

'Quite,' I said. 'And what are the authorities doing about it?'

'There's no evidence ... look, Ty, there's nothing you can put your finger on. Just a string of coincidences.'

'Like Bert Checkov's articles?' I suggested.

He was startled. 'All right, then. Yes. I heard it on good authority that he was going to be asked to explain them. But then he fell out of the window ...'

'Tell me about the nonrunners,' I said.

He looked gloomily at the note from his wife, which he still clutched in his hand. He took a deep swallow and shrugged heavily. The caution barriers were right down.

'There was this French horse, Polyxenes, which they made favourite for the Derby. Remember? All last winter and spring there was a stream of information about it, coming out of France ... how well he was developing, how nothing could stay with him on the gallops, how he made all the three year olds look like knock-kneed yearlings? Every week, something about Polyxenes.'

'I remember,' I said. 'Derry Clark wrote him up for the *Blaze*.'

Colly Gibbons nodded. 'So there we are. By Easter, six to one favourite for the Derby. Right? They leave him in through all the forfeit stages. Right? They declare him at the four day declarations. Right? Two days later he's taken out of the race. Why? He knocked himself out at exercise and his leg's blown up like a football. Can't run a lame horse. Too bad, everybody who'd backed him. Too bad. All their money down the drain. All right. Now I'll tell you something, Ty. That Polyxenes, I'll never believe he was all that good. What had he ever done? Won two moderate races as a two year old at St Cloud. He didn't run this year before the Derby. He didn't run the whole season in the end. They said his leg was still bad. I'll tell you what I think. He never was good enough to win the Derby, and from the start they never meant him to run.'

'If he were as bad as that they could have run him anyway. He wouldn't have won.'

'Would you risk it, if you were them? The most fantastic outsiders *have* won the Derby. Much more certain not to run at all.'

'Someone must have made thousands,' I said slowly.

'More like hundreds of thousands.'

'If they know it's going on, why don't the racing authorities do something about it?'

'What *can* they do? I told you, no evidence. Polyxenes *was* lame, and he stayed lame. He was seen by dozens of vets. He had a slightly shady owner, but no shadier than some of ours. Nothing, absolutely nothing, could be proved.

After a pause I said, 'Do you know of any others?'

'God, Ty, you're a glutton. Well .. yes ...'

Once started, he left little out. In the next half hour I listened to the detailed case histories of four more ante-post favourites who hadn't turned up on the day. All could have been bona fide hard luck stories. But all, I knew well, had been over-praised by Bert Checkov.

He ran down, in the end, with a faint look of dismay.

'I shouldn't have told you all this.'

'No one will know.'

'You'd get information out of a deaf mute.'

I nodded. 'They can usually read and write.'

'Go to hell,' he said. 'Or rather, don't. You're four behind me. You aren't trying.' He waved the bottle in my direction and I went over and took it from him. It was empty.

'Got to go home,' I said apologetically.

'What's the hurry?' He stared at the letter in his hand. 'Will your wife give you gip if you're late? or will she be running off with some bloody Yankee colonel?'

'No,' I said unemotionally. 'She won't.'

He was suddenly very sober. '*Christ*, Ty ... I forgot.'

He stood up, as steady as a rock. Looked forlornly round his comfortable wifeless sitting room. Held out his hand.

'She'll come back,' I said uselessly.

He shook his head. 'I don't think so.' He sighed deeply. 'Anyway, I'm glad you came. Needed someone to talk to, you know. Even if I've talked too much ... better than getting drunk alone. And I'll think of you, this evening. You ... and your wife.'

I got hung up in a jam at Swiss Cottage and arrived home at eight minutes past seven. An hour and a half's overtime. Mrs Woodward was delighted.

'Isn't she sweet?' Elizabeth said when she had gone. 'She never minds when you are late. She never complains about having to stay. She's so nice and kind.'

'Very,' I said.

As usual I spent most of Thursday at home, writing Sunday's article. Mrs Woodward went out to do the week's shopping and to take and collect the laundry. Sue Davis came in and made coffee for herself and Elizabeth. Elizabeth's mother telephoned to say she might not come on Sunday, she thought she could be getting a cold.

No one came near Elizabeth with a cold. With people on artificial respiration, colds too often meant pneumonia, and pneumonia too often meant death.

If Elizabeth's mother didn't come on Sunday, I couldn't go to Virginia Water. I spent too much of the morning unproductively trying to persuade myself it would be better if the cold developed, and knowing I'd be wretched if it did.

Luke-John galloped through the article on nonstarting favourites, screwed his eyes up tight and leaned back in his chair with his face to the ceiling. Symptoms of extreme emotion. Derry reached over, twitched up the typewritten sheets and read them in his slower intense short-sighted looking way. When he'd finished he took a deep breath.

'Wowee,' he said. 'Someone's going to love this.'

'Who?' said Luke-John, opening his eyes.

'The chap who's doing it.'

Luke-john looked at him broodingly. 'As long as he can't sue, that's all that matters. Take this down to the lawyers and make sure they don't let it out of their sight.'

Derry departed with a folded carbon copy of the article and Luke-John permitted himself a smile.

'Up to standard, if I may say so.'

'Thanks,' I said.

'Who told you all this?'

'Couple of little birds.'

'Come off it, Ty.'

'Promised,' I said. 'They could get their faces pushed in, one way or another.'

'I'll have to know. The Editor will want to know.'

I shook my head. 'Promised.'

'I could scrub the article altogether ...'

'Tut, Tut,' I said. 'Threats, now?'

He rubbed his larynx in exasperation. I looked round the vast busy floor space, each section, like the Sports Desk, collecting and sorting out its final copy. Most of the feature stuff went down to the compositors on Fridays, some even on Thursdays, to be set up in type. But anything like a scoop stayed under wraps upstairs until after the last editions of the Saturday evening papers had all been set up and gone to press. The compositors were apt to make the odd ten quid by selling a red hot story to reporters on rival newspapers. If the legal department and the Editor both cleared my article, the print shop wouldn't see it until too late to do them any good. The *Blaze* held its scandalous disclosures very close to its chest.

Derry came back from the lawyers without the article.

'They said they'd have to work on it. They'll ring through later.'

The *Blaze* lawyers were of Counsel standard on the libel laws. They needed to be. All the same they were true *Blaze* men with 'publish and be damned' engraved on their hearts. The *Blaze* accountants allowed for damages in their budget as a matter of course. The *Blaze's* owner looked upon one or two court cases a year as spendid free advertising, and watched the sales graphs rise. There had however been four actions in the past six months and two more were pending. A mild memo had gone round, saying to cool it just a fraction. Loyal for ever, Luke-John obeyed even where he disapproved.

'I'll take this in to the Editor,' he remarked. 'See what he says.'

Derry watched his retreating back with reluctant admiration.

'Say what you like, the sports pages sell this paper to people who otherwise wouldn't touch it with gloves on. Our Luke-John, for all his stingy little ways, must be worth his weight in gumdrops.

Our Luke-John came back and went into a close huddle with a soccer correspondent. I asked Derry how the funeral had been, on the Wednesday.

'A funeral's a funeral.' He shrugged. 'It was cold. His wife wept a lot. She had a purple nose, blue from cold and red from crying.'

'Charming.'

He grinned. 'Her sister told her to cheer up. Said how lucky it was Bert took out all that extra insurance.'

'He did what?'

'Yeah. I thought you'd like that. I chatted the sister up a bit. Two or three weeks ago Bert trebled his life insurance. Told his wife they'd be better off when he retired. Sort of self-help pension scheme.'

'Well, well,' I said.

'So it had to be an accident,' Derry nodded. 'In front of witnesses. The insurance company might not have paid up if he'd fallen out of the window with no one watching.'

'I wonder if they'll contest it.'

'Don't see how they can, when the inquest said misadventure.'

The Editor's secretary came back with my piece. The Editor's secretary was an expensive package tied up with barbed wire. No one, reputedly, had got past the prickles to the goodies.

The Editor had scrawled 'O.K. on the lawyer's say so' across the top of the page. Luke-John stretched out a hand for it, nodded in satisfaction, and slid it into the lockable top drawer of his desk, talking all the while to the soccer man. There was no need for me to stay longer. I told Derry I'd be at home most of the day if they wanted me and sketched a goodbye.

I was half-way to the door when Luke-John called after me.

'Ty ... I forgot to tell you. A woman phoned, wanted you.'

'Mrs Woodward?'

'Uhuh. Let's see, I made a note ... oh, yes, here it is. A Miss Gail Pominga. Would you ring her back. Something about *Tally* magazine.'

He gave me the slip of paper with the telephone number. I went across to the under-populated News Desk and picked up the receiver. My hands were steady. My pulse wasn't.

'The Western School of Art. Can I help you?'

'Miss Pominga ...'

Miss Pominga was fetched. Her voice came on the line, as cool and uninvolved as at the railway station.

'Are you coming on Sunday?' Crisp. Very much to the point.

'I want to.' Understatement. 'It may not be possible to get away.'

'Well ... I've been asked out to lunch.'

'Go, then,' I said, feeling disappointment lump in my chest like a boulder.

'Actually, if you are coming I will stay at home.'

Damn Elizabeth's mother, I thought. Damn her and her cold.

'I want to come. I'll come if I possibly can,' I said.

There was a short silence before she said, 'When can you let me know for sure?'

'Not until Sunday, really. Not until I go out to catch the train.'

'Hmm ...' she hesitated, then said decisively, 'Ring me in any case, whether you can come or whether you can't. I'll fix it so that I can still go to lunch if you aren't coming.'

'That's marvellous,' I said, with more feeling than caution.

She laughed. 'Good. Hope to see you, then. Any time after ten. That's when Harry and Sarah go off to golf.'

'It would be eleven-thirty or so.'

She said 'All right,' and 'Goodbye,' and disconnected. I went home to write up Colly Gibbons for *Tally* and to have lunch with Elizabeth and Mrs Woodward. It was fish again: unspecified variety and not much flavour. I listened to Elizabeth's sporadic conversation and returned her smiles and hoped fiercely not to be there with her forty-eight hours later. I ate automatically, sightlessly. By the end of that meal, treachery tasted of salt.

Chapter Six

Time was running short, *Tally*-wise. With their deadline only two days ahead I went to Heathbury Park races on Saturday to meet Dermot Finnegan, an undistinguished jockey with an undistinguished mount in the Lamplighter.

For a while I couldn't understand a word he said, so impenetrable was his Irish accent. After he had sipped unenthusiastically at a cup of lunch counter coffee for ten minutes he relaxed enough to tell me he always spoke worse when he was nervous, and after that we got by with him having to repeat some things twice, but not four or five times, as at the beginning.

Once past the language barrier, Dermot unveiled a resigned wit and an accepting contented way of life. Although by most standards his riding success was small, Dermot thought it great. His income, less than a dustman's, seemed to him princely compared with the conditions of his childhood. His father had fed fourteen children on the potatoes he had grown on two and a half exhausted acres. Dermot, being neither the strong eldest nor the spoilt youngest, had usually had to shove for his share and hadn't always got it. At nineteen he tired of the diet and took his under-developed physique across the sea to Newmarket, where an Irish accent, irrespective of previous experience, guaranteed him an immediate job in the labour-hungry racing industry.

He had 'done his two' for a while in a flat racing stable, but couldn't get a ride in a flat race because he hadn't been apprenticed. Philosophically he moved down the road to a stable which trained jumpers as well, where the 'Governor' gave him a chance in a couple of hurdle races. He still worked in the same stable on a part-time basis, and the 'Governor' still put him up as his second string jockey. How many rides? He grinned, showing spaces instead of teeth. Some seasons, maybe thirty. Two years ago, of course, it was only four, thanks to breaking his leg off a brainless divil of a knock-kneed spalpeen.

Dermot Finnegan was twenty-five, looked thirty. Broken nosed and weatherbeaten, with bright sharp blue eyes. His ambition, he said, was to take a crack at Aintree. Otherwise he was all right with what he had: he wouldn't want to be a classy top jockey, it was far too much responsibilty. 'If you only ride the scrubbers round the gaffs at the back end of the season, see, no one expects much. They they gets a glorious surprise if you do come in.'

He had ridden nineteen winners in all, and he could remember each of them in sharp detail. No, he didn't think he would do much good in the Lamplighter, not really, as he was only in it because his stable was running three. 'I'll be on the pacemaker, sure. You'll see me right up there over the first, and maybe for a good while longer, but then my old boy will run out of steam and drop out of the back door as sudden as an interrupted burglar, and if I don't have to pull him up it'll be a bloody miracle.'

Later in the afternoon I watched him start out on some prospective ten-year-old dog-meat in a novice chase. Horse and rider disappeared in a flurry of legs into the second open ditch, and when I went to check on his injuries some time after the second race I met Dermot coming out of the ambulance room wearing a bandage and a grin.

'It's only a scratch' he assured me cheerfully. 'I'll be there for the Lamplighter sure enough.'

Further investigation led to the detail of a finger nail hanging on by a thread. 'Some black divil' had leant an ill-placed hoof on the Finnegan hand.

To complete the *Tally* round-up I spent the last half of the afternoon in the Clerk of the Course's office, watching him in action.

Heathbury Park, where the Lamplighter was to be held a fortnight later, had become under his direction one of the best organized courses in the country. Like the handicapper, he was ex-forces, in his case R.A.F., which was unusual in that the racing authorities as a rule leant heavily towards the Army and the Navy for their executives.

Wing Commander Willy Ondroy was a quiet effective shortish man of forty-two who had been invalided out after fracturing his skull in a slight mishap with a Vulcan bomber. He still, he said, suffered from blackouts, usually at the most inconvenient, embarrassing and even obscene moments.

It wasn't until after racing had finished for the day that he was really ready to talk, and even then he dealt with a string of people calling into his office with statistics, problems and keys.

The Lamplighter was his own invention, and he was modestly proud of it. He'd argued the Betting Levy Board into putting up most of the hefty stake money, and then drawn up entry conditions exciting enough to bring a gleam to the hardest-headed trainer's eye. Most of the best horses would consequently be coming. They should draw an excellent crowd. The gate receipts would rise again. They'd soon be able to afford to build a warm modern nursery room, their latest project, to attract young parents to the races by giving them somewhere to park their kids.

Willy Ondroy's enthusiasm was of the enduring, not the bubbling kind. His voice was as gentle as the expression in his amber eyes, and only the small self-mockery in his smile gave any clue to the steel within. His obvious lack of any need to assert his authority in any forceful way was finally explained after I'd dug, or tried to dig, into his history. A glossed over throw-away phrase about a spot of formation flying turned out to be his version of three years as a Red

Arrow, flying two feet away from the jet pipe of the aircraft in front. 'We did two hundred displays in one year,' he said apologetically. 'Entertaining at air shows. Like a concert party on Blackpool pier, no difference really.'

He had been lucky to transfer to bombers when he was twenty-six, he said. So many R.A.F. fighter and formation pilots were grounded altogether when their reaction times began to slow. He'd spent eight years on bombers, fifteen seconds knowing he was going to crash, three weeks in a coma, and twenty months finding himself a civilian job. Now he lived with his wife and twelve-year-old twins in a house on the edge of the racecourse, and none of them wanted to change.

I caught the last train when it was moving and made a start on Dermot and Willy Ondroy on the way back to London.

Mrs Woodward departed contentedly at a quarter to seven, and I found she had for once left steaks ready in the kitchen. Elizabeth was in good spirits. I mixed us a drink each and relaxed in the armchair, and only after a strict ten minutes of self denial asked her casually if her mother had telephoned.

'No, she hasn't.' She wouldn't have.

'So you don't know if she's coming?'

'I expect she'll ring, if she doesn't.'

'I suppose so,' I said. Damn her eyes, couldn't she at least settle it, one way or another?

Trying to shut my mind to it I worked on the *Tally* article: cooked the supper: went back to *Tally*: stopped to settle Elizabeth for the night; and returned to the typewriter until I'd finished. It was then half past two. A pity, I thought, stretching, that I wrote so slowly, crossed out so much. I put the final version away in a drawer with only the fair copy to be typed the next day. Plenty of time for that even if I spent the rest of it on the primrose path making tracks for Gail.

I despised myself. It was five before I slept.

Elizabeth's mother came. Not a sniffle in sight.

I had spent all morning trying to reconcile myself to her nonappearance at ten-fifteen her usual time of arrival. As on past occasions, I had turned a calm and everyday face to Elizabeth and found I had consciously to stifle irritation at little tasks for her that normally I did without thought.

At ten-seventeen the door bell rang, and there she was, a well groomed good-looking woman in her mid-fifties with assisted tortoiseshell hair and a health farm figure. When she showed surprise at my greeting I knew I had been too welcoming. I damped it down a little to more normal levels and saw that she felt more at home with that.

I explained to her, as I had already done to Elizabeth, that I still had people to interview for *Tally*, and by ten-thirty I was walking away down the mews feeling as though a safety valve was blowing fine. The sun was shining too. After a sleepless night, my conscience slept.

Gail met me at Virginia Water, waiting outside in the estate car. 'The train's late,' she said calmly, as I sat in beside her. No warm, loving, kissing hello. Just as well, I supposed.

'They work on the lines on Sunday. There was a delay at Staines.'

She nodded, let in the clutch, and cruised the three quarters of a mile to her uncle's house. There she led the way into the sitting-room and without asking poured two beers.

'You aren't writing today,' she said, handing me the glass.

'No.'

She gave me a smile that acknowledged the purpose of my visit. More businesslike about sex than most women. Certainly no tease. I kissed her mouth lightly, savouring the knowledge that the deadline of the Huntersons' return was three full hours ahead.

She nodded as if I'd spoken. 'I approve of you,' she said.

'Thanks.'

She smiled, moving away. Her dress that day was of a pale cream colour which looked wonderful against the gilded coffee skin. She was no darker, in fact, than many southern Europeans or heavily sun-tanned English: her mixed origin was distinct only in her face. A well, proportioned, attractive face, gathering distinction from the self assurance within. Gail, I imagined, had had to come to terms with herself much earlier and more basically than most girls. She had done almost too good a job.

A copy of the *Sunday Blaze* lay on the low table, open at the sports page. Editors or sub-editors write all the headlines, and Luke-John had come up with a beauty. Across the top of my page, big and bold, it said 'Don't back Tiddely Pom—YET'. Underneath, he'd left in word for word every paragraph I'd written. This didn't necessarily mean he thought each word was worth its space in print, but was quite likely because there weren't too many advertisements that week. Like all newspapers, the *Blaze* lived on advertising: if an advertiser wanted to pay for space, he got it, and out went the deathless prose of the columnists. I'd lost many a worked on sentence to the late arrival of spiels on Whosit's cough syrup or Wammo's hair tonic. It was nice to see this intact.

I looked up at Gail. She was watching me.

'Do you always read the sports page?' I asked.

She shook her head. 'Curiosity,' she said. 'I wanted to see what you'd written. That article ... it's disturbing.'

'It's meant to be.'

'I mean, it leaves the impression that you know a great deal more than you've said, and it's all bad, if not positively criminal.'

'Well,' I said, 'it's always nice to hear one has done exactly what one has intended.'

'What usually happens when you write in this way?'

'Repercussions? They vary from a blast from the racing authorities about minding my own business to abusive letters from nut cases.'

'Do wrongs get righted?'

'Very occasionally.'

'Sir Galahad,' she mocked.

'No. We sell more papers. I apply for a raise.'

She laughed with her head back, the line of her throat leading tautly down into her dress. I put out my hand and touched her shoulder, suddenly wanting no more talk.

She nodded at once, smiling, and said, 'Not on the rug. More comfortable upstairs.'

Her bedroom furnishings were pretty but clearly Sarah's work. Fitted cupboards, a cosy armchair, book shelves, a lot of pale blue carpet, and a single bed.

At her insistence, I occupied it first. Then while I watched, like the time before, she took off her clothes. The simple, undramatized, unselfconscious undressing was more ruthlessly arousing than anything one could every pay to see. When she had finished she stood still for a moment near the window, a pale bronze naked girl in a shaft of winter sun.

'Shall I close the curtains?'

'Whichever you like.'

She screwed my pulse rate up another notch by stretching up to close them, and then in the mid-day dusk she came to bed.

At three she drove me back to the station, but a train pulled out as we pulled in. We sat in the car for a while, talking, waiting for the next one.

'Do you come home here every night?' I asked.

'Quite often not. Two of the other teachers share a flat, and I sleep on their sofa a night or two every week, after parties, or a theatre, maybe.'

'But you don't want to live in London all the time?'

'D'you think it's odd, that I stay with Harry and Sarah? Quite frankly, it's because of money. Harry won't let me pay for living here. He says he wants me to stay. He's always been generous. If I had to pay for everything myself in London my present standard of living would go down with a reverberating thump.'

'Comfort before independence,' I commented mildly.

She shook her head. 'I have both.' After a considering pause she said, 'Do you live with your wife? I mean, have you separated, or anything?'

'No, we've not separated.'

'Where does she think you are today?'

'Interviewing someone for my *Tally* article.'

She laughed. 'You're a bit of a bastard.'

Nail on the head. I agreed with her.

'Does she know you have ... er ... outside interests? Has she ever found you out?'

I wished she would change the subject. However, I owed her quite a lot, at least some answers, which might be the truth and nothing but the truth, but would certainly not be the whole truth.

'She doesn't know,' I said.

'Would she mind?'

'Probably.'

'But if she won't ... sleep with you ... well, why don't you leave her?'

I didn't answer at once. She went on, 'You haven't any children, have you?' I shook my head. 'Then what's to stop you? Unless, of course, you're like me.'

'How do you mean?'

'Staying where the living is good. Where the money is.'

'Oh ...' I half laughed, and she misunderstood me.

'How can I blame you,' she sighed, 'When I do it myself? So your wife is rich . .'

I thought about what Elizabeth would have been condemned to without me: to hospital ward routine, hospital food, no privacy, no gadgets, no telephone, lights out at nine and lights on at six, no free will at all, for ever and ever.

'I suppose you might say,' I agreed slowly, 'that my wife is rich.'

Back in the flat I felt split in two, with everything familiar feeling suddenly unreal. Half my mind was still down in Surrey. I kissed Elizabeth and thought of Gail. Depression had clamped down like drizzle in the train and wouldn't be shaken off.

'Some man wants to talk to you,' Elizabeth said. 'He telephoned three times. He sounded awfully angry.'

'Who?'

'I couldn't understand much of what he said. He was stuttering.'

'How did he get our number?' I was irritated, bored; I didn't want to have to deal with angry men on the telephone. Moreover our number was ex-directory, precisely so that Elizabeth should not be bothered by this sort of thing.

'I don't know. But he did leave his number for you to ring back, it was the only coherent thing he said.'

Elizabeth's mother handed me a note pad on which she had written down the number.

'Victor Roncey,' I said.

'That's right,' agreed Elizabeth with relief. 'That sounds like it.'

I sighed, wishing that all problems, especially those of my own making, would go away and leave me in peace.

'Maybe I'll call him later,' I said. 'Right now I need a drink.'

'I was just going to make some tea,' said Elizabeth's mother reprovingly, and in silent fury I doubled the quantity I would normally have taken. The bottle was nearly empty. Gloomy Sunday.

Restlessly I took myself off into my writing room and started the clean unscribbled-on retype for *Tally*, the mechanical task eventually smoothing out the rocky tensions of my guilt-ridden return home. I couldn't afford to like Gail too much, and I did like her. To come to love someone would be too much hell altogether. Better not to visit Gail again. I decided definitely not to. My body shuddered in protest, and I knew I would.

Roncey rang again just after Elizabeth's mother had left.

'What the devil do you mean about this ... this trash in the paper? Of course my horse is going to run. How dare you ... how dare you suggest there's anything shady going on?'

Elizabeth had been right: he was stuttering still, at seven in the evening. He took a lot of calming down to the point of admitting that nowhere in the article was it suggested that he personally had anything but good honest upright intentions.

'The only thing is, Mr Roncey, as I said in the article, that some owners have in the past been pressurized into not running their horses. This may even happen to you. All I was doing was giving punters several good reasons why they would be wiser to wait until half an hour before big races to put their money on. Better a short starting price than losing their money in a swindle.'

'I've read it,' he snapped. 'Several times. And no one, believe me, is going to put pressure on *me*.'

'I very much hope not,' I said. I wondered whether his antipathy to his elder sons extended to the smaller ones; whether he would risk their safety or happiness for the sake of running Tiddely Pom in the Lamplighter. Maybe he would. The stubborn streak ran through his character like iron in granite.

When he had calmed down to somewhere near reason I asked him if he'd mind telling me how he'd got my telephone number.

'I had the devil's own job, if you want to know. All that exdirectory piffle. The enquiries people refused point blank to tell me, even though I said it was urgent. Stupid. I call it, but I wasn't to be put off by that. If you want to know, your colleague on the paper told me. Derrick Clark.'

'I see,' I said resignedly, thinking it unlike Derry to part so easily with my defences. 'Well, thank you. Did the *Tally* photographer find you all right?'

'He came on Friday. I hope you haven't said anything in *Tally* about...' His anger was on its way up again.

'No,' I said decisively. 'Nothing like that at all.'

'When can I be sure?' He sounded suspicious.

'That edition of *Tally* is published on the Tuesday before the Lamplighter.'

'I'll ask for an advance copy from the Editor. Tomorrow. I'll demand to see what you've written.'

'Do that,' I agreed. Divert the buck to Arnold Shankerton. Splendid.

He rang off still not wholly pacified. I dialled Derry's number and prepared to pass the ill temper along to him.

'*Roncey?*' He said indignantly. 'Of course I didn't give your number to Roncey.' His baby girl was exercising her lungs loudly in the background. 'What did you say?'

'I said, who *did* you give it to?'

'Your wife's uncle.'

'My wife hasn't got any uncles.'

'Oh Christ. Well, he said he was your wife's uncle, and that your wife's aunt had had a stroke, and that he wanted to tell you, but he'd lost your number.'

'Lying crafty bastard,' I said with feeling. 'And he accused me of misrepresenting facts.'

'I'm sorry, Ty.'

'Never mind. Only check with me first, next time, huh? Like we arranged.'

'Yeah. Sure. Sorry.'

'How did he get hold of your number, anyway?'

'It's in the directory of the British Turf, unlike yours. My mistake.'

I put the receiver back in its special cradel near to Elizabeth's head and transferred to the armchair, and we spent the rest of the evening as we usually did, watching the shadows on the goggle box. Elizabeth never tired of it, which was a blessing, though she complained often about the shut-downs in the day time between all the child-oriented programmes. Why couldn't they fill them, she said, with interesting things for captive adults.

Later I made some coffee and did the vapour rubs and other jobs for Elizabeth, all with a surface of tranquil domesticity, going through my part with my thoughts somewhere else, like an actor at the thousandth performance.

On the Monday morning I took my article to the *Tally* offices and left the package at the reception desk, virtuously on the deadline.

After that I caught the race train to Leicester, admitting to myself that although it was technically my day off I did not want to stay in the flat. Also the Huntersons' raffle horse Egocentric was to have its pre-Lamplighter warm-up, which gave me an excellent overt reason for the journey.

Raw near-mist was doing its best to cancel the proceedings and only the last two fences were visible. Egocentric finished fourth without enough steam left to blow a whistle, and the jockey told the trainer that the useless bugger had made a right bloody shambles of three fences on the far side and couldn't jump for peanuts. The trainer didn't believe him and engaged a different jockey for the Lamplighter. It was one of those days.

The thin Midland crowd of cloth caps and mufflers strewed the ground with betting slips and newspapers and ate a couple of hundredweight of jellied eels out of little paper cups. I adjourned to the bar with a colleague from the *Sporting Life*, and four people commented on my non-starters with varying degrees of belief. Not much of a day. One, on the whole, to forget.

The journey home changed all that. When I forget it, I'll be dead.

Chapter Seven

Thanks to having left before the last race I had a chance in the still empty and waiting train of a forward facing window-seat in a nonsmoker. I turned the heating to 'hottest', and opened the newspaper to see what Spyglass had come up with in the late editions.

'Tiddely Pom will run, trainer says. But is your money really safe?'

Amused, I read to the end. He'd cribbed most of my points and rehashed them. Complimentary. Plagiary is the sincerest form of flattery.

The closed door to the corridor slid open and four bookmakers' clerks lumbered in, stamping their feet with cold and discussing some luckless punter who had lost an argument over a betting slip.

'I told him to come right off it, who did he think he was kidding? We may not be archangels, but we're not the ruddy mugs he takes us for.'

They all wore navy blue overcoats which after a while they shed on to the luggage racks. Two of them shared a large packet of stodgy looking sandwiches and the other two smoked. They were all in the intermediate thirty-forties, with London-Jewish accents in which they next discussed their taxi drive to the station in strictly non Sabbath day terms.

'Evening,' they said to me, acknowledging I existed, and one of them gestured with his cigarette to the nonsmoking notice on the window and said, 'O.K. with you chum?'

I nodded, hardly taking them in. The train rocked off southwards, the misty day turned to foggy night, and five pairs of eyeballs fell gently shut.

The door to the corridor opened with a crash. Reluctantly I opened one eye a fraction, expecting the ticket collector. Two men filled the opening, looking far from bureaucratic. Their effect on my four fellow travellers was a spine-straightening mouth-opening state of shock. The larger of the newcomers stretched out a hand and pulled the blinds down on the insides of the corridor-facing windows. Then he gave the four clerks a contemptuous comprehensive glance, jerked his head towards the corridor and said with simplicity, 'Out.'

I still didn't connect any of this as being my business, not even when the four men meekly took down their navy blue overcoats and filed out into the train. Only when the large man pulled out a copy of the *Blaze* and pointed to my article did I have the faintest prickle on the spine.

'This is unpopular in certain quarters,' remarked the larger man. Thick sarcastic Birminghan accent. He pursed his lips, admiring his own heavy irony. 'Unpopular.'

He wore grubby overalls from shoes to throat, with above that a thick neck, puffy cheeks, a small wet mouth and slicked down hair. His companion, also in overalls, was hard and stocky with wide eyes and a flat topped head.

'You shouldn't do it, you shouldn't really,' the large man said. 'Interfering and that.'

He put his hand into his pocket and it reappeared with a brass ridge across the knuckles. I glanced at the other man. Same thing.

I came up with a rush, grabbing for the communication cord. Penalty for improper use, twenty-five pounds. The large man moved his arm in a professional short jab and made havoc of my intention.

They had both learned their trade in the ring, that much was clear. Not much else was. They mostly left my head alone, but they knew where and how to hit to hurt on the body, and if I tried to fight off one of them, the other had a go. The most I achieved was a solid kick on the smaller man's ankle which drew from him four letters and a frightening kidney punch. I collapsed on to the seat. They leant over me and broke the Queensberry Rules.

It crossed my mind that they were going to kill me, that maybe they weren't meaning to, but they were killing me. I even tried to tell them so, but if any sound came out, they took no notice. The larger one hauled me bodily to my feet and the small one broke my ribs.

When they let go I crumpled slowly on to the floor and lay with my face against cigarette butts and the screwed up wrappings of sandwiches. Stayed quite motionless, praying to a God I had no faith in not to let them start again.

The larger one stooped over me.

'Will he cough it?' the smaller one said.

'How can he? We ain't ruptured nothing, have we? Careful, aren't I? Look out the door, time we was off.'

The door slid open and presently shut, but not for a long time was I reassured that they had completely gone. I lay on the floor breathing in coughs and jerky shallow breaths, feeling sick. For some short time it seemed in a weird transferred way that I had earned such a beating not for writing a newspaper article but because of Gail; and to have deserved it, to have sinned and deserved it, turned it into some sort of expurgation. Pain flowed through me in a hot red tide, and only my guilt made it bearable.

Sense returned, as sense does. I set about the slow task of picking myself up and assessing the damage. Maybe they had ruptured nothing: I had only the big man's word for it. At the receiving end it felt as though they had ruptured pretty well everything, including self respect.

I made it up to the seat, and sat vaguely watching the lights flash past, fuzzy and yellow from fog. Eyes half shut, throat closing with nausea, hands nerveless and weak. No one focus of pain, just too much. Wait, I thought, and it will pass.

I waited a long time.

The lights outside thickened and the train slowed down. London. All change. I would have to move from where I sat. Dismal prospect. Moving would hurt.

The train crept into St. Pancras and stopped with a jerk. I stayed where I was, trying to make the effort to stand up and not succeeding, telling myself that if I didn't get up and go I could be shunted into a siding for a cold uncomfortable night, and still not raking up the necessary propulsion.

Again the door slid open with a crash. I glanced up, stifling the beginnings of panic. No man with heavy overalls and knuckleduster. The guard.

Only when I felt the relief wash through me did I realize the extent of my fear, and I was furious with myself for being so craven.

'The end of the line,' the guard was saying.

'Yeah,' I said.

He came into the compartment and peered at me. 'Been celebrating, have you sir?' He thought I was drunk.

'Sure,' I agreed. 'Celebrating.'

I made the long delayed effort and stood up. I'd been quite right about it. It hurt.

'Look mate, do us a favour and don't throw up in here,' said the guard urgently.

I shook my head. Reached the door. Rocked into the corridor. the guard anxiously took my arm and helped me down on to the platform and as I walked carefully away I heard him behind me say to a bunch of porters, half laughing. 'Did you see that one? Greeny grey and sweating like a pig. Must have been knocking it back solid all afternoon.'

I went home by taxi and took my time up the stairs to the flat. Mrs Woodward for once was in a hurry for me to come, as she was wanting to get home in case the fog thickened. I apologized. 'Quite all right, Mr Tyrone, you know I'm usually glad to stay...' The door closed behind her and I fought down a strong inclination to lie on my bed and groan.

Elizabeth said, 'Ty, you look terribly pale,' when I kissed her. Impossible to hide it from her completely.

'I fell,' I said. 'Tripped. Knocked the breath out of myself, for a minute or two.'

She was instantly concerned; with the special extra anxiety for herself apparent in her eyes.

'Don't worry,' I comforted her. 'No harm done,'

I went into the kitchen and held on to the table. After a minute or two I remembered Elizabeth's pain killing tablets and took the bottle out of the cupboard. Only two left. There would be. I swallowed one of them, tying a mental knot to remind me to ring the doctor for another prescription. One wasn't quite enough, but better than nothing. I went back into the big room and with a fair stab at normality poured our evening drinks.

By the time I had done supper and the jobs for Elizabeth and got myself undressed and into bed, the main damage had resolved itself into two or possibly three cracked ribs low down on my left side. The rest slowly subsided into a blanketing ache. Nothing ruptured, like the man said.

I lay in the dark breathing shallowly and trying not to cough, and at last took time off from simply existing to consider the who and why of such a drastic roughing up, along with the pros and cons of telling Luke-John. He'd make copy of it, put it on the front page, plug it for more than it was worth, write the headlines himself. My feelings would naturally be utterly disregarded as being of no importance compared with selling papers. Luke-John had no pity. If I didn't tell him and he found out later, there would be frost and fury and a permanent atmosphere of distrust. I couldn't afford that. My predecessor had been squeezed off the paper entirely as a direct result of having concealed from Luke-John a red hot scandal in which he was involved. A rival paper got hold of it and scooped the *Blaze*. Luke-John never forgave, never forgot.

I sighed deeply. A grave mistake. The cracked ribs stabbed back with unnecessary vigour. I spent what could not be called a restful, comfortable, sleep-filled night, and in the morning could hardly move. Elizabeth watched me get up and the raw anxiety twisted her face.

'Ty!'

'Only a bruise or two, honey. I told you, I fell over.'

'You look ... hurt.'

I shook my head. 'I'll get the coffee ...'

I got the coffee. I also looked with longing at Elizabeth's last pill, which I had no right to take. She still suffered sometimes from terrible cramp, and on these occasions had to have the pills in a hurry. I didn't need any mental knots to remind me to get some more. When Mrs Woodward came, I went.

Doctor Antonio Perelli wrote the prescription without hesitation and handed it across.

'How is she?'

'Fine. Same as usual.'

'It's time I went to see her.'

'She'd love it,' I said truthfully. Perelli's visits acted on her like champagne. I'd met him casually at a party three years earlier, a young Italian doctor in private practice in Welbeck Street. Too handsome, I'd thought at once. Too feminine, with those dark, sparkling, long lashed eyes. All bedside manner and huge fees, with droves of neurotic women patients paying to have their hands held.

Then just before the party broke up someone told me he specialized in chest complaints, and not to be put off by his youth and beauty, he was brilliant: and by coincidence we found ourselves outside on the pavement together, hailing the same taxi, and going the same way.

At the time I had been worried about Elizabeth. She had to return to hospital for intensive nursing every time she was ill, and with a virtual stamping out of polio, the hospitals geared to care for patients on artificial respiration were becoming fewer and fewer. We had just been told she could not expect to go back any more to the hospital that had always looked after her.

I shared the taxi with Perelli and asked him if he knew of anywhere I could send her quickly if she ever needed it. Instead of answering directly he invited me into his tiny bachelor flat for another drink, and before I left he had acquired another patient. Elizabeth's general health had improved instantly under his care and I paid his moderate fees without a wince.

I thanked him for the prescription and put it in my pocket.

'Ty ... are the pills for Elizabeth, or for you?'

I looked at him, startled. 'Why?'

'My dear fellow, I have eyes. What I see in your face is ... severe.'

I smiled wryly. 'All right. I was going to ask you. Could you put a bit of strapping on a couple of ribs?'

He stuck me up firmly and handed me a small medicine glass containing, he said, disprins dissolved in nepenthe, which worked like a vanishing trick: now you feel it, now you don't.

'You haven't told Elizabeth?' he said anxiously.

'Only that I fell and winded myself.'

He relaxed, moving his head in a gesture of approval. 'Good.'

It had been his idea to shield her from worries which ordinarily women could cope with in their stride. I had thought him unduly fussy at first, but the strict screening he had urged had worked wonders. She had become far less nervous, much happier, and had even put on some badly needed weight.

'And the police? Have you told the police?'

I shook my head and explained about Luke-John.

'Difficult. Um. suppose you tell this Luke-John simply that those men threatened you? You'll not be taking your shirt off in the office.' He smiled in the way that made Elizabeth's eyes shine. 'These two men, they will not go about saying they inflicted so much damage.'

'They might.' I frowned, considering. 'It could be a good idea if I turned up in perfect health at the races today and gave them the lie.'

With an assenting gesture he mixed me a bottle full of the disprin and nepenthe. 'Don't eat much,' he said, handing it over. 'And only drink coffee.'

'O.K.'

'And do nothing that would get you another beating like this.'

I was silent.

He looked at me with sad understanding. 'That is too much to give up for Elizabeth?.

'I can't just ... crawl away,' I protested. 'Even for Elizabeth.'

He shook his head. 'It would be best for her. But ...' He shrugged, and held out his hand in goodbye. 'Stay out of trains, then.'

I stayed out of trains. For ninety-four minutes. Then I caught the race train to Plumpton and travelled down safely with two harmless strangers and a man I knew slightly from the B.B.C.

Thanks to Tonio's mixture I walked about all day and talked and laughed much the same as usual. Once I coughed. Even that caused only an echo of a stab. For maximum effect I spent a good deal of my time walking about the bookmakers' stalls, inspecting both their prices and their clerks. The fraternity knew something had happened. Their heads swivelled as I passed and they were talking behind my back, nudging each other. When I put ten shillings on a semi-outsider with one of them he said, 'You feeling all right, chum?'

'Why not?' I said in surprise. 'It's a nice enough day.'

He looked perplexed for a second, and then shrugged. I walked on looking at faces, searching for a familiar one. The trouble was I'd paid the four clerks in the compartment so little attention that I wasn't sure I'd recognize any one of them again, and I wouldn't have done, if he hadn't given himself away. When he saw me looking at him, he jerked, stepped down off his stand, and bolted.

Running was outside my repertoire. I walked quietly up behind him an hour later when he had judged it safe to go back to his job.

'A word in your ear,' I said at his elbow.

He jumped six inches. 'It was nothing to do with me.'

'I know that. Just tell me who the two men were. Those two in overalls.'

'Do me a favour. Do I want to end up in hospital?'

'Twenty quid?' I suggested.

'I dunno about that ... How come you're here today?'

'Why not?'

'When those two've seen to someone ... they stay seen to.'

'Is that so? They seemed pretty harmless.'

'No, straight up,' he said curiously, 'didn't they touch you?'

'No.'

He was puzzled.

'A pony. Twenty-five quid,' I said. 'For their names, or who they work for.'

He hesitated. 'Not here, mate, On the train.'

'Not on the train.' I was positive. 'In the Press Box. And now.'

He got five minutes off from his grumbling employer and went in front of me up to the eyrie allotted to newspapers. I gave a shove-off sign to the only press man up there, and he obligingly disappeared.

'Right,' I said. 'Who were they?'

'They're Brummies,' he said cautiously.

'I know that. You could cut their accents.'

'Bruisers,' he ventured.

I stopped myself just in time from telling him I knew that too.

'They're Charlie Boston's boys.' It came out in a nervous rush.

'That's better. Who's Charlie Boston?'

'So who hasn't heard of Charlie Boston? Got some betting shops, hasn't he, in Birmingham and Wolverhampton and such like.'

'And some boys on race trains?'

He looked more puzzled than ever. 'Don't you owe Charlie no

money? So what did they want, then? It's usually bad debts they're after.'

'I've never heard of Charlie Boston before, let alone had a bet with him.' I took out my wallet and gave him five fivers. He took them with a practised flick and stowed them away in a pocket like Fort Knox under his left armpit. 'Dirty thieves,' he explained. 'Taking precautions, aren't I?'

He scuttled off down the stairs, and I stayed up in the press box and took another swig at my useful little bottle, reflecting that when Charlie Boston unleashed his boys on me he had been very foolish indeed.

Luke-John reacted predictably with a bridling 'They can't do that to the *Blaze'* attitude.

Wednesday morning. Not much doing in the office. Derry with his feet up on the blotter, Luke-John elbow deep in the Dailies' sports pages, the telephone silent, and every desk in the place exhibiting the same feverish inactivity.

Into this calm I dropped the pebble of news that two men, adopting a threatening attitude, had told me not to interfere in the nonstarters racket. Luke-John sat up erect like a belligerent bull frog, quivering with satisfaction that the article had produced tangible results. With a claw hand he pounced on the telephone.

'Manchester office? Give me the Sports Desk . . . That you, Andy? Luke Morton. What can you tell me about a bookmaker called Charlie Boston? Has a string of betting shops around Birmingham.'

He listened to a lengthy reply with growing intensity.

'That adds up. Yes. Yes. Fine. Ask around and let me know.'

He put down the receiver and rubbed his larynx. 'Charlie Boston changed his spots about a year ago. Before that he was apparently an ordinary Birmingham bookmaker with about six shops and a reasonable reputation. Now, Andy says he's expanded a lot and become a bully. He says he's been hearing too much about Charlie Boston lately. Seems he hires two ex-boxers to collect unpaid debts from his credit customers, and as a result of all this he's coining it.'

I thought it over. Charlie Boston of Birmingham with his betting shops and bruisers didn't gel at all with the description Dembley had given me of a quiet gentleman in a Rolls with a chauffeur and a Greek, Dutch or Scandinavian accent. They even seemed an unlikely pair as shoulder to shoulder partners. There might of course be two separate rackets going on, and if so, what happened if they clashed? And by which of them had Bert Checkov been seduced? But if they were all one outfit, I'd settle for the Rolls gent as the brains and Charlie Boston the muscles. Setting his dogs on me had been classic muscle-bound thinking.

Luke-John's telephone rang and he reached out a hand. As he listened his eyes narrowed and he turned his head to look straight at me.

'What do you mean, he was pulped? He certainly was not. He's here in the office at this moment and he went to Plumpton races yesterday. What your paper needs is a little less imagination . . . If you don't believe me, talk to him yourself.' He handed me the receiver, saying with a grimace 'Connersley. Bloody man.'

'I heard,' said the precise malicious voice on the phone, 'that some Birmingham heavies took you to pieces on the Leicester race train.'

'A rumour,' I said with boredom. 'I heard it myself yesterday at Plumpton.'

'According to my informant you couldn't have gone to Plumpton.'

'Your informant is unreliable. Scrap him.'

A small pause. Then he said 'I can check if you were there.'

'Check away.' I put the receiver down with a brusque crash and thanked my stars I had reached Luke-John with my version first.

'Are you planning a follow-up on Sunday?' he was asking. Connersley had planted no suspicions: was already forgotten. 'Hammer the point home. Urge the racing authorities to act. Agitate. You know the drill.'

I nodded. I knew the drill. My bruises gave me a protesting nudge. No more, they said urgently. Write a nice mild piece on an entirely different, totally innocuous subject.

'Get some quotes,' Luke-John said.

'O.K.'

'Give with some ideas,' he said impatiently. 'I'm doing all your ruddy work.'

I sighed. Shallowly and carefully. 'How about us making sure Tiddely Pom starts in the Lamplighter? Maybe I'll go fix it with the Ronceys . . .'

Luke-John interrupted, his eyes sharp. 'The *Blaze* will see to it that Tiddely Pom runs. Ty, that's genius. Start your piece with that. The *Blaze* will see to it . . . Splendid. Splendid.'

Oh God, I thought. I'm the world's greatest bloody fool. Stay out of race trains, Tonio Perelli had said. Nothing about lying down on the tracks.

Chapter Eight

Nothing had changed at the Ronceys'. Dead leaves, cobwebs, still in place. No dripping meat on the kitchen table: two unplucked pheasants sagged with limp necks there instead. The sink overflowed with unwashed dishes and the wellington smell had intensified.

I arrived unannounced at two-thirty and found Roncey himself out in the yard watching Pat and the old man saw up a large hunk of dead tree. He received me with an unenthusiastic glare but eventually took me through into the sitting room with a parting backwards instruction to his son to clean out the tackroom when he'd finished the logs.

Madge was lying on the sofa, asleep. Still no stockings, still the blue slippers, still the yellow dress, very dirty now down the front. Roncey gave her a glance of complete indifference and gestured me to one of the armchairs.

'I don't need help from the *Blaze*,' he said, as he'd said outside in the yard. 'Why should I?'

'It depends on how much you want Tiddely Pom to run in the Lamplighter.'

'Of course he's going to run.' Roncey looked aggressive and determined. 'I told you. Anyone who tries to tell me otherwise had another think coming.'

'In that case,' I said mildly, 'one of two things will happen. Either the men operating the racket will abandon the idea of preventing Tiddely Pom from running, as a result of all the publicity they've been getting. Or they will go ahead and stop him. If they've any sense they'll abandon the idea. But I don't see how one can count on them having any sense.'

'They won't stop him.' Pugnacious jaw, stubborn eyes.

'You can be sure they will, one way or another, if they want to.'

'I don't believe you.'

'But would you object to taking precautions, just in case? The *Blaze* will foot the bills.'

He stared at me long and hard. 'This is not just a publicity stunt to cover your sensation-hunting paper with glory?'

'Dual purpose,' I said. 'Half for you and betting public. Half for us. But only one object: to get Tiddely Pom safely off in the Lamplighter.'

He thought it over.

'What sort of precautions?' he said at last.

I sighed inwardly with mixed feelings, a broken ribbed skier at the top of a steep and bumpy slope, with only myself to thank.

'There are three main ones,' I said. 'The simplest is a letter to Weatherbys, stating your positive intention to run in the Lamplighter, and asking them to check carefully with you if they should receive any instructions to strike out the horse either before or after the four day declaration stage next Tuesday. You do realize, don't you, that I or anyone else could send a telegram or telex striking out the horse, and you would have a bit of a job getting him put back again?'

His mouth dropped open. '*Anyone?*'

'Anyone signing your name. Of course. Weatherbys receive hundreds of cancellations a week. They don't check to make sure the trainer really means it. Why should they?'

'Good God,' he said, stunned. 'I'll write at once. In fact I'll ring them up.' He began to stand up.

'There won't be that much urgency,' I said. 'Much more likely a cancellation would be sent in at the last moment, in order to allow as much time as possible for ante-post bets to be made.'

'Oh ... quite.' A thought struck him as he sat down again. 'If the *Blaze* declares it is going to make Tiddely Pom safe and then he *doesn't* run for some reason, you are going to look very silly.'

I nodded. 'A risk. Still ... We'll do our best. But we do need your whole-hearted cooperation, not just your qualified permission.'

He made up his mind. 'You have it. What next?'

'Tiddely Pom will have to go to another stable.'

That rocked him. 'Oh no.'

'He's much too vulnerable here.'

He swallowed. 'Where then.'

'To one of the top trainers. He will still be expertly prepared for the race. He can have the diet he's used to. We'll give you a report on him every day.'

He opened and shut his mouth several times, speechless.

'Thirdly,' I said, 'Your wife and at least your three youngest sons must go away for a holiday.'

'They can't,' he protested automatically.

'They must. If one of the children were kidnapped, would you set his life against running Tiddely Pom?'

'It isn't possible,' he said weakly.

'Just the threat might be enough.'

Madge got up and opened her eyes. They were far from dreamy. 'Where and when to we go?' she said.

'Tomorrow. You will know where after you get there.'

She smiled with vivid delight. Fantasy had come to life. Roncey himself was not enchanted.

'I don't like it,' he said frowning.

'Ideally, you should all go. The whole lot of you,' I said.

Roncey shook his head. 'There are other horses, and the farm. I can't leave them. And I need Pat here, and Peter.'

I agreed to that, having gained the essentials. 'Don't tell the children they are going.' I said to Madge. 'Just keep them home from school in the morning, and someone will call for you at about nine. You'll need only country clothes. And you'll be away until after the race on Saturday week. Also, please do not on any account write any letters straight to here, or let the children send any. If you want to write, send the letters to us at the *Blaze*, and we will see that Mr Roncey gets them.'

'But Vic can write to us?' Madge said.

'Of course ... but also via the *Blaze*. Because he won't know where you are.'

They both protested, but in the end saw the sense of it. What he didn't know, he couldn't give away, even by accident.

'It won't only be people working the racket who might be looking for them,' I explained apologetically. 'But one or two of our rival newspapers will be hunting for them, so as to be able to black the *Blaze's* eye. And they are quite skilled at finding people who want to stay hidden.'

I left the Ronceys looking blankly at each other and drove the van back to London. It seemed a very long way, and too many aches redeveloped on the journey. I'd finished Tonio's mixture just before going into the office in the morning and was back on Elizabeth's pills, which were not as good. By the time I got home I was tired, thirsty, hurting and apprehensive.

Dealt with the first three: armchair and whisky. Contemplated the apprehension, and didn't know which would be worse, another encounter with the Boston boys or a complete failure with Tiddely Pom. It would likely be one or the other. Could even be both.

'What's the matter, Ty?' Elizabeth looked and sounded worried.

'Nothing.' I smiled at her. 'Nothing at all, honey.'

The anxious lines relaxed in her face as she smiled back. The pump hummed and thudded, pulling air into her lungs. My poor, poor Elizabeth. I stretched my hand over and touched her cheek in affection, and she turned her head and kissed my fingers.

'You're a fantastic man, Ty,' she said. She said something like it at least twice a week. I twitched my nose and made the usual sort of answer, 'You're not so bad yourself.' The disaster that a virus had made of our lives never got any better. Never would. For it was total and absolute: for me there were exits, like Gail. When I took them, the guilt I felt was not just the ordinary guilt of an unfaithful husband, but that of a deserter. Elizabeth couldn't leave the battlefield: but when it got too much for me, I just slid out and left her.

At nine o'clock the next morning Derry Clark collected Madge and the three Roncey boys in his own Austin and drove them down to Portsmouth and straight on to the Isle of White car ferry.

At noon I arrived at the farm with a car and Rice trailer borrowed from the city editor, whose daughters went in for show jumping. Roncey showed great reluctance at parting with Tiddely Pom, and loaded the second stall of the trailer with sacks of feed and bales of hay, adding to these the horse's saddle and bridle, and also three dozen eggs and a crate of beer. He had written out the diet and training regime in four page detail scattered with emphatic underlinings. I assured him six times that I would see the new trainer followed the instructions to the last full stop.

Pat helped with the loading with a twisting smile, not unhappy that his father was losing control of the horse. He gave me a quick look full of ironic meaning when he saw me watching him, and said under his breath as he humped past with some hay, 'Now he knows what it feels like.'

I left Victor Roncey standing disconsolately in the centre of his untidy farmyard watching his one treasure depart, and drove carefully away along the Essex lanes, heading west to Berkshire. About five miles down the road I stopped near a telephone box and rang up the Western School of Art.

Gail said 'Surprise, surprise.'

'Yes,' I agreed. 'How about Sunday?'

'Um.' She hesitated. 'How about tomorrow?'

'Won't you be teaching?'

'I meant,' she explained, 'tomorrow night.'

'Tomorrow ... *all* night?'

'Can you manage it?'

I took so deep a breath that my sore ribs jumped. It depended on whether Mrs Woodward could stay, as she sometimes did.

'Ty?' she said. 'Are you still there?'

'Thinking.'

'What about?'

'What to tell my wife.'

'You slay me,' she said. 'Is it yes or no?'

'Yes,' I said with a sigh. 'Where?'

'A hotel, I should think.'

'All right,' I agreed. I asked her what time she finished work, and arranged a meeting point at King's Cross railway station.

When I called the flat, Elizabeth answered.

'Ty! Where are you?'

'On the road. There's nothing wrong. It's just that I forgot to ask Mrs Woodward before I left if she could stay with you tomorrow night ... so that I could go up to Newcastle ready for the races on Saturday.' Louse, I thought. Mean, stinking louse. Lying, deceiving louse. I listened miserably to the sounds of Elizabeth asking Mrs Woodward and found no relief at all in her answer.

'She says yes, Ty, she could manage that perfectly. You'll be home again on Saturday?'

'Yes, honey. Late, though.'

'Of course.'

'See you this evening.'

'Bye, Ty,' she said with a smile in her voice. 'See you.'

I drove all the way to Norton Fox's stable wishing I hadn't done it. Knowing that I wouldn't change it. Round and round the mulberry bush and a thumping headache by Berkshire.

Norton Fox looked curiously into the trailer parked in the private front drive of his house.

'So that's the great Tiddely Pom. Can't say I think much of him from this angle.'

'Nor from any other,' I agreed. 'It's good of you to have him.'

'Happy to oblige. I'm putting him in the box next to Zig Zag, and Sandy Willis can look after both of them.'

'You won't tell her what he is?' I asked anxiously.

'Of course not.' He looked resigned at my stupidity. 'I've recently bought a chaser over in Kent ... I've just postponed collecting it for a while, but Sandy and all the other lads think Tiddely Pom is him.'

'Great.'

'I'll just get my head lad to drive the trailer into the yard and unload. You said on the phone that you wanted to stay out of sight ... come inside for a cuppa.'

Too late, after I'd nodded, I remembered the near black tea of my former visit. The same again. Norton remarked that his housekeeper had been economizing, he never could get her to make it strong enough.

'Did the *Tally* photographer get here all right?' I asked as he came in from the yard, filled his cup, and sat down opposite me.

He nodded. 'Took dozens of pics of Sandy Willis and thrilled her to bits.' He offered me a slice of dry looking fruit cake and when I said no, ate a large chunk himself, undeterred. 'That article of yours last Sunday,' he said past the currants, 'that must have been a bombshell in certain quarters.'

I said, 'Mm, I hope so.'

'Brevity ... that Champion Hurdler of mine ... that was definitely one of the nonstarters you were talking about, wasn't it? Even though you didn't mention it explicitly by name?'

'Yes, it was.'

'Ty, did you find out *why* Dembley struck his horse out, and then sold out of racing altogether?'

'I can't tell you why, Norton,' I said.

He considered this answer with his head on one side and then nodded as if satisfied. 'Tell me one day, then.'

I smiled briefly. 'When and if the racket is extinct.'

'You go on the way you are, and it will be. If you go on exposing it publicly, the ante-post market will be so untrustworthy that we'll find ourselves doing as the Americans do, only betting on a race on the day of the race, and never before. They don't have any off-the-course betting at all, over there, do they?'

'Not legally.'

He drank in big gulps down to the tea leaves. 'Might shoot our attendances up if punters had to go to the races to have a bet.'

'Which would shoot up the prize money too ... did you see that their champion jockey earned well over three million dollars last year? Enough to make Gordon Richards weep.'

I put down the half-finished tea and stood up. 'Must be getting back, Norton. Thank you again for your help.'

'Anything to prevent another Brevity.'

'Send the accounts to the *Blaze*.'

He nodded. 'And ring the sports desk every day to give a report, and don't speak to anyone except you or Derry Clark or a man called Luke-John Morton. Right?'

'Absolutely right,' I agreed. 'Oh ... and here are Victor Roncey's notes. Eggs and beer in Tiddely Pom's food every night.'

'I've one owner,' Norton said, 'who sends his horse champagne.'

I drove the trailer back to the city editor's house, swapped it for my van, and went home. Ten to seven on the clock. Mrs Woodward was having a grand week for overtime and had cooked chicken à la king for our supper, leaving it ready and hot. I thanked her. 'Not at all, Mr Tyrone, a pleasure I'm sure. Ta ta, luv, see you tomorrow, I'll bring my things for stopping the night.'

I kissed Elizabeth, poured the drinks, ate the chicken, watched a TV programme, and let a little of the day's tension trickle away. After supper there was my Sunday article to write. Enthusiasm for the project: way below zero. I went into the writing room determined to put together a calm played-down sequel to the previous week, with a sober let's-not-rush-our-fences approach. Somewhere along the line most of these good intentions vanished. Neither Charlie Boston nor the foreign gent in the Rolls was going to like the result.

Before setting off to the office in the morning I packed an overnight bag, with Elizabeth reminding me to take my alarm clock and a clean shirt.

'I hate it when you go away,' she said. 'I know you don't go often, probably not nearly as much as you ought to. I know you try not to get the far away meetings ... Derry nearly always does them, and I feel so guilty because his wife has those tiny children to look after all alone...'

'Stop worrying,' I said, smiling. 'Derry likes to go.' I had almost convinced myself that I really was taking the afternoon train to Newcastle. Gail was hours away, unreal. I kissed Elizabeth's cheek three times and dearly regretted leaving her. Yet I left.

Luke-John and Derry were both out of the office when I arrived. Luke-John's secretary handed me a large envelope which she said had come for me by hand just after I left on Wednesday. I opened it. The galley-proofs of my *Tally* article: please would I read and O.K. immediately.

'*Tally* telephoned for you twice yesterday,' Luke-John's secretary said. 'They go to press today. They wanted you urgently.'

I read the article. Arnold Shankerton had changed it about here and there and had stamped his own slightly pedantic views of grammar all over it. I sighed. I didn't like the changes, but a hundred and fifty guineas plus expenses softened the impact.

Arnold Shankerton said in his perfectly modulated tenor, with a mixture of annoyance and apology, 'I'm afraid we've had to go ahead and print, as we hadn't heard from you.'

'My fault. I've only just picked up your letter.'

'I see. Well, after I'd worked on it a little I think it reads very well, don't you? We're quite pleased with it. We think it will be a success with our readers. They like that sort of intimate human touch.'

'I'm glad,' I said politely. 'Will you send me a copy?'

'I'll make a note of it,' he said suavely. I thought I would probably have to buy one on a bookstall. 'Let me have your expenses. Small, I hope?'

'Sure,' I agreed. 'Tiny.'

Luke-John and Derry came back as I disconnected and Luke-John, without bothering to say good morning, stretched out a hand for my Sunday offering. I took it out of my pocket and he unfolded it and read it.

'Hmph,' he said. 'I expected a bit more bite.'

Derry took one of the carbon copies from me and read it.

'Any more bite and he'd have chewed up the whole page,' he said, disagreeing.

'Couldn't you emphasize a bit more that only the *Blaze* knows where Tiddely Pom is?' Luke-John said. 'You've only implied it.'

'If you think so.'

'Yes, I do think so. As the *Blaze* is footing the bills we want all the credit we can get.'

'Suppose someone finds him ... Tiddely Pom?' I asked mildly. 'Then we'd look right nanas, hiding him, boasting about it, and then having him found.'

'No one will find him. The only people who know where he is are us three and Norton Fox. To be more precise, only you and Fox know *exactly* where he is. Only you and Fox know which in that yard full of sixty horses is Tiddely Pom. Neither of you is going to tell anyone else. So how is anyone going to find him? No, no, Ty. You make that article absolutely definite. The *Blaze* is keeping the horse safe, and only the *Blaze* knows where he is.'

'Charlie Boston may not like it,' Derry observed to no one in particular.

'Charlie Boston can stuff it,' Luke-John said impatiently.

'I meant,' Derry explained, 'that he might just send his thug-uglies to take Ty apart for so obviously ignoring their keep-off-the-grass.'

My pal. Luke-John considered the possibility for two full seconds before shaking his head. 'They wouldn't dare.'

'And even if they did,' I said, 'it would make a good story and you could sell more papers.'

'Exactly.' Luke-John started nodding and then looked at me suspiciously. 'That was a joke?'

'A feeble one.' I sighed, past smiling.

'Change the intro, then, Ty. Make it one hundred per cent specific.' He picked up a pencil and put a line through the first paragraph. Read the next, rubbed his larynx thoughtfully, let that one stand. Axed the next. Turned the page.

Derry watched sympathetically as the pencil marks grew. It happened to him, too, often enough. Luke-John scribbled his way through to the end and then returned to the beginning, pointing out each alteration that he wanted made. He was turning my moderately hard hitting original into a bulldozing battering ram.

'You'll get me slaughtered,' I said, and I meant it.

I worked on the rewrite most of the morning, fighting a rear-guard action all the way. What Luke-John finally passed was a compromise between his view and mine, but still left me so far out on a limb as to be balancing on twigs. Luke-John took it in to the Editor, stayed there while he read it, and brought it triumphantly back.

'He liked it. Thinks it's great stuff. He liked Derry's piece yesterday too, summing up the handicap. He told me the sports desk is a big asset to the paper.'

'Good,' Derry said cheerfully. 'When do we get our next raise?'

'Time for a jar at the Devereux,' Luke-John suggested, looking at his watch. 'Coming today, Ty?'

'Norton Fox hasn't rung through yet.'

'Call him then.'

I telephoned to Fox. Tiddely Pom was fine, ate his feed the previous evening, had settled in well, had done a mile at a working canter that morning, and no one had looked at him twice. I thanked him and relayed the news to Roncey, who sounded both agitated and depressed.

'I don't like it,' he said several times.

'Do you want to risk having him at home?'

He hesitated, then said, 'I suppose not. No. But I don't like it. Don't forget to ring tomorrow evening, I'll be at Kempton races all afternoon.'

'The Sports Editor will ring,' I assured him. 'And don't worry.'

He put the receiver down saying an explosive 'Huh.' Luke-John and Derry were already on the way to the door and I joined them to go to lunch.

'Only a fortnight since Bert Checkov died,' observed Derry, sitting on a bar stool. 'Only ten days since we spotted the nonstarters. Funny.'

Hilarious. And eight more days to go to the Lamplighter. This Monday, I decided, I would stay safely tucked away at home.

'Don't forget,' I said to Derry. 'Don't tell any one my phone number.'

'What brought that on all of a sudden?'

'I was thinking about Charlie Boston. My address isn't in the phone book . .'

'Neither Derry nor I will give your address to any one,' Luke-John said impatiently. 'Come off it Ty, any one would think you were frightened.'

'Any one would be so right,' I agreed, and they both laughed heartily into their pints.

Derry was predictably pleased that I wanted to go to Newcastle instead of Kempton, leaving the London meeting for once for him.

'Is it all right,' he said, embarrassed. 'With your wife, I mean?'

I told him what Elizabeth had said, but as usual anything to do with her made him uncomfortable. Luke-John said dutifully, 'How is she?' and I said 'Fine.'

I kicked around the office all the afternoon, arranging a travel warrant to Newcastle, putting in a chit for expenses for Heatherbury Park, Leicester and Plumpton, and collecting the case from Accounts. Luke-John was busy with a football columnist and the golfing correspondent, and Derry took time off from working out his tips for every meeting in the following week to tell me about taking the Roncey kids to the Isle of Wight.

'Noisy little devils,' he said disapprovingly. 'Their mother has no control over them at all. She seemed to be in a dream most of the time. Anyway, none of them actually fell off the ferry, which was a miracle considering Tony, that was the eldest one, was trying to lean over far enough to see the paddles go round. I told him they were under the water. Made no difference.'

I made sympathetic noises, trying not to laugh out of pity for my ribs. 'They were happy enough, then?'

'Are you kidding? No school and a holiday and the sea? Tony said he was going to bathe, November or no November. His mother showed no signs of stopping him. Anyway, they settled into the boarding house all right though I should think we shall get a whacking bill for damage, and they thought it tremendous fun to change their names to Robinson, no trouble there. They thought Robinson was a smashing choice, they could all pretend they were cast away on a desert island . . . Well, I tell you, Ty, by the time I left them I was utterly exhausted.'

'Never mind. You can look forward to bringing them back.'

'Not me,' he said fervently. 'Your turn for that.'

At four I picked up my suitcase and departed for King's Cross. The Newcastle train left at five. I watched it go.

At five forty-eight she came up from the Underground, wearing a beautifully cut darkish blue coat and carrying a creamy white suitcase. Several heads turned to look at her, and a nearby man who had been waiting almost as long as I had watched her steadfastly until she reached the corner where I stood.

'Hallo,' she said. 'Sorry I'm late.'

'Think nothing of it.'

'I gather,' she said with satisfaction, 'that you fixed your wife.'

Chapter Nine

She moved against me in the warm dark and put her mouth on the thin skin somewhere just south of my neck. I tightened my arms round her, and buried my nose in her clean, sweet-scented hair.

'There's always something new,' she said sleepily. 'Broken ribs are quite a gimmick.'

'I didn't feel them.'

'Oh yes you did.'

I stroked my hands slowly over her smooth skin and didn't bother to answer. I felt relaxed and wholly content. She had been kind to my ribs, gentle to my bruises. They had even in an obscure way given her pleasure.

'How did it happen?'

'What?'

'The black and blue bit.'

'I lost an argument.'

She rubbed her nose on my chest. 'Must have been quite a debate.'

I smiled in the dark. The whole world was inside the sheets, inside the small private cocoon wrapping two bodies in intimate primeval understanding.

'Ty?'

'Mm?'

'Can't we stay together all weekend?'

I said through her hair, 'I have to phone in a report from Newcastle. Can't avoid it.'

'Damn the *Blaze*.'

'There's Sunday, though.'

'Hurrah for the Golf Club.'

We lay quiet for a long while. I felt heavy with sleep and fought to stay awake. There were so few hours like this. None to waste.

For Gail time was not so precious. Her limbs slackened and her head slid down on to my arm, her easy breath fanning softly against my chest. I thought of Elizabeth lying closely curled against me like that when we were first married, and for once it was without guilt, only with regret.

Gail woke of her own accord a few hours later and pulled my wrist round to look at the luminous hands on my watch.

'Are you awake?' she said. 'It's ten to six.'

'Do you like it in the morning?'

'With you, Ty, any time.' Her voice smiled in the darkness. 'Any old time you care to mention.'

I wasn't that good. I said, 'Why?'

'Because you're normal, maybe. Nice bread and butter love.' She played the piano down my stomach. 'Some men want the weirdest things...'

'Let's not talk about them.'

'O.K.' she said. 'Let's not.'

I caught the Newcastle express at eight o'clock with ten seconds in hand. It was a raw cold morning with steam hissing up from under the train. Hollow clanking noises and unintelligible station announcements filled the ears, and bleary-eyed shivering passengers hurried greyly through the British Standard dawn.

I took my shivering bleary-eyed self into the dining car and tried some strong black coffee, but nothing was going to shift the dragging depression which had settled in inexorably as soon as I left Gail. I imagined her as I had left her, lying warm and luxuriously lazy in the soft bed and saying Sunday was tomorrow, we could start again where we'd left off. Sunday was certainly tomorrow, but there was Saturday to get through first. From where I sat it looked like a very long day.

Four and a half hours to Newcastle. I slept most of the way, and spent the rest remembering the evening and night which were gone. We had found a room in a small private hotel near the station and I had signed the register Mr and Mrs Tyrone. No one there had shown any special interest in us: they had presently shown us to a clean uninspiring room and given us the key, had asked if we wanted early tea, had said they were sorry they didn't do dinners, there were several good restaurants round about. I paid them in advance, explaining that I had an early train to catch. They smiled, thanked me, withdrew, asked no questions, made no comment. Impossible to know what they guessed.

We talked for a while and then went out to a pub for a drink and from there to an Indian restaurant where we took a long time eating little, and an even longer time drinking coffee. Gail wore her usual air of businesslike poise and remained striking-looking even when surrounded by people of her own skin colour. I, with my pale face, was in a minority.

Gail commented on it. 'London must be the best place in the world for people like me.'

'For anyone.'

She shook her head. 'Especially for people of mixed race. In so many countries I'd be on the outside looking in. I'd never get the sort of job I have.'

'It never seems to worry you, being of mixed race,' I said.

'I accept it. In fact I wouldn't choose now to be wholly white or wholly black, if I could alter it. I am used to being me. And with people like you, of course, it is easy, because you are unaffected by me.'

'I wouldn't say that, exactly,' I said, grinning.

'Damn it, you know what I mean. You don't mind me being brown.'

'You're brown and you're beautiful. A shattering combination.'

'You're not being serious,' she complained.

'And you're glossy to the bone.'

Her lips curved in amusement. 'If you mean I've a hard core instead of a soft centre, then I expect you're right.'

'And one day you'll part from me without a twinge.'

'Will we part?' No anxiety, no involvement.

'What do you think?'

'I think you wouldn't leave your wife to live with me.'

Direct, no muddle, no fluffy wrappings.

'Would you?' she asked, when I didn't quickly answer.

'I'll never leave her.'

'That's what I thought. I like to get things straight. Then I can enjoy what I have, and not expect more.'

'Hedging your bets.'

'What do you mean?' she asked.

'Insuring against disappointment.'

'When people desperately want what they can never have, they *suffer*. Real grinding misery. That's not for me.'

'You will be luckier than most,' I said slowly, 'if you can avoid it altogether.'

I'll have a danmed good try.'

One day uncontrollable emotion would smash up all that organized level-headedness. Not while I was around, if I could help it. I prized it too much. Needed her to stay like that. Only while she demanded so little could I go on seeing her, and since she clearly knew it, we had a good chance of staying safely on the tightrope for as long as we wanted.

With the coffee we talked, as before, about money. Gail complained that she never had enough.

'Who has?' I said sympathetically.

'Your wife, for one.' There was a faint asperity in her voice, which made me stifle my immediate impulse to deny it.

'Sorry,' she said almost at once. 'Shouldn't have said that. What your wife has is quite irrelevant. It's what I haven't got that we're talking about. Such as a car of my own, a sports car, and not having to borrow Harry's all the time. And a flat of my own, a sunny one overlooking a park. Never having to budget every penny. Buying lavish presents for people if I feel like it. Flying to Paris often for a few days, and having a holiday in Japan . . .'

'Marry a millionaire,' I suggested.

'I intend to.'

We both laughed, but I thought she probably meant it. The man she finally didn't part with would have to have troubles with his surtax. I wondered what she would do if she knew I could only afford that dinner and the hotel bill because *Tally's* fee would be plugging for a while the worst holes in the Tyrone economy. What would she do if she knew that I had a penniless paralysed wife, not a rich one. On both counts, wave a rapid goodbye, probably. For as long as I could, I wasn't going to give her the opportunity.

I missed the first Newcastle race altogether and only reached the press stand halfway through the second. Delicate probes among colleagues revealed that nothing dramatic had happened in the hurdle race I had spent urging the taxi driver to rise above twenty. Luke-John would never know.

After the fourth race I telephoned through a report, and another after the fifth, in which one of the top northern jockeys broke his leg. Derry came on the line and asked me to go and find out from the trainer who would be riding his horse in the Lamplighter instead, and I did his errand thanking my stars I had had the sense actually to go to Newcastle, and hadn't been tempted to watch the racing on television and phone through an 'on-the-spot' account from an armchair three hundred miles away, as one correspondent of my acquaintance had been known to do.

Just before the last race someone touched my arm. I turned. Collie Gibbons, the handicapper, looking harassed and annoyed,

'Ty. Do me a favour.'

'What?'

'You came by train? First class?'

I nodded. The *Blaze* wasn't mean about comfort.

'Then swap return tickets with me.' He held out a slim booklet which proved to be an air ticket. Newcastle to Heathrow.

'There's some damn meeting been arranged here which I shall have to go to after this race,' He explained. 'And I won't be able to catch the plane. I've only just found out and . . . it's most annoying. There's a later train . . . I particularly want to get to London tonight.'

'Done,' I said. 'Suits me fine.'

He smiled, still frowning simultaneously. 'Thanks. And here are the keys to my car. It's in the multi-storey park opposite the Europa building.' He told me its number and position. 'Drive yourself home.'

'I'll drive to your house and leave the car there,' I said. 'Easier than bringing it over tomorrow.'

'If you're sure...' I nodded, giving him my train ticket.

'A friend who lives up here was going to run me back to the airport,' he said. 'I'll get him to take you instead.'

'Have you heard from your wife?' I asked.

'That's just it ... she wrote to say we'd have a trial reconciliation and she'd be coming home today. If I stay away all night she'll never believe I had a good reason ... She'll be gone again.'

'Miss the meeting,' I suggested.

'It's too important, especially now I've got your help. I suppose you couldn't explain to her, if she's there, that I'm on my way?'

'Of course,' I said.

So the friend whisked me off to the airport, and I flew to Heathrow, collected the car, drove to Hampstead, explained to Mrs Gibbons, who promised to wait, and arrived home two and a half hours early. Elizabeth was pleased, even if Mrs Woodward wasn't.

Sunday morning. Elizabeth's mother didn't come.

Ten fifteen, ten thirty. Nothing. At eleven someone telephoned from the health farm and said they were so sorry, my mother-in-law was in bed with a virus infection, nothing serious, don't worry, she would ring her daughter as soon as she was a little better.

I told Elizabeth. 'Oh well,' she said philosophically, 'we'll have a nice cosy day on our own.'

I smiled at her and kept the shocking disappointment out of my face.

'Do you think Sue Davis would pop along for a moment while I get us some whisky?' I asked.

'She'd get it for us.'

'I'd like to stretch my legs...'

She smiled understandingly and rang Sue, who came at twelve with flour down the sides of her jeans. I hurried round corners to the nearest phone box and gave the Huntersons' number. The bell rang there again and again, but no one answered. Without much hope I got the number of Virginia Water station and rang there: no, they said, there was no young woman waiting outside in an estate car. They hadn't seen one all morning. I asked for the Huntersons' number again. Again, no reply.

Feeling flat I walked back to our local pub and bought the whisky, and tried yet again on the telephone too publicly installed in the passage there.

No answer. No Gail.

I went home.

Sue Davis had read out to Elizabeth my piece in the *Blaze*.

'Straight between the eyeballs,' she observed cheerfully. 'I must say, Ty, no one would connect the punch you pack in that paper with the you we know.'

'What's wrong with the him you know?' asked Elizabeth with real anxiety under the surface gaiety. She hated people to think me weak for staying at home with her. She never told any one how much nursing she needed from me: always pretended Mrs Woodward did everything. She seemed to think that what I did for her would appear unmanly to others; she wanted in public a masculine never-touch-the-dishes husband, and since it made her happy I played that role except when we were alone.

'Nothing's wrong with him,' Sue protested. She looked me over carefully. 'Nothing at all.'

'What did you mean, then?' Elizabeth was smiling still, but she wanted an answer.

'Oh ... only that this Ty is so quiet, and that one ...' she pointed to the paper, 'bursts the eardrums.' She put her head on one side, summing me up, then turned to Elizabeth with the best of motives and said: 'This one is so gentle ... that one is tough.'

'Gentle nothing,' I said, seeing the distress under Elizabeth's laugh. 'When you aren't here, Sue, I throw her round the room and black her eyes regularly on Fridays.' Elizabeth relaxed, liking that. 'Stay for a drink,' I suggested to Sue, 'Now that I've fetched it.'

She went, however, back to her half-baked Yorkshire pudding, and I avoided discussing what she had said by going out to the kitchen and rustling up some omelettes for lunch. Elizabeth particularly liked them, and could eat hers with the new feeding gadget, up to a point. I helped her when her wrist tired, and made some coffee and fixed her mug in its holder.

'Do you really know where the horse is?' she asked.

'Tiddely Pom? Yes, of course.'

'Where is it?'

'Dark and deadly secret, honey,' I said. 'I can't tell anyone, even you.'

'Oh go on,' she urged. 'You know I won't tell either.'

'I'll tell you next Sunday.'

Her nose wrinkled. 'Thanks for nothing.' The pump heaved away, giving her breath. 'You don't think anyone would try to ... well ... *make* you tell. Where he is, I mean.' More worry, more anxiety. She couldn't help it. She was always on the edge of a precipice, always on the distant look out for anything which would knock her over.

'Of course not, honey, How could they?'

'I don't know,' she said; but her eyes were full of horrors.

'Stop fussing,' I said with a smile. 'If anyone threatened me with anything really nasty, I'd say quick enough where he is. No horse is worth getting in too deep for.' Echoes of Dembley. The matrix which nurtured the germ. No one would sacrifice themselves or their families for the sake of running a horse.

Elizabeth detected the truth in my voice and was satisfied. She switched on the television and watched some fearful old movie which bored me to death. Three o'clock came and went. Even if I'd gone to

Virginia Water, I would have been on the way back again. And I'd had Friday night. Rare, unexpected Friday night. Trouble was, the appetite grew on what it fed on, as someone else once said. The next Sunday was at the wrong end of a telescope.

Drinks, supper, jobs for Elizabeth, bed. No one else called, no one telephoned. It crossed my mind once or twice as I lazed in the armchair in our customary closed-in little world, that perhaps the challenge implicit in my column had stirred up, somewhere, a hive of bees.

Buzz buzz, busy little bees. Buzz around the *Blaze*. And don't sting me.

I spent all Monday in and around the flat. Washed the van, wrote letters, bought some socks, kept off race trains from Leicester.

Derry telephoned twice to tell me (a) that Tiddely Pom was flourishing, and (b) The Roncey children had sent him a stick of peppermint rock.

'Big deal,' I said.

'Not bad kids.'

'You'll enjoy fetching them.'

He blew a raspberry and hung up.

Tuesday morning I walked to the office. One of those brownish late November days, with saturated air and a sour scowl of fog to come. Lights shone out brightly at 11 a.m. People hurried along Fleet Street with pinched, mean eyes working out whose neck to scrunch on the next rung of the ladder, and someone bought a blind man's matches with a poker chip.

Luke-John and Derry wore moods to match.

'What's the matter?' I asked mildly.

'Nothing's happened,' Derry said.

'So?'

'So where's our reaction?' Luke-John inquired angrily. 'Not a letter. No one's phoned, even. Unless,' be brightened, 'Unless Charlie Boston's boys have called on you with a few more threats?'

'They have not.'

Relapse into gloom for the Sports Desk. I alone wasn't sorry the article had fallen with a dull thud. If it had. I thought it was too soon to be sure. I said so.

'Hope you're right, Ty,' Luke-John said sceptically. 'Hope it hasn't all been a coincidence ... Bert Checkov and the nonstarters ... hope the *Blaze* hasn't wasted its time and money for nothing on Tiddely Pom ...'

'Charlie Boston's boys were not a coincidence.'

'I suppose not.' Luke-John sounded as though he thought I might have misunderstood what the Boston boys had said.

'Did your friend in Manchester find out any more about Charlie B?' I asked.

Luke-John shrugged. 'Only that there was some talk about his chain of betting shops being taken over by a bigger concern. But it doesn't seem to have happened. He is still there, anyway, running the show.'

'Which bigger concern?'

'Don't know.'

To pass the time we dialled four of the biggest London bookmaking businesses which had chains of betting shops all over the country. None of them admitted any immediate interest in buying out Charlie Boston. But one man was hesitant, and when I pressed him, he said, 'We did put out a feeler, about a year ago. We understood there was a foreign buyer also interested. But Boston decided to remain independent and turned down both offers.'

'Thanks,' I said, and Luke-John commented that that took us a long way, didn't it. He turned his attention crossly to a pile of letters which had flooded in contradicting one of the football writers, and Derry began to assess the form for the big race on Boxing Day. All over the vast office space the Tuesday picking of teeth and scratching of scabs proceeded without haste, the slow week still slumbering. Tuesday was gossip day. Wednesday planning. Thursday, writing. Friday, editing. Saturday, printing. Sunday, *Blaze* away. And on Mondays the worked-on columns lit real fires or wrapped fish and chips. No immortality for a journalist.

Tuesday was also *Tally* day. Neither at home nor at the office had a copy come for me by post. I went downstairs to the next-door magazine stand, bought one, and went back inside the *Blaze*.

The pictures were off-beat and rather good, the whole article well presented. One had to admit that Shankerton knew his stuff. I forgave him his liberties with my syntax.

I picked up Derry's telephone and got through to the *Tally* despatch department. As expected, they didn't send free copies to the subjects of any articles: not their policy. Would they send them? Oh sure, give us the addresses, we'll let you have the bill. I gave them the six addresses, Huntersons, Ronceys, Sandy Willis, Collie Gibbons, Dermot Finnegan, Willie Ondroy.

Derry picked up the magazine and plodded through the article, reading at one third Luke-John's wide angled speed.

'Deep, deep,' he said ironically, putting it down. 'One hundred and fifty fathoms.'

'Sixty will go in tax.'

'A hard life,' Derry sighed. 'But if you hadn't picked on Roncey, we would never have cottoned on to this nonstarter racket.'

Nor would I have had any cracked ribs. With them, though, the worst was over. Only coughing, sneezing, laughing, and taking running jumps were sharply undesirable. I had stopped eating Elizabeth's pills. In another week, the cracks would have knitted.

'Be seeing you,' I said to Derry. Luke-John waved a freckled farewell hand. Carrying *Tally* I went down in the lift and turned out of the front door up towards the Strand, bound for a delicatessen shop which sold Austrian apple cake which Elizabeth liked.

Bought the cake. Came out into the street. Heard a voice in my ear. Felt a sharp prick through my coat abeam the first lumbar vertebra.

'It's a knife, Mr Tyrone.'

I stood quite still. People could be stabbed to death in busy streets and no one noticed until the body cluttered up the fairway. Killers vanished into crowds with depressing regularity.

'What do you want?' I said.

'Just stay where you are.'

Standing on the Fleet Street pavement, holding a magazine and a box of apple cake. Just stay where you are. For how long?

'For how long?' I said.

He didn't answer. But he was still there, because his knife was. We stood where we were for all of two minutes. Then a black Rolls rolled to a silent halt at the kerb directly opposite where I stood. The door to the back seat swung open.

'Get in,' said the voice behind me.

I got in. There was a chauffeur driving, all black uniform and a stolid acne-scarred neck. The man with the knife climbed in after me and settled by my side. I glanced at him, knew I'd seen him somewhere before, didn't know where. I put *Tally* and the apple cake carefully on the floor. Sat back. Went for a ride.

Chapter Ten

We turned north into the Aldwych and up Drury Lane to St Giles' Circus. I made no move towards escape, although we stopped several times at traffic lights. My companion watched me warily, and I worked on where I had seen him before and still came up with nothing. Up Tottenham Court Road. Left, right, left again. Straight into Regent's Park and round the semicircle. Stopped smoothly at the turnstile entrance to the Zoo.

'Inside,' said my companion, nodding.

We stepped out of the car, and the chauffeur quietly drove off.

'You can pay,' I remarked.

He gave me a quick glance, tried to juggle the money out of his pocket one handed, and found he couldn't manage it if he were to be of any use with his knife.

'No,' he said. 'You pay. For us both.'

I paid, almost smiling. He was nowhere near as dangerous as he wanted to be thought.

We checked through the turnstiles. 'Where now?' I said.

'Straight ahead. I'll tell you.'

The Zoo was nearly empty. On that oily Tuesday November lunch time, not even the usual bus loads from schools. Birds shrieked mournfully from the aviary and a notice board said the vultures would be fed at three.

A man in a dark overcoat and black homburg hat was sitting on a seat looking towards the lions' outdoor compounds. The cages were empty. The sun-loving lions were inside under the sun lamps.

'Over there,' said my companion, nodding.

We walked across. The man in the black homburg watched us come. Every line of his clothes and posture spoke of money, authority, and high social status, and his manner of irritating superiority would have done credit to the Foreign Office. As Dembley had said, his subject matter was wildly at variance with his appearance.

'Did you have any trouble?' he asked.

'None at all,' said the knife man smugly

A bleak expression crept into pale grey eyes as cold as the stratosphere. 'I am not pleased to hear it.'

The accent in his voice was definite but difficult. A thickening of some consonants, a clipping of some vowels.

'Go away, now,' he said to the knife man. 'And wait.'

My nondescript abductor in his nondescript raincoat nodded briefly and walked away, and I nearly remembered where I'd seen him. Recollection floated up, but not far enough.

'You chose to come,' the man in the homburg said flatly.

'Yes and no.'

He stood up. My height, but thicker. Yellowish skin, smooth except for a maze of wrinkles round his eyes. What I could see of his hair was nearly blond, and I put his age down roughly as five or six years older than myself.

'It is cold outside. We will go in.'

I walked with him round inside the Big Cats' House, where the strong feral smell seemed an appropriate background to the proceedings. I could guess what he wanted. Not to kill: that could have been done in Fleet Street or anywhere on the way. To extort. The only question was how.

'You show too little surprise,' he said.

'We were waiting for some ... reaction. Expecting it.'

'I see.' He was silent, working it out. A bored-looking tiger blinked at us lazily, claws sheathed inside rounded pads, tail swinging a fraction from side to side. I sneered at him. He turned and walked three paces and three paces back, round and round, going nowhere.

'Was last week's reaction not enough for you?'

'Very useful,' I commented. 'Led us straight to Charlie Boston. So kind of you to ask. That makes you a side kick of his.'

He gave me a blazingly frosty glare. 'I *employ* Boston.'

I looked down, not answering. If his pride were as easily stung as that he might give me more answers than I gave him.

'When I heard about it I disapproved of what they did on the train. Now, I am not so sure.' His voice was quiet again, the voice of culture, diplomacy, tact.

'You didn't order it, then.'

'I did not.'

I ran my hand along the thick metal bar which kept visitors four feet away from the animals' cages. The tiger looked tame, too gentle to kill. Too indifferent to maul, to maim, to scrape to the bone.

'You know what we want,' said the polite tiger by my side. 'We want to know where you have hidden the horse.'

'Why?' I said.

He merely blinked at me.

I sighed. 'What good will it do you? Do you still seriously intend to try to prevent it from running? You would be much wiser to forget the whole thing and quietly fold your tent and steal away.'

'You will leave that decision entirely to me.' Again, the pride stuck out a mile. I didn't like it. Few enemies were as ruthless as those who feared a loss of face. I began to consider before how wide an acquaintanceship the face had to be preserved. The wider, the worse for me.

'Where is it?'

'Tiddely Pom?' I said.

'Tiddely Pom.' He repeated the name with fastidious disgust. 'Yes.'

'Quite safe.'

'Mr Tyrone, stop playing games. You cannot hide for ever from Charlie Boston.'

I was silent. the tiger yawned, showing a full set of fangs, Nasty.

'They could do more damage next time,' he said.

I looked at him curiously, wondering if he seriously thought I would crumble under so vague a threat. He stared straight back and was unmoved when I didn't answer. My heart sank slightly. More to come.

'I suspected,' he said conversationally, 'when I heard that you were seen at Plumpton races the day following Boston's ill-judged attack, that physical pressure would run us into too much difficulty in your case. I see that this assessment was correct. I directed that a different lever should be found. We have, of course, found it. And you will tell us where the horse is hidden.'

He took out the black crocodile wallet and removed from it a small sheet of paper, folded once. He gave it to me. I looked. He saw the deep shock in my face and he smiled in satisfaction.

It was a photo-copy of the bill of the hotel where I had stayed with Gail. Mr and Mrs Tyrone, one double room.

'So you see, Mr Tyrone, that if you wish to keep this interesting item of news from your wife, you must give us the address we ask.'

My mind tumbled over and over like a dry-cleaning machine and not a useful thought came out.

'So quiet, Mr Tyrone? You really don't like that, do you? So you will tell us. You would not want your wife to divorce you, I am sure. And you have taken such pains to deceive her that we are certain you know she would throw you out if she discovered this . . .' He pointed to the bill. 'How would she like to know that your mistress is coloured? We have other dates, too. Last Sunday week, and the Sunday before that. Your wife will be told it all. Wealthy women will not stand for this sort of thing, you know.'

I wondered numbly how much Gail had sold me for.

'Come along, Mr Tyrone. The address.'

'I need time,' I said dully.

'That's right,' he said calmly. 'It takes time to sink in properly, doesn't it? Of course you can have time. Six hours. You will telephone to us precisely seven o'clock this evening.' He gave me a plain white card with numbers on it. 'Six hours is all, Mr Tyrone. After that, the information will be on its way to your wife, and you will not be able to stop it. Do you clearly understand?'

'Yes.' I said. The tiger sat down and shut its eyes. Sympathetic.

'I thought you would.' He moved away from me towards the door. 'Seven o'clock precisely. Good day, Mr Tyrone.'

With erect easy assurance he walked straight out of the Cat House, turned a corner, and was gone. My feet seemed to have become disconnected from my body. I was going through the disjointed floating feeling of irretrievable disaster. A disbelieving part of my mind said that if I stayed quite still the nutcracker situation would go away.

It didn't, of course. But after a while I began to think normally instead of in emotional shock waves; began to look for a hole in the net. I walked slowly away from the tiger, out into the unwholesome air and down towards the gate, all my attention turned inward. Out of the corner of my eye I half caught sight of my abductor in his raincoat standing up a side path looking into an apparently empty wire-netted compound, and when I'd gone out of the turnstile on the road it hit me with a thump where I'd seen him before. So significant a thump that I came to a rocking halt. Much had urgently to be understood.

I had seen him at King's Cross station while I waited for Gail. He had been standing near me: had watched her all the way from the Underground until she had reached me. Looking for a lever. Finding it.

To be watching me at King's Cross, he must have followed me from the *Blaze*.

Today, he had picked me up outside the *Blaze*.

I walked slowly, thinking about it. From King's Cross in the morning I had gone on the train to Newcastle, but I hadn't come back on my return ticket. Collie Gibbons had. I'd taken that unexpected roundabout route home, and somewhere, maybe back at Newcastle races, I'd shaken off my tail.

Someone also must either have followed Gail, or have gone straight into the hotel to see her after I had left. I baulked at thinking she would sell me out with my imprint still on our shared sheets. But maybe she would. It depended on how much they had offered her, I supposed. Five hundred would have tempted her mercenary heart too far.

No one but Gail could have got a receipt from the hotel. No one but Gail knew of the two Sunday afternoons, No one but Gail thought my wife was rich. I coldly faced the conclusion that I had meant little to her. Very little indeed. My true deserts. I had sought her out because she could dispense sex without involvement. She had been consistent. She owed me nothing at all.

I reached the corner and distinctively turning my plodding steps towards home. Not for twenty paces did I realize that this was a desperate mistake.

Gail didn't know where I lived. She couldn't have told them. They didn't know the true facts about Elizabeth: they thought she was a rich woman who would divorce me. *They picked me up this morning outside the Blaze* ... At the same weary place I turned right at the next crossing.

If the man in the black homburg didn't know where I lived, the Raincoat would be following to find out. Round the next corner I stopped and looked back through the thick branches of a may bush, and there he was, hurrying. I went on slowly as before, heading round imperceptibly towards Fleet Street.

The Homburg Hat had been bluffing. He couldn't tell Elizabeth about Gail, because he didn't know where to find her. Ex-directory telephone. My address in none of the reference books. By sheer luck I twice hadn't led them straight to my own front door.

All the same, it couldn't go on for ever. Even if I fooled them until after the Lamplighter, one day, somehow, they would tell her what I'd done.

First they buy you, then they blackmail, Bert Checkov had said. Buy Gail, blackmail me. All of a piece. I thought about blackmail for three long miles back to the *Blaze*.

Luke-John and Derry were surprised to see me back. They made no comment on a change in my appearance. I supposed the inner turmoil didn't show.

'Have any of the crime reporters a decent pull with the police?' I asked.

Derry said 'Jimmy Sienna might have. What do you want?'

'To trace a car number.'

'Someone bashed that ancient van of yours?' Luke-John asked uninterestedly.

'Hit and run,' I agreed with distant accuracy.

'We can always try,' Derry said with typical helpfulness. 'Give me the number, and I'll go and ask him.'

I wrote down for him the registration of Homburg Hat's Silver Wraith.

'A London number,' Derry remarked. 'That might make it easier.' He took off across the room to the Crime Desk and consulted a mountainous young man with red hair.

I strolled over to the deserted News Desk and with a veneer of unconcern over a thumping heart dialled the number Homburg Hat told me to ring at seven. It was three-eighteen. More than two hours gone out of six.

A woman answered, sounding surprised.

'Are you sure you have the right number?' she said.

I read it out to her.

'Yes, that's right. How funny.'

'Why is it funny?'

'Well, this is a public phone box. I had just shut the door and was going to make a call when the phone started ringing ... Are you *sure* you have the right number?'

'I can't have,' I said. 'Where is this phone box, exactly?'

'It's one of a row in Piccadilly undergound station.'

I thanked her and rang off. Not much help.

Derry came back and said Jimmy Sienna was doing what he could, good job it was Tuesday, he was bored and wanted something to pass the time with.

I remembered that I had left my copy of *Tally* and Elizabeth's apple cake on the floor of the Rolls. Debated whether or not to get replacements. Decided there was no harm in it, and went out and bought them. I didn't see Raincoat, but that didn't mean he wasn't there, or that they hadn't swapped him for someone I wouldn't know.

Derry said Jimmy Sienna's police friend was checking the registration number but would use his discretion as to whether it was suitable to pass on to the *Blaze*. I sat on the side of Derry's desk and bit my nails.

Outside, the fog which had been threatening all day slowly cleared right away. It would. I thought about unobserved exits under the bright Fleet Street lights.

At five, Luke-John said he was going home, and Derry apologetically followed. I transferred myself to Jimmy Sienna's desk and bit my nails there instead. When he too was lumbering to his feet to leave, his telephone finally rang. He listened, thanked, scribbled.

'There you are,' he said to me. 'And good luck with the insurance. You'll need it.'

I read what he'd written. The Silver Wraith's number had been allocated to an organization called 'Hire Cars Lucullus.'

I left the *Blaze* via the roof. *Tally*, apple cake and mending ribs complicated the journey, but after circumnavigating ventilation shafts and dividing walls I walked sedately in through the fire door of the next door newspaper, a popular daily in the full flood of going to press.

No one asked me what I was doing. I went down in the lift to the basement and out to the huge garage at the rear where rows of yellow vans stood ready to take the wet ink bundles off to the trains. I knew one of the drivers slightly, and asked him for a lift.

'Sure, if you want Paddington.'

'I do.' I wanted anywhere he was going.

'Hop in, then.'

I hopped in, and after he was loaded he drove briskly out of the garage, one indistinguishable van among a procession. I stayed with him to Paddington, thanked him, and back tracked home on the underground, as certain as I could be that no one had followed.

I beat Mrs Woodward to six by two minutes but had no heart for the game.

From six-thirty to seven I sat in the armchair holding a glass of whisky and looking at Elizabeth, trying to make up a beleaguered mind.

'Something worrying you, Ty,' she said, with her ultra-sensitive feeling for trouble.

'No, honey.'

The hands galloped round the clock. At seven o'clock precisely I sat absolutely still and did nothing at all. At five past I found I had clenched my teeth so hard that I was grinding them. I imagined the telephone box in Piccadilly Circus, with Homburg Hat or Raincoat or the chauffeur waiting inside it. Tiddely Pom was nothing compared with Elizabeth's piece of mind, and yet I didn't pick up the receiver. From seven onwards the clock hands crawled.

At half-past Elizabeth said again, with detectable fear, 'Ty, there *is* something wrong. You never look so ... so bleak.'

I made a great effort to smile at her as usual, but she wasn't convinced. I looked down at my hands and said with hopeless pain. 'Honey, how much would it hurt you if I went ... and slept with a girl?'

There was no answer. After an unbearable interval I dragged my head up to look at her. Tears were running down her cheeks. She was swallowing, trying to speak.

From long, long habit I pulled a tissue out of the box and wiped her eyes, which she couldn't do for herself.

'I'm sorry,' I said uselessly. 'I'm sorry ...'

'Ty ...' She never had enough breath for weeping. Her mouth strained open in her need for more air.

'Honey, don't cry. Don't cry. Forget I said it. You know I love you, I'd never leave you. Elizabeth, honey, dear Elizabeth, don't cry ...'

I wiped her eyes again and cursed the whim which had sent me down to the Huntersons for *Tally*. I could have managed without Gail. Without anyone. I had managed without for most of eleven years.

'Ty.' The tears had stopped. Her face looked less strained. 'Ty.' She gulped, fighting for more breath. 'I can't bear to think about it.'

I stood beside her, holding the tissue, wishing she didn't have to.

'We never talk about sex,' she said. The Spirashell heaved up her chest, let it drop, rhythmically. 'I don't want it any more ... you know that ... but sometimes I remember ... how you taught me to like it ...' Two more tears welled up. I wiped them away. She said, 'I haven't ever asked you ... about girls ... I couldn't, somehow.'

'No,' I said slowly.

'I've wondered sometimes ... if you ever have, I mean ... but I didn't really want to know ... I know I would be too jealous ... I decided I'd never ask you ... because I wouldn't want you to say yes ... and yet I know that's selfish ... I've always been told men are different, they need women more . . . is it true?'

'Elizabeth,' I said helplessly.

'I didn't expect you ever to say anything . . . after all these years . . . yes, I would be hurt, if I knew . . . I couldn't help it . . . Why did you ask me? I wish you hadn't.'

I would never have said anything,' I said with regret, 'but someone is trying to blackmail me.'

'Then . . . you *have* . . . ?'

'I'm afraid so.'

'Oh.' She shut her eyes. 'I see.'

I waited, hating myself. The tears were over. She never cried for long. She physically couldn't. If she progressed into one of her rare bursts of rebellious anger she would utterly exhaust herself. Most wives could scream or throw things. Elizabeth's furies were the worse for being impotent. It must have been touch and go, because when she spoke her voice was low, thick, and deadly quiet.

'I suppose you couldn't afford to be blackmailed.'

'No one can.'

'I know it's unreasonable of me to wish you hadn't told me. To wish you hadn't done it at all. Any man who stays with a paralysed wife ought to have *something* . . . So many of them pack up and leave altogether . . . I know you say you never will and I do mostly believe it, but I must be such an unbearable burden to you . . .'

'That,' I said truthfully, 'is just not true.'

'It must be. Don't tell me . . . about the girl.'

'If I don't, the blackmailer will.'

'All right . . . get it over quickly . . .'

I got it over quickly. Briefly. No details. Hated myself for having to tell her, and knew that if I hadn't, Homburg Hat wouldn't have stopped his leverage with the whereabouts of Tiddely Pom. Blackmailers never did. Don't sell your soul, Bert Checkov said. Don't sell your column. Sacrifice your wife's peace instead.

'Will you see her again?' she asked.

'No.'

'Or . . . anyone else?'

'No.'

'I expect you will,' she said. 'Only if you do . . . don't tell me . . . Unless of course someone tries to blackmail you again . . .'

I winced at the bitterness in her voice. Reason might tell her that total lifelong celibacy was a lot to demand, but emotion had practically nothing to do with reason, and the tearing emotions of any ordinary wife on finding her husband unfaithful hadn't atrophied along with her muscles. I hadn't expected much else. She would have to have been a saint or a cynic to have laughed it off without a pang, and she was neither of those things, just a normal human being trapped in an abnormal situation. I wondered how suspicious she would be in the future of my most innocent absences; how much she would suffer when I was away. Reassurance, always tricky, was going to be doubly difficult.

She was very quiet and depressed all evening. She wouldn't have any supper, wouldn't eat the apple cake. When I washed her and did the rubs and the other intimate jobs I could almost feel her thinking about the other body my hands had touched. Hands, and much else. She looked sick and strained, and for almost the first time since her illness, embarrassed. If she could have done without me that evening, she would have.

I said, meaning it, 'I'm sorry, honey.'

'Yes.' She shut her eyes. 'Life's just bloody, isn't it.'

Chapter Eleven

The uncomfortable coolness between Elizabeth and myself persisted in the morning. I couldn't go on begging for a forgiveness she didn't feel. At ten I said I was going out, and saw her make the first heart-rending effort not to ask where.

'Hire Cars Lucullus' hung out in a small plushy office in Stratton Street, off Piccadilly. Royal blue wilton carped, executive type acre of polished desk, tasteful prints of vintage cars on dove grey walls. Along one side, a wide gold upholstered bench for wide gold, upholstered clients. Behind the desk, a deferential young man with Uriah Heep eyes.

For him I adopted a languid voice and my best imitation of the homburg hat manners. I had, I explained, left some property in one of his firm's cars, and I hoped he could help me get it back.

We established gradually that no, I had not hired one of their cars, and no, I did not know the name of the man who had, he had merely been so kind as to give me a lift. Yesterday.

Ah. Then had I any idea which car . . . ?

A Rolls-Royce, a Silver Wraith.

They had four of those. He briefly checked a ledger, though I suspected he didn't need to. All four had been out on hire yesterday. Could I describe the man who had given me a lift? 'Certainly. Tallish, blondish, wearing a black homburg. Not English. Possibly South African.'

'Ah. Yes.' He had no need to consult the ledger this time. He put his spread finger tips carefully down on the desk. 'I regret, sir, I cannot give you his name.'

'But surely you keep records?'

'This gentleman puts great store on privacy. We have been instructed not to give his name and address to anyone.'

'Isn't that a bit odd?' I said, raising eyebrows.

He considered judicially. 'He is a regular customer. We would, of course, give him any service he asked for, without question.'

'I suppose it wouldn't be possible to ... um ... purchase the information?'

He tried to work some shock into his deference. It was barely skin deep.

'Was your lost property very valuable?' he asked.

Tally and apple cake. 'Very,' I said.

'Then I am sure our client will return it to us. If you would let us have your own name and address, perhaps we could let you know?'

I said the first name I thought of, which nearly came out as Kempton Park. 'Kempton Jones. 31 Cornwall Street.'

He wrote it down carefully on a scratch pad. When he had finished, I waited. We both waited.

After a decent interval he said, 'Of course, if it is really important, you could ask in the garage ... they would let you know as soon as the car comes in, whether your property is still in it.'

'And the garage is where?' The only listed number and address of the Lucullus Cars had been the office in Stratton Street.

He studied his finger tips. I produced my wallet and resignedly sorted out two fivers. The twenty-five for the bookmaker's clerk's information about Charlie Boston's boys I had put down to expenses and the *Blaze* had paid. This time I could be on my own. Ten pounds represented six weeks' whisky, a month's electricity, three and a half days of Mrs Woodward, one and a half weeks' rent.

He took it greedily, nodded, gave me a hypocritical obsequious smile, and said 'Radnor Mews, Lancaster Gate.'

'Thanks.'

'You do understand, sir, that it's more than my job is worth to give you our client's name?'

'I understand,' I said. 'Principles are pretty things.'

Principles were luckily not so strongly held in Radnor Mews. The foreman sized me up and another tenner changed hands. Better value for money this time.

'The chauffeur comes here to collect the car, see? We never deliver it or supply a driver. Unusual, that. Still, the client is always right, as long as he pays for it, I always say. This foreigner, see, he likes to travel in style when he comes over here. 'Course, most of our trade is like that. Americans mostly. They hire a car and a driver for a week, two weeks, maybe three. We drive them all over, see, Stratford, Broadway, the Cotswold run most often, and Scotland a good deal too. Never have all the cars in here at once, there'd hardly be room, see, four Silver Wraiths for a start, and then two Austin Princesses, and three Bentleys and a couple of large Wolseleys.'

I brought him back gently to the Silver Wraith in question.

'I'm telling you, aren't I?' he protested. 'This foreign chap, he takes a car, always a Rolls mind you, though of course not always the same one, whenever he's over here. Started coming just over a year ago, I'd say. Been back several times, usually just for three or four days. Longer this time, I'd say. Let's see, the chauffeur came for a car last week. I could look it up ... Wednesday. Yes, that's right. What they do, see, is, the chauffeur flies over first, picks up the car and then drives out to Heathrow to fetch his gent off the next flight. Neat, that. shows money, that does.'

'Do you know where they fly from?'

'From? Which country? Not exactly. Mind, I think it varies. I know once it was Germany. But usually further than that, from somewhere hot. The chauffeur isn't exactly chatty, but he's always complaining how cold it is here.'

'What is the client's name?' I asked patiently.

'Oh sure, hang on a minute. We always put the booking in the chauffeur's name, see, it's easier, being Ross. His gent's name is something chronic. I'll have to look back.'

He went into his little boarded cubicle of an office and looked back. It took hom nearly twenty minutes, by which time he was growing restive. I waited, making it plain I would wait all day. For ten pounds he could keep on looking. He was almost as relieved as I when he found it.

'Here it is, look.' He showed me a page in a ledger, pointing to a name with a black rimmed finger nail. 'That one.'

There was a pronunciation problem, as he'd said.

Vjoersterod.

'Ross is easier,' the foreman repeated. 'We always put Ross.'

'Much easier,' I agreed. 'Do you know where I could find them, or where they keep the car while they're in England?'

He sniffed meditatively, shutting the ledger with his finger in the page.

'Can't say as I do, really. Always a pretty fair mileage on the clock, though. Goes a fair way in the three or four days, see? But then that's regular with our cars, most times. Mind you, I wouldn't say that this Ross and his gent go up to Scotland, not as far as that.'

'Birmingham?' I suggested.

'Easily. Could be, easily. Always comes back immaculate, I'll say that for Ross. Always clean as a whistle. Why don't you ask in the front office, if you want to find them?'

'They said they couldn't help me.'

'That smarmy crumb,' he said disgustedly, 'I'll bet he knows, though. Give him his due, he's good at that job, but he'd sell his grandmother if the price was right.'

I started to walk in the general direction of Fleet Street, thinking. Vjoersterod had to be the real name of Homburg Hat. Too weird to be an alias. Also, the first time he had hired a Silver Wraith from Hire Cars Lucullus he would have had to produce cast iron references and a passport at least. The smarmy crumb was no fool. He wouldn't let five thousand pounds' worth of machinery be driven away without being certain he would get it back.

Vjoersterod. South African of Afrikaner stock.

Nothing like Fleet Street if one wanted information. The only trouble was, the man who might have heard of Vjoersterod worked on the racing page of a deadly rival to the *Blaze*. I turned into the first telephone box and rang his office. Sure, he agreed cautiously, he would meet me in the Devereux for a pint and a sandwich. He coped manfully with stifling any too open speculation about what I wanted. I smiled, and crossed the road to catch a bus. A case of who pumped who. He would be trying to find out what story I was working on, and Luke-John would be slightly displeased if he were successful and scooped the *Blaze*.

Luke-John and Derry were both among the crowd in the Devereux. Not so, Mike de Jong. I drank a half-pint while Luke-John asked what I planned to write for Sunday.

'An account of the Lamplighter, I suppose.'

'Derry can do that.'

I lowered my glass, shrugging. 'If you like.'

'Then you,' said Luke-John, 'can do another follow-up to the Tiddely Pom business. Whether he wins or loses, I mean. Give us a puff for getting him to the starting gate.'

'He isn't there yet.' I pointed out.

Luke-John sniffed impatiently. 'There hasn't been a vestige of trouble. No reaction at all. We've frightened them off, that's what's happened.'

I shook my head, wishing he had. Asked about the reports on Tiddely Pom and the Roncey children.

'All O.K.,' said Derry cheerfully. 'Everything going smoothly.'

Mike de Jong appeared in the doorway, a quick, dark, intense man with double strength glasses and a fringe of black beard outlining his jaw. Caution rolled over him like a sea mist when he saw who I was with, and most of the purposefulness drained out of his stride. It took too much manoeuvring to get Luke-John and Derry to go into the other bar to eat without me, and Luke-John left looking back over his shoulder with smouldering suspicion, wanting to know why.

Mike joined me, his sharp face alight with appreciation.

'Keeping secrets from the boss, eh?'

'Sometimes he's butter-fingered with other people's T.N.T.'

Mike laughed. The cogs whirred round in his high-speed brain. 'So what you want is private? Not for the *Blaze*?'

I dodged a direct answer. 'What I want is very simple. Just anything you may have heard about a fellow countryman of yours.'

'Who?' His accent was a carbon copy, clipped and flat.

'A man called Vjoersterod.'

There was a tiny pause while the name sank in, and then he choked on his beer. Recovered, and pretended someone had jogged his elbow. Made a playing-for-time fuss about brushing six scattered drops off his trouser leg. Finally he ran out of alibis and looked back at my face.

'Vjoersterod?' His pronunciation was subtly different from mine. The real thing.

'That's right,' I agreed.

'Yes ... well, Ty ... why do you ask me about him?'

'Just curiosity.'

He was silent for thirty seconds. Then he said carefully again, 'Why are you asking me about him?' Who pumped who.

'Oh come on,' I said in exasperation, 'What's the big mystery? All I want is a bit of gen on a harmless chap who goes racing occasionally...'

'*Harmless*. You must be mad.'

'Why?' I sounded innocently puzzled.

'Because he's ...' He hesitated, decided I wasn't on to a story, and turned thoroughly helpful. 'Look here, Ty, I'll give you a tip, free, gratis and for nothing. Just steer clear of anything to do with that man. He's poison.'

'In what way?'

'He's a bookmaker, back home. Very big business, with branches in all the big cities and a whole group of them round Johannesburg. Respectable enough on the surface. Thousands of perfectly ordinary people bet with him. But there have been some dreadful rumours...'

'About what?'

'Oh ... blackmail, extortion, general high powered thuggery. Believe me, he is not good news.'

'Then why don't the police...?' I suggested tentatively.

'Why don't they? Don't be so naïve, Ty. They can't find anyone to give evidence against him, of course.'

I sighed. 'He seemed so charming.'

Mike's mouth fell open and his expression became acutely anxious. 'You've *met* him?'

'Yeah.'

'Here ... in England?'

'Well, yes, of course.'

'Ty ... for God's sake ... keep away from him.'

'I will,' I said wih feeling. 'Thanks a lot, Mike. I'm truly grateful.'

'I'd hate anyone I liked to tangle with Vjoersterod,' he said, the genuine friendship standing out clear in his eyes, unexpectedly affecting. Then with a born newspaper man's instinct for the main chance, a look of intense curiosity took over.

'What did he want to talk about with you?' he asked.

'I really don't know,' I said, sounding puzzled.

'Is he going to get in touch with you again?'

'I don't know that, either.'

'Hm ... give me a ring if he does, and I'll tell you something else.'

'Tell me now.' I tried hard to make it casual.

He considered, shrugged, and friendship won again over journalism. 'All right. It's nothing much. Just that I too saw him here in England; must have been nine or ten months ago, back in the Spring.' He paused.

'In that case,' I said, 'why ever were you so horrified when I said I'd met him?'

'Because when I saw him he was in the buffet bar on a race train, talking to another press man. Bert Checkov.'

With an enormous effort, I kept my mildly puzzled face intact.

Mike went on without a blink. 'I warned Bert about him later, just like I have you. In here, actually. Bert was pretty drunk. He was always pretty drunk after that.'

'What did he say?' I asked.

'He said I was three months too late.'

Mike didn't know any more. Bert had clammed up after that one indiscretion and had refused to elaborate or explain. When he fell out of the window, Mike wondered. Violent and often unexplained deaths among people who had had dealings with Vjoersterod were not unknown, he said. When I said I had met Vjoersterod, it had shocked him. He was afraid for me. Afraid I could follow Bert down on to the pavement.

I put his mind at rest. After what he'd told me, I would be forewarned, I said.

'I wonder why he got his hooks into Bert . . .' Mike said, his eyes on the middle distance, all the cogs whirring.

'I've no idea,' I said, sighing, and distracted his attention on to another half-pint and a large ham sandwich. Luke-John's thin freckled face loomed over his shoulder, and he turned to him with a typical bounce, as if all his body were made of springs.

'So how's the Gospel Maker? What's cooking on the *Blaze*?'

Luke-John gave him a thin smile. He didn't care for his Fleet Street nickname; nor for puns in general. Nor, it seemed for Mike de Jong's puns in particular. Mike received the message clearly, sketched me a farewell, and drifted over to another group.

'What did he want?' Luke-John asked sharply.

'Nothing,' I said mildly. 'Just saying hello.'

Luke-John gave me a disillusioned look, but I knew very well that if I told him at that stage about Vjoersterod he would dig until he stumbled on the blackmail, dig again quite ruthlessly to find out how I could have been blackmailed, and then proceed to mastermind all subsequent inquiries with a stunning absence of discretion. Vjoersterod would hear his steam roller approach clean across the country. Luke-John was a brilliant Sports Editor. As a Field Marshal his casualty list would have been appalling.

He and Derry drank around to closing time at three, by which time the crowd had reduced to Sunday writers only. I declined their invitation to go back with them to the doldrums of the office, and on reflection telephoned to the only member of the racing authorities I knew well enough for the purpose.

Eric Youll at thirty-seven was the youngest and newest of the three stewards of the National Hunt Committee, the ruling body of Steeplechasing. In two years, by natural progression, he would be Senior Steward. After that, reduced to the ranks until re-elected for another three-year term. As a Steward he made sense because until recently he had himself ridden as an amateur, and knew at first hand all the problems and mechanics of racing. I had written him up in the *Blaze* a few times and we had been friendly acquaintances for years. Whether he either could or would help me now was nonetheless open to doubt.

I had a good deal of trouble getting through to him, as he was a junior sprig in one of the grander merchant banks. Secretaries with bored voices urged me to make an appointment.

'Right now,' I said, 'will do very well.'

After the initial shock the last voice conceded that right now Mr Youll could just fit me in. When I got there, Mr Youll was busily engaged in drinking a cup of tea and reading the *Sporting Life*. He put them both down without haste, stood up, and shook hands.

'This is unexpected,' he said. 'Come to borrow a million?'

'Tomorrow, maybe.'

He smiled, told his secretary on the intercom to bring me some tea, offered me a cigarette, and leaned back in his chair, his manner throughout one of indecision and uncertainty. He was wary of me and of the purpose of my visit. I saw that uneasy expression almost every day of my life: the screen my racing friends erected when they weren't sure what I was after, the barrier that kept their secrets from publication. I didn't mind that sort of withdrawal. Understood it. Sympathized. And never printed anything private, if I could help it. There was a very fine edge to be walked when ones friends were ones raw material.

'Off the record,' I assured him. 'Take three deep breaths and relax.'

He grinned and tension visibly left his body. 'How can I help you then?'

I waited until the tea had come and been drunk, and the latest racing news chewed over. Then, without making much of it, I asked him if he'd ever heard of a bookmaker called Vjoersterod.

His attention pin-pointed itself with a jerk.

'Is that what you've come to ask?'

'For openers.'

He drummed his fingers on the desk. 'Someone showed me your column last week and the week before ... Stay out of it, Ty.'

'If you racing bigwigs know what's going on and who is doing it, why don't you stop him?'

'How?'

The single bald word hung in the air, cooling. It told me a lot about the extent of their knowledge. They should have known how.

'Frankly,' I said at last, 'that's your job, not mine. You could of course ban all ante-post betting, which would knock the fiddle stone dead.'

'That would be highly unpopular with the Great British Public. Anyway your articles have hit the ante-post market badly enough as it is. One of the big firms was complaining to me bitterly about you a couple of hours ago. Their Lamplighter bets are down by more than twenty per cent.'

'Then why don't they do something about Charlie Boston?'

He blinked. 'Who?'

I took a quiet breath. 'Well, now ... just what do the Stewards know about Vjoersterod?'

'Who is Charlie Boston?'

'You first,' I said.

'Don't you trust me?' He looked hurt.

'No,' I said flatly. 'You first.'

He sighed resignedly and told me that all the Stewards knew about Vjoersterod was hearsay, and scanty at that. None of them had ever actually seen him, and wouldn't know him if they did. A member of the German horse racing authorities had sent them a private warning that Vjoersterod was suspected of stage managing a series of non-starting ante-post favourites in big races in Germany, and that they had heard rumours he was now beginning to operate in England. Pursuit had almost cornered him in Germany. He was now moving on. The British Stewards had noted the alarming proportion of nonstarters in the past months and were sure the German authorities were right, but although they had tried to find out the facts from various owners and trainers, they had been met with only a brick wall of silence everywhere.

'It's a year since Vjoersterod came here first,' I remarked. 'A year ago he bought out Charlie Boston's string of betting shops around Birmingham and started raking in the dough. He also found a way to force Bert Checkov to write articles which persuaded ante-post punters to believe they were on to a good thing. Vjoersterod chose a horse, Checkov wrote it up, Vjoersterod stopped it running, and Bingo, the deed was done.'

His face was a mixture of astonishment and satisfaction. 'Ty, are you sure of your facts?'

'Of course I am. If you ask me, both the bookmakers and the authorities have been dead slow on the trail'.

'And how long exactly have you been on it?'

I grinned, conceding the point. I said 'I met Vjoersterod yesterday. I referred to Charlie Boston being his partner and he told me he owned Charlie Boston. Vjoersterod wanted to know where Tiddely Pom was.'

He stared. 'Would you . . . um . . . well, if necessary, testify to that?'

'Certainly. But it would be only my word against his. No corroboration.'

'Better than anything we've had before.'

'There might be a quicker way to get results, though.'

'How?' he asked again.

'Find a way to shut Charlie Boston's shops, and you block off Vjoersterod's intakes. Without which there is no point in him waiting around to stop any favourites. If you can't get him convicted in the Courts, you might at least freeze him out, back to South Africa.'

There was another long pause during which he thought complicated thoughts. I waited, guessing what was in his mind. Eventually, he said it.

'How much do you want for your help?'

'An exclusive for the *Blaze*.'

'As if I couldn't guess . . .'

'It will do,' I conceded, 'if the *Blaze* can truthfully claim to have made the ante-post market safe for punters to play in. No details. Just a few hints that but for the libel laws, all would and could be revealed.'

'Why ever do you waste your time with that dreadful rag?' he exclaimed in exasperation.

'Good pay,' I said.' It's a good paper to work for. And it suits me.'

'I'll promise you one thing,' he said smiling. 'If through you personally we get rid of Vjoersterod, I'll take it regularly.'

From Eric Youll's bank, I went home. If the youngest Steward did his stuff, Vjoersterod's goose was on its way to the oven and would soon be cooked. He might of course one day read the *Blaze* and send someone to carve up the chef. It didn't trouble me much. I didn't believe it would happen.

Elizabeth had had Mrs Woodward put her favourite rose pink, white-embroidered sheets on the bed. I looked at her searchingly. Her hair had been done with particular care. Her makeup was flawless.

'You look pretty,' I said tentatively.

Her expression was a mixture of relief and misery. I understood with a sudden rocking wince what had led her to such scenery painting: the increased fear that if she were bitchy I would leave her. No matter if I'd earned and deserved the rough side of her tongue; I had to be placated at all costs, to be held by the best she could do to appear attractive, to be obliquely invited, cajoled, entreated to stay.

'Did you have a good day?' Her voice sounded high and near to cracking point.

'Quite good ... how about a drink?'

She shook her head, but I poured her one all the same, and fixed it in the clip.

'I've asked Mrs Woodward to find someone to come and sit with me in the evenings,' she said. 'So that you can go out more.'

'I don't want to go out more,' I protested.

'You must do.'

'Well, I don't.' I sat down in the armchair and took a hefty mouthful of nearly neat whisky. At best, I thought, in an unbearable situation alcohol offered postponement. At worst, aggravation. And anyway it was too damned expensive, nowadays, to get drunk.

Elizabeth didn't answer. When I looked at her, I saw she was quietly crying again. The tears rolled down past her ears and into her hair. I took a tissue out of the box and dried them. Had she but known it, they were harder for me to bear than any amount of fury.

'I'm getting old,' she said. 'And you still look so young. You look ... strong ... and dark ... and young.'

'And you look pale and pretty and about fifteen. So stop fretting.'

'How old is ... that girl?'

'You said you didn't want to hear about her.'

'I suppose I don't, really.'

'Forget her,' I said. 'She is of no importance. She means nothing to me. Nothing at all.' I sounded convincing, even to myself. I wished it were true. In spite of the scope of her betrayal, in a weak inner recess I ached to be able to sleep with her again, I sat with the whisky glass in my hand and thought about her on the white rug and in her own bed and in the hotel, and suffered dismally from the prospect of the arid future.

After a while I pushed myself wearily to my feet and went to fix the supper. Fish again. Mean little bits of frozen plaice. I cooked and ate them with aversion and fed Elizabeth when her wrist tired on the gadget. All evening she kept up the pathetic attempt to be nice to me, thanking me exaggeratedly for every tiny service, apologizing for needing me to do things for her which we had both for years taken for granted, trying hard to keep the anxiety, the embarrassment and the unhappiness out of her eyes and voice, and nowhere near succeeding. She couldn't have punished me more if she had tried.

Late that evening Tiddely Pom developed violent colic.

Norton Fox couldn't get hold of Luke-John or Derry, who had both long gone home. The *Blaze* never divulged home addresses, however urgent the inquiry. Norton didn't know my telephone number either; didn't know anyone who did.

In a state of strong anxiety, and on his vet's advice, he rang up Victor Roncey and told him where his horse was, and what they were doing to save its life.

Chapter Twelve

I heard about it in the morning. Roncey telephoned at ten thirty, when I was sitting in the writing room looking vacantly at the walls and trying to drum up some preliminary gems for my column on Sunday. Mrs Woodward had gone out to the launderette, and Elizabeth called me to the telephone with two rings on the bell over my head: two rings for come at once but not an emergency. Three rings for 999. Four for panic.

Roncey had calmed down from the four ring stage he had clearly been in the night before. He was calling, he said, from Norton Fox's house, where he had driven at once after being given the news. I sorted out that he had arrived at 2 a.m. to find that the vet had got Tiddely Pom over the worst, with the stoppage in the horse's gut untangling into normal function. Norton Fox had given Roncey a bed for the rest of the night, and he had just come in from seeing Tiddely Pom walk and trot out at morning exercise. The horse was showing surprisingly few ill effects from his rocky experience, and it was quite likely he would be fit enough to run in the Lamplighter on Saturday.

I listened to his long, brisk detailed saga with uncomfortable alarm. There were still two whole days before the race. Now that Roncey knew where he was, Tiddely Pom's safety was halved. When he had come to the end of the tale I asked him whether anyone had tried to find out from him at home where his horse had gone.

'Of course they did,' he said. 'Exactly as you said. Several other newspapers wanted to know. Most of them telephoned. Three or four actually turned up at the farm, and I know they asked Peter and Pat as well as me. Some of their questions were decidedly tricky. I thought at the time you'd been quite right, we might have let it slip if we'd known ourselves.'

'When did these people come to the farm? What did they look like?'

'They didn't look like anything special. Just nondescript. One of them was from the *Evening Peal*, I remember. All the inquiries were on Sunday and Monday, just after your article came out.'

'No one turned up in a Rolls?' I asked.

He laughed shortly. 'They did not.'

'Were any of your visitors tallish, thickish, blondish, with a faintly yellow skin and a slightly foreign accent?'

'None that I saw were like that. One or two saw only the boys, because they called while I was in Chelmsford. You could ask them, if you like.'

'Maybe I will,' I agreed. 'No one tried any threats?'

'No, I told your Sports Editor that. No one has tried any pressure of any sort. To my mind, all your elaborate precautions have been a waste of time. And now that I know where Tiddely Pom is, you may as well tell me where my family is too...'

'I'll think about it,' I said. 'Would you ask Norton Fox if I could have a word with him?'

He fetched Norton, who apologized for bursting open the secrecy, but said he didn't like the responsibility of keeping quiet when the horse was so ill.

'Of course not. It can't be helped,' I said. 'As long as it goes no further than Roncey himself it may not be too bad, though I'd prefer...'

'His sons knew, of course,' Norton interrupted. 'Though I don't suppose that matters.'

'*What?*' I said.

'Roncey told one of his sons where he was. He telephoned him just now. He explained to me that he couldn't remember your telephone number, but he'd got it written down somewhere at home, from having rung you up before sometime. So he rang his son ... Pat, I think he said ... and his son found it for him. I think he, the son, asked Roncey where he was calling from, because Roncey said that as everyone had stopped inquiring about where the horse was, he didn't see any harm in his son knowing, so he told him.'

'Damn it,' I said. 'The man's a fool.'

'He might be right.'

'And he might be wrong,' I said bitterly. 'Look, Norton, I suppose there was no question of Tiddely Pom's colic being a misjudged case of poisoning?'

'For God's sake Ty ... no. It was straighforward colic. How on earth could he have been poisoned? For a start, no one knew then who he was.'

'And now?' I asked. 'How many of your lads know now that he is Tiddely Pom?'

There was a brief, supercharged silence.

'All of them,' I said flatly.

'Some of them knew Roncey by sight,' he explained. 'And they'd all read the *Blaze*. So they put two and two together.'

One of them would soon realize he could earn a fiver by ringing up a rival newspaper. Tiddely Pom's whereabouts would be as secret as the Albert Memorial. Tiddely Pom, at that moment, was a certain nonstarter for the Lamplighter Gold cup.

Even if Victor Roncey thought that the opposition had backed out of the project, I was certain they hadn't. In a man like Vjoersterod, pride would always conquer discretion. He wouldn't command the same respect in international criminal circles if he turned out and ran just because of a few words in the *Blaze*. He wouldn't, therefore, do it.

At the four day declaration stage, on the Tuesday, Roncey had confirmed with Weatherbys that his horse would be a definite runner. If he now withdrew him, as he could reasonably do because of the colic, he would forfeit his entry fee, a matter of fifty pounds. If he left his horse at Norton's still intending to run, he would forfeit a great deal more.

Because I was certain that if Tiddely Pom stayed where he was, he would be lame, blind, doped or dead by Saturday morning.

Norton listened in silence while I outlined these facts of life.

'Ty, don't you think you are possibly exaggerating ...?'

'Well,' I said with a mildness I didn't feel, 'how many times will you need to have Brevity – or any other of your horses – taken out of the Champion Hurdle at the last moment without any explanation, before you see any need to do something constructive in opposition?'

There was a short pause. 'Yes,' he said. 'You have a point.'

'If you will lend me your horsebox, I'll take Tiddely Pom off somewhere else.'

'Where?'

'Somewhere safe,' I said noncommittally. 'How about it?'

'Oh, all right,' he sighed. 'Anything for a quiet life.'

'I'll come as soon as I can.'

'I'll repel boarders until you do.' The flippancy in his voice told me how little he believed in any threat to the horse. I felt a great urge to leave them to it, to let Roncey stew in his own indiscretion, to let Vjoersterod interfere with the horse and stop it running, just to prove I was right. Very childish urge indeed. It didn't last long, because in my way I was as stubborn as Vjoersterod. I wasn't going to turn and run from him either, if I could help it.

When I put the telephone receiver back in its special cradle, Elizabeth was looking worried with a more normal form of anxiety.

'That Tiddely Pom,' I said lightly, 'is more trouble than a bus load of eleven-year-old boys. As I expect you gathered, I'll have to go and shift him off somewhere else.'

'Couldn't someone else do it?'

I shook my head. 'Better be me.'

Mrs Woodward was still out. I filled in the time until her return by ringing up Luke-John and giving him the news that the best laid plan had gone astray.

'Where are you taking the horse, then?'

'I'll let you know when I get there.'

'Are you sure it's necessary . . . ?' he began.

'Are you,' I interrupted, 'sure the *Blaze* can afford to take any risk, after boasting about keeping the horse safe?'

'Hm.' He sighed. 'Get on with it, then.'

When Mrs Woodward came back I took the van and drove to Berkshire. With me went Elizabeth's best effort at a fond wifely farewell. She had even offered her mouth for a kiss, which she did very rarely, as mouth to mouth kissing interfered with her frail breathing arrangements and gave her a feeling of suffocation. She liked to be kissed on the cheek or forehead, and never too often.

I spent most of the journey worrying whether I should not after all have allowed myself to be blackmailed: whether any stand against pressure was luxury when compared with the damage I'd done to Elizabeth's weak hold on happiness. After all the shielding, which had improved her physical condition, I'd laid into her with a bulldozer. Selfishly. Just to save myself from a particularly odious form of tyranny. If she lost weight or fretted to breakdown point it would be directly my fault; and either or both seemed possible.

A hundred and fifty guineas, plus expenses, less tax. A study in depth. *Tally* had offered me the deeps. And in I'd jumped.

On the outskirts of London I stopped to make a long and involved telephone call, arranging a destination and care for Tiddely Pom. Norton Fox and Victor Roncey were eating lunch when I arrived at the stables, and I found it impossible to instil into either of them enough of a feeling for urgency to get them to leave their casseroled beef.

'Sit down and have some,' Norton said airily.

'I want to be on my way.'

They didn't approve of my impatience and proceeded to gooseberry crumble and biscuits and cheese. It was two o'clock before they agreed to amble out into the yard and see to the shifting of Tiddely Pom.

Norton had at least had his horsebox made ready. It stood in the centre of the yard with the ramp down. As public an exit as possible. I sighed resignedly. The horsebox driver didn't like handing over to a stranger and gave me some anxious instructions about the idiosyncratic gear change.

Sandy Willis led Tiddely Pom across the yard, up the ramp, and into the centre stall of the three-stall box. The horse looked worse than ever, no doubt because of the colic. I couldn't see him ever winning any Lamplighter Gold Cup. Making sure he ran in it seemed a gloomy waste of time. Just as well, I reflected, that it wasn't to Tiddely Pom himself that I was committed, but to the principle that if Roncey wanted to run Tiddely Pom, he should. Along the lines of 'I disagree that your horse has the slightest chance, but I'll defend to the death your right to prove it.'

Sandy Willis finished tying the horse into his stall and took over where the box driver left off. Her instructions on how Tiddely Pom was to be managed were detailed and anxious. In her few days with the horse she had already identified herself with its well-being. As Norton had said, she was one of the best of his lads. I wished I could take her too, but it was useless expecting Norton to let her go, when she also looked after Zig Zag.

She said, 'He will be having proper care, won't he?'

'The best,' I assured her.

'Tell them not to forget his eggs and beer.'

'Right.'

'And he hates having his ears messed about with.'

'Right.'

She gave me a long searching look, a half smile, and a reluctant farewell. Victor Roncey strode briskly across to me and unburdened himself along similar lines.

'I want to insist that you tell me where you are taking him.'

'He will be safe.'

'Where?'

'Mr Roncey, if you know where, he is only half as safe. We've been through all this before...'

He pondered, his glance darting about restlessly, his eyes not meeting mine. 'Oh very well,' he said finally, with impatience. 'But it will be up to you to make sure he gets to Heathbury Park in good time on Saturday.'

'The *Blaze* will arrange that,' I agreed. 'The Lamplighter is at three. Tiddely Pom will reach the racecorse stables by noon, without fail.'

'I'll be there,' he said. 'Waiting.'

I nodded. Norton joined us, and the two of them discussed this arrangement while I shut up the ramp with the help of the hovering box driver.

'What time do you get Zig Zag to Heathbury?' I asked Norton, pausing before I climbed into the cab.

'Mid-day,' he said. 'It's only thirty-two miles ... He'll be setting off at about eleven.'

I climbed into the driving seat and looked out of the window. The two men looked back, Roncey worried, Norton not. To Norton I said, 'I'll see you this evening, when I bring the horsebox back.' To Roncey, 'Don't worry, he'll be quite safe. I'll see you on Saturday.

Ring the *Blaze*, as before, if you'd like to be reassured tonight and tomorrow.'

I shut the window, sorted out the eccentric gears, and drove Tiddely Pom gently out of the yard and up the lane to the village. An hour later than I intended, I thought in disgust. Another hour for Mrs Woodward. My mind shied away from the picture of Elizabeth waiting for me to come back. Nothing would be better. Nothing would be better for a long time to come. I felt the first stirrings of resentment against Elizabeth and at least had the sense to realize that my mind was playing me a common psychological trick. The guilty couldn't stand the destruction of their self-esteem involved in having to admit they were wrong, and wriggled out of their shame by transferring it into resentment against the people who had made them feel it. I resented Elizabeth because I had wronged her. Of all ridiculous injustices. And of all ridiculous injustices, one of the most universal.

I manoeuvred the heavy horsebox carefully through the small vilage and set off north eastwards on the road over the Downs, retracing the way I had come from London. Wide rolling hills with no trees except a few low bushes leaning sideways away from the prevailing wind. No houses. A string of pylons. Black furrows in a mile of plough. A bleak early December sky, a high sheet of steel grey cloud. Cold, dull, mood-matching landscape.

There was very little traffic on the unfenced road, which served only Norton's village and two others beyond. A blue-grey Cortina appeared on the brow of the next hill, coming towards me, travelling fast. I pulled over to give him room, and he rocked past at a stupid speed for the space available.

My attention was so involved with Elizabeth that it was several seconds before the calamity got through. With a shattering jolt the casually noticed face of the Cortina's driver kicked my memory to life. It belonged to one of Charlie Boston's boys from the train. The big one. With the brass knuckles.

December couldn't stop the prickly sweat which broke out on my skin. I put my foot on the accelerator and felt Tiddely Pom's weight lurch behind me from the sudden spurt. All I could hope for was that the big man had been too occupied judging the width of his car to look up and see me.

He had, of course, had a passenger.

I looked in the driving mirror. The Cortina had gone out of sight over the hill. Charlie Boston's boys hurrying towards Norton Fox's village was no mild coincidence; but Tiddely Pom's whereabouts must have been transmitted with very little delay for them to be here already, especially if they had had to come from Birmingham. Just who, I wondered grimly, had told who where Tiddely Pom was to be found. Not that it mattered much at the moment. All that mattered was to get him lost again.

I checked with the driving mirror. No Cortina. The horsebox was pushing sixty-five on a road wiser for forty. Tiddely Pom's hooves clattered inside his stall. He didn't like the swaying. He would have to put up with it until I got him clear of the Downs road, which was far too empty and far too visible from too many miles around.

When I next looked in the mirror there was a pale speck on the horizon two hills behind. It might not be them, I thought. I looked again. It was them. I swore bitterly. The speedometer needle crept to sixty-eight. That was the lot. My foot was down on the floor boards. And they were gaining. Easily.

There was no town close enough to get lost in, and once on my tail they could stay there all day, waiting to find out where I took Tiddely Pom. Even in a car it would have been difficult to lose them: in a lumbering horsebox, impossible. Urgent appraisal of a depressing situation came up with only a hope that Charlie Boston's boys would again be propelled by more aggression than sense.

They were. They came up fast behind me, leaning on the horn. Maybe they thought I hadn't had time to see *them* as they went past me the other way, and wouldn't know who wanted to pass.

If they wanted to pass, they didn't want to follow. I shut my teeth. If they wanted to pass, it was now, it was here, that they meant to make certain that Tiddely Pom didn't run in the Lamplighter. What they intended to do about me was a matter which sent my mending ribs into a tizzy. I swallowed. I didn't want another hammering like the last time, ahd this time they might not be so careful about what they did or didn't rupture.

I held the horsebox in the centre of the road so that there wasn't room enough for their Cortina to get by. They still went on blowing the horn. Tiddely Pom, kicked his stall. I took my foot some way off the accelerator and slowed the proceedings down to a more manageable forty-five. They would guess I knew who they were. I didn't see that it gave them any advantage.

A hay lorry appeared round a hill ahead with its load overhanging the centre of the road. Instinctively I slowed still further, and began to pull over. The Cortina's nose showed sharply in the wing mirror, already up by my rear axle. I swung the horsebox back into the centre of the road, which raised flashing headlights from the driver of the advancing hay lorry. When I was far too close to a radiator to radiator confrontation he started blowing his horn furiously as well. I swung back to my side of the road when he was almost stationary from standing rigidly on his brakes, and glimpsed a furious face and a shaking fist as I swerved past. Inches to spare. Inches were enough.

The Cortina tried to get past in the short second before the horsebox was re-established on the crown of the road. There was a bump this time, as I cut across its bows. It dropped back ten feet, and stayed there. It would only stay there, I thought despairingly, until Charlie Boston's boys had got what they came for.

Less than a mile ahead lay my likely Waterloo, in the shape of a crossroads. A halt sign. It was I who would have to halt. Either that or risk hitting a car speeding legitimately along the major road, risk killing some innocent motorist, or his wife, or his child ... Yet if I stopped, the Cortina with its faster acceleration would pass me when I moved off again, whether I turned right, as I had intended to, or left, back to London, or went straight on, to heaven knew where.

There wouldn't be anyone at the crossroads to give me any help. No police car sitting there waiting for custom. No A.A. man having a smoke. No life-saving bystander of any sort. No troop of United States cavalry to gallop up in the nick of time.

I changed down into second to climb a steepish hill and forgot Norton's box driver's instructions. For a frightening moment the gears refused to mesh and the horsebox's weight dragged it almost to a standstill. Then the cogs slid together, and with a regrettable jolt we started off again. Behind me, Charlie Boston's boys still wasted their energy and wore out their battery by almost non-stop blasts on their horn.

The horsebox trundled to the top of the hill, and there already, four hundred yards down the other side, was the crossroads.

I stamped on the accelerator. The horsebox leaped forward. Charlie Boston's boys had time to take in the scene below, and to realize that I must be meaning not to halt at the sign. In the wing mirror, I watched him accelerate to keep up, closing enough to stick to me whatever I did at the crossroads.

Two hundred yards before I got there, I stood on the brake pedal as if the road ended in an abyss ten yards ahead. The reaction was more than I'd bargained for. The horsebox shuddered and rocked and began to spin. Its rear slewed across the road, hit the verge, rocked again. I feared the whole high-topped structure would overturn. Instead, there was a thudding, crunching, anchoring crash as the Cortina bounced on and off at the rear.

The horsebox screeched and slid to a juddering stop. Upright. Facing the right way.

I hauled on the hand brake and was out of the cab on the road before the glass from the Cortina had stopped tinkling on to the tarmac.

The grey-blue car had gone over on to its side and was showing its guts to the wind. It lay a good twenty yards behind the horsebox, and from the dented look of the roof it had rolled completely over before stopping. I walked back towards it, wishing I had a weapon of some sort, and fighting an inclination just to drive off and leave without looking to see what had happened to the occupants.

There was only one of them in the car. The big one; the driver. Very much alive, murderously angry, and in considerable pain from having his right ankle trapped and broken among the pedals. I turned my back on him and ignored his all too audible demands for assistance. Revenge, I assessed, would overcome all else if I once got within reach of his hands.

The second Boston boy had been flung out by the crash. I found him on the grass verge, unconscious and lying on his face. With anxiety I felt for his pulse, but he too was alive. With extreme relief I went back to the horsebox, opened the side door, and climbed in to take a look at Tiddely Pom. He calmly swivelled a disapproving eye in my direction and began to evacuate his bowels.

'Nothing much wrong with you, mate,' I said aloud. My voice came out squeaky with tension. I wiped my hand round my neck tried to grin, felt both like copying Tiddely Pom's present action and being sick.

The horse really did not seem any the worse for his highly unorthodox journey. I took several deep breaths, patted his rump, and jumped down again into the road. Inspection of the damage at the back of the horsebox revealed a smashed rear light and a dent in the sturdy off rear wing no larger than a soup plate. I hoped that Luke-John would agree to the *Blaze* paying for the repairs. Charlie Boston wouldn't want to.

His unconscious boy was beginning to stir. I watched him sit up, put his hands to his head, begin to remember what had happened. I listened to his big colleague still shouting furiously from inside the car. Then with deliberate nonhaste I climbed back into the cab of the horsebox, started the engine, and drove carefully away.

I had never intended to go far. I took Tiddely Pom to the safest place I could think of; the racecourse stables at Heathbury Park. There he would be surrounded by a high wall and guarded by a security patrol at night. Everyone entering racecourse stables had to show a pass: even owners were not allowed in unless accompanied by their trainer.

Willy Ondroy, consulted on the telephone, had agreed to take in Tiddely Pom, and to keep his identity a secret. The stables would in any case be open from mid-day and the guards would be on duty from then on: any time after that, he said. Tiddely Pom would be just one of a number of horses arriving for the following day's racing. Horses which came from more than a hundred miles away normally travelled the day before their race and stayed overnight in the racecourse stables. A distant stable running one horse on Friday and another on Saturday would send them both down on Thursday and leave them both at the racecourse stables for two nights, or possibly even three. Tiddely Pom's two nights' stay would be unremarkable and inconspicuous. The only oddity about him was that he had no lad to look after him, an awkward detail to which Willy Ondroy had promised to find a solution.

He was looking out for me and came across the grass outside the stable block to forestall me from climbing down from the cab. Instead, he opened the door on the passenger side, and joined me.

'Too many of these lads know you by sight,' he said, waving an arm to where two other horseboxes were unloading. 'If they see you, they will know you would not have brought any other horse but Tiddely Pom. And as I understand it, you don't want to land us with the security headache of a bunch of crooks trying to injure him. Right?'

'Right,' I agreed thankfully.

'Drive down this road, then. First left. In through the white gate posts, fork left, park outside the rear door of my house. Right?'

'Right,' I said again, and followed his instructions, thankful for his quick grasp of essentials and his jet formation pilot's clarity of decision.

'I've had a word with the racecourse manager,' he said. 'The stables and security are his pigeon really. Had to enlist his aid. Hope you don't mind. He's a very sound fellow, very sound indeed. He's fixing up a lad to look after Tiddely Pom. Without telling him what the horse is, naturally.'

'That's good,' I said with relief.

I stopped the horsebox and we both disembarked. The horse, Willy Ondroy said, could safely stay were he was until the racecourse manager came over for him. Meanwhile, would I care for some tea? He looked at his watch. Three fifty. He hesitated. Or a whisky, he added.

'Why a whisky?' I asked.

'I don't know. I suppose because you look as though you need it.'

'You may be right,' I said, dredging up a smile. He looked at me assessingly, but how could I tell him that I'd just risked killing two men to bring Tiddely Pom safe and unfollowed to his door. That I had been extremely lucky to get away with merely stopping them. That only by dishing out such violence had I avoided a second beating of proportions I couldn't contemplate. It wasn't really surprising that I looked as if I needed a whisky. I did. It tasted fine.

Chapter Thirteen

Norton Fox was less than pleased when I got back.

He heard me rumble into the yard and came out of his house to meet me. It was by then full dark, but there were several external lights on, and more light flooded out of open stable doors as the lads bustled around with the evening chores. I parked, climbed stifffly down from the cab and looked at my watch. Five-fifty. I'd spent two hours on a roundabout return journey to fool the box driver over the distance I'd taken Tiddely Pom. Heathbury Park and back was probably the driver's most beaten track: he would know the mileage to a hundred yards, recognize it instantly if he saw it on the clock, know for a certainty where the horse was, and make my entire afternoon a waste of time.

'You're in trouble, Ty,' Norton said, reaching me and frowning. 'What in God's name were you thinking of? First the man delivering my hay gets here in a towering rage and says my horsebox drove straight at him with some maniac at the wheel and that there'd be an accident if he was any judge, and the next thing is we hear there has been an accident over by Long Barrow crossroads involving a horsebox and I've had the police here making inquiries ...'

'Yes.' I agreed. 'I'm very sorry, Norton. Your horsebox has a dent in it, and a broken rear light. I'll apologize to the hay lorry driver. And I guess I'll have to talk to the police.'

Dangerous driving. Putting it mildly. Very difficult to prove it was a case of self-preservation.

Norton looked near to explosion. 'What on earth were you *doing*?'

'Playing cowboys and Indians,' I said tiredly. 'The Indians bit the dust.'

He was not amused. His secretary came out to tell him he was wanted on the telephone, and I waited by the horsebox until he came back, gloomily trying to remember the distinction between careless, reckless and dangerous, and the various penalties attached. Failing to stop. Failing to report an accident. How much for those?

Norton came back less angry than he went. 'That was the police,' he said abruptly. 'They still want to see you. However it seems the two men involved in the crash have vanished from the casualty department in the hospital and the police have discovered that the Cortina was stolen. They are less inclined to think that the accident was your fault, in spite of what the hay lorry driver told them.'

'The men in the Cortina were after Tiddely Pom,' I said flatly, 'And they damn nearly got him. Maybe you could tell Victor Roncey that there is some point to our precautions, after all.'

'He's gone home,' he said blankly. I began to walk across the dark stable yard to where I'd left my van, and he followed me, giving me directions about how to find the police station.

I stopped him. 'I'm not going there. The police can come to me. Preferably on Monday. You tell them that.'

'Why on Monday?' He looked bewildered. 'Why not now?'

'Because,' I spelled it out, 'I can tell them roughly where to find those men in the Cortina and explain what they were up to. But I don't want the police issuing any warrants before Monday, otherwise the whole affair will be sub judice and I won't be able to get a squeak into the *Blaze*. After all this trouble, we've earned our story for Sunday.'

'You take my breath away,' he said sounding as if I had. 'And the police won't like it.'

'For God's sake, don't tell them,' I said in exasperation. 'That was for your ears only. If and when they ask you where I am, simply say I will be getting in touch with them, that you don't know where I live, and that they could reach me through the *Blaze*, if they want me.'

'Very well,' he agreed doubtfully. 'If you're sure. But it sounds to me as though you're landing yourself in serious trouble. I wouldn't have thought Tiddely Pom was worth it.'

'Tiddely Pom. Brevity, Polyxenes, and all the rest . . . individually none of them was worth the trouble. That's precisely why the racket goes on.'

His disapproving frown lightened into a half-smile. 'You'll be telling me next that the *Blaze* is more interested in justice than sensationalism.'

'It says so. Often,' I agreed sardonically.

'Huh,' said Norton. 'You can't believe everything you read in the papers.'

I drove home slowly, tired and depressed. Other times, trouble has been a yeast lightening the daily bread. A positive plus factor. Something I needed. But other times, trouble hadn't bitterly invaded my marriage or earned me such a savage physical attack.

This time, although I was fairly confident that Tiddely Pom would start in his race, the successful uncovering and extermination of a racing scandal was bringing me none of the usual upsurging satisfaction. This time, dust and ashes. This time, present grief and grey future.

I stopped on the way and rang the *Blaze*. Luke-John had left for the day. I got him at home.

'Tiddely Pom is in the racecourse stables at Heathbury,' I said. 'Guarded by an ex-policeman and a large Alsatian. The Clerk of the Course and the racecourse manager both know who he is, but no one else does. O.K.?'

'Very, I should think.' He sounded moderately pleased, but no more. 'We can take it as certain now that Tiddely Pom will start in the Lamplighter. It's made a good story, Ty, but I'm afraid we exaggerated the danger.'

I disillusioned him. 'Charlie Boston's boys were three miles from Norton Fox's stable by two thirty this afternoon.'

'Christ,' he said. 'So it's really true ...'

'You've looked at it so far as a stunt for the *Blaze*.'

'Well ...'

'Well, so it it,' I agreed. 'Anyway, Charlie Boston's boys had a slight accident with their car, and they are now back to square one as they don't know where I took Tiddely Pom.'

'What sort of accident?'

'They ran into the back of the horsebox. Careless of them. I put the brakes on rather hard, and they were following a little too close.'

A shocked silence. Then he said, 'Were they killed?'

'No. Hardly bent.' I gave him an outline of the afternoon's events. Luke-John's reaction was typical and expected, and the enthusiasm was alive again in his voice.

'Keep away from the police until Sunday.'

'Sure thing.'

'This is great, Ty.'

'Yeah.' I said.

'Knock out a preliminary version tonight and bring it in with you in the morning,' he said. 'Then we can discuss it tomorrow, and you can phone in the final touches from Heathbury after the Lamplighter on Saturday.'

'All right.'

'Oh, and give Roncey a ring, would you, and tell him the horse is only safe thanks to the *Blaze*.'

'Yes,' I said. 'Maybe I will.'

I put down the receiver and felt like leaving Roncey severely alone.

I was tired and I wanted to go home. And when I got home, I thought drearily, there would be no let off, only another dose of self hate and remorse.

Roncey answered the telephone at the first ring and needed no telling. Norton Fox had already been through.

'Tiddely Pom is safe and well looked after,' I assured him.

'I owe you an apology,' he said abruptly.

'Be my guest,' I said.

'Look here, there's something worrying me. Worrying me badly.' He paused, swallowing a great deal of pride. 'Do you ... I mean, have you any idea ... how those men appeared so quickly on the scene?'

'The same idea as you.' I agreed. 'Your son, Pat.'

'I'll break his neck,' he said, with real and unfatherly viciousness.

'If you've any sense, you'll let him ride your horses in all their races, not just the unimportant ones.'

'What are you talking about?'

'About Pat's outsize sense of grievance. You put up anyone except him, and he resents it.'

'He's not good enough,' he protested.

'And how will he ever be, if you don't give him the experience? Nothing teaches a jockey faster than riding a good horse in a good race.'

'He might lose,' he said pugnaciously.

'He might win. When did you ever give him the chance?'

'But to give away the secret of Tiddely Pom's whereabouts ... what would he expect to gain?'

'He was getting his own back, that's all.'

'*All!*'

'There's no harm done.'

'I hate him.'

'Then send him to another stable. Give him an allowance to live on and let him see if he's going to ride well enough to turn professional. That's what he wants. If you stamp on people's ambitions too hard, it's not frantically astonishing if they bite back.'

'It's a son's duty to work for his father. Especially a farmer's son.'

I sighed. He was half a century out of date and no amount of telling from me was going to change him. I said I'd see him on Sunday, and disconnected.

Like his father, I took no pleasure at all in Pat Roncey's vengeful disloyalty. Understand, maybe. Admire, far from it.

One of the men who came to inquire at Roncey's farm must have sensed Pat's obvious disgruntlement and have given him a telephone number to ring if he ever found out where Tiddely Pom had gone, and wanted to revenge himself on his father. One might give Pat the benefit of enough doubt to suppose that he'd thought he was only telling a rival newspaperman to the *Blaze*: but even so he must have known that a rival paper would spread the information to every corner of the country. To the ears which waited to hear. Exactly the same in the end. But because of the speed with which Charlie Boston's boys had reached Norton Fox's village, it must have been Raincoat or the chauffeur, or even Vjoersterod himself who had talked to Pat at the farm.

It had to be Pat. Norton Fox's stable lads might have passed the word on to newspapers, but they couldn't have told Vjoersterod or Charlie Boston because they didn't know they wanted to know, and probably didn't even know they existed.

I drove on, back to London. Parked the van in the garage downstairs. Locked up. Walked slowly and unenthusiastically up to the flat.

'Hi,' said Elizabeth brightly.

'Hi yourself.' I kissed her cheek.

It must have looked, to Mrs Woodward, a normal greeting. Only the pain we could read in each other's eyes said it wasn't.

Mrs Woodward put on her dark blue coat and checked the time again to make sure it was ten to, not ten after. She'd had three hours extra, but she wanted more. I wondered fleetingly if I could charge her overtime to the *Blaze*.

'We've had our meal,' Mrs woodward said. 'I've left yours ready to warm up. Just pop it in the oven, Mr Tyrone.'

'Thanks.'

''Night, then, luv,' she called to Elizabeth.

''Night.'

I opened the door for her and she nodded briskly, smiled, and said she'd be there on the dot in the morning. I thanked her appreciatively. She would indeed be there on the dot. Kind, reliable, necessary Mrs Woodward. I hoped the *Tally* cheque wouldn't be too long coming.

Beyond that first greeting Elizabeth and I could find little to say to each other. The most ordinary inquiries and remarks seemed horribly brittle, like a thin sheet of glass over a pit.

It was a relief to both of us when the door bell rang.

'Mrs Woodward must have forgotten something,' I said. It was barely ten minutes since she had left.

'I expect so,' Elizabeth agreed.

I opened the door without a speck of intuition. It swung inward with a rush, weighted and pushed by a heavy man in black. He stabbed a solid leather gloved fist into my diaphragm and when my head came forward chopped down with something hard on the back of my neck.

On my knees, coughing for breath, I watched Vjoersterod appear in the doorway, take in the scene, and walk past me into the room. A black-booted foot kicked the door shut behind him. There was a soft whistling swish in the air and another terrible thump high up between my shoulder blades. Elizabeth cried out. I staggered to my feet and tried to move in her direction. The heavy man in black, Ross, the chauffeur, slid his arm under mine and twisted and locked my shoulder.

'Sit down, Mr Tyrone,' Vjoersterod said calmly. 'Sit there.' He pointed to the tapestry-covered stool Mrs Woodward liked to knit on as there were no arms or back to get in the way of her busy elbows.

'Ty,' Elizabeth's voice rose high with fear. 'What's happening?'

I didn't answer. I felt stupid and sunk. I sat down on the stool when Ross released my arm and tried to work some control into the way I looked at Vjoersterod.

He was standing near Elizabeth's head, watching me with swelling satisfaction.

'So now we know just where we are, Mr Tyrone. Did you really have the conceit to think you could defy me and get away with it? No one does, Mr Tyrone. No one ever does.'

I didn't answer. Ross stood beside me, a pace to the rear. In his right hand he gently swung the thing he had hit me with, a short elongated pear-shaped truncheon. Its weight and crushing power made a joke of Charlie Boston's boy's knuckledusters. I refrained from rubbing the aching places below my neck.

'Mr Tyrone,' Vjoersterod said conversationally, 'Where is Tiddely Pom?'

When I still didn't answer immediately he half turned, looked down, and carefully put the toe of his shoe under the switch of the electric point. From there the cable led directly to Elizabeth's breathing pump. Elizabeth turned her head to follow my eyes and saw what he was doing.

'No,' she said. It was high pitched, terrified. Vjoersterod smiled.

'Tiddely Pom?' he said to me.

'He's in the racecourse stables at Heathbury Park.'

'Ah.' He took his foot away, put it down on the floor. 'You see how simple it is? It's always a matter of finding the right lever. Of applying the right pressure. No horse, I find, is ever worth a really serious danger to a loved one.'

I said nothing. He was right.

'Check it,' Ross said from behind me.

Vjoersterod's eyes narrowed. 'He couldn't risk a lie.'

'He wouldn't be blackmailed. He was out to get you, and no messing. Check it.' There was advice in Ross's manner, not authority. More than a chauffeur. Less than an equal.

Vjoersterod shrugged but stretched out a hand and picked up the receiver. Telephone inquiries. Heathbury Park racecourse. The Clerk of the Course's house? that would do very well.

Willie Ondroy himself answered. Vjoersterod said 'Mr Tyrone asked me to call you to check if Tiddely Pom had settled in well . . .'

He listened to the reply impassively, his pale yellow face immobile. It accounted for the fact, I thought inconsequentially, that his skin was unlined. He never smiled: seldom frowned. The only wrinkles were around his eyes, which I suppose he screwed up against his native sun.

'Thank you so much,' he said. His best Foreign Office voice, courteous and charming.

'Ask him which box the horse is in,' Ross said. 'The number.'

Vjoersterod asked. Willie Ondroy told him.

'Sixty eight, Thank you. Goodnight.'

He put the receiver carefully back in its cradle and let a small silence lengthen. I hoped that since he had got what he came for he would decently go away again. Not a very big hope to start with, and one which never got off the ground.

He said, studying his finger nails, 'It is satisfactory, Mr Tyrone, that you do at last see the need to cooperate with me.' Another pause. 'However in your case I would be foolish to think that this state of affairs would last very long if I did nothing to convince you that it must.'

I looked at Elizabeth. She didn't seem to have followed Vjoersterod's rather involved syntax. Her head lay in a relaxed way on the pillow and her eyes were shut. She was relieved that I had told where the horse was: she thought that everything was now all right.

Vjoersterod followed my glance and my thought. He nodded. 'We have many polio victims on respirators in my country. I understand about them. About the importance of electricity. The importance of constant attendance. The razor edge between life and death. I understand it well.'

I said nothing. He said, 'Many men desert wives like this. Since you do not, you would care if harm came to her. Am I right? You have, in fact, just this minute proved it, have you not? You wasted so little time in telling me correctly what I wanted to know.'

I made no comment. He waited a fraction, then went smoothly on. What he said, as Dembly had found out, was macabrely at variance with the way he said it.

'I have an international reputation to maintain. I simply cannot afford to have pipsqueak journalists interfering with my enterprises and trying to hold me up to ridicule. I intend to make it clear to you once and for all, to impress upon you indelibly, that I am not a man to be crossed.'

Ross moved a pace at my side. My skin crawled. I made as good a job as I could of matching Vjoersterod's immobility of expression.

Vjoersterod had more to say. As far as I was concerned, he could go on all night. The alternative hardly beckoned.

'Charlie Boston reports to me that you have put both his men out of action. He too cannot afford such affronts to his reputation. Since all you learned from his warning attentions on the train was to strike back, we will see if my chauffeur can do any better.'

I tucked one foot under the stool, pivotted on it, and on the way to my feet struck at Ross with both hands, one to the stomach, one to the groin. He bent over, taken by surprise, and I wrenched the small truncheon out of his and, raising it to clip him on the head.

'Ty . .' Elizabeth's voice rose in an agonized wail. I swung round with the truncheon in my hand and met Vjoersterod's fiercely implacable gaze.

'Drop it.'

He had his toe under the switch. Three yards between us.

I hesitated, boiling with fury, wanting above anything to hit him, knock him out, get rid of him out of my life and most particularly out of the next hour of it. I couldn't risk it. One tiny jerk would cut off the current. I couldn't risk not being able to reach the switch again in time, not with Vjoersterod in front of it and Ross behind me. Under the weight of the Spirashell she would suffocate almost immediately. If I resisted any more I could kill her. He might really do it. Let her die. Leave me to explain her death and maybe even be accused of slaughtering her myself. The unwanted wife bit ... He didn't know I knew his name or anything about him. He would think he could kill Elizabeth with reasonable safety. I simply couldn't risk it.

I put my arm down slowly and dropped the truncheon on the carpet. Ross, breathing heavily, bent and picked it up.

'Sit down, Mr Tyrone,' Vjoersterod said. 'And stay sitting down. Don't get up again. Do I make myself clear?'

He still had his toe under the switch. I sat down, seething inside, rigid outside, and totally apprehensive. Twice in a fortnight was definitely too much.

Vjoersterod nodded to Ross, who hit me solidly with the truncheon on the back of the shoulder. It sounded horrible. Felt worse.

Elizabeth cried out. Vjoersterod looked at her without pity and told Ross to switch on the television. They both waited while the set warmed up. Ross adjusted the volume to medium loud and changed the channel from a news magazine to song and dance. No neighbours, unfortunately, would call to complain about the noice. The only ones who lived near enough were out working in a night club.

Ross had another go with his truncheon. Instinctively I started to stand up ... to retaliate, to escape, heaven knows.

'Sit down,' Vjoersterod said.

I looked at his toe. I sat down. Ross swung his arm and that time I fell forward off the stool on to my knees.

'Sit.' Vjoersterod said. Stiffly I returned to where he said.

'Don't,' Elizabeth said to him in a wavering voice. 'Please don't.'

I looked at her, met her eyes. She was terrified. Scared to death. And something else. Beseeching. Begging me. With a flash of blinding understanding I realized she was afraid I wouldn't take any more, that I wouldn't think she was worth it, that I would somehow stop them hurting me even if it meant switching off her pump. Vjoersterod knew I wouldn't. It was ironic, I thought mordantly, that Vjoersterod knew me better than my own wife.

It didn't last a great deal longer. It had anyway reached the stage where I no longer felt each blow separately but rather as a crushing addition to an intolerable whole. It seemed as though I had the whole weight of the world across my shoulders. Atlas wasn't even in the race.

I didn't see Vjoersterod tell Ross to stop. I had the heels of my hands against my mouth and my fingertips in my hair. Some nit on television was advising everyone to keep their sunny side up. Ross cut him off abruptly in mid note.

'Oh God,' Elizabeth said. 'Oh God.'

Vjoersterod's smooth voice dryly comforted her. 'My dear Mrs

Tyrone, I assure you that my chauffeur knows how to be a great deal more unpleasant than that. He has, I hope you realize, left your husband his dignity.'

'Dignity,' Elizabeth said faintly.

'Quite so. My chauffeur used to work in the prison service in the country I come from. He knows about humiliation. It would not have been suitable, however, to apply certain of his techniques to your husband.'

'Russia?' she asked. 'Do you come from Russia?'

He didn't answer her. He spoke to me.

'Mr Tyrone, should you try to cross me again, I would allow my chauffeur to do anything he liked. Anything at all. Do you understand?'

I was silent. He repeated peremptorily, 'Do you understand?'

I nodded my head.

'Good. That's a start. But only a start. You will also do something more positive. You will work for me. You will write for me in your newspaper. Whatever I tell you to write, you will write.'

I detached my hands slowly from my face and rested my wrists on my knees.

'I can't,' I said dully.

'I think you will find that you can. In fact you will. You must. And neither will you contemplate resigning from your paper.' He touched the electric switch with his brown polished toe cap. 'You cannot guard your wife adequately every minute for the rest of her life.'

'Very well,' I said slowly. 'I will write what you say.'

'Ah.'

Poor old Bert Checkov. I thought drearily. Seven floors down to the pavement. Only I couldn't insure myself for enough to compensate Elizabeth for having to live for ever in a hospital.

'You can start this week,' Vjoersterod said. 'You can say on Sunday that what you have written for the last two weeks turns out to have no foundation in fact. You will restore the situation to what it was before you started interfering.'

'Very well.'

I put my right hand tentatively over my left shoulder. Vjoersterod watched me and nodded.

'You'll remember that,' he said judiciously. 'Perhaps you will feel better if I assure you that many who have crossed me are now dead. You are more useful to me alive. As long as you write what I say, your wife will be safe, and my chauffeur will not need to attend to you.'

His chauffeur, did he but know it, had proved to be a pale shadow of the Boston boys. For all my fears, it now seemed to me that the knuckledusters had been worse. The chauffeur's work was a bore, a present burden, yet not as crippling as before. No broken ribs. No all-over weakness. This time I would be able to move.

Elizabeth was close to tears. 'How can you,' she said, 'How can you be so ... beastly.'

Vjoersterod remained unruffled. 'I am surprised you care so much for your husband after his behaviour with that coloured girl.'

She bit her lip and rolled her head away from him on the pillow. He stared at me calmly. 'So you told her.'

There was no point in saying anything. If I'd told him where Tiddely Pom had been on Tuesday, when he first tried to make me, I would have saved myself a lot of pain and trouble. I would have saved Elizabeth from knowing about Gail. I would have spared her all this fear. Some of Bert Checkov's famous last words floated up from the past ... 'It's the ones who don't know when to give in who get the worst clobbering ... in the ring, I mean ...'

I swallowed. The ache from my shoulders was spreading down my back. I was dead tired of sitting on that stool. Mrs Woodward could keep it. I thought scrappily. I wouldn't want it in the flat any more.

Vjoersterod said to Ross, 'Pour him a drink.'

Ross went over to where the whisky bottle stood on its tray with two glasses and the Malvern Water. The bottle was nearly half full. He unscrewed the cap, picked up one of the tumblers, and emptied into it all the whisky. It was filled to the brim. Vjoersterod nodded. 'Drink it.'

Ross gave me the glass. I stared at it.

'Go on,' Vjoersterod said. 'Drink it.'

I took a breath to protest. He moved his toe towards the switch. I put the glass to my lips and took a mouthful. Jump through hoops when the man said.

'All of it,' he said. 'Quickly.'

I had eaten nothing for more than twenty four hours. In spite of a natural tolerance, a tumbler full of alcohol on an empty stomach was not my idea of fun. I had no choice. Loathing Vjoersterod, I drank it all.

'He seems to have learned his lesson,' Ross said.

Chapter Fourteen

They stood in silence for nearly fifteen minutes, watching me. Then Vjoersterod said, 'Stand up.'

I stood.

'Turn round in a circle.'

I turned. Lurched. Staggered. Swayed on my feet.

Vjoersterod nodded in satisfaction. 'That's all, Mr Tyrone. All for today. I expect to be pleased by what you write in the paper on Sunday. I had better be pleased.'

I nodded. A mistake. My head swam violently. I overbalanced slightly. The whisky was being absorbed into my bloodstream at a disastrous rate.

Vjoersterod and Ross let themselves out unhurriedly and without another word. As soon as the door closed behind them I turned and made tracks for the kitchen. Behind me Elizabeth's voice called in a question, but I had no time to waste and explain. I pulled the tin of salt from the shelf, poured two inches of it into a tumbler and splashed in an equal amount of water.

Stirred it with my fingers. No time for a spoon. Seconds counted. Drank the mixture. It tasted like the Seven Seas rolled into one. Scorched my throat. An effort to get more than one mouthful down. I was gagging over the stuff even before it did its work and came up again, bringing with it whatever of the whisky hadn't gone straight through my stomach wall.

I leaned over the sink, retching and wretched. I had lurched for Vjoersterod more than was strictly necessary, but the alcohol had in fact taken as strong and fast a hold as I had feared it would. I could feel its effects rising in my brain, disorganizing coordination, distorting thought. No possible antidote except time.

Time. Fifteen minutes, maybe, since I had taken the stuff. In ten minutes more, perhaps twenty, I would be thoroughly drunk.

I didn't know whether Vjoersterod had made me drink for any special purpose or just from bloody-mindedness. I did know that it was a horrible complication to what I had planned to do.

I rinsed my mouth out with clean water and straightened up. Groaned as the heavy yoke of bruises across my shoulders reminded me I had other troubles besides drink. Went back to Elizabeth concentrating on not knocking into the walls and doors, and picked up the telephone.

A blank. Couldn't remember the number.

Think.

Out it came. Willie Onroy answered.

'Willie,' I said. 'Move that horse out of box sixty eight. That was the opposition you were talking to earlier. Put on all the guards you can, and move the horse to another box. Stake out sixty eight and see if you can catch any would-be nobblers in the act.'

'Ty! Will do.'

'Can't stop, Willie. Sorry about this.'

'Don't worry. We'll see no one reaches him. I think like you, that it's essential that he should be kept safe until the race.'

'They may be determined ...'

'So am I.'

I put the receiver back in its cradle with his reassurance shoring me up, and met Elizabeth's horrified gaze.

'Ty,' she said faintly, 'What are you doing?'

I sat down for a moment on the arm of the chair. I felt terrible. Battered, sick and drunk.

I said, 'Listen, honey. Listen well. I can't say it twice. I can't put things back to where they were before I wrote the articles.'

'You told him you would,' she interrupted in bewilderment.

'I know I did. I had to. But I can't. I've told the Stewards about him. I can't go back on that. In fact I won't. He's utter poison, and he's got to be stopped.'

'Let someone else do it.'

'That's the classic path to oppression.'

'But why you?' A protesting wail, but a serious question.

'I don't know ... someone has to.'

'But you gave in to him ... you let him ...' She looked at me with wide, appalled eyes, struck by sudden realization. 'He'll come back.'

'Yes. When he finds out that Tiddely Pom has changed boxes and the whole stable is bristling with guards, he'll guess I warned them, and he'll come back. So I'm moving you out of here. Away. At once.'

'You don't mean now?'

'I do indeed.'

'But Ty ... all that whisky ... Wouldn't it be better to leave it until the morning?'

I shook my head. The room began spinning. I held on to the chair and waited for it to stop. In the morning I would be sore and ill, much worse than at the moment; and the morning might anyway be too late. Heathbury and back would take less than three hours in a Rolls.

'Ring up Sue Davis and see if Ron can come along to help. I'm going downstairs to get the van out. O.K.?'

'I don't want to go.'

I understood her reluctance. She had so little grasp on life that even a long-planned daytime move left her worried and insecure. This sudden bustle into the night seemed the dangerous course to her, and staying in a familiar warm home the safe one. Whereas they were the other way round.

'We must.' I said. 'We absolutely must.'

I stood up carefully and concentrated on walking a straight path to the door. Made it with considerable success. Down the stairs. Opened the garage doors, started the van, and backed it out into the mews. A new set of batteries for Elizabeth's pump were in the garage. I lifted them into the van and put them in place. Waves of giddiness swept through me every time I bent my head down. I began to lose hope that I could retain any control of my brain at all. Too much whisky sloshing about in it. Too much altogether.

I went upstairs again. Elizabeth had the receiver to her ear and her eyes were worried.

'There isn't any reply. Sue and Ron must be out.'

I swore inwardly. Even at the best of times it was difficult to manage to transfer to the van on my own. This was far from the best of times.

I took the receiver out of the cradle, disconnected the Davis's vainly ringing number, and dialled that of Antonio Perelli. To my bottomless relief, he answered.

'Tonio, will you call the nursing home and tell them I'm bringing Elizabeth over.'

'Do you mean now, tonight?'

'Almost at once, yes.'

'Bronchial infection?' He sounded brisk, preparing to be reassuring, acknowledging the urgency.

'No. She's well. It's a different sort of danger. I'll tell you later. Look . . . could you possibly down tools and come over here and help me with her?'

'I can't just now, Ty. Not if she isn't ill.'

'But life and death, all the same,' I said with desperate flippancy.

'I really can't, Ty. I'm expecting another patient.'

'Oh. Well, just ring the nursing home, huh?'

'Sure,' he said. 'And . . . er . . . bring Elizabeth here on the way. Would you do that? It isn't much of a detour. I'd like just to be sure she's in good shape. I'll leave my patient for a few minutes, and just say hello to her in the van. All right?'

'All right,' I said. 'Thanks, Tonio.'

'I'm sorry . . .'

'Don't give it a thought,' I said. 'Be seeing you.'

The room whirled when I put the receiver down. I held on to the bedhead to steady myself, and looked at my watch. Couldn't focus on the dial. The figures were just a blur. I made myself see. Concentrated hard. The numbers and the hands came back sharp and clear. Ten thirty-seven. As if it mattered.

Three more trips to make up and down the stairs: Correction; five. Better start, or I'd never finish. I took the pillows and blankets off the bed, folded them as I would need them in the van, and took them down. When I'd made up the stretcher bed ready for Elizabeth, I felt an overpowering urge to lie down on it myself and go to sleep. Dragged myself back to the stairs instead.

Ridiculous, I thought. Ridiculous to try to do anything in the state I was in. Best to unscramble the eggs and go to bed. Wait till morning. Go to sleep. Sleep.

If I went to sleep I would sleep for hours. Sleep away our margin of safety. Put it into the red time-expired section. Cost us too much.

I shook myself out of it. If I walked carefully, I could stop the world spinning round me. If I thought slowly, I could still think. There was a block now somewhere between my brain and my tongue, but if the words themselves came out slurred and wrong, I still knew with moderate clarity what I had intended them to be.

'Honey.' I said to Elizabeth. 'I'm going to take the pump down first. Then you and the Shira . . . Spira.'

'You're drunk,' she said miserably.

'Not surprising,' I agreed. 'Now listen, love. You'll have to breathe on your own. Four minutes. You know you can do it eash . . . easily.' She did four minutes every day, while Mrs Woodward gave her a bed bath.

'Ty, if you drop the pump . . .'

'I won't,' I said, 'I won't . . . drop . . . the pump.'

The pump was the only one we had. There was no replacement. Always we lived in the shadow of the threat that one day its simple mechanism would break down. Spares were almost impossible to find, and they had discontinued making them. If the pump needed servicing, Mrs Woodward and I worked the bellows by hand while it was being done in the flat. Tiring for an hour. Impossible for a lifetime. If I dropped the pump and punctured the bellows, Elizabeth's future could be precisely measured.

Four minutes.

'We'd better,' I said, considering, 'Pack some things for you first. Clean nightdress, f'rinstance.'

'How long ... will we be going for?' She was trying hard to keep the fear out of her voice, to treat our flight on a rational, sensible basis. I admired her, understood her effort, liked her for it, loved her, had to make and keep her safe ... and I'd never do it, I thought astringently, if I let my mind dribble on in that silly way.

How long? I didn't know how long. Until Vjoersterod had been jailed or deported. Even then, it would be safer to find another flat.

'A few days,' I said.

I fetched a suitcase and tried to concentrate on what she needed. She began to tell me, item by item, realizing I couldn't think.

'Washing things. Hair brush. Make-up. Bedsocks. Hot water bottle. Cardigans. Pills ...' She looked with longing at the Possum machine and all the gadgets.

'I'll come soon ... come back soon for those,' I promised. With company, just in case.

'You'll need some things yourself,' she said.

'Hm?' I squinted at her. 'Yeah ...'

I fetched toothbrush, comb, electric razor. I would sleep in the van, dressed, on the stretcher bed. Better take a clean shirt. And a sweater. Beyond that, I couldn't be bothered. Shoved them into a grip. Packing done.

'Could you leave a note for Mrs Woodward?' she asked. 'She'll be so worried if we aren't here in the morning.'

A note for Mrs Woodward. Found some paper. Ball point pen in my pocket. Note for Mrs Woodward. 'Gone away for few days. Will write to you.' Didn't think she would be much less worried when she read that, but didn't know what else to put. The writing straggled upwards, as drunk as I felt.

'All set,' I said.

The packing had postponed the moment we were both afraid of. I looked at the pump. Its works were encased in a metal cabinet of about the size of a bedside table, with a handle at each side for carrying. Like any large heavy box, it was easy enough for two to manage, but difficult for one. I'd done it often enough before, but not with a whirling head and throbbing bruises. I made a pratice shot at picking it up, just to find out.

I found out.

Elizabeth said weakly, 'Ty ... you can't do it.'

'Oh yes ... I can.'

'Not after ... I mean, it's hurting you.'

'The best thing about being drunk,' I said carefully, 'is that what you feel you don't feel, and even if you feel it you don't care.'

'What did you say?'

'Live now, hurt later.'

I pulled back her sheets and my fingers fumbled on the buckle which unfastened the Spirashell. That wouldn't do, I thought clearly. If I fumbled the buckle I'd never have a chance of doing the transfer in four minutes. I paused, fighting the chaos in my head. Sometimes in my youth I'd played a game against alcohol, treating it like an opponent, drinking too much of it and then daring it to defeat me. I knew from experience that if one concentrated hard enough it was possible to carry out quite adequately the familiar jobs one did when sober. This time it was no game. This time, for real.

I started again on the buckle, sharpening every faculty into that one simple task. It came undone easily. I lifted the Spirashell off her chest and laid it over her knees, where it hissed and sucked at the blankets.

Switched off the electricity. Unplugged the lead. Wound it onto the lugs provided. Disconnected the flexible tube which led to the Spirashell.

Committed now. I tugged the pump across the floor, pulling it on its rocky old casters. Opened the door. Crossed the small landing. The stairs stretched downwards. I put my hand on the wall to steady myself and turned round to go down backwards.

Step by step. One foot down. Lift the pump down one step. Balance it. One foot down. Lift the pump. Balance ...

Normally, if Ron or Sue or Mrs Woodward were not there to help, I simply carried it straight down. This time, if I did that, I would fall. I leaned against the wall. One foot down. Lift the pump down. Balance it ... It overhung the steps. Only its back two casters were on the ground, the others out in space ... If it fell forward, it would knock me down the stairs with it ...

Hurry. Four minutes. half way down it seemed to me with an uprush of panic that the four minutes had already gone by. That I would be still on the stairs when Elizabeth died. That I would never, never get it to the bottom unless I fell down there in a tangled heap.

Step by deliberate step, concentrating acutely on every movement, I reached the ground below. Lugged the pump across the small hall, lifted it over the threshold on to the street. Rolled it to the van.

The worst bit. The floor of the van was a foot off the ground. I climbed in, stretched down, grasped the handles, and tugged. I felt as if I'd been torn apart, like the old Chinese torture of the two trees. The pump came up, in through the door, on to the floor of the van. The world whirled violently round my head. I tripped over the end of the stretcher and fell backwards still holding the pump by one handle. It rocked over, crashed on its side, broke the glass over the gauge which showed the pressures and respirations per minute.

Gasping, feeling I was clamped into a hopeless nightmare, I bent over the pump and lifted it upright. Shoved it into its place. Fastened the straps which held it. Pushed the little wedges under its wheels. Plugged in the leads to and from the batteries. Couldn't believe I had managed it all, and wasted several seconds checking through again.

If it didn't work ... If some of the broken glass was inside ... If it rubbed a hole in its bellows . . . I couldn't think straight, didn't know what to do about it, hoped it would be all right.

Up the stairs. Easy without the pump. Stumbled over half the steps, reached the landing on my knees.

Elizabeth was very frightened, her eyes wide and dark, looking at death because I was drunk. When she had to do her own breathing she had no energy or air left for talking, but this time she managed an appalled, desperate word.

'Hurry.'

I remembered not to nod. Picked her up, one arm under her knees, one arm round her shoulders, pulling her towards me so that she could rest her head against my shoulder. Like one carries a baby.

She was feather light, but not light enough. She looked at my face and did my moaning for me.

'Hush.' I said. 'Just breathe.'

I went down the stairs leaning against the wall, one step at a time, refusing to fall. Old man alcohol was losing the game.

The step up into the van was awful. More trees. I laid her carefully on the stretcher, puting her limp limbs straight.

Only the Spirashell now. Went back for it, up the stairs. Like going up a down escalator, never ending, moving where it should have been still. Picked up the Spirashell. The easiest burden. Very nearly came to grief down the stairs through tripping over the long concertina connecting tube. Stumbled into the van and thrust it much too heavily on to Elizabeth's knees.

She was beginning to labour, the tendons in her neck standing out like strings under her effort to get air.

I couldn't get the tube to screw into its connection in the pump. Cursed, sweated, almost wept. Took a deep breath, choked down the panic, tried again. The tricky two-way nut caught and slipped into a crossed thread, caught properly at last, fastened down firmly. I pressed the battery switch on the pump. The moment of truth.

The bellows nonchalantly swelled and thudded. Elizabeth gave the smallest sound of inexpressible relief. I lifted the Spirashell gently on to her chest, slipped the strap underneath her, and couldn't do up the buckle because my fingers were finally trembling too much to control. I just knelt there holding the ends tight so that the Spirashell was close enough for its vacuum to work. It pulled her chest safely up and down, up and down, filling her lungs with air. Some of the agonized apprehension drained out of her face, and some fragile colour came back.

Sixteen life-giving breaths later I tried again with the buckle. Fixed it after two more attempts. Sat back on the floor of the van, rested my elbow on my bent knees, and my head on my hands. Shut my eyes. Everything spun in a roaring black whirl. At least, I thought despairingly, at least I had to be nearly as drunk as I was going to get. Which, thanks to having got some of the stuff up, might not now be paralytic.

Elizabeth said with effortful calm, 'Ty, you aren't fit to drive.'

'Never know what you can do till you try.'

'Wait a little while. Wait till you're better.'

'Won't be better for hours.' My tongue slipped on the words, fuzzy and thick. It sounded terrible. I opened my eyes, focused carefully on the floor in front of me. The swimming gyrations in my head gradually slowed down to manageable proportions. Thought about the things I still had to do.

'Got to get the shoot . . . suitcases.'

'Wait, Ty. Wait a while.'

She didn't understand that waiting would do no good. If I didn't keep moving I would go to sleep. Even while I thought it I could feel the insidious languor tempting me to do just that. Sleep. Sleep deadly sleep.

I climbed out of the van, stood holding on to it, waiting for some sort of balance to come back.

'Won't be long,' I said. Couldn't affort to be long. She couldn't be left alone. In case.

Coordination had again deteriorated. The stairs proved worse than ever. I kept lifting my feet up far higher than was necessary, and half missing the step when I put them down. Stumbled upwards, banging into the walls. In the flat, propped up the note for Mrs Woodward so she couldn't miss it. Tucked Elizabeth's hot water bottle under my arm, carried the suitcases to the door, switched off the light, let myself out. Started down the stairs and dropped the lot. It solved the problem of carrying them, anyway. To prevent myself following them I finished the journey sitting down, lowering myself from step to step.

I picked up the hot water bottle and took it out to Elizabeth.

'I thought . . . Did you fall?' she was acutely anxious.

'Dropped the cases.' I felt an insane urge to giggle. 'S'all right.' Dropped the cases, but not the pump, not Elizabeth. Old man alcohol could stuff it.

I fetched the bags and put them on the floor of the van. Shut the doors. Swayed round to the front and climbed into the driving seat. Sat there trying very hard to be sober. A losing battle, but not yet lost.

I looked at Elizabeth. Her head was relaxed on the pillows, her eyes shut. She'd reached the stage, I supposed, when constant fear was too much of a burden and it was almost a relief to give up hope and surrender to disaster. She'd surrendered for nothing, if I could help it.

Eyes front. Method needed. Do things by numbers, slowly. Switched off the light inside the van. Suddenly very dark. Switched it on again. Not a good start. Start again.

Switched on the side lights. Much better. Switch on ignition. Check fuel. Pretty low after the run to Berkshire, but enough for five miles. Pull out the choke. Start engine. Turn out light inside van.

Without conscious thought I found the gear and let out the clutch. The van rolled forward up the mews.

Simple.

Stopped at the entrance, very carefully indeed. No one walking down the pavement, stepping out in front of me. Turned my head left and right, looking for traffic. All the lights in the road swayed and dipped. I couldn't see anything coming. Took my foot off the clutch. Turned out into the road. Gently accelerated. All clear so far.

Part of my mind was stone cold. In that area, I was sharply aware that to drive too slowly was as obvious a giveaway as meandering all over the road. To drive too fast meant no margin for a sudden stop. My reaction times were a laugh. Hitting someone wouldn't be.

As long as I kept my head still and my eyes front, it wasn't impossible. I concentrated fiercely on seeing pedestrian crossings, stationary cars, traffic lights. Seeing them in time to do something about them. I seemed to be looking down a small cone of clarity: everything in my peripheral vision was a shimmering blur.

I stopped without a jerk at some red lights. Fine. Marvellous. They changed to green. A sudden hollow void in my stomach. I couldn't remember the way. Knew it well, really. The man in the car behind began flashing his headlights. thought of the old joke ... What's the definition of a split second? The interval between the lights going green and the man behind hooting or flashing. Couldn't afford to sit there doing nothing. Let in the clutch and went straight on, realizing that if I strayed off course and got lost I would be sunk. The small print on my maps was for other times. Couldn't ask anyone the way, they might turn me over to the police. Breathalysers, and all that. I'd turn the crystals black.

Ten yards over the crossing I remembered the way to Welbeck Street. I hadn't gone wrong. A vote of thanks to the unconscious mind. Hip hip hooray. For God's sake mind that taxi ... U-turns in front of drunken drivers ought to be banned ...

Too much traffic altogether. Cars swimming out of side roads like shiny half-seen fish with yellow eyes. Cars with orange rear direction blinkers as blinding as the sun. Buses charging across to the kerb and pulling up in six feet at the stops. People running where they shouldn't cross, saving the seconds and risking the years.

Fight them all. Defeat the inefficiency of crashing. Stamp on the enemy in the blood, beat the drug confusing the brain ... Stop the world spinning, hold tight to a straight and steady twenty miles an hour through an imaginary earthquake. Keep death off the roads. Arrive alive. Fasten your safety belts. London welcomes careful drivers ...

I wouldn't like to do it again. Apart from the sheer physical exertion involved in keeping control of my arms and legs there was also a surging recklessness trying to conquer every care I took. An inner voice saying, 'spin the wheel largely, go on, you can straighten out fine round the bend' and an answering flicker saying faintly, 'Careful, careful, careful, careful ...'

Caution won. Mainly, I imagine, through distaste at what would happen to me if I were caught. Only pulling up safely at the other end could possibly justify what was to all intents a crime. I knew that, and clung to it.

Welbeck Street had receded since I went there last.

Chapter Fifteen

Tonio must have been looking out for us, because he opened the front door and came out on to the pavement before I had climbed out of the van. True, I had been a long time climbing out of the van. The waves of defeated intoxication had swept in as soon as I'd put on the brakes. Not defeated after all. Just postponed.

I finally made it on to the road, put one foot in front of the other round the front of the van, leaned against the near side wing.

Tonio peered at me with absolute incredulity.

'You're drunk.'

'You're so right.'

'Elizabeth ...' he said anxiously.

I nodded my head towards the van and wished I hadn't. Hung on to the wing mirror. Still liable for drunk in charge, even on his pavement.

'Ty,' he said, 'for God's sake, man. Pull yourself together.'

'You try,' I said. 'I can't.'

He gave me a withering look and went round to the back of the van to open the doors. I heard him inside, talking to Elizabeth. Tried hard not to slither down the wing and fold up into the gutter. Remotely watched a man in a raincoat get out of a taxi away down the street and cross into a telephone box. The taxi waited for him. Knew I couldn't drive any further, would have to persuade Tonio to do it, or get someone else. No use thinking any more that one could remain sober by will power. One couldn't. Old Bloody man alcohol sneaked up on you just when you thought you'd got him licked.

Tonio reappeared at my elbow.

'Get in the passenger seat,' he said. 'And give me the keys, so that you can't be held to be in charge. I'll drive you to the nursing home. But I'm afraid you'll have to wait ten minutes or so, because I still have that patient with me and there's a prescription to write ... Are you taking in a word I say?'

'The lot.'

'Get in, then.' He opened the door for me, and put his hand on my arm when I rocked. 'If Elizabeth needs me, blow the horn.'

'Right.'

I sat in the seat, slid down, and put my head back. Sleep began to creep in round the edges.

'You all right?' I said to Elizabeth.

Her head was behind me. I heard her murmur quietly, 'Yes.'

The pump hummed rhythmically, aiding and abetting the whisky. The sense of urgency drifted away. Tonio would drive us ... Elizabeth was safe. My eyelids gave up the struggle. I sank into a pit, whirling and disorientated. Not an unpleasant feeling if one didn't fight it.

Tonio opened the door and shook me awake.

'Drink this,' he said. A mug of coffee, black and sweet. 'I'll be with you in a minute.'

He went back into the house, propping the door open with a heavy wrought-iron facsimile of the Pisa Tower. The coffee was too hot. With exaggerated care I put the mug down on the floor. Straightened up wishing the load of ache across my shoulder would let up and go away, but was much too full of the world's oldest anaesthetic to feel it very clearly.

I had been as drunk as that only once before, and it wasn't the night they told me Elizabeth would die, but four days later when they said she would live. I'd downed uncountable double whiskies and I'd eaten almost nothing for a week. It was odd to remember the delirious happiness of that night because of course it hadn't after all been the end of an agony but only the beginning of the years of pain and struggle and waste...

I found myself staring vacantly at the off-side wing mirror. If I conshen ... well, concentrated ... very hard, I thought bemusedly, I would be able to see what it reflected. A pointless game. It simply irritated me that I couldn't see clearly if I wanted to. Looked obstinately at the mirror and waited for the slowed-down focusing process to come right. Finally, with a ridiculous smile of triumph, I saw what it saw down the street. Nothing much. Nothing worth the trouble. Only a silly old taxi parked by the kerb. Only a silly man in a raincoat getting into it.

Raincoat.

Raincoat.

The alarm bells rang fuzzily in my sluggish head. I opened the door and fumbled my way on to the pavement, kicking the coffee over in the process. Leaned against the side of the van and looked down towards the taxi. It was still parked. By the telephone box. Where the man in the raincoat had been ringing someone up.

They say sudden overwhelming disaster sobers you, but it isn't true. I reeled across the pavement and up the step to Tonio's door. Forgot all about blowing the car horn. Banged the solid knocker on his door, and called him loudly. He appeared at the top of the stairs, which led to his consulting room on the first floor and his flat above that.

'Shut up, Ty,' he said. 'I won't be long.'

'Shome ... someone's followed us,' I said. 'It's dangerous.' He wouldn't understand, I thought confusedly. He wouldn't know what I was talking about. I didn't know where to start explaining.

Elizabeth, however, must have told him enough.

'Oh. All right, I'll be down in one minute.' His head withdrew round the bend in the stairs and I swivelled unsteadily to take another look down the street. Taxi still there, in the same place. Light out, not for hire. Just waiting. Waiting to follow us again if we moved. Waiting to tell Vjoersterod where we'd gone.

I shook with futile rage. Vjoersterod hadn't after all been satisfied that Ross's truncheon and the threats against Elizabeth had been enough to ensure a permanent state of docility. He'd left Raincoat outside to watch. Just in case. I hadn't spotted him. Had been much too drunk to spot anything. But there he was. Right on our tail.

I'll fix him, I thought furiously. I'll fix him properly.

Tonio started to come down the stairs, escorting a thin, bent, elderly man whose breath rasped audibly through his open mouth. Slowly they made it to the bottom. Tonio held his arm as they came past me, and helped him over the threshold and down the step to the pavement. An almost equally elderly woman emerged from the Rover parked directly behind my van. Tonio handed him over, helped him into the car, came back to me.

'He likes to come at night,' he explained. 'Not so many fumes from the traffic, and easier parking.'

'Lord Fore ... Fore something,' I said.

'Forlingham,' Tonio nodded. 'Do you know him?'

'Used to go racing. Poor old thing.' I looked wuzzily up the street. 'See that taxi?'

'Yes.'

'Following us.'

'Oh.'

'So you take 'Lizabeth on to the nursing home. I'll stop the taxi.' A giggle got as far as the first ridiculous note. 'What's worse than raining cats and dogs? I'll tell you ... hailing taxis.'

'You're drunk,' Tonio said. 'Wait while I change my coat.' He was wearing formal consultants' dress and looked young and glamorous enough to be a pop singer. 'Can we wait?'

I swung out a generous arm in a wide gesture. 'The taxi,' I said owlishly, 'is waiting for *us*.'

He went to change his coat. I could hear Elizabeth's pump thudding safely away; wondered if I ought to go and reassure her; though that in my state I probably couldn't. The Forlinghams started up and drove away. The taxi went on waiting.

At first I thought what I saw next was on the pink elephant level. Not really there. Couldn't be there. But this time, no hallucination. Edging smoothly round the corner, pulling gently into the kerb, stopping behind the taxi, one Silver Wraith, property of Hire Cars Lucullus.

Raincoat emerged from the taxi and reported to the Rolls. Two minutes later we returned to the taxi, climbed in, and was driven away.

Tonio ran lightly down the stairs and came to a halt beside me in a black sweater instead of a coat.

'Let's get going,' he said.

I put my hand clumsily on his arm.

'Shee ... I mean, see that Rolls down there, where the taxi was.'

'Yes.'

'In that,' I said carefully, 'is the man who ... oh God, why can't I think ... who said he would ... kill ... 'Lizabeth if I didn't do what he wanted ... well ... he might ... he might not ... but can't rish ... risk it. Take her ... Take her. I'll stop ... him following you.'

'How?' Tonio said unemotionally.

I looked at the Tower of Pisa holding the door open.

'With that.'

'It's heavy,' he objected, assessing my physical state.

'Oh for God's sake stop arguing,' I said weakly. 'I want her to go where they can't find her. Please ... please get going ... go on, Tonio. And drive away slowly.'

He hesitated, but finally showed signs of moving. 'Don't forget,' he said seriously, 'that you are no use to Elizabeth dead.'

''Spose not.'

'Give me your coat,' he said suddenly. 'Then they'll think it's still you in the van.'

I took off my coat obediently, and he put it on. He was shorter than me. It hung on him. Same dark head, though. They might mistake us from a distance.

Tonio gave a riproaring impression of my drunken walk, reeling right round the back of the van on his way to the driving seat. I laughed. I was that drunk.

He started the van and drove slowly away. I watched him give one artistic weave across the road and back. Highly intelligent fellow, Tonio Perelli.

Down the road, the Silver Wraith began to move. Got to stop him, I thought fuzzily. Got to stop him smashing up our lives, smashing up other people's lives. Someone, somewhere, had to stop him. In Welbeck Street, with a doorstop. Couldn't think clearly beyond that one fact. Had to stop him.

I bend down and picked up the Leaning Tower by its top two storeys. As Tonio had said, it was heavy. Bruised-muscle-tearingly heavy. Tomorrow its effects would be awful. Fair enough. Tomorrow would be much more awful if I put it down again ... or if I missed.

The Rolls came towards me slowly as Tonio had driven away. If I'd been sober I'd have had all the time in the world. As it was, I misjudged the pace and all but let him go cruising by.

Down one step. Don't trip. Across the pavement. Hurry. Swung the wrought-iron Tower round with both hands as if I was throwing the hammer and forgot to leave go. Its weight and momentum pulled me after it; but although at the last moment Ross saw me and tried to swerve away, the heavy metal base crashed exactly where I wanted it. Drunks' luck. Dead centre of the windscreen.

Scrunch went the laminated glass in a radiating star. Silver cracks streaked across Ross's vision. The huge car swerved violently out into the centre of the road and then towards the kerb as Ross stamped on the brakes. A screech of tyres, a scraping jolt. The Rolls stopped abruptly at a sharp angle to the pavement with its rear end inviting attention from the police. No police appeared to pay attention. A great pity. I wouldn't have minded being scooped in for being drunk and disorderly and disturbing the peace . . .

I had rebounded off the smooth side of the big car and fallen in a heap in the road. The Rolls had stopped, and that was that. Job done. No clear thought of self-preservation spearheaded its way through the mist in my head. I didn't remember that Tonio's solid front door stood open only a few yards away. Jelly had taken over from bone in my legs. Welbeck Street had started revolving around me and was taking its time over straightening out.

It was Ross who picked me up. Ross with his truncheon. I was past caring much what he did with it: and what he intended, I don't know, because this time I was saved by the bell in the shape of a party of people in evening dress who came out into the street from a neighbouring house. The had cheerful gay voices full of a happy evening, and they exclaimed in instant sympathy over the plight of the Rolls.

'I say, do you need any help . . .?'

'Shall we call anyone . . . the police, or anything?'

Can we give you a lift . . . ?'

'Or call a garage?'

'No thank you,' said Vjoersterod in his most charming voice. 'So kind of you . . . but we can manage.'

Ross picked me to my feet and held on grimly to my arm. Vjoersterod was saying, 'We've been having a little trouble with my nephew. I'm afraid he's very drunk . . . still, once we get him home everything will be all right.'

They murmured sympathetically. Began to move away.

'S'not true,' I shouted. 'They'll prob'ly kill me.' My voice sounded slurred and much too melodramatic. They paused, gave Vjoersterod a group of sympathetic, half-embarrassed smiles, and moved off up the street.

'Hey,' I called. 'Take me with you.'

Useless. They didn't even look back.

'What now?' Ross said to Vjoersterod.

'We can't leave him here. Those people would remember.'

'In the car?'

While Vjoersterod nodded he shoved me towards the Rolls, levering with his grasp on my right arm. I swung at him with the left, and missed completely. I could see two of him, which made it difficult. Between them they more or less slung me into the back of the car and I sprawled there face down, half on and half off the seat, absolutely furious that I still could not climb out of that crippling alcoholic stupor. There was a ringing in my head like the noise of the livid green corridors of gas at the dentist's. But no stepped-up awakening to daylight and the taste of blood. Just a continuing extraordinary sensation of being conscious and unconscious, not alternately, but both at once.

Ross knocked out a few of the worst-cracked pieces of the windscreen and started the car.

Vjoersterod, sitting beside him, leaned over the back of his seat and said casually, 'Where to, Mr Tyrone? Which way to your wife?'

'Round and round the mulberry bush,' I mumbled indistinctly. 'And goodnight to you too.'

He let go with four-letter words which were much more in keeping with his character than his usual elevated chat.

'It's no good,' Ross said disgustedly. 'He won't tell us unless we take him to pieces and even then . . . if we did get it out of him . . . what good would it to? He'll never write for you. Never.'

'Why not?' said Vjoersterod obstinately.

'Well, look at it this way. We threatened to kill his wife. Does he knuckle under? Yes, as long as we're there. The moment our backs are turned, first thing he does is move her out. We follow, find her, he shifts her off again . . . That could go on and on. All we can do more is actually kill her, and if we do that we've no hold on him anyway. So he'll never write for you, whatever we do.'

Full marks, I said to myself fatuously. Masterly summing up of the situation. Top of the class.

'You didn't hit him hard enough,' Vjoersterod said accusingly, sliding out of the argument.

'I did.'

'You can't have.'

'If you remember,' Ross said patiently, 'Charlie Boston's boys made no impression either. They either do or don't respond to the treatment. This one doesn't. Same with the threats. Same with the drink. Usually one method is enough. This time we use all three, just to make sure. And where do we get? We get nowhere at all. Just like Gunther Braunthal last year.'

Vjoersterod grunted. I wondered remotely what had become of Gunther Braunthal. Decided I didn't really want to know.

'I can't affort for him to get away with it,' Vjoersterod said.

'No,' Ross agreed.

'I don't like disposals in England,' Vjoersterod went on in irritation. 'Too much risk. Too many people everywhere.'

'Leave it to me,' Ross said calmly.

I struggled up into a sitting position, propping myself up on my hands. Looked out of the side window. Lights flashing past, all one big whirl. We weren't going very fast, on account of the broken windscreen, but the December night air swept into the car in gusts, freezing me in my cotton shirt. In a minute, when my head cleared a fraction, I would open the door and roll out. We weren't going very fast . . . If I waited for a bit of main street, with people . . . couldn't wait too long. Didn't want Ross attending to my disposal.

Vjoersterod's head turned round my way. 'You've only yourself to thank, Mr Tyrone. You shouldn't have crossed me. You should have done what I said. I gave you your chance. You've been very stupid, Mr Tyrone. Very stupid indeed. And now, of course, you'll be paying for it.'

'Huh?' I said.

'He's still drunk,' Ross said. 'He doesn't understand.'

'I'm not so sure. Look what he's done in the past hour. He's got a head like a bullet.'

My eyes suddenly focused on something outside. Something I knew, that everyone knew. The Aviary in Regent's Park, pointed angular wire opposite the main entrance to the Zoo. Been there before with Vjoersterod. He must be staying somewhere near there, I thought. Must be taking me to where he lived. It didn't matter that it was near the Zoo. What did matter was that this was also the way to the nursing home where Tonio had taken Elizabeth. It was less than a mile ahead.

I thought for one wild horror-stricken moment that I must have told Vjoersterod where to go; then remembered and knew I hadn't. But he was much too close. Much too close. Supposing his way home took him actually past the nursing home, and he saw the van ... saw them unloading Elizabeth even ... He might change his mind and kill her and leave me alive ... which would be unbearable, totally and literally unbearable.

Distract his attention.

I said with as much clarity as my tongue would allow: 'Vjoersterod and Ross. Vjoersterod and Ross.'

'*What?*' said Vjoersterod.

The shock to Ross resulted in a swerve across the road and a jolt on the brakes.

'Go back to South Africa before the bogies get you.'

Vjoersterod had twisted round and was staring at me. Ross had his eyes too much on the mirror and not enough on the road. All the same, he started his indicator flashing for the right turn which led over the bridge acros Regent's Canal and then out of the Park. Which led straight past the nursing home, half a mile ahead.

'I told the Stewards,' I said desparately. 'I told the Stewards ... all about you. Last Wednesday. I told my paper ... it'll all be there on Sunday. So you'll remember me too, you'll remember ...'

Ross turned the wheel erratically, sweeping wide to the turn. I brought my hands round with a wholly uncoordinated swing and clamped them hard over his eyes. He took both of his own hands off the wheel to try and detach them and the car rocked straight half way through the turn and headed across the road at a tangent, taking the shortest distance to the bank of the Canal.

Vjoersterod shouted frantically and pulled with all his strength at my arm, but my desperation was at least the equal of his. I hauled Ross's head back towards me harder still, and it was their own doing that I was too drunk to care where or how the car crashed.

'Brake,' Vjoersterod screamed. 'Brake, you stupid fool.'

Ross put his foot down. He couldn't see what he was doing. He put his foot down hard. On the accelerator.

The Rolls leaped across the pavement and on to the grass. The bank sloped gently and then steeply down to the Canal, with saplings and young trees growing here and there. The Rolls scrunched sideways into one trunk and ricochetted into a sapling which it mowed down like corn.

Vjoersterod grabbed the wheel, but the heavy car was now pointed downhill and going too fast for any change of steering. The wheel twisted and lurched out of his hand under the jolt of the front wheel hitting another tree and slewing sideways. Branches cracked around the car and scraped and stabbed at the glossy coachwork. Vjoersterod fumbled in the glove shelf and found the truncheon, and twisted round in his seat and began hitting my arm in panic-stricken fury.

I let go of Ross. It was far too late for him both to assess the situation and do anything useful about it. He was just beginning to reach for the hand brake when the Rolls crashed down over the last sapling and fell into the Canal.

The car slewed convulsively on impact, throwing me around like a rag doll in the back and tumbling Vjoersterod and Ross together in the front. Black water immediately poured through the broken windscreen and began filling the car with lethal speed.

How to get out ... I fumbled for a door handle in the sudden dark, couldn't find one, and didn't know what I had my feet on, didn't know which way up I was. Didn't know if the car was on its back or its nose ... Didn't know anything except that it was sinking.

Vjoersterod began screaming as the water rose up his body. His arm was still flailing about and knocking into me. I felt the truncheon still in his hand. Snatched it from him and hit it hard against where I thought the rear window must be. Connected only with material. I Felt around wildly with my hand, found glass above my head and hit at that.

It cracked. Laminated and tough. Cursed Rolls-Royce for their standards. Hit again. Couldn't get a decent swing. Tried again. Crunched a hole. Water came through it. Not a torrent, but too much. The window was under the surface. Not far under. Tried again. Bash, bash. Made a bigger hole but still not enough ... and water fell through it and over me and from the front of the car the icy level was rising past my waist.

Great to die when you're dead drunk, I thought. And when I die don't bury me at all, just pickle my bones in alcohol ... Crashed the truncheon against my hole. Missed. My arm went right up through it. Felt it up there in the air, out of the water. Stupid. Silly. Drowning in less than an inch of Regent's Canal.

Pulled my arm back and tried again. Absolutely no good. Too much water, too much whisky. One outside, one in. No push in my battered muscles and not much comprehension in my mind. Floating off on the river of death ... sorry, Elizabeth

Suddenly there were lights shining down over me. Hallucinations, I thought. Hallelujah hallucinations. Death was a blinding white light and a crashing noise in the head and a shower of water and glass and voices calling and arms grasping and pulling and raising one up . . . up . . . into a free cold wind . . .

'Is there anyone else in the car?' a voice said. A loud urgent voice, speaking to me. The voice of earth. Telling me I was alive. Telling me to wake up and do something. I couldn't adjust. Blinked at him stupidly.

'Tell us,' he said. 'Is there anyone else in the car?' He shook my shoulder. It hurt. Brought me back a little. He said again, 'Is there anyone else?'

I nodded weakly. 'Two.'

'Christ,' he muttered. 'What a hope.'

I sitting on the grass on the Canal bank, shivering. Someone put a coat round my shoulders. There were a lot of people and more coming, black figures against the reflection of the dark water, figures lit on one side only by the headlights of the car which had come down the path ploughed by the Rolls. It was parked there on the edge, with its lights on the place where the Rolls had gone. You could see the silver rim of the rear window shimmering just below the surface, close to the bank. You could see the water sliding shallowly through the gaping hole my rescuers had pulled me through. You could see nothing inside the car except darkness and water.

A youngish man had stripped to his underpants and was proposing to go through the rear window to try to rescue the others. People tried to dissuade him, but he went. I watched in a daze, scarcely feeling. His head came back through the window into the air, and several hands bent over to help him.

They pulled Vjoersterod out and laid him on the bank.

'Artificial respiration,' one said. 'Kiss of life.'

Kiss Vjoersterod . . . if they wanted to, they were welcome.

The diver went back for Ross. He had to go down twice. A very brave man. The Rolls could have toppled over on to his side at any moment and trapped him inside. People, I thought groggily, were amazing.

They put Ross beside Vjoersterod, and kissed him too.

Neither of them responded.

Cold was seeping into every cell of my body. From the ground I sat on it rose, from the wind it pierced, from my wet clothes it clung clammily to my skin. Bruises stiffen fast in those conditions. Everything started hurting at once, climbing from piano to fortissimo. The noises in my head were deafening. A fine time for the drink to begin dying out of me, I thought. Just when I needed it most.

I lay back on the grass, and someone put something soft under my head. Their voices sprayed over me, questioning and solicitous.

'How did it happen?'

'We've sent for an ambulance . . .'

'What he needs is some good hot tea . . .'

'We're so sorry about your friends . . .'

'Can you tell us your name?'

I didn't answer them. Didn't have enough strength. Could let it all go, now. Didn't have to struggle any more. Old man alcohol could have what was left.

I shut my eyes. The world receded rapidly.

'He's out cold,' a tiny faraway voice said.

It wasn't true at that moment. But a second later, it was.

Chapter Sixteen

I was in a dim long room with a lot of bodies laid out in white. I too was in white, being painfully crushed in a cement sandwich. My head, sticking out of it, pulsed and thumped like a steam hammer.

The components of this nightmare gradually sorted themselves out into depressing reality. Respectively, a hospital ward, a savage load of bruises, and an Emperor-sized hangover.

I dragged my arm up and squinted at my watch. Four-fifty. Even that small movement had out-of-proportion repercussions. I put my hand down gently on top of the sheets and tried to duck out by going to sleep again.

Didn't manage it. Too many problems. Too many people would want too many explanations. I'd have to edit the truth here and there, juggle the facts a little. Needed a clear head for it, not a throbbing dehydrated morass.

I tried to sort out into order exactly what had happened the evening before, and wondered profitlessly what I would have done if I hadn't been drunk. Thought numbly about Vjoersterod and Ross being pulled from the wreck. If they were dead, which I was sure they were, I had certainly killed them. The worst thing about that was that I didn't care.

If I shut my eyes the world still revolved and the ringing noise in my head grew more persistent. I thought wearily that people who poisoned themselves with alcohol for pleasure had to be crazy.

At six they woke up all the patients, who shook my tender brain with shattering decibels of coughing, spitting, and brushing of teeth. Breakfast was steamed haddock and weak tea. I asked for water and something for a headache, and thought sympathetically about the man who said he didn't like Alka-seltzers because they were so noisy.

The hospital was equipped with telephone trolleys, but for all my urging I couldn't get hold of one until nine-thirty. I fed it with coins salvaged from my now drying trousers and rang Tonio. Caught him luckily in his consulting room after having insisted his receptionist tell him I was calling.

'Ty! Deo gratia ... where the hell have you been?'

'Swimming,' I said. 'I'll tell you later. Is Elizabeth O.K.?'

'She's fine. But she was extremely anxious when you didn't turn up again last night ... Where are you now? Why haven't you been to find out for yourself how she is?'

'I'm in University College Hospital. At least, Im here for another few hours. I got scooped in here last night, but there's not much damage.'

'How's the head?'

'Lousy.'

He laughed. Charming fellow.

I rang the nursing home and talked to Elizabeth. There was no doubt she was relieved to hear from me, though from the unusual languor in her voice it was clear they had given her some sort of tranquillizer. She was almost too calm. She didn't ask me what happened when Tonio had driven her away; she didn't want to know where I was at the moment.

'Would you mind staying in the nursing home for a couple of days?' I asked. 'Just till I get things straight.'

'Sure,' she said. 'Couple of days. Fine.'

'See you soon, honey.'

'Sure,' she said again, vaguely. 'Fine.'

After a while I disconnected and got through instead to Luke-John. His brisk voice vibrated loudly through the receiver and sent javelins through my head. I told him I hadn't written my Sunday column yet because I'd been involved in a car crash the night before, and held the receiver six inches away while he replied.

'The car crash was yesterday afternoon.'

'This was another one.'

'For God's sake, do you make a habit of it?'

'I'll write my piece this evening and come in with it in the morning before I go to Heathbury for the Lamplighter. Will that do?'

'It'll have to, I suppose,' he grumbled. 'You weren't hurt in the second crash, were you?' He sounded as if an affirmative answer would be highly unpopular.

'Only bruised,' I said, and got a noncommittal unsympathetic grunt.

'Make that piece good,' he said. 'Blow the roof off.'

I put down the receiver before he could blow the roof off my head. It went on thrumming mercilessly. Ross's target area also alternately burned and ached and made lying in bed draggingly uncomfortable. The grim morning continued. People came and asked me who I was. And who were the two men with me, who had both drowned in the car? Did I know their address?

No, I didn't.

And how had the accident happened?

'The chauffeur had a blackout,' I said.

A police sergeant came with a notebook and wrote down the uninformative truth I told him about the accident. I didn't know Mr Vjoersterod well: he was just an acquaintance. He had insisted on taking me in his car to the nursing home where my wife was at present a patient. The chauffeur had had a blackout and the car had run off the road. It had all happened very quickly. I couldn't remember clearly, because I was afraid I had had a little too much to drink. Mr Vjoersterod had handed me something to smash our way out of the car with, and I had done my best. It was very sad about Mr Vjoersterod and the chauffeur. The man who had fetched them out ought to have a medal. The Sergeant said I would be needed for the inquest, and went away.

The doctor who came to examine me at mid-day sympathized with my various discomforts and said it was extraordinary sometimes how much bruising one could sustain through being thrown about in a somersaulting car. I gravely agreed with him and suggested I went home as soon as possible.

'Why not?' he said. 'If you feel like it.'

I felt like oblivion. I creaked into my rough-dried crumpled shirt and trousers and left my face unshaven, my hair unbrushed and my tie untied, because lifting my arms up for those jobs was too much trouble. Tottered downstairs and got the porter to ring for a taxi, which took me the short distance to Welbeck Street and decanted me on Tonio's doorstep. Someone had picked up the Leaning Tower and put it back in place. There wasn't a mark on it. More than could be said for the Rolls. More than could be said for me.

Tonio gave me one penetrating look, an armchair, and a medicine glass of disprin and nepenthe.

'What's this made of?' I asked, when I'd drunk it.

'Nepenthe? A mixture of opium and sherry.'

'You're joking.'

He shook his head. 'Opium and sherry wine. Very useful stuff. How often do you intend to turn up here in dire need of it?'

'No more,' I said. 'It's finished.'

He wanted to know what had happened after he had driven Elizabeth away, and I told him, save for the one detail of my having blacked out the chauffeur myself. He was no fool, however. He gave me a twisted smile of comprehension and remarked that I had behaved like a drunken idiot.

After that he fetched my jacket from his bedroom and insisted on driving me and the van back to the flat on the basis that Elizabeth needed me safe and sound, not wrapped round one of the lamp posts I had miraculously missed the night before. I didn't argue. Hadn't the energy. He put the van in the garage for me and walked away up the mews to look for a taxi, and I slowly went up the stairs to the flat feeling like a wet dishcloth attempting the Matterhorn.

The flat was stifling hot. I had left all the heaters on the night before and Mrs Woodward hadn't turned them off. There was a note from her on the table. 'Is everything all right? Have put milk in fridge. Am very anxious. Mrs W.'

I looked at my bed. Nothing on it but sheets. Remembered all the blankets and pillows were still downstairs on the stretcher in the van. Going down for them was impossible. Pinched Elizabeth's. Spread one pink blanket roughly on the divan, lay down on it still dressed, pulled another over me, put my head down gingerly on the soft cool pillow.

Bliss.

The world still spun. And otherwise, far too little to put out flags for. My head still manufactured its own sound track. And in spite of the nepenthe the rest of me still felt fresh from a cement mixer. But now there was luxuriously nothing more to do except drift over the edge of the precipice into a deep black heavenly sleep . . .

The telephone bell rang sharply, sawing the dream in half. It was Mrs Woodward, Lancashire accent very strong under stress, sounding touchingly relieved that no unbearable disaster had happened to Elizabeth.

'It's me that's not well,' I said. 'My wife's spending a couple of days in the nursing home. If you'll ring again I'll let you know when she'll be back . . .'

I put the receiver down in its cradle and started across to my bed. Took two steps, yawned, and wondered if I should tell Victor Roncey to go fetch Madge and the boys. Wondered if I should tell Willie Ondroy to slacken the ultra-tight security. Decided to leave things as they were. Only twenty-four more hours to the race. Might as well be safe. Even with Vjoersterod dead, there was always Charlie Boston.

Not that Tiddely Pom would win. After all the trouble to get him there his chances were slender, because the bout of colic would have taken too much out of him. Charlie Boston would make his profit, just as if they'd nobbled him as planned.

I retraced the two steps back to the telephone and after a chat with inquiries put through a personal call to Birmingham.

'Mr Boston?'

'Yers.'

'This is James Tyrone.'

There was a goggling silence at the other end punctuated only by some heavy breathing.

I asked, 'What price are you offering on Tiddely Pom?'

No answer except a noise half way between a grunt and a growl.

'The horse will run,' I commented.

'That's all you know,' he said. A rough, bad tempered voice. A rough, bad tempered man.

'Don't rely on Ross or Vjoersterod,' I said patiently. 'You won't be hearing from them again. The poor dear fellows are both dead.'

I put down the receiver without waiting for the Boston reactions. Felt strong enough to take off my jacket. Made it back to bed and found the friendly precipice still there, waiting. Didn't keep it waiting any longer.

A long while later I woke up thirsty and with a tongue which felt woolly and grass green. The nepenthe had worn off. My shoulders were heavy, stiffly sore, and insistent. A bore. All pain was a bore. It was dark. I consulted my luminous watch. Four o'clock, give or take a minute. I'd slept twelve hours.

I yawned. Found my brain no longer felt as if it was sitting on a bruise and remembered with a wide-awakening shock that I hadn't written my column for the *Blaze*. I switched on the light and took a swig of Tonio's mixture, and after it had worked went to fetch a notebook and pencil and a cup of coffee. Propped up the pillows, climbed back between the blankets, and blew the roof off for Luke-John.

'The lawyers will have a fit,' he said.

'As I've pointed out, the man who ran the racket died this week, and the libel laws only cover the living. The dead can't sue. And no one can sue for them. Also you can't accuse or try the dead. Not in this world, anyway. So nothing they've done can be sub judice. Right?'

'Don't quote *Blaze* dictums to me, laddie. I was living by them before you were weaned.' He picked up my typed sheets as if they would burn him.

'Petrified owners can come out of their caves,' he read aloud. 'The reign of intimidation is over and the scandal of the nonstarting favourites can be fully exposed.'

Derry lifted his head to listen, gave me a grin, and said, 'Our troubleshooter loosing the big guns again?'

'Life gets tedious otherwise,' I said.

'Only for some.'

Luke-John eyed me appraisingly. 'You look more as if you'd been the target. I suppose all this haggard-eyed stuff is the result of a day spent crashing about in cars.' He flicked his thumb against my article. 'Did you invent this unnamed villain, or did he really exist? and if so who was he?'

If I didn't tell, Mike de Jong in his rival newspaper might put two and two together and come up with a filling-in-the-gaps story that Luke-John would never forgive me for. And there was no longer any urgent reason for secrecy.

I said, 'He was a South African called Vjoersterod, and he died the night before last in the second of those car crashes.'

Their mouths literally fell open.

'Dyna ... *mite*,' Derry said.

I told them most of what had happened. I left Gail and Ross's truncheon out altogether but put in the threat to Elizabeth. Left out the drunken driving and the hands over Ross's eyes. Made it bald and factual. Left out the sweat.

Luke-John thought through the problem and then read my article again.

'When you know what you've omitted, what you've included seems pale. But I think this is enough. It'll do the trick, tell everyone the pressure's off and that they can safely bet ante-post again, thanks entirely to investigations conducted by the *Blaze*.'

'That's after all what we wanted.'

'Buy the avenging *Blaze*,' said Derry only half sardonically. 'Racket-smashing a speciality.'

Luke-John gave him a sour look for a joke in bad taste, as usual taking the *Blaze's* role with unrelieved seriousness. I asked him if he would ring up a powerful bookmaking friend of his and ask him the present state of the Lamplighter market, and with raised eyebrows but no other comment he got through. He asked the question, listened with sharpening attention to the answer, and scribbled down some figures. When he had finished he gave a soundless whistle and massaged his larynx.

'He says Charlie Boston has been trying to lay off about fifty thousand on Tiddely Pom since yesterday afternoon. Everyone smells a sewer full of rats because of your articles and the *Blaze's* undertaking to keep the horse safe and they're in a tizzy whether to take the bets or not. Only one or two of the biggest firms have done so.'

I said, 'If Boston can't lay off and Tiddely Pom wins, he's sunk without trace, but if Tiddely Pom loses he'll pocket all Vjoersterod's share of the loot as well as his own and be better of than if we'd done nothing at all. If he manages to lay off and Tiddely Pom wins, he'll be smiling, and if he lays off and Tiddely Pom loses he'll have thrown away everything the crimes were committed for.'

'A delicate problem,' said Derry judicially. 'Or what you might call the antlers of a dilemma.'

'Could he know about the colic?' Luke-John asked.

We decided after picking it over that as he was trying to lay off he probably couldn't. Luke-John rang back to his bookmaker friend and advised him to take as much of the Boston money as he could.

'And after that,' he said gloomily, as he put down the receiver, 'every other bloody horse will fall, and Tiddely Pom will win.'

Derry and I went down to Heathbury Park together on the race train. The racecourse and the sponsors of the Lamplighter had been smiled on by the day. Clear, sunny, still, frosty: a perfect December morning. Derry said that fine weather was sure to bring out a big crowd, and that he thought Zig Zag would win. He said he thought I looked ill. I said he should have seen me yesterday. We completed the journey in our usual relationship of tolerant acceptance and I wondered why it had never solidified into friendship.

He was right on the first count. Heathbury Park was bursting at the seams. I went first to Willie Ondroy's office beside the weighing-room and found a scattered queue of people wanting a word with him, but he caught my eye across the throng and waved a beckoning hand.

'Hey,' he said, swinging round in his chair to talk to me behind his shoulder. 'Your wretched horse has caused me more bother ... that Victor Roncey, he's a bloody pain in the neck.'

'What's he been doing?'

'He arrived at ten this morning all set to blow his top if the horse arrived a minute after twelve and when he found he was there already he blew his top anyway and said he should have been told.'

'Not the easiest of characters,' I agreed.

'Anyway, that's only the half of it. The gate-man rang me at about eight this morning to say there was a man persistently trying to get in.

He'd offered him a bribe and then increased it and had tried to slip in unnoticed while he, the gate-man, was having an argument with one of the stable lads. So I nipped over from my house for a reccy, and there was this short stout individual walking along the back of the stable block looking for an unguarded way in. I marched him round to the front and the gate-man said that was the same merchant, so I asked him who he was and what he wanted. He wouldn't answer. Said he hadn't committed any crime. I let him go. Nothing else to do.'

'Pity.'

'Wait a minute. My racecourse manager came towards us as the man walked away, and the first thing he said to me was, 'What's Charlie Boston doing here?'

'What?'

'Ah. I thought he might mean something to you. But he was extraordinarily clumsy, if he was after Tiddely Pom.'

'No brains and no brawn,' I agreed.

He looked at me accusingly. 'If Charlie Boston was the sum total of the threat to Tiddely Pom, haven't you been over-doing the melodrama a bit?'

I said dryly. 'Read the next thrilling instalment in the *Blaze*.'

He laughed and turned back decisively to his impatient queue. I wandered out into the paddock, thinking of Charlie Boston and his futile attempt to reach the horse. Charlie Boston who thought with his muscles. With other people's muscles, come to that. Having his boys on the sick list and Vjoersterod and Ross on the dead, he was as naked and vulnerable as an opened oyster.

He might also be desperate. If he was trying to lay off fifty thousand pounds, he had stood to lose at least ten times that – upwards of half a million – if Tiddely Pom won. A nosedive of epic proportions. A prospect to induce panic and recklessness in ever-increasing intensity as the time of the race drew near.

I decided that Roncey should share the care of his horse's safety, and began looking out for him in the throng. I walked round the corner with my eyes scanning sideways and nearly bumped into someone standing by the Results-at-other-Meetings notice board. The apology was half way to my tongue before I realized who it was.

Gail.

I saw the pleasure which came first into her eyes, and the uncertainty afterwards. Very likely I was showing her exactly the same feeling. Very likely she, like me, felt a thudding shock at meeting. Yet if I'd considered it at all, it was perfectly reasonable that she should come to see her uncle's horse run in the Lamplighter.

'Ty?' she said tentatively, with a ton less than her usual poise.

'Surprise, surprise.' It sounded more flippant than I felt.

'I thought I might see you,' she said. Her smooth black hair shone in the sun and the light lay along the bronze lines of her face, touching them with gold. The mouth I had kissed was a rosy pink. The body I had liked naked was covered with a turquoise coat. A week today, I thought numbly. A week today I left her in bed.

'Are Harry and Sarah here?' I said. Social chat. Hide the wound which hadn't begun to form scar tissue. I'd no right to be wounded in the first place. My own fault. Couldn't complain.

'They're in the bar,' she said. Where else?

'Would you like a drink?'

She shook her head, 'I want to ... to explain. I see that you know ... I have to explain.'

'No need. A cup of coffee, perhaps?'

'Just listen.'

I could feel the rigidity in all my muscles and realized it extended even to my mouth and jaw. With a conscious effort I loosened them and relaxed.

'All right.'

'Did she ... I mean, is she going to divorce you?'

'No.'

'Ohhhh.' It was a long sigh. 'Then I'm sorry if I got you into trouble with her. But why did she have you followed if she didn't want to divorce you?'

I stared at her. The wound half healed in an instant.

'What's the matter?' she said.

I took a deep breath. 'Tell me what happened after I left you. Tell me about the man who followed me.'

'He came up and spoke to me in the street just outside the hotel.'

'What did he look like?'

'He puzzled me a bit. I mean, he seemed too ... I don't know ... civilized, I suppose is the word, to be a private detective. His clothes were made for him, for instance. He had an accent of some sort and a yellowish skin. Tall. About forty, I should think.'

'What did he say?'

'He said your wife wanted a divorce and he was working on it. He asked me for ... concrete evidence.'

'A bill from the hotel?'

She nodded, not meeting my eyes. 'I agreed to go in again and ask for one.'

'Why, Gail?'

She didn't answer.

'Did he pay you for it?'

'God, Ty,' she said explosively. 'Why not? I needed the money. I'd only met you three times and you were just as bad as me, living with your wife just because she was rich.'

'Yes,' I said. 'Well, how much?'

'He offered me fifty pounds and when I'd got used to the idea that he was ready to pay I told him to think again, with all your wife's money she could afford more than that for her freedom.'

'And then what?'

'He said ... if I could give him full and substantial facts, he could raise the payment considerably.' After a pause, in a mixture of defiance and shame, she added, 'He agreed to a thousand pounds, in the end.'

I gave a gasp which was half a laugh.

'Didn't your wife tell you?' she asked.

I shook my head. 'He surely didn't have that much money on him? Did he give you a cheque?'

'No. He met me later, outside the Art School, and gave me a brown carrier bag . . . Beautiful new notes, in bundles. I gave him the bill I'd got, and told him . . . everything I could.'

'I know,' I said.

'Why did he pay so much, if she doesn't want a divorce?' When I didn't answer at once she went on, 'It wasn't really only the money . . . I thought if she wanted to divorce you, why the hell should I stop her. You said you wouldn't leave her, but if she sort of left *you*, then you would be free, and maybe we could have more than a few Sundays . . .'

I thought that one day I might appreciate the irony of it.

I said, 'It wasn't my wife who paid you that money. It was the man himself. He wasn't collecting evidence for a divorce, but evidence to blackmail me with.'

'Ohh.' It was a moan. 'Oh no, Ty. Oh God, I'm so sorry.' Her eyes widened suddenly. 'You must have thought . . . I suppose you thought . . . that I sold you out for *that*.'

'I'm afraid so,' I apologized. 'I should have known better.'

'That makes us quits, then.' All her poise came back at one bound. She said, with some concern but less emotional disturbance, 'How much did he take you for?'

'He didn't want money. He wanted me to write my column in the *Blaze* every week according to his instructions.'

'How extraordinary. Well, that's easy enough.'

'Would you design dresses to dictation by threat?'

'Oh.'

'Exactly. Oh. So I told my wife about you myself. I had to.'

'What . . . what did she say?'

'She was upset,' I said briefly. 'I said I wouldn't be seeing you again. There'll be no divorce.'

She slowly shrugged her shoulders. 'So that's that.'

I looked away from her, trying not to mind so appallingly much that that was that. Tomorrow was Sunday. Tomorrow was Sunday and I could be on my own, and there was nothing on earth that I wanted so much as to see her again in her smooth warm skin and hold her close and tight in the half dark . . .

She said thoughtfully, 'I suppose if that man was a blackmailer it explains why I thought he was so nasty.'

'Nasty? He was usually fantastically polite.'

'He spoke to me as if I'd crawled out of the cracks. I wouldn't have put up with it . . . except for the money.'

'Poor Gail,' I said sympathetically. 'He was South African.'

She took in the implication and her eyes were furious. 'That explains it. A beastly Afrikaner. I wish I'd never agreed.'

'Don't be silly,' I interrupted. 'Be glad you cost him so much.'

She calmed down and laughed. 'I've never even been to Africa. I didn't recognize his accent or give it a thought. Stupid, isn't it?'

A man in a check tweed suit came and asked us to move as he wanted to read the notices on the board behind us. We walked three or four steps away, and paused again.

'I suppose I'll see you sometimes at the races,' she said.

'I suppose so.'

She looked closely at my face and said, 'If you really feel like that, why ... *why* don't you leave her?'

'I can't.'

'But we could ... you want to be with me. I know you do. Money isn't everything.'

I smiled twistedly. I did after all mean something to her, if she could ever say that.

'I'll see you sometimes,' I repeated emptily. 'At the races.'

Chapter Seventeen

I caught Victor Roncey coming out of the luncheon room and told him that the danger to Tiddely Pom was by no means over.

'He's here, isn't he?' he said squashingly.

'He's here thanks to us,' I reminded him. 'And there are still two hours to the race.

'What do you expect me to do? Hold his hand?'

'It wouldn't hurt,' I said flatly.

There was the usual struggle between aggressive independence and reasonable agreement. He said grudgingly, 'Peter can sit outside his box over in the stables.'

'Where is Peter now?'

He waved a hand behind him. 'Finishing lunch.'

'You'll have to take him in yourself, if he hasn't got a stable lad's pass.'

He grumbled and agreed, and went back to fetch his son. I walked over to the stables with them and checked with the man on the gate who said he'd had the usual number of people trying to get in, but not the man he'd turned away in the morning. Wing Commander Ondroy had told him to sling that man in the storeroom and lock him in, if he came sniffing round again.

I smiled appreciatively and went in with Roncey to look at the horse. He stood patiently in his box, propped on one hip, resting a rear leg. When we opened the door he turned his head lazily and directed on us an unexcited eye. A picture of a racehorse not on his toes, not strung up by the occasion, not looking ready to win Lamplighter Gold Cups.

'Is he always like this before a race?' I said. 'He looks doped.'

Roncey gave me a horrified glance and hurried to his horse's head. He looked in his mouth and eyes, felt his neck and legs and kicked open and studied a small pile of droppings. Finally he shook his head.

'No dope that I can see. No signs of it.'

'He never has nerves,' Peter observed. 'He isn't bred for it.'

He looked bred for a milk cart. I refrained from saying so. I walked back into the paddock with Roncey and got him to agree to saddle up his horse in the stables, not the saddling boxes, if the Stewards would allow it.

The Stewards, who included Eric Youll, didn't hesitate. They said only that Tiddely Pom would have to walk the three stipulated times round the parade ring for the public to see him before the jockey mounted, but were willing for him to walk six feet in from the rails and be led and guarded by Peter and myself.

'All a waste of time,' Roncey muttered. 'No one will try anything here.'

'Don't you believe it,' I said. 'You'd try anything if you stood to lose half a million you hadn't got.'

I watched the first two races from the Press Box and spent the time in between aimlessly wandering about in the crowd trying to convince myself that I wasn't really looking out for another glimpse of Gail.

I didn't see her. I did see Dermot Finnegan. The little Irish jockey walked in front of me and gave me a huge gap-toothed grin. I took in, as I was supposed to, that he was dressed in colours, ready to ride in a race. The front of his jacket was carefully unbuttoned. I added up the purple star on the pink and white horizontal stripes and he laughed when he saw my astonishment.

'Be Jasus, and I'm almost as staggered as yourself,' he said. 'But there it is, I've got my big chance on the Guvnor's first string and if I make a mess of it may God have mercy on my soul because I won't.'

'You won't make a mess of it.'

'We'll see,' he said cheerfully. 'That was a grand job you made of me in *Tally*, now. Thank you for that. I took that when it came and showed it to the Guvnor but he'd already seen it, he told me. And you know I wouldn't be certain that it wasn't the magazine that put him in mind of putting me up on Rockville, when the other two fellows got hurt on Thursday. So thank you for that too.'

When I told Derry about it in the Press Box during the second race he merely shrugged. 'Of course he's riding Rockville. Don't you read the papers?'

'Not yesterday.'

'Oh, Well yes, he's got as much as he can chew this time. Rockville's a difficult customer, even with the best of jockeys, and our Dermot isn't that.' He was busy polishing the lenses of his race glasses. 'Luke-John's bookmaker friend must have accepted a good deal of Boston's fifty thousand, because the price on Tiddely Pom has come crashing down like an express lift from 100 to 8 to only 4 to 1. That's a stupid price for a horse like Tiddely Pom, but there you are.'

I did a small sum. If Boston had taken bets at 10 or 12 to 1 and had only been able to lay them off at 4 to 1, that left him a large gap of 6 or 8 to 1. If Tiddely Pom won, that would be the rate at which he would have to pay: which added up still to more than a quarter of a million pounds and meant that he would have to sell off the string of betting shops to pay his debts. Dumb Charlie Boston, trying to play with the big boys and getting squeezed like a toothpaste tube.

There was no sign of him in the paddock. Roncey saddled his horse in the stables and brought him straight into the parade ring very shortly before the time for the jockeys to mount. Peter led him round and I walked along by his quarters: but no one leaned over the rails to squirt him with acid. No one tried anything at all.

'Told you so,' Roncey muttered. 'All this fuss.' He put up his jockey, slapped Tiddely Pom's rump, and hurried off to get a good position on the trainers' stand. Peter led the horse out on to the course and let him go, and Tiddely Pom cantered off unconcernedly with the long lopping stride so at variance with his looks. I sighed with relief and went up to join Derry in the Press Box to watch the race.

'Tiddely Pom's favourite,' he said. 'Then Zig Zag, then Rockville. Zig Zag should have it in his pocket.' He put his race glasses to his eyes and studied the horses milling round at the start. I hadn't taken my own glasses as I'd found the carrying strap pressed too heavily on tender spots. I felt lost without them, like a snail without antennae. The start for the Lamplighter was a quarter of a mile down the course from the stands. I concentrated on sorting out the colours with only force four success.

Derry exclaimed suddenly, 'What the devil . . .'

'Tiddely Pom,' I said fearfully. Not now. Not at the very post. I should have foreseen . . . should have stationed someone down there . . . But it was so public. So many people walked down there to watch the start. Anyone who tried to harm a horse there would have a hundred witnesses.

'There's someone hanging on to his rein. No, he's been pulled off. Great God . . .' Derry started laughing incredulously. 'I can't believe it. I simply can't believe it.'

'What's happening?' I said urgently. All I could see was a row of peacefully lining up horses, which miraculously included Tiddely Pom, and some sort of commotion going on in the crowd on the far side of the rails.

'It's Madge . . . Madge Roncey. It must be. No one else looks like that . . . She's rolling about on the grass with a fat little man . . . struggling. She pulled him away from Tiddely Pom . . . Arms and legs are flying all over the place . . .' He stopped, laughing too much. 'The boys are with her . . . they're all piling on to the poor little man in a sort of rugger scrum . . .'

'It's a pound to a penny the poor little man is Charlie Boston,' I said grimly. 'And if it's Madge and not the *Blaze* who's saved the day, we'll never hear the end of it from Victor Roncey.'

'Damn Victor Roncey,' Derry said. 'They're off.'

The line of horses bounded forward, heading for the first jump.

Seventeen runners, three and a half miles, and a gold trophy and a fat cheque to the winner.

One of them crumpled up over the first. Not Tiddely Pom, whose scarlet and white chevrons bobbed in a bunch at the rear. Not Zig Zag, already positioned in the fourth place, from where he usually won. Not Egocentric, leading the field up past the stands to give the Huntersons their moment of glory. Not Rockville, with Dermot Finnegan fighting for his career in a battle not to let the horse run away with him.

They jumped the water jump in front of the stands. A gasp from the crowd as one of them splashed his hind legs right into it. The jockey in orange and green was dislodged and rolled.

'That horse always makes a balls of the water,' Derry said dispassionately. 'They should keep it for hurdles.' No tremor excitement in his voice or hands. It had cost him nothing to get Tiddely Pom on to the track. It had cost me too much.

They swept round the top bend and started out round the circuit. Twice round the course to go. I watched Tiddely Pom all the way, expecting him to fall, expecting him to drop out at the back and be pulled up, expecting him to be too weak from colic to finish the trip.

They came round the bottom bend and up over the three fences in the straight towards the stands. Egocentric was still in front. Zig Zag still fourth. Dermot Finnegan had Rockville in decent control somewhere in the middle, and Tiddely Pom was still there and not quite last.

Over the water. Zig Zag stumbled, recovered, raced on. Not fourth any more, though. Sixth or seventh. Tiddely Pom scampered over it with none of the grace of Egocentric but twice the speed. Moved up two places.

Out they went again into the country. Derry remarked calmly, 'Tiddely Pom has dropped his bit.'

'Damn,' I said. The jockey was working with his arms, urging the horse on. Hopeless. And half the race still to run.

I shut my eyes. Felt the fatigue and illness come swamping back. Wanted to lie down somewhere soft and sleep for a week and escape from all the problems and torments and disillusionments of weary life. A week alone, to heal in. A week to give a chance for some energy for living to come creeping back. I needed a week at least. If I were lucky, I'd have a day.

'There's a faller at that fence.' The race commentator's amplified voice jerked my eyes open. 'A faller among the leaders. I think it was Egocentric ... yes, Egocentric is down ...'

Poor Huntersons. Poor Harry, poor Sarah.

Gail.

I didn't want to think about her. Couldn't bear to, and couldn't help it.

'He's still going,' Derry said. 'Tiddely Pom.'

The red and white chevrons were too far away to be clear. 'He's made up a bit,' Derry said. 'He's taken a hold again.'

They jumped the last fence on the far side and began the sweeping bend round into the straight, very strung out now, with great gaps between little bunches. One or two staggered fifty yards in the rear. There was a roar from the crowd and the commentator's voice rose above it . . . 'And here is Zig Zag coming to the front . . . opening up a commanding lead . . .'

'Zig Zag's slipped them,' Derry said calmly. 'Caught all the others napping.'

'Tiddely Pom . . .?' I asked.

'He's well back. Still plodding on, though. Most we could expect.'

Zig Zag jumped the first fence in the straight five seconds clear of the rest of the field.

'Nothing will catch him,' Derry said. I forgave him the satisfaction in his voice. He had tipped Zig Zag in his column. It was nice to be right. 'Tiddely Pom's in the second bunch. Can you see him? Even if he hasn't won, he's not disgraced.'

Zig Zag jumped the second last fence well ahead, chased after an interval by four horses more or less abreast. After these came Tiddely Pom, and behind him the other half dozen still standing. If we had to settle for that, at least the ante-post punters had had some sort of run for their money.

It was a clear twenty yards from the last fence that Zig Zag was meeting it wrong. The jockey hesitated fatally between pushing him on to lengthen his stride and take off sooner or shortening the reins to get him to put in an extra one before he jumped. In the end he did neither. Simply left it to the horse to sort himself out. Some horses like to do that. Some horses like to be told what to do. Zig Zag went into the fence like a rudderless ship, took off too late and too close, hit the fence hard with his forelegs slewed round in mid air, crashed down in a tangle of hooves, and treated his rider to a well deserved thump on the turf.

'Stupid *bastard*,' Derry said, infuriatedly lowering his glasses. 'An apprentice could have done better.'

I was watching Tiddely Pom. The four horses ahead of him jumped the last fence. One of them swerved to avoid Zig Zag and his supine jockey and bumped heavily into the horse next to him. Both of them were thoroughly unbalanced and the jockey of one fell off. When Tiddely Pom came away from the fence to tackle the straight he was lying third.

The crowd roared. 'He's got a chance,' Derry yelled. 'Even now.'

He couldn't quicken. The low lolloping stride went on at the same steady pace and all the jockey's urging was having no constructing effect. But one of the two in front of him was tiring and rolling about under pressure. Tiddely Pom crept up on him yard by yard but the winning post was coming nearer and there was still one more in front.

I looked at the leader, taking him in for the first time. A jockey in pink and white stripes, riding like a demon on a streak of brown, straining, hard-trained muscle. Dermot Finnegan on Rockville, with all his future in his hands.

While I watched he swept conclusively past the post, and even from the stands one could see that Irish grin bursting out like the sun.

Three lengths behind, Tiddely Pom's racing heart defeated the colic and put him second. A genuine horse, I thought thankfully. Worth all the trouble. Or at least, worth some of it.

'All we need now,' said Derry, 'is an objection.'

He wrapped the strap round his race glasses, put them in their case, and hurriedly made for the stairs. I followed him more slowly down and edged gingerly through the crowd milling round the unsaddling enclosure until I reached the clump of other press men waiting to pick up something to print. There was a cheer as Rockville was led through into the winner's place. Another cheer for Tiddely Pom. I didn't join in. Had nothing to contribute but a dead feeling of anti-climax.

All over. Tiddely Pom hadn't won. What did I expect?

The crowd parted suddenly like the Red Sea and through the gap struggled a large, untidy earth mother surrounded by planets. Madge Roncey and her sons.

She walked purposefully across the comparatively empty unsaddling enclosure and greeted her husband with a gentle pat on the arm. He was astounded to see her and stood stock still with his mouth open and Tiddely Pom's girth buckles half undone. I went across to join them.

'Hullo,' Madge said. 'Wasn't that splendid?' The faraway look in her eyes had come a few kilometres nearer since fact had begun to catch up on fantasy. She wore a scarlet coat a shade to small. Her hair floated in its usual amorphous mass. She had stockings on. Laddered.

'Splendid,' I agreed.

Roncey gave me a sharp look. 'Still fussing?'

I said to Madge, 'What happened down at the start?'

She laughed. 'There was a fat little man there going absolutely berserk and screaming that he would stop Tiddely Pom if it was the last thing he did.'

Roncey swung round and stared at her. 'He started hanging on to Tiddely Pom's reins,' she went on, 'and he wouldn't let go when the starter told him to. It was absolutely crazy. He was trying to kick Tiddely Pom's legs. So I just ducked under the rails and walked across and told him it was our horse and would he please stop it, and he was frightfully rude ...' A speculative look came into her eye. 'He used some words I didn't know.'

'For God's sake,' said Roncey irritably. 'Get on with it.'

She went on without resentment, 'He still wouldn't let go so I put my arms round him and lifted him up and carried him off and he was so surprised he dropped the reins, and then he struggled to get free and I let him fall down on the ground and rolled him under the rails, and then the boys and I sat on him.'

I said, trying to keep a straight face, 'Did he say anything after that?'

'Well, he hadn't much breath,' she admitted judiciously. 'But he did say something about killing you, as a matter of fact. He didn't seem to like you very much. He said you'd smashed everything and stopped him getting to Tiddely Pom, and as a matter of fact he was so hysterical he was jolly nearly in tears.'

'Where is he now?' I asked.

'I don't know exactly. When I let him get up, he ran away.'

Roncey gave me a mean look. 'So it took my wife to save my horse, not the *Blaze*.'

'Oh no, dear,' she said placidly. 'If Mr Tyrone hadn't been looking after him, the little man would have been able to reach him sooner, and if I hadn't come back from the Isle of Wight because I thought it would be quite safe if no one knew, and we all wanted to see the race, if I hadn't been there at the starting gate, someone else would have taken the little man away. Lots of people were going to. It was just that I got to him first.' She gave me a sweet smile. 'I haven't had so much fun for years.'

The day fragmented after that into a lot of people saying things to me that I didn't really hear. Pieces still stick out: Dermot Finnegan being presented with a small replica of the Lamplighter Gold Cup and looking as if he'd been handed the Holy Grail. Willie Ondroy telling me that Charlie Boston had been slung off the racecourse, and Eric Youll outlining the Stewards' plan for warning him off permanently, which would mean the withdrawal of his betting licence and the closing of all his shops.

Derry telling me he had been through to Luke-John, whose bookmaker friend had taken all of Charlie Boston's fifty thousand and was profoundly thankful Tiddely Pom hadn't won.

Collie Gibbons asking me to go for a drink. I declined. I was off drink. He had his wife with him, and not an American colonel in sight.

Pat Roncey staring at me sullenly, hands in pockets. I asked if he'd passed on my own telephone number along with the whereabouts of Tiddely Pom. Belligerently he tried to justify himself: the man had been even more keen to know where I lived than where the horse was. What man? The tall yellowish man with some sort of accent. From the *New Statesman*, he'd said. Didn't Pat know that the *New Statesman* was the one paper with no racing page? Pat did not.

Sandy Willis walking past leading Zig Zag, giving me a worried smile. Was the horse all right, I asked. She thought so, poor old boy. She muttered a few unfeminine comments on the jockey who had thrown the race away. She said she'd grown quite fond of Tiddely Pom, she was glad he'd done well. She'd won a bit on him, as he'd come in second. Got to get on, she said, Zig Zag needed sponging down.

The Huntersons standing glumly beside Egocentric while their trainer told them their raffle horse had broken down badly and wouldn't run again for a year, if ever.

The message got through to me razor sharp and clear. no Egocentric racing, No Huntersons at the races. No Gail at the races.

Not even that.

I'd had enough. My body hurt. I understood the full meaning of the phrase sick at heart. I'd been through too many mangles, and I wasn't sure it was worth it. Vjoersterod was dead, Bert Checkov was dead, the nonstarter racket was dead ... until someone else tried it, until the next wide boy came along with his threats and his heavies. Someone else could bust it next time. Not me. I'd had far, far more than enough.

I wandered slowly out on to the course and stood beside the water jump, looking down into the water. Couldn't go home until the race train went, after the last race. Couldn't go home until I'd phoned in to Luke-John for a final check on what my column would look like the next day. Nothing to go home to, anyway, except an empty flat and the prospect of an empty future.

Footsteps swished towards me through the grass. I didn't look up. Didn't want to talk.

'Ty,' she said.

I did look then. There was a difference in her face. She was softer; less cool, less poised. Still extraordinarily beautiful. I badly wanted what I couldn't have.

'Ty, why didn't you tell me about your wife?'

I shook my head. Didn't answer.

She said, 'I was in the bar with Harry and Sarah, and someone introduced us to a Major Gibbons and his wife, because he had been in your *Tally* article too, like Harry and Sarah. They were talking about you ... Major Gibbons said it was such a tragedy about your wife ... I said, what tragedy ... and he told us ...'

She paused. I took a deep difficult breath: said nothing.

'I said it must be some help that she was rich, and he said what do you mean rich, as far as I know she hasn't a bean because Ty is always hard up with looking after her, and he'd be reasonably well off if he put her in a hospital and let the country pay for her keep instead of struggling to do it himself...'

She turned half away from me and looked out across the course. 'Why didn't you tell me?'

I swallowed and loosened my mouth. 'I don't like ... I didn't want ... consolation prizes.'

After a while she said, 'I see.' It sounded as if she actually did.

There was a crack in her cool voice. She said, 'If it was me you'd married, and I'd got polio ... I can see that you must stay with her. I see how much she needs you. If it had been me ... and you left me ...' She gave a small laugh which was half a sob. 'Life sure kicks you in the teeth. I find a man I don't want to part with ... a man I'd live on crumbs with ... and I can't have him ... even a little while, now and then.'

Chapter Eighteen

I spent Sunday alone in the flat, mostly asleep. Part of the time I pottered around tidying things up, trying to put my mind and life into order along with my house. Didn't have much success.

On Monday morning I went to fetch Elizabeth. She came home in an ambulance, with two fit uniformed men to carry her and the pump upstairs. They laid her on the bed I had made up freshly for her, checked that the pump was working properly, helped replace the Spirashell on her chest, accepted cups of coffee, agreed that the weather was raw and cold but what could you expect in December, and eventually went away.

I unpacked Elizabeth's case and made some scrambled eggs for lunch, and fed her when her wrist packed up, and fixed another mug of coffee into the holder.

She smiled and thanked me. She looked tired, but very calm. There was a deep difference in her, but for some time I couldn't work out what it was. When I finally identified it, I was surprised. She wasn't anxious any more. The long-established, deep-rooted insecurity no longer looked out of her eyes.

'Leave the dishes, Ty,' she said. 'I want to talk to you.'

I sat in the armchair. She watched me. 'It still hurts ... what that man did.'

'A bit,' I agreed.

'Tonio told me they were both killed that night ... trying to find me again.'

'He did, did he?'

She nodded. 'He came to see me yesterday. We had a long talk. A long, long talk. He told me a lot of things ...'

'Honey,' I said, 'I ...'

'Shut up, Ty. I want to tell you ... what he said.'

'Don't tire yourself.'

'I won't. I am tired, but it feels different from usual. I feel just ordinarily tired, not ... not *worried* tired. Tonio did that. And you I mean, he made me understand what I saw on Thursday, that you would let yourself be smashed up ... that you would drive when you were drunk and risk going to prison ... that you would do anything, however dangerous ... to keep me safe ... He said, if I'd seen that with my own eyes, why did I doubt ... why did I ever doubt that you would stay with me ... It was such a relief ... I felt as if the whole world were lighter ... I know you've always told me ... but now I do believe it, through and through.'

'I'm glad,' I said truthfully. 'I'm very glad.'

She said, 'I talked to Tonio about ... that girl.'

'Honey ...'

'Hush,' she said. 'I told him about the blackmail. We talked for ages ... He was so understanding. He said of course I would be upset, anyone would, but that I shouldn't worry too much ... He said you were a normal, healthy man and if I had any sense I would see that the time to start worrying would be if you *didn't* want to sleep with someone.' She smiled. 'He said if I could face it, we would both be happier if I didn't mind if sometimes ... He said you would always come home.'

'Tonio said a great deal.'

She nodded. 'It made such sense. I haven't been fair to you.'

'Elizabeth,' I protested.

'No. I really haven't. I was so afraid of losing you, I couldn't see how much I was asking of you. But I understand now that the more I can let you go, the easier you will find it to live with me ... and the more you will want to.'

'Tonio said that?.

'Yes, he did.'

'He's very fond of you,' I said.

She grinned. 'He said so. He also said some pretty ear-burning things about you, if you want to know.' She told me some of them, her mouth curving up at the corners and the new security gleaming in her eyes.

'Exaggeration,' I said modestly.

She laughed. A breathy giggle. Happy.

I got up and kissed her on the forehead and on the cheek. She was the girl I'd married. I loved her very much.

On Tuesday morning, when Mrs Woodward came back, I went out along the mews, round the corner and into the telephone box, and dialled the number of the Western School of Art.

HIGH STAKES

Chapter One

I looked at my friend and saw a man who had robbed me. Deeply disturbing. The ultimate in rejection.

Jody Leeds looked back at me, half smiling, still disbelieving.

'You're *what*?'

'Taking my horses away,' I said.

'But ... I'm your *trainer.*' He sounded bewildered. Owners, his voice and expression protested, never deserted their trainers. It simply wasn't done. Only the eccentric or the ruthless shifted their horses from stable to stable, and I had shown no signs of being either.

We stood outside the weighing room of Sandown Park racecourse on a cold windy day with people scurrying past us carrying out saddles and number cloths for the next steeplechase. Jody hunched his shoulders inside his sheepskin coat and shook his bare head. The wind blew straight brown hair in streaks across his eyes and he pulled them impatiently away.

'Come on, Steven,' he said. 'You're kidding me.'

'No.'

Jody was short, stocky, twenty-eight, hardworking, clever, competent and popular. He had been my constant adviser since I had bought my first racehorse three years earlier, and right from the beginning he had robbed me round the clock and smiled while doing it.

'You're crazy,' he said. 'I've just won you a race.'

We stood, indeed, on the patch of turf where winners were unsaddled: where Energise, my newest and glossiest hurdler, had recently decanted his smiling jockey, had stamped and steamed and tossed his head with pride and accepted the crowd's applause as simply his due.

The race he had won had not been important, but the way he had won it had been in the star-making class. The sight of him sprinting up the hill to the winning post, a dark brown streak of rhythm, had given me a rare bursting feeling of admiration, of joy ... probably even of love. Energise was beautiful and courageous and chockfull of will to win and it was because he had won, and won in that fashion, that my hovering intention to break with Jody had hardened into action.

I should, I suppose, have chosen a better time and place.

'I picked out Energise for you at the Sales,' he said.

'I know.'

'And all your other winners.'

'Yes.'

'And I moved into bigger stables because of you.'

I nodded briefly.

'Well ... You can't let me down now.'

Disbelief had given way to anger. His bright blue eyes sharpened to belligerance and the muscles tightened round his mouth.

'I'm taking the horses away,' I repeated. 'And we'll start with Energise. You can leave him here when you go home.'

'You're mad.'

'No.'

'Where's he going then?'

I actually had no idea. I said, 'I'll make all the arrangements. Just leave him in the stable here and go home without him.'

'You've no right to do this.' Full-scale anger blazed in his eyes. 'You're a bloody rotten *shit*.'

But I had every right. He knew it and I knew it. Every owner had the right at any time to withdraw his custom if he were dissatisfied with his trainer. The fact that the right was seldom exercised was beside the point.

Jody was rigid with fury. 'I am taking that horse home with me and nothing is going to stop me.'

His very intensity stoked up in me an answering determination that he should not. I shook my head decisively. I said, 'No, Jody. The horse stays here.'

'Over my dead body.'

His body, alive, quivered with pugnaciousness.

'As of this moment,' I said, 'I'm cancelling your authority to act on my behalf, and I'm going straight into the weighing room to make that clear to all the authorities who need to know.'

He glared. 'You owe me money,' he said. 'You can't take your horses away until you've paid.'

I paid my bills with him on the nail every month and owed him only for the current few weeks. I pulled my cheque book out of my pocket and unclipped my pen.

'I'll give you a cheque right now.'

'No you bloody well won't.'

He snatched the whole cheque book out of my hand and ripped it in two. Then in the same movement he threw the pieces over his shoulder, and all the loose halves of the cheques scattered in the wind. Faces turned our way in astonishment and the eyes of the Press came sharply to life. I couldn't have chosen anywhere more public for what was developing into a first class row.

Jody looked around him. Looked at the men with notebooks. Saw his allies.

His anger grew mean.

'You'll be sorry,' he said. 'I'll chew you into little bits.'

The face that five minutes earlier had smiled with cheerful decisive friendliness had gone for good. Even if I now retracted and apologized, the old relationship could not be re-established. Confidence, like Humpty Dumpty couldn't be put together again.

His fierce opposition had driven me further than I had originally meant. All the same I still had the same objective, even if I had to fight harder to achieve it.

'Whatever you do,' I said, 'you won't keep my horses.'

'You're ruining me,' Jody shouted.

The Press advanced a step or two.

Jody cast a quick eye at them. Maliciousness flooded through him and twisted his features with spite. 'You big rich bastards don't give a damn who you hurt.'

I turned abruptly away from him and went into the weighing room, and there carried out my promise to disown him officially as my trainer. I signed forms cancelling his authority to act for me, and for good measure also included a separate handwritten note to say that I had expressly forbidden him to remove Energise from Sandown Park. No one denied I had the right: there was just an element of coolness towards one who was so vehemently and precipitately ridding himself of the services of the man who had ten minutes ago given him a winner.

I didn't tell them that it had taken a very long time for the mug to face the fact that he was being conned. I didn't tell them how I had thrust the first suspicions away as disloyalty and had made every possible allowance before being reluctantly convinced.

I didn't tell them either that the reason for my determination now lay squarely in Jody's first reaction to my saying I was removing my horses.

Because he hadn't, not then or afterwards, asked the one natural question.

He hadn't asked *why*.

When I left the weighing room, both Jody and the Press had gone from the unsaddling enclosure. Racegoers were hurrying towards the stands to watch the imminent steeplechase, the richest event of the afternoon, and even the officials with whom I'd just been dealing were dashing off with the same intent.

I had no appetite for the race. Decided, instead, to go down to the racecourse stables and ask the gatekeeper there to make sure Energise didn't vanish in a puff of smoke. But as the gatekeeper was there to prevent villainous strangers walking *in*, not any bona fide racehorses walking *out*, I wasn't sure how much use he would be, even if he agreed to help.

He was sitting in his sentry box, a middle-aged sturdy figure in a navy blue serge uniform with brass buttons. Various lists on clipboards hung on hooks on the walls, alongside an electric heater fighting a losing battle against the December chill.

'Excuse me,' I said. 'I want to ask you about my horse...'

'Can't come in here,' he interrupted bossily. 'No owners allowed in without trainers.'

'I know that,' I said. 'I just want to make sure my horse stays here.'

'What horse is that?'

He was adept at interrupting, like many people in small positions of power. He blew on his fingers and looked at me over them without politeness.

'Energise,' I said.

He screwed up his mouth and considered whether to answer. I supposed that he could find no reason against it except natural unhelpfulness, because in the end he said grudgingly, 'Would it be a black horse trained by Leeds?'

'It would.'

'Gone, then,' he said.

'Gone?'

'S'right. Lad took him off, couple of minutes ago.' He jerked his head in the general direction of the path down to the area where the motor horseboxes were parked. 'Leeds was with him. Ask me, they'll have driven off by now.' The idea seemed to cheer him. He smiled.

I left him to his sour satisfaction and took the path at a run. It led down between bushes and opened abruptly straight on to the gravelled acre where dozens of horseboxes stood in haphazard rows.

Jody's box was fawn with scarlet panels along the sides: and Jody's box was already manoeuvring out of its slot and turning to go between two of the rows on its way to the gate.

I slid my binoculars to the ground and left them, and fairly sprinted. Ran in front of the first row of boxes and raced round the end to find Jody's box completing its turn from between the rows about thirty yards away, and accelerating straight towards me

I stood in its path and waved my arms for the driver to stop.

The driver knew me well enough. His name was Andy-Fred. He drove my horses regularly. I saw his face, looking horrified and strained, as he put his hand on the horn button and punched it urgently.

I ignored it, sure that he would stop. He was advancing between a high wooden fence on one side and the flanks of parked horseboxes on the other, and it wasn't until it became obvious that he didn't know what his brakes were for that it occurred to me that maybe Energise was about to leave over *my* dead body, not Jody's.

Anger, not fear, kept me rooted to the spot.

Andy-Fred's nerve broke first, thank God, but only just. He wrenched the wheel round savagely when the massive radiator grille was a bare six feet from my annihilation and the diesel throb was a roar in my ears.

He had left it too late for braking. The sudden swerve took him flatly into the side of the foremost of the parked boxes and with screeching and tearing sounds of metal the front corner of Jody's box ploughed forwards and inwards until the colliding doors of the cabs of both vehicles were locked in one crumpled mess. Glass smashed and tinkled and flew about with razor edges. The engine stalled and died.

The sharp bits on the front of Jody's box had missed me but the smooth wing caught me solidly as I leapt belatedly to get out of the way. I lay where I'd bounced, half against the wooden fence, and wholly winded.

Andy-Fred jumped down unhurt from the unsmashed side of his cab and advanced with a mixture of fear, fury and relief.

'What the bloody hell d'you think you're playing at?' he yelled.

'Why . . .' I said weakly, 'didn't . . . you . . . stop?'

I doubt if he heard me. In any case, he didn't answer. He turned instead to the exploding figure of Jody, who arrived at a run along the front of the boxes, the same way that I had come.

He practically danced when he saw the crushed cabs and rage poured from his mouth like fire.

'You stupid *bugger*,' he shouted at Andy-Fred. 'You stupid sodding effing . . .'

The burly box driver shouted straight back.

'He stood right in my way.'

'I told you not to stop.'

'I'd have killed him.'

'No you wouldn't.'

'I'm telling you. He stood there. Just stood there . . .'

'He'd have jumped if you'd kept on going. You stupid bugger. Just look what you've done. You stupid . . .'

Their voices rose, loud and acrimonious, into the wind. Further away the commentator's voice boomed over the tannoy system, broadcasting the progress of the steeplechase. On the other side of the high wooden fence the traffic pounded up and down the London to Guildford road. I gingerly picked myself off the cold gravel and leaned against the weathered planks.

Nothing broken. Breathing coming back. Total damage, all the buttons missing from my overcoat. There was a row of small right-angled tears down the front where the buttons had been. I looked at them vaguely and knew I'd been lucky.

Andy-Fred was telling Jody at the top of a raucous voice that he wasn't killing anyone for Jody's sake, he was bloody well not.

'You're fired,' Jody yelled.

'Right.'

He took a step back, looked intensely at the mangled horseboxes, looked at me, and looked at Jody. He thrust his face close to Jody's and yelled at him again.

'*Right.*'

Then he stalked away in the direction of the stables and didn't bother to look back.

Jody's attention and fury veered sharply towards me. He took three or four purposeful steps and yelled, 'I'll sue you for this.'

I said, 'Why don't you find out if the horse is all right?'

He couldn't hear me for all the day's other noises.

'What?'

'Energise,' I said loudly. 'Is he all right?'

He gave me a sick hot look of loathing and scudded away round the side of the box. More slowly, I followed. Jody yanked open the groom's single door and hauled himself up inside and I went after him.

Energise was standing in his stall quivering from head to foot and staring wildly about with a lot of white round his eyes. Jody had packed him off still sweating from his race and in no state anyway to travel and the crash had clearly terrified him: but he was none the less on his feet and Jody's anxious search could find no obvious injury.

'No thanks to you,' Jody said bitterly.

'Nor to you.'

We faced each other in the confined space, a quiet oasis out of the wind.

'You've been stealing from me,' I said. 'I didn't want to believe it. But from now on . . . I'm not giving you the chance.'

'You won't be able to prove a thing.'

'Maybe not. Maybe I won't even try. Maybe I'll write off what I've lost as the cost of my rotten judgement in liking and trusting you.'

He said indignantly, 'I've done bloody well for you.'

'And out of me.'

'What do you expect? Trainers aren't in it for love, you know.'

'Trainers don't all do what you've done.'

A sudden speculative look came distinctly into his eyes. 'What have I done, then?' he demanded.

'You tell me,' I said. 'You haven't even pretended to deny you've been cheating me.'

'Look, Steven, you're so bloodly unwordly. All right, so maybe I have added a bit on here and there. If you're talking about the time I charged you travelling expenses for Hermes to Haydock the day they abandoned for fog before the first . . . well, I know I didn't actually *send* the horse . . . he went lame that morning and couldn't go. But trainer's perks. Fair's fair. And you could afford it. You'd never miss thirty measly quid.'

'What else?' I said.

He seemed reassured. Confidence and a faint note of defensive wheedling seeped into his manner and voice.

'Well . . .' he said. 'If you ever disagreed with the totals of your bills, why didn't you query it with me? I'd have straightened things out at once. There was no need to bottle it all up and blow your top without warning.'

Ouch, I thought. I hadn't even checked that all the separate items on the monthly bills did add up to the totals I'd paid. Even when I was sure he was robbing me, I hadn't suspected it would be in any way so ridiculously simple.

'What else?' I said.

He looked away for a second, then decided that I couldn't after all know a great deal.

'Oh all right,' he said, as if making a magnanimous concession. 'It's Raymond, isn't it?'

'Among other things.'

Jody nodded ruefully. 'I guess I did pile it on a bit, charging you for him twice a week when some weeks he only came once.'

'And some weeks not at all.'

'Oh well . . .' said Jody deprecatingly. 'I suppose so, once or twice.'

Raymond Child rode all my jumpers in races and drove fifty miles some mornings to school them over fences on Jody's gallops. Jody gave him a fee and expenses for the service and added them to my account. The twice a week schooling session fees had turned up regularly for the whole of July, when in fact, as I had very recently and casually discovered, no horses had been schooled at all and Raymond himself had been holidaying in Spain.

'A tenner here or there,' Jody said persuasively. 'It's nothing to you.'

'A tenner plus expenses twice a week for July came to over a hundred quid.'

'Oh.' He tried a twisted smile. 'So you really have been checking up.'

'What did you expect?'

'You're so easy going. You've always paid up without question.'

'Not any more.'

'No . . . Look, Steven, I'm sorry about all this. If I give you my word there'll be no more fiddling on your account . . . If I promise every item will be strictly accurate . . . why don't we go on as before? I've won a lot of races for you, after all.'

He looked earnest, sincere and repentant. Also totally confident that I would give him a second chance. A quick canter from confession to penitence, and a promise to reform, and all could proceed as before.

'It's too late,' I said.

He was not discouraged; just piled on a bit more of the ingratiating manner which announced 'I know I've been a bad boy but now I've been found out I'll be angelic.'

'I suppose having so much extra expense made me behave stupidly,' he said. 'The mortgage repayments on the new stables are absolutely bloody, and as you know I only moved there because I needed more room for all your horses.'

My fault, now, that he had had to steal.

I said, 'I offered to build more boxes at the old place.'

'Wouldn't have done,' he interrupted hastily: but the truth of it was that the old place had been on a plain and modest scale where the new one was frankly opulent. At the time of the move I had vaguely wondered how he could afford it. Now, all too well, I knew.

'So let's call this just a warning, eh?' Jody said cajolingly. 'I don't want to lose your horses, Steven. I'll say so frankly. I don't want to lose them. We've been good friends all this time, haven't we? If you'd just *said* . . . I mean, if you'd just said, "Jody, you bugger, you've been careless about a bill or two . . ." Well, I mean, we could have straightened it out in no time. But . . . well . . . When you blew off without warning, just said you were taking your horses away, straight after Energise won like that . . . well, I lost my temper real and proper. I'll admit I did. Said things I didn't mean. Like one does. Like everyone does when they lose their temper.'

He was smiling in a counterfeit of the old way, as if nothing at all had happened. As if Energise were not standing beside us sweating in a crashed horsebox. As if my overcoat were not turn and muddy from a too close brush with death.

'Steven, you know me,' he said. 'Got a temper like a bloody rocket.'

When I didn't answer at once he took my silence as acceptance of his explanations and apologies, and briskly turned to practical matters.

'Well now, we'll have to get this lad out of here.' He slapped Energise on the rump. 'And we can't get the ramp down until we get this box moved away from that other one.' He made a sucking sound through his teeth. 'Look, I'll try to back straight out again. Don't see why it shouldn't work.'

He jumped out of the back door and went round to the front of the cab. Looking forward through the stalls I could see him climb into the driver's seat, check the gear lever, and press the starter: an intent, active, capable figure dealing with an awkward situation.

The diesel starter whirred and the engine roared to life. Jody settled himself, found reverse gear, and carefully let out the clutch. The horsebox shuddered and stood still. Jody put his foot down on the accelerator.

Through the windscreen I could see two or three men approaching, faces a mixture of surprise and anger. One of them began running and waving his arms about in the classic reaction of the chap who comes back to his parked car to find it dented.

Jody ignored him. The horsebox rocked, the crushed side of the cab screeched against its mangled neighbour, and Energise began to panic.

'Jody, stop,' I yelled.

He took no notice. He raced the engine harder, then took his foot off the accelerator, then jammed it on again. Off, on, repeatedly.

Inside the box it sounded as if the whole vehicle were being ripped in two. Energise began whinnying and straining backwards on his tethering rope and stamping about with sharp hooves. I didn't know how to begin to soothe him and could hardly get close enough for a pat, even if that would have made the slightest difference. My relationship with horses was along the lines of admiring them from a distance and giving them carrots while they were safely tied up. No one had briefed me about dealing with a hysterical animal at close quarters in a bucketing biscuit tin.

With a final horrendous crunch the two entwined cabs tore apart and Jody's box, released from friction, shot backwards. Energise slithered and went down for a moment on his hindquarters and I too wound up on the floor. Jody slammed on the brakes, jumped out of the cab and was promptly clutched by the three newcomers, one now in a full state of apoplectic rage.

I stood up and picked bits of hay off my clothes and regarded my steaming, foamflaked, terrified, four-footed property.

'All over, old fellow,' I said. It sounded ridiculous. I smiled, cleared my throat, tried again.

'You can cool off, old lad. The worst is over.'

Energise showed no immediate signs of getting the message. I told him he was a great horse, he'd won a great race, he'd be king of the castle in no time and that I admired him very much. I told him he would soon be rugged up nice and quiet in a stable somewhere though I hadn't actually yet worked out exactly which one, and that doubtless someone would give him some excessively expensive hay and a bucket of nice cheap water and I dared say some oats and stuff life that. I told him I was sorry I hadn't a carrot in my pocket at that moment but I'd bring him one next time I saw him.

After a time this drivel seemed to calm him. I put out a hand and gave his neck a small pat. His skin was wet and fiery hot. He shook his head fiercely and blew out vigorously through black moist nostrils, but the staring white no longer showed round his eye and he had stopped trembling. I began to grow interested in him in a way which had not before occurred to me: as a person who happened also to be a horse.

I realized I had never before been alone with a horse. Extraordinary, really, when Energise was the twelfth I'd owned. But racehorse owners mostly patted their horses in stables with lads and trainers in attendance, and in parade rings with all the world looking on, and in unsaddling enclosures with friends pressing round to congratulate. Owners who like me were not riders themselves and had nowhere of their own to turn horses out to grass seldom ever spent more than five consecutive minutes in a horse's company.

I spent longer with Energise in that box than in all the past five months since I'd bought him.

Outside, Jody was having troubles. One of the men had fetched a policeman who was writing purposefully in a notebook. I wondered with amusement just how Jody would lay the blame on my carelessness in walking in front of the box and giving the driver no choice but to swerve. If he thought he was keeping my horses, he would play it down. If he thought he was losing them, he'd be vitriolic. Smiling to myself I talked it over with Energise.

'You know,' I said, 'I don't know why I haven't told him yet that I know about his other fraud, but as it turns out I'm damn glad I haven't. Do you know?' I said. 'All those little fiddles he confessed to, they're just froth.'

Energise was calm enough to start drooping with tiredness. I watched him sympathetically.

'It isn't just a few hundred quid he's pinched,' I said. 'It's upwards of thirty-five thousand.'

Chapter Two

The owner of the crunched box accepted my apologies remembered he was well insured and decided not to press charges. The policeman sighed, drew a line through his notes and departed. Jody let down the ramp of his box, brought out Energise and walked briskly away with him in the direction of the stables. And I returned to my binoculars, took off my battered coat and went thoughtfully back towards the weighing room.

The peace lasted for all of ten minutes – until Jody returned from the stables and found that I had not cancelled my cancellation of his authority to act.

He sought me out among the small crowd standing around talking on the weighing room verandah.

'Look, Steven,' he said. 'You've forgotten to tell them I'm still training for you.'

He showed no anxiety, just slight exasperation at my oversight. I weakened for one second at the thought of the storm which would undoubtedly break out again and began to make all the old fatal allowances : he *was* a good trainer, and my horses *did* win, now and again. And I could keep a sharp eye on the bills and let him know I was doing it. And as for the other thing ... I could easily avoid being robbed in future.

I took a deep breath. It had to be now or never.

'I haven't forgotten,' I said slowly. 'I meant what I said. I'm taking the horses away.'

'*What*?'

'I am taking them away.'

The naked enmity that filled his face was shocking.

'You *bastard*,' he said.

Heads turned again in our direction.

Jody produced several further abusive epithets, all enunciated very clearly in a loud voice. The Press notebooks sprouted like mushrooms in little white blobs on the edge of my vision and I took the only way I knew to shut him up.

'I backed Energise today on the Tote,' I said.

Jody said. 'So what?' very quickly in the second before the impact of what I meant hit him like a punch.

'I'm closing my account with Ganser Mays,' I said.

Jody looked absolutely murderous, but he didn't ask *why*. Instead he clamped his jaws together, cast a less welcoming glance at the attentive Press and said very quietly and with menace, 'If you say anything I'll sue you for libel.'

'Slander,' I said automatically.

'What?'

'Libel is written, slander is spoken.'

'I'll have you,' he said, 'if you say anything.'

'Some friendship,' I commented.

His eyes narrowed. 'It was a pleasure,' he said, 'To take you for every penny I could.'

A small silence developed. I felt that racing had gone thoroughly sour and that I would never get much fun from it again. Three years of uncomplicated enjoyment had crumbled to disillusionment.

In the end I simply said, 'Leave Energise here. I'll fix his transport,' and Jody turned on his heel with a stony face and plunged in through the weighing room door.

The transport proved no problem. I arranged with a young owner-driver of a one-box transport firm that he should take Energise back to his own small transit yard overnight and ferry him on in a day or two to whichever trainer I decided to send him.

'A dark brown horse. Almost black,' I said. 'The gatekeeper will tell you which box he's in. But I don't suppose he'll have a lad with him.'

The owner-driver, it transpired, could provide a lad to look after Energise. 'He'll be right as rain,' he said. 'No need for you to worry.' He had brought two other horses to the course, one of which was in the last race, and he would be away within an hour afterwards, he said. We exchanged telephone numbers and addresses and shook hands on the deal.

After that, more out of politeness than through any great appetite for racing, I went back to the private box of the man who had earlier given me lunch and with whom I'd watched my own horse win.

'Steven, where have you been? We've been waiting to help you celebrate.'

Charlie Canterfield, my host, held his arms wide in welcome, with a glass of champagne in one hand and a cigar in the other. He and his eight or ten other guests sat on dining chairs round a large central table, its white cloth covered now not with the paraphernalia of lunch, but with a jumble of half full glasses, race cards, binoculars, gloves, handbags and betting tickets. A faint haze of Havana smoke and the warm smell of alcohol filled the air, and beyond, on the other side of snugly closed glass, lay the balcony overlooking the fresh and windy racecourse.

Four races down and two to go. Mid afternoon. Everyone happy in the interval between coffee-and-brandy and cake-and-tea. A cosy little roomful of chat and friendliness and mild social smugness. Well-intentioned people doing no one any harm.

I sighed inwardly and raised a semblance of enjoyment for Charlie's sake, and sipped champagne and listened to everyone telling me it was *great* that Energise had won. They'd all backed it, they said.

Lots of lovely lolly, Steven dear. Such a clever horse ... and such a clever little trainer, Jody Leeds.

'Mm,' I said, with a dryness no one heard.

Charlie waved me to the empty chair between himself and a lady in a green hat.

'What do you fancy for the next race?' he asked.

I looked at him with a mind totally blank.

'Can't remember what's running,' I said.

Charlie's leisured manner skipped a beat. I'd seen it in him before, this split-second assessment of a new factor and I knew that therein lay the key to his colossal business acumen. His body might laze, his bonhomie might expand like softly whipped cream, but his brain never took a moment off.

I gave him a twisted smile.

Charlie said 'Come to dinner.'

'Tonight, do you mean?'

He nodded.

I bit my thumb and thought about it. 'All right.'

'Good. Let's say Parkes, Beauchamp Place, eight o'clock.'

'All right.'

The relationship between Charlie and me had stood for years in that vague area between acquaintanceship and active friendship where chance meetings are enjoyed and deliberate ones seldom arranged. That day was the first time he had invited me to his private box. Asking me for dinner as well meant a basic shift to new ground.

I guessed he had misread my vagueness, but all the same I liked him, and no one in his right mind would pass up a dinner at Parkes. I hoped he wouldn't think it a wasted evening.

Charlie's guests began disappearing to put on bets for the next race. I picked up a spare race card which was lying on the table and knew at once why Charlie had paid me such acute attention: two of the very top hurdlers were engaged in battle and the papers had been talking about it for days.

I looked up and met Charlie's gaze. His eyes were amused.

'Which one, then?' he asked.

'Crepitas.'

'Are you betting?'

I nodded. 'I did it earlier. On the Tote.'

He grunted. 'I prefer the bookmakers. I like to know what odds I'm getting before I lay out my cash,' And considering his business was investment banking that was consistent thinking. 'I can't be bothered to walk down, though.'

'You can have half of mine, if you like,' I said.

'Half of how much?' he said cautiously.

'Ten pounds.'

He laughed. 'Rumour says you can't think in anything less than three noughts.'

'That was an engineering joke,' I said, 'which escaped.'

'How do you mean?'

'I sometimes use a precision lathe. You can just about set it to an accuracy of three noughts ... point nought nought nought one. One ten thousandth of an inch. That's my limit. Can't think in less than three noughts.'

He chuckled. 'And you never have a thousand on a horse?'

'Oh, I did that too, once or twice.'

He definitely did, that time, hear the arid undertone. I stood up casually and moved towards the glass door to the balcony.

'They're going down to the post,' I said.

He came without comment, and we stood outside watching the two stars, Crepitas and Waterboy, bouncing past the stands with their jockeys fighting for control.

Charlie was a shade shorter than I, a good deal stouter, and approximately twenty years older. He wore top quality clothes as a matter of course and no one hearing his mellow voice would have guessed his father had been a lorry driver. Charlie had never hidden his origins. Indeed he was justly proud of them. It was simply that under the old education system he'd been sent to Eton as a local boy on Council money, and had acquired the speech and social habits along with the book learning. His brains had taken him along all his life like a surf rider on the crest of a roller, and it was probably only a modest piece of extra luck that he'd happened to be borne within sight of the big school.

His other guests drifted out on to the balcony and claimed his attention. I knew none of them well, most of them by sight, one or two by reputation. Enough for the occasion, not enough for involvement.

The lady in the green hat put a green glove on my arm. 'Waterboy looks wonderful, don't you think.'

'Wonderful,' I agreed.

She gave me a bright myopic smile from behind thick lensed glasses. 'Could you just tell me what price they're offering now in the ring?'

'Of course.'

I raised my binoculars and scanned the boards of the bookmakers ranged in front of a sector of stands lying some way to our right. 'It looks like evens Waterboy and five to four Crepitas, as far as I can see.'

'So kind,' said the green lady warmly.

I swung the binoculars round a little to search out Ganser Mays: and there he stood, half way down the row of bookmakers lining the rails separating the Club Enclosure from Tattersall's, a thin man of middle height with a large sharp nose, steel-rimmed spectacles and the manner of a high church clergyman. I had never liked him enough to do more than talk about the weather, but I had trusted him completely, and that had been foolish.

He was leaning over the rails, head bent, talking earnestly to someone in the Club Enclosure, someone hidden from me by a bunch of other people. Then the bunch shifted and moved away and the person behind them was Jody.

The anger in Jody's body came over sharp and clear and his lower jaw moved vigorously in speech. Ganser Mays' responses appeared more soothing than fierce and when Jody finally strode furiously away, Ganser Mays raised his head and looked after him with an expression more thoughtful than actively worried.

Ganser Mays had reached that point in a bookmaker's career where outstanding personal success began to merge into the status of a large and respectable firm. In gamblers' minds he was moving from an individual to an institution. A multiplying host of betting shops bore his name from Glasgow southwards, and recently he had announced that next Flat season he would sponsor a three-year-old sprint.

He still stood on the rails himself at big meetings to talk to his more affluent customers and keep them faithful. To open his big shark jaws and suck in all the new unwary little fish.

With a wince I swung my glasses away. I would never know exactly how much Jody and Ganser Mays had stolen from me in terms of cash, but in terms of dented self-respect they had stripped me of all but crumbs.

The race started, the super-hurdlers battled their hearts out, and Crepitas beat Waterboy by a length. The Tote would pay me a little because of him, and a great deal because of Energise, but two winning bets in one afternoon weren't enough to dispel my depression. I dodged the tea-and-cakes, thanked Charle for the lunch and said I'd see him later, and went down towards the weighing room again to see if inspiration would strike in the matter of a choice of trainers.

I heard hurrying footsteps behind me and a hand grabbed my arm.

'Thank goodness I've found you.'

He was out of breath and looking worried. The young owner-driver I'd hired for Energise.

'What is it? Box broken down?'

'No . . . look, you did say your horse was black, didn't you? I mean, I did get that right, didn't I?'

Anxiety sharpened my voice. 'Is there anything wrong with him?'

'No . . . at least . . . not with him, no. But the horse which Mr Leeds has left for me to take is . . . well . . . a chestnut mare.'

I went with him to the stables. The gatekeeper still smiled with pleasure at things going wrong.

'S'right,' he said with satisfaction. 'Leeds went off a quarter of an hour ago in one of them hire boxes, one horse. Said his own box had had an accident and he was leaving Energise here, instructions of the owner.'

'The horse he's left is not Energise,' I said.

'Can't help that, can I?' he said virtuously.

I turned to the young man. 'Chestnut mare with a big white blaze?'

'That's Asphodel. She ran in the first race today. Jody Leeds trains her. She isn't mine.'

'What will I do about her then?'

'Leave her here,' I said. 'Sorry about this. Send me a bill for cancellation fees.'

He smiled and said he wouldn't, which almost restored my faith in human nature. I thanked him for bothering to find me instead of keeping quiet, taking the wrong horse and then sending me a bill for work done. He looked shocked that anyone could be so cynical, and I reflected that until I learnt from Jody, I wouldn't have been.

Jody had taken Energise after all.

I burnt with slow anger, partly because of my own lack of foresight. If he had been prepared to urge Andy-Fred to risk running me down I should have known that he wouldn't give up at the first setback. He had been determined to get the better of me and whisk Energise back to his own stable and I'd underestimated both his bloody-mindedness and nis nerve.

I could hardly wait to be free of Jody. I went back to my car and drove away from the racecourse with no thoughts but of which trainer I would ask to take my horses and how soon I could get them transferred from one to the other.

Charlie smiled across the golden polished wood of the table in Parkes and pushed away his empty coffee cup. His cigar was half smoked, his port half drunk, and his stomach, if mine were anything to go by, contentedly full of some of the best food in London.

I wondered what he had looked like as a young man, before the comfortable paunch and the beginning of jowls. Big businessmen were all the better for a little weight, I thought. Lean-and-hungry was for the starters, the hotheads in a hurry. Charlie exuded maturity and wisdom with every excess pound.

He had smooth greying hair, thin on top and brushed back at the sides. Eyes deep set, nose large, mouth firmly straight. Not conventionally a good-looking face, but easy to remember. People who had once met Charlie tended to know him next time.

He had come alone, and the restaurant he had chosen consisted of several smallish rooms with three or four tables in each; a quiet place where privacy was easy. He had talked about racing, food, the Prime Minister and the state of the Stock Market, and still had not come to the point.

'I get the impression,' he said genially, 'that you are waiting for something.'

'You've never asked me to dine before.'

'I like your company.'

'And that's all?'

He tapped ash off the cigar. 'Of course not,' he said.

'I thought not,' I smiled. 'But I've probably eaten your dinner under false pretences.'

'Knowingly.'

'Maybe. I don't know exactly what's in your mind.'

'Your vagueness,' he said. 'When someone like you goes into a sort of trance...'

'I thought so,' I sighed. 'Well, that was no useful productive otherwhereness of mind, that was the aftermath of a practically mortal row I'd just had with Jody Leeds.'

He sat back in his chair. 'What a pity.'

'Pity about the row, or a pity about the absence of inspiration?'

'Both, I dare say. What was the row about?'

'I gave him the sack.'

He stared. 'What on earth for?'

'He said if I told anyone that, he'd sue me for slander.'

'Oh, did he indeed!' Charlie looked interested all over again, like a horse taking fresh hold of its bit. 'And could he?'

'I expect so.'

Charlie sucked a mouthful of smoke and trickled it out from one corner of his mouth.

'Care to risk it?' he said.

'Your discretion's better than most . . .'

'Absolute,' he said. 'I promise.'

I believed him. I said, 'He found a way of stealing huge sums from me so that I didn't know I was being robbed.'

'But you must have known that *someone* . . .'

I shook my head. 'I dare say I'm not the first the trick's been played on. It's so deadly simple.'

'Proceed,' Charlie said. 'You fascinate me.'

'Right. Now suppose you are basically a good racehorse trainer but you've got a large and crooked thirst for unearned income.'

'I'm supposing,' Charlie said.

'First of all, then,' I said, 'you need a silly mug with a lot of money and enthusiasm and not much knowledge of racing.'

'You?' Charlie said.

'Me.' I nodded ruefully. 'Someone recommends you to me as a good trainer and I'm impressed by your general air of competence and dedication, so I toddle up and ask you if you could find me a good horse, as I'd like to become an owner.'

'And do I buy a good horse cheaply and charge you a fortune for it?'

'No. You buy the very best horse you can. I am delighted, and you set about the training and very soon the horse is ready to run. At this point you tell me you know a very reliable bookmaker and you introduce me to him.'

'Oh hum.'

'As you say. The bookmaker however is eminently respectable and respected and as I am not used to betting in large amounts I am glad to be in the hands of so worthy a fellow. You, my trainer, tell me the horse shows great promise and I might think of a small each way bet on his first race. A hundred pounds each way, perhaps.'

'A small bet!' Charlie exclaimed.

'You point out that that is scarcely more than three weeks' training fees,' I said.

'I do?'

'You do. So I gulp a little as I've always bet in tenners before and I stake a hundred each way. But sure enough the horse does well and finishes third, and the bookmaker pays out a little instead of my paying him.'

I drank the rest of my glass of port. Charlie finished his and ordered more coffee.

'Next time the horse runs,' I went on, 'you say it is really well and sure to win and if I ever want to have a big bet, now's the time, before everyone else jumps on the bandwagon. The bookmaker offers me a good price and I feel euphoric and take the plunge.'

'A thousand?'

I nodded. 'A thousand.'

'And?'

'The word goes round and the horse starts favourite. It is not his day, though. He runs worse that the first time and finishes fifth. You are very upset. You can't understand it. I find myself comforting you and telling you he is bound to run better next time.'

'But he doesn't run better next time?'

'But he does. Next time he wins beautifully.'

'But you haven't backed it?'

'Yes, I have. The price this time isn't five to two as it was before, but six to one. I stake five hundred pounds and win three thousand. I am absolutely delighted. I have regained all the money I had lost and more besides, and I have also gained the prize money for the race. I pay the training bills out of the winnings and I have recouped part of the purchase price of the horse, and I am very happy with the whole business of being an owner. I ask you to buy me another horse. Buy two or three, if you can find them.'

'And this time you get expensive duds?'

'By no means. My second horse is a marvellous two-year-old. He wins his very first race. I have only a hundred on him, mind you, but as it is at ten to one, I am still very pleased. So next time out, as my horse is a hot favourite and tipped in all the papers, you encourage me to have a really big bet. Opportunities like this seldom arise, you tell me, as the opposition is hopeless. I am convinced, so I lay out three thousand pounds.'

'My God,' Charlie said.

'Quite so. My horse sprints out of the stalls and takes the lead like the champion he is and everything is going splendidly. But then half way along the five furlongs a buckle breaks on the saddle and the girths come loose and the jockey has to pull up as best he can because by now he is falling off.'

'Three thousand!' Charlie said.

'All gone,' I nodded. 'You are inconsolable. The strap was new, the buckle faulty. Never mind, I say kindly, gulping hard. Always another day.'

'And there is?'

'You're learning. Next time out the horse is favourite again and I have five hundred on. He wins all right, and although I have not this time won back all I lost, well, it's the second time the horse has brought home a decent prize, and taking all in all I am not out of pocket and I have had a great deal of pleasure and excitement. And I am well content.'

'And so it goes on?'

'And so, indeed, it goes on. I find I get more and more delight from watching horses. I get particular delight if the horses are my own, and although in time of course my hobby costs me a good deal of money, because owners on the whole don't make a profit, I am totally happy and consider it well spent.'

'And then what happens?'

'Nothing really,' I said. 'I just begin to get these niggling suspicions and I thrust them out of my head and think how horribly disloyal I am being to you, after all the winners you have trained for me. But the suspicions won't lie down. I've noticed, you see, that when I have my biggest bets, my horses don't win.'

'A lot of owners could say the same,' Charlie said.

'Oh sure. But I tot up all the big bets which didn't come up, and they come to nearly forty thousand pounds.'

'Good God.'

'I am really ashamed of myself, but I begin to *wonder*. I say to myself, suppose . . . just suppose . . . that every time I stake anything over a thousand, my trainer and my bookmaker conspire together and simply keep the money and make sure my horse doesn't win. Just suppose . . . that if I stake three thousand, they split it fifty fifty, and the horse runs badly, or is left, or the buckle on the girth breaks. Just suppose that next time out my horse is trained to the utmost and the race is carefully chosen and he duly wins, and I am delighted . . . just suppose that this time my bookmaker and my trainer are betting on the horse themselves . . . with the money they stole from me last time.'

Charlie looked riveted.

'If my horse wins, they win. If my horse loses, they haven't lost their money, but only mine.'

'Neat.'

'Yes. So the weeks pass and now the Flat season is finished, and we are back again with the jumpers. And you, my trainer, have found and bought for me a beautiful young hurdler, a really top class horse. I back him a little in his first race and he wins it easily. I am thrilled. I am also worried, because you tell me there is a race absolutely made for him at Sandown Park which he is certain to win, and you encourage me to have a very big bet on him. I am by now filled with horrid doubts and fears, and as I particularly admire this horse I do not want his heart broken by trying to win when he isn't allowed to . . . which I am sure happened to one or two of the others . . . so I say I will not back him.'

'Unpopular?'

'Very. You press me harder than ever before to lay out a large stake. I refuse. You are obviously annoyed and warn me that the horse will win and I will be sorry. I say I'll wait till next time. You say I am making a big mistake.'

'When do I say all this?'

'Yesterday.'

'And today?' Charlie asked.

'Today I am suffering from suspicion worse than ever. Today I think that maybe you will let the horse win if he can, just to prove I was wrong not to back him, so that next time you will have no difficulty at all in persuading me to have a bigger bet than ever.'

'Tut tut.'

'Yes. So today I don't tell you that a little while ago ... because of my awful doubts ... I opened a credit account with the Tote, and today I also don't tell you that I have backed my horse for a thousand pounds on my credit account.'

'Deceitful of you.'

'Certainly.'

'And your horse wins,' Charlie said, nodding.

'He looked superb ...' I smiled wryly. 'You tell me after the race that it is my own fault I didn't back him. You say you did try to get me to. You say I'd do better to take your advice next time.'

'And then?'

'Then,' I sighed, 'all the weeks of suspicion just jelled into certainty. I knew he'd been cheating me in other ways too. Little ways. Little betrayals of friendship. Nothing enormous. I told him there wasn't going to be a next time. I said I would be taking the horses away?'

'What did he say to that?'

'He didn't ask why.'

'Oh dear,' Charlie said.

Chapter Three

I told Charlie everything that had happened that day. All amusement died from his expression and by the end he was looking grim.

'He'll get away with it,' he said finally.

'Oh yes.'

'You remember, I suppose, that his father's a member of the Jockey Club?'

'Yes.'

'Above suspicion, is Jody Leeds.'

Jody's father, Quintus Leeds, had achieved pillar-of-the-Turf status by virtue of being born the fifth son of a sporting peer, owning a few racehorses and knowing the right friends. He had a physically commanding presence, tall, large and handsome, and his voice and handshake radiated firm confidence. He was apt to give people straight piercing looks from fine grey eyes and to purse his mouth thoughtfully and shake his head as if pledged to secrecy when asked for an opinion. I privately thought his appearance and mannerisms were a lot of glossy window-dressing concealing a marked absence of goods, but there was no doubting that he was basically well-meaning and honest.

He was noticeably proud of Jody, puffing up his chest and beaming visibly in unsaddling enclosures from Epsom to York.

In his father's eyes, Jody, energetic, capable and clever, could do no wrong. Quintus would believe in him implicitly, and for all his suspect shortness of intelligence he carried enough weight to sway official opinion.

As Jody had said, I couldn't prove a thing. If I so much as hinted at theft he'd slap a lawsuit on me, and the bulk of the Jockey Club would be ranged on his side.

'What will you do?' Charlied said.

'Don't know.' I half smiled. 'Nothing, I suppose.'

'It's bloody unfair.'

'All crime is bloody unfair on the victim.'

Charlie made a face at the general wickedness of the world and called for the bill.

Outside we turned left and walked down Beauchamp Place together, having both, as it happened, parked our cars round the corner in Walton Street. The night was cold, cloudy, dry and still windy. Charlie pulled his coat collar up round his ears and put on thick black leather gloves.

'I hate the winter,' he said.

'I don't mind it.'

'You're young,' he said. 'You don't feel the cold.'

'Not that young. Thirty-five.'

'Practically a baby.'

We turned the corner and the wind bit sharply with Arctic teeth. 'I hate it,' Charlie said.

His car, a big blue Rover 3500, was parked nearer than my Lamborghini. We stopped beside his and he unlocked the door. Down the street a girl in a long dress walked in our direction, the wind blowing her skirt sideways and her hair like flags.

'Very informative evening,' he said, holding out his hand.

'Not what you expected, though,' I said, shaking it.

'Better, perhaps.'

He opened his door and began to lower himself into the driver's seat. The girl in the long dress walked past us, her heels brisk on the pavement. Charlie fastened his seat belt and I shut his door.

The girl in the long dress stopped, hesitated and turned back.

'Excuse me,' she said. 'But I wonder . . .' She stopped, appearing to think better of it.

'Can we help you?' I said.

She was American, early twenties, and visibly cold. Round her shoulders she wore only a thin silk shawl, and under that a thin silk shirt. No gloves. Gold sandals. A small gold mesh purse. In the street lights her skin looked blue and she was shivering violently.

'Get in my car,' Charlie suggested, winding down his window, 'out of the wind.'

She shook her head. 'I guess . . .' She began to turn away.

'Don't be silly,' I said. 'You need help. Accept it.'

'But . . .'

'Tell us what you need.'

She hesitated again and then said with a rush, 'I need some money.'

'Is that all?' I said and fished out my wallet. 'How much?'

'Enough for a taxi . . . to Hampstead.'

I held out a fiver. 'That do?'

'Yes. I . . . where shall I send it back to?'

'Don't bother.'

'But I must.'

Charlie said, 'He's got wads of the stuff. He won't miss it.'

'That's not the point,' the girl said. 'If you won't tell me how to repay it, I can't take it.'

'It is ridiculous to argue about morals when you're freezing,' I said. 'My name is Steven Scott. Address, Regent's Park Malthouse. That'll find me.'

'Thanks.'

'I'll drive you, if you like. I have my car.' I pointed along the street.

'No thanks,' she said. 'How d'you think I got *into* this mess?'

'How then?'

She pulled the thin shawl close. 'I accepted a simple invitation to dinner and found there were strings attached. So I left him at the soup stage and blasted out, and it was only when I was walking away that I realised that I'd no money with me. He'd collected me, you see.' She smiled suddenly, showing straight white teeth. 'Some girls are dumber than others.'

'Let Steven go and find you a taxi, then,' Charlie said.

'Okay.'

I took me several minutes, but she was still huddled against the outside of Charlie's car, sheltering as best she could from the worst of the wind, when I got back. I climbed out of the taxi and she climbed in and without more ado and drove away.

'A fool and his money,' Charlie said.

'That was no con trick.'

'It would be a good one,' he said. 'How do you know she's not hopping out of the cab two blocks away and shaking a fiver out of the next Sir Galahad?'

He laughed, wound up the window, waved and pointed his Rover towards home.

Monday morning brought the good news and the bad.

The good was a letter with a five pound note enclosed. Sucks to Charlie, I thought.

Dear Mr Scott,

I was so grateful for your help on Saturday night. I guess I'll never go out on a date again without the cab fare home.

Yours sincerely,

Alexandra Ward.

The bad news was in public print: comments in both newspapers delivered to my door (one sporting, one ordinary) about the disloyalty of owners who shed their hardworking trainers. One said:

> Particularly hard on Jody Leeds that after all he had done for Mr Scott the owner should see fit to announce he would be sending his horses elsewhere. As we headlined in this column a year ago, Jody Leeds took on the extensive Berksdown Court Stables especially to house the expanding Scott string. Now without as much as half an hour's warning, the twenty-eight-year-old trainer is left flat, with all his new liabilities still outstanding. Treachery may sound a harsh word. Ingratitude is not.

And the other, in more tabloid vein:

> Leeds (28 smarting from the sack delivered by ungrateful owner Steven Scott (35) said at Sandown on Saturday, 'I am right in the cart now. Scott dumped me while still collecting backslaps for the win on his hurdler Energise, which I trained. I am sick at heart. You sweat your guts out for an owner, and he kicks you in the teeth.'
>
> High time trainers were protected from this sort of thing. Rumour has it Leeds may sue.

All those Press note books, all those extended Press ears, had not been there for nothing. Very probably they did all genuinely believe that Jody had had a raw deal, but not one single one had bothered to ask what the view looked like from where I stood. Not one single one seemed to think that there might have been overpowering reason for my action.

I disgustedly put down both papers, finished my breakfast and settled down to the day's work, which as usual consisted mostly of sitting still in an armchair and staring vacantly into space.

Around mid-afternoon, stiff and chilly, I wrote to Miss Ward.

> Dear Miss Ward,
>
> Thank you very much for the fiver. Will you have dinner with me? No strings attached. I enclose five pounds for the cab fare home.
>
> Yours sincerely,
>
> Steven Scott.

In the evening I telephoned three different racehorse trainers and offered them three horses each. They all accepted, but with the reservations blowing cool in their voices. None actually asked why I had split with Jody though all had obviously read the papers.

One, a blunt north countryman, said 'I'll want a guarantee you'll leave them with me for at least six months, so long as they don't go lame or something.'

'All right.'

'In writing.'

'If you like.'

'Ay, I do like. You send 'em with a guarantee and I'll take 'em.'

For Energise I picked a large yard in Sussex where hurdlers did especially well, and under the guarded tones of the trainer Rupert Ramsey I could hear that he thought almost as much of the horse as I did.

For the last three I chose Newmarket, a middle-sized stable of average achievement. No single basket would ever again contain all the Scott eggs.

Finally with a grimace I picked up the receiver and dialled Jody's familiar number. It was not he who answered, however, but Felicity, his wife.

Her voice was sharp and bitter. 'What do you want?'

I pictured her in their luxuriously furnished drawing-room, a thin positive blonde girl, every bit as competent and hardworking as Jody. She would be wearing tight blue jeans and an expensive shirt, there would be six gold bracelets jingling on her wrist and she would smell of a musk-based scent. She held intolerant views on most things and stated them forthrightly, but she had never, before that evening, unleashed on me personally the scratchy side of her mind.

'To talk about transport,' I said.

'So you really are kicking our props away.'

'You'll survive.'

'That's bloody complacent claptrap,' she said angrily. 'I could kill you. After all Jody's done for you.'

I paused. 'Did he tell you why I'm breaking with him?'

'Some stupid little quarrel about ten quid on a bill.'

'It's a great deal more than that,' I said.

'Rubbish.'

'Ask him,' I said. 'In any case, three horseboxes will collect my horses on Thursday morning. The drivers will know which ones each of them has to take and where to take them. You tell Jody that if he mixes them up he can pay the bills for sorting them out.'

The names she called me would have shaken Jody's father to the roots.

'Thursday,' I said. 'Three horseboxes, different destinations. And goodbye.'

No pleasure in it. None at all.

I sat gloomily watching a play on television and hearing hardly a word. At nine forty-five the telephone interrupted and I switched off.

'. . . Just want to know, sir, where I stand.'

Raymond Child. Jump jockey. Middle-ranker, thirty years old, short on personality. He rode competently enough, but the longer I went racing and the more I learnt, the more I could see his shortcomings. I was certain also that Jody could not have manipulated my horses quite so thoroughly without help at the wheel.

'I'll send you an extra present for Energise,' I said. Jockeys were paid an official percentage of the winning prize money through a central system, but especially grateful owners occasionally came across with more.

'Thank you, sir.' He sounded surprised.

'I had a good bet on him.'

'Did you, sir?' The surprise was extreme. 'But Jody said ...' He stopped dead.

'I backed him on the Tote.'

'Oh.'

The silence lengthened. He cleared his throat. I waited.

'Well, sir. Er ... about the future...'

'I'm sorry,' I said, half meaning it. 'I'm grateful for the winners you've ridden. I'll send you the present for Energise. But in the future he'll be ridden by the jockey attached to his new stable.'

This time there was no tirade of bad language. This time, just a slow defeated sigh and the next best thing to an admission.

'Can't really blame you, I suppose.'

He disconnected before I could reply.

Tuesday I should have had a runner at Chepstow, but since I'd cancelled Jody's authority he couldn't send it. I kicked around my rooms unproductively all morning and in the afternoon walked from Kensington Gardens to the Tower of London. Cold grey damp air with seagulls making a racket over the low-tide mud. Coffee-coloured river racing down on the last of the ebb. I stood looking towards the City from the top of little Tower Hill and thought of all the lives that had ended there under the axe. December mood, through and through. I bought a bag of roast chestnuts and went home by bus.

Wednesday brought a letter.

Dear Mr Scott,

When and where?

Alexandra Ward.

She had kept the five pound note.

On Thursday evening the three new trainers confirmed that they had received the expected horses; on Friday I did a little work and on Saturday I drove down to Cheltenham races. I had not, it was true, exactly expected a rousing cheer, but the depth and extent of the animosity shown to me was acutely disturbing.

Several backs were turned, not ostentatiously but decisively. Several acquaintances lowered their eyes in embarrassment when talking to me and hurried away as soon as possible. The Press looked speculative, the trainers wary and the Jockey Club coldly hostile.

Charlie Canterfield alone came up with a broad smile and shook me vigorously by the hand.

'Have I come out in spots?' I said.

He laughed. 'You've kicked the underdog. The British never forgive it.'

'Even when the underdog bites first?'

'Underdogs are never in the wrong.'

He led me away to the bar. 'I've been taking a small poll for you. Ten per cent think it would be fair to hear your side. Ten per cent think you ought to be shot. What will you drink?'

'Scotch. No ice or water. What about the other eighty per cent?'

'Enough righteous indignation to keep the Mothers' Union going for months.' He paid for the drinks. 'Cheers.'

'And to you too.'

'It'll blow over,' Charlie said.

'I guess so.'

'What do you fancy in the third?'

We discussed the afternoon's prospects and didn't refer again to Jody, but later, alone, I found it hard to ignore the general climate. I backed a couple of horses on the Tote for a tenner each, and lost. That sort of day.

All afternoon I was fiercely tempted to protest that it was I who was the injured party, not Jody. Then I thought of the further thousands he would undoubtedly screw out of me in damages if I opened my mouth, and I kept it shut.

The gem of the day was Quintus himself, who planted his great frame solidly in my path and told me loudly that I was a bloody disgrace to the good name of racing. Quintus, I reflected, so often spoke in clichés.

'I'll tell you something,' he said. 'You would have been elected to the Jockey Club if you hadn't served Jody such a dirty trick. Your name was up for consideration. You won't be invited now, I'll see to that.'

He gave me a short curt nod and stepped aside. I didn't move.

'Your son is the one for dirty tricks.'

'How dare you!'

'You'd best believe it.'

'Absolute nonsense. The discrepancy on your bill was a simple secretarial mistake. If you try to say it was anything else...'

'I know,' I said. 'He'll sue.'

'Quite right. He has a right to every penny he can get.'

I walked away. Quintus might be biased, but I knew I'd get a straight answer from the Press.

I asked the senior columnist of a leading daily, a fiftyish man who wrote staccato prose and sucked peppermints to stop himself smoking.

'What reason is Jody Leeds giving for losing my horses?'

The columnist sucked and breathed out a gust of sweetness.

'Says he charged you by mistake for some schooling Raymond Child didn't do.'

'That's all?'

'Says you accused him of stealing and were changing your trainer.'

'And what's your reaction to that?'

'I haven't got one.' He shrugged and sucked contemplatively. 'Others … The consensus seems to be it was a genuine mistake and you've been unreasonable … to put it mildly.'

'I see,' I said. 'Thanks.'

'Is that all? No story?'

'No,' I said. 'Sorry.'

He put another peppermint in his mouth, nodded noncommittally, and turned away to more fertile prospects. As far as he was concerned, I was last week's news. Others, this Saturday, were up for the chop.

I walked thoughtfully down on the Club lawn to watch the next race. It really was not much fun being cast as everyone's villain, and the clincher was delivered by a girl I'd once taken to Ascot.

'Steven dear,' she said with coquettish reproof, 'You're a big rich bully. That poor boy's struggling to make ends meet. Even if he did pinch a few quid off you, why get into such a tizz? So uncool, don't you think?'

'You believe the rich should lie down for Robin Hood?'

'What?'

'Never mind.'

I gave it up and went home.

The evening was a great deal better. At eight o'clock I collected Miss Alexandra Ward from an address in Hampstead and took her to dinner in the red and gold grill room of the Café Royal.

Seen again in kinder light, properly warm and not blown to rags by the wind, she was everything last week's glimpse had suggested. She wore the same long black skirt, the same cream shirt, the same cream silk shawl. Also the gold sandals, gold mesh purse and no gloves. But her brown hair was smooth and shining, her skin glowing, her eyes bright, and over all lay the indefinable extra, a typically American brand of grooming.

She opened the door herself when I rang the bell and for an appreciable pause we simply looked at each other. What she saw was, I supposed, about six feet of solidly built chap, dark hair, dark eyes, no warts to speak of. Tidy, clean, housetrained and dressed in a conventional dinner jacket.

'Good evening,' I said.

She smiled, nodded as if endorsing a decision, stepped out through the door, and pulled it shut behind her.

'My sister lives here,' she said, indicating the house. 'I'm on a visit. She's married to an Englishman.'

I opened the car door for her. She sat smoothly inside, and I started the engine and drove off.

'A visit from the States?' I asked.

'Yes. From Westchester ... outside New York.'

'Executive ladder-climbing country?' I said, smiling.

She gave me a quick sideways glance. 'You know Westchester?'

'No. Been to New York a few times, that's all.'

We stopped at some traffic lights. She remarked that it was a fine night. I agreed.

'Are you married?' she said abruptly.

'Did you bring the fiver?'

'Yes, I did.'

'Well ... No, I'm not.'

The light changed to green. We drove on.

'Are you truthful?' she said.

'In that respect, yes. Not married now. Never have been.'

'I like to know,' she said with mild apology.

'I don't blame you.'

'For the sakes of the wives.'

'Yes.'

I pulled up in due course in front of the Café Royal at Piccadilly Circus, and helped her out of the car. As we went in she looked back and saw a small thin man taking my place in the driving seat.

'He works for me,' I said. 'He'll park the car.'

She looked amused. 'He waits around to do that?'

'On overtime, Saturday nights.'

'So he likes it?'

'Begs me to take out young ladies. Other times I do my own parking.'

In the full light inside the hall she stopped for another straight look at what she'd agreed to dine with.

'What do you expect of me?' she said.

'Before I collected you, I expected honesty, directness and prickles. Now that I've know you for half an hour I expect prickles, directness and honesty.'

She smiled widely, the white teeth shining and little pouches of fun swelling her lower eyelids.

'That isn't what I meant.'

'No ... So what do you expect of me?'

'Thoroughly gentlemanly conduct and a decent dinner.'

'How dull.'

'Take it or leave it.'

'The bar,' I said, pointing, 'is over there. I take it.'

She gave me another flashing smile, younger sister to the first, and moved where I'd said. She drank vodka martini, I drank scotch, and we both ate a few black olives and spat out the stones genteelly into fists.

'Do you usually pick up girls in the street?' she said.

'Only when they fall.'

'Fallen girls?'

I laughed. 'Not those, no.'

'What do you do for a living?'

I took a mouthful of scotch. 'I'm a sort of engineer.' It sounded boring.

'Bridges and things?'

'Nothing so permanent or important.'

'What then?'

I smiled wryly. 'I make toys.'

'You make ... *what*?'

'Toys. Things to play with.'

'I know what toys are, damn it.'

'What do you do?' I asked, 'In Westchester.'

She gave me an amused glance over her glass. 'You take it for granted that I work?'

'You have the air.'

'I cook, then.'

'Hamburgers and French fries?'

Her eyes gleamed. 'Weddings and stuff. Parties.'

'A lady caterer.'

She nodded. 'With a girl friend, Millie.'

'When do you go back?'

'Thursday.'

Thursday suddenly seemed rather close. After a noticeable pause she added almost defensively, 'It's Christmas, you see. We've a lot of work then and around New Year. Millie couldn't do it all alone.'

'Of course not.'

We went into dinner and ate smoked trout and steak wrapped in pastry. She read the menu from start to finish with professional interest and checked with the head waiter the ingredients of two or three dishes.

'So many things are different over here,' she explained.

She knew little about wine. 'I guess I drink it when I'm given it, but I've a better palate for spirits.' The wine waiter looked sceptical, but she wiped that look off his face later by correctly identifying the brandy he brought with the coffee as Armagnac.

'Where is your toy factory?' she asked

'I don't have a factory.'

'But you said you made toys.'

'Yes, I do.'

She looked disbelieving. 'You don't mean you actually *make* them. I mean, with your own hands?'

I smiled. 'Yes.'

'But ...' She looked round the velvety room with the thought showing as clear as spring water: if I worked with my hands how could I afford such a place.

'I don't often make them,' I said. 'Most of the time I go to the races.'

'Okay,' she said. 'I give in. You've got me hooked. Explain the mystery.'

'Have some more coffee.'

'Mr Scott ...' She stopped. 'That sounds silly, doesn't it?'

'Yes, Miss Ward, it does.'

'Steven …'

'Much better.'

'My mother calls me Alexandra, Millie calls me Al. Take your pick.'

'Allie?'

'For God's sakes.'

'I invent toys,' I said. 'I patent them. Other people manufacture them. I collect royalties.'

'Oh.'

'Does "oh" mean enlightenment, fascination, or boredom to death?'

'It means oh how extraordinary, oh how interesting, and oh I never knew people did things like that.'

'Quite a lot do.'

'Did you invent Monopoly?'

I laughed. 'Unfortunately not.'

'But that sort of thing?'

'Mechanical toys, mostly.'

'How odd …' She stopped, thinking better of saying what was in her mind. I knew the reaction well, so I finished the sentence for her.

'How odd for a grown man to spend his life in toyland?'

'You said it.'

'Children's minds have to be fed.'

She considered it. 'And the next bunch of leaders are children today?'

'You rate it too high. The next lot of parents, teachers, louts and layabouts are children today.'

'And you are fired with missionary zeal?'

'All the way to the bank.'

'Cynical.'

'Better than pompous.'

'More honest,' she agreed. Her eyes smiled in the soft light, half mocking, half friendly, greeny-grey and shining, the whites ultra white. There was nothing wrong with the design of her eyebrows. Her nose was short and straight, her mouth curved up at the corners, and her cheeks had faint hollows in the right places. Assembled, the components added up not to a standard type of beauty, but to a face of character and vitality. Part of the story written, I thought. Lines of good fortune, none of discontent. No anxiety, no inner confusion. A good deal of self assurance, knowing she looked attractive and had succeeded in the job she'd chosen. Definitely not a virgin: a girl's eyes were always different, after.

'Are all your days busy,' I asked, 'Between now and Thursday?'

'There are some minutes here and there.'

'Tomorrow?'

She smiled and shook her head. 'Not a chink tomorrow. Monday if you like.'

'I'll collect you,' I said. 'Monday morning, at ten.'

Chapter Four

Rupert Ramsey's voice on the telephone sounded resigned rather than welcoming.

'Yes, of course, do come down to see your horses, if you'd like to. Do you know the way?'

He gave me directions which proved easy to follow, and at eleven thirty, Sunday morning, I drove through his white painted stone gateposts and drew up in the large gravelled area before his house.

He lived in a genuine Georgian house, simple in design, with large airy rooms and elegant plaster-worked ceilings. Nothing self-consciously antique about the furnishings: all periods mingled together in a working atmosphere that was wholly modern.

Rupert himself was about forty-five, intensely energetic under a misleadingly languid exterior. His voice drawled slightly. I knew him only by sight and it was to all intents the first time we had met.

'How do you do?' He shook hands. 'Care to come into my office?'

I followed him through the white painted front door, across the large square hall and into the room he called his office, but which was furnished entirely as a sitting-room except for a dining table which served as a desk, and a grey filing cabinet in one corner.

'Do sit down.' He indicated an armchair. 'Cigarette?'

'Don't smoke.'

'Wise man.' He smiled as if he didn't really think so and lit one for himself.

'Energise,' he said, 'Is showing signs of having had a hard race.'

'But he won easily,' I said.

'It looked that way, certainly.' He inhaled, breathing out through his nose. 'All the same, I'm not too happy about him.'

'In what way?'

'He needs building up. We'll do it, don't you fear. But he looks a bit thin at present.'

'How about the other two?'

'Dial's jumping out of his skin. Ferryboat needs a lot of work yet.'

'I don't think Ferryboat likes racing any more.'

The cigarette paused on its way to his mouth.

'Why do you say that?' he asked.

'He's had three races this autumn. I expect you'll have looked up his form. He's run badly every time. Last year he was full of enthusiasm and won three times out of seven starts, but the last of them took a lot of winning ... and Raymond Child cut him raw with his whip ... and during the summer out at grass Ferryboat seems to have decided that if he gets too near the front he's in for a beating, so it's only good sense *not* to get near the front ... and he consequently isn't trying.'

He drew deeply on the cigarette, giving himself time.

'Do you expect me to get better results than Jody?'

'With Ferryboat, or in general?'

'Let's say ... both.'

I smiled. 'I don't expect much from Ferryboat. Dial's a novice, an unknown quantity. Energise might win the Champion Hurdle.'

'You didn't answer my question,' he said pleasantly.

'No ... I expect you to get different results from Jody. Will that do?'

'I'd very much like to know why you left him.'

'Disagreements over money,' I said. 'Not over the way he trained the horses.'

He tapped ash off with the precision that meant his mind was elsewhere. When he spoke, it was slowly.

'Were you always satisfied with the way your horses ran?'

The question hovered delicately in the air, full of inviting little traps. He looked up suddenly and met my eyes and his own widened with comprehension. 'I see you understand what I'm asking.'

'Yes. But I can't answer. Jody says he will sue me for slander if I tell people why I left him, and I've no reason to doubt him.'

'That remark in itself is a slander.'

'Indubitably.'

He got cheerfully to his feet and stubbed out the cigarette. A good deal more friendliness seeped into his manner.

'Right then. Let's go out and look at your horses.'

We went out into his yard, which showed prosperity at every turn. The thin cold December sun shone on fresh paint, wall-to-wall tarmac, tidy flower tubs and well-kept stable lads. There was none of the clutter I was accustomed to at Jody's; no brooms leaning against walls, no rugs, rollers, brushes and bandages lying in ready heaps, no straggles of hay across the swept ground. Jody like to give owners the impression that work was being done, that care for the horses was nonstop. Rupert, it seemed, preferred to tuck the sweat and toil out of sight. At Jody's, the muck heap was always with you. At Rupert's it was invisible.

'Dial is here.'

We stopped at a box along a row outside the main quadrangle, and with an unobtrusive flick of his fingers Rupert summoned a lad hovering twenty feet away.

'This is Donny,' he said. 'Looks after Dial.'

I shook hands with Donny, a young tough-looking boy of about twenty with unsmiling eyes and you-can't-con-me expression. From the look he directed first at Rupert and then later at the horse I gathered that this was his overall attitude to life, not an announcement of no confidence in me personally. When we'd looked at and admired the robust little chestnut I tried Donny with a fiver. It raised a nod of thanks, but no smile.

Further along the same row stood Ferryboat, looking out on the world with a lacklustre eye and scarcely shifting from one leg to the other when we went into his box. His lad, in contrast to Donny, gave him an indulgent smile, and accepted his gift from me with a beam.

'Energise is in the main yard,' Rupert said, leading the way. 'Across in the corner.

When we were half way there two other cars rolled up the drive and disgorged a collection of men in sheepskin coats and ladies in furs and jangly bracelets. They saw Rupert and waved and began to stream into the yard.

Rupert said, 'I'll show you Energise in just a moment.'

'It's all right,' I said. 'You tell me which box he's in. I'll look at him myself. You see to your other owners.'

'Number fourteen, then. I'll be with you again shortly.'

I nodded and walked on to number fourteen. Unbolted the door. Went in. The near-black horse was tied up inside. Ready, I supposed, for my visit.

Horse and I looked at each other. My old friend, I thought. The only one of them all with whom I'd ever had any real contact. I talked to him, as in the horsebox, looking guiltily over my shoulder at the open door, for fear someone should hear me and think me nuts.

I could see at once why Rupert had been unhappy about him. He looked thinner. All that crashing about in the horsebox could have done him no good.

Across the yard I could see Rupert talking to the newcomers and shepherding them to their horses. Owners came en masse on Sunday mornings.

I was content to stay where I was. I spent probably twenty minutes with my black horse, and he instilled in me some very strange ideas.

Rupert came back hurrying and apologising. 'You're still here ... I'm so sorry.'

'Don't be,' I assured him.

'Come into the house for a drink.'

'I'd like to.'

We joined the other owners and returned to his office for lavish issues of gin and scotch. Drinks for visiting owners weren't allowable as a business expense for tax purposes unless the visiting owners were foreign. Jody had constantly complained of it to all and sundry while accepting cases of the stuff from me with casual nods. Rupert poured generously and dropped no hints, and I found it a refreshing change.

The other owners were excitedly making plans for the Christmas meeting at Kempton Park. Rupert made introductions, explaining that Energise, too, was due to run there in the Christmas Hurdle.

'After the way he won at Sandown,' remarked one of the sheepskin coats, 'he must be a cast-iron certainty.'

I glanced at Rupert for an opinion but he was busy with bottles and glasses.

'I hope so,' I said.

The sheepskin coat nodded sagely.

His wife, a cosy-looking lady who had shed her ocelot and now stood five-feet-nothing in bright green wool, looked from him to me in puzzlement.

'But George honey, Energise is trained by that nice young man with the pretty little wife. You know, the one who introduced us to Ganser Mays.'

She smiled happily and appeared not to notice the poleaxed state of her audience. I must have stood immobile for almost a minute while the implications fizzed around my brain, and during that time the conversation between George-honey and the bright green wool had flowed on into the chances of their own chaser in a later race. I dragged them back.

'Excuse me,' I said, 'but I didn't catch your names.'

'George Vine,' said the sheepskin coat, holding out a chunky hand, 'and my wife, Poppet.'

'Steven Scott,' I said.

'Glad to know you.' He gave his empty glass to Rupert, who amiably refilled it with gin and tonic. 'Poppet doesn't read the racing news much, so she wouldn't know you've left Jody Leeds.'

'Did you say,' I asked carefuly, 'that Jody Leeds introduced you to Ganser Mays?'

'Oh no' Poppet said, smiling. 'His wife did.'

'That's right,' George nodded. 'Bit of luck.'

'You see,' Poppet explained conversationally, 'the prices on the Tote are sometimes so awfully small and it's all such a lottery isn't it? I mean, you never know really what you're going to get for your money, like you do with the bookies.'

'Is that what she said?' I asked.

'Who? Oh ... Jody Leeds' wife. Yes, that's right, she did. I'd just been picking up my winnings on one of our horses from the Tote, you see, and she was doing the same at the next window, the Late-Pay window that was, and she said what a shame it was that the Tote was only paying three to one when the bookies' starting price was five to one, and I absolutely agreed with her, and we just sort of stood there chatting. I told her that only last week we had bought the steeplechaser which had just won and it was our first ever racehorse, and she was so interested and explained that she was a trainer's wife and that sometimes when she got tired of the Tote paying out so little she bet with a bookie. I said I didn't like pushing along the rows with all those men shoving and shouting and she laughed and said she meant one on the rails, so you could just walk up to them and not go through to the bookies' enclosure at all. But of course you have to know them, I mean, they have to know *you*, if you see what I mean. And neither George nor I knew any of them, as I explained to Mrs Leeds.'

She stopped to take a sip of gin. I listened in fascination.

'Well,' she went on, 'Mrs Leeds sort of hesitated and then I got this great idea of asking her is she could possibly introduce us to *her* bookie on the rails.'

'And she did?'

'She thought it was a great idea.'

She would.

'So we collected George and she introduced us to dear Ganser Mays. And,' she finished triumphantly, 'he gives us much better odds than the Tote.'

George Vine nodded several times in agreement.

'Trouble is,' he said, 'you know what wives are, she bets more than ever.'

'George honey.' A token protest only.

'You know you do, love.'

'It isn't worth doing in sixpences,' she said smiling. 'You never win enough that way.'

He patted her fondly on the shoulder and said man-to-man to me, 'When Ganser Mays' account comes, if she's won, she takes the winnings, and if she's lost, I pay.'

Poppet smiled happily. 'George honey, you're sweet.'

'Which do you do most?' I asked her. 'Win or lose?'

She made a face. 'Now that's a naughty question, Mr Scott.'

Next morning, ten o'clock to the second, I collected Allie from Hampstead.

Seen in daylight for the first time she was sparkling as the day was rotten. I arrived at her door with a big black umbrella holding off slanting sleet, and she opened it in a neat white mackintosh and knee-high black boots. Her hair bounced with new washing, and the bloom on her skin had nothing to do with Max Factor.

I tried a gentlemanly kiss on the cheek. She smelled of fresh flowers and bath soap.

'Good morning,' I said.

She chuckled. 'You English are so formal.'

'Not always.'

She sheltered under the umbrella down the path to the car and sat inside with every glossy hair dry and in place.

'Where are we going?'

'Fasten your lap straps,' I said. 'To Newmarket.'

'Newmarket?'

'To look at horses.' I let in the clutch and pointed the Lamborghini roughly north-east.

'I might have guessed.'

I grinned. 'Is there anything you'd really rather do?'

'I've visited three museums, four picture galleries, six churches, one Tower of London, two Houses of Parliament and seven theatres.'

'In how long?'

'Sixteen days.'

'High time you saw some real life.'

The white teeth flashed. 'If you'd lived with my two small nephews for sixteen days you couldn't wait to get away from it.'

'Your sister's children?'

She nodded. 'Ralph and William. Little devils.'

'What do they play with?'

She was amused. 'The toy maker's market research?'

'The customer is always right.'

We crossed the North Circular road and took the A1 towards Baldock.

'Ralph dresses up a doll in soldier's uniforms and William makes forts on the stairs and shoots dried beans at anyone going up.'

'Healthy aggressive stuff.'

'When I was little I hated being given all those educational things that were supposed to be good for you.'

I smiled. 'It's well known there are two sorts of toys. The ones that children like and the ones their mothers buy. Guess which there are more of?'

'You're cynical.'

'So I'm often told,' I said. 'It isn't true.'

The wipers worked overtime against the sleet on the windscreen and I turned up the heater. She sighed with what appeared to be contentment. The car purred easily across Cambridgeshire and into Suffolk, and the ninety minute journey seemed short.

It wasn't the best of weather but even in July the stable I'd chosen for my three young flat racers would have looked depressing. There were two smallish quadrangles side by side, built tall and solid in Edwardian brick. All the doors were painted a dead dull dark brown. No decorations, no flowers, no grass, no gaiety of spirit in the whole place.

Like many Newmarket yards it led straight off the street and was surrounded by houses. Allie looked around without enthusiasm and put into words exactly what I was thinking.

'It looks more like a prison.'

Bars on the windows of the boxes. Solid ten foot tall gates at the road entrance. Jagged glass set in concrete along the top of the boundary wall. Padlocks swinging on every bolt on every door in sight. All that was missing was a uniformed figure with a gun, and maybe they had those too, on occasion.

The master of all this security proved pretty dour himself. Trevor Kennet shook hands with a smile that looked an unaccustomed effort for the muscles involved and invited us into the stable office out of the rain.

A bare room; linoleum, scratched metal furniture, strip lighting and piles of paper work. The contrast between this and the grace of Rupert Ramsey was remarkable. A pity I had taken Allie to the wrong one.

'They've settled well, your horses.' His voice dared me to disagree.

'Splendid,' I said mildly.

'You'll want to see them, I expect.'

As I'd come from London to do so, I felt his remark silly.

'They're doing no work yet, of course.'

'No,' I agreed. The last Flat season had finished six weeks ago. The next lay some three months ahead. No owner in his senses would have expected his Flat horses to be in full work in December. Trevor Kennet had a genius for the obvious.

'It's raining,' he said. 'Bad day to come.'

Allie and I were both wearing macs, and I carried the umbrella. He looked lengthily at these preparations and finally shrugged.

'Better come on, then.'

He himself wore a raincoat and a droopy hat that had suffered downpours for years. He led the way out of the office and across the first quadrangle with Allie and me close under my umbrella behind him.

He flicked the bolts on one of the dead chocolate doors and pulled both halves open.

'Wrecker,' he said.

We went into the box. Wrecker moved hastily away across the peat which covered the floor, a leggy bay yearling colt with a nervous disposition. Trevor Kennet made no effort to reassure him but stood four square looking at him with an assessing eye. Jody for all his faults had been good with young stock, fondling them and talking to them with affection. I thought I might have chosen badly, sending Wrecker here.

'He needs a gentle lad,' I said.

Kennet's expression was open scorn. 'Doesn't do to mollycoddle them. Soft horses win nothing.'

End of conversation.

We went out into the rain and he slammed the bolts home. Four boxes further along he stopped again.

'Hermes.'

Again the silent appraisal. Hermes, from the experience of two full racing seasons, could look at humans without anxiety and merely stared back. Ordinary to look at, he had won several races in masterly fashion . . . and lost every time I'd seriously backed him. Towards the end of the Flat season he had twice trailed in badly towards the rear of the field. Too much racing, Jody had said. Needed a holiday.

'What do you think of him?' I asked.

'He's eating well,' Kennet said.

I waited for more, but nothing came. After a short pause we trooped out again into the rain and more or less repeated the whole depressing procedure in the box of third colt, Bubbleglass.

I had great hopes of Bubbleglass. A late-developing two-year-old, he had run only once so far, and without much distinction. At three, though, he might be fun. He had grown and filled out since I'd seen him last. When I said so, Kennet remarked that it was only to be expected.

We all went back to the office, Kennet offered us coffee and looked relieved when I said we'd better be going.

'What an utterly dreary place,' Allie said, as we drove away.

'Designed to discourage owners from calling too often, I dare say.'

She was surprised. 'Do you mean it?'

'Some trainers think owners should pay their bills and shut up.'

'That's crazy.'

I glanced sideways at her.

She said positively, 'If I was spending all that dough, I'd sure expect to be welcomed.'

'Biting the hand that feeds is a national sport.'

'You're all nuts.'

'How about some lunch?'

We stopped at a pub which did a fair job for a Monday, and in the afternoon drove comfortably back to London. Allie made no objections when I pulled up outside my own front door and followed me in through it with none of the prickly reservations I'd feared.

I lived in the two lower floors of a tall narrow house in Prince Albert Road overlooking Regent's Park. At street level, garage, cloakroom, workshop. Upstairs, bed, bath, kitchen and sittingroom, the last with a balcony half as big as itself. I switched on lights and led the way.

'A bachelor's pad if ever I saw one,' Allie said, looking around her. 'Not a frill in sight.' She walked across and looked out through the sliding glass wall to the balcony. 'Don't you just hate all that traffic?'

Cars drove incessantly along the road below, yellow sidelights shining through the glistening rain.

'I quite like it,' I said. 'In the summer I practically live out there on the balcony ... breathing in great lungfuls of exhaust fumes and waiting for the clouds to roll away.'

She laughed, unbuttoned her mac and took it off. The red dress underneath looked as unruffled as it had at lunch. She was the one splash of bright colour in that room of creams and browns, and she was feminine enough to know it.

'Drink?' I suggested.

'It's a bit early ...' She looked around her as if she had expected to see more than sofas and chairs. 'Don't you keep any of your toys here?'

'In the workshop,' I said. 'Downstairs.'

'I'd love to see them.'

'All right.'

We went down to the hall again and turned towards the back of the house. I opened the civilized wood-panelled door which led straight from carpet to concrete, from white collar to blue, from champagne to tea breaks. The familiar smell of oil and machinery waited there in the dark. I switched on the stark bright lights and stood aside for her to go through.

'But it *is* ... a factory.' She sounded astonished.

'What did you expect?'

'Oh, I don't know. Something much smaller, I guess.'

The workshop was fifty feet long and was the reason I had bought the house on my twenty-third birthday with money I had earned myself. Selling off the three top floors had given me enough back to construct my own first floor flat, but the heart of the matter lay here, legacy of an old-fashioned light engineering firm that had gone bust.

The pulley system that drove nearly the whole works from one engine was the original, even if now powered by electricity instead of steam, and although I had replaced one or two and added another, the old machines still worked well.

'Explain it to me,' Allie said.

'Well ... this electric engine here ...' I showed her its compact floor-mounted shape. '... drives that endless belt, which goes up there round that big wheel.'

'Yes.' She looked up where I pointed.

'The wheel is fixed to that long shaft which stretches right down the workshop, near the ceiling. When it rotates, it drives all those other endless belts going down to the machines. Look, I'll show you.'

I switched on the electric motor and immediately the big belt from it turned the wheel, which rotated the shaft, which set the other belts circling from the shaft down to the machines. The only noises were the hum of the engines, the gentle whine of the spinning shaft and the soft slapping of the belts.

'It looks alive,' Allie said. 'How do you make the machines work?'

'Engage a sort of gear inside the belt, then the belt revolves the spindle of the machine.'

'Like a sewing machine,' Allie said.

'More or less.'

We walked down the row. She wanted to know what job each did, and I told her.

'That's a milling machine, for flat surfaces. That's a speed lathe; I use that for wood as well as metal. That tiny lathe came from a watchmaker for ultra fine work. That's a press. That's a polisher. That's a hacksaw. And that's a drilling machine; it bores holes downwards.'

I turned round and pointed to the other side of the workshop.

'That big one on its own is an engine lathe, for heavier jobs. It has its own electric power.'

'It's incredible. All this.'

'Just for toys?'

'Well ...'

'These machines are all basically simple. They just save a lot of time.'

'Do toys have to be so ... well ... *accurate*?'

'I mostly make the prototypes in metal and wood. Quite often they reach the shops in plastic, but unless the engineering's right in the first place the toy's don't work very well, and break easily.'

'Where do you keep them?' She looked around at the bare well-swept area with no work in sight.

'Over there. In the righthand cupboard.

I went over with her and opened the big double doors. She pulled them wider with outstretched arms.

'Oh!' She looked utterly astounded.

She stood in front of the shelves with her mouth open and her eyes staring, just like a child.

'Oh,' she said again, as if she could get no breath to say anything else. 'Oh ... They're the Rola toys!'

'Yes, that's right.

'Why didn't you say so?'

'Habit, really. I never do.'

She gave me a smile without turning her eyes away from the bright coloured rows in the cupboard. 'Do so many people ask for free samples?'

'It's just that I get tired of talking about them.'

'But I played with them myself.' She switched her gaze abruptly in my direction, looking puzzled. 'I had a lot of them in the States ten or twelve years ago.' Her voice plainly implied that I was too young to have made those.

'I was only fifteen when I did the first one,' I explained. 'I had an uncle who had a workshop in his garage ... he was a welder, himself. He'd show me how to use tools from the time I was six. He was pretty shrewd. He made me take out patents before I showed my idea to anyone, and he raised and lent me the money to pay for them.'

'Pay?'

'Patents are expensive and you have to take out one for each different country, if you don't want your idea pinched. Japan, I may say, costs the most.'

'Good heavens.' She turned back to the cupboard, put out her hand and lifted out the foundation of all my fortunes, the merry-go-round.

'I had the carousel,' she said. 'Just like this, but different colours.' She twirled the centre spindle between finger and thumb so that the platform revolved and the little horses rose and fell on their poles. 'I simply can't believe it.'

She put the merry-go-round back in its slot and one by one lifted out several of the others, exclaiming over old friends and investigating the strangers. 'Do you have a Rola-base down here?'

'Sure,' I said, lifting it from the bottom of the cupboard.

'Oh do let me ... please?' She was as excited as if she'd still been little. I carried the base over to the workbench and laid it there, and she came over with four of the toys.

The Rola-base consisted of a large flat box, in this case two feet square by six inches deep, though several other sizes had been made. From one side protruded a handle for winding, and one had to have that side of the Rola-base aligned with the edge of the table, so that winding was possible. Inside the box were the rollers which gave the toy its phonetic Rola name; wide rollers carrying a long flat continuous belt inset with many rows of sideway facing cogwheel teeth. In the top of the box were corresponding rows of holes: dozens of holes altogether. Each of the separate mechanical toys, like the merry-go-round and a hundred others, had a central spindle which protruded down from beneath the toy and was grooved like a cog-wheel. When one slipped any spindle through any hole it engaged on the belt of cog teeth below, and when one turned the single handle in the Rola-base, the wide belt of cog teeth moved endlessly round and all the spindles rotated and all the toys performed their separate tasks. A simple locking device on the base of each toy engaged with stops by each hole to prevent the toy rotating as a whole.

Allie had brought the carousel and the roller-coaster from the fairground set, and a cow from the farm set, and the firing tank from the army set. She slotted the spindles through random holes and turned the handle. The merry-go-round went round and round, the trucks went up and down the roller-coaster, the cow nodded its head and swished its tail, and he tank rotated with sparks coming out of its gun barrel.

She laughed with pleasure.

'I don't believe it. I simply don't believe it. I never dreamt you could have made the Rola toys.'

'I've made others, though.'

'What sort?'

'Um . . . the latest in the shops is a coding machine. It's doing quite well this Christmas.'

'You don't mean the Secret Coder?'

'Yes.' I was surprised she knew of it.

'Do show me. My sister's giving one each to the boys, but they were already gift-wrapped.'

So I showed her the coder, which looked like providing me with racehorses for some time to come, as a lot of people besides children had found it compulsive. The new adult version was much more complicated but also much more expensive, which somewhat increased the royalties.

From the outside the children's version looked like a box, smaller than a shoe box, with a sloping top surface. Set in this were letter keys exactly like a conventional typewriter, except that there were no numbers, no punctuations and no space bar.

'How does it work?' Allie asked.

'You type your message and it comes out in code.'

'Just like that?'

'Try it.'

She gave me an amused look, turned so that I couldn't see her fingers, and with one hand expertly typed about twenty-five letters. From the end of the box a narrow paper strip emerged, with letters typed on it in groups of five.

'What now?'

'Tear the strip off,' I said.

She said that. 'It's like ticker-tape,' she said.

'It is. Same size, anyway.'

She held it out to me. I looked at it and came as close to blushing as I'm ever likely to.

'Can you read it just like that?' she exclaimed. 'Some coder, if you can read it at a glance.'

'I invented the damn thing,' I said. 'I know it by heart.'

'How does it work?'

'There's a cylinder inside with twelve complete alphabets on it, each arranged in a totally random manner and all different. You set this dial here ... see,' I showed her, 'to any numbers from one to twelve. Then you type your message. Inside the keys don't print the letter you press on the outside, but the letter that's aligned with it inside. There's an automatic spring which jumps after every five presses, so the message comes out in groups of five.'

'It's fantastic. My sister says the boys have been asking for them for weeks. Lots of children they know have them, all sending weird secrete messages all over the place and driving their mothers wild.

'You can make more involved codes by feeding the coded message through again, or backwards,' I said. 'Or by switching the code number every few letters. All the child receiving the message needs to know is the numbers he has to set on his own dial.'

'How do I decode this?'

'Put that tiny lever ... there ... down instead of up, and just type the coded message. It will come out as it went in, except still in groups of five letters, of course. Try it.'

She herself looked confused. She screwed up the tape and laughed, 'I guess I don't need to.'

'Would you like one?' I asked diffidently.

'I sure would.'

'Blue or red?'

'Red.'

In another cupboard I had a pile of manufactured coders packed like those in the shops. I opened one of the cartons, checked the contents had a bright red plastic casing and handed it over.

'If you write me a Christmas message,' she said, 'I'll expect it in code number four.'

I took her out to dinner again as I was on a bacon-and-egg level myself as a cook, and she was after all on holiday to get away from the kitchen.

There was nothing new in taking a girl to dinner. Nothing exceptional, I supposed, in Allie herself. I liked her directness, her naturalness. She was supremely easy to be with, not interpreting occasional silences as personal insults, not coy or demanding, nor sexually a tease. Not a girl of hungry intellect, but certainly of good sense.

That wasn't all, of course. The spark which attracts one person to another was there too, and on her side also, I thought.

I drove her back to Hampstead and stopped outside her sister's house.

'Tomorrow?' I said.

She didn't answer directly. 'I go home on Thursday.'

'I know. What time is your flight?'

'Not till the evening. Six-thirty.'

'Can I drive you to the airport?'

'I could get my sister ...'

'I'd like to.'

'Okay.'

We sat in a short silence.

'Tomorrow,' she said finally. 'I guess ... If you like.'

'Yes.'

She nodded briefly, opened the car door, and spoke over her shoulder. 'Thank you for a fascinating day.'

She was out on the pavement before I could get round to help her. She smiled. Purring and contented, as far as I could judge.

'Good night.' She held out her hand.

I took it, and at the same time leant down and kissed her cheek. We looked at each other, her hand still in mine. One simply cannot waste such opportunities. I repeated the kiss, but on her lips.

She kissed as I'd expected, with friendliness and reservations. I kissed her twice more on the same terms.

'Good night,' she said again, smiling.

I watched her wave before she shut her sister's front door, and drove home wishing she were still with me. When I got back I went into the workshop and retrieved the screwed up piece of code she'd thrown in the litter bin. Smoothing it, I read the jumbled up letters again.

No mistake. Sorted out, the words were still a pat on the ego.

The toy man is as great as his toys.

I put the scrap of paper in my wallet and went upstairs to bed feeling the world's biggest fool.

Chapter Five

On Wednesday morning Charlie Canterfield telephoned at seven-thirty. I stretched a hand sleepily out of bed and groped for the receiver.

'Hullo?'

'Where the hell have you been?' Charlie said. 'I've been trying your number since Sunday morning.'

'Out.'

'I know that.' He sounded more amused than irritated. 'Look ... can you spare me some time today?'

'All of it, if you like.'

My generosity was solely due to the unfortunate fact that Allie had felt bound to spend her last full day with her sister, who had bought tickets and made plans. I had gathered that she'd only given me Monday and Tuesday at the expense of her other commitments, so I couldn't grumble. Tuesday had been even better than Monday, except for ending in exactly the same way.

'This morning will do,' Charles said. 'Nine-thirty?'

'Okay. Amble along.'

'I want to bring a friend.'

'Fine. Do you know how to get here?'

'A taxi will find it,' Charlie said and disconnected.

Charlie's friend turned out to be a large man of Charlie's age with shoulders like a docker and language to match.

'Bert Huggerneck,' Charlie said, making introductions.

Bert Huggerneck crunched my bones in his muscular hand. 'Any friend of Charlie's is a friend of mine,' he said, but with no warmth or conviction.

'Come upstairs,' I said. 'Coffee? Or breakfast?'

'Coffee,' Charlie said. Bert Huggerneck said he didn't mind, which proved in the end to be bacon and tomato ketchup on toast twice, with curried baked beans on the side. He chose the meal himself from my meagre store cupboard and ate with speed and relish.

'Not a bad bit of bleeding nosh,' he observed, 'considering.'

'Considering what?' I asked.

He gave me a sharp look over a well-filled fork and made a gesture embracing both the flat and its neighbourhood. 'Considering you must be a rich bleeding capitalist, living here.' He pronounced it "ca*pit*alist", and clearly considered it one of the worst of insults.

'Come off it,' Charlie said amiably. 'His breeding's as impeccable as yours and mine.'

'Huh.' Total disbelief didn't stop Bert Huggerneck accepting more toast. 'Got any jam?' he said.

'Sorry.'

He made do with half a jar of marmalade.

'What's that about breeding?' he said suspiciously to Charlie. 'Ca*pit*alists are all snobs.'

'His grandfather was a mechanic,' Charlie said. 'Same as mine was a milkman and yours a navvie.'

I was amused that Charlie had glossed over my father and mother, who had been school teacher and nurse. Far more respectable to be able to refer to the grandfather-mechanic, the welder-uncle and the host of card-carrying cousins. If politicians of all sorts searched diligently amongst their antecedents for proletarianism and denied aristocratic contacts three times before cockcrow every weekday morning, who was I to spoil the fun? In truth the two seemingly divergent lines of manual work and schoolmastering had given me the best of both worlds, the ability to use my hands and the education to design things for them to make. Money and experience had done the rest.

'I gather Mr Huggerneck is here against his will,' I observed.

'Don't you believe it,' Charlie said. 'He wants your help.'

'How does he act if he wants to kick you in the kidneys?'

'He wouldn't eat your food.'

Fair enough, I thought. Accept a man's salt, and you didn't boot him. Times hadn't collapsed altogether where that still held good.

We were sitting round the kitchen table with Charlie smoking a cigarette and using his saucer as an ashtray and me wondering what he considered so urgent. Bert wiped his plate with a spare piece of toast and washed that down with coffee.

'What's for lunch?' he said.

I took it as it was meant, as thanks for breakfast.

'Bert,' said Charlie, coming to the point, 'is a bookie's clerk.'

'Hold on,' Bert said. 'Not is. Was.'

'Was,' Charlie conceded, 'and will be again. But at the moment the firm he worked for is bankrupt.'

'The boss went spare,' Bert said, nodding. 'The bums come and took away all the bleeding office desks and that.'

'And the bleeding typists?'

'Here,' said Bert, his brows suddenly lifting as a smile forced itself at last into his eyes. 'You're not all bad, then.'

'Rotten to the core,' I said. 'Go on.'

'Well, see, the boss got all his bleeding sums wrong, or like he said, his mathematical computations were based on a misconception.'

'Like the wrong horse won?'

Bert's smile got nearer. 'Cotton on quick, don't you? A whole bleeding row of wrong horses. Here, see, I've been writing for him for bleeding years. All the big courses, he has . . . well, he had . . . a pitch in Tatt's and down in the Silver Ring too, and I've been writing for him myself most of the time, for him personally, see?'

'Yes.' Bookmakers always took a clerk to record all bets as they were made. A bookmaking firm of any size sent out a team of two men or more to every allowed enclosure at most race meetings in their area: the bigger the firm, the more meetings they covered.

'Well, see, I warned him once or twice there was a leary look to his book. See, after bleeding years you get a nose for trouble, don't you? This last year or so he's made a right bleeding balls-up more than once and I told him he'd have the bums in if he went on like that, and I was right, wasn't I?'

'What did he say?'

'Told me to mind my own bleeding business,' Bert said. 'But it was my bleeding business, wasn't it? I mean, it was my job at stake. My livelihood, same as his. Who's going to pay my H.P. and rent and a few pints with the lads, I asked him, and he turned round and said not to worry, he had it all in hand, he knew what he was doing.' His voice held total disgust.

'And he didn't,' I remarked.

'Of course he bleeding didn't. He didn't take a blind bit of notice of what I said. Bleeding stupid, he was. Then ten days ago he really blew it. Lost a bleeding packet. The whole works. All of us got the push. No redundancy either. He's got a bleeding big overdraft in the bank and he's up to the eyeballs in debt.'

I glanced at Charlie who seemed exclusively interested in the ash on his cigarette.

'Why,' I asked Bert, 'did your boss ignore your warnings and rush headlong over the cliff?'

'He didn't jump over no cliff, he's getting drunk every night down the boozer.'

'I meant...'

'Hang on, I get you. Why did he lose the whole bleeding works? Because someone fed him the duff gen, that's my opinion. Cocky as all get out, he was, on the way to the races. Then coming home he tells me the firm is all washed up and down the bleeding drain. White as chalk, he was. Trembling, sort of. So I told him I'd warned him over and over. And that day I'd warned him too that he was laying too much on that Energise and not covering himself, and he'd told me all jolly like to mind my own effing business. So I reckon someone had told him Energise was fixed not to win, but it bleeding did win, and that's what's done for the firm.'

Bert shut his mouth and the silence was as loud as bells. Charlie tapped the ash off and smiled.

I swallowed.

'Er ...' I said eventually.

'That's only half of it,' Charlie said, interrupting smoothly. 'Go on, Bert, tell him the rest.'

Bert seemed happy to oblige. 'Well, see, there I was in the boozer Saturday evening. Last Saturday, not the day Energise won. Four days ago, see? After the bums had been, and all that. Well, in walks Charlie like he sometimes does and we had a couple of jars together, him and me being old mates really on account of we lived next door to each other when we were kids and he was going to that la-di-da bleeding Eton and someone had to take him down a peg or two in the holidays. So, anyway, there we were in the boozer and I pour out all my troubles and Charlie says he has another friend who'd like to hear them, so ... well ... here we are.'

'What are the other troubles, then?' I asked.

'Oh ... Yeah. Well, see, the boss had a couple of betting shops. Nothing fancy, just a couple of betting shops in Windsor and Staines, see. The office, now, where the bailifs came and took everything, that was behind the shop in Staines. So there's the boss holding his head and wailing like a siren because of all his bleeding furniture's on its way out, when the phone rings. Course by this time the phone's down on the floor because the desk it was on is out on the pavement. So the boss squats down beside it and there's some geezer on the other end offering to buy the lease.'

He paused more for dramatic effect than breath.

'Go on,' I said encouragingly.

'Manna from Heaven for the boss, that was,' said Bert, accepting the invitation. 'See, he'd have had to go on paying the rent for both places even if they were shut. He practically fell on the neck of this geezer in a manner of speaking, and the geezer came round and paid him in cash on the nail, three hundred smackers, that very morning and the boss has been getting drunk on it ever since.'

A pause. 'What line of business' I asked, 'is this geezer in?'

'Eh?' said Bert, surprised. 'Bookmaking, of course.'

Charlie smiled.

'I expect you've heard of him,' Bert said. 'Name of Ganser Mays.'

It was inevitable, I supposed.

'In what way,' I asked, 'do you want me to help?'

'Huh?'

'Charlie said you wanted my help.'

'Oh that. I dunno, really. Charlie just said it might help to tell you what I'd told him, so I done it.'

'Did Charlie tell you,' I asked, 'who owns Energise?'

'No, Charlie didn't,' Charlie said.

'What the bleeding hell does it matter who owns it?' Bert demanded.

'I do,' I said.

Bert looked from one of us to the other several times. Various thoughts took their turn behind his eyes, and Charlie and I waited.

'Here,' he said at last. 'Did you bleeding fix that race?'

'The horse ran fair and square, and I backed it on the Tote,' I said.

'Well, how come my boss thought...'

'I've no idea,' I said untruthfully.

Charlie lit another cigarette from the stub of the last. They were his lungs, after all.

'The point is,' I said, 'who gave your boss the wrong information?'

'Dunno.' He thought it over, but shook his head. 'Dunno.'

'Could it have been Ganser Mays?'

'Blimey!'

'Talk about slander,' Charlie said. 'He'd have you for that.'

'I merely ask,' I said. 'I also ask whether Bert knows of any other small firms which have gone out of business in the same way.'

'Blimey,' Bert said again, with even more force.

Charlie sighed with resignation, as if he hadn't engineered the whole morning's chat.

'Ganser Mays,' I said conversationally, 'has opened a vast string of betting shops during the past year or so. What has happened to the opposition?'

'Down the boozer getting drunk,' Charlie said.

Charlie stayed for a while after Bert had gone, sitting more comfortably in one of my leather armchairs and reverting thankfully to his more natural self.

'Bert's a great fellow,' he said. 'But I find him tiring.' His Eton accent, I noticed, had come back in force and I realized with mild surprise how much he tailored voice and manner to suit his company. The Charlie Canterfield I knew, the powerful banker smoking a cigar who thought of a million as everyday currency, was not the face he had shown to Bert Huggerneck. It occurred to me that of all the people I had met who had moved from one world to another, Charlie had done it with most success. He swam through big business like a fish in water but he could still feel completely at home with Bert in a way that I, who had made a less radical journey, could not.

'Which is the villain,' Charlie asked. 'Ganser Mays or Jody Leeds?'

'Both.'

'Equal partners?'

We considered it. 'No way of knowing at the moment,' I said.

'At the moment?' His eyebrows went up.

I smiled slightly. 'I thought I might have a small crack at . . . would you call it justice?'

'The law's a bad thing to take into your own hands.'

'I don't exactly aim to lynch anyone.'

'What, then?'

I hesitated. 'There's something I ought to check. I think I'll do it today. After that, if I'm right, I'll make a loud fuss.'

'Slander actions notwithstanding?'

'I don't know.' I shook my head. 'It's infuriating.'

'What are you going to check?' he asked.

Telephone tomorrow morning and I'll tell you.'

Charlie, like Allie, asked before he left if I would show him where I made the toys. We went down to the workshop and found Owen Idris, my general helper, busy sweeping the tidy floor.

'Morning, Owen.'

'Morning, sir.'

'This is Mr Canterfield, Owen.'

'Morning, sir.'

Owen appeared to have swept without pause but I knew the swift glance he had given Charlie was as good as a photograph. My neat dry little Welsh factotum had a phenomenal memory for faces.

'Will you want the car today, sir?' he said.

'This evening.'

'I'll just change the oil, then.'

'Fine.'

'Will you be wanting me for the parking?'

I shook my head. 'Not tonight.'

'Very good, sir.' He looked resigned. 'Any time,' he said.

I showed Charlie the machines but he knew less about engineering than I did about banking.

'Where do you start, in the hands or in the head?'

'Head,' I said. 'Then hands, then head.'

'So clear.'

'I think of something, I make it, I draw it.'

'Draw it?'

'Machine drawings, not an artistic impression.'

'Blue prints,' said Charlie, nodding wisely.

'Blue prints are copies . . . The originals are black on white.'

'Disillusioning.'

I slid open one of the long drawers which held them and showed him some of the designs. The fine spidery lines with a key giving details of materials and sizes of screw threads looked very different from the bright shiny toys which reached the shops, and Charlie looked from design to finished article with a slowly shaking head.

'Don't know how you do it.'

'Training,' I said. 'Same way that you switch money round ten currencies in half an hour and end up thousands richer.'

'Can't do that so much these days,' he said gloomily. He watched me put designs and toys away. 'Don't forget though that my firm can always find finances for good ideas.'

'I won't forget.'

'There must be a dozen merchant banks,' Charlie said, 'all hoping to be nearest when you look around for cash.'

'The manufacturers fix the cash. I just collect the royalties.'

He shook his head. 'You'll never make a million that way.'

'I won't get ulcers, either.'

'No ambition?

'To win the Derby and get even with Jody Leeds.'

I arrived at Jody's expensive stable uninvited, quietly, at half past midnight, and on foot. The car lay parked half a mile behind me, along with prudence.

Pale fitful moonlight lit glimpses of the large manor house with its pedimented front door and rows of uniform windows. No lights shone upstairs in the room Jody shared with Felicity, and none downstairs in the large drawing-room beneath. The lawn, rough now and scattered with a few last dead leaves, stretched peacefully from the house to where I stood hidden in the bushes by the gate.

I watched for a while. There was no sign of anyone awake or moving, and I hadn't expected it. Jody like most six-thirty risers was usually asleep by eleven at the latest, and telephone calls after ten were answered brusquely if at all. On the other hand he had no reservations about telephoning others in the morning before seven. He had no patience with life-patterns unlike his own.

To the right and slightly to the rear of the house lay the dimly gleaming roofs of the stables. White railed paddocks lay around and beyond them, with big planned trees growing at landscaped corners. When Berksdown Court had been built, cost had come second to excellence.

Carrying a large black rubber-clad torch, unlit, I walked softly up the drive and round towards the horses. No dogs barked. No all-night guards sprang out to ask my business. Silence and peace bathed the whole place undisturbed.

My breath, all the same, came faster. My heart thumped. It would be bad if anyone caught me. I had tried reassuring myself that Jody would do me not actual physical harm, but I hadn't found myself convinced. Anger, as when I'd stood in the path of the horsebox, was again thrusting me into risk.

Close to the boxes one could hear little more than from a distance. Jody's horses stood on sawdust now that straw prices had trebled, and made no rustle when they moved. A sudden equine sneeze made me jump.

Jody's yard was not a regular quadrangle but a series of three-sided courts of unequal size and powerful charm. There were forty boxes altogether, few enough in any case to support such a lavish establishment, but since my horses had left I guessed there were only about twenty inmates remaining. Jody was in urgent need of another mug.

He had always economized on labour, reckoning that he and Felicity between them could do the work of four. His inexhaustible energy in fact ensured that no lads stayed in the yard very long as they couldn't stand the pace. Since the last so-called head lad had left in dudgeon because Jody constantly usurped his authority, there had been no one but Jody himself in charge. It was unlikely, I thought, that in present circumstances he would have taken on another man, which meant that the cottage at the end of the yard would be empty.

There were at any rate no lights in it, and no anxious figure came scurrying out to see about the stranger in the night. I went with care to the first box in the first court and quietly slid back the bolts.

Inside stood a large chestnut mare languidly eating hay. She turned her face unexcitedly in the torchlight. A big white blaze down her forehead and nose. Asphodel.

I shut her door, inching home the bolts. Any sharp noise would carry clearly through the cold calm air and Jody's subconscious ears would never sleep. The second box contained a heavy bay gelding with black points, the third a dark chestnut with one white sock. I went slowly round the first section of stables, shining the torch at each horse.

Instead of settling, my nerves got progressively worse. I had not yet found what I'd come for, and every passing minute made discovery more possible. I was careful with the torch. Careful with the bolts. My breath was shallow. I decided I'd make a rotten burglar.

Box number nine, in the next section, contained a dark brown gelding with no markings. The next box housed an undistinguished bay, the next another and the next another. After that came an almost black horse, with a slightly Arab looking nose, another very dark horse, and two more bays. The next three boxes all contained chestnuts, all unremarkable to my eyes. The last inhabited box held the only grey.

I gently shut the door of the grey and returned to the box of the chestnut next door. Went inside. Shone my torch over him carefully inch by inch.

I came to no special conclusion except that I didn't know enough about horses.

'I'd done all I could. Time to go home. Time for my heart to stop thudding at twice the speed of sound. I turned for the door.

Lights came on in a blaze. Startled I took one step towards the door. Only one.

Three men crowded into the opening.

Jody Leeds.

Ganser Mays.

Another man whom I didn't know, whose appearance scarcely

inspired joy and confidence. He was large, hard and muscular, and he wore thick leather gloves, a cloth cap pulled forward and, at two in the morning, sunglasses.

Whomever they had expected, it wasn't me. Jody's face held a mixture of consternation and anger, with the former winning by a mile.

'What the bloody hell are you doing here?' he said.

There was no possible answer.

'He isn't leaving,' Ganser Mays said. The eyes behind the metal rims were narrowed with ill intent and the long nose protruded sharply like a dagger. The urbane manner which lulled the clients while he relieved them of their cash had turned into the naked viciousness of the threatened criminal. Too late to worry that I'd cast myself in the role of threat.

'What?' Jody turned his face to him, not understanding.

'He isn't leaving.'

Jody said 'How are you going to stop him?'

Nobody told him. Nobody told me, either. I took two steps towards the exit and found out.

The large man said nothing at all, but it was he who moved. A large gloved fist crashed into my ribs at the business end of a highly efficient short jab. Breath left my lungs faster than nature intended and I had difficulty getting it back.

Beyond schoolboy scuffles I had never seriously had to defend myself. No time to learn. I slammed an elbow at Jody's face, kicked Ganser Mays in the stomach and tried for the door.

Muscles in cap and sunglasses knew all that I didn't. An inch or two taller, a stone or two heavier, and warmed to his task. I landed one respectable punch on the junction of his nose and mouth in return for a couple of bangs over the heart, and made no progress towards freedom.

Jody and Ganser Mays recovered from my first onslaught and clung to me like limpets, one on each arm. I staggered under their combined weight. Muscles measured his distance and flung his bunched hand at my jaw. I managed to move my head just in time and felt the leather glove burn my cheek. Then the other fist came round, faster and crossing, and hit me square. I fell reeling across the box, released suddenly by Ganser Mays and Jody, and my head smashed solidly into the iron bars of the manger.

Total instant unconsciousness was the result.

Death must be like that, I suppose.

Chapter Six

Life came back in an incomprehensible blur.

I couldn't see properly. Couldn't focus. Heard strange noises. Couldn't control my body, couldn't move my legs, couldn't lift my head. Tongue paralysed. Brain whirling. Everything disconnected and hazy.

'Drunk,' someone said distinctly.

The word made no sense. It wasn't I who was drunk.

'Paralytic.'

The ground was wet. Shining. Dazzled my eyes. I was sitting on it. Slumped on it, leaning against something hard. I shut my eyes against the drizzle and that made the whirling noise. I could feel myself falling. Banged my head. Cheek in the wet. Nose in the wet. Lying on the hard wet ground. There was a noise like rain.

'Bloody amazing,' said a voice.

'Come on, then, 'let's be having you.'

Strong hands slid under my armpits and grasped my ankles. I couldn't struggle. Couldn't understand where I was or what was happening.

It seemed vaguely that I was in the back of a car. I could smell the upholstery. My nose was on it. Someone was breathing very loudly. Almost snoring. Someone spoke. A jumbled mixture of sounds that made no words. It couldn't have been me. Couldn't have been.

The car jerked to a sudden stop. The driver swore. I rolled off the seat and passed out.

Next thing, bright lights and people carrying me as before.

I tried to say something. It came out in a jumble. This time I knew the jumble came from my own mouth.

'Waking up again,' someone said.

'Get him out of here before he's sick.'

March, march. More carrying. Loud boots on echoing floors.

'He's bloody heavy.'

'Bloody nuisance.'

The whirling went on. The whole building was spinning like a merry-go-round.

Merry-go-round.

The first feeling of identity came back. I wasn't just a lump of weird disorientated sensations. Somewhere, deep inside, I was ... somebody.

Merry-go-rounds swam in and out of consciousness. I found I was lying on a bed. Bright lights blinded me every time I tried to open my eyes. The voices went away.

Time passed.

I began to feel exceedingly ill. Heard someone moaning. Didn't think it was me. After a while, I knew it was, which made it possible to stop.

Feet coming back. March march. Two pairs at least.

'What's your name?'

What was my name? Couldn't remember.

'He's soaking wet.'

'What do you expect? He was sitting on the pavement in the rain.'

'Take his jacket off.'

They took my jacket off, sitting me up to do it. I lay down again. My trousers were pulled off and someone put a blanket over me.

'He's dead drunk.'

'Yes. Have to make sure though. They're always an infernal nuisance like this. You simply can't risk that they haven't bumped their skulls and got a hairline fracture. You don't want them dying on you in the night.'

I tried to tell him I wasn't drunk. Hairline fracture ... Christ ... I didn't want to wake up dead in the morning.

'What did you say?'

I tried again. 'Not drunk,' I said.

Someone laughed without mirth.

'Just smell his breath.'

How did I know I wasn't drunk? The answer eluded me. I just knew I wasn't drunk ... because I knew I hadn't drunk enough ... or any ... alcohol. How did I know? I just knew. How did I know?

While these hopeless thought spiralled around in the chaos inside my head a lot of strange fingers were feeling around in my hair.

'He *has* banged his head, damn it. There's quite a large swelling.'

'He's no worse than when they brought him in, doc. Better, if anything.'

'Scott,' I said suddenly.

'What's that?'

'Scott.'

'Is that your name?'

I tried to sit up. The lights whirled giddily.

'Where ... am I?'

'That's what they all say.'

'In a cell, my lad, that's where.'

In a cell.

'What?' I said.

'In a cell at Savile Row police station. Drunk and incapable.'

I couldn't be.

'Look, constable, I'll just take a blood test. Then I'll do those other jobs, then come back and look at him, to make sure. I don't think we've a fracture here, but we can't take the chance.'

'Right, doc.'

The prick of a needle reached me dimly. Waste of time, I thought. Wasn't drunk. What was I ... besides ill, giddy, lost and stuck in limbo? Didn't know. Couldn't be bothered to think. Slid without struggling into a whirling black sleep.

The next awakening was in all ways worse. For a start, I wasn't ready to be dragged back from the dark. My head ached abominably, bits of my body hurt and good deal and over all I felt like an advanced case of seasickness.

'Wakey, wakey, rise and shine. Cup of tea for you and you don't deserve it.'

I opened my eyes. The bright light was still there but now identifiable not as some gross moon but as a simple electric bulb near the ceiling.

I shifted my gaze to where the voice had come from. A middle-aged policeman stood there with a paper cup in one hand. Behind him, an open door to a corridor. All round me, the close walls of a cell. I lay on a reasonably comfortable bed with two blankets keeping me warm.

'Sobering up, are you?'

'I wasn't ... drunk.' My voice came out hoarse and my mouth felt as furry as a mink coat.

The policeman held out the cup. I struggled on to one elbow and took it from him.

'Thanks.' The tea was strong, hot and sweet. I wasn't sure it didn't make me feel even sicker.

'The doc's been back twice to check on you. You were drunk all right. Banged your head, too.'

'But I wasn't...'

'You sure were. The doc did a blood test to make certain.'

'Where are my clothes?'

'Oh yeah. We took 'em off. They were wet. I'll get them.'

He went out without shutting the door and I spent the few minutes he was away trying to sort out what was happening. I could remember bits of the night, but hazily. I knew who I was. No problem there. I looked at my watch: seven-thirty. I felt absolutely lousy.

The policeman returned with my suit which was wrinkled beyond belief and looked nothing like the one I'd set out in.

Set out ... Where to?

'Is this ... Savile Row? West end of London?'

'You remember being brought in then?'

'Some of it. Not much.'

'The patrol car picked you up somewhere in Soho at around four o'clock this morning.'

'What was I doing there?'

'I don't know, do I? Nothing, as far as I know. Just sitting dead drunk on the pavement in the pouring rain.'

'Why did they bring me here if I wasn't doing anything?'

'To save you from yourself,' he said without rancour. 'Drunks make more trouble if we leave them than if we bring them in, so we bring them in. Can't have drunks wandering out into the middle of the road and causing accidents or breaking their silly skulls falling over or waking up violent and smashing shop windows as some of them do.'

'I feel ill.'

'What do expect? If you're going to be sick there's a bucket at the end of the bed.'

He gave me a nod in which sympathy wasn't entirely lacking, and took himself away.

About an hour later I was driven with three other gentlemen in the same plight to attend the Marlborough Street Magistrates' Court. Drunks, it seemed, were first on the agenda. Every day's agenda.

In the interim I had become reluctantly convinced of three things.

First was that even though I could not remember drinking, I had at four a.m. that morning been hopelessly intoxicated. The blood test, analysed at speed because of the bang on my head, had revealed a level of two hundred and ninety milligrammes of alcohol per centilitre of blood which, I had been assured, meant that I had drunk the equivalent of more than half a bottle of spirits during the preceding few hours.

The second was that it would make no difference at all if I could convince anyone that at one-thirty I had been stone cold sober seventy miles away in Berkshire. They would merely say I had plenty of time to get drunk on the journey.

And the third and perhaps least welcome of all was that I seemed to have collected far more sore spots than I could account for.

I had remembered, bit by bit, my visit to Jody. I remembered trying to fight all three men at once, which was an idiotic sort of thing to attempt in the first place, even without the casual expertise of the man in sunglasses. I remembered the squashy feel when my fist connected with his nose and I knew all about the punches he'd given me in return. Even so . . .

I shrugged. Perhaps I didn't remember it all, like I didn't remember getting drunk. Or perhaps . . . Well, Ganser Mays and Jody both had reason to dislike me, and Jody had been wearing jodhpur boots.

The court proceedings took ten minutes. The charge was 'drunk in charge'. In charge of what, I asked. In charge of the police, they said.

'Guilty or not guilty?'

'Guilty,' I said resignedly.

'Fined five pounds. Do you need time to pay?'

'No, sir.'

'Good. Next, please.'

Outside, in the little office where I was due to pay the fine, I telephoned Owen Idris. Paying after all had been a problem, as there had proved to be no wallet in my rough-dried suit. No cheque book either, nor, when I came to think of it, any keys. Were they all by any chance at Savile Row, I asked. Someone telephoned. No, they weren't. I had had nothing at all in my pockets when picked up. No means of identification, no money, no keys, no pen, no handkerchief.

'Owen? Bring ten pounds and a taxi to Marlborough Street Court.'
'Very good, sir.'
'Right away.'
'Of course.'
I felt hopelessly groggy. I sat in an upright chair to wait and wondered how long it took for half a bottle of spirits to dry out.
Owen came in thirty minutes and handed me the money without comment. Even his face showed no surprise at finding me in such a predicament and unshaven into the bargain. I wasn't sure that I appreciated his lack of surprise. I also couldn't think of any believable explanation. Nothing to do but shrug it off, pay the five pounds and get home as best I could. Owen sat beside me in the taxi and gave me small sidelong glances every hundred yards.
I made it upstairs to the sitting-room and lay down flat on the sofa. Owen had stayed downstairs to pay the taxi and I could hear him talking to someone down in the hall. I could do without visitors, I thought. I could do without everything except twenty-four hours of oblivion.
The visitor was Charlie.
'Your man says you're in trouble.'
'Mm.'
'Good God.' He was standing beside me, looking down. 'What on earth have you been doing?'
'Long story.'
'Hm. Will your man get us some coffee?'
'Ask him ... he'll be in the workshop. Intercom over there.' I nodded towards the far door and wished I hadn't. My whole brain felt like a bruise.
Charlie talked to Owen on the intercom and Owen came up with his ultra polite face and messed around with filters in the kitchen.
'What's the matter with you?' Charlie asked.
'Knocked out, drunk and ...' I stopped.
'And what?'
'Nothing.'
'You need a doctor.'
'I saw a police surgeon. Or rather ... he saw me.'
'You can't see the state of your eyes,' Charlie said seriously. 'And whether you like it or not, I'm getting you a doctor.' He went away to the kitchen to consult Owen and I heard the extension bell there tinkling as he kept his promise. He came back.
'What's wrong with my eyes?'
'Pinpoint pupils and glassy daze.'
'Charming.'
Owen brought the coffee, which smelled fine, but I found I could scarcely drink it. Both men looked at me with what I could only call concern.
'How did you get like this?' Charlie said.
'Shall I go, sir?' Owen said politely.
'No. Sit down, Owen. You may as well know too ...' He sat

comfortably in a small armchair, neither perching on the front nor lolling at ease in the depths. The compromise of Owen's attitude to me was what made him above price, his calm understanding that although I paid for work done, we each retained equal dignity in the transaction. I had employed him for less than a year: I hoped he would stay till he dropped.

'I went down to Jody Leeds' stable, last night, after dark,' I said. 'I had no right at all to be there. Jody and two other men found me in one of the boxes looking at a horse. There was a bit of a struggle and I banged my head ... on a manger, I think ... and got knocked out.'

I stopped for breath. My audience said nothing at all.

'When I woke up, I was sitting on a pavement in Soho, dead drunk.'

'Impossible,' Charlie said.

'No. It happened. The police scooped me up, as they apparently do to all drunks littering the footpaths. I spent the remains of the night in a cell and got fined five pounds, and here I am.'

There was a long pause.

Charlie cleared his throat. 'Er ... various questions arise.'

'They do indeed.'

Owen said calmly, 'The car, sir. Where did you leave the car?' The car was his especial love, polished and cared for like silver.

I told him exactly where I'd parked it. Also that I no longer had its keys. Nor the keys to the flat or the workshop, for that matter.

Both Charlie and Owen showed alarm and agreed between themselves that the first thing Owen would do, even before fetching the car, would be to change all my locks.

'I made those locks,' I protested.

'Do you want Jody walking in here while you're asleep?'

'No.'

'Then Owen changes the locks.'

I didn't demur any more. I'd been thinking of a new form of lock for some time, but hadn't actually made it. I would soon, though. I would patent it and make it as a toy for kids to lock up their secrets, and maybe in twenty years time half the doors in the country would be keeping out burglars that way. My lock didn't need keys or electronics, and couldn't be picked. It stood there, clear and sharp in my mind, with all its working parts meshing neatly.

'Are you all right?' Charlie said abruptly.

'What?'

'For a moment you looked ...' He stopped and didn't finish the sentence.

'I'm not dying, if that's what you think. It's just that I've an idea for a new sort of lock.'

Charlie's attention sharpened as quickly as it had at Sandown.

'Revolutionary?' he asked hopefully.

I smiled inside. The word was apt in more ways than one, as some of the lock's works would revolve.

'You might say so,' I agreed.

'Don't forget ... my bank.'

'I won't.'

'No one but you would be inventing things when he's half dead.'

'I may look half dead,' I said, 'but I'm not.' I might feel half dead, too, I thought, but it would all pass.

The door bell rang sharply.

'If it's anyone but the doctor,' Charlie told Owen, 'tell them our friend is out.'

Owen nodded briefly and went downstairs, but when he came back he brought not the doctor but a visitor less expected and more welcome.

'Miss Ward, sir.'

She was through the door before he had the words out, blowing in like a gust of fresh air, her face as smooth and clean and her clothes as well-groomed as mine were dirty and squalid. She looked like life itself on two legs, her vitality lighting the room.

'Steven!'

She stopped dead a few feet from the sofa, staring down. She glanced at Charlie and at Owen. 'What's the matter with him?'

'Rough night on the tiles,' I said. 'D'you mind if I don't get up?'

'How do you do?' Charlie said politely. 'I am Charlie Canterfield. Friend of Steven's.' He shook hands with her.

'Alexandra Ward,' she replied, looking bemused

'You've met,' I said.

'What?'

'In Walton Street.'

They looked at each other and realized what I meant. Charlie began to tell Allie how I had arrived in this sorry state and Owen went out shopping for locks. I lay on the sofa and drifted. The whole morning seemed disjointed and jerky to me, as if my thought processes were tripping over cracks.

Allie pulled up a squashy leather stool and sat beside me, which brought recovery nearer. She put her hand on mine. Better still.

'You're crazy,' she said.

I sighed. Couldn't have everything.

'Have you forgotten. I'm going home this evening?'

'I have not,' I said. 'Though it looks now as though I'll have to withdraw my offer of driving you to the airport. I don't think I'm fit. No car, for another thing.'

'That's actually what I came for.' She hesitated. 'I have to keep peace with my sister ...' She stopped, leaving a world of family tensions hovering unspoken. 'I came to say goodbye.'

'What sort of goodbye?'

'What do you mean?'

'Goodbye for now,' I said, 'or goodbye for ever?'

'Which would you like?'

Charlie chuckled. 'Now there's a double-edged question if I ever heard one.'

'You're not supposed to be listening,' she said with mock severity.

'Goodbye for now,' I said.

'All right.' She smiled the flashing smile. 'Suits me.'

Charlie wandered round the room looking at things but showed no signs of going. Allie disregarded him. She stroked my hair back from my forehead and kissed me gently. I can't say I minded.

After a while the doctor came. Charlie went down to let him in and apparently briefed him on the way up. He and Allie retired to the kitchen where I heard them making more coffee.

The doctor helped me remove all my clothes except underpants. I'd have been much happier left alone. He tapped my joints for reflexes, peered through lights into my eyes and ears and prodded my many sore spots. Then he sat on the stool Allie had brought, and pinched his nose.

'Concussion,' he said. 'Go to bed for a week.'

'Don't be silly,' I protested.

'Best,' he said succinctly.

'But the jump jockeys get concussion one minute and ride winners the next.'

'The jump jockeys are bloody fools.' He surveyed me morosely. 'If you'd been a jump jockey I'd say you'd been trampled by a field of horses.'

'But as I'm not?'

'Has someone been beating you?'

It wasn't the sort of question that one expected one's doctor to ask. Certainly not as matter-of-factly as this.

'I don't know,' I said.

'You must do.'

'I agree it feels a bit like it, but if they did, I was unconscious.'

'With something big and blunt,' he added. 'They're large bruises.' He pointed to several extensive reddening patches on my thighs, arms and trunk.

'A boot?' I said.

He looked at me soberly. 'You've considered the possibility?'

'Forced on me.'

He smiled. 'Your friend, the one who let me in, told me you say you got drunk also while unconscious.'

'Yes. Tube down the throat?' I suggested.

'Tell me the time factors.'

I did, as nearly as I could. He shook his head dubiously. 'I wouldn't have thought pouring neat alcohol straight into the stomach would produce that amount of intoxication so quickly. It takes quite a while for a large quantity of alcohol to be absorbed into the bloodstream through the stomach wall.' He pondered, thinking aloud. 'Two hundred and ninety milligrammes ... and you were maybe unconscious from the bang on the head for two hours or a little more. Hm.'

He leaned forward, picked up my left forearm and peered at it closely, front and back. Then he did the same with the right, and found what he was looking for.

'There,' he exclaimed. 'See that? The mark of a needle. Straight into the vein. They've tried to disguise it by a blow on top to bruise all the surrounding tissue. In a few more hours the needle mark will be invisible.'

'Anaesthetic?' I said dubiously.

'My dear fellow. No. Probably gin.'

'*Gin!*'

'Why not? Straight into the bloodstream. Much more efficient than a tube to the stomach. Much quicker results. Deadly, really. And less effort, on the whole.'

'But ... how? You can't harness a gin bottle to a hypodermic.'

He grinned. 'No, no. You'd set up a drip. Sterile glucose saline drip. Standard stuff. You can buy it in plastic bags from any chemist. Pour three quarters of a pint of gin into one bag of solution, and drip it straight into the vein.'

'But, how long would that take?'

'Oh, about an hour. Frightful shock to the system.'

I thought about it. If it had been done that way I had been transported to London with gin dripping into my blood for most of the journey. There hadn't been time to do it first and set off after.

'Suppose I'd started to come round?' I asked.

'Lucky you didn't, I dare say. Nothing to stop someone bashing you back to sleep, as far as I can see.'

'You take it very calmly,' I said.

'So do you. And it's interesting, don't you think?'

'Oh very,' I said dryly.

Chapter Seven

Charlie and Allie stayed for lunch, which meant that they cooked omelettes for themselves and found some reasonable cheese to follow. Out in the kitchen Charlie seemed to have been filling in gaps because when they carried their trays into the sitting-room it was clear that Allie knew all that Charlie did.

'Do you feel like eating?' Charlie asked.

'I do not.'

'Drink?'

'Shut up.'

'Sorry.'

The body rids itself of alcohol very slowly, the doctor had said. Only at a rate of ten milligrammes per hour. There was no way of hastening the process and nothing much to be done about hangovers except endure them. People who normally drank little suffered worst, he said, because their bodies had no tolerance. Too bad, he'd said, smiling about it.

Two hundred and ninety milligrammes came into the paralytic bracket. Twenty-nine hours to be rid of it. I'd lived through about ten so far. No wonder I felt so awful.

Round a mouthful of omelette Charlie said, 'What are you going to do about all this?' He waved his fork from my heels to my head, still prostrate on the sofa.

'Would you suggest going to the police?' I asked neutrally.

'Er . . .'

'Exactly. The very same police who gave me hospitality last night and know for a certainty that I was so drunk that anything I might complain of could be explained away as an alcoholic delusion.'

'Do you think that's why Jody and Ganser Mays did it?'

'Why else? And I suppose I should be grateful that all they did was discredit me, not bump me right off altogether.'

Allie looked horrified, which was nice. Charlie was more prosaic.

'Bodies are notoriously difficult to get rid of,' he said. 'I would say that Jody and Ganser Mays made a rapid assessment and reckoned that dumping you drunk in London was a lot less dangerous than murder.'

'There was another man as well,' I said, and described my friend with sunglasses and muscles.

'Ever seen him before?' Charlie asked.

'No, never.'

'The brawn of the organization?'

'Maybe he has brain, too. Can't tell.'

'One thing is sure,' Charlie said, 'If the plan was to discredit you, your little escapade will be known all round the racecourse by tomorrow afternoon.'

How gloomy, I thought. I was sure he was right. It would make going to the races more uninviting than ever.

Allie said, 'I guess you won't like it, but if I were trying to drag your name through the mud I'd have made sure there was a gossip columnist in court this morning.

'Oh hell.' Worse and worse.

'Are you just going to lie there,' Charlie said, 'and let them crow?'

'He's got a problem,' Allie said with a smile. 'How come he was wandering around Jody's stable at that time anyway?'

'Ah,' I said. 'Now that's the nub of the matter, I agree. And if I tell you, you must both promise me on your souls that you will not repeat it.'

'Are you serious?' Allie said in surprise.

'You don't sound it,' Charlie commented.

'I am though. Deadly serious. Will you promise?'

'You play with too many toys. It's childish.'

'Many civil servants swear an oath of secrecy.'

'Oh all right,' Charlie said in exasperation. 'On my soul.'

'And on mine,' Allie said lightheartedly. 'Now do get on with it.'

'I own a horse called Energise,' I said. They both nodded. They knew. 'I spent half an hour alone with him in a crashed horsebox at

Sandown.' They both nodded again. 'Then I sent him to Rupert Ramsey and last Sunday morning I spent half an hour with him again.'

'So what?' Charlie said.

'So the horse at Rupert Ramsey's is not Energise.'

Charlie sat bolt upright so quickly that his omelette plate fell on the carpet. He bent down, feeling around for bits of egg with his astounded face turned up to mine.

'Are you sure?'

'Definitely. He's very like him, and if I hadn't spent all that time in the crashed horsebox I would never have known the difference. Owners often don't know which their horse is. It's a standing joke. But I *learnt* Energise that day at Sandown. So when I visited Rupert Ramsey's I knew he had a different horse.'

'So,' said Charlie slowly, 'you went to Jody's stable last night to see if Energise was still there.'

'Yes.'

'And is he?'

'Yes.'

'Absolutely certain?'

'Positive. He has a slightly Arab nose, a nick near the tip of his left ear, a bald spot about the size of a twopenny piece on his shoulder. He was in box number thirteen.'

'Is that where they found you?'

'No. You remember, Allie, that we went to Newmarket?'

'How could I forget?'

'Do you remember Hermes?'

She wrinkled her nose. 'Was that the chestnut?'

'That's right. Well, I went to Trevor Kennet's stable that day with you because I wanted to see if I could tell whether the Hermes he had was the Hermes Jody had had ... if you see what I mean.'

'And was he?' she said, fascinated.

'I couldn't tell. I found I didn't know Hermes well enough and anyway if Jody did switch Hermes he probably did it before his last two races last summer, because the horse did no good at all in those and trailed in at the back of the field.'

'Good God,' Charlie said. 'And did you find Hermes at Jody's place too?'

'I don't know. There were three chestnuts there. No markings, same as Hermes. All much alike. I couldn't tell if any of them was Hermes. But it was in one of the chestnut's boxes that Jody and the others found me, and they were certainly alarmed as well as angry.'

'But what would he get out of it?' Allie asked.

'He owns some horses himself,' I said. 'Trainers often do. They run them in their own names, then if they're any good, they sell them at a profit, probably to owners who already have horses in the stable.'

'You mean ...' she said, 'that he sent a horse he owned himself to Rupert Ramsey and kept Energise. Then when Energise wins another big race he'll sell him to one of the people he trains for, for a nice fat sum, and keep on training him himself?'

'That's about it.'

'Wow.'

'I'm not so absolutely sure,' I said with a sardonic smile, 'that he hasn't in the past sold me my own horse back after swopping it with one of his own.'

'Je-*sus*,' Charlie said.

'I had two bay fillies I couldn't tell apart. The first one won for a while, then turned sour. I sold her on Jody's advice and bought the second, which was one of his own. She started winning straight away.'

'How are you going to prove it?' Allie said.

'I don't see how you can,' said Charlie. 'Especially not after this drinking charge.'

We all three contemplated the situation in silence.

'Gee, dammit,' said Allie finally and explosively. 'I just don't see why that guy should be allowed to rob you and make people despise you and get away with it.'

'Give me time,' I said mildly, 'and he won't.'

'Time?'

'For thinking,' I explained. 'If a frontal assault would land me straight into a lawsuit for slander, which it would, I'll have to come up with a sneaky scheme which will creep up on him from the rear.'

Allie and Charlie looked at each other.

Charlie said to her, 'A lot of the things he's invented as children's toys get scaled up very usefully.'

'As if Cockerell had made the first Hovercraft for the bath tub?'

'Absolutely.' Charlie nodded at her with approval. 'And I dare say it was a gentle-seeming man who thought of gunpowder.'

She flashed a smiling look from him to me and then looked suddenly at her watch and got to her feet in a hurry.

'Oh golly! I'm late. I should have gone an hour ago. My sister will be so mad. Steven...'

Charlie looked at her resignedly and took the plates out to the kitchen. I shifted my lazy self off the sofa and stood up.

'I wish you weren't going,' I said.

'I really have to.'

'Do you mind kissing an unshaven drunk?'

It seemed she didn't. It was the best we'd achieved.

'The Atlantic has shrunk,' I said, 'since Columbus.'

'Will you cross it?'

'Swim, if necessary.'

She briefly kissed my bristly cheek, laughed and went quickly. The room seemed darker and emptier. I wanted her back with a most unaccustomed fierceness. Girls had come and gone in my life and each time afterwards I had relapsed thankfully into singleness. Maybe at thirty-five, I thought fleetingly, what I wanted was a wife.

Charlie returned from the kitchen carrying a cup and saucer.

'Sit down before you fall down,' he said. 'You're saying about like the Empire State.'

I sat on the sofa.

'And drink this.'

He had made a cup of tea, not strong, not weak, and with scarcely any milk. I took a couple of sips and thanked him.

'Will you be all right if I go?' he said. 'I've an appointment.'

'Of course, Charlie.'

'Take care of your damned silly self.'

'Yeah.'

He buttoned his overcoat, gave me a sympathetic wave and departed. Owen had long since finished changing the locks and had set off with a spare set of keys to fetch the car. I was alone in the flat. It seemed much quieter than usual.

I drank the rest of the tea, leaned back against the cushions, and shut my eyes, sick and uncomfortable from head to foot. Damn Jody Leeds, I thought. Damn and blast him to hell.

No wonder, I thought, that he had been so frantically determined to take Energise back with him from Sandown. He must already have had the substitute in his yard, waiting for a good moment to exchange them. When I'd said I wanted Energise to go elsewhere immediately he had been ready to go to any lengths to prevent it. I was pretty sure now that had Jody been driving the horsebox instead of Andy-Fred I would have ended up in hospital if not in the morgue.

I thought about the passports which were the identity cards of British thoroughbreds. A blank passport form bore three stylised outlines of a horse, one from each side and one from head on. At the time when a foal was named, usually as a yearling or two-year-old, the veterinary surgeon attending the stable where he was being trained filled in his markings on the form and completed a written description alongside. The passport was then sent to the central racing authorities who stamped it, filed it and sent a photocopy back to the trainer.

I had noticed from time to time that my horses had hardly a blaze, star or white sock between them. It had never struck me as significant. Thousands of horse had no markings. I had even preferred them without.

The passports, once issued, were rarely used. As far as I knew, apart from travelling abroad, they were checked only once, which was on the day of the horse's very first race; and that not out of suspicion, but simply to make sure the horse actually did match the vet's description.

I didn't doubt that the horse now standing instead of Energise at Rupert Ramsey's stable matched Energise's passport in every way. Details like the shape of the nose, the slant of the stomach, the angle of the hock, wouldn't be on it.

I sighed and shifted a bit to relieve various aches. Didn't succeed. Jody had been generous with his boots.

I remembered with satisfaction the kick I'd landed in Ganser Mays' stomach. But perhaps he too had taken revenge.

It struck me suddenly that Jody wouldn't have had to rely on Raymond Child to ride crooked races. Not every time, anyway. If he had a substitute horse of poor ability, all he had to do was send him instead of the good one whenever the race had to be lost.

Racing history was packed with rumours of ringers, the good horses running in the names of the bad. Jody, I was sure, had simply reversed things and run bad horses in the names of good.

Every horse I'd owned, when I looked back, had followed much the same pattern. There would be at first a patch of sporadic success, but with regular disasters every time I staked a bundle, and then a long tailoff with no success at all. It was highly likely that the no success was due to my now having the substitute, which was running way out of its class.

It would explain why Ferryboat had run badly all autumn. Not because he resented Raymond Child's whip, but because he wasn't Ferryboat. Wrecker, too. And at least one of the three older horses I'd sent up north.

Five at least, that made. Also the filly. Also the first two, now sold as flops. Eight. I reckoned I might still have the real Dial and I might still have the real Bubbleglass, because they were novices who had yet to prove their worth. But they too would have been matched, when they had.

A systematic fraud. All it needed was a mug.

I had been ignorantly happy. No owner expected to win all the time and there must have been many days when Jody's disappointment too had been genuine. Even the best-laid bets went astray if the horses met faster opposition.

The money I'd staked with Ganser Mays had been small change compared with the value of the horses.

Impossible ever to work out just how many thousands had vanished from there. It was not only that the resale value of the substitutes after a string of bad races was low, but there was also the prize money the true horses might have won for me and even, in the case of Hermes, the possibility of stud fees. The real Hermes might have been good enough. The substitute would fail continually as a four-year-old and no one would want to breed from him. In every way, Jody had bled every penny he could.

Energise . . .

Anger deepened in me abruptly. For Energise I felt more admiration and affection than for any of the others. He wasn't a matter of cash value. He was a person I'd got to know in a horsebox. One way or another I was going to get him back.

I moved restlessly, standing up. Not wise. The headache I'd had all day began imitating a piledriver. Whether it was still alcohol, or all concussion, it made little difference to the wretched end result. I went impatiently into the bedroom, put on a dressing-gown over shirt and trousers and lay down on the bed. The short December afternoon began to close in with creeping grey shadows and I reckoned it was twelve hours since Jody had dumped me in the street.

I wondered whether the doctor was right about the gin dripping into my vein. The mark he had said was a needle prick had, as predicted, vanished into a large area of bruising. I doubted whether it had ever been there. When one thought it over it seemed an unlikely method because of one simple snag: the improbability of Jody just happening to have a bag of saline lying around handy. Maybe it was true one could but it from any chemist, but not in the middle of the night.

The only all-night chemists were in London. Would there have been time to belt up the M4, buy the saline, and drip it in while parked in central London? Almost certainly not. And why bother? Any piece of rubber tubing down the throat would have done instead.

I massaged my neck thoughtfully. No soreness around the tonsils. Didn't prove anything either way.

It was still less likely that Ganser Mays, on a visit to Jody, would be around with hypodermic and drip. My absolutely stinking luck, I reflected gloomily, that I had chosen to snoop around on one of the rare evenings Jody had not been to bed by ten thirty. I supposed that for all my care the flash of my torch had been visible from outside. I supposed that Jody had come out of his house to see off his guests and they'd spotted the wavering light.

Ganser Mays. I detested him in quite a different way from Jody because I had never at any time liked him personally. I felt deeply betrayed by Jody, but the trust I'd given Ganser Mays had been a surface thing, a matter of simple expectation that he would behave with professional honour.

From Bert Huggerneck's description of the killing-off of one small bookmaking business it was probable Ganser Mays had as much professional honour as an octopus. His tentacles stretched out and clutched and sucked the victim dry. I had a vision of a whole crowd of desperate little men sitting on their office floors because the bailifs had taken the furniture, sobbing with relief down their telephones while Ganser Mays offered to buy the albatross of their lease for peanuts: and another vision of the same crowd of little men getting drunk in dingy pubs, trying to obliterate the pain of seeing the bright new shop fronts glowing over the ashes of their closed books.

Very likely the little men had been stupid. Very likely they should have had more sense than to believe even the most reliable-seeming information, even though the reliable-seeming information had in the past proved to be correct. Every good card-sharper knew that the victim who had been allowed to win to begin with would part with the most in the end.

If on a minor level Ganser Mays had continually worked that trick on me, and others like me, then how much more had he stood to gain by entangling every vulnerable little firm he could find. He'd sucked the juices, discarded the husks, and grown fat.

Proof, I thought, was impossible. The murmurs of wrong information could never be traced and the crowd of bankrupt little men probably thought of Ganser Mays as their saviour, not the architect of the skids.

I imagined the sequence of events as seen by Jody and Ganser

Mays when Energise ran at Sandown. To begin with, they must have decided that I should have a big bet and the horse would lose. Or even ... that the substitute would run instead. Right up until the day before the race, that would have been the plan. Then I refused to bet. Persuasion failed. Quick council of war. I should be taught a lesson, to bet when my trainer said so. The horse ... Energise himself ... was to run to win.

Fine. But Bert Huggerneck's boss went off to Sandown expecting, positively *knowing*, that Energise would lose. The only people who could have told him so were Ganser Mays and Jody. Or perhaps Raymond Child. I thought it might be informative to find out just when Bert Huggerneck's boss had been given the news. I might get Bert to ask him.

My memory wandered to Rupert Ramsey's office and the bright green wool of Poppet Vine. She and her husband had started to bet with Ganser Mays and Felicity Leeds had engineered it. Did Felicity, I wondered sourly, know all about Jody's plundering ways? I supposed that she must, because she knew all their horses. Lads might come and go, discouraged by having to work too hard, but Felicity rode out twice every morning and groomed and fed in the evenings. Felicity assuredly would know if a horse had been switched.

She might be steering people to Ganser Mays out of loyalty, or for commission, or for some reason unguessed at; but everything I heard or learned seemed to make it certain that although Jody Leeds and Ganser Mays might benefit in separate ways, everything they did was a joint enterprise.

There was also, I supposed, the third man, old muscle and sunglasses. The beef of the organization. I didn't think I would ever forget him: raincoat over heavy shoulders, cloth cap over forehead, sunglasses over eyes ... almost a disguise. Yet I hadn't known him. I was positive I'd never seen him anywhere before. So why had he needed a disguise at one-thirty in the morning when he hadn't expected to be seen by me in the first place?

All I knew of him was that at some point he had learned to box. That he was of sufficient standing in the trio to make his own decisions, because neither of the others had told him to hit me: he'd done it of his own accord. That Ganser Mays and Jody felt they needed his extra muscle, because neither of them was large, though Jody in his way was strong, in case any of the swindled victims cut up rough.

The afternoon faded and became night. All I was doing, I thought, was sorting through the implications and explanations of what had happened. Nothing at all towards getting myself out of trouble and Jody in. When I tried to plan that, all I achieved was a blank.

In the silence I clearly heard the sound of the street door opening. My heart jumped. Pulse raced again, as in the stable. Brain came sternly afterwards like a schoolmaster, telling me not to be so bloody silly.

No one but Owen had the new keys. No one but Owen would be

coming in. All the same I was relieved when the lights were switched on in the hall and I could hear his familiar tread on the stairs.

He went into the dark sitting-room.

'Sir?'

'In the bedroom,' I called.

He came into the doorway, silhouetted against the light in the passage.

'Shall I turn the light on?'

'No, don't bother.'

'Sir . . .' His voice suddenly struck me as being odd. Uncertain. Or distressed.

'What's the matter?'

'I couldn't find the car.' The words came out in a rush. The distress was evident.

'Go and get yourself a stiff drink and come back and tell me about it.'

He hesitated a fraction but went away to the sitting-room and clinked glasses. I fumbled around with an outstretched hand and switched on the bedside light. Squinted at my watch. Six-thirty. Allie would be at Heathrow, boarding her aeroplane, waving to her sister, flying away.

Owen returned with two glasses, both containing scotch and water. He put one glass on my bedside table and interrupted politely when I opened my mouth to protest.

'The hair of the dog. You know it works, sir.'

'It just makes you drunker.'

'But less queasy.'

I waved towards my bedroom armchair and he sat in it easily as before, watching me with a worried expression. He held his glass carefully, but didn't drink. With a sigh I propped myself on one elbow and led the way. The first sip tasted vile, the second passable, the third familiar.

'Okay,' I said. 'What about the car?'

Owen took a quick gulp from his glass. The worried expression intensified.

'I went down to Newbury on the train and hired a taxi, like you said. We drove to where you showed me on the map, but the car didn't seem to be there. So I got the taxi driver to go along every possible road leading away from Mr Leeds' stable and I still couldn't find it. The taxi driver got pretty ratty in the end. He said there wasn't anywhere else to look. I got him to drive around in a larger area, but you said you'd walked from the car to the stables so it couldn't have been more than a mile away, I thought.'

'Half a mile, no further,' I said.

'Well, sir, the car just wasn't there.' He took another swig. 'I didn't really know what to do. I got the taxi to take me to the police in Newbury, but they knew nothing about it. They rang around two or three local nicks because I made a bit of a fuss, sir, but no one down there had seen hair or hide of it.'

I thought a bit. 'They had the keys, of course.'

'Yes, I thought of that.'

'So the car could be more or less anywhere by now.'

He nodded unhappily.

'Never mind,' I said. 'I'll report it stolen. It's bound to turn up somewhere. They aren't ordinary car thieves. When you come to think of it we should have expected it to be gone, because if they were going to deny I had ever been in the stables last night they wouldn't want my car found half a mile away.'

'Do you mean they went out looking for it?'

'They would know I hadn't dropped in by parachute.'

He smiled faintly and lowered the level in his glass to a spoonful. Shall I get you something to eat, sir?'

'I don't feel...'

'Better to eat. Really it is. I'll pop out to the take-away.' He put his glass down and departed before I could argue and came back in ten minutes with a wing of freshly roasted chicken.

'Didn't think you'd fancy the chips,' he said. He put the plate beside me, fetched knife, fork and napkin, and drained his own glass.

'Be going now, sir,' he said, 'if you're all right.'

Chapter Eight

Whether it was Owen's care or the natural course of events, I felt a great deal better in the morning. The face peering back at me from the bathroom mirror, though adorned now with two days' stubble, had lost the grey look and the dizzy eyes. Even the bags underneath were retreating to normal.

I shaved first and bathed after, and observed that at least twenty per cent of my skin was now showing bruise marks. I supposed I should have been glad I hadn't been awake when I collected them. The bothersome aches they had set up the day before had more or less abated, and coffee and breakfast helped things along fine.

The police were damping on the matter of stolen Lamborghinis. They took particulars with pessimism and said I might hear something in a week or so; then within half an hour they were back on the line bristling with irritation. My car had been towed away by colleagues the night before last because I'd parked it on a space reserved for taxis in Leicester Square. I could find it in the pound at Marble Arch and there would be a charge for towing.

Owen arrived at nine with a long face and was hugely cheered when I told him about the car.

'Have you seen the papers, sir?'

'Not yet.'

He held out one of his own. 'You'd better know,' he said.

I unfolded it. Allie had been right about the gossip columnist. The paragraph was short and sharp and left no one in any doubt.

> Red-face day for Steven Scott (35), wealthy racehorse owner, who was scooped by police from a Soho gutter early yesterday. At Marlborough Street Court, Scott, looking rough and crumpled, pleaded guilty to a charge of drunk and incapable. Save your sympathy. Race-followers will remember Scott recently dumped Jody Leeds (28), trainer of all his winners, without a second's notice.

I looked through my own two dailies and the *Sporting Life*. They all carried the story and in much the same vein, even if without the tabloid heat. Smug satisfaction that the kicker-of-underdogs had himself bitten the dust.

It was fair to assume that the story had been sent to every newspaper and that most of them had used it. Even though I'd expected it, I didn't like it. Not a bit.

'It's bloody unfair,' Owen said, reading the piece in the *Life*.

I looked at him with surprise. His usually noncommittal face was screwed into frustrated anger and I wondered if his expression was a mirror-image of my own.

'Kind of you to care.'

'Can't help it, sir.' The features returned more or less to normal, but with an effort. 'Anything I can do sir?'

'Fetch the car?'

He brightened a little. 'Right away.'

His brightness was short-lived because after half an hour he came back whitefaced and angrier than I would have thought possible.

'Sir!'

'What is it?'

'The car, sir. The car.'

His manner said it all. He stammered with fury over the details. The nearside front wing was crumpled beyond repair. Headlights smashed. Hub cap missing. Bonnet dented. All the paintwork on the nearside scratched and scored down to the metal. Nearside door a complete right-off. Windows smashed, handle torn away.

'It looks as if it was driven against a brick wall, sir. Something like that.'

I thought coldly of the nearside of Jody's horsebox, identically damaged. My car had been smashed for vengeance.

'Were the keys in it?' I asked.

He shook his head. 'It wasn't locked. Couldn't be, with one lock broken. I looked for your wallet, like you said, but it wasn't there. None of your things, sir.'

'Is the car drivable?'

He calmed down a little. 'Yes, the engine's all right. It must have been going all right when it was driven into Leicester Square. It looks a proper wreck, but it must be going all right, otherwise how could they have got it there?'

'That's something, anyway.

'I left it in the pound, sir. It'll have to go back to the coach builders, and they might as well fetch it from there.'

'Sure,' I agreed. I imagined he couldn't have borne to have driven a crumpled car through London; he was justly proud of his driving.

Owen took his tangled emotions down to the workshop and I dealt with mine upstairs. The fresh blight Jody had laid on my life was all due to my own action in creeping into his stable by night. Had it been worth it, I wondered. I'd paid a fairly appalling price for a half-minute's view of Energise: but at least I now *knew* Jody had swapped him. I was a fact, not a guess.

I spent the whole morning on the telephone straightening out the chaos. Organizing car repairs and arranging a hired substitute. Telling my bank manager and about ten assorted others that I had lost my cheque book and credit cards. Assuring various enquiring relatives, who had all of course read the papers, that I was neither in jail nor dipsomaniac. Listening to a shrill lady, whose call inched in somehow, telling me it was disgusting for the rich to get drunk in gutters. I asked her if it was okay for the poor, and if it was, why should they have more rights than I. Fair's fair, I said. Long live equality. She called me a word rude and rang off. It was the only bright spot of the day.

Last of all I called Rupert Ramsey.

'What do you mean, you don't want Energise to run?' His voice sounded almost as surprised as Jody's at Sandown.

'I thought,' I said diffidently, 'that he might need more time. You said yourself he needed building up. Well, it's only a week or so to that Christmas race and I don't want him to run below his best.'

Relief distinctly took the place of surprise at the other end of the wire.

'If you feel like that, fine,' he said. 'To be honest, the horse has been a little disappointing on the gallops. I gave him a bit of fast work yesterday upsides a hurdler he should have made mincemeat of, and he couldn't even lie up with him. I'm a bit worried about him. I'm sorry not to be able to give you better news.'

'It's all right,' I said. 'If you'll keep him and do your best, that'll be fine with me. But don't run him anywhere. I don't mind waiting. I just don't want him raced.'

'You made your point.' The smile came down the wire with the words. 'What about the other two?'

'I'll leave them to your judgement. Nothing Ferryboat does will disappoint me, but I'd like to bet on Dial whenever you say he's ready.'

'He's ready now. He's entered at Newbury in a fortnight. He should run very well there, I think.'

'Great,' I said.

'Will you be coming?' There was a load of meaning in the question.

He too had read the papers.

'Depends on the state of my courage,' I said flippantly. 'Tell you nearer the day.'

In the event, I went.

Most people's memories were short and I received no larger slice than I expected of the cold shoulder. Christmas had come and gone, leaving perhaps a trace of goodwill to all men even if they had been beastly to poor Jody Leeds and got themselves fined for drunkenness. I collected more amused sniggers than active disapproval, except of course from Quintus Leeds, who went out of his way to vent himself of his dislike. He told me again that I would certainly never be elected to the Jockey Club. Over his dead body, he said. He and Jody were both addicted to the phrase.

I was in truth sorry about the Jockey Club. Whatever one thought of it, it was still a sort of recognition to be asked to become a member. Racing's freedom of the city: along those lines. If I had meekly allowed Jody to carry on robbing, I would have been in. As I hadn't, I was out. Sour joke.

Dial made up for a lot by winning the four-year-old hurdle by a length, and not even Quintus telling everyone it was solely due to Jody's groundwork could dim my pleasure in seeing him sprint to the post.

Rupert Ramsey, patting Dial's steaming sides, sounded all the same apologetic.

'Energise isn't his old self yet, I'm afraid.'

Truer than you know, I thought. I said only, 'Never mind. Don't run him.'

He said doubtfully, 'He's entered for the Champion Hurdle. I don't know if it's worth leaving him in at the next forfeit stage.'

'Don't take him out,' I said with haste. 'I mean ... I don't mind paying the extra entrance fee. There's always hope that he'll come right.'

'Ye-es.' He was unconvinced, as well he might be. 'As you like, of course.'

I nodded. 'Drink?' I suggested.

'A quick one, then. I've some other runners.'

He gulped his scotch in friendly fashion, refused a refill, and cantered away to the saddling boxes. I wandered alone to a higher point in the stands and looked idly over the cold windy racecourse.

During the past fortnight I'd been unable to work out just which horse was doubling for Energise. Nothing on Jody's list of horses-in-training seemed to match. Near-black horses were rarer than most, and none on his list were both the right colour and the right age. The changeling at Rupert's couldn't be faulted on colour, age, height, or general conformation. Jody, I imagined, hadn't just happened to have him lying around: he would have had to have searched for him diligently. How, I wondered vaguely, would one set about buying a ringer? One could hardly drift about asking if anyone knew of a spitting image at bargain prices.

My wandering gaze jolted to a full stop. Down among the crowds among the row of bookmakers' stands I was sure I had seen a familiar pair of sunglasses.

The afternoon was grey. The sky threatened snow and the wind searched every crevice between body and soul. Not a day, one would have thought, for needing to fend off dazzle to the eyes.

There they were again. Sitting securely on the nose of a man with heavy shoulders. No cloth cap, though. A trilby. No raincoat; sheepskin.

I lifted my race glasses for a closer look. He had his back towards me with his head slightly turned to the left. I could see a quarter profile of one cheek and the tinted glasses which showed plainly as he looked down to a race card.

Mousey brown hair, medium length. Hands in pigskin gloves. Brownish tweed trousers. Binoculars slung over one shoulder. A typical racegoer among a thousand others. Except for those sun specs.

I willed him to turn round. Instead he moved away, his back still towards me, until he was lost in the throng. Impossible to know without getting closer.

I spent the whole of the rest of the afternoon looking for a man, any man, wearing sunglasses, but the only thing I saw in shades was an actress dodging her public.

Inevitably, at one stage, I came face to face with Jody.

Newbury was his local meeting and he was running three horses, so I had been certain he would be there. A week earlier I had shrunk so much from seeing him that I had wanted to duck going, but in the end I had seen that it was essential. Somehow or other I had to convince him that I had forgotten most of my nocturnal visit, that the crack on the head and concussion had between them wiped the memory slate clean.

I couldn't afford for him to be certain I had seen and recognized Energise and knew about the swap. I couldn't afford it for exactly the same reason that I had to failed to go to the police. For the same reason that I had quite seriously sworn Charlie and Allie to secrecy.

Given a choice of prosecution for fraud and getting rid of the evidence, Jody would have jettisoned the evidence faster than sight. Energise would have been dead and dogmeat long before an arrest.

The thought that Jody had already killed him was one I tried continually to put out of my head. I reasoned that he couldn't be sure I'd seen the horse, or recognized him even if I had. They had found me down one of the line of boxes: they couldn't be sure that I hadn't started at that far end and was working back. They couldn't really be sure I had been actually searching for a ringer, or even that I suspected one. They didn't know for certain why I'd been in the yard.

Energise was valuable, too valuable to destroy in needless panic. I guessed, and I hoped, that they wouldn't kill him unless they had to. Why else would they have gone to such trouble to make sure my word would be doubted. Transporting me to London and making me drunk had given them ample time to whisk Energise to a safer place, and I was sure that if I'd gone belting back there at once with the police I would have been met by incredulous wide-eyed innocence.

'Come in, come in, search where you like,' Jody would have said.

No Energise anywhere to be seen.

'Of course, if you were drunk, you dreamt it all, no doubt.'

End of investigation, and end of Energise, because after that it would have been too risky to keep him.

Whereas if I could convince Jody I knew nothing, he would keep Energise alive and somehow or other I might get him back.

I accidentally bumped into him outside the weighing room. We both half-turned to each other to apologize, and recognition froze the words in our mouths.

Jody's eyes turned stormy and I suppose mine also.

'Get out of my bloody way,' he said.

'Look, Jody,' I said, 'I want your help.'

'I'm as likely to help you as kiss your arse.'

I ignored that and put on a bit of puzzle. 'Did I, or didn't I, come to your stables a fortnight ago?'

He was suddenly a great deal less violent, a great deal more attentive.

'What d'you mean?'

'I know it's stupid ... but somehow or other I got drunk and collected concussion from an almighty bang on the head, and I thought ... it seemed to me, that the evening before, I'd set out to visit you, though with things as they are between us I can't for the life of me think why. So what I want to know is, did I arrive at your place, or didn't I?'

He gave me a straight narrow-eyed stare.

'If you came, I never saw you,' he said.

I looked down at the ground as if disconsolate and shook my head. 'I can't understand it. In the ordinary way I never drink much. I've been trying to puzzle it out ever since, but I can't remember anything between about six one evening and waking up in a police station next morning with a frightful headache and a lot of bruises. I wondered if you could tell me what I'd done in between, because as far as I'm concerned it's a blank.'

I could almost feel the procession of emotions flowing out of him, Surprise, elation, relief and a feeling that this was a totally unexpected piece of luck.

He felt confident enough to return to abuse.

'Why the bloody hell should you have wanted to visit me? You couldn't get shot of me fast enough.'

'I don't know,' I said glumly. 'I suppose you didn't ring me up and ask me...'

'You're so right I didn't. And don't you come hanging round. I've had a bellyful of you and I wouldn't have you back if you crawled.'

He scowled, turned away and strode off, and only because I knew what he must really be thinking could I discern the twist of satisfied smile that he couldn't entirely hide. He left me in much the same state. If he was warning me so emphatically to stay away from his stables there was the best of chances that Energise was back there, alive and well.

I watched his sturdy backview threading through the crowd, with people smiling at him as he passed. Everyone's idea of a bright young trainer going places. My idea of a ruthless little crook.

At Christmas I had written to Allie in code four.

'Which is the first night you could have dinner with me and where ? I enclose twenty dollars for cab fare home.'

On the morning after Newbury races I received her reply, also in groups of five letters, but not in code four. She had jumbled her answer ingeniously enough for it to take me two minutes to unravel it. Very short messages were always the worst, and this was brief indeed.

'January fifth in Miami.'

I laughed aloud. And she had kept the twenty bucks.

The *Racing Calendar* came in the same post. I took it and a cup of coffee over to the big window on the balcony and sat in an armchair there to read. The sky over the Zoo in Regent's Park looked as heavy and grey as the day before, thick with the threat of snow. Down by the canal the bare branches of trees traced tangled black lines across the brown water and grassy banks, and the ribbon traffic as usual shattered the illusion of rural peace. I enjoyed this view of life which, like my work, was a compromise between old primitive roots and new glossy technology. Contentment, I thought, lay in being succoured by the first and cosseted by the second. If I'd had a pagan god, it would have been electricity, which sprang from the skies and galvanised machines. Mysterious lethal force of nature, harnessed and insulated and delivered on tap. My welder-uncle had made electricity seem a living person to me as a child. 'Electricity will catch you if you don't look out.' He said it as a warning; and I thought of Electricity as a fiery monster hiding in the wires and waiting to pounce.

The stiff yellowish pages of the *Racing Calendar* crackled familiarly as I opened their double spread and folded them back. The *Calender*, racing's official weekly publication, contained lists of horses entered for forthcoming races, pages and pages of them, four columns to a page. The name of each horse was accompanied by the name of its owner and trainer, and also by its age and the weight it would have to carry if it ran.

With pencil in hand to act as insurance against skipping a line with the eye, I began painstakingly, as I had the previous week and the week before that, to check the name, owner, and trainer of every horse entered in hurdle races.

Grapevine (*Mrs R. Wantage*) *B. Fritwell*	6	11	11
Pirate Boy (*Lord Dresden*) *A. G. Barnes*	10	11	4
Hopfield (*Mr Paul Hatheleigh*) *K. Poundsgate*	5	11	2

There were reams of them. I finished the Worcester entries with a sigh. Three hundred and sixty-eight down for one novice hurdle and three hundred and forty-nine for another, and not one of them what I was looking for.

My coffee was nearly cold. I drank it anyway and got on with the races scheduled for Taunton.

Hundreds more names, but nothing.

Ascot, nothing. Newcastle, nothing. Warwick, Teesside, Plumpton, Doncaster, nothing.

I put the *Calendar* down for a bit and went out onto the balcony for some air. Fiercely cold air, slicing down to the lungs. Primeval arctic air carrying city gunge: the mixture as before. Over in the Park the zoo creatures were quiet, sheltering in warmed houses. They always made more noise in the summer.

Return to the task.

Huntingdon, Market Rasen, Stratford on Avon ... I sighed before starting Stratford and checked how many more still lay ahead. Nottingham, Carlisle and Wetherby. I was in for another wasted morning, no doubt.

Turned back to Stratford, and there it was.

I blinked and looked again carefully, as if the name would vanish if I took my eyes off it.

Half way down among sixty-four entries for the Shakespeare Novice Hurdle.

Padellic (*Mr J. Leeds*) *J. Leeds*	5	10	7

Padellic.

It was the first time the name had appeared in association with Jody. I knew the names of all his usual horses well, and what I had been searching for was a new one, an unknown. Owned, if my theories were right, by Jody himself. And here it was.

Nothing in the *Calendar* to show Padellic's colour or markings. I fairly sprinted over to the shelf where I kept a few form books and looked him up in every index.

Little doubt, I thought. He was listed as a black or brown gelding, five years old, a halfbred by a thoroughbred sire out of a hunter mare. He had been trained by a man I'd never heard of and he had run three times in four-year-old hurdles without being placed.

I telephoned to the trainer at once, introducing myself as a Mr Robinson trying to buy a cheap novice.

'Padellic?' he said in a forthright Birmingham accent. 'I got shot of that bugger round October time. No bloody good. Couldn't run fast enough to keep warm. Is he up for sale again? Can't say as I'm surprised. He's a right case of the slows, that one.'

'Er ... where did you sell him?' I asked tentatively.

'Sent him to Doncaster mixed sales. Right bloody lot they had there. He fetched four hundred quid and I reckon he was dear at that. Only the one bid, you see. I reckon the bloke could've got him for three hundred if he'd tried. I was right pleased to get four for him, I'll tell you.'

'Would you know who bought him?'

'Eh?' He sounded surprised at the question. 'Can't say. He paid cash to the auctioneers and didn't give his name. I saw him make his bid, that's all. Big fellow. I'd never clapped eyes on him before. Wearing sunglasses. I didn't see him after. He paid up and took the horse away and I was right glad to be shot of him.'

'What is the horse like?' I asked.

'I told you, bloody slow.'

'No, I mean to look at.'

'Eh? I thought you were thinking of buying him.'

'Only on paper, so to speak. I thought,' I lied, 'that he still belonged to you.'

'Oh, I see. He's black, then. More or less black, with a bit of brown round the muzzle.'

'Any white about him?'

'Not a hair. Black all over. Black 'uns are often no good. I bred him, see? Meant to be bay, he was, but he turned out black. Not a bad looker, mind. He fills the eye. But nothing there where it matters. No speed.'

'Can he jump?'

'Oh ay. In his own good time. Not bad.'

'Well, thanks very much.'

'You'd be buying a monkey,' he said warningly. 'Don't say as I didn't tell you.'

'I won't buy him,' I assured him. 'Thanks again for your advice.'

I put down the receiver reflectively. There might of course be dozens of large untraceable men in sunglasses going round the sales paying cash for slow black horses with no markings; and then again there might not.

The telephone rang under my hand. I picked up the receiver at the first ring.

'Steven?'

No mistaking that cigar-and-port voice. 'Charlie.'

'Have you lunched yet?' he said. 'I've just got off a train round the corner at Euston and I thought...'

'Here or where?' I said.

'I'll come round to you.'

'Great.'

He came, beaming and expansive, having invested three million somewhere near Rugby. Charlie, unlike some merchant bankers, liked to see things for himself. Reports on paper were all very well, he said, but they didn't give you the smell of a thing. If a project smelt wrong, he didn't disgorge the cash. Charlie followed his nose and Charlie's nose was his fortune.

The feature in question buried itself gratefully in a large scotch and water.

'How about some of that nosh you gave Bert?' he suggested, coming to the surface. 'To tell the truth I get tired of eating in restaurants.'

We repaired amicably to the kitchen and ate bread and bacon and curried baked beans and sausages, all of which did no good at all to anyone's waistline, least of all Charlie's. He patted the bulge affectionately. 'Have to get some weight off, one of these days. But not today,' he said.

We took coffee back to the sitting-room and settled comfortably in armchairs.

'I wish I lived the way you do,' he said. 'So easy and relaxed.'

I smiled. Three weeks of my quiet existence would have driven him screaming to the madhouse. He thrived on bustle, big business, fast decisions, financial juggling and the use of power. And three weeks of all *that*, I thought in fairness, would have driven me mad even quicker.

'Have you made that lock yet?' he asked. He was lighting a cigar round the words and they sounded casual, but I wondered all of a sudden if that was why he had come.

'Half,' I said.

He shook his match to blow it out. 'Let me know,' he said.

'I promised.'

He drew a lungful of Havana and nodded, his eyes showing unmistakably now that his mind was on duty for his bank.

'Which would you do most for,' I asked. 'Friendship or the lock?'

He was a shade starled. 'Depends what you want done.'

'Practical help in a counter-offensive.'

'Against Jody?'

I nodded.

'Friendship,' he said. 'That comes under the heading of friendship. You can count me in.'

His positiveness surprised me. He saw it and smiled.

'What he did to you was diabolical. Don't forget, I was here. I saw the state you were in. Saw the humiliation of that drink charge, and the pain from God knows what else. You looked a little below par and that's a fact.'

'Sorry.'

'Don't be. If it was just your pocket he'd bashed, I would probably be ready with cool advice but not active help.'

I hadn't expected anything like this. I would have thought it would have been the other way round, that the loss of property would have angered him more on the loss of face.

'If you're sure . . .' I said uncertainly.

'Of course.' He was decisive. 'What do you want done?'

I picked up the *Racing Calendar*, which was lying on the floor beside my chair, and explained how I'd looked for and found Padellic.

'He was bought at Doncaster sales for cash by a large man in sunglasses and he's turned up in Jody's name.

'Suggestive.'

'I'd lay this house to a sneeze,' I said, 'that Rupert Ramsey is worrying his guts out trying to train him for the Champion Hurdle.'

Charlie smoked without haste. 'Rubert Ramsey has Padellic, but thinks he has Energise. Is that right?'

I nodded.

'And Jody is planning to run Energise at Stratford on Avon in the name of Padellic?'

'I would think so,' I said.

'So would I.'

'Only it's not entirely so simple.'

'Why not?'

'Because,' I said, 'I've found two other races for which Padellic is entered, at Nottingham and Lingfield. All the races are ten to fourteen days ahead and there's no telling which Jody will choose.'

He frowned. 'What difference does it make, which he chooses?'

I told him.

He listened with his eyes wide open and the eyebrows disappearing upwards into his hair. At the end, he was smiling.

'So how do you propose to find out which race he's going for?' he asked.

'I thought,' I said, 'that we might mobilize your friend Bert. He'd do a lot for you.'

'What, exactly?'

'Do you think you could persuade him to apply for a job in one of Ganser Mays' betting shops?'

Charlie began to laugh. 'How much can I tell him?'

'Only what to look for. Not why.'

'You slay me, Steven.'

'And another thing,' I said, 'how much do you know about the limitations of working hours for truck drivers?'

Chapter Nine

Snow was falling when I flew out of Heathrow, thin scurrying flakes in a driving wind. Behind me I left a half-finished lock, a half-mended car and a half-formed plan.

Charlie had telephoned to say Bert Huggerneck had been taken on at one of the shops formerly owned by his ex-boss and I had made cautious enquiries from the auctioneers at Doncaster. I'd had no success. They had no record of the name or the person who'd bought Padellic. Cash transactions were common. They couldn't possibly remember who had bought one particular cheap horse three months earlier. End of enquiry.

Owen had proclaimed himself as willing as Charlie to help in any way he could. Personal considerations apart, he said, whoever had bent the Lamborghini deserved hanging. When I came back, he would help me build the scaffold.

The journey from snow to sunshine took eight hours. Seventy-five degrees at Miami airport and only a shade cooler outside the hotel on Miami Beach; and it felt great. Inside the hotel the air-conditioning brought things nearly back to an English winter, but my sixth-floor room faced straight towards the afternoon sun. I drew back the closed curtains and opened the window, and let heat and light flood in.

Below, round a glittering pool, tall palm trees swayed in the sea wind. Beyond, the concrete edge to the hotel grounds led immediately down to a narrow strip of sand and the frothy white waves edging the Atlantic, with mile upon mile of deep blue water stretching away to the lighter blue horizon.

I had expected Miami Beach to be garish and was unprepared for its beauty. Even the ranks of huge white slabs of hotels with rectangular windows piercing their façades in a uniform geometrical pattern held a certain grandeur, punctuated and softened as they were by scattered palms.

Round the pool people lay in rows on day beds beside white fringed sun umbrellas, soaking up ultraviolet like a religion. I changed out of my travel-sticky clothes and went for a swim in the sea, paddling lazily in the warm January water and sloughing off cares like dead skin. Jody Leeds was five thousand miles away, in another world. Easy, and healing, to forget him.

Upstairs again, showered and dressed in slacks and cotton shirt I checked my watch for the time to telephone Allie. After the letters we had exchanged cables, though not in code because the cable company didn't like it.

I sent, 'What address Miami.'

She replied: 'Telephone four two six eight two after six any evening.'

When I called her it was five past six on January fifth, local time. The voice which answered was not hers and for a soggy moment I wondered if the Western Union had jumbled the message as they often did, and that I should never find her.

'Miss Ward? Do you mean Miss Alexandra?'

'Yes,' I said with relief.

'Hold the line, please.'

After a pause came the familiar voice, remembered but suddenly fresh. 'Hallo?'

'Allie ... It's Steven.'

'Hi.' Her voice was laughing. 'I've won close on fifty dollars if you're in Miami.'

'Collect it,' I said.

'I don't believe it.'

'We have a date,' I said reasonably.

'Oh sure.'

'Where do I find you?'

'Twelve twenty-four Garden Island,' she said. 'Any cab will bring you. Come right out, it's time for cocktails.'

Garden Island proved to be a shady offshoot of land with wide enought channels surrounding it to justify its name. The cab rolled slowly across twenty yards of decorative iron bridge and came to a stop outside twelve twenty-four. I paid off the driver and rang the bell.

From the outside the house showed little. The whitewashed walls were deeply obscured by tropical plants and the windows by insect netting. The door itself looked solid enough for a bank.

Allie opened it. Smiled widely. Gave me a noncommittal kiss.

'This my cousin's house,' she said. 'Come in.'

Behind its secretive front the house was light and large and glowing with clear, uncomplicated colours. Blue, sea-green, bright pink, white and orange; clean and sparkling.

'My cousin Minty,' Allie said, 'and her husband, Warren Barbo.'

I shook hands with the cousins. Minty was neat, dark and utterly self-possessed in lemon-coloured beach pyjamas. Warren was large, sandy and full of noisy good humour. They gave me a tall, iced, unspecified drink and led me into a spacious glass-walled room for a view of the setting sun.

Outside in the garden the yellowing rays fell on a lush lawn, a calm pool and white painted lounging chairs. All peaceful and prosperous and a million miles from blood, sweat and tears.

'Alexandra tells us you're interested in horses,' Warren said, making host-like conversation. 'I don't know how long you reckon on staying, but there's a racemeet at Hialeah right now, every day this week. And the bloodstock sales, of course, in the evenings. I'll be going myself some nights and I'd be glad to have you along.'

The idea pleased me, but I turned to Allie.

'What are your plans?'

'Millie and I split up,' she said without visible regret. 'She said when we were through with Christmas and New Year she would be off to Japan for a spell, so I grabbed a week down here with Minty and Warren.'

'Would you come to the races, and the sales?'

'Sure.'

'I have four days,' I said.

She smiled brilliantly but without promise. Several other guests arrived for drinks at that point and Allie said she would fetch the canapés. I followed her to the kitchen.

'You can carry the stone crabs,' she said, putting a large dish into my hands. 'And okay, after a while we can sneak out and eat some place else.'

For an hour I helped hand round those understudies for a banquet, American-style canapés. Allie's delicious work. I ate two or three and like a true male chauvinist meditated on the joys of marrying a good cook.

I found Minty at my side, her hand on my arm, her gaze following mine.

'She's a great girl,' she said. 'She swore you would come.'

'Good,' I said with satisfaction.

Her eyes switched sharply to mine with a grin breaking out. 'She told us to be careful what we said to you, because you always understood the implications, not just the words. And I guess she was right.'

'You've only told me that she wanted me to come and thought I liked her enough to do it.'

'Yeah, but ...' She laughed. 'She didn't actually say all that.'

'I see what you mean.'

She took out of my hands a dish of thin pastry boats filled with pink chunks of lobster in pale green mayonnaise. 'You've done more than your duty here,' she smiled 'Get on out.'

She lent us her car. Allie drove it northwards along the main boulevard of Collins Avenue and pulled up at a restaurant called Stirrup and Saddle.

'I thought you might feel at home here,' she said teasingly.

The place was crammed. Every table in sight was taken, and as in many American restaurants, the tables were so close together that only emaciated waiters could inch around them. Blow-ups of racing scenes decorated the walls and saddles and horseshoes abounded.

Dark decor, loud chatter and, to my mind, too much light.

A slightly harassed head waiter intercepted us inside the door.

'Do you have reservations, sir?'

I began to say I was sorry, as there were dozens of people already waiting round the bar, when Allie interrupted.

'Table for two, name of Barbo.'

He consulted his lists, smiled, nodded. 'This way, sir.'

There was miraculously after all one empty table, tucked in a corner but with a good view of the busy room. We sat comfortably in dark wooden-armed chairs and watched the head waiter turn away the next customers decisively.

'When did you book this table?' I asked.

'Yesterday. As soon as I got down here.' The white teeth gleamed. 'I got Warren to do it; he likes this place. That's when I made the bets. He and Minty said it was crazy, you wouldn't come all the way from England just to take me out to eat.'

'And you said I sure was crazy enough for anything.'

'I sure did.'

We ate bluepoint oysters and barbecued baby ribs with salad alongside. Noise and clatter from other tables washed around us and waiters towered above with huge loaded trays. Business was brisk.

'Do you like it here?' Allie asked, tackling the ribs.

'Very much.'

She seemed relieved. I didn't add that some quiet candlelight would have done even better. 'Warren says all horse people like it, the same way he does.'

'How horsey is Warren?'

'He owns a couple of two-year-olds. Has them in training with a guy in Aiken, North Carolina. He was hoping they'd be running here at Hialeah but they've both got chipped knees and he doesn't know if they'll be any good any more.'

'What are chipped knees?' I asked.

'Don't you have chipped knees in England?'

'Heaven knows.'

'So will Warren.' She dug into the salad, smiling down at the food. 'Warren's business is real estate but his heart beats out there where the hooves thunder along the homestretch.'

'Is that how he puts it?'

Her smile widened. 'It sure is.'

'He said he'd take us to Hialeah tomorrow, if you'd like.'

'I might as well get used to horses, I suppose.' She spoke with utter spontaneity and then in a way stood back and looked at what she'd said. 'I mean . . .' she stuttered.

'I know what you mean,' I said smiling.

'You always do, dammit.'

We finished the ribs and progressed to coffee. She asked how fast I'd recovered from the way she had seen me last and what had happened since. I told her about the gossip columns and the car, and she was fiercely indignant; mostly, I gathered, because of the car.

'But it was so beautiful!'

'It will be again.'

'I'd like to murder that Jody Leeds.'

She scarcely noticed, that time, that she was telling me what she felt for me. The sense of a smoothly deepening relationship filled me with contentment: and it was also great fun.

After three cups of dawdled coffee I paid the bill and we went out to the car.

'I can drop you off at your hotel,' Allie said. 'It's quite near here.'

'Certainly not. I'll see you safely home.'

She grinned. 'There isn't much danger. All the alligators in Florida are a hundred miles away in the Everglades.'

'Some alligators have two feet.'

'Okay, then.' She drove slowly southwards, the beginnings of a smile curling her mouth all the way. Outside her cousin's house she put on the handbrake but left the engine running.

'You'd better borrow this car to go back. Minty won't mind.'

'No, I'll walk.'

'You can't. It's all of four miles.'

'I like seeing things close. Seeing how they're made.'

'You sure are nuts.'

I switched off the engine, put my arm round her shoulders and kissed her the same way as at home, several times. She sighed deeply, but not, it seemed, with boredom.

I hired an Impala in the morning and drove down to Garden Island.

A cleaner answered the door and showed me through to where Warren and Minty were in swimsuits, standing by the pool in January sunshine as warm as July back home.

'Hi,' said Minty in welcome. 'Alexandra said to tell you she'll be right back. She's having her hair fixed.'

The fixed hair, when it appeared, looked as smooth and shining as the girl underneath. A black-and-tan sleeveless cotton dress did marvellous things for her waist and stopped in plenty of time for the legs. I imagine appreciation was written large on my face because the wide smile broke out as soon as she saw me.

We sat by the pool drinking cold orange juice while Warren and Minty changed into street clothes. The day seemed an interlude, a holiday, to me, but not to the Barbos. Warren's life, I came to realize, was along the lines of perpetual summer vacation interrupted by short spells in the office. Droves of sharp young men did the legwork of selling dream retirement homes to elderly sunseekers and Warren, the organizer, went to the races.

Hialeah Turf Club was a sugar-icing racecourse, as pretty as lace. Miami might show areas of cracks and rust and sun-peeled poverty on its streets, but in the big green park in its suburb the lush life survived and seemingly flourished.

Bright birds in cages beguiled visitors the length of the paddock, and a decorative pint-sized railway trundled around. Tons of ice cream added to weight problems and torn up Tote tickets fluttered to the ground like snow.

The racing itself that day was moderate, which didn't prevent me losing my bets. Allie said it served me right, gambling was a nasty habit on a par with jumping off cliffs.

'And look where it's got you,' she pointed out.

'Where?'

'In Ganser Mays' clutches.'

'Not any more.'

'Which came first,' she said, 'the gamble or the race?'

'All life's a gamble. The fastest sperm fertilizes the egg.'

She laughed. 'Tell that to the chickens.'

It was the sort of day when nonsense made sense. Minty and Warren met relays of drinking pals and left us much alone, which suited me fine, and at the end of the racing programme we sat high up on the stands looking over the course while the sunlight died to yellow and pink and scarlet. Drifts of flamingoes on the small lakes in the centre of the track deepened from pale pink to intense rose and the sky on the water reflected silver and gold.

'I bet it's snowing in London,' I said.

After dark and after dinner Warren drove us round to the sales paddock on the far side of the racecourse, where spotlights lit a scene that was decidely more rustic than the stands. Sugar icing stopped with the tourists: horsetrading had its feet on the grass.

There were three main areas linked by short undefined paths and well-patronized open-fronted bars; there was the sale ring, the parade ring and long barns lined with stalls, where the merchandise ate hay and suffered prods and insults and people looking at its teeth.

Warren opted for the barns first and we wandered down the length of the nearest while he busily consulted his catalogue. Minty told him they were definitely not buying any more horses until the chipped knees were all cleared up. 'No dear,' Warren said soothingly, but with a gleam in his eye which spelt death to the bank balance.

I looked at the offerings with interest. A mixed bunch of horses which had been raced, from three years upwards. Warren said the best sales were those for two-year-olds at the end of the month and Minty said why didn't he wait awhile and see what they were like.

The lights down the far end of the barn were dim and the horse in the last stall of all was so dark that at first I thought the space was empty. Then an eye shimmered and a movement showed a faint gleam on a rounded rump.

A black horse. Black like Energise.

I looked at him first because he was black, and then more closely with surprise. He was indeed very like Energise. Extremely like him.

The likeness abruptly crystallized an idea I'd already been turning over in my mind. A laugh fluttered in my throat. The horse was a gift from the gods and who was I to look it in the mouth.

'What have you found?' Warren asked, advancing with good humour.

'I've a hurdler like this at home.'

Warren looked at the round label stuck onto one hind-quarter which bore the number sixty-two.

'Hip number sixty-two,' he said, flicking the pages of the catalogue. 'Here it is. Black Fire, five-year-old gelding. Humph.' He read quickly down the page through the achievements and breeding. 'Not much good and never was much good, I guess.'

'Pity.'

'Yeah.' He turned away. 'Now there's a damned nice looking chestnut colt along there...'

'No, Warren,' said Minty despairingly.

We all walked back to look at the chestnut colt. Warren knew no more about buying horses than I did, and besides, the first thing I'd read on the first page of the catalogue was the clear warning that the auctioneers didn't guarantee the goods were of merchantable quality. In other words, if you bought a lame duck it was your own silly fault.

'Don't pay no attention to that,' said Warren expansively. 'As long as you don't take the horse out of the sales paddock, you can get a veterinarian to check a horse you've bought, and if he finds anything wrong you can call the deal off. But you have to do it within twenty-four hours.'

'Sounds fair.'

'Sure. You can have x-rays even. Chipped knees would show on an x-ray. Horses can walk and look okay with chipped knees but they sure can't race.'

Allie said with mock resignation. 'So what exactly are chipped knees?'

Warren said 'Cracks and compressions at the ends of the bones at the knee joint.'

'From falling down?' Allie asked.

Warren laughed kindly. 'No. From too much hard galloping on dirt. The thumping does it.'

I borrowed the sales catalogue from Warren again for a deeper look at the regulations and found the twenty-four hour inspection period applied only to brood mares, which wasn't much help. I mentioned it diffidently to Warren. 'It says here,' I said neutrally, 'that it's wise to have a vet look at a horse for soundess before you bid. After is too late.'

'Is that so?' Warren retrieved his book and peered at the small print. 'Well, I guess you're right.' He received the news good-naturedly. 'Just shows how easy it is to go wrong at horse sales.'

'And I hope you remember it,' Minty said with meaning.

Warren did in fact seem a little discouraged from his chestnut colt but I wandered back for a second look at Black Fire and found a youth in jeans and grubby sweat shirt bringing him a bucket of water.

'Is this horse yours?' I asked.

'Nope. I'm just the help.'

'Which does he do most, bite or kick?'

The boy grinned. 'Reckon he's too lazy for either.'

'Would you take him out of that dark stall so I could have a look at him in the light?'

'Sure.' He untied the halter from the tethering ring and brought Black Fire out into the central alley, where the string of electric lights burned without much enthusiasm down the length of the barn.

'There you go, then,' he said, persuading the horse to arrange its legs as if for a photograph. 'Fine looking fella, isn't he?'

'What you can see of him,' I agreed.

I looked at him critically, searching for differences. But there was no doubt he was the same. Same height, same elegant shape, even the same slightly dished Arab-looking nose. And black as coal, all over. When I walked up and patted him he bore it with fortitude. Maybe his sweet nature, I thought. Or maybe tranquillizers.

On the neck or head of many horses the hair grew in one or more whorls, making a pattern which was entered as an identifying mark on the passports. Energise had no whorls at all. Nor had Padellic. I looked carefully at the forehead, cheeks, neck and shoulders of Black Fire and ran my fingers over his coat. As far as I could feel or see in that dim light, there were no whorls on him either.

'Thanks a lot,' I said to the boy, stepping back.

He looked at me with surprise. 'You don't aim to look at his teeth or feel his legs?'

'Is there something wrong with them?'

'I guess not.'

'Then I won't bother,' I said and left unsaid the truth understood by us both, that even if I'd inspected those extremities I wouldn't have been any the wiser.

'Does he have a tattoo number inside his lip?' I asked.

'Yeah, of course.' The surprise raised his eyebrows to peaks, like a clown. 'Done when he first raced.'

'What is it?'

'Well, gee, I don't know.' His tone said he couldn't be expected to and no one in his senses would have bothered to ask.

'Take a look.'

'Well, okay.' He shrugged and with the skill of practice opened the horses's mouth and turned down the lower lip. He peered closely for a while during which time the horse stood suspiciously still, and then let him go.

'Far as I can see there's an F and a six and some others, but it's not too light in here and anyway the numbers get to go fuzzy after a while, and this fella's five now so the tattoo would be all of three years old.'

'Thanks anyway.'

'You're welcome.' He pocketed my offered five bucks and took the very unfiery Black Fire back to his stall.

I turned to find Allie, Warren and Minty standing in a row, watching. Allie and Minty both wore indulgent feminine smiles and Warren was shaking his head.

'That horse has won a total of nine thousand three hundred dollars in three years' racing,' he said. 'He won't have paid the feed bills.' He held out the catalogue opened at Black Fire's page, and I took it and read the vaguely pathetic record for myself.

At two, unplaced. At three, three wins, four times third. At four, twice third. Total: three wins, six times third, earned $9,326.'

A modest success as a three-year-old, but all in fairly low-class races. I handed the catalogue back to Warren with a smile of thanks, and we moved unhurriedly out of that barn and along to the next. When even Warren had had a surfeit of peering into stalls we went outside and watched the first entries being led into the small wooden-railed collecting ring.

A circle of lights round the rails lit the scene, aided by spotlights set among the surrounding trees. Inside, as on a stage, small bunches of people anxiously added the finishing touches of gloss which might wring a better price from the unperceptive. Some of the horses' manes were decorated with a row of bright wool pompoms, arching along the top of the neck from ears to withers as if ready for the circus. Hip No. 1, resplendent in scarlet pompoms, raised his long bay head and whinnied theatrically.

I told Allie and the Barbos I would be back in a minute and left them leaning on the rails. A couple of enquiries and one misdirection found me standing in the cramped office of the auctioneers in the sale ring building.

'A report from the veterinarian? Sure thing. Pay in advance, please. If you don't want to wait, return for the report in half an hour.'

I paid and went back to the others. Warren was deciding it was time for a drink and we stood for a while in the fine warm night near one of the bars drinking Bacardi and coke out of throwaway cartons.

Brilliant light poured out of the circular sales building in a dozen places through open doors and slatted windows. Inside, the banks of canvas chairs were beginning to fill up, and down on the rostrum in the centre the auctioneers were shaping up to starting the evening's business. We finished the drinks, duly threw away the cartons and followed the crowd into the show.

Hip No. 1 waltzed in along a ramp and circled the rostrum with all his pompoms nodding. The auctioneer began his sing-song selling, amplified and insistent, and to me, until my ears adjusted, totally unintelligible. Hip No. 1 made five thousand dollars and Warren said the prices would all be low because of the economic situation.

Horses came and went. When Hip No. 15 in orange pompoms had fetched a figure which had the crowd murmuring in excitement I slipped away to the office and found that the veterinary surgeon himself was there, dishing out his findings to other enquirers.

'Hip number sixty-two?' he echoed. 'Sure, let me find my notes.' He turned over a page or two in a notebook. 'Here we are. Dark bay or brown gelding, right?'

'Black,' I said.

'Uh, uh. Never say black.' He smiled briefly, a busy middle-aged man with an air of a clerk. 'Five years. Clean bill of health.' He shut the notebook and turned to the next customer.

'Is that all?' I said blankly.

'Sure,' he said briskly. 'No heart murmur, legs cool, teeth consistent with given age, eyes normal, range of movement normal, trots sound. No bowed tendons, no damaged knees.'

'Thanks,' I said.

'You're welcome.'

'Is he tranquillized?'

He looked at me sharply, then smiled. 'I guess so. Acepromazine probably.'

'Is that usual, or would he be a rogue?'

'I wouldn't think he'd had much. He should be okay.'

'Thanks again.'

I went back to the sale ring in time to see Warren fidgeting badly over the sale of the chestnut colt. When the price rose to fifteen thousand Minty literally clung on to his hands and told him not to be a darned fool.

'He must be sound,' Warren protested, 'to make that money.'

The colt made twenty-five thousand in thirty seconds' brisk bidding and Warren's regrets rumbled on all evening. Minty relaxed as if the ship of state of state had safely negotiated a killing reef and said she would like a breath of air. We went outside and leaned again on the collecting ring rails.

There were several people from England at the sales. Faces I knew, faces which knew me. No close friends, scarcely acquaintances, but people who would certainly notice and remark if I did anything unexpected.

I turned casually to Warren.

'I've money in New York,' I said. 'I can get it tomorrow. Would you lend me some tonight?'

'Sure,' he said good-naturedly, fishing for his wallet. 'How much do you need?'

'Enough to buy that black gelding.'

'What?' His hand froze and his eyes widened.

'Would you buy it for me?'

'You're kidding.'

'No.'

He looked at Allie for help. 'Does he mean it?'

'He's sure crazy enough for anything,' she said.

'That's just what it is,' Warren said. 'Crazy. Crazy to buy some goddamned useless creature, just because he looks like a hurdler you've got back home.'

To Allie this statement suddenly made sense. She smiled vividly and said, 'What are you going to do with him?'

I kissed her forehead. 'I tend to think in circles,' I said.

Chapter Ten

Warren, enjoying himself hugely, bought Black Fire for four thousand six hundred dollars. Bid for it, signed for it, and paid for it.

With undiminished good nature he also contracted for its immediate removal from Hialeah and subsequent shipment by air to England.

'Having himself a ball,' Minty said.

His good spirits lasted all the way back to Garden Island and through several celebratory nightcaps.

'You sure bought a stinker,' he said cheerfully, 'But boy, I haven't had so much fun in years. Did you see that guy's face, the one I bid against? He thought he was getting it for a thousand.' He chuckled. 'At four thousand five he sure looked mad and he could see I was going on for ever.'

Minty began telling him to make the most of it, it was the last horse he'd be buying for a long time, and Allie came to the door to see me off. We stood outside for a while in the dark, close together.

'One day down. Three to go,' she said.

'No more horses,' I promised.

'Okay.'

'And fewer people.'

A pause. Then again, 'Okay.'

I smiled and kissed her good night and pushed her indoors before my best intentions should erupt into good old-fashioned lust. The quickest way to lose her would be to snatch.

She said how about Florida Keys and how about a swim and how about a picnic. We went in the Impala with a cold box of goodies in the boot and the Tropic of Cancer flaming away over the horizon ahead.

The highway to Key West stretched for mile after mile across a linked chain of causeways and small islands. Palm trees, sand dunes, sparkling water and scrubby grass. Few buildings. Sun-bleached wooden huts, wooden landing stages, fishing boats. Huge skies, hot sun, vast seas. Also Greyhound buses on excursions and noisy families in station wagons with Mom in pink plastic curlers.

Allie had brought directions from Warren about one of the tiny islands where he fished, and when we reached it we turned off the highway on to a dusty side road that was little more than a track. It ended abruptly under two leaning palms, narrowing to an Indian file path though sand dunes and tufty grass towards the sea. We took the picnic box and walked, and found outselves surprisingly in a small sandy hollow from which neither the car nor the road could be seen.

'That,' said Allie, pointing at the sea, 'is Hawk Channel.'

'Can't see any hawks.'

'You'd want cooks in Cook Strait.'

She took off the loose white dress she'd worn on the way down and dropped it on the sand. Underneath she wore a pale blue and white bikini, and underneath that, warm honey coloured skin.

She took the skin without more ado into the sea and I stripped off shirt and trousers and followed her. We swam in the free warm-cool water and it felt the utmost in luxury.

'Why are these islands so uninhabited?' I asked.

'Too small, most of them. No fresh water. Hurricanes, as well. It isn't always so gentle here. Sizzling hot in the summer and terrible storms.

The wind in the palm trees looked as if butter wouldn't melt in its mouth. We splashed in the shallows and walked up the short beach to regain the warm little hollow, Allie delivering on the way a fairly non-stop lecture about turtles, bonefish, marlin and tarpon. It struck me in the end that she was talking fast to hide that she was feeling self-conscious.

I fished in my jacket pocket and brought out a twenty dollar bill. 'Bus fare home,' I said, holding it out to her.

She laughed a little jerkily. 'I still have the one you sent from England.'

'Did you bring it?'

She smiled, shook her head, took the note from me, folded it carefully and pushed it into the wet top half of her bikini.

'It'll be safe there,' she said matter-of-factly. 'How about a vodka martini?'

She had brought drinks, ice and delicious food. The sun in due course shifted thirty degrees round the sky, and I lay lazily basking in it while she put the empties back in the picnic box and fiddled with spoons.

'Allie?'

'Mm?'

'How about now?'

She stopped the busy rattling. Sat back on her ankles. Pushed the hair out of her eyes and finally looked at my face.

'Try sitting here,' I said, patting the sand beside me with an unemphatic palm.

She tried it. Nothing cataclysmic seemed to happen to her in the way of fright.

'You've done it before,' I said persuasively, stating a fact.

'Yeah ... but...'

'But what?'

'I didn't really like it.'

'Why not?'

'I don't know. I didn't like the boy enough, I expect.'

'Then why the hell sleep with him?'

'You make it sound so simple. But at college, well, one sort of had to. Three years ago, most of one summer. I haven't done it since. I've been not exactly afraid to, but afraid I would ... be unfair ...' She stopped.

'You can catch a bus whenever you like,' I said.

She smiled and bit by bit lay down beside me. I knew she wouldn't have brought me to this hidden place if she hadn't been willing at least to try. But acquiescence, in view of what she'd said, was no longer enough. If she didn't enjoy it, I couldn't.

I went slowly, giving her time. A touch. A kiss. An undemanding smoothing of hand over skin. She breathed evenly through her nose, trusting but unaroused.

'Clothes off?' I suggested. 'No one can see us.'

'... Okay.'

She unhitched the bikini top, folded it over the twenty dollars, and put it on the sand beside her. The pants in a moment followed. Then she sat with her arms wrapped round her knees, staring out to sea.

'Come on,' I said, my shorts joining hers. 'The fate worse than death isn't all that bad.'

She laughed with naturalness and lay down beside me, and it seemed as if she'd made up her mind to do her best, even if she found it unsatisfactory. But in a while she gave the first uncontrollable shiver of authentic pleasure, and after that it became not just all right but very good indeed.

'Oh God,' she said in the end, half laughing, half gasping for air. 'I didn't know...'

'Didn't know what?' I said, sliding lazily down beside her.

'At college ... he was clumsy. And too quick.'

She stretched out her hand, fumbled in the bikini and picked up the twenty dollar note.

She waved it in the air, holding it between finger and thumb. Then she laughed and opened her hand, and the wind blew her fare home away along the beach.

Chapter Eleven

London was cold enough to encourage emigration. I arrived back early Tuesday morning with sand in my shoes and sympathy for Eskimos, and Owen collected me with a face pinched and blue.

'We've had snow and sleet and the railways are on strike,' he said, putting my suitcase in the hired Cortina. 'Also the mild steel you ordered hasn't come and there's a cobra loose somewhere in Regent's Park.'

'Thanks very much.'

'Not at all, sir.

'Anything else?'

'A Mr Kennet rang from Newmarket to say Hermes has broken down. And ... sir ...'

'What?' I prompted, trying to dredge up resignation.

'Did you order a load of manure, sir?'

'Of course not.'

The total garden in front of my house consisted of three tubs of fuchsia, an old walnut tree and several square yards of paving slabs. At the rear, nothing but workshop.

'Some has been delivered, sir.'

'How much?'

'I can't see the dustmen moving it.'

He drove steadily from Heathrow to home, and I dozed from the jet-lag feeling that it was midnight. When we stopped it was not in the driveway but out on the road, because the driveway was completely blocked by a dunghill five feet high.

It was even impossible to walk round it without it sticking to one's shoes. I crabbed sideways with my suitcase to the door, and Owen drove off to find somewhere else to park.

Inside, on the mat, I found the delivery note. A postcard handwritten in ball point capitals, short and unsweet.

'*Shit to the shit.*'

Charming little gesture. Hardly original, but disturbing all the same, because it spoke so eloquently of the hatred prompting it.

Felicity, I wondered?

There was something remarkably familiar about the consistency of the load. A closer look revealed half rotted horse droppings mixed with a little straw and a lot of sawdust. Straight from a stable muck heap, not from a garden supplier: and if it looked exactly like Jody's own familiar muck heap, that wasn't in itself conclusive. I dared say one vintage was much like another.

Owen came trudging back and stared at the smelly obstruction in disgust.

'If I hadn't been using the car to go home, like you said, I wouldn't have been able to get out of the garage this morning to fetch you.'

'When was it dumped?'

'I was here yesterday morning, sir. Keeping an eye on things. Then this morning I called round to switch on the central heating, and there it was.'

I showed him the card. He looked, read, wrinkled his nose in distaste, but didn't touch.

'There'll be fingerprints on that, I shouldn't wonder.'

'Do you think it's worth telling the police?' I asked dubiously.

'Might as well, sir. You never know, this nutter might do something else. I mean, whoever went to all this trouble is pretty sick.'

'You're very sensible, Owen.'

'Thank you, sir.'

We went indoors and I summoned the constabulary, who came in the afternoon, saw the funny side of it, and took away the card in polythene.

'What are we going to do with the bloody stuff?' said Owen morosely. 'No one will want it on their flower beds, it's bung full of undigested hay seeds and that means weeds.'

'We'll shift it tomorrow.'

'There must be a ton of it.' He frowned gloomily.

'I didn't mean spadeful by spadeful,' I said. 'Not you and I. We'll hire a grab.'

Hiring things took the rest of the day. Extraordinary what one could hire if one tried. The grab proved to be one of the easiest on a long list.

At about the time merchant bankers could reasonably be expected to be reaching for their hats, I telephoned to Charlie.

'Are you going straight home?' I asked.

'Not necessarily.'

'Care for a drink?'

'On my way,' he said.

When he arrived, Owen took his Rover to park it and Charlie stood staring at the much heap, which looked no more beautiful under the street lights and was moreover beginning to ooze round the edges.

'Someone doesn't love me,' I said with a grin. 'Come on in and wipe your feet rather thoroughly on the mat.'

'What a stink.'

'Lavatory humour,' I agreed.

He left his shoes alongside mine on the tray of newspaper Owen had prudently positioned near the front door and followed me upstairs in his socks.

'Who?' he said, shaping up to a large scotch.

'A shit is what Jody's wife Felicity called me after Sandown.'

'Do you think she did it?'

'Heaven knows. She's a capable girl.'

'Didn't anyone see the ... er ... delivery?'

'Owen asked the neighbours. No one saw a thing. No one ever does, in London. All he discovered was that the much wasn't there at seven yesterday evening when the man from two doors along let his labrador make use of my fuchsia tubs.'

He drank his whisky and asked what I'd done in Miami. I couldn't stop the smile coming. 'Besides that,' he said.

'I bought a horse.'

'You're a glutton for punishment.'

'An understudy,' I said, 'for Energise.'

'Tell all to your Uncle Charlie.'

I told, if not all, most.

'The trouble is though, that although we must be ready for Saturday at Stratford, he might choose Nottingham on Monday or Lingfield on Wednesday,' I said.

'Or none of them.'

'And it might freeze.'

'How soon would we know?' Charlie asked.

'He'll have to declare the horse to run four days before the race, but he then has three days to change his mind and take him out again. We wouldn't know for sure until the runners are published in the evening papers the day before. And even then we need the nod from Bert Huggerneck.'

He chuckled. 'Bert doesn't like the indoor life. He's itching to get back on the racecourse.'

'I hope he'll stick to the shop.'

'My dear fellow!' Charlie lit a cigar and waved the match. 'Bert's a great scrapper by nature and if you could cut him in on the real action he'd be a lot happier. He's taken a strong dislike to Ganser Mays, and he says that for a ca*pit*alist you didn't seem half bad. He knows there's something afoot and he said if there's a chance of anyone punching Ganser Mays on the long bleeding nose he would like it to be him.'

I smiled at the verbatim reporting. 'All right. If he really feels like that, I do indeed have a job for him.'

'Doing what?'

'Directing the traffic.'

He puffed at the cigar. 'Do you know what your plan reminds me of?' he said. 'Your own Rola toys. There you are, turning the single handle, and all the little pieces will rotate on their spindles and go through their allotted acts.'

'You're no toy,' I said.

'Of course I am. But at least I know it. The real trick will be programming the ones who don't.'

'Do you think it will all work?'

He regarded me seriously. 'Given ordinary luck, I don't see why not.'

'And you don't have moral misgivings?'

His sudden huge smile warmed like a fire. 'Didn't you know that merchant bankers are pirates under the skin?'

Charlie took Wednesday off and spent the whole day prospecting the terrain. We drove from London to Newbury, from Newbury to Stratford on Avon, from Stratford to Nottingham, and from Nottingham back to Newbury. By that time the bars were open, and we repaired to the Chequers for revivers.

'There's only the one perfect place,' Charlie said, 'and it will do for both Stratford and Nottingham.'

I nodded. 'By the fruit stall.'

'Settle on that, then?'

'Yes.'

'And if he isn't down at either of those courses we spend Sunday surveying the road to Lingfield?'

'Right.'

He smiled vividly. 'I haven't felt so alive since my stint in the army. However, this turns out, I wouldn't have missed it for the world.'

His enthusiasm was infectious and we drove back to London in good spirits.

Things had noticeably improved in the garden. The muck heap had gone and Owen had sloshed to some effect with buckets of water, though without obliterating the smell. He had also stayed late, waiting for my return. All three of us left our shoes in the hall and went upstairs.

'Too Japanese for words,' Charlie said.

'I stayed, sir,' Owen said, 'because a call came from America.'

'Miss Ward?' I said hopefully.

'No, sir. About a horse. It was a shipping firm. They said a horse consigned to you would be on a flight to Gatwick Airport tonight as arranged. Probable time of arrival, ten a.m. tomorrow morning. I wrote it down.' He pointed to the pad beside the telephone. 'But I thought I would stay in case you didn't see it. They said you would need to engage transport to have the horse met.'

'You,' I said, 'will be meeting it.'

'Very good, sir,' he said calmly.

'Owen,' Charlie said, 'If he ever kicks you out, come to me.'

We all sat for a while discussing the various arrangements and Owen's part in them. He was as eager as Charlie to make the plan work, and he too seemed to be plugged into some inner source of excitement.

'I'll enjoy it, sir,' he said, and Charlie nodded in agreement. I have never thought of either of them as being basically adventurous and I had been wrong.

I was wrong also about Bert Huggerneck, and even in a way about Allie, for they too proved to have more fire than reservations.

Charlie brought Bert with him after work on Thursday and we sat round the kitchen table poring over a large scale map.

'That's the A34,' I said, pointing with a pencil to a red line running south to north. 'It goes all the way from Newbury to Stratford. For

Nottingham, you branch off just north of Oxford. The place we've chosen is some way south of that. Just here ...' I marked it with the pencil. 'About a mile before you reach the Abingdon by-pass.'

'I know that bleeding road,' Bert said. 'Goes past the Harwell atomic.'

'That's right.'

'Yeah. I'll find that. Easy as dolly-birds.'

'There's a roadside fruit stall there,' I said. 'Shut, at this time of year. A sort of wooden hut.'

'Seen dozens of 'em,' Bert nodded.

'It has a good big space beside it for cars.'

'Which side of the road?'

'On the near side, going north.'

'Yeah. I get you.'

'It's on a straight stretch after a fairly steep hill. Nothing will be going very fast there. Do you think you could manage?'

'Here,' he complained to Charlie. 'That's a bleeding insult.'

'Sorry,' I said.

'Is that all I do, then? Stop the bleeding traffic?' He sounded disappointed; and I'd thought he might have needed to be persuaded.

'No,' I said. 'After that you do a lot of hard work extremely quickly.'

'What, for instance?'

When I told him, he sat back on his chair and positively beamed.

'That's more bleeding like it,' he said. 'Now that's a daisy, that is. Now you might think I'm slow on my feet, like, with being big, but you'd be bleeding wrong.'

'I couldn't do it at all without you.'

'Hear that?' he said to Charlie.

'It might even be true,' Charlie said.

Bert at that point described himself as peckish and moved in a straight line to the store cupboard. 'What've you got here, then? Don't you ever bleeding eat? Do you want this tin of ham?'

'Help yourself,' I said.

Bert made a sandwich inch-deep in mustard and ate it without blinking. A couple of cans of beer filled the cracks.

'Can I chuck the betting shop, then?' he asked between gulps.

'What have your learned about Ganser Mays?'

'He's got a bleeding nickname, that's one thing I've learned. A couple of smart young managers run his shops now, you'd never know they was the same place. All keen and sharp and not a shred of soft heart like my old boss.'

'A soft-hearted bookmaker?' Charlie said. 'There's no such thing.'

'Trouble was,' Bert said, ignoring him, 'he had a bleeding soft head and all.'

'What is Ganser Mays' nickname?' I asked.

'Eh? Oh yeah. Well, these two smart alecs, who're sharp enough to cut themselves, they call him Squeezer. Squeezer Mays. When they're talking to each other, of course, that is.'

'Squeezer because he squeezes people like your boss out of business?'

'You don't hang about, do you? Yeah, that's right. There's two sorts of squeezer. The one they did on my boss, telling him horses were fixed to lose when they wasn't. And the other way round, when the smart alecs know a horse that's done no good before is fixed to win. Then they go round all the little men putting thousands on, a bit here and a bit there, and all the little men think it's easy pickings because they think the bad horse can't win in a month of bleeding Sundays. And then of course it does, and they're all down the bleeding drain.'

'They owe Ganser Mays something like the National Debt.'

'That's right. And they can't raise enough bread. So then Mr pious bleeding Mays comes along and says he'll be kind and take the shop to make up the difference. Which he does.'

'I thought small bookies were more clued up nowadays,' I said.

'You'd bleeding well think so, wouldn't you? They'll tell you they are, but they bleeding well aren't. Oh sure, if they find afterwards there's been a right fiddle, like, they squeal blue murder and refuse to pay up, but take the money in the first place, of course they do. Like bleeding innocent little lambs.'

'I don't think there would be any question of anyone thinking it a fiddle, this time,' I said.

'There you are, then. Quite a few would all of a bleeding sudden be finding they were swallowed up by that smarmy bastard. Just like my poor old boss.'

I reflected for a minute or two. 'I think it would be better if you stayed in the betting shop until we're certain which day the horse is going to run. I don't imagine they would risk letting him loose without backing him, so we must suppose that his first race is IT. But if possible I'd like to be sure. And you might hear something, if you're still in the shop.

'Keep my ears flapping, you mean?'

'Absolutely. And eyes open.'

'Philby won't have nothing on me,' Bert said.

Charlie stretched out to the makings of the sandwich and assembled a smaller edition for himself.

'Now, transport,' I said. 'I've hired all the vehicles we need from a firm in Chiswick. I was there this morning, looking them over. Owen took a Land-Rover and trailer from there to Gatwick to meet Black Fire and ferry him to his stable, and he's coming back by train. Then there's the caravan for you, Charlie, and the car to pull it. Tomorrow Owen is driving those to Reading and leaving them in the station car park, again coming back by train. I got two sets of keys for the car and caravan, so I'll give you yours now.' I went through to the sitting-room and came back with the small jingling bunch. 'Whichever day we're off, you can go down to Reading by train and drive from there.'

'Fine,' Charlie said, smiling broadly.

'The caravan is one they hire out for horse shows and exhibitions and things like that. It's fitted out as a sort of office. No beds or cookers, just a counter, a couple of desks, and three or four folding chairs. Owen and I will load it with all the things you'll need before he takes it to Reading.'

'Great.'

'Finally there's the big van for Owen. I'll bring that here tomorrow and put the shopping in it. Then we should be ready.'

'Here,' said Bert. 'How's the cash, like?'

'Do you want some, Bert?'

'It's only, well, seeing as how you're hiring things left right and centre, well, I wondered if it wouldn't be better to hire a car for me too, like. Because my old banger isn't all that bleeding reliable, see? I wouldn't like to miss the fun because of a boiling bleeding radiator or some such.'

'Sure,' I said. 'Much safer.' I went back to the sitting-room, fetched some cash, and gave it to Bert.

'Here,' he said. 'I don't need that much. What do you think I'm going to hire, a bleeding golden coach.'

'Keep it anyway.'

He looked at me dubiously. 'I'm not doing this for bread, mate.'

I felt humbled. 'Bert . . . Give me back what you don't use. Or send it to the Injured Jockeys' Fund.'

His face lightened. 'I'll take my old boss down the boozer a few times. Best bleeding charity there is!'

Charlie finished his sandwich and wiped his fingers on his handkerchief. 'You won't forget the sign-writing, will you?' he said.

'I did it today,' I assured him. 'Want to see?'

We trooped down to the workshop, where various painted pieces of the enterprise were standing around drying.

'Blimey,' Bert said. 'They look bleeding real.'

'They'd have to be,' Charlie nodded.

'Here,' Bert said, 'seeing these makes it seem, well, as if it's all going to happen.'

Charlie went home to a bridge-playing wife in an opulent detached in Surrey and Bert to the two-up two-down terraced he shared with his fat old mum in Staines. Some time after their departure I got the car out and drove slowly down the M4 to Heathrow.

I was early. About an hour early. I had often noticed that I tended to arrive prematurely for things I was looking forward to, as if by being there early one could make them happen sooner. It worked in reverse that time. Allie's aeroplane was half an hour late.

'Hi,' she said, looking as uncrushed as if she'd travelled four miles, not four thousand. 'How's cold little old England?'

'Warmer since you're here.'

The wide smile had lost none of its brilliance, but now there was also a glow in the eyes, where the Miami sun shone from within.

'Thanks for coming,' I said.

'I wouldn't miss this caper for the world.' She gave me a kiss full of excitement and warmth. 'And I haven't told my sister I'm coming.'

'Great,' I said with satisfaction; and took her home to the flat.

The change of climate was external. We spent the night, our first together, warmly entwined under a goosefeather quilt: more comfortable, more relaxed and altogether more cosy than the beach or the fishing boat or my hotel bedroom on an air-conditioned afternoon in Miami.

We set off early next morning while it was still dark, shivering in the chill January air and impatient for the car heater to make an effort. Allie drove, concentrating fiercely on the left-hand business, telling me to watch out that she didn't instinctively turn the wrong way at crossings. We reached the fruit stall on the A34 safely in two hours and drew up there in the wide sweep of car-parking space. Huge lorries ground past on the main route from the docks at Southampton to the heavy industry area at Birmingham; a road still in places too narrow for its traffic.

Each time a heavy truck breasted the adjoining hill and drew level with us, it changed its gears, mostly with a good deal of noise. Allie raised her voice. 'Not the quietest of country spots.'

I smiled. 'Every decibel counts.'

We drank hot coffee from a thermos flask and watched the slow grey morning struggle from gloomy to plain dull.

'Nine o'clock,' said Allie, looking at her watch. 'The day sure starts late in these parts.'

'We'll need you here by nine,' I said.

'You just tell me when to start.'

'Okay.'

She finished her coffee. 'Are you certain sure he'll come this way?'

'It's the best road the most direct, and he always does.'

'One thing about having an ex-friend for an enemy,' she said. 'You know his habits.'

I packed away the coffee and we started again, turning south.

'This is the way you'll be coming,' I said. 'Straight up the A34.'

'Right.'

She was driving now with noticeably more confidence, keeping left without the former steady frown of anxiety. We reached a big crossroads and stopped at the traffic lights. She looked around and nodded. 'When I get here, there'll only be a couple of miles to go.'

We pressed on for a few miles, the road climbing and descending over wide stretches of bare downlands, bleak and windy and uninviting.

'Slow down a minute,' I said. 'See that turning there, to the left? That's where Jody's stables are. About a mile along there.'

'I really hate that man,' she said.

'You've never met him.'

'You don't have to know snakes to hate them.'

We went round the Newbury by-pass, Allie screwing her head round alarmingly to learn the route from the reverse angle.

'Okay,' she said. 'Now what?'

'Still the A34. Signposts to Winchester. But we don't go that far.'

'Right.'

Through Whitchurch, and six miles beyond we took a narrow side road on the right, and in a little while turned into the drive of a dilapidated looking country house with a faded paint job on a board at the gate.

Hantsford Manor Riding School.
First class instruction. Residential Accommodation.
Ponies and horses for hire or at livery.

I had chosen it from an advertisement in the *Horse and Hound* because of its location, to make the drive from there to the fruit stall as simple as possible for Allie, but now that I saw it, I had sinking doubts.

There was an overall air of life having ended, of dust settling, weeds growing, wood rotting and hope dead. Exaggerated, of course. Though the house indoors smelt faintly of fungus and decay, the proprietors were still alive. They were two much-alike sisters, both about seventy, with thin wiry bodies dressed in jodhpurs, hacking jackets and boots. They both had kind faded blue eyes, long strong lower jaws, and copious iron grey hair in businesslike hairnets.

They introduced themselves as Miss Johnston and Mrs Fairchild-Smith. They were glad to welcome Miss Ward. They said they hoped her stay would be comfortable. They never had many guests at this time of year. Miss Ward's horse had arrived safely the day before and they were looking after him.

'Yourselves?' I asked doubtfully.

'Certainly, ourselves.' Miss Johnston's tone dared me to imply they were incapable. 'We always cut back on staff at this time of year.'

They took us out to the stables, which like everything else were suffering from advancing years and moreover appeared to be empty. Among a ramshackle collection of wooden structures whose doors any self-respecting toddler could have kicked down, stood three or four brick-built boxes in a sturdy row; in one of these we found Black Fire.

He stood on fresh straw. There was clean water in his bucket and good-looking hay in his net, and he had his head down to the manger, munching busily at oats and bran. All too clear to see where any profits of the business disappeared: into the loving care of the customers.

'He looks fine,' I said, and to myself, with relief, confirmed that he really was indeed the double of Energise, and that in the warm distant Miami night I hadn't been mistaken.

Allie cleared her throat. 'Er ... Miss Johnston, Mrs Fairchild-Smith ... tomorrow morning I may be taking Black Fire over to some friends, to ride with them. Would that be okay?'

'Of course,' they said together.

'Leaving at eight o'clock?'

'We'll see he's ready for you, my dear,' said Miss Johnston.

'I'll let you know for sure when I've called my friends. If I don't go tomorrow, it may be Monday, or Wednesday.'

'Whenever you say, my dear.' Miss Johnston paused delicately. 'Could you give us any idea how long you'll be staying?'

Allie said without hesitation. 'I guess a week's board would be fair, both for Black Fire and me, don't you think? We may not be here for all of seven days, but obviously at this time of year you won't want to be bothered with shorter reservations.'

The sisters looked discreetly pleased and when Allie produced cash for the bulk of the bill in advance, a faint flush appeared on their thin cheeks and narrow noses.

'Aren't they the weirdest?' Allie said as we drove out of the gates. 'And how do you shift these damned gears?'

She sat this time at the wheel of the Land-Rover I'd hired from Chiswick, learning her way round its unusual levers.

'That one with the red knob engages four-wheeled drive, and the yellow one is for four ultra-low gears, which you shouldn't need as we're not aiming to cross ploughed fields or drag tree stumps out of the ground.'

'I wouldn't rule them out when you're around.'

She drove with growing ease, and before long we returned to hitch on the two-horse trailer. She had never driven with a trailer before and reversing, as always, brought the worst problems. After a fair amount of swearing on all sides and the part of an hour's trundling around Hampshire she said she guessed she would reach the fruit stall if it killed her. When we returned to Hantsford Manor after refuelling she parked with the Land-Rover's nose already facing the road, so that at least she wouldn't louse up the linkage, as she put it, before she'd even started.

'You'll find the trailer a good deal heavier with a horse in it,' I said.

'You don't say.'

Without encountering the sisters we returned to Black Fire, and I produced from an inner pocket a haircutting gadget in the form of a razor blade incorporated into a comb.

'What are you going to do with that?' Allie said.

'If the two old girls materialize, keep them chatting,' I said. 'I'm just helping the understudy to look like the star.'

I went into the box and as calmly as possible approached Black Fire. He wore a head collar, but was not tied up, and the first thing I did was attach him to the tethering chain. I ran my hand down his neck and patted him a few times and said a few soothing nonsenses. He didn't seem to object to my presence, so rather gingerly I laid the edge of the hair-cutting comb against his black coat.

I had been told often that nervous people made horses nervous also. I wondered if Black Fire could feel my fumbling inexperience. I thought that after all this I would really have to spend more time with horses, that owning them should entail the obligation of intimacy.

His muscles twitched. He threw his head up and down. He whinneyed. He also stood fairly still, so that when I'd finished my delicate scraping he had a small bald patch on his right shoulder, the same size and in the same place as the one on Energise.

Allie leant her elbows on the closed bottom half of the stable door and watched through the open top half.

'Genius,' she said smiling, 'Is nine te almost familiarly, and shook my head. 'Genius is infinite pain,' I said. 'I'm happy. Too bad.'

'How do you know, then? About genius being pain?'

'Like seeing glimpses of a mountain from the valley.'

'And you'd prefer to suffer on the peaks?'

I let myself out of the loose box and carefully fastened all the bolts.

'You're either issued with climbing boots, or you aren't,' I said. 'You can't choose. Just as well.'

The sisters reappeared and invited us to take sherry: a double thimbleful in unmatched cut glasses. I looked at my watch and briefly nodded, and Allie asked if she might use the telephone to call the friends.

In the library, they said warmly. This way. Mind the hole in the carpet. Over there, on the desk. They smiled, nodded and retreated.

Beside the telephone stood a small metal box with a stuck-on notice. *Please pay for calls.* I dialled the London number of the Press Association and asked for the racing section.

'Horses knocked out of the novice hurdle at Stratford?' said a voice. 'Well, I suppose so, but we prefer people to wait for the evening papers. These enquiries waste our time.'

'Arrangements to make as soon as possible ...' I murmured.

'Oh, all right. Wait a sec. Here we are ...' He read out about seven names rather fast. 'Got that?'

'Yes, thank you very much,' I said.

I put down the telephone slowly, my mouth suddenly dry. Jody had declared Padellic as a Saturday Stratford runner three days ago. If he had intended not to go there, he would have had to remove his name by a Friday morning deadline of eleven o'clock ...

Eleven o'clock had come and gone. None of the horses taken out of the novice hurdle had been Padellic.

'Tomorrow,' I said. 'He runs tomorrow.'

'Oh.' Allie's eyes were wide. 'Oh golly!'

Chapter Twelve

Eight o'clock, Saturday morning.

I sat in my hired Cortina in a lay-by on the road over the top of the Downs, watching the drizzly dawn take the eyestrain out of the passing headlights.

I was there much too early because I hadn't been able to sleep. The flurry of preparations all Friday afternoon and even had sent me to bed still in top gear and from then on my brain had whirred relentlessly, thinking of all the things which could go wrong.

Snatches of conversation drifted back.

Rupert Ramsey expressing doubts and amazement on the other end of the telephone.

'You want to do *what*?'

'Take Energise for a ride in a horsebox. He had a very upsetting experience in a horsebox at Sandown, in a crash . . . I thought it might give him confidence to go for an uneventful drive.'

'I don't think it would do much good,' he said.

'All the same I'm keen to try. I've asked a young chap called Pete Duveen, who drives his own box, just to pick him up and take him for a ride. I thought tomorrow would be a good day. Pete Duveen says he can collect him at seven thirty in the morning. Would you have the horse ready?'

'You're wasting your money,' he said regretfully. 'I'm afraid there's more wrong with him than nerves.'

'Never mind. And . . . will you be at home tomorrow evening?'

'After I get back from Chepstow races, yes.'

The biggest race meeting of the day was scheduled for Chepstow, over on the west side of the Bristol Channel. The biggest prizes were on offer there and most of the top trainers, like Rupert, would be going.

'I hope you won't object,' I said, 'but after Energise returns from his ride, I'd like to hire a security firm to keep an eye on him.'

Silence from the other end. Then his voice, carefully polite. 'What on earth for?'

'To keep him safe,' I said reasonably. 'Just a guard to patrol the stable and make regular checks. The guard wouldn't be a nuisance to anybody.'

I could almost feel the shrug coming down the wire along with the resigned sigh. Eccentric owners should be humoured. 'If you want to, I suppose . . . But why?'

'If I called at your house tomorrow evening,' I suggested diffidently, 'I could explain.'

'Well . . .' He thought for a bit. 'Look, I'm having a few friends to dinner. Would you care to join us?'

'Yes, I would,' I said positively. 'I'd like that very much.'

I yawned in the car and stretched. Despite anorak, gloves and thick socks the cold encroached on fingers and toes, and through the drizzle-wet windows the bare rolling Downs looked thoroughly inhospitable. Straight ahead through the windscreen wipers I could see a good two miles of the A34. It came over the brow of a distant hill opposite, swept down into a large valley and rose again higher still to cross the Downs at the point where I sat.

A couple of miles to my rear lay the crossroads with the traffic lights, and a couple of miles beyond that, the fruit stall.

Bert Huggerneck, wildly excited, had telephoned at six in the evening.

'Here, know what? There's a squeezer on tomorrow!'

'On Padellic?' I said hopefully.

'What else? On bleeding little old Padellic.'

'How do you know?'

'Listened at the bleeding door,' he said cheerfully. 'The two smart alecs was talking. Stupid bleeding gits. All over the whole bleeding country Ganser Mays is going to flood the little bookies' shops with last minute bets on Padellic. The smart alecs are all getting their girl friends, what the little guys don't know by sight, to go round putting on the dough. Hundreds of them, by the sound of it.'

'You're a wonder, Bert.'

'Yeah,' he said modestly. 'Missed my bleeding vocation.'

Owen and I had spent most of the afternoon loading the big hired van from Chiswick and checking that we'd left nothing out. He worked like a demon, all energy and escaping smiles.

'Life will seem flat after this,' he said.

I had telephoned Charlie from Hantsford Manor and caught him before he went to lunch.

'We're off,' I said. 'Stratford, tomorrow.'

'Tally bloody ho!'

He rang me from his office again at five. 'Have you seen the evening papers?'

'Not yet,' I said.

'Jody has two definite runners at Chepstow as well.'

'Which ones?'

'Cricklewood in the big race and Asphodel in the handicap chase.'

Cricklewood and Asphodel both belonged to the same man, who since I'd left had become Jody's number one owner. Cricklewood was now also ostensibly the best horse in the yard.

'That means,' I said, 'that Jody himself will almost certainly go to Chepstow.'

'I should think so,' Charlie agreed. 'He wouldn't want to draw attention to Padellic by going to Stratford, would you think?'

'No, I wouldn't.'

'Just what we wanted,' Charlie said with satisfaction. 'Jody going to Chepstow.'

'We thought he might.'

Charlie chuckled. '*You* thought he might.' He cleared his throat. 'See you tomorrow, in the trenches. And Steven...'

'Yes?'

'Good luck with turning the handle.'

Turning the handle...

I looked at my watch. Still only eight-thirty and too early for any action. I switched on the car's engine and let the heater warm me up.

All the little toys, revolving on their spindles, going through their programmed acts. Allie, Bert, Charlie and Owen. Felicity and Jody

Leeds, Ganser Mays. Padellic and Energise and Black Fire. Rupert Ramsey and Pete Duveen.

And one little toy I knew nothing about.

I stirred, thinking of him uneasily.

A big man who wore sunglasses. Who had muscles, and knew how to fight.

What else?

Who had bought Padellic at Doncaster Sales?

I didn't know if he had bought the horse after Jody had found it, or if he knew Energise well enough to look for a double himself; and there was no way of finding out.

I'd left no slot for him in today's plan. If he turned up like a joker, he might entirely disrupt the game.

I picked up my raceglasses which were lying on the seat beside me and started watching the traffic crossing the top of the opposite distant hill. From two miles away, even with strong magnification, it was difficult to identify particular vehicles, and in the valley and climbing the hill straight towards me they were head-on and foreshortened.

What looked like a car and trailer came over the horizon. I glanced at my watch. If it was Allie, she was dead on time.

I focussed on the little group. Watched it down into the valley. Definitely a Land-Rover and animal trailer. I got out of the car and watched it crawling up the hill, until finally I could make out the number plate. Definitely Allie.

Stepping a pace on to the road, I flagged her down. She pulled into the lay-by, opened her window, and looked worried.

'Something wrong?'

'Not a thing.' I kissed her. 'I got here too early, so I thought I'd say good morning.'

'You louse. When I saw you standing there waving I thought the whole darned works were all fouled up.'

'You found the way, then.'

'No problem.'

'Sleep well?'

She wrinkled her nose. 'I guess so. But oh boy, that's some crazy house. Nothing works. If you want to flush the john you have to get Miss Johnston. No one else has the touch. I guess they're really sweet, though, the poor old ducks.'

'Shades of days gone by,' I said.

'Yeah, that's exactly right. They showed me their scrap books. They were big in the horse world thirty-forty years ago. Won things at shows all over. Now they're struggling on a fixed income and I guess they'll soon be starving.'

'Did they say so?'

'Of course not. You can see it, though.'

'Is Black Fire all right?'

'Oh sure. They helped me load him up, which was lucky because I sure would have been hopeless on my own.'

'Was he any trouble?'

'Quiet as a little lamb.'

I walked round to the back of the trailer and looked in over the three-quarter door. Black Fire occupied the left-hand stall. A full hay net lay in the right. The ladies might starve, but their horses wouldn't.

I went back to Allie. 'Well ...' I said. 'Good luck.'

'To you to.'

She gave me the brilliant smile, shut the window and with care pulled out of the lay-by into the stream of northbound traffic.

Time and timing, the two essentials.

I sat in the car metaphorically chewing my nails and literally looking at my watch every half minute.

Padellic's race was the last of the day, the sixth race, the slot often allotted to that least crowd-pulling of events, the novice hurdle. Because of the short January afternoon, the last race was scheduled for three-thirty.

Jody's horses, like those of most other trainers, customarily arrived at a racecourse about two hours before they were due to run. Not often later, but quite often sooner.

The journey by horsebox from Jody's stable to Stratford on Avon racecourse took two hours. The very latest, therefore, that Jody's horsebox would set out would be eleven-thirty.

I thought it probable it would start much sooner than that. The latest time allowed little margin for delays on the journey or snags on arrival and I knew that if I were Jody and Ganser Mays and had so much at stake, I would add a good hour for contingencies.

Ten-thirty ... But suppose it was earlier ...

I swallowed. I had had to guess.

If for any reason Jody had sent the horse very early and it had already gone, all our plans were for nothing.

If he had sent it the day before ... If he had sent it with another trainer's horses, sharing the cost ... If for some unimaginable reason the driver took a different route ...

The ifs multiplied like stinging ants.

Nine-fifteen.

I got out of the car and extended the aerial of a large efficient walkie-talkie. No matter that British civilians were supposed to have permission in triple triplicate before operating them: in this case we would be cluttering the air for seconds only, and lighting flaming beacons on hilltops would have caused a lot more fuss.

'Charlie?' I said, transmitting.

'All fine here.'

'Great.' I paused for five seconds, and transmitted again. 'Owen?.'

'Here, sir.'

'Great.'

Owen and Charlie could both hear me but they couldn't hear each other, owing to the height of the Downs where I sat. I left the aerial extended and the switches to 'receive', and put the gadget back in the car.

The faint drizzle persisted, but my mouth was dry.

I thought about the five of us, sitting and waiting. I wondered if the others like me were having trouble with their nerves.

The walkie-talkie crackled suddenly. I picked it up.

'Sir?'

'Owen?'

'Pete Duveen just passed me.'

'Fine.'

I could hear the escaping tension in my own voice and the excitement in his. The on-time arrival of Pete Duveen signalled the real beginning. I put the walkie-talkie down again and was disgusted to see my hand shaking.

Pete Duveen in his horsebox drove into the lay-by nine and half minutes after he had passed Owen, who was stationed in sight of the road to Jody's stable. Pete owned a pale blue horsebox with his name, address and telephone number painted in large black and red letters on the front and back. I had seen the box and its owner often at race meetings and it was he, in fact, whom I had engaged at Sandown on my abortive attempt to prevent Jody taking Energise home.

Pete Duveen shut down his engine and jumped from the cab.

'Morning, Mr Scott.'

'Morning,' I said, shaking hands. 'Glad to see you.'

'Anything to oblige.' He grinned cheerfully, letting me know both that he thought I was barmy and also that I had every right to be, as long as I was harmless and, moreover, paying him.

He was well-built and fair, with weatherbeaten skin and a threadbare moustache. Open-natured, sensible and honest. A one-man transport firm, and making a go of it.

'You brought my horse?' I said.

'Sure thing.'

'And how has he travelled?'

'Not a peep out of him the whole way.'

'Mind if I take a look at him?' I said.

'Sure thing,' he said again. 'But honest, he didn't act up when we loaded him and I wouldn't say he cared a jimmy riddle one way or another.'

I unclipped and opened the part of the side of the horsebox which formed the entrance ramp for the horses. It was a bigger box than Jody's, but otherwise much the same. The horse stood in the front row of stalls in the one furthest across from the ramp, and he looked totally uninterested in the day's proceedings.

'You never know,' I said, closing the box again. 'He might be all the better for the change of routine.'

'Maybe,' Pete said, meaning he didn't think so.

I smiled. 'Like some coffee?'

'Sure would.'

I opened the boot of my car, took out a thermos, and poured us each a cup.

'Sandwich?' I offered.

Sandwich accepted. He ate beef-and-chutney with relish. 'Early start,' he said, explaining his hunger. 'You said to get here soon after nine-thirty.'

'That's right,' I agreed.

'Er . . . why so early?'

'Because,' I said reasonably, 'I've other things to do all the rest of the day.'

He thought me even nuttier, but the sandwich plugged the opinion in his throat.

The sky began to brighten and the tiny-dropped drizzle dried away. I talked about racing in general and Stratford on Avon in particular, and wondered how on earth I was to keep him entertained if Jody's box should after all not leave home until the last possible minute.

By ten-fifteen we had drunk two cups of coffee each and he had run out of energy for sandwiches. He began to move restively and make ready-for-departure signs of which I blandly took no notice. I chatted on about the pleasures of owning racehorses and my stomach bunched itself into anxious knots.

Ten-twenty. Ten twenty-five. Ten-thirty. Nothing.

It had all gone wrong, I thought. One of the things which could have sent everything awry had done so.

Ten thirty-five.

'Look,' Pete said persuasively. 'You said you had a great deal to do today, and honestly, I don't think . . .'

The walkie-talkie crackled.

I practically leapt towards the front of the car and reached in for it.

'Sir?'

'Yes, Owen.'

'A blue horsebox just came out of his road and turned south.'

'Right.'

I stifled my disappointment. Jody's two runners setting off to Chepstow, no doubt.

'What's that?' Pete Duveen said, his face appearing at my shoulder full of innocent enquiry.

'Just a radio.'

'Sounded like a police car.'

I smiled and moved away back to the rear of the car, but I had hardly got Pete engaged again in useless conversation when the crackle was repeated.

'Sir?'

'Go ahead.'

'A fawn coloured box with a red slash, sir. Just turned north.' His voice trembled with excitement.

'That's it, Owen.'

'I'm on my way.'

I felt suddenly sick. Took three deep breaths. Pressed the transmit button.

'Charlie?'

'Yes.'

'The box is on its way.'

'Halle-bloody-lujah.'

Pete was again looking mystified and inquisitive. I ignored his face and took a travelling bag out of the boot of my car.

'Time to go,' I said pleasantly. 'I think, if you don't mind, I'd like to see how my horse behaves while going along, so could you start the box now and take me up the road a little way?'

He looked very surprised, but then he had found the whole expedition incomprehensible.

'If you like,' he said helplessly. 'You're the boss.'

I made encouraging signs to him to get into his cab and start the engine and while he was doing it I stowed my bag on the passenger side. The diesel engine whirred and coughed and came to thunderous life, and I went back to the Cortina.

Locked the boot, shut the windows, took the keys, locked the door, and stood leaning against the wing holding binoculars in one hand and walkie-talkie in the other.

Pete Duveen had taken nine and a half minutes from Jody's road to my lay-by and Jody's box took exactly the same. Watching the far hill through raceglasses I saw the big dark blue van which contained Owen come over the horizon, followed almost immediately by an oblong of fawn.

Watched them down into the valley and on to the beginning of the hill.

I pressed the transmit button.

'Charlie?'

'Go ahead.'

'Seven minutes. Owen's in front.'

'Right.'

I pushed down the aerial of the walkie-talkie and took it and myself along to the passenger door of Pete's box. He looked across and down at me enquiringly, wondering why on earth I was still delaying.

'Just a moment,' I said, giving no explanation, and he waited patiently, as if humouring a lunatic.

Owen came up the hill, changed gears abreast of the lay-by, and slowly accelerated away. Jody's horsebox followed, doing exactly the same. The scrunched nearside front had been hammered out, I saw, but respraying lay in the future. I had a quick glimpse into the cab: two men, neither of them Jody, both unknown to me; a box driver who had replaced Andy-Fred and the lad with the horse. Couldn't be better.

I hopped briskly up into Pete's box.

'Off we go, then.'

My sudden haste looked just as crazy as the former dawdling, but again he made no comment and merely did what I wanted. When he had found a gap in the traffic and pulled out on to the road there were four or five vehicles between Jody's box and ourselves, and this seemed to me a reasonable number.

I spent the next four miles trying to look as if nothing in particular was happening while listening to my heart beat like a discotheque. Owen's van went over the traffic lights at the big crossroads a half second before they changed to amber and Jody's box came to a halt as they showed red. The back of Owen's van disappeared round a bend in the road.

Between Jody's box and Pete's there were three private cars and one small van belonging to an electrical firm. When the lights turned green one of the cars peeled off to the left and I began to worry that we were getting too close.

'Slow down just a fraction,' I suggested.

'If you like ... but there's not a squeak from the horse.' He glanced over his shoulder to where the back head looked patiently forward through a small observation hatch, as nervous as a suet pudding.

A couple of private cars passed us. We motored sedately onwards and came to the bottom of the next hill. Pete changed his gears smoothly and we lumbered noisily up. Near the top, his eye took in a notice board on a tripod at the side of the road.

'Damn,' he said.

'What is it?' I asked.

'Did you see that?' he said. 'Census point ahead.'

'Never mind, we're not in a hurry.'

'I suppose not.'

We breasted the hill. The fruit stall lay ahead on our left, with the sweep of the car park beside it. Down the centre of the road stood a row of the red and white cones used for marking road obstructions and in the northbound lane, directing the traffic, stood a large man in navy blue police uniform with a black and white checked band round his cap.

As we approached he waved the private cars past and then directed Pete into the fruitstall car park, walking in beside the horsebox and talking to him through the window.

'We'll keep you only a few minutes, sir. Now, will you pull right round in a circle and park facing me just here, sir?'

'All right,' Pete said resignedly and followed the instructions. When he pulled the brake on we were facing the road. On our left, about ten feet away, stood Jody's box, but facing in the opposite direction. On the far side of Jody's box was Owen's van. And beyond Owen's van, across about twenty yards of cindery park, lay the caravan, its long flat windowless side towards us.

The Land-Rover and trailer which Allie had brought stood near the front of Jody's box. There was also the car hitched to the caravan and the car Bert had hired, and all in all the whole area looked populated, official, and busy.

A second large notice on a tripod faced the car park from just outside the caravan.

Department of the Environment
Census point

and near a door at one end of the caravan a further notice on a stand said '*Way In*.'

Jody's horsebox driver and Jody's lad were following its directions, climbing the two steps up to the caravan and disappearing within.

'Over there, please sir.' A finger pointed authoritatively. 'And take your driving licence and log book, please.'

Pete shrugged, picked up his papers, and went. I jumped out and watched him go.

The second he was inside Bert slapped me on the back in a most unpolicemanlike way and said 'Easy as Blackpool tarts.'

We zipped into action. Four minutes maximum, and a dozen things to do.

I unclipped the ramp of Jody's horsebox and let it down quietly. The one thing which would bring any horsebox driver running, census or no census, was the sound of someone tampering with his cargo; and noise, all along, had been one of the biggest problems.

Opened Pete Duveen's ramp. Also the one on Allie's trailer.

While I did that, Bert brought several huge rolls of three-inch thick latex from Owen's van and unrolled them down all the ramps, and across the bare patches of car park in between the boxes. I fetched the head collar bought for the purpose from my bag and stepped into Jody's box. The black horse looked at me incuriously, standing there quietly in his travelling rug and four leg-guards. I checked his ear for the tiny nick and his shoulder for the bald pennyworth, and wasted a moment in patting him.

I knew all too well that success depended on my being able to persuade this strange four-footed creature to go with me gently and without fuss, and wished passionately for more expertise. All I had were nimble hands and sympathy, and they would have to be enough.

I unbuckled his rug at high speed and thanked the gods that the leg-guards Jody habitually used for travelling his horses were not laboriously wound-on bandages but lengths of plastic-backed foam rubber fastened by strips of velcro.

I had all four off before Bert had finished the soundproofing. Put the new head collar over his neck; unbuckled and removed his own and left it swinging, still tied to the stall. Fitted and fastened the new one, and gave the rope a tentative tug. Energise took one step, then another, then with more assurance followed me sweetly down the ramp. It felt miraculous, not nothing like fast enough.

Hurry. Get the other horses, and hurry.

They didn't seem to mind walking on the soft spongy surface, but they wouldn't go fast. I tried to take them calmly, to keep my urgency to myself, to stop them taking fright and skittering away and crashing those metal-capped feet on to the car park.

Hurry. Hurry.

I had to get Energise's substitute into his place, wearing the right rug, the right bandages, and the right head collar, before the box driver and the lad came out of the caravan.

Also his hooves ... Racing plates were sometimes put on by the blacksmith at home, who then rubbed on oil to obliterate the rasp marks on the file and give the feet a well-groomed appearance. I had brought hoof oil in my bag in case Energise had already had his shoes changed and he had.

'Hurry for gawd's sake,' said Bert, seeing me fetch the oil. He was running back to the van with relays of re-rolled latex and grinning like a Pools winner.

I painted the hooves a glossy dark. Buckled on the swinging head collar without disturbing the tethering knot, as the lad would notice if it were tied differently. Buckled the rug round the chest and under the belly. Fastened the velcro strips on all four leg-guards. Shut the folding gates to his stall exactly as they had been before, and briefly looked back before closing the ramp. The black head was turned incuriously towards me, the liquid eye patient and unmoved. I smiled at him involuntarily, jumped out of the box, and with Bert's help eased shut the clips on the ramp.

Owen came out of the caravan, ran across, and fastened the ramp on the trailer. I jumped in with the horse in Pete's box. Bert lifted the ramp and did another silent job on the clips.

Through the windscreen of Pete's box the car park looked quiet and tidy.

Owen returned to the driving seat of his van and Bert walked back towards the road.

At the same instant Jody's driver and lad hurried out of the caravan and tramped across to their horsebox. I ducked out of sight, but I could hear one of them say, as he re-embarked, 'Right lot of time-wasting cobblers, that was.'

Then the engine throbbed to life, the box moved off, and Bert considerately held up a car or two so that it should have a clear passage back to its interrupted journey. If I hadn't had so much still to do I would have laughed.

I fastened the rug. Tied the head collar rope. Clipped on the leg guards. I'd never worked so fast in my life.

What else? I glanced over my beautiful black horse, seeking things undone. He looked steadfastly back. I smiled at him, too, and told him he was a great fellow. Then Pete came out of the caravan and I scrambled through to the cab, and tried to sit in the passenger seat as if bored with waiting instead of sweating with effort and with a heart racing like tappets.

Pete climbed into his side of the cab and threw his log book and licence disgustedly on to the glove shelf.

'They're always stopping us nowadays. Spot check on log books. Spot check on vehicles. Half an hour a time, those. And now a census.'

'Irritating,' I agreed, making my voice a lot slower than my pulse.

His usual good nature returned in a smile. 'Actually the checks are a good thing. Some lorries, in the old days, were death on wheels. And some drivers, I dare say.' He stretched his hand towards the ignition. 'Where to?' he said.

'Might as well go back. As you say, the horse is quiet. If you could take me back to my car?'

'Sure thing,' he said. 'You're the boss.'

Bert shepherded us solicitously on to the southbound lane, holding up the traffic with a straight face and obvious enjoyment. Pete drove steadfastly back to the lay-by and pulled in behind the Cortina.

'I expect you think it a wasted day,' I said. 'But I assure you from my point of view it's been worth it.'

'That's all that matters,' he said cheerfully.

'Take good care of this fellow going home,' I said, looking back at the horse. 'And would you remind the lads in Mr Ramsey's yard that I've arranged for a security guard to patrol the stable at night for a while? He should be arriving there later this afternoon.'

'Sure,' he said, nodding.

'That's all then, I guess.' I took my bag and jumped down from the cab. He gave me a final wave through the window and set off again southwards along the A34.

I leaned against the Cortina, watching him go down the hill, across the valley, and up over the horizon on the far side.

I wondered how Energise would like his new home.

Chapter Thirteen

Charlie, Allie, Bert and Owen were all in the caravan when I drove back there, drinking coffee and laughing like kids.

'Here,' Bert said, wheezing with joy. 'A bleeding police car came along a second after I'd picked up the census notices and all those cones. Just a bleeding second.'

'It didn't stop, I hope.'

'Not a bleeding chance. Mind you, I'd taken off the fancy clobber. First thing. The fuzz don't love you for impersonating them, even if your hatband is only a bit of bleeding ribbon painted in checks.'

Charlie said more soberly. 'It was the only police car we've seen.'

'The cones were only in the road for about ten minutes,' Allie said. 'It sure would have been unlucky if the police had driven by in that time.'

She was sitting by one of the desks looking neat but unremarkable in a plain skirt and jersey. On the desk stood my typewriter, uncovered, with piles of stationery alongside. Charlie, at the other desk, wore an elderly suit, faintly shabby and a size too small. He had parted his hair in the centre and brushed it flat with water, and had somehow contrived a look of middling bureaucracy instead of world finance. Before him, too, lay an impressive array of official forms and other literature and the walls of the caravan were drawing-pinned with exhortative Ministry posters.

How did you get all this bleeding junk?' said Bert, waving his hand at it.

'Applied for it,' I said. 'It's not difficult to get government forms or information posters. All you do is ask.'

'Blimey.'

'They're not census forms, of course. Most of them are application forms for driving licences and passports and things like that. Owen and I just made up the census questions and typed them out for Charlie, and he pretended to put the answers on the forms.'

Owen drank his coffee with a happy smile and Charlie said, chuckling, 'You should have seen your man here putting on his obstructive act. Standing there in front of me like an idiot and either answering the questions wrong or arguing about answering them at all. The two men from the horsebox thought him quite funny and made practically no fuss about being kept waiting. It was the other man, Pete Duveen, who was getting tired of it, but as he was at the back of the queue he couldn't do much.'

'Four minutes,' Owen said. 'You said you needed a minimum of four. So we did our best.'

'You must have given me nearer five,' I said gratefully. 'Did you hear anything?'

Allie laughed. 'There was so much darned racket going on in here. Owen arguing, me banging away on the typewriter, the traffic outside, pop radio inside, and that heater ... How did you fix that heater?'

We all looked at the calor gas heater which warmed the caravan. It clattered continually like a broken fan.

'Screwed a small swinging flap up at the top here, inside. The rising hot air makes it bang against the casing.'

'Switch it off,' Charlie said. 'It's driving me mad'.

I produced instead a screwdriver and undid the necessary screws. Peace returned to the gas and Charlie said he could see the value of a college education.'

'Pete Duveen knew the other box driver,' Allie said conversationally. 'Seems they're all one big club.'

'See each other every bleeding day at the races,' Bert confirmed. 'Here, that box driver made a bit of a fuss when I said the lad had to go into the caravan too. Like you said, they aren't supposed to leave a racehorse unguarded. So I said I'd bleeding guard it for him. How's that for a laugh? He said he supposed it was okay, as I was the police. I said I'd got instructions that everyone had to go into the census, no exceptions.'

'People will do anything if it looks official enough,' Charlie said, happily nodding.

'Well ...' I put down my much needed cup of coffee and stretched my spine. 'Time to be off, don't you think?'

'Right,' Charlie said. 'All this paper and stuff goes in Owen's van.'

They began moving slowly, the reminiscent smiles still in place, packing the phoney census into carrier bags. Allie came out with me when I left.

'We've had more fun ...' she said. 'You can't imagine.'

I supposed that I felt the same way, now that the flurry was over. I gave her a hug and a kiss and told her to take care of herself, and she said you, too.

'I'll call you this evening,' I promised.

'I wish I was coming with you.'

'We can't leave that here all day,' I said, pointing to the Land-Rover and the trailer.

She smiled. 'I guess not. Charlie says we'd all best be gone before anyone starts asking what we're doing.'

'Charlie is a hundred per cent right.'

I went to Stratford on Avon races.

Drove fast, thinking of the righting of wrongs without benefit of lawyers. Thinking of the ephemeral quality of racehorses and the snail pace of litigation. Thinking that the best years of a hurdler's life could be wasted in stagnation while the courts deliberated to whom he belonged. Wondering what Jody would do when he found out about the morning's work and hoping that I knew him well enough to have guessed right.

When I drew up in the racecourse car park just before the first race, I saw Jody's box standing among a row of others over by the entrance to the stables. The ramp was down and from the general stage of activity I gathered that the horse was still on board.

I sat in my car a hundred yards away, watching through raceglasses. I wondered when the lad would realize he had the wrong horse. I wondered if he would realize at all, because he certainly wouldn't expect to set off with one and arrive with another, and he would quite likely shrug off the first stirring of doubt. He was new in the yard since I had left and with average luck, knowing Jody's rate of turnover, he would be neither experienced nor very bright.

Nothing appeared to be troubling him at that moment. He walked down the ramp carrying a bucket and a bundle of other equipment and went through the gate to the stables. He looked about twenty. Long curly hair. Slight in build. Wearing flashy red trousers. I hoped he was thinking more of his own appearance than his horse's. I put the glasses down and waited.

My eye was caught by a woman in a white coat striding across the car park towards the horse boxes, and it took about five seconds before I realized with a jolt who she was.

Felicity Leeds.

Jody might have taken his knowing eyes to Chepstow, but Felicity had brought hers right here.

I hopped out of the car as if stung and made speed in her direction.

The lad came out of the stable, went up the ramp and shortly reappeared, holding the horse's head. Felicity walked towards him as he began to persuade the horse to disembark.

'Felicity,' I called.

She turned, saw me, looked appalled, threw a quick glance over her shoulder at the descending horse and walked decisively towards me.

When she stopped I looked over her shoulder and said with the sort of puzzlement which takes little to tip into suspicion, 'What horse is that?'

She took another hurried look at the black hind-quarters now disappearing towards the stable and visibly gathered her wits.

'Padellic. Novice hurdler. Not much good.'

'He reminds me of ...' I said slowly.

'First time out, today,' Felicity said hastily. 'Nothing much expected.'

'Oh,' I said, not sounding entirely reassured. 'Are you going into the stables to see him, because I ...'

'No,' she said positively. 'No need. He's perfectly all right.' She gave me a sharp nod and walked briskly away to the main entrance to the course.

Without an accompanying trainer no one could go into the racecourse stables. She knew I would have to contain my curiosity until the horse came out for its race and until then, from her point of view, she was safe.

I, however, didn't want her visiting the stables herself. There was no particular reason why she should, as trainers mostly didn't when the journey from home to course was so short. All the same I thought I might as well fill up so much of her afternoon that she scarcely had time.

I came up with her again outside the weighing room, where she vibrated with tension from her patterned silk headscarf to her high-heeled boots. There were sharp patches of colour on her usually pale cheeks and the eyes which regarded me with angry apprehension were as hot as fever.

'Felicity,' I said. 'Do you know anything about a load of muck that was dumped in my front garden?'

'A what?' The blank look she gave me was not quite blank enough.

I described at some length the component parts and all-over consistency of the obstruction and remarked on their similarity to the discard pile at her own home.

'All muck heaps are alike,' she said. 'You couldn't tell where one particular load came from.'

'All you'd need is a sample for forensic analysis.'

'Did you take one?' she said sharply.

'No,' I admitted.

'Well, then.'

'You and Jody seem the most likely to have done it.'

She looked at me with active dislike. 'Everyone on the racecourse knows what a shit you've been to us. It doesn't surprise me at all that someone has expressed the same opinion in a concrete way.'

'It surprises me very much that anyone except you should bother.'

'I don't intend to talk about it,' she said flatly.

'Well I do,' I said, and did, at some length, repetitively.

The muck heap accounted for a good deal of the afternoon, and Quintus, in a way, for the rest.

Quintus brought his noble brow and empty mind on to the stands and gave Felicity a peck on the cheek, lifting his hat punctiliously. To me he donated what could only be called a scowl.

Felicity fell upon him as if he were a saviour.

'I didn't know you were coming!' She sounded gladder than glad that he had.

'Just thought I would, you know, my dear.'

She drew him away from me out of earshot and began talking to him earnestly. He nodded, smiling, agreeing with her. She talked some more. He nodded benignly and patted her shoulder.

I homed in again like an attacking wasp.

'Oh for God's sake, leave the bloody subject alone,' Felicity exploded.

'What's the fella talking about?' Quintus said.

'A muck heap on his doorstep.'

'Oh,' Quintus said. 'Ah...'

I described it all over again. I was getting quite attached to it, in retrospect.

Quintus was distinctly pleased. Chuckles quivered in his throat and his eyes twinkled with malice.

'Serves you right, what?' he said.

'Do you think so?'

'Shit to a shit,' he said, nodding with satisfaction.

'*What* did you say?'

'Er ... nothing.'

Realization dawned on me with a sense of fitness. 'You did it yourself,' I said with conviction.

'Don't be ridiculous.' He was still vastly amused.

'Lavatory humour would be just your mark.'

'You are insulting.' Less amusement, more arrogance.

'And the police took away the card you left to test it for fingerprints.'

His mouth opened and shut. He looked blank. 'The police?'

'Fellows in blue,' I said.

Felicity said furiously, 'Trust someone like you not to take a joke.'

'I'll take an apology,' I said mildly. 'In writing.'

Their objections, their grudging admissions and the eventual drafting of the apology took care of a lot of time. Quintus had hired a tip-up truck for his delivery and had required his gardener to do the actual work. Jody and Felicity had generously contributed the load. Quintus had supervised its disposal and written his message.

He also, in his own hand and with bravado-ish flourishes, wrote the apology. I thanked him courteously and told him I would frame it, which didn't please him in the least.

By that time the fifth race was over and it was time to saddle the horses for the sixth.

Felicity, as the trainer's wife, was the natural person to supervise the saddling of their runner, and I knew that if she did she would know she had the wrong horse.

On the other hand if she did the saddling she couldn't stop me, as a member of the public, taking a very close look, and from her point of view that was a risk she didn't want to take.

She solved her dilemma by getting Quintus to see to the saddling.

She herself, with a superhuman effort, laid her hand on my arm in a conciliatory gesture and said, 'All right. Let bygones be bygones. Let's go and have a drink.'

'Sure,' I said, expressing just the right amount of surprise and agreement. 'Of course, if you'd like.'

So we went off to the bar where I bought her a large gin and tonic and myself a scotch and water, and we stood talking about nothing much while both busy with private thoughts. She was trembling slightly from the force of hers, and I too had trouble preventing mine from showing. There we were, both trying our darnedest to keep the other away from the horse, she because she thought it was Energise and I because I knew it wasn't. I could feel the irony breaking out in wrinkles round my eyes.

Felicity dawdled so long over her second drink that the horses were already leaving the parade ring and going out to the course when we finally made our way back to the heart of things. Quintus had understudied splendidly and was to be seen giving a parting slap to the horse's rump. Felicity let her breath out in a sigh and dropped most of the pretence of being nice to me. When she left me abruptly to rejoin Quintus for the race, I made no move to stop her.

The horse put up a good show, considering.

There were twenty-two runners, none of them more than moderate, and they delivered the sort of performance Energise would have left in the next parish. His substitute was running in his own class and finished undisgraced in sixth place, better than I would have expected. The crowd briefly cheered the winning favourite, and I thought it time to melt prudently and inconspicuously away.

I had gone to Stratford with more hope than certainty that the horse would actually run without the exchange being noticed. I have been prepared to do anything I reasonably could to achieve it, in order to give Ganser Mays the nasty shock of losing every penny he'd laid out on his squeezer.

What I hadn't actually bargained for was the effect the lost race would have on Felicity.

I saw her afterwards, though I hadn't meant to, when she went to meet her returning horse. The jockey, a well-known rider who had doubtless been told to win, was looking strained enough, but Felicity seemed on the point of collapse.

Her face was a frightening white, her whole body shook and her eyes looked as blank as marbles.

If I had ever wanted any personal revenge, I had it then, but I drove soberly away from the racecourse feeling sorry for her.

Chapter Fourteen

Rupert Ramsey met me with a stony face, not at all the expression one would normally expect from a successful trainer who had invited one of his owners to dinner.

'I'm glad you're early,' he said forbiddingly. 'Please come into the office.'

I followed him across the hall into the familiar room which was warm with a living log fire. He made no move to offer me a drink and I thought I might as well save him some trouble.

'You're going to tell me,' I said, 'that the horse which left here this morning is not the one which returned.'

He raised his eyebrows. 'So you don't deny it?'

'Of course not.' I smiled. 'I wouldn't have thought all that much of you if you hadn't noticed.'

'The lad noticed. Donny. He told the head lad, and the head lad told me, and I went to see for myself. And what I want is an explanation.'

'And it had better be good,' I added, imitating his schoolmasterly tone. He showed no amusement.

'This is no joke.'

'Maybe not. But it's no crime, either. If you'll calm down a fraction, I'll explain.'

'You have brought me a ringer. No trainer of any sense is going to stand for that.' His anger was cold and deep.

I said, 'The horse you thought was Energise was the ringer. And I didn't send him here, Jody did. The horse you have been trying to train for the Champion Hurdle and which left here this morning, is a fairly useless novice called Padellic.'

'I don't believe it.'

'As Energise,' I pointed out, 'you have found him unbelievably disappointing.'

'Well ...' The first shade of doubt crept into his voice.

'When I discovered the wrong horse had been sent here, I asked you expressly not to run him in any races, because I certainly did not want you to be involved in running a ringer, nor myself for that matter.

'But if you knew ... why on earth didn't you immediately tell Jody he had made a mistake?'

'He didn't,' I said simply. 'He sent the wrong one on purpose.'

He walked twice around the room in silence and then still without a word poured us each a drink.

'Right,' he said, handing me a glass. 'Pray continue.'

I continued for quite a long while. He gestured to me to sit down and sat opposite me himself, he listened attentively with a serious face.

'And this security firm ...' he said at the end. 'Are you expecting Jody to try to get Energise back?'

I nodded. 'He's an extremely determined man. I made the mistake once of underestimating his vigour and his speed, and that's what lost me Energise in the first place. I think when he got home from Chepstow and heard what Felicity and the box driver and the lad had to say, he would have been violently angry and would decide to act at once. He's not the sort to spend a day or so thinking about it. He'll come tonight. I think and hope he will come tonight.'

'He will be sure Energise is here?'

'He certainly should be,' I said. 'He'll ask his box driver about the journey and his box driver will tell him about the census. Jody will question closely and find that Pete Duveen was there too. Jody will, I think, telephone to ask Pete Duveen if he saw anything unusual and Pete, who has nothing to hide, will tell him he brought a black horse from here. He'll tell him he took a black horse home again. And he'll tell him I was there at the census point. I didn't ask him not to tell and I am sure he will, because of his frank and open nature.'

Rupert's lips twitched into the first hint of a smile. He straightened it out immediately. 'I don't really approve of what you've done.'

'Broken no laws,' I said neutrally, neglecting to mention the shadowy area of Bert's police-impression uniform.

'Perhaps not.' He thought it over. 'And the security firm is here both to prevent the theft of Energise and to catch Jody red-handed?'

'Exactly so.'

'I saw them in the yard this evening. Two men. They said they were expecting instructions from you when you arrived, though frankly at that point I was so angry with you that I was paying little attention.'

'I talked to them on my way in,' I agreed. 'One will patrol the yard at regular intervals and the other is going to sit outside the horse's box. I told them both to allow themselves to be enticed from their posts by any diversion.'

'To *allow*?'

'Of course. You have to give the mouse a clear view of the cheese.'

'Good God.'

'And I wondered ... whether you would consider staying handy, to act as a witness if Jody should come a-robbing.'

It seemed to strike him for the first time that he too was Jody's victim. He began to look almost as Charlie had done, and certainly as Bert had done, as if he found countermeasures attractive. The tugging smile reappeared.

'It depends of course on what time Jody comes ... if he comes at all ... but two of my guests tonight would be the best independent witnesses you could get. A lady magistrate and the local vicar.'

'Will they stay late?' I asked.

'We can try.' He thought for a bit. 'What about the police?'

'How quickly can they get here if called?'

'Um . . . Ten minutes. Quarter of an hour.'

'That should be all right.'

He nodded. A bell rang distantly in the house, signalling the arrival of more guests. He stood up, paused a moment, frowned and said, 'If the guard is to allow himself to be decoyed away, why plant him outside the horse's door in the first place?'

I smiled. 'How else is Jody to know which box to rob?'

The dinner party seemed endless, though I couldn't afterwards remember a word or a mouthful. There were eight at table, all better value than myself, and the vicar particularly shone because of his brilliance as a mimic. I half heard the string of imitated voices and saw everyone else falling about with hysterics and could think only of my men outside in the winter night and of the marauder I hoped to entice.

To groans from his audience the vicar played Cinderella at midnight and took himself off to shape up to Sunday, and three others shortly followed. Rupert pressed the last two to say for nightcaps: the lady magistrate and her husband, a quiet young colonel with an active career and a bottomless capacity for port. He settled happily enough at the sight of a fresh decanter, and she with mock resignation continued a mild flirtation with Rupert.

The wheels inside my head whirred with the same doubts as in the morning. Suppose I had been wrong. Suppose he did come, but came unseen, and managed to steal the horse unseen, and managed to steal the horse successfully.

Well . . . I'd planned for that, too. I checked for the hundredth time through the ifs. I tried to imagine what I hadn't already imagined, see what I hadn't seen, prepare for the unprepared. Rupert cast an amused glance or two at my abstracted expression and made no attempt to break it down.

The door bell rang sharply, three long insistent pushes.

I stood up faster than good manners.

'Go on,' Rupert said indulgently. 'We'll be right behind you, if you need us.'

I nodded and departed, and crossed the hall to open the front door. My man in a grey flannel suit stood outside, looking worried and holding a torch.

'What is it?'

'I'm not sure. The other two are patrolling the yard and I haven't seen them for some time. And I think we have visitors, but they haven't come in a horsebox.'

'Did you see them? The visitors?'

'No. Only their car. Hidden off the road in a patch of wild rhododendrons. At least . . . there is a car there which wasn't there half an hour ago. What do you think?'

'Better take a look,' I said.

He nodded. I left the door of Rupert's house ajar and we walked together towards the main gate. Just inside it stood the van which had brought the security guards, and outside, less than fifty yards along the road, we came to the car in the bushes, dimly seen even by torchlight.

'It isn't a car I recognize,' I said. 'Suppose it's just a couple of lovers?'

'They'd be inside it on a night like this, not out snogging in the freezing undergrowth.'

'You're right.'

'Let's take the rotor arm, to make sure.'

We lifted the bonnet and carefully removed the essential piece of electrics. Then, shining the torch as little as possible and going on grass whenever there was a choice, we hurried back towards the stable. The night was windy enough to swallow small sounds, dark enough to lost contact at five paces and cold enough to do structural damage to brass monkeys.

At the entrance to the yard we stopped to look and listen.

No lights. The dark heavy bulk of buildings was more sensed than seen against the heavily overcast sky.

No sounds except our own breath and the greater lungs of the wind. No sign of our other two guards.

'What now?'

'We'll go and check the horse,' I said.

We went into the main yard and skirted round its edges, which were paved with quieter concrete. The centre was an expanse of crunchy gravel, a giveaway even for cats.

Box fourteen had a chair outside it. A wooden kitchen chair planted prosaically with its back to the stable wall. No guard sat on it.

Quietly I slid back the bolts on the top half of the door and looked inside. There was a soft movement and the sound of a hoof rustling the straw. A second's flash of torch showed the superb black shape patiently standing half-asleep in the dark, drowsing away the equine night.

I shut the door and made faint grating noises with the bolt.

'He's fine,' I said. 'Let's see if we can find the others.'

He nodded. We finished the circuit of the main yard and started along the various branches, moving with caution and trying not to use the torch. I couldn't stop the weird feeling growing that we were not the only couple groping about in the dark. I saw substance in shadows and reached out fearfully to touch objects which were not there, but only darker patches in the pervading black. We spent five or ten minutes feeling our way, listening, taking a few steps, listening, going on. We completed the tour of the outlying rows of boxes, and saw and heard nothing.

'This is no good,' I said quietly. 'There isn't a sign of them, and has it occurred to you that they are hiding from us, thinking we are the intruders?'

'Just beginning to wonder.'

'Let's go back to the main yard.'

We turned and retraced our steps, taking this time a short cut through a narrow alleyway between two sections of boxes. I was in front, so it was I who practically tripped over the huddled bundle on the ground.

I switched on the torch. Saw the neat navy uniform and the blood glistening red on the forehead. Saw the shut eyes and the lax limbs of the man who should have been sitting on the empty kitchen chair.

'Oh God,' I said desperately, and thought I would never ever forgive myself. I knelt beside him and fumbled for his pulse.

'He's alive,' said my friend in the grey flannel suit. He sounded reassuring and confident. 'Look at him breathing. He'll be all right, you'll see.'

All I could see was a man who was injured because I'd stationed him in the path of danger. I'll get a doctor,' I said, standing up.

'What about the horse?'

'Damn the horse. This is more important.'

'I'll stay here with him till you get back.'

I nodded and set off anxiously towards the house, shining the torch now without reservations. If permanent harm came to that man because of me . . .

I ran.

Burst in through Rupert's front door and found him standing there in the hall talking to the lady magistrate and the colonel, who were apparently just about to leave. She was pulling a cape around her shoulders and Rupert was holding the colonel's coat. They turned and stared at me like a frozen tableau.

'My guard's been attacked. Knocked out,' I said. 'Could you get him a doctor?'

'Sure,' Rupert said calmly. 'Who attacked him?'

'I didn't see.'

'Job for the police?'

'Yes, please.'

He turned to the telephone, dialling briskly. 'What about the horse?'

'They didn't come in a horsebox.'

We both digested implications while he got the rescue services on the move. The colonel and the magistrate stood immobile in the hall with their mouths half open and Rupert, putting down the telephone, gave them an authoritative glance.

'Come out into the yard with us, will you?' he said. 'Just in case we need witnesses?'

They weren't trained to disappear rapidly at the thought. When Rupert hurried out of the door with me at his heels they followed more slowly after.

Everything still looked entirely quiet outside.

'He's in a sort of alley between two blocks of boxes,' I said.

'I know where you mean,' Rupert nodded. 'But first we'll just check on Energise.'

'Later.'

'No. Now. Why bash the guard if they weren't after the horse?'

He made straight for the main yard, switched on all six external lights, and set off across the brightly illuminated gravel.

The effect was like a flourish of trumpets. Noise, light and movement filled the space where silence and dark had been total.

Both halves of the door of box fourteen swung open about a foot, and two dark figures catapulted through the gap.

'Catch them!' Rupert shouted.

There was only one way out of the yard, the broad entrance through which we had come. The two figures ran in curving paths towards the exit, one to one side of Rupert and me, one to the other.

Rupert rushed to intercept the smaller who was suddenly, as he turned his head to the light, recognizable as Jody.

I ran for the larger. Stretched out. Touched him.

He swung a heavy arm and threw out a hip and I literally bounced off him, stumbling and falling.

The muscles were rock hard. The sunglasses glittered.

The joker was ripping through the pack.

Jody and Rupert rolled on the gravel, one clutching, one punching, both swearing. I tried again at Muscles with the same useless results. He seemed to hesitate over going to Jody's help, which was how I'd come to be able to reach him a second time, but finally decided on flight. By the time I was again staggering to my feet he was on his way to the exits with the throttle wide open.

A large figure in navy blue hurtled straight at him from the opposite direction and brought him down with a diving hug round the knees. The sunglasses flew off in a shiny arc and the two large figures lay in a writhing entwined mass, the blue uniform uppermost and holding his own. I went to his help and sat on Muscles' ankles, crushing his feet sideways with no compunction at all. He screeched with pain and stopped struggling, but I fear I didn't immediately stand up.

Jody wrenched himself free from Rupert and ran past me. The colonel, who with his lady had been watching the proceedings with astonishment, decided it was time for some soldierly action and elegantly stuck out his foot.

Jody tripped over and fell sprawling. The colonel put more energy into it, leant down and took hold of the collar of Jody's coat. Rupert, rallying, came to his aid, and between them they too more or less sat on Jody, pinning him to the ground.

'What now?' Rupert panted.

'Wait for the police,' I said succinctly.

Muscles and Jody both heaved about a good deal at this plan but didn't succeed in freeing themselves. Muscles complained that I'd broken his ankle. Jody, under the colonel's professional ministrations, seemed to have difficulty saying anything at all. The colonel was in fact so singlehandedly efficient that Rupert stood up and dusted himself down and looked at me speculatively.

I jerked my head in the direction of box fourteen, where the door was still stood half open, showing only darkness within. He nodded slowly and went that way. Switched on the light. Stepped inside. He came back with a face of stone and three bitter words.

'Energise is dead.'

Chapter Fifteen

Rupert fetched some rope with which he ignominiously tied Jody's hands behind his back before he and the colonel let him get up, and the colonel held the free end of rope so that Jody was to all intents on a lead. Once up, Jody aimed a kick at the colonel and Rupert told him to stop unless he wanted his ankles tied as well.

Rupert and my man in blue uniform did a repeat job on Muscles, whose ankles were not in kicking shape and whose language raised eyebrows even on the lady magistrate, who had heard more than most.

The reason for Muscles' ubiquitous sunglasses was at once apparent, now that one could see his face. He stood glowering like a bull, seething with impotent rage, hopping on one foot and pulling against the tethering rope which led back from his wrists to my man in blue. His eyelids, especially the lower, were grossly distorted, and even in the outside lighting looked bright pink with inflammation. One could pity his plight, which was clearly horrid.

'I know you,' Rupert said suddenly, looking at him closely. 'What's the matter with your eyes?'

'Mind your own effing business.'

'Macrahinish. That's what your name is. Macrahinish.'

Muscles didn't comment. Rupert turned to me. 'Don't you know him? Perhaps he was before your time. He's a vet. A struck-off vet. Struck off the vets' register and warned off the racecourse. And absolutely not allowed to set foot in a racing stable.'

Muscles-Macrahinish delivered himself of an unflattering opinion of racing in general and Rupert in particular.

Rupert said, 'He was convicted of doping and fraud and served a term in jail. He ran a big doping ring and supplied all the drugs. He looks older and there's something wrong with his eyes, but that's who this is, all right. Macrahinish.'

I turned away from the group and walked over to the brightly lit loosebox. Swung the door wide. Looked inside.

My beautiful black horse lay flat on his side, legs straight, head flaccid on the straw. The liquid eye was dull and opaque, mocking the sheen which still lay on his coat, and he still had pieces of unchewed hay half in and half out of his mouth. There was no blood, and no visible wound. I went in and squatted beside him, and patted him sadly with anger and regret.

Jody and Macrahinish had been unwillingly propelled in my wake. I looked up to find them inside the box, with Rupert, the colonel, his wife, and the man in blue effectively blocking the doorway behind them.

'How did you kill him?' I asked, the bitterness apparent in my voice.

Macrahinish's reply did not contain the relevant information.

I straightened up and in doing so caught sight of a flat brown attaché case half hidden in the straw by the horse's tail. I bent down again and picked it up. The sight of it brought a sound and a squirm from Macrahinish, and he began to swear in earnest when I balanced it on the manger and unfastened the clips.

The case contained regular veterinarian equipment, neatly stowed in compartments. I touched only one thing, lifting it carefully out.

A plastic bag containing a clear liquid. A bag plainly proclaiming the contents to be sterile saline solution.

I held it out towards Jody and said, 'You dripped alcohol straight into my veins.'

'You were unconscious,' he said disbelievingly.

'Shut up, you stupid fool,' Macrahinish screamed at him.

I smiled. 'Not all the time. I remember nearly everything about that night.'

'He said he didn't,' Jody said defensively to Macrahinish and was rewarded by a look from the swollen eyes which would have made a nonstarter of Medusa.

'I went to see if you still had Energise,' I said. 'And I found you had.'

'You don't know one horse from another,' he sneered. 'You're just a mug. A blind greedy mug.'

'So are you,' I said. 'The horse you've killed is not Energise.'

'It is!'

'Shut up,' screamed Macrahinish in fury. 'Keep your stupid sodding mouth shut.'

'No,' I said to Jody. 'The horse you've killed is an American horse called Black Fire.'

Jody looked wildly down at the quiet body.

'It damn well is Energise,' he insisted. 'I'd know him anywhere.'

'Jesus,' Macrahinish shouted. 'I'll cut your tongue out.'

Rupert said doubtfully to me, 'Are you sure it's not Energise?'

'Positive.'

'He's just saying it to spite me,' said Jody furiously. 'I know it's Energise. See that tiny bald patch on his shoulder?' That's Energise.'

Macrahinish, beyond speech, tried to attack him, tied hands and dicky ankle notwithstanding. Jody gave him a vague look, concentrating only on the horse.

'You are saying,' Rupert suggested, 'that you came to kill Energise and that you've done it.'

'Yes,' said Jody triumphantly.

The word hung in the air, vibrating. No one said anything. Jody looked round at each watching face, at first with defiant angry pride, then with the first creeping of doubt, and finally with the realization of what Macrahinish had been trying to tell him, that he should never have been drawn into admitting anything. The fire visibly died into glum and chilly embers.

'I didn't kill him,' he said sullenly. 'Macrahinish did. I didn't want to kill him at all, but Macrahinish insisted.'

A police car arrived with two young and persistent constables who seemed to find nothing particularly odd in being called to the murder of a horse.

They wrote in their notebooks that five witnesses, including a magistrate, had heard Jody Leeds admit that he and a disbarred veterinary surgeon had broken into a racing stable after midnight with the intention of putting to death one of the horses. They noted that a horse was dead. Cause of death, unknown until an autopsy could be arranged.

Hard on their heels came Rupert's doctor, and elderly man with a paternal manner. Yawning but uncomplaining, he accompanied me to find my security guard, who to my great relief was sitting on the ground with his head in his hands, awake and groaning healthily. We took him into Rupert's office, where the doctor stuck a plaster on the dried wound on his forehead, gave him some tablets and told him to lay off work for a couple of days. He smiled weakly and said it depended if his boss would let him

One of the young policemen asked if he'd seen who had hit him.

'Big man with sunglasses. He was creeping along behind me, holding a ruddy great chunk of wood. I heard something . . . I turned and shone my torch, and there he was. He swung at my head. Gave me a right crack, he did. Next thing I knew, I was lying on the ground.'

Reassured by his revival I went outside again to see what was happening.

The magistrate and the colonel seemed to have gone home, and Rupert was down in the yard talking to some of his own stable staff who had been woken by the noise.

Macrahinish was hopping about on one leg, accusing me of having broken the other and swearing he'd have me prosecuted for using undue force to protect my property. The elderly doctor phlegmatically examined the limb in question and said that in his opinion it was a sprain.

The police had rashly untied the Macrahinish wrists and were obviously relying on the leg injury to prevent escape. At the milder word sprain they produced handcuffs and invited Macrahinish to stick out his arms out. He refused and resisted and because they, as I had done, underestimated both his strength and his violence, it took a hectic few minutes for them to make him secure.

'Resisting arrest,' they panted, writing it in the notebooks. 'Attacking police officers in the course of their duty.'

Macrahinish's sunglasses lay on the gravel in the main yard, where he had lost them in the first tackle. I walked down to where they shone in the light and picked the up. Then I took them slowly back to him and put them in his handcuffed hands.

He stared at me through the raw-looking eyelids. He said nothing. He put the sunglasses on, and his fingers were trembling.

'Ectropion,' said the doctor, as I walked away.

'What?' I said.

'The condition of his eyes. Ectropion. Poor fellow.'

The police made no mistakes with Jody. He sat beside Macrahinish in the back of the police car with handcuffs on his wrists and the Arctic in his face. When the police went to close the doors ready to leave, he leant forwards and spoke to me through rigid lips.

'You *shit*,' he said.

Rupert invited the rest of my security firm indoors for warmth and coffee and in his office I introduced them to him.

'My friend in grey flannel,' I said, 'is Charlie Canfield. My big man in blue is Bert Huggerneck. My injured friend with the dried blood on his face is Owen Idris.'

Rupert shook hands with each and they grinned at him. He sensed immediately that there was more in their smiles than he would have expected, and he turned his enquiring gaze on me.

'Which firm do they come from?' he asked.

'Charlie's a merchant banker, Bert's a bookies' clerk, and Owen helps in my workshop.'

Charlie chuckled and said in his fruitiest Eton, 'We also run a nice line in a census, if you should ever need one.'

Rupert shook his head helplessly and fetched the brandy and glasses from a cupboard.

'If I ask questions,' he said, pouring lavishly, 'will you answer them?'

'If we can,' I said.

'That dead horse in the stable. Is it Energise?'

'No. Like I said, it's a horse I bought in the States called Black Fire.'

'But the bald patch ... Jody was so certain.'

'I did that bald patch with a razor blade. The horses were extraordinarily alike, apart from that. Especially at night, because of being black. But there's one certain way of identifying Black Fire. He has his American racing number tattooed inside his lip.'

'Why did you bring him here?'

'I didn't want to risk the real Energise. Before I saw Black Fire in America I couldn't see how to entice Jody safely. Afterwards, it was easier.'

'But I didn't get the impression earlier this evening,' Rupert said pensively, 'that you expected them to kill the horse.'

'No ... I didn't know about Macrahinish. I mean, I didn't know he was a vet, or that he could overrule Jody. I expected Jody just to try to steal the horse and I wanted to catch him in the act. Catch him physically committing a positive criminal act which he couldn't possibly explain away. I wanted to force the racing authorities, more than the police, to see that Jody was not the innocent little underdog they believed.'

Rupert thought it over. 'Why didn't you think he would kill him?'

'Well ... it did cross my mind, but on balance I thought it unlikely, because Energise is such a good horse. I thought Jody would want to hide him away somewhere so that he could make a profit on him later, even if he sold him as a point-to-pointer. Energise represents money, and Jody has never missed a trick in that direction.'

'But Macrahinish wanted him dead,' Rupert said.

I sighed. 'I suppose he thought it safer.'

Rupert smiled. 'You had put them in a terrible fix. They couldn't risk you beeing satisfied with getting your horse back. They couldn't be sure you couldn't somehow prove they had stolen it originally. But if you no longer had it, you would have found it almost impossible to make allegations stick.'

'That's right,' Charlie agreed. 'That's exactly what Steven thought.'

'Also,' I said, 'Jody wouldn't have been able to bear the thought of me getting the better of him. Apart from safety and profit, he would have taken Energise back simply for revenge.'

'You know what?' Charlie said, 'it's my guess that he probably put his entire bank balance on Padellic at Stratford, thinking it was Energise, and when Padellic turned up sixth he lost the lot. And that in itself is a tidy little motive for revenge.'

'Here,' Bert said appreciatively. 'I wonder how much Ganser bleeding Mays is down the drain for! Makes you bleeding laugh, don't it? There they all were, thinking they were backing a ringer, and we'd gone and put the real Padellic back where he belonged.'

'Trained by Rupert,' I murmured, 'to do his best.'

Rupert looked at us one by one and shook his head. 'You're a lot of rogues.'

We drank our brandy and didn't dispute it.

'Where did the American horse come from?' Rupert asked.

'Miami.'

'No ... This morning.'

'A quiet little stable in the country,' I said. 'We had him brought to the census point ...'

'And you should have bleeding seen him,' Bert interrupted gleefully. 'Our ca*pit*alist here, I mean. Whizzing those three horses in and out of horseboxes faster than the three card trick.'

'I must say,' Rupert said thoughtfully, 'that I've wondered just how he managed it.'

'He took bleeding Energise out of Jody's box and put it in the empty stall of the trailer which brought Black Fire. Then he put Padellic where Energise had been, in Jody's box. Then he put bleeding Black Fire where Padellic had been, in your box, that is. All three of them buzzing in a circle like a bleeding merry-go-round.'

Charlie said, smiling, 'All change at the census. Padellic started from here and went on to Stratford. Black Fire started from the country and came here. And Energise started from Jody's . . .' He stopped.

'And went to where?' Rupert asked.

I shook my head. 'He's safe, I promise you.' Safe with Allie at Hantsford Manor, with Miss Johnston and Mrs Fairchild-Smith. 'We'll leave him where he is for a week or two.'

'Yeah,' Bert said, explaining. 'Because, see, we've had Jody Leeds and that redeyed hunk of muscle of his exploding all over us with temper-temper, but what about that other one? What about that other one we've kicked right where it hurts, eh? We don't want to risk Energise getting the chop after all from Mr Squeezer bleeding Ganser down the bleeding drain Mays.'

Chapter Sixteen

Owen and I went back to London. I drove, with him sitting beside me fitfully dozing and pretending in between times that he didn't have a headache.

'Don't be silly,' I said. 'I know what it feels like. You've got a proper thumper and notwithstanding that snide crack to the doctor about your boss not letting you take a couple of days off, that's what you're going to get.'

He smiled.

'I'm sorry about your head,' I said.

'I know.'

'How?'

'Charlie said.'

I glanced across at him. His face in the glow from the dashboard looked peaceful and contented. 'It's been,' he said drowsily, 'a humdinger of a day.'

It was four in the morning when we reached the house and pulled into the driveway. He woke up slowly and shivered, his eyes fuzzy with fatigue.

'You're sleeping in my bed,' I said, 'and I'm taking the sofa.' He opened his mouth. 'Don't argue,' I added.

'All right.'

I locked the car and we walked to the front door, and that's where things went wrong.

The front door was not properly shut. Owen was too sleepy to realize at once, but my heart dropped to pavement level the instant I saw it.

Burglars, I thought dumbly. Today of all days.

I pushed the door open. Everything was quiet. There was little furniture in the hall and nothing looked disturbed. Upstairs, though, it would be like a blizzard...

'What is it?' said Owen, realizing that something was wrong.

'The workshop door,' I said, pointing.

'Oh no!'

That too was ajar, and there was no question of the intruder having used a key. The whole lock area was split, the raw wood showing in jagged layers up and down the jamb.

We walked along the carpeted passage, pushed the door wider, and took one step through on to concrete.

One step, and stopped dead.

The workshop was an area of complete devastation.

All the lights were on. All the cupboard doors and drawers were open, and everything which should have been in them was out and scattered and smashed. The work benches were overturned and the racks of tools were torn from their moorings and great chunks of plaster had been gouged out of the walls.

All my designs and drawings had been ripped to pieces. All the prototype toys seemed to have been stamped on.

Tins of oil and grease had been opened, and the contents emptied on to the mess, and the paint I'd used on the census notices was splashed on everything the oil had missed.

The machines themselves...

I swallowed. I was never going to make anything else on those machines. Not ever again.

Not burglars, I thought aridly.

Spite.

I felt too stunned to speak and I imagine it was the same with Owen because for an appreciable time we both just stood there, immobile and silent. The mess before us screamed out its message of viciousness and evil, and the intensity of the hate which had committed such havoc made me feel literally sick.

On feet which seemed disconnected from my legs I took a couple of steps forward.

There was a flicker of movement on the edge of my vision away behind the half-open door. I spun on my toe with every primeval instinct raising hairs in instant alarm, and what I saw allowed no reassurance whatsoever.

Ganser Mays stood there, waiting like a hawk. The long nose seemed a sharp beak, and his eyes behind the metal-rimmed spectacles glittered with mania. He was positioning his arms for a scything downward swing, which was the movement I'd seen, and in his hands he held a heavy long-handled axe.

I leapt sideways a thousandth of a second before the killing edge swept through the place where I'd been standing.

'Get help,' I shouted breathlessly to Owen. 'Get out and get help.'

I had a blurred impression of his strained face, mouth open, eyes huge, dried blood still dark on his cheek. For an instant he didn't move and I thought he wouldn't go, but when I next caught a glimpse of the doorway, it was empty.

Whether or not he'd been actively lying in wait for me, there was no doubt that now that I was there Ganser Mays was trying to do to me what he'd already done to my possessions. I learned a good deal from him in the next few minutes. I learned about mental terror. Learned about extreme physical fear. Learned that it was no fun at all facing unarmed and untrained a man with the will and the weapon for murder.

What was more, it was my own axe.

We played an obscene sort of hide and seek round the wrecked machines. It only needed one of the ferocious chops to connect, and I would be without arm or leg if not without life. He slashed whenever he could get near enough, and I hadn't enough faith in my speed or strength to try to tackle him within slicing range. I dodged always and precariously just out of total disaster, circling the ruined lathe ... the milling machine ... the hacksaw ... back to the lathe ... putting the precious bulks of metal between me and death.

Up and down the room, again and again.

There was never a rigid line between sense and insanity and maybe by some definitions Ganser Mays was sane. Certainly in all that obsessed destructive fury he was aware enough that I might escape through the door. From the moment I'd first stepped past him into the workshop, he gave me no chance to reach safety that way.

There were tools scattered on the floor from the torn-down racks, but they were mostly small and in any case not round the machines but on the opposite side of the workshop. I could leave the shelter of the row of machines and cross open space to arm myself ... but nothing compared in weight or usefulness with that axe, and chisels and saws and drill bits weren't worth the danger of exposure.

If Owen came back with help, maybe I could last out...

Shortage of breath ... I was averagely fit, but no athlete ... couldn't pull in enough oxygen for failing muscles ... felt fatal weaknesses slowing my movements ... knew I couldn't afford to slip on the oil or stumble over the bolts mooring the base plates to the floor or leave my hands holding on to anything for more than a second for fear of severed fingers.

He seemed tireless, both in body and intent. I kept my attention more on the axe than his face, but the fractional views I caught of his fixed, fanatical and curiously rigid expression gave no room for hope that he would stop before he had achieved his object. Trying to reason with him would have been like arguing with an avalanche. I didn't even try.

Breath sawed through my throat. Owen ... why didn't he bloody well hurry . . . if he didn't hurry he might as well come back tomorrow for all the good it would do me . . .

The axe crashed down so close to my shoulder that I shuddered from imagination and began to despair. He was going to kill me. I was going to feel the bite of that heavy steel . . . to know the agony and see the blood spurt . . . to be chopped and smashed like everything else.

I was up at one end, where the electric motor which worked all the machines was located. He was four feet away, swinging, looking merciless and savage. I was shaking, panting and still trying frantically to escape, and it was more to distract him for a precious second than from any devious plan that I took the time to kick the main switch from off to on.

The engine hummed and activated the main belt, which turned the big wheel near the ceiling and rotated the long shaft down the workshop. All the belts to the machines began slapping as usual, except that this time half of them had been cut right through and the free ends flapped in the air like streamers.

It took his eye off me for only a blink. I circled the electric motor which was much smaller than the machines and not good cover, and he brought his head back towards me with a snap.

He saw that I was exposed. A flash of triumph crossed his pale sweating face. He whipped the axe back and high and struck at me with all his strength.

I jumped sideways in desperation and slipped and fell, and thought as I went down that this was it . . . this was the end . . . he would be on me before I could get up.

I half saw the axe go up again. I lunged out with one foot in a desperate kick at his ankles. Connected. Threw him a fraction off balance. Only a matter of a few inches: and it didn't affect the weight of his downward swing, but only its direction. Instead of burying itself in me, the blade sank into the main belt driving the machines, and for one fatal moment Ganser Mays hung on to the shaft. Whether he thought I had somehow grasped the axe and was trying to tug it away from him, heaven knows. In any case he gripped tight, and the whirling belt swept him off his feet.

The belt moved at about ten feet a second. It took one second for Ganser Mays to reach the big wheel above. I dare say he let go of the shaft at about that point, but the wheel caught him and crushed him in the small space between itself and the ceiling.

He screamed . . . a short loud cry of extremity, chokingly cut off.

The wheel inexorably whirled him through and out the other side. It would have taken more than a soft human body to stop a motor which drove machine tools.

He fell from the high point and thumped sickeningly on to the concrete not far from where I was still scrambling to get up. It had happened at such immense speed that he had been up to the ceiling and down again before I could find my feet.

The axe had been dislodged and had fallen separately beside him. Near his hand, as if all he had to do was stretch out six inches and he would be back in business.

Mr Ganser Mays was never going to be back in business. I stood looking down at him while the engine hummed and the big killing wheel rotated impersonally as usual, and the remaining belts to the machines slapped quietly as they always did.

There was little blood. His face was white. The spectacles had gone and the eyes were half open. The sharp nose was angled grotesquely sideways. The neck was bent at an impossible angle; and whatever else had broken, that was enough.

I stood there for a while panting for breath and sweating and trembling from fatigue and the screwed tension of past fear. Then whatever strength I had left drained abruptly away and I sat on the floor beside the electric motor and drooped an arm over it for support like a wilted lily. Beyond thought. Beyond feeling. Just dumbly and excruciatingly exhausted.

It was the moment that Owen returned. The help he'd brought wore authentic navy blue uniform and a real black and white checkered band on his cap. He took a long slow look and summoned reinforcements.

Hours later, when they had all gone, I went back downstairs to the workshop.

Upstairs nothing, miraculously, had been touched. Either our return had interrupted the programme before it had got that far, or the workshop had been the only intended target. In any case my first sight of the peaceful sitting-room had been a flooding relief.

Owen and I had flopped weakly around in armchairs while the routine police work ebbed and flowed, and after lengthy question-and-answer sessions and the departure of the late Mr Mays we had found ourselves finally alone.

It was already Sunday morning. The sun, with no sense of fitness, was brightly shining. Regent's Park sparkled with frost and the puddles were glazed with ice.

'Go to bed,' I said to Owen.

He shook his head. 'Think I'll go home.'

'Come back when you're ready.'

He smiled. 'Tomorrow,' he said. 'For a spot of sweeping up.'

When he'd gone I wandered aimlessly about, collecting coffee cups and emptying ashtrays and thinking disconnected thoughts. I felt both too tired and too unsettled for sleep, and it was then that I found myself going back to the devastation in the workshop.

The spirit of the dead man had gone. The place no longer vibrated with violent hate. In the morning light it looked a cold and sordid shambles, squalid debris of a spent orgy.

I walked slowly down the room, stirring things with my toe. The work of twenty years lay there in little pieces. Designs torn like confetti. Toys crushed flat. Nothing could be mended or saved.

I suppose I could get duplicates at least of the design drawings if I tried, because copies were lodged in the patents' office. But the originals, and all the hand-made prototype toys, were gone for good.

I came across the remains of the merry-go-round which I had made when I was fifteen. The first Rola; the beginning of everything. I squatted down and stirred the pieces, remembering that distant decisive summer when I'd spent day after day in my uncle's workshop with ideas gushing like newly-drilled oil out of a brain that was half child, half man.

I picked up one of the little horses. The blue one, with a white mane and tail. The one I'd made last of the six.

The golden barley-sugar rod which had connected it to the revolving roof was snapped off jaggedly an inch above the horse's back. One of the front legs was missing, and one of the ears.

I turned it over regretfully in my hands and looked disconsolately around at the mess. Poor little toys. Poor beautiful little toys, broken and gone.

It had cost me a good deal, one way and another, to get Energise back.

Turn the handle, Charlie had said, and all the little toys would revolve on their spindles and do what they should. But people weren't toys, and Jody and Macrahinish and Ganser Mays had jumped violently off their spindles and stripped the game out of control.

If I hadn't decided to take justice into my own hands I wouldn't have been kicked or convicted of drunkenness. I would have saved myself the price of Black Fire and a host of other expenses. I wouldn't have put Owen at risk as a guard, and I wouldn't have felt responsible for the ruin of Jody and Felicity, the probable return to jail of Macrahinish, and the death of Ganser Mays.

Pointless to say that I hadn't meant them so much harm, or that their own violence had brought about their own doom. It was I who had given them the first push.

Should I have done it?

Did I wish I hadn't?

I straightened to my feet and smiled ruefully at the shambles, and knew the answer to both questions was no.

Epilogue

I gave Energise away.

Six weeks after his safe return to Rupert's stable he ran in the Champion Hurdle and I took a party to Cheltenham to cheer him on. A sick tycoon having generously lent his private box, we went in comfort, with lunch before and champagne after and a lot of smiling in between.

The four newly-registered joint-owners were having a ball and slapping each other on the back with glee: Bert, Allie, Owen and Charlie, as high in good spirits as they'd been at the census.

Charlie had brought the bridge-playing wife and Bert his fat old mum, and Owen had shyly and unexpectedly produced an unspoiled daughter of sixteen. The oddly mixed party proved a smash-hit success, my four conspirators carrying it along easily on the strength of liking each other a lot.

While they all went off to place bets and look at the horses in the parade ring, I stayed up in the box. I stayed there most of the afternoon. I had found it impossible, as the weeks passed, to regain my old innocent enthusiasm for racing. There was still a massive movement of support and sympathy for Jody, which I supposed would never change. Letters to sporting papers spoke of sympathy for his misfortunes and disgust for the one who had brought them about. Racing columnists, though reluctantly convinced of his villainy, referred to him still as the 'unfortunate' Jody. Quintus, implacably resentful, was ferreting away against me in the Jockey Club and telling everyone it was my fault his son had made 'misjudgements'. I had asked him how it could possibly be my fault that Jody had made the misjudgement of taking Macrahinish and Ganser Mays for buddy-buddies, and had received no answer.

I had heard unofficially the results of the autopsy on Black Fire. He had been killed by a massive dose of chloroform injected between the ribs straight into the heart. Quick, painless, and positively the work of a practised hand.

The veterinary bag found beside the dead horse had contained a large hypodermic syringe with a sufficient length of needle; traces of chloroform inside the syringe and Macrahinish's fingerprints outside.

These interesting facts could not be generally broadcast on account of the forthcoming trial, and my high-up police informant had made me promise not to repeat them.

Jody and Macrahinish were out on bail, and the racing authorities had postponed their own enquiry until the law's verdict should be known. Jody still technically held his trainer's licence.

The people who to my mind had shown most sense had been Jody's other owners. One by one they had melted apologetically away, reluctant to be had for mugs. They had judged without waiting around for a jury, and Jody had no horses left to train. And that in itself, in many eyes, was a further crying shame to be laid at my door.

I went out on the balcony of the kind tycoon's box and stared vacantly over Cheltenham racecourse. Moral victory over Jody was impossible, because too many people still saw him, despite everything, as the poor hardworking little man who had fallen foul of the rich robber baron.

Charlie came out on the balcony in my wake.

'Steven? What's the matter? You're too damned quiet.'

'What we did,' I said sighing, 'has changed nothing.'

'Of course it has,' he said robustly. 'You'll see. Public opinion works awful slowly. People don't like doing about-turns and admitting they were fooled. But you trust your Uncle Charlie, this time next year, when they've got over their red faces, a lot of people will quietly be finding you're one of their best friends.'

'Yeah.'

'Quintus,' he said positively, 'is doing himself a lot of personal no good just now with the hierarchy. The *on dit* round the bazaars is that if Quintus can't see his son is a full-blown criminal he is even thicker than anyone thought. I tell you, the opinion where it matters is one hundred per cent for you, and our little private enterprise is the toast of the cigar circuit.'

I smiled. 'You make me feel better even if you do lie in your teeth.'

'As God's my judge,' he said, virtuously, and spoiled it by glancing a shade apprehensively skywards.

'I saw Jody,' I said. 'Did you know?'

'No!'

'In the City,' I nodded. 'Him and Felicity, coming out of some law offices.'

'What happened?'

'He spat,' I said.

'How like him.'

They had both looked pale and worried and had stared at me in disbelief. Jody's ball of mucus landed at my feet, puncuation mark of how he felt. If I'd known they were likely to be there I would have avoided the district by ten miles, but since we were accidentally face to face I asked him straight out the question I most wanted answered.

'Did you send Ganser Mays to smash my place up?'

'He told him how to make you suffer,' Felicity said spitefully. 'Serves you right.'

She cured in that one sentence the pangs of conscience I'd had about the final results of the Energise shuttle.

'You're a bloody fool, Jody,' I said. 'If you'd dealt straight with me I'd've bought you horses to train for the Classics. With your ability, if you'd been honest, you could have gone to the top. Instead, you'll be warned off for life. It is you, believe me, who is the mug.'

They had both stared at me sullenly, eyes full of frustrated rage. If either of them should have a chance in the future to do me further bad turns I had no doubt that they would. There was no one as vindictive as the man who'd done you wrong and been found out.

Charlie said beside me, 'Which do you think was the boss? Jody or Macrahinish or Ganser Mays?'

'I don't know,' I said. 'How does a triumvirate grab you?'

'Equal power?' He considered. 'Might well be, I suppose. Just three birds of a feather drawn to each other by natural evil, stirring it in unholy alliance.'

'Are all criminals so full of hate?'

'I dare say. I don't know all that many. Do you?'

'No.'

'I should think,' Charlie said, 'that the hate comes first. Some people are just natural haters. Some bully the weak, some become anarchists, some rape women, some steal with maximum mess . . . and all of them enjoy the idea of the victim's pain.'

'Then you can't cure a hater,' I said.

'With hardliners, not a chance.'

Charlie and I contemplated this sombre view and the others came back waving Tote tickets and bubbling over with good humour.

'Here,' Bert said, slapping me on the back. 'Know what I just heard? Down in the ring, see. All those bleeding little bookies that we saved from going bust over Padellic, they're passing round the bleeding hat.'

'Just what, Bert,' said Allie, 'do you bleeding mean?'

'Here!' A huge grin spread across Bert's rugged features. 'You're a right smashing bit of goods, you are, Allie, and that's a fact. What I mean is, those little guys are making a bleeding collection all round the country, and every shop the smart alecs tried it on with, they're all putting a fiver in, and they're going to send it to the Injured Jockey's bleeding Fund in honour of the firm of Scott, Canterfield, Ward, Idris and Huggerneck, what saved them all from disappearing down the bleeding plughole.'

We opened a bottle of champagne on the strength of it and Charlie said it was the eighth wonder of the world.

When the time came for the Champion Hurdle we all went down to see Energise saddled. Rupert, busy fastening buckles, looked at the ranks of shining eyes and smiled with the indulgence of the long-time professional. The horse himself could scarcely stand still, so full was he of oats and health and general excitement. I patted his elegant black neck and he tossed his head and sprayed me with a blow through his nostrils.

I said to Rupert, 'Do you think I'm too old to learn to ride?'

'Racehorses?' He pulled tight the second girth and fastened the buckle.

'Yes.'

He slapped the black rump. 'Come down Monday morning and make a start.'

'In front of all the lads?'

'Well?' He was amused, but it was an exceptional offer. Few trainers would bother.

'I'll be there,' I said.

Donny led Energise from the saddling boxes to the parade ring, closely followed by Rupert and the four new owners.

'But you're coming as well,' Allie said, protesting.

I shook my head. 'Four owners to one horse is enough.'

Bert and Charlie tugged her with them and they all stood in a little smiling group with happiness coming out of their ears. Bert's mum, Owen's daughter and Charlie's wife went off to plunder the Tote, and I, with the most reputable bookmaking firm in the business, bet five hundred pounds to three thousand that Energise would win.

We watched him from the balcony of the private box with hearts thumping like jungle drums. It was for this that we had gone to so much trouble, this few minutes ahead. For the incredible pleasure of seeing a superb creature do what he was bred, trained, endowed and eager for. For speed, for fun, for exhilaration, for love.

The tapes went up and they were away, the fourteen best hurdlers in Britain out to decide which was king.

Two miles of difficult undulating track. Nine flights of whippy hurdles. They crossed the first and second and swept up the hill past the stands, with Energise lying sixth and moving easily, his jockey still wearing my distinctive bright blue colours because none of his new owners had any.

'Go on, boyo,' Owen said, his fact rapt. 'Slaughter the bloody lot of them.' Generations of fervent Welshmen echoed in his voice.

Round the top of the course. Downhill to the dip. More jumps, then the long climb on the far side. One horse fell, bring a gasp like a gale from the stands and a moan from Allie that she couldn't bear to watch. Energise flowed over the hurdles with the economy of all great jumpers and at the top of the far hill he lay fourth.

'Get your bleeding skates on,' muttered Bert, whose knuckles showed white with clutching his raceglasses. 'Don't bleeding hang about.'

Energise obeyed the instructions. Down the leg-testing slope she swooped like a black bird, racing level with the third horse, level with the second, pressing on the leader.

Over the next, three of them in line like a wave. Round the last bend swept all three of them in a row, with nothing to choose and all to be fought for over the last of the hurdles and the taxing, tiring, pull-up to the winning post.

'I can't bear it,' Allie said. 'Oh come on, you great . . . gorgeous . . .'

'Slaughter them, boyo . . .'

'Shift, you bleeding . . .'

The voices shouted, the crowd yelled, and Charlie had tears in his eyes.

They came to the last flight all in a row, with Energise nearest the rails, furthest from the stands. He met it right, and jumped it cleanly and I had stopped breathing.

The horse in the middle hit the top of the hurdle, twisted in the air, stumbled on landing, and fell in a skidding, sliding, sprawling heap. He fell towards Energise, who had to dodge sideways to avoid him.

Such a little thing. A half-second's hesitation before he picked up his stride. But the third of the three, with a clear run, started away from the hurdle with a gain of two lengths.

Energise put his soul into winning that race. Stretched out and fought for every inch. Showed what gut and muscle could do on the green turf. Shortened the gap and closed it, and gained just a fraction at every stride.

Allie and Owen and Bert and Charlie were screaming like maniacs, and the winning post was too near, too near.

Energise finished second, by a short head.

It's no good expecting fairytale endings, in racing.

TWICE SHY

With love and thanks
to my son
FELIX

An excellent shot
who teaches physics

PART ONE

Jonathan

Chapter One

I told the boys to stay quiet while I went to fetch my gun.

It usually worked. For the five minutes that it took to get to the locker in the common-room and to return to the classroom, thirty fourteen-year-old semi-repressed hooligans could be counted on to be held in a state of fragile good behaviour, restrained only by the promise of a lesson they'd actually looked forward to. Physics in general they took to be unacceptably hard mental labour, but what happened when a gun spat out a bullet ... that was *interesting*.

Jenkins delayed me for a moment in the common-room: Jenkins with his sour expression and bad-tempered moustache, telling me I could teach momentum more clearly with chalk on a blackboard, and that an actual firearm was on my part simply self-indulgent dramatics.

'No doubt you're right,' I said blandly, edging around him.

He gave me his usual look of frustrated spite. He hated my policy of always greeting him, which was of course, why I did it.

'Excuse me,' I said, retreating, 'Four A are waiting.'

Four A, however, weren't waiting in the hoped-for state of gently simmering excitement. They were, instead, in collective giggles fast approaching mild hysteria.

'Look,' I said flatly, sensing the atmosphere with one foot through the door, 'steady down, or you'll copy notes....'

This direst of threats had no result. The giggles couldn't be stifled. The eyes of the class darted between me and my gun and the blackboard, which was still out of my sight behind the open door, and upon every young face there was the most gleeful anticipation.

'OK,' I said, closing the door, 'so what have you writ—'

I stopped.

They hadn't written anything.

One of the boys stood there, in front of the blackboard, straight and still: Paul Arcady, the wit of the class. He stood straight and still because, balanced on his head, there was an apple.

The giggles all around me exploded into laughter, and I couldn't myself keep a straight face.

'Can you shoot it off, sir?'

The voices rose above a general hubbub.

'William Tell could, sir.'

'Shall we call an ambulance, sir, just in case?'

'How long will it take a bullet to get through Paul's skull, sir?'

'Very funny,' I said repressively, but indeed it *was* very funny, and they knew it. But if I laughed too much I'd lose control of them, and control of such a volatile mass was always precarious.

'Very clever, Paul,' I said. 'Go and sit down.'

He was satisfied. He'd produced his effect perfectly. He took the apple off his head with a natural elegance and returned in good order to his place, accepting as his due the admiring jokes and the envious catcalls.

'Right then,' I said, planting myself firmly where he had stood, 'by the end of this lesson you'll all know how long it would take for a bullet travelling at a certain speed to cross a certain distance....'

The gun I had taken to the lesson had been a simple air-gun, but I told them also how a rifle worked, and why in each case a bullet or a pellet came out fast. I let them handle the smooth metal: the first time many of them had seen an actual gun, even an air-gun, at close quarters. I explained how bullets were made, and how they differed from the pellets I had with me. How loading mechanisms worked. How the grooves inside a rifle barrel rotated the bullet, to send it out spinning. I told them about air friction, and heat.

They listened with concentration and asked the questions they always did.

'Can you tell us how a bomb works, sir?'

'One day,' I said.

'A nuclear bomb?'

'One day.'

'A hydrogen ... cobalt ... neutron bomb?'

'One day.'

They never asked how radio waves crossed the ether, which was to me a greater mystery. They asked about destruction, not creation; about power, not symmetry. The seed of violence born in every male child looked out of every face, and I knew how they were thinking, because I'd been there myself. Why else had I spent countless hours at their age practising with a .22 cadet rifle on a range, improving my skill until I could hit a target the size of a thumbnail at fifty yards, nine times out of ten. A strange, pointless, sublimated skill, which I never intended to use on any living creature, but had never since lost.

'Is it true, sir,' one of them said, 'that you won an Olympic medal for rifle shooting?'

'No, it isn't.'

'What then, sir?

'I want you all to consider the speed of a bullet compared to the speed of other objects you are familiar with. Now, do you think that you could be flying along in an aeroplane, and look out of the window, and see a bullet keeping pace with you, appearing to be standing still just outside the window?'

The lesson wound on. They would remember it all their lives, because of the gun. Without the gun, whatever Jenkins might think, it would have faded into the general dust they shook from their shoes every afternoon at four o'clock. Teaching, it often seemed to me, was as much a matter of image-jerking as of imparting actual information. The facts dressed up in jokes were the ones they got right in exams.

I liked teaching. Specifically I liked teaching physics, a subject I suppose I embraced with passion and joy, knowing full well that most people shied away in horror. Physics was only the science of the unseen world, as geography was of the seen. Physics was the science of all the tremendously powerful invisibilities – of magnetism, electricity, gravity, light, sound, cosmic rays ... Physics was the science of the mysteries of the universe. How could *anyone* think it dull?

I had been for three years head of the physics department of the East Middlesex Comprehensive, with four masters and two technicians within my domain. My future, from my present age of thirty-three, looked like a possible deputy headmastership, most likely with a move involved, and even perhaps a headship, though if I hadn't achieved that by forty I could forget it. Headmasters got younger every year; mostly, cynics suggested, because the younger the man they appointed, the more the authorities could boss him about.

I was, all in all, contented with my job and hopeful of my prospects. It was only at home that things weren't so good.

Four A learned about momentum and Arcady ate his apple when he thought I wasn't looking. My peripheral vision after ten years of teaching was, however, so acute that at times they thought I could literally see out of the back of my head. I did no harm: it made control easier.

'Don't drop the core on the floor, Paul,' I said mildly. It was one thing to let him eat the apple – he'd deserved it – but quite another to let him think I hadn't seen. Keeping a grip on the monsters was a perpetual psychological game, but also priority number one. I'd seen stronger men than myself reduced to nervous breakdowns by the hunting-pack instincts of children.

When the end-of-lesson bell rang, they did me the ultimate courtesy of letting me finish what I was saying before erupting into the going-home stampede. It was, after all, the last lesson on Friday – and God be thanked for weekends.

I made my way slowly round the four physics laboratories and the two equipment rooms, checking that everything was in order. The two technicians, Louisa and David, were dismantling and putting away all apparatus not needed on Monday, picking Five E's efforts at radio-circuitry to pieces and returning the batteries, clips, bases and transistors to the countless racks and drawers in the equipment rooms.

'Shooting anyone special?' Louisa said, eyeing the gun which I was carrying with me.

'Didn't want to leave it unattended.'

'Is it loaded?' Her voice sounded almost hopeful. By late Friday, she was always in the state in which one never asked her for an extra favour: not, that is, unless one was willing to endure a weepy ten minutes of 'you don't realize how much this job entails', which, on most occasions, I wasn't. Louisa's tantrums, I reckoned, were based on her belief that life had cheated her, finding her at forty as a sort of storekeeper (efficient, meticulous and helpful) but not a Great Scientist. 'If I'd gone to college . . .' she would say, leaving the strong impression that if she had, Einstein would have been relegated. I dealt with Louisa by retreating at the warning signs of trouble, which was maybe weak, but I had to live with her professionally, and bouts of sullenness made her slow.

'My list for Monday!' I said, handing it to her.

She glanced disparagingly down it. 'Martin has ordered the oscilloscopes for third period.'

The school's shortage of oscilloscopes was a constant source of friction.

'See what you can manage,' I said.

'Can you make do with only two?'

I said I supposed so, smiled, hoped it would keep fine for her gardening, and left for home.

I drove slowly with the leaden feeling of resignation clamping down, as it always did on the return journey. Between Sarah and me there was no joy left; no springing love. Eight years of marriage, and nothing to feel but a growing boredom.

We had been unable to have children. Sarah had hoped for them, longed for them, pined for them. We'd been to every conceivable specialist and Sarah had had countless injections and pills and two operations. My own disappointment was bearable, though none the less deep. Hers had proved intractable and finally disabling in that she had gone into a state of permanent depression from which it seemed nothing could rescue her.

We'd been told by encouraging therapists that many childless marriages were highly successful, husband and wife forging exceptionally strong bonds through their misfortune, but with us it had worked in reverse. Where once there had been a passion there was now politeness; where plans and laughter, now a grinding hopelessness; where tears and heartbreak, silence.

I hadn't been enought for her, without babies. I'd been forced to face the fact that to her motherhood mattered most, that marriage had been but the pathway, that many a man would have done. I wondered unhappily from time to time how soon she would have divorced me had it been I who had proved infertile: and it was profitless also to guess that we would have been contented enough for ever if she herself had been fulfilled.

I dare say it was a marriage like many another. We never quarrelled. Seldom argued. Neither of us any longer cared enough for that; and as a total, prolonged way of life it was infinitely dispiriting.

It was a homecoming like thousands of others. I parked outside the closed garage doors and let myself into the house with arms full of airgun and exercise books. Sarah, home as usual from her part-time job as a dentist's receptionist, sat on the sofa in the sitting-room reading a magazine.

'Hullo,' I said.

'Hullo. Good day?'

'Not bad.'

She hadn't looked up from her pages. I hadn't kissed her. Perhaps for both of us it was better than total loneliness, but not much.

'There's ham for supper,' she said. 'And coleslaw. That all right?'

'Fine.'

She went on reading; a slim fair-haired girl, still arrestingly pretty but now with a settled resentful expression. I was used to it, but in flashes suffered unbearable nostalgia for the laughing eagerness of the early days. I wondered sometimes if she noticed that the fun had gone out of me, too, although I could sometimes feel it still bubbling along inside, deeply buried.

On that particular evening I made an effort (as I did more and more rarely) to jog us out of our dimness.

'Look, let's just dump everything and go out to dinner. Maybe to Florestan's, where there's dancing.'

She didn't look up. 'Don't be silly.'

'Let's just go.'

'I don't want to.' A pause. 'I'd rather watch television.' She turned a page, and added with indifference, 'And we can't afford Florestan's prices.'

'We could, if you'd enjoy it.'

'No, I wouldn't.'

'Well,' I sighed, 'I'll make a start on the books, then.'

She nodded faintly. 'Supper at seven.'

'All right.'

I turned to go.

'There's a letter for you from William,' she said with boredom in her voice. 'I put it upstairs.'

'Oh? Well, thanks.'

She went on reading, and I took my stuff up to the third and smallest of our bedrooms, which I used as a sort of study-cum-office. The estate agent who had shown us the house had brightly described the room as 'just right for the nursery', and had nearly lost himself the sale. I'd annexed the place for myself and made it as masculine as possible, but I was aware that for Sarah the spirit of unborn children still hovered there. She rarely went in. It was slightly unusual that she should have put the letter from my brother on my desk.

It said:

Dear Jonathan,

Please can I have thirty pounds? It's for going to the farm at half-term. I wrote to Mrs Porter, and she'll have me. She says her rates have gone up because of inflation. It can't be for what I eat, as she mostly gives me bread and honey. (No complaints.) Also actually I need some money for riding, in case they won't let me earn any more rides at the stables by mucking out, they were a bit funny about it last time, something to do with the law and exploiting juveniles, I ask you. Roll on sixteen. Anyway, if you could make it fifty quid it would be fine. If I can earn my riding, I'll send the extra twenty back, because if you don't want your dough lifted at this high-class nick you have to have it embedded in concrete. Half term is a week on Friday, early this term, so could you send it pronto?

Did you notice that Clinker did win the Wrap-Up 'chase at Stratford? If you don't want me to be a jockey, how about a tipster?

Hope you are well. And Sarah.

William.

P.S. Can you come for sports day, or for Blah-Blah day? I've got a prize for two plus two, you'll be astounded to hear.

Blah-Blah day was Speech Day, at which the school prizes were handed out. I'd missed every one of William's for one reason or another. I would go this time, I thought. Even William might sometimes feel lonely with no one close to him ever to see him collect his prizes, which he did with some monotony.

William went to public school thanks to a rich godfather who had left him a lot of money on trust 'for his education and vocational training, and good luck to the little brat'. William's trustees regularly paid his fees to the school and maintenance for clothes and etceteras to me, and I passed on cash to William as required. It was an arrangement which worked excellently on many counts, not least that it meant that William didn't have to live with Sarah and me. Her husband's noisy and independent-minded brother was not the child she wanted.

William spent his holidays on farms, and Sarah occasionally said that it was most unfair that William should have more money than I had and that William had been spoiled rotten from the day my mother had discovered she was pregnant again at the age of forty-six. Sarah and William, whenever they met, behaved mostly with wary restraint and only occasionally with direct truth. William had learned very quickly not to tease her, which was his natural inclination, and she had accepted that doling out sarcastic criticism invited a cutting response. They circled each other, in consequence, like exactly matched opponents unwilling to declare open war.

For as long as he could remember William had been irresistably attracted to horses and had long affirmed his intention to be a jockey, of which Sarah strongly and I mildly disapproved. Security, William said, was a dirty word. There were better things in life than a safe job. Sarah and I, I suppose, were happier with pattern and order and achievement. William increasingly as he grew through thirteen, fourteen, and now fifteen, seemed to hunger for air and speed and uncertainty. It was typical of him that he proposed to spend the week's mid-term break in riding horses instead of working for the eight 'O' Level exams he was due to take immediately afterwards.

I left his letter on my desk to remind myself to send him a cheque and unlocked the cupboard where I kept my guns.

The air-gun that I'd taken to school was little more than a toy and needed no licence or secure storage, but I also owned two Mauser 7.62s, an Enfield No. 4 7.62 and two Anschütz .22s around which all sorts of regulations bristled, and also an old Lee Enfield .303 dating back from my early days which was still as lethal as ever if one could raise the ammunition for it. The little I had, I hoarded, mostly out of nostalgia. There were no more .303 rounds being made, thanks to the army switching to 7.62 mm in the sixties.

I put the air-gun back in its rack, checked that everything was as it should be, and locked the doors on the familiar smell of oil.

The telephone bell rang downstairs and Sarah answered it. I looked at the pile of exercise books which would all have to be read and corrected and handed out to the boys again on Monday, and wondered why I didn't have a fixed-hours job that one didn't have to take home. It wasn't only for the pupils that homework was a drag.

I could hear Sarah's telephone-answering voice, loud and bright.

'Oh. Hallo, Peter. How nice ...'

There was a long pause while Peter talked, and then from Sarah a rising wail.

'Oh, *no*! Oh, my *God*! Oh, no, Peter ...' Horror, disbelief, great distress. A quality, anyway, which took me straight downstairs.

Sarah was sitting stiffly upright on the sofa, holding the telephone at the end of its long cord. 'Oh, no,' she was saying wildly. 'It can't be true. It just *can't*.'

She stared at me unseeingly, neck stretched upwards, listening with even her eyes.

'Well, of course ... of course we will ... Oh, Peter, yes, of course ... Yes, straight away. Yes ... yes ... we'll be there. ...' She glanced at her watch. 'Nine o'clock. Perhaps a bit later. Will that do? ... All right then ... and Peter, give her my love ...'

She clattered the receiver down with shaking hands.

'We'll have to go,' she said. 'Peter and Donna—'

'Not tonight,' I protested. 'Whatever it is, not tonight. I'm damned tired and I've got all those books ...'

'Yes, at once, we must go at once.'

'It's a hundred miles.'

'I don't *care* how far it is. We must go *now. Now!*'

She stood up and practically ran towards the stairs. 'Pack a suitcase,' she said. 'Come on.'

I followed her more slowly, half exasperated, half moved by her urgency. 'Sarah, hold on a minute, what exactly has happened to Peter and Donna?'

She stopped four stairs up, and looked down at me over the bannister. She was already crying, her whole face screwed into agonised disorder.

'Donna.' The words were indistinct. 'Donna...'

'Has she had an accident?'

'No ... not...'

'What, then?'

The question served only to increase the tears. 'She . . . needs . . . me.'

'You go, then.' I said, feeling relieved at the solution. 'I can manage without the car for a few days. Until Tuesday anyway. Monday I can do by bus.'

'No. Peter wants you, too. He begged me ... both of us.'

'Why?' I said, but she was already running again up the stairs, and wouldn't answer.

I won't like it, I thought abruptly. Whatever had happened she knew that I wouldn't like it and that my instincts would all be on the side of non-involvement. I followed her upwards with reluctance and found her already gathering clothes and toothpaste onto the bed.

'Donna has parents, hasn't she?' I said. 'And Peter, too? So if something terrible's happened, why in God's name do they need *us*?'

'They're our friends.' She was rushing about, crying and gulping and dropping things. It was much, much more than ordinary sympathy for any ill that might have befallen Donna: there was a quality of extravagance that both disturbed and antagonized.

'It's beyond the bounds of friendship,' I said, 'to go charging off to Norfolk hungry and tired and not knowing why. And I'm not going.'

Sarah didn't seem to hear. The haphazard packing went ahead without pause and the tears developed into a low continuous grizzle.

Where once we had had many friends, we now had just Donna and Peter, notwithstanding that they no longer lived five miles away and played squash on Tuesdays. All our other friends from before and after marriage had either dropped away or coupled and bred; and it was only Donna and Peter who, like us, had produced no children. Only Donna and Peter, who never talked nursery, whose company Sarah could bear.

She and Donna had once been long-time flatmates. Peter and I, meeting for the first time as their subsequent husbands, had got on together amicably enough for the friendship to survive the Norfolk removal, though it was by now more a matter of birthday cards and telephone calls than of frequent house-to-house visits. We had spent a boating holiday together once on the canals. 'We'll do it again next year,' we'd all said: but we didn't.

'Is Donna ill?' I said.

'No...'

'I'm not going,' I said.

The keening grizzle stopped. Sarah looked a mess, standing there with vague reddened eyes and a clumsily folded nightdress. She stared down at the pale green froth that she wore against the chill of separate beds and the disastrous news finally burst out of her.

'She was arrested,' she said.

'Donna ... arrested?' I was astounded. Donna was mouselike. Organized. Gentle. Apologetic. Anything but likely to be in trouble with the police.

'She's home now,' Sarah said. 'She's ... Peter says she's ... well ... *suicidal*. He says he can't cope with it.' Her voice was rising. 'He says he needs us ... *now* ... this minute. He doesn't know what to do. He says we're the only people who can help.'

She was crying again. Whatever it was, was too much.

'What,' I said slowly, 'has Donna done?'

'She went out shopping,' Sarah said, trying at last to speak clearly. 'And she stole ... She stole ...'

'Well, for heaven's sake,' I said, 'I know it's bloody for them, but thousands of people shoplift. So why all this excessive drama?'

'You don't listen,' Sarah shouted. 'Why don't you *listen*?'

'I—'

'She stole a *baby*.'

Chapter Two

We went to Norwich.

Sarah had been right. I didn't like the reason for our journey. I felt a severe aversion to being dragged into a highly-charged emotional situation where nothing constructive could possibly be done. My feelings of friendship towards Peter and Donna were nowhere near strong enough. For Peter, perhaps. For Donna, definitely not.

All the same, when I thought of the tremendous forces working on that poor girl to impel her to such an action it occurred to me that perhaps the unseen universe didn't stop at the sort of electromagnetics that I taught. Every living cell, after all, generated electric charges: especially brain cells. If I put baby-snatching on a par with an electric storm, I could be happier with it.

Sarah sat silently beside me for most of the way, recovering, readjusting, preparing. She said only once what must have been in both of our minds.

'It could have been me.'

'No,' I said.

'You don't know ... what it's like.'

There was no answer. Short of having been born female and barren, there was no way of knowing. I had been told about five hundred times over the years in various tones from anguish to spite that I didn't know what it was like, and there was no more answer now than there had been the first time.

The long lingering May evening made the driving easier than usual, although going northwards out of London in the Friday night exodus was always a beast of a journey.

At the far, far end of it lay the neat new box-like house with its big featureless net-curtained windows and its tidy oblong of grass. One bright house in a street of others much the same. One proud statement that Peter had reached a certain salary-level and still aspired to future improvement. A place and a way of life that I understood and saw no harm in: where William would suffocate.

The turmoil behind the uninformative net curtains was much as expected in some ways and much worse in others.

The usually meticulously tidy interior was in much disarray, with unwashed cups and mugs making wet rings on every surface and clothes and papers scattered around. The trail, I came to realize, left by the in-and-out tramp of officialdom over the past two days.

Peter greeted us with gaunt eyes and the hushed voice of a death in the family; and probably for him and Donna what had happened was literally hurting them worse than a death. Donna herself sat in a silent huddle at one end of the big green sofa in their sitting-room and made no attempt to respond to Sarah when she rushed to her side and put her arms round her in almost a frenzy of affection.

Peter said helplessly, 'She won't talk . . . or eat.'

'Or go to the bathroom?'

'*What?*'

Sarah looked at me with furious reproach, but I said mildly, 'If she goes off to the bathroom when she feels the need, it's surely a good sign. It's such a *normal* act.'

'Well, yes,' Peter said limply. 'She does.'

'Good, then.'

Sarah clearly thought that this was another prime example of what she called my general heartlessness, but I had meant only to reassure. I asked Peter what exactly had taken place, and he wouldn't tell me in front of Donna herself we removed to the kitchen.

In there, too, the police and medics and court officials and social workers had made the coffee and left the dishes. Peter seemed not to see the mess that in past times would have set both him and Donna busily wiping up. We sat at the table with the last remnants of daytime fading to dusk, and in that gentle light he slowly unlocked the horrors.

It was on the previous morning, he said, that Donna had taken the baby from its pram and driven off with it in her car. She had driven seventy odd miles north-east to the coast, and had at some point abandoned the car with the baby inside it, and had walked off along the beach.

The car and the baby had been traced and found within hours, and Donna herself had been discovered on the sand in pouring rain, speechless and stunned.

The police had arrested her, taken her to the station for a night in the cells, and paraded her before a magistrate in the morning. The bench had called for psychiatric reports, set a date for a hearing a week ahead and, despite protests from the baby's mother, set Donna free. Everyone had assured Peter she would only be put on probation, but he still shuddered from their appalling future of ignominy via the press and the neighbourhood.

After a pause, and thinking of Donna's trancelike state, I said, 'You told Sarah she was suicidal.'

He nodded miserably. 'This afternoon I wanted to warm her. To put her to bed. I ran the bath for her.' It was a while before he could go on. It seemed that the suicide attempt had been in deadly earnest: he had stopped her on the instant she plunged herself and her switched-on hairdrier into the water. 'And she still had all her clothes on,' he said.

It seemed to me that what Donna urgently needed was some expert and continuous psychiatric care in a comfortable private nursing-home, all of which she was probably not going to get.

'Come on out for a drink,' I said.

'But I *can't*.' He was slightly trembling all the time, as if his foundations were in an earthquake.

'Donna will be all right with Sarah.'

'But she might try . . .'

'Sarah will look after her.'

'But I can't face . . .'

'No,' I said. 'We'll buy a bottle.'

I bought some Scotch and two glasses from a philosophical publican just before closing time, and we sat in my car to drink in a quiet tree-lined street three miles from Peter's home. Stars and street lights between the shadowy leaves.

'What are we going to do?' he said despairingly.

'Time will pass.'

'We'll never get over it. How can we? It's bloody . . . impossible.' He choked on the last word and began to cry like a a boy. An outrush of unbearable, pent-up, half-angry grief.

I took the wobbling glass out of his hand. Sat and waited and made vague sympathetic noises and wondered what to God I would have done if, like she said, it had been Sarah.

'And to happen now,' he said at length, fishing for a handkerchief to blow his nose, 'of all times.'

'Er . . . oh?' I said.

He sniffed convulsively and wiped his cheeks. 'Sorry about that.'

'Don't be.'

He sighed. 'You're always so calm.'

'Nothing like this has happened to me.'

'I'm in a mess,' he said.

'Well, it'll get better.'

'No, I mean, besides Donna. I didn't know what to do . . . before . . . and now, after, I can't even *think*.'

'What sort of mess? Financial?'

'No. Well, not exactly.' He paused uncertainly, needing a prompt.

'What then?'

I gave him his glass back. He looked at it vaguely, then drank most of the contents in one mouthful.

'You don't mind if I burden you?' he said.

'Of course not.'

He was a couple of years younger than I, the same age as both Donna and Sarah; and all three of them, it had sometimes seemed to me, saw me not only as William's elder brother but as their own. At any rate it was as natural to me as to Peter that he should tell me his troubles.

He was middling tall and thin and had recently grown a lengthy moustache which had not given him the overpoweringly macho appearance he might have been aiming for. He still looked an ordinary inoffensive competent guy who went around selling his computer know-how to small businesses on weekdays and tinkered with his boat on Sundays.

He dabbed his eyes again for several minutes took slow deep calming breaths.

'I got into something which I wish I hadn't,' he said.

'What sort of thing?'

'It started more or less as a joke.' He finished the last inch of drink and I stretched across and poured him a refill. 'There was this fellow. Our age, about. He'd come up from Newmarket, and we got talking in that pub you bought the whisky from. He said it would be great if you could get racing results from a computer. And we both laughed.'

There was a silence.

'Did he know you worked with computers?' I said.

'I'd told him. You know how one does.'

'So what happened next?'

'A week later I got a letter. From this fellow. Don't know how he got my address. From the pub, I suppose. The barman knows where I live.' He took a gulp from his drink and was quiet for a while, and then went on, 'The letter asked if I would like to help someone who was working out a computer program for handicapping horses. So I thought, why not? All handicaps for horse races are sorted out on computers, and the letter sounded quite official.'

'But it wasn't?'

He shook his head. 'A spot of private enterprise. But I still thought, why not? Anyone is entitled to work out his own program. There isn't such thing as *right* in handicapping unless the horses pass the post in the exact order that the computer weighted them, which they never do.'

'You know a lot about it,' I said.

'I've learnt, these past few weeks.' The thought brought no cheer. 'I didn't even notice I was neglecting Donna, but she says I've hardly spoken to her for ages.' His throat closed and he swallowed audibly. 'Perhaps if I hadn't been so occupied...'

'Stop feeling guilty,' I said. 'Go on about the handicapping.'

After a while he was able to.

'He gave me pages and pages of stuff. Dozens of them. All handwritten in diabolical handwriting. He wanted it organized into programs that any fool could run on a computer.' He paused. 'You do know about computers.'

'More about microchips than programming, which isn't saying much.'

'The other way round from most people, though.'

'I guess so,' I said.

'Anyway, I did them. Quite a lot of them. It turned out they were all much the same sort of thing. They weren't really very difficult, once I'd got the hang of what the notes all meant. It was understanding those which was the worst. So, anyway, I did the programs and got paid in cash.' He stopped and moved restlessly in his seat, glum and frowning.

'So what is wrong?' I asked.

'Well, I said it would be best if I ran the programs a few times on the computer he was going to use, because so many computers are different from each other, and although he'd told me the make of computer he'd be using and I'd made allowances, you never can really tell you've got no bugs until you actually try things out on the actual type of machine. But he wouldn't let me. I said he wasn't being reasonable and he told me to mind my own business. So I just shrugged him off and thought if he wanted to be so stupid it was his own affair. And then these other two men turned up.'

'What other two men?'

'I don't know. They just sneered when I asked their names. They told me to hand over to them the programs I'd made on the horses. I said I had done. They said they were nothing to do with the person who'd paid for the job, but all the same I was to give them the programs.

'And did you?'

'Well, yes – in a way.'

'But, Peter—' I said.

He interrupted, 'Yes, I know, but they were so bloody *frightening*. They came the day before yesterday – it seems years ago – in the evening. Donna had gone out for a walk. It was still light. About eight o'clock, I should think. She often goes for walks. . . .' He trailed off again and I gave his glass a nudge with the bottle. 'What?' he said. 'Oh no, no more, thanks. Anyway, they came, and they were so *arrogant*, and they said I'd regret it if I didn't give them the programs. They said Donna was a pretty little missis, wasn't she, and they were sure I'd like her to stay that way.' He swallowed. 'I'd never have believed . . . I mean, that sort of thing doesn't *happen*. . . .'

It appeared, however, that it had.

'Well,' he said, rallying, 'what I gave them was all that I had in the house, but it was really only first drafts, so to speak. Pretty rough. I'd written three or four trial programs out in longhand, like I often do. I know a lot of people work on typewriters or even straight onto a computer, but I get on better with pencil and rubber, so what I gave them *looked* all right, especially if you didn't know the first thing about programming, which I should think they didn't, but not much of it would run as it stood. And I hadn't put the file names on anyway, or any REMS or anything, so even if they debugged the programs they wouldn't know what they referred to.'

Disentangling the facts from the jargon, it appeared that what he had done had been to deliver to possibly dangerous men a load of garbage, knowing full well what he was doing.

'I see,' I said slowly, 'what you meant by a mess.'

'I'd decided to take Donna away for a few days, just to be safe. I was going to tell her as a nice surprise when I got home from work yesterday, and then the police turned up in my office, and said she'd taken ... taken ... Oh Christ, how *could* she?'

I screwed the cap onto the bottle and I looked at my watch. 'It's getting on for midnight,' I said. 'We'd better go back.'

'I suppose so.'

I paused with my hand on the ignition key. 'Didn't you tell the police about your two unpleasant visitors?' I said.

'No, I didn't. I mean, how could I? They've been in and out of the house, and a policewoman too, but it was all about Donna. They wouldn't have listened, and anyway ...'

'Anyway what?'

He shrugged uncomfortably. 'I got paid in cash. Quite a lot. I'm not going to declare it for tax. If I told the police ... well, I'd more or less have to.'

'It might be better,' I said.

He shook his head. 'It would cost me a lot to tell the police, and what would I gain? They'd make a note of what I said and wait until Donna got bashed in the face before they did anything. I mean, they can't go around guarding everyone who's been vaguely threatened night and day, can they? And as for guarding *Donna* – well, they weren't very nice to her, you know. Really rotten, most of them were. They made cups of tea for each other and spoke over her head as if she was a lump of wood. You'd think she'd poked the baby's eyes out, the way they treated her.'

It didn't seem unreasonable to me that official sympathy had been mostly on the side of the baby's frantic mother, but I didn't say so.

'Perhaps it would be best, then,' I said, 'if you did take Donna away for a bit, straight after the hearing. Can you get leave?'

He nodded.

'But what she really needs is proper psychiatric care. Even a spell in a mental hospital.'

'No,' he said.

'They have a high success rate with mental illness nowadays. Modern drugs, and hormones, and all that.'

'But she's not—' He stopped.

The old taboos died hard. 'The brain is part of the body,' I said.

'It's not separate. And it goes wrong sometimes, just like anything else. Like the liver. Or the kidneys. You wouldn't hesitate if it was her kidneys.'

He shook his head, however, and I didn't press it. Everyone had to decide things for themselves. I started the car and wheeled us back to the house, and Peter said as we turned into the short concrete driveway that Donna was unusually happy on their boat, and he would take her away on that.

The weekend dragged on. I tried surreptitiously now and then to mark the inexorable exercise books, but the telephone rang more or less continuously and, as answering it seemed to be the domestic chore I was best fitted for, I slid into a routine of chat. Relatives, friends, press, officials, busybodies, cranks and stinkers, I talked with the lot.

Sarah cared for Donna with extreme tenderness and devotion and was rewarded with wan smiles at first and, gradually, low-toned speech. After that came hysterical tears, a brushing of hair, a tentative meal, a change of clothes, and a growth of invalid behaviour.

When Peter talked to Donna it was in a miserable mixture of love, guilt and reproach, and he found many an opportunity of escaping into the garden. On Sunday morning he went off in his car at pub-opening time and returned late for lunch, and on Sunday afternoon I said with private relief that I would now have to go back home ready for school on Monday.

'I'm staying here,' Sarah said. 'Donna needs me. I'll ring my boss and explain. He owes me a week's leave anyway.'

Donna gave her the by now ultra-dependent smile she had developed over the past two days, and Peter nodded with eager agreement.

'OK,' I said slowly, 'but take care.'

'What of?' Sarah said.

I glanced at Peter, who was agitatedly shaking his head. All the same, it seemed sensible to take simple precautions.

'Don't let Donna go out alone,' I said.

Donna blushed furiously and Sarah was instantly angry, and I said helplessly, 'I didn't mean ... I meant keep her safe ... from people who might want to be spiteful to her.'

Sarah saw the sense in that and calmed down, and a short while later I was ready to leave.

I said goodbye to them in the house because there seemed to be always people in the street staring at the windows with avid eyes, and right at the last minute Peter thrust into my hand three cassettes for playing in the car if I should get bored on the way home. I glanced at them briefly: *The King and I*, *Oklahoma*, and *West Side Story*. Hardly the latest rave, but I thanked him anway, kissed Sarah for appearances, kissed Donna ditto, and with a regrettable lightening of spirits took myself off.

It was on the last third of the way home, when I tried *Oklahoma* for company, that I found that what Peter had given me wasn't music at all, but quite something else.

Instead of 'Oh What a Beautiful Morning,' I got a loud vibrating scratchy whine interspersed with brief bits of one-note plain whine. Shrugging, I wound the tape forward a bit, and tried again.

Same thing.

I ejected the tape, turned it over and tried again. Same thing. Tried *The King and I* and *West Side Story*. All the same.

I knew that sort of noise from way back. One couldn't forget it, once one knew. The scratchy whine was made by two tones alternating very fast so that the ear could scarcely distinguish the upper from the lower. The plain whine indicated simply an interval with nothing happening. On *Oklahoma*, fairly typically, the stretches of two-tone were lasting anywhere from ten seconds to three minutes.

I was listening to the noise a computer produced when its programs were recorded onto ordinary cassette tape.

Cassettes were convenient and widely used, especially with smaller computers. One could store a whole host of different programs on casette tapes, and simply pick out whichever was needed, and use it: but the cassettes were still, all the same, just ordinary cassettes, and if one played the tape straightforwardly in the normal way on a cassette player, as I had done, one heard the vibrating whine.

Peter had given me three sixty-minute tapes of computer programs: and it wasn't so very difficult to guess what those programs would be about.

I wondered why he had given them to me in such an indirect way. I wondered, in fact, why he had given them to me at all. With a mental shrug I shovelled the tapes and their misleading boxes onto the glove shelf and switched on the radio instead.

School on Monday was a holiday after the greenhouse emotions in Norfolk, and Louisa-the-technician's seemed moths' wings besides Donna's.

On Monday evening, while I was watching my own choice on the television and eating cornflakes and cream with my feet on the coffee table, Peter telephoned.

'How's Donna?' I said.

'I don't know where she'd be without Sarah.'

'And you?'

'Oh, pretty fair. Look, Jonathan, did you play any of those tapes?' His voice sounded tentative and half apologetic.

'A bit of them,' I said.

'Oh. Well, I expect you'll know what they are?'

'Your horse-handicapping programs?'

'Yes ... er ... Will you keep them for me for now?' He gave me no chance to answer and rushed on, 'You see, we're hoping to go off to the boat straight after the hearing on Friday. Well, we do have to believe Donna will get probation, even the nastiest of those officials said it would be so in such a case, but obviously she'll be terribly upset with having to go to court and everything and so we'll go away as soon as we can, and I didn't like the thought of leaving those cassettes lying around in the office, which they were, so I went over to fetch them yesterday morning, so I could give them to you. I mean, I didn't really think it out. I could have put them in the bank, or anywhere. I suppose what I really wanted was to get those tapes right out of my life so that if those two brutes came back asking for the programs I'd be able to say I hadn't got them and that they'd have to get them from the person I made them for.'

It occurred to me not for the first time that for a computer programmer Peter was no great shakes as a logical thinker, but maybe the circumstances were jamming the circuits.

'Have you heard from those men again?' I asked.

'No, thank God.'

'They probably haven't found out yet.'

'Thanks very much,' he said bitterly.

'I'll keep the tapes safe,' I said. 'As long as you like.'

'Probably nothing else will happen. After all, I haven't done anything illegal. Or even faintly wrong.'

The 'if-we-don't-look-at-the-monster-he'll-go-away' syndrome, I thought. But maybe he was right.

'Why didn't you tell me what you were giving me?' I enquired. 'Why *The King and I* dressing, and all that?'

'What?' His voice sounded almost puzzled, and then cleared to understanding. 'Oh, it was just that when I got home from the office, you were sitting down to lunch, and I didn't get a single chance to catch you away from the girls, and I didn't want to have to start explaining in front of them, so I just shoved them into those cases to give to you.'

The faintest twitch of unease crossed my mind, but I smothered it. Peter's world since Donna took the baby had hardly been one of general common sense and normal behaviour. He had acted pretty well, all in all, for someone hammered from all directions at once, and over the weekend I had felt an increase of respect for him, quite apart from liking.

'If you want to play those programs,' he said, 'you'll need a Grantley computer.'

'I don't suppose ...' I began.

'They might amuse William. He's mad on racing, isn't he?'

'Yes, he is.'

'I spent so much time on them. I'd really like to know how they work in practice. I mean, from someone who knows horses.'

'All right,' I said. But Grantley computers weren't scattered freely round the landscape and William had his exams ahead, and the prospect of actually using the programs seemed a long way off.

'I wish you were still here,' he said. 'All the telephone calls, they're really getting me down. And did you have any of those poisonous abusive beastly voices spitting out hate against Donna, when you were answering.'

'Yes, several.'

'But they've never even *met* her.'

'They're unbalanced. Just don't listen.'

'What did you say to them?'

'I told them to take their problems to a doctor.'

There was a slight uncomfortable pause, then he said explosively, 'I wish to God Donna had gone to a doctor.' A gulp. 'I didn't even *know* ... I mean, I knew she'd wanted children, but I thought, well, we couldn't have them, so that was that. I never *dreamed* ... I mean she's always so quiet and wouldn't hurt a fly. She never showed any signs ... We're pretty fond of each other, you know. Or at least I thought...'

'Peter, stop it.'

'Yes ...' A pause. 'Of course, you're right. But it's difficult to think of anything else.'

We talked a bit more, but only covering the same old ground, and we disconnected with me feeling that somehow I could have done more for him than I had.

Two evenings later, he went down to the river to work on his two-berth cabin cruiser, filling its tanks with water and fuel, installing new cooking-gas cylinders and checking that everything was in working order for his trip with Donna.

He had been telling me earlier that he was afraid the ship's battery was wearing out and that if he didn't get a new one they would run it down flat with their lights at night and in the morning find themselves unable to start the engine. It had happened once before, he said.

He wanted to check the battery still had enough life in it.

It had.

When he raised the first spark, the rear half of the boat exploded.

Chapter Three

Sarah told me.

Sarah on the telephone with the stark over-controlled voice of exhaustion.

'They think it was gas, or petrol vapour. They don't know yet.'

'Peter...'

'He's dead,' she said. 'There were people around. They saw him moving ... with his clothes on fire. He went over the side into the water ... but when they got him out ...' A sudden silence, then, slowly, 'We weren't there. Thank God Donna and I weren't there.'

I felt shaky and slightly sick. 'Do you want me to come?' I said.

'No. What time is it?'

'Eleven.' I had undressed, in fact, to go to bed.

'Donna's asleep. Knockout drops.'

'And how ... how is she?'

'Christ, how would you expect?' Sarah seldom spoke in that way: a true measure of the general awfulness. 'And Friday,' she said, 'the day after tomorrow, she's due in court.'

'They'll be kind to her.'

'There's already been one call, just now, with some beastly woman telling me it served her right.'

'I'd better come,' I said.

'You can't. There's school. No, don't worry. I can cope. The doctor at least said he'd keep Donna heavily sedated for several days.'

'Let me know, then, if I can help.'

'Yes,' she said. 'Goodnight, now. I'm going to bed. There's a lot to do tomorrow. Goodnight.'

I lay long awake in bed and thought of Peter and the unfairness of death: and in the morning I went to school and found him flicking in and out of my mind all day.

Driving home I saw that his cassettes were still lying in a jumble on the glove shelf. Once parked in the garage, I put the tapes back into their boxes, slipped them in my jacket pocket, and carried my usual burden of books indoors.

The telephone rang almost at once, but it was not Sarah, which was my first thought, but William.

'Did you send my cheque?' he said.

'*Hell*, I forgot.' I told him why, and he allowed that forgetting in such circs could be overlooked.

'I'll write it straight away, and send it direct to the farm.'

'OK. Look, I'm sorry about Peter. He seemed a nice guy, that time we met.'

'Yes.' I told William about the computer tapes, and about Peter wanting his opinion on them.

'Bit late now.'

'But you still might find them interesting.'

'Yeah,' he said without much enthusiasm. 'Probably some nutty betting system. There's a computer here somewhere in the maths department. I'll ask what sort it is. And look, how would it grab you if I didn't go to university?'

'Badly.'

'Yeah. I was afraid so. Anyway, work on it, big brother. There been a lot of guff going on this term about choosing a career, but I reckon it's the career that chooses *you*. I'm going to be a jockey. I can't help it.'

We said goodbyes and I put the receiver down thinking that it wasn't much good fighting to dissuade someone who at fifteen already felt that a vocation had him by the scruff of the neck.

He was slim and light: past puberty but still physically a boy, with the growth into man's stature just ahead. Perhaps nature, I thought hopefully, would take him to my height of six feet and break his heart.

Sarah rang almost immediately afterwards, speaking crisply with her dentist's-assistant voice. The shock had gone, and the exhaustion. She spoke to me with edgy bossiness, a leftover, I guessed, from a very demanding day.

'It seems that Peter should have been more careful,' she said. 'Everyone who owns a boat with an inboard engine is repeatedly told not to start up until they are sure that no gas of petrol or petrol vapour has accumulated in the bilge. Boats blow up every year. He must have known. You wouldn't think he would be so stupid.'

I said mildly, 'He had a great deal else on his mind.'

'I suppose he had, but all the same everyone says...'

If you could blame a man for his own death, I thought, it diminished the chore of sympathy. 'It was his own fault ...' I could hear the sharp voice of my aunt over the death of her neighbour ... 'He shouldn't have gone out with that cold.'

'The insurance company,' I said to Sarah, 'may be trying to wriggle out of paying all they might.'

'What?'

'Putting the blame onto the victim is a well-known ploy.'

'But he should have been more careful.'

'Oh sure. But for Donna's sake, I wouldn't go around saying so.'

There was a silence which came across as resentful. Then she said, 'Donna wanted me to tell you ... She'd rather you didn't come here this weekend. She says she could bear things better if she's alone with me.'

'And you agree?'

'Well, yes, frankly, I do.'

'OK, then.'

'You don't mind?' She sounded surprised.

'No. I'm sure she's right. She relies on you.' And too much, I thought. 'Is she still drugged?'

'Sedated.' The word was a reproof.

'Sedated, then.'

'Yes, of course.'

'And for the court hearing tomorrow?' I asked.

'Tranquillisers,' Sarah said decisively. 'Sleeping pills after.'

'Good luck with it.'

'Yes,' she said.

She disconnected almost brusquely, leaving me with the easement of having been let off an unpleasant task. Once upon a time, I supposed, we would have clung together to help Donna. At the beginning our reactions would have been truer, less complicated, less distorted by our own depressions. I mourned for the dead days, but undoubtedly I was pleased not to be going to spend the weekend with my wife.

On the Friday I went to school still with the computer tapes in my jacket pocket and, feeling that I owed it to Peter at least to try to play them, sought out one of the maths masters in the common-room. Ted Pitts, short-sighted, clear-headed, bilingual in English and algebra.

'That computer you've got tucked away somewhere in a cubby hole in the maths department,' I said, 'It's your especial baby, isn't it?'

'We all use it. We teach the kids.'

'But it's you who plays it like Beethoven while the rest are still at chopsticks?'

He enjoyed the compliment in his quiet way. 'Maybe,' he said.

'Could you tell me what make it is?' I asked.

'Sure. It's a Harris.'

'I suppose,' I said unhopefully, 'that you couldn't run a tape on it that was recorded on a Grantley?'

'It depends,' he said. He was earnest and thoughtful, twenty-six, short on humour, but full of good intentions and ideals of fair play. He suffered greatly under the sourly detestable Jenkins who was head of maths department and extracted from his assistants the reverential attitude he never got from me.

'The Harris has no language built into it,' Ted said. 'You can feed it any computer language, Fortran, Cobol, Algol, Z-80, Basic, you name it, the Harris will take it. Then you can run any programs written in those languages. But the Grantley is a smaller affair which comes all ready pre-programmed with its own form of Basic. If you had a Grantley Basic language tape, you could feed it into our Harris's memory, and then you could run Grantley Basic programs.' He paused. 'Er, is that clear?'

'Sort of.' I reflected. 'How difficult would it be to get a Grantley Basic language tape.'

'Don't know. Best to write to the firm direct. They might send you one. And they might not.'

'Why might they not?'

He shrugged. 'They might say you'd have to buy one of their computers.'

'For heaven's sake,' I said.

'Yeah. Well, see, these computer firms are very awkward. All the smaller personal computers use Basic, because it's the easiest language and also one of the best. But the firms making them all build in their own variations, so that if you record your programs from their machines, you can't run them on anyone else's. That keep you faithful to *them* in the future, because if you change to another make, all your tapes will be useless.'

'What a bore,' I said.

He nodded. 'Profits getting the better of common sense.'

'Like all those infuriatingly incompatible video-recorders.'

'Exactly. But you'd think the computer firms would have more sense. They may hang on to their own customers by force, but they're sure as Hades not going to persuade anyone else to switch.'

'Thanks anyway,' I said.

'You're welcome.' He hesitated. 'Do you actually have a tape that you want to use?'

'Yes.' I fished in my pocket and produced *Oklahoma*. 'This one and two others. Don't be misled by the packaging, it's got computer noise all right on the tape.'

'Were they recorded by an expert or an amateur?'

'An expert. Does it make any difference?'

'Sometimes.'

I explained about Peter making the tapes for a client who had a Grantley, and I added that the customer wouldn't let Peter try out the programs on the machine they were designed to run on.

'Oh, really?' Ted Pitts seemed happy with the news. 'In that case, if he was a conscientious and careful chap, it's just possible that he recorded the machine language itself on the first of the tapes. TOMS can be very touchy. He might have thought it would be safer.'

'You've lost me,' I said. 'What are TOMS?'

'Computers.' He grinned. 'Stands for Totally Obedient Moron.'

'You've made a joke,' I said disbelievingly.

'Not mine though.'

'So why should it be safer?'

He looked at me reproachfully, 'I thought you knew more about computers than you appear to.'

'It's ten years at least since I knew more. I've forgotten and they've changed.'

'It would be safer,' he said patiently, 'because if the client rang up and complained that the program wouldn't run, your friend could tell them how to stuff into their computer a brand-new version of its own language, and then your friend's programs *would* run from that. Mind you,' he added judiciously, 'you'd use up an awful lot of computer space putting the language in. You might not have much room for the actual programs.'

He looked at my expression, and sighed

'OK,' he said. 'Suppose a Grantley has a 32K store, which is a pretty normal size. That means it has about forty-nine thousand store-slots, of which probably the first seventeen thousand are used in providing the right circuits to function as Basic. That would leave you about thirty-two thousand store-slots for punching in your programs. Right?'

I nodded. 'I'll take it on trust.'

'But then if you feed in the language all over again it would take up another seventeen thousand store-slots, which would leave you with under fifteen thousand store-slots to work with. And as you need one store-slot for every letter you type, and one for every number, and one for every space, and comma, and bracket, you wouldn't be able to do a great deal before all the store-slots were used and the whole thing was full up. And at that point the computer would stop working.' He smiled. 'So many people think computers are bottomless pits. They're more like bean bags. Once they're full you have to empty the beans out before you can start to fill them again.'

'Is that what you teach the kids.'

He looked slightly confused. 'Er ... yes. Same words. One gets into a rut.'

The bell rang for afternoon registration and he stretched out his hand for the tape. 'I could try that,' he said, 'if you like.'

'Yes. If it isn't an awful bother.'

He shook his head encouragingly, and I gave him *The King and I* and *West Side Story* for good measure.

'Can't promise it will be today,' he said. 'I've got classes all afternoon and Jenkins wants to see me at four.' He grimaced. 'Jenkins. Why we can't call him Ralph and be done with it?'

'There's no hurry,' I said, 'with the tapes.'

Donna got her probation.

Sarah reported, again sounding tired, that even the baby's mother had quietened down because of Peter being killed, and Donna had gently wept in court, and even some of the policemen had been fatherly.

'How is she?' I said.

'Miserable. It's just hitting her, I think, that Peter's really gone.' Her voice sounded sisterly, motherly, protective.

'No more suicide?' I asked

'I don't think so, but the poor darling is so *vulnerable*. So easily hurt. She says its like living without skin.'

'Have you enough money?' I said.

'That's just like you!' she exclaimed. 'Always so damned practical.'

'But ...'

'I've got my bank card.'

I hadn't wanted to wallow too long in Donna's emotions and it had irritated her. We both knew it. We knew each other too well.

'Don't let her wear you out,' I said.

Her voice came back, still sharp, 'I'm perfectly all right. There's no question of wearing me out. I'm staying here for a week or two longer at least. Until after the inquest and the funeral. And after that, if Donna needs me. I've told my boss, and he understands.'

I wondered fleetingly whether I might not become too fond of living alone if she were away a whole month. I said, 'I'd like to be there at the funeral.'

'Yes. Well, I'll let you know.'

I got a tart and untender goodnight: but then my own to her hadn't been loving. We wouldn't be able to go on, I thought, if ever the politeness crumbled.

The building had long been uninhabited, and we were only a short step from demolition.

On Saturday I put the Mausers and the Enfield No. 4 in the car and drove to Bisley and let off a lot of bullets over the Surrey ranges.

During the past few months, my visits there had become less constant, partly of course because there was no delight during the winter in pressing one's stomach to the cold earth, but mostly because my intense love of the sport seemed to be waning.

I had been a member of the British rifle team for several years but now never wore any of the badges to prove it. I kept quiet in the bar after shooting and listened to others analyse their performances and spill the excitement out of their systems. I didn't like talking of my own scores, present or past.

A few years back, I had taken a sideways jump of entering for the Olympics, which was a competition for individuals and quite different from my normal pursuits. Even the guns were different (at that time all small bore) and all the distances the same (300 metres). It was a world dominated by the Swiss, but I had shot luckily and well in the event and had finished high for a Briton in the placings, and it had been marvellous. The day of a lifetime; but it had faded into memory, grown fuzzy with time passing.

In the British team, which competed mostly against the old Commonwealth countries and often won, one shot 7.62 mm guns at varying distances – 300, 500, 600, 900 and 1000 yards. I had always taken immense delight in accuracy, in judging wind velocity and air temperature and getting the climate variables exactly right. But now, both internally and externally, the point of such skill was fading.

The smooth elegant Mausers that I cherished were already within sight of being obsolete. Only long-distance assassins, these days seemed to need totally accurate rifles, and *they* used telescopic sights, which were banned and anathema to target shooters. Modern armies tended to spray out bullets regardless. None of the army rifles shot absolutely straight and in addition, every advance in effective killing-power was a loss to aesthetics. The present standard issue self-loading rifle, with its gas-powered feed of twenty bullets per magazine and its capability of continuous fire, was already a knobby untidy affair with half of it made of plastic for lightness. On the horizon was a rifle without a stock, unambiguously designed to be shot from waist level if necessary with no real pretence at precise aim: a rifle with infrared sights for night use, all angular protuberances. And beyond cordite and lead, what? Neutron missiles fired from ground launchers which would halt an invading tank army literally in its tracks. A new sort of battery which would make hand-held ray guns possible.

The marksman's special skill was drifting towards sport, as archery had, as swordplay had, as throwing the javelin and the hammer had; the commonplace weapon of one age becoming the Olympic medal of the next.

I didn't shoot very well on that particular afternoon and found little appetite afterwards for the camaraderie in the clubhouse. The image of Peter stumbling over the side of his boat on fire and dying made too many things seem irrelevant. I was pledged to shoot in the Queen's Prize in July and in a competition in Canada in August, and I reflected driving home that if I didn't put in a little more practice I would disgrace myself.

The trips overseas came up at fairly regular intervals, and because of the difficulties involved in transporting guns from one country to another, I had had built my own design of carrying case. About four feet long and externally looking like an ordinary extra-large suitcase, it was internally lined with aluminium and divided into padded shock-absorbing compartments. It held everything I needed for competitions, not only three rifles but all the paraphernalia; score-book, ear-defenders, telescope, rifle sling, shooting glove, rifle oil, cleaning rod, batman jag, roll of flannelette patches, cleaning brush, wool mop for oiling the barrel, ammunition, thick jersey for warmth, two thin olive-green protective boiler suits, and a supporting canvas and leather jacket. Unlike many people, I usually carried the guns fully assembled and ready to go, legacy of having missed my turn once through traffic hold-ups, a firearm still in pieces and fingers trembling with haste. I was not actually supposed to leave them with the bolt in place, but I often did. Only when the special gun suitcase went onto aeroplanes did I strictly conform to regulations, and then it was bonded and sealed and hedged about with red tape galore; and perhaps also because it didn't look like what it was, I'd never lost it.

Sarah, who had been enthusiastic at the beginning and had gone with me often to Bisley, had in time got tired of the bang bang bang, as most wives did. She had tired also of my spending so much time and money and had been only partly mollified by the Games. All the jobs I applied for, she had pointed out crossly, let us live south of London, convenient for the ranges. 'But if I could ski,' I'd said, 'it would be silly to move to the tropics.'

She had a point, though. Shooting wasn't cheap, and I wouldn't have been able to do as much as I did without support from indirect sponsors. The sponsors expected in return that I would not only go to the international competitions, but go to them practised and fit: conditions that until very recently I'd been happy to fulfil. I was getting old, I thought. I would be thirty-four in three months.

I drove home without haste and let myself into the quiet house which was no longer vibrant with silent tensions. Dumped my case on the coffee table in the sitting-room with no one to suggest I take it straight upstairs. Unclipped the lock and thought of the pleasant change of being able to go through the cleaning and oiling routine in front of the television without tight-lipped disapproval. Decided to postpone the clean-up until I'd chosen what to have for supper and poured out a reviving scotch.

Chose a frozen pizza. Poured the scotch.

The front doorbell rang at that point I went to answer it. Two men, olive skinned, dark haired, stood on the doorstep: and one of them held a pistol.

I looked at it with a sort of delayed reaction, not registering at once because I'd been looking at peaceful firearms all day. It took me at least a whole second to realise that this one was pointing at my midriff in a thoroughly unfriendly fashion. A Walther .22, I thought: as if it mattered.

My mouth, I dare say, opened and shut. It wasn't what one expected in a moderately crime-free suburb.

'Back,' he said.

'What do you want?'

'Get inside.' He prodded towards me with the long silencer attached to the automatic and because I certainly respected the blowing-away power of hand guns, I did as he said. He and his friend advanced through the front door and closed it behind them.

'Raise your hands,' said the gunman.

I did so.

He glanced towards the open door of the sitting-room and jerked his head towards it.

'Go in there.'

I went slowly, and stopped, and turned, and said again, 'What do you want?'

'Wait,' he said. He glanced at his companion and jerked his head again, this time at the windows. The companion switched on the lights and then went across and closed the curtains. It was not yet dark outside. A shaft of evening sunshine pierced through where the curtains met.

I thought: why aren't I desperately afraid? They looked so purposeful, so intent. Yet I still thought they had made some weird mistake and might depart if nicely spoken to.

They seemed younger than myself, though it was difficult to be sure. Italian, perhaps, from the south. They had the long straight nose, the narrow jaw, the black-brown eyes. The sort of face which went fat with age, grew a moustache and became a godfather.

That last thought shot through my brain from nowhere and seemed as nonsensical as a pistol

'What do you want?' I said again.

'Three computer tapes.'

My mouth no doubt went again through the fish routine. I listened to the utterly English sloppy accent and thought that it couldn't have less matched the body it came from.

'What ... what computer tapes?' I said, putting on bewilderment.

'Stop messing. We know you've got them. Your wife said so.'

Jesus, I thought. The bewilderment this time needed no acting.

He jerked the gun a fraction. 'Get them,' he said. His eyes were cold. His manner showed he despised me.

I said suddenly dry mouth, 'I can't think why my wife said ... why she thought ...'

'Stop wasting time,' he said sharply.

'But—'

'*The King and I*, and *West Side Story*,' he said impatiently, 'and *Okla-fucking-homa*.'

'I haven't got them.'

'Then that's too bad, buddy boy,' he said, and there was in an instant in him an extra dimension of menace. Before, he had been fooling along in second gear, believing no doubt that a gun was enough. But now I uncomfortably perceived that I was not dealing with someone reasonable and safe. If these were the two who had visited Peter, I understood what he had meant by frightening. There was a volatile quality, an absence of normal inhibition, a powerful impression of recklessness. The brakes-off syndrome which no legal deterrents deterred. I'd sensed it occasionally in boys I'd taught, but never before at such magnitude.

'You've got something you've no right to,' he said. 'And you'll give it to us.'

He moved the muzzle of the gun an inch or two sideways and squeezed the trigger. I heard the bullet zing past close to my ear. There was a crash of glass breaking behind me. One of Sarah's mementos of Venice, much cherished.

'That was a vase,' he said. 'Your television's next. After that, you. Ankles and such. Give you a limp for life. Those tapes aren't worth it.'

He was right. The trouble was that I doubted if he would believe that I really hadn't got them.

He began to swing the gun round to the television.

'OK.' I said.

He sneered slightly. 'Get them, then.'

With my capitulation he relaxed complacently and so did his obedient and unspeaking assistant, who was standing a pace to his rear. I walked the few steps to the coffe table and lowered my hands from the raised position.

'They're in the suitcase,' I said.

'Get them out.'

I lifted the lid of the suitcase a little and pulled out the jersey, dropping it on the floor.

'Hurry up,' he said.

He wasn't in the least prepared to be faced with a rifle; not in that room, in that nighbourhood, in the hands of the man he took me for.

It was with total disbelief that he looked at the long deadly shape and heard the double click as I worked the bolt. There was a chance he would realize that I'd never transport such a weapon with a bullet up the spout, but then if he took his own shooter around loaded, perhaps he wouldn't.

'Drop the pistol,' I said. 'You shoot me, I'll shoot you both, and you'd better believe it. I'm a crack shot.' There was a time for boasting, perhaps; and that was it.

He wavered. The assistant looked scared. The rifle was an ultra scary weapon. The silencer slowly began to point downwards, and the automatic thudded to the carpet. The anger could be felt.

'Kick it over here,' I said. 'And gently.'

He gave the gun a furious shove with his foot. It wasn't near enough for me to pick up, but too far for him also.

'Right,' I said. 'Now you listen to me. I haven't got those tapes. I've lent them to somebody else, because I thought they were music. How the hell should I know they were computer tapes? If you want them back, you'll have to wait until I get them. The person I lent them to has gone away for the weekend and I've no way of finding out where. You can have them without all this melodrama, but you'll have to wait. Give me an address, and I'll send them to you. I frankly want to get shot of you. I don't give a damn about those tapes or what you want them for. I just don't want you bothering me ... or my wife. Understood?'

'Yeah.'

'Where do you want them sent?'

His eyes narrowed.

'And it will cost you two quid,' I said, 'for packing and postage.'

The mundane detail seemed to convince him. With a disgruntled gesture he took two pounds from his pocket and dropped them at his feet.

'Cambridge main post office,' he said. 'To be collected.'

'Under what name?'

After a pause he said, 'Derry.'

I nodded. 'Right,' I said. A pity, though, that he'd given my own name. Anything else might have been informative. 'You can get out, now.'

Both pairs of eyes looked down at the automatic now on the carpet.

'Wait in the road,' I said. 'I'll throw it to you through the window. And don't come back.'

They edged to the door with an eye on the sleek steel barrel following them, and I went out after them into the hall. I got the benefit of two viciously frustrated expressions before they opened the front door and went out, closing it again behind them.

Back in the sitting-room I put the rifle on the sofa and picked up the Walther to unclip it and empty its magazine into an ashtray. Then I unscrewed the silencer from the barrel, and opened the window.

The two men stood on the pavement, balefully staring across twenty feet of grass. I threw the pistol so that it landed in a rose bush not far from their feet. When the assistant had picked it out and scratched himself on the thorns, I threw the silencer into the same place.

The gunman, finding he had no bullets, delivered a verbal parting shot.

'You send those tapes, or we'll be back.'

'You'll get them next week. And stay out of my life.'

I shut the window decisively and watched them walk away, every line of their bodies rigid with discomfiture.

What on *earth*, I wondered intensely, had Peter programmed onto those cassettes?

Chapter Four

'Who,' I said to Sarah, 'asked for computer tapes?'

'What?' She sounded vague, a hundred miles away on this planet but in another world.

'Someone,' I said patiently, 'must have asked you for some tapes.'

'Oh, you mean cassettes?'

'Yes, I do.' I tried to keep any grimness out of my voice; to sound merely conversational.

'But you can't have got his letter already,' she said, puzzled. 'He only came this morning.'

'Who was he?' I said.

'Oh!' she exclaimed. 'I suppose he telephoned. He could have got our number from enquiries.'

'Sarah . . .'

'Who was he? I've no idea. Someone to do with Peter's work.'

'What sort of a man?' I asked.

'What do you mean? Just a man. Middle-aged, grey-haired, a bit plump.' Sarah herself, like many naturally slim people, saw plumpness as a moral fault.

'Tell me what he said,' I pressed.

'If you insist. He said he was so sorry about Peter. He said Peter had brought home a project he'd been working on for his firm, possibly in the form of handwritten notes, possibly in the form of cassettes. He said the firm would be grateful to have it all back, because they would have to reallocate the job to someone else.'

It all sounded a great deal more civilised than frighteners with waving guns.

'And then?' I prompted.

'Well, Donna said she didn't know of anything Peter had in the house, though she did of course know he'd been working on *something*. Anyway, she looked in a lot of cupboards and drawers, and she found those three loose cassettes, out of their boxes, stacked between the gin and the Cinzano in the drinks cupboard. Am I boring you?'

She sounded over-polite and as if boring had been her intention, but I simply answered fervently, 'No, you're not. Please do go on.'

The shrug travelled almost visibly down the wire. 'Donna gave them to the man. He was delighted until he looked at them closely. Then he said they were tapes of musicals and not what he wanted, and please would we look again.'

'And then either you or Donna remembered—'

'I did,' she affirmed. 'We both saw Peter give them to you, but he must have got them mixed up. He gave you his firm's cassettes by mistake.'

Peter's firm . . .

'Did the man give you his name?' I said.

'Yes,' Sarah said. 'He introduced himself when he arrived. But you know how it is. He mumbled it a bit and I've forgotten it. Why? Didn't he tell you when me rang up?'

'No visiting card?'

'Don't tell me,' she said with exasperation, 'that you didn't take his address. Wait a minute, I'll ask Donna.'

She put the receiver down on the table and I could hear her calling Donna. I wondered why I hadn't told her of the nature of my visitors, and decided it was probably because she would try to argue me into going to the police. I certainly didn't want to do that, because they were likely to take unkindly to my waving a rifle about in such a place. I couldn't prove to them that it had been unloaded, and it did not come into the category of things a householder could reasonably use to defend his property. Bullets fired from a Mauser 7.62 didn't at ten paces smash vases and embed themselves in the plaster, they seared straight through the wall itself and killed people outside walking their dogs.

Firearms certificates could be taken away faster than given.

'Jonathan?' Sarah said, coming back.

'Yes.'

She read out the full address of Peter's firm in Norwich and added the telephone number.

'Is that all?' she said.

'Except . . . you're both still all right?'

'I am, thank you. Donna's very low. But I'm coping.'

We said our usual goodbyes: almost formal, without warmth, deadly polite.

Duty took me back to Bisley the following day: duty and restlessness and dreadful prospects on the box. I shot better and thought less about Peter, and when the light began to fade I went home and corrected the ever-recurring exercise books: and on Monday Ted Pitts said he hadn't yet done anything about my computer tapes but that if I cared to stay on at four o'clock, we could both go down to the computer room and see what there was to see.

When I joined him he was already busy in the small side-room that with its dim cream walls and scratchily polished floor had an air of being everyone's poor relation. A single light hung without a shade from the ceiling, and the two wooden chairs were regulation battered school issue. Two nondescript tables occupied most of the floorspace, and upon them rested the uninspiring-looking machines which had cost a small fortune. I asked Ted mildly why he put up with such cramped, depressing quarters.

He looked at me vaguely, his mind on his task. 'You know how it is. You have to teach boys individually on this baby to get good results. There aren't enough classrooms. This is all that's available. It's not too bad. And anyway, I never notice.'

I could believe it. He was a hiker, an ex-youth-hosteller, an embracer of earnest discomforts. He perched on the edge of the hard wooden chair and applied his own computer-like brain to the one on the tables.

There were four separate pieces of equipment. A box like a small television set with a typewriter keyboard protruding forward from the lower edge of the screen. A cassette player. A large upright uninformative black box marked simply 'Harris', and something which looked at first sight like a typewriter, but which in fact had no keys. All four were linked together, and each to its own wall socket, by black electric cables.

Ted Pitts put *Oklahoma* into the cassette player and typed CLOAD

'BASIC' on the keyboard. CLOAD 'BASIC' appeared in small white capital letters high up on the left of the television screen, and two asterisks appeared, one of them rapidly blinking on and off, up on the right. On the cassette player, the wheels of the tape-reels quickly revolved.

'How much do you remember?' Ted said.

'About enough to know you're searching the tape for the language, and the CLOAD means LOAD from the cassette.'

He nodded and pointed briefly to the large upright box. 'The computer already has its own BASIC stored in there. I put it in at lunchtime. Now just let's see ...' He hunched himself over the keyboard, pressing keys, stopping and starting the cassette player and punctuating his activity with grunts.

'Nothing useful,' he muttered, turning the tapes over and repeating the process. 'Let's try ...' A fair time passed. He shook his head now and then, and said finally, 'Give me those other two tapes. It must logically be at the *beginning* of one of the sides – unless of course he added it at the end simply because he had space left ... or perhaps he didn't do it at all....'

'Won't the programs run on your own version of BASIC?'

He shook his head. 'I tried before you came. The only response you get is ERROR IN LINE 10. Which means that the two versions aren't compatible.' He grunted again and tried *West Side Story*, and towards the end of the first side he sat bolt upright and said, 'Well, now.'

'It's on there?'

'Can't tell yet. But there's something filed under "Z". Might just try that.' He flicked a few more switches and sat back beaming. 'Now all we do is wait a few minutes while that...' he pointed at the large upright box ... 'soaks up whatever is on the tape under "z", and if it should happen to be Grantley Basic, we'll be in business.'

'Why does "z" give you hope.'

'Instinct. Might be a hundred per cent wrong. But it's a much longer recording than anything else I've found so far on the tapes, and it feels the right length. Four and a quarter minutes. I've fed BASIC into the Harris thousands of times.'

His instinct proved reliable. The word READY suddenly appeared on the screen, white and bright and promising. Ted sighed heavily with satisfaction and nodded three times.

'Sensible fellow, your friend,' he said. 'So now we can see what you've got.'

When he ran *Oklahoma* again, the file names came up clearly beside the flashing asterisk at the top right of the screen, and although some of them were mysterious to me, some of them were definitely not.

DONCA EDINB EPSOM FOLKE FONTW GOODW HAMIL HAYDK. HEREF HEXHM

'Names of towns,' I said. 'Towns with racecourses.'

Ted nodded. 'Which would you like to try?'

'Epsom.'

'OK.' he said. He rewound the tape with agile fingers and typed CLOAD 'EPSOM' on the keyboard. 'This puts the program filed under EPSOM into the computer, but you know that, of course, I keep forgetting.'

The encouraging word READY appeared again, and Ted said, 'Which do want to do, List it or Run it?'

'Run,' I said.

He nodded and typed RUN on the keyboard, and in bright little letters the screen enquired WHICH RACE AT EPSOM? TYPE NAME OF RACE AND PRESS 'ENTER'.

'My God,' I said. 'Let's try the Derby.'

'Stands to reason,' Ted said, and typed DERBY. The screen promptly responded with TYPE NAME OF HORSE AND PRESS 'ENTER'.

Ted typed JONATHAN DERRY and again pressed the double-sized key on the keyboard marked 'Enter', and the screen obliged with:

EPSOM: THE DERBY

HORSE: JONATHAN DERRY.

TO ALL QUESTIONS ANSWER YES OR NO AND PRESS 'ENTER'.

A couple of inches lower down there was a question:

HAS HORSE WON A RACE?

Ted typed YES and pressed 'Enter'. The first three lines remained, but the question was replaced with another.

HAS HORSE WON THIS YEAR?

Ted typed NO. The screen responded:

HAS HORSE WON ON COURSE?

Ted typed NO. The screen responded:

HAS HORSE RUN ON COURSE?

Ted typed YES.

There were questions about the horse's sire, its dam, its jockey, its trainer, the number of days since its last run, and its earnings in prize money; and one final question:

IS HORSE QUOTED ANTE-POST AT 25-1 OR LESS?

Ted typed YES, and the screen said merely,

ANY MORE HORSES?

Ted typed YES again, and we found ourselves back at

TYPE NAME OF HORSE AND PRESS 'ENTER'.

'That's not handicapping,' I said.

'Is that what it's supposed to be?' Ted shook his head. 'More like statistical probabilities, I should have thought. Let's got through it again and answer NO to ANY MORE HORSES?'

He typed TED PITTS for the horse's name and varied the answers, and immediately after his final NO we were presented with a cleared screen and a new display.

HORSE'S NAME	WIN FACTOR
JONATHAN DERRY	27
TED PITTS	12

'You've *no* chance,' I said. 'You might as well stay in the stable.'

He looked a bit startled, and then laughed. 'Yes. That's what it is. A guide to gamblers.'

He typed LIST instead of RUN, and immediately the bones of the program appeared, but scrolling upwards too fast to read, like flight-information changes at airports. Ted merely hummed a little and typed LIST 10–140, and after some essential flickering the screen presented the goods.

```
LIST 10–140
10 PRINT "WHICH RACE AT EPSOM? TYPE NAME OF RACE AND PRESS 'ENTER'"
20 INPUT A$
30 IF A$ = "DERBY" THEN 330
40 IF A$ = "OAKS" THEN 340
50 IF A$ = "CORONATION CUP" THEN 350
60 IF A$ = "BLUE RIBAND STAKES" THEN 360
```

The list went down to the bottom of the screen in this fashion, and Ted gave it one appraising look and said, 'Dead simple.'

The dollar sign, I seemed to remember, meant that the Input had to be in the form of letters. Input A, without the dollar sign, would have asked for numbers.

Ted seemed perfectly happy. He typed LIST 300–380 and got another set of instructions.

At 330 the program read: LET A = 10: B = 8: C = 6: D = 2: D1 = 2. Lines 332, 334, and 336 looked similar, with numbers being ascribed to letters.

'That's the weighting,' Ted said. 'The value given to each answer. Ten points for the first question, which was ... um ... has the horse won a race. And so on. I see that 10 points are given also for the last question, which was about ... er ... ante-post odds, wasn't it?'

I nodded.

'There you are, then,' he said. 'I dare say there's a different weighting for every race. There might of course be different *questions* for every race. Ho hum. Want to see?'

'If you've the time,' I said.

'Oh sure. I've always got time for TOMSS. Love 'em, you know.'

He went on typing LIST followed by various numbers and came up with such gems as:

```
520 IF N$ = "NO" THEN GOTO 560: X = X + B
530 INPUT N$: AB = AB + I
540 IF N$ = "NO" THEN GOTO 560: X = X + M
550 T = T + G2
560 GOSUB 4000
```

'What does all that mean?' I asked.

'Um ... well. It's much easier to *write* a program than to read and understand someone else's. Programs are frantically individual. You can get the same results by all sorts of different routes. I mean, if you're going from London to Bristol you go down the M4 and it's called M4 all the way, but on a computer you can call the road anything you like, at any point on the journey, and *you* might know that at different moments L2, say, or RQ3 or B7(2) equalled M4, but no one else would.'

'Is that also what you teach the kids?'

'Er, yes. Sorry, it's a habit.' He glanced at the screen. 'I'd guess that those top lines are to do with skipping some questions if previous answers make them unnecessary. Jumping to later bits of program. If I printed the whole thing out onto paper I could work out their exact meaning.'

I shook my head. 'Don't trouble. Let's try a different racecourse.'

'Sure.'

He rewound the tape to the beginning and typed CLOAD 'DONCA', AND WHEN THE SCREEN SAID READY, typed RUN.

Immediately we were asked WHICH RACE AT DONCASTER? TYPE NAME OF RACE AND PRESS 'ENTER'.

'OK.' Ted said, pressing switches. 'What about further down the tape? Say, GOODW?'

We got WHICH RACE AT GOODWOOD? TYPE NAME OF RACE AND PRESS 'ENTER'.

'I don't know any races at Goodwood,' I said.

Ted said, 'That's easy,' and typed LIST 10–140. When the few seconds of flickering had stopped, we had:

```
LIST 10–140
10 PRINT "WHICH RACE AT GOODWOOD? TYPE NAME OF RACE AND
PRESS 'ENTER'"
20 INPUT A$
30 IF A$ = "GOODWOOD STAKES" THEN 330
40 IF A$ = "GOODWOOD CUP" THEN 340
```

There were fifteen races listed altogether.

'What happens if you type in the name of a race there's no program for?' I asked.

'Let's see,' he said. He typed RUN, and we were back to WHICH RACE AT GOODWOOD? He typed DERBY, and the screen informed us THERE IS NO INFORMATION FOR THIS RACE.

'Neat and simple,' Ted said.

We sampled all the sides of the three tapes, but the programs were all similar. WHICH RACE AT REDCAR? WHICH RACE AT ASCOT? WHICH RACE AT NEWMARKET?

There were programs for about fifty racecourses, with varying numbers of races listed at each. Several lists contained not actual titles of races but general categories like STRAIGHT 7 FURLONGS FOR 3 YR OLDS AND UPWARDS, or THREE MILE WEIGHT-FOR-AGE STEEPLECHASE: and it was not until quite late that I realized with amusement that *none* of the races were handicaps. There were no questions at all about how many lengths a horse had won by, while carrying such and such a weight.

All in all, there was provision for scoring for any number of horses in each of more than eight hundred named races, and in an unknown quantity of *un*named races. Each race had its own set of weightings and very often its own set of questions. It had been a quite monumental task.

'It must have taken him days,' Ted said.

'Weeks, I think. He had to to it in his spare time.'

'They're not complicated programs, of course,' Ted said. 'Nothing really needing an expert. It's more organization than anything else. Still, he hasn't wasted much space. Amateurs write very long programs. Experts get to the same nitty-gritty in a third of the time. It's just practice.'

'We'd better make a note of which side of which tape contains the Grantley Basic,' I said.

Ted nodded. 'It's at an end. After York. Filed under 'z'. He checked that he had the right tape, and wrote on its label in pencil.

For no particular reason I picked up the other two tapes and briefly looked at the words I had half-noticed before: the few words Peter had pencilled onto one of the labels.

'Programs compiled for C. Norwood.'

Ted, glancing over, said, 'That's the first side you're looking at. Ascot and so on.' He paused. 'We might just as well number the sides properly, one to six. Get them in order.'

Order, to him as to me, was a habit. When he'd finished the numbering he put the cassettes back in their gaudy boxes and handed them over. I thanked him most profoundly for his patience and took him out for a couple of beers; then over his pint, 'Will you be trying them out?'

'Trying what out?'

'Those races, of course. It's the Derby next month, some time. If you like we could work out the scores for all the Derby horses, and see if the program comes up with the winner. I'd actually quite *like* to do it. Wouldn't you?'

'I wouldn't begin to know the answers to all those questions.'

'No.' He sighed. 'Pity. The info must be *somewhere*, but unearthing it might be a bore.

'I'll ask my brother,' I said, explaining about William. 'He sometimes mentions form books. I'd guess the answers would be in those.'

Ted seemed pleased with the idea, and I didn't immediately ask him which he was keener to do, to test the accuracy of the programs or to make a profit. He told me, however.

He said tentatively, 'Would you mind very much ... I mean ... would you mind if I took a *copy* of those tapes?'

I looked at him in faint surprise and he smiled awkwardly.

'The fact is Jonathan, I could do with a boost to the economy. I mean, if those tapes actually come up with the goods, why not use them?' He squirmed a little on his seat, and when I didn't rush to answer he went on, 'You know how bloody small our salaries are. It's no fun with three kids to feed, and their clothes, their shoes cost a bomb, and the little devils grow out of them before you've paid for them, practically. I'm never under my limit on my credit cards. Never.'

'Have another beer,' I said.

'It's better for you,' he said gloomily, accepting the offer. 'You've no children. It isn't so hard for you to manage on a pittance. And you earn more anyway, with being a head of department.'

I said thoughtfully, 'I don't see why you shouldn't make copies, if you want to.'

'Jonathan!' He was clearly delighted.

'But I wouldn't use them,' I said, 'without finding out if they're any good. You might lose a packet.'

'I'll be careful,' he said, but his eyes gleamed behind his black-rimmed spectacles and I wondered uneasily if I were seeing the birth of a compulsion. There was always a slight touch of the fanatic about Ted. 'Can you ask your brother where I can get a form book?' he said.

'Well ...'

He scanned my face. 'You're regretting saying I could copy them. Do you want them for yourself, now, is that it?'

'No. I just thought ... gambling's like drugs. You can get addicted and go down the drain.'

'But all I want—' He stopped and shrugged. He looked disappointed but nothing more.

I sighed and said, 'OK. But for God's sake be sensible.'

'I will,' he said fervently. He looked at me expectantly and I took the tapes out of my pocket and gave them back to him.

'Take good care of them,' I said.

'With my life.'

'Not that far.' I thought briefly of gun-toting visitors and of much I didn't understand, and I added slowly, 'While you're about it, make copies for me too.'

He was puzzled. 'But you'll have the originals.'

I shook my head. 'They'll belong to someone else. I'll have to give them back. But I don't see why, if copies are possible, I shouldn't also keep what I return.'

'Copies are dead easy,' he said. 'Also they're prudent. All you do is load the program into the computer, from the cassette, like we did, then change to a fresh cassette and load the program back from the computer onto the new tape. You can make dozens of copies, if you like. Any time I've written a program I especially don't want to lose, I record it onto several different tapes. That way, if one tape gets lost or some idiot re-records on top of what you've done, you've always got a backup.'

'I'll buy some tapes, then,' I said.

He shook his head. 'You give me the money, and I'll get them. Ordinary tapes are OK if you're pushed, but special digital cassettes made for computer work are better.'

I gave him some money, and he said he would make the copies the following day, either at lunch or after school. 'And get the form book,' he reminded me, 'won't you?'

'Yes,' I said; and later, from home, I telephoned the farm and spoke to William.

'How's it going?'

'What would you say if I tried for a racing stable in the summer?'

'I'd say stick to farms,' I said.

'Yeah. But the hunters are all out at grass in July and August, and this riding school here's cracking up, they've sold off the best horses, there's nothing much to ride, and there's weeds and muck everywhere. Mr Askwith's taken to drink. He comes roaring out in the mornings clutching the hard stuff and swearing at the girls. There are only two of them left now, trying to look after fourteen ponies. It's a mess.'

'It sounds it.'

'I've been reduced to doing some revision for those grotty exams.'

'Things must be bad,' I said.

'Thanks for the cheque.'

'Sorry it was late. Listen, I've a friend who wants a racing form book. How would he get one?'

William, it transpired, knew of about six different types of form book. Which did my friend want?

One which told him a horse's past history, how long since it had last raced and whether its ante-post odds were less than 25-1. Also its sire's and dam's and jockey's and trainer's history, and how much it had won in prize money. For starters.

'Good grief,' said my brother. 'You want a combination of the form book and *The Sporting Life*.'

'Yes, but *which* form book.'

'*The* form book,' he said. '*Raceform* and *Chaseform*. *Chaseform*'s the jumpers. Does he want jumpers as well?'

'I think so.'

'Tell him to write to Turf Newspapers, then. The form book comes in sections; a new updated section every week. Best on earth. I covet it increasingly, but it costs a bomb. Do you think the trustees would consider it vocational training?' He spoke, however, without much hope.

I thought of Ted Pitt's financial state and inquired for something cheaper.

'Hum,' said William judiciously. 'He could try the weekly *Sporting Record*, I suppose.' A thought struck him. 'This wouldn't be anything to do with your friend Peter and his betting system, would it? You said he was dead.'

'Same system, different friend.'

'There isn't a system born,' William said, 'that really works.'

'You'd know, of course,' I said dryly.

'I do read.'

We talked a little more and said goodbye in good humour, and I found myself regretting, after I'd put down the receiver, that I hadn't asked him if he'd like to spend the week with me rather than on the farm. But I didn't suppose he would have done. He'd have found even the drunken Mr Askwith more congenial than the decorum of Twickenham.

Sarah telephoned an hour later, sounding strained and abrupt.

'Do you know anyone called Chris Norwood?' she said.

'No, I don't think so.' The instant I'd said it I remembered Peter's handwriting on the cassette. 'Program compiled for C. Norwood'. I opened my mouth to tell her, but she forestalled me.

'Peter knew him. The police have been here again, asking questions.'

'But what—' I began in puzzlement.

'I don't *know* what it's all about, if that's what you're going to ask. But someone called Chris Norwood has been shot.'

Chapter Five

Ignorance seemed to surround me like a fog.

'I thought Peter might have mentioned him to you,' Sarah said. 'You always talked with him more than to Donna and me.'

'Doesn't Donna know this Norwood?' I asked, ignoring the bitter little thrust.

'No, she doesn't. She's still in shock. It's all too much.'

Fogs could be dangerous, I thought. There might be all manner of traps waiting, unseen.

'What did the police actually say?' I said.

'Nothing much. Only that they were enquiring into a death, and wanted any help Peter could give.'

'*Peter!*'

'Yes, Peter. They didn't know he was dead. They weren't the same as the ones who came before. I think they said they were from Suffolk. What does it matter?' She sounded impatient. 'They'd found Peter's name and address on a pad beside the telephone. This Norwood's telephone. They said that in a murder investigation they had to follow even the smallest lead.'

'Murder...'

'That's what they said.'

I frowned and asked, 'When was he killed?'

'How do I know? Sometime last week. Thursday. Friday. I can't remember. They were talking to Donna, really, not to me. I kept telling them she wasn't fit, but they wouldn't listen. They wouldn't see for ages that the poor darling is too dazed to care about a total stranger, however he died. And to crown it all, when they did finally realize, they said they might come back when she was better.'

After a pause I said, 'When's the inquest?'

'How on earth should I know.'

'I mean, on Peter.'

'Oh.' She sounded disconcerted. 'On Friday. We don't have to go. Peter's father is giving evidence of identity. He won't speak to Donna. He somehow thinks it was her fault that Peter was careless with the boat. He's been perfectly beastly.'

'Mm,' I said noncommittally.

'A man from the insurance came here, asking if Peter had ever had problems with leaking gas lines and wanting to know if he always started the engine without checking for petrol vapour.'

Peter hadn't been careless, I thought. I remembered that he'd been pretty careful on the canals, opening up the engine compartment every morning to let any trapped vapour escape. And that had been diesel, not petrol: less inflammable altogether.

'Donna said she didn't know. The engine was Peter's affair. She was always in the cabin unpacking food and so on while he was getting ready to start up. And anyway,' Sarah said, 'why all this fuss about vapour? It isn't as if there was any actual *petrol* sloshing about. They say there wasn't.'

'It's the vapour that explodes,' I said. 'Liquid petrol won't ignite unless it's mixed with air.'

'Are you serious?'

'Absolutely.'

'Oh.'

There was a pause: a silence. Some dying-fall goodbyes. Not with a bang, I thought, but with a yawn.

On Tuesday, Ted Pitts said he hadn't yet had a chance to buy the tapes for the copies and on Wednesday I sweet-talked a colleague into taking my games duty for the afternoon and straight after morning school set off to Norwich. Not to see my wife, but to visit the firm where Peter had worked.

It turned out to be a three-room two-men-and-a-girl affair tucked away in a suite of offices in a building on an industrial estate: one modest component among about twenty others listed on the directory-board in the lobby: MASON MILES ASSOCIATES, COMPUTER CONSULTANTS rubbing elbows with DIRECT ACCESS DISTRIBUTION SERVICES and SEA MAGIC, DECORATIVE SHELL IMPORTERS.

Mason Miles and his Associates showed no signs of overwork but neither was there any of the gloom which hangs about a business on the brink. The inactivity, one felt, was normal.

The girl sat at a desk reading a magazine. The younger man fiddled with a small computer's innards and hummed in the manner of Ted Pitts. The older man, beyond a wide open door labelled Mason Miles, lolled in a comfortable chair with an arm-stretching expanse of newspaper. All three looked up without speed about five seconds after I'd walked through their outer unguarded defences.

'Hullo,' the girl said. 'Are you for the job?'

'Which job?'

'You're not, then. Not Robinson, D.F.?'

'Afraid not.'

'He's late. Dare say he's not coming.' She shrugged. 'Happens all the time.'

'Would that be Peter Keithley's job?' I asked.

The young man's attention went back to his eviscerated machine.

'Sure is,' said the girl. 'If you're not for his job, er, how can we help you?'

I explained that my wife, who was staying in Peter's house, was under the impression that someone from the firm had visited Peter's widow, asking for some tapes he had been working on.

The girl looked blank. Mason Miles gave me a lengthy frown from the distance. The young man dropped a screwdriver and muttered under his breath.

The girl said, 'None of us has been to Peter's house. Not even before the troubles.'

Mason Miles cleared his throat and raised his voice. 'What tapes are you talking about? You'd better come in here.'

He put down the newspaper and stood up reluctantly, as if the effort was too much for a weekday afternoon. He was not in the least like Sarah's description of a plump grey-haired ordinary middle-aged man. There was a crinkly red thatch over a long white face, a lengthy stubborn-looking upper lip and cheekbones, of Scandinavian intensity; the whole extra-tall body being, as far as I could judge, still under forty.

'Don't let me disturb you,' I said without irony.

'You are not.'

'Would anyone else from your firm,' I asked, 'have gone to Peter's house, asking on your behalf for the tapes he was working on?'

'What tapes were those?'

'Cassettes with programs for evaluating racehorses.'

'He was working on no such project.'

'But in his spare time?' I suggested.

Mason Miles shrugged and sat down again with the relief of a traveller after a wearisome journey. 'Perhaps. What he did in his spare time was his own affair.'

'And do you have a grey-haired middle-aged man on your staff?'

He gave me a considering stare and then said merely, 'We employ no such person. If such a person has visited Mrs Keithley purporting to come from here, it is disturbing.'

I looked at his totally undisturbed demeanour and agreed.

'Peter was writing the programs for someone called Chris Norwood,' I said. 'I don't suppose you've ever heard of him?' I made it a question but without much hope, and he shook his head and suggested I ask his Associates in the outer office. The Associates also showed nil reactions to the name of Chris Norwood, but the young man paused from his juggling of microchips long enough to say that he had put everything Peter had left concerning his work in a shoebox in a cupboard, and he supposed it would do no harm if I wanted to look.

I found the box, took it out, and began to sift through the handwritten scraps of notes which it contained. Nearly all of them concerned his work and took the form of mysterious memos to himself. 'Remember to tell RT of modification to PET.' 'Pick up floppy discs for LMP.' 'Tell ISCO about L's software package.' 'The bug in R's program must be a syntax error in the subroutine.' Much more of the same, and none of it of any use.

There was a sudden noise and flurry at the outer door, and a wild-eyed breathless heavily flushed youth appeared, along with a suitcase, a holdall, an overcoat and a tennis racket.

'Sorry,' he panted. 'The train was late.'

'Robinson?' the girl said calmly. 'D.F.?'

'What? Oh. Yes. Is the job still open?'

I looked down at another note, the writing as neat as all the others: 'Borrow Grantley Basic tape from GF.' Turned the piece of paper over. On the back he'd written, 'C. Norwood, Angel Kitchens, Newmarket.'

I persevered to the bottom of the box, but there was nothing else that I understood. I put all the scrappy notes back again, and thanked the Associates for their trouble. They hardly listened. The attention of the whole firm was intently fixed on D.F. Robinson, who was wilting under the probing questions. Miles, who had beckoned them all into the inner office, was saying, 'How would you handle a client who made persistently stupid mistakes but blamed *you* for not explaining his system thoroughly?'

I sketched a farewell which nobody noticed, and left.

Newmarket lay fifty miles to the south of Norwich, and I drove there through the sunny afternoon thinking that the fog lay about me as thick as ever. Radar, perhaps, would be useful. Or a gale. Or some good clarifying information. Press on, I thought: press on.

Angel Kitchens, as listed in the telephone directory in the post office, were to be found in Angel Lane, to which various natives directed me with accuracy varying from vague to absent, and which proved to be a dead-end tarmac tributary to the east of the town, far from the mainstream of High Street.

The Kitchens were just what they said: the kitchens of a mass food-production business, making frozen gourmet dinners in single-portion foil pans for the upper-end of the market. 'Posh nosh' one of my route-directors had said. 'Fancy muck,' said another. 'You can buy that stuff in the town, but give me a hamburger any day' from another, and 'Real tasty' from the last. They'd all known the product, if not the location.

At a guess the Kitchens had been developed from the back half and outhouses of a defunct country mansion; they had that slightly haphazard air, and were surrounded by mature trees and the remnants of a landscaped garden. I parked in the large but well-occupied expanse of concrete outside a new-looking white single-storey construction marked Office, and pushed my way through its plate-glass double-door entrance.

Inside, in the open-plan expanse, the contrast to Mason Miles Associates was complete. Life was taken at a run, if not a stampede. The work in hand, it seemed, would overwhelm the inmates if they relaxed for a second.

My tentative inquiry for someone who had been a friend of Chris

Norwood reaped me a violently unexpected reply.

'That *creep*? If he had any friends, they'd be down in Veg Preparation, where he worked.'

'Er, Veg Preparation?'

'Two-storey grey stone building past the freezer sheds.'

I went out to the car park, wandered around and asked again.

'Where them carrots is being unloaded.'

Them carrots were entering a two-storey grey stone building by the sack-load on a fork-lift truck, the driver of which mutely pointed me to a less cavernous entrance round a corner.

Through there one passed through a small lobby beside a large changing-room where rows of outdoor clothing hung on pegs. Next came a white-tiled scrub-up room smelling like a hospital, followed by a swing door into a long narrow room lit blindingly by electricity and filled with gleaming stainless steel, noisily whirring machines and people dressed in white.

At the sight of me standing there in street clothes a large man wearing what looked like a cotton undervest over a swelling paunch advanced with waving arms and shooed me out.

'Cripes, mate, you'll get me sacked,' he said, as the swing-door swung behind us.

'I was directed here,' I said mildly.

'What do you want?'

With less confidence than before I inquired for any friend of Chris Norwood.

The shrewd eyes above the beer-stomach appraised me. The mouth pursed. The chef's hat sat comfortably over strong dark eyebrows.

'He's been murdered,' he said. 'You from the press?'

I shook my head. 'He knew a friend of mine, and he got both of us into a bit of trouble.'

'Sounds just like him.' He pulled a large white handkerchief out of his white trousers and wiped his nose. 'What exactly do you want?'

'I think just to talk to someone who knew him. I want to know what he was like. Who he knew. Anything. I want to know why and how he got us into trouble.'

'I knew him,' he said. He paused, considering. 'What's it worth?'

I sighed. 'I'm a schoolmaster. It's worth what I can afford. And it depends *what* you know.'

'All right then,' he said judiciously. 'I finish here at six. I'll meet you in the Purple Dragon, right? Up the lane, turn left, quarter of a mile. You buy me a couple of pints and we'll take it from there. OK?'

'Yes,' I said. 'My name is Jonathan Derry.'

'Akkerton.' He gave a short nod, as if sealing a bargain. 'Vince,' he added as an afterthought. He gave me a last unpromising inspection and barged back through the swing doors. I heard the first of the words he sprayed into the long busy room, 'You, Reg, you get back to work. I've only to take my eyes off you . . .'

The door closed discreetly behind him.

* * *

I waited for him at a table in the Purple Dragon, a pub a good deal less colourful than its name, and at six-fifteen he appeared, dressed now in grey trousers and a blue and white shirt straining at its buttons. Elliptical views of hairy chest appeared when he sat down, which he did with a wheeze and a licking of lips. The first pint I bought him disappeared at a single draught, closely followed by half of the second.

'Thirsty work, chopping up veg,' he said.

'Do you do it by hand?' I was surprised, and sounded it.

'Course not. Washed, peeled, chopped, all done by machines. But nothing hops into a machine by itself. Or out, come to that.'

'What, er ... veg?' I said.

'Depends what they want. Today, mostly carrots, celery, onions, mushrooms. Regular ever day, that lot. Needed for Burgundy Beef. Our best seller, Burgundy Beef. Chablis Chicken, Pork and Port, next best. You ever had any?'

'I don't honestly know.'

He drank deeply with satisfaction. 'It's good food,' he said seriously, wiping his mouth, 'All fresh ingredients. No mucking about. Pricey, mind you, but worth it.'

'You enjoy the job?' I asked.

He nodded. 'Sure. Worked in kitchens all my life. Some of them, you could shake hands with the cockroaches. Big as rats. Here, so clean you'd see a fruit fly a mile off. I've been in Veg three months now. Did a year in Fish but the smell hangs in your nostrils after a while.'

'Did Chris Norwood,' I said, 'chop up veg?'

'When we were pushed. Otherwise he cleaned up, checked the input, and ran errands.' His voice was assured and positive: a man who had no need to guard his tongue.

'Er, checked the input?' I said.

'Counted the sacks of veg as they were delivered. If there were twenty sacks of onions on the day's delivery note, his job to see twenty sacks arrived.' He inspected the contents of the pint glass. 'Reckon it was madness giving him that job. Mind you, it's not millionaire class, knocking off sacks of carrots and onions, but it seems he was supplying a whole string of bleeding village shops with the help of the lorry drivers. The driver would let the sacks fall off the lorry on the way here, see, and Chris Norwood would count twenty where there was only sixteen. They split the profits. It goes on everywhere, that sort of thing, in every kitchen I've ever worked in. Meat too. Sides of ruddy beef. Caviar. You name it, it's been nicked. But Chris wasn't just your usual opportunist. He didn't know what to keep his hands off.'

'What didn't he keep his hands off?' I asked.

Vince Akkerton polished off the liquid remains and put down his glass with suggestive loudness. Obediently I crossed to the bar for a refill, and once there had been a proper inspection of the new froth and a sampling of the first two inches, I heard what Chris Norwood had stolen.

'The girls in the office said he pinched their cash. They didn't cotton on for ages. They thought it was one of the women there that they didn't like. Chris was in and out all the time, taking in the day-sheets and chatting them up. He thought a lot of himself. Cocky bastard.'

I looked at the well-fleshed worldly-wise face and thought of chief petty officers and ships' engineers. The same easy assumption of command: the ability to size men up and put them to work. People like Vince Akkerton were the indispensible getters of things done.

'How old,' I said, 'was Chris Norwood?'

'Thirtyish. Same as you. Difficult to say, exactly.' He drank. 'What sort of trouble did he get you in?'

'A couple of bullies came to my house looking for something of his.'

Fog, I thought.

'What sort of thing?' said Akkerton.

'Computer tapes.'

If I'd spoken in Outer Mongolian, it couldn't have meant less to him. He covered his bewilderment with beer and in disappointment I drank some of my own.

'Course,' said Akkerton, rallying, 'there's a computer or some such over in the office. They use it for keeping track of how many tons of Burgundy Beef and so on they've got on order and in the freezers, stuff like that. Working out how many thousands of ducks they need. Lobsters. Even coriander seeds.' He paused and with the first glint of humour said, 'Mind you, the results are always wrong, on account of activities on the side. There was a whole shipment of turkeys missing once. Computer error, they said.' He grunted. 'Chris Norwood with his carrots and onions, he was peanuts.'

'These were computer tapes to do with horseracing,' I said.

The dark eyebrows rose. 'Now that makes more sense. Every bleeding thing in this town practically is to do with horseracing. I've heard they think the knacker's yard has a direct line to our Burgundy Beef. It's a libel.'

'Did Chris Norwood bet?'

'Everyone in the firm bets. Cripes, you couldn't live in this town and not bet. It's in the air. Catching, like the pox.'

I seemed to be getting nowhere at all and I didn't know what else to ask. I cast around and came up with, 'Where was Chris Norwood killed?'

'Where? In his room. He rented a room in a council house from a retired old widow who goes out cleaning in the mornings. See, she wasn't supposed to take in lodgers, the council don't allow it, and she never told the welfare, who'd been doling out free meals, that she was earning, so the fuss going on now is sending her gaga.' He shook his head. 'Next street to me, all this happened.'

'What *did* exactly happen?'

He showed no reluctance to tell. More like relish.

'She found Chris dead in his room when she went in to clean it. See, she thought he'd have gone to work; she always went out before him in the mornings. Anyway, there he was. Lot of blood, so I've heard. You don't know what's true and what isn't, but they say he had bullets in his *feet*. Bled to death.'

Christ Almighty . . .

'Couldn't walk, you see,' Akkerton said. 'No telephone. Back bedroom. No one saw him.'

With a dry mouth I asked, 'What about . . . his belongings?'

'Dunno, really. Nothing stolen, that I've heard of. Seems there were just a few things broken. And his stereo was shot up proper, same as him.'

What do I do, I thought. Do I go to the police investigating Chris Norwood and tell them I was visited by two men who threatened to shoot my television and my ankles? Yes, I thought, this time I probably do.

'When . . .' My voice sounded hoarse. I cleared my throat and tried again. 'Which day did it happen?'

'Last week. He didn't show up Friday morning, and it was bloody inconvenient as we were handling turnips that day and it was his job to chop the tops and roots off and feed them into the washer.'

I felt dazed. Chris Norwood had been dead by Friday morning. It had been *Saturday afternoon* when I'd flung my visitors' Walther out into the rose bush. On Saturday they had been still looking for the tapes, which meant . . . dear God . . . that they hadn't got them from Chris Norwood. They'd shot him, and left him, and they still hadn't got the tapes. He would have given them to them if he'd had them: to stop them shooting him; to save his life. The tapes weren't worth one's life: they truly weren't. I remembered the insouciance with which I faced that pistol, and was in retrospect terrified.

Vince Akkerton showed signs of feeling it was time he was paid for his labours. I mentally tossed between what I could afford and what he might expect and decided to try him with the least possible. Before I could offer it, however, two girls came into the bar and prepared to sit at the next table. One of them, seeing Akkerton, changed course abruptly and fetched up at his side.

'Hullo, Vince,' she said. 'Do us a favour. Stand us a rum and coke and I'll pay you tomorrow.'

'I've heard that before,' he said indulgently, 'but this friend of mine's buying.'

Poorer by two rum and cokes, another full pint and a further half (for me), I sat and listened to Akkerton explaining that the girls worked in the Angel Kitchens office.

Carol and Janet. Young, medium bright, full of chatter and chirpiness, expecting from minute to minute the arrival of their boyfriends.

Carol's opinion of Chris Norwood was straightforwardly indignant. 'We all worked out it had to be him dipping into our handbags, but we couldn't *prove* it, see? We were just going to set a trap for him when he got killed, and I suppose I should feel sorry for him, but I don't. He couldn't keep his hands off anything. I mean, not anything. He'd take your last sandwich when you weren't looking and laugh at you while he ate it.'

'He didn't see anything wrong in pinching things,' Janet said.

'Here,' Akkerton said, leaning forward for emphasis, 'young Janet here, she works the computer. You ask her about those tapes.'

Janet's response was a raised-eyebrow thoughtfulness.

'I didn't know he had any actual tapes,' she said. 'But of course he was always *around*. It was his job, you know, collecting the day-sheets from all the departments and bringing them to me. He'd always hang around a bit, especially the last few weeks, asking how the computer worked, you know? I showed him how it came up with all the quantities, how much salt, you know, and things like that, had to be shifted to each department, and how all the orders went through, mixed container loads to Bournemouth or Birmingham, you know. The whole firm would collapse you know, without the computer.'

'What make is it?' I said.

'What *make*?' They all thought it an odd question, but I'd have gambled on the answer.

'A Grantley,' Janet said.

I smiled at her as inoffensively as I knew how and asked her if she would have let Chris Norwood run his tapes through her Grantley if he'd asked her nicely, and after some guilty hesitation and a couple of downward blushes into her rum and coke, said she might have done, you know, at one time, before they discovered, you know, that it was Chris who was stealing their cash.

'We should have guessed it ages ago,' Carol said, 'but then the things he took, like our sandwiches and such, and things out of the office, staples, envelopes, rolls of sticky tape, well we *saw* him take those, we were used to it.'

'Didn't anyone ever complain?' I said.

Not officially, the girls said. What was the use? The firm never sacked people for nicking things, if they did there would be a strike.

'Except that time, do you remember, Janet?' Carol said. 'When that poor old lady turned up, wittering on about Chris stealing things from her house. *She* complained, all right. She came back three times, making a fuss.'

'Oh sure,' Janet nodded. 'But it turned out it was only some odd bits of paper she was on about, you know, nothing like money or valuables, and anyway Chris said she was losing her marbles, and had thrown them away, most like, and it all blew over, you know.'

I said, 'What was the old lady's name?'

The girls looked at each other and shook their heads. It was weeks ago, they said.

Akkerton said he hadn't known of that, he'd never heard about the old lady, not down with his veg.

The girls' boyfriends arrived at that moment and there a general reshuffle round the tables. I said I would have to be going, and by one of those unspoken messages Akkerton indicated that I should see him outside.

'O'Rorke,' said Carol suddenly.

'What?'

'The old lady's name,' she said. 'I've remembered. It was Mrs O'Rorke. She was Irish. Her husband had just died, and she'd been paying Chris to carry logs in for her fire, and things like that that she couldn't manage.'

'I don't suppose you remember where she lived?'

'Does it matter? It was only a great fuss over nothing.'

'Still...'

She frowned slightly with obliging concentration, though most of her attention was on her boyfriend, who was tending to flirt with Janet.

'Stretchworth,' she exclaimed. 'She complained about the taxi fare.' She gave me a quick glance. 'To be honest, we were glad to be rid of her in the end. She was an awful old nuisance, but we couldn't be too unkind because of her old man dying, and that.'

'Thanks very much,' I said.

'You're welcome.' She moved away from me and sat herself decisively between her boyfriend and Janet, and Akkerton and I went outside to settle our business.

He looked philosophically at what I gave him, nodded and asked me to write my name and address on a piece of paper in case he thought of anything else to tell me. I tore a page out of my diary, wrote, and gave it to him thinking that our transaction was over, but when I'd shaken his hand, said goodbye and walked away from him he called after me.

'Wait, lad.'

I turned back.

'Did you get your money's worth?' he said.

More than I'd bargained for, I thought. I said, 'Yes, I think so. Can't really tell yet.'

He nodded, pursing his lips. Then with an uncharacteristically awkward gesture he held out half of the cash. 'Here,' he said. 'You take it. I saw into your wallet in the pub. You're nearly cleaned out. Enough's enough.' He thrust his gift towards my hand, and I took it back with gratitude. 'Teachers,' he said, pushing open the pub door. 'Downtrodden underpaid lot of bastards. Never reckoned much to school myself.' He brushed away my attempt at thanks and headed back to the beer.

Chapter Six

By map and in spite of misdirections, I eventually found the O'Rorke house in Stretchworth. Turned into the driveway. Stopped the engine. Climbed out of the car, looking at what lay ahead.

A large rambling untidy structure; much wood, many gables, untrained creeper pushing tendrils onto the slated roof, and sash window frames long ago painted white. The garden in the soft evening light seemed a matter of grasses and shrubs growing wherever they liked; and a large bush of lilac, white and sweet-scented, almost obliterated the front door.

The bell may have rung somewhere deep inside in response to my finger on the button, but I couldn't hear it. I rang again, and tried a few taps on the inadequate knocker, and when the blank seconds mounted to minutes, I stepped back a few paces, looking up at the windows for signs of life.

I didn't actually see the door open behind the lilac bush, but a sharp voice spoke to me from among the flowers.

'Are you Saint Anthony?' it said.

'Er, no.' I stepped back into the line of sight and found standing in the shadowy half-open doorway and short white-haired old woman with yellowish skin and wild-looking eyes.

'About the fate?' she said.

'Whose fate?' I asked, bewildered.

'The church's, of course.'

'Oh,' I said. 'The *fête*.'

She looked at me as if I were totally stupid, which from her point of view I no doubt was.

'If you cut the peonies tonight,' she said, 'they'll be dead by Saturday.'

Her voice was distinguishably Irish, but with the pure vowels of education, and her words were already a dismissal. She was holding onto the door with one hand and its frame with the other, and was on the point of irrevocably rejoining them.

'Please,' I said hastily, 'show me the peonies ... so that I'll know which to pick ... on Saturday.'

The half-begun movement was arrested. The old woman considered for a moment and then stepped out past the lilac into full view, revealing a waif-thin frame dressed in a rust-coloured jersey, narrow navy blue trousers, and pink and green checked bedroom slippers.

'Round the back,' she said. She looked me up and down, but

apparently saw nothing to doubt. 'This way.'

She led me round the house along a path whose flat sunken paving stones merged at the edges with the weedy overgrowth of what might once have been flowereds. Past a shoulder-high stack of sawn logs, contrastingly neat. Past a closed side door. Past a greenhouse filled with the straggly stalks of many dead geraniums. Past a wheelbarrow full of cinders, about whose purpose one could barely guess. Round an unexpected corner, through a too-small gap in a vigorously growing hedge, and finally into the riotous mess of the back garden.

'Peonies,' she said, pointing, though indeed there was no need. Around the ruin of a lawn huge swathes of the fat luxurious blowsy heads, pink, crimson, frilly white, raised themselves in every direction from a veritable ocean of glossy dark leaves, the sinking sun touching all with gold. Decay might lie in the future but the present was a triumphant shout in the face of death.

'They're magnificent,' I said, slightly awed. 'There must be thousands of them.'

The old woman looked around without interest. 'They grow every year. Liam couldn't have enough. You can take what you like.'

'Um.' I cleared my throat. 'I'd better tell you I'm not from the church.'

She looked at me with the same sort of bewilderment as I'd recently bent on her. 'What did you want to see the peonies for, then?'

'I wanted to talk to you. For you not to go inside and shut your door when you learned what I want to talk about.'

'Young man,' she said severely, 'I'm not buying anything. I don't give to charities. I don't like politicians. What do you want?'

'I want to know,' I said slowly, 'about the papers that Chris Norwood stole from you.'

Her mouth opened. The wild eyes raked my face like great watery searchlights. The thin body shook with powerful but unspecified emotion.

'Please don't worry,' I said hastily. 'I mean you no harm. There's nothing at all to be afraid of.'

'I'm not afraid. I'm angry.'

'You did have some papers, didn't you, that Chris Norwood took?'

'Liam's papers. Yes.'

'And you went to Angel Kitchens to complain?'

'The police did nothing. Absolutely nothing. I went to Angel Kitchens to make that beastly man give them back. They said he wasn't there. They were lying. I know they were.'

Her agitation was more than I was ready to feel guilty for. I said calmly. 'Please, could we just sit down ...' I looked around for a garden bench, but saw nothing suitable. 'I don't want to upset you. I might even help.'

'I don't know you. It's not safe.' She looked at me for a few more unnerving seconds with full beam, and then turned and began to go back the way we had come. I followed reluctantly, aware that I'd been clumsy but still not knowing what else to have done. I had lost her, I thought. She would go in behind the lilac and shut me out.

Back through the hedge, past the cinders, past the cemetery in the greenhouse: but not past the closed side door. To my slightly surprised relief she stopped there and twisted the knob.

'This way,' she said, going in. 'Come along. I think I'll trust you. You look all right. I'll take the risk.'

The house was dark inside and smelled of disuse. We seemed to be in a narrow passage, along which she drifted ahead of me, silent in her slippers, light as a sparrow.

'Old women living alone,' she said, 'should never take men they don't know into their houses.' As she was addressing the air in front of her, the admonishment seemed to be to herself. We continued along past various dark-painted closed doors, until the passage opened out into a central hall where such light as there was filtered through high-up windows of patterned stained glass.

'Edwardian,' she said, following my upward gaze. 'This way.'

I followed her into a spacious room whose elaborate bay window looked out onto the glory in the garden. Indoors, more mutedly, there were deep-blue velvet curtains, good-looking large rugs over the silver-grey carpet, blue velvet sofas and armchairs – and dozens and dozens of seascapes crowding the walls. Floor to ceiling. Billowing sails. Four-masters. Storms and seagulls and salt spray.

'Liam's,' she said briefly, seeing my head turn around them.

When Liam O'Rorke liked something, I thought fleetingly, he liked a lot of it.

'Sit down,' she said, pointing to an armchair. 'Tell me who you are and why you've come here.' She moved to a sofa where, to judge from the book andglass onthe small table adjacent, she had been sitting before I arrived, and perched her small weight on the edge as if ready for flight.

I explained about Peter's link with Chris Norwood, saying that Chris Norwood had given what I thought might be her husband's papers to Peter for him to organize into computer programs. I said that Peter had done the job, and had recorded the programs on tape.

She brushed aside the difficult technicalities and came straight to the simple point. 'Do you mean,' she demanded, 'that your friend Peter has my papers?' The hope in her face was like a light.

'I'm afraid not. I don't know where the papers are.'

'Ask your friend.'

'He's been killed in an accident.'

'Oh.' She stared at me, intensely disappointed.

'But the tapes,' I said. 'I do know where those are – or at least I know where copies of them are. If the knowledge that's on them is yours, I could get them for you.'

She was a jumble of renewed hope and puzzlement. 'It would be wonderful. But these tapes, wherever they are, didn't you bring them with you?'

I shook my head. 'I didn't know you existed until an hour ago. It was a girl called Carol who told me about you. She works in the office of Angel Kitchens.'

'Oh yes.' Mrs O'Rorke made a small movement of embarrassment. 'I screeched at her. I was so *angry*. They wouldn't tell me where to find Chris Norwood in all those buildings and sheds. I'd said I'd scratch his eyes out. I've an Irish temper, you know.I can't always control it.'

I thought of the picture she must tave presented to those girls, and reckoned their description of her 'Making a fuss' had been charitable.

'The trouble is,' I said slowly, 'that someone else is looking for those tapes.' I told her a watered-down version of the visit to my house of the gunmen, to which she listened with open-mouthed attention. 'I don't know who they are,' I said, 'or where they come from. I began to think that so much ignorance might be dangerous. So I've been trying to find out what's going on.'

'And if you know?'

'Then I'll know what *not* to do. I mean, one can do such stupid things, with perhaps appalling consequences, just through not knowing some simple fact.'

She regarded me steadily with the first glimmer of a smile. 'All you're asking for, young man, is the secret that has eluded *homo sapiens* from day one.'

I was startled not so much by the thought as by the words she phrased it in, and as if sensing my surprise she said with dryness, 'One does not grow silly with age. If one was silly when young, one may be silly when old. If one were acute when young, why should acuteness wane?'

'I have done you,' I said slowly, 'an injustice.'

'Everyone does,' she said indifferently. 'I look in my mirror. I see an old face. Wrinkles. Yellow skin. As society is now constituted, to present this appearance is to be thrust into a category. Old woman, therefore silly, troublesome, can be pushed around.'

'No,' I said. 'It's not true.'

'Unless, of course,' she added as if I hadn't spoken, 'one is an *achiever*. Achievement is the saviour of the very old.'

'And are you not . . . an achiever?'

She made a small regretful movement with hands and head. 'I wish I were. I am averagely intelligent, but that's all. It gets you nowhere. It doesn't save you from rage. I apologize for my reaction in the garden.'

'But don't,' I said. 'Theft's an assault. Of course you'd be angry.'

She relaxed to the extent of sitting back into the sofa, where the cushions barely deflated under her weight.

'I will tell you as much as I can of what has happened. If it saves you from chasing Moses across the Red Sea, so much the better.'

To know what *not* to do . . .

I grinned at her.

She twitched her lips and said, 'What do you know about racing?'

'Not a great deal.'

'Liam did. My husband. Liam lived for the horses all his life. In Ireland, of course, when we were children. Then here. Newmarket,

Epsom, Cheltenham, that's where we've lived. Then back here to Newmarket. Always the horses.'

'Were they his job?' I asked.

'In a way. He was a gambler.' She looked at me calmly. 'I mean a professional gambler. He lived on his winnings. I still live on what's left.'

'I thought it wasn't possible,' I said.

'To beat the odds?' The words sounded wrong for her appearance. It was true, I thought, what she'd said about categories. Old women weren't expected to talk gambling; but this one did. 'In the old days it was perfectly possible to make a good living. Dozens did it. You worked on a profit expectation of ten per cent on turnover, and if you had any judgement at all, you achieved it. Then they introduced the Betting Tax. It took a slice off all the winnings, reduced the profit margin to almost nil, killed off all the old pros in no time. Your ten per cent was all going into the Revenue, do you see?'

'Yes,' I said.

'Liam had always made more than ten per cent. He took a pride in it. He reckoned he could win one race out of three. That means that every third bet, on average, would win. That's a very high percentage, day after day, year after year. And he *did* beat the tax. He tried new ways, added new factors. With his statistics, he said, you could always win in the long run. None of the bookies would take his bets.'

'Er, what?' I said.

'Didn't you know?' She sounded surprised. 'Bookmakers won't take bets from people who repeatedly win.'

'But I thought that's what they were in business for. I mean, to take people's bets.'

'To take bets from ordinary mug punters, yes,' she said. 'The sort who may win occasionally but never do in the end. But if you have an account with almost any bookie and you keep winning, he'll close your account.

'Good grief,' I said weakly.

'At the races,' she said, 'all the bookies knew Liam. If they didn't know him to talk to, they knew him by sight. They'd only let him bet in cash at starting price, and then as soon as he'd got his money on they'd tic-tac it round the ring and they'd all reduce the price of that horse to ridiculously small odds, making the starting price very low, so that he wouldn't win much himself, and so that the other racegoers would be put off backing that horse, and stake their money on something else.'

There was a longish pause while I sorted out and digested what she'd said.

'And what,' I said, 'about the Tote?'

'The Tote is unpredictable. Liam didn't like that. Also the Tote in general pays worse odds than the bookies. No, Liam liked betting with the bookies. It was a sort of war. Liam always won, though most times the bookies didn't know it.'

'Er,' I said, 'how do you mean?'

She sighed. 'It was a lot of work. We had a gardener. A friend really. He lived here in the house. Down that passage where we came in just now, those were his rooms. He used to like driving round the country, so he'd take Liam's cash and drive off to some town or other, and put it all on in the local betting shops, bit by bit, and if the horse won, which it usually did, he'd go round and collect, and come home. He and Liam would count it all out. So much for Dan – that was our friend – and so much for the working funds, and the rest for us. No more tax to pay, of course. No income tax. We went on for years like that. Years. We all got on so well together, you see.'

She fell silent, looking into the gentle past with those incongruously wild eyes.

'And Liam died?' I said.

'Dan died. Eighteen months ago, just before Christmas. He was ill for only a month. It was so quick.' A pause. 'And Liam and I, we didn't realize until after—We didn't know how much we depended on Dan, until he wasn't there. He was so strong. He could lift things ... and the garden ... Liam was eighty-six, you see, and I'm eighty-eight, but Dan was younger, not over seventy. He was a blacksmith from Wexford, way back. Full of jokes, too. We missed him so much.'

The golden glow of sunlight outside had faded from the peonies, the great vibrant colours fading to greys in the approaching dusk. I listened to the young voice of the old woman telling the darker parts of her life, clearing the fog from my own.

'We thought we'd have to find someone else to put the bets on,' she said. 'But who could we trust? Some of the time last year Liam tried to do it himself, going round betting shops in places like Ipswich and Colchester, places where they wouldn't know him, but he was too old, he got dreadfully exhausted. He had to stop it, it was too much. We had quite a bit saved, you see, and we decided we'd have to live on that. And then this year a man we'd heard of, but never met, came to see us, and he offered to *buy* Liam's methods. He said to Liam to write down how he won so consistently, and he would buy what he'd written.'

'And those notes,' I said, enlightened, 'were what Chris Norwood stole?'

'Not exactly,' she said, sighing. 'You see there was no need for Liam to write down his method. He'd written it down years ago. All based on statistics. Quite complicated. He used to update it when necessary. And, of course, add new races. After so many years, he could bet with a thirty-three per cent chance of succes in nearly a thousand particular races every year.'

She coughed suddenly, her white thin face vibrating with the muscular spasm. A fragile hand stretched out to the glass on the table, and she took a few sips of yellowish liquid.

'I'm so sorry,' I said contritely. 'Making you talk.'

She shook her head mutely, taking more sips, then put down the glass carefully and said, 'It's great to talk. I'm glad you're here, to give me an opportunity. I have so few people to talk to. Some days I don't talk at all. I do miss Liam, you know. We chattered all the time. He was a terrible man to live with. Obsessive, do you see? When he had something in his mind he'd go on and on and on with it. All these sea pictures, it drove me mad when he kept buying them, but now he's gone, well, they seem to bring him close again, and I won't move them, not now.'

'It wasn't so very long ago, was it, that he died?' I said.

'On March 1st,' she said. She paused, but there were no tears, no welling distress. 'Only a few days after Mr Gilbert came. Liam was sitting there . . .' She pointed to one of the blue armchairs, the only one which showed rubbed dark patches on the arms and a shadow on its high back. '. . . and I went to make us some tea. Just a cup. We were thirsty. And when I came back he was asleep.' She paused again. 'I thought he was asleep.'

'I'm sorry,' I said.

She shook her head. 'It was the best way to go. I'm glad for him. We'd both loathed the thought of dying in hospital stuck full of tubes. If I'm lucky and if I can manage it I'll die here too, like that, one of these day. I'll be glad to. It is comforting, do you see?'

I did see, in a way, though I had never before thought of death as a welcome guest to be patiently awaited, hoping that he would come quietly when one was asleep.

'If you'd like a drink,' she said in exactly the same matter-of-fact tone, 'there's a bottle and some glasses in the cupboard.'

'I have to drive home . . .'

She didn't press it. She said. 'Do you want to hear about Mr Gilbert? Mr Harry Gilbert?'

'Yes, please. If I'm not tiring you.'

'I told you. Talking's a *pleasure*.' She considered, her head to one side, the white hair standing like a fluffy halo round the small wrinkled face. 'He owns bingo halls,' she said, and there was for the first time in her voice the faintest hint of contempt.

'You don't approve of bingo?'

'It's a mugs game.' She shrugged. 'No skill in it.'

'But a lot of people enjoy it.'

'And pay for it. Like mug punters. The wins keep them hooked but they lose in the end.'

The same the world over, I thought with amusement: the professional's dim view of the amateur. There was nothing amateur, however, about Mr Gilbert.

'Bingo made him rich,' the old woman said. 'He came here one day to see Liam, just drove up in a Rolls and said he was buying a chain of betting shops. He wanted to buy Liam's system so he'd always be six jumps ahead of the mugs.'

I said curiously, 'Do you always think of a gambler as a mug?'

'Mr Gilbert does. He's a cold man. Liam said it depends what they want. If they want excitement, OK, they're mugs but they're getting their money's worth. If they want profit and they still bet on instinct, they're just mugs.'

She coughed again, and sipped again, and after a while gave me the faint smile, and continued.

'Mr Gilbert offered Liam a lot of money. Enough for us to invest and live on comfortably for the rest of our days. So Liam agreed. It was wisest. They argued a bit about the price, of course. They spent almost a week ringing each other up with offers. But in the end it was settled.' She paused. 'Then before Mr Gilbert paid the money, and before Liam gave him all the papers, Liam died. Mr Gilbert telephoned me to say he was sorry, but did the bargain still stand, and I said yes it did. It certainly did. I was very pleased to be going to be without money anxieties, do you see?'

I nodded.

'And then,' she said, and this time with anger, 'that *hateful* Chris Norwood stole the papers out of Liam's office ... Stole all his life's work.' Her body shook. It was the fact of *what* had been stolen which infuriated her, I perceived, more than the fortune lost. 'We'd both been glad to have him come here, to carry coal and logs and clean the windows, and then I'd begun to wonder if he'd been in my handbag, but I'm always pretty vague about how much I have there ... and then Liam died.' She stopped, fighting against agitation, pressing a thin hand to her narrow chest, squeezing shut those wide-staring eyes.

'Don't go on,' I said, desperately wanting her to.

'Yes, yes,' she said, opening her eyes again. 'Mr Gilbert came to collect the papers. He brought the money all in cash. He showed it to me, in a briefcase. Packets of notes. He said to spend it, not invest it. That way there would be no fuss with tax. He said he would give me more if I ever needed it, but there was enough, you know, for years and years, living as I do ... And then we went along to Liam's office, and the papers weren't there. Nowhere. Vanished. I'd put them all ready, you see, the day before, in a big folder. There were so many of them. Sheets and sheets, all in Liam's spiky writing. He never learned to type. Always wrote by hand. And the only person who'd been in there besides Mrs Urquart was Chris Norwood. The only person.'

'Who,' I said, 'is Mrs Urquart?'

'What? Oh, Mrs Urquart comes to clean for me. Or she did. Three days a week. She can't now, she says. She's in trouble with the welfare people, poor thing.'

Akkerton's voice in the pub floated back: '... she never told the welfare she was earning ...'

I said 'Was it in Mrs Urquart's house that Chris Norwood lodged?'

'Yes, that's right.' She frowned. 'How did you know?'

'Something someone said.' I sorted through what I had first said to her to explain my visit and belatedly realized that I'd taken for granted she'd known something which I now saw that perhaps she didn't.

'Chris Norwood ...' I said slowly.

'I'd like to strangle him.'

'Didn't your Mrs Urquart tell you ... what had happened?'

'She rang in a great fuss. Said she wasn't coming any more. She sounded very upset. Saturday morning, last week.'

'And that was all she said, that she wasn't coming any more?'

'We hadn't been very good friends lately, not with Chris Norwood stealing Liam's papers. I didn't want to quarrel with her. I needed her, for the cleaning. But since that hateful man stole from us, she was very defensive, almost rude. But she needed the money, just like I needed her, and she knew I'd never give her away.'

I looked out towards the peonies, where the greys were darkening to night, and debated whether or not to tell her what had befallen Chris Norwood. Decided against, because hearing of the murder of someone one knew, even someone one disliked, could be incalculably shattering. To thrust an old lady living alone in a big house into a state of shock and fear couldn't do any possible good.

'Do you read newspapers?' I said.

She raised her eyebrows over the oddness of the question but answered simply enough. 'Not often. The print's too small. I've good eyes, but I like big-print books.' She indicated the fat red-and-white volume on her table. 'I read nothing else, now.' She looked vaguely round the dusk-filled room. 'Even the racing pages. I've stopped reading those. I just watch the results on television.'

'Just the results? Not the races?'

'Liam said watching the races was the mug's way of betting. Watch the results, he said, and add them to statistical probabilities. I do watch the races, but the results are more of a habit.'

She stretched out a stick-thin arm and switched on the table-light beside her, shutting the peonies instantly into blackness and banishing the far corners of the room into deep shadow. On herself the instant effect was to enhance her physical degeneration, putting skin-folds cruelly back where the dusk had softened them, anchoring the ageless mind into the old, old body.

I looked at the thin, wizened yellow face, at the huge eyes that might once have been beautiful, at the white unstyled hair of Liam O'Rorke's widow, and I suggested that maybe, if I gave her the computer tapes, she could still sell the knowledge that was on them to her friend Mr Gilbert.

'It did cross my mind,' she said, nodding, 'when you said you had them. I don't really understand what they are, though. I don't know anything about computers.'

She'd been married to one, in a way. I said, 'They are just cassettes – like for a cassette player.'

She thought for a while, looking down at her hands. Then she said, 'If I pay you a commission, will you do the deal for me? I'm not so good at dealing as Liam, do you see? And I don't think I have the strength to haggle.'

'But wouldn't Mr Gilbert pay the agreed price?'

She shook her head doubtfully. 'I don't know. That deal was struck three months ago, and now it isn't the papers themselves I'm selling, but something else. I don't know. I think he might twist me into corners. But you *know* about these tapes, or whatever they are. You could talk to him better than me.' She smiled faintly. 'A proper commission, young man. Ten per cent.'

It took me about five seconds to agree. She gave me Harry Gilbert's address and telephone number, and said she would leave it all to me. I could come back and tell her when it was done. I could bring her all the money, she said, and she would pay me my share, and everything would be fine.

'You trust me?' I said.

'If you steal from me, I'll be no worse off than I am at present.'

She came with me to the lilac-shrouded front door to let me out, and I shook her thistledown hand and drove away.

The Red Sea parted for Moses, and he walked across.

Chapter Seven

On Thursday I trundled blearily round school, inneffective from lack of the sleep I'd forfeited in favour of correcting the Upper V's exercise books. They too, like William, had decisive exams ahead. One of the most boring things about myself, I'd discovered, was this sense of commitment to the kids.

Ted Pitts didn't turn up. Jenkins, when directly asked, said scratchily that Pitts had laryngitis, which was disgraceful as it put the whole Maths department's timetable out of order.

'When will he be back?'

Jenkins gave me a sour sneer, not for any particular reason but because it was an ingrained mannerism.

'His wife telephoned,' he said. 'Pitts has lost his voice. When he regains it, doubtless he will return.'

'Could you give me his number.'

'He isn't on the telephone,' Jenkins said repressively. 'He says he can't afford it.'

'His address, then.'

'You should ask in the office.' Jenkins said . 'I can't be expected to remember where my assistant masters live.'

The school secretary was not in his office when I went to look for him during morning break, and I spent the last two periods before lunch (Five C, magnetism; Four D, electrical power) fully realizing that if I didn't send computer tapes to Cambridge on that very day they would not arrive by Saturday: and if no computer tapes arrived at Cambridge main post office by Saturday I could expect another and much nastier visit from the man behind the Walther.

At lunchtime, food came low on the priorities. Instead I first went out of school along to the nearest row of shops and bought three blank sixty-minute cassettes. They weren't of the quality beloved by Ted Pitts, but for my purpose they were fine then I sought out one of Ted Pitts's colleagues and begged a little help with the computer.

'Well,' he said hesitantly. 'OK, if it's only for ten minutes. Straight after school. And don't tell Jenkins, will you?

'Never.'

His laugh floated after me as I hurried down the passage towards the coin-box telephone in the main entrance hall. I rang up Newmarket police station (via Directory Enquiries) and asked for whoever was in charge of the investigation into the murder of Chris Norwood.

That would be Detective Superintendent Irestone, I was told. He wasn't in. Would I care to talk to Detective Sergeant Smith? I said I supposed so, and after a few clicks and silences a comfortable Suffolk voice asked me what he could do for me.

I had mentally rehearsed what to say, but it was still difficult to begin. I said tentatively, 'I might know a bit about why Chris Norwood was murdered and I might know perhaps roughly who did it, but I also might easily be wrong, it's just that...'

'Name, sir?' he said, interrupting. 'Address? Can you be reached there, sir? At what time can you be reached there, sir? Detective Chief Superintendent Irestone will get in touch with you, sir. Thank you for calling.'

I put the receiver down not knowing whether he had paid extra-fast attention to what I'd said, or whether he had merely given the stock reply handed out to every crackpot who rang up with his/her pet theory. In either case, it left me with just enough time to catch the last of the hamburgers in the school canteen and to get back to class on the dot.

At four, I was held up by Louise's latest grudge (apparatus left out all over the benches – Martin would never do that) and I was fearful as I raced along the corridors the boys were not allowed to run in, and slid down the stairs with both hands on the on the bannisters and my feet touching only about every sixth tread (a trick I had learned in my far-back youth), that Ted Pitts's colleague would have tired of waiting, and gone home.

To my relief, he hadn't he was sitting in front of the familiar screen shooting down little random targets with the zest of a seven-year-old.

'What's that?' I said, pointing at the game.

'"Starstrike". Want a go?'

'Is it yours?'

'Something Ted made up to amuse and teach the kids.'

'Is it in BASIC?' I asked.

'Sure. BASIC, graphics and special characters.'

'Can you list it?'

'Bound to be able to. He'd never stuff it into ROM if he wanted to teach from it.'

'What exactly,' I said frustratedly, 'is ROM?'

'Read Only Memory. If a program is in ROM you can only Run it, you can't List it.'

He typed LIST, and Ted's game scrolled up the screen to seemingly endless flickering rows.

'There you are,' Ted's colleague said.

I looked at part of the last section of the program, which was now at rest on the screen:

```
410 RESET (RX, RY): RX = RX–RA: RY–8
420 IF RY > 2 SET (RX, RY): GOTO 200
430 IF ABS (1* 8–RX) > 4 THEN 150
460 FOR Q = 1 TO 6: PRINT @ 64 + 4 * V, "****";
```

A right load of gibberish to me, though poetry to Ted Pitts.

To his colleague I said, 'I came down here to ask you to record something . . . anything . . . on these cassettes.' I produced them. 'Just so they have computer noise on them, and a readable program. They're for, er, demonstration.'

He didn't query it.

I said, 'Do you think Ted would mind me using his game?'

He shrugged. 'I shouldn't think so. Two or three of the boys have got tapes of it. It's no secret.'

He took the cassettes out of my hands and said, 'Once on each tape?'

'Er no. Several times on each side.'

His eyes widened, 'What on earth for?'

'Um.' I thought in circles. 'To demonstrate searching through file names.'

'Oh. All right.' He looked at his watch. 'I'd leave you to do it, but Jenkins goes mad if one of the department doesn't check the computer's switched off and put the door key in the common-room. I can't stay long anyway, you know.'

He put the first of the tapes obligingly into the recorder, however, typed CSAVE 'A', and pressed 'Enter'. When the screen announced READY, he typed CSAVE 'B', and after that CSAVE'C', and so on until the first side of the tape was full of repeats of 'Starstrike'.

'This is taking ages,' he muttered.

'Could you do one side of each tape, then?' I asked.

'OK.'

He filled one side of the second tape and approximately half of a side on the third before his growing restiveness overcame him.

'Look, Jonathan, that's enough. It's taken nearer an hour than ten minutes.'

'You're a pal.'

'Don't worry, I'll hit you one of these days for my games duty.'

I picked up the cassettes and nodded agreement. Getting someone else to do games duty wasn't only the accepted way of wangling Wednesday afternoons off, it was also the coin in which favours were paid for.

'Thanks a lot,' I said.

'Any time.'

He began putting the computer to bed and I took the cassettes out to my car to pack them in a padded envelope and send them to Cambridge, with each filled side marked 'Play this side first.'

Since there was a Parents' Evening that day, I went for a pork pie with some beer in a pub, corrected books in the common-room, and from eight to ten, along with nearly the whole complement of staff (as these occasions involved a three-line whip) reassured the parents of all the fourth forms that their little horrors were doing splendidly. The parents of Paul apple-on-the-head Arcady asked if he would make a research scientist. 'His wit and style will take him far,' I said. noncommittally, and they said 'He enjoys your lessons', which was a nice change from the next parent I talked to who announced belligerently, 'My lad's wasting his time in your class.'

Placate, agree, suggest, smile: above all, show concern. I supposed Those evenings were a Good Thing, but after a long day's teaching they were exhausting. I drove home intending to flop straight into bed but when I opened the front door I found the telephone on the boil.

'Where have you been?' Sarah said, sounding cross.

'Parents' meeting.'

'I've been ringing and ringing. Yesterday too.'

'Sorry.'

With annoyance unmollified she said, 'Did you remember to water my house plants?'

Hell, I thought. 'No, I didn't.'

'It's so *careless*.'

'Yes. Well, I'm sorry.'

'Do them now. Don't leave it.'

I said dutifully, 'How's Donna.'

'Depressed.' The single word was curt and dismissive. 'Try not to forget,' she said acidly, 'the croton in the spare bedroom.'

I put the receiver down thinking that I positively didn't want her back. It was an uncomfortable, miserable, thought. I'd loved her once so much. I'd have died for her, literally. I thought purposefully for the first time about divorce and in the thinking found neither regret nor guilt, but relief.

At eight in the morning when I was juggling coffee and toast the telephone rang again, and this time it was the police. A London accent very polite.

'You rang with a theory, sir, about Christopher Norwood.'

'It's not exactly a theory. It's ... at least ... a coincidence.' I had had time to cut my words down to essentials. I said, 'Christopher Norwood commissioned a friend of mine, Peter Keithly, to write some computer programs. Peter Keithly did them, and recorded them on cassette tapes which he gave to me. Last Saturday, two men came to my house, pointed a gun at me, and demanded the tapes. They threatened to shoot my television set and my ankles if I didn't hand them over. Are you, er, interested?'

There was a silence, then the same voice said, 'Wait a moment, sir.'

I drank some coffee and waited, and finally a different voice spoke in my ear, a bass voice, slower, less stilted, asking me to repeat what I'd said to the inspector.

'Mm,' he said, when I'd finished. 'I think. 'I'd better see you. How are you placed?'

School, he agreed, was unavoidable. He would come to my house in Twickenham at four-thirty.

He was there before me, sitting not in a labelled and light-flashing police car, but in a fast four-door saloon. When I'd braked outside the garage he was already on his feet, and I found myself appraising a stocky man with a craggy young-old face, black hair dusting grey, unwavering light brown eyes and a sceptical mouth. Not a man, I thought, to save time for fools.

'Mr Derry?'

'Yes.'

'Detective Chief Superintendent Irestone.' He briefly produced a flip-over wallet and showed me his certification. 'And Detective Inspector Robson.' He indicated a second man emerging from the car, dressed casually like himself in grey trousers and sports jacket. 'Can we go inside, sir?'

'Of course.' I led the way in. 'Would you like coffee – or tea?'

They shook their heads and Irestone plunged straight into the matter in hand. It appeared that what I'd told them so far did indeed interest them intensely. They welcomed, it seemed, my account of what I'd learned on my trek via Angel Kitchens to Mrs O'Rorke. Irestone asked many questions, including how I persuaded the gunmen to go away empty-handed.

I said easily, 'I didn't have the tapes here, because I'd lent them to a friend. I said I'd get them back and post them to them and luckily they agreed to that.'

His eyebrows rose, but he made no comment. It must have seemed to him merely that I'd been fortunate.

'And you'd no idea who they were?' he said.

'None at all.'

'I don't suppose you know what sort of pistol it was?'

He spoke without expectation, and it was an instant before I answered: 'I think ... a Walther .22. I've seen one before.'

He said intently, 'How certain are you?'

'Pretty certain.'

He reflected. 'We'd like you to go to your local station to see if you can put together Identikit pictures.'

'Of course, I will,' I said, 'but you might be able to see these men themselves, if you're lucky.'

'How do you mean?'

'I did send them some tapes, but not until yesterday. They were going to pick them up from Cambridge main post office, and I should think there's a chance they'll be there tomorrow.'

'That's helpful.' He sounded unexcited, but wrote it all down. 'Anything else?'

'They aren't the tapes they wanted. I still haven't got those back. I sent them some other tapes with a computer game on.'

He pursed his lips. 'That wasn't very wise.'

'But the real ones morally belong to Mrs O'Rorke. And those gunmen won't come stampeding back here while they think they've got the goods.'

'And how long before they find out?'

'I don't know. But if they're the same two people who threatened Peter, it might be a while. He said they didn't seem to know much about computers.'

Irestone thought aloud. 'Peter Keithly told you that two men visited him on the Wednesday evening, is that right?' I nodded. 'Christopher Norwood was killed last Friday morning. Eight and a half days later.' He rubbed his chin. 'It might be unwise too suppose it will take them another eight and a half days to discover what you've done.'

'I could always swear those *were* the tapes Peter Keithly gave me.'

'And I don't think,' he said flatly, 'that this time they'd believe you.' He paused. 'The inquest on Peter Keithly was being held today, wasn't it?'

I nodded.

'We consulted with the Norwich police. There's no room to doubt your friend's death was an accident. I dare say you've wondered?'

'Yes, I have.'

'You don't need to. The insurance inspector's report says the explosion was typical. There were no arson devices. No dynamite or plastics. Just absence of mind and rotten bad luck.'

I looked at the floor.

'Your gunmen didn't do it,' he said.

I thought that maybe he was trying to defuse any hatred I might be brewing, so that my testimony might be more impartial, but in fact what he was giving me was a kind of comfort, and I was grateful.

'If Peter hadn't died,' I said, looking up, 'they might have gone back to him when they found what they'd got from him was useless.'

'Exactly,' Irestone said dryly. 'Do you have friends you could stay with for a while?'

On Saturday morning, impelled, I fear, by Mrs O'Rorke's ten-per-cent promise, I drove to Welwyn Garden City to offer her tapes to Mr Harry Gilbert.

Not that I exactly had the tapes with me as they were still locked up with Ted Pitts's laryngitis, but at least I had the knowledge of their existence and contents, and that should be enough, I hoped, for openeners.

From Twickenham to Welwyn was twenty miles in a direct line but far more in practice and tedious besides, round the North Circular Road and narrow shopping streets. In contrast the architects' dream city, when I got there, was green and orderly, and I found the Gilbert residence in an opulent cul-de-sac. Bingo, it seemed, had kept poverty a long way from his doorstep, which was reproduction Georgian, flanked with two pillars and surrounded by a regular regiment of windows. A house of red, white and sparkle on a carpet of green. I pressed the shiny brass doorbell thinking it would be a bore if the inhabitants of this bijou mansion were out.

Mr Gilbert, however, was in.

Just.

He opened his front door to my ring and said whatever I wanted I would have to come back later, as he just off to play golf. Clubs and a cart for transporting them stood just inside the door, and Mr Gilbert's heavy frame was clad appropriately in check trousers, open-necked shirt and blazer.

'It's about Liam O'Rorke's betting system,' I said.

'What?' he said sharply.

'Mrs O'Rorke asked me to come. She says she might be able to sell it to you after all.'

He looked at his watch; a man of about fifty, in appearance unimpressive, more like a minor official than a peddlar of pinchbeck dreams.

'Come in,' he said. 'This way.'

His voice was no-nonsense middle-of-the-road, nearer the bingo hall than Eton. He led me into an unexpectedly functional room furnished with a desk, typewriter, wall maps with coloured drawing pins dotted over them, two swivel chairs, one tray of drinks and five telephones.

'Fifteen minutes,' he said. 'So come to the point.' He made no move to sit down or offer me a seat, but he was not so much rude as indifferent. I saw what Mrs O'Rorke had meant about him being a cold man. He didn't try to clothe the bones of his thoughts with social top-dressing. He'd have made a lousy schoolmaster, I thought.

'Liam O'Rorke's notes were stolen,' I began.

'I know that,' he said impatiently. 'Have they turned up?'

'Not his notes, no. But computer programs made from them, yes.'

He frowned. 'Mrs O'Rorke has these programs?'

'No. I have. On her behalf. To offer to you.'

'And your name?'

I shrugged. 'Jonathan Derry. You can check with her, if you like.' I gestured to the rank of telephones. 'She'll vouch for me.'

'Did you bring these ... programs with you?'

'No,' I said. 'I thought we should make a deal first.

'Humph.'

Behind his impassive face, a fierce amount of consideration seemed to be taking place, and at length I had a powerful feeling that he couldn't make up his mind.

I said, 'I wouldn't expect you to buy them without a demonstration. But I assure you they're the real thing.'

It produced no discernible effect. The interior debate continued; and it was resolved not by Gilbert or myself but by the arrival of someone else.

A car door slammed outside and there were footsteps on the polished parquet in the hall. Gilbert's head lifted to listen, and a voice outside the open door called 'Dad?'

'In here,' Gilbert said.

Gilbert's son came in. Gilbert's son, who had come to my house with his pistol.

I must have looked as frozen with shock as I felt: but then so did he. I glanced at his father, and it came to me too late that this was the man Sarah had described – middle-aged, ordinary, plump – who had gone to Peter's house asking for the tapes. The one to whom she had said, 'My husband's got them.'

I seemed to have stopped breathing. It was as if life itself had been punched out of me. To know what *not* to do...

For all my instinct that ignorance was dangerous, I had not learned enough. I hadn't learned the simple fact that would have stopped me from walking into that house: that Mr Bingo Gilbert had a marauding Italian-looking son.

It was never a good idea to pursue Moses across the Red Sea....

'My son, Angelo,' Gilbert said.

Angelo made an instinctive movement with his right hand towards his left armpit as if reaching for his gun, but he wore a bloused suede jerkin over his jeans, and was unarmed. Thank the Lord, I thought, for small mercies.

In his left hand he carried the package I had sent to Cambridge. It had been opened, and he was holding it carefully upright to save the cassettes from falling out.

He recovered his voice faster than I did. His voice and his arrogance and his sneer.

'What's this mug doing here?' he said.

'He came to sell me the computer tapes.'

Angelo laughed derisively. 'I told you we'd get them for nothing. This mug sent them. I told you he would.' He lifted the package jeeringly. 'I told you you were an old fool to offer that Irish witch any cash. You'd have done better to let me shake the goods out of her the minute her old man died. You've no clue, Dad. You should have cut me in months ago, not tell me when it's already a mess.'

His manner, I thought, was advanced son-parent rebellion: the young bull attacking the old. And part of it, I suspected, was for my benefit. He was showing off. Proving that even if I'd got the better of him the last time we'd met, it was he, Angelo, who was the superior being.

'How did this creep get here?' he demanded.

Gilbert either ignored the peacockery or indulged it. 'Mrs O'Rorke sent him,' he said.

Neither of them thought to ask the very awkward question of how I knew Mrs O'Rorke. I'd have given few chances for my health if they'd worked it through. I reckoned that this was one exceptional occasion when ignorance was emphatically the safest path, and that in prudence I should be wholly ignorant of the life and death of Chris

Norwood.

'How come he still has the tapes to sell,' Angelo said cunningly, 'if he's already sent them to me?'

Gilbert's eyes narrowed and his neck stiffened, and I saw that his unprepossessing exterior was misleading: that it was indeed a tough bull Angelo was challenging, one who still ruled his territory.

'Well?' he said to me.

Angelo waited with calculation and triumph growing in his eyes and throughout his face like an intoxication, the scarifying lack of inhibition ballooning as fast as before. It was his utter recklessness, I thought, which was to be feared above all.

'I sent a copy,' I said. I pointed to the package in his hand. 'Those are copies.'

'Copies?' It stopped Angelo for a moment. Then he said suspiciously, 'Why did you send copies?'

'The originals belonged to Mrs O'Rorke. They weren't mine to give you. But I certainly didn't want you and your friend coming back again waving your gun all over the place, so I did send some tapes. I had no idea I would ever see you again. I just wanted to be rid of you. I had no idea you were Mr Gilbert's son.'

'Gun?' Gilbert said sharply. '*Gun?*'

'His pistol.'

'Angelo—' There was no mistaking the anger in the father's voice. 'I've forbidden you – *forbidden* you, do you hear, to carry that gun. I sent you to *ask* for those tapes. To ask. To buy.'

'Threats are cheaper,' Angelo said. 'And I'm not a child. The days when I took your orders are over.'

They faced each other in unleashed antagonism.

'That pistol is for protection,' Gilbert said intensely. 'And it is mine. You are not to threaten people with it. You are not to take it out of this house. You still depend on me for a living, and while you work for me and live in this house you'll do what I say. You'll leave that gun strictly alone.'

God in Heaven, I thought: *he doesn't know about Chris Norwood*

'You taught me to shoot,' Angelo said defiantly.

'But as a sport,' Gilbert said, and didn't understand that sport for his son was a living target.

I interrupted the filial battle and said to Gilbert, 'You've got the tapes. Will you pay Mrs O'Rorke?'

'Don't be bloody stupid,' Angelo said.

I ignored him. To his father I said, 'You were generous before. Be generous now.'

I didn't expect him to be. I wanted only to distract him, to keep his mind on something trivial, not to let him *think*.

'Don't listen to him,' Angelo said. 'He's only a mug.'

Gilbert's face mirrored his son's words. He looked me up and down with the same inner conviction of superiority, the belief that everyone was a mug except himself.

If Gilbert felt like that, I thought, it was easy to see why Angelo did.

Parental example. I would often at school know the father by the behaviour of the son.

I shrugged. I looked defeated. I let them get on with their ill-will. I wanted above all to get out of that house before they started putting bits of knowledge together and came up with a picture of me as a real towering threat to Angelo's liberty. I didn't know if Gilbert would stop his son – or *could* stop him – if Angelo wanted me dead: and there was a lot of leafy Welwyn Garden City lying quietly in the back garden.

'Mrs O'Rorke's expecting me,' I said, 'to know how I got on.'

'Tell her nothing doing,' Angelo said.

Gilbert nodded.

I edged past Angelo to the door, looking suitably meek under his scathing sneer.

'Well,' I said weakly, 'I'll be going.'

I walked jerkily through the hall, past the attendant golf clubs and out of the open front door, taking with me a last view of Gilbert locking psychological horns with meance that would one day overthrow him.

I was sweating. I wiped the palms of my hands on my trousers, fumbled open the car door, put a faintly trembling hand on the ignition key and started the engine.

If they hadn't been so busy fighting each other...

As I turned out of the drive into the cul-de-sac itself I had a glimpse of the two of them coming out onto the step to stare after me, and my mouth was uncomfortably dry until I was sure Angelo hadn't leapt into his car to give chase.

I had never felt my heart flutter that way before. I had never, I supposed, felt real fear. I couldn't get it to subside. I felt shaky, restless, short of breath, slightly sick.

Reaction, no doubt.

Chapter Eight

Somewhere between Welwyn and Twickenham, I pulled into a parking space to work out where to go.

I could go home, collect my guns, and drive to Bisley. I looked down at my hands. On present form, I'd miss the target by a yard. No point in wasting the money on the ammunition.

It should take a fair while for the Gilberts to discover that they had 'Starstrike' instead of racing programs, but not as long as that to work out that while I had the original tapes, they had no exclusive control of Liam's system. I needed somewhere they wouldn't find me when they came looking. Pity, I thought, that Sarah and I had so few friends.

I walked across the road to a public telephone box and telephoned to William's farm.

'Well, of course, Jonathan,' Mrs Porter said. 'Of course, I'd have you. But William's gone. He got fed up with no horses to ride here and he packed up and went off to Lambourn this morning. He'd a friend there, he said, and he's going straight back to school from there tomorrow evening.'

'Was he all right?'

'So much *energy*!' she said. 'But he won't eat a thing. Says he wants to keep his weight down, to be a jockey.'

I sighed. 'Thanks anyway.'

'It's a pleasure to have him,' she said. 'He makes me laugh.'

I rang off and counted the small stack of coins I had left, and public-spiritedly spent them on the Newmarket police.

'Chief Superintendent Irestone isn't here, sir,' they said. 'Do you want to leave a message?'

I hesitated, but in the end all I said was, 'Tell him Jonathan Derry called. I have a name for him. I'll get in touch with him later.'

'Very good, sir.'

I got back into the car, consulted a slip of paper in my wallet and drove to Northolt to visit Ted Pitts, knowing that quite likely he wouldn't be pleased to see me. When I had finally tracked down the school secretary, he had parted with the requested information reluctantly, saying that the masters' addresses were sacrosanct to save them from over-zealous parents. Ted Pitts, he said, had particularly made him promise not to divulge.

'But I'm not a parent.'

'Well, no.'

I'd had to persuade, but I got it. And one could see, I thought, why Ted wanted to guard his privacy, because where he lived, I found, was in a mobile home on a caravan site. Neat enough, but not calculated to impress some of the social-climbers in the P.T.A.

Ted's wife, who opened the door to my knock, looked surprised but not unwelcoming. She was as earnest as Ted, small, bright-eyed, an occasional visitor to school football matches, where Ted tore up and down the pitches refereeing. I sought for a name and thought 'Jane', but wasn't sure. I smiled hopefully instead.

'How's Ted?' I said.

'Much better. His voice is coming back.' She opened the door wider. 'He'd like to see you, I'm sure, so do come in.' She gestured to the inside of the caravan, where I couldn't yet see, and said – 'It's a bit of a mess. We didn't expect visitors.'

'If you'd rather I didn't—'

'No. Ted will want you.'

I stepped up into the van and saw what she meant. In every direction spread an untidy jumble of books and newspapers and clothes and toys, all the normal clutter of a large family but condensed into a very small space.

Ted was in the miniscule sitting-room with his three little girls, sitting on a sofa and watching while they played on the floor. When he saw me he jumped to his feet in astonishment and opened his mouth, but all that came out was a squeaky croak.

'Don't talk,' I said. 'I just came to see how you are.' Any thoughts I had about cadging a bed from him had vanished. It seemed silly, indeed, to mention it.

'I'm better.' The words were recognizable, but half a whisper, and he gestured for me to sit down. His wife offered coffee and I accepted. The children squabbled and he kicked them gently with his toe.

'Jane will take them out soon,' he said huskily.

'I'm being a nuisance.'

He shook his head vigorously. 'Glad you came.' He pointed to a ledge running high along one wall and said, 'I bought your new tapes. They're up there, with your cassettes, out of reach. The children climb so. Haven't done the copying yet, though. Sorry.' He rubbed his throat as if massage would help, and made a face of frustration.

'Don't talk,' I said again, and passed on William's information about form books. He seemed pleased enough but also subdued, as if the knowledge no longer interested.

Jane returned with one mug of coffee and offered sugar. I shook my head and took a sip of the liquid which looked dark brown but tasted weak.

I said, more to make conversation than anything else, 'I don't suppose either of you know where I could put up for a night or two? Somewhere not too expensive. I mean, not a hotel.' I smiled lop-sidedly. 'I've spent so much on petrol and other things this week that I'm a bit short.'

'End of the month,' Ted said, nodding. 'Always the same.'

'But your house!' Jane said. 'Ted says you've got a house.'

'Er . . . um . . . er . . . I haven't been getting on too well with Sarah.' The convenient half-truth arrived just in time and they made small sad noises in sympathetic comprehension. Ted, all the same, shook his head, sorry not to be able to help.

'Don't know of anywhere,' he said.

Jane, standing straight, tucking her elbows into her sides and clasping her hands tightly together said, 'You could stay here. On the sofa.'

Ted looked extremely surprised but his wife tensely said, 'Would you pay us?'

'Jane!' Ted said despairingly: but I nodded.

'In advance?' she said rigidly, and I agreed again. I gave her two of the notes I'd got from the bank a day earlier and asked if it was enough. She said yes, looking flushed, and bundled the three children out of the room, out of the caravan, and down towards the road. Ted, hopelessly awkward and embarrassed, stuttered a wheezy apology.

'We've had a bad month . . . they've put the land rent up here . . . and I had to pay for new tyres, and for the car licence. I must have the car and it's falling to bits – and I'm overdrawn. . . .'

'Do stop, Ted,' I said. 'I know all about being broke. Not starving broke. Just penniless.'

He smiled weakly. 'I suppose we've never had the bailiffs ... but this week we've been living on bread mostly. Are you sure you don't mind?'

'Positive.'

So I stayed with the Pitts. Watched television, built bright brick towers for the children, ate the egg supper my money had bought, took Ted for a pint.

The talking couldn't have done his throat much good, but between the froth and dregs I learned a good deal about the Pitts. He'd met Jane one summer in a youth hostel in the Lake District, and they'd married while he was still at college because the oldest of the little girls was imminent. They were happy, he said, but they'd never been able to save a deposit for a house. Lucky to have a mobile home. Hire purchase, of course. During the holidays, he looked after the children while Jane took temporary secretarial jobs. Better for the family income. Better for Jane. He still went hiking on his own, though, one week every year. Backpacking. Sleeping in a tent, in hilly country; Scotland or Wales. He gave me a shy look through the black-framed glasses. 'It sorts me out. Keeps me sane.' It wasn't everyone, I thought, who was his own psychotherapist.

When we got back, the caravan was tidy and the children asleep. One had to be quiet, Ted said, going in: they woke easily. The girls all slept, it appeared, in the larger of the two bedrooms, with their parents in the smaller. There was a pillow, a car travelling rug and a clean sheet awaiting me, and although the sofa was a bit short for comfort it was envelopingly soft.

It was only on the point of sleep, far too late to bother, that I remembered that I hadn't called back to talk to Irestone. Oh well, I thought, yawning, tomorrow would do.

In the morning I did call from a telephone box near the public park where Ted and I took the children to play on the swings and seesaw.

Irestone, as usual, wasn't in. Wasn't he *ever* in, I asked. A repressive voice told me the Chief Superintendent was off-duty at present, and would I please leave a message. I perversely said that no, I wouldn't, I wanted to speak to the Chief Superintendent personally. If I would leave a number, they said, he would in due course call me. Impasse, I thought: Ted Pitts had no telephone.

'If I call you at nine tomorrow morning,' I said, 'will Chief Superintendent Irestone be there? If I call at ten? At eleven? At midday?'

I was told to wait and could hear vague conversations going on in the background, and going on for so long that I had to feed more coins into the box, which scarcely improved my patience. Finally, however, the stolid voice returned. 'Detective Chief Superintendent Irestone will be in the Incident Room tomorrow morning from ten o'clock onwards. You may call him at the following number.'

'Wait a minute.' I unclipped my pen and dug out the scrap of paper which held Ted's address. 'OK.'

He gave me the number, and I thanked him fairly coolly, and that was that.

Ted was pushing his tiniest girl carefully round on a sort of turntable, holding her close to him and laughing with her. I wished quite surprisingly fiercely that I could have had a child like that, that I could have taken her to a sunny park on Sunday mornings, and hugged her little body and watched her grow. Sarah, I thought. Sarah – this is the way you've ached, perhaps; and for the baby to cuddle, and the young woman to see married. This is the loss. This, that Ted Pitts has. I watched his delight in the child and I envied him with all my heart.

We sat on a bench a bit later while the girls played in a sandpit, and for something to say I asked him why he'd lost his first intense interest in the racing form-books.

He shrugged, looking at his children, and said in the husky voice which was slowly returning to normal, 'You can see how it is. I can't risk the money, I can't afford to buy the form books. I couldn't even afford to buy a set of tapes for myself this week, to copy the programs onto. I bought some for you with the money you gave me, but I just didn't have enough. ... I told you, we've been down to counting pennies for food, and although next month's pay will be in the bank tomorrow I still haven't paid the electricity.'

'It's the Derby soon,' I said.

He nodded morosely. 'Don't think I haven't thought of it. I look at those tapes sitting up on that shelf, and I think, shall I or shan't I? But I've had to decide not to. I can't risk it. How could I possibly explain to Jane if I lost? We need every pound, you know. You can see we do.'

It was ironic, I thought. On the one hand there was Angelo Gilbert, who was prepared to kill to get those tapes, and on the other, Ted Pitts, who had them and set them lower than a dust-up with his wife.

'The programs belong to an old woman called O'Rorke,' I said. 'Mrs Maureen O'Rorke. I went to see her this week.'

Ted showed only minor signs of interest.

'She said a few things I thought you'd find amusing.'

'What things?' Ted said.

I told him about the bookmakers closing the accounts of regular winners, and about the system the O'Rorkes had used with their gardener, Dan, going round betting shops to put their money on anonymously.

'Great heavens,' Ted said. 'What a palaver.' He shook his head. 'No Jonathan, it's best to forget it.'

'Mrs O'Rorke said her husband could bet with an overall certainty of winning once every three times. How does that strike you statistically?'

He smiled. 'I'd need a hundred per cent certainty to bet on the Derby.'

One of the children threw sand in the eyes of another and he got up in a hurry to scold, to comfort, to dig around earnestly with the corner of his handerchief.

'By the way,' I said, when order was restored, 'I took some copies of your game "Starstrike", I hope you don't mind.'

'You're welcome,' he said. 'Did you play it? You have to type in F or S at the first question mark. I haven't written the instructions out yet, but I'll let you have them when I do. The kids,' he looked pleased and a touch smug, 'say it's neat.'

'Is it your best?'

'My best?' He smiled a fraction and shrugged, and said, 'I teach from it. I had to write it so that the kids could understand the program and how it worked. Sure, I could write a far more sophisticated one, but what would be the point?'

A pragmatist, Ted Pitts, not a dreamer. We collected the children together, with Ted brushing them down and emptying sand from their shoes, and drove back to the caravan to home-made hamburgers for lunch.

In the afternoon under Ted's commiserating eyes I corrected the load of exercise books which I happened not to have carried into my house on Friday night. Five B had Irestone to thank for that. And on Monday morning with Ted's voice in good enough shape, he thought, to quell the monsters in the third form, we both went back to school.

We each drove our own cars. I felt I'd used up my welcome in the caravan and although Jane said I could stay if I liked I could see I was no longer a blessing from heaven. The new pay cheque would be in the bank. There would be more than bread this week, and I would have to think of somewhere else.

Ted stretched up in the last minutes before we left and plucked the six cassettes from the high shelf. 'I could do these at lunchtime today,' he said, 'if you like.'

'That would be great,' I said. 'Then you can keep one set and the others will be Mrs O'Rorke's.'

'But don't you want some yourself?'

'Maybe later I could get copies of yours, but I can't see me chasing round betting shops for the rest of my life.'

He laughed. 'Nor me. Though I wouldn't have minded a flutter...' A sort of longing gleamed in his eyes again, and was quickly extinguished. 'Ah well,' he said, 'forward to the fray.' He kissed Jane and the little girls, and off we went.

During the mid-morning break I yet again tried to reach Chief Superintendent Irestone, this time from the coin box in the common-room. Even with the new number, I got no joy. Chief Superintendent Irestone wasn't available at that time.

'This is boring,' I said. 'I was told he would be.'

'He was called away, sir. Will you leave a message?'

I felt like leaving a couple of round oaths. I said, 'Tell him Jonathan Derry called.'

'Very good, sir. Your message time at ten thirty-three.'

To hell with it, I thought.

I had taken about five paces down the room in the direction of the coffee machine when the telephone bell rang behind me. It was the time of day when masters' wives tended to ring up to get their dear ones to run errands on their way home, and the nearest to the bell answered its summons as a matter of course. My wife, at least, I thought, wouldn't be calling, but someone shouted, 'Jonathan, it's for you.'

Surprised, I retraced my steps and picked up the receiver.

'Hullo,' I said.

Jonathan,' Sarah said. 'Where *have* you been? Where in God's name have you *been?*'

She sounded hysterical. Her voice was high, vibrating with tension, strung tighter than I'd ever heard before. Near snapping point. Frightening.

'What's happened?' I asked. I was aware that my voice sounded too calm, but I couldn't help it. It always seemed to come out that way when there was a jumbled turmoil going on inside.

'Oh my *Christ*!' She still had time to be exasperated with me, but no time to say more.

After the shortest of pauses another voice spoke, and this time every hair of my body rose in protest.

'Now you listen to me, creep. . . .'

Angelo Gilbert.

'You listen to me,' he said. 'Your little lady wifey's sitting here snug as you like. We tied her to a chair so's not to hurt her.' He sniggered. 'Her friend too, the wet little bird. Now you listen, mug, because you're going to do just what I tell you. Are you listening?'

'Yes,' I said. I was in fact listening with all my might and with one hand clamped over my other ear because of the chatter and coffee cups all around me. It was macabre. It also seemed to have divorced me from any feeling in my feet.

'That was your last runaround, that was,' Angelo said, 'sending us those duff tapes. This time you'll give us the real ones, get it?'

'Yes,' I said mildly.

'You wouldn't like to get your little wifey back with her face all smashed up, would you?'

'No.'

'All you got to do is give us the tapes.'

'All right,' I said.

'And no bloody runaround.' He seemed disappointed that I'd shown so little reaction to his dramatics but even in that dire moment it seemed second nature to use on him the techniques I'd unconsciously developed in the years of teaching: to deflate the defiance, to be bored by the super-ego, to kill off the triumphant cruelty by an appearance of indifference.

It worked on the kids, it worked a treat on Jenkins, and it had already worked twice on Angelo. He should have learned by now, I thought, that I didn't rise to sneers or arrogance: not visibly anyway. He was too full of himself to believe that someone might not show the fear he felt the urge to induce. He might not be ultra-bright, but he was incalculably dangerous.

He held the receiver to Sarah's mouth, and against her I had fewer defences.

'Jonathan...' It was half anger, half fright: high and vehement. 'They came yesterday. *Yesterday*. Donna and I have been tied up here all *night*. Where have you damned well *been*?'

'Are you in Donna's house?' I said anxiously.

'*What*? Yes, of *course*. Of *course*, we are. Don't ask such damn silly questions.'

Angelo took the phone back again. 'Now you listen, mug. Listen good. This time there's to be no messing. This time we want the real McCoy, and I'm telling you, it's your last chance.'

I didn't answer.

'Are you there?' he said sharply.

'Sure,' I said.

'Take the tapes to my father's house in Welwyn. Have you got that?'

'Yes. But I haven't got the tapes.'

'Then *get* them.' His voice was nearly a screech. 'Do you hear?' he demanded. 'Get them.'

'It'll take some time,' I said.

'You haven't got time, creep.'

I took a deep breath. He wasn't safe. He wasn't reasonable. He wasn't a schoolchild. I simply couldn't play him too far.

'I can get the tapes today,' I said. 'I'll take them to your father when I get them. It might be late.'

'Sooner,' he said.

'I can't. It's impossible.'

I didn't know exactly why I wanted to delay. It was an instinct. To work things out; not to rush in. This time the Egyptians would have more sense.

'When you get there,' he said, seeming to accept it, 'my father will test the tapes. On a computer. A Grantley computer. Get it, mug? My father bought a Grantley computer, because that's the sort of computer those tapes were written for. So no funny tricks like last time. He'll try the tapes, see? And they'd better be good.'

'All right,' I said again.

'When my father is satisfied,' he said, 'he'll ring me here. Then I'll leave your little wifey and the wet chick tied up here, and you can come and rescue them like a right little Galahad. Got it?'

Yes,' I said.

'Don't you forget, creep, any funny stuff and your little wifey will keep the plastic surgery business in work for years. Starting with her nice white teeth, creep.'

He apparently again held the receiver for Sarah because it was her voice which came next. Still angry, still frightened, still high.

'For God's sake, get those tapes.'

'Yes I will,' I said. 'Has Angelo got his pistol?'

'Yes. Jonathan, do as he says. *Please* do as he says. Don't fool about.' It was an order just as much as a prayer.

'The tapes,' I said with an attempt at reassurance, 'are not worth a tooth. Keep him calm if you can. Tell him I'll do what he says. Tell him I've promised you.'

She didn't answer. It was Angelo who said. 'That's all, creep. That's enough. You get those tapes. Right?'

'All right,' I said, and the line abruptly went dead.

I felt pretty dead myself.

The common-room had emptied and I was already going to be late for the Lower VI. I picked up the necessary books mechanically and propelled myself on unfelt feet along the passages to the laboratories.

Get the tapes . . .

I couldn't get them until I could find Ted Pitts, which would probably not be until lunchtime at twelve fifteen. I had an hour and a half until then in which to decide what to do.

The Lower VI were studying radioactivity. I told them to continue the set of experiments with alpha particles that they had started last week and I sat on my high stool by the blackboard from where I often taught, and watched the Geiger counters counting with my mind on Angelo Gilbert.

Options, I thought.

I could yet once again ring the police. I could say an unstable man is holding my wife hostage at gunpoint. I could say I thought it was he who had killed Christopher Norwood. If I did, they might go chasing out to the Keithly house and try to make Angelo surrender – and then Sarah could be a hostage not for three little cassettes, but for Angelo's personal liberty. An escalation not to be thought of.

No police.

What, then?

Give Harry Gilbert the tapes. Trust that Angelo would leave Sarah and Donna undamaged. Do, in fact, precisely what I'd been told, and believe that Angelo wouldn't wait for me to walk into Donna's house and then leave three dead bodies behind when he walked out of it.

It wasn't logically likely, but it was possible.

It would have been better if I could have thought of a good valid logical reason for the murder of Chris Norwood. He hadn't given Angelo the finished computer programs because if he had there would have been no need for Angelo to come to *me*. I had speculated, not for the first time, on exactly what had happened to Liam O'Rorke's original notes, and what had happened to the tapes Peter told me he had sent to the person who had commissioned them. To C. Norwood, Angel Kitchens, Newmarket.

To Chris Norwood, comprehensive thief. Cocky little bastard, Akkerton had said. Vegetable chef Akkerton, feeding his paunch in the pub.

I supposed that Chris Norwood, when first faced with Angelo, had simply said that Peter Keithly was writing the programs and had all the notes, and that Angelo should get them from *him*. Angelo had then gone threateningly to Peter, who had been frightened into giving him programs which he knew were incomplete. By the time the Gilberts discovered they were useless, Peter was dead. Back Angelo must have gone to Chris Norwood, this time waving a gun. And again Chris Norwood must have said Peter Keithly had the programs on tapes. That if he was dead, they were in his house. He would have told him that, I thought, *after* Angelo had shot up the stereo. He would have begun to be really frightened: but he would have still wanted to keep the programs if he could, because he knew they were a meal ticket for life.

Chris Norwood, I guessed, had twice not given Angelo what he wanted; and Chris Norwood was dead.

I also had fooled and obstructed Angelo twice, and I couldn't be sure that I wasn't alive because I'd had a handy rifle. Without his father there to restrain him, Angelo could still be as volatile as the petrol vapour that had killed Peter, even if he thought he finally had his hands on the treasure he'd been chasing for so long.

Some of the Lower VI were getting their nuclei into knots. Automatically I descended from the heights of the stool and reminded them that cloud chambers didn't cloud if one neglected to add dry ice.

No more runarounds, Angelo had said.

Well...

What tools did I have, I thought. What skills that I could use?

I could shoot.

I couldn't on the other hand shoot Angelo. Not while he had a Walther to Sarah's head. Not without landing myself in jail for manslaughter at the least.

Shooting Angelo was out.

I had the knowledge that Physics had given me. I could construct a radio, a television, a thermostat, a digital clock, a satellite tracker and, given the proper components, a laser beam, a linear accelerator and an atomic bomb. I couldn't exactly make an atomic bomb before lunch.

The two boys who were using the alpha-particle-scattering analogue were arguing over the apparatus, which consisted of one large magnet bombarded by a host of small ones. One boy insisted that the power of permanent magnets decayed with time and the other said it was rubbish, permanent meant permanent.

'Who's right, sir?' they asked.

'Permanent is relative,' I said. 'Not absolute.'

There was a flash of impermanent electrical activity at that moment in my brain. The useful knowledge was to hand.

God bless all boys, I thought.

Chapter Nine

Ted Pitts hunched over the Harris all through lunchtime, making and testing the copies on the new tapes.

'There you are,' he said finally, rubbing his neck. 'As far as I can see they're perfect.'

'Which set do you want?' I said.

He peered at me earnestly through the black frames. 'Don't you mind?'

'Choose which you like,' I said. 'I'll take the others.'

He hesitated, but decided on the originals. 'If you're sure?'

'Certain,' I said. 'But give me the original boxes, *Oklahoma* and so on. It might be better if I hand them over in the right wrappings.'

I slid the copies into the gaudy boxes, thanked Ted, returned to the common-room, and told my four long-suffering lieutenants that I had developed a stupefying sick shivery headache and would they please take my afternoon classes between them. There were groans, but it was a service we regularly did for each other when it was unavoidable. I was going home, I said. With luck, I would be back in the morning.

Before I left I made a detour to the prep room where Louisa was counting out springs and weights for the 2nd form that afternoon. I told her about the headache and got scant sympathy, which was fair. While she took the load of batteries through into one of the laboratories to distribute them along the benches I opened one of her tidy cupboards and helped myself to three small objects, hiding them smartly in my pocket.

'What are you looking for?' Louisa asked, coming back and seeing me in front of the still open doors.

'Nothing particular,' I said vaguely. 'I don't really know.'

'Get home to bed,' she said sighing, casting herself for martyrdom. 'I'll cope with the extra work.'

My absence meant in reality less work for her, not more, but there was nothing to be gained by pointing it out. I thanked her profusely to keep her in a good mood for the others, and went out to the car to drive home.

No need to worry about Angelo being there: he was in the Keithly's house a hundred miles away in Norfolk.

Everything felt unreal. I thought of the two girls, tied to the chairs, uncomfortable, scared, exhausted. Don't fool about, Sarah had said. Do what Angelo says.

Somewhere in one of the sideboard drawers we had a photograph album, thrust out of sight since we had lost the desire to record our joyless life. I dug it out and turned the pages, looking for the picture I had taken once of Peter, Donna and Sarah standing out on the pavement in front of Peter's house. The sun had been shining, I found. All three were smiling, looking happy. A pang to see Peter's face, no moustache, looking so pleased with himself and young. Nothing special about that photograph: just people, a house, a street. Reassuring to me, however, at that moment.

I went upstairs to my own small room, unlocked the gun cupboard and took out one of the Mauser 7.62s and also one of the Olympic-type rifles,the Anschütz .22. Packed them both into the special suitcase along with some ammunition of both sizes. Carried the case down to the car and locked it into the boot.

Reflected and went upstairs to fetch a large brown bathtowel from the linen cupboard. Locked that also into the boot.

Locked the house.

After that I sat in the car for three or four minutes thinking things out, with the result that I went back into the house yet again, this time for a tube of extra-strength glue.

All I didn't have enough of, I thought, was time.

I started the engine and set off not to Welwyn, but to Norwich.

Propelled by demons, I did the trip in a shorter time than usual, but it was still four-thirty when I reached the city outskirts. Six hours since Angelo had telephoned. Six long hours for his hostages.

I drew up beside a telephone box in a shopping parade not far from Donna's house and dialled her number. Praying, I think, that Angelo would answer: that all would be at least no worse than it had been in the morning.

'Hullo,' he said. Eagerly, I thought. Expecting his father.

'It's Jonathan Derry,' I said. 'I've got the tapes.'

'Let me talk to my father.'

'I'm not at your father's house. I haven't gone there yet. It's taken me all day to get the tapes.'

'Now you listen, creep ...' He was roughly, nastily angry. 'I warned you ...'

'It's taken me all day, but I've got them,' I interrupted insistently. 'I've got the tapes. I've got the tapes.'

'All *right*,' he said tautly. 'Now take them to my father. Take them there, do you hear?'

'Yes,' I said. 'I'll go there straightaway, but it'll take me some time. It's a long way.'

Angelo muttered under his breath and then said, 'How long? Where are you? We've been waiting all fucking night and all fucking day.'

'I'm near Bristol.'

'*Where?*' It was a yell of fury.

'It'll take me four hours,' I said, 'to reach your father.'

There was a brief silence. Then Sarah's voice, tired beyond tears, numb with too much fright.

'Where are you?' she said.

'Near Bristol.'

'Oh my God.' She sounded no longer angry, but hopeless. 'We can't stand much more of this . . .'

The receiver was taken away from her in mid-sentence, and Angelo came back on the line.

'Get going, creep,' he said; and disconnected.

Breathing space, I thought. Four hours before Angelo expected the message from his father. Instead of pressure mounting inexorably, dangerously, in that house, there would at worst, I hoped, be a bearable irritation, and at best a sort of defusing of suspense. They wouldn't for another four hours be strung up with a minute-to-minute expectation.

Before getting back into the car I opened the boot, took the telescope and the two rifles out of their non-jolt beds in the suitcase and wrapped them more vulnerably in the brown towel. Put them into the car on the brown upholstery of the back seat. Put the boxes of bullets beside them, also hidden by towel. Looked then at my fingers. No tremors. Not like in my heart.

I drove round into the road where the Keithly house stood and stopped at the kerb just out of sight of the net-curtained window. I could see the roof, part of a wall, most of the front garden – and Angelo's car in the driveway.

There weren't many people in the street. The children would be home from school, indoors having tea. The husbands wouldn't be back yet from work: there was more space than cars outside the houses. A peaceful suburban scene. Residential street, middle-income prosperous, not long built. An uncluttered street with no big trees and no forests of electricity and telegraph poles: new-laid cables tended to run underground for most of their journey, emerging only occasionally into the daylight. In the photograph of Peter's house, there had been one telegraph pole nearby with wires distributing from it to the individual houses all around, but not much else. No obstructions. Neat flat asphalt pavements, white kerbstones, tar-and-chipping roadway. A few neat little hedges bordering some of the gardens. A lot of neat green rectangular patches of repressed grass. Acres of net curtains ready to twitch. I-can-see-out-but-you-can't-see-in.

The first essential for pin-point rifle shooting was to know how far one was from the target. On ranges the distances were fixed, and always the same. I was accustomed to precisely three, four, and five hundred yards. To nine hundred and a thousand yards, both of them further than half a mile. The distance affected one's angle of aim: the longer the distance, the further above the target one had to aim in order to hit it.

Olympic shooting was all done at three hundred metres, but from different body positions: standing, kneeling and lying prone. In Olympic shooting also one was allowed ten sighters in each position – ten chances of adjusting one's sights before one came to the forty rounds which counted for scoring.

In that street in Norwich I was not going to get ten sighters. I could afford barely one.

No regular lines of telegraph poles meant no convenient help with measuring the distance. The front gardens, though, I reckoned, should all be of more or less the same width because all the houses were identical, so as inconspicuously and casually as possible I slipped out of the car and paced slowly along the street, going away from Peter's house.

Fourteen paces per garden. I did some mental arithmetic and came up with three hundred yards meaning twenty-two houses.

I counted carefully. There were only twelve houses between me and my target – say one hundred and seventy yards. The shorter distance would be to my advantage. I could reckon in general to hit a target within one minute of a degree of arc: or in other words to hit a circular target of about one inch wide at a hundred yards, two inches wide at two hundred, three inches wide at three hundred, and so on to a ten-inch dinner plate at a thousand.

My target on that evening was roughly rectangular and about four inches by six, which meant that I mustn't be further away from it than four hundred yards. The main problem was that from where I stood, even if I used the telescope, I couldn't see it.

An old man came out of the house against whose kerbside I was parked and asked if I wanted anything.

'Er, no,' I said. 'Waiting for someone. Stretching my legs.'

'My son wants to park there,' he said, pointing to where my car was. 'He'll be home soon.'

I looked at the stubborn old face and knew that if I didn't move he would be staring at me through the curtains, watching whatever I did. I nodded and smiled, got into the car, reversed into his next-door driveway, and left the street by the way I'd come.

All right, I thought, driving around. I have to come into the street from the opposite end. I have to park where I can see the target. I do not, if possible, park outside anyone's house fully exposed to one of those blank-looking one-way viewing screens. I do not park where Angelo can see me. I count the houses carefully to get the distance right; and above all I don't take much time.

It's a cliché in movies that when an assassin looks through the telescopic sight, steadies the crossed lines on the target and squeezes the trigger, the victim drops dead. Quite often the assassin will perform his feat while standing up, and nearly always it will be with his first shot: all of which makes serious marksmen laugh, or wince, or both. The only film I ever saw that got it right was *The Day of the Jackal*, where the gunman went into a forest to pace out his distance, to strap his rifle to a tree for steadiness, to adjust his sights and take two or three trial shots at a head-sized melon before transferring it all to the place of execution. Even then, there was no allowance for wind – but one can't have everything.

I drove into the top end of Peter's road, with which I was less familiar, and between two of the houses came across the wide entrance gates to the old estate upon which the new estate had been built. The double gates themselves, wrought iron, ajar, led to a narrow road that disappeared into parkland, and they were set not flush with the roadway or even with the fronts of the houses, but slightly further back. Between the gates and the road there was an area of moderately well-kept gravel and a badly weathered notice board announcing that all the callers to the Paranormal Research Institute should drive in and follow the arrows to Reception.

I turned without hesitation onto the gravel area and stopped the car. It was ideal. From there, even with the naked eye, I had a clear view of the target. A slightly sideways view certainly, but good enough.

I got out of the car and counted the houses which stretched uniformly along the street: the Keithlys' was the fourteenth on the opposite side of the road and my target was one house nearer.

The road curved slightly to my right. There was a slight breeze from the left. I made the assessments almost automatically and eased myself into the back of the car.

I had gone through long patches of indecision over which rifle to use. The 7.62 bullets were far more destructive, but if I missed the target altogether with the first shot, I could do terrible damage to things or people I couldn't see. People half a mile away, or more. The .22 was much lighter: still potentially deadly if I missed the target, but not for such a long distance.

In a car I obviously couldn't lie flat on my stomach, the way I normally fired the Mauser. I could kneel, and I was more used to kneeling with the .22. But when I knelt in the car I wouldn't have to support the rifle's weight ... I could rest it on the door and shoot through the open window.

For better or worse I chose the Mauser. The stopping power was so much greater, and if I was going to do the job, it was best done properly. Also I could see the target clearly and it was near enough to make hitting it with the second shot a certainty. It was the *first* shot that worried.

A picture of Paul Arcady rose in my mind. 'Could you shoot the apple off his head, sir?' What I was doing was much the same. One slight mistake could have unthinkable results.

Committed, I wound down the rear window and then fitted the sleek three-inch round of ammunition into the Mauser's breech. I took a look at the target through the telescope, steadying that too on the window ledge, and what leapt to my eye was a bright, clear, slightly oblique close-up of a flat shallow box, fixed high up and to one side on the telegraph pole: grey, basically rectangular, fringed with wires leading off to all the nearby houses.

The junction box.

I was sorry for all the people who were going to be without telephones for the rest of that day, but not too sorry to put them out of order.

I lowered the telescope, folded the brown towel, and laid it over the door frame to make a non-slip surface. Wedged myself between the front and rear seats firmly as possible, and rested the barrel of the Mauser on the towel.

I thought I would probably have to hit the junction box two or three times to be sure. 7.62 mm bullets tended to go straight through things, doing most of the damage on the way out. If I'd cared to risk shooting the junction box *through the pole* one accurate bullet would have blown it apart, but I would have to have been directly behind it, and I couldn't get there unobserved.

I set the sights to what I thought I would need for that distance, lowered my body into an angle that felt right, corrected a fraction for the breeze, and squeezed the trigger. Hit the pole, I prayed. High or low, hit the pole. The bullet might indeed go through it, but with the worst of its impetus spent.

7.62 calibre rifles make a terrific noise. Out in the street it must have cracked like a bull whip. In the car it deafened me like in the old days before ear-defenders.

I reloaded. Looked through the telescope. Saw the bullet hole, round and neat, right at the top of the grey junction box casing.

Allelujah, I thought gratefully, and breathed deeply from relief.

Lowered the sight a fraction, keeping my body position unchanged. Shot again. Reloaded. Shot again. Looked through the telescope.

The second and third holes overlapped, lower down than the first, and, maybe because I wasn't shooting at it directly face-on but from a little to one side, the whole casing seemed to have split.

It would have to do. It was all too noisy.

I put the guns and telescopes on the floor with the towel over them and scrambled through onto the front seat.

Started the engine, reversed slowly onto the road and drove away at a normal pace, seeing in the rear-view mirror a couple of inhabitants come out inquiringly into the street. The net curtains must all have been twitching, but no one shouted after me, no one pointed and said 'That's the man.'

And Angelo – what would he think? And Sarah – who knew the sound of a rifle better than church bells? I hoped to God she'd keep quiet.

Going out of Norwich I stopped for petrol and used the telephone there to ring Donna's number.

Nothing.

A faint humming noise, like wind in the wires.

I blew out a lungful of air and wondered with a smile what the repair men would say when they climbed the pole on the morrow. Unprintable, most like.

There were perhaps ways of interfering with incoming calls by technical juggling, by ringing a number, waiting for it to be answered, saying nothing, waiting for the receiver to be put down, and then not replacing one's own receiver, leaving the line open and making it impossible for the number to ring again. I might have trusted that method for a short while, but not for hours: and with some exchanges it didn't work.

Further along the road I again stopped, this time to tidy and reorganize the car. I returned the Mauser and the telescope to their beds in the suitcase in the boot, along with the 7.62 mm ammunition; then broke all my own and everyone else's rules and loaded a live .22 round into the breech of the Anschütz.

I laid the towel on the back seat and rolled the Olympic rifle in it lengthways, and then stowed it flat on the floor behind the front seats. The towel blended well enough with the brown carpet, and I reckoned that if I didn't accelerate or brake or corner too fast, the gun should travel without moving.

Next I put four extra bullets into my right-hand pocket, because the Anschütz had no magazine and each round had to be loaded separately. After so many years of practice I could discharge the spent casing and load a new bullet within the space of two seconds, and even faster if I held the fresh bullet in my right palm. The two rifles were physically the same size, and I'd taken the Mauser with its available magazine if it hadn't been for its horrific power in a domestic setting. The .22 would kill, but not the people in the next house.

After that I juggled around a bit with the cassettes and their boxes and the glue and the bits I'd pinched from school, and finally drove on again, this time to Welwyn.

Harry Gilbert was expecting me. From the way he came bustling out of his house the moment I turned into his driveway he had been expecting me for a long time and had grown thoroughly tired of it.

'Where have you *been*?' he said. 'Did you bring the tapes?'

He had come close to me as I emerged from the car, thrusting his chin forward belligerently, sure of his power over a man at a disadvantage.

'I thought you didn't approve of Angelo threatening people with your pistol,' I said.

Something flickered in a muscle in his face.

'There are times when only threats will do,' he said. 'Give me the tapes.'

I took the three tapes out of my pocket and showed them to him; the three tapes themselves, out of their boxes.

I said, 'Now ring Angelo and tell him to untie my wife.'

Gilbert shook his head. 'I try the tapes first. Then I ring Angelo. And Angelo leaves your wife tied up until you yourself go to release her. That is the arrangement. It's simple. Come into the house.'

We went again into his functional office, which this time had an addition in the shape of a Grantley computer sitting on his desk.

'The tapes.' He held his hand out for them, and I gave them to him. He slotted the first one into the recorder which stood beside the computer and began to fumble around with the computer's typewriter-like keys in a most disorganized fashion.

'How long have you had that computer?' I said.

'Shut up.'

He typed RUN, and not surprisingly nothing happened, as he hadn't fed the program in from the cassette. I watched him pick up the instruction book and begin leafing through it, and if there had been all the time in the world I would have let him stew in it longer. But every minute I wasted meant one more dragging minute for Donna and Sarah, so I said, 'You'd better take lessons.'

'Shut *up*.' He gave me a distinctly bull-like glare and typed RUN again.

'I want Angelo out of that house,' I said, 'so I'll show you how to run the tapes. Otherwise we'll be here all night.'

He would have given much not to allow me the advantage, but he should have done his homework first.

I ejected the tape to see which side we'd got, then reinserted it and typed CLOAD "EPSOM". The asterisks began to blink at the top right hand corner as the computer searched the tape, but at length it found "EPSOM", loaded the Epsom program and announced READY.

'Now type RUN and press "Enter",' I said.

Gilbert did so, and immediately the screen said:

WHICH RACE AT EPSOM?

TYPE NAME OF RACE AND PRESS 'ENTER'.

Gilbert typed DERBY, and the screen told him to type the name of the horse. He typed in "ANGELO", and made the same sort of fictional replies Ted Pitts and I had done. Angelo's win factor was 46, which must have been maximum. It also said quite a lot about Gilbert's estimate of his son.

'How do you get Ascot?' he said.

I ejected the tape and inserted the first side of all. Typed CLOAD "ASCOT", pressed 'Enter', and waited for READY.

'Type RUN, press "Enter",' I said.

He did so, and at once got WHICH RACE AT ASCOT? TYPE NAME OF RACE AND PRESS 'ENTER'.

He typed GOLD CUP and looked enthralled by the ensuing questions, and I thought that he'd played with it long enough.

'Telephone Angelo,' I said. 'You must surely be satisfied that this time you've got the real thing.'

'Wait,' he said heavily. 'I'll try all the tapes. I don't trust you. Angelo was insistent that I don't trust you.'

I shrugged. 'Test what you like.'

He tried one or two programs on each of the sides, finally realizing that CLOAD plus the first five letters of the racecourse required, inserted between inverted commas, would unlock the goodies.

'All right,' I said at length. 'Now ring Angelo. You can run the programs all you like when I'm gone.'

He could find no further reason for putting it off. With a stare to which his own natural arrogance was fast returning he picked up one of the telephones, consulted a note pad beside it, and dialled the number.

Not surprisingly he didn't get through. He dialled again. Then, impatiently, again. Then, muttering under his breath he tried one of the other telephones with ditto nil results.

'What is it?' I said.

'The number doesn't ring.'

'You must be dialling it wrong,' I said. 'I've got it here.'

I fished into my jacket pocket for my diary and made a show of fluttering through the leaves. Came to the number. Read it out.

'That's what I dialled,' Gilbert said.

'It can't be. Try again.' I'd never thought of myself as an actor but I found it quite easy to pretend.

Gilbert dialled again, frowning, and I thought it time to be agitated and anxious.

'You *must* get through,' I said. 'I've worried and rushed all day to get those tapes here, and now you *must* ring Angelo, he *must* leave my wife.'

In experience of command he had tough years of advantage, but then I too was accustomed to having to control wily opponents, and when I took a step towards him it was clear to both of us that physically I was taller and fitter and quite decisively stronger.

He said hastily, 'I'll try the operator,' and I fidgetted and fumed around him in simulated anxiety while the operator tried without success and reported the number out of order.

'But it can't be,' I yelled. '*You've got to ring Angelo.*'

Harry Gilbert simply stared at me, knowing that it was impossible. I cut the decibels a shade but looked as furious as I could, and said, 'We'll have to go there.'

'But Angelo said . . .'

'I don't give a damn what Angelo said,' I said forcefully. 'He won't leave that house until he knows you've got the tapes, and now it seems you can't tell him you have. So we'll bloody well have to go there and tell him. And I'm absolutely fed up with all this buggering about.'

'You can go,' Gilbert said. 'I'm not coming.'

'Yes you are. I'm not walking up to that house alone with Angelo inside it with that pistol. He said I was to give the tapes to *you*, and that's what I've done, and you've got to come with me to tell him so. And I promise you,' I said threateningly, warming to the part, 'that I'll take you with me one way or another. Knocked out or tied up or just sitting quietly in the front seat beside me. Because you're the only one Angelo will listen to.' I snatched up the cassettes lying beside the computer. 'If you want these tapes back you'll come with me.'

He agreed to come. He hadn't much choice. I pulled the cases for the tapes out of my pocket and showed him the labels, *Oklahoma*, *The King and I*, *West Side Story*. Then I ejected the cassette which was still in the recorder and put all three of the tapes into their cases. 'And we'll take these,' I said, 'to prove to Angelo that you have them.'

He agreed to that also. He came out with me to my car, slamming his own front door behind him, and sat in the front passenger seat.

'I'll hold the tapes,' he said.

I put them, however, on the glove shelf out of his immediate reach and told him he could have them once we got to Norwich.

It was a strange journey.

He was a far more powerful man than I would normally have thought of opposing, yet I was discovering that I had probably always thought of myself as being weaker than I was. For the whole of my life I had gone in awe of headmasters; as a pupil, as a student, as a teacher. Even when I'd disagreed or despised or rebelled, I'd never tried actively to defeat. One could easily be chucked out of school and out of college and out of the better jobs in physics.

Harry Gilbert couldn't chuck me out of anything, and perhaps that was the difference. I could face his belief in his own superiority and not be intimidated by it. I could use my wits and my muscles to get him to do what I wanted. It was heady stuff. Have to be careful, I reflected, not to develop delusions of grandeur of my own.

Angelo, I thought suddenly, feels just as I do. Feels the spreading of the wings of internal power. Feels he can do more than he realized. Sees his world isn't as constricting as he thought. Angelo too was emerging into a new conception of ability ... but in him there were no brakes.

'There is someone there with Angelo,' I said. 'My wife said "they".' I spoke neutrally, without aggression.

Gilbert sat heavily silent.

'When Angelo came to my house,' I said, 'there was another man with him. Very like Angelo in looks. Did what Angelo told him.'

After a pause Gilbert shrugged and said, 'Eddy. Angelo's cousin. Their mothers were twins.'

'Italian?' I said.

Another pause. Then, 'We are all Italian by descent.'

'But born in England?'

'Yes. Why do you ask?'

I sighed. 'Just to pass the journey.'

He grunted, but gradually a good deal of his resentment of my behaviour subsided. I had no idea whether or not he considered it justified.

Anxiety on my part didn't need to be acted. I found myself drumming my fingers on the steering wheel when stopped by red lights and cursing long lorries which delayed my passing. By the time we got to Norwich, it would be over the four hours I'd warned Angelo to expect, and of all things that I didn't want, it was Angelo ballooning into premature rage.

'Will you pay Mrs O'Rorke anything for these tapes?' I said.

A pause. 'No.'

'Not even without Angelo knowing?'

He gave me a fierce sideways glare. 'Angelo does what I tell him. Whether I pay or don't pay Mrs O'Rorke is nothing to do with him.'

If he believed all that, I thought, he was deluding himself. Or perhaps he still wanted to believe what had so far been true. Perhaps he truly didn't see that his days of domination over Angelo were ticking away fast.

Just let them last, I thought, for another two hours.

Chapter Ten

The long lingering evening was slowly dying by the time we reached Norwich, though it wouldn't be totally dark for another hour. I drove into the Keithlys' road from the direction that would place Gilbert nearest to the house when I pulled up at the kerb: Angelo had seen my car at his father's house as I had seen his, and the sight of it would alarm him.

'Please get out of the car as soon as I stop,' I said to Gilbert. 'So that Angelo can see you.'

He grunted, but when I pulled up he opened the door as I'd suggested, and gave any watchers from behind the curtains a full view of his lumbering exit from the front seat.

'Wait,' I said, standing up on my own side and talking to him across the top of the car. 'Take the tapes.' I reached across the top of the car and gave them to him. 'Hold them up,' I said, 'so that Angelo can see them.'

'You give too many orders.'

'I don't trust your son any more than he trusts me.'

He gave me a bullish stare of fully revived confidence, but he did in fact turn and lift the tapes, showing them to the house.

Behind his back I leant down and picked up the towel-wrapped rifle, holding it longways with the stock to my chest and the flap of my jacket falling over it.

Angelo opened the front door, shielding himself half behind it.

'Go in,' I said to Gilbert. 'This street is full of people watching through the curtains.'

He gave an automatically alarmed look at being spied on and began to walk towards his son. I slid round the car fast and walked close behind him, almost stepping on his heels.

'Explain,' I said urgently.

His head lifted ominously, but he said loudly to Angelo, 'Your telephone's out of order.'

'*What?*' Angelo exclaimed, opening the door a fraction wider. 'It can't be.'

Gilbert said impatiently, 'It is. Don't be a fool. Why else would I come all this way?'

Angelo turned away from the door and strode into the sitting-room, which was where the telephone was located. I heard him pick up the receiver and rattle the cradle, and slam the instrument down again.

'But he brought the tapes,' Gilbert said, walking to the sitting-room and showing the bright cases. 'I tried them. All of them. This time they're the real thing.'

'Come in here, you, creep,' Angelo called.

I propped the wrapped rifle, barrel downwards to the carpet, against the small chest of drawers which stood within arm's reach of the sitting-room door, and showed myself in the doorway.

The sitting-room furniture was all pushed awry. Sarah and Donna sat back-to-back in the centre of the room, with their wrists and ankles strapped to the arms and legs of two of the chairs from the dining room. To one side stood Angelo, holding the Walther, with, beyond the two girls, his look-alike, Eddy. There were glasses and plates sprinkled about, and the smell of long hours of cigarette smoke.

Sarah was facing me.

We looked at each other with a curious lack of emotion, I noticing almost distantly the dark smudges under her eyes, the exhausted sag of her body, the strain and pain round her mouth.

She said nothing. No doubt she considered I was showing too little concern and was too calm as usual: the message on her face wasn't love and relief but relief and disgust.

'Go home,' I said warily to Angelo. 'You've got what you wanted.'

I prayed for him to go. To be satisfied, to be sensible, to be ruled by his father, to be approximately normal.

Harry Gilbert began to turn from his son back towards me, saying, 'That's it, then, Angelo. We'd best be off.'

'No', Angelo said.

Gilbert stopped. 'What did you say?' he said.

'I said, no,' Angelo said. 'This creep's going to pay for all the trouble he's put me to. You come here, creep.'

Gilbert said, 'No, Angelo.' He gestured to the girls. 'This is enough.'

Angelo pointed his pistol with its bulbous silencer straight at Donna's head. 'This one,' he said viciously, 'has been screaming at me for hours that they'll report me to the police, the stupid little bitch.'

'They won't,' I said quickly.

'Dead right they won't.'

Even to Gilbert his meaning was clear. Gilbert made movements of extreme disapproval and active fear and said, 'Put down the gun. Angelo, put it down.' His voice thundered with parental command and from long long habit Angelo began to obey. Even in the same second he visibly reversed his instinct; and I knew that for me it was then or never.

I stretched out my right arm, thrust my hand down into the towel and grasped the stock of the rifle. Swung the towel off the barrel and in the same fluid movement stood in the doorway with the barrel pointing straight at Angelo and the safety catch unlocking with a click.

'Drop it,' I said.

They were all utterly astounded but perhaps Angelo most of all because I'd twice played the same trick on him. The three men stood there as if frozen, and I didn't look at Sarah, not directly.

'Drop the pistol,' I said. He was still pointing it towards Donna.

He couldn't bear to drop it. Not to lose that much face.

'I'll shoot you,' I said.

Even then he hesitated. I swung the barrel to the ceiling and squeezed the trigger. The noise crashed in the small room. Pieces of plaster fell from the ceiling. The sharp smell of cordite prevailed over stale cigarette, and all the mouths were open, like fish. The rifle was pointing back at his heart with the next round in the breech almost before he'd moved an inch, and he looked at it with dazed disbelief.

'Drop the pistol,' I said. '*Drop it.*'

He was still undecided. I'll have to hit him, I thought despairingly. I don't want to. Why won't he drop the bloody thing, there's nothing he can gain.

The air seemed to be still ringing with the aftermath of explosion, but it was into silence that Sarah spoke.

With a sort of sullen ferocity, which seemed as much directed at me as at Angelo, she said loudly, 'He shot in the Olympic Games.'

Angelo's eyes developed doubt.

'Drop the pistol,' I said quietly, 'or I'll shoot your hand.'

Angelo dropped it.

His face was full of fury and hate and I thought him capable of flinging himself upon me regardless of consequences. I looked at him stolidly, showing no triumph, showing nothing to inflame.

'You've got the tapes,' I said. 'Get in the car, all three of you, and get out of my life. I'm sick of your faces.' I stepped back a pace into the hall and nodded with my head towards the front door.

'Just get out,' I said. 'One at a time. Angelo first.'

He came towards me with his dark eyes like pits in the olive face, the light too dim now to give them wicked life. I stood back a few steps further and followed his progress to the front door, as in my own house, with the black barrel.

'I'll get you,' he said.

I didn't answer.

He pulled open the door with the force of rage and stepped outside.

'Now you,' I said to Harry Gilbert.

He was almost as angry as his son, but perhaps it was fanciful of me to guess that there was also some recognition that I'd been able to stop Angelo where he couldn't, and that that had been a good thing.

He followed Angelo out onto the driveway and I saw them both opening the doors of Angelo's car.

'Now you,' I said to Eddy. 'You pick up Angelo's gun. Pick it up by the silencer. Do you know how to unload it?'

Eddy the carbon-copy nodded miserably.

'Do it, then,' I said. 'Very carefully.'

He looked at the rifle and at Angelo getting into the car, and shook the bullets out of the clip, letting them drop on the carpet.

'Right,' I said. 'Take the pistol with you.' I gestured with the rifle barrel and jerked my head towards the open front door, and of the three of them it was Eddy who left with the least reluctance and the most speed.

From inside the hall I watched Angelo start the engine, slam the gears into reverse and make a rough exit into the road. Once there he deliberately side-swiped my car, damaging his own rear wing in the process, and accelerated down the street as if to prove his superior manhood.

With a feeling of terrible tension I closed the front door and went into the sitting-room. Crossed to Sarah, looked at the rubber straps which fastened her wrists and unbuckled them. Unbuckled them. Unbuckled those round her ankles. Then those round Donna.

Donna started crying. Sarah shoved herself stiffly off the chair and collapsed onto the softer contours of the sofa.

'Do you realize how long we've been sitting there?' she demanded bitterly. 'And before you damned well ask, yes, they did untie us now and then for us to go to the bathroom.'

'And to eat?'

'I hate you,' she said.

'I really wanted to know.'

'Yes, to eat. Twice. He made me cook.'

Donna said between sobs, 'It's been awful. *Awful.* You've no idea.'

'They didn't . . .?' I began anxiously.

'No they didn't,' Sarah said flatly. 'They just sneered.'

'*Hateful*,' Donna said. 'Called us mugs.' She hobbled across the carpet and lowered herself gingerly into an armchair. 'I hurt all over.' Tears trickled down her cheeks. I thought of Angelo's description of 'wet chick' and stifled it quickly.

'Look,' I said, 'I know you don't feel like it, but I'd be much happier if you'd stuff a few things into a suitcase and we all left this house.'

Donna helplessly shook her head, and Sarah said 'Why?' with mutiny.

'Angelo hated having to go. You saw him. Suppose he comes back? When he thinks we're off guard . . . he might.'

The idea alarmed them as much as me and also angered Sarah. 'Why did you give them the pistol?' she demanded. 'That was *stupid.* You're such a *fool.*'

'Are you coming?'

'You can't expect us . . .' Donna wailed.

I said to Sarah, 'I have to make a phone call. I can't do it from here.' I indicated the dead telephone. 'I'm going away in the car to do it. Do you want to come, or not?'

Sarah took stock of that rapidly and said that yes, they were coming, and despite Donna's protests she drove her stiffly upstairs. They came down a few minutes later carrying a holdall each, and I noticed that Sarah had put on some lipstick. I smiled at her with some of the old pleasure in seeing her resurfacing briefly, and she looked both surprised and confused.

'Come on, then,' I said, and took the holdalls from them to put in the boot. 'Best be off.' I fetched the rifle, once again wrapped loosely in towel to confuse the neighbours, and stowed it in the suitcase. Checked that Donna had brought the door keys: shut the front door; drove away.

'Where are we going?' Sarah said.

'Where would you like.'

'What about *money*?'

'Credit cards,' I said.

We drove a short way in a silence broken only by Donna's occasional sniffs and sobs, going along with lights on everywhere and the long soft evening turning to full dark.

I pulled up beside a telephone box and put a reversed charge call to the Suffolk police.

'Is Detective Superintendent Irestone there?' I said. Hopeless question, but had to be asked.

'Your name, sir?'

'Jonathan Derry.'

'One moment.'

I waited through the usual mutterings and clicks, and then a voice that was still not Irestone's said, 'Mr Derry, Chief Superintendent Irestone left instructions that if you telephoned again, your message was to be taken down in full and passed on to him directly. Chief Superintendent Irestone asked me to say that owing to ... er ... a hitch in communications he was not aware that you had tried to reach him so often, not until this afternoon. I am Detective Inspector Robson. I came to your house with the Chief Superintendent, if you remember.'

'Yes,' I said. A man nearing forty, fair-headed, reddish skin.

'If you tell me why you rang, sir?'

'You'll take notes?'

'Yes, sir. And a recording.'

'Right. Well – the man who came to my house with a pistol is called Angelo Gilbert. His father is Harry Gilbert, who runs bingo halls all over Essex and north-east London. The man who came with Angelo is his cousin Eddy – don't know his last name. He does what Angelo tells him.'

I paused and Inspector Robson said, 'Is that the lot, sir?'

'No, it isn't. At this moment all three of them are travelling from Norwich in Angelo's car.' I told him the make, the colour, the number, and that it had a bashed-in nearside rear wing. 'They are probably going to Harry Gilbert's house in Welwyn Garden City. I think Angelo also lives there, but perhaps not Eddy.' I gave him the address. 'They should arrive there in about an hour and a quarter to an hour and a half. In the car there is a Walther .22 pistol with a silencer. There may or may not be bullets in it. It may or may not be the pistol which Angelo waved at me, but it looks identical. It might be the pistol which killed Christopher Norwood.'

'That's very useful, sir,' Robson said.

'There's one more thing ...'

'Yes?'

'I don't think Harry Gilbert knows anything at all about Chris Norwood's death. I mean, I don't think he even knows he's dead. If you go to arrest Angelo, Harry Gilbert won't know why.'

'Thank you, sir.'

'That's all,' I said.

'Er,' he said, 'the Chief Superintendent will be in touch with you.'

'All right, but—' I hesitated.

'Yes, sir?'

'I'd be glad to know ...'

'Just a minute, sir,' he interrupted, and kept me hanging on through some lengthy unintelligible background talk. 'Sorry, sir, you were saying.'

'You remember I sent Angelo some computer tapes with games on?'

'Yes, I do. We went to Cambridge main post office and alerted the man whose job it was to hand out letters-to-be-called-for, but unfortunately he went for his tea-break without mentioning it to anyone, and during that short period your package was collected. A girl clerk handed it over. We didn't find out until it was too late. It was ... infuriating.'

'Mm,' I said. 'Well, Angelo came back with more threats, demanding the real tapes, and I've just given them to him. Only ...'

'Only what, sir?'

'Only they won't be able to run them on their computer. I think when they get home they might try those tapes straight away, and when they find they don't work they might ... well they *might* set out to look for me. I mean—'

'I know *exactly* what you mean,' he said dryly.

'So, er, I'd be glad to know if you plan to do anything about Angelo this evening. And if you think there's enough to hold him on.'

'Instructions have already gone off,' he said. 'He'll be picked up tonight as soon as he reaches the house in Welwyn. We have some fingerprints to match ... and some girls who saw two men arrive at Norwood's. So don't worry, once we've got him, we won't let him go.'

'Could I ring up to find out?'

'Yes.' He gave me a new number. 'Call there. I'll leave a message. You'll get it straight away.'

'Thank you,' I said gratefully, 'very much.'

'Mr Derry?'

'Yes?'

'What's wrong with the tapes this time?'

'Oh, I stuck magnets into the cases.'

He laughed. 'I'll see you later, perhaps,' he said. 'And thanks. Thanks a lot.'

I put the receiver down smiling, thinking of the three powerful

Magnadur magnets distorting the programs on the tapes. The permanent magnets which were black and flat; two inches long, three-quarters of an inch wide, three-sixteenths of an inch thick. I'd stuck one into the side of each case, flat on the bottom, black as the plastic, looking like part of the case itself. I'd taken the tapes and the cases separately to Harry Gilbert's – the tapes in the one pocket, the cases in another – and only after he'd played them had I married them all together. Sandwiching electromagnetic recording tapes between such magnets was like wiping a blackboard roughly with wet sponge: there would be traces of what had been recorded there, but not enough to make sense.

It might take Angelo all the way home to see what I'd done, because the magnets did look as if they belonged there.

Or it might not.

I drove wearily in the direction of home. I seemed to have been driving for ever. It had been a very long day. Extraordinary to think it was only that morning that I'd set out from Ted Pitts's.

Both of the girls went to sleep as the miles unrolled, the deep sleep of release and exhaustion. I wondered briefly what would become of us in the future, but mostly I just thought about driving and keeping my own eyelids open.

We stayed in a motel on the outskirts of London and slept as if dead. The alarm call I'd asked for dragged me from limbo at seven in the morning and, yawning like a great white shark, I got through to the number Inspector Robson had given me.

'Jonathan Derry,' I said. 'Am I too early?'

It was a girl's voice which answered, fresh and unofficial. 'No, it's not too early,' she said. 'John Robson asked me to tell you that Angelo Gilbert and his cousin Eddy are in custody.'

'Thank you very much.'

'Any time.'

I put the receiver down with a steadily lightening heart and shook Sarah awake in the next bed.

'Sorry,' I said, 'but I've got to be in school by nine o'clock.'

Chapter Eleven

There was a period when Sarah went back to work and Donna drooped around our house trying to come to terms with the devastation of her life. Sarah's manner to her grew gradually less over-protective and more normal, and when Donna found she was no longer indulged and pampered every minute she developed a pout in place of the invalid smile, and went home. Home to sell her house, to collect Peter's insurance money, and to persuade her Probation Officer to take Sarah's psychological place.

On the surface, things between myself and Sarah continued much as before: the politeness, the lack of emotional contact, the daily meetings of strangers. She seldom met my eye and seemed only to speak when it was essential, but I slowly realized that the deeply embittered set of her mouth, which had been so noticeable before the day we set off to Norwich, had more or less gone. She looked softer and more as she had once been and although it didn't seem to have altered her manner towards me it was less depressing to look at.

In my inner self a lot had changed. I seemed to have stepped out of a cage. I did everything with more confidence and more satisfaction. I shot better. I taught with zest. I even found the wretched exercise books less of a drag. I felt that one day soon I would stretch the spreading wings, and fly.

One night as we lay in the dark, each in our frostily separate cocoon, I said to Sarah, 'Are you awake?'

'Yes.'

'You know that at the end of term I'm going to Canada with the rifle team?'

'Yes.'

'I'm not coming back with them.'

'Why not?'

'I'm going to the United States. Probably for the rest of the school holidays.'

'Whatever for?'

'To see it. Perhaps to live there, eventually.'

She was silent for a while: and what she said in the end seemed only obliquely to have anything to do with my plans.

'Donna talked to me a lot, you know. She told me all about the day she stole that baby.'

'Did she?' I said noncommittally.

'Yes. She said that when she saw it lying there in its pram, she had an overpowering urge to pick it up and cuddle it. So she did. She just did. Then when she had it in her arms she felt as if it belonged to her, as if it was hers. So she carried it to her car, which was just there, a few steps away. She put the baby on the front seat beside her and drove off. She didn't know where she was going. She said it was a sort of dream, in which she had at last had the baby she'd pined for for so long.'

She stopped. I thought of Ted Pitts's little girls and the protective curve of his body as he held his smallest one close. I would have wept for Sarah, for Donna, for every unwillingly barren parent.

'She drove for a long way,' Sarah said. 'She got to the sea and stopped there. She took the baby into the back of the car and it was perfect. She was in utter bliss. It was still like a dream. And then the baby woke up.' She paused. 'I suppose it was hungry. Time for its next feed. Anyway it began to cry, and it wouldn't stop. It cried and cried and cried. She said that it cried for an hour. The noise started driving her mad. She put her hand over its mouth, and it cried harder. She tried to hug its face into her shoulder so that it would stop, but it didn't. And then she found that its nappies were dirty, and the brown stuff had oozed down the baby's leg and was on her dress.'

Another long pause, then Sarah's voice, 'She said she didn't know babies were like that. Screaming and smelly. She'd thought of them as sweet and smiling at her all the time. She began to hate that baby, not love it. She said she sort of threw it down onto the back seat in a rage, and then she got out of the car and just left it. Walked away. She said she could hear the baby crying all the way down the beach.'

This time the silence was much longer.

'Are you still awake?' Sarah said.

'Yes.'

'I'm reconciled now to not having a child. I grieve . . . but it can't be helped.' She paused and then said, 'I've learned a lot about myself these past weeks, because of Donna.'

And I, I thought, because of Angelo.

After another long while she said, 'Are you still awake?'

'Yes.'

'I don't really understand, you know, all that happened. I mean, I know that that hateful Angelo has been arrested for murder, of course I do, and that you have been seeing the police, but you've never told me exactly what it was all about.'

'You seriously want to know?'

'Of course I do, otherwise I wouldn't ask.' The familiar note of impatience rang out clearly. She must have heard it herself, because she immediately said more moderately, 'I'd like you to tell me. I really would.'

'All right,' I said, and I told her pretty well everything, starting from the day that Chris Norwood set it all going by stealing Liam O'Rorke's notes. I told her events in their chronological order, not in the jumbled way I learned of them, so that a clear pattern emerged of Angelo's journeyings in search of the tapes.

When I'd finished, she said slowly, 'You knew all through that day when he had us tied up that he was a murderer.'

'Mm.'

'My God.' She paused. 'Didn't you think he might kill us? Donna and me?'

'I thought he *might*. I thought he might do it any time after he knew his father had the tapes. I thought he might kill all three of us, if he felt like it. I couldn't tell . . . but couldn't risk it.'

A long silence. Then she said, 'I think, looking back, that he did mean to. Things he said . . .' She paused. 'I was glad to see you.'

'And angry.'

'Yes, angry. You'd been so *long* . . . and Angelo was so bloody *frightening*.'

'I know.'

'I heard the rifle shots. I was in the kitchen cooking.'

'I was afraid you might tell Angelo you heard them.'

'I only spoke to him when I absolutely had to. I loathed him. He was so *arrogant*.'

'You shook him,' I said, 'telling him I'd shot in the Games. It was the clincher.'

'I just wanted to ... to kick him in the ego.'

I smiled in the darkness. Angelo's ego had taken quite a pummelling at the hands of the Derrys.

'Do you realize,' I said, 'that we haven't talked like this for months?'

'Such a lot has happened. And I feel ... different.'

Nothing like a murderer, I thought, for changing one's view of the world. He'd done a good job for both of us.

'Do you want to come, then,' I said, 'to America?'

To America. To go on together. To try a bit longer. I didn't really know which I wanted: to clear out, cut loose, divorce, start again, remarry, have children, or to make what one might of the old dead love, to pour commitment into the shaky foundations, to rebuild them solid.

It was Sarah, I thought, who would have to decide.

'Do you want us to stay together?' I asked.

'You've thought of divorce?'

'Haven't you?'

'Yes.' I heard her sigh. 'Often lately.'

'It's pretty final, being divorced,' I said.

'What then?'

'Wait a bit,' I said slowly. 'See how we go. See what we both really want. Keep on talking.'

'All right,' she said. 'That'll do.'

INTERVAL

Letter from Vince Akkerton to Jonathan Derry.

Angel Kitchens,
Newmarket.
July 12th

Dear Mr Derry,

You remember you were asking about Chris Norwood, that day back in May? I don't know if you're still interested in those computer tapes you were talking about, but they've turned up here at the Kitchens. We were clearing out the room we change from outdoor clothes in, prior to it being repainted, you see, and there was this bag there that everyone said didn't belong to them. So I looked in it, and there were a lot of old papers of writing and three cassettes. I thought I'd give them a run on my cassette player because they didn't have any labels on saying what was on them, but all that came out was a screeching noise. Well, a mate of mine who heard it said don't throw them away, because I was going to, that's computer noise, he said. So I took the tapes in to Janet to see what she could make of them, but she said the firm has got rid of their old computer, it wasn't big enough for all it was having to do, and they've now got a company computer or something with disc drives, she says, and it doesn't use cassettes.

So, anyway, I remembered about you all of a sudden, and I found I'd still got your address, so I thought I'd ask you if you thought this was what you were talking about. I threw the pages of writing into the rubbish, and that's that, they're gone, but if you want these tapes, you send me a tenner for my trouble and you can have them.

Yours truly,
Vince Akkerton

Letter from the executors of Mrs Maureen O'Rorke to Jonathan Derry.

September 1st

Dear Sir,

We are returning the note you wrote to Mrs O'Rorke, together with your enclosure of three cassettes.

Unfortunately Mrs O'Rorke had died peacefully in her sleep at home three days before your gift was posted. In our opinion, therefore, the contents of the package should be regarded as belonging to yourself, and we herewith return them.

We are,
Yours faithfully,
Jones, Pearce and Block, Solicitors

Letter from the University of Eastern California selection board to Jonathan Derry.

London
October 20th

Dear Mr Derry,

Subsequent to your interview in London last week, we have pleasure in offering you a three-year teaching post in the Department of Physics. Your salary for the first year will be Scale B (attached) to be reviewed thereafter. One full semester's notice to be given in writing on either side.

We understand that you will be free to take up the post on January 1st next, and we await your confirmation that you accept this offer.

Further details and instructions will be sent to you upon receipt of your acceptance.

Welcome to the University!
Lance K. Barowska, D.Sc.
Director of Selections, Science Faculty,
University of Eastern California

Letter from Harry Gilbert to Marty Goldman Ltd, Turf Accountants.

October 15th

Dear Marty,

In view of what has happened, I'm asking you to release me from the transfer that we had agreed. I haven't the heart, old friend, to build any more kingdoms. With Angelo jailed for life, there's no point in me buying all your betting shops. You knew, of course, that they were for him – for him to manage, anyway.

I know you had some other offers, so I hope you won't be coming after me for compensation.

Your old friend,
Harry

Excerpt from a private letter from the Governor of Albany Prison, Parkhurst, Isle of Wight to his friend the Governor of Wakefield Prison, Yorkshire.

Well, Frank, we're letting Angelo Gilbert out on parole this week, and I wish between you and me that I felt better about it. I'd like to have advised against it, but he's served fourteen years and there's been a lot of pressure from the Reformers group on the Home Sec. to release him. It's not that Gilbert's actively violent or even hostile, but he's been trying hard to get this parole so for the last two years there's been no breath of trouble.

But as you know with some of them they're never stable however meek they look, and I've a feeling Gilbert's like that. You remember, when you had him about five years ago, you felt just the same. It isn't on the cards, I suppose, to keep him locked up for life, but I just hope to God he doesn't go straight out and shoot the first person who crosses him.

See you soon Frank,
Donald

PART TWO

William

Chapter Twelve

I put my hand on Cassie's breast, and she said 'No, William. No.'
'Why not?' I said.
'Because it's never good for me, twice, so soon. You know that.'
'Come one,' I said.
'No.'
'You're lazy,' I said.
'And you're greedy.' She picked my hand off and gave it back to me.
I replaced it. 'At least, let me hold you,' I said.
'No.' She threw my hand off again. 'With you, one thing leads to another. I'm going to get some orange juice and run the bath, and if you're not careful, you'll be late.'
I rolled onto my back and watched her walk about the bedroom, a tall thin girl with too few curves and very long feet. Seen like that in all her angular nakedness, she still had the self-possessed quality which had first attracted me: a natural apartness, a lack of cling. Her self-doubts, if any, were well hidden, even from me. She went downstairs and came back carrying two glasses of orange.
'William,' she said, 'stop staring.'
'I like to.'
She walked to the bathroom to turn on the taps and came back brushing her teeth.
'It's seven o'clock,' she said.
'So I've noticed.'
'You'll lose that cushy job of yours if you're not out on the gallops in ten minutes.'
'Twenty will do.'
I rose up, however, and pinched the bath first, drinking the orange juice as I went. Count your blessings, I said to myself, soaping. Count Cassandra Morris, a better girl than I'd ever had before; seven months bedded, growing more essential every day. Count the sort of job that no one could expect to be given at twenty-nine. Count enough money, for once, to buy a car that wasn't everyone's cast-off held together by rust and luck.
The old ache to be a jockey was pretty well dead, but I supposed there would always be regret. It wasn't as if I'd never ridden in races; I had, from sixteen to twenty, first as an amateur, then a professional, during which time I'd won eighty-four steeplechases, twenty-three hurdle races, and wretchedly cursed my unstoppably lengthening

body. At six foot one I'd broken my leg in a racing fall, been imprisoned in traction for three months, and grown two more inches in bed.

It had been practically the end. There *had* been very tall jump jockeys in the past, but I'd progressively found that even if I starved to the point of weakness I couldn't keep my weight reliably below eleven stone. Trainers began saying I was too tall, too heavy, sorry lad, and employing someone else. So at twenty I'd got myself a job as an assistant trainer, and at twenty-three I'd worked for a bloodstock agent, and at twenty-six on a stud farm, which kept me off the racecourse too much. At twenty-seven I'd been employed in a sort of hospital for sick racehorses which went out of business because too many owners preferred to shoot their liabilities, and after that there had been a spell of selling horse cubes, and then a few months in the office of a bloodstock auctioneer, which had paid well but bored me to death; and each time between jobs I'd spent the proceeds of the last one in wandering round the world, drifting homewards when the cash ran out and casting around for a new berth.

It had been at one of the points of no prospects that Jonathan had sent the cable.

'Catch the next flight. Good job in English racing possible if you interview here immediately. Jonathan.'

I'd turned up on his Californian doorstep sixteen hours later and early the next morning he had sent me off to see 'a man I met at a party'. A man, it transpired, of middle height, middle years and middling grey hair: a man I knew instantly by sight. Everyone in racing, worldwide, knew him by sight. He ran his racing as a big business, taking his profits in the shape of bloodstock, selling his stallions for up to a hundred times more than they'd earned on the track.

'Luke Houston,' he said neutrally, extending his hand.

'Yes, sir,' I said, retrieving some breath. 'Er . . . William Derry.'

He offered me breakfast on a balcony overlooking the Pacific, eating grapefruit and boiled eggs and giving me smiling genial glances which were basically as casual as X-rays.

'Warrington Marsh, my racing manager in England, had a stroke four days ago,' he said. 'Poor guy, he's doing well – I have bulletins every a.m. – but it is going to be some time, a long time, I'm afraid, before he'll be active again.' He gestured to my untouched breakfast. 'Eat your toast.'

'Yes, sir.'

'Tell me why I should give you his job. Temporarily, of course.'

Good grief, I thought. I hadn't the experience or the connections of the stricken revered maestro. 'I'd work hard,' I said.

'You know what it entails?'

'I've seen Warrington Marsh everywhere, on the racecourse, at the sales. I know what he does, but not the extent of his authority.'

He cracked his second egg. 'Your brother says you've gotten a lot of general know-how. Tell me about it.'

I listed the jobs, none of which sounded any more impressive than they had in fact been.

He said, 'College degrees?' pleasantly.

'No, I left school at seventeen, and didn't go to university.'

'Private income?' he said. 'Any?'

'My Godfather left some money for my schooling. There's still enough for food and clothes. Not enough to live on.'

He drank some coffee and hospitably poured me a second cup.

'Do you know which trainers I have horses with in the British Isles?'

'Yes, sir. Shell, Thompson, Miller, and Sanlache in England and Donavan in Ireland.'

'Call me Luke,' he said. 'I prefer it.'

'Luke,' I said.

He stirred sweetener into his coffee.

'Could you handle the finance?' he said. 'Warrington always has full responsibility. Do millions frighten you?'

I looked out at the vast blue ocean and told the truth. 'I think they do in a way, yes. It's too easy in the upper reaches to think of a nought or two as not mattering one way or another.'

'You need to spend to buy good horses,' he said. 'Could you do it?'

'Yes.'

'Go on,' he said mildly.

'Buying potentially good horses isn't the problem. Looking at a great yearling, seeing it move, knowing its breeding is as near perfect as you can predict, and being able to afford it, that's almost easy. It's picking the excellent from among the second rank and the unknowns, that's where the judgement comes in.'

'Could you guarantee that every horse you bought for me, or advised my trainers to buy, would win?'

'No, I couldn't,' I said. 'They wouldn't.'

'What percentage would you expect to win?'

'About fifty per cent. Some would never race, others would disappoint.'

He unaggressively, quietly, slowly and without pleasure asked me questions for almost an hour, sorting out what I'd done, what I knew, how I felt about taking ultimate powers of decision over trainers who were older than myself, how I felt about dealing with the racing authorities, what I'd learnt about book-keeping, banking and money markets, whether I could evaluate veterinarian and nutritive advice. By the end I felt inside out; as if no cranny of my mind stayed gently unprobed. He would choose someone older, I thought.

'How do you feel,' he said finally, 'about a steady job, nine to five, weekends off, pension at the end of it?'

I shook my head from deep instinct, without thinking it out. 'No,' I said.

'That came from the heart, fella,' he observed.

'Well ...'

'I'll give you a year and a ceiling beyond which you're not to spend.

I'll be looking over your shoulder, but I won't interfere unless you get in a fix. Want to take it?'

I drew and deep breath and said, 'Yes.'

He leaned smilingly forward to shake my hand. 'I'll send you a contract,' he said, 'but go right on home now and take over at once. Things can fall apart too fast with no one in charge. So you go straight to Warrington's house, see his wife Nonie, I'll call her you're coming, and you operate from the office he's gotten there until you find a place of your own. Your brother told me you're a wanderer, but I don't mind that.' He smiled again. 'Never did like tame cats.'

Like so much else in American life the contract, when it swiftly followed me over the Pond, was in complete contrast to the relaxed approach of the man who'd offered it. It set out in precise terms what I must do, what I had discretion to do, what I must not do. It stated terms of reference I'd never have thought of. He had given me a great deal of freedom in some ways and none at all in others; but that, I supposed, was fair enough. He wouldn't want to stake his whole British operation on an unknown factor without enforceable safeguards. I took it to a solicitor who read it and whistled and said it had been drawn up by corporation lawyers who were used to munching managers as snacks.

'But do I sign it?' I said.

'If you want the job, yes. It's tough, but as far as I can see, fair.'

That had been eight months ago. I had come home to widespread and understandable disbelief that such a plum should have fallen my way. I had survived Nonie Marsh's resentment and Warrington's incoherent unhelpfuleness; had sold several of Luke's unpromising two-year-olds without great loss, had cajoled the trainers into provisionally accepting me and done nothing sweat-makingly disastrous. Despite all the decisions and responsibility, I'd enjoyed every minute.

Cassie appeared in the doorway.

'Aren't you going to get out of that bath?' she demanded. 'Just sitting there smiling.'

'Life's good.'

'And you'll be late.'

I stood up in the water and as she watched me straighten she said automatically, 'Mind your head.' I stepped out onto the floor, and kissed her, dripping down her neck.

'For God's sake, get dressed,' she said. 'And you need a shave.' She gave me a towel. 'The coffee's hot, and we're out of milk.'

I flung on a few clothes and went downstairs, dodging beams and low doorways on the way. The cottage we'd rented in the village of Six Mile Bottom (roughly six miles south of Newmarket) had been designed for seventeenth-century man, who hadn't suffered the dietetic know-how of the twentieth. And would seven feet, I wondered, ducking into the kitchen, be considered normal in the twenty-fifth?

We had lived in the cottage all summer and in spite of its low ceilings it suited us fine. There were apples now in the garden, and mists in the mornings, and sleepy wasps trying to find warm cracks in the eaves. Red tiled floors and rugs downstairs, dining-room surrendered to office, sitting-room cosy round an as yet untried hearth; red-checked curtains, rocking chairs, corn dollies and soft lights. A townspeople's country toy, but enough, I sometimes thought, to make one want to put down roots.

Bananas Frisby had found it for us. Bananas, longtime friend, who kept a pub in the village. I'd called in there one day on my way back to Newmarket and told him I was stuck for somewhere to live.

'What's wrong with your old boat?'

'I've grown out of it.'

He gave me a slow glance. 'Mentally?'

'Yeah. I've sold it. And I've met a girl.'

'And this one,' he suggested, 'isn't ecstatic about rubbing down dead varnish?'

'Far from.'

'I'll keep it in mind,' he said, and indeed he called me a week later at Warrington's house and said there was a tarted-up cottage down the road from him that I could go and look at: the London-baseed owners didn't want to sell but could do with some cash, and they'd be willing to let it to someone who wouldn't stay for ever.

'I told them you'd the wanderlust of an albatross,' he said. 'I know them, they're nice people, don't let them down.'

Bananas personally owned his almost equally old pub, which was very slowly crumbling under his policy of neglect. Bananas had no family, no heirs, no incentive to preserve his worldly goods; so when each new patch of damp appeared inside his walls he bought a luxurious green potted plant to hide it. Since I'd known him, the shiny-leafed camouflage had multiplied from three to eight: and there was a vine climbing now through the windows. If anyone ever remarked about the dark patches on the walls, Bananas said the plants had caused them, and strangers never realized it was the other way round.

Bananas' main pride and joy was the small restaurant, next door to the bar, in which he served *cuisine minceur* of such perfection that half the passing jockeys of England ate there religiously. It had been over his dried, crisp, indescribable roast duck that I'd first met him, and like a mark well hooked had become an addict. Couldn't count the *délices* I'd paid for since.

He was already up as usual when I waved to him on my way to the gallops: sweeping out, cleaning up, opening his windows wide to get rid of the overnight fug. A fat man himself, he nonetheless had infinite energy, and ran the whole place with the help of two women, one in the bar and one in the kitchen, both of whom he bossed around like a feudal lord. Betty in the kitchen cooked stolidly under his eagle eye and Bessie in the bar served drinks with speed bordering on sleight-of-hand. Bananas was head-waiter and every other sort of waiter, collecting orders, delivering food, presenting bills, cleaning and relaying tables, all with a deceptive show of having all day to chat. I'd watched him at it so often that I knew his system; he practically never wasted time by going into the kitchen. Food appeared from Betty through a vast serving hatch shielded from the public view, and dirty dishes disappeared down a gentle slide.

'Who washes up?' I'd said once in puzzlement.

'I do,' Bananas said. 'After closing time I feed it all through the washer.'

'Don't you ever sleep?'

'Sleep's boring.'

He needed, it seemed, only four hours a night.

'And why work so hard? Why not have more help?'

He looked at me pityingly. 'Staff cause as much work as they do,' he said. And I'd found out later that he closed the restaurant every year towards the end of November and took off to the West Indies returning in late March when the Flat racing stirred back to life. He hated the cold, he said: worked at a gallop for eight months for four months' palm trees and sun.

That morning on the Limekilns, Simpson Shell was working his best young prospect and looking smug. The eldest of Luke Houston's five trainers, he had been resigned to me least and still had hang-ups which showed on his face every day.

'Morning, William,' he said, frowning.

'Morning, Sim.' I watched him with the rangy colt upon whom the Houston hope of a classic next season was faintly pinned. 'He's moving well,' I said.

'He always does.' The voice was slighting and impatient. I smiled to myself. Neither compliments nor soft soap, he was saying, were going to change his opinion of the upstart who had overruled him in the matter of selling two two-year-olds. He had told me he disagreed strongly with my weeding-out policy, even though I'd put it to him beforehand and discussed every dud to be discarded. 'Warrington never did that,' he'd thundered, and he'd warned me he was writing to Luke to complain.

I never heard the result. Either he'd never written or Luke had backed me up; but it had consolidated his Derry-wards hostility, not least because although I had saved Luke Houston a stack of pointless training fees I had at the same time deprived Simpson Shell. He was waiting, I knew, for the duds to win for their new owners so that he could crow, and it was my good luck that so far they hadn't.

Like all Luke's trainers, he trained for many other owners besides. Luke's horses at present constituted about a sixth of his string, which was too high a percentage for him to risk losing them altogether: so he was civil to me, but only just.

I asked him about a filly who had some heat in her leg the previous evening, and he grumpily said it was better. He hated me to take a close interest in his eight Houston horses, yet I guessed that if I didn't, another letter would be winging to California complaining that I was neglecting my duties. Sim Shell, I thought ruefully, couldn't be pleased.

Over in the Bury Road, Mort Miller, younger, neurotic, fingers snapping like firecrackers, told me that Luke's ten darlings were eating well and climbing the walls with eagerness to slaughter the opposition. Mort had considered the sale of three no-gooders a relief, saying he hated the lazy so-and-sos and grudged them their oats. Mort's horses were always as strung up as he was, but they certainly won when it mattered.

I dropped in on Mort most days because it was he, for all his positive statements, who in fact asked my opinion most.

Once a week, usually fitting in with race meetings, I visited the other two trainers, Thompson and Sandlache, who lived thirty miles from each other on the Berkshire Downs, and about once a month I spent a couple of days with Donavan in Ireland. With them all, I had satisfactory working arrangements, they on their part admitting that the two-year-olds I'd got rid of were of no benefit to themselves, and I promising that I would spend the money I'd saved on the training fees on extra yearlings in October.

I would be sorry, I thought, when my year was over.

Driving home from Mort's, I stopped in the town to collect a radio I'd been having repaired, and again to fill up with petrol, and again at Bananas' pub to pick up some beer.

Bananas was in the kitchen prodding some marinating veal. Opening time still lay an hour ahead. Everything in the place was gleaming and fresh and the plants grew damply in their pots.

'There was a fellow looking for you,' Bananas said.

'What sort of fellow?'

'Big man. Didn't know him. I told him where your cottage was.' He scowled at Betty, who was obliviously peeling grapes. 'I told him you were out.'

'Did he say what he wanted?'

'Nope.'

He shed an apron and took his bulk into the bar. 'Too early for you?' he said, easing behind the counter.

'Sort of.'

He nodded and methodically assembled his usual breakfast; a third of a tumbler of brandy topped with two scoops of vanilla-walnut ice cream.

'Cassie went off to work,' he said, reaching for a spoon.

'You don't miss much.'

He shrugged. 'You can see that yellow car a mile off, and I was out front cleaning the windows.' He stirred the ice cream into the brandy and with gourmand enjoyment shovelled the first instalment into his mouth. 'That's better,' he said.

'It's no wonder you're fat.'

He merely nodded. He didn't care. He told me once that his size made his fat customers feel better and spend more, and that his fat customers in search of a miracle outnumbered the thin.

He was a natural eccentric, himself seeing nothing unusual in anything he did. In various late-night sessions, he'd unbuttoned a little of his inner self, and under the surface geniality I'd had glimpses of a deep pessimism, a moroseness which looked with despair at the inability of the human race to live harmoniously on the beautiful earth. He had no politics, no god, no urge to agitate. People, he said, were known to starve on rich fertile tropical earth; people stole their neighbours' lands; people murdered people from racial hate; people tortured and murdered in the name of freedom. It sickened him, he said. It had been going on from prehistory, and it would go on until the vindictive ape was wiped out.

'But you yourself seem happy enough,' I'd once said.

He looked at me darkly. 'You're a bird. Always on the wing. You'd be a sparrowhawk if you hadn't such long legs.'

'And you?'

'The only option is suicide,' he said. 'But right now it's not necessary.' He'd deftly poured himself another brandy, and lifted the glass in a sort of salute. 'Here's to civilisation, damn it.'

His real fore-names, written over the pub doorway were John James, but his nickname was a pudding. 'Bananas Frisby,' a hot fluffy confection of eggs, rum, bananas and orange, was an item nearly always on his menu, and 'Bananas' he himself had become. It suited his outer perona well, but his inner, not at all.

'You know what?' he said.

'What?'

'I'm growing a beard.'

I looked at the faint shadow on the dark jaw. 'It needs compost,' I said.

'Very funny. The days of the big fat slob are over. What you see is the start of the big fat distinguished innkeeper.' He took a large spoonfull of ice cream and drank some of the liquid as a chaser, wiping the resulting white moustache off on the back of his hand.

He wore his usual working clothes: open-necked shirt, creaseless grey flannels, old tennis shoes. Thinning dark hair scattered his scalp haphazardly, with one straight lock falling over an ear, and as Frisby in the evenings wasn't all that different from Frisby in the mornings I couldn't see a beard transforming the image. Particularly not, I thought interestedly, while it grew.

'Can you spare a tomato or two?' I said. 'Those Italian ones?'

'For your lunch?'

'Yeah.'

'Cassie doesn't feed you.'

'It's not her job.'

He shook his head over the waywardness of our domestic arrangements, but if he had had a wife I wondered which one of them would have cooked. I paid for the beer and the tomatoes, promised to bring Cassie to admire the whiskers, and drove home.

Life for me was good, as I'd told Cassie. Life at that moment was a long way from Bananas' world of horrors.

I parked in front of the cottage and walked up the path juggling radio, beer and tomatoes in one hand and fishing for keys with the other.

One doesn't expect people to leap out of nowhere waving baseball bats. I had merely a swift glimpse of him, turning my head towards the noise of his approach, seeing the solid figure, the savagery, the raised arm. I hadn't even the time to think incredulously that he was going to hit me before he did it.

The crashing blow on my moving head sent me dazed and headlong, shedding radio, beer cans, tomatoes on the way. I fell half on the path and half on a bed of pansies and lay in a pulsating semi-consciousness in which I could smell the earth but couldn't think.

Rough fingers twined themselves into my hair and pulled my head up from its face-down position. As if from a great distance away from my closed eyes a harsh deep voice spoke nonsensical words.

'You're not—' he said. '*Fuck* it.'

He dropped my head suddenly and the second small knock finished the job. I wasn't aware of it. In my conscious mind, things simply stopped happening.

The next thing that impinged was that someone was trying to lift me up, and that I was trying to stop him.

'All right, lie there,' said a voice. 'If that's how you feel.'

How I felt was like a shapeless form spinning in a lot of outer space. He tried again to pick me up and things inside the skull suddenly shook back into order.

'Bananas,' I said weakly, recognizing him.

'Who else? What happened?'

I tried to stand up and staggered a bit, trampling a few more long-suffering pansies.

'Here,' Bananas said, catching me by the arm, 'come into the house.' He semi-supported me, and found the door was locked.

'Keys,' I mumbled.

'Where are they?'

I waved a vague arm, and he let go of me to look for them. I leant against the doorpost and throbbed. Bananas found the keys and came towards me and said in anxiety. 'You're covered in blood.'

I looked down at my red-stained shirt. Fingered the cloth. 'That blood's got pips in.' I said.

Bananas peered at my chest. 'Your lunch.' He sounded relieved. 'Come on.'

We went into the cottage where I collapsed into a chair and began to sympathize with migraine sufferers. Bananas searched in random cupboards and asked plaintively for the brandy.

'Can't you wait until you get home?' I said without criticism.

'It's for you.'

'None left.'

He didn't press it. He may have remembered that it had been he, a week ago, who'd emptied the bottle.

'Can you make tea?' I said.

He said resignedly, 'I suppose so,' and did.

While I drank the resulting nectar, he told me that he'd seen a car driving away from the direction of the cottage at about eighty miles an hour down the country road. It was the car, he said, of the man who'd asked for me earlier. He had been at first puzzled and then disquieted, and had finally decided to amble down to see if everything was all right.

'And there you were,' he said, 'looking like a pole-axed giraffe.'

'He hit me,' I said.

'You don't say.'

'With a baseball bat.'

'So you saw him,' Bananas said.

'Yeah. Just for a second.'

'Who was he?'

'No idea.' I drank some tea. 'Mugger.'

'How much did he take?'

I put down the tea and patted the hip pocket in which I carried a small notecase. The wallet was still there. I pulled out and looked inside. Nothing much in there, but also nothing missing.

'Pointless,' I said. 'What did he want?'

'He asked for you,' Bananas said.

'So he did.' I shook my head which wasn't a good idea as it sent little daggers in all cranial directions. 'What exactly did he say?'

Bananas gave it some thought. 'As far as I can remember, he said, "Where does Derry live?"'

'Would you know him again?' I asked.

He pensively shook his head. 'I shouldn't think so, I mean, I've a general impression – not young, not old, roughish accent – but I was busy, I didn't pay all that much attention.'

Oddly enough, though I'd seen him for only a fraction of the time Bananas had, I had a much clearer recollection of my attacker. A freeze view, like a snapshot, standing framed in my mind. A thick-set man with yellowish skin, greyish about the head, intent eyes darkly shadowed. The blur on the edge of the snapshot was the downward slash of his arm. Whether the memory was reliable, or whether I'd know him again, I couldn't tell.

Bananas said, 'Are you all right to leave?'

'Sure.'

'Betty will finish those grapes and stare into space,' he said. 'The old cow's working to rule. That's what she says. Working to rule, I ask you. She doesn't belong to a union. She's invented her own bloody rules. At the moment rule number one is that she doesn't do anything I don't directly tell her to.'

'Why not?'

'More pay. She wants to buy a pony to ride on the Heath. She can't ride, and she's damn near sixty.'

'Go on back,' I said smiling. 'I'm OK.'

He semi-apologetically made for the door. 'There's always the doctor, if you're pushed.'

'I guess so.'

He opened the door and peered out into the garden. 'There are beer cans in your pansies.'

He went out saying he would pick them up, and I shoved myself off the chair and followed him. When I got to the door he was standing on the path holding three beer cans and a tomato and staring intently at the purple and yellow flowers.

'What is it?' I said.

'Your radio.'

'I've just had it fixed.'

He looked up at me. 'Too bad.'

Something in his tone made me totter down the path for a look. Sure enough, my radio lay in the pansies: what was left of it. Casing, dials, circuits, speaker, all had been comprehensively smashed.

'That's nasty,' Bananas said.

'Spite,' I agreed. 'And a baseball bat.'

'But *why*?'

'I think,' I said slowly, 'that maybe he thought I was someone else. After he'd hit me, he seemed surprised. I remember him swearing.'

'Violent temper,' said Bananas, looking at the radio.

'Mm.'

'Tell the police,' he said.

'Yeah.'

I took the beer from him and sketched a wave as he walked briskly up the road. Then I stared for a while at the shattered radio thinking slightly disturbing thoughts: like what would my head have looked like if he hadn't stopped after one swipe.

With a mental shiver, I went back indoors and applied my concussion to writing up my weekly report sheet for Luke Houston.

Chapter Thirteen

I never did get around to consulting the doctor or calling the police. I couldn't see anything productive coming from spending the time.

Cassie took the whole affair philosophically but said that my skull must be cracked if I didn't want to make love.

'Double ration tomorrow,' I said.

'You'll be lucky.'

I functioned on two cylinders throughout the next day and in the evening Jonathan rang, as he sometimes did, keeping a long-distance finger on little brother's pulse. He had never grown out of the *in loco parentis* habit and nor, to be honest, did I want him to. Jonathan, six thousand miles away, was still my anchor, my most trusted friend.

A pity about Sarah, of course. I would have seen more of Jonathan if I could have got on better with Sarah. She irritated me like an allergy rash with her bossiness and her sarcasm, and I'd never been able to please her. I'd thought at one time that their marriage was on its way to the cemetery and I hadn't grieved much, but somehow or other they'd retreated from the brink. She certainly seemed softer with Jonathan nowadays, but when I was around the old acid rose still in her voice, and I never stayed long in their house. Never staying long in one place was in fact, according to her, one of my least excusable faults. I ought to buckle down, she said, and get a proper job.

She was looking splendid these days, slender as a girl and tawny with the sun. Many, I supposed, seeing the fair hair, the good bones, the still tight jawline, the grace of movement, would have envied Jonathan his young-at-forty-five wife. And all, as far as I knew, without the plastic surgeon's knife.

'How's Sarah?' I said automatically. I'd been asking after her religiously most of my life, and not caring a jot. The truce she and I maintained for Jonathan's sake was fragile; a matter of social form, of empty politeness, of unfelt smiles, of asking after health.

'She's fine,' he said. 'Just fine.' His voice after all these years had taken on a faint inflection and many of the idioms of his adopted country. 'She sends you her best.'

'Thanks.'

'And you?' he said.

'Well enough considering some nutter hit me on the head.'

'What nutter?'

'Some guy who came here and lay in wait, and took a bash at me.'

'Are you all right?'

'Yeah. No worse than a racing fall.'

'Who was he?' he asked.

'No idea. He asked for directions from the pub, but he'd got the wrong man. Maybe he asked for Terry ... it sounds much the same. Anyway, he blasted off when he found he'd made a slight error, so that's that.'

'And no harm done?' he asked insistently.

'Not to me, but you should see the radio.'

'What?'

'When he found I was the wrong guy, he took it out on my radio. I wasn't awake, mind you, at that point. But when I came round, there it was, smashed.'

There was a silence on the other end, and I said, 'Jonathan? Are you still there?'

'Yes,' he said. 'Did you seem the man? What did he look like?'

I told him: fortyish, greyish, yellowish. 'Like a bull,' I said.

'Did he say anything?'

'Something about me not being who he expected, and fuck it.'

'How did you hear him if you were knocked out?'

I explained. 'But all that's left is a sore spot for the hair brush,' I said, 'so don't give it another thought.'

We talked about this and that for the rest of our customary six minutes, and at the end he said, 'Will you be in tomorrow night?'

'Yes, I should think so.'

'I might call you back,' he said.

'OK.' I didn't bother to ask him why. He had a habit of not answering straightforward questions with straightforward answers if it didn't suit him, and his noncommittal announcement told me that this was one of those times.

We said amicable goodbyes and Cassie and I went to bed and renewed our normal occupation.

'Do you think we'll ever be tired of it?' she said.

'Ask me when we're eighty.'

'Eighty is impossible,' she said, and indeed it seeed so to us both.

Cassie went to Cambridge every day in her little yellow car to spend eight hours behind a building society desk discussing mortgages. Cassie's mind was full of terms like with-profits endowment and early redemption charges, and I thought it remarkable, sometimes, that she'd never suggested a twenty-five year millstone round my own neck.

I'd once before tried living with someone: nearly a year with a cuddly blonde who wanted marriage and nestlings. I'd felt stifled and gone off to South America and behaved abominably, according to her parents. But Cassie wasn't like that: if she wanted the same things she didn't say so, and maybe she realized, as I did, that I always came back to England, that the homing instinct was fairly strong. One day, I thought, one *distant* day ... and maybe with Cassie ... I might, just perhaps, and with all options open, buy a house.

One could always sell it again, after all.

Jonathan did telephone again the following evening, and came straight to the point.

'Do you,' he said, 'remember that summer when Peter Keithly got killed in his boat?'

'Of course, I do. One doesn't actually forget one's own brother being tangled up in a murder.'

'It's fourteen years ago,' he said doubtfully.

'Things that happen when you're fifteen stay sharp in your mind for ever.'

'I guess you're right. Anyway, you know who I mean by Angelo Gilbert.'

'The bumper-off,' I said.

'As you say. I think the man who hit you on the head may be Angelo Gilbert.'

A great one, my brother, for punching the air out. On a distinctly short breath I said, 'You sound very calm about it.' But then of course he would. He was always calm. In the scariest crisis it would be Jonathan who spoke and acted as if nothing unusual was happening. He'd carried me out of a fire once as a small child and I'd thought that somehow nothing was the matter, nothing was really wrong with the flames and the roaring and crashing all around us, because he'd looked down at me and smiled.

'I checked up,' he said. 'Angelo Gilbert got out of prison seventeen days ago, on parole.'

'Out—'

'It would take him a while to orientate himself and to find you. I mean, if it was him, he would have thought you were me.'

I sorted my way through that and said, 'What makes you think it was him?'

'Your radio, really. He seemed to enjoy destroying things like that. Televisions. Stereos. And he'd be forty now, and his father reminded me of a bull. What you said took me right back.'

'Good grief.'

'Yes.'

'You really think it was him?'

'I'm afraid it's possible.'

'Well,' I said, 'now that he knows he got the wrong guy, maybe he won't bother me again.'

'Monsters don't go away if you don't look at them.'

'What?'

'He may come back.'

'Thanks very much.'

'William, take it seriously. Angelo was dangerous in his twenties and it sounds as if he still is. He never did get the computer programs he killed for, and he didn't get them because of me. So take care.'

'It might not have been him.'

'Act as if it was.'

'Yeah,' I said. 'So long, Professor.' The wryness in my voice must have been plain to him.

'Keep off horses,' he said.

I put the receiver down ruefully. Horses, to him, meant extreme risk.

'What's the matter?' Cassie said. 'What did he say?'

'It's all a very long story.'

'Tell it.'

I told it on and off over the next few hours, remembering things in pieces and not always in the order they'd happened, much as Jonathan had told it to me all those years ago. Before going off to Canada to shoot he had collected me straight from school at the end of that summer term and we'd gone to Cornwall, just the two of us, for a few days' sailing. We'd had great holidays there two or three times before, but that year it blew a gale and poured with rain continuously, and to amuse me while we sat and stared through the dripping yacht club windows waiting for the improvement which never came, he'd told me about Mrs O'Rorke and Ted Pitts and the Gilberts, and how he'd stuck magnets in the cassettes. I'd been so fascinated that I hadn't minded missing the sailing.

I wasn't sure that I'd been shown every alley of the labyrinth; my quiet schoolmasterly brother had been reticent in patches and I'd always guessed that it was because probably in some way he'd used his guns. He never would let me touch them, and the only thing I ever knew him to be scared of was having his precious firearms certificate taken away.

'So there you are,' I said finally. 'Jonathan got Angelo tossed into clink. And now he's out.'

Cassie had listened with alternating alarm and amusement, but it was doubt that remained in the end.

'So what now?' she said.

'So now, if Angelo's on the rampage, hostilities may be resumed.'

'Oh no.'

'And there are certain disadvantages that Derry number two may have to contend with.' I ticked them off on my fingers. 'One, I can't shoot. Two, I know practically nothing about computers. And three, if Angelo's come charging out of jail intending to track down his lost crock of gold, I've no idea where it is or even if it still exists.'

She frowned. 'Do you think that's what he wants?'

'Wouldn't you?' I said gloomily. 'You spend fourteen years in a cell brooding over what you lost and dreaming of vengeance and yes, you're going to come out looking for both – and a small detail like having attacked the wrong man isn't going to put you off.'

'Come to bed,' Cassie said.

'I wonder if he thinks the way he used to.' I looked at her increasingly loved face. 'I don't want him busting in here to hold you hostage.'

'With no Jonathan to cut the telephone wires and send for the posse? Come to bed.'

'I wonder how he did it?'

'What?'

'Cut the wires. It isn't that easy.'

'Climbed the pole with a pair of scissors,' she said.

'You can't climb a pole. There aren't any footholds except at the top.'

'Why are you wondering about it after all these years? Come to bed.'

'Because of a bang on the head.'

She said, 'Are you really anxious?'

'Uneasy.'

'You must be. I've mentioned bed three times and you're still sitting down.'

I grinned at her and rose to my feet – and at that moment an almighty crash on the front door burst it open with splintering wood and a broken lock.

Angelo stood in the gap. Stood for less than a second regaining his balance from the kick which had brought him in, stood with the baseball bat swinging and his face rigid with ill intent.

Neither Cassie nor I had to time to protest or yell. He waded straight in, laying about him, smashing anything near him, a lamp, some corn dollies, a vase, a picture . . . the television. Like a whirlwind demented, he devastated the pretty interior, and when I leapt at him I met a fist in the face and a fast knee which missed my groin, and I smelled his sweat and heard his breath rasp from exertion and took in what he was grittily saying: and it was just my name and Jonathan's, over and over.

'Derry – Derry – Fucking *Derry*.'

Cassie tried to help me, and he slashed at her with the heavy wooden bat and connected with her arm. I saw her stumble from the pain of it and in a fury I put one of my own arms round his neck and tried to yank his head back, to hurt him enough to make him drop his weapon and probably if the truth were told to throttle him. But he knew more about dirty fighting than I'd ever learned and it took him about two elbow jabs and a scrunching backhand jerk of my fingers to prise me loose. He shook me off with such force that I half fell, but still clung to his clothes with octopus tentacles, not wanting to be thrown clear so that he could get another swing with that bat.

We crashed around the broken room with me sticking to him with at least his equal ferocity and him struggling to get free; and it was Cassie, in the end, who finished it. Cassie who had grabbed the brass coal scuttle from the hearth by its shining handle and swung it in an arc at arm's length, aiming at Angelo's head. I saw the flash of its gleaming surface and felt the jolt though Angelo's body: and I let go of him as he fell in a sprawl on the carpet.

'Oh, God,' Cassie was saying. 'Oh, God.' There were tears on her face and she was holding her left arm away from her body in a way I knew all too well.

Angelo was visibly breathing. Stunned only. Soon to awake.

'Have to tie him,' I said breathlessly. 'What've we got?'

Cassie painfully said, 'Washing line,' and before I could stop her she'd vanished into the kitchen, returning almost at once with a new line still in its package. Wire wrapped in plastic, the bright label said. Strong enough, indeed for a bull.

While I was still uncoiling it with unsteady fingers, there was the sound outside of someone thudding up the path and I had time for a feeling of absolute despair before I saw who it was.

Bananas came to the dark doorway with a rush and there stood stock still taking in the ravaged scene.

'I saw his car come back. I was just closing up . . .'

'Help me tie him,' I said, nodding at Angelo, who was stirring ominously. 'He did all this. He's coming round.

Bananas turned Angelo onto his face and held his hands together behind his back while I built knots around his wrists, and then continued with the job himself, leading the line down from the wrists to join it to two more knots around the ankles.

'He's broken Cassie's arm,' I said.

Bananas looked at her and at me and at Angelo, and walked purposefully over to where the telephone stood miraculously undamaged on its little table.

'Wait,' I said. 'Wait.'

'But Cassie needs a doctor. And I'll get the police. . . .'

'No,' I said, 'not yet.'

'But you must.'

I wiped my nose on the back of my hand and looked remotely at the resulting smear of blood. 'There's some pethedine and a syringe in the bathroom,' I said. 'It'll do a lot to stop Cassie hurting.'

He nodded in understanding and said he would fetch it.

'Bring the box marked "Emergency". It's on the shelf over the bath taps.'

While he went and came back with his ever-surprising speed, I helped Cassie to sit on a chair and to rest her left arm on a cushion which I put on the telephone table. It was the forearm, I found, which was broken: both bones, probably, from the numb uselessness of her hand.

'William,' she said whitely, 'don't. It hurts. Don't.'

'Darling . . . darling . . . It has to have support. Just let it lie there. Don't fight it.'

She did mutely what I said and looked paler than ever.

'I didn't feel it,' she said. 'Not like this . . . not at first.'

Bananas brought the emergency box and opened it. I tore the syringe out of its sterile package and filled it from the ampoule of pethedine. Pulled Cassie's skirt up high over the sun-browned legs and fed the muscle-relaxing painkiller into the long muscle of her thigh.

'Ten minutes,' I said, pulling the needle out and rubbing the place with my knuckles. 'A lot of the pain will go. Then we'll be able to take you to the casualty department of Cambridge hospital to get it set. Nowhere nearer will be open at this time of night.'

She nodded slightly with the first twitch of a smile, and on the floor Angelo began trying the kick.

Bananas again walked towards the telephone and again I stopped him.

'But William—'

I looked around at the jagged evidence of a passionate need for revenge; the explosion of fourteen years of pent-up hate.

I said, 'He did this because my brother got him jailed for murder. He's out on parole. If we call the police he'll be back inside.'

'Then, of *course*,' Bananas said, picking up the receiver.

'No,' I said. 'Put it down.'

He looked bewildered. Angelo on the floor began mumbling as if in delirium; a mixture of atrocious swear words and loud incomprehensible unfinished sentences.

'That's stir talk,' said Bananas, listening.

'You've heard it before?'

'You hear everything in the end in my trade.'

'Look,' I said. 'I get him sent back to jail and then what happens? It wouldn't be so long next time before he was out, and he'd have a whole new furious grudge to avenge. And by that time he might have learned some sense and not come waving a piece of wood and going off half-cock, but wait until he'd managed to get a pistol, and sneak up on me one day, three, four years from now, and finish me off. This ...' I waved a hand, 'isn't an act of reason. I'm only Jonathan's brother. I myself did him no harm. This is anger against life. Blind, colossal, ungovernable rage. I can do without him focusing it all on me personally in the future.' I paused. 'I have to find a better ... a final solution. If I can.'

'You can't mean ...' Bananas said tentatively.

'What?'

'To ... to ... No, you couldn't.'

'Not that final a solution, no. Though it's quite a thought. Cement wellingtons and a downwards trip in the North Sea.'

'Tankful of piranhas,' Cassie said.

Bananas looked at her with relief and almost laughed, and finally put the telephone receiver back in its cradle.

Angelo stopped mumbling and came fully awake. When he realized where he was and in what condition, the skin, which had until then been pale, became redly suffused: the face, the neck, even the hands. He rolled halfway over onto his back and filled the room with the intensity of his rage.

'If you start swearing,' I said, 'I'll gag you.'

With an effort he said nothing, and I looked at his face squarely and fully for the first time. There wasn't a great deal left of the man whose picture I had once pored over in the newspaper; not youth, not black hair, not narrow jaw, not long thin nose. Age, heredity, prison food, all had given him fatty deposits to blur the outlines of the head and bulk the body.

Average brains, Jonathan had said. Not clever. Relies on his frightening-power, and gets his results from that. Despises everyone. Calls them creeps and mugs.

'Angelo Gilbert,' I said.

He jerked, and looked surprised, as if he thought I wouldn't know him: and nor would I have, if Jonathan hadn't called.

'Let's get it straight,' I said. 'It was not my brother who sent you to prison. You did it to yourself.'

Cassie murmured, 'Criminals in jail are there voluntarily.'

Bananas looked at her in surprise.

'My arm feels better,' she said.

I stared down at Angelo. 'You chose jail when you shot Chris Norwood. Those fourteen years were your own fault, so why take it out on *me*?'

It made no impression. I hadn't really thought it would. Blaming one's troubles on someone else was average human nature.

Angelo said, 'Your fucking brother tricked me. He stole what was mine.'

'He stole nothing of yours.'

'He did.' The words were bass-voiced, fierce and positive, a growl in the throat. Cassie shivered at the menace Angelo could generate even tied up in ignominy on a cottage floor.

The crock of gold, I thought suddenly, might have its uses.

Angelo seemed to be struggling within himself but in the end the words tore out of him, furious, frustrated, still bursting with an anger that had nowhere to go. '*Where is he?*' he said. 'Where's your fucking brother? I can't find him.'

Saints alive . . .

'He's dead,' I said coldly.

Angelo didn't say whether or not he believed me but the news did nothing for his general temper. Bananas and Cassie displayed a certain stillness, but thankfully kept quiet.

I said to Bananas, 'Could you watch him for a minute while I make a phone call?'

'Hours if you like.'

'Are you all right?' I asked Cassie.

'That stuff's amazing.'

'Won't be long.' I picked the whole telephone off the table beside her and carried it into the office, closing the door as I went.

I called California, thinking that Jonathan would be anywhere but home, that I'd get Sarah, that it would be siesta time under the golden sun. But Jonathan was in, and he answered.

'I just had a thought,' I said. 'Those tapes that Angelo Gilbert wanted, have you still got them?'

'Good grief,' he said. 'I shouldn't think so.' A pause while he reflected. 'No, we cleared everything out when we left Twickenham. You remember, we sold the furniture and bought new out here. I got rid of pretty well everything. Except the guns, of course.'

'Did you throw the tapes away?'

'Um,' he said. 'There was a set I sent to Mrs O'Rorke and got back again. Oh yes, I gave them to Tedd Pitts. If anyone still has them it would be Ted. But I shouldn't think they'd be much use after all these years.'

'The tapes themselves, or the betting system?'

'The system. It must be long out of date.'

It wouldn't matter too much, I thought.

'There are a lot of computer programs out here now for helping you win on horses,' Jonathan said. 'Some of them work, they say.'

'You haven't tried them?'

'I'm not a gambler.'

'Oh yeah?'

'What do you want the tapes for?' he said.

'To tie Angelo up in knots again.'

'Take care.'

'Sure. Where would I find Ted Pitts?'

He told me doubtfully to try the East Middlesex Comprehensive, where they'd both been teaching, but said it was unlikely he was still there. They hadn't been in touch with each other at all since he'd emigrated. Perhaps I could trace Ted through the Schoolmasters Union, who might have his address.

I thanked him and disconnected, and went back into the sitting-room, where everyone looked much as I'd left them.

'I have a problem,' I said to Bananas.

'Just one?'

'Time.'

'Ah. The essence.'

'Mm.' I stared at Angelo. 'There's a cellar under this cottage.'

Angelo had no fear: one had to give him that. I could see quite clearly that he understood I meant not to let him go, yet his only reaction was aggressive and set him struggling violently against the washing line.

'Watch him,' I said to Bananas. 'There's some stuff in the cellar. I'm going to clear it out. If he looks like getting free, give him another bash on the head.'

Bananas looked at me as if he'd never seen me before; and perhaps he hadn't. I put a quick apologetic hand on Cassie's shoulder as I went, and in the kitchen opened the latched wooden door which led to the steps to the cellar.

Down there it was cool and dry: a brick-lined room with a concrete floor and a single light bulb swinging from the ceiling. When we had come to the cottage we had found the garden chairs stacked in there, but they were now outside on the grass, leaving only oddments like a paraffin stove, some tins of paint, a step-ladder and a stack of fishing gear. I carried everything in relays up the steps and dumped it all in the kitchen.

When I'd finished there was nothing in the cellar to help a captive; yet I would still have to keep him tied because of the nature of the lockless door. It was simply of upright planks with bracing bars across the top, centre and bottom, the whole screwed together with the screwheads thankfully on the kitchen side. Across near the top there were six thumb-sized holes, presumably for ventilation. A good enought barrier against most contingencies, but not to be trusted to withstand the sort of kick with which the enemy had battered his initial way in.

'Right,' I said, going back into the sitting-room. 'Now you, Angelo, are going into the cellar. Your only alternative is an immediate return to jail, as all this ...' I indicated the room '... and that ...' Cassie's arm '... will cancel your parole and send you straight back behind bars.'

'You bloody can't,' he said furiously.

'I bloody can. You started this. You damn well take the consequences.'

'I'll get you *busted*.'

'Yeah. You try it. You got it wrong, Angelo. I'm not my brother. He was clever and wily and he tricked you silly, but he would never use physical force; and I will, you mug, I will.'

Angelo used words that made Bananas wince and glance apprehensively at Cassie.

'I've heard them before,' she said.

'You've a choice, Angelo,' I said. 'Either you let my friend and me carry you carefully down the steps without you struggling, or you struggle and I pull you down by the legs.'

The loss of face in not struggling proved too much. He tried to bite me as I bent down to put my arms under his armpits, so I did what I'd said; grasped the line tying his ankles and dragged him feet foremost out of the sitting-room, through the kitchen and down the cellar steps, with him yelling and swearing the whole way.

Chapter Fourteen

I tugged him well away from the stairs, let go of his legs and returned to the kitchen. He shouted after me blasphemously and I could still hear him when the door was shut. Let him get on with it, I thought callously; but I left on the single light, whose switch was outside on the kitchen wall.

I wedged the latch shut by sliding a knife handle through the slot, and for good measure stacked the step-ladder, the table and a couple of chairs into a solid line between the refrigerator and the cellar door, making it impossible for it to open normally into the kitchen.

In the sitting-room and without hustling, I said, 'OK. Decision time, mates.' I looked at Bananas. 'It's not your fight. If you'd rather, you can go back to your dishwashing and forget this ever happened.'

He looked resignedly round the room. 'I promised you'd leave this place as you found it. Practically pledged my soul.'

'I'll replace what I can. Pay for the rest. And grovel. Will that do?'

'You can't manage that brute on your own.' He shook his head. 'How long do you mean to keep him?'

'Until I find a man called Pitts.' I explained to him and Cassie what I wanted to do and why, and Bananas sighed and said it seemed fairly sensible in the circs, and that he would help where he could.

We shoe-horned Cassie gently into my car and I drove her to Cambridge while Bananas in his effective way set himself to tidy the sitting-room. There wasn't a great deal one could do at that point about the splintered and unclosable front door, and he promised to stay in the cottage until we got back.

In the event it was only I who returned. I sat with Cassie through the long wait in the silent hospital while they tried to find someone to X-ray her arm, but it seemed that after midnight the radiology department was firmly shut, with all the radiologists asleep in their own homes, and only the direst surgical emergency would recall them.

Cassie was given a careful splint from shoulder to fingernails and also another painkiller and a bed: and when I kissed her and left she said, 'Don't forget to feed the bull,' which the nurses put down to drug-induced light-headedness.

Bananas was asleep when I got back, flat out on the sofa and dreaming I dare say of palm trees. The mess I'd left behind was miraculously cleared with every broken fragment out of sight. There were many things missing but overall it looked more like a room the owners would recognize. Gratefully I went quietly into the kitchen and found my barricade altered and strengthened with four planks which had been lying in the garage, the door was wedged shut from top to bottom.

The light switch was up. Except for whatever dim rays were crawling through the ventilation holes, Angelo was lying in the dark.

Although I'd been quiet I'd woken Bananas, who was sitting up pinching the bridge of his nose and blinking heavy eyelids open and shut.

'All the pieces are in the garage,' he said. 'Not in the dustbin. I reckoned you might need them, one way or another.'

'You're great,' I said. 'Did Angelo try to get out?'

Bananas made a face. 'He's a horrible man, that.'

'You talked to him?'

'He was shouting through the door that you'd stopped his circulation by tying his wrists too tight. I went to see, but you hadn't, his fingers were pink. He was halfway up the stairs and he tried to knock me over. Tried to sweep my legs from under me and make me fall. God knows what he thought it would achieve.'

'Probably to scare me into letting him go.'

Bananas scratched himself around the ribs. 'I came up into the kitchen and shut the door on him, and switched his light off, and he went on howling for ages about what he'd do to you when he got out.'

Keeping his courage up, I thought.

I looked at my watch. Five o'clock. Soon be light. Soon be Friday with all its problems. 'I guess,' I said yawning, 'that a couple of hours shut-eye would do not harm.'

'And that one?' He jerked his head towards the kitchen.

'He won't suffocate.'

'You're a revelation to me,' Bananas said.

I grinned at him and I think he thought me as ruthless as our visitor. But he was wrong. I was fairly sure that Angelo that night had come back to kill, to finish off what he had earlier started, knowing by then who I was and not expecting a Cassie. I was soft compared with him.

Bananas walked home to his dishwasher and I took his place on the sofa, feeling the bedroom too far away out of touch. Despite the hectic night I went to sleep immediately and woke with mind-protesting reluctance to switch off the alarm at seven o'clock. The horses would be working on the Heath. Simpson Shell had set up a trial of two late-developing three-year-olds, and if I wasn't there to watch he'd be writing to Luke Houston to say I was a shirker ... and I wanted anyway, Angelo or no Angelo, to see how those horses went.

I loved the Heath in the early mornings with the manes blowing under the wide skies. My affection for horses was so deep and went back so far that I couldn't imagine life without them. They were a friendly foreign nation living in our land, letting their human neighbours tend them and feed them, accepting them as servants as much as masters. Fast, fascinating, essentially untamed, they were my landscape, my old shoes, the place to where my heart returned, as necessary to me as the sea to sailors.

Even on that morning as they lifted my spirits and I watched the trial with a concentration Angelo couldn't disrupt. One of the three-year-olds finished most decisively fast and Simpson said with careful civility that he hoped that I would report to Luke how well the colt was looking.

'I'll tell Luke you've done wonders with him. Remember how unbalanced he looked in May? He'll win next week, don't you think?'

He gave me the usual ambivalent stare, needing my approbation but hating it. I smiled internally and left him to drive the short distance to where Mort was directing his string.

'All OK?' I said.

'Well, yes,' Mort said. 'Genotti's still shaping up well for the Leger.' He flicked his fingers six times rapidly. 'Can you come back to the house for breakfast? The Bungay filly is still not eating well, and I thought we might discuss what we could do. You sometimes have ideas. And there's Luke's bill. I want to explain one or two items before you query them.'

'Mort,' I interrupted him regretfully, 'could we postpone it for a day or two? Something's come up that I'll have to deal with first.'

'Oh? Oh,' he sounded put out, because I'd never refused him before. 'Are you sure?'

'Really sorry,' I said.

'I might see you this afternoon,' he said, fidgetting badly.

'Um, yes. Of course.'

He nodded with satisfaction and let me go with good grace, and I doubted whether I would in fact turn up on Newmarket racecourse for that day's programme, even though three of Luke's horses were running.

On my way back through the town I stopped at a few shops which were open early and did some errands on my prisoner's account, buying food and one or two small comforts. Then I rocketed the six miles to the village and stopped first at the pub.

Bananas, looking entirely his usual self, had done his dishes, cleaned the bar, and put Betty's back up by saying she was too old to start learning to ride.

'The old cow's refusing to make the celery mousse for lunch. Working to her stupid rules.' He disgustedly assembled his breakfast, adding chopped ginger as a topping to the ice cream and pouring brandy lavishly over the lot. 'I went down to the cottage again. Not a peep from our friend.' He stirred his mixture with anticipation. 'You can't hear him from outside, however loud he yells. I found that out last night. You'll be all right if you keep any callers in the garden.'

'Thanks.'

'When I've finished this, I'll come and help you.'

'Great.'

I hadn't wanted to ask him, but I was most thankful for his offer. I drove on down to the cottage and unloaded all the shopping into the kitchen, and Bananas appeared in his tennis shoes while I was packing food into a carrier. He looked at the small heap of things I'd put ready by the door.

'Let's get it over,' he said. 'I'll carry this lot.'

I nodded. 'He'll be blinded at first by the light, so even if he's got himself free we should have the advantage.'

We began to remove the barricade from against the door, and when it would open satisfactorily I took the knife out of the latch, picked up the carrier, switched on the cellar light and went into the cage.

Angelo was lying face down in the middle of the floor, still trussed the way we'd left him: arms behind his back, white clothes line leading slackly between tied wrists and tied ankles.

'It's morning,' I said cheerfully.

Angelo barely moved. He said a few low words of which 'turd' was the only one distinguishable.

'I've brought you some food.' I dumped in one corner the carrier bag which in fact contained two sliced loaves, several cartons of milk, some water in a plastic bottle, two large cooked chickens, some apples and a lot of various candy bars and chocolate. Bananas silently dumped his own load which consisted of a blanket, a cheap cushion, some paperback books and two disposal polystyrene chamber pots with lids.

'I'm not letting you out,' I said to Angelo, 'but I'll untie you.'

'Fuck you,' he said.

'Here's your watch.' I had slipped it off his wrist the evening before to make the tying easier. I took it out of my pocket and put it on the floor near his head. 'Lights out tonight at eleven,' I said.

It seemed prudent at that point to search Angelo's pockets, but all he was carrying was money. No knives, no matches, no keys: nothing to help him escape.

I nodded to Bananas and we both began to untie the knots, I the wrists, Bananas the ankles, but Angelo's struggles had so tightened our original work that it took time and effort to remove it. Once Angelo was free we coiled the line and retreated up the stairs, from where I watched him move stiffly into a kneeling position with his arms loose and not yet working properly.

The air in the celler had seemed quite fresh. I closed the door and fixed the latch and Bananas restacked the barricade with methodical thoroughness.

'How much food did you give him?' he asked.

'Enough for two to four days. Depends on how fast he eats it.'

'He's used to being locked up, there's that about it.'

Bananas, I thought, was busy stifling remaining doubts. He shoved the four planks into place between the cellar door and the refrigerator, casually remarking that during the night he'd sawn the wood to fit.

'More secure that way,' he said. 'He'll not get out.'

'Hope you're right.'

Bananas stood back, hands on hips, to contemplate his handiwork, and indeed I was as sure as one could be that Angelo couldn't kick his way out, particularly as he would have to try it while standing on the stairs.

'His car must be here somewhere,' I said. 'I'll look for it after I've phoned the hospital.'

'You phone, I'll look,' Bananas said, and went on the errand.

Cassie, I was told, would be having her arm set under anaesthetic during the morning. I could collect her at six that evening if all went well.

'May I speak to her?'

'One moment.'

Her voice came slowly and sleepily onto the line. 'I'm pie-eyed with pre-med,' she said. 'How's our guest?'

'Happy as a kangaroo with blisters.'

'Hopping ... mad?'

'That pre-med isn't working,' I said.

'Sure is. My body's floating but my brain's fizzing along in zillions of sparks. It's weird.'

'They say I can fetch you at six.'

'Don't ... be late.'

'I might be,' I said.

'You don't love me.'

'Yeah.'

'Sweet William,' she said. 'A pretty flower.'

'Cassie, go to sleep.'

'Mm.'

She sounded infinitely drowsy. 'Goodbye,' I said, but I don't think she heard.

I telephoned next to her office, told her boss she'd fallen down the cellar steps and broken her arm, and that she'd probably be back at work sometime the next week.

'How irritating,' he said. 'Er ... for her, of course.'

'Of course.'

Bananas came back as I was putting down the receiver and said that Angelo's car was parked harmlessly at the top of the lane where the hard surface petered out into muddy cart track. Angelo had left the keys in the ignition. Bananas dumped them on the table.

'Want anything, shout,' he said. I nodded gratefully and he padded off, a power-house in a suit of blubber.

I set about the task of finding Ted Pitts, telephoning first to Jonathan's old school, the East Middlesex Comprehensive. A female voice there crisply told me that no one of that name was presently on the staff, and that none of the present staff could help me as they were not there: the new term would not start for another week. The only master who had been teaching in the school fourteen years ago would be, she imagined, Mr Ralph Jenkins, assistant headmaster, but he had retired at the end of the summer term and in any case it would be unlikely that any of his past assistants would have kept in touch with him.

'Why not?' I asked curiously.

After the faintest of hesitations the voice said levelly, 'Mr Jenkins himself would have discouraged it.'

Or in other words, I thought, Mr Jenkins had been a cantankerous old bastard. I thanked her for as little as I had realistically expected and asked if she could tell me the address of the Schoolmasters Union.

'Do you want their number as well?'

'Yes please.'

She told me both, and I put through a call to their offices. Ted Pitts? Edward? I suppose so, I said. Could I wait? Yes, I could.

The answering voice, a man's this time, shortly told me that Edward Farley Pitts was no longer a member. He had resigned his membership five years previously. His last known address was still in Middlesex. Did I want it? Yes please, I said.

Again I was given a telephone number along with the address. Another female voice answered it, this time with music and children's voices loud in the background.

'What?' she said, 'I can't hear you.'

'Ted Pitts,' I shouted. 'Can you tell me where he lives?'

'You've got the wrong number.'

'He used to live in your house.'

'What? Wait a minute ... shut up, you lousy kids. What did you say?'

'Ted Pitts ...'

'Terry, shut off that bleeding stereo. Can't hear myself think. Shut it off. Go on, shut it off.'

The music suddenly stopped.

'What did you say?' she said again.

I explained that I wanted to find my lost friend, Tedd Pitts.

'Guy with three daughters?'

'That's right.'

'We bought this house off him. Terry, you knock Michelle's head on that wall one more time and I'll rattle your teeth. Where was I? Oh yes, Ted Pitts. He gave us an address to send things on to but it's years ago and I don't know where my husband put it.'

It was really important, I said.

'Well if you hold on I'll look. Terry, *Terry*!' There was the sound of a slap and a child's wail. The joys of motherhood, I thought.

I held on for an age listening to the scrambled noise of the squabbling siblings, held on so long that I thought she had forgotten all about me and left me off the hook, but in the end she did come back.

'Sorry I've been so long, but you can't put your hand on a thing in this house. Anyway, I've found where he moved to.'

'You're a doll,' I said, writing it down.

She laughed in a pleased fashion. 'Want to call round? I'm fed up to the teeth with these bloody kids.'

'School starts next week.'

'Thank the Lord.'

I disconnected and tried the number she had given me, but to this one there was no reply. Ten minutes later, again no reply.

I went to the kitchen. All quiet from the cellar. I ate some cornflakes, padded restlessly about and tried the number again.

Zilch.

There was something, I thought, looking at it, that I could immediately do about the front door. It wouldn't at the moment even fit into the frame, but given a chisel and some sandpaper . . . I fetched them from the tool-rack in the garage and reduced the sharply splintered patches to smooth edges, shutting the door finally by totally removing the broken lock. It looked all right from the outside but swung inward at a touch: and we had sweet but inquisitive neighbours who called sometimes to sell us honey.

I again dialled Ted Pitts's possible number. No reply.

Shrugging, I tugged a small chest of drawers across inside the front door and climbed out through the dining-room window. Drove down to the pub: told Bananas the way in.

'Do you expect *me*—'

'Not really. Just in case.'

'Where are you going?' he asked.

I showed him the address. 'It's a chance.'

The address was in Mill Hill on the northern outskirts of London. I drove there with my mind resolutely on the traffic and not on Cassie, unconscious, and Angelo, captive. Crunching the car at that point could be the ultimate disaster.

The house, when I found it, proved to be a middle-sized detached affair in a street of trees and somnolence; and it was empty.

I went up the driveway and looked through the windows. Bare wall, bare floors, no curtains.

With sinking spirits I rang the bell of the house next door, and although it was clearly occupied there was no one in there either. I tried several more houses, but none of the people I spoke to knew anything more of Tedd Pitts than yes, perhaps they had seen some girls going in and out, but of course with all the shrubs and trees one was shielded from one's neighbours, which meant, of course, that also one couldn't see them.

It was in one of the houses obliquely opposite, from where only a corner of the Pittses' front garden was visible, that in the end I found some help. The front door was opened a foot by a large woman in pink hair rollers with a pack of assorted small dogs roaming round her legs.

'If you're selling, I don't want it,' she said.

I exercised on her the story I had by then invented, saying that Ted Pitts was my brother, he'd sent me his new address but I'd lost it, and I wanted to get in touch with him urgently. After six repetitions, I almost believed it.

'I didn't know him,' she said, not opening the door any wider. 'He didn't live there long. I never even saw him, I don't think.'

'But, er, you noticed them move in . . . and out.'

'Walking the dogs, you see.' She looked fondly down at the pack. 'I go past there every day.'

'Do you remember how long ago they left?'

'It must be ages. Funny your brother didn't tell you. The house was for sale for weeks after they'd gone. It's only just been sold, as a matter of fact. I saw the agents taking the board down just last week.'

'You don't happen to remember,' I said carefully, 'the name of the agents?'

'Goodness,' she said. 'I must have walked past it a hundred times. Just let me think.' She stared at her pets, her brow wrinkled with concentration. I could still see only half of her body but I couldn't tell whether the forbidding angle of the door was designed to keep the dogs in or me out.

'Hunt bleach' she exclaimed.

'What?'

'Hunt comma BLEACH.' She spelled it out. 'The name of the agents. A yellow board with black lettering. You'll see it all over the place, if you look.'

I said fervently, 'Thank you very much.'

She nodded the pink rollers and shut herself in, and I drove around until I found a yellow board with Hunt, Bleach's local address: Broadway, Mill Hill.

The brother story brought its by now familiar crop of sympathetic and/or pitying looks, but finally gained results. A slightly sullen-looking girl said she thought the house had been handled by their Mr Jackman who was now away on his holidays.

'Could you look in the files?'

She took advice from various colleagues, who doubtfully agreed under my urging that perhaps in the circumstances she might. She went into an inner office, and I heard cabinet drawers begin to open and shut.

'Here you are, Mr Pitts,' she said, returning, and it took me a fraction to realize that of course I too would be Pitts. 'Ridge View, Oaklands Road.'

She didn't give me a town. I thought; he's still *here*.

'Could you tell me how to get there?' I said.

She shook her head unhelpfully, but one of the colleagues said, 'You go back up Broadway, right round the roundabout until you're pointing towards London, then first left, up the hill, turn right, that's

Oaklands Road.'

'Terrific.' I spoke with heartfelt relief which they took as appropriate, and I followed their directions faithfully and found the house. It looked a small brown affair; brownish bricks, brown tiled roof, a narrow window each side of an oak front door, bushes screening much else. I parked in what seemed an oversized driveway outside a closed double garage, and doubtfully rang the doorbell.

There was no noise from inside the house. I listened to the distant hum of traffic and the nearer hum of bees round a tub of dark red flowers, and pressed the bell again.

No results. If I hadn't wanted to find Ted Pitts so much I would have given up and driven away at that point. It wasn't even the sort of road where one could enquire at a neighbour's: there were houses only on one side, with a steep wooded hillside rising on the other, and the houses themselves were far-spaced and reclusive, drawing themselves back from public view.

I rang a third time out of indecisiveness, thinking that I could wait or come back, or leave a note begging Pitts to call me.

The door opened. A pleasant-looking girl-woman stood there; not young, not yet middle-aged, wearing a loosely flowing green sundress with broad straps over suntanned shoulders.

'Yes?' she said inquiringly. Dark curly hair, blue eyes, the brown glowing face of summer leisure.

'I'm looking for Ted Pitts,' I said.

'This is his house.'

'I've been trying to locate him. I'm the brother of an old friend of his. A friend he had years ago, I mean. Could I see him, do you think?'

'He isn't here at the moment.' She looked at me doubtfully. 'What's your brother's name?'

'Jonathan Derry.'

After the very slightest pause her face changed from watchfulness to welcome; a smile in remembrance of time past.

'Jonathan! We haven't heard from him for years.'

'Are you ... Mrs Pitts?'

She nodded. 'Jane. She opened the door wide and stepped back. 'Come in.'

'I'm William,' I said.

'Weren't you ...' she frowned, 'away at school?'

'One does tend to grow.'

She looked up at me, 'I'd forgotten how long it was.' She led me across a cool dark hall. 'This way.'

We came to a wide stairway of shallow green-carpeted steps leading downwards, and I saw before me what had been totally invisible from the higher roadway, that the house was large, ultra-modern, built into the side of the hill and absolutely stunning.

The stairs led directly down to a huge room whose ceiling was half-open to the sky and whose floor was partly green carpet and partly swimming pool. There were sofas and coffee tables nearest the stairs and lounging chairs, bamboo with pink, white and green cushions, dotting the far poolside, out in the sun; and on either side wings of house spread out protectively, promising bedrooms and comfort and a life of delight. I looked at the spectacular and pretty room and thought no schoolmaster on earth could afford it.

'I was sitting over there,' Jane Pitts said, pointing to the sunny side. 'I nearly didn't answer the doorbell. I don't always bother.'

We walked around there, passing white trellised alcoves filled with plants and cushioned bamboo sofas with bathing towels casually thrown down. The pool water looked sea-green and peaceful, gleaming and inviting after my trudging search.

'Two of the girls are around somewhere,' Jane said. 'Melanie, our eldest, is married, of course. Ted and I will be grandparents quite soon.'

'Incredible.'

She smiled. 'We married at college.' She gestured to the chairs and I sat on the edge of one of the loungers while she spread out voluptuously on another. Beyond the house the lawn sloped grassily away to a wide sweeping view over north-west London, the horizon lost in misty purples and blues.

'This place is fantastic,' I said.

She nodded. 'We were so lucky to get it. We've only been here three months, but I think we'll stay for ever.' She pointed to the open roof. 'This all closes over, you know. There are solar panels that slide across. They say the house is warm all winter.'

I admired everything sincerely and asked if Ted were still teaching. She said without strain that he sometimes taught University courses in computer programming and that unfortunately he wouldn't be home until quite late the following evening. He would be sorry to have missed me, she said.

'I would quite urgently like to talk to him.'

She gently shook her head. 'I don't honestly know where he is, except somewhere up near Manchester. He went this morning, but he didn't know where he'd be staying. In a motel somewhere, he said.'

'What time would he be back tomorrow?'

'Late. I don't know.'

She looked at the concern which must have shown plainly on my face and said apologetically, 'You could come early on Sunday, if you like, if it's that important.'

Chapter Fifteen

Saturday crawled.

Cassie wandered around with her plastered arm in a sling and Bananas jogged down to the cottage three or four times, both of them worried by the delay and not saying so. It had seemed reasonable on Thursday night to incarcerate Angelo with his handiwork still appalling us in the sitting-room and Cassie in pain, but by Saturday evening she and Bananas had clearly progressed through reservations and uneasiness to downright anxiety.

'Let him go,' Bananas said when he came late after closing time. 'You'll be in real trouble if anyone finds out. He knows now that you're no pushover. He'd be too scared to come back.'

I shook my head. 'He's too arrogant to be scared. He'd want his revenge, and he'd come back to take it.'

They stared miserably at each other. 'Cheer up,' I said. 'I was ready to keep him for a week – two weeks – as long as it took.'

'I just don't know,' Bananas said, 'how you could calmly go to the races.'

I'd gone uncalmly to the races. Also to the gallops in the morning and to Mort's for breakfast, but no one I had seen could have guessed what was going on at home. Behind a public front I found it was fairly easy to hide an ongoing crime: hundreds of people did it, after all.

'I suppose he's still alive,' Cassie said.

'He was up by the door swearing at four o'clock.' Bananas looked at his watch. 'Nine and a half-hours ago. I shouted at him to shut up.'

'And did he?'

'Just swore back.'

I smiled. 'He's not dead.'

As if to prove it Angelo started kicking the door and letting go with the increasingly familiar obscenities. I went into the kitchen and stood close to the barricade, and when he drew breath for the next verbal onslaught I said loudly, 'Angelo.'

There was a brief silence, then a fierce furious growling shout: '*Bastard.*'

'The light's going out in five minutes,' I said.

'I'll kill you.'

Maybe the heavily savage threat should have raised my goose bumps, but it didn't. He had been murderous too long, was murderous by nature, and I already knew it. I listened to his continuing rage and felt nothing.

'Five minutes,' I said again, and left him.

In the sitting-room Bananas was looking mildly piratical in his open-necked shirt and his sneakers and his four days' growth of harsh black beard, but he himself would never have made anyone walk the plank. The gloom and doom in his mind deplored what I was doing even while he condoned it, and I could almost sense him struggling anew with the old anomaly that to defeat aggression one might have to use it.

He sat on the sofa and in short order drank two stiff brandies with his arm round Cassie, who never minded. He was tired, he'd said, of us being out of his favourite tipple: he'd brought the bottle himself. 'Have some ice-cream with it?' Cassie had suggested, and he'd said seriously, 'What flavour?'

I gave Angelo his five minutes and switched off the light, and there was a baleful silence from the cellar.

Bananas gave Cassie a bristly kiss, said she looked tired, said every plate in the pub needed washing, said 'Barbados!' as a toast, and tossed back his drink. 'God rest all prisoners. Good night.'

Cassie and I watched his disappearing back. 'He's half sorry for Angelo,' she said.

'Mm. A fallacy always to think that because you feel sorry for the tiger in the zoo he won't eat you, given the chance. Angelo doesn't understand compassion. Not other people's for him. He feels none himself. In others he sees it as a weakness. So never, my darling, be kind to Angelo expecting kindness in return.'

She looked at me. 'You mean that as a warning, don't you?'

'You've a soft heart.'

She considered for a moment, then found a pencil and wrote a message to herself in large letters on the white plaster.

REMEMBER TIGERS.

'Will that do?'

I nodded. 'And if he says his appendix is bursting or he's suffering from bubonic plague feed him some aspirins through the ventilation holes, and do it in a roll of paper, and not with your fingers.'

'He hasn't thought of that yet.'

'Give him time.'

We went upstairs to bed but as on the previous night I slept only in brief disturbed snatches, attuned the whole time to any noise from the cellar. Cassie slept more peacefully than before, the cast becoming less of a problem as she grew used to it. Her arm no longer hurt, she said; she simply felt tired. She said play would be resumed when the climate got better.

I watched the dark sky lighten to streaks of navy-blue clouds across a sombre orange glow, a strange brooding dawn like the aura of the man downstairs. Never before, I thought, had I entered a comparable clash of wills; never tested so searchingly my willingness to command. I had never thought of myself as a leader, and yet, looking back, I'd never had much stomach to be led.

In recent months I had found it easier than I'd expected to deal with Luke's five trainers, the power seeming to develop as the need arose. The power to keep Angelo in the cellar, that too had arisen, not merely physically, but also in my mind. Perhaps one's capacity always expanded to meet the need: but what did one do when the need was gone? What did generals do with their full-grown hubris when the war was over? When the whole world no longer obeyed when they said jump?

I thought: unless one could adjust one's power-feelings perpetually to the current need, one could be headed for chronic dissatisfaction with the hall of fate. One could grow sour, power-hungry, despotic. I would shrink back, I thought, to the proper size, once Angelo was solved, once Luke's year was over. If one saw that one had to, perhaps one might.

The fierce sky slowly melted to mauve-grey clouds drifting over a sea of gold and lingeringly then to gentle white over palest blue, and I got up and dressed, thinking the sky's message was false: problems didn't fade with the sun and Cain was still downstairs.

Cassie's eyes, when I left, were saying all that her tongue wasn't. Hurry. Come back. I don't feel safe here with Angelo.

'Sit by the telephone,' I said. 'Bananas will run.'

She swallowed. I kissed her and drove away, burning up the empty Sunday-early roads to Mill Hill. It was still only eight-thirty when I turned into Oaklands Road, the very earliest that Jane Pitts had said I could arrive, but she was already up and in a wet bathing dress to answer the doorbell.

'Come in,' she said. 'We're in the pool.'

'We' were two lithely beautiful teenage girls and a stringy man going bald who swam without splashing, like a seal. The roof was open to the fair sky and a waiting breakfast of cereals and fruit stood ready on one of the low bamboo tables, and none of the Pittses seemed to mind or notice that the new day was still cool.

The stringy man slithered out onto the pool's edge in a sleek economical movement and stood shaking the water from his head and looking approximately in my direction.

'I'm Ted Pitts,' he said, holding out a wet hand. 'I can't see a damn thing without my glasses.'

I shook the hand and smiled into the unfocussed eyes. Jane walked round with some heavy black frames which converted the brown fish into an ordinary shortsighted mortal, and he dripped round the pool beside me to where his towel lay on a lounging chair.

'William Derry?' he said, blotting water out of his ears.

'That's right.'

'How's Jonathan?'

'Sends his regards.'

Ted Pitts nodded, towelled his chest vigorously and then stopped abruptly and said, 'It was you who told me where to get the form books.'

All those years ago ... information so casually given. I glanced around the amazing house and asked the uppermost question. 'The betting system on those tapes,' I said. 'Did it really work?'

Ted Pitts's smile was of comprehensive contentment. 'What do you think?' he said.

'All this—'

'All this.'

'I never believed in it,' I said, 'until I came here the other day.'

He towelled his back. 'It's fairly hard work, of course. I shunt around a good deal. But with this to come back to ... most rewarding.'

'How long ...' I said slowly.

'How long have I been gambling? Ever since Jonathan gave me the tapes. That first Derby ... I borrowed a hundred quid with my car as security to raise some stake-money. I was madness, you know. I couldn't have afforded to lose. Sometimes in those days we had hardly enough to eat. It was pretty well desperation that made me do it, but of course the system looked mathematically OK and it had already worked for years for the man who invented it.'

'And you won?'

He nodded. 'Five hundred. A fortune. I'l never forget that day, never. I felt sick.' He smiled vividly, the triumph still childlike in its simplicity. 'I didn't tell anybody. Not Jonathan. Not even Jane. I didn't mean to do it again, you see. I was so grateful it had turned out all right, but the *strain* ...' He dropped the damp towel over the arm of a chair. 'And then, you know, I thought, why not?'

He watched his daughters dive into the pool with their arms round each other's waists. 'I only taught for one more term,' he said calmly. 'I couldn't stand the Head of Maths department. Jenkins, his name was.' He smiled. 'It seems odd now, but I felt oppressed by that man. Anyway, I promised myself that if I won enough during the summer holidays to buy a computer, I would leave at Christmas, and if I didn't, I'd stay and use the school's computer still, and be content with a wager now and then.'

Jane joined us, carrying a pot of coffee. 'He's telling you how he started betting? I thought he was crazy.'

'But not for long.'

She shook her head, smiling. 'When we moved out of our caravan into a house – bought it outright with Ted's winnings – then I began to believe it would last, that it was safe. And now here we are, so well off it's embarrassing, and it's all thanks to your dear brother Jonathan.'

The girls climbed dripping out of the pool and were introduced as Emma and Lucy, hungry for breakfast. I was offered bran flakes, natural yoghurt, wheat germ and fresh peaches, which they all ate sparingly but with enjoyment.

I ate as well, but thought inescapably of Angelo and of Cassie alone with him in the cottage. Those planks would hold ... they'd kept him penned in for two whole days. No reason to think they'd fail this morning ... no reason, just a strong feeling that I should have persuaded her to wait with Bananas.

It was over coffee, when the girls were again swimming and Jane had disappeared into the house, that Ted said, 'How did you find me?'

I looked at him. 'Don't you mean why?'

'I suppose so. Yes.'

'I came to ask you to let me have copies of those tapes.'

He breathed deeply and nodded. 'That's what I thought.'

'And will you?'

He looked at the shimmering pool for a while and then said, 'Does Jonathan know you're asking?'

'Yeah. I asked him where the tapes were now, and he said if anyone knew, you would. You and only you, he said.'

Ted Pitts nodded again and made up his mind. 'It's fair. They're his, really. But I haven't got any spare tapes.'

'I brought some,' I said. 'They're out in the car. Can I fetch them?'

'All right.' He nodded decisively. 'I'll change into dry clothes while you're getting them.'

I fetched the computer-type tapes I'd brought for the purpose, and he said, 'Six? You'll only need three.'

'Two sets?' I suggested.

'Oh. Well, why not?' He turned away. 'The computer's downstairs. Would you like to see it?'

'Very much.'

He led the way into the body of the house and we went down some carpeted stairs to a lower floor. 'Office,' he said succinctly, leading the way into a normal-sized room from which one could see the same wide view of London as upstairs. 'It's a bedroom really. Bathroom through there,' he pointed. 'Spare bedroom beyond.'

The office was more accurately a sitting-room with armchairs, television, bookshelves and pinewood panelling. On an upright chair by one wall stood a pair of well-used mountain climbing boots, with the latest in thermal sleeping bags still half in its carton on the floor beside them. Ted followed my glance. 'I'm off to Switzerland in a week or two. Do you climb?'

I shook my head.

'I don't attempt the peaks,' he said earnestly. 'I prefer walking, mostly.' He pulled open a section of the pine panelling to reveal a long counter upon which stood a host of electronic equipment. 'I don't need all this for the racing programs,' he said, 'but I enjoy computers . . .' and he ran his fingers caressingly over the metal surfaces with the ardour of a lover.

'I've never seen those racing programs,' I said.

'Would you like to?'

'Please.'

'All right.' With the speed of long dexterity he fed a tape into a cassette recorder and explained he was putting the machine to search for the file 'Epsom'. 'How much do you know about computers?' he said.

'There was one at school, way back. We played "Space Invader" on it.'

He glanced at me pityingly. 'Everyone in this day and age should be able to write a simple program. Computer language is the universal tongue of the new world, as Latin was of the old.'

'Do you tell your students that?'

'Eh ... yes.'

The small screen suddenly announced 'READY?' Ted pressed some keys on the keyboard and the screen asked 'WHICH RACE AT EPSOM?' Ted typed DERBY, and the screen in a flash presented:

EPSOM: THE DERBY.

NAME OF HORSE?

He put in his own name and randomly answered the ensuing questions, ending with:

TED PITTS. WIN FACTOR: 24

'Simple,' I said.

He nodded. 'The secret is in knowing which questions to ask, and in the weighting given to the answers. There's nothing mysterious about it. Anyone could evolve such a system, given the time.'

'Jonathan says there are several of them in the United States.'

Ted nodded. 'I've got one of them here.' He opened a drawer and brought out what looked like a pocket calculator. 'It's a baby computer with quite elegant programs,' he said. 'I bought it out of curiosity. It only works on American racing, of course, because one of its bases is that all tracks are identical in shape, left-handed ovals. It is geared chiefly to prize money. I understand that if you stick to its instruction book religiously you can certainly win, but of course like Liam O'Rorke's system you have to work at it to get results.'

'And never back a hunch?'

'Absolutely not,' he said seriously. 'Hunches are hopelessly unscientific.'

I looked at him curiously. 'How often do you go to the races?'

'To the races themselves? Practically never. I watch them, of course on television, sometimes. But you don't need to, to win. All you need are the form books and objectivity.'

It seemed to me a dry view of the world where I spent my life. Those beautiful creatures, their speed, their guts, their determination, all reduced to statistical probabilities and microchips.

'These copies of yours,' he said, 'do you want them open, so that anyone can use them?'

'How do you mean?'

'If you like, you can have them with passwords, so that they wouldn't work if anyone stole them from you.'

'Are you serious?'

'Of course,' he said, as if he were never anything else. 'I've always put passwords on all my stuff.'

'Er, how do you do it?'

'Easiest thing in the world. I'll show you.' He flicked a few switches and the screen suddenly announced 'READY?'

'You see that question mark,' Ted said. 'A question mark always means that the computer operator must answer it by typing something. In this case, if you don't type in the correct sequence of letters the program will stop right there. Try it. See what happens.'

I obediently typed EPSOM. Ted pressed the key marked 'Enter'. The screen gave a sort of flick and went straight back to 'READY?'

Ted smiled. 'The password on this tape is QUITE. Or it is at the moment. One can change the password easily.' He typed QUITE and pressed 'Enter' and the screen flashed into WHICH RACE AT EPSOM?

'See the question mark?' Ted said. 'It always needs an answer.'

I thought about question marks and said I'd better not have passwords, if he didn't mind.

'Whatever you say.'

He typed BREAK and LIST 10–80, and the screen suddenly produced a totally different looking format.

'This is the program itself,' Ted said. 'See Line 10?'

Line 10 read INPUT A$: IF A$ = "QUITE" THEN 20 ELSE PRINT "READY?"

Line 20 read PRINT "WHICH RACE AT EPSOM?"

'If you don't type QUITE,' Ted said, 'You never get to line 20.'

'Neat,' I agreed. 'But what's to prevent you looking at the program, like we are now, and seeing that you need to type QUITE?'

'It's quite easy to make it impossible for anyone to List the program. If you buy other people's programs, you can practically never List them. Because if you can't List them you can't make copies, and no one wants their work pinched in that way.'

'Um,' I said. 'I'd like tapes you *can* List, and without passwords.'

'OK.'

'How do you get rid of the password?'

He smiled faintly, typed 10 and then pressed 'Enter'. Then he typed LIST 10–80 again, but this time when the program appeared on the screen there was no Line 10 at all. Line 20 was the first.

'Elementary, you see,' he said.

'So it is.'

'It will take me quite a while to get rid of the passwords and make the copies,' he said. 'So why don't you go and sit upstairs by the pool. To be honest, I'd get on faster on my own.'

Pleased enough to agree, I returned to the lazy bamboo loungers and listened to Jane talking about her daughters. An hour crawled by before Ted reappeared bearing the cassettes, and even then I couldn't leave without an instructional lecture.

'To run those tapes, you'll need either an old Grantley personal computer, and there aren't many of them about nowadays, they're obsolete, or any type of company computer, as long as it will load from a cassette recorder.'

He watched my incomprehension and repeated what he'd said.

'Right,' I said.

He told me how to load Grantley BASIC, which was the first item on Side 1 of the tapes, into a company computer, which had no language of its own built in. He again told me twice.

'Right.'

'Good luck with them,' he said.

I thanked him wholeheartedly, and Jane also, and as quickly as decently possible set off on the drive home.

Half a mile down the road, compelled by a feeling of dread, I stopped by a telephone box and called Cassie. She answered at the very first ring and sounded uncharacteristically shaky.

'I'm so glad it's you,' she said. 'How long will you be?'

'About an hour.'

'Do hurry.'

'Is Angelo . . .?'

'He's been banging ever since you left and wrenching at the door. I've been in the kitchen. He's shaking those planks, he'll have the door off its hinges if he goes on and on. I can't strengthen the barricade. I've tried, but with one arm—'

'Cassie,' I said. 'Go up to the pub.'

'But—'

'Darling, go. Please do.'

'What if he gets out?'

'If he gets out I want you safe up the road with Bananas.'

'All right.'

'I'll see you,' I said, and disconnected. Drove like the furies towards home, taking a chance here and there and getting away with it. Across Royston Heath like a streak, weaving through pottering Sunday-outing traffic. Through the town itself; snarling down the last stretch crossing the M11 motorway, and finally branching off the main road into Six Mile Bottom village.

Wondering all the way what Angelo would do if he did get free. Smash up the cottage? Set fire to it? Lie in wait somewhere for me to return.

The one thing he would not do was to go meekly away.

Chapter Sixteen

I walked carefully up the path to the lockless front door which we now no longer guarded with the chest because Cassie found climbing through the window too difficult.

The birds were singing in the garden. Would they sing if Angelo were among them, hidden in the bushes? No they wouldn't. I reached the door and pushed it open.

The cottage lay silent as if long deserted, and with spirits sinking I went through to the kitchen.

Angelo had ripped away one of the main timbers of the door and had dislodged two of the extra planks which had been wedging it shut. The door in fact was still closed, but the knife had gone from the latch.

The hole in the door was large enough to shove an arm through, but not to allow the passage of a grown man. The table and chairs and the two lowest planks hadn't shifted, but with progress he'd made their stopping power was temporary. I had come not a minute too soon.

'Angelo,' I said.

He appeared almost instantly at the hole in the door, scowling furiously at my return. He put both hands into the gap and violently tried to wrench away the wood from each side, and I saw that he had already been bleeding from his exertions.

'I'm going to let you out,' I said. 'You can save your strength.'

'I'll get you.' The deep growl again. The statement of intent.

'Yeah,' I said. 'I dare say. Now listen, because you'll want to hear.'

He waited, eyes black with ferocity in the shadows.

I said, 'You believe that my brother cheated you out of some computer tapes. They weren't yours to start with, but we'll not argue about that. At this moment *I* have those tapes. They're here in the cottage. It's taken me a a good while to get them, which is why you've stayed here this long in the cellar. I'll give you those tapes. Are you listening?'

He wouldn't say so, but his attention was rivetted.

'You spent fourteen years brooding over the fortune you lost. I'll give it to you. Fourteen years swearing to kill my brother. He's dead. You came here to do violent damage, and for that you could lose your parole. I'm prepared not to report you. In return for the computer tapes and for your continued freedom you can clear out of here and henceforward leave me strictly alone.'

He stared through the door with little change of expression; certainly without joy.

I said, 'You may have been brooding over your revenge for so many years that you can't face not having the prospect of it there any longer to keep you going. You may fall apart from lack of purpose.' I shrugged. 'But *if* I give you liberty and the treasure you want, I'll expect the slate to be wiped clean between you and me.' I paused. 'Do you understand?'

He still said absolutely nothing.

'If you agree that what I'm offering is OK,' I said, 'you can throw out that knife you took from the door latch, and I will give you the three tapes and the keys to your car, which is still where you left it.'

Silence.

'If you choose not to accept that offer,' I said, 'I'll telephone to the police to come and fetch you, and they'll hear all about you breaking my friend's arm.'

'They'll have you for keeping me in here.'

'Maybe. But if they do, you'll never get those tapes. And I mean it. *Never*. I'll destroy them immediately.'

He went away from behind the door but after a long minute he reappeared.

'You'll trick me,' he said. 'Like your brother.'

I shook my head. 'It's not worth it. I want you out of my life altogether and permanently.'

He made a fierce thrusting movement with his unshaven chin, a gesture which could be taken as assent.

'All right, then,' he said. 'Hand them over.'

I nodded. Turned away from him. Went into the sitting-room and sorted out one copy of each tape, shutting the three spares into a chest of drawers. When I returned Angelo was still standing by the door; still suspicious, still wary.

'Tapes.' I showed him. 'Car keys.' I held them up. 'Where's the knife?'

He raised his hand and let me see it: a dinner knife, not very sharp, but destructive enough to be counted.

I laid the three cassettes on a small tray and held it out to him, and he put his arm through the hole to snatch them up.

'Now the knife,' I said.

He dropped it out onto the tray. I slid it into my hand and replaced it with the keys.

'All right,' I said. 'Go down the steps. I'll undo the barricade. Then you can come up and go out. And if you've any thoughts of rushing me, just remember your parole.'

He nodded sullenly.

'Have you still got that computer you bought fourteen years ago?'

'Dad smashed it. When I got sent down. Out of rage.'

Like son, like father ... 'The tapes are still in the same computer language,' I said. 'Grantley Basic. The language itself is there, on Side 1. You'll need to know that.

He scowled. Beyond him entirely to be placated, let alone pleased.

'Go on,' I said. 'I'll unbar the door.'

He disappeared from the impromptu window and I tugged away the effective planks and pulled the table and chairs from their stations, and stood finally out of his arms' reach behind them.

'Come up,' I called. 'Undo the latch and be on your way.'

He came out fast, clutching the cassettes in one bloodstained hand and the keys in the other: gave me a brief hard stare which nonetheless held little of the former menace, and disappeared through the sitting-room towards the door. I followed and watched him go down the path, first quickening his step and almost running as he turned into the lane and then fairly sprinting out of sight towards where he'd left his car. In short time he came blasting back again, driving as if he feared I would still somehow stop him; but in truth all I did want was to be rid of him once and for all.

The empty cellar stank like a lair of an animal.

I looked into it briefly and decided it was a job for a shovel, a hose, a broom and some strong disinfectant, and while I was collecting those things Bananas and Cassie walked anxiously along from the pub.

'We saw you come,' she said, 'and we saw him go. I wanted to be here but Bananas said it might snarl things up.'

'He was right.' I kissed her soundly, both from love and tension released. 'Angelo hates to lose face.'

'You gave him the tapes?' Bananas asked.

'Yeah.'

'And may they choke him,' Cassie said.

I smiled. 'They may not. I'd guess Ted Pitts is worth a million.'

'Really?' Her eyebrows shot up. 'Then why don't *we*—?'

'It takes time and work. Ted Pitts lives right at the London end of the M1, half a mile off the country's biggest artery. I'll bet he spends countless days beating up that road to towns in the north, traipsing round betting shops, sucking his honey. It's what I guess he does, anyway. He was near Manchester yesterday, his wife said. A different town every day, so that no one gets to know him.'

'What difference would that make?' Bananas said.

I explained what happened to constant winners. 'I'll bet there isn't a single bookie who knows Ted Pitts by sight.'

'If *you* did it,' Bananas said thoughtfully, 'I suppose they'd know you at once.'

I shook my head. 'Only on the racecourse. Round the backstreet betting shops in any big town I'd be just another mug.'

They both looked at me expectantly.

'Yeah,' I said. 'I can just see me spending my life that way.'

'Think of the loot,' Bananas said.

'And no tax,' said Cassie.

I thought of Ted Pitts's splendid house and of my own lack of amassed goods. Thought of him walking the upper slopes of Swiss mountains, restoring his spirit, wandering but coming home. Thought of my lack of a settled life-pattern and my hatred of being tied down. Thought of the way I'd enjoyed the past months, making decisions, running a business, knowing all the time it was just for a year, not a lifetime, and being reassured by such impermanency. Thought of spending hot summer days and wet winter afternoons in betting shops, playing the percentages, joylessly, methodically making a million.

'Well?' Bananas said.

'Maybe one day, when I'm hungry.'

'You've no sense.'

'You do it then,' I said. 'Give up the pub. Give up the cooking. Take to the road.'

He stared at me while he thought about it, then grimaced and said, 'There's more to life than making money. Not a lot, but some.'

'One of these days,' said Cassie with sweet certainty, 'you'll both do it. Not even a saint could sit on a goldmine and be too lazy to pick up the nuggets.'

'You think it's just lazy—'

'I sure do. Where's your buccaneering heart? Where's the glint of piracy? What about the battlecry of those old north-country industrialists – where there's muck there's brass?' She looked alight with enthusiasm, a glow I guessed derived as much from Angelo's absence as from the thought of an available fortune.

'If you feel the same when I've finished for Luke Houston,' I said, 'I'll give it a trial. Just for a while.'

'Picky,' she said. 'That's what you are.'

All the same it was in better spirits that I set about cleaning the cellar and making it fit for fishing gear to live in; and in the late afternoon, all three of us sat in the sun on the cottage grass while Cassie and Bananas discussed how they would spend the lolly they thought I would inevitably chase.

They already felt as I did that Angelo's revengeful lust had been at last dissipated, and they said he had even done us a favour as without his violent attack I would never have sought out Ted Pitts.

'Good can come of bad,' Cassie said with satisfaction.

And bad of good, I thought. Jonathan's conjuring tricks had trapped Angelo thoroughly and made it certain that he would be convicted empty handed. Had ensured that for fourteen years Angelo would be unable to kill anyone else. But that particular good sequence of actions which had seemed so final at the time had proved to be only a plug for a simmering volcano. The psychopathic young man had at length erupted as a full-blown coarsened thug, no longer as Jonathan had described him, occasionally high on the drug of recklessness, but more plainly, comprehensively, violent.

Time changed perspectives. From disasters could come successes, and from successes, disasters. A pity, I thought, that one could never perceive whether to weep or cheer at the actual event.

Our lives gradually quietened to sensible proportions. Cassie went back to work in a sling and Bananas invented a new delight involving liquid spiced beef: and I began a series of forays to stud farms to take preliminary peeks at the yearlings soon to be offered at the sales, all too aware that the climax of my year was approaching, the test by which Luke would judge me, looking back. To buy young stock that would win would be satisfactory; to buy a colt to sire a dynasty would be luck. Somewhere between the two lay an area in which judgement would turn out to have been good, indifferent or absent, and it was there that I hoped to make as few mistakes as possible.

For about a week I mosied around all over the place with detours to race meetings and to Luke's two trainers in Berkshire, and spent every spare waking minute with the Stud Book. Sim Shell said severely that he wished to be present and in full consultation whenever I bought anything for him personally to train, and Mort with every nerve twitching asked for Sir Ivor, Nijinsky and Northern Dancer, all at once, and at the very least.

Cassie came with me to the evening session on the first day of the sales, roaming about on the forever legs and listening engrossed to the gossip. Every year Newmarket sale ring saw fortunes lost quicker than crashing stock markets, but the talk was all of hope and expectation, of slashing speed and breeding potential, all first-day euphoria and unspent cheques.

'What excitement,' Cassie said. 'You can see it in every face.'

'The joy of acquisition. Disillusion comes next week. Then optimistic gloom. Then, if you're lucky, complacent relief.'

'But today ...'

'Today,' I nodded. 'There's still the chance of buying the winner of the Derby.'

I bought two colts and a filly on that evening for staggering sums, reassured to a point by having competed against top echelons of bloodstock agents but pursued by the sapping fear that it was I who had pressed on too far, not they who had stopped too soon.

We stayed to the end of the programme, partly because of Cassie's fascination with a new world but also because it was when the big buyers had gone home that a bargain sometimes arose, and I did in fact buy the last lot of the day, a thin-looking pony-like creature, because I liked his bright eyes.

The breeder thanked me. 'Is it really for Luke Houston?'

'Yes,' I said.

'He won't be sorry. He's intelligent, that little colt.'

'He looks it.'

'He'll grow, you know,' he told me earnestly. 'His dam's family are all late growers. Come and have a drink. It isn't every day I sell one to Luke Houston.'

We went back, however, to drink and eat with Bananas, and from there to the cottage, where I sent off a telexed report to Luke, for whom our midnight was three in the afternoon.

Luke liked telexes. If he wanted to discuss what I'd sent he would telephone after his evening dinner, catching me at six in the morning before I left for the gallops, but more normally he would reply by telex or not at all.

The dining-room was filled with equipment provided by Luke: a video-disc recorder for rewatching and analysing past races, a print-out calculator, photo-copier, a row of filing cabinets, an electric typewriter, the telex machine and a complicated affair which answered the telephone, took messages, gave messages, and recorded every word it heard, including my own live conversations. It worked on a separate line from the telephone in the sitting room, a good arrangement which most simply divorced our private calls from his business, allowing me to pay for one and him the other. All he hadn't given me – or had had me collect from an unwilling Warrington Marsh – was a computer.

When I came down the following morning I found the telex had chattered during the night.

'Why didn't you buy the Fischer colt? Why did you buy the cheap colt? Give my best to Cassie.

He had never actually met Cassie but only talked to her a few times on the telephone. The politeness was his way of saying that his questions were simply questions, not accusations. Any telexes which came without 'best to Cassie' were jump-to-it matters.

I telexed back. 'Two private owners who detest each other,

Schubman and Mrs Crickington, beat each other up to three hundred and forty thousand for the Fisher colt, way beyond its sensible value. The cheap colt might surprise you yet. Regards, William.'

Cassie these days was being collected and brought back by a slightly too friendly man who lived near the pub and worked a street away from Cassie in Cambridge. She said he was putting his hand on her knee instead of the steering wheel increasingly often and she would be extremely glad to be rid of both him and the plaster. In other respects than driving the cast had been accommodated, and our night-time activities were back to their old joy.

By day we slowly repaired or replaced everything which had been smashed, using as references the pieces Bananas had stacked in the garage. Television, vases, lamps, all as near as possible to the originals. Even six corn dollies hung again in their mobile group, dollies freshly and intricately woven from the shiny stalks of the new harvest by an elderly ethnic-smock lady who said you had to cut the corn for them specially nowadays by hand, because combine harvesters chopped the straw too short.

Bananas thought that replacing the corn dollies might be going too far, but Cassie said darkly that they represented pagan gods who should be placated – and deep in the countryside *you never knew*.

I carpentered new pieces into both the damaged doors and fitted a new lock to the front. All traces of Angelo gradually vanished, all except his baseball bat which lay along the sill of the window which faced the road. We had consciously kept it there to begin with as a handy weapon in case he should come back, but even as day after peaceful day gave us a growing sense of ease we let it lie: another hostage to the evil eye, perhaps.

Jonathan telephoned me one evening and although I was sure he wouldn't approve of what I'd done I told him everything that had happened.

'You kept him in the *cellar*?'

'Yeah.'

'Good God.'

'It seems to have worked.'

'Mm. I can't help being sorry that Angelo has that system after all.'

'I know. I'm sorry too, after all you did to keep it from him. I really hated giving it to him. But you were right, he's dangerous, and I don't want to vanish to California, the life I want is right here on the English turf. And about the system ... Don't forget, it isn't enough just to possess it, you'd have to operate it discreetly. Angelo knows just about nothing about racing, and he's impetuous and undisciplined, not cunning and quiet.'

'He may also,' Jonathan said, 'think that the system gives a winner every time, which it doesn't. Old Mrs O'Rorke said it steadily gave an average of one winner in three.'

'Angelo versus the bookies should be quite a match. And by the way, I told him you were dead.'

'Thanks very much.'

'Well you didn't want him turning up one day on your sunny doorstep, did you?'

'He'd never get a visa.'

'You can walk across the Canadian border,' I said, 'without anyone being the wiser.'

'And the Mexican,' he agreed.

I told him in detail about Ted Pitts's house, and he sounded truly pleased. 'And the little girls? How are they?'

'Grown up and pretty.'

'I envied him those children.'

'Did you?' I said.

'Yes. Well ... there you are. It's the way life turns out.'

I listened to the regret in his voice and understood how much he himself wanted a daughter, a son ... and I thought that I too would regret it one day if I didn't ... and that maybe it would be terrific fun if Cassie ...'

'Are you still there?' he said.

'Yeah. If I get married, will you come over to the wedding?'

'I don't believe it.'

'You never know. I haven't asked her yet. She might not want to.'

'Keep me posted.' He sounded amused.

'Yeah. How's Sarah?'

'Fine, thanks.'

'So long,' I said, 'So long,' and I put down the receiver with the usual feeling of thankfulness that I had a brother, and specifically that he was Jonathan.

More days passed. By the end of the first week's sales I'd bought twelve yearlings for Luke and lost five more to higher bidders, and I'd consulted with Sim until he was sick of it and given Mort a filly that was on her toes if not actually a dancer, and spent two evenings in the Bedford Arms with the Irish trainer Donavan, listening to his woes and watching him get drunk.

'There's more good horses in Ireland than ever come out,' he said, wagging an unsteady finger under my nose.

'I'm sure.'

'You want to come over, now. You want to poke around them studs, now, before you go to the sales.'

'I'll come over soon,' I said. 'Before the next sales, two weeks from now.'

'You do that.' He nodded sagely. 'There's a colt I have my eye on, way down below Wexford. I'd like to train that colt, now. I'd like for you to buy that little fella for Luke, that I would.'

In that particular year, as a trial, the first Newmarket Yearling Sales had been held early, at the beginning of September. The Premium Sales, when most of the bluest-blooded youngsters would come under the hammer, were as usual at the end of the month. The colt Donavan had his eye on was due to be sold two weeks ahead, but unfortunately not only Donavan had his eye on it. The whole of Ireland and most of England seemed also to have their optics swivelled that way. Even allowing for Irish exaggeration, that colt seemed the best news of the season.

'Luke would want that fella, now,' Donavan said.

'I'll bid for it,' I said mildly.

He peered boozily into my face. 'What you want to do, now, is to get Luke to say there's no ceiling. No ceiling, that's the thing.'

'I'll go to Luke's limit.'

'You're a broth of a boy, now. And it's write to Luke I did, I'll admit it, to say you were as green as a pea and no good to man nor horse, not in the job he'd given you.'

'Did you?'

'Well now, if you get me that little colt I'll write again and say I was wrong.' He nodded heavily and half fell off the bar stool. He was never drunk on the gallops or at the races or indeed by the sale-ring itself, but at all other times – probably. The owners didn't seem to mind and nor did the horses: drunk or sober, Donavan produced as many winners year by year as anyone in Ireland. I didn't like or dislike him. I did business with him before ten in the morning and listened intently in the evenings, the time when through clouds of whisky he spoke the truth. Many thought him uncouth, and so he was. Many thought Luke would have chosen a smoother man with tidier social manners, but perhaps Luke had seen and heard Donavan's intimate way with horses, as I now had, and preferred the priceless goods to a gaudier package. I had come to respect Donavan. Two solid days of his company were quite enough.

When the flood of purchasing trainers and agents and go-it-alone owners had washed out of the town temporarily, Sim gave a brown short-necked filly a final workout and afterwards rather challenging told me she was as ready as could be to win the last race on St Leger day, on Saturday.

'She looks great,' I said. 'A credit to your care.'

Sim half scowled. 'You'll be going to Doncaster, I suppose?'

I nodded. 'Staying up there, Friday night. Mort's running Genotti in the St Leger.'

'Will you help me saddle mine up? ' Sim said.

I tried to hide my astonishment at this olive branch of epic proportions. He usually attempted to keep me as far from the runners as possible.

'Be glad to,' I said.

He nodded with customary brusqueness. 'See you there, then.'

'Good luck.'

He was going up on the Wednesday for the whole of the four-day meeting but I didn't particularly want to, not least because Cassie still found it difficult to manage on her own with the rigid arm. I left her on the Friday, though, and drove to Doncaster, and almost the first person I saw as I walked through the racecourse gates was Angelo.

I stopped abruptly and turned aside, willing him not to spot me, not to speak.

He was buying two racecards from one of the booths near the

entrance, holding up the queue while he sorted out coins.

I supposed it was inevitable I would one day see him if he took to racegoing at all often, but somehow it was still a shock. I was glad when he turned away from the booth in the opposite direction to where I stood: there might be a truce between us but it was fragile at best.

I watched while he barged his way through the swelling crowd with elbows like battering rams and thighs like rocks: he was heading not to anywhere where he could place a bet but towards the less populated area near the rails of the track itself, where supporters had not yet flocked to see the first race. Reaching the rails, he stopped beside an elderly man in a wheelchair and unceremoniously thrust one of the racecards into his hands. Then he turned immediately on his heel and bullied his way purposefully towards the serried ranks of bookmakers inside the stands, where I lost sight of him, thankfully, for the rest of the day.

He was back, however, on the Saturday. Although I seldom bothered with gambling, I decided to have a small bet on Genotti in the St Leger, infected no doubt by Mort's fanatical eagerness, and as I stood near a little Welsh bookmaker whom I'd long known, I saw Angelo, thirty feet away, frowning heavily over a small notebook.

'Genotti,' my bookmaker friend said to his clerk who wrote down (in the book) every transaction, 'Three tenners at fives, William Derry.'

'Thanks, Taff,' I said.

Along the row Angelo began arguing about a price on offer, which was apparently less than he thought fair.

'Everyone else is at five to one.' His voice was a growl which I knew all too well.'

'Try someone else, then. It's fours to you, *Mister* Gilbert.'

With half my mind I was satisfied that Angelo was indeed rushing in stupidly with the system where Liam O'Rork and Ted Pitts had taken care not to tread, but also I was uneasy that he should be arousing opposition so soon. I positively needed for him to win for a while. I'd never envisaged him sticking to the anonymous drudgery required for long-term success, but the honeymoon period should not already have been over.

Taff-the-bookmaker glanced over his shoulder at the altercation and gave his clerk an eyes-to-heaven gesture.

'What's all the fuss about?' I asked.

'He's a right git, that man.' Taff divided his comment impartially between him, his clerk, and the world in general.

'Angelo Gilbert.'

Taff's gaze sharpened on me directly. 'Know him, do you?'

'Somebody pointed him out . . . he murdered somebody, years ago.'

'That's right. Just out of the jug, he is. And *stupid* – you wouldn't credit it.'

'What's he done?'

'He came up to York last week with a fistful of banknotes, laying it about as if there were no tomorrow, and us not knowing who he was at that moment. And there's us thinking we were all taking lollipops off a baby when whammo, this outsider he'd invested about six big ones on comes cantering in from nowhere and we're all paying out and wincing and scratching our heads over where he got the info, because the trainer hadn't had as much as a quid on, as far as we knew. So Lancer, that bloke along there arguing with this Gilbert, he asks this geezer straight out who'd put him onto the winner, and the stupid git smirked and said Liam O'Rorke did.'

Taff peered at my face, which I felt must have mirrored my feeling of inner shock, but apparently it merely looked blank because Taff, who was a good sixty-plus, made a clicking sound with his mouth and said, 'Before your time, I suppose.'

'What was?'

Taff's attention was torn away by several customers who crowded to place bets, and he seemed vaguely surprised to see me still there when they'd gone.

'Are you that interested?' he asked.

'Got nothing else to do.'

Taff glanced along to where Angelo had been, but Angelo had gone. 'Thirty years ago. Thirty-five. Time does go quick. There was this old Irishman, Liam O'Rorke, he'd invented the only system I ever knew that would guarantee you'd win. Course, once we'd cottoned to him we weren't all that keen to take his bets. I mean, we wouldn't be, would we, knowing he had the edge on us somehow. Anyway, he would never part with his secret, how he did it, and it went with him to the grave, and good riddance, between you and me.'

'And now?'

'And now here's this geezer rocking us back on our heels with this huge win at York and then he's sneering at us and calling us mugs, and saying we don't know what's hit us yet, and what he's using on us is Liam O'Rorke's old system resurrected, and now he's all indignant and complaining that we won't give him a good price. Acting all hurt and angry.' Taff laughed contemptuously. 'I mean how stupid can you get?'

Chapter Seventeen

Genotti won the St Leger by an easy four lengths.

Mort's excitement afterwards seemed to levitate him visibly off the ground, the static electricity about him crackling in the dry September sunshine. He wrung my hand with bone-scrunching enthusiasm and danced round the unsaddling enclosure giving rapturous responses to all who congratulated him, reacting with such uncomplicated delight to his victory that he had all the crowd smiling. It was easy, I reflected, to think of Mort as simple through and through, whereas, as I had gradually discovered, he traversed mental mazes of tortuous routes where pros battled cons like moves on a chessboard, and the plans and solutions which seemed so obvious once they had turned out to be right were the fruits of the mazes.

I collected my winnings from Taff, who gloomily said he would never have given anyone five to one if he'd known beforehand that Genotti was Angelo Gilbert's fancy.

'Did Angelo win?' I asked.

'Of course, he did. He must have had a grand on. None of us would take his money at the finish.'

'So he didn't get fives?'

'More like evens,' he said sourly

At evens, Angelo would still have doubled his money, but for Angelo that might not be enough. Grievance, I could see, might raise a very ugly head.

'No system could win ever single time,' I said. 'Angelo won't.'

'I dare say not,' Taff said with obstinancy. 'But you can take it from me that no bookie on the racecourse will in future give that arrogant so-and-so much more than evens, even if what he's backing is lame on three legs, carrying two stone overweight and ridden by my old dad.'

'At evens, he wouldn't win over all,' I said.

'So who's crying? We're not in the loving-kindness business, you know.'

'Fleece the mugs?'

'You got it.'

He began paying out other successful punters with the rapidity of long practice but it was seldom that he would go home from a racecourse with less cash than he'd brought. Few bookmakers were gamblers at heart and only the good mathematicians survived.

I drifted away from him and drank some champagne with the similarly fizzing Mort and a little later helped Sim to saddle the filly, who made it another hooray-for-Houston day by a short head. Sim took it more calmly than Mort, but with a satisfaction at least as deep, and he seemed to be admitting and acknowledging at last that I was not an ignorant bossy upstart but a well-meaning colleague and that all Luke's successes worked for our joint good. I wasn't sure how or why his attitude had changed, I knew only that a month earlier a friendly drink together in a racecourse bar to celebrate a Houston winner would have been unthinkable.

Thinking more of Mort and Sim and the horses than of the still active spectre of Angelo, I drove from Doncaster to collect Cassie, and from there to late dinner with Bananas. He too, it appeared, had backed Genotti, more than doubling my own winnings.

'I had a hundred on,' he said.

'I didn't know you ever bet.'

'On the quiet, now and then. Hearing all I do, how could I not?'

'So what did you hear about Genotti?'

He looked at me pityingly. 'Every time you've seen that colt work on the gallops, you've come back like a kid with tickets to the Cup Final.'

'More to the point,' Cassie said, 'if you'd used Liam O'Rorke's system, would it have come up with Genotti?'

'Ah.' I read Bananas's new menu and wondered what he meant by Prisoner Chicken. Said casually, 'Angelo Gilbert backed him.'

'*What?*'

I explained about Angelo, the bookmakers, and stupidity in general.

'He's blown it,' Cassie said, not without satisfaction.

I nodded. 'Into fragments.'

Bananas looked at me thoughtfully. 'What's it going to do for the dear man's temper?'

'It's not William's fault,' Cassie said.

'That trifle didn't stop him before.'

Cassie looked frowningly alarmed. 'What's Prisoner Chicken?' I said.

Bananas smirked. 'Breast of chicken marinated in lemon juice and baked under match-stick thin bars of herb pastry.'

'It sounds dry,' I said with jaundice.

'Bread and water are optional extras.'

Cassie laughed and Angelo retreated a little. We ate the Prisoner Chicken which was predictably a delight of juice and flavour and reminded us not at all of its inspiration.

'I'm going to Ireland tomorrow,' I said to Cassie. 'Like to come?'

'Ireland? There and back?'

I nodded. 'To see a man about a horse.'

'What else?'

So we spent some of my winnings on her fare, and went down south of Wexford to see the colt all the world wanted: and half the world, it seemed, was there on the same errand, standing around an untidy stable yard with blank faces all carefully not expressing identical inner thoughts.

Cassie watched as the beautifully coupled brown yearling skittered around under the calming hands of the stud groom and unprofessionally pronounced him 'sweet'.

'A money machine on the hoof,' I said. 'Look at the greed in all those shuttered faces.'

'They just seem uninterested to me.'

'Enthusiasm puts the price up.'

One or two of the bored-looking onlookers advanced to run exploratory hands down the straight young bones, stepping back with poker-playing non-committal eyes, the whole procedure hushed as if in church.

'Aren't you going to feel its legs?' Cassie asked.

'Might as well.'

I took my turn in the ritual, and found like everyone else that the young limbs were cool and firm with tendons like fiddle strings in all the right places. There was also a good strong neck, a well-shaped quarter and most importantly a good depth of chest. Quite apart from his pedigree, which resounded with Classic winners, one couldn't I thought, even imagine a better-looking animal: all of which meant that the bidding at the sale on Wednesday would rise faster than Bananas Frisby.

We flew thoughtfully back to England and I sent a telex to Luke. 'Bidding for the Hansel colt will be astronomical. I've seen him. He is without fault. How high do you want me to go?'

To which, during the night, I received a reply. 'It's your job, fella. You decide.'

Ouch, I thought. Where is the ceiling? How high is disaster?

Newmarket filled up again for the new week of sales, the most important programme of yearling sales of the whole season. Everyone in racing with money to spend brought determination and dreams, and the four-legged babies came in horseboxes from just up the road, from Kent and the Cotswolds, from Devon and Scotland, from across the Irish Sea.

The Hansel colt from Wexford was due to be sold at the prime time of seven-thirty on the Wednesday evening and by seven the high-rising banks of seats of the sale ring were invisible under a sea of bodies, Cassie somewhere among them. Down near the floor in the pen reserved for probable bidders, Donavan was breathing heavily at my elbow as he had been all afternoon, determinedly sober and all the gloomier for it.

'Now you get that little colt, now, you get him for me.' If he'd said it once he'd said it a hundred times, as if repetition of desire could somehow make the purchase certain.

They brought the colt into the ring in the sudden hush of a host of lungs holding back their breath all at once, and the light gleamed on the walking gem and he did in truth look like a prince who could sire a dynasty.

The bidding for him started not in thousands but in tens of thousands, leaping in seconds to the quarter million and racing away beyond. I waited until the first pause and raised the price by a giant twenty-five thousand, to be immediately capped by a decisive nod from an agent along to my right. I raised another twenty-five and lost it as quickly, and another, and another: and I could go on nodding, I thought, until my head fell off. Nothing easier in the world than spending someone else's money as fast as noughts running through the meter on a petrol pump.

At eight hundred thousand quineas I just stopped. The auctioneer looked at me inquiringly. I didn't blink. 'Against you, sir,' he said.

'Go on,' said Donavan, thinking I'd merely overlooked that it was my turn. 'Go on, go on.'

I shook my head. Donavan turned and literally punched me on the arm in an agony of fear that my dithering would lose him the colt. 'Go on, it's you. Bid, you bugger, bid.'

'Any more, sir?' the auctioneer said.

I again shook my head. Donavan kicked my leg. The auctioneer looked around the silent sale ring. 'All done, then?' he said: and after a lifetime's pause his gavel came down sharply, the clap of opportunity gone forever. 'Sold to Mr O'Flaherty. Next lot, please.'

Under the buzz of comment that followed the super-colt out of the ring, Donavan thrust a furious purple face towards mine and yelled uninhibitedly, 'You buggering *bastard.* Do you know who bought that colt?'

'Yes I do.'

'I'll kill you, so I will.'

Shades of Angelo . . .

'There's no reason,' I said, 'why Luke should pay for your feud with Mick O'Flaherty.'

'That colt will win the Derby.'

I shook my head. 'You're *afraid* it will.'

'I'll write to Luke, so I will. I'll tell him it's you who's afraid. Bloody English. I'd kill the lot of you.'

He stalked away with rage pouring visibly from every pore, and I watched him with regret because I would indeed have liked to buy him his little fellow and seen him croon over him to make him a champion.

'Why did you stop?' Cassie asked, taking my arm.

'Does it worry you?'

She blinked. 'You know what they're saying?'

'That I didn't have the nerve to go on?'

'It was just that I heard . . .'

I smiled lopsidedly. 'My first big battle, and I retreated. Something like that?'

'Something.'

'O'Flaherty and Donavan hate each other so much it curdles their judgement. I meant to go as far as seven hundred and fifty thousand guineas and I thought I'd get the colt, I really did, because that's an extremely high price for any yearling. I went one bid higher still, but it wasn't enough. O'Flaherty was standing behind his agent prodding him in the back to make him carry on. I could see him. O'Flaherty was absolutely determined to buy the colt. To spite Donavan, I think. It isn't sense to go on bidding against someone compelled by raw emotion, so I stopped.'

'But what if he *does* win the Derby?'

'About ten thousand thoroughbred colts were born last year in the British Isles alone. Then there's France and America too. *One* colt from that huge crop will win the Derby the year after next, when he's three. The odds are against it being this one.'

'You're so cool.'

'No,' I said truthfully. 'Bruised and disgruntled.'

We drove home and I sent the telex to Luke. 'Regret underbidder at eight hundred and forty thousand pounds excluding tax for Hansel colt. Donavan's deadly rival Mick O'Flaherty successful at eight hundred and sixty-six thousand two fifty. Donavan furious. Sack me if you like. Regards, William.'

The return message came within an hour. 'If the colt wins the Derby you owe me ten million pounds otherwise you are still employed. Best to Cassie.'

'Thank God for that,' she said. 'Let's go to bed.'

Two busy days later I dropped her at work and drove on south-westwards to Berkshire to visit Luke's other trainers during the morning and to go on to see three of their horses race at Newbury in the afternoon; and there again on the racecourse was Angelo.

This time he saw me immediately before I had time to dodge: came charging across a patch of grass, took roughly hold of my lapel, and told me the betting system didn't work.

'You sold me a pup. You'll be sorry.' He looked quickly around as if hoping to find us both on deserted moorland, but as there was only concrete well populated, he smothered his obvious wish to slaughter me there and then. He was physically tougher, I thought. Less pale, less puffy; the effects of long imprisonment giving way to a healthy tan and tighter muscles, the bull-like quality of the body intensifying. The black eyes . . . cold as ever. I looked at his re-emerging malevolence and didn't like it a bit.

I pulled his hand off my lapel and dropped it. 'There's nothing wrong with the system,' I said. 'It's not my fault you've been trampling all over it like a herd of elephants.'

His voice came back in the familiar bass register, 'If I'm still losing by five tomorrow, I'll *know* you've conned me. And I'll come after you. That's a promise.'

He turned away abruptly and strode off towards the stands, and in a while I went in search of Taff among the bookmakers.

'The latest on Angelo Gilbert?' he looked down at me from his raised position on an inverted beer crate. 'He's nuts.'

'Are you still offering him rotten odds?'

'Look you, Mr Derry, I'm too busy to talk now.' He was indeed surrounded by eager customers holding out cash. 'If you want to know, buy me a pint after the last race.'

'Right,' I said, 'it's a deal.' And at the end of the afternoon he came with me into the crowded bar and shouted the unexpected news into my attentive ear.

'That man Angelo's gone haywire. He won big money at York, like I told you, and a fair amount at Doncaster, but before York it seems he lost a packet at Epsom and last Monday he kissed goodbye to a fortune at Goodwood, and today he's plunged on two horses who finished out of sight. So we're all back to giving him regular odds. Old Lancer – he works for Joe Glickstein, Honest Joe, you must have seen his stands at all the tracks?' I nodded. 'Well, Old Lancer, he took a thousand in readies this afternoon off that Angelo on Pocket Handbook, what couldn't win if it started yesterday. I mean, the man's a screwball. He's no more playing Liam O'Rorke's system than I'm a bleeding fairy.'

I watched him drink his beer, feeling great dismay that Angelo couldn't manage the system even to the extent of letting it find him the right horses. He had to be guessing some of the answers to the multifarious questions instead of looking them up accurately in the form books: skipping the hard work out of laziness and still trusting the scores which the computer returned. But a computer couldn't advise him, couldn't tell him that omitting an answer here and an answer there would upset all those delicately balanced weightings and inevitably distort the all-important win factors.

Angelo was dumb, dim, stupid.

Angelo would think it was my fault.

'They say his father's getting tired of it,' Taff said.

'Who?'

'That Angelo person's father. Old Harry Gilbert. Made a packet out of bingo halls, they say, before he got struck.'

'Er, struck?'

Taff brought a lined brown outdoor face out of the beer mug. 'Struck down with arthritis, I think it is. He can't hardly walk, anyway. Comes to the races sometimes in a wheel chair, and it's him what has the cash.'

Enlightened, I thought back to the previous week at Doncaster, seeing in memory Angelo giving a racecard to an elderly chairbound man. Angelo's father, still indulgent, still supportive, still paying for his deadly middle-aged son.

I thanked Taff for his information. 'What's this Angelo to you?' he said.

'A long-time no friend of my brother's.'

He made an accepting motion with his head, looked at his watch and finished his beer at a gulp, saying he'd left his clerk looking after the day's takings and he'd be happer having his mitts on them himself. 'We've all had a good day,' he said cheerfully, 'with those two odds-on favourites getting stuffed.'

I drove homewards and collected Cassie who was waiting at the hospital after what they had called a progress assessment.

'Plaster off next week,' she complained. 'I wanted it off this afternoon, but they wouldn't.'

The plaster was by then itching badly, the 'REMEMBER TIGERS' was fading, Cassie was insisting that her arm *felt* mended and impatience had definitely set in.

We again went to the sales: I seemed to have spent half a lifetime round that sale ring, and Luke now owned twenty-eight yearlings he had not yet seen. I had signed cheques on his behalf for nearly two million pounds and was tending to dream about it at night. There was only the Saturday morning left now, an undistinguished programme according to the catalogue, the winding-down after the long excitements of the week. I went early by habit and with only short premeditation bought very cheaply the first lot of the day, an undistinguished-looking liver chestnut colt whose blood lines were sounder to the inspection than his spindly legs. One couldn't have foretold on that misty autumn morning that *this* was the prince who would sire a dynasty, but that in the end was what happened. My mind, as I signed for him and arranged for him to be sent along the road to Mort's stable, was more immediately on the conversation I'd had with Jonathan on the telephone the evening before.

'I want to talk to Angelo's father,' I said. 'Do you remember where he lived?'

'Of course I do. Welwyn Garden City. If you give me a minute, I'll find the street and the number.' There was a pause while he searched. 'Here we are. Seventeen, Pemberton Close. He may have moved, of course, and don't forget, William, he won't be in the least pleasant. I heard he was threatening all sorts of dire revenges against me after Angelo was convicted, but I didn't hang around long enough for him to get going.'

'Angelo seems to depend on him for cash,' I said.

'That figures.'

'Angelo's making a right balls-up of the betting system. He's losing his father's money and he's blaming me for it, and stoking up again towards volcanic eruption with me as the designated target for the lava flow.'

'He's an absolute pest.'

'He sure is. How does one rid oneself of a monster that won't go away? Don't answer that. Engineering Angelo back into jail permanently is all I can think of, and even then I would need to do it so that he didn't know who'd done it, and would it even on the whole be fair?'

'Provocation? Put a crime in his way and invite him to commit it?'

'As you say.'

'No, it wouldn't exactly be fair.'

'I was afraid you wouldn't think so,' I said.

'Nothing much short of murder would put him back inside for the whole of his life. Anything less and he'd be out breathing fire again, as you said before. And however could you line up a living victim?'

'Mm,' I said, 'it's impossible. I still think the only lasting solution is to make Angelo prosper, so I'll see if I can persuade his old dad to that effect.'

'His dad is an old rattlesnake, don't forget.'

'His old dad is in a wheelchair.'

'Is he?' Jonathan seemed surprised. 'All the same, remember that rattlesnakes don't have legs.'

I reckoned that on that Saturday afternoon Angelo would still be blundering around the bookies on Newbury racecourse and that his father might have stayed at home, so it was then that I drove to Welwyn Garden City, leaving Cassie wandering around the cottage with a duster and an unaccustomedly domestic expression.

The house at number seventeen Pemberton Close proved to be inhabited not by Harry Gilbert but by a stockbroker, his chatty wife and four noisy children on roller skates, all of them out in the garden.

'Harry Gilbert?' said the wife, holding a basket of dead roses. 'He couldn't manage the stairs with his illness. He built himself a bungalow full of ramps.'

'Do you know where?'

'Oh sure. On the golf course. He used to play, poor man. Now he sits at a window and watches the foursomes go by on the fourteenth green. We often wave to him when we're playing.'

'Does he have arthritis?' I asked.

'Good Lord, no.' She made a grimace of sympathy. 'Multiple sclerosis. He's had it for years. We've seen him slowly get worse . . . We used to live four doors away, but we always liked this house. When he put it up for sale, we bought it.'

'Could you tell me how to find him?'

'Sure.' She gave me brisk clear instructions. 'You do know, don't you, not to talk about his son?'

'Son?' I said vaguely.

'His only son is in prison for murder. So sad for the poor man. Don't talk about it, it distresses him.'

'Thanks for warning me,' I said.

She nodded and smiled from a kind and unperceiving heart and went back to tidying her pretty garden. Surely goodness and mercy all thy days shall follow thee, I thought frivolously, and no monsters who won't go away shall gobble thee up. I left the virtuous and went in search of the sinner, and found him, as she'd said, sitting in his wheelchair by a big bay window, watching the earnest putters out on the green.

The wide double front doors of the large and still new-looking one-storey building were opened to me by a man so like Angelo at first sight that I thought for a fearsome moment that he hadn't after all gone to the races; but it was only the general shape and colouring that was the same, the olive skin, greying hair, unfriendly dark eyes, tendency to an all-over padding of fat.

'Eddy,' a voice called. 'Who is it? Come in here.'

The voice was as deep and harsh as Angelo's, the words themselves slightly slurred. I walked across the polished wood of the entrance hall and then across the lush drawing room with its panoramic view, and not until I was six feet away from Harry Gilbert did I stop and say I was William Derry.

Vibrations could almost be felt. Eddy, behind me, audibly hissed from the air leaving his lungs. The much older version of Angelo's face which looked up from the wheelchair went stiff with strong but unreadable emotions, guessed at as anger and indignation, but possibly not. He had thinning grey hair, a grey moustache, a big body in a formal grey suit with a waistcoat. Only in the lax hands was the illness visible, and only then when he moved them; and from his polished shoes to the neat parting across his scalp it seemed to me that he was denying the weaknesses, presenting an outwardly uncrumbled façade so as to announce to the world that authority still lived within.

'You're not welcome in my house,' he said.

'If your son would stop threatening me, I wouldn't be here.'

'He says you tricked us like your brother.'

'No.'

'The betting system doesn't work.'

'It worked for Liam O'Rorke,' I said. 'Liam O'Rorke was quiet, clever, careful and a statistician. Is Angelo any of those things?'

He gave me a cold stare. 'A system should work for everyone alike.'

'A horse doesn't run alike for every jockey,' I said.

'There's no similarity.'

'Engines run sweetly for some drivers and break down for others. Heavy-handedness is always destructive. Angelo is trampling all over that system. No wonder it isn't producing results.'

'The system is wrong,' he said stubbornly.

'It may,' I said slowly, 'be slightly out of date.' Yet for Ted Pitts it was purring along still: but then Ted Pitts too was quiet, clever; a statistician.

It seemed that I had made the first impression upon Harry Gilbert. He said with faint note of doubt, 'It should not have changed with the years. Why should it?'

'I don't know. Why shouldn't it? There may be a few factors that Liam O'Rorke couldn't take into account because in his time they didn't exist.'

A depressed sort of grimness settled over him.

I said, 'And if Angelo has been hurrying through the programs, skipping some of the questions or answering them inaccurately, the scores will come out wrong. He's had some of the answers right. You won a lot at York, so I'm told. And you'd have won more on the St Leger if Angelo hadn't scared the bookmakers with his boastfulness.'

'I don't understand you.' The slur in his speech, the faint distortion of all his words was, I realized, the effect of his illness. Articulation might be damaged but the chill awareness in his eyes said quite clearly that his intelligence wasn't.

'Angelo told all the bookmakers at York that he would henceforth fleece them continually, because it was he who possessed Liam O'Rorke's infallible system.'

Harry Gilbert closed his eyes. His face remained unmoved.

Eddy said belligerently, 'What's wrong with that? You have to show people who's boss.'

'Eddy,' Harry Gilbert said, 'you don't know anything about anything and you never will.' He slowly opened his eyes. 'It makes a difference,' he said.

'They gave him evens on the St Leger winner. The proper price was five to one.'

Harry Gilbert would never thank me: not if I gave him life-saving advice, not if I helped him win a fortune, not if I kept his precious son out of jail. He knew, all the same, what I was saying. Too much of a realist, too old a businessman, not to. Angelo in too many ways was a fool, and it made him more dangerous, not less.

'What do you expect me to do?' he said.

'I expect you to tell your son that if he attacks me again, or any of my friends or any of my property, he'll be back behind bars so fast he won't know what hit him. I expect you to make him work the betting system carefully and quietly, so that he wins. I expect you to warn him that the system guarantees only one win in three, not a winner every single time. Making the system work is a matter of strict application and careful persistence, not of flamboyance and anger.'

He stared at me expressionlessly.

'Angelo's character,' I said, 'is as far different from Liam O'Rorke's as it's possible to get. I expect you to make Angelo aware of that fact.'

They were all expectations, I saw, that were unlikely to be achieved. Harry Gilbert's physical weakness, though he disguised it, was progressive, and his imperfect control of Angelo would probably only last at all for exactly as long as Angelo needed financing.

A tremor shook his body but no emotion showed in his face. He said however with a sort of throttled fury, 'All our problems are your brother's fault.'

The uselessness of my visit swamped me. Harry Gilbert was after all only an old man blindly clinging like his son to an old obsession. Harry Gilbert was not any longer a man of reason, even if he had ever been.

I tried all the same, once more. I said, 'If you had paid Mrs O'Rorke all those years ago, if you had bought Liam's system from her, as you had agreed, you would legally have owned it and could have profited from it ever since. It was because you refused to pay Mrs O'Rorke that my brother saw to it that you didn't get the system.'

'She was too old,' he said coldly.

I stared at him. 'Are you implying that her age was a reason for not paying her?'

He didn't answer.

'If I stole your car from you,' I said, 'would you consider me justified on the grounds that you were too ill to drive it?'

'You prattle,' he said. 'You are nothing.'

'Mug,' Eddy said, nodding.

Harry Gilbert said wearily, 'Eddy, you are good at pushing wheelchairs and cooking meals. On all other subjects, shut up.'

Eddy gave him a look which was half-defiant, half-scared, and I saw that he too was dependent on Harry for his food and shelter, that it couldn't be all that easy out in the big cynical world for murderers' assistants to earn a cushy living, that looking after Harry wasn't a job to be lightly lost.

To Harry Gilbert I said, 'Why don't you do what you once intended? Why don't you buy Angelo a betting shop and let the system win for him there?'

I got another stretch of silent unmoving stare. Then he said, 'Business is a talent. I have it. It is, however, uncommon.'

I nodded. It was all the answer he would bring himself to make. Certainly he wouldn't admit to me of all people that he thought Angelo would bankrupt any sensible business in a matter of weeks.

'Keep your son away from me,' I said. 'I've done more for you in getting you that system than you deserve. You've no rights to it. You've no right to demand that it makes you a fortune in five minutes. You've no right to blame me if it doesn't. You keep your son away from me. I can play as rough as he does. For your own sake, and for his, you keep him off me.'

I turned away from him without waiting for any sort of answer, and walked unhurriedly out of the room and across the hall.

Footsteps pattered after me on the polished wood.

Eddy.

I didn't look round. He caught up with me as I opened the front doors and stepped outside, and he put his hand on my arm to make me pause. He looked back guiltily over his shoulder to where his uncle sat mutely by his splendid window, knowing the old man wouldn't approve of what he was doing. Then as he saw Harry was looking out again steadfastly to the golf, he turned on me a nasty self-satisfied smirk.

'Mug,' he said, speaking with prudent quietness. 'Angelo won't like you coming here.'

'Too bad.' I shook his hand off my sleeve. He sneered back in a poisonous mixture of slyness and malice and triumph, and half-whispered his final enjoyable words.

'Angelo's bought a pistol,' he said.

Chapter Eighteen

'Why are you so thoughtful?' Cassie asked.

'Uneasy.'

We were sitting as so often at a table in Bananas' dining room with him moving about lightfootedly in his sneakers seeming never to hurry yet keeping everyone fed. The plants grew with shining healthy leaves in the opulent gloom of his designedly intimate lighting, glasses and silverware gleaming in candlelight and mould spreading slowly in the dark.

'It's not like you,' Cassie said.

I smiled at her thin suntanned uncomplicated face and said that I didn't want above all things a return visit from Angelo.

'Do you really think he'd come?'

'I don't know.'

'We'd never get any more corn dollies,' she said. 'It's too late now for decent straw.'

Her arm in its plaster lay awkwardly on the table. I touched the bunched fingertips peeping out. 'Would you consider leaving me for a while?' I asked.

'No, I wouldn't.'

'Suppose I said I was tired of you?'

'You're not.'

'Are you so sure?'

'Positive,' she said contentedly. 'And anyway, for how long?'

I drank some wine. For how long was an absolute puzzle. 'Until I get Angelo stabilized,' I said. 'And don't ask me how long, because I don't know. But the first thing to do, I think, is persuade Luke he needs a computer right here in Britain.'

'Would that be difficult?'

'It might be. He has one in California ... he might say he didn't need two.'

'What do you want it for, the betting system?'

I nodded. 'I think,' I said, 'that I'll try to rent one. Or some time on one. I want to find out what the winners should be according to O'Rorke, and what Angelo's doing wrong. And if I can put him *right*, perhaps that will keep him quiet.'

'You'd have thought just giving him the tapes would be enough.'

'Yes, you would.'

'He's like a thistle,' she said. 'You're sure you've got rid of him and he grows back.

Thistles, I thought, didn't go out to buy guns.

Bananas reverently bore his eponymous soufflé to the people at the next table, the airy peaks shining light and luscious and pale brown. The old cow, whose skill had produced it, must have stopped working to rule: Bananas himself, joining us later for coffee, gloomily admitted it. 'She took an hour to shred carrots. Did them by hand. Ten seconds in the processor. She said processors were dangerous machinery and she'd have to negotiate a new rate for all jobs with machinery.'

Bananas' new beard had grown curly which was unforeseen in view of the lank straight locks further up but seemed to me to be in accord with the doubleness of his nature.

'Historically,' he said, 'it's seldom a good idea to appease a tyrant.'

'The old cow?'

'No. Angelo Gilbert.'

'What do you suggest, then?' I asked. 'Full-scale war?'

'You have to be sure you'll win. Historically, full scale war's a toss up.'

'The old cow might leave,' Cassie said, smiling.

Bananas nodded. 'Tyrants always want more next time. I dare say next year she'll turn to motor racing.'

'I suppose you don't know anyone who has a computer you can feed any language into?' I said.

'Turkish? Indo-Chinese? That sort of stuff?'

'Yeah. Gibberish, double-speak, jargonese, and gobble-de-gook.'

'Try the sociologists.'

I tried, however, Ted Pitts, early the following morning, and reached Jane instead.

'Ted isn't here,' she said. 'I'm afraid he's still in Switzerland. Can I help?'

I explained I wanted to borrow a good computer to run a check on the racing programs and she said sadly that she couldn't really lend me Ted's, not without him being there; she knew he was working on a special program for his classes and if anyone touched the computer at present his work could be lost, and she couldn't risk that.

'No,' I agreed. Did she know of anyone else whose computer I could use?

She thought it over. 'There's Ruth,' she said doubtfully. 'Ruth Quigley.'

'Who?'

'She was a pupil of Ted's. Actually he says there's nothing he can teach her now, and when she comes here I can't understand a word they say to each other, it's like listening to creatures from outer space.'

'Would she have a computer of her own?'

'She's got everything,' Jane said without envy. 'Born rich. Only child. Only has to ask, and it's hers. And on top of that, she's brainy. Doesn't seem fair, does it?'

'Beautiful as well?'

'Oh.' She hesitated. 'Not bad. I don't really know. It's not the sort of thing you *notice* about Ruth.'

'Well, um, where could I find her?'

'In Cambridge. That's why I thought of her, because she lives over your way. She writes programs for teaching-machines. Would you like me to ring her? When do you want to go?'

I said 'Today', and half an hour later I'd had my answer and was on my way, seeking out a flat in a modern block on the outskirts of the town.

Ruth Quigley proved to be young: very early twenties, I guessed. I could see also what Jane meant about not noticing her looks, because the first overpowering and lasting impression she gave was of the speed of her mind. There were light eyes, light brown extra-curly hair and long slender neck, but mostly there was an impatient jerk of the head and a stumblingly rapid diction as if to her utter disgust her tongue couldn't speak her thoughts fast enough.

'Yes. Come in. Did you bring your tapes?' She wasted no precious words on any other greeting. 'This way. Old Grantley Basic, Jane said. You've got the language with you. Do you want to load it, or shall I?'

'I'd be glad if—'

'Hand them over, then. Which side?'

'Er, first program on Side 1.'

'Right. Come along.'

She moved with the same inborn rapidity, disappearing down a short passage and through a doorway before I'd even managed a step. She must always find, I thought, that the rest of the world went along intolerably in slow motion.

The room into which I finally followed her must originally have been designed as a bedroom, which it now in no way resembled. There was a quiet, felt-like pale green floor covering, track-lighting with spotlights, a roller blind at the window, matt white walls – and long benches of machines more or less like Ted Pitts's, only double.

'Workroom,' Ruth Quigley said.

'Eh, yes.'

It was cooler in there than out on the street. I identified a faint background hum as air-conditioning, and remarked on it.

She nodded, not lifting her eyes from the already almost completed job of loading Grantley Basic into a machine that would accept it. 'Dust is like gravel to computers. Heat, damp, all makes them temperamental. They're thoroughbreds, of course.'

Racing programs ... thoroughbred computers. Excellence won. Pains taken gave one the edge. I was beginning to think like her, I thought.

'I'm wasting your time,' I said apologetically.

'Glad to help. Always do anything for Jane and Ted. They know that. Did you bring the form books? You'll need them. Simple programs, but facts must be right. Most teaching-machines, just the same. They bore me quite often. Multiple-choice questions. Then the child takes half an hour to get it right and I put it in a bright remark like. "Well done, aren't you clever." Nothing of the sort. Encouragement, they say, is all. What do you think?'

'Are they gifted children?'

She gave me a flashing glance. 'All children are gifted. Some more so. They need the best teaching. They often don't get it. Teachers are jealous, did you know?'

'My brother always said it was intensely exciting to have a very bright boy in the class.'

'Like Ted, generous. There you are, fire away. I'll be in and out, don't let me disturb you. I'm working on a sort-listing of string arrays. They said it was taking them eighteen minutes, I ask you. I've got it down to five seconds, but only one dimension. I need two dimensions if I'm not to scramble the data. I'm poking a machine-language program into the memory from BASIC, then converting the machine code into assembly-language economics. Am I boring you?'

'No,' I said. 'I just don't understand a word of it.'

'Sorry. Forgot you weren't like Ted. Well, carry on.'

I had brought in a large briefcase the tapes, the racing form books, all sorts of record books and all the recent copies of a good racing paper, and with a feeling that by Ruth Quigley's standards it was going to take a very long time I set about working out which horses were *likely* to have won according to Liam O'Rorke, and checking them against those which had actually reached the post first. I still needed a list of horses which Angelo had backed, but I thought I might get that from Taff and from Lancer on the following day: and *then* I might be able to figure out where Angelo had messed everything up.

FILE NAME?

CLOAD DONCA, I typed. Pressed the 'Enter' key, and watched the asterisks; waited for READY. Pressed 'Enter' again and got my reward.

WHICH RACE AT DONCASTER?

ST LEGER, I typed.

DONCASTER: ST LEGER. TYPE NAME OF HORSE AND PRESS 'ENTER'.

GENOTTI, I typed. Pressed 'Enter'.

DONCASTER: ST LEGER.

GENOTTI.

ANSWER ALL QUESTIONS YES OR NO OR WITH A NUMBER AND PRESS 'ENTER'.

HAS HORSE WON AS A TWO YEAR OLD?

YES, I typed. The screen flashed a new question leaving the headings intact.

HAS HORSE WON AS A THREE YEAR OLD?

YES, I typed.

HOW MANY DAYS SINCE HORSE LAST RAN?

I consulted the daily newspaper which always gave that precise information, and typed in the number which had appeared there on St Leger day: 23.

HAS HORSE WON OVER DISTANCE: ONE MILE SIX FURLONGS?

NO, I typed.

HAS HORSE RUN OVER DISTANCE: ONE MILE SIX FURLONGS?

NO.

TYPE LONGEST DISTANCE IN FURLONGS OVER WHICH HORSE HAS WON.

12

HAS HORSE RUN ON COURSE?

NO.

TYPE IN PRIZE MONEY WON IN CURRENT SEASON.

I consulted the form books and typed Genotti's winnings, which had been fairly good but not stupendous.

HAS HORSE'S SIRE SIRED WINNERS AT THE DISTANCE?

I looked it up in the breeding records, which took much longer, but the answer was YES.

DAM ditto?

YES.

IS HORSE QUOTED ANTE-POST AT TWELVE TO ONE OR LESS?

YES.

HAS JOCKEY PREVIOUSLY WON A CLASSIC?

YES.

HAS TRAINER PREVIOUSLY WON A CLASSIC?

YES.

ANY MORE HORSES?

YES.

I found myself back at the beginning and repeated the program for every horse which had run in the race. The questions weren't always precisely the same, because different answers produced alternative queries, and for some horses there were far more questions than for others. It took me a good hour to look everything up, and I thought that if I ever did begin to do it all seriously I would make myself a whole host of more easily accessible tables than those available in the record books. When I at last answered NO to the final question ANY MORE HORSES? I got the clear reply that left no doubt about Liam O'Rorke's genius.

Genotti headed the win factor list. An outsider turned up on it in second place, with the horse that had started favourite in third: and the St Leger result had been those three horses in that order exactly.

I could hardly believe it.

Ruth Quigley said suddenly, 'Got the wrong result? You look flummoxed.'

'No – the right one.'

'Disturbing.' She grinned swiftly. 'If I get the results I expect, I check and check and check. Doesn't do to be complacent. Like some coffee?'

I accepted and she made it as fast as she did everything else.

'How old are you?' I said.

'Twenty-one. Why?'

'I'd have thought you'd have been at the university.'

'Degree at twenty plus one month. Nothing unusual. Cheated my way in, of course. Everything's so slow nowadays. Forty years ago, degrees at nineteen or less were possible. Now they insist on calendar age. Why? Why hold people back? Life's terribly short as it is. Masters degree at twenty plus six months. Did the two courses simultaneously. No one knew. Don't spread it around. Doing my doctorate now. Are you interested?'

'Yes,' I said truthfully.

She smiled like a summer's day, come and gone. 'My father says I'm a bore.

'He doesn't mean it.'

'He's a surgeon,' she said, as if that explained much. 'So's my mother. Guilt complexes, both of them. Give to mankind more than you take. That sort of thing. They can't help it.'

'And you?'

'I don't know yet. I can't give much. I can't get jobs I can do. They look at the years I've been alive and make judgements. Quite deadly. Time has practically nothing to do with anything. They'll give me the jobs when I'm thirty that I could do better now. Poets and mathematicians are best before twenty-five. What chance have they got?'

'To work alone,' I said.

'My God. Do you understand? You're wasting time, get on with your programs. Don't show me what I should do. I've got a research fellowship. What do I seek for? What is there to seek? Where is the unknown, what is not known, what's the question?'

I shook my head helplessly, 'Wait for the apple to fall on your head.'

'It's true. I can't contemplate. Sitting under the apple trees. Metaphorical apples trees. I've tried. Get on with your nags.'

Philosophically I loaded YORK and worked through the three races for which there were programs and found that in two of them the highest-scoring horse had won. Three winners from the four races I'd worked through. Incredible.

With a feeling of unreality I loaded EPSOM and went painstakingly through the four races for which there were programs; and this time came up with no winners at all. Frowning slightly I loaded NEWBU for Newbury and from a good deal of hard accurate work came up with the win factors of the race in which Angelo had backed the absolute no-hoper Pocket Handbook.

Pocket Handbook, who had finished exhausted and tailed-off by at least thirty lengths, was at the top of the win-factor list by a clear margin.

I stared distrustfully at the rest of the scores, which put the race's actual winner second from the bottom with negligible points.

'What's the matter?' Ruth Quigley said, busy at her own machine and not even glancing my way.

'Parts of the system are haywire.'

'Really?'

I loaded GOODW and sorted through fives races. All the top scorers were horses which in the events had finished no nearer than second.

'Are you hungry?' Ruth said. 'Three-thirty. Sandwich?'

I thanked her and went with her into her small kitchen where I was interested to see that her speed stopped short of dexterity with slicing tomatoes. She quite slowly, for her, made fat juicy affairs of cheese, chutney, tomatoes and corned beef which toppled precariously on the plate and had to be held in both hands for eating.

'Logical explanations exist,' she said, looking at my abstracted expression. 'Human logic's imperfect. Absolute logic isn't.'

'Mm,' I said. 'Ted showed me how easy it is to add and delete passwords.'

'So?'

'It would be pretty easy, wouldn't it, to change other things besides?'

'Unless it's in ROM. Then it's difficult.'

'ROM?'

'Read Only Memory. Sorry.'

'He showed me how to List things.'

'You've got RAM, then. Random Access Memory. Change what you like. Kids' stuff.'

We finished the sandwiches and returned to the keyboards. I loaded the Newbury file, chose the Pocket Handbook race and listed the program piece by piece.

LIST 1200–1240 I typed, and in front of the resulting screenful of letters, numbers and symbols sat figuring out the roots of trouble.

```
1200 PRINT "TYPE IN PRIZE MONEY IN CURRENT SEASON"
1210 INPUT W: IF W < 1000 THEN T = T + 20
```

```
1220 IF W < 1000 THEN T = T: IF W > 5000 T = T
1230 IF W > 10000 THEN T = T: IF W > 15000 THEN T = T
1240 GOSUB 6000
```

Even to my ignorant and untutored eyes it was nonsense. Liam O'Rorke wouldn't have meant it, Peter Keithly wouldn't have written it, Ted Pitts would never have used it. In plain language, what it was saying was that if the season's winnings of a horse were *less* than one thousand pounds, the win factor score should be increased by 20, and if they were *more* than one thousand, and however much more, the win factor score would not increase at all. The least successful horses would therefore score most highly on that particular point. The weighting was topsy-turvey and the answers would come out wrong.

With the hollow certainty of what had happened staring me in the face, I loaded the Epsom file and searched the Lists of the programs for the four races on which Angelo had lost. In two cases the weightings for prize money were upside down.

Tried Goodwood. In three of the five listed races, the same thing.

Depressed beyond measure, I loaded the files for Leicester and Ascot, where races were to be held during the week ahead. Typed in the names of all the races to be run there and found there were programs for eight of them: one at Leicester, seven at Ascot. Listed each of the eight programs in sections, and found that in four of them the score for amassing much prize money was nought, and the score for prize money of under one thousand pounds was anything up to 20.

There were programs for some races at all the tracks which I knew for a certainty were not fourteen years old. Modern races, introduced since Liam O'Rorke had died.

The programs were no longer pure O'Rorke, but O'Rorke according to Pitts. O'Rorke updated, expanded, renewed. O'Rorke, on these particular tapes, interfered with, falsified, mangled. Ted Pitts – one had to face it – had wrecked the system before he'd handed it to me ... and had delivered me defenceless to the wrath of Angelo Gilbert.

I thanked the frustrated and brilliant Miss Quigley for her day-long patience and drove home to Cassie.

'What's the matter?' she said immediately.

I said wearily, 'The ess aitch I tee has hit the fan.'

'What do you *mean*?'

'Angelo thinks I've tricked him. That the betting system I gave him is wrong. That it produces too many losers. Well so it does. Normally it must be all right but on these tapes it's been altered. Ted Pitts has rigged so many of the programs that anyone using them will fall flat on his greedy face.' And I explained about the reversed scores for winning, which produced scatty results. 'He may also have changed some of the other weightings to get the same effect. I've no way of knowing.'

She looked as stunned as I felt. 'Do you mean Ted Pitts did it on *purpose*?'

'He sure did.' I thought back to the time he'd taken to make me 'copies'; to the hour I'd spent sitting by his pool talking to Jane, leaving him, at his own request, to work alone.

'But why?' Cassie said.

'I don't know.

'You didn't tell him, did you, what you wanted the tapes for?'

'No, I didn't.'

She said doubtfully, 'Perhaps it might have been better if you'd said how vital they were.'

'And perhaps he wouldn't have given them to me at all if he'd known I had Angelo locked in the cellar. I mean, I thought he might not want to be *involved.* Most people wouldn't, with something like that. And then, if he was like Jonathan, he might have changed the weightings anyway, just to prevent Angelo from profiting. You never know. Jonathan himself would somehow have tricked Angelo again. I'm sure of it.'

'You don't think Ted Pitts asked Jonathan what he should do, do you?'

I thought back and shook my head. 'It was before nine in the morning when I went to the Pitts's house. That would make it about one a.m. in California. Even if he had his number, which I doubt, I don't think he would have telephoned Jonathan in the middle of the night ... and Jonathan anyway sounded truly disappointed when I told him I'd given Angelo the tapes. No, Ted must have done it for his own reasons, and by himself.'

'Which doesn't help much.'

I shook my head.

I thought of the certainty with which I'd gone to Harry Gilbert's house on the previous day. Hell's teeth, how wrong could one be, how naïve could one get?

If I wanted Angelo not to use the tapes in the week ahead he would be sure I had tricked him and was scared to death of his revenge.

If I didn't warn him not to use the tapes, he would most likely lose again and be more sure than ever that I'd tricked him ...

If I wrung the right answers out of Ted Pitts and told them to Angelo, he would still think I had deliberately given him useless tapes – on which he had already lost.

Ted Pitts was in Switzerland walking up mountains.

'Would you care,' I said to Cassie, 'for a long slow cruise to Australia?'

Chapter Nineteen

Jane Pitts on the telephone said, 'No, terribly sorry, he moves about and stops in different places every night. Quite often he sleeps in his tent. Is it important?'

'Horriby,' I said.

'Oh dear. Could I help?'

'There's something wrong with those tapes he made for me. Could you by any chance lend me his own?'

'No, I simply can't. I'm frightfully sorry but I don't know where he keeps anything in that room and he positively hates his things being touched.' She thought for a few minutes, puzzled but not unwilling, friendly, anxious to help. 'Look, he's sure to call me one day soon to say when he'll be home. Would you like me to ask him to ring you?'

'Yes please,' I said fervently. 'Or ask him where I can reach him, and I'll call him. Do tell him it's really urgent, beg him for me, would you? Say it's for Jonathan's sake more than mine.'

'I'll tell him,' she promised, 'as soon as he rings.'

'You're unscrupulous,' Cassie said as I put down the receiver. 'It's for your sake, not Jonathan's.'

'He wouldn't want to weep on his brother's grave.'

'*William!*'

'A joke,' I said hastily. 'A joke.'

Cassie shivered, however. 'What are you going to do?'

'Think,' I said.

The basic thought was that the more Angelo lost, the angrier he would get, and that the first objective was therefore to stop him betting. Taff and the others could hardly be persuaded not to accept such easy pickings, which left the source of the cash, Harry Gilbert himself. Precisely what, I wondered, could I say to Harry Gilbert which would cut off the stake money without sending Angelo straight round to vent his rage?

I could tell him that Liam O'Rorke's system no longer existed: that I'd got the tapes in good faith but had been tricked myself. I could tell him a lot of half-truths, but whether he would believe me, and whether he could restrain Angelo even if he himself were convinced, of those imponderables there was no forecast.

Realistically there was nothing else to do.

I didn't particularly want to try to trap Angelo into being sent back to jail: fourteen years was enough for any man. I only wanted, as I had all along, for him to leave me alone. I wanted him deflated defused ... docile. What a hope.

A night spent with my mind on pleasanter things produced no cleverer plan. A paragraph in the *Sporting Life*, read over a quick breakfast after an hour with the horses on the Heath, made me wish that Angelo would solve my problems himself by bashing someone else on the head: about as unlikely as him having a good week on the system. Lancer the bookmaker said the paper, had been mugged on his own doorstep on returning from Newbury races on Friday evening. His wallet, containing approximately fifty-three pounds, had been stolen. Lancer was OK, police had no leads: poor old Lancer, too bad.

I sighed. Who, I wondered, could I get Angelo to bash?

Besides, of course, myself.

On account of the knee-groper, I was driving Cassie to work whenever possible, and on that morning after I'd dropped her I went straight on to Welwyn Garden City, not relishing my prospects but with not much alternative. I hoped to persuade both Harry Gilbert and Angelo that the havoc the years had caused to the O'Rorke system couldn't be undone, that it was blown, no longer existed, couldn't be recovered. I was going to tell them again that any violence from Angelo would find him back in a cell; to try to make them believe it ... to fear it.

I was taller than Angelo and towered over a man in a wheelchair. I intended slightly to crowd them, faintly to intimidate, certainly to leave a physical impression that it was time for them to back off. Even on Angelo, who must have known how to frighten from childhood, it might have some effect.

Eddy opened the front doors and tried at once to close them again when he saw who had called. I pushed him with force out of my way.

'Harry isn't dressed,' he said fearfully, though whether the fear was of me or of Harry wasn't clear.

'He'll see me,' I said.

'No. You can't.' He tried to bar my way to one of the wide doors at the side of the entrance hall, thereby showing me which way to go, and I walked over there with Eddy trying to edge me out of my path by leaning on me.

I thrust him again aside and opened the door, and found myself in a short passage which led into a large bedroom which was equipped first and most noticeably with another vast window looking out to the golf.

Harry Gilbert lay in a big bed facing the window, ill and growing old but still in some indefinable way not defenceless, even in pyjamas.

'I tried to stop him,' Eddy was saying ineffectually.

'Take this tray and go away,' Harry Gilbert said to him, and Eddy picked off the bedclothes the half-eaten breakfast which I had interrupted. 'Shut the door.' He waited until Eddy had retreated and then frostily to me said, 'Well?'

'I've discovered,' I said with urgency, 'that Liam O'Rorke's betting system has the equivalent of smallpox. It should be treated like the plague. It'll bring trouble to all who touch it. The old system has been through too many hands, been adulterated by the years. It's gone bad. If you want to save your cash, you'll stop Angelo using it, and it's pointless getting angry with me on any counts. I got the system for you in good faith and I'm furious to find it's useless. Bring Angelo in here and let me tell him.'

Harry Gilbert stared at me with his usual unreadable face, and it was without any visible consternation that he said in his semi-slurred way, 'Angelo isn't here. He is cashing my cheque at the bank. He is going to Leicester races.'

'He will lose,' I said. 'I didn't need to warn you. I'm warning you. Your money will be lost.'

Thoughts must have traversed the brain behind the cold eyes but nothing much showed. Finally, and it must have been with an inner effort, he said, 'Can you stop him?'

'Stop the cheque,' I said. 'Call the bank.'

He glanced at a clock beside him. 'Too late.'

'I can go to Leicester,' I said. 'I'll try to find him.'

After a pause he said, 'Very well.'

I nodded briefly and left him, and drove towards Leicester feeling that even if I had managed to convince Harry, which was in itself uncertain, I was facing the impossible with Angelo. The impossible all the same had to be tried: and at least, I thought, he wouldn't actually attack me on a busy racecourse.

Leicester races on that cold autumn day turned out to be as busy as a well-smoked beehive, with only a scattering of dark-coated figures trudging about doggedly, head-down to the biting wind. As sometimes happened on city-based tracks on weekdays, the crowd was thin to the point of embarrassment, the whole proceedings imbued with the perfunctory and temporary air of a ritual taking place without fervour.

Taff was stamping about by his beer crate, blowing on his fingers and complaining that he would have done better business if he'd gone to the day's other meeting at Bath.

'But there's the Midlands Cup here,' he said. 'It'll be a good race. I thought it would pull them – and look at them, not enough punters to sing auld lang syne round a teapot.' The Welsh accent was ripe with disgust.

'What are you making favourite?' I said smiling.

'Pink Flowers.'

'And what about Terrybow?'

'Who?'

'Runs in the Midlands Cup,' I said patiently. Terrybow, the computer's choice, top of the win factors. Terrybow with a habit of finishing tenth of twelve, or seventh of eight, or fifteenth of twenty: never actually last but a long way from success.

'Oh, Terrybox.' He consulted a notebook. 'Twenties, if you like.'

'Twenty to one?'

'Twenty-fives then. Can't say fairer than twenty-five. How much do you want?'

'How much would you take?'

'Whatever you like,' he said cheerfully. 'No limit. Not unless you know something I don't, like it's stuffed to the eyeballs with rocket dust.'

I shook my head and looked along the row of cold disgruntled bookmakers who were doing a fraction of their usual trade. If Angelo had been among them I would have seen him easily, but there was no sign of him. The Midlands Cup was the fourth race on the programme and still and hour ahead, and if Angelo was sticking rigidly to the disaster-laden system, Terrybow would be the only horse he would back.

'Have you seen Angelo Gilbert here today, Taff?' I asked.

'No.' He took a bet from a furtive-looking man in a raincoat and gave him a ticket. 'Ten at threes, Walkie-Talkie,' he told his clerk.

'How's Lancer?' I asked. 'Can't see him here.'

'Cursing muggers and rubbing a lump.' He took another tenner from a purposeful woman in glasses. 'Ten at eights, Engineer. Some kids rolled old Lancer on his own doorstep. I ask you, he carries thousands around the racecourse, pays it in to his firm at the end of the day, and then goes and gets himself done for fifty quid.'

'Did he see who robbed him?'

'One of Joe Glick's other boys who's here said it was a bunch of teenagers.'

Not Angelo, I thought. Well, it wouldn't have been. But if only he *would* . . .

I looked speculatively at Taff, who worked for himself and did carry his takings home at the end of the day. Pity one couldn't catch Angelo in the act of trying to retrieve his stake money after Terrybow had lost . . . pity one couldn't arrange for the police to be on hand when Angelo mugged Taff on the way home.

I'm down to fantasies, I thought: it's depressing.

The time passed and Angelo, who had been so ubiquitous when I had been trying to avoid him, was nowhere to be seen. I walked among the bookmakers and asked others besides Taff, but none of them had seen Angelo all that afternoon, and there was still no sign of him during the run-up to the Midlands Cup. If he had gone to Bath after all, I thought, I was wasting my time – but the only race that day on the O'Rorke tapes was the Midlands Cup; it's only designated horse, Terrybow.

With less than five minutes to go, when the horses were already cantering down to the start, a tremendous burst of tic-tac activity galvanised the men with white gloves high on the stands who semaphored changes of odds. With no direct link like telephones or radio the bookmakers relied on tic-tac to tell them if large sums had been placed with their firms on any particular horse, so that they could bring down the offered price. Taff, watching his man signalling frenziedly, rubbed out the 20 written against Terrybow on his blackboard and with his piece of chalk wrote in 14. Along the row all the other bookies were similarly engaged. Terrybow fell again to 12.

'What's happening?' I said to Taff urgently.

He cast an abstracted eye in my direction. 'Someone down in the cheap ring is piling a stack on Terrybow.'

'*Damn*,' I said bitterly. I hadn't thought of looking for Angelo anywhere but round his usual haunts: certainly not in the comfortless far enclosure away down the course where the entrance fee was small, the view of the races moderate, and the expectation of the few bookmakers trading there modest to the point of not being worth standing in the cold all afternoon. And even if I'd thought of it I wouldn't have gone there, because it would have meant risking missing Angelo in the paddock. Damn and blast, I thought. Damn Angelo today and all days and for the whole of his life.

'You knew something about this Terrybow,' Taff said to me accusingly.

'I didn't back it,' I said.

'Yeah, that's right, so you didn't. So what's going on?'

'Angelo Gilbert,' I said. 'He's betting where he isn't known in case you wouldn't give him a good price up here.'

'What? Really?' He laughed, rubbed out the 12 against Terrybow and replaced it with 20. A small rush of punters resulted and he took their money with relish.

I went up on the stands and watched in a fury while Terrybow ran true to his form and drifted in twelfth of fifteen. Ted Pitts, I thought bleakly, might as well have shoved me under the wheels of a truck.

I did see Angelo that afternoon, and so did practically everyone else who hadn't gone home before the sixth race.

Angelo was the angrily shouting epicentre of a fracas going on near the weighing-room; a row involving several bookmakers, a host of racegoers and some worried looking officials. Disputes between bookmakers and clients were traditionally dealt with on that spot by one particular Jockey Club official, the Ring Inspector. Angelo appeared to have punched him in the face.

The milling crowd parted a little and shifted and I found myself standing near the front of the onlookers with a clear view of the performance. The Ring Inspector was holding his jaw and trying to argue around his winces, six bookmakers were declaring passionately that money once wagered was lost for ever, and Angelo, waving his hard bunched fist, was insisting they gave it back.

'You tricked me,' he shouted. 'The whole bloody lot of you, you stole my cash.'

'You bet it fair and square,' yelled a bookmaker, wagging a finger forcefully in Angelo's face.

Angelo bit his finger. The bookmaker yelled all the harder.

A man standing next to me laughed but most of the onlookers had less objectively taken sides and it seemed that a general brawl needed only a flashpoint. Into the ugliness and among the angrily gesturing hands and violent voices walked two uniformed policemen, both very young, both slight, both looking poor opponents in size and forcefulness for the prison-taught Angelo. The Ring Inspector said something to one of them which was inaudible to me in the hubbub and to his immense and visible surprise Angelo suddenly found himself wearing, on the wrist he happened not to be waving in the air at that moment, a handcuff.

His bellow of rage fluttered the pigeons off the weighing-room roof. He tugged with his whole weight and the boy-policeman whose own wrist protruded from the other cuff was jerked off his feet onto his knees. It looked not impossible that Angelo could pick him up bodily and simply run off with him, but the second constable came to his rescue, saying something boldly to Angelo and pulling his radio-communicator out of the front of his uniform jacket to bring up reinforcements.

Angelo looked at the ring of spectators through which he had little real hope of pushing and at his unexpectedly adroit captor, now rising from his knees, and at the seething bookmakers who were showing signs of satisfaction, and finally straight at me.

He took a step towards me which such strength that the half-risen policeman lost his balance again and fell on his back, his arm twisting awkwardly over his head, stretching in the handcuff. There was about Angelo suddenly such an extraordinary growth of menace, something so different from a mere racecourse argument, that the thronging voices fell away to silence and eyes looked at him with age-old fright. The monstrous recklessness seemed to swell his whole body, and even if his words were banal his gritty voice vibrated with a darkness straight out of myth.

'You,' he said deliberately, 'you and your fucking brother.'

There was an awareness in his face of the attentive crowd of witnesses around us and he didn't say aloud what was in his mind, but I could hear it as clearly as if he'd woken the sleeping hills.

I'll kill you. *I'll kill you.*

It was a message not so much new as newly intense. More than ever implacable. A promise, not a threat.

I stared back at him as if I hadn't heard, as if it wasn't there looking at me out of his eyes. He nodded however as if savagely satisfied and turned with a contemptuous shrug to the rising policeman, jerking him the last few inches upright; and he went, after that, without fighting, walking away between the two constables towards a police car which was driving in through the gates. The car halted. They put him in the back seat between them and presently rolled away, and the now strangely quiet crowd began to spread open and disperse.

A voice in my ear, the Welsh voice of Taff, said, 'You know what set all that off?'

'What?' I said.

'The bookies down in the cheap ring told Angelo he was a right mug. They were laughing at him, it seems. Joshing him, but friendly like to start with. They said they'd be happy to keep on taking his money because if he thought he'd bought Liam O'Rorke's old system he'd been robbed, duped, bamboozled, made a fool of and generally conned from here to Christmas.'

Dear God.

'So then this Angelo sort of exploded and started trying to get his stake back.'

'Yes,' I said.

'Well,' Taff said cheerfully. 'It all makes a change, though I reckon those goons in the cheap ring would have done better to keep their mouths shut. That Angelo was a bit of a golden goose and after this he won't lay no more golden eggs.'

I drove home with a feeling that the seas were closing over my head. Whatever I did to try to disentangle myself from Angelo it seemed that I slid further into the coils.

He was never, after this, going to believe that I hadn't tricked him on purpose. Even if I could at last get him the real correct system, he wouldn't forgive me the bets lost, the sneers of the bookmakers, the click of those handcuffs.

The police might hold him overnight, I thought, but not much longer: I doubted if one punch and a few yells would upset his parole. But to the tally in his mind would be added a night in the cells to rankle with those in my cellar – and if he'd come out of prison angry enough to attack me with nothing against me but the fact of my being Jonathan's brother, how much more would he now come swinging.

Cassie had long been home when I finally got there and was buoyantly pleased with the prospect of having the plaster off her arm on the following afternoon. She had arranged a whole day off from work and had thanked the groper for the last time, confident that she would be able to drive more or less at once. She was humming in the kitchen while I cooked some spaghetti for supper and I kissed her abstractedly and thought of Angelo and wished him dead with all my heart.

Before we had finished eating, the telephone rang and, most unexpectedly, it was Ted Pitts calling from Switzerland. His voice, on the whole, was as cool as the Alps.

'Thought I'd better apologize,' he said.

'It's kind of you.'

'Jane's disgusted with me. She told me to ring you at once. She said it was urgent. So here I am. Sorry, and all that.'

'I just wondered,' I said hopelessly, 'why you did it.'

'Mashed up the weightings?'

'Yes.'

'You'll think I'm mean. Jane says I'm so mean she's ashamed of me. She's furious. She says all our wealth is due to Jonathan, and I've played the most rotten trick on Jonathan's brother. She's hardly speaking to me she's so cross.'

'Well ... *why?*' I said.

He did at least seem to want me to understand. He spoke earnestly, explaining, excusing, telling me the destructive truth. 'I don't know.

It was an impulse. I was making those copies and I suddently thought I don't want to part with this system. I don't want anyone else to have it. It's mine. Not Jonathan's, just mine. He didn't even want it, and I've had it to myself all these years, and I've added to it and made it my own. It belongs to me. It's *mine*. And there you were, just asking for it as if I would give it to you as of right, and I suddenly thought why should I? So I just quickly changed a lot of the weightings. I didn't have time to test them. I had to guess. I altered just enough, I thought, but it seems I did too much. Otherwise you wouldn't have checked ... I intended that when you used the system, you wouldn't win enough to think it worth all the work, and you'd get tired of it.' He paused. 'I was jealous of you having it, if you really want to know.'

'I wish you'd told me ...'

'If I'd said I didn't want to give it to you, Jane would have made me. She says I must now. She's so cross.'

'If you would,' I said, 'you might save me a lot of grief.'

'Make your fortune, you mean.' The apology, it seemed, hadn't come from the heart: he still sounded resentful that I should be learning his secrets.

I thought again about telling him about Angelo but it still seemed to me that he might think it the best reason for *not* giving me the system that I could devise, so I said merely, 'It could work for two people, couldn't it? If someone else had it, it wouldn't stop you yourself winning as much as ever.'

'I suppose,' he said grudgingly, 'that that's true.'

'So ... when do you come home?'

'The week after next.'

I was silent. Appalled. By the week after next heaven knew what Angelo would have done.

Ted Pitts said with half-suppressed annoyance, 'I suppose you've betted heavily on the wrong horses and lost too much, and now you need bailing out a lot sooner than the week after next?'

I didn't dispute it.

'Jane's furious. She's afraid I've cost you more than you can afford. Well, I'm sorry.' He didn't truly sound it.

'Could she find the tapes to give to me?' I said humbly.

'How soon do you need them?'

'More or less at once. Tonight, if possible.'

'Hmph.' He thought for a few moments. 'All right. All right. But you can save yourself the journey, if you like.'

'Er, how?'

'Do you have a tape recorder?'

'Yes.'

'Jane can play the tapes to you over the telephone. They'll sound like a lot of screeching. But if you've a half-way decent recorder the programs will run all right on a computer.'

'Good heavens.'

'A lot of computer programs whiz round the world on telephones every day,' he said. 'And up to the satellites and down again. Nothing extraordinary in it.'

To me it did seem extraordinary, but then I wasn't Ted Pitts. I thanked him with more intensity than he knew for his trouble in ringing me up.

'Thank Jane,' he said.

I did thank her, sincerely, five minutes later.

'You sounded in such *trouble*,' she said. 'I told Ted I'd sent you to Ruth because you'd wanted to check the tapes, and he *groaned*, so I asked him why ... and when he told me what he'd done I was just *furious*. To think of you wasting your precious money when everything we have is thanks to Jonathan.'

Her kindness made me feel guilty. I said, 'Ted said you could play the real tapes to me over the telephone – if you wouldn't mind.'

'Oh yes, all right. I've seen Ted do it often. He and Ruth are always swopping programs that way. I've got the tapes here beside me. I made Ted tell me where to find them. I'll go and get the recorder now, if you'll hang on, and then I'll play them to you straight away.'

I had called her from the office because of the message-recorder already fitted to that telephone, and when she returned I recorded the precious programs on Luke's supply of fresh unused tapes which might not have been of prime computer standard but were all the same a better bet, I reckoned, than trying to record a new machine language on top of old.

Cassie came into the office and listened to the scratchy whining noises running on and on.

'Horrible,' she said: but to me, sweet music. A ransom to the future. Passport to a peaceful world. In a sudden uprush of optimism entirely at variance with the gloom of my drive home from Leicester, I convinced myself that this time, now that we had the genuine article, our troubles would come to an end. The solution was still, as it had always been, to make Angelo rich, and at last it could be done.

'I'll give these tapes to Angelo,' I said, 'and we'll go away from the cottage for just a while, a few weeks, just until he's won enough not to want his revenge. And we'll be free of him at last, thank God.'

'Where shall we go?'

'Not far. Decide tomorrow.'

When the three tapes were full and the noises fell quiet I switched off the recording part of the machine and spoke again to Jane.

'I'm grateful,' I said. 'More than I can say.'

'My dear William, I'm so sorry ...'

'Don't be,' I said. 'You've saved my life.' Quite literally, probably, I thought. 'Everything,' I said, 'will be all right.'

One shouldn't say such things. One really shouldn't.

Chapter Twenty

Cassie came with me in the early morning to see the horses work on the Heath, shivering a little in boots, trousers and padded husky jacket, but glad, she said, to be alive in the free air and the wide spaces. Her breath, like mine, like that of all the horses, spurted out in lung-shaped plumes of condensing vapour, chilled and gone in a second and quickly renewed, cold transformed to heat within the miracle of bodies.

We had already in a preliminary fashion left the cottage, having packed clothes and necessaries and stowed the suitcases in my car. I had also brought along a briefcase containing the precious tapes and a lot of Luke's paperwork and had re-routed my telephone calls by a message on the answer-system, and it remained only to make a quick return trip to pick up the day's mail and arrange for future postal deliveries to be left at the pub.

We hadn't actually decided where we would sleep that night or for many nights to come, but we did between us have a great many friends who might be cajoled, and if the traditional open-house generosity of the racing world failed us, we could for a while afford a hotel. I felt freer and more light-hearted than I had for weeks.

Sim was positively welcoming on the gallops and Mort asked us to breakfast. We shivered gratefully into his house and warmed up with him on toast and coffee while he slit open his letters with a paper-knife and made comments on what he was at the same time reading in the *Sporting Life*. Mort never did one thing at a time if he could do three.

'I've re-routed my telephone messages to you,' I told him. 'Do you mind?'

'Have you? No, of course not. Why?

'The cottage,' I said, 'is at the moment uninhabitable.'

'Decorators?' He sounded sympathetic and it seemed simplest to say yes.

'There won't be many calls,' I promised. 'Just Luke's business.'

'Sure,' he said. He sucked in a boiled egg in two scoops of a spoon. 'More coffee?'

'How are the yearlings settling?' I asked.

'Come and see them. Come this afternoon, we'll be lungeing them in the paddock.'

'What's lungeing?' Cassie said.

Mort gave her a fast forgiving smile and snapped his fingers a few times. 'Letting them run round in a big circle on the end of a long rein.

Gives them exercise. No one rides them yet. They've never been saddled. Too young.'

'I'd like that,' Cassie said, looking thoughtfully at the plaster and clearly wondering about the timing.

'Where are you staying?' Mort asked me. 'Where can I find you?'

'Don't know yet,' I said.

'Really? What about here? There's a bed here, if you like.' He crunched his teeth across half a piece of toast and ate it in one gulp. 'You could answer your own phone calls. Makes sense.'

'Well,' I said. 'For a night or two . . . very grateful.'

'Settled then.' He grinned cheerfully at Cassie. 'My daughter will be pleased. Got no wife, you know. She scarpered. Miranda gets bored, that's my daughter. Sixteen, needs a girl's company. Stay for a week. How long do you need?'

'We don't know,' Cassie said.

He nodded briskly. 'Take things as they come. Very sensible.' He casually picked up the paperknife and began cleaning his nails with it, reminding me irresistibly of Jonathan who throughout my childhood had done his with the point of a rifle bullet.

'I thought I'd go to Ireland at the weekend,' I said, 'and try to make peace with Donavan.'

Mort gave me a blinding grin, 'I hear you're a turd and an ignorant bastard, and should be dragged six times round the Curragh by your heels. At the least.'

The telephone standing on the table by his elbow rang only once, sharply, before Mort was shouting 'Hullo?' down the receiver. 'Oh,' he said, 'Hullo, Luke.' He made signalling messages to me with his eyebrows. 'Yes, he's here right now, having breakfast.' He handed over the receiver, saying, 'Luke rang your number first, he says.'

'William,' Luke said, sounding relaxed and undemanding. 'How are the new yearlings?'

'Fine. No bad reports.'

'Thought I'd come over to see them. See what you've gotten me. I feel like a trip. Listen fella, do me a favour, make me some reservations at the Bedford Arms for two nights, fourteenth and fifteenth October?'

'Right' I said.

'Best to Cassie,' he said. 'Bring her to dinner at the Bedford on the fourteenth, OK? I'd sure like to meet her. And fella, I'll be going on to Dublin. You aiming to go to the Ballsbridge Sales?'

'Yeah, I thought to. Ralph Finnigan died . . . they're selling all his string.'

Luke sounded appreciative. 'What would you pick, fella? What's the best?'

'Oxidise. Two years old, well bred, fast, a prospect for next June's Derby and bound to be expensive.'

Luke gave a sort of rumbling grunt. 'You'd send it to Donavan?'

'I sure would.'

The grunt became a chuckle. 'See you, fella, on the fourteenth.'

There was a click and he was gone. Mort said, 'Is he coming?' and I nodded and told him when. 'Most years he comes in October,' Mort said.

He asked if we'd like to see the second lot exercise but I was anxious to be finished at the cottage so Cassie and I drove the six miles back to the village and stopped first at the pub. Mine host, who had been invisible earlier, was now outside in his shirtsleeves sweeping dead leaves off his doorstep.

'Aren't you cold?' Cassie said.

Bananas, perspiring in contrast to our huskies, said he had been shifting beer barrels in his cellar.

We explained about going away for a while, and why.

'Come inside,' he said, finishing the leaves. 'Like some coffee?'

We drank some with him in the bar but without the ice cream and brandy he stirred into his own. 'Sure,' he said amiably. 'Ill take in your mail. Also papers, milk, whatever you like. Anything else?'

'How absolutely extravagantly generous are you feeling?' Cassie said.

He gave her a sideways squint over his frothy mugful, 'Spill it,' he said.

'My little yellow car is booked in today for a service and its road test, and I just wondered . . .'

'If I'd drive it along to that big garage for you?'

'William will bring you back,' she said persuasively.

'For you, Cassie, anything,' he said. 'Straightaway.'

'Plaster off this afternoon,' she said happily, and I looked at her clear grey eyes and thought that I loved her so much it was ridiculous. Don't ever leave me, I thought. Stay around for ever. It would be lonely now without you . . . It would be agony.

We all went in my car along to the cottage and I left it out in the road because of Cassie wanting Bananas to back her little yellow peril out of the garage onto the driveway. She and he walked towards the garage doors to open them and I, half watching them, went across to unlock the front door and retrieve the letters which would have fallen on the mat just inside.

The cottage lay so quiet and still that our precautions seemed unnecessary, like crowd barriers on the moon.

Angelo is unpredictable, I told myself. Unstable as Mount St Helens. One might as well expect reasonable behaviour from an earthquake, even if one does ultimately wish him to prosper.

REMEMBER TIGERS.

There was a small banging noise out by the garage. Nothing alarming. I paid little attention.

Six envelopes lay on the mat. I bent down, picked them up, shuffled through them. Three bills for Luke, a rate demand for the cottage, an advertisement for books and a letter to Cassie from her mother in Sydney. Ordinary mundane letters, not worth dying for.

I gave one final glance round the pretty sitting-room, seeing the red check frills on the curtains and the corn dollies moving gently in the breeze through the door. It wouldn't be so long, I thought, before we were back.

The kitchen door stood open, the light from the kitchen window lying in a reflecting gleam on the white paint: and across the gleam a shadow moved.

Bananas and Cassie, I thought automatically, coming in through the kitchen door. But they couldn't. It was locked.

There was hardly time even for alarm, even for primeval instinct, even for rising hair. The silencer of a pistol came first into the room, a dark silhouette against the white paint, and then Angelo, dressed in black, balloon-high with triumph, towering with malice, looking like the devil.

There was no point in speech. I knew conclusively that he was going to shoot me, that I was looking at my own death. There was about him such an intention of action, such a surrender to recklessness, such an intoxication of destructiveness, that nothing and no one could have talked him out of it.

With a thought so light-fast that it wasn't even conscious, I reached out to the baseball bat which still lay on the window sill. Grasped its handle end with the dexterity of desperation and swung towards Angelo in one continuous movement from twisting foot through legs, trunk, arm and hand to bat, bringing the weight of the wood down towards the hand which held the pistol with the whole force of my body.

Angelo fired straight at my chest from six feet away. I felt a jerking thud and nothing else and wasn't even astonished and it didn't even a fraction deflect my swing. A split second later the bat crunched down onto Angelo's wrist and hand and broke them as thoroughly as he'd broken Cassie's arm.

I reeled from the force of that impact and spun across the room, and Angelo dropped the gun on the carpet and hugged his right arm to his body, yelling one huge shout at the pain of it and doubling over and running awkwardly out of the front door and down the path to the road.

I watched him through the window. I stood in a curious sort of inactivity, knowing that there was a future to come that had not yet arrived, a consequence not yet felt but inexorable, the fact of a bullet through my flesh.

I thought: Angelo has finally bagged his Derry. Angelo has taken his promised revenge. Angelo knows his shot hit me straight on target. Angelo will be convinced that he has done right, even if it costs him a lifetime in prison. In Angelo, despite his smashed wrist, despite his prospects, there would be at that moment an overpowering, screaming, unencompassable delirium of joy.

The battle was over, and the war. Angelo would be satisfied that in every physical, visible way, he had won.

Bananas and Cassie came running through the front door and looked enormously relieved to see me standing there, leaning a little against a cupboard but apparently unhurt.

'That was Angelo!' Cassie said.

'Yeah.'

Bananas looked at the baseball bat which lay on the floor and said, 'You bashed him.'

'Yeah.'

'Good,' Cassie said with satisfaction. 'His turn for the dreaded plaster.'

Bananas saw Angelo's gun and leaned to pick it up.

'Don't touch it,' I said.

He looked up enquiringly, still half bent.

'Fingerprints,' I said. 'Jail him for life.'

'But—'

'He shot me,' I said.

I saw the disbelief on their faces begin to turn to anxiety.

'Where?' Cassie said.

I made a fluttery movement with my left hand towards my chest. My right arm felt heavy and without strength, and I thought unemotionally that it was because some of the muscles needed to lift it were torn.

'Shall I get an ambulance?' Bananas said.

'Yes.'

They didn't understand, I thought, how bad it was. They couldn't see any damage, and I was concerned mostly about how to tell them without frightening Cassie to death.

It wasn't that at that point it felt so terrible, but I still knew in a detached fashion that it soon would be. There was an internal disintegration going on like the earth shifting, like foundations slipping away. Accelerating, but still slowly.

I said, 'Ring Cambridge hospital.'

It all sounded so calm.

I slid down, without meaning to, to my knees, and saw the anxiety on their faces turn to horror.

'You're really hurt,' Cassie said with spurting alarm.

'It's ... er ... er ...' I couldn't think what to say.

She was suddenly beside me, kneeling, finding with terrified scarlet fingers that the entry wound that didn't show through the front of my padded husky jacket led to a bigger bleeding exit at the back.

'Oh my *God*,' she said in stunned absolute shock.

Bananas strode over for a look and I could see from both their faced that they did know now, there was no longer any need to seek the words.

He turned grim-faced away and picked up the telephone, riffling urgently through the directory and dialling the number.

'Yes,' he was saying. 'Yes, it's an emergency. A man's been shot. Yes, I did say shot ... through the chest ... Yes, he's alive ... Yes, he's conscious ... No, the bullet can't be in him.' He gave the address of the cottage and brief directions. 'Look, stop asking damn fool questions ... tell them to shift their arse ... Yes, it does look *bloody* serious, for God's sake stop wasting time ... *My* name? Christ

Almighty, John Frisby.' He crashed the receiver down in anger and said, 'They want to know if we've reported it to the police. What the hell does it matter?'

I couldn't be bothered to tell him that all gunshot wounds had to be reported. Breathing, in fact, was becoming more difficult. Only words that needed to be said were worth the effort.

'That pistol,' I said. 'Don't put it . . . in a plastic bag. Condensation . . . destroys . . . the prints.'

Bananas looked surprised and I thought that he didn't realize I was telling him because quite soon I might not be able to. I was beginning to feel most dreadfully ill, with clamminess creeping over my skin and breaking into a sweat on my forehead. I gave a smallish cough and wiped a red streak from my mouth onto the back of my hand. An enveloping wave of weakness washed through me and I found myself sagging fairly comprehensively against the cupboard and then half lying on the floor.

'Oh, William,' Cassie said. 'Oh *no*.'

If I'd ever doubted she loved me, I had my answer. No one could have acted or feigned the extremity of despair in her voice and in her body.

'Don't . . . worry,' I said. I tried to smile. I don't suppose it came off. I coughed again, with worse results.

I was trying to breathe, I thought, through a lake. A lake progressively filling, fed by many springs. It was happening faster now. Much faster. Too fast. I wasn't ready. Who was ever ready?

I could hear Bananas saying something urgent but I didn't know quite what. My wits started drifting. Existence was ceasing to be external. I'm dying, I thought, I really am. Dying too fast.

My eyes were shut and then open again. The daylight looked odd. Too bright. I could see Cassie's face wet with tears.

I tried to say, 'Don't cry,' but I couldn't get the breath. Breathing was becoming a sticky near-impossibility.

Bananas was still talking, distantly.

There was a feeling of everything turning to liquid, of my body dissolving, of a deep subterranean river overflowing its banks and carrying me away.

Dim final astringent thought . . . I'm drowning, God damn it, in my own blood.

Chapter Twenty-One

Cassie's face was the next thing I saw, but not for more than a day, and it was no longer weeping but asleep and serene. She was sitting by a bed with me in it, surrounded by white things and glass and chromium and a lot of lights. Intensive care, and all that.

I woke by stages over several hours to the pain I hadn't felt from the shot, and to tubes carrying liquids into and away from my log of clay and to voices telling me over and over that I was lucky to be there; that I had died and was alive.

I thanked them all, and meant it.

Thanked Bananas, who had apparently picked me up and put me in my own car and driven me at about a hundred miles an hour to Cambridge because it was quicker than waiting for the ambulance.

Thanked two surgeons who it seemed had worked all day and then again half the night to staunch and tidy the wreckage of my right lung and stop blood dripping out of the drainage as fast as the tranfusions flowed into my arm.

Thanked the nurses who clattered about with deft hands and noisy machinery, and in absentia thanked the donors of blood type 'O' who had refilled my veins.

Thanked Cassie for her love and for sitting beside me whenever they'd let her.

Thanked the fates that the destructive lump of metal had missed my heart. Thanked everyone I could for anything I could think of in gratitude for my life.

The long recurring dreams that had come during unconsciousness faded, receded, seemed no longer to be vivid fact. I no longer saw the Devil pacing beside me, quiet but implacable, the master waiting for my soul. I no longer saw him, the Fallen Angel, the Devil with Angelo's face, the yellow face with frosted hair and black empty holes where the eyes should have been. The Presence had gone. I was back to the daft real enjoyable world where tubes were what mattered, not concepts of evil.

I didn't say how close I had been to death because they were saying it for me, roughly every five minutes. I didn't say I had looked on the spaces of eternity and seen the everlasting Darkness and had known it had a meaning and a face. The visions of the dying and the snatched-from-death were suspect. Angelo was a living man, not the Devil, not an incarnation or a house or a dwelling place. It was delirium, the confusion of the brain's circuits, that had shown me the one as the other, the other as the One. I said nothing for fear of ridicule: and later nothing from feeling that I had in truth been mistaken and that the dreams were indeed ... merely dreams.

'Where is Angelo?' I said.

'They said not to tire you.'

I looked at the evasion in Cassie's face. 'I'm lying down,' I pointed out. 'So give.'

She said reluctantly, 'Well ... he's here.'

'*Here*? In this hospital?'

She nodded. 'In the room next door.'

I was bewildered. 'But why?'

'He crashed his car.' She looked at me anxiously for signs I supposed of relapse, but was seemingly reassured. 'He drove into a bus about six miles from here.'

'After he left the cottage?'

She nodded. 'They brought him here. They brought him into the emergency unit while Bananas and I were waiting there. We couldn't believe it.'

It wasn't over. I closed my eyes. It was never ever going to be over. Wherever I went, it seemed that Angelo would follow, even onto the slab.

'William?' Cassie said urgently.

'Mm?'

'Oh. I thought ...'

'I'm all right.'

'He was nearly dead,' she said. 'Just like you. He's still in a coma.'

'What?'

'Head injuries,' she said.

I learned bit by bit over the next few days that the hospital people hadn't believed it when Bananas and Cassie told them it was Angelo who had shot me. They had fought as long and hard to save his life as mine, and apparently we had been placed side by side in the Intensive Care Unit until Cassie told them I'd have a heart attack if I woke and found him there.

The police had more moderately pointed out that if it was Angelo who woke first he might complete the job of murdering me: and Angelo was now in his unwaking sleep along the hallway, guarded by a constable night and day.

It was extraordinary to think of him being there, lying there so close. Unsettling in a fundamental way. I wouldn't have thought it would have affected me so badly, but my pulse started jumping every time anyone opened the door. Reason said he wouldn't come. The subconscious feared it.

Bodies heal amazingly quickly. I was free of tubes, moved to a side ward, on my feet, walking about within a week: creeping a bit, sure, and stiff and sore, but positively, conclusively alive. Angelo too, it seemed, was improving. On the way up from the depths. Opening unseeing eyes, showing responses.

I heard it from the nurses, from the cleaners, from the woman who pushed a trolly of comforts, and all of them watched me curiously to see how I would take it. The piquancy of the situation hit first the local paper and then the national dailies, and the constables guarding Angelo started drifting in to chat.

It was from one of them that I learned how Angelo had lost control of his car while going round a roundabout, how a whole queue of people at a bus stop had seen him veer towards the bus as if unable to turn the steering wheel, how he'd been going too fast in any case, and how he had seemed at first to be *laughing*.

Bananas, when he heard it, said trenchantly, 'He crashed because you broke his wrist.'

'Yes,' I said.

He sighed deeply. 'The police must know it.'

'I expect so.'

'Have they bothered you?'

I shook my head. 'I told them what happened. They wrote it down. No one has said much.'

'They collected the pistol.' He smiled. 'They put it in a paper bag.'

I left the hospital after twelve days, walking slowly past Angelo's room but not going in. Revulsion was too strong even though I knew he was still lightly unconscious and wouldn't be aware I was there. The damage he had caused in my life and Cassie's might be over but my body carried his scars, livid still and still hurting, too immediate for detachment.

I dare say I hated him. Perhaps I feared him. I certainly didn't want to see him again, then or ever.

For the next three weeks I mooched around the cottage doing paperwork, getting fitter every day and persuading Bananas at first to drive me along to the Heath to watch the gallops. Cassie went to work, the plastered arm a memory. My blood had washed almost entirely off the sitting-room carpet and the baseball bat was in the cellar. Life returned more or less to normal.

Luke came over from California, inspected the yearlings, met Cassie, listened to Sim and Mort and the Berkshire trainers, visited Warrington Marsh, and went off to Ireland. It was he, not I, who bid for Oxidise at Ballsbridge and sent the colt to Donavan, and he who in some way smoothed the Irish trainer's feelings.

He came back briefly to Newmarket before leaving for home, calling in at the cottage and drinking a lunchtime scotch.

'Your year's nearly through,' he said.

'Yeah.'

'Have you enjoyed it?'

'Very much.

'Want another?'

I lifted my head. He watched me through a whole minute of silence. He didn't say, and nor did I, that Warrington Marsh was never going to be strong enough again to do the job. That wasn't the point: the point was permanence ... captivity.

'One year,' Luke said. 'It's not for ever.'

After another pause I said, 'One year, then. One more.'

He nodded and drank his drink, and it seemed to me that somewhere he was smiling. I had a presentiment of him coming over again the next year and offering the same thing. One year. One year's contract at a time, leaving the cage door open but keeping his bird imprisoned: and as long as I could go, I thought, I might stay.

Cassie, when she came home, was pleased. 'Mort told him he'd be mad to lose you.'

'Did he?'

'Mort likes you.'

'Donavan doesn't.'

'You can't have everything,' she said.

I had quite a lot, it was true; and then the police telephoned and asked me to see Angelo.

'No,' I said.

'That's a gut reaction,' a voice said calmly. 'But I'd like you to listen.'

He talked persuasively for a long time, cajoling again every time I protested, wearing down my opposition until in the end I reluctantly agreed to do what he wanted.

'Good,' he said finally. 'Wednesday afternoon.'

'That's only two days—'

'We'll send a car. We don't expect you to be driving yet.'

I didn't argue. I could drive short distances but I tended to get tired. In another month, they'd said, I'd be running.

'We're grateful,' the voice said.

'Yeah . . .'

I told Cassie and Bananas, in the evening.

'How awful,' Cassie said. 'It's too much.'

The three of us were having dinner alone in the dining-room as the restaurant didn't officially open these days on Mondays: the old cow had negotiated Mondays off. Bananas had done the cooking himself, inventing a soufflé of white fish, herbs, orange and nuts to try out on Cassie and me: a concoction typically and indescribably different, an unknown language, a new horizon of taste.

'You could have said you wouldn't go,' Bananas said, heaping his plate to match ours.

'With what excuse?'

'Selfishness,' Cassie said. 'The best reason in the world for not doing things.'

'Never thought of it.'

Bananas said, 'I hope you insisted on a bulletproof vest, a six-inch-thick plate glass screen and several rolls of barbed wire.'

'They did assure me,' I said mildly, 'that they wouldn't let him leap at my throat.'

'Too kind,' Cassie murmured.

We poured Bananas's exquisite sauce over his soufflé and said that when we had to leave the cottage we would camp in his garden.

'And will you bet?' he asked.

'What do you mean?'

'On the system.'

I thought blankly that I'd forgotten all about that possibility: but we did have the tapes. We did have the choice.

'We don't have a computer,' I said.

'We could soon pay for one,' Cassie said.

We all looked at each other. We were happy enough with our own jobs; with what we had. Did one always, inevitably, stretch out for more?

Yes, one did.

'You work the computer,' Bananas said, 'and I'll do the betting. Now and then. When we're short.'

'As long as it doesn't choke us.'

'I don't want diamonds,' Cassie said judiciously, 'or furs, or a yacht ... but how soon can we have a pool in our sitting-room?'

Whatever Luke said to my brother when he got home to California I never knew, but it resulted in Jonathan telephoning that night to say he would be arriving at Heathrow on Wednesday morning.

'What about your students?'

'Sod the students. I've got laryngitis.' His voice bounced the distance strongly and healthy. 'I'll see you.'

He came in a hired car looking biscuit-coloured from the sun and anxious about what he would find, and although I was by then feeling well again it didn't seem to reassure him.

'I'm alive,' I pointed out. 'One thing at a time. Come back next month.'

'What exactly happened?'

'Angelo happened.'

'Why didn't you tell me?' he demanded.

'I'd have told you if I'd died. Or someone would.'

He sat in one of the rockers and looked at me broodingly.

'It was all my fault,' he said.

'Oh, sure.' I was ironic.

'And that's why you didn't tell me.'

'I'd probably have told you one day.'

'Tell me now.'

I told him, however, where I was going that afternoon, and why, and he said in his calm positive way that he would come with me. I had thought he would: had been glad he was coming. I told him over the next few hours pretty well everything which had happened between Angelo and me, just as he had told me all those years ago in Cornwall.

'I'm sorry,' he said, at the end.

'Don't be.'

'You'll use the system?'

I nodded. 'Pretty soon.'

'I think old Mrs O'Rorke would be glad. She was proud of Liam's work. She wouldn't want it wasted.' He reflected for a bit and then said, 'What make of pistol, do you know?'

'I believe ... the police said ... a Walther .22?'

He smiled faintly. 'True to form. And just as well. If it had been a .38 or something like that you'd have been in trouble.'

'Ah,' I said dryly. 'Just as well.'

The car came for us as threatened and took us to a large house in Buckinghamshire. I never did discover exactly what it was: a cross between a hospital and a civil service institution, all long wide corridors and closed doors and hush.

'Down there,' we were directed. 'Right along at the end. Last door on the right.'

We walked unhurriedly along the parquet flooring, our heels punctuating the silence. At the far end there was a tall window, floor to ceiling, casting not quite enough daylight; and silhouetted against the window were two figures, a man in a wheelchair with another man pushing him.

Those two and Jonathan and I in due course approached each other, and as we drew nearer I saw with unwelcome shock that the man in the wheelchair was Harry Gilbert. Old, grey, bowed, ill Harry Gilbert who still consciously repelled compassion.

Eddy, who was pushing, faltered to a halt, and Jonathan and I also stopped, we staring at Harry and Harry staring at us over a space of a few feet. He looked from me to Jonathan, glancing at him briefly at first and then looking longer, more carefully, seeing what he didn't believe.

He switched to me. 'You said he was dead,' he said.

I nodded slightly.

His voice was cold, dry, bitter, past passion, past hope, past strength to avenge. 'Both of you,' he said. 'You destroyed my son.'

Neither Jonathan nor I answered. I wondered about the genetics of evil, the chance that bred murder, the predisposition which lived already at birth. The biblical creation, I thought, was also the truth of evolution. Cain existed, and in every species there was survival of the ruthless.

It was only by luck that I had lived; by Bananas's speed and surgeon's dedication. Abel and centuries of other victims were dead: and in every generation, in many a race, the genes still threw up the killer. The Gilberts bred their Angelos for ever.

Harry Gilbert jerked his head back, aiming at Eddy, signalling that he wanted to go; and Eddy the look-alike, Eddy the easily led, Eddy the sheep from the same flock, wheeled his uncle quietly away.

'Arrogant old bastard,' Jonathan said under his breath, looking back at them.

'The breeding of racehorses,' I said, 'is interesting.'

Jonathan's gaze came round very slowly to my face. 'And do rogues,' he asked, 'beget rogues?'

'Quite often.'

He nodded and we went on walking along the corridor, up to the window, to the last door on the right.

The room into which we went must once have been finely proportioned but with the insensitivity of government departments it had been hacked into two for utility. The result was one long narrow room with a window and another inner long narrow room without one.

In the outer room, which was furnished only by a strip of mud-coloured carpet on the parquet leading to a functional desk and two hard chairs, were two men engaged in what looked like unimportant passing of the time. One sat behind the desk, one sat on it, both fortyish, smallish, smooth, bored-looking and with an air of wishing to be somewhere else.

The looked enquiringly as we went in.

'I'm William Derry,' I said.

'Ah.'

The man sitting on the desk rose to his feet, came towards me, shook hands, and looked enquiring at Jonathan.

'My brother, Jonathan Derry,' I said.

'Ah.'

He shook hands with him too. 'I don't think,' he said neutrally, 'that we'll need to bother your brother.'

I said, 'Angelo is more likely to react violently to Jonathan than to me.'

'But it was you he tried to kill.'

'Jonathan got him jailed . . . fourteen years ago.'

'Ah.'

He looked from one of us to the other, his head tilted slightly back to accommodate our height. We seemed to be in some way not what he'd expected, though I didn't know why. Jonathan did certainly look pretty distinguished, especially since age had given him such an air of authority, and he had always of the two of us had the straighter features; and I, I supposed, looked less of a victim that I might have. I wondered vaguely if he'd been expecting a shuffling little figure in a dressing gown and hadn't reckoned on clothes like his own.

'I think I'll just go and *explain* about your brother,' he said at last. 'Will you wait?'

We nodded and he opened the door to the inner room parsimoniously and eeled himself through the gap, closing it behind him. The man behind the desk went on looking bored and offered no comment of any sort, and presently his colleague slid back through the same sized opening and said they were ready for us inside and would we please go in.

The inner room was lit brightly and entirely by electricity and contained four people and a great deal of electrical equipment with multitudinous dials and sprouting wires. I saw Jonathan give them a swift sweep of the eyes and supposed he could identify the lot, and he said afterwards that they had all seemed to be standard machines for measuring body changes – cardiograph, encephalograph, gauges for temperature, respiration and skin moisture – and there had been at least two of each.

One of the four people wore an identifying white coat and introduced himself quietly as Tom Course, doctor. A woman in similar white moved among the machines, checking their faces. A third person, a man, seemed to be there specifically as an observer, since that was what he did, without speaking, during the next strange ten minutes.

The fourth person, sitting in a sort of dentist's chair with his back towards us, was Angelo.

We could see only the top of his bandaged head, but also his arms, which were strapped by the wrists to the arms of the chair.

There was no sign of any plaster on the arm I'd broken: mended no doubt. His arms were bare and covered sparsely with dark hairs, the hands lying loose, without tension. From every part of his body it seemed that wires led backwards to the machines, which were all ranked behind him. In front of him there was nothing but a stretch of empty brightly lit room.

Dr Course, young, wiry, bolstered by certainties, gave me an enquiring glance and said in the same quiet manner, 'Are you ready?'

As ready, I supposed, as I ever would be.

'Just walk round in front of him. Say something. Anything you like. Stay there until we tell you it's enough.'

I swallowed. I had never wanted to do anything less in all my life. I could see them all waiting, polite, determined, businesslike . . . and too damned understanding. Even Jonathan, I noticed, was looking at me with a sort of pity.

Intolerable.

I walked slowly round the machines and the chair and stopped in front of Angelo, and looked at him.

He was naked to the waist. On his head, below a cap of fawn crêpe bandage, there was a band of silvery metal like a crown. His skin everywhere gleamed with grease and his face, his neck, his chest, arms and abdomen were fastened an army of electrodes. No one, I imagined, could have been more comprehensively wired; no flicker of change could have gone unmonitored.

He seemed as well-fleshed and as healthy as ever, despite his earlier two weeks in a coma. The muscles looked as strong, the trunk as tank-like, the mouth as firm. The hard man. The frightener. The despiser of mugs. Apart from his headdress and the wires he looked just the same. I breathed a shade deeply and looked straight into his black eyes, and it was there that one saw the difference. There was nothing in the eyes, nothing at all. It was extraordinary, like seeing a stranger in a long-known face. The house was the same . . . but the monster slept.

It was five weeks all but a day since we had last faced each other; since we had brought each other near to death, one way or another. Even though I had been prepared, seeing him again affected me powerfully. I could feel my heart thudding: could actually hear it in the expectant room.

'Angelo,' I said. My tongue felt sticky in my dry mouth. 'Angelo, you shot me.'

In Angelo, nothing happened.

He was looking at me in complete calm. When I took a pace to one side, his eyes followed. When I stepped back he still watched.

'I am ... William Derry,' I said. 'I gave you ... Liam O'Rorke's betting system.' I said the words slowly, clearly, deliberately, trying to control my own uneven breath.

From Angelo there was no reaction at all.

'If you hadn't shot me ... you'd have been free now ... and rich.'

Nothing. Absolutely nothing.

I found Jonathan standing beside me and after a pause Angelo's gaze wandered from me to him.

'Hullo, Angelo,' Jonathan said. 'I'm Jonathan, do you remember? William told you I was dead. It wasn't true.'

Angelo said nothing.

'Do you remember?' Jonathan said. 'I tricked you sideways.'

Silence. A dull absence of all we had endured for so long. No fury. No sneers, no threats, no towering hurricane of hate.

Silence, it seemed to me, was all that was appropriate. Jonathan and I stood there together in front of the shell of our enemy and there was nothing in the world left to say.

'Thank you,' Tom Course said, coming round the chair to join us. 'That should do it.'

Angelo looked at him.

'Who are you?' he said.

'Dr Course. We talked earlier, while we were fixing the electrodes.'

Angelo made no comment but instead looked directly at me.

'You were talking,' he said. 'Who are you?'

'William Derry.'

'I don't know you.'

'No.'

His voice was as deep and as gritty as ever, the only remnant, it seemed, of the old foe.

Dr Course said heartily, 'We'll take all those wires off you now. I expect you'll be glad to get rid of them.'

'Who did you say you are?' Angelo said, frowning slightly.

'Dr Course.'

'Who?'

'Never mind. I'm here to take the wires off.'

'Can I have tea?' Angelo said.

Dr Course left the taking-off of the the wires to his woman colleague and led us round to look at the results on the machines. The observer, I noticed, was also consulting them acutely, but Course paid him scant attention.

'There we are,' he said, holding out a yard long strip of paper. 'Not a flicker. We had him stabilized for an hour before his visitors came. Breathing, pulse rate, everything rock steady. Quiet in here, you see. No interruptions, no intrusions, no noise. That mark, that's the point at which he saw *you*,' he nodded at me, 'and as you can see, nothing altered. This is the skin temperature chart. Always rises if someone's lying. And here ...' he moved across to a different machine. 'Heart rate unchanged. And here ...' to another. 'Brain activity, very faint alteration. He couldn't have seen *you*, his hated victim, suddenly and unexpectedly standing in front of him, and yet show no strong body or brain changes, not if he'd known you. Absolutely impossible.'

I thought of my own unrecorded but pretty extreme responses, and knew that it was true.

'Is this state permanent?' Jonathan asked.

Tom Course gave him a swift look. '*I* think so. It's *my* opinion, yes. See, they dug pieces of skull out of his brain tissue. Brilliant repair job on the bone structure, have to hand it to them. But there you are, you can see, no memory. Many functions unimpaired. Eat, talk, walk, he can do all that. He's continent. He'll live to be old. But he can't remember anything for longer than about fifteen minutes, sometimes not even that. He lives in the absolute present. Loss of capacity for memory is not all that rare, you know, after severe brain damage. But with this one, there were *doubts*. Not *my* doubts, official doubts. They said he was faking, that he knew he'd go to a hospital, not a prison, if he could persuade everyone he'd lost his memory.'

Tom Course waved a hand around the machines. 'He couldn't have faked today's results. Conclusive. Settle the arguments once and for all. Which is why we're all here, of course. Why they gave us this facility.'

His woman colleague had taken the silver band off Angelo's forehead and the straps off his wrists, and was wiping the grease from his skin with pieces of cotton wool.

'Who are you?' he said to her, and she answered, 'Just a friend.'

'Where will he go?' I asked.

Tom Course shrugged. 'Not my decision. But I'd be careful. I'm not a civil servant. My advice, I don't suppose, will be taken.' His remark was clearly aimed at the observer, who remained obstinately impassive.

I said slowly, 'Could he still be violent?'

Tom Course gave me a swift sideways glance. 'Can't tell. He might be. Yes, he might be. He lookes harmless. He'll never *hate* anyone, he can't remember anyone long enough. But the sudden impulse ...' he shrugged again. 'Let's say, I wouldn't turn my back on him if we were alone.'

'Not ever?'

'How old is he? Forty?' He pursed his mouth. 'Not for another ten years. Twenty perhaps. You can't tell.'

'Lightning?' I said.

'Just like that.'

The woman finished wiping the grease and was holding out a grey shirt for Angelo to put on.

'Have we had tea?' he said.

'Not yet.'

'I'm thirsty.'

'You'll have tea soon.'

I said to Tom Course, 'His father was outside ... did Angelo see him?'

Course nodded. 'No reaction. Nothing on the machines. Conclusive tests, the whole lot of them.' He looked slyly at the observer. 'They can stop all the arguing.'

Angelo stood up out of the chair, stretching upright, seeming strong with physical life but fumbling with the buttons on his shirt, moving without total coordination, looking around vaguely as if not quite sure what he should be doing next.

His wandering gaze came to rest on Jonathan and me.

'Hullo,' he said.

The doors from the outer room opened wide and two white-coated male nurses and a uniformed policeman came through it.

'Is he ready?' the policeman said.

'All yours.'

'Let's be off, then.'

He fastened a handcuff round Angelo's left wrist and attached him to one of the nurses.

Angelo didn't seem to mind. He looked at me uninterestedly for the last time with the black holes where the eyes should have been and walked as requested to the door.

Diminished, defused ... perhaps even docile.

'Where's my tea?' he said.